Rich

Solitaire

GRAHAM MASTERTON OMNIBUS

Rich
Solitaire

GRAHAM MASTERTON

A *Time Warner* Paperback

This omnibus edition first published in Great Britain by
Time Warner Paperbacks in 2004
Graham Masterton Omnibus Copyright © Graham Masterton 2004

Previously published separately:
Rich first published in Great Britain by Hamish Hamilton 1979
Published by Sphere Books Ltd 1979
Reprinted 1980 (four times), 1981, 1983, 1984, 1985, 1986
Copyright © 1979 by Graham Masterton

Solitaire first published in Great Britain by Hamish Hamilton Ltd 1982
Published by Sphere Books Ltd 1984
Copyright © 1982 by Graham Masterton

The moral right of the author has been asserted.

A CIP catalogue record for this book
is available from the British Library.

ISBN 0 7515 3601 6

Printed and bound in Great Britain by
Clays Ltd, St Ives plc

Time Warner Paperbacks
An imprint of
Time Warner Books UK
Brettenham House
Lancaster Place
London WC2E 7EN

www.TimeWarnerBooks.co.uk

Rich

For Wiescka, my wife, with love,
and for Marty Asher, with very
special thanks.

1900

A WONDERFUL GARDEN PARTY

THREE HUNDRED FIFTY DOLLARS RAISED
FOR SICK CHILDREN

By Our Society Correspondent

Mr Frank Edmunds of Broughton threw a scintillating garden party for 250 celebrities and guests at his home on Saturday last, and $350.23 was raised for the sick children of Broughton and surrounding environs.

A notable newcomer to Broughton's social circles was a New Yorker, Mr J. Cornelias, who has recently arrived in these parts to consider business investment.

—*The Broughton Sentinel,*
August 14, 1900

It was one of those days when the heat comes in suffocating waves, and you only had to leave your house and walk a few yards down Main Street, just to Scully's Hardware for a bag of beans or some washing soda, or maybe down to the little fish stall on the corner of Galveston Street for some snapper, and your clothes began to feel hot and sticky and uncomfortable, and your boots too tight, and you started to think about ice-cream sodas or lemon water ice, sipped at the shady tables of Howard's Refreshment Parlor.

There was no such person as Howard, never had been. The parlour was run by a small birdlike widow called Mrs Grey, who ran up and down behind her high marble-topped counter in a rigid white apron, serving up sundaes and milk shakes in moulded glass dishes. She served advice, too, if you needed it, or even if you didn't. Mrs Grey considered that the free dissemination of worldly wisdom was part and parcel of the function of selling ices.

When Janet stepped across the scrubbed wooden floor that afternoon in August, the place was crowded, and the conversation tumbled warm and lazy through the cool filtered sunlight. Mrs Grey was piling the last creamy layer onto a seven-layer strawberry ice, and talking to a big, sweaty-looking man in a worn blue jacket and patched-up trousers.

'If you want my opinion, young feller,' she was saying, as she popped a final cherry on top, 'you'll take yourself up North, and find yourself a factory to work in. There's regular employment up there, I hear the wages are better than ever. Things move slow down here, always have, and always will.'

The man didn't seem to be listening. He was drawing invisible patterns on the cold marble counter with his blunt, workingman's finger.

'These days,' said Mrs Grey, 'you have to know your onions if you want to make anything out of yourself. Time was, a pick and a shovel and a broad back was good enough. But these days, if you don't know your onions, you'll finish your

3

life as poor as you started it, and folks don't come any poorer than that.'

A calendar on the pine-boarded wall flapped and flickered in the warm breeze that eddied into the parlour from the open front door. It read August 13, 1900.

'Janet,' said Mrs Grey in her hoarse old voice, 'I do believe you come to indulge yourself again, at your mistress's expense.'

It was a long-standing joke between them, but the big sweaty man at the counter obviously didn't realize, and stood back to look at Janet the way you'd look at someone's pet poodle when it wouldn't behave itself.

Mrs Grey laid her hand on his arm. 'It's a hot day,' she explained, 'and this here's just about halfway between the stores and the houses, and it ain't surprisin' that serving maids find themselves tempted.'

Janet smiled. 'It sure is hot, Mrs Grey. I reckon a blackcurrant ice, with sweet syrup and a cherry on top, that'll do me. I swear I thought I'd melt to a puddle before I got here.'

'Young girls like you shouldn't feel the heat,' said Mrs Grey, digging into the chilled blackcurrant sherbet. There was a delicious musty sour smell of blackcurrant leaves. 'Wear more underthings, that's what I always say.'

As she prattled on, the heavy-built stranger shifted himself around and took a long look at Janet. She was quite aware that he was watching, because she blushed slightly and lowered her eyes, but she didn't look back his way. Apart from anything else at all, he was a common workingman, and Mrs Mulliner had spoken to Janet very severely about what she called 'addressing herself' to butcher's roundsmen and general roughnecks. Janet thought it made her sound like an untidy parcel that insisted on being posted wherever it thought fit.

Janet was eighteen, and a housemaid for Mr and Mrs Mulliner, on Beaumont Street, where the houses were detached and painted white, and set back among palms and acacia and shady creepers. Down in the railroad area of town, they called it 'The Racetrack', on account of its white-painted fences and its neatly trimmed turf, and the well-dressed young fillies who pranced up and down it. Mrs Mulliner was one of the better-known fillies, even though she was a married woman. She went to Houston two or three times a year, and on every trip she bought herself several hundred dollars' worth of fashionable clothes. Janet had heard that last season she paid nearly twenty dollars for one dress alone. But Mr Mulliner didn't seem to mind his wife's extravagance; he was a good ten years older than she was, with peppery whiskers, and perhaps he thought his beautiful consort was worth a sizeable slice of his profits. He ran a respectable and successful law partnership on Fifth Street, in the business district, and was considered a rich man.

Janet liked working for the Mulliners, and her contentment showed. She was a short girl, only five-feet-four in her military-heeled boots, and she had a pretty chubbiness about her that made her master's houseguests want to give her affectionate squeezes, especially after the brandy had been passed around for the third time. She had wispy brown hair that floated under her wide-brimmed straw leghorn in irrepressible clouds. Her cheeks were freckly, her lips were pert and pink, and she had wide slate-coloured eyes that made her look permanently surprised at what she saw. In her cream percale skirt and her pink German linen blouse, she had a round-breasted curviness that made housepainters whistle as she bounced her way past, and retired gentlemen raise their eyeglasses for a longer and more appreciative look.

The heavy-built man in Howard's Refreshment Parlor was being more than appreciative, though. He was openly staring at Janet with his pale bulgy eyes in a way that made her wonder if her blouse was unfastened, or there was an unsightly smudge on the tip of her nose. He had a red, Dutch-looking face, with protruding ears as thick as gammon rinds, and rubbery lips. His hair was yellow and thinning on top; but for all his brutishness and his coarseness, there was something very powerful and masculine about him. He looked the kind of man who would see you out of trouble, or lift your cart out of a muddy rut with the strength of his own broad back.

He didn't say a word as Mrs Grey topped off Janet's blackcurrant sherbet with syrup and cherries, tucked a long-handled spoon into the dish and handed it across the counter. Janet, still blushing, opened her purse and dropped five cents on the marble-topped counter. Mrs Grey rang the money on the cash register, and gave her two cents change.

'Now, you make haste consuming that, Miss Janet, or else

you'll get a scolding when you get yourself back. I just thank heavens you ain't my housemaid, or else I'd be after you with a floor brush.'

Janet gave her a tight little smile and carried her dish of ice across to one of the tables She chose it because it was the only spare seat, and she didn't want the heavy-built workingman to sit down next to her and make a nuisance of himself. She bent her head over her plate, and ate as quickly as she could. All of a sudden, all the pleasure seemed to have drained out of Howard's Refreshment Parlor, and she didn't even dare to look up, in case the fellow was still staring at her.

There were two young clerks at her table. She recognized them from Okram's Quantity Goods Store on Eighth Street. At first they were talking about fishing down at Harness Creek, but after a while they started making pointed remarks about her, as if she wasn't there. While she could usually have taken this kind of teasing in good part, and flirt back, she really didn't care for it today, and almost lost her temper.

'You have to make *one* concession,' remarked one of the clerks, a redheaded boy in a tight brown suit. 'She dresses nobby, even though she's working in the kitchen.'

'Nobby?' said the other, who had dark wavy hair and plenty of dandruff. 'She's a picture, I'd say, the kind men like.'

She left her ice unfinished, which in actual fact she thought was a rather adult thing to do. Only small children and dogs licked the plate. She pushed back her bentwood chair, gathered up her shopping bag, and walked out. She didn't even turn around to call good-bye to Mrs Grey, in case the red-faced workingman was looking, but she told herself that Mrs Grey was probably too busy scooping out fresh dishes of ice cream to notice. Outside, on the boardwalk, the heat and the glare were like a great furnace door opening up.

Well, she thought to herself, *I'm glad I work for a respectable household. The way men behave, they're like wild dogs, only chasing after one thing. How can they be so brutish? They only have to sniff a pretty girl, and they turn into crude and horrible beasts. They treat a woman like a piece of raw meat.*

She crossed Main Street at the corner of Tenth Street, and walked in the shade of the wooden buildings, her heels rapping on the boardwalk and her long skirt rustling. A messenger boy on a bicycle whistled at her as he pedalled past, but she tilted her chin up and ignored him. From now

6

on, she decided, she wasn't going to have anything to do with men. They could stare and slaver as much as they wanted to She couldn't stop that. But she could make sure that they didn't receive the slightest pinch of encouragement.

As she walked, she glanced at her reflection in the store windows, and saw a pretty little girl in a high-crowned straw hat and a crisp pink blouse. She straightened her back to make herself look taller, and to lift her breasts. A sizeable frontage was fashionable this year, and she was quite proud of hers.

She waited at the corner of Ninth Street while a horse-drawn runabout rattled briskly past, and then she stepped out onto the hard-baked road. But she had only walked a few steps when she felt a strong hand pull at her left arm. She jolted her head up with surprise, and said: 'Oh!'

It was the heavyset man with the red face. The crude brute had had the all-fired temerity to trail her down the street! Janet tugged her sleeve away, and said in a very high-pitched voice: 'Take your hands off of me, you crude brute!'

The man actually laughed. 'Come on,' he said, reaching out his hand. 'Let's cross the street first. I don't want myself sent sprawling by one of your local bumpkins on a bicycle.'

Janet lifted her nose, picked up her skirts, and strutted across the street without looking left or right. When she reached the boardwalk on the other side, she was just about to keep strutting on, but the man grabbed her arm again and swung her around.

'Don't touch me!' she snapped, slapping his hand away. 'If you don't leave me alone, and quit pestering, I'll shout out for help!'

The man blocked her way. 'Listen,' he said in quite a calm, reasonable voice. 'I'm not trying to have my way with you. I recognize you from some place, that's all, and when I saw you back there in Howard's, I was just trying to think where it was.'

Janet turned her head away and did her best to look offended. In truth, she was quite intrigued to know where this mysterious stranger might have laid eyes on her before.

'I'll thank you,' she said with a little quaver in her voice, 'to let me pass by.'

The stranger stepped out of her way. 'I'm not detaining you, ma'am,' he said.

Janet looked at him and frowned. He was simply standing there, with a smile on his thick lips and a tiny mocking twinkle in his eyes.

'Well,' she said uncomfortably, 'thank you.'

'It's my pleasure,' he said.

She brushed her skirt down and adjusted her shopping bag. This man was too irritating! First he behaved like a brute, and wouldn't keep himself to himself; but now, when it seemed that he probably wasn't a brute, he kept himself to himself too much.

'I suppose you're not going to tell me,' she said in the loftiest accents she could manage.

The man grinned. 'I'm not going to pester you,' he said obliquely.

'But you're not going to tell me, either?'

'Not unless you want to hear.'

'Well,' she said, giving in, 'I can't remember having seen *you* before.'

The man gently took her arm. 'Let me tell you about it while we stroll along. I know you have an errand to run.'

Janet was quite embarrassed, walking along Main Street with this big red-faced man in his working clothes, but she tried to look as composed as she could. She had seen Mrs Mulliner going in to dinner with doddering old men, and if Mrs Mulliner could escort unlikely-looking people with grace, then so could she.

'You work for Beatrice Mulliner, don't you?' asked the man. 'I saw you out at Frank Edmunds' garden party on Saturday afternoon, but correct me if I'm wrong.'

Janet blushed, for no reason at all. Perhaps it was the way the stranger referred to Mrs Mulliner as 'Beatrice'.

'That's right,' she said. 'I'm housemaid at Mr and Mrs Mulliner's. I can't say I saw you at the garden party.'

The man laughed. 'No, I don't suppose you did. Not looking this way, anyhow. When I go to garden parties, I don't wear my working clothes.'

She stared at him. 'You mean . . . you went as a *guest*?'

He stopped walking, and gave a little bow. 'In manner of speaking. Actually, I gate-crashed. I thought the food was good enough, but the conversation pretty dull. Still, I guess I'm going to have to put up with it if I want to get on in local

8

society. Is that whiskery old gent really Mrs Mulliner's husband?'

Janet suppressed a smile. 'Mr Mulliner is older than Mrs Mulliner, yes, by a good few years. He runs a law business down on Fifth. He's a very amiable man, you know'

'Oh, sure,' said the stranger reflectively. 'I didn't say he wasn't.'

Janet watched him for a while. She had never met such a curious person in her whole life. She knew she had to go, or else she'd be late back for the washing, but somehow she was reluctant to leave – at least until she had a clue about his identity and his extraordinary behaviour. Why was a man who gate-crashed society parties walking around Main Street dressed like a common labourer? He was ugly and yet strangely fascinating, and she felt he had a power that was all his own. It wasn't just physical power, either. It was some kind of inside strength; some clear-cut definition of purpose that would never be deflected or slowed. The man ran his hand through his thinning yellow hair and looked back at Janet with a friendly grimace.

'Janet,' he said, 'I wonder if you could do a little thing to help me.'

'It depends what it is.'

'Well ... I've been around this town for four or five days now, taking a look about. It strikes me that it could be the best place to set up business, and that's what I want to do.'

Janet frowned. 'There isn't anyone who's going to stop you.'

The man moved aside to let a lad from the grocer's go past with a sack of potatoes. 'I know that,' he said. 'But setting up business involves more than people tolerating you. They have to help you, as well. I need to know what goes on in this town, as far as business and society are both concerned, because I need to move fast and sure. Now, that's where your favour comes in.'

'What is it?' asked Janet. 'There isn't much I can do. I'm only the housemaid.'

The man smiled. 'You can spread a little gossip, that's what you can do. You can tell your mistress that an important fellow just came in from New York, aiming to set up business here, and that his name is Johann Cornelius. That's all you need to say. Give it time, and everyone in town will want to know who I am, and where to find me.'

9

'Is that all?' said Janet. 'Just to say that Mr Cornelius came to town and aims to set up shop?'

The stranger nodded. 'That's all you have to do.'

There was an odd pause. For a moment Janet wondered if Mr Cornelius was going to give her some money, but when he kept smiling, and didn't make any kind of move to go for his pockets, it was plain that he expected the favour *gratis*.

She said slowly: 'Don't think I'm not being neighbourly, Mr Cornelius, but free favours is something you do for your friends.'

He smiled. 'Aren't you my friend?'

'I've only known you for five minutes! Friendship is like a sheltering tree, Mr Cornelius, but you can't shade yourself under half a twig.'

He thought for a while. Then he said: 'Okay, let's *make* friends. If you have a day off this week, I'll take you down to the meadow carnival.'

She widened those surprised grey eyes. 'Mr Cornelius . . . you'll have to give me time to think about that. I do have . . well, another admirer.'

He took her hand and kissed it. It was a bit like being kissed by the red rubber ring around a pear-preserving jar. She glanced nervously around the busy streets to see if anyone noticed.

'Janet,' he said. 'All men, when they see you, are your admirers. Leave a message round at Howard's when you've made up your mind. Meanwhile, I have work to do, and so do you. It's been a great and cordial pleasure to meet you, and I look forward to seeing you again.'

He smiled one brief smile, and then he strode off down the boardwalk, disappearing at the corner of Eighth. Janet stood staring after him for a whole minute, and then walked with uncertain steps toward Scully's Hardware.

'Something on your mind?' said Scully in the dim, soapy-smelling depths of the store.

Janet shook her head. 'I'm not sure, Mr Scully,' she said quietly. 'I think I just met someone very strange. Either that, or a villain. Or maybe both. I hope I don't ever have to find out which.'

At lunchtime, hot and hungry, Johann Cornelius went into Parsons' Lunch Rooms on Second Street, on the peeling and impoverished side of the business district, and sat at a bare wooden table with a white basin of salt beef and dumplings, price eight cents.

Parsons' was a workingman's place, and unlike the middle-class restaurants in town, where conversation buzzed over the midday meal like a swarm of bluebottles, Parsons' was silent, as exhausted and ravenous men hunched over their food. Johann joined them, digging his cheap spoon into the solid dumplings, and breaking his rough brown bread with his hands.

He knew now, as a fact of life, that starting afresh in a new world was neither romantic nor exciting. It was, instead, as lonely and painful and dispiriting as any human condition could be. Today – August 13, 1900 – Johann Cornelius was twenty-seven years old, but the family celebrations that would have given his birthday any joy were absent, and so he studiously tried to think of it as an ordinary day, with no special significance at all. Growing older was not so important as surviving, and in any case the span of his life was already known and determined by the Lord, and nothing he could do would ever alter that. His only mission now was to set up in business and make money. The Lord helps those who help themselves.

Johann had been in America for a little over two years. He hardly thought at all about his family now, except in odd, unpredictable, and highly romanticized fragments. Johann, as a boy, had always had a passion for engineering – for anything mechanical, complex, and mathematical. His father, a dairy hand at Amersfoort, Holland, had worked for years to put Johann through school, so that he might become a great engineer. The year that Johann graduated, his father had a paralyzing stroke, for no apparent reason at all, while crossing a thundery field to fetch his cows. Johann had sacrificed his great engineering career to work at home and care for his mother, his debilitated father, and his six younger brothers and sisters.

No one knew how he really felt. No one knew that for all those years he sweated and laboured in the dairy with a terrible gnawing frustration and bitterness, regretting his lost chance like a magnificently wrapped gift box that turns out to contain nothing but a badly knitted pair of khaki mittens. One day in 1897 he took his lunch of cheese and

11

black bread from his mother, walked down the puddly lane, turned right instead of left, and never went home again. He still had dreams about his tired, plain-faced mother and his nodding, grunting, paralyzed father, but in the daytime he shut out such guilty visions with brightly coloured pictures of Holland with red-brick pavements, black-and-white cows, and pretty skies of chintz blue and puffy white clouds.

He had cadged a ride from a cheese wagon bound for 's-Gravenhage, and from there he walked to Scheveningen, and spent his last guilders on a boat ride to England. He knew two words of English – 'yes' and 'tolerance'. 'Tolerance' was an engineering word, and had nothing to do with religious freedom, which was why most Dutch people left their own country. He had found a job in Balham, a suburb of London, as a toolmaker and engineer, going back at night to a damp room which smelled of leaking gas and dirty bed linen. He remembered London for its huddled rooftops of rain-slicked slate, its yellow smoky skies, and a desperate feeling that life was always going to be like this.

In 1897, one rainy night in November, in Garratt Lane, Balham, he saw a poster in the window of a bootmaker's shop advertising passage to New York. There was a stirring etching of a White Star steamer, pennants flapping, bounding over a millpond sea on its way to the New World. The ships left Liverpool every Wednesday, and the steerage passage was four pounds. Johann went home that evening, opened up his tin money box, and discovered he had twenty-five shillings saved.

Through December, January, and February – a bitter London winter of deep snow and endlessly lead-coloured skies – Johann starved himself for the price of a ticket. On Christmas Day 1897 he sat alone in his room and ate thin barley soup. By St Valentine's Day 1898 he had the last threepence he needed, and the following day he went to the White Star office and bought his ticket.

The etching of the Royal Mail steamer sailing happily through calm waters turned out to be a product of artistic licence. On a sloping, heaving Atlantic, Johann huddled under a sodden blanket, listening to the wretched crying of sick children, the coughing of old men, and the ceaseless pounding of the engines that bore them all relentlessly

12

toward their unknown destiny. He felt exhausted and lonely, and he spent night after night in prayer.

With hundreds of other immigrants he was herded through Ellis Island. On his first day in New York, it rained from dawn until nightfall, and he was soaked through. But with time, and miles of painful walking, he found himself a job downtown with Nathaniel's Engineering, a small corporation that made brake systems for locomotives. Old man Nathaniel, an iron-haired German immigrant with half-glasses and a liking for canary-coloured vests, had grown to like Johann, and had told him a few things about business, and particularly engineering business.

'It don't matter how good you are, you may be a genius,' he used to say, lighting up his pungent meerschaum pipe. 'What you have to do in engineering is make people think they can't do without you. Make them think you're indispensable. As soon as they start thinking that, you will be. Also, make yourself a lot of friends. It don't matter if you hate the sight of them. In this country, people give a helping hand to friends before they give a clenched fist to strangers, because this, my lad, is a country full of strangers.'

Johann had kept his mouth shut, and nodded, and learned. In the late afternoon, when old man Nathaniel had gone home, he used to take out the corporation's accounting books and pore over them for hours at a time, until he knew the financial structure of Nathaniel's Engineering like the wallpaper next to his own bed. He learned the price of labour and the price of steel; the price of springs, screws, bolts, and spare parts.

At nine o'clock every evening he went to a night school on the Bowery, learning English from a fat Dutch spinster who wore black flannel dresses and black veiled hats. Over the weekends he took a brown paper bag with bread and sausage and walked around the streets of New York, keeping his eyes and his ears open. He explored the Battery and the ghetto; he pushed his way through the colourful crowds on Grand Street, and he mingled with the Italian festivities in Chatham Square. He also walked uptown and stood outside the magnificent mansions of the American rich. Once, outside 26 Broadway, he saw John D. Rockefeller himself, in his dark, perfectly tailored morning suit, and his heavy whiskers. What gave him the strangest feeling of all was that Rockefeller, so incredibly rich, was just the same size as he was – shorter, in fact.

During the months that he spent in New York, Johann tried as hard as he could to suppress his nostalgia for Holland, although one summer evening he sat in Van Cortlandt Park with tears running down his cheeks. He visited the Dutch graves on Staten Island, too, for no reason but to read their inscriptions under his breath.

He was desperately lonely, but he felt that his loneliness was an essential part of his destiny. Being alone enabled him to work twice as hard, with twice the intensity and the dedication. He made two friends at work – a young Irishman called Danny O'Sullivan and a Jewish boy with a stutter called Ira Greenbaum – and sometimes they went out and ate their lunch together down at the docks. He also went out twice with a plump Italian girl he met at night school. The first time they went to a variety concert on Broadway; the second time she took him home to Washington Street to meet her parents. They fed him with *dolma*, plied him with muscatel, and then congratulated him, to his complete amazement, on his forthcoming marriage to their daughter. He skipped night school for two weeks after that, and when he plucked up the nerve to attend again, she was no longer there.

In the early summer of 1900 he was making $6.35 a week, and old man Nathaniel, one June morning, made a hint about promotion. That weekend he took a long walk up to the mid-Fifties, on Fifth Avenue, and for a whole Saturday afternoon he wandered among expensive carriages with top-hatted coachmen; women in furs and feathers and diamonds; men in starched white shirts and handmade shoes. He sat on one of the stone benches outside the Forty-second Street Library, with pigeons strutting around his ankles, and ate dry biscuits from his pockets. He made up his mind right then that he was going to be rich.

Johann had saved enough at Nathaniel's for two important things. One was a steam-packet ticket to Galveston, Texas. The other was a secondhand dress suit and shirt, which he bought from a pushcart on the East Side. He packed his worn-out brown suitcase and left New York without giving his notice and without saying good-bye to anyone.

Now, on his birthday, he sat in Parsons' Lunch Rooms, in

14

Broughton, Texas, as poor as before but with his ambitions sharply defined. Not only his ambitions, but his techniques, too. As far as he saw it, the barrier between the rich and the poor was obvious. It was not much to do with hard work, and it was nothing at all to do with luck. To be rich, you needed to start off rich. Money could never be made without money. Wealth was created by the shrewd use of money itself; and great wealth could only be created by the use of lesser wealth. Once you had dollars that didn't need to be earmarked for shelter, clothing, and basins of salt beef and dumplings, you had the means to lift yourself out of penury and into plentitude. In finance, you needed money as your tool just as much as a carpenter needs his hammer.

Johann's problem was that he *had* no money. He had eleven dollars that he saved from his months of work in New York, and that was going to have to feed him and keep him for at least a month. But he had made up his mind that, in the absence of real dollars, imaginary dollars would have to do. He would give the appearance of reasonable wealth and hope that the illusion would be enough to attract the real thing. That's why he had gate-crashed the local society party on Saturday, painstakingly dressed in his carefully pressed suit and shirt, and that's why he was doing his best to make the acquaintance of everybody in Broughton who meant anything at all. The Mulliners, he decided, were a good bet.

The man next to him, a greasy-faced railroad worker, was covetously staring at Johann's piece of bread. He was obviously hoping that Johann had had enough to eat and would leave some behind. Johann raised his eyes and saw him. The man didn't look away. He had sunken cheeks and thin, calloused hands.

Slowly and obviously Johann stuffed his bread into his own mouth and chewed it. The railroad worker watched every chew, as if Johann might change his mind halfway through masticating it and let him have a piece. Only when Johann swallowed did the railroad worker drop his eyes and carry on eating his thin red-cabbage soup.

Johann had made himself an unbending rule Dollars could never be made by those who gave away pennies He knew from his reading that if the richest man in America brought everyone in the whole country just one steak dinner each, he would go bankrupt overnight Making money and *using* money was, in the long run, a far more charitable act. Even though the railroad worker stared at him resentfully, Johann knew that the Lord would understand, and was unshakeably on his side.

He left his boardinghouse the next morning in his best suit. The house was a clean but shabby clapboard building on the corner of Lubbock Street, overlooking the stockyards. Broughton, above all, had been founded on the sale and transportation of cattle, although these days it also boasted a light engineering works that made kitchen ranges, and the T. F. Pusey Rifle Company. Johann had already been around to both of these factories, loitering near the gates in his workingmen's clothes, and had formed some opinions about their production, their capacity, and their needs.

He was nervous, and he couldn't help sweating. At Sixth Street he took out his ragged white handkerchief and wiped his hands. Then he turned the corner into Fifth and made his way toward the Broughton National Bank, a solid and respectable-looking orange-brick building on the north side of the street. He pushed through the mahogany swing doors into the musty, marble-floored interior, and walked up to the high counter.

A clerk in spectacles said: 'Yes?'

Johann said brusquely: 'I have an appointment with Mr Greaves. My name is Cornelius.'

'Yes, sir,' said the clerk, and went to tap on the manager's door.

Mr Greaves was a tall, thin, and fidgety man with a habit of putting his glasses on and taking them off every few seconds, and of taking his pocket watch out of his vest and lifting the lid and snapping it shut, and then tucking it away again, and running his hand hurriedly through his thin grey hair, and coughing, and crossing and uncrossing his legs. He ushered Johann into his office, and offered him a seat, and then sat down himself behind his large leather-topped desk.

'Well, Mr Cornelius, I've heard about you,' said Mr Greaves, shifting in his chair.

Johann raised his eyebrows. News obviously travelled very fast in a small town like Broughton. He lowered his eyes modestly and said: 'Good things, I hope, Mr Greaves?'

Mr Greaves smiled. 'Well enough, Mr Cornelius. Well enough.'

Johann smiled back. He knew that he was sitting too rigid in his chair, and that his hands were clenched tight on the brim of his hat. But he also knew that this interview could mean the difference between wealth and poverty. As he said years later to one of his children: 'It was "the crunch". It was one of those moments when you know your whole life is at stake, and there is nothing you can do but fight for your own survival.'

Johann tried to relax. He gripped the brim of his stiff black hat and said quietly: 'I'm an engineer.'

Mr Greaves smiled patiently. 'Yes. I heard you were.'

'I'm thinking of starting up in business in Broughton. I came from New York, where I was a partner in a locomotive brake company, and I heard that Texas was short on engineers, so down I came.'

'I see,' said Mr Greaves in the manner of a man who patently doesn't.

'Texas, I heard, was a boom state. There's cattle, and oil, and a great need for good transportation.'

'That's so,' said Mr Greaves. He crossed his legs, then changed his mind and uncrossed them, and looked at Johann with an odd, impatient look, as if he wished he would finish what it was he had to say, and leave him alone to fidget in peace.

'I ... er ... I believe ...'

Johann couldn't seem to find the words. Mr Greaves twitched and fiddled and fidgeted, and the more he fidgeted, the more difficult Johann found it was to speak. He suddenly realized the enormity of what he was trying to do, and it seemed so impossible and ludicrous that he almost felt like apologizing, saying 'good day,' and walking out backward while the going was good.

'I ... er ... believe there's a healthy need in Broughton for a maintenance works ...'

Mr Greaves raised his eyebrows. 'Maintenance works?'

'Yes ... I mean for engineering ... there's all these machines – locomotives and lathes and steam presses and so forth – and I guess they break down quite often. They need maintenance, which is just where I come in.'

Johann paused. He felt uncertain and embarrassed. He was trying to make a play for more money than he'd ever seen in his whole life before, and he couldn't even find the words to

17

speak a simple sentence. He felt feverish and sweaty, and Mr Greaves's neat little office seemed as airless and claustrophobic as a closed safe.

Mr Greaves opened a silver cigarette box, passed it over, and said: 'Smoke?'

Johann shook his head.

'I . . . er . . . feel that . . . er . . .'

'Yes, Mr Cornelius?' said Mr Greaves, lighting a cigarette himself and puffing smoke. The smell of it made Johann feel sweatier than ever, and he had a strong desire to walk out, leave the bank altogether, and stand in the street to breathe some fresh air. *Get yourself together*, he thought, staring at the brim of his hat. *Get yourself together and tell this man what you want. If you don't succeed now, you never will.*

'I believe that there's a need for such a works in Broughton,' said Johann slowly. 'And because of that, I'd like to get one going. I've spent a few days here now, and I've toured the factories and sounded out some real-estate agents, and I believe the whole thing's feasible. Not only feasible, but potentially profitable.'

He spoke the abstract words he had learned in night school with immaculate care.

Mr Greaves rested back in his chair, smoking. Even when he was relaxed he couldn't stay still, and he passed the cigarette from one hand to the other, and twiddled it around and around, and sucked at it with the habit-ridden disinterest of a caged monkey sucking a grape.

Johann remained rigid, his back straight and his feet neatly together. His polished shoes were side by side, as if they were still in the box.

'Well,' sniffed Mr Greaves. 'How much do you want to borrow?'

Johann licked his lips. It seemed, for one strange moment, as if he might actually get what he wanted. Magically and without fuss. But he reminded himself that lending money was, after all, a bank manager's job. Just because he was asking how much Johann wanted to borrow, that didn't mean he approved of Johann's ideas, or considered that Johann's credentials were adequate.

'About . . . ten thousand dollars.'

'*About* ten thousand dollars? I see. Give or take how much?'

Johann nodded. 'Give or take a nickel.'

18

The bank manager laughed, until his laugh turned to splutters, and his splutters into a hacking cough.

'Excuse me,' he said, wiping his mouth with his big green handkerchief. 'I shouldn't smoke.'

Johann shrugged nervously. 'I've heard it's bad for the heart,' he said. It was all he could think of to say.

Mr Greaves said: *'Everything* about being a bank manager is bad for the heart. My doctor says I ought to spend six months on the Gulf, recuperating. He tells me to give up brandy-sodas and Havana cigars, and run around the goddamned lawn every evening. If I did what my doctor told me, I'd be dead in three days. I take sweet spirits of nitre six times a day, and essence of pepsin four times a day, and I still feel sick as a dog.'

Johann smiled politely. 'Er . . . about this ten thousand dollars . . .'

Mr Greaves crossed his legs again and gave two or three sage and serious nods of the head to show that they were back to business.

'Well,' he said. 'Ten thousand dollars is a great deal of money. I presume you have some kind of prospectus for this maintenance works of yours. Financial profiles, estimates of labour and materiél, employment requirements, that kind of thing.'

Johann reached into his coat pocket. Out of a clean manila envelope he had bought yesterday afternoon, he took the pages of neat financial statistics he had laboriously prepared in New York, many of them based on the workings of Nathaniel's. He passed them across the desk, and for five silent minutes Mr Greaves went through them, a tiny frown creasing the middle of his bony forehead, his fingers twitching the edges of the pages.

Johann relaxed a little and looked around the bank manager's office. There was an elaborately decorated six-hundred-pound Fireking safe in one corner, with a sepia photograph of Mr Greaves's wife on top of it. In another corner stood a tall filing cabinet, with the names of local businesses on neat handwritten labels. Once you had your name in there, thought Johann, you were respectable. You had money. You had started off on your way to wealth. Sitting in front of Mr Greaves as he was now, he felt like a shabby pauper, a penniless immigrant with nothing but the clothes he stood up in. He didn't yet understand the meaning of true wealth, but he knew, without any question, the meaning of poverty. He closed his eyes for a moment, and clenched his hands together, and prayed silently to God for guidance.

There was a rustle of papers. 'Mr Cornelius?' said Mr Greaves. Johann, embarrassed, opened his eyes.

'These financial estimates seem to be excellent,' said Mr Greaves. 'I haven't seen sounder prospectus work for years. Usually they come along with a few numbers scribbled on the back of an old sugar bag and expect me to lend them money on the basis of that.'

He chuckled, and Johann, tense as a cat trying to stalk a bird twice its own size, chuckled with him.

'You say you've been talking to real-estate agents?' asked Mr Greaves.

Johann nodded again. 'There's an empty store down on Fourth Street that looks pretty useful. I went to see it yesterday. They're asking three dollars and nineteen cents a week.'

Mr Greaves sucked at his cigarette. 'Well,' he said, 'I guess you could always beat them down a bit. Fourth Street isn't exactly millionaires' row.'

'No, it isn't. But it's near the railroad yards and it's close to the factories, and that's what counts.'

Mr Greaves nodded. 'Sure. Now, what about *security*?'

This was the crucial moment. Johann felt his heart rising and falling, and there seemed to be so much tight breath in his body he could hardly say anything sensible.

'We're not talking about an *unsecured loan*, I hope,' chuckled Mr Greaves, as if the idea of unsecured loans was the funniest thing since the Yellow Kid.

Johann tried to laugh, too. But then he had to say in a small, dry voice: 'Mr Greaves, I realize I'm asking you to take a great deal on trust, but the fact of the matter is that I am asking for ten thousand dollars without security.'

There was a silence. Mr Greaves stared at him for a moment, and then shook his head.

'Mr Cornelius, I'm *very* sorry—'

Johann said: 'Please. Don't tell me you're sorry. Please just listen to what I've worked out.'

Mr Greaves sighed. 'Well, of course I'll listen. But you know, Mr Cornelius, that we can never lend money without some kind of guarantee that it will ultimately find its way back to us. We take risks, like everyone else; but if I were to give you ten thousand dollars, on your say-so alone, well, then, everybody and anybody would be doing it, and where would I stand then? I'd have an empty bank.'

Johann said: 'Mr Greaves, I am not "anybody".'

Mr Greaves smiled. 'I know you're not in *your* eyes, Mr Cornelius, and I assure you that you're not in mine. But in the eyes of the bank's board of governors, I regret that you are. You don't even have an account here.'

Johann took out his last ten dollars, ten creased one-dollar bills, and dropped them on Mr Greaves's desk. 'If that's your objection, I'll open one now.'

Mr Greaves shook his head. 'That's not the objection, Mr Cornelius. I have heard favourable things about you from several people in this town already. I'm sure you are a man of reasonable substance. But ten thousand dollars . . .'

Johann laid his hand firmly on Mr Greaves's leather-topped desk. 'Mr Greaves,' he said, 'if you lend me ten thousand dollars, you will be doing something you will never, in the whole of your life, regret.'

'With respect, Mr Cornelius, if I lend you ten thousand dollars unsecured, and my governors get to hear of it, I may never even *live* to regret it.'

'I will bring you a note,' said Johann stubbornly.

'What kind of a note?'

'I will bring you a note from all the businessmen in Broughton, all the men who will want to use my maintenance works. Between them, they will guarantee your loan of ten thousand dollars.'

Mr Greaves sat back, twiddling his thumbs together, and thought about that.

'I think you're underestimating the businessmen of Broughton, Mr Cornelius. They're a hard-baked bunch.'

A week later Johann walked down Beaumont Street, head bent, like a man on his way to discuss his mother's funeral. The weather was cooler, and a fresh breeze was blowing from the Gulf, making the palms rustle, and the delicate flowers tremble on their creepers. He was dressed in the same dark suit he had worn to the bank, and the same stiff black derby hat, and his black shoes were very brightly polished.

21

He reached number 15 and stopped. It was a secluded, graceful house, surrounded by trees and white-painted wooden palings, with a wooden colonnade and a shaded veranda. There was a heavy scent of flowers, and from the leafy retreats of the garden a Negro woman was singing 'Ella Speed'. Johann walked up to the gate, looked up the pathway at the imposing entrance, and not for the first time felt a deep pang of hesitation and anxiety.

> Come on, and ta-ake heed,
> Let me tell ya 'bout poor Ella Speed . . .

He clicked open the gate and walked up the path. Out of his breast pocket he took a clean white card, and then he rang at the gleaming brass bell pull. Somewhere inside the house a chime went *binggg-bonggg*. He stood fidgeting on the veranda, tapping his card against his hand, waiting for someone to answer the door. A small tufty bird flittered onto the veranda rail beside him, chirped, and flew off.

The Negro voice sang:

> Ella Speed was downtown, she was havin' her lovin'
>   fun . . .
> Let me tell ya what Bill Morton done . . .

The glossy black door opened up just a crack, and a white-faced parlourmaid stared out.

'Yes?' she asked sharply.

'I've, er . . . I've come to call on Mr and Mrs Mulliner.'

The maid opened the door a fraction more. She was a peaky little girl with a lacy apron and bright red ears.

'Mr Mulliner isn't at home, and Mrs Mulliner is resting.'

Johann coughed. 'Well, I only came to leave this.'

He held out his card. He had had fifty printed, in the hope that they would give his name more authority. They read, in copperplate script: 'Johann Cornelius, Gentleman Engineer.'

The maid took the card and read it, moving her lips as she read. Then she said brusquely: 'Very well, sir. I'll see that Mr Mulliner receives it. Good day, sir.'

Johann said: 'Good day.'

The door closed, and he was left on his own on the veranda. He coughed, and turned around, and made his way back down the path, his head still bent, and a persistent frown on his forehead. He was beginning to acquire the look of a man who, despite years of hopeful struggle, has come at last to realize that time is running out, and that his great and golden opportunity may never arrive. With his two years' work in New York, Johann had bought himself the chance of starting afresh, and of building the foundations of a fortune. But now, with only three dollars and seventy-five cents left, he was sliding inexorably toward that moment when he would be forced back into daily employment, for the basic wants of food, drink and a place to sleep. If it was God's will, though, he would have to bear it.

Johann was not an easy man to understand because he hardly understood himself. He was both shy and stubborn; ambitious and cautious; aggressive and defensive. He believed in his own strength and his own determination, but he was also resigned to the casual and even arbitrary intervention of God in his affairs. He never spared himself any discomfort; and he didn't particularly sympathize with the discomfort of others. But at the same time he was wholly entranced by visions of great wealth, and all the comforts and privileges that great wealth could muster. He didn't even stop to wonder whether he might *enjoy* riding in carriages, or drinking vintage wines, or dining like a gourmet, or not. He had no education in art and music, and very little understanding of history and culture. He knew a good tune when he heard it, and he knew the importance of a clean collar, but that was almost as far as his taste extended itself. When you talked to Johann Cornelius, you felt that inside his mind there was an unbending sense of belief, but after a while you began to ask – *in what?*

He stood on the corner of Beaumont Street, the shady and well-turfed racetrack of Broughton's superior citizens, and tried to decide what to do next. The truth was, he had spent four days making appointments with factory managers and railroad chiefs, and every one had turned him down. It was not that they weren't interested in the idea of a maintenance works. It was simply that investment money was short; and they would rather risk their capital in their own businesses than in his. Thomas F. Pusey, the riflemaker, had stroked his ginger whiskers shaken his head slowly, and said: 'If I had ten thousand dollars to set to chance, I'd just as soon take a ride on a Mississippi steamer, and gamble it all on faro.'

Now, as a final effort, Johann was trying to make the acquaintance of Broughton's high society, in the struggling hope that someone of substance might underwrite his loan.

He was just about to cross the road when he heard a high-pitched voice calling his name. He turned around, and there was the parlourmaid from number 15, and she was running toward him with her heavy skirts held up, waving his little white card.

'Mr Cornelius! Mr Cornelius!'

She reached him, panting and flushed. 'Mr Cornelius,' she said. 'I gave your card to Mrs Mulliner, and Mrs Mulliner asked if you would care to take some morning coffee with her.'

Johann raised his eyebrows. 'Coffee – now?'

'Yes, sir. And she said she'd be terribly disappointed if you couldn't come.'

Johann said slowly: 'Well, then, I guess I mustn't disappoint her. I thought you said she was resting.'

'She was, sir,' said the parlourmaid. 'But when she heard who it was who had called, she changed her mind, and decided to quit resting, and take some coffee.'

'I'm flattered,' said Johann as he walked with the parlour maid back to the house. 'I believe I'm flattered.'

The inside of the Mulliner house was dim, musty, and sumptuously high-Victorian. Dwarfing the hallway was a massive oak sideboard with ornate carving all over its doors and feet, fluting down its front, and brass handles in the shape of seashells. There was an umbrella stand made from an elephant's foot and a rigid-looking chair. On the walls hung a series of gloomy etchings of Canadian forests, and an oil painting of an elk with some anatomical problem to do with its neck. Johann was led by the parlourmaid into the morning room, and requested to wait. Mrs Mulliner was 'fixing herself', and would be down in a trice.

If the hallway was supposed to be impressive, the morning room was the *salle de résistance*. Heavily figured drapes of dark wine-red hung at the windows, and behind these were *point d'esprit* lace curtains, embroidered with baskets of roses, to strain out all but the mellowest of sunlights. Over the mantelshelf was a drape of green velour, decorated with

24

a pond-lily pattern and trimmed with a knotted silk fringe. The shelf was crowded with daguerreotypes, pottery figurines, spider plants, paperweights, chiming clocks, silver candelabra, and souvenir knick-knacks. The five-piece parlour furniture suite – upright settee, armchairs, and rocker – was carved out of gloomy and grotesquely Gothic oak, upholstered in crimson velour, and as uncomfortable to sit on as it was to look at. The walls were papered in a busy brown floral motif, and clustered with etchings, silhouettes, and embroidered samplers. It was clear that Mrs Mulliner, apart from her talents with interior decor, also considered herself accomplished with needles and coloured thread.

Looking about the morning room, Johann found himself knee-deep in occasional tables, aspidistra pots, side tables, parlour stands, and china cabinets – marooned amidst the washed-up flotsam of middle-class Texan taste. There was a cloying fragrance like pot-pourri, and an airlessness that made him perspire.

Johann waited for five minutes, pacing the Brussels rug, before Beatrice Mulliner swished aside the portière and made her entrance.

'Mr *Cornelius*,' she breathed, greeting him like a long-lost friend, and lifting her hand to be kissed. 'How *lovely* of you to call.'

Johann touched his lips to her diamonds and sapphires, and attempted a bow. 'The pleasure is all mine, Mrs Mulliner. I was passing, that's all, and I remembered you and your husband from the Edmundses' party, and how charming you'd been, and wished to pay my respects.'

'*Respects?*' said Beatrice Mulliner, fluttering her eyelashes. 'What a wonderful man you are. Please sit down. I've heard so much about you, and I'm absolutely *agog* to hear more.'

They sat – Johann very upright on the settee, and Beatrice Mulliner, with elegant poise, on a nearby armchair.

'Do you like walnut cake?' said Mrs Mulliner in her provocative, husky voice. 'I just *adore* it. I could eat it until I explode. But I must watch my figure, you know. I mustn't *always* overindulge myself.'

Johann thought Beatrice Mulliner had a remarkable figure. She was a brunette, of medium height, with a thin, well-boned, and almost beautiful face. Her eyes were very large, with long lashes, and they had a feline tilt to them. Her mouth was a little weak, but her long and creamy-white neck, decorated with a seven-strand choker of sparkling jet beads, more than made up for it. She wore a cashmere tea gown of Chinese blue, with a wide lace-trimmed collar that reached to her shoulders, full sleeves and lace-trimmed cuffs. The gown was tied with ribbon at the neck, and a ribbon at the back drew it into her tiny waist. Johann could just see her toes, in grey silk slippers, peeping out from under her hem.

There was a quality about Beatrice Mulliner that, on first sight, attracted and disturbed Johann greatly. She was respectable, well-off, and an honourable lady member of Broughton's middle-class society. Yet she was magnetically and immediately attractive, sensuous and suggestive; the last woman you'd expect to find in a one-and-a-half-horse town in south Texas, married to a whiskery old buffer more than ten years her senior. There was no doubt at all that Beatrice Mulliner was a puzzle; although whether she was the kind of puzzle that a man would be able to solve in a God-fearing manner was another question altogether.

The parlourmaid brought in coffee and walnut cake on rose-decorated plates and set them up on a parlour stand. Mrs Mulliner dismissed her, and insisted on pouring the coffee herself. Johann, who expected a high degree of formality from upper-class society, was mildly concerned about this.

'You have a fine household here, Mrs Mulliner,' he said stiffly.

Beatrice Mulliner smiled, and Johann noticed that she had gaps between her teeth.

'You mustn't call me Mrs Mulliner. That sounds too stuffy for words. Call me Beatrice, or Bea if you like. Some people do call me Bea when they're feeling *affectionate*.'

'Oh,' said Johann, taking a cake plate and resting it on his knee. There was something in Beatrice Mulliner's manner that made him feel extremely awkward and gauche.

'Mind you,' breathed Beatrice, 'in my firmament there is never very much affection. Do you believe, Johann, that people can be starved of love, just as much as they can be starved of walnut cake?'

Johann had his mouth full. When he tried to answer, crumbs dropped on his lap, and he blushed.

'I don't know,' he said, swallowing hard.

Beatrice sighed. 'I believe that love is food, Johann. You

don't mind me calling you Johann, do you? I believe that love is as much like food as beef, and curly kale.'

'I'm sorry,' said Johann. 'I don't understand

Beatrice shook her head. Her upswept hair was pinned and brushed, and shone in the soft sunlight that fell through the decorated lace curtains.

'It doesn't matter. It's one of those things that is of no particular consequence. Liddy, you see, doesn't *enjoy* discussing love, and so I have to do the best that I can.'

'Liddy?'

'Oh – that's my husband. I call him Liddy but his real name is Lidmore. Isn't it strange? Mind you, his parents were Irish, and the Irish are quite capable of anything. Do you know that he sings in his sleep?'

Johann sipped coffee. 'No,' he said. 'I didn't know that.'

'He has a penchant for popular songs.' Beatrice sighed. 'The other night, after a dinner party with the Greaveses, he lay in bed and sang "I'm Old, But I'm Awfully Tough." And, can you believe it, he was deep asleep, and when I told him in the morning, he didn't remember a thing.'

Johann laid down his coffee cup. 'Mrs Mulliner – Beatrice – I can't help wondering if you're teasing me some. Pulling my leg.'

Beatrice smiled. 'A little, perhaps. But it's so nice to have a man's company. I mean a real man. I suppose I get silly, and carried away.'

Johann said: 'I don't know much about ladies' interests myself. I guess I've always had to put other things first.'

Beatrice looked interested. 'Really? What on earth could you put before *that*?'

Johann lowered his eyes. He didn't answer.

Beatrice suddenly leaned forward and touched his hand with hers, and said: 'Janet, my housemaid, said you chased after her down the street. She said you were dressed like a workingman. She was quite disgusted. Especially when you wouldn't give her any money to spread your little rumour.'

Johann looked up. 'She told you about that?'

'Of course she did. Janet's a little bit silly sometimes, and she's always slacking; but she and I get on quite well, considering we're mistress and servant. Janet doesn't even appreciate herself how good she is at keeping me informed. I like to know, you see, what's going on.'

Johann laid his tea plate on the occasional table next to him 'And what did you conclude?' he asked. 'I mean . . . after Janet had told you?'

Beatrice said: 'I didn't conclude anything, except that everything everyone was saying about you was inconclusive, I've been watching you, you know, ever since you gate-crashed the Edmundses' garden party. You're an odd duck, if you don't mind my saying so.'

Johann smiled.

'I think,' went on Beatrice, still touching his hand, 'that you're one of two things.'

'Oh? What?'

'Well,' said Beatrice, 'I think that you're either very rich, and that you've come to Broughton to sweep us off our feet and shake us all up, or else . . .'

Beatrice paused. There was almost a look of regret in her eyes.

'Or else what?' said Johann throatily.

'Or else . . . you're extremely poor,' said Beatrice in a very quiet voice.

There was a long silence. Beatrice looked at Johann, and Johann looked down at the small piece of uneaten walnut cake on his plate. The clocks on the mantelshelf, three of them, began to chime the hour of eleven. At last Johann said: 'Beatrice, your husband is a man of means.'

'Yes. Why? That's about all.'

'All?'

Beatrice twisted a ring on her finger and smiled. 'Poor Liddy – all means and no beans.'

Johann coughed. 'I'd rather not—'

'I know you'd rather not,' interrupted Beatrice. 'Everybody in the whole world would rather not. Liddy is a dear, respected gentleman. He is a pillar of Broughton society, and at Thanksgiving we include him in our prayers. Everybody would rather not say anything about Liddy, because Liddy is a saint.'

'You sound bitter. What do you have to be bitter about?'

Beatrice gave a hard little laugh. 'Material possessions, my dear Johann, are no consolation for emotional impoverishment. Look at this room. It's wonderful, isn't it? Grand luxury, the best that Liddy's money can buy. It has everything, and for your information we are even buying a horseless carriage. What it doesn't have is very much in the way of love.'

Johann said: 'Beatrice, I don't think . . .'

She sighed. 'I know. I'm talking about love again. You must think I'm such a bore. You wanted to talk about money, didn't you? Money is so much more fascinating than love.'

'I was simply trying to see if Liddy – your husband – might be interested in some investment.'

Beatrice said: 'Investment?'

'Yes – that's right. I'm starting an engineering works in Broughton, and I'm looking for investors.'

'Do you want some more coffee?'

'What?'

'Do you want more coffee? There's plenty left.'

Johann held out his cup. 'Thank you, yes. You see, I was wondering if your husband—'

Beatrice shook her head. 'Liddy is not interested in investment. Liddy is not really interested in anything. You can try to persuade him, but you won't get very far. Are you taking Janet to the carnival?'

Johann watched Beatrice closely while she poured his coffee. He was beginning to feel suspicious about her motives in asking him here. She was obviously playing some kind of game with him, but he didn't have enough experience with women to be able to sense the tack of their devious ploys. He stirred his coffee with his tiny silver spoon, and didn't say anything at all.

'Janet said that you promised to take her,' said Beatrice lightly. 'As a kind of reward for spreading your reputation about.'

'Well—' said Johann, but Beatrice interrupted him.

'Why *do* you want your reputation spread about, Johann? Is it that you're trying to make us believe something that's true? Or is it that you're trying to make us believe something that's *not* true? Do tell, I've been dying to know.'

Johann coughed and lowered his head. Once again he felt like an amateur. He knew what he wanted out of his life, and he hoped he knew how to get it. But he had a great deal to learn about business techniques and intricate social man-oeuvres. Beatrice evidently knew where this conversation and this questioning were leading; but Johann didn't have an inkling, and simply stumbled suspiciously along behind her, hoping he would sense the inevitable ambush before it was sprung.

'I'm a businessman,' he told her quite bluntly. 'Every businessman wants his reputation spread around. You know what they say – "early to work, early to rise, stick to your job and advertise." '

Beatrice laughed. Then she gazed at Johann very seriously, with her feline eyes wide open. She knew she looked her best when she made big eyes like that, and Johann felt an errant surge of attraction for her. There was no question that Beatrice Mulliner was a disturbing woman – both to look at and to know.

'Johann,' she said in a throaty voice, 'do you believe in the sanctity of marriage?'

He frowned. 'I don't understand.'

She leaned closer. 'Johann, do you think it's right for married women, sometimes, to entertain admirers?'

'Well . . . I guess it depends.'

'There's no love in my life, Johann. Liddy is a true and honest man, and he cares for me well. In every way except one.'

'Mrs Mulliner, I think this conversation is on dangerous ground.'

She widened her eyes again. 'Dangerous? There's nothing dangerous about me, Johann. Nothing dangerous happens in this house. This house is safe and secure and respectable.'

Johann said nothing. The more he talked to Beatrice, and the more she coaxed and flirted with him, the more unsettled he became. He felt he could quite easily kiss her. He felt he could quite easily do more than that. But she was a temptation that the Lord had, quite deliberately, placed in his path, and he knew that if he succumbed to the urges of his flesh, he would probably be lost forever. Nonetheless, he had to place his saucer discreetly over his lap.

Beatrice stood up and went to the window. The thin sunlight made flower-basket patterns across her cheeks.

'I will be perfectly candid with you, Johann. I am a lonely woman who is craving for affection. I knew when I first saw you that you were a strong and affectionate man. You were drinking champagne at the Edmundses' garden party, and you were standing in the shade of that old tree at the end of the lawns. The tree was strong and so were you. I compared you with that tree, and I think, in a way, that I fell in love with you. You're not a pretty man, are you, Johann?'

Johann almost imperceptibly, shook his head.

'We' said Beatrice, 'I have no time for pretty men. I like men with their masculinity hewn on every feature. That's a lovely word, isn't it – *hewn*? Rough men, ambitious men, powerful men. Men with big hands and strong chests. Men with sturdy thighs. Those are the kind of men I like.'

Johann sipped coffee. 'And what about Liddy?' he asked softly.

'Liddy?' said Beatrice. She came away from the window and rested her hand on the back of her chair, facing Johann with a wry, sad expression. 'Liddy is a wealthy, genteel, well-spoken, well-educated, respectable bag of bones. I married him when I was seventeen. My parents lived in Galveston, you see, and Liddy was there for a lengthy trial. He saw me on the street, found out where I lived, and paid court. My father and mother were delighted, because I was a problem girl, and they always warned me that I would end up in trouble. They had no place in their lives for anyone passionate. They were mean-minded and shallow, and my life with them was nothing but conflict and frustration. I suppose I was just as glad to get away from them as they were to get rid of me. I never loved Liddy. But he was wealthy, and he gave me presents, and he made me feel like a grown-up woman. We were married in three months, and he brought me back here to Broughton. I have been here ever since, the prettiest lady on the Broughton social circuit, as well as one of the wealthiest. I'm young, well-dressed, over-indulged, and miserable. Can you imagine, Johann, how bored and lonely I am here? I have been here for nearly ten years, and nothing has happened. A whole decade, passed by, and nothing to show for it!'

'No children?' asked Johann uncomfortably.

Beatrice closed her eyes. She spoke with them closed, as if reciting a well-known psalm.

'Liddy told me the night we were married that he did not believe in the pleasures of the body, and that he hoped I agreed with him. He said that there was no greater virtue for a woman than to return to heaven as unsullied as when she left it. I have never *known* my husband, Johann. Do you understand that? All the happiness I have ever had has come from admirers. *Lovers*, if you prefer the word the local gossips use.'

Johann knew what was coming next. His chest went tight, and he tried to remain as calm as he possibly could. But this sultry, husky-voiced lady in her Chinese-blue tea gown and her provocative perfume was stirring sensations inside him that he had never felt with such intensity before.

'Beatrice . . .' he said. 'Beatrice, I feel I ought to leave.'

Beatrice smiled. 'You can leave if you like. But I know that you'll be back.'

He stood up, brushing the crumbs from his best pants.

'I believe I know what you're going to suggest,' he said, 'and it cannot be. I must . . . I must thank you for the coffee.'

Beatrice stood in his way, her hands on her hips

'*What* was I going to suggest?' she said huskily

'I can hardly—'

'What? What was it that you're so sure I was going to suggest? You can hardly walk out without explaining yourself.'

Johann turned away. 'Beatrice – Mrs Mulliner – I think things have gotten a little out of hand. It's really better if I . . .'

He heard a rustle of skirts. He turned around again, and stopped in mid-sentence. His heavy mouth hung open like a startled porpoise's.

Beatrice Mulliner, standing by the coffee table, had raised her blue tea gown up to her waist. Underneath, apart from her grey silk slippers, she was wearing nothing at all. Her white legs were slim and shapely, and between her thighs was a dark triangular smudge. That was all Johann saw before he looked away again and covered his eyes with his hand.

'Mrs Mulliner,' he said. 'Please lower your gown.'

She didn't. She came up to him, with her skirts still raised, and stood only inches away. He could smell her perfume, feel the warmth of her body, and he had no idea of what he was going to do.

'Johann,' she whispered. 'Look at me. Do I look like the kind of woman who should lead a life like this?'

He didn't answer. He shut his eyes tight, and prayed earnestly that God would erase the persistent image of Beatrice Mulliner's nudity that kept swimming across his vision.

'Johann,' said Beatrice again, 'I liked you from the moment I very first saw you. I knew you were the kind of man for me. Johann, please say you like me. That's all you have to say.'

'Mrs Mulliner,' he said, *please.*'

There was a moment's silence. Then she dropped her dress and brushed it straight.

'All right,' she said. 'But don't think you've gotten away with it.'

When he was sure that she was decent, he turned around again. 'I don't understand what you mean,' he said heavily. 'Mrs Mulliner, this isn't right. It's all so *unusual.*'

She sat down. It amazed Johann that she could seem so matter-of-fact just after displaying to him the most intimate parts of her body. She poured herself another cup of coffee, and even cut herself a fresh slice of cake.

'Of course it's unusual,' she said, without turning his way. 'The whole trouble with Broughton is that it's so *usual*. Liddy is usual, this house is usual, my life is usual. And so, it seems, are you. Have you ever had a love affair, Johann?'

He shook his head.

'Well, you ought to,' she said. 'If you were a man of any passion, you would have thrown me down on the rug and possessed me. Does that shock you, my saying that?'

Johann nodded. 'Yes, I think it does. I have always tried to be a man of Christian principles.'

She shrugged. 'Well, if it shocks you, then I don't know what I can do to persuade you otherwise. But you must remember, Johann, that happiness is paramount. God did not create us to lead frustrated and worthless lives.'

'Beatrice, your life is not worthless. Think what you mean to Liddy.'

She laughed. 'I know what I mean to Liddy. Liddy is possessive to the point of illness. To Liddy I am the pure lily of the valley, his one and only, his dream wife. Liddy would die without me.'

'Does Liddy know? I mean . . . about your admirers?'

Beatrice shook her head. 'If he even guessed, he would have taken to his sickbed and died of a broken heart.'

Johann was silent for a while. Then he said: 'Beatrice, I consider you a beautiful and remarkable woman. You have shocked me, and upset me, but I don't want you to feel that, because of what's happened today, I think any the worse of you. I know what anguish you must feel, and I only hope that God gives you the strength to overcome it.'

Beatrice didn't answer.

'You are a lovely woman, Beatrice,' said Johann gently.

She looked up at him. There was a kind smile on her face, but it wasn't a smile of trust or belief.

'Many men have told me that, Johann.'

He shrugged. 'Yes, I suppose they have. But I want you to know that I'm not offended, and I hope we can continue our social intercourse.'

'At a distance?'

He nodded. 'I think it's better.'

'Johann,' she said. 'How much money do you need?'

'What do you mean?'

She looked serious. 'We had dinner with the Greaveses the other night. I mentioned you to Mr Greaves, and he told me that you were trying to start an engineering company, a maintenance works, in Broughton. It seemed to me that you had asked him for money.'

'Well?' said Johann.

'Well . . . is it impertinent of me to ask how much you need?'

Johann sat down.

'I think you have fathomed me,' he said. 'I am not a rich man. In fact, I am very poor. The reason I tried to get Janet to spread rumours about me was that I had little hope left of making myself wealthy and respectable. I come from a poor Dutch family, and that is about all. I have no connections, no friends, and no money. I was trying to borrow ten thousand dollars from Mr Greaves to start an engineering business, yes. But so far, I can find nobody to underwrite my loan, and it looks as if I will never get the money.'

Beatrice looked at him thoughtfully.

'I knew you weren't rich,' she said. 'I suppose that was part of your attraction. Other people may not have noticed, but I did. Rich men don't wear seven-cent collars and cuffs, and rich men don't eat cream cake with their fingers. I watched you at the garden party, remember? This,' she said, lifting it up from the parlour stand, 'is a cake fork.'

Johann stared at the broad-tined fork, and felt more deflated by that than almost anything else Beatrice Mulliner had done.

'I see,' he said dully.

'I wish,' said Beatrice Mulliner, 'that you would leave Liddy to me. As far as investments are concerned, anyway. If you're good to me, Johann, I'm sure that I can persuade Liddy to assist you.'

'Good?'

Beatrice smiled wanly. 'That's right, good. Are you still taking Janet to the carnival?'

Johann stood up. 'I think I'd better go,' he said hurriedly 'I think, really, I'd better go.'

Beatrice kept on smiling. 'Remember what I said,' she told him huskily. 'One good turn deserves another.'

Johann called for his hat, and stood silent and rigid while it was brought. Beatrice Mulliner remained in her chair, a slight smile on her lips, while he stood there. He kept trying not to remember that she was stark naked underneath her tea gown.

When his hat was brought, Johann said 'Good day,' and Beatrice Mulliner offered her hand, silently, for a kiss.

Janet, in her frilly white maid's cap, was waiting for him by the front gate. He doffed his hat to her and smiled as much as he could.

'Tomorrow's my afternoon off,' she said brightly. 'And you *did* promise that you'd take me to the carnival.'

He thought about his remaining three dollars and seventy-five cents. Then he smiled and said: 'All right. I'll meet you at the pasture at three. Wear the brightest dress you have. I think we ought to celebrate.'

Janet cocked her head on one side. 'Celebrate what?'

Johann put his hat on again and straightened it. 'Either the beginning,' he said quietly, 'or the very end.'

The offices of Belliveau, Jackson, Strich & Mulliner, on Fifth Street, were imposing and respectable. Their shingle was painted in funereal black, with classic gold lettering, and it hung over a wooden portico and mahogany swing doors with shiny brass doorplates. Johann pushed his way in, and the swing doors swished quietly closed behind him. It was just after lunch, and the whole of Broughton was quiet and sleepy in the hot afternoon sun. A young law clerk in a green eyeshade was dozing behind the reception desk, head nodding

35

over the racing papers, while flies hummed fitfully around the ceiling.

Johann pinged the bell on the clerk's counter. The boy blinked his eyes and raised his eyeshade.

'Sir?'

Johann took off his black hat and wiped his red perspiring forehead with his handkerchief. 'I'd like to see Mr Mulliner, if he's available.'

The clerk stood up and tugged down his fancy vest. 'I think he's still taking luncheon, sir. But you'll find him at Cade's Restaurant, on Sixth, if it's urgent.'

'Thank you,' said Johann. 'I believe it is.'

He walked back out into the glaring midday sunlight. Broughton was always sleepy at this hour, and there was nothing stirring in the street but a slow-moving business wagon and a dog disturbed by flies. Johann turned left at the end of the street, up to Sixth Street, and found the frosted-glass front of Cade's Restaurant about fifty yards along, on the right.

Cade's was one of the respectable restaurants in Broughton. Its front was freshly painted in green and gold, and there were heavy green drapes at the windows. It was a regular meeting-place for lawyers, gentlemen of property, merchants, and cattle owners. When Johann stepped in, most of the tables were taken. Men in flourishing whiskers sat over the green-check tablecloths, finishing their cigars and their coffee, and there was a rich aroma of steak and fried potatoes around.

A bald waiter in a long white apron came up and said: 'You wanted a table? We have a table for one right down the back here.'

Johann shook his head. 'I'm looking for Mr Mulliner. His office said he'd be here.'

The waiter nodded. 'Sure – he's right over there, with Mr Croxton. Can I get you anything?'

Johann shook his head. 'Not just now.' With the money he had in his pocket, he couldn't even afford to sit down in this place. He made his way through the tables, until he reached Mr Mulliner, and he stood beside him and coughed.

Mr Mulliner, a tall and scrawny man with bushy grey whiskers, a long hooked nose, and receding hair, was deeply engaged in conversation with Mr Croxton. Johann looked at

Mr Mulliner, at the hair sprouting out of his ears, at his shrunken body and his piercing, near-together eyes, and wondered how Beatrice could ever have considered marrying him, even for the sake of escaping from her parents. He was forty years old, but he looked ten years older Almost old enough to have been Beatrice's father, or her doddering old uncle. Johann tried hard not to think about Liddy and Beatrice Mulliner together in bed, and almost prayed his relief at Liddy's sexual puritanism. Johann believed in God, and the institution of marriage, but he also believed that marriage should be reserved for those who were physically and emotionally suitable, or no good would come of it. The marriage of Liddy and Beatrice Mulliner was a pertinent example.

'I *told* him,' Mr Mulliner was saying intensely. 'I *told* him that if he attempted to bring an action, I would sue him from Dallas to next Wednesday, and I did. He settled for eight hundred dollars, and left the whole thing open.'

Mr Croxton, a cheerful and overweight Texan with a bootlace tie and a sweat-stained linen jacket, nodded his approval.

'I think you did the correct thing there, Lidmore. I always said he was all mouth and no spunk. Didn't I always say that?'

Johann coughed again, more pointedly. Mr Mulliner heard him and turned around. The whiskered face that Johann saw then was the face of a hard, professional, and relentless lawyer. It didn't do much to ease his discomfiture, or his feelings of uncertainty and nervousness.

'You want something, sir?' said Mulliner. 'Or are you just coughing from the dust?'

Mr Croxton grinned. 'I always take menthol drops myself,' he said humorously. 'Menthol drops and a stiff dose of rye. It don't do my cough no good, but it keeps me happy.'

Johann attempted a smile. 'I didn't mean to interrupt your luncheon, Mr Mulliner, but the truth is that I have something important to discuss with you.'

Mulliner shrugged. 'Well, is it pressing? This luncheon I've been promising to Mr Croxton here for nigh on twelve months.'

'It would only take a couple of minutes,' said Johann. 'But I think you ought to know as soon as possible.'

37

Mulliner frowned. 'Know what? There isn't anything wrong, is there? Nothing wrong at home?'

'Oh, no – it's nothing like that. But I feel it would be best for everyone.'

Mr Croxton said: 'Lidmore, if you want to spend a minute or two in private with this gentleman, I'm willing to occupy the next table for that time.'

Johann said: 'You're very kind, sir.'

Mr Mulliner sighed. 'Okay, then, if it's only a couple of minutes. But you'll have to stop when the jambalaya comes, because I'm good and hungry.'

Mr Croxton moved to the next table, Johann sat in his place. He laced his hands together and tried to look as earnest and serious as possible.

'Well,' said Mr Mulliner. 'Spit it out.'

Johann coughed. 'It's about business, sir. My name's Johann Cornelius, and I'm an engineer. You may remember me from the Edmundses' garden party.'

Mr Mulliner nodded. 'I recall your face. Carry on.'

'I came into Broughton to help out a few of the factories here. I want to set up an engineering maintenance works, because that's my line of business. The kind of work I can do is repairing machinery, testing new equipment, designing special parts. At the moment, Pusey's and Welward's and even the locomotive people have to send all their lathes and stuff away off to Austin, or even Houston. I can do that kind of work right here, and save them all time and money.'

Mr Mulliner sniffed and tugged at his whiskers. 'I see. What's that to do with me?'

Johann bit his lip. 'It's kind of delicate, sir. You see, I dropped by your house this morning to leave my card, in the hope of visiting you sometime and maybe discussing some investment in this works.'

Mr Mulliner said: 'Yes?'

'Well,' said Johann, 'I'm a little short of the total capital I require for starting up, and I was hoping that a few local people might be interested in chipping in. Yourself included.'

Mr Mulliner said: 'I don't quite see what you're driving at.'

'Investment, sir,' explained Johann a little desperately. 'What I'm looking for is people who want to help me start up. People with money.'

A waiter came past with a tin tray, bearing plates of Creole sausage and squab. Johann smelled the savoury waft of food and felt distinctly hungry. All he had eaten all day was a rough breakfast of *flash un kas*, and if he didn't manage to settle his future soon, it looked as though dinner was out of the question.

Mr Mulliner said: '*Money*? How much money?'

'Er . . . ten thousand, just about.'

Mr Mulliner puffed his breath out. 'Ten thousand? That's a *lot* of money. You won't find many people around here with ten thousand in loose dollars, just lying around. Most people have invested their loose money already.'

'The bank has ten thousand,' said Johann.

Mr Mulliner nodded. 'Sure they do. If you're prepared to offer the bank the right kind of security, you can borrow as much as you like.'

'That's the problem.'

'What's the problem?'

'I don't *have* the security, and I'm looking for local people to underwrite me.'

'Is that why you've come to me? You want a note for ten thousand dollars?'

Johann shook his head. 'Not exactly. It's your wife.'

Mr Mulliner squinted his near-together eyes and said: 'My wife? What has my wife got to do with this?'

Johann knew he was blushing. But it was better to try to forestall any sticky difficulties by telling Mr Mulliner the truth than have Beatrice Mulliner ensnare him in her seductive ambush. His throat constricting, he said: 'Your wife . . . invited me in this morning . . . and offered me coffee. I took coffee with her . . . and told her about my schemes.'

'Yes?' said Mr Mulliner, looking sharp and intent.

'Well,' said Johann, 'I think she became a little overenthusiastic. I think she might try to persuade you to invest in my idea.'

Mr Mulliner pursed his lips. 'I see.'

Johann reached for his handkerchief and wiped his perspiring forehead.

'I just want you to know,' he said unsteadily, 'that I did nothing to encourage her interest. In other words, I don't want you to get the wrong idea.'

Mr Mulliner toyed with his knife and fork Then he arranged the cut-glass salt and pepper pots side by side on

39

the green-check tablecloth, and lined up a bottle of sauce between them. All the time, he didn't take his glittering near-together eyes away from Johann's face. Johann sat upright in his chair and tried not to look shifty.

Finally Mr Mulliner said: 'My wife, Mr Cornelius, is a woman who has bursts of enthusiasm.' He made 'bursts of enthusiasm' sound like boils on the neck. 'She takes an idea into her mind, and chatters about it for days at a time, and then as soon as she has thought of it, it disappears. She is young still, and her mind is not constant. She is the same with people. She will take a fancy to someone, and for a while they will occupy the whole of her energies. But, like as not, they will soon be dropped for someone fresh.'

He stroked his whiskers like a man stroking a particularly unpleasant pet cat.

'I want you to understand, Mr Cornelius, that while your concern for my wife's excitement is appreciated, it is unnecessary. I am also afraid that I must let you know that I am not a man who cares to speculate, and that I could not even consider underwriting your loan, no matter how much enthusiasm my wife brings to bear on me.'

Johann swallowed. 'I understand,' he said quietly. 'However, I did think I was doing the right thing by bringing this matter to your attention.'

Mr Mulliner nodded. Johann thought the lawyer had a strangely artificial quality about him, like a stuffed goat in a glass case. The bald waiter arrived with plates of jambalaya and hoecake, and Johann had to get up to leave.

'Despite everything,' said Mr Mulliner as Johann put his hat on again, 'I want you to know that you have my very best wishes for the future.'

Johann said: 'Thank you. I hope I haven't disturbed your luncheon.' Then he made his way through the crowded restaurant, and out into the street, before the fragrant smell of ham and tomatoes and prawns got too much for him.

That night, lying in his narrow iron bed under the sloping ceiling of his boardinghouse room, he heard a locomotive in the yards outside, sneezing and clanking as it waited for its boxcars. Reflections from the railroad lamps stalked and stirred across the wall, and he felt exhausted and empty. There is a dream of wealth in all men, and in Johann

Cornelius its fulfilment was essential to his progress in life Lying there, in his patched and faded blue nightshirt, he mumbled a short prayer to God for guidance and help, and hoped that God wouldn't think him too impertinent.

On the very brink of ruin, though, Johann somehow felt more hopeful about his future success than ever before. Perhaps he needed crisis to stir him into bold and desperate action. He slept for a while, and had a long dream in which he was being given stocks and bonds of immense value, only to discover that they were nothing more than instruction leaflets for patent medicines.

He woke again, and lay there for almost an hour thinking about Beatrice Mulliner. She disturbed him a great deal, and he kept trying to imagine the incongruity of Lidmore and Beatrice side by side in the same bed. They were actually there now, not more than a half a mile away. The stuffed goat and the goddess. Johann closed his eyes, and before he slept again, had a brief and haunting vision of Beatrice's thighs.

The next day was grey and thundery. The dust from the streets was whipped up into stinging clouds, and the horses tethered outside the Main Street stores were restless and bothersome. As Johann strode along the boardwalk past Seventh Street, he was beginning to wonder if he ought to invest a dollar-ten in an umbrella. Everybody else was carrying one, and the surreys and business wagons rattled past with their black hoods up.

He held his hat on his head as he crossed the breezy street past Howard's Refreshment Parlor and headed out towards Kyle's Pasture. The pasture was a small scrubby field on the outskirts of Broughton, surrounded by rustling windswept trees, where Barnet and Shenton's Meadow Carnival, according to the posters, was enjoying its second stupendous week.

When Johann reached the pasture, the carnival was almost deserted. The sideshows were open, but men were tugging tarpaulins over the sawdust rings where the trained dogs danced, and they were blowing out the popcorn lamps and tying down the tent flaps for a storm. A fresh metallic breeze was blowing out of the west, and the sky was the colour of steel.

Johann walked across the tufted grass, looking around for Janet. She had promised to meet him at three, and it was

41

already five past, according to the clock on Broughton's white-painted town hall. There was a greasy aroma of hot franks and onions, which reminded Johann that he hadn't eaten since yesterday morning. A few couples were wandering around the wind-blown stands and sideshows, but the weather was too brisk for crowds.

He looked around the back of the Mississippi Steamboat Ride, and into the boxing tent, where two fat bald pugilists were drinking bottled beer and laughing; he walked the whole length of the sideshows, where gypsy girls sat behind hoop-las and shooting galleries, chattering in high Romanian voices. Eventually he had covered the whole carnival, and there was no sign of Janet at all. Maybe the thundery weather had put her off. Maybe her mistress had forbidden her to go. Johann resigned himself to another tedious afternoon on his own, and started to walk toward the exit.

The flap of a small striped marquee was pushed open, not far away, and a woman stepped out. Johann glanced at her, then stopped in mid-stride and looked again. She was wearing a neat brown velvet-collared coat that reached to her hips, and a long brown skirt with braid patterns around the hem. Over her upswept brunette hair she wore an elegant turban hat decorated with feathers. It was Beatrice Mulliner. She smiled at him and gave him a little wave.

Johann stayed where he was while she approached him. In her walking-out clothes she looked even more attractive than she had yesterday. Her cheeks were flushed with a touch of *rouge de theatre*, but apart from that her face was elegantly white. She walked with a graceful sway of her skirts that showed beyond doubt she was a prime filly from The Racetrack.

'*Johann*,' she said, extending her cream-gloved hand to be kissed. 'What an unusual coincidence.'

Johann lifted his hat. 'Yes,' he said flatly. 'Is Janet coming, or have you come in her stead?'

Beatrice smiled. 'Janet was indisposed, and sends her sincere regrets. I thought it would be most unkind if you were left on your own at the carnival. You must forgive me for keeping you waiting, but I just had to go and have my fortune read. That palmist is really quite a remarkable lady.'

She took Johann's sleeve and they strolled arm in arm towards the roadway. Johann tried to remain as stiff and proper as possible, and held Beatrice Mulliner's arm as if it was a French loaf.

'Do you know what she said?' said Beatrice brightly

'Do I know what who said?'

'The palmist, my dear! The palmist said I was to have a lucky day today, and that all who were dear to me would benefit from my affection.'

'I see.'

Beatrice stopped walking and looked up at Johann with a frown.

'Johann . . . I have the distinct impression that you are displeased.'

Johann coughed. 'Yes, Beatrice, I think I am.'

'Don't you enjoy my company?' she said. 'Isn't it just as good as Janet's?'

Johann nodded. 'Of course.'

'Then what's the matter? Are you worried that it might rain? Have you only one pair of socks? Have your shares fallen?'

Johann lowered his head. 'I have two pairs of socks and no shares,' he said quietly. 'I am concerned that you are trying to use me for your own amusement.'

Beatrice widened those feline eyes of hers. 'Johann! I don't know how you could say such a thing!'

They resumed walking. Johann said: 'I went to see your husband yesterday.'

'Yes, I know.'

'You know?'

'Of course. You don't think that Liddy isn't going to cross-question me about any man of whom I show the slightest enthusiasm, do you? He was quite annoyed, as a matter of fact, and said I had no right to invite a single man in for coffee without a chaperone.'

Johann didn't answer. They reached the edge of Kyle's Pasture and began to walk back toward the town. Behind them, the steam calliope suddenly started up, and the roundabout with its red-and-gold-painted horses began to turn around, with nobody on it except one serious small boy in a sailor suit. His nanny, a dour woman in grey flannel, watched him go around and around with equal seriousness, and Johann, seeing them, wondered why the pleasure of others was always such a grave business. Certainly the pleasure of

Beatrice Mulliner was a serious affair, in every sense of the word.

'You know something,' said Beatrice, lifting her brown skirts out of the dust, 'you are the first man about whom I can truthfully say that your financial situation means nothing to me.'

'Does it usually matter?'

Beatrice laughed. 'Of course it matters, my dear! The poor, besides having no use for toiletries, are not such good lovers as the wealthy. The poor man returns home each night exhausted from his toil, and if he does feel the needs of love, he satisfies them as quickly as possible. The wealthy man, however, likes to take his time, and dally awhile, and that is what makes him a more competent beau.'

Johann said: 'You speak very frankly, Beatrice, for a woman I hardly know.'

Beatrice laughed again. 'Is it necessary to know someone to feel fond of them?'

'I think so,' Johann said. 'Is that rain? We ought to hurry.'

'I knew you were worried about the rain,' said Beatrice.

'I am not worried about the rain. I am worried about what people may think. What did your husband say to you yesterday?'

'He said I was to be more discreet, or people would think I was behaving immodestly. He's a prudish old woman, and you mustn't mind him. And nor must you mind what people think. That's the first lesson in success. You want success, don't you?'

'I suppose so. It depends on the price.'

Beatrice looked up at him. 'Success costs nothing to the successful. You really ought to understand that success is always won from other people's failure.'

They turned the corner into Main Street, and Johann began to feel distinctly nervous in case they were spotted by a friend of Lidmore Mulliner's, or even Lidmore himself. If he was going to have any chance of raising his ten thousand dollars, he couldn't afford the slightest twitching of local eyebrows, or the slightest whisper of gossip. Small towns like Broughton had a way of making life intolerably hostile and uncomfortable for unwelcome strangers. 'Beatrice,' he said, 'I will walk you home to Beaumont Street, and then I believe it will be wiser if we do not see each other alone again.'

'*Johann,*' she said, pretending to be deeply hurt, 'you are being so cruel to me today.' She smiled politely at a passing friend, who made no pretence of her interest in Johann 'Hello, Mrs Westmore!'

'This is very embarrassing,' whispered Johann. 'What if word gets back to your husband?'

Beatrice nodded to another friend. 'Don't worry about Liddy. I know how to handle him, you know, even when he's really mad. You must have more courage, my dear, if you are going to make a fortune. Raise a little hell, my dear, that's my advice.'

Johann said nothing. He didn't know what to say. As they passed Seventh Street arm in arm, he felt as sinful and outrageous as he ever had done in his whole life. He hoped that God would forgive him for this loose behaviour, and he even tried to pray as they walked and talked.

'Johann,' said Beatrice, 'I do believe you're not listening.'

'Of course I am. I'm just . . . concerned.'

'Concerned? Or scared? Do I frighten you? You're not very smooth with ladies, Johann – did you know that?'

'I have no pretensions to smoothness.'

'Johann, you're in such a dither! I *do* scare you, don't I? But do I do more than that? Do I make you feel good, as well? Do I make you feel lionhearted, and bold, and perhaps even savage?'

Johann was sweating. 'I really can't say, Beatrice. I don't think we ought to speak like this.'

'You don't like to talk about your passions, do you, Johann? But you must! I can see your passions boiling inside you! Why don't you let them out? Release them! They want to be free!'

'Beatrice,' said Johann quietly, 'please don't torment me.'

They had reached the corner of Beaumont Street. It was quiet there. The sky was dull, and a few spots of rain were beginning to rattle among the leaves of the trees in the spacious Racetrack yards.

Johann took both her hands and said: 'I must leave you here. It will do no good, otherwise.'

She looked so beautiful standing there, with her dark uptilted eyes, her trim brown coat, and her neat figure, that it was as much as Johann could do to say those words. He was not used to emotional situations, and because of that, his feelings came on him like a storm of grit, unmanageable and

45

unexpected. He had tears in his eyes, for no reason that he could even think of.

'I shall think of you,' said Beatrice, 'as one of those strange possibilities that never happened. Can I tell you something?'

'Of course.'

'You are a man who doesn't even recognize the half of his potential. You are struggling for ten thousand dollars when you should be considering millions. You have the power, but right now you don't have the courage. You have the determination, but you haven't yet discovered what it is you should be determined about. All your energy is being wasted, because you are trying to live by other people's rules. I know what I'm talking about, Johann, because it has happened to me. I'm not the free, wild lady you think I am. I am as much trapped by this town and its narrow-minded people as you are.'

Johann shook his head. 'Beatrice—'

'I know,' she said, a little sadly. 'You have no money and you have to start somewhere. You and I, we have more in common than any of these dull and worthy townsfolk could ever understand. By God, I hate this place. I could raze it to the ground, and I would laugh while I was doing it.'

Johann said: 'I think we'd better say good-bye.'

'Must we?' asked Beatrice. But then she took her hands away and said: 'I know we must.'

She paused for a moment, then stood on tiptoe and kissed his cheek. She smelled of heliotrope, and her cheek was so soft that he remembered what it felt like for days afterwards.

'I will do you a favour,' she said.

'A favour? I don't understand.'

'Like all favours,' she said gently, 'it will have a condition attached. You see, you really need to learn that nobody, ever, does anything for nothing.'

Johann took off his hat. The wind blew his thinning hair up and down like a semaphore signal.

'What is it? The favour?'

She smiled faintly. 'You won't discover that until later. But the condition is that, in return, you never turn me away.'

'What?'

'The condition is that, if I come looking for you, at any time, in any place, you never turn me away.'

Johann stood stock-still and silent. He felt numb, like he

46

felt when the New York dentist gave him chloroform to tug out his aching tooth.

'All right,' he said hoarsely. He didn't understand at all.

Beatrice looked at him with a warm, regretful expression for a moment, and then she turned around and walked off down Beaumont Street. The last that Johann saw of her, she was turning into the gate of number 15. She didn't look around, and didn't wave. It occurred to him that they hadn't even said good-bye.

He stood there for two or three minutes. Then he placed his hat on his head and made his way back to the boardinghouse. That evening he had just enough money left for a plate of pork-and-apple pie down at Parsons'. He ate it very slowly, to make it last, and licked every scrap from his knife and fork

The boy rapped cheerfully on the door of his boardinghouse room and stepped in. Johann was packing his white dress shirt and collars into his battered brown suitcase, and didn't take kindly to being interrupted. When it came to folding clothes, he was clumsy and awkward, and somehow they always emerged from his suitcase looking as if they had been worn as loincloths by a whole tribe of unwashed Kiowa.

'Message for Mr Corny-eely-ass!' said the boy cheekily.

'That's me,' said Johann. The boy handed him a long crisp envelope sealed with red wax.

'Who's it from?'

'Dunno,' said the boy. 'Gave me a quarter for doing it, though.'

Johann looked up. The boy was leaning against the door-jamb, obviously expecting the same financial favour from him.

'I'm sorry. I don't have a nickel. When I leave here, I guess I'll have to go live in a gopher hole.'

The boy wrinkled his nose in disgust. 'Don't ya believe in free enterprise?' he asked with high-pitched insolence

'Sure,' said Johann. 'And that's why I'm not going to pay you for it.'

'Oh, swell,' said the boy, and went off, slamming the door so hard behind him that plaster dust drifted down to the floor.

Johann went to the window, where the light was better, and picked the red seal off the envelope. He opened it up and took out an official-looking letter. It was headed 'Belliveau,

47

Jackson, Strich & Mulliner, Attorneys-at-Law,' but it was penned by hand. The writing was scratchy and intense, and the writer had obviously stopped after every few words to dip his nib into the inkpot.

'Sir,' said the letter. 'It has been brought to my attention that you have been making advances to my wife of a kind considered improper in respectable society. I have had the matter out with her, and it seems you have compounded the offence by encouraging her to fall into an affectionate humour as regards yourself. I consider it essential for my wife's good name, and the name of my business and my family, that you should leave the town of Broughton forthwith. In order to enable you to do so with the minimum of commotion, I have already spoken to Mr Greaves at the Broughton National Bank, and informed him that I am prepared to guarantee your loan of ten thousand dollars, subject to those conditions required by state and federal law. Needless to say, I am only doing this under considerable personal duress, as the lesser of two evils, and my feelings are that you behaved like a roughneck of no character, and an adventurer. My wife wishes me to communicate to you that she has no further feelings of anything except revulsion and regret, and she trusts she will never lay eyes on you again.'

The letter was signed 'Lidmore Mulliner.' It was a fierce, angry signature that must almost have snapped the nib.

Johann read the letter again, and then laid it down carefully on the green-painted wooden dresser. Outside, in the weak sunlight, a locomotive was moving out through the yards with a train of cattle. The pale sun gleamed on the crisscrossing rails, and long after the locomotive had puffed heavily northward, the boxcars clattered and rattled across the points. Fragments of steam and smoke drifted away between the fences and the telegraph posts, and across the untidy sidings and overgrown grass.

Johann stood there for a long time, silent and still. Then he turned back to his dress shirt, and with as much care and skill as he could, he started to fold it. There were wet stains on it where his tears fell, but even as he wept, he promised himself that he would never cry over anything ever again.

1902

THE EXCELSIOR HOTEL
'Where Nobs Stay'

offers

Accommodation of the
PLUSHEST SORT
Clean Beds, Hot Water
Flushing Closets

and

Our Special Steak Breakfast
with Two Eggs
Any Style

The sun had only just risen across the wide, windblown prairie when the motorcar crossed the rutted track that led across the Grant cattle spread and puttered its way westward by the water pump and the Mexican lean-tos in a plume of ochre dust. It was six o'clock on a March morning, and even though the breeze was dry and warm, the man at the wheel of the motorcar was dressed in a long white overcoat, with a knitted scarf and glass goggles, and his hands grasped the upright steering wheel in huge brown leather gauntlets. He had left Edgar, Texas, while it was still dark, and he wanted to be in Amarero in time for breakfast, which meant that he had travelled fifteen miles already in the chill of the false dawn.

His car squeaked and creaked over the ruts, but it was running well. It was a 1901 New Orleans 3½ which he had bought for one hundred dollars from the managing director of a bankrupt British shipping company in Galveston two months ago. He had painstakingly tuned up the single-cylinder 704cc engine; he had refurbished the two brass coaching lamps and the striped paintwork on the hood; he had nourished the buttoned leather seats with saddle polish; and he had rebalanced the elegant spoked wheels with their narrow white thirty-inch tyres. This was his first long trip in it, and even though the leaf springs didn't do much to cushion his backside from the sun-baked Texas tracks, he felt magnificent, like a kind of motorized Nemesis bearing down on the horse-and-buggy world that science would soon sweep away.

As he passed the Grant spread, a herd of rangy-looking cattle, their coats ruffled in the wind, eyed him mournfully. The fut-fut-fut-fut of his engine rose and fell across the prairies, and a coopful of chickens squawked and squittered in fright

Two Mexican workers in faded dungarees, trudging up to the house to hoe Mrs Grant's vegetable patch, dropped

51

abruptly to their knees as this unearthly mechanical apparition appeared around the corner by the paint store and roared past them in a blinding cloud of dust. They remained kneeling for almost five minutes, gaping towards the horizon where the car had disappeared, as if Jesus had just whizzed by on His way to a second coming, and had forgotten to say *buenos dias.*

But in his personal cyclone of sandy-coloured dust, the automobilist himself felt cheerful. He liked to surprise people these days. In fact, he had gotten himself quite a reputation for it. He had surprised the whole township of Edgar, which was a roughish place with a pretty high threshold of surprise, when he had first moved in two years ago from nowhere at all and opened up the best-equipped machine-maintenance shop for hundreds of miles around. He had surprised his chief competitors, the sleepy and disorganized Perrot Oil-Rig Company, by purchasing 40 percent of their stock and 43 percent of their bonds and forcing them to sell out to him. He had surprised his landlady, old Mrs Ottilie Hermann, by buying her rambling wooden boardinghouse from her for fifteen hundred dollars, by having it repainted red and replumbed with flushing toilets, and by letting it out again for five times the rent she used to charge in the old days. And he had surprised everybody even more by going to church not just once on Sundays but three times, and praying deeply and silently in his own pew, and by never drinking whiskey and by never paying court to any of the local girls, even though some of them were very pretty and all of them were extremely frustrated. They said about him in Edgar that he was a man who was destined for something, although they could never decide quite what. It didn't occur to them, of course, that he was dedicated to the making of money by scientific means; that he believed in luck and he believed in chance, but that most of all he believed in method and determination, those two, and that any man with the correct method who applied it with sufficient determination would become rich, as inevitably as any young man who visited Nelly Jones's fun house on Amarillo Street, Edgar, would catch himself a fearful dose of crabs.

Although he had a staff of two trained engineers, Sam Chivers and Jack Beak, and although he had three mechanics and a black man called Winston who oiled the lathes and swept up, he appeared to have no friends at all, and in company he was reticent and standoffish. They invited him everywhere, of course, because he was one of the most prosperous men in town. But at bake-offs and fêtes, at church teas and men's social evenings, he stood large and quiet, as if he had his mind on other things; and if he hadn't been the fastest and most efficient supplier around of drill bits, Corliss valves, dynamos, Neurnst lamps, and Vernier transit compasses, and if he hadn't been able to repair oil-drilling equipment sounder and better than anyone in the whole of the Lone Star State, then they probably would never have invited him anyplace at all.

On this warm March morning, he crossed the prairie under an empty sky, with empty horizons stretching out on every side, and he felt chosen, and alone. And as the hours and the prairie went by, hours of jolting and bouncing and dust and flies, he sang to himself in a deep, croaky voice, which nobody had ever heard him do. He sang 'Where the Sweet Magnolias Bloom.'

While he sang, on the horizon, great castles of cumulus clouds grew, pile upon pile of elaborate white towers, and terraces, and boiling bridges. His eyes were sore from the dust, and his arms ached from clutching the automobile's steering wheel for so long, but he felt an inspirational strength, and he sang louder.

It took four hours of bumping and squeaking through the dust and the heat before Amarero appeared in the distance – a shabby clutter of wooden houses, stores and hotels, surrounded on all sides by oil rigs. The rigs from several miles away looked like the masts of a strange fleet of ships which had anchored mysteriously on the prairie. Oily black smoke smudged across the sky, and Johann, stopping his automobile on a low and eroded ridge, knew that he was back in wildcat country.

He took out his handkerchief and dabbed his grimy face. Johann had been fascinated by the oil operations in Amarero ever since he had first visited the town last year, trundling an overhauled rotary power force pump on the back of his horse-drawn business wagon. It was a hard-bitten town, populated by oilmen, whores, and shopkeepers, apart from a doctor who drank and a priest who appeared to be under the impression that he was Saint Sebastian. Up until the fall of 1901, Amarero had been nothing but a railhead for West Texas cattle, and the woodburning locomotives used to come up from Broughton and the Gulf only four or five times a year. There used to be little more than an auction room, a boardinghouse, a diner that offered pork and beans or sausage and beans only (home fries extra), and a railroad yard that didn't amount to more than a few rickety cattle enclosures and a rusted set of buffers. Then a middle-aged wildcat prospector named Kyle Lennox arrived in town – a man with great black droopy whiskers, brocade vests, and an unpleasant reputation for brawling and taking his teeth out during poker games. He had drilled in the area for four or five months, as well as drinking himself insensible every night and having an intermittent and very noisy affair with the widow of the auctioneer before last, who lived in a peeling house on her own at the northwest end of Main Street, which was the only street there was. One morning in October, miraculously, Kyle Lennox's drill bits released the Amarero Number One well, a moderate-sized gusher that eventually pumped out thirty-five thousand barrels a day The only problem was that the land on which Lennox was drilling belonged to the widow, and to safeguard his interests he had to run up Main Street in the heat of the eleven o'clock sun, burst into her house, and fall on his knees on her Berlinwork rug in his oily dungerees to propose marriage. She clucked at him for making the rug dirty, but when he promised her ten thousand rugs, she said yes.

Kyle Lennox and the woman he still called 'the widow' had sold out Amarero Number One to a young businessman from Houston called Jimmy Makepiece, who together with an investment group from New York had promptly founded Amarero Oil. As a bonus, Lennox was guaranteed dividends and lump sums, and appointed president of the company, which didn't give him much influence but conveniently meant that he had to stay in Amarero, well out of Makepiece's way. From his low vantage point on the ridge, Johann could already see Lennox's three-storey Gothic house, set a quarter-mile out of town to the north, with its gilded dragonscale roof gleaming in the morning sun.

The discovery of oil had transformed Amarero overnight. Johann arrived on Main Street with his New Orleans automobile fut-futting and his goggles thick with dust. He pulled up opposite the Excelsior, applied his brake, and shut off the engine. There was a hot, swallowing silence, interrupted only by the click of his car as it cooled down, and the wind swinging the sign saying 'Excelsior Hotel – Good Eats & Clean Beds.' He took off his gauntlets and his goggles and unbuttoned his motoring coat.

An old fellow with a white walrus moustache and dusty breeches came walking up the boardwalk next to him, and stopped. He was smoking an eagle's-claw pipe, and he wore a weather-faded derby hat. He said: 'How do,' without taking his pipe out from between his teeth.

'How do you do,' replied Johann, smiling briefly in acknowledgment. He was looking tanned and healthy these days, although his cheeks were blotchy from the sun, and his thin blond hair, under a panama hat with a green puggaree, was stuck down with lavender pomade. Beneath his motoring coat he was wearing a light linen suit, with a green bow tie and a fresh percale shirt.

The old man inspected Johann's car. Then he said: 'Happen you're looking for John Kummer.'

Johann lifted his mock-alligator briefcase out of the back seat of the car. He didn't answer.

The old man said: 'You ain't the first, of course. There's been creditors galore. Grocer's men for the chuck he ate; haberdasher's men for the overalls he wore; dry-goods men for the dry goods; and hardware men for the nails and God alone knows what else. Why, he's even run hisself a slate up over yonder.'

Johann turned and looked at the Excelsior Hotel, a wooden monstrosity painted green and gold. On the first-floor balcony, shaded from the morning sun by a parasol, was a young prostitute with red wavy hair and a black basque which forced her breasts into a low and provocative line. She waved her fingers at Johann, and he turned away.

'Do you know where to find him?' asked Johann.

The old man coughed. 'I can tell you something,' he said 'I once scouted for Robert E. Lee.'

Johann stepped into the cooler shadow of the boardwalk. 'You and every other old storyteller this side of the Brazos. Is he out at the oil camp, do you know, or has he come into town?'

55

The old man took off his derby hat and knocked it back into shape.

'Could do with a fill,' he said uncommunicatively.

Johann said: 'I'll give you a nickel for a fill if you tell me where he is; but you tell me first.'

The old man thought about that. He wasn't in any particular hurry.

Kummer was one of many wildcatters who hadn't struck it rich out at Amarero, and he owed Johann $732.08 for maintenance work, gasoline engines, and spares. This trip was a debt-collecting trip, and Johann intended to get his money.

'Well,' said the old man at last, 'how about a fill and a slug?'

'A fill,' said Johann. 'And not until you tell me.'

The old man shrugged. Then he said: 'It sure wasn't like this in the old days, you know, when folks recalled the war. There was a time when you only had to say to someone that you'd seen Robert E. Lee hisself, and more than that I once touched his coattails, which I did. I touched his coattails and said "God bless you, general," and he looked down with that gentle bearded face of his, this was in Pennsylvania, and do you know what he said to me?'

'No,' said Johann wearily, 'I don't.'

'Lee said to me, "Take your goddamned filthy fingers off of my coat," and that was all. And that's why I ain't been too partial to great heroes ever since, because they never go around making great and gentle speeches like they're supposed to.'

Johann leaned forward and laid his hand on the old man's shoulder.

'Supposing you just tell me where John Kummer is, huh?'

The old man nodded. 'You could try the oil camp.'

'And what if he isn't there, like I suspect he's not?'

'Then you could try the church. Maybe he's praying to God to make it rain money.'

Johann shook his head.

The old man sighed. 'You could, if you had a mind to, try Room 26 at the Excelsior Hotel, where you might find a man who's almost packed and ready to leave town with his sweetheart, who's a reformed whore of sorts, name of Dolly Jarvis, from Abilene originally.'

56

Johann gave the old man's shoulder an affectionate pat. Then he reached in his vest pocket and produced a nickel, which he pressed into the creases of the old man's leathery hand. He then straightened his tie, picked up his briefcase, and walked across the hot morning street to the entrance of the Excelsior Hotel.

Next door, the front of the firehouse was open, and the fire chief, in shirtsleeves and suspenders, was polishing the steam-pumper. He was sweating so profusely that his withered crimson face looked as if it were jewelled with rhinestones. It was hot in the firehouse because the pumper had to be connected at all times to the basement boiler, and it was only when it was called out to a fire that the chief would toss an incendiary rocket into the pumper's own furnace to set it alight.

Johann paused for a moment to watch the fire chief at work. There was a hot smell of horses, brass polish, steam, and incandescent coal that made the firehouse seem like the waiting room to hell. After a while the fire chief came over to the door, wiping his hands on a rag.

'Howdy,' he said, admiring his handiwork and hardly glancing at Johann.

Johann nodded. 'How do you do. Looks like hot work.'

'You bet.'

Johann walked around the gleaming pumper respectfully. In every handle and bracket and pipe he could see his own face, brass-coloured and distorted, and he could even see a ghostly red image of himself in the shining scarlet paintwork. The chief continued to wipe his hands.

Johann said: 'You keep this thing polished all by yourself?'

'Sure do.'

'Seems like an awful lot of unproductive time. I mean, if they made pumpers with less brass and more steel, you wouldn't have to furbish them up so much, would you? There's your helmet, too. That doesn't have to be brass. Up in New York they have black leather.'

The fire chief rested his hands on his hips and stared at Johann with the expression of a man who's just taken a mouthful of cold coffee and doesn't quite know in which direction to spit it.

'Mister,' he said, 'a fire pumper without brass just ain't what a fire pumper *is*. Anyhow, using up time, that's what

57

it's all *there* for. It's there to keep me busy, in between fires. A fireman's life ain't all chasing after burning chimney stacks and spraying water around the shop. No, sir! As they said to me back in the old days – a fireman's duty is to keep a good firehouse, and that's what counts.'

Johann almost felt embarrassed at being so crassly ignorant of firehouse ethics. He said: 'I'm sorry. I'm not an expert you know. I don't know much about fires.'

The fire chief hung up his rag. He was scrawny and potbellied, like a tough old turkey. 'Well, friend,' he said, 'you'd learn yourself a great deal about fires if you stuck around here.'

'Why's that?'

'Huh! Firetraps, these houses are. It only takes some drunken foreman from out at the camp to snooze off to sleep with his pipe going, and you've got yourself roast family before you can spit in the wind.'

'Sounds dangerous.'

'It sure is, and that's what I'm here for. Aside from the polishing, of course.'

Johann stepped out into the street again and squinted up at the Excelsior. 'That place must be a worry to you,' he said.

The fire chief was blowing his nose. 'What place?' he asked.

'The Excelsior, next door.'

'Oh, that! That's the devil's own playground, that place is. We've had three fires there this year already, and one of 'em real serious. A fellow from Amarero Two was up there with a lady, and they was tussling around or something of the kind, her foot kicked the oil lamp by the bedside and spilled oil over his back, and set him alight like a torch! That whole room smelled like pork cutlets for days.'

Johann wiped the sweat from his forehead with the back of his hand. 'If I was *in* that hotel,' he said, 'and I wanted to get *out* of there quick, because of a fire or suchlike, where would I go?'

The fire chief came out into the street too. He pointed with his polish-whitened fingers up to the second-floor balcony.

'That's easy,' he said. 'That balcony runs around the back of the building, and round the back there's an iron fire escape, bought from the old Magnificent Hotel at Dallas when they pulled it down, or it fell down, I don't recall which.'

Johann nodded. 'Thank you,' he said. 'And I wish you well with your fires.'

'Won't you come in for a shot?' asked the fire chief. 'Or there's some ginger wine if you're a temperance man.'

'Thank you, no,' said Johann gently. 'I have some business to attend to.'

He left the firehouse and walked around to the front of the Excelsior Hotel. The front doors of mahogany and patterned glass were hooked ajar to create a draught, and in the gloomy lobby Johann could see potted aspidistras, plush red sofas, and two or three well-dressed men standing around talking and smoking cigars. At the long marble-topped desk, which ran along the length of the right-hand wall, a desk clerk in a grey uniform braided with fraying gold cord was picking his nose. Johann stepped in, and walked with measured footsteps across the black-and-white-tiled floor. The desk clerk, a greasy-faced man with a brilliantined moustache, didn't even look in his direction. Johann pinged the bell.

'When you've finished prospecting for oil up that nose of yours, perhaps I can have some service,' he said loudly.

The desk clerk turned, eyed him up and down, and said: 'Okay, mister. Don't get yourself all riled up. What's it to be?'

'What's on offer?'

The desk clerk shrugged. 'Well, that depends if you're staying or if you're just passing through, and it depends on whether you want breakfast with bacon and cream in your coffee, and it depends on how long it's been since you last got your leg over a lady. Where did you come from?'

'Edgar.'

'And how did you come?'

'By automobile.'

'Well, in that case, I guess you won't be as keyed up for a woman as some of them that have come all the way from Abilene by horse.'

Johann rested his elbow on the counter and beckoned the desk clerk nearer. Then, when the man was close enough, he said: 'A dollar bill says I'm looking for John Kummer.'

The desk clerk stared at him without answering for almost

half a minute. Then he said: 'Five dollars has already said he ain't in.'

Johann thought for a while, then stood up straight and nodded. 'That's all right. Just make sure he knows that Johann Cornelius called and that Johann Cornelius won't be put off his debt for any longer.'

'You ain't raising the ante?'

'Why should I? I'll catch him, sooner or later. That's what I came here for.'

The desk clerk looked at Johann's muscular shoulders and thick-lipped, determined face and said: 'Yes, I guess you will.' Then he said, more cheerfully: 'I don't suppose I can interest you in our latest acquisition?'

'What's that?'

The desk clerk made a clumsy circle out of finger and thumb and kissed the air. 'It's a peach, if you must know. A quadroon girl from Piedras Negras. Twelve years old and willing to learn anything you want to teach her. A clean slate, so to speak.'

Johann looked at the man but said nothing. A tiny nerve pulled at the underside of his left eye, but otherwise he remained motionless.

'There she is now,' said the desk clerk, leaning across the marble counter and pointing toward the far end of the lobby. Johann turned.

She was sitting in the faded light that fell through the frosted glass window onto the plush settees. The 'Ex' of 'Excelsior,' a shadow from the hotel's name on the grimy pane, was patterned across her soft dusky cheek. There was another girl down there – a bleached blonde with dark roots and mottled acne scars on her cheeks – but the quadroon girl sat by herself, staring at the tiled floor as if she were waiting patiently for a train that was already four hours late. She was exceptionally pretty, with long dark eyelashes and curved pouting lips, and she was dressed in an incongruously quiet and elegant lace-waist dress of coppery brown Japanese silk, with elbow sleeves and collar trimmed with Valenciennes lace. Her black hair was brushed upwards and tied with brown ribbons, leaving one or two stray curls around her ears. She did not look up when Johann first turned around, but after she became aware that he was staring at her, she lifted a small white Marcelaine silk fan and gazed at him bashfully over the top of it.

Johann turned back to the desk clerk.

'That girl there? She's a . . . ?'

The desk clerk smoothed his moustache. 'Most certainly is. Twelve years old and very clean. Ready for anything, if you want to know.'

Johann felt an extraordinary sensation in his stomach that he had never felt before. He also found he was short of breath. He looked again at the girl, fascinated and horrified at the same time. She was so pretty, and so young, and so unspoiled, that it seemed electrifyingly disturbing to him that she should be a whore, and that she should be available to whatever stinking greasy middle-aged oilman wanted to put her price down on the desk clerk's counter. How could she allow herself to do it? She looked so delicate and respectable, she should have been sewing in a milliner's or still learning her lessons at school. Did she enjoy it, or was it the only way she knew how to make money? She was so poised, as if she came from a good family, and that was what made it even worse.

'Well?' said the clerk, drumming his fingers idly on the open register. 'What's it to be? Two dollars fifty the half hour, eight dollars all night.'

Johann said huskily: 'I didn't come here for that. I came here for John Kummer. Just tell him I'm here in town, and if he wants me I'll be waiting outside in my automobile.'

'Automobile, huh?' said the clerk. 'Pretty fancy! Wish I was in the debt-collecting business.'

Johann ignored his gibing, and turned around to leave the hotel lobby and return to the street. But when he reached the doors, he couldn't resist one last look back at the quadroon girl, who was still sitting there meek and pretty in the slanting light of the sun. She saw him looking, and this time she didn't hide her face behind her fan, but returned his gaze boldly.

He stepped out onto the boardwalk and took a deep breath. Then he straightened his panama hat and walked slowly around the side of the hotel to the alley where the kitchens were, and where the hotel laundry was dripping on long washing lines to dry in the noon sun. The kitchen door was open, and Johann could hear the clattering of pans on the

61

range, and when he passed he saw a black kitchen-hand turning the handle of a bread mixer and singing 'Tenting on the Old Camp Ground.'

He checked his pocket watch. It was getting on for ten o'clock. When he had found John Kummer, he was going to get himself some late breakfast, and with any luck John Kummer would be picking up the check. He squinted up at the shabby back of the Excelsior Hotel, and he could see where the ornate fire escape ran down from the second floor into the backyard.

Kummer was even more predictable than Johann could have hoped for. It was at moments like this that Johann knew, without question, that he had that radiantly simple view of life that makes millionaires what they are. While ordinary mortals sweated and struggled to enmesh themselves in more and more complications, Johann Cornelius refused to perceive any problem as complicated, and he dealt with everything in a straightforward way that was sometimes crude but always brought the hogs home with their noses clipped and their ears marked. He knew that subtlety was something that only those who were content to remain poor could possibly afford. That was why he was standing at the back of the hotel, perspiring slightly in the prairie sun, as John Kummer came hurrying around the second-floor balcony in a cheap check summer suit and a haircloth hat, carrying a bulging carpetbag. Just behind him, with flouncing red skirts and all her possessions stuffed into a worn velvet bag, came a big-nosed girl with reddish hair all awry, and Johann gathered this to be the whore of sorts, Dolly Jarvis.

John Kummer came clanging down the iron fire escape, and Dolly Jarvis came clanging down after him. They pushed their way through the lines of wet bedsheets hanging on the washing lines, and reached the alley hand-in-hand, looking back up at the hotel as they went, for fear that Johann Cornelius had already discovered their room was empty and that they had taken to their heels.

Johann was standing there with his hands in his pants pockets, and John Kummer almost bumped into him. Johann said: 'Hallo, John! Nice of you to come down so prompt.'

Kummer was a bulging-eyed man with a sad moustache and enormous ears. He was so startled when he saw Johann

62

that he froze in a pose of complete shock, like someone playing statues at a birthday party, and Dolly Jarvis stared at both him and Johann in complete bewilderment.

'I was thinking of taking some breakfast,' said Johann calmly. 'I drove over from Edgar this morning in the New Orleans, and I haven't had a bite since last night's supper. Won't you join me?'

Kummer licked his lips. He had a marked Minnesota accent when he spoke, which didn't improve his general desirability, and made him seem even shiftier and cheaper than he really was.

'That's real nice of you, Mr Cornelius. But the fact is, the train's in from Broughton before too long, and I really have to catch it.'

Johann took out his watch again. 'I don't want to detain you,' he said, 'but the Broughton train isn't due until three this afternoon, and I usually reckon that five hours is enough for breakfast, don't you?'

'John,' put in Dolly Jarvis, 'is this that Cornelius man? Is this him? Tell him to get lost!'

John Kummer patted her arm and gave her an uneasy little smirk. 'It's okay, Dolly. Mr Cornelius here is a very understanding man.'

Johann smiled at Dolly and nodded. 'I'm known for my understanding,' he told her.

'In that case,' she said, 'why are you keeping us here? We want to catch that train, and we've got a lot to do beforehand, so unless you've got anything important to say, I suggest you get out of the way and let us get on with it.'

Johann adjusted his panama hat. 'John,' he said quietly, 'I can't let you go without the money.'

John Kummer said: 'Money?'

'The seven hundred and thirty-two dollars and eight cents. The money you owe me for rig maintenance and two four-stroke gasoline engines and everything you put into that dud oil well of yours and never paid me for.'

John Kummer smiled and then abruptly stopped smiling.

'I'd appreciate settlement before you get on the train,' said Johann. 'Broughton's a long way off, and Mexico's even longer.'

Dolly Jarvis said shrilly: 'What do you know about Mexico? Who said we were going there?'

'Ma'am,' replied Johann, raising his hat, 'it's the natural place for anyone to go that owes seven hundred and thirty-two dollars and eight cents, and doesn't have the necessary capital to pay for it.'

John Kummer suddenly said: 'All right, Cornelius. That's enough. Out of our way.'

'Not without the money, John,' warned Johann.

'With or without. I'll pay you next month. Just get out of the way, that's all.'

There was always a kind of code to arguments like these, but Johann didn't obey it. Instead of waiting for John Kummer to provoke him any further, he took one step forward and punched him, as hard as he could, in the mouth. He felt Kummer's teeth on his knuckles, and then Kummer fell over backwards into the dust and lay there like a checkered log. Dolly Jarvis lifted her hands in surprise and shock, but all she could manage to say was a squeaky little 'Oh! You've killed him!'

Johann inspected his knuckle, which was bleeding. 'Oh, no,' he told her, 'I haven't done that.'

John Kummer sat up. He didn't look at all well, and he spat three teeth, in strings of blood, onto the dusty alleyway. Oh, fuck,' he moaned.

Johann hunkered down beside him, and spoke in very soft, insistent tones. 'John,' he said, 'I've invited you to breakfast and I recommend that you come. If you don't have the money to pay me, then I think we're going to have to work out a deal between us that satisfies everyone, especially me. You could use some ice water on that mouth, anyway.'

'Oh, my God,' said Dolly Jarvis. 'Oh, my God, you're so *brutal*. Do you hear that? You're a brute!'

Johann turned around and looked at her. 'I may be a brute, ma'am, but you're a harlot, and speaking for myself, I'd rather make my money through honest brutality than spurious love.'

'John!' shrieked Dolly Jarvis, pointing a grubby white glove at Johann. 'Hit him!'

John Kummer wiped his mouth and climbed painfully to his feet.

'Hit him!' snapped Dolly. 'Go on!'

John Kummer shook his head 'Come on, Dolly, let's just be sensible, huh? If I try to hit him he's going to knock my head off, and for that pleasure I wouldn't exactly walk a mile.'

'What are you?' said Dolly. 'Some kind of a coward?'

Johann said: 'I think he has a right to be, Miss Jarvis. I intend to get my money out of him even if I have to boil him down and sell him for laundry soap. I also have an Iver Johnson revolver in my automobile, and I will shoot him if necessary. A man's property and money may not mean much in Minnesota, but it's the law down here in Texas, and whatever people here may think of me, they've accepted me as a Texan.'

'You're big enough and dumb enough,' said Dolly sarcastically.

Without much further argument, they walked across the street to the Amarero Lunch Parlor. It was only two or three buildings away from where Johann had left his automobile, which was not being solemnly inspected by half a dozen scruffy small boys and a man in a plaid shirt and black Texas Ranger pants who looked like the Amarero idiot.

The lunch parlour was quiet at this time of day. It was a small white-painted place that used to be a hay-and-feed store, with white-painted wooden tables and bentwood chairs. There was a high counter with a glass case of pastries and crackers at one end, and an elaborate stack of cans of Doris Brand molasses at the other. As they sat down, a big woman with forearms like Kentucky hams came out from behind the counter and set down three glasses of ice water. In one corner of the parlour, a thin man in a derby hat sucked his coffee out of his saucer.

John Kummer was distinctly not hungry, although Dolly Jarvis ordered corned-beef hash and beans because she knew from experience that if you didn't eat free meals when they were offered you might end up paying for the next one. Johann asked for pancakes, bacon, Virginia links, fried eggs, hash, syrup, and cream. His taste in food was as straightforward and unpretentious as his business technique, but that didn't prevent him from eating a great deal of it.

Kummer was looking pale and bruised, particularly in the pallid light of the lunch parlour, which was filtered by cream paint that came halfway up the windows. He sipped his ice water and winced and Dolly Jarvis sighed and crossed her legs and turned away as if to say that at least he could have

65

been a man and taken *one* swing at Johann Cornelius, even if it had missed.

While they waited for the food, Johann lifted his alligator briefcase onto the table and opened it.

'John,' he said seriously, 'I've got a proposition to make to you. You can take it or leave it, but if you leave it, I'll have to warn you that you'll go straight down to the sheriff's office and I'll have you thrown in jail for taking money by fraud.'

John Kummer gave a seasick smile.

'I'm glad you're giving me the option,' he said weakly, and Dolly Jarvis sighed dramatically and clucked and flounced even more.

'You have a hundred and six acres of land out there at Sweetwater Trail,' said Johann. 'You're entitled to it, all correct and legal, although I did hear that it was Indian land once, and that you didn't exactly pay them a whole mint for it.'

John Kummer shook his head. 'I paid two dollars an acre, fair and square. They took it, and if they took it, that's their problem, not mine.'

Johann shrugged. 'Your love of your fellow man really doesn't interest me. What I am interested in is how you're going to pay me back. I suggest that it might be fair and square if you *gave* me those hundred and six acres. I work that out at six dollars and ninety cents an acre, exclusive of rigs and engines and other equipment which I'm repossessing anyway, and when you look at it that way, you realize that you've actually made a profit of four dollars and ninety cents an acre, which is five hundred and nineteen dollars and forty cents.'

John Kummer put down his glass of ice water. He appeared to be a little confused.

'You're telling me that I've actually made a *profit* of five hundred and nineteen dollars?'

'That's correct.'

'So how come I wind up with no land, no machinery, and no cash? If I made five hundred and nineteen dollars, where is it? Huh? I don't have any five hundred and nineteen dollars.'

'And forty cents,' added Johann.

Dolly Jarvis protested vociferously at this. 'What kind of

adding up is that?' she said harshly. 'You're a first-quality, out-and-out stickup artist, and that's the whole truth of the matter in one word!'

Johann didn't even look at her. As the big woman with the muscular forearms brought their plates of food, with soda bread and fresh tomato salad, he picked up his knife and fork and said to John Kummer in a level and utterly calm voice: 'There's your choice, John. Give me the land and get yourself out of Amarero a free man, or else it's down to the lock-up as soon as breakfast's over.'

John Kummer looked miserable. He said: 'What about my other creditors? What are they going to say? I might be paying *you* off, Mr Cornelius, but I owe for the food and the clothes and the tools I used, and a whole lot more besides.'

Johann crammed his mouth with pancake and sausages. 'That's all right,' he said. 'No need to worry about that. You just go around to the people you owe, and tell them to come to me, and I'll pay them off in full.'

Dolly Jarvis, who was forking up corned-beef hash as voraciously as if she expected to find a diamond necklace underneath it, stopped eating for a moment and regarded Johann suspiciously.

'You'll pay off all his debts?'

'That's what I said.'

'How much are your debts, John?'

'Oh, I don't know. Four, five hundred bucks.'

Dolly Jarvis wiped her mouth with her hand, and stared at Johann hard. Johann simply smiled at her affably, like a man on a pleasant Sunday-afternoon trolley ride smiling at his fellow passengers.

'Oh, you're a rat and a half,' she said softly.

Johann kept on smiling.

'You're the sneakiest low-down dirty rat that ever took breath,' she continued.

John Kummer frowned at her and said: 'Come on, now, Dolly. Mr Cornelius has made an offer that's going to get us out of trouble. Don't let's strain the *entente cordiale* around here. Please?'

Dolly pushed away her half-eaten plate of corned beef.

'Are you so dumb, John Kummer, that you don't realize what game this man is playing?' she said scathingly. 'Don't

67

you understand what he's doing, and don't you understand what a mistake you're making?'

John Kummer scratched his head. Dolly gave an exasperated cluck, and then turned back to Johann. 'You know something that John doesn't know, don't you, Mr Cornelius?' she said. 'You know that there's oil out there at Sweetwater Trail, and just because John ain't found it yet, that doesn't mean to say it ain't there. The minute we step on that train for Broughton, you're going to be out there with your pick and your shovel, and you're going to make yourself so much money that four or five hundred dollars won't seem like nothing more worthwhile than a red cent.'

Johann neatly mopped up the egg yolk from the side of his plate. 'You should have been a businesswoman, Miss Jarvis,' he said warmly.

'You forget,' said Dolly Jarvis, 'I am.'

John Kummer didn't like that. 'You mean you *were*,' he told her. 'You said you were giving it up.'

Dolly turned and snapped: 'How can I give it up when I'm hanging around with a penniless no-good booby like you? This is the first time in your whole life you ever made a profit, and besides the fact that you've spent it already, you have to give away a gusher to get it! You dumb bastard!'

Johann finished his meal and called for some fresh coffee.

'You can shout and scream all you want, Miss Jarvis,' he said blandly, 'but even if you kept that land for yourselves, you'd never find that oil in a million years, even if you knew where to look. You don't think I'm that simple, do you, that I'd give you the slightest inkling of what I was doing if I thought you'd be able to prospect it for yourselves? I like things plain and honest and out in the open, and what I'm saying is that I'll take the land in lieu of my debt, but that if the debt isn't paid, I'll make sure our mutual friend here spends the rest of his life breaking up rocks for the county.'

John Kummer said: 'It's hopeless, Dolly. I'm going to have to give it to him. Listen, Mr Cornelius, I've got the papers here. There's an attorney on the next block, and he'll fix it for us.'

'You worm,' said Dolly Jarvis.

Kummer turned on her and banged the table with his fist. 'Don't you call me no worm, you henna-haired whore! I'm doing this because I don't have no option! If you're so all-

68

fired courageous, how come you're not back in Abilene, giving yourself up to the bail bondsmen?'

'Oh, nuts,' said Dolly Jarvis.

Johann Cornelius stood up, took his hat off the hatstand by the wall, and pushed his chair back in.

'Thanks for the breakfast, Dolly,' he said. 'You're a generous woman.'

Dolly glanced at the empty plates and cups and then back up at Johann, and flushed.

'What do you mean?' she said. 'I thought this was *your* treat, not mine!'

'Let's just put it this way,' Johann said. 'It's sometimes easier to shell out for a late breakfast than it is to find a bounty hunter on your doorstep looking for ten percent of your bail money.'

Dolly opened her purse, took out a dollar, and laid it on the table. She said quietly: 'They used to tell me in Sunday school, when they found me behind the bushes with my drawers down and all the little boys looking, that I didn't have no morals. Until I met you, Mr Johann Cornelius, I believed them. But now I've met someone who has no more morals than this table, and it's a frightening thing.'

Johann didn't reply at first, but tipped his hat to the woman behind the counter, and ushered Dolly Jarvis and John Kummer out into the street. He stood for a moment on the boardwalk, screwing up his eyes against the glaring sun and the heat of approaching noon.

'I'll tell you something about morals, Miss Jarvis,' he said as he watched a horse-drawn runabout jangle past, driven by a fierce-looking woman in an old-style bonnet and a floral print dress. 'Morals are a way of anticipating the divine justice of the Lord on earth, in the hope that when the Day of Judgment finally arrives, that our hearts and our affairs will be in reasonable order. I live my life by a far greater morality than you because I have a far greater task to perform, and one day you will be able to think to yourself, with a considerable amount of pleasure, that you bought me my breakfast.'

Dolly Jarvis gave Johann a long, expressionless stare, as if trying to capture this moment on some Lumière dry plate in her mind. 'Come on,' she said. 'Let's get this over. The sooner we send the Reverend Cornelius on his way, the better I'll like it.'

'The attorney's just down this way,' said John Kummer.

Johann nodded. 'If you're so anxious to be rid of me, I suppose we'd better go.'

Dolly Jarvis, walking arm-in-arm with John Kummer, the heels of her button-up boots tapping on the boardwalk, turned around and looked at Johann and gave a sardonic little laugh.

'Oh, I'm not anxious to be rid of you,' she said. 'I just hope that one day the Lord grants me the pleasure of having you as a customer, and then, by God, I'll bite you where it hurts, and you won't forget Dolly Jarvis in a particular rush.'

Johann said: 'You shouldn't talk that way, you know. You're making our mutual friend nervous. A man should never be nervous when signing away his rights to anything, don't you agree? It makes the nib tremble, and forever after the deeds will show just how frightened he *really* was.'

At three, Johann saw Dolly Jarvis and John Kummer off on the southbound train, and he stood by the side of the track, his thumbs in his belt, until the locomotive and its three-carriage train had almost disappeared into the distance, leaving nothing but a ringing reverberation in the rails and a series of black puffs of smoke which drifted away westward, expanding and opening like funeral plumes.

Then he left Amarero station, with its freshly painted signal box and its new maroon ticket office, and crossed the sun-baked yard to where his automobile was waiting. He took out the starting handle, cranked her up, and then climbed aboard to go and inspect his property.

It took twenty minutes to reach Sweetwater Trail, a remnant of one of the old cattle trails that had made fortunes for beef barons in the days before gasoline engines and lubricants. Johann stopped his car by a slabby butte that protruded out of the prairie, and sat there for ten minutes or more, looking around the hundred sloping acres of scrub and dust that a large sign optimistically announced as 'Kummer One.' It was a blazing afternoon, with only a few clouds on the horizon, and there wasn't more than a warm whisper of wind to relieve the heat. Johann took off his panama and wiped the sweatband with his handkerchief.

About six or seven hundred yards away, John Kummer's main drilling rig stood, silent and deserted. There was a small hut with a tin chimney stack, a wagon with a broken wheel, and a litter of ropes and tackle and abandoned tools There were no shadows, and only lizards moved in the sun, staring at Johann with blank beady eyes. ,

There was only one job to do today. He got down from the car, making its springs creak, and walked over to the sign that said 'Kummer One.' He pushed and pulled it backward and forward until it eventually fell flat, with a clatter that seemed unnaturally loud. Then he went back to the automobile and took from the back floor a black-and-white sign that he had painted for himself three days ago. He found a hammer among the abandoned tools, and banged the new sign into the ground just a few feet away from the drilling rig. The sign said: 'Cornelius Oil.'

He used his sleeve to mop the sweat off his forehead. Then he swung the hammer around and threw it in a long tumbling parabola toward the oil camp. It struck the side of the hut with a hollow thump.

He knew there was oil out here. It would take him a little while to locate the best site for drilling, but he had already done enough casual experimental surveys around Sweetwater and Amarero to convince him that there was more black gold under the ground here than Kyle Lennox and all the other wildcatters dreamed of. Johann believed in science, not the hard-bitten spit-in-the-wind type of guesswork that had brought in Amarero One and most of the other wells in this part of the prairie. That was why he had spent a few hours of every visit to Amarero with a seismograph, popping off small charges of dynamite here and there, and recording his readings in a carefully written notebook – the same notebook that he had used to write down his analyses of Nathaniel's Engineering in New York. There wasn't any sense in buying a new notebook until this one was used up. They cost two cents each.

Johann had studied the whole subject of oil prospecting for almost two years – ever since he had arrived in Edgar. With weighty geological books imported from Europe by Kernbaum's Bookstore, he had spent night after night sitting in his apartment in the old red rambling house on Grange Street, gradually learning by the light of his glass reading lamp that the presence of oil was indicated by underground salt domes. American opinion was that these salt domes were formed by the expansion of salt crystals or deposits from rising columns of brine which came up from deep and volcanic sources. But European theory attested that the salt flowed because of the weight of overhanging rocks. Johann read more and more, and eventually came to understand what geological features to look for, and how to use a seismograph, a torsion balance, and a gravimeter to test the formation of underground soil structures. It was the crust of the earth which told you whether there was likely to be oil under the ground or not, and Johann made sure that he could systematically and accurately find out where it was.

It was five months ago, on his last trip out to Amarero, that he had set off charges not far from Sweetwater. He had suspected then that John Kummer was in financial difficulties, and apart from being academically interested in whether there was oil under Kummer's property or not, Johann was also trying to safeguard the cash that Kummer owed him. He still wasn't sure how copious a well was there, and he wasn't at all certain where to start drilling. But the stuff was there all right, and he counted himself lucky that there were more than four million square feet in one hundred and six acres, and that John Kummer had picked all the wrong ones to drill in.

He stood there for a while, hands on his hips, looking around the dusty land in the afternoon heat. This was his beginning. This was where he came in with a chance to make some real money. He kicked the ground like a man testing a cartwheel to see if it was sound. He felt pleased, but at the same time he felt calm and detached. It wasn't luck that had brought him John Kummer's land. It was the culmination of all his years of planning and study and hard work, plus the ten thousand dollars that Lidmore Mulliner had paid him to get out of Broughton and never return.

After a while he went back to his automobile and started it up. He backed the New Orleans up the slope by the butte, paused for a couple of minutes just to take a last satisfied look at the fresh-painted sign that said 'Cornelius Oil,' and then engaged the gears and drove northward in a billowing trail of dust.

He hadn't, to begin with, aimed at going back to Amarero.

There was a shortcut he could have taken two or three miles outside of town, where the northbound track divided and one branch wended its way diagonally east across scrub and sand to join the Edgar trail not far from the ridge where Johann had sat that same morning, looking at Amarero from way off. The shortcut would have saved him a good two miles, but when he reached the turnoff he kept heading due north, despite the nagging in the back of his mind that said *What are you doing? What are you doing?*

As he bounced over the rough track in his automobile, he kept telling himself that he needed to go to Amarero to top up his spare gasoline can. He was pretty sure he had enough fuel to get home, but you never knew for sure with automobiles. They were temperamental devices at the best of times. The last thing he wanted to do was camp out on the prairie all night with an empty gas tank.

It was only when he was actually driving down Main Street that he began to admit to himself what he was really doing. Even then, he felt as if he was completely helpless, completely unable to change the course of events by turning around and going straight home. Usually, he felt as if he was the master of his own destiny, but when it came to women, he lost his grip like a swimmer in the Colorado rapids losing his grip on a lifeline, and he was swirled away into the current.

He drew up right outside the Excelsior Hotel, and left his motor running. He stepped inside through the decorated glass doors, removing his hat, and walked up to the counter along the wall, where the desk clerk was now reading a copy of *The Broughton Sentinel* and picking his nose with even more industry than before. The quadroon girl was not there, and the plushy sofas were empty. An abandoned cigar butt still burned in a brown onyx ashtray, its blue smoke twiddling and twirling in the late-afternoon sunlight that fell through the windows.

Johann pinged the bell. The desk clerk looked up.

'Oh,' he said, 'you're back.'

Johann felt cold and sweaty, and desperately uncertain about what he was going to say. The desk clerk waited expectantly for him to state his business, twisting the brilliantined hairs of his left moustache and blinking with disconcerting regularity.

'It occurred to me,' said Johann, 'that you might be open to certain financial arrangements.'

The desk clerk raised an eyebrow.

'The thing is,' Johann continued, 'I wish to make you a proposition. This is only if it's economically suitable to you, and, well, romantically suitable to the person in question.'

The desk clerk said: 'Romantically?'

Johann nodded. 'That's the only way I can think of to say it.'

'I see,' said the desk clerk.

Johann fingered the brim of his panama hat nervously. 'This may be impossible,' he said. 'I'm not a usual visitor to this kind of establishment, and so I'm not sure of the etiquette. It may be out of the question.'

The desk clerk said: 'You're quite right. It may.'

Johann swallowed. 'On the other hand,' he said, 'the person in question may be amenable to it, and find it a satisfactory way to settle all sides of the problem.'

The desk clerk dug in the corner of his eye with the end of his forefinger and then examined the speck of sleep that he had excavated, with apparent connoisseurship. 'It sounds to me like you've got someone in mind,' he suggested. 'A lady?'

Johann fumbled with his hat. 'A lady, yes. The . . . the young one. The quadroon who was down here earlier.'

The desk clerk swivelled around in his chair and checked the clock on the wall behind him. 'You're too late, I'm afraid.'

'Too late? You mean she's already—'

'She's gone for her supper. She'll be back soon '

'Listen,' said Johann. 'I want to buy her.'

The desk clerk sniffed. 'All right. How long for?'

Johann came forward up to the counter and said: 'You don't understand. I don't just want her for half an hour.'

'All right,' said the clerk. 'It's eight dollars the night.'

'No,' said Johann. 'I didn't mean that, either.'

The desk clerk, pen poised over his guest book, looked up at Johann warily. 'I can give you the night for seven-fifty,' he said. 'But no less. Not a cent less.'

'You don't understand,' said Johann, flushing. 'I don ⁺ want her for just one night. I want her for good. I want to buy her from you completely.'

The desk clerk laid down his pen. 'In other words, you

74

want to book her every single night? Three hundred sixty-five nights a year? Mister, that's going to cost you. I ain't so sure she's worth it. She's only twelve, you know, and she don't have that much experience. Not much meat on her, either.'

'Well,' said Johann, smiling a little with embarrassment, 'I expect the meat will fatten up later. But you still don't understand what I mean. I want to purchase her for myself. I want to take her away from here, and have her live with me.'

At that, the desk clerk stared at Johann as if he thought he was quite mad. In most ways, Johann thought he probably was. But he knew this was one compulsion which he would have to follow through. The quadroon girl had somehow moved him so deeply that he *had* to have her. He didn't know if he wanted to save her from her sordid fate or if he wanted her to satisfy his own fleshly desires. He would have to think about that later. At the moment, all that concerned him was taking her away.

'Mister,' said the desk clerk cagily, 'that girl belongs to Mr Kyle Lennox, the same way this hotel does, and the same way most of this town does. I don't believe that Mr Lennox would take too kindly to the downright sale of one of his girls. I don't believe that at all.'

Johann said: 'In other words, you don't want to take the responsibility?'

'Well, no, sir, I'm not sure that I do.'

'In that case,' said Johann, 'I'll go speak to Mr Kyle Lennox myself. Do you happen to know if he's in town today?'

The desk clerk nodded, and closed his guest book. 'Mr Lennox is always in town. But take it from me, I don't think he's going to take too kindly to the downright sale of one of his girls.'

'Well, leave that to me,' said Johann. 'Tell the girl to wait, and not to go with any customers, and I'll be back in a half hour.'

'Okay,' said the desk clerk. 'It's your funeral.'

Johann left the hotel and climbed aboard his automobile. It was growing cooler now, and the sun was touching the top of the Red Star Stores & Ironmongery opposite. The dusty street was striped with shadows, and someone in an upstairs

75

room was playing a trumpet. A surrey clattered past with its horse sniffling and jangling its bridle. There was a dry, aromatic smell of prairie in the air, mingled with the strong aroma of fatback and beans.

With a loud backfire, Johann's automobile jerked forward and futtered up the street. He steered the motorcar out through the few stables and stores that dotted the northern boundary of the town, and then drove across the hard prairie track that led to Kyle Lennox's mansion.

It was a three-storey Gothic house of uncomely proportions. Kyle Lennox had ordered it built from a drawing in a magazine, and while the Amarero carpenter had done his best, he was more used to putting oil rigs together, and the house had finished up impressive enough but oddly disturbing to look at. None of the windows seemed to be in quite the right place; none of the doors were sufficiently wide; and the carvings and decorations were only as good as an enthusiastic stick whittler could have done with a small penknife. The front yard was surrounded by a neat green pale, although nothing grew there but three or four tough, stunted bushes.

Johann switched off his engine, dismounted from his car, and went up to the front gate. He paused for a moment before he walked up the red-ash path, and he thought about the risk of what he was doing. He was well-known around these parts, and respected. It wasn't that he cared what anyone thought of him; it was just that for now, he depended too much on local approbation and support in his efforts to make money. If the tale of this day's conversations got around, and there was always a risk of that, he wasn't at all sure that he could still command the same influence in Edgar, or anywhere about. When he struck oil, the townsfolk of Edgar could choke themselves with their own tongues as far as he cared, but tonight called for discretion.

He squinted at the fading sun. The trouble was, he didn't even feel that he had any choice. The moment he had set eyes on that girl, he had known that he wanted her. There wasn't any question of going back now.

He walked up the path, mounted the two wooden steps that led to the porch, and knocked on the narrow mulberry-coloured door. Inside, he heard a dog barking, and the sound of footsteps.

76

It was Kyle Lennox himself who opened the door. Johann had seen tintypes of him in *The Amarero Citizen*, but he had never met him in person. He looked older and oilier than he had in print – a fat dissolute man in a purple silk smoking jacket, with a broad sweaty face and a heavy walrus moustache. He was smoking a cigar and carrying a cut-glass tumbler of bourbon, and he stood there looking at Johann as if he'd been expecting him, but wasn't quite sure if he was real.

'Mr Cornelius,' he said, in a phlegmy voice. 'How grand of you to call.'

Johann took off his hat. 'The hotel called you, did they, on the telephone? I saw the wires, and wondered.'

'Well, actually, they did,' grunted Kyle Lennox. 'But I would have known you anyway. The reputation of Johann Cornelius has made itself felt in these parts, and don't you know it.'

'May I come in?' asked Johann.

Kyle Lennox swung wide the door, and Johann stepped past him. Lennox's breath stank of drink and anchovies, and as he bowed with mock formality to welcome Johann into his house, Johann could see that his hair was dyed black and was growing silver at the roots.

The hall was musty and dark, as if nobody ever opened a window. It was hung with florid late-Victorian oil paintings of women with immense thighs and cascading bosoms; and the furniture, though sparse, was dark and immense. A German shepherd with one ear bitten to shreds was lying panting on the rose-patterned carpet next to the umbrella stand. Even though the usual annual rainfall in Amarero was something less than four inches, the stand was crowded with gold- and silver-knobbed umbrellas. In society magazines, Kyle Lennox had seen umbrellas in the homes of all the leading socialites, and he considered at least ten of them essential equipment in any high-class residence.

'The widow's resting, I regret,' explained Kyle Lennox, following Johann unsteadily into the drawing room. 'She has *turns* these days, not being as young as she was, and she finds the only way to get rid of them is to lie in bed with drapes drawn, and cover her face with Creme de Java.'

'I'm sorry about that,' said Johann politely, looking around the room.

'I'm not,' said Kyle Lennox. 'It gives me a chance to read my French magazines. Do you want a drink?'

'No, thank you.'

'A cigar? They're good, you know. An old gambling buddy of mine brings them direct from Havana.'

'No, no. I don't smoke.'

Kyle Lennox sat himself down in a big red plush Morris rocker with swan's necks carved on the arms. The whole drawing room was furnished in this style, with a massive davenport of quarter-sawed oak, a gigantic gondola couch, and various armchairs of ill-assorted sizes. There were more paintings and engravings on the walls, but they were so awkwardly arranged that it always looked as if some were missing, or there was one too many. The carpet was dark tan with a floral pattern and pictures of castles on it.

'Well,' said Kyle Lennox, crossing his fat legs in their grey grease-spotted pants. 'You don't drink, and you don't smoke. I gather you're a first-class attender of church too.'

Johann sat down on the edge of the davenport, with his hat on his knee, and said nothing. Kyle Lennox eyed him, and puffed more smoke into the stale drawing-room air.

'If you're as good a fellow as all that,' said Lennox, 'what *do* you do for fun?'

Johann coughed. 'If they've already called you on the telephone, Mr Lennox, they would have told you why I'm here. I want to make this as brief and as modest as possible.'

'I'm sure you do.'

'The fact is, you employ a young quadroon girl down at the Excelsior Hotel. I would like to employ her myself, permanently, as a housekeeper and companion. This would be subject, of course, to her approval, and to whatever price you would care to ask for her transfer.'

Kyle Lennox scrutinized Johann with an amused smile.

'I want you to know,' added Johann, 'that she would be well looked after. She would be cared for, and fed, and her general education would be continued.'

'Aha,' said Kyle Lennox.

'I can pay well,' said Johann, 'and I would hope that between us we could reach a quiet and satisfactory settlement. A gentleman's agreement to the benefit of all concerned.'

Kyle Lennox swallowed some more bourbon, and then

stretched back in his chair, setting it rocking on its lion's-claw feet. The whole idea of Johann Cornelius wanting to buy one of his girls seemed to tickle him enormously.

'Mr Cornelius,' he said, 'you don't seem to grasp the nature of the girl's business. As the old saying goes, whoring is the world's greatest industry. You have something, you then sell it, but having sold it, you still have it to sell again. Carina is not a cake of kitchen soap or a half-pound of cheese. She's going to make money for me for the next twenty or thirty years, until her hair goes white and her teeth drop out and she has to spend the rest of her days fornicating with circus mules to make a few pennies for food. That's the way it is, and that's the way it always will be.'

Johann said: 'How much do you anticipate that she will make for you in her working lifetime?'

Kyle Lennox noticed the tenseness in his voice, and looked less amused than before.

He said: 'Twenty dollars a night for three hundred sixty-five nights is seven thousand three hundred dollars. Seven thousand three hundred dollars times twenty years is one hundred and forty-six thousand dollars. The girl, you see, is a little gold mine.'

'You're not saying that you want a hundred and forty-six thousand dollars?'

'You're a friend. You can have her for one hundred and forty.'

Johann lowered his eyes. 'That's out of the question.'

Kyle Lennox laughed. 'Let's face up to it, Mr Cornelius. You just can't afford her.'

'I could pay you by instalments.'

'In which case, I would give her to you by instalments. A few minutes each week at first, and only full-time when you had paid everything off. Mr Cornelius, it's only fair.'

Johann rubbed his chin thoughtfully for a moment, and then stood up.

'I don't think we can do business, Mr Lennox,' he said huskily. 'You'll excuse me for taking up your time.'

Kyle Lennox shrugged. 'Well, if you can't see your way to the price, that's very sad.'

'Will you show me out?'

Kyle Lennox didn't answer, but puffed at his cigar, with a frown on his face, the frown of a man who is trying to work out something complicated in spite of three-quarters of a bottle of bourbon.

'Will you show me out?' repeated Johann.

'Wait a moment,' said Lennox, waving his hand. 'Supposing we put it this way. Supposing you give me ten percent of whatever you find on the Kummer land out at Sweetwater Trail. Supposing you agree to do that.'

'Then you'd give me the girl?'

'Certainly. No question about it.'

Johann looked at Kyle Lennox closely. There was a toad-like look about him that Johann found repulsively fascinating. If ever a man had his character advertised on his face, it was the oil magnate of Amarero. But as Johann had already discovered, it didn't do in Texas to hide any of your lights under any of your barrels, and if Kyle Lennox was going to do business like a toad, then it was all the better if he looked like one.

'You think there's oil there?' asked Johann.

'No doubt about it,' said Kyle Lennox. 'If there wasn't, why should you want it?'

Johann kept his eyes on the floor. 'It could be that I'm thinking of raising myself a few cows.'

'At Sweetwater? Don't make a sick man laugh. What are they going to eat out at Sweetwater? Lizard mornay, with cactus juice for dessert?'

Johann still didn't look up. 'Could be that I'm thinking of opening myself a new engineering works.'

'Sure,' admitted Kyle Lennox. 'Except that you don't go looking for building land with dynamite charges and a seismograph. When you go looking with dynamite charges and a seismograph, you're looking for oil, in the approved fancy up-to-the-minute Frenchified way.'

Johann, looking thoughtful, walked back across the drawing room to the window. This side of the house faced west, and the dazzling orange sun was sinking toward the horizon in a haze of indigo dusk. Almost silhouetted against it, the thin outline of Kyle Lennox's Negro gardener worked at the dried-up rows of broccoli with a spindly hoe, and the chop of metal against hard soil reached Johann where he stood. He glanced down at the small carved side table beside him, and there was an open copy of *La Vie Parisienne*, with a two-tone drawing of a pretty girl pleasurably startled by two butterflies suckling her nipples.

'Eight percent,' said Johann in a low but decisive voice.

Kyle Lennox didn't turn around.

'Nine,' he said, by way of reply.

Johann came away from the window, and sat down again on the edge of the davenport. He looked Kyle Lennox straight in the eye, and he said softly: 'Mr Lennox, you care for money so far above the welfare of the girls you own, and you are so convinced that there is oil out at Sweetwater Trail, that you know in your heart and your mind that eight percent is more than a generous price.'

'Eight and a half?' suggested Kyle Lennox.

Johann sat back and simply stared at him without any expression at all. Kyle Lennox looked back at him twitchily for a few moments, and then uncrossed his legs and said: 'All right. Eight percent it is.'

Johann extended his hand. 'Let's shake on that, Mr Lennox, and let me say one more thing.'

'What's that?' joked Lennox. 'Seven and a half percent?'

'No, the price is agreed. But I just want to say that this is a private bargain, between men of honour. If you so much as whisper the news of this to anyone at all, I shall be round here in what I can only call a less than forgiving humour.'

'You have a fine way of putting it, Mr Cornelius,' said Kyle Lennox. 'Would you care for a drink?'

'No, thank you. If you would just kindly call the Excelsior, and tell the girl to get ready, I will collect her on my way back to Edgar.'

Kyle Lennox set down his bourbon glass and walked out to the hallway where a five-magnet telephone in a heavily decorated mahogany case was hung on the wall. He picked it up and gave his instructions to the desk at the Excelsior in a soft mutter, in case the widow heard from her sickbed upstairs. Johann heard him saying: 'That's right, trunk, hatboxes, and all. In ten minutes.'

Lennox then came back into the drawing room and stood for a while with his cigar in his mouth and his hands in his smoking-jacket pockets, smiling at Johann in an odd kind of way, as if he couldn't make out what manner of person this Cornelius fellow was at all.

81

Johann said: 'I shall be off, then,' and he put on his panama.

Kyle Lennox kept on smiling. 'I wish I knew what you were going to do with our young Carina,' he said. ' A man like you – well, it doesn't seem usual, somehow. Mind you, the priest around here, Father Pankhurst, he's had a few strange moments. Maybe it's all those years of going without.'

'Mr Lennox,' said Johann, 'what I now do with Carina is none of your business. Our deal is settled.'

'Okay,' replied Lennox. 'I get the hint. But you can take your little girl along in the happy knowledge that anything you want her to do, she'll do. Why, if you even asked her to open that pretty mouth of hers so's you could—'

'I said, it's none of your business!' snapped Johann.

'Okay, okay, no offence meant,' said Lennox soothingly, raising his hands in mock surrender.

Johann said: 'I apologize. I didn't mean to lose my temper. I'd better go now.'

Together they walked through the hallway to the front door. As Johann stepped outside into the warm evening air, Kyle Lennox stood by the porch rail and breathed in the aroma of dust and weed. 'Can't say I care too much for oxygen,' he said. 'I've heard that it rots the mind!'

Johann walked down the ash path to the gate and opened it.

'I'll say good-bye, then.'

Lennox gave him a wave of the hand. 'Good-bye, Mr Cornelius. It's been a pleasure to do trade with you. I hope you're happy with your goods, and I know that I'm going to be happy with my eight percent.'

'Yes,' said Johann, and went across to his automobile.

As he mounted the step and sat down in the driving seat of the car, something moved him to lift his eyes from the purple figure of Kyle Lennox on the porch and glance up at a lace curtain that was twitched in an upstairs window. For a few seconds he saw a pale unlovely face peering out at him through the glass, and then the curtain fell back again. He looked down at Kyle Lennox, who was still grinning and waving, and he felt terribly disturbed. If Lennox had condemned himself to live in this grotesque house on the prairie, with this wan woman in her face creams, then his dissolution and his greed for money must have surpassed anything that Johann had ever felt. He just hoped that, in his own way, he wasn't another Kyle Lennox in the making. Often the ugliest visions are the visions which appear in the mirror. He didn't wave at all, but turned his automobile and drove back into the centre of Amarero with the sun on his right cheek and the first chill of evening on his left.

He pulled the New Orleans to a shuddering stop right outside the hardware store and stepped down. The proprietor, a tall mournful young man with a brown storekeeper's apron and a heavily scented walrus moustache, came out onto the boardwalk wiping his hands. He stood there and looked at the New Orleans and said nothing. Then he looked at Johann and said nothing. The pale evening sky was reflected in the store window behind him, and a price tag on a Dutch hoe handle whirred and flapped in the breeze.

'You stock gasoline?' asked Johann at length.

The young man nodded. 'We surely do. You want some? We got some good cheese, too, just came in from the coast.'

'Just the gasoline, thanks.'

'You're the boss,' said the young man, and walked around the back of the store to bring the gasoline. While he was gone, Johann paced up and down the boardwalk, checking his watch again. If he'd had a mind to, he could have bought a long-tine alfalfa fork for sixty-nine cents.

The young proprietor came back around the store with a red-painted enamel can of gasoline and a brass funnel. Johann unscrewed the cap of the fuel tank for him, and he began to pour the gasoline in.

'How'd you like her?' he asked. 'Reckon she's pretty bumpy out on these roads.'

Johann wasn't really listening, and he said: 'What?'

'Pretty bumpy,' repeated the young man.

Johann frowned at him, and brushed back his straying hair with his hand. 'Oh, sure. I see what you mean. No, she's not too bad.'

The proprietor sniffed, and jerked his head over to the north-west. 'Old Jack Hulton, one of his boys had one. I don't know what make it was. But the first time he took it out, it overturned in a dry ditch and he busted his neck. It didn't kill him, mind, but they have to wheel him around in a basket chair now, and feed him with mushed-up oats.'

Johann gave a brief, uninterested smile. The gasoline gurgled and splashed into the automobile's tank, and the simmering fumes distorted the darkening evening air.

'Saw a fellow was killed in Broughton, too, by his own machine. Got himself run over.'

Johann said impatiently: 'Listen – how long is this going to take? I have to meet someone.'

The young man sniffed. 'You want it filled up, don't you? I have to take it slow, on account of it's inflexible.'

'Inflammable, not inflexible.'

'You bet. You sure you don't want some cheese?'

Johann shook his head. 'Just fill the car and I'll get going.'

Eventually the young man had emptied the red-painted can. He shook out the last few drops with a flourish, and then screwed the top back on.

'There you are, sir. Filled to the brim. Just mind you don't do what that fellow in Broughton did. Squashed flat like a bug, he was.'

Johann paid him, and then climbed back up into the driving seat to set the spark and the throttle. The hardware-store man watched him, and added: 'It just goes to show, doesn't it, that God can strike you down no matter what kind of man you are, storekeeper or sodbuster or attorney-at-law.'

Johann raised his head. 'Attorney-at-law? What made you say that?'

The proprietor blinked, as if he couldn't even remember what he'd been talking about. 'Well,' he said slowly, 'the fellow in Broughton that was squashed flat, he was an attorney-at-law. Least, that's what it says in the *Sentinel*.'

'Do you have a copy?'

'Well, uh . . . sure. It's inside.'

'Will you go get it for me?'

Puzzled, the storekeeper disappeared inside the doorway of his store, ducking down to avoid the cheese graters and nutmeg scrapers and Hunter's Old Reliable flour sifters that festooned the frame. He came back with a crumpled copy of *The Broughton Sentinel* on which somebody had obviously been blacking their boots, and handed it over. He pointed to a story at the foot of the front page, and then stood back and watched with undisguised curiosity while Johann read it.

For a while the only sounds in the street were the flapping of the newspaper in the breeze and the fitful whirring of the price ticket on the hoe.

The headlines read 'Tragic Automobile Accident Kills Broughton Lawyer,' 'Crushed to Death by Own Vehicle,' 'A Most Heart-Rending Scene on Beaumont Street.'

The man who had died was Lidmore Mulliner. According to the newspaper, which was written in the most flowery and melodramatic way, he had been taking his wife, Mrs Beatrice Mulliner, for a first run in his new Pierce Arrow, just delivered. Toward the end of Beaumont Street the automobile had stalled, and Mr Mulliner had climbed out of the car to restart it. Just as he had managed to get the engine going again, the emergency hand brake had slipped, and the automobile had jumped forward and knocked Mr Mulliner to the ground, running over his chest with its right front wheel. By the time three passing accountants had been able to lift the Pierce Arrow from his prostrate body, he was at the point of death, and had expired without even passing on the combination of his office safe.

Johann laid the newspaper down. His face showed no emotion at all, but inside he felt as if something extraordinary had happened, as if pages had fallen from the calendar in scores, as if the sun had come up again, and set again, as if the ground beneath his feet had stirred.

He handed the paper back to the hardware-store proprietor. Farther along the street, in the gathering shadows, he saw the door of the Hotel Excelsior open, and a small figure step out onto the boardwalk. He said in a distant voice: 'Thank you. I appreciate your kindness.'

The hardware proprietor said nothing as Johann started up his automobile and moved off down the street toward the corner. But he stood there and watched for a long while before ducking back into the shady, soap-and-leather-smelling interior of his store to light up the lamps.

She was waiting for him on the hotel steps. She was wearing the same brown dress of Japanese silk, only this time she wore a fawn spring cape over her shoulders, decorated with brown piping, and a brown mushroom hat with ribbons. At her feet were two hatboxes and a smallish basswood trunk. The faded light of evening made her look even younger and slimmer than Johann remembered her, and as he drew his automobile up to the corner and applied the brake, she turned toward him with the intensely beautiful face of a dark child, and he felt that same shortness of breath that he had felt before.

He climbed down from the car. He was broad and heavy, while she, even in her velvet-and-patent Blucher boots, was only a little over five feet. He held out his big hand and said as gently as he could: 'Carina? I'm Johann Cornelius.'

She nodded, without speaking.

'Are these your boxes? Your trunk?'

She nodded again.

'Okay, then,' he said uncomfortably, and he picked up the luggage and stowed it along with his briefcase in the back seat of the New Orleans. Then he turned and helped her to mount to the front passenger seat, where she sat with her hands demurely together on her lap.

He climbed aboard himself, and released the brake. 'You're not frightened, are you?' he asked her. 'This thing's noisy as all hell, and if you're not used to it, it can shake you up. But it won't hurt you.'

Carina looked at him, and inclined her head almost imperceptibly to show that she understood.

'All right, then,' said Johann, revving up the automobile's engine and engaging the gears, 'let's get going.'

He was ready to start when the desk clerk appeared at the door of the Excelsior Hotel, waving a piece of paper. Johann disengaged the gears again and turned around in his seat. The desk clerk came down the hotel steps with a particularly insolent smile.

'What's this?' said Johann, as the clerk handed him the paper.

'Speaks for itself,' answered the clerk, and then said: 'Good-bye, Carina. Have fun!'

Johann took off one of his gauntlets and unfolded the paper. It was a regular bill from the 'Hotel Excelsior, Fine Food & The Telephone, 27 Main Street, Amarero, Where Nobs Stay.' On it was written: 'For one girl, 8% gross oil rights at Sweetwater Trail rec'd with Thanks.'

When he read that, Johann felt for the first time in his

life that he had gone against God. He tucked the bill away, and drove off.

They drove for hours across the prairie. The moon hadn't risen yet, and they had been making their way by the dim yellowish light of the automobile's lamps, bouncing and creaking over ruts and hard-baked cattle tracks, and almost choked sometimes by dust. Carina had taken off her hat and wrapped a fascinator around her head, although she remained silent, and hadn't said a single word to Johann since he had first collected her from the hotel steps.

Sometimes they saw lights of homesteads and ranch houses from way off. They twinkled through the huge prairie night like the lights of ships far away at sea, with the whole night sky glittering with stars above them. The wind was cooler, but still gentle, and the barking of dogs carried for miles.

Johann cleared the dust from his throat and said: 'It makes you feel lonely, doesn't it, out here at night-time?'

Carina said nothing. He could see by the reflected sparkle of the lamps in her eyes that she wasn't asleep. But she didn't even turn her head or acknowledge that he had spoken.

He drove for a while longer, and then he said: 'I discovered today that someone had died, someone whose death could have meant a lot to me, if it had happened a while sooner. I was thinking about death, too, and how it must leave you all alone, like being on this prairie at night. I was thinking . . .'

He paused. She didn't even seem to be listening. But then he said: 'I was thinking that you have to take your chances when and where you can find them. I mean, your chances of not being alone.'

He didn't know what else to say after that, so he fell silent. Over the lip of the prairie, a curve of light appeared, as white as a frightened face, as the moon came up.

Not long before they saw the lights of Edgar, Carina unexpectedly reached her hand over and touched his thigh. It wasn't a sensual touch; but more a touch that sought reassurance, and companionship. Johann turned his head and saw that her eyes were glistening with tears. She was muffled up in her knitted fascinator, and he could hardly see

87

her face, but he suddenly realized that her long silence had not been hostility, or aloofness. She was a twelve-year-old girl who had been packed off without warning with a hefty twenty-nine-year-old engineer, and even though she might have been a prostitute, and been prepared to do anything at all with anyone, Johann wondered how much of that was simply because she knew nothing about life and what was expected of her, and had no friends.

'Was it someone you loved?' she asked him. She had a soft, lisping Mexican accent.

He squeezed her hand kindly. 'Not really. I met him once, but I didn't know him well. It's nothing to worry about. It was a shock, that's all.'

'I thought . . .' she said, and then stopped herself.

'What did you think?'

'When you went to Kyle Lennox, and bought me, I thought you loved nobody. But you do, don't you?'

Johann steered the automobile across a rough patch of rocks and ruts. 'What do you know about love?' he asked her.

'I don't know much,' she said, shaking her head.

They drove in silence for a little while longer, and then Johann said: 'Did it surprise you, when you heard what I'd done?'

'A little. I was frightened, though, because some men are very strange.'

'You've known . . . a lot of men? *Muchos hombres?*'

She nodded.

Johann, in spite of the empty feeling that her nod provoked in his stomach, attempted a smile.

'Well,' he said as cheerfully as he could, 'that *was* your business.'

'You don't like it,' she said.

'I didn't say that. I just said, that *was* your business.'

She dropped the fascinator so that the wind and the dust blew in her dark upswept hair. 'You are jealous, though, aren't you? You want everything to be your own, to belong to you. You don't like to think that I went with many men.'

'I didn't say that either.'

'You didn't have to. I can see.'

Johann said: 'It doesn't matter now, anyway. It's all in the past. It's forgotten.'

'I can't forget,' argued Carina. 'All those men, I was with them. I can't forget them.'

'Well, you'll have to try.'

'Why? Because you want me to? You bought my body. That was all. You didn't buy what's in here.' She tapped her head.

He looked at her wildly. 'It's for your own goddamned good! The sooner you . . . wipe those things out of your memory—'

'The better you'll like it?'

He looked at her again, and he suddenly realized she was deliberately teasing him. He started to laugh, and then they were both laughing. He was laughing so much he almost drove into a scrub of bushes, and he had to twist the wheel around to get himself back on the track.

'You must stop yourself from feeling jealous,' she said, holding his arm. 'If you want me to live with you, you must stop yourself. I cannot change what happened now. All those men who put themselves inside me, nothing can change that.'

Johann said: 'Was it many? I mean, was it fifty, or a hundred?'

Carina stroked his chin with her hand. 'Does it matter?' she asked him. 'Why is a hundred worse than fifty?'

'I just—'

She raised her hand so that it sealed his mouth. Then she leaned over and said quietly: 'Don't worry. If you have bought me, then I will learn how to love you. You can teach me.'

Johann drove in silence for a while, and then he turned to gaze with increasing strangeness and wonder at her gentle profile, her soft parted lips, and the tears that sparkled in her eyes. He felt terribly afraid, as if he had stepped off the straightforward path that God had set for him, and indulged desires without regard for anyone's feelings but his own. He knew that he had committed a sin by buying Carina, although he wasn't quite sure which sin it was. He didn't lust after her or even want to touch her. He just wanted to *own* her because she was a beautiful thing. He knew without question that he was going to pay for this day's disobedience, and yet his desire to have Carina was so strong that he never once considered turning back to Amarero, delivering her back with her trunk and hatboxes to the Excelsior Hotel, and forgetting that she had ever taken his eye.

'I don't know,' he said, 'if I can teach you love. I have had very little love myself. I can teach you friendship.'

She touched his hand. 'Perhaps we can learn it together. Two people who don't know, trying to learn!'

'You're so young,' he said. He coughed in the clinging dust.

'Young!' she exclaimed. 'I'm thirteen next week!'

He stared at her uneasily. 'But that's so young. You're nothing more than a child.'

She sat there in her cape and fascinator, so upright and ladylike, and said: 'I *used* to be young. I was young when I started. I was ten when I started. My tenth birthday! But now I know more. I've found out which men are the sons of bitches and which men aren't.'

Johann said: 'I'm afraid there's more to life than that.'

'You think so?' she answered. 'I don't think so. I think if you can tell a man for a son of a bitch the first time you lay your eyes on him, then that is all you have to know.'

'What about me? Am I a son of a bitch?'

Carina put her head on one side and smiled at him sweetly.

'Yes,' she said. 'You are the biggest son of a bitch of all.'

He laughed. 'What makes you say that?'

'Because you will always get what you want, no matter what, and you will always get it cheap. Mostly, you will get it for nothing.'

'I didn't get *you* for nothing.'

'What did you pay? Can I ask?'

Johann said: 'Of course you can ask. I gave Kyle Lennox eight percent of the oil rights to the hundred acres I own out at Sweetwater Trail.'

'And how much is that?'

'It depends. It might make him a wealthy man for the rest of his days, it might not. Until we bring the well in, we don't have any idea how much crude is down there at all.'

'And, just for me, you will give him all that?'

'That was the deal.'

She lowered her head. 'I didn't think I was worth a fortune.'

Johann was embarrassed. 'Don't flatter yourself,' he said. 'He was originally asking for ten, and I knocked him down.'

'Ah,' she said, 'but that is the way you are. In the end, you'll see you will get me for nothing. No – I don't mind. That is just the kind of man you are. One day, I think you will be very rich.'

'Well, let's hope so. Look – there's the lights of Edgar. Now let's see wat you think of the way a budding rich man lives.'

Carina leaned closer against him, and held him near as he drove, and he was glad for the sake of his reputation that Edgar's streets were almost deserted as they drove in, and that the lighting on most corners was dim enough to make it difficult for anyone whose curtains parted to see what that goddamned futtering was – at this time of night for Lord's sake – or to make out who they were.

He pulled up on Grange Street, by the white fence of his big red house with white shutters, and he reached into his vest pocket to find his front-door key. As they reached the porch, Carina turned and smiled at him happily, excited with her new life, and that made him feel even guiltier than ever.

Johann, being the owner, had the largest apartment in the house. He occupied the whole of the third floor, which included a sitting room, a dining room which he usually used as a study, a kitchen, a bathroom, a main bedroom, and a smaller bedroom which opened out into the Gothic turret on the northwest corner of the house. Carina went up the stairs first, carrying her hatboxes, and Johann came clumping up behind with her basswood trunk and his brief-case.

The door from the landing opened straight into Johann's cramped little hallway, with an ugly hall stand that was all protruding coat hooks and cheap varnish. He dropped everything there, and ushered Carina through to the sitting room, where he went around lighting the lamps and opening the two wide windows. This evening he drew the red velvet drapes as well, although he wasn't in the habit of it. What does a puritanical engineer do on his own that any passerby is going to find of burning prurient interest?

The floors in the apartment were dark-stained oak, laid with red-and-brown rugs which he had picked up as a bargain from a travelling carpet salesman. In the sitting room, the walls were papered in green fleur-de-lis patterns, and hung with black-framed sepia photographs of views of Holland. Johann's furniture was all solid, functional business pieces which he had bought at an auction of effects from a cattle broker's office at the respectable end of Amarillo Street. Brown leather armchairs, each uglier than the last, were crowded around an enormous golden oak desk with brass handles, a high-backed davenport in brown plush, and other odd and uncomfortable knick-knacks that belonged more in an office than a private home, like a Bank of England swivel chair and a varnished filing cabinet.

Across the corridor, as she peeked around the apartment, Carina could see the small dining room. The table was piled high with engineering books, and a greasy part of a steam piston lay on the sideboard on a piece of folded-up newspaper.

'The first thing to do is get yourself into the tub,' said Johann. 'Have yourself a good long bath, and get rid of the dust. There's no scented soap, I'm afraid, only plain, but I'll put a clean towel out for you, and you can borrow the bathrobe that's hanging on the back of the door if you need it.'

While Johann lit the cylindrical gasoline water heater beside the bath, Carina unpacked her trunk in the small turret bedroom. There was a narrow brass bed in there, and a veneered wardrobe which smelled of mothballs, and a rag carpet. A print of Loch Lomond hung above the bed. Carina hung up her six silky dresses and put away her shoes. She had stockings to put away, too, and petticoats; but no underclothes, because she never wore them. On the windowsill she laid her cheap Russian-bristle hairbrush and comb, and a creased and faded photograph of a Mexican woman peering into harsh sunlight.

Johann rapped on the door and said: 'Water's hot now, Carina.'

After Carina had padded into the bathroom, and rather disconcertingly left the door ajar, Johann went into the kitchen and stoked up the cooker with corn cobs ready for supper. He was only a bachelor cook, but he could put together a good plateful of bacon and eggs, with hunks of bread and fresh butter from his little ice chest, and that was the fanciest food that anyone could want after jolting on automobile springs all the way from Amarero.

The cobs were burning up nicely when the bell in the

hallway rang. Wiping his hands on a grubby towel, Johann went out and opened the front door of his apartment, and said: 'Yes?'

A woman was standing alone on the landing, in a large plumed black hat and a black spring coat.

Johann peered into the shadow under the veiled brim of her hat.

'Yes?' he said again.

The woman didn't move. She remained dark as a raven on the landing, accoutred in jet beads and black gloves, like a visitation from the grave.

'I don't know you,' said Johann. 'Did you want another apartment?'

The woman shook her head very slightly.

'Never,' she said. 'Never in a *thousand* years could I want another apartment. Don't you recognize me, Johann? It's Beatrice.'

Without another word she stepped into the apartment, funereal and regal, and into the sitting room. Johann closed the door and went after her as quickly as he could.

She was standing in the warm lamplight, already removing her mourning hat and peeling off her black leather gloves. She turned to him, and although she looked a little older, and a little more tired, it was the same slender brunette Beatrice, with her beautiful slanting eyes and her sensuous lips. He could even smell that same fragrance on her that he had smelled the last time he saw her, at the Broughton carnival. Heliotrope, delicate and nostalgic.

Johann stood there unable to speak. His chest felt like a steam boiler under extreme pressure, and he could hardly draw breath.

'Johann,' said Beatrice, reaching out her hands. 'It's so good to see you. You look so well.'

'Beatrice,' said Johann hoarsely.

She came up and took his wrists, and kissed him on the cheek. Her lips were warm and moist, but his own jaw appeared to be paralyzed, as if he had kept it in the ice chest all night, and his eyes were wide open and staring.

'I'm staying with an old friend of Liddy's, just three streets away, here in Edgar. Do you know Mrs Elvira Russell? She's been so sweet to me. I moved in yesterday. Mrs Elvira

Russell said I should wait, but I had to see you. You're looking so prosperous!'

'Yes,' he said faintly. 'Times are better.'

'I thought it would be so wonderful to be near you while I mourned. I need your strength, Johann, just like you once needed mine. And when my year's over, when I put aside the black—'

The sitting-room door creaked slightly. Johann raised his head at the sound and looked across the room. The door creaked again, and then opened.

Beatrice looked up, too.

It was Carina, and she was quite nude. Her body was slim and dusky-skinned, with tiny brown-nippled breasts, narrow hips, and only the tiniest curls between her legs. Her hair was dripping wet, and hung over her shoulder in ragged tails. She wore a single gold chain around her bare stomach.

'Sir?' she asked, obviously intimidated by Beatrice. 'Sir? I think I have nits.'

1903

CORNELIUS (ENGINEERS)
of Edgar, Texas

Specialists in the supply and repair of equipment for the prospecting of oil and the survey of land, and General Engineers for farm and railroad machinery.

Propr: J. Cornelius

He walked across Main Street with the edgy, restrained step of a man who has set out for an appointment too early, and has to file away at each long and obstinate minute with the rough edge of his own impatience. He stopped at the drugstore on the corner, and in the dim interior, shaded at this time of day by green blinds, he went up to the candy counter, with all its glossy home-dipped toffee apples and twists of jawbreaking barley sugar, and paid two cents for a small pack of violet cachous, which he opened as he stepped back out onto the boardwalk, and crunched between his teeth.

As he continued his walk to Kearney Street, the dust filmed the toes of his well-polished shoes. He was unusually smart today, even for such a visit. He wore a light grey linen suit, and a dove-grey hat. He smelled of Roberts' Cologne, and carried a cane. Several townsfolk, as they passed him by, said: 'How do, Mr Cornelius,' but most of them seemed to mutter it out of the corner of their mouths, and all of them stopped in their tracks once he had passed, and stared at him. He was, after all, the richest man they had ever known.

On the corner of Kearney Street, he raised his hat to Miss Beckinsale, from the Edgar Town School. She was a young, pale woman much given to black-and-white shepherd-check skirts and wide, plain hats.

She said, in her wan voice: 'You're looking finer than ever, Mr Cornelius. Life seems to agree with you here.'

'I wish love did, as well as life.' He smiled.

Miss Beckinsale sighed. 'You know what Lord Byron wrote, Mr Cornelius. He wrote that "man's love is of man's life a thing apart, but 'tis woman's whole existence." '

Johann smiled uncomfortably. 'Perhaps I should remember that,' he said, and raised his hat again. Miss Beckinsale looked at him for a moment, as plain as a clothespin on which someone had painted a face, and then sighed quite loudly and went on her way.

As he continued his walk, Johann felt disturbed, but not unpleasantly. It occurred to him that his increasing wealth and his greater experience in dealing with people and business was giving him a mastery of himself which made him more interesting and attractive – in spite of his continuing tendency to hit first and ask questions later, and in spite of the fact that he was obdurately male rather than handsome.

A horse-drawn buggy rattled past, taking sacks of corn-meal out to the Mesquite Ranch, and he put another violet cachou between his front teeth and bit it.

Beatrice had timed her afternoon promenade to the second, and was waiting for him on the corner of Kearney and Maple. She was dressed in black, as always, although she was shielding her pale complexion from the sun with a grey parasol. She smiled when she saw him, and lifted her hand, delicately and perhaps a little mockingly limp-wristed, so that he could take it and press his lips to her black cotton glove.

They were walking now, arm-in-arm, back along Kearney Street toward Main Street, where they would go into the lounge of Edgar's only hotel, the Superior, and take tea. It was a ritual they observed two or three times each week, during these long, respectable months of Beatrice's mourning. Beatrice may have been sexually outrageous by the standards of many of the citizens of western Texas, but never openly, and even during her most impassioned affairs when she was married to Lidmore, she had maintained the outward appearance of a woman of the correctest kind. Now that she was living in Edgar, which was a far smaller town than Broughton, she had to make particularly sure that she conducted herself by the standards of Christian etiquette, and that meant keeping her friendship with Johann within circumscribed limits, at least until a prudent period of time had passed. Johann did not really see the necessity for postponing his courtship for so long, but he tended to forget that Beatrice was not as thick-skinned as he was, and that she needed, as a woman, to have a leading place in Edgar's social circle, such as it was. So while she had made it known to the ladies of the town that she was an old friend of Johann's, and that she was staying in Edgar under his protection, she remained at the house on Kearney Street of 'he widowed Mrs Elvira Russell, who had been a playmate of Liddy's sister back in the '70s, and who had albums and albums of sepia pictures of Lidmore as a serious young man.

As they crossed the square toward the pillared wooden frontage of the Superior, they were greeted with polite 'how dos' and 'good afternoons' from almost everyone they passed. Johann opened the swing door of the hotel, and they went inside.

The Superior in Edgar was as much like the Excelsior in Amarero as a loofah resembled a saguaro. It had a creaky carpeted floor, plenty of aspidistras in pedestalled planters, a high mahogany desk, and ceiling fans that went around and around tirelessly and uselessly. The whole place smelled of Garland's glycerine antiseptic soap, known as 'the farmer's bar,' and Johann often complained that even the tea tasted of it. They went through glass doors into the hotel lounge, where some of Edgar's leading ladies were already perched on their bentwood chairs nibbling at sand tarts, and a waitress in a long black skirt and white apron showed them to their accustomed table by the northern window, away from the sun.

'Well,' said Beatrice, setting her reticule at her feet, 'have you had a good day?'

Johann shrugged. 'I'm seeing Phil McKeogh in a few days. He's been stock-taking, assessing how much the whole business is worth. Oil, engineering, the lot. He says we already have liquid assets well over half a million dollars.'

'My dear,' rejoined Beatrice. 'Does that mean you could be a millionaire?'

Johann shook out his napkin. 'I suppose it's possible.'

'But you don't seem very excited.'

'Why should I be? It's what I set out to do.'

Beatrice reached across the table and took his hand. 'But, my dear – a millionaire! It's simply wonderful!'

He lowered his eyes. 'I suppose it is, yes.'

'Oh, my darling,' she said, in the quietest voice she could, so that the sharpened ears of Mrs Dunphy couldn't pick up her endearment from the next table. 'I'm so glad for you. So very glad. I always knew that you had it in you.'

He looked up at her. Her expression was very soft and gentle, but somehow, for some reason he couldn't quite grasp, she seemed curiously distant. He said: 'Millionaires are supposed to get what they want.'

She paused. She could guess what was coming next. The pause was communicated to the people at the next table, and Mrs Whitehead, a bulky woman in taut lavender satin, with the profile of Geronimo, turned obtrusively in her chair to see what was afoot. Johann glanced across at her and gave her a vinegary little grin. She turned away.

'I have to admit you've been very patient,' said Beatrice. 'I want you to know that I admire you for that.'

'It's been well over a year now,' insisted Johann. 'And you told me yourself that Lidmore wasn't much of a husband to you.'

She nodded absently. 'I know.'

'Well, if you *know*,' insisted Johann, 'then why don't you come out of mourning? I love you, Beatrice. You're quite aware of that. I believe you love me. You came here, didn't you, to be close to me? The moment you say the word, we can marry, and you can come live with me.'

She looked at him. A carriage went past outside their window, with jingling harness. Johann could see the tall waitress sweeping toward them, bearing their tea tray. He coughed.

'Once you say the word,' he continued, 'I can go out and buy us a house. A real mansion. Or have one built to order. But you have to say the word.'

The waitress set down their teacups, their plate of cookies, their thin-sliced bread and butter. Beatrice poured, her hand perfectly steady, and then replaced the rose-patterned teapot on its china teapot stand.

'I don't want to appear to be *hasty*,' she said, without looking at Johann. 'After all, I'm chairman of the Women's Art League.'

'What does the Art League have to do with us getting married?'

She put her finger to her lips. 'Please, my dear. Not so loud. I couldn't bear gossip.'

'What does the Art League have to do with us?' Johann hissed. 'I don't want to marry the goddamned Art League. I want to marry you.'

She brushed one of her high-curved eyebrows with the tips of her fingers, as if she had a slight headache. 'I'm not sure,' she said at last.

'You do *love* me, don't you? You still love me?'

She looked up at him, and smiled tenderly.

'I think I'm just afraid,' she said.

'Afraid? Afraid of what?'

'Afraid of getting married again. Afraid of being caged up. The little blackbird in the wicker lantern.'

Johann stirred his tea, and tapped the spoon once against the rim of the cup.

'You can't mourn forever,' he said in a husky voice.

'Well, I know that. But I don't want to rush. And, please, I don't want you to rush me.'

'I'm not rushing you. I've waited more than a year already.'

Beatrice turned her head. Johann sat there and watched her, looking at the way the pale light from the north window touched her high, curved forehead, her long upswept eyelashes, and the perfect curves of her lips. At her throat was a black velvet ribbon with a black carved flower of ebony, set in silver.

He said: 'I love you.'

She didn't turn back. Instead, she lowered her head, and he suddenly realized that her eyes were moist.

He said: 'You're crying. Beatrice, you're crying.'

She reached down for her reticule, and took out a black-edged handkerchief. 'It's nothing,' she said. 'It's simply the dust.'

'It must be something.'

'I don't know,' she whispered. 'I'm just being ridiculous.'

'You're never ridiculous.'

She wiped her eyes. 'Oh, yes I am. All human beings are ridiculous sometimes.'

'Not you.'

Beatrice stared at him with watery eyes. There was a sad smile on her face. 'I need time,' she said. 'That's all.'

'Time for what? More mourning?'

'No, I'm past mourning. Past real mourning. But I'm still not sure about myself. I thought when Liddy died that all my problems were over; but it was only after a few weeks that I realized they were just beginning. You can't solve any problem by trying to destroy the cause of it. We are all wedded to our problems, Johann, until we overcome them by our own human logic and our own human strength. Liddy died, but now there is you. That's one of the reasons I'm holding back. I couldn't bear it if you became Liddy, all over again.'

The muscles in Johann's jaw tensed, and then slowly relaxed. He laid the fingertips of all ten fingers on the edge of the table, as if he were trying to push it away from him, and then he said: 'Do you want me to show you?'

Beatrice looked pale. 'Show me what?'

'Show you that I'm not like Liddy.'

'I don't know what you mean.'

'Of course you do. You remember that day you invited me into your parlour.'

She touched her forehead. 'That was different,' she said quickly.

'Why was it different? Don't you think I haven't had that picture of you burned onto my eyes ever since? If you looked into my eyes now, you could still see it.'

'Johann,' she said weakly, 'I think I feel faint.'

He grasped her wrist. The fierceness of his gesture didn't go unnoticed at Mrs Whitehead's table. Scarcely moving his lips, he whispered: 'I adore you, Beatrice. I need you. Don't you understand how much I have to possess you?'

Beatrice blinked. She looked at him like a woman who has just been rescued from drowning in a public boating pool.

'I think you're too much for me, Johann. Perhaps that's the truth. You have so much . . . energy. So much power. And yet you lay it all at my feet, as if it meant nothing. I'm not at all sure that I'm capable of controlling it. All my lovers before you were such boys.'

Johann released her wrist. 'I'm not your lover,' he said baldly. 'I only wish that I were.'

Beatrice took a sand tart from the dish, and laid it on her plate. She made no attempt to eat it. The lounge of the Superior was very hushed, and Johann wondered if they'd been talking too loud. On the far wall was a print of Winan's 'Mud Digger' locomotive of 1844, and for some reason it made Johann strangely nostalgic for his days in New York. He felt churned up inside – passionate, aroused, but fearful, too, because he did desperately love and worship Beatrice, and the thought that she might not love him, the idea that she might be slipping away, receding from him with every month that passed, almost made his millionaireship seem worthless.

Two nights later, after he had closed the green-and-gold door of his workshop behind him, Johann went to the corner drugstore and drank, standing up, a single cold glass of lemonade. Then, instead of turning right as he left the store toward Grange Street, where his red-and-white house was, he kept walking straight ahead, along Mountolive Street, where the houses were smaller, but neater, and fenced off with white-painted palings.

A few houses along, he stopped, and looked up and down the street. Then he opened the gate of a tidy one-storey weatherboard cottage, and went up to the front door, in the shadow of a narrow veranda. He took out a key from the breast pocket of his brown suit and let himself in.

Carina was waiting for him in the small parlour, which was decorated with figured wallpaper of emerald green, and crowded with knickknacks which she had collected during her months as Johann's protégée. There were cases of South American butterflies and moths, bedraggled stuffed warbling vireos in dusty glass domes, mournful prints of villages in Portugal, and ugly china plates with chipped edges. Everything was treasure to Carina, as long as it looked exotic and colourful, and Johann often complained that her cottage was more like an auction room than a young girl's home.

She was sitting gracefully in a small curved chair, her hair pinned up with a glittering cut-glass slide, dressed in a pink tafetta gown with net over the sleeves. Her face was as oval and mystically beautiful as ever, and her dark eyes were lifted to Johann with such mesmerizing liquidity that he could only stand by the door when he first came in, and smile at her. A porcelain clock, heavily over-decorated with fruit and cherubs, chimed on the mantelpiece.

'I expected you at seven,' she said, with very young solemnity.

'Yes,' he said, setting his hat down on a side table, next to a collection of seashells glued into the shapes of frogs and horses. 'I had a late order for the Amarero rig. I have to get over there next week. Amarero, I mean.'

She stood up from her chair with a rustle of petticoats,

and came over to kiss his cheek. He bent forward so that she could do it.

'Would you care for a drink?' he asked her. 'I brought a bottle of port wine.'

'All right.' She smiled.

There was an easy, relaxed silence between them as he went to the corner cabinet and took out two crystal wine-glasses. He uncorked the port and poured them each a modest half-glassful; and then he came over and sat down beside her next to the brick fireplace.

'What shall we drink to?' she said.

He shrugged, still smiling. 'I don't know. Maybe to friends.'

'Why not to business?' she asked him. 'You love your business.'

'The business is taking pretty good care of itself right now. And in any case, I love you, too.'

She looked wistful. 'Not properly.'

'Of course, properly.'

She gazed down at the amethyst and carnelian rings on her thin, delicate fingers.

'Not as a husband might,' she said softly.

He sat back, tugging up the knees of his pants so that they wouldn't get baggy. He sipped his wine and looked across at her with an expression of gentleness and concern that would have amazed and disconcerted most of his friends and business colleagues. Beatrice saw Johann's face when he was trying to express his adoration of her. Only Carina saw the face of simple, uncomplicated affection.

Turning his glass between his thick fingers, he said: 'I like to think that I rescued you. How could I treat you the same way as the people I saved you from?'

'You never thought of making love to me?'

He looked away.

'Love ... making love ... doesn't always have to be painful,' she said in a voice so calm and demure that he didn't realize what she was saying at first.

He cleared his throat. 'I know. But regardless of what most people seem to think, there are other things that a man may want from a young girl like you, apart from making love. I bought you, Carina, but the day I brought you here, I made you a gift of yourself. You're not my property. I ask only to be your good friend.'

'You are my good friend,' she said, gently reaching across and touching the back of his hand. 'You are.'

He was silent for a while, and then he stood up and paced around the room, picking up odd paperweights and postcards that Carina had arranged on the shelves and tables.

'I may be deceiving you, and I may be deceiving myself,' he said in a thick voice. 'Perhaps, when I bought you, I was just trying to prove to myself that anything could be bought. An oil well, or an automobile, or a girl. I can't pretend that money isn't important to me, Carina, and that I don't want all the power and the luxury that money can bring. You know, when I first came to Texas, I went to a bank with my cap in my hand asking for ten thousand dollars, and they refused. Last week, the same bank manager came back and asked me if I would care to deposit any of my funds there '

'What did you say? Something nasty?'

'Not really. I just told him that he seemed to have forgotten his own lesson – neither a borrower nor a lender be. Then I accidentally, or maybe not accidentally, trod on his foot.'

Carina laughed. 'You make me feel so safe,' she said.

He shook his head. 'None of us are really safe. But money can make us safe from some things. Like hunger. Or humiliation.'

Carina frowned. It was growing dark now, and the duskiness of her skin seemed to be part of the grainy shadows in the over-decorated parlour. Johann had the strangest feeling that, many years from now, he would remember this day, remember this moment, and think of it with unbearable sadness.

Carina said: 'Are you that much afraid of Beatrice?'

'I don't know. Maybe it's not Beatrice at all. Maybe it's just my feelings that make me concerned. Whenever we're together, I can't stop myself from acting like an idiot.'

Carina set down her wine, and turned in her chair so that she could look at him with that soft, tender warmth that he treasured her for. She was still very young, which made her direct and naïve; but her years of selling herself for the clumsy and rancid satisfaction of old men had given her a sharpness and sense of human absurdity from which Johann often unashamedly learned. She rode around town in her dogcart every evening after the heat of the day had cooled, her matchless profile held high, her expression unalterably calm and self-possessed, and she relished every whispered word, every turned head, and every frown of Baptist disapproval. They knew, you see, that she had something to do with Johann, but they could never quite figure out what. And sometimes she stopped at the drugstore to buy herself peppermint ices, which to the townsfolk seemed to make matters even worse. Whenever she met Johann after work, she would tell him about everything that had amused her, and she described some of Edgar's most sober citizens so wickedly that he laughed until he almost choked.

He loved Carina's company in the way that some men grow to love the company of college friends; but even more than that, she was like a younger sister. She was precious to him, and yet approachable. She brought out in him a capacity for warmth and a feeling of delightful kinship that he could hardly contain. He had no desire to marry her, or to make love to her. That would break the feyness of her spell. But he knew that if he lost her, he would probably lose the dearest person he had ever known. He couldn't describe or understand it any more than that.

Although Edgar was a small town, where gossip flew faster than dry alfalfa in a September wind, Johann's regular visits to Mountolive Street had fortunately escaped Beatrice's attention. She knew of Carina, of course; but only as the orphaned daughter of a Mexican wildcatter to whom, as the man lay crushed under a collapsed rig, Johann had once faithfully promised to act as Carina's protector and guardian. That was the explanation he had given Beatrice the night she arrived to find Carina naked in his apartment ('Poor child, she was filthy from neglect'), and that was the explanation he continued to give, with occasional minor elaborations. It wasn't surprising that Beatrice knew nothing of the whispers and the raised eyebrows that followed Carina wherever her dogcart trotted. The ladies of Edgar were as keen to keep themselves in her good books as she was keen to keep herself in theirs, and apart from that they were extremely fearful of what Johann might do if Beatrice were told the truth. Johann had the kind of intolerant masculinity that made them all flutter and tremble and wish (in their wilder moments) that they weren't already married.

Carina said: 'I can never understand why Beatrice frightens you. You're not scared of anybody else. Everybody else is scared of you.'

Johann took another sip of wine, and stood before a cracked case of hawkmoths with an expression of resignation.

'She's a beautiful woman,' said Carina. 'But she never makes you happy, does she? She never will, either, because she doesn't really love you. Not as I do.'

'You don't think so?' asked Johann, turning. 'I don't know.'

'If I were her, and I loved you as she says she does, I would come out of mourning tonight. I would show you all the tricks that I ever learned with men, and make you happier than you could ever dream. Have you heard of the trick called the Mohawk Claw?'

'Carina,' Johann admonished her.

'But it's true,' insisted Carina. 'When she refuses to come out of mourning, that means that she doesn't love you.'

Johann blew some of the dust from the glass moth case. 'She's frightened, that's all. She can't make up her mind.'

'But how can she love you, if she treats you so bad?'

'She doesn't treat me bad. She's just confused.'

Carina smiled, and shook her head. 'She doesn't love you, Johann. One day you'll have to face it.'

Johann looked away. He suspected that what Carina was saying was true. But somehow, with the dogged refusal to surrender that characterizes those who love but are not loved in return, he supposed, he guessed, that Beatrice was shy, or that she was simply uncertain, or that maybe Liddy's death had affected her more than she had ever revealed.

'Carina,' he said huskily.

She came over and held his arm. He pressed his fingers to his forehead, and he had to swallow before he spoke again.

'She made me shed tears once,' he told her. 'I hope I won't ever have to shed tears again.'

'Johann,' whispered Carina, 'you're not a man of wood and iron. You're a man of skin and blood, like all the rest. You mustn't drive yourself this way.'

He looked at her, and then, very gently, he kissed her braided hair.

'To be rich, I have to be made of wood and iron. Men of skin and blood stay poor.'

She stroked his cheek. She said: 'Tonight, will you stay?'

In the gloom of the parlour, he could see a tear on her cheek, glistening like the reflection of a single star on a dark beach. She kissed his cheek, soft lips against the taut gloss of close shaving.

He put down his empty glass. He answered: 'No,' so quietly that she wasn't sure he had spoken at first.

Early the next morning, he dressed in a blue wool suit and a derby hat, and went out to be shaved at Tatum's Barbershop. This was his sole extravagance, his only self-indulgence, and he would sit back in the big leather-and-iron chair while Jack Tatum lathered his blond prickly chin with a badger brush and then shaved him close and sharp with one of George Wostenholm's Original and True hollow-ground pipe razors. In later years, Johann would often remember Tatum's place at odd and unpredictable times; the sharp smell of the surgical alcohol in which Tatum soaked his teeth at night, the clipping of shears, the bland aroma of shaving soap and the way the early-morning sun fell across the mirror and across the Brown & Bigelow calendar of 'Colette'; and the reason he recalled it was that having himself shaved each morning by a barber was his first outward display of wealth. After Jack Tatum, nothing on which he spent his money would ever have quite the same tang of success.

Freshened up, he walked down Congress Street to the workshop. It was a corner premises, with green-painted window frames and handsome gold lettering that said 'Cornelius (Engineers).' When he opened the front door, the bell tinkled, and Sam Chivers came out to the front counter in his greasy brown apron, bald but whiskery, his half-glasses perched on the end of his reddened nose, like Santa Claus making some last-minute adjustments to his sleigh.

'Hallo, Sam,' said Johann quietly. He closed the door behind him, and walked across the worn boards of the shop toward the counter, taking off his coat as he came. Sam raised the flap for him, and he came through into the inner office, which in turn led out to the stores and the workshops. There was a reverberating clang of hammers on metal, and when he glanced through the glass windows of the office, Johann could see that work on his latest oil-pumping equipment was well-advanced.

Phil McKeogh, his accountant, was sitting waiting for him. He was a painfully thin young man with brilliantined hair and silk socks, and he held his briefcase on his lap like a pet spaniel. Johann said: 'You're up early. I thought accountants slept until sunset.'

McKeogh snickered. 'Today, you'll be glad I didn't. I finished your valuations last night.'

Sam should have gone back to the workshop, but he knew how crucial these evaluations were, and he waited there, his wrench held loose in his hand, and looked at Johann expectantly.

Johann sat down. On his desk was a leather-edged blotter, a brass calendar with yesterday's date on it, a ledger, and a jar of pencils. He clasped his big hands together on top of the blotter and said: 'Well?'

McKeogh grinned, opened his briefcase, and handed over a sheaf of accounts. 'Congratulations,' he said. 'You're a millionaire.'

Johann took the papers and flicked through them. He didn't feel elated, but then this moment had been anticipated for so long, through so many months of hard work and setbacks, that he hadn't expected to. What he did feel, though, was a sense of self-vindication, a sense that he was right, and that God *knew* that he was right.

'It was that well you spudded on the eastern edge of the site that clinched it,' explained McKeogh. 'That's brought up more barrels of crude in two months than the rest of them have in six. And having those new storage tanks is going to help plenty.'

Johann couldn't help smiling. He said: 'Well, Sam, that's it. We made it.'

Sam reached out his hand. 'I'm real pleased for you. I'd just like to say that I hope it brings you what you want.'

'Let's have some brandy,' Johann suggested.

'Not for me,' said McKeogh. 'I have old man Sharp's books to go through this morning, and I can tell you for nothing they need the concentration of Hercules himself.'

They shook hands all around, and then Phil McKeogh left, leaving the doorbell jangling behind him. Johann went to his veneered filing cabinet, took out a bottle of brandy and three glasses, and poured a nip into each.

'Let's have Jack in here, shall we?' he asked Sam. 'I think this is one day we ought to celebrate.'

Sam wiped his hands on his apron. He said: 'You're happy?'

Johann filled the last glass, and then looked up, puzzled. 'Why shouldn't I be?'

'I don't know. It's just that you've been pretty glum of late. And folks are beginning to ask how long the widow-woman of yours is going to stay in her weeds.'

Johann raised his eyebrows. 'So that's it.'

Sam looked a little embarrassed. 'I don't mean to pry. You know that. But we've been working together for a long time now. And I sometimes wonder if you might do yourself some good unburdening yourself. It helps to have a friend to talk to.'

There was an awkward silence, and then Johann said: 'Yes, Sam, I know.'

Sam sat on the edge of Johann's desk. He picked up one of the glasses of brandy, but he didn't drink any. He said: 'You're a rich man now, Johann. You can travel anyplace you want, meet any woman you want. It doesn't seem to make much sense, fretting over a widow-woman like that.'

'Sam, I love her.'

Sam sniffed. 'Maybe you do. But does she love you? That's what folks are asking.'

Johann got up from his desk and walked across to the window that overlooked the workshop. He could see Jack Beak, thin and wiry with dundreary whiskers, hammering away at a metal crossbeam. He said: 'Sam, there's love in her heart somewhere. I know there is. But the woman's a goddess.'

'No woman's a goddess, Johann.'

Johann swiftly shook his head. 'This one is. She has the strength of a man, and the wit of a man, and yet she's a beautiful woman. She scares me to death sometimes. I don't know if I hate her or worship her. But she's got me right here, Sam, right in my heart and my mind, and I can't do anything about it.'

Sam put down his brandy. 'It isn't any of my business, Johann. I'm only trying to tell you what it seems like to me. And it seems like to me that you're chasing after some kind of shadow that isn't there.'

110

'Well, maybe I am.'

Sam reached into his apron pocket and took out a briar pipe. He slowly packed the bowl with negrohead tobacco, and then he struck a match on the window and lit up.

'Have you bedded her?' he asked softly.

Johann shook his head. 'She wouldn't have it. Not till her mourning's over.'

'Well, do you think it might be some kind of idea to try?'

Johann's eyes widened, but he didn't look up.

Sam said: 'I know it sounds blunt. But a cousin of mine in New York was after a widowed lady in much the same way, and it was only because he got himself drunk one Washington's birthday and took her off to bed that he ever found out she was feared of the physical side of things, not having had them for so long.'

Johann grunted. 'I'm not a drinker. One glass of brandy is enough for me.'

'I'm just giving you help, Johann. Sometimes us old people look at things a little more salty than you young ones. There's a time for manners and there's a time for going out there and taking what you want.'

'Sam, you just don't know Beatrice. You don't know her.'

'All women are pretty much alike. It's only moonstruck lovers think they're different.'

'Sam, for Christ's sake!'

Sam shrugged and put his pipe back in his mouth. Then he took it out again and said: 'Listen, I'll have one more word on the subject. If you want to get yourself around to Mrs Mulliner's place one evening, and you want a few hours uninterrupted, I'll ask Mrs Elvira Russell to step out with me for the fiddle concert. I reckon she's always cast an appreciative eye my way, and that's the best I can do.'

Johann lifted his glass. 'That's what I call devotion, Sam I don't think I'd step out with Mrs Elvira Russell any more than I'd step out with a bald eagle.'

'Do you want me to do it?'

There was a long silence. Then Johann said: 'I don't know, Sam. I don't think so.'

Sam stuck his thumbs in his apron. 'Okay, Johann. But the offer's always there.'

'Anyway,' said Johann, 'I believe I'm more interested in business right now. It's time I went to New York.'

111

'New York? What about the business here?'

'Slobodien's quite capable of looking after the oil rigs.'

'But this place?'

Johann frowned, and looked around the workshop. 'You can run this place for a couple of months, can't you? You and Jack? You can always call on Phil McKeogh if you have trouble with the books.'

'I don't understand why you're going. Just when you're doing so good.'

Johann stood up. 'It's very simple. I have a million dollars and it's time to make use of them. If you stay still, you get rusty. I want to keep going, keep making more. I want to get into insurance, and shipping, and maybe buy some railroad stock. I want to fix up a better price for refining my crude. I want to find out what goes on in Wall Street. I want to stop being a rich rube and start being a businessman.'

'What about Beatrice?'

Johann paused. 'Well, I don't know. Maybe she'll want to come along. Maybe she'll wait here. A couple of months without me might help her to make up her mind.'

'You really think so?'

Johann looked at him. 'I don't know what I think. But I'll have to find out, won't I? I can't keep dancing on the end of her mourning ribbons.'

Sam leaned forward on the desk. 'Listen, Johann, just let me ask Mrs Elvira Russell to step out with me. Just let me do that once. Then, when you're alone with Beatrice, seize your chance. Do it before you go away to New York.'

'Sam—'

Sam tilted his head on one side. 'I know what you're thinking. You're thinking that I don't understand how sacred this lady is to you, that I don't understand anything at all. But sooner or later you're going to have to do something, Johann. You can't spend the rest of your natural life standing around like a cigar-store Indian.'

Johann fingered the edges of the valuation reports which told him he was a millionaire. Then he said: 'You'd better call Jack. Let's celebrate before we spend it.'

Late the following evening, Thursday, he was still at his desk by the time it grew dark. The last act of the day was to write a long letter, by hand, to the headquarters of Amarero

Oil in New York. Ever since he'd struck crude out at Sweetwater Trail, Johann's relationships with Amarero Oil had been cordial and constructive. He had lent them equipment on several occasions, and he was on good terms with their crews and their foremen. He did little business with them. All his crude oil he sold to the Colton Oil company for refining, simply because Colton's prices were better. But he had the kind of business mentality that looks way ahead into the future, and it occurred to him that the day might come when he needed to buy an outfit like Amarero Oil, and it would help if they were already amenable.

The letter concerned Kylē Lennox. It was a friendly letter that belied what Johann was actually trying to do. Now that Johann was worth well over a million dollars, and now that Jerry Slobodien had reported that the eight rigs out at Sweetwater Trail were bringing in twenty-five thousand barrels a day, Kyle Lennox's eight percent was fast becoming a small fortune in its own right. It was not that Johann begrudged Carina her price. It was just that enough was enough, especially as far as a cheap toad like Kyle Lennox was concerned, and after Phil McKeogh's valuations Johann had made up his mind to elbow Lennox out of his way.

In sentence after sentence, he praised Kyle Lennox's abilities as a manager, even though he was quite aware that Amarero Oil considered him unreliable and disagreeable. He called Lennox 'upstanding and discerning' and said that he was 'worth his salt.' And then, almost as an afterthought, he asked if Amarero Oil would care to help him out by transferring Lennox's contract to Cornelius Oil, and thus affording Johann the services of a 'true veteran of the oilfields.'

He sealed the letter, addressed it, and then put on his coat and closed up the workshop for the night. He knew that Amarero Oil would find his suggestion irresistible, and he was even humming to himself as he turned down the lamps on his desk. Once he had Lennox's contract in his own safe, things would begin to look very different. Lennox's eight percent would be discontinued immediately, and if Lennox complained – well, the circuit judges didn't think much of employees who griped about their employers, especially when their employers were as rich and as potentially influential as Johann.

He left the office and locked the door behind him. Out on the dark street, a cool evening breeze was blowing, and there was a distant yowling of wild dogs. He heard a footstep on the boardwalk, and he turned around to see Sam Chivers leaning against the veranda post, smoking his pipe.

'Sam. I didn't see you there.'

'I haven't been here long.'

'Why didn't you come inside? There was some brandy left over from yesterday.'

Sam stepped forward, and the light from an upstairs window fell across his brushed velour hat and a smart powder-blue suit that Johann had never seen him wearing before. He smelled strongly of lavender.

'To tell you the truth,' he said, 'I was kind of embarrassed.'

Johann smiled, a little quirkily. 'You look like you're dressed for a Spanish funeral.'

'Well, not quite. But I *am* dressed up to take Mrs Elvira Russell out for an evening stroll.'

'I thought you were taking her out to a fiddle concert.'

Sam prodded at the bowl of his pipe. Across the street, in the shadows, a tethered horse restlessly shook its harness. Sam said: 'The fiddle concert isn't till Wednesday next. I thought you needed your help a little more urgent than that.'

'Sam,' said Johann, 'I'm *not* going around there. You can walk Mrs Elvira Russell till your legs drop off. But I can't go near Beatrice with any kind of personal proposition until she comes out of mourning. And that's all.'

Sam sighed. 'Johann,' he said, 'you're pretty dumb for a millionaire. Can't you get it through that head of yours that Beatrice is chewing the strings of her stays, just waiting for you to go around there and pull her out of those widow's weeds headfirst? She wants you to do it, Johann. She *needs* you to do it. Otherwise there won't be any feeling that she's been chased, and catched. A woman needs to be catched, Johann, and that's one of the first facts of life.'

Johann took a deep breath. 'I'm taking this letter to the Wells Fargo office, and then I'm going across to Walsh's for supper. After that, I'm going home to bed, and I'm going to go through the cracking analyses until I fall to sleep.'

Sam gripped his arm. Under the shadow of his hat, Johann could just make out the rheumy gleam of his eyes. The old-timer paused for a moment, not certain what kind of words could cajole Johann into taking a chance with Beatrice, but then he said dryly: 'How old are you, Johann?'

'Thirty. Why?'

'Just asking. It seems to me that thirty's kind of old to stay unwed. What happens if you pass away without an heir for all that money of yours?'

'I'm not planning on passing away.'

'Nobody ever is.'

'Well, even if I do, I won't be too worried about my money, will I? I'll be dead.'

Sam sighed again. 'You take a hell of a lot of persuading.'

'I'm not going to see Beatrice tonight, Sam, and that's my last word.'

'You'd let me suffer a whole evening with Elvira Russell for nothing? I've promised her now. I can't go back on my promise.'

'Sam, I'm not going.'

'You're scared.'

'Maybe I am.'

Sam pushed back his hat. 'Well, will you walk along with me to Mrs Elvira Russell's door? I kind of hate to face the old crow alone.'

Johann looked at him for a while, and then nodded. 'Okay. But next time, ask me first before you go asking old ladies out for decoy walks.'

They stepped off the veranda and crossed the street in the cold light of an early moon. There was a smell of sausage and dust and mesquite in the night air. A piano was tinkling 'My Love from Level-land,' and someone in an upstairs room was arguing loudly.

'I was thinking,' said Sam, as they walked side by side down Kearney Street. 'This town is too small for you now, when you come to consider it. I guess you're right to think of New York.'

Johann was looking ahead, toward the lighted veranda of Mrs Elvira Russell's two-storey weatherboard house. He said: 'It's not so much New York, Sam. It's the whole world.'

They walked up to the front door, and Sam rang the bell that hung down beside it. 'I was considering taking Mrs Russell down to the church hall. I hear there's a singing practice tonight.'

115

Johann smiled. 'Rather you than me.'

They heard footsteps inside the house, and then Mrs Russell appeared at the door. She was a very tall woman with wide shoulders, from which her high-buttoned dresses were draped across her bustless chest like a tarpaulin over an old gun carriage. Her face was big as a buffalo's, and her hair was twisted and knotted into an iron-grey confusion of braids. She saw Sam, and pursed her lips in incongruous flirtation.

'Sam Chivers! And early, too. And you too, Mr Cornelius! I didn't know you were coming along.'

Johann coughed. 'Well, I'm not. I was just taking a short stroll with Sam. I'll say good night now.'

'I'll fetch my wrap.' Mrs Russell bustled. 'Do you step inside here, Sam Chivers. I won't be more than a moment.'

Johann said: 'Good night, Sam. Good night, Mrs Russell,' and he was about to turn to leave when he heard Beatrice's voice call: 'Johann! Is that Johann?'

Johann turned, and glanced at Sam tautly. Sam hesitated for a moment, and then said: 'That's right, Mrs Mulliner. He's just leaving.'

Beatrice came through the lamplit hallway, and paused by the front door. She was wearing a long simple dress of dark brown cotton, which for some reason reminded Johann of the dress that Carina had worn the first day he found her. In the glow of the oil lamps, Beatrice looked more goddesslike and more beautiful than ever.

'Don't go,' she said. 'Why not stay for a sherry-wine?'

Mrs Elvira Russell was busily arranging a fringed wrap around her broad shoulders, and pinning her hat on. 'If Mr Cornelius stays, Beatrice, then I'll have to stay, too, and I must say that I'm not inclined to. I've been looking forward to this walk with Mr Chivers all the day.'

'He can stay for five minutes, Aunt Elvira. I *am* a grown woman.'

'That's what your cousin Coreen used to say, and she was assaulted by fish porters.'

Beatrice gave that small, mystic smile. 'Aunt Elvira, there are no fish porters for three hundred miles.'

'Very well. But for five minutes only. I don't want my house connected with scandal.'

116

Johann, hat in hand, felt disturbed and discomfited. He said: 'I have some work to catch up on, as a matter of fact.'

'You can spare five minutes,' insisted Beatrice. 'Come inside, and let me have your hat.'

Sam, as he passed, gave him a quick squeeze on his elbow. He paused in mid-step, uncertain, but then he followed Beatrice inside, and into the dowdy little parlour. The windows had been closed all day, and the parlour was uncomfortably stuffy.

Beatrice sat down at one end of the leatherette settee and said: 'The sherry-wine is to your left of the two decanters. A small one will be quite enough for me.'

Johann opened the cabinet, took down two glasses, and poured the sherry. Beatrice said: 'I was thinking of you today.'

He looked around. 'Oh, yes?'

She smiled briefly. 'I was thinking of how you came into my life, in need of my assistance; and how I came back into yours, in need of your assistance. It shows that life has a certain ironic balance, don't you think?'

Johann handed Beatrice her glass. Behind him, the front door slammed shut as Sam Chivers and Mrs Elvira Russell went off for their stroll and their singing practice. Johann wondered how long they were going to stay out. He coughed, and perched himself on the opposite end of the settee.

'Here's to your million,' said Beatrice, raising her glass.

'And here's to you,' replied Johann, much more quietly, raising his.

They drank, and then exchanged embarrassed smiles.

'It seems strange to be on our own,' remarked Beatrice. 'I am so used to having Aunt Elvira hovering over me. She is very particular, you know. I sometimes wonder what on earth she would have thought about all those misbehaviours of mine.'

'Does the brown dress mean that you're out of mourning?'

Beatrice glanced down at it. Then she shook her head. 'No, it means that all my black dresses are in the laundry.'

Johann looked down at his glass. 'Why don't you consider it?' he asked her.

'Consider what?'

'You know what I mean. Coming out of mourning.'

'But I've told you. I'm simply not ready.'

Johann lifted his eyes. 'I have to go to New York, you know.'

She gave him a quick sideways glance. 'New York?'

'I can't stay in Edgar forever. This place has been good to me, but there's more to business than pumping up a little oil and mending broken-down compressors.'

'Well . . .' said Beatrice. She sounded put out. 'I suppose it had to be.'

Johann didn't answer. Beatrice put down her drink and stood up, brushing the creases out of her dress. She went to the fireplace and looked at herself in the mirror over the mantelpiece. She saw, in her own eyes, the face of a woman who was probably born too comely, at least for the life she was destined to lead. And seeing herself in this dingy parlour, with this rich but clumsy man, she suddenly felt very sorry for herself. When she looked down at her hands, she was twisting her wedding ring around and around with almost feverish nervousness.

'Well,' she said, 'I expect I shall get used to it.'

'Used to what?'

She turned, with a tight smile. 'Used to living out my life in godforsaken towns in the west of Texas, taking my tea by myself, and wondering whether life ever did have anything else to offer me.'

'Beatrice – life has a whole storehouse of things to offer you.'

She lifted her hands as if it was all hopeless. 'You're a man,' she said. 'A man is a free agent. He can go where he pleases, do what he likes. He can go to saloons and drink. He can drive automobiles, and curse out loud. He can vote. But what can a woman do, even if she has the spirit? She has to rely on a husband for all things. She even has to rely on him to provide her the means to be unfaithful.'

Johann rubbed his chin. He didn't know what to say.

Beatrice came over and offered her hands. She said, more gently this time: 'I don't mean to hurt you, Johann. You know that, don't you? But I'm no longer sure of my feelings. Your work and your money seem to mean so much to you. I feel when I'm with you that your mind is always somewhere else, always thinking about business, always thinking about making more money. If we're to have any kind of life together, if I'm to have any kind of life with you, I must

118

know that you're not going to lock me up in a house on my own, fretting for love, while you go off to New York and Washington and San Francisco, chasing your dollars and forgetting your wife. That's what happened with Lidmore. He put me in prison while he went off to work. Don't you see that a woman can only be free when her husband's there beside her?'

Johann cleared his throat. 'You don't think that I could make you happy?'

'Johann – I need *reassurance*. I need to know that you wouldn't treat me like Liddy. I need to believe that, whatever happens, your feelings for me will always come before business. *Always*, without question.'

He looked at her, confused. He couldn't understand her at all. She had come to live in Edgar so that they could be close during her mourning, and eventually marry. At least, that was the way he had believed things to be. Yet she had prolonged her mourning indefinitely, and as the months went by, he had gradually grown to believe that he would be best occupied in making as much money as he possibly could and biding his time. Now that he was off to New York, however, she seemed to have changed her mind altogether, and was actually setting out her terms for marrying him.

What he didn't know was that Beatrice was deeply afraid. She had privately postponed the day that she was to come out of mourning again and again; not because she was afraid of marriage, but because she was afraid of marriage to Johann. He was a different man from the poor young hopeful she had first coquettishly entertained in her parlour. Since then, he had made his own money, and learned to handle it, and grown sharper and quicker and wiser. Whereas she had once been able to control him, and twist him around her finger, he was now quite capable of doing the same to her, and would have done if he had realized just how pale her influence over him had faded. He still adored her, still loved her, but she knew that once he saw real society, and real wealth, she would probably lose him forever.

The alternatives kept her awake nights. If Johann left her behind in Edgar, she would be beached in this stuffy plains community without means, apart from what Liddy had left her, and without an escort. But if she married him and went with him, she knew that her social skills, no matter how grand they seemed to the ladies of Edgar, would seem hopelessly gauche in comparison to the celestial etiquette of big-city hostesses. Only Beatrice herself knew how overwhelming her fear of social humiliation was. It was almost greater than her fear of being left alone.

She said: 'I need to feel protected, Johann, and cosseted as a wife should be. I need the security of my own house, and to know that you're not going to leave me alone while you go off on business. I don't want to be an oil-well widow, or a compressor widow, or even a Wall Street widow. If we are to marry, I want you to be here by my side, as my attentive husband.'

Johann reached out for her hand. 'Haven't I been attentive up until now?'

'You're attentive to your business, too.'

'Of course. What man isn't?'

Beatrice smiled sadly. 'I told you when I first met you that I was starved of affection. I am an affectionate woman, Johann. But a woman cannot decently go in *search* of affection, as a man can, and that is why I need to know that you will build me a house, and in that house be constantly more attentive to me than anything or anybody else in your life. You want me to be faithful, don't you?'

'Of course.'

'Of course! But that means that I want you to be equally faithful to me!'

'I shall be. I swear it.'

She sat down next to him on the leatherette settee, grasped his hands, and kissed him, very lightly, on the end of his nose.

'Then you won't go to New York?'

He looked at her narrowly. 'I *have* to.'

'Even if it means we can't marry?'

'Beatrice, I don't understand!'

'Johann, it has to *be*! I have been mistreated in love all my life! I have never known what it is like to live with pride and affection with the man I desire! I need to be loved, Johann, all the hours and all the minutes and all the seconds of my life! If you wish to marry me, if you wish me to cast aside my weeds, then you will have to promise that love forever and ever!'

Johann was silent. He could feel his own heart beating,

120

tight and slow. The brass clock on the mantelpiece whirred softly and then began a ridiculously elaborate chiming that went on for almost a minute.

Beatrice whispered: 'You may kiss me, if you wish.'

He blinked at her.

'Do you want me to prove myself to you?' she asked, her voice soft but heated. 'Are you concerned that your love will be demanded but not returned?'

'I don't know,' he said uncertainly. 'It seems that you're not yourself. One moment it was almost impossible to persuade you to talk about marriage, and now you're insisting on it.'

'Perhaps I've realized what a prize might be slipping out of my grasp. Perhaps I've made up my mind.'

'Made up your mind about what?'

'You. That you're really the man I need.'

'I don't understand what made you suddenly—'

She smiled, and then gave an odd little laugh. 'Does it matter? Does anything matter except for us?'

'Well . . . some things do.'

She shifted herself nearer to him, and he could feel that tightness in his heart squeeze even tighter. That perfume of hers, that heady scent of heliotrope, seemed to affect his mind. Through the brown cotton of her dress, her body felt very warm and enticing, and he felt, quite unexpectedly, a sensation of passion for her that soaked over his emotions like syrup over a stack of dry pancakes.

'You won't go, will you?' she whispered.

'Beatrice, Bea, you can't hold back the natural course of a river. If I have to go to New York, I have to go. It's what my life is about. It's *me*.'

She put her arm around his neck. He felt very short of breath.

'Don't you love me?' she coaxed him. 'You said you adored me.'

'My God, I do.'

'Then say you won't go. Say you'll marry me, and stay with me forever. Promise me that much.'

'Beatrice, that's *everything*.'

'Won't you give me everything? Don't you adore me?'

'Of course. More than my life. Don't you believe me?'

She kissed him, first his cheek and then his lips. Her

121

mouth was indescribably soft and luscious to him, a sweet fruit that he wanted to bite into and devour. He could feel her breasts against him, heavy and taut in their stays. Deep down, he had a hotness and a hardness that threatened to overwhelm him.

He held her back. His hair was ruffled, and he felt as if he were trying to hold back a landslide.

'Your mourning,' he breathed. 'What about your mourning?'

'It's over,' she said. 'All you have to do is say it, say you'll marry me, say you'll stay with me, promise, promise, promise, and it'll be over.'

Her fingers brushed against the tautness in his lap, and he shivered.

'Oh, my darling Johann,' she whispered, holding him close again, and licking at his ear. 'All you have to do is promise.'

'Beatrice, that's—'

His head dropped, and he shut his eyes tight. He was torn inside by such lusts and such fears that he could hardly think.

'Promise,' she said softly. 'Please promise.'

He opened his eyes. 'You're asking for everything,' he told her in a croaky voice. 'I love you, Beatrice. You can't even understand how much I love you. But you're asking for everything.'

She nestled closer. 'Oh, promise,' she begged him. Her hand stroked his thigh, and her wrist kept touching his hardest and most sensitive spot. He took a deep breath, and raised his head.

'Look,' she said, and she reached her hand inside his coat and took out his brown leather wallet. She had given it to him herself, last Christmas, and had admonished him to fill it to bursting. She opened it up now, and took out his money – five or six hundred dollars in singles, fives, and tens, and twenties. She stood up, clutching the money in her hand.

'Is *this* what you want, instead of me? More of this? Don't you have enough already? You're a millionaire! You have oil wells! If you stay here in Edgar, if you marry me, you can have us both! Money and me – both!'

Bright-eyed, she tossed the money up into the air, and the parlour was filled with floating, swooping bills. Then, as they scattered over the rug she raised her brown dress, and sat down among them, a saucy curtsy amidst a shower of greenbacks.

Johann looked at her, electrified. Her long, well-shaped legs were gleaming in their black silk stockings. Then he could see her black stocking supporters, and the lace-trimmed edge of her corset cover. She wore no bloomers, and against the dull carpet he could make out the faintest suggestion of dark curls.

She smiled at him. 'Oh, Johann. Don't change. Let's be just the way we were, on that day you first came to tea. We had walnut cake, remember?'

He stood up. His head was pounding. He tugged off his coat; then, even more rapidly, he unbuttoned his vest, and loosened his cuff links. As he did so, Beatrice lay back in the litter of money, and held up her arms towards him, enticing him. His muscles were trembling with anticipation, and his broad chest was flushed. He felt as if he had completely lost control of himself, and was acting like a stiff and jerky puppet in a paper theatre. Dressed in nothing but his close-fitting white cotton underwear, with the front of his fly unfastened, his red hardness bare, he knelt down on the rustling dollars and grasped her silk-sheathed thighs in both of his broad muscular hands, parting them wider.

'Take me now,' coaxed Beatrice. 'I have had so many, Johann, but none like you. Take me now.'

He leaned over her, panting with strain and passion, and presented his crimson head to her moist black curls. She pulled his face down toward her, and kissed him, savagely and fiercely, as if she wanted to tear his ears off, or rip the flesh in tatters from his cheeks.

'Promise,' she gasped, as he was about to thrust for the first time. 'Promise you'll stay. Promise you'll love me, and keep me, and promise you'll never go away. Promise you won't go to New York.'

Johann's eyes were tight shut. He felt as if he were nearer to Beatrice than he could ever imagine possible, and yet a thousand thousand miles away. He loved her so much that he could scarcely take a breath, and he could feel her warmth and wetness touching his glans like a siren's kiss.

'*Promise*,' she insisted.

He made a noise that, even to him, sounded like a suppressed sob. Then he said: 'I promise,' and she opened herself up to him, and he pushed inside her so hard and so big that she actually jumped.

It was short, greedy, loud, and so overwhelming that both of them screamed at each other in their lust The dollar bills, fives and tens and twenties, flurried around them as Johann thrust and thrust and thrust with all of his masculine strength, thrusting against everything that had been crowded inside his mind for so long, thrusting against the passion he felt for Beatrice, thrusting against the world that threatened to fall in on him and crush him.

Then Beatrice shrieked like a coyote bitch, and tore her fingernails all the way up his back, inside his cotton combinations, and the pain of it triggered off an endlessly sharp, pumping ejaculation that finally, finally, when the last tremors had shaken him, left him feeling as if he had departed the world altogether, left Texas, and spun around distant stars.

The next he knew, Beatrice was lying beside him, kissing him over and over, and saying: 'You promised. Oh, you're beautiful. You promised.'

Johann felt stunned, elated, and awash on waves of love and disbelief. He held her in his arms, touching the miraculous softness of her face and her ears. He kissed her with great tenderness, and whispered hoarsely, 'I love you. My God, Beatrice, I love you more than I could ever say.'

Beatrice's lashes were moist with tears. She kissed him back, as lightly as a butterfly alighting on his lips. There was a slight mark of worry on her forehead, but she was flushed pink with the excitement and the exertion of their lovemaking, and no matter what fears the future held, she knew that she could never explain to Johann what it was to have a man after so long.

'We'd better dress now,' she said softly. 'Aunt Elvira will be back soon.'

Johann kissed her again, and held her face against his chest. 'I was beginning to think this would never happen,' he told her

Beatrice sat on the floor, with one silken calf bared, while he collected his clothes and his money and dressed. As he tied his necktie in the glass above the mantelpiece, she said: 'I shall announce tomorrow that my mourning is over, and that we are courting. Then perhaps we can look for a place to build our house.'

He tugged at the bows of his necktie, and then turned around to look at her. He was about to say something when there was a knock at the front door.

'That must be Aunt Elvira. She's forgotten ner key Quick, Johann – let her in, while I button up my dress. Look, you've left some money on the floor there.'

Johann went to the front door and opened it. On the porch, in the dim light of the moth-riddled lamp, stood a Western Union boy with cockeyed spectacles and tousled blond hair. He stiffly held out an envelope and said: 'Wire, sir, from New Orleans. Addressed to Mrs Mulliner.'

Johann frowned, and reached into his vest for a nickel. He didn't know that Beatrice was acquainted with anyone in New Orleans, let alone anyone who might send her a wire.

The boy, quite gratuitously, said: 'Her sister is dead. Died of consumption. They're sending her nephew up to stay here in Edgar.'.

Beatrice, pinning up her hair, came out into the hall and said: 'Who is it, Johann? What's happened?'

Johann turned, and handed her the wire with a cold feeling of misgiving. 'Before you open that,' he said, 'I want you to know that I love you.'

The boy stood on the boardwalk of Broughton railroad station in his tan double-breasted English suit with elasticated breeches, his shoes brightly polished and a clean white handkerchief poking from his top pocket, and all around him the long shadows of a fall evening in Texas stretched across the street. Beside him was a cardboard valise with cheap tin locks. It had a manila label, as did the boy. The train had long since clanked and chuffed its way out of the station, and disappeared around the bend by the sun-bleached palings and the freight yards. Since the boy had been waiting, almost two hours, the sky had darkened from clear blue to dusky indigo.

The man who served as master of the station, as collector of fares, and as sweeper and sluicer of the station premises, a friendly ginger-haired fellow with a peaked cap and a large railroad watch, came out from the station building and approached the boy slowly, his hands planted irremovably

125

in his pockets, and he stood for a while just a few yards away, whistling 'Who Put the Overalls in Mrs Murphy's Chowder?' through the gap in his front teeth.

'Your folks coming to get you?' asked the stationmaster. 'Seems to me you've been waiting a powerful long time.'

The boy looked up. He was pale and serious, and about nine years old. He touched his tan rep cap before he answered, which showed the stationmaster he was well-reared. He had very blue eyes. He looked tired and thirsty.

'A friend is coming to collect me, sir. My aunt's new gentleman, in his automobile.'

The stationmaster rocked backward and forward on his heels. He had an elderly mother at home, senile but still blessed with a hilarious line in piano-salesman stories. He said: 'So that's it. Well, you can bet your pants to a pile of snow that he's broke down. I always said those automobiles wouldn't stand the pace, because I'm a railroad man myself, and I don't believe in travel without rails. My pappy was a railroad man before I was, Texas and Pacific, in the days of Dodge, and he used to say that if folks was intended to travel wherever and whenever the mood took them, then God would have laid rails here, there, and every which place.'

'The name of my aunt's new gentleman is Mr Cornelius, sir,' said the boy to the stationmaster.

The stationmaster turned and looked down at him. Then he looked around and said, 'Come inside.'

He picked up the boy's valise in case anyone should take a fancy to it, which was unlikely, since it contained only clean undervests and a book that the boy's father had given him when he was six, about famous desperadoes of the West. Then he pushed open the brass-handled door of his office, which was a dusty and stifling little room with a cluttered rolltop desk and dozens and dozens of railroad dockets and timetables pinned to the walls in curled-up sheaves. There was a gloomy railroad clock which measured time so grudgingly that the boy kept thinking it was about to stop, but it never did.

'Sit down,' suggested the stationmaster. There was a wooden crate of oil-rig spares by the side of the desk, and the boy did so. The stationmaster opened and shut almost every drawer until he found a box of stale Spanish-peanut candy. He offered some to the boy, but the boy declined, and so he chewed off a piece himself, and everything he said was accompanied by a great deal of munching and swallowing and sticking his little finger between his teeth to clear out the sticky pieces.

'I guess your aunt is Mrs Beatrice Mulliner, the widow lady,' said the stationmaster.

The boy whispered: 'Yes.'

The stationmaster leaned forward and read the boy's label. 'Well, that's a good guess. "Master Daniel Forster, c/o Mrs Beatrice Mulliner, Kearney Street, Edgar, Texas. To be collected." '

The boy said: 'Is there anything wrong? Has something gone wrong?'

The stationmaster sat back in his swivel chair. 'Not in so many words, Master Daniel Forster. But I guess you're old enough to know what folks hereabouts think of Mr Cornelius, your aunt's new gentleman, and you'd be well-advised to hold it in mind.'

Sitting on the crate, the boy suddenly began to think of his mother, and even though he was listening to the ginger-haired stationmaster, he began to feel an uncomfortable lump in his throat, as if he were going to cry. After waiting outside the station for two hours, he was beginning to miss his usual teatime milk, and he couldn't help feeling a painful yearning for the quiet house in the genteel suburbs of New Orleans with its orchards and rambling gardens, and if he closed his eyes he could almost see the blue gingham table-cloth where he used to sit and drink his beaker of milk before going out for a last play.

'You mustn't think I'm being ill-natured,' said the stationmaster, 'but I like you. You're a good old boy, and I guess forewarned is usually forearmed, and I reckon you could do with some of that forearming. You take my word for it, J. Cornelius is a hard man, hard as rocks, hard as nails. He's rich as all hell, but the way I heard it, he got that way more through cheating than hard work, and anyone who gets in his way gets pulled up and tossed aside like tumbleweed. I've heard some odd tales of his tricks, I can tell you, and I reckon you'd be doing yourself a favour, and Mrs Mulliner too, if you kept your ear to the rail '

The boy said anxiously: 'Nothing's gone wrong, has it?'

The stationmaster sucked at his teeth to get out the candy

'Not in so many words. But you go see for yourself. Now you're forewarned, you won't let nothing take you by surprise. And if you ever feel the need, pass a note to Jack Beak, he's an old railroad buddy of mine, from the Santa Fe, and Jack'll make sure it gets to me.'

Biting his lip, the boy said: 'I'm not quite sure what you've warned me about. I'm afraid I don't quite understand.'

The stationmaster reached over and laid his hand on the boy's shoulder. 'Master Daniel Forster,' he said, 'you've got yourself a whole lot of growing up to do before I can tell you all there is. But you keep your ear to the rail, and you'll be ready when the train comes.'

Almost at the moment, there was the regurgitating sound of a motor horn outside. The stationmaster said: 'That'll be him. Are you ready now?'

The boy said: 'I'm afraid, a little.'

'No you're not,' chided the stationmaster. 'Here, take this. Keep it by you, and in emergencies, blow it like billy-o.'

He handed Daniel a real metal railroad whistle, with a brass ring and a green cord. Daniel took it hesitantly, but then he realized it was actually his, and he put it eagerly into the pocket of his tan suit. He said formally: 'Thank you, sir. Your generosity is much appreciated.'

The stationmaster cuffed him lightheartedly. 'You get along now. Here's your bag. And remember your old friend if you ever feel unhappy, and come down here and see me again soon. The name's K. Jones, stationmaster.'

Daniel solemnly shook hands with the stationmaster, and then hefted his valise and walked out into the late-afternoon sunlight. Johann's automobile was waiting in the yard, juddering and shaking as its engine ticked over, and Johann himself was sitting at the wheel in his white motoring coat, his eyes concealed by small dark-tinted goggles. Especially after K. Jones's dire warning, his aunt's new gentleman appeared to Daniel like some kind of bizarre ogre, and it didn't help the boy's nerve much when Johann sat there, silent and unmoving, while he tried to lift his valise into the back of the car.

Daniel climbed up to the front seat, and sat there waiting for something to happen. Over at the station door, the stationmaster stood with his hands in his pockets whistling his favourite tune and watching what went on.

128

Johann said dryly: 'Do you know who I am?'

Daniel said: 'Yes, sir,' in a very small voice.

'What did you say?' asked Johann, louder.

I said, "Yes, sir."'

Johann regarded the boy for a long moment, his eyes invisible behind his dark goggles. He said: 'Well, if you know who I am, why don't you raise your cap?'

The boy coloured, and raised his cap. 'Sorry, sir.'

Johann, quite unexpectedly, gave a small, lopsided smile He said: 'You don't have to say sorry. I was taught to do the same when I was a boy, and cuffed when I didn't. When you're a boy, manners are worth having. They help you survive in a world made for grown-ups.'

Daniel was completely perplexed. But he didn't have much time to think about Johann's peculiar words, for Johann said: 'Hold tight!' released the hand brake, engaged the gears, and drove out of the railroad yard with three loud backfires.

Johann drove as if there were only two possible speeds – halted or flat out – and over the ruts and gullies of Broughton's sun-hardened roads, Daniel bounced up and down in his seat like the needle bar on top of a sewing machine. He had never travelled in an automobile before, and he was thoroughly alarmed by the dust and the noise and the terrible speed. Beside him, Johann was hunched over the four-spoke steering wheel as if bending double was an essential part of increasing the automobile's velocity.

'The fastest machine around!' shouted Johann, as they came clattering around the corner into Broughton's main street. 'What do you think of it?'

Daniel, white-faced, could do nothing but stare at Johann and try to smile.

They drove through Broughton's neat and respectable centre, past Howard's Refreshment Parlor, past houses and stores and stables, and headed northward across flat ranch country, under an engulfing sky the colour of purple laundry ink, the wind and the dust blowing in their faces. Daniel had to screw up his eyes to prevent the road grit from making them smart, and keep his pocket handkerchief pressed to his nose and mouth.

Johann said 'There's nothing like it for blowing out

129

cobwebs, a ride in an automobile. You don't have time to be gloomy, like you would in a carriage.'

Daniel didn't know what to say to that, or whether he was expected to say anything at all. Whatever K. Jones had told him about his aunt's new gentleman, Johann Cornelius appeared to be tolerably dashing, and quite friendly. Whether he was really as hard as rocks was another matter, but Daniel was old enough to suppose that a man could be as hard as rocks to his business partners, and yet civil and amiable to his friends.

'I think Texas looks very wild,' he ventured to say. 'Are there still desperadoes here?'

Johann thought about that, and then laughed. 'There are always desperadoes here,' he said, 'and not all of them have guns.'

Daniel waited for Johann to say something else, or explain what he meant, but that seemed to be all. They drove in silence for another two or three miles, across a breezy plateau with only a faint violet smudge on the horizon to suggest there might be mountains in the distance, or clouds, and then Johann suddenly reached in his pocket and handed Daniel a greaseproof-paper packet.

'Cold beef sandwiches. Beatrice made them for you.'

Daniel took them gratefully, and opened them up. 'Would you like one, sir?' he asked politely. Although Johann didn't say very much, and seemed to speak in conundrums whenever he did decide to talk, Daniel was beginning to like him. He was a man's man. He drove and drove at top speed, and there was something larger than life and heroic about him.

Johann said: 'Much obliged,' and took a sandwich, and crammed it into his mouth as he drove. Daniel bit into his, and made a neat semicircle with his teeth.

Johann said, with his mouth full: 'This place is going to be good for you, do you know that? It's wild all right, and that's just what you need. Start up a new life, put all the past behind you. I'll help you. Forget about the sad things that happened before, and start fresh.'

Daniel swallowed his sandwich before he spoke, the way his mother had taught him. It seemed strange that Johann should be so insistent on him raising his cap, and yet could blithely talk and eat at the same time. He said: 'The stationmaster told me you were hard as rocks.'

Johann turned and looked at him with those piggy-eyed goggles.

'He said that? Those were his actual words?'

'Yes, sir. "Hard as rocks," he said. And he said you cheated people.'

'Cheated people? What did he mean by that?'

Daniel frowned. He wasn't sure now that he should have betrayed K. Jones's confidence. But at the same time, Johann was Beatrice's gentleman, wasn't he? And if Beatrice was fond of him, and if Daniel himself felt that he was friendly, then what could be the harm? Maybe K. Jones had exchanged cross words with Johann Cornelius, and bore a grudge. You could never tell with stationmasters.

'I'm not sure,' he told Johann uncertainly. 'He didn't really explain himself.'

Johann looked at Daniel for one moment more, and then turned his attention back to the wheel of the car. The last glowering rays of the sun touched his goggles, and sparked off them as if his eyes were godly lances of fire.

'Well,' he said at last, 'I suppose what he says is true.'

Daniel took another bite of sandwich, and then quickly had to put it down and cling to his seat. The track across the plateau was crusted with the hoofprints of cattle, baked into the mud, and the automobile shook and rattled as it crossed over them.

'This is a land of hard men,' said Johann. 'They came here when there was nothing but prairie and dust. They're proud of their hardness, and if you want to best them, you have to be harder still. I've been trying to make my fortune here, Daniel, and that's why I conduct myself the way that I do.'

He was silent for a while, and then he said: 'When I came to America, I had nothing and nobody. I was worse off than you are now, because I didn't even have aunts or friends. Well, when you're alone like that, and you have to make your way up from the basement, you learn to keep yourself to yourself, and to show nobody that you're hurt, or disappointed, or angry, or even when you're happy, if you ever are. If you do show them, just once, then they'll turn your weaknesses against you, and you'll be back down to the basement before you know.'

Daniel believed that he understood this. He would have liked to hear more, but Johann didn't seem to have any more to say, and so for the next few miles they sat side by side without speaking.

'Is Aunt Beatrice well, sir?' Daniel asked at last.

Johann glanced at him. He had been thinking about Carina. He said: 'Saddened by your mother's death, but otherwise well

'Is she a good friend of yours, sir? A very good friend?'

Johann took out his handkerchief and loudly blew dust out of his nose. 'We were to marry, as a matter of fact,' he said, sniffing.

'Were to, sir? Does that mean you won't?'

'Well, I'm not so sure. We couldn't wed up until now because she was mourning your uncle Lidmore. Now she's mourning your mother, and that has postponed things for a while longer. I suppose we shall marry eventually. She's a very attractive and self-willed lady, your aunt.'

'I don't know Aunt Beatrice very well, sir. She only came down to see us once, and I was just a child then.'

Johann nodded. 'You'll get to know her now. She's a lady in a hundred thousand, I can promise you that.'

Daniel looked serious. 'You do sound as if you like her, sir, I must say.'

Johann didn't turn around this time. He remained bent over his wheel, his eyes fixed on the dusky distance.

'Well,' he answered, 'that's as may be.'

It was almost dark by the time they arrived in Edgar. Daniel thought it looked a very shabby and broken-down place indeed; but then, he was used to the lush tropical gardens and elegant wrought iron of New Orleans. A few men in unfashionable suits were talking on a street corner, and when Johann passed in his white coat and goggles, they swivelled on their heels and stared until he was out of sight. Daniel turned and looked back at them once, and he was surprised to see that they didn't appear friendly at all. Perhaps Johann had treated some of them as hard as rocks, and they didn't like him for it.

They turned off at the main square, and puttered slowly down Kearney Street. It looked, to Daniel's eyes, a very desolate little row of weatherboard houses, and he had to swallow very hard to stop the tears from filling his eyes. Johann said: 'Here we are. This one on the left, with the lighted porch,' and slowed the automobile down

As they came nearer, and drew up outside, they saw that another car was already parked there, around the side of the house. It was a white Daimler-Benz, coated with dust, as if it had been driven very far and very fast. Johann, climbing down from the New Orleans, pulled off his goggles and stared at it hard.

He was still looking at it when the front door of the house opened and Beatrice came out with Mrs Elvira Russell. Beatrice called: 'Daniel, my poor little boy!' and came down the veranda steps toward him, her arms outstretched.

Beatrice was wearing a black evening dress of silk mull, overlaid with wide Gibson shoulders, Her soft dark hair was pinned up as usual; and when Daniel reached the veranda and caught the scent of her perfume, which seemed so like his mother's, he burst immediately into tears, and clung around her waist, trying uselessly to blot out what had happened.

Johann stood a little way away, holding Daniel's cheap valise and regarding the Daimler-Benz with a humourless face. Mrs Russell called out: 'You have a visitor, Mr Cornelius. He tried to find you at home, but you were still out, so one of your tenants directed him here.'

Johann brushed the dust from his motoring coat as he came up to the porch. Beatrice smiled and lifted her head from comforting Daniel to give him a light kiss on the cheek. She said: 'It's Mr Lennox, from Amarero. I don't know what he wants. He said he had to talk to you urgently.'

'Yes,' said Johann, and Beatrice frowned briefly as he walked past her into the house, and set down Daniel's case in the hall with an expression of darkly engraved anger.

Kyle Lennox was waiting in the parlour with a glass of sherry. He looked sweaty and red, as if he'd been drinking. Johann came into the room and stood there silently for almost a minute, while Lennox eyed him with greasy discomfort.

'Well,' said Johann, taking off his motoring coat. 'What do *you* want?'

Kyle Lennox grinned and sat back. He was even more dishevelled than Johann remembered him, with a food-spotted vest of shiny quilted green silk, and his hair pomaded flat to his head. He said: 'That's a hard drive, that, Mr

Cornelius, from Amarero. Lots of dust, lots of flies. It's one of those trips you'd only make if you had to.'

'Oh, yes?' asked Johann guardedly

Kyle Lennox raised his glass of sherry, and then tipped it all down his throat in one swallow. He wiped his mouth on the back of his sleeve. 'A nice sherry-wine, that,' he said. 'Widow-women always keep a good sherry-wine, and I speak from experience.'

Johann stayed where he was, his pale blue eyes fixed on Lennox's sweat-glossed face. He said nothing.

Lennox sniffed. 'The truth is,' he said, lacing his fingers together, and then waggling his long black fingernails. 'The truth is that something appears to have gone awry. You know what I mean by awry?'

Johann almost imperceptibly shook his head.

'Well,' said Lennox, taking out a cigar, 'what I mean by *awry* is not so much *awry* as *astray*. Something seems to have gone astray. Not a cow in this case, nor a girl, but a payment. A payment of eight percent, as agreed between us, and which was regularly placed in my bank until now.'

Johann raised an eyebrow 'You drove all the way from Amarero to tell me that?'

Lennox tugged at his earlobe. 'I wouldn't have, not normally. But then I heard rumours.'

'I always say that people who listen to rumours get to hear what they deserve,' said Johann quite coldly.

Kyle Lennox shrugged. 'Maybe you're right. But maybe I deserved to know that you'd fixed my contract before it got to *be* a rumour, and maybe I deserved to hear that you'd decided to welsh on our deal.'

At that moment, Beatrice came in. She said: 'Would you like another drink, Mr Lennox? Johann, what about you?'

'Is Daniel all right?' asked Johann.

'Oh, I think so. He's tired, mostly, and overwrought. Aunt Elvira's cooking him ham and eggs in the kitchen. Poor little child. He was so fond of Sally, and she was so fond of him. I could cry for him.'

Johann said tightly: 'Mr Lennox is just leaving, so he won't need another drink.'

Kyle Lennox raised his empty glass. 'On the contrary, I'd love one. I wasn't planning on leaving straightaway.'

'What you're planning and what you're going to do are quite different kettles of fish,' said Johann.

Beatrice looked at him anxiously. 'Is something wrong?' she asked. 'Have you two had an argument?'

Johann shook his head. 'Mr Lennox is leaving, that's all Right away.'

Kyle Lennox's smile looked a little more rigid, but he didn't move from the leatherette settee.

'We have a small matter of eight percent to settle first. I won't leave here without it, nor without your signed bond that you won't default again. I know what you've done with my contract, Mr Cornelius, but there's a law in the Lone Star State, and that law says that a man has to have rendered unto him what is rightly his.'

Johann didn't answer. Beatrice had never seen him looking so fierce, and she was almost frightened of him herself. But Kyle Lennox didn't seem impressed. He sat there picking his variegated teeth, still watching Johann in the way that a toad watches a mountain lion: *You may eat me, but by hell you won't like the taste.*

'Surely eight percent is not such a great amount,' suggested Beatrice, trying to be conciliatory.

Kyle Lennox flicked a scornful glance at her. 'Eight percent of a million dollars is eighty thousand dollars,' he said in a dry voice. 'And if it strikes you that eighty thousand dollars is not such a great amount, then I'd say that you probably owe me even more than you're admitting to.'

Beatrice turned to Johann, flushed and confused, but Johann didn't take his eyes off Lennox, although he reached out and held her wrist in a strong, comforting grasp. He said quietly: 'Mr Lennox is right. But eighty thousand dollars, whether we admit to it or not, is eighty thousand dollars more than he's going to get.'

Lennox stuck his cigar between his teeth, took out a match, and struck it against the sole of his shoe. As he lit up, he watched Johann coldly and unblinkingly through the clouds of blue smoke. For a moment, all three of them were motionless, and Johann felt again that strange sense of destiny, as if the history of his life was bearing down on them all, and he knew that what was going to happen next was as unavoidable as his purchase of Carina. This, for some arcane reason, was a crucial moment in Johann's career.

Kyle Lennox said: 'You're forgetting yourself, aren't you? You're forgetting what those eighty thousand dollars paid for.'

'I suggest you get out of here, before you cause this lady any further offence.'

'Offence? You're talking to me about offence? Does the lady know what favour I did you that was worth all that amount of money?'

Johann could feel his heart beating in slow, suffocating bumps. He knew then that he loved Beatrice more than he had ever imagined possible, and it was all he could do not to look down at the rug where he had actually possessed her, for the first and only time. He held her wrist so tight that he hurt her, and when she prised his fingers off her, he had the dreary, frightening sensation that he had touched her for the last time.

She said to Lennox: 'Favour? What favour? What are you talking about? What possible favour could Mr Cornelius have wanted from you?'

Kyle Lennox stood up. It was only then that they realized how drunk he was. He leaned toward Beatrice at an alarming angle, and pushed back his greasy hair with his ring-covered fingers

'Ask Mr Cornelius. He's your beau, madam, unless the gossip has it wrong. Surely a beau shouldn't have secrets from his lady '

Beatrice glanced at Johann uneasily. 'Johann?' she asked. 'What is this favour? What does he mean?'

Johann said slowly: 'It was a small private matter which Mr Lennox, on careful reflection, has decided not to speak about '

'Johann, insisted Beatrice, 'I want to know. Surely we shouldn't hide anything at all from each other. Not if we're to—'

'It's a matter of no importance,' snapped Johann. 'Now Lennox, you can leave. And I mean *now*.'

'Oh, no.' Lennox laughed, and then coughed thickly. 'You don't get rid of me that easy. I want your signed note right here in my hand, or I don't take a single step.'

'You're my employee now. Don't forget that. And you're not getting a brass button. Now, get out before I toss you out.'

Lennox picked up the sherry decanter and poured himself another drink with hands that shook so badly that Beatrice was afraid he was going to shatter both his glass and the crystal decanter. Then he raised his glass, contemptuously toasted Johann, and downed the sherry in one

'You don't leave me much of a choice, Mr Cornelius. No choice at all. I've tried to play the game, tried to do it fair, but if you don't stick to your bargains, then there's nothing else for it.'

Beatrice said: 'This is absurd! Surely we can know what this favour was supposed to have been?'

Kyle Lennox coughed, sniffed, and then grinned. 'It seems, since we haven't been paid for holding our tongues, that we *can*. The favour, if you can call it a favour—'

Johann took a deep breath. '*Lennox*,' he warned.

But Kyle Lennox was too drunk with whiskey and sherry, and the intoxicating sensation of taunting the richest man in Broughton County. 'The favour,' he said with a sloping smile, 'was a girl.'

Beatrice frowned, and blinked.

'She was a young quadroon girl, from Piedras Negras,' continued Lennox. 'She was sent to me for employment in my hotel, the Excelsior, as a common prostitute. As *fodder*, if you know what I mean, for the baser tastes of the Amarero oilmen.'

The silence was as thick as dusty velvet drapes.

Kyle Lennox continued: 'The girl was said to be thirteen years old, but the wetbacks don't know counting from horse manure. I saw her myself, and she was eleven or twelve at most.'

Lennox glanced up at Johann, and gave a little smirk. It was part pleasure, and part fear. Johann's face was stiff with suppressed rage, and Lennox knew that he was going to hit him.

Strangely, though, the atmosphere changed. Lennox glanced toward the door, and Johann, turning, saw Daniel standing there, pale-faced, in his shirtsleeves and tan breeches.

Daniel looked from Lennox to Johann to Beatrice, and then said in a small voice: 'Aunt Elvira sent me to say good night.'

137

Beatrice said quickly: 'Good night, Daniel. I'll be up in a moment to tuck you in. I just have to—'

Lennox drunkenly raised a finger. 'Even though she was only eleven or twelve,' he continued, his voice very slurred. 'Even though she was only eleven or twelve—'

'*Lennox!*' shouted Johann. He reached forward and tried to seize Kyle Lennox's lapels, but Lennox was so ridiculously drunk that he fell sideways on the leatherette settee, and then slipped onto the floor. Beatrice pulled Daniel protectively into her skirts, and screamed: 'Johann! *No!*'

But in any case, Johann couldn't reach Lennox in time. Lennox staggered up onto his knees and shouted: 'He bought her! For eight percent of his oil! That was the favour! He bought the girl and he set her up here in Edgar! He gave her a house and fancy clothes! And better than that, he uses her night after night in the way she is accustomed to!'

Johann barked like a mad dog. He took one stiff stride across the room, seized Kyle Lennox by his green vest, and flung him back against the fireplace. Lennox half-climbed to his feet again, but it was then that Johann reached back his arm and punched Lennox so hard in the mouth that teeth and blood burst out of Johann's fist like a magic trick. Lennox said: 'Grargh,' and dropped back onto the floor, but Johann was insane with rage and wouldn't let him go. He plucked the man up and hit him in the face again, dislocating his jaw. Then he hurled him back against the glass-fronted cabinet, and in a shower of broken teacups he kicked Kyle Lennox again and again in the testicles until Lennox shrieked like a woman in labour.

Beatrice was screaming: '*No! No! Johann! No!*' and Daniel was whimpering in terror. But Johann was ablaze with fury, guilt, and grief, and he was unreachable and unstoppable. He stood over Kyle Lennox, who was twisted under a chair, and he raised the heel of his coltskin shoe and stepped on Lennox's nose with his entire weight. There was a snap as loud as a chicken's leg breaking, and blood ran over Lennox's upturned face in a dark spidery gush.

Johann turned around. Beatrice was standing there, her hands raised in almost comic horror, and Daniel was clinging to her skirt.

'Do you see that man?' quaked Johann. 'Do you see that filth beneath my feet?'

Beatrice said: 'My God, I'm sure you've killed him. Oh, my God.'

'Killed him?' shouted Johann. 'And what if I have?'

'He said   he said you *bought* that girl . '

'Yes!'

'Johann . . .'

'You want to know if it's true? Is that it?'

'Johann, you must calm yourself. Johann, please.'

'You want to know if it's true? You want to know if I've deceived you? You don't trust my honour? Is that it?'

'Johann, no!'

Johann turned away, still breathing heavily. He looked down at the glass-littered floor for a moment, and then at his swollen knuckles. He said in a low, quiet voice: 'It's true. Her name is Carina, and I bought her from Lennox for an eight-percent share in the oil pumped up from Sweetwater Trail. She wasn't the daughter of a Mexican oil worker at all, not like I told you. That was just a way of making it easier for you to understand.'

There was a white, rigid silence. Then Beatrice said: 'And do you *use* her, as Mr Lennox said? Is that why you bought her? To *use* her?'

On the floor, Kyle Lennox gargled and groaned.

Johann said: 'I suppose I bought her because I needed affection, and I needed love. I also bought her because she is very beautiful, and I couldn't bear the thought of her spending her life in that fleabitten hotel, being abused by oil workers, night after night, and getting old before her time. I bought her because . . .' He paused, searching for ways to explain to Beatrice the sad mystical sensations that Carina gave him. But all he could say was: 'I bought her because I wanted to have her, like a possession.'

'Then she's your mistress?'

Johann shook his head numbly.

'Then she's *not* your mistress?'

He looked up at her, cautious and suddenly tired.

'I promise you, I have never touched her,' he said.

Beatrice stood there with her face as white as an alabaster statue. She whispered: 'My God,' and then she raised her arm to her forehead and fell to the floor in a rustle of black silk, swooning gracefully across the tasteless carpet. Daniel, distraught, fell on his knees beside her, and patted her cheeks in a vain attempt to wake her up.

Johann took three or four deep breaths, and then walked over to Beatrice. He gently pushed Daniel aside

'She's dead,' wept Daniel. 'She's dead!'

Johann said: 'No, she's not. I just think she couldn't face any more. She's fainted.'

Quite unexpectedly, Daniel took out his real railroad whistle and blew a long and piercing blast. Johann stared at him in amazement. He said: 'What was that for?'

'It's an emergency,' said Daniel. 'The stationmaster told me to blow it in case of emergency.'

Johann lowered his eyes back to Beatrice. 'I don't think all the whistles in the world could help with this emergency,' he said, so softly that Daniel could hardly hear.

At that moment, Mrs Elvira Russell appeared in the doorway, her hair tied up in curling papers. She looked around her ravaged parlour, and at Beatrice and Kyle Lennox, and whispered: 'Heavens. Is anything wrong?'

Johann stood up. 'There's nothing wrong, ma'am, that a good earthquake couldn't set right. I think you'd better call for the doctor.'

He waited until the doctor came, and stood uselessly by while Kyle Lennox's nose was examined and pronounced crushed, and while Mrs Elvira Russell climbed furiously up and down stairs with hot towels and sal volatile for Beatrice. At last, at ten o'clock, Mrs Elvira Russell frostily suggested that he might have outstayed his welcome, and he found his hat and left.

He drove around to Carina's cottage, and parked outside. All the lights were out, which must have meant that Carina was asleep. He desperately wanted someone to talk to, but he didn't want to wake her. So he sat in his silent automobile in the cool Texas night, listening to the wind from the prairie and wishing that the needle-pointed stars would drop from the sky. The metal hood of his automobile ticked and pinged as it cooled down.

He knew what he had done to Beatrice. He supposed that the only surprise was that she had taken so long to find out. Even though it hadn't really mattered up until now, because nobody in Edgar had had the nerve to say anything openly about it, he knew that Beatrice would find it intolerable to live with the pity and the mockery that she would sense behind every smile.

He didn't cry. He had promised himself that he would never cry again. But he felt such misery that anyone passing by that night would have heard a single, held-back sob, and known that Johann Cornelius was hurt.

The following afternoon, Friday, he called around at Mrs Elvira Russell's house just after luncheon. He was dressed in a plain blue suit and a blue hat, and he was carrying a box of crystallized fruit tied up with yellow ribbons. He was surprised to see that Kyle Lennox's white Daimler-Benz was no longer parked outside, but he presumed that his toadlike adversary of the previous night had driven off back to Amarero and his washed-out wife.

Mrs Elvira Russell was not amused by his call. She stood in the doorway and said: 'Yes?'

Johann coughed. 'If it's possible, I'd like to see Beatrice. I think I need to apologize. And to you, too.'

'She's not in.'

'Are you sure? It would mean a lot if I could. I think there were a whole lot of misunderstandings last night.'

'Yes. But she's not in.'

Johann held out the fruit with a stiff arm. 'Could you give her this candy, then?'

Mrs Elvira Russell made no move to take it.

'Please?' asked Johann.

Mrs Elvira Russell said: 'It won't do you no good. She's left for permanent.'

'Permanent? What do you mean?'

'She left with Mr Lennox this morning. She said to tell you it was all she could do. She wasn't going to stay here to be laughed at. She's going to put up with Mr and Mrs Lennox for a while, in Amarero, then she's taking young Daniel to the Gulf, and you won't see hide nor hair of them from then on.'

Johann stared at her in horror. 'She left with *Lennox*?' he asked her.

'That's right. Mr Lennox kindly offered to take her home, and take care of Daniel, too.'

'When did they leave?'

141

'An hour since. You won't catch them.'

Johann stood on the porch, numbed. How could she leave him without even a letter or a message? How could she leave him for *Lennox*? He lifted his box of sugared fruits and looked at them bitterly. She hadn't even given him time to explain.

He said: 'I'd better pay you for the broken cabinet.'

Mrs Elvira Russell shook her head. 'You needn't trouble.'

'But that's ten dollars' worth of damage there.'

'That's all right. I found twenty dollars under the settee a while back, and I guessed whose it was, and how it got to be there. So that will see me right.'

Johann bit his lip. Behind him, out of the shade of the porch, it was a bright clear day, with a sky as blue and wide as America's best. He turned and, without a word, walked back to his automobile.

Friday afternoon was a bad day to travel to Amarero. It was the day that the Amarero Oil Company and the Cornelius Oil Company paid their men, and those that didn't go straight to the marble-and-mahogany fastnesses of the Wonderful Elk saloon to watch themselves fade into drunken gloom in the mirrors that surmounted the bar, like underexposed photographs of long-forgotten faces, took themselves to the Hotel Excelsior for quick sexual relief. Friday night was a rowdy night, with fights and fires and oilmen having bizarre accidents, like the time an Oklahoma-born wildcatter had leaped from the second-floor window of the Red Star Ironmongery to greet an old drilling buddy from Damnright who was passing in the street below, and he died impaled on the upright handles of three self-wringing mops that were standing on the boardwalk.

But Beatrice had been determined, with the kind of determination that only those who have been gravely humiliated can understand. And with Kyle Lennox impressed to take the wheel, regardless of his grotesquely bandaged nose, she had sat straight-spined all day in the rear seat of the Daimler-Benz, with Daniel beside her, as they travelled across the miles and miles of dusty deserted prairie between Edgar and Amarero, and the sun circled above them like the gleaming arc of a polished sextant

It was a day of heat, blowflies, and dust. They ate chicken

that Mrs Elvira Russell had prepared for them, and drank tepid lemonade from a stone bottle, although Kyle Lennox had two quarts of bourbon in his carpetbag, and he consulted them more and more frequently as the doctor's pain-suppressing tablets wore off. By the time they saw Amarero in the distance, under a distended red sun that was fat from the week's shining, Lennox was singing 'I'm Wearing My Heart Away for You' in a high nasal trill, and the white Daimler-Benz was bouncing and jolting from one side of the track to the other.

Beatrice attempted several times to shake Kyle Lennox back to sensibility, but as the sun finally settled behind the low distant hills, he was scarcely able to drive at more than a stuttering crawl, and the automobile's motor cut out time and time again. Eventually, only half a mile away from the rundown shacks and stables that surrounded the town, the car veered into a low, stony gully and came to a sharp halt against the fallen truck of a checkered-bark juniper. Lennox fell face-forward over his steering wheel and began to snore loudly, a long string of bloody saliva hanging from his open lips. Beatrice stood up in the car, the evening wind blowing the ribbons of her hat, and Daniel sat worriedly beside her, holding his valise against his knees.

'We shall have to abandon him here,' announced Beatrice. 'I am sorry for the poor man, but his condition *was* rather self-inflicted. We can always send someone back to fetch him.'

'Where shall we go?' asked Daniel.

Beatrice descended from the automobile, her skirts held up in case the hem was snagged by the Daimler's brake handle.

'Hand down the cases,' she said. 'We shall walk to the railroad station and inquire about suitable lodging for the night.'

As evening faded into darkness, Beatrice and Daniel, hand-in-hand, hurried as fast as they could along the dusty track into Amarero. Beatrice turned around once, but she could hardly make out the white shape of Kyle Lennox's car, and it was plain that he hadn't stirred.

Ahead of them, in the mournful prairie night, they could see the lights of the Excelsior and the Wonderful Elk, and they could hear shouting and shrieking and every now and then a volley of pistol shots. It was an ordinary Friday night in Amarero, and Beatrice felt a tug of alarm and anticipation, because even an ordinary Friday night in Amarero was riotous. She clutched Daniel's hand tighter, and tried not to think about her fear, even when she heard a woman screaming and screaming in the distance, out by the old Indian huts. Daniel said: 'Can we go slower? My legs are quite tired.' But although she slackened her pace for a little while, her anxiety soon got the better of her, and she began to hurry along as quickly as before.

To reach Main Street, they had to pass through the dark and shadowy tangle of huts and rundown stables where Amarero and the even prairie reached an untidy compromise. Old ramshackle doors and windows creaked and banged in the steady wind, and the sun-whitened remnants of fences and signposts poked through the darkness like the bones of a carcass. Beatrice gripped Daniel's hand so tightly that he cried out, and held her shawl to her throat as if it could protect her from whatever demons, human or supernatural, might lurk in the night.

She felt afterwards, in what afterwards there was, that she willed her fate upon herself by being so frightened. She wondered if her fear gave off a scent that men could detect; or if it glowed luridly in the dark. But the inevitability of what happened was more to do with her broken association with Johann Cornelius than it was to do with her own fear.

She remembered very little. A bunch of men in plaid shirts and working trousers were gathered at the corner of the old livery stables, laughing and jostling each other and passing a bottle around. She saw the bottle shine, and heard the liquid sound as the men lifted it up to their bearded lips. She remembered that she made up her mind to pass them by without looking at them and without comment. They were probably ten or eleven of them, and they looked a hard-bitten bunch. They were drunk already, and one of them was singing a coarse and raucous song about drilling for oil There was a smell of rough pipe tobacco on the wind.

As Beatrice and Daniel hurried past, one of the men called out: 'Hoi!'

Beatrice didn't turn around, but tugged Daniel along even faster.

'Hoi, lady!' shouted the man again.

Beatrice started to run. She held up her black silk skirts and went as fast as she could along the soft dusty track. Daniel ran beside her, panting.

She thought she had escaped; but the men, though drunk were faster. She heard them running up behind her, and almost as she reached the rhomboids of lamplight that fell across the street from the Wonderful Elk saloon, she was seized by the skirts, and she fell, shrieking and beating her fists, into the dusty roadway. Curious faces, whiskery and red, appeared at the windows of the saloon, but nobody attempted to come out and help her. She shrieked: 'Leave me be, for the love of Our Lord!' but two of the sweaty and sour-breathed oilmen lifted her bodily up from the ground and carried her, with legs kicking and petticoats flying, back into the darkness. There was only Daniel, whining and crying as he ran around and around, helpless and desperate, hitting at the legs of the oilmen while they made away with his aunt. One of them – a black-bearded fellow in a balding beaver hat – eventually turned around and went after Daniel like a bow-legged spider, and snatched him by the arm.

'Let her go!' wept Daniel. 'Let her go! She's not yours!'

The man in the beaver hat shook Daniel hard and said roughly: 'We didn't never say she was, boy! We didn't never say she was! All we aim to do is to borrow a lend of her for just a while!'

Daniel kicked at the man's shins with his pointed boot, and the man boxed Daniel's ears so hard that the boy fell over backwards in the dust. His head sang, and he ripped his tan breeches on a stray tag of barbed wire.

Singing and laughing, the bunch of oilmen carried their prize away into the shadows behind the dilapidated livery stables, and they only laughed the more when she shrieked for mercy in the names of her saints, Saint Agnes and Saint Bartholomew, in her high, well-bred voice.

Daniel picked himself up and trotted, his cheeks smudged with tears, to the building where he thought they had taken her. Even though the men were making such a row, he trod as carefully as he could so that they wouldn't hear him. He skirted around the stables, and down a narrow alleyway overgrown with tough wild grass. Something shifted suspiciously in the shadows – a prairie rat or a disturbed lizard – and the boy went cold all over with fright. But now.

145

through the gaps in the dried-out timber walls of the livery stable, he could see the darting beam of an Ever Ready flashlight, and heard the men roar and guffaw, and Beatrice beg all the more insistently for clemency. So he tried to ignore his fear of the invisible creatures in the dark, and he stepped up to the shaky old wall and put his eye to the knothole.

By the quixotic light of the electric torch, the scene he saw was of such extraordinary vividness that he remained still and silent, a boy poured from alabaster. It was the *colours* that he would remember for so many years afterwards, as if what he saw was a rich Rembrandt tableau, a painted anatomy lesson in the murky night of a Texan oil town in the 1900's. He did not recognize what he saw, because he was an innocent boy, as boys could be in those times, and he knew his catechism better than he knew what rabbits did when their tails twitched. But he was luridly conscious of the grisly desecration that was taking place before him, and although he remained still, his spirits sank within him until he felt that he was lost to the real world forever.

He saw Beatrice's legs raised, in their shiny grey silk stockings, and parted wide. He saw a dark motif of hair, and what appeared to him to be a glistening scarlet wound. Her black dress was bunched up around her waist, so that he could not see her face. The oilmen appeared to have tied her with frayed cord to the top of an old kitchen table. They were huddled around her, with sweaty and bearded faces of strangely gentle curiosity. One after another, as they passed the bottle around and some of them sang, they unbuckled their heavy belts and dropped their pants to their knees. Then they stood between Beatrice's opened thighs, and from his spy place at the knothole Daniel could see their big hairy buttocks jerking backward and forward in a way that disturbingly brought to mind a wooden monkey he had been given by his mother as a smaller boy, which jerked its way up a string. Beatrice prayed at first, in a quiet voice, but after the fourth or perhaps the fifth oilman had presented himself between her legs, she remained silent, except for an occasional mewl. The Ever Ready flashlight was directed at her red and shining gash between each bout of monkey-

146

climbing, and Daniel saw that it was basted with gelatinous white.

This proceeding went on for two or three hours. and the oilmen were as unconcerned and jocular about it as if they were crowded in the ginger-beer tent of a meadow carnival. They opened more bottles of whiskey, and sang some more; and one of them even produced a mouth harp and played a few bars of a popular song. Now and then, one of them would return to Beatrice and stand between her legs again, although as time wore on their exertions grew less vigorous, and they panted and puffed, and sometimes gave up with shouts of self-derogatory laughter. Several times Daniel heard Beatrice say: 'Please, I'm a widow.' But all they did was grin and tell her: 'That's all right, ma'am. In that event, your husband won't mind, will he?'

Towards midnight the oilmen grew so drunk that two or three of them passed out on the ground and began to snore. One of them was violently and noisily sick, and because of this, the others decided to make their way back to the Excelsior Hotel, since they still had sufficient money for paid fornication, their first relief of the evening having been free. Daniel heard them stumble away, and after half an hour he was quite certain that they had gone. It was only then that he stood away from the knothole, his arms by his sides, his face blank and shocked. He was not a boy who found it easy to hate people, or even to dislike them. Although he was only nine, he had a precociously developed sense of pity and forgiveness, which may have come from his mother's constant and eventually terminal illness. He did not blame the oilmen for what had happened so much as he blamed Johann for having obliged a defenceless widow and a small boy to venture into a rowdy boom town on pay night. He saw Johann as the author of everything bad that had happened.

He heard Beatrice sighing. Long, extended sighs. He tugged at one of the boards, and it came out with a squeak of rusty nails. Then he squeezed through the wall into the livery stable, and approached Beatrice softly and gently, averting his eyes from her lifted skirts and the bloody smears of fluid on her parted thighs.

He held her hand. He whispered: 'Beatrice, it's Daniel.'

She turned and stared at him. There was only moonlight

147

now, from a freshly risen moon, and she wasn't sure if he was real or not. She said: 'Daniel?'

He pulled at the cords which bound her and eventually worked them loose enough for her to get free. She laid a heavy hand on his shoulder as she lifted herself painfully up from the kitchen table, and stood in the gloom of the stables, breathing in irregular gasps. The mess of her rape slid stickily down her legs, and she felt as if she was going to vomit, but she held her head high, and said to Daniel in an unsteady and husky voice: 'You must find the sheriff.'

In New York, in the opulent smoking room of a substantial stone house overlooking the East River, two men sat crouched over a table and spoke to each other in soft, carefully enunciated whispers. The room was enormous and suffused with brown afternoon light. One wall was ranked with green and crimson leather books, all with gold lettering on their figured spines. A globe rested in antique mahogany gimbals. What seemed strange about the way the two men were huddled together was that the smoking room was empty apart from them, and nobody could possibly have overheard what they were saying. The man with the hand-carved meerschaum pipe and the round, brandy-mottled face was none other than Percy F. Colton, the oil millionaire, and the man with the pale grey suit and the unfashionably clipped moustaches was Arnie Styvers, who had been acquitted only last month of the manslaughter of the Polish actress Irena Womack. Styvers was known to his friends as 'The Vent,' for the way in which he talked without apparently moving his lips.

They met together seldom. It was not in Percy Colton's interest to have it known that he was a friend of Styvers', and in any event both men had enough messengers and minions to keep up an almost daily dialogue. As they talked, Styvers kept looking at his long clean fingernails. He hardly ever looked up.

'I talked to Jimmy Makepiece today,' said Percy Colton quietly.

'Umh-humh?'

'Amareror's fine, by all accounts.'

Styvers splayed his fingers, and then buffed his nails on

his lapel. He didn't answer. He knew that Percy Colton had more to say.

'The only problem seems to be Cornelius Oil. Have you heard of Cornelius Oil?'

'No.'

Percy Colton picked up his pipe from the leather-topped table and stuck it between his teeth. Right now, he didn't know whether he was going to light it or not. He said: 'Cornelius Oil is bringing up twenty-five thousand barrels a day, maybe more. They're pumping oil from the same pool as Amarero One. It's a snappy little outfit, from what I hear.'

'Who's in charge?'

'His name's Johann Cornelius. One of your hardheaded immigrant types. Strong-tempered, by all accounts. It seems he makes it a specialty to lease or buy up land where other wildcatters have run out on their luck. He uses his head, you see, and a whole lot of fancy instruments, and he brings up oil where other people can only find gophers.'

'You're worried?'

Colton shook his head. 'Not really. He doesn't have the refining. All of his crude he sells to us. If he gets too uppity, or too lucky, we can simply smile and say sorry. I'd rather give him some rope, though – let him keep spudding wells while fortune smiles in his direction. Then, when he's up to his ears in crude, we can refuse to buy any more.'

'Sounds sensible.'

Colton took his pipe out of his mouth and sat back. 'It's known as forward planning, so they tell me.'

Styvers nodded vaguely. 'What do you want me to do?'

Colton produced a small gold penknife from his vest pocket and began to dig at the caked dottle in his pipe bowl. 'Nothing at the moment,' he said. 'That's the essence of forward planning.'

'You sound like you've got something up your sleeve.'

Colton chuckled. 'I shouldn't really tell you.'

'Is it that bad?'

'It's bad enough.'

Styvers waited for Colton to tell him. He was a patient man. A ship hooted on the flat silvery river outside.

'You know Kyle Lennox, don't you?' asked Percy Colton, his voice crammed with amusement.

'Sure. Big whiskers, bad taste in vests. He started off with a three-card table on Hester Street. Years ago, that was. Then he went west and gambled on the riverboats. He's Jimmy's manager down in Amarero, isn't he?'

'That's right. And that's what makes this whole thing so funny

'Go on, said Styvers, without moving his lips.

Percy Colton leaned forward conspiratorially 'Kyle Lennox sold Johann Cornelius a twelve-year-old girl.'

Styvers' eyes flickered, but he didn't seem particularly surprised. He wasn't the most shockable man in New York City.

Colton leaned back again. 'For some reason, Cornelius took a fancy to this twelve-year-old girl down at Lennox's cathouse, and he made Lennox a deal. The deal was that Cornelius took the girl, and in return Lennox got eight percent of his gross profits.'

Styvers glanced up. 'Eight percent of twenty-five thousand barrels a day? For a twelve-year-old girl?'

Colton said: 'Ours not to reason why – ours but to take advantage. It just seems that Cornelius felt a burning need for this young lady – if that's not too polite a description of her – and that was the price he was prepared to pay. For a while, anyway. When the oil really started to gush up, he wanted out. His accountants wrote to us here in New York a very serious and solemn letter saying how much Cornelius Oil would like to take Kyle Lennox off our hands, and use Lennox's expert talents in Amarero for themselves. This, of course, was before we found out about the girl.'

Styvers grunted in amusement. 'Poor old Kyle. So you let Cornelius have him?'

'Of course! Lennox is nothing but a drunken vegetable these days. It was a pleasure to see him go.'

Styvers scrutinized his fingernails with even greater concentration. 'That's not all, though, is it?'

Colton grinned. 'Oh, no, that's not all. Lennox got to hear what Cornelius had done, and so he paid him a visit, and understandably protested, and Cornelius understandably broke Lennox's nose and four of his ribs.'

Styvers said: 'I've heard they're very uncultured out west.'

'Wait!' said Colton with overflowing pleasure. 'What happened after that was even better. Cornelius had his fiancée with him, and his fiancée's young nephew, a boy of eight or nine, and they were so scandalized by his behaviour that they decided to leave Edgar, and travel to Amarero with Lennox. On the way into Amarero they were set upon by a gang of rowdies, and the fiancée, can you believe it, was raped. Not once, which would have been bad enough, but *twenty* times, with the boy watching. Or so Jimmy informs me. Now, don't you think that's distressing?'

Styvers didn't appear to be particularly distressed. 'Sure, it's distressing,' he said. 'Where do I send the flowers?'

Colton tapped his head. 'You have to think, Arnie. Think! And you have to know that Johann Cornelius is in a real interesting situation right now. He's fixed his eyes on three more plots of land, two to lease and one to buy. Even if he strikes a runt of a well, he's going to have thirty or forty thousand barrels of crude every day for refining.'

'And that's more crude than you can refine for him?'

'Can or will.'

'And what does that mean?'

Colton opened his desk drawer and took out a Delft tobacco jar. 'It means that all the crude he can't refine he has to store. Storage is very expensive, even if you can find the tanks. And oil has to be transported from the well to the tanks, and that's expensive too. And all the time you're storing crude, you're making no more money out of it than you would be if it was still lying in the ground, and so you run out of fluid cash and you go bankrupt.'

Styvers considered this. Then he said: 'Okay, but Cornelius must know this as well. So what's his way out?'

Colton was so pleased with himself that he couldn't stop himself from smiling. 'He can do one of several things, Arnie. He can sell out his business to us for a fair and reasonable price, and make something out of it, which is better than nothing at all. Or else he can store up his crude in the slender hope that we'll change our minds, or that Shell or someone else will agree to refine it. Or else he can do what he's doing now, and that's try to interest the Houston-West Refinery into starting a partnership. He's on his way to New York right now, so Jimmy tells me, to talk to their major shareholders.'

'Houston-West? Who are they?'

'They used to be a branch of Schmettens Oil. Schmettens went to the wall, but the Houston-West plant was bought up by a small group who were looking for investment in petroleum products.'

Styvers said: 'You've lost me. What does all this have to do with Lennox getting his nose busted and Cornelius' fiancée getting herself raped?'

Colton rose from his seat like a classical conductor bringing his orchestra into the last movement of Beethoven's Seventh. 'It has plenty to do with it. Especially when you know that the small investment group who bought Houston-West are all Quakers, and that if they ever discovered they were doing business with a molester of twelve-year-old children, or a monster who could surrender an innocent woman into the hands of a gang of drunken rapists, they would consider their deal at a very firm end. When Cornelius arrives here, I shall have him discreetly informed that we know all about his aberrations, and that his wisest course of action would be to forget about Houston-West and enter into some kind of amicable arrangement with us.'

Styvers' fingernails traced out the gilt leaf patterns that bordered the desk. 'Amicable, huh?'

'Of course! You think I'm going to upset such a talented discoverer of oil? I shall be happy for him to continue what he's doing, employed by Colton Oil, and to pay him five hundred dollars a month.'

Styvers said: 'That's good money. Unless you happen to own the wells yourself. Do you think he'll agree?'

'That's where you come in,' said Colton. 'Cornelius has an obvious weakness, and the weakness is his twelve-year-old girl. When they arrive in New York, I want you to abduct her for just as long as it takes to persuade Johann Cornelius to change his mind.'

'And if he doesn't?'

'He has to.'

'But if he doesn't?'

'Then the East River is deep and wide.'

Styvers was silent for a moment, and then he rose from his chair and neatly pushed it back under the table. He was a slight man, with an appearance of almost constant tiredness, as if he had to keep books late at night, or send a promising young daughter through ballet school. He ran fifteen gambling-and-booze dens in New York City alone, and three of the most notorious bawdy houses. He often

152

dined with the mayor, and he occasionally went fishing with the chief of police. There had been several incidents of death by shooting or drowning which had been rumoured to be 'Styvers' jobs,' but the judges had always looked down favourably so far on a man who did so much for New York commerce, and whose fingernails were always so immaculately clean.

Styvers said: 'Keep in touch about the timing. When Cornelius is expected to arrive, and so forth. Then leave all the rest of it to me.'

Colton said: 'I still have some of that good brandy, if you'd care for a snort.'

Styvers shook his head. 'Save it for yourself, Percy. The cunningest bastard deserves the finest drink.'

They had arrived in the foyer of their hotel, the old Plaza on Fifty-ninth Street, amid mahogany and marble and brass, and they stood with their trunks at their feet, severe and quiet, not speaking to each other because each was submerged in different and particular thoughts. They were booked into two separate but adjacent rooms as Mr J. Cornelius and Daughter. They did not look like father and daughter, but neither did they look like man and whore.

Johann was dressed in a light grey fall overcoat with black velveteen lapels, and a light grey hat. He carried a black cane, and his pointed shoes were black and grey. Carina wore a black turban-style hat decorated with German braid and spangled jet, with a black lace veil across her face, and she was sophisticated and discreet in a plainly cut black coat. They held their heads high in the way that close friends do as they wait in the foyers of strange hotels.

Later, they dined by lamplight on oysters and plain roasted quail at Eduard's, a fashionable restaurant that Johann had once passed by when he worked for Nathaniel's Engineering. The waiters had starched white fronts, and plied them with sauces and vegetables as if they were children to be spoiled. Carina said very little, but ate a black-cherry bombe in enchanted silence. A violinist with white wiry hair stood next to an aspidistra and carefully sliced up Mozart like a grocer's assistant slicing up ham. At the next table, a ginger-haired man in a high white collar was saying 'That Hetty Green is the meanest woman alive. Mean! She has more

153

ready cash than J. P. Morgan, some say, and yet she walks around like a ragbag, and argues over sixteen cents for a pair of shoes.'

His companion, a finely dressed young lady with a very large nose, laid her white hand on his sleeve and said: 'Yes, dear. But wouldn't it be marvellous to be able to *afford* such meanness?'

Johann listened, and watched. His face was alive with quick secret smiles. He was back in New York, but now he was sitting on the solvent side of the window, and he wanted to learn names and connections and prices. He wanted to discover who had power and who had not. He wanted to know who could be levered and who was strong. He was quite aware that in this city of Cabots, and Coltons, and Rockefellers, and Vanderbilts, his one million dollars was inestimably puny. Hetty Green was conservatively valued at one hundred million, despite her parsimony and the aged black dress she wore day after day and year after year. And lesser though his fortune was, J. P. Morgan, with his passions for yachts and European art treasures, was worth at least sixty-eight million. Johann was conscious of his own brute ambition and his almost religious fervour for making himself rich; but he was also conscious that the wealth of New York's four hundred dominated every industrial endeavour and every hall of politics and influence, and that he needed more than fervour to break into the fortressed walls of trusts and monopolies and fixed prices.

Carriages clattered outside the restaurant window, and appeared to blaze in the reflected flames from a flambé dish across the room. There was an aroma of cigars and grilled lobster and Benedictine which Johann inhaled as if the very inhalation of it could enhance his wealth. Carina said: 'I love New York. It makes me very happy.'

Johann was not aware of any particular sensation of happiness; but he was certainly aware of feelings of renewed strength. There had been many days in Texas when he had been ready to despair. Days when the dusty wind blew, and he was short of money and work. But now he felt that real wealth was within his grasp. He had producing oil wells, and a billfold of ready cash, and when he tied up his first big-business deal with Houston-West next week, he would be ready to take over more land, and more oil, and he would be blizzarded with dollars like a Yukon prospector struggling through the snow. He was unnaturally excited, and flushed.

He held Carina's thin wrist across the starched tablecloth and said: 'I'm pleased that you're happy. Sometimes you seem a little sad.'

'Yes,' she said simply.

He didn't ask her why she was sometimes sad, because he knew. He lifted his glass of mineral water and drank it slowly, watching her face in the light of the table lamp, his eyes giving nothing away.

She said: 'Will we ever be elegant, like these other couples in here?'

He smiled. It was a wistful smile, which she hardly ever saw.

She said anxiously: 'You'll try to love me, won't you? As long as I know that you'll try.'

He used his napkin to pat away the perspiration which glistened on his forehead. He shook his head. He asked for the check. For the oysters and the plain roasted quail, as well as the bombe and the mineral waters and the coffee, the total was twelve dollars and six cents. This was more than Carina used to earn for giving herself to a drunken oilman. They rose and walked with dignity through the tables of laughing and chattering people. It was eight-thirty, and Carina was surprised that so many people were up so late. The waiter came hurrying after them and said: '*Monsieur, le pour-boire.*'

Johann frowned at him. 'What?'

'The gratuity, monsieur. You have left no tip.'

Johann looked down at the expectant silver plate. A few of the people at nearby tables could see what was going on, and they were watching with amused interest.

The waiter said: 'It is customary, monsieur.'

Johann reached into his inside pocket and produced his billfold. He undid the snap fastener and carefully removed a single dollar bill. He held it between finger and thumb, and waved it slowly backward and forward in front of the waiter's nose.

'This dollar,' he said. 'was not earned by begging. It won't be spent on beggars, either.'

Then he returned the bill to his wallet, took Carina by the arm, and walked out of the restaurant to collect his hat and his coat. There was a murmur of shock and laughter behind him, but he took no notice. In this life, nobody deserved anything for free. He had once refused bread to a railroad worker, three years ago in Parsons' Lunch Rooms, in Broughton, and he certainly didn't intend to betray himself or that railroad worker by handing out free money.

The restaurant manager, a short Armenian with a gleaming bald head, caught his arm as he pushed his way out of the front door.

'Sir, excuse me . . .'

Johann turned. From the uncompromising expression of Johann's face, the manager could see that it was probably advisable to let go of his arm. He said in a high voice: 'Sir, I regret you are no longer welcome here.'

Johann stared at the man for a long while with a look that was both patient and violent. Then he said: 'What is the name of this place?'

The manager said: 'Eduard's, sir.'

Johann nodded. 'Very well,' he said. 'I shall make a particular point of buying this place in the near future, and of throwing you out on your ear.'

The manager gave a high, supercilious laugh. 'Empty threats don't worry us here, sir. We expect a gentleman to behave like a gentleman. Now, please go.'

Johann led Carina out into the night. He hailed a cab, and they returned uptown through the dimly lit streets. Halfway back, Carina asked: 'What will you do with a restaurant?'

Johann looked at her. 'You really believe that I'll buy it?'

'Yes.'

Johann squeezed her hand and laughed. 'You're right,' he said. 'I probably shall.'

She kissed his cheek. He thought nothing of the kiss at the time, except that it was pleasantly affectionate, but like many human events of which we think nothing at the time, it was the last. She would never kiss him again, nor would he ever kiss her. He saw her smiling to herself in the occasional squares of light that fell across her face. Outside, a shower began to spot the streets. It was the third Friday in October, 1903.

They abducted her with efficiency and skill. In the first slate coloured light of morning, there was a knock at Johann's door, and a bellhop entered with a sealed envelope on a tray. Johann, tousled and bad-tempered, took the envelope and tore it open. The boy waited for a nickel. Johann read the letter slowly while the boy waited, and then ripped back his bedsheets and stalked, in his long striped nightshirt, to the connecting door which joined his room to Carina's. He banged on it loudly.

The bellhop said: 'I must be cutting along now, sir'

Johann ignored him. He banged on Carina's door again. He shouted roughly. *'Carina!'*

There was no reply. Johann stormed furiously back across the room and tugged open his wardrobe door. The boy hovered nervously in the background, anxious to leave but unaccustomed to anyone who didn't tip. He cleared his throat, although it didn't need clearing.

Johann turned to him and snapped: 'Get the hell out of here!'

The bellhop was almost grateful. He went quietly and closed the door, while Johann struggled out of his nightshirt and pulled on his black pants. He was angry and frightened, but his expression was one of sour determination. When he was dressed, he went into the bathroom and ran the faucets to shave. This might be an emergency, but he wasn't going to face any extortionist with a stubbled chin and a soiled collar. He worked up a lather in his rose-decorated shaving mug and began to spread the soap on his chin with his badger brush.

The letter was written on good vellum paper by a type-writer. It said: *'Your lady companion is safe with us. You will proceed instanter to the Waldorf Hotel, where you will be met by our representative and negotiations for her release commenced. Come at eight. Do not inform the police.'*

He looked at his red, lathered face in the steamed-up mirror. He said to himself, quite loudly: 'Stay calm,' but calmness was impossible. The best he could do was suppress his fear and keep his hands steady while he shaved. He knew Carina would probably be safe. After all, it must be his money they wanted, and they certainly wouldn't get any if they harmed her. But she was so precious, so much his own, that he felt as if his whole emotional life had been burgled and ransacked, and his dearest secret spoiled.

157

Carina, and the affection she so freely gave him, were all that he had of the world in which people liked and loved each other. Without her, now that Beatrice nad left him he was alone, with only his sense of historic mission to keep him going. And even for a financial demigou there were plenty of empty and lonesome hours when a sense of historic mission was a pretty cold substitute for a laughing dinner companion, although Johann may have been hard put to admit it.

His Tree-brand razor cut through the shaving soap in quick, geometric patterns, and he thought of Beatrice, too. Perhaps he should have been kinder that terrible night in Edgar. Perhaps he should have curbed his temper, or tried to lie his way out of it. He knew that he still adored her, but he wasn't sure now whether he could have married her. She was a woman of strange, tantalizing force. Maybe they would have been happy together, once she had learned to love him again; or maybe they would have quarrelled and fought until they sought divorce, or chosen to live together in icy noncommunication. He wondered where she was this minute, and what she was doing. He had left Edgar early Saturday morning, taking Carina with him, and had driven to Broughton for the noon train east. He knew nothing of Beatrice's rape, and he certainly wasn't aware that news of his private affairs had preceded his arrival in New York.

He finished dressing, tucked the typewritten letter in his pocket, and left his room. As he crossed the foyer, the bellhop who had woken him that morning blew a raspberry, and was promptly cuffed by the bell captain.

He arrived at the Waldorf a little before eight. He entered the hotel cautiously, and with an upright back. Although it was quite early, the foyer was crowded with fifty or sixty gentlemen in frock coats who had assembled for no apparent reason, and were talking to each other in almost embarrassing earnestness. Johann kept away from the crowd, and circled the lobby slowly, his eyes flickering around in search of his mysterious correspondent.

When a hand touched his elbow, he knew that his correspondent had found him. He did not turn around at once, but said in a quiet voice: 'You are risking your neck, I hope you know.'

An equally quiet and composed voice replied: 'I trust we

won't have to risk *anyone's* neck, yours or the girl's. This is something we can settle with great promptitude.'

'You wish to speak here?' asked Johann.

'Here is the best place possible,' answered the voice This is a meeting of numismatists. They have it annually. Nobody will notice that out of all these enthusiasts, only we are discussing coinage of a different breed.'

Johann coughed. 'Is this extortion?'

The voice chuckled. 'Certainly not. Not unless you consider that all business is extortion of one kind or another.'

Johann at last turned around. The man he saw was Arnie Styvers, 'The Vent,' in a sagging morning suit. He looked the gangster up and down without saying a word.

'Do you want to open discussions?' asked Styvers. 'Or do you want to be heroic? It's up to you, really.'

'What do you want?' asked Johann hoarsely.

Styvers smiled. He still didn't open his lips, though, and Johann considered that he probably had rotten teeth. There was a diamond stickpin in Styvers' necktie that was probably worth eight or nine thousand dollars. It could have been more; Styvers' weedy physique had the effect of cheapening everything he wore.

'Let's sit down,' Styvers suggested. He indicated two gilt-painted tapestry chairs, either side of a potted palm. He sat himself down on one of them, and waited for Johann to sit down on the other.

Johann said: 'I want to know where the girl is.'

Styvers examined his fingernails. 'Of course you do. That's why I'm keeping mum. If you agree to the deal, you get the girl back unharmed. If not, we'll have to think of some way to parcel things up. You understand that, don't you? It's not businesslike to leave loose ends.'

'You'll kill her?'

'I didn't say that.'

'I know. But you meant it, didn't you?'

Styvers looked almost coy.

'All right,' said Johann. 'Tell me what you came here to say.'

'I wish you'd sit down,' said Styvers. Johann, testily, sat. Then Styvers said: 'It's a question of financial cooperation. It's a sound plan, when you consider it, and there's no reason why you should lose out. All I need is your say-so.'

'What's the plan?'

'It's like this,' said Styvers. 'A friend of mine hears you're in town to talk to some people called Houston-West. It seems like, in Texas, you're striking oil just about everyplace you park your automobile, and you're looking for refinery facilities.'

'What if I am?'

Styvers gave a sickly shrug. 'I keep telling you, it's very easy. Houston-West are mainly Quakers, and the way I hear it, they don't take too kindly to doing business with people who lead immoral or scandalous lives. If you try to do a deal with Houston-West, then the chances are that they're going to find out about the girl, and also about the rape.'

Johann squinted at him. 'Rape? What are you talking about? What rape?'

Styvers smiled. 'You know what rape,' he said sardonically.

Johann stood up. 'Now, listen here,' he said fiercely. 'Whatever you say about the girl, there's never been any question of rape.'

Two bespectacled numismatists turned and blinked at him. Johann said: 'Listen, mister, you'd better spit out what you've got to say pretty damned quick, or I'm going to tear your head right off your shoulders.'

Styvers started to clean his ear out with his finger. 'I don't advise it. Not all of these people are coin collectors. One or two of them work for me, and they can all shoot straight when it's called for.'

Johann turned and stared ferociously around at the assembled men. It was impossible to tell if Styvers was telling the truth or not. But the way he had things organized, he probably was. A man who could silently kidnap a girl from under his nose was bound to make sure that he had a bodyguard. He took a deep breath and then sat down again.

'I know what you mean about the girl,' he said quietly. 'But I don't know what you mean about the rape.'

Styvers examined the end of his finger. 'Maybe my information is awry,' he said blandly. 'But the way I heard it, you KO'd Kyle Lennox, and then your old lady got herself raped twenty times by a bunch of oilmen, out in the streets.'

Johann s face went grey. He said: 'Beatrice?'

'I don't know,' said Styvers, unconcerned. 'Twenty times,

though – that's what they said. Just after you belted Kyle Lennox.'

Johann stared at his feet. He felt numb. He whispered: 'I didn't know

Styvers began to clean out the other ear. 'Well, that's too bad But whether you knew or not, Houston-West ain't going to like it '

'You're going to tell them?'

'If we have to.'

'And what's the alternative?'

Styvers grinned. 'The alternative is actually very attractive. The alternative is that you sell up to Colton Oil for a favourable price and leave all your cares and woes to good old Percy F. Colton.'

Johann stuck his hands in his pockets and let out a long breath. 'I see. It's Percy Colton.'

'He's only trying to do you a favour,' put in Styvers. 'He knows that you've struck more crude oil than you know what to do with, and he knows you've been looking for someone to take it all off your hands.'

Johann nodded. Then he said: 'How long do I have?'

'What do you mean?'

'Well, Colton doesn't expect me to make my mind up right away, does he? I need a few hours to think.'

Styvers took out his pocket watch. 'We've got the girl, you know,' he reminded Johann. 'Any dawdling, and she's a stuffed goose.'

'Just a couple of hours.'

Styvers thought about it. 'All right,' he said after a few moments. 'Call this telephone number at eleven o'clock on the nose, and give them your answer. If it's yes, then you get the girl back straightaway. If it's no – then she's a stuffed goose.'

Johann said gently: 'I understand.'

He rose from his seat, and without looking back at Styvers, he walked through the numismatists with the straight back and set of a man who has reached a terrible crisis in his life, from which he may not turn back. In the street outside, an unpleasant crosswind was blowing, and a news butcher on the intersection was trying to hold down his flapping placard and keep a hand on his cap at the same time. Johann ignored the Waldorf's doorman, who tried to hail him a cab, and walked uptown toward the park, his hands dug deep in his overcoat pockets.

During those three hours of grace, he did several things. He sent a cable to Mrs Elvira Russell's address in Edgar, beseeching Beatrice to cable him back with news that she was safe. He also wired Sam Chivers, inquiring 'How's tricks?' He took his Iver Johnson revolver out of his suitcase, loaded it, and put it into the bedside drawer of his hotel room. He telephoned the nearest police precinct and informed them that his half-caste adopted daughter was late in returning from a walk in the park, and that he was worried. The desk sergeant told him to remain optimistic, and to call again if she hadn't returned by midafternoon. Then he walked down to the Dutch church on Forty-fourth Street and sat for ten minutes in silent prayer. At eleven o'clock 'on the nose' he telephoned the number that Arnie Styvers had given him, and said he needed more time. The soothing voice on the other end of the line gave him two more hours to think it over, but that was going to be all. There was a lengthy silence, and then the telephone went dead.

He never discovered what really happened, although he was still paying private investigators three years later to look into it. He was only ten minutes away from calling up and surrendering to Styvers when the telephone rang and a police officer told him that his adopted daughter may have been found. Unfortunately, the circumstances were not happy. His throat went very dry, and he sat on the edge of his bed like a man who has just woken up from a bad dream to discover that reality is worse. His adopted daughter (if it was actually she) had apparently fallen or jumped from a sixth-floor window on Fifty-fifth Street, two doors away from the Gotham Hotel, where a young man called John Warde would leap to his death from a seventeenth-floor ledge in 1938. His adopted daughter had suffered from fractured ribs which had pierced her lungs, and she had died on the way to the hospital. The police were very sorry. A Jewish pediatrician who had attended her while she lay on the sidewalk had reported that she said only two things – first, that she had gotten away from them (whoever 'they' were); and second, that she should have stayed where she belonged

Johann heard these words with such pain that he bent forward as the policeman told him, clutching his chest as if he had agonizing heartburn.

It took him a long time to recover from the shock. He stood by the hotel window for almost an hour, not moving. Then he checked his watch and realized it was almost time for him to leave. He went to the door of his room as if his leg and arm joints had seized up from lack of use. Only as he walked along the long carpeted corridor did he begin to understand what Carina had saved him from, whether she had died accidentally or sacrificed herself deliberately. Without Carina, Colton had no proof of any misbehaviour whatever; and even if the news about Beatrice were true, it was hardly enough on its own to stand up against him.

He went down in the elevator and asked the doorman in a whisper to hail him a cab.

As he had expected, no one had spoken to the board of Houston-West. Their office was darkly panelled, and their elderly faces were almost invisible in the gloom of this October morning. Behind them, a brass-faced, long-case clock chimed every half hour, and their discussions had to pause each time while the chimes died away. Johann sat at the far end of the massive oak directors' table with his papers and plans spread out before him, and explained his operations and his finances; and after three hours of careful examination of his written plans and detailed schedules, the board agreed informally to a working partnership to refine his crude oil from Sweetwater, Emmett Heights, and the West Amarero fields. They shook hands with him Their hands were old and dry.

The morgue was chilly and tiled in olive green. He didn't stay for long. A German student in a white coat folded back the sheet over Carina's body and Johann identified her at once. She looked quite peaceful, and he remarked on it. The student said that falling from a height was quite a happy death, compared for instance with burning or mangling. She had been so heavily concussed that she probably never felt any pain. Johann thought of her sitting next to him in his automobile, her beautiful face framed by her fascinator. Here in the morgue she was no longer quite so beautiful;

163

but whether it was her life with Johann that had done that, or her fall from the window on Fifty-fifth Street, he couldn't be sure.

Outside, in an uncomfortable draught, he was interviewed by a policeman. He was able to give an exact account of his own movements at the time of Carina's death, and to produce his telephone accounts from the Plaza to prove it. The policeman made copious notes in very round handwriting with a blunt pencil, and then let him go. He went straight to the Plaza to pack.

He knelt by his bed when his suitcases were all closed, and said a short prayer for Carina. He told her he loved her dearly, and he gave her soul to the Lord. He said a prayer, too, for Beatrice, hoping that she was safe, and that she would understand and forgive him. Before he left, he took a last look around the rooms to make sure that he hadn't forgotten anything. On the bathroom shelf, next to the mirror, was one of Carina's hair slides, in the shape of a butterfly. He picked it up and put it in his pocket; but then changed his mind, and set it back on the shelf. Maybe some other young girl would find it, and wear it in unconscious memory of someone who had made him realize that love is often more magical than human beings can bear.

1909

CORNELIUS OIL PAYS TWO
MILLION FOR EAST INDIANA
CHEMICALS

'A bargain buy'

Ninety new jobs for local men and women

From P. K. Lomas, Industry Reporter

Cornelius Oil, the wealthy and expanding concern from Texas, has paid almost two million dollars in stocks and bonds for the East Indiana Chemical Corporation, and has immediate plans for expanding the factory's production of nitrates and phosphates.

Mr Johann Cornelius, the millionaire owner of Cornelius Oil, expressed the opinion to this correspondent that the price he had paid for East Indiana was 'of the bargain-basement variety.'

–*Indianapolis Star & Citizen*,
February 9 1909

They had been walking through the trees almost all afternoon, and eventually, when the sun began to lose its warmth, they meandered back toward the house across the long wild meadow where the poppies blew, and through the squeaky iron gate into the walled kitchen garden. There, they went hand-in-hand along the mellow brick pathways, talking in quiet, affectionate voices; while the June breeze rustled the leaves of ripening corn and summer squash, and butterflies danced around the beans and sweet potatoes, and rosemary and thyme and tarragon nodded in their separate beds like enthusiastic operagoers in a private box.

Reaching the lean-to greenhouse, where pale Polish tomatoes were fattening behind the misted glass, she spread her skirts and sat on a low wall; and he stood protectively beside her, and took his pipe from the breast pocket of his linen jacket, and began to pack it with tobacco.

She said: 'You've made me so happy, Jack. I can hardly believe that it's true.'

He smiled and said: 'Ellie.' He didn't have to say much else, because she knew for a factual certainty that he felt the same way. Only three hours previous, he had knelt on the mossy floor of the woods that skirted her parents' home, as the green stain on his pants still bore witness; and he had taken her hand and kissed it once, and asked her to be his bride. Since then, they had walked and talked about love, and money, and where they were going to live, and the day had circled its shadows around them like a pleased parent encircling them with her arms. Now, in the kitchen garden, a few hundred yards away from the white-painted plantation house where she had lived all her life, they basked in that gingery evening light that is almost peculiar to Williamsburg County in South Carolina, and the birds chirped and the bees droned and their happiness was so ridiculously full that they spoke with tears in their eyes sometimes, and sometimes with laughter, and once, on the

167

sloping hill that led away towards the neighbouring estates, they had waltzed together, an impromptu waltz that had taken them around and around until they collapsed breathless and hilarious in the waving grass.

He took out matches and steadily lit his pipe. After three matches, the rich aroma of Balkan tobacco mingled with the scent of climbing roses, and after a couple of satisfied puffs he rested his elbow on his knee, and took the pipe from his mouth, and looked at her tenderly.

'Making you happy, that's what I'm here for,' he said. 'And besides, making you happy makes me happier still, and so I guess that I'm only being selfish anyway.'

'Oh, come on. You're *never* selfish.'

He leaned forward and kissed her forehead. A gentle, reassuring kiss that barely touched her. He said: 'I'm sure of my love for you, Ellie, and that's the way it's going to stay. Because if I thought that our love would go sour, the way that their love did; if I thought we were going to scrap all the time, and wind up scratching each other's eyes out, then I'd take up my hat right now, and I'd turn on my heel, and I'd be three hundred miles away from here before the week was out.'

'Jack' she whispered. 'Nobody could stop us loving each other but the devil himself.'

He kept on smiling, so pleased and so happy that he couldn't stop himself. Ellie looked deliciously cute and grave, sitting on the wall in her blue-check gingham jumper, with her coppery hair brushed up into a gingham bow, and he had to touch her soft cheek to convince himself that she was real, and that she was really his. She was the prettiest of Earle Jackson's four daughters, and the youngest, and that meant she'd been spoiled all her life, but spoiling hadn't spoiled her, and as her father used to say, in a low voice so that she wouldn't hear: 'She hands out twice what she's handed, and in my accounts that's credit.' She was a small girl, with a round, almost childish face; and her eyes were wide and grey and dreamy. But her manner was confident and poised, and her voice was vibrant, and the words that she spoke could raise even sceptical eyebrows; so that when a man talked to Ellie Jackson, he knew he was talking to a woman. Maybe, at nineteen, she was precocious. Maybe she rode her chestnut

168

mare a little too showily; and maybe the French that her governess had taught her was a little too flamboyant. But the Jackson family possessed both gentility and gentleness, and their wealth and fortune had been long enough established in South Carolina for them to find social savagery unnecessary. Maybe they weren't as rich as they'd been in antebellum days, when Earle Jackson's grandfather had seen the hills of Fortuna so thick with slaves that a visitor could have believed they were growing black wool instead of white cotton; and maybe life in the South had lost some of its elegance as the century had turned and the automobile had opened up the countryside. But in this summer of 1909, the days were still balmy, and the dresses still swept the well-cropped lawns, and there were still parties with parasols and punts on the lake, and Ellie Jackson was pretty and kind, and more than anything, happy.

'We'd better get going,' said Jack, opening up his watch. 'Your mother wanted us back for tea.'

'Tea and wedding cakes?'

He kissed her. 'That'll come soon enough. And then you'll be Mrs Jack Field, and you'll have tea parties of your own.'

'Tea parties? I shall have champagne parties, every day. Just to show people how happy I am.'

'Not on my salary, you won't. Not until Father makes me a partner.'

'Well, it's time he did,' asserted Ellie. 'You're doing very important work now.'

'Defending a squatter charged with stealing two hundred head of cabbage isn't exactly Supreme Court stuff.'

'Yes, but you're going to Rhode Island to enter that plea for Husman and Welch.'

'I wish I weren't. I'm going to miss you.'

Her eyes softened. 'I'm going to miss you, too. But one day you're going to be a great and famous attorney, and we won't regret it then.'

He took her hand, and they left the kitchen garden and walked across the grass to the back veranda. The house, Fortuna, was shadowed by elms, but the sinking sun lit up the figures of Ellie's mother and father and sisters as they sat admiring the gardens, and they looked in their white lawn dresses and wide white hats like famous society figures on the deck of a yacht. Ellie waved, and her father waved back.

Earle Jackson had been cautious of Jack at first. The boy had seemed determined and energetic, but inclined to rush at whatever he wanted to do without thinking first. He was a handsome boy, yes. He was tall with wavy brown hair and a fine straight nose, and his dark eyes rarely seemed to lose their humour. His father had sent him to Harvard, and he had returned to the South with a reasonable degree in law and a reputation for healthy practical-joking. But what had disturbed the conservative Mr Jackson when Jack and Ellie had first exchanged glances at a coming-out dance for Ellie's sister Annette was that Jack had made it plain he wanted to practice law out West, in Texas or Oklahoma, where the big oil companies were. He had told Mr Jackson with intense conviction that 'If the future of business is to be steeped in oil, then the future of business attorneys is bound to be steeped alongside of it.'

Mr Jackson hadn't denied the truth of what young Jack Field was saying: but with Ellie so sweet on the boy, there was always a chance that he would ask for her hand; and Mr Jackson knew that he wouldn't be able to find it in himself to refuse his darling baby Ellie anything. However, he couldn't take to the notion of Ellie being marooned in a Texas cowtown or one of those wildcat shanties on the Oklahoma Red Beds, and no more could Mrs Jackson, who was warm and sympathetic to the flutter and flush of true love, but knew how important it was for her daughter to take her place in South Carolina society.

So behind today's proposal of matrimony, there had been a little friendly manoeuvring. Mr Jackson had invited Jack's father, Duncan P. Field, the respected Kingstree attorney, to have lunch at his country club; and there, over a damask tablecloth and filet of sole marguery à la Diamond Jim, Mr Jackson had broached the suggestion that if Jack had marriage to Ellie in mind, then he might do better to remain in South Carolina for a while, particularly if part of Ellie's dowry were to include the passing of all Mr Jackson's legal business to the offices of Field, Field & Sobers, of Kingstree.

Mr Field hadn't wanted to sell his son down the river, not even for the price of ten or twelve thousand dollars' worth of new business. But for his part he had always believed that Jack would be wise to pick up a few years' legal experience in Carolina before he tried to take on the boisterous law of the oilfields; and there was something else, too, which he rarely spoke about, and that was his own painful and martyred marriage to Jack's mother, who had died of pleurisy when Jack was ten. He wanted Jack to be happy, above all, and he knew that Ellie could make him so.

Now, as Jack and Ellie came across the lawn toward the house, Mr Jackson stood up from his seat on the veranda and raised a glass of champagne. 'I am drinking to your future good fortune,' he announced. 'And so would your mother, but she feels she may have already had sufficient.'

Mrs Jackson, a poised, straight-backed woman in a white summer shirtwaister and a picture hat with white roses on it, let out a tinkly laugh. She approved of Jack, partly because he was easy on the eye, and relaxed, and would make himself a respectable amount of money, and partly because he smoked a pipe, which she always found irresistibly masculine.

'Sit down, sit down,' invited Mr Jackson. 'We have apees and butter drops if you're partial, and gingersnaps if you're not.'

The table on the veranda was laid with a white lace cloth, and was elegantly set out with dishes of cookies, a Georgian silver tea service, and a magnum of Bollinger, green and beaded with dew, in a large silver cooler. Annette was there, and Esther, the oldest of the four sisters, and Esther's two-year-old son, Christopher, was perched on three cushions, with a huge white napkin tucked into his neck to save his white Russian romper suit from crumbs. They were all excited and flushed, and they had all been drinking champagne, and Jack found himself bubbled along on a tide of laughter and flirtatious admiration from Mrs Jackson and her daughters, and irrepressible friendliness from her husband.

'When Earle came to my father and asked for my hand,' said Mrs Jackson in her cultured Southern accent, 'my father said, "You couldn't take her sister Alexandra instead, could you? She's the one who really gets on my nerves." '

They all laughed, and Ellie poured some Darjeeling tea,

and under the cool roof of the veranda and the whispering leaves of the flowering clematis they spent the afternoon in family celebration. For Jack, having a family like this was something completely new; and even though he started off with caution and reserve, he soon found himself brought so affectionately into the Jackson circle that he felt as if he'd known them for most of his life.

Earle Jackson rose to his feet. He wasn't a tall man; in his light grey summer suit he stood about five-feet-nine. He tousled the hair of his grandson, whose mouth was now brown as a nigger minstrel's from eating chocolate cake, and he spoke in a low, happy voice. He said: 'I just want to drink a toast to us, because we're real contented today at Ellie's betrothal to Jack. I know that Jack had his heart set on going out West and making his fortune in the oilfields, but I think Jack realizes now that by staying here in Carolina he's going to prepare himself mighty well for any future challenge that he might encounter. To my mind, one of the best preparation's he's making – and I'm highly biased – is marrying Ellie. Ellie, like Annette and Esther and Caroline, has been brought up to live her life fully and to give her heart to everything she does. Well, I'm pleased to see that she's finally given her heart to a young man that we can all be proud of, and we wish all of ourselves happiness because of it.'

Jack, a little dizzy from champagne, and blushing, got to his feet. He said: 'I want to thank you for your words, sir. I know that I'm going to do my best to fulfil them, because you've all shown me kindness that's over and above what anyone could have expected. I love Ellie, and I'm going to do everything I can to make her happy; and I hope that by making her happy, I'll make you happy, too.'

He sat down, and Ellie kissed him, and they all laughed some more and applauded, and maybe for the first time in his life Jack began to have some kind of inkling of what happiness really meant.

'Well,' said Margaret Jackson, 'we're going to have to settle a date. Sometime in the spring, of course.'

'And guests,' enthused Annette. 'We'll have to decide on guests. My Lord, there are going to be hundreds!'

'What about the cake?' asked Esther. 'How many tiers?'

Ellie went pink. 'We haven't even *thought* about children

172

yet. Jack said as long as they're healthy, and have all their toes, then he's quite content.'

They stayed on the veranda until it began to grow cool, and then the ladies went inside to change for dinner, while Earle Jackson took Jack into the smoking room, and they stood by the tall window looking out over the trees and the fields of Fortuna plantation, and talked of money and law.

Earle Jackson said: 'You're off to Rhode Island tomorrow, then.'

'That's right, sir. It's a special hearing. One of our oldest clients got himself mixed up in a land-restraining order up there. It's going to be big stuff. Well, for me, anyway.'

Earle Jackson coughed. 'That's good. I always like to see a keen young man getting ahead. As a matter of fact, though, I was wondering if I could impose on you while you're up in those parts. I have some valuables, jewellery and paintings and suchlike, that I inherited from my mother when she died last year. I've been meaning to take them up to New York for auction, but I haven't had the occasion, and the way things are going it looks as though I won't for some time. Short-staffed, you know, especially out in the fields. Perhaps when you've finished in Rhode Island, you could stop off in New York for a few days and taken them along to the auctioneer's for me. All expenses paid for, of course'

Jack was a little embarrassed. He hadn't made himself any firm commitments for the rest of the summer vacation, but apart from stepping out with Ellie as often as possible, he'd also been planning to fish in Lake Marion with a college chum who was working for the season in Columbia.

'Well, sir,' he said, 'I'm not sure that I can.'

Earle Jackson shrugged. 'If you can't, then I'm out of luck. But it would have helped. It would only take a few days – just long enough to see the jewellery sold, and you could stay with some friends of mine at the Ritz-Carlton on Forty-sixth Street. The Forbeses, you'd like them.'

Jack had to admit that the trip sounded pretty tempting. He'd only been to New York twice – once as a small boy, and once from Harvard – and the idea of staying at the Ritz-Carlton and taking a look around the city with all his costs paid for was a darn sight more attractive than angling for lake fish with Oliver Talmadge, who was good fun when

173

you had nothing better to do than sit in a small boat and hope the trout would bite, because he could do bird calls and moose calls and imitate President Taft, but when you *did* have something better to do, which was almost always, Oliver Talmadge was one of those pests who didn't know when he wasn't required. He'd miss Ellie, of course; but Earle Jackson had been so generous and friendly that it seemed pretty churlish to say no.

'I'd have to make a few rearrangements,' said Jack. 'But it sounds like kind of a pleasant diversion. I'd like to do it.'

'Well, I'm pleased,' Earle Jackson smiled. 'I wouldn't like to trust that jewellery to the mails or the railroads, and in any case I need someone to take it around to Parke-Bernet personal. And since I have a beautiful hostage waiting for you here, I'm pretty sure you're not going to run off with it.'

Jack grinned. 'The day I run away from Ellie is the day I lose my senses.'

An engraved brass clock on the mantelpiece struck seven, in prissy, whirring chimes. Earle Jackson said: 'How about a bourbon before we change for dinner? I have my own special blend brought down from Kentucky, and if anything ever made your hair stand to attention, this will.'

That night, after a rich dinner of turtle soup, ham mousse, baby turkey bordelaise, and orange sherbet, and after a lot more laughter and champagne, Jack and Ellie took their coffee on the veranda, with Mr and Mrs Jackson sitting a discreet distance away, and they watched the fireflies dancing in the darkness, and listened to the sad rustle of the trees and the distant sound of fiddle music from the servants' cottages, across by the stables.

Ellie, in an evening gown of lace over alice-blue silk, sat as straight-backed as her mother, and Jack relaxed with his pipe and watched her with all the secret pleasure of a man who's newly in love. It seemed to him then that she was just perfect. Those wide-open eyes, the tilt of that nose, those slightly parted lips. The light from the veranda lamps reflected from her diamond-and-sapphire engagement ring, a spark of blue fire on the small hand that lay in the shadows of her lap.

She said: 'Do you ever feel scared?'

'Scared of what?'

She turned and looked at him, and the moths that flickered around the lamps threw patterns across her cheek. 'Scared of growing up. Scared of having to fend for yourself.'

'I don't think so. I've been fending for myself for a long time.'

She said: 'I'm scared of being a woman, in a way. Instead of a girl, I mean.'

'I don't believe there's anything to be worried about. And in any event, you'll have a husband to care for you.'

She smiled. 'I don't want you to care for me *too* much. That's one of the things that I'm scared about. It just seems to me that women should be more independent these days. We're not wax dolls, you know, to be wrapped up in tissue paper and kept at home. I think women should do their best to match their husbands.'

Jack sucked at his pipe doubtfully. 'You don't mean *work*, surely? I wouldn't expect a wife of mine to work.'

'Of course not. But I'm sure I could find plenty of respectable and profitable things to do. I'm very educated, you know. I can breed horses and I can grow flowers, and I can even sail a dinghy.'

'You'll be saying you want to vote next.'

'Well, don't be surprised, that could come. I bet I know more about politics than most men. I take an *interest*, Jack, and I want to be the kind of woman you can talk to, and respect, as well as love.'

He tamped down the tobacco in his pipe. 'I'd still love you, even if you couldn't speak a word.'

She reached across and touched his face, as if she was touching something very rare and precious, and she gently wound his hair around her finger. 'You won't object, though, if I try to have a mind of my own? It won't ever mean that I'm less loving, or that I won't obey you as the marriage vows say. But Mama and Papa have always brought us up to have opinions, and tastes, and to think for ourselves.'

Jack held her wrist, and then leaned forward and softly kissed her lips. 'Whether I liked it or not,' he said, 'nothing could stop you from being my own dear Ellie. It's just for yourself that I want to marry you, and if you have opinions on anything, whether it's American foreign policy in the

Caribbean, or the colour of a baby's layette, then whatever you say will be as welcome in our home as you are.'

He sat back in his high-backed wicker seat and looked at her warmly. 'As a matter of fact, I've been concerned about what you were going to do all day, once we were married, and once I was off working at the office. I used to see my mother sitting around in her housecoat, reading library books and eating candies all day, as bored and fretful as a mouse in a cage; and when my father came home she used to burst out with all of her stored-up boredom and all of her fretfulness, just because she was too idle to get up and do something interesting on her own account.'

He stopped, and looked away. He hadn't meant to slight his mother, but it was so difficult to explain what he was and how he felt without bringing her into it. He said quietly: 'I love you, Ellie. If you want to breed horses or grow flowers or even climb mountains, I'll help you. I want to know that you're happy, and that you're doing what you want to do. I can't say that I won't ever be jealous of you, or that I won't feel protective toward you. But I promise you that I won't try to coop you up, or make you live a life that you secretly despise.'

She kissed him, glancing quickly over her shoulder to make sure that her mother and father weren't watching. Then she whispered: 'And what would you do if I was very naughty, and wouldn't behave?'

'Independent girls aren't supposed to *be* naughty.'

'Oh, they are sometimes. Just because I have a mind of my own, that doesn't mean that I don't want to be treated like a defenceless female sometimes.'

He grinned. Then he said: 'Well ... if you're naughty ... I shall have to reprimand you.'

She giggled. 'And what if you reprimand me, and I'm still naughty?'

He pretended to think deeply. Then he kissed her on the tip of the nose and said: 'In that event, I shall be obliged to spank you.'

Her eyelids drooped coquettishly. 'I shall have to be naughty quite a lot then, won't I? After we've talked about your work, and the political situation, and the colour of baby's layette.'

They looked at each other for a long, silent moment, both

with perplexed expressions. Then they burst out laughing, so loud and so long that they had tears in their eyes and Mr Jackson came across the veranda and stood over them with an amused face, not understanding their hilarity at all, but pleased with their joy, so pleased that he turned back to grin at his wife, Margaret, as if to say: Look at this happiness that we ourselves created.

Johann Cornelius came out on deck just after the steamship had passed Shutes Folly Island in Charleston harbour, and was beating its way out to sea. He stood for a while holding the varnished rail, the cool Atlantic breeze ruffling his hair, and he watched the afternoon sun sparkling on the water, and the tree-lined shore of James Island sliding slowly past. A small tugboat with a shiny brass ring around its funnel bounced over the waves on their starboard side, pooping its whistle with a puff of white steam that chased away inland; and seagulls wheeled and dived all around them. He took out a green handkerchief and solemnly blew his nose.

Although the railroad was quicker, he still preferred to travel from Texas by sea. He had two first-class suites, complete with a desk and a comfortable bed, and he could keep in touch with any part of the continent by ship's telegraph. What was more, apart from a coaling stop at Charleston, the SS *Galveston Bay* remained at sea, and he could keep himself isolated from pests and spongers and litigious rivals. To his fellow travellers, he appeared like a dour and wealthy eccentric, whiling away his time on a small coastal steamer, and whenever they politely inquired why he spent so many hours secluded in his cabins, he would simply reply: 'Canasta,' as if that answered everything. But in reality his cabins, while he journeyed to New York, were the headquarters of the whole of Cornelius Oil, and from his huge mahogany desk, with its green-shaded lamps and its single sepia photograph of a sad-looking woman in a boa, he kept daily and nightly reins on his oil properties in Texas and Oklahoma and California, his insurance interests in New York, his chemical works in Indiana and Illinois, and his political involvements in Washington. There were many Republican senators and congressmen who were beginning to notice his steady

177

financial rise with interest, although the Rockefellers didn't like him one bit, and J. P. Morgan had once said that 'given the choice of having Johann Cornelius on this earth or of not having Johann Cornelius on this earth, it would take me several hours of considered thought to put up any kind of argument in favour of the former, and then I'd be damned if I could get myself to agree.'

Johann was living between a large white house at the better end of Washington Avenue, Houston, and a seventh-floor suite at the two-year-old Plaza Hotel in New York which he was increasingly anxious to move out of, partly because it cost one hundred dollars a day even when he wasn't there; and partly because Mrs Clara Bell Walsh, widow of the Royal typewriter tycoon Julius Walsh, lived right along the corridor, and insisted on keeping a motley collection of dogs which yapped when he was trying to work. He had already been upstate a couple of times to view a number of mansions, and he liked the look of a sober, symmetrical house on Lynwood's Island, in the Hudson.

During these years before the Great War, he seemed more remote to those who knew him than at any time before or after. Only two people stayed close beside him – his oil manager, Jerry Slobodien, a sarcastic professional rig worker with a thin, chiselled face, a permanent five-o'clock shadow, and a taste for ruby signet rings and shoestring ties; and his manservant, Carl, a baffled white-faced Swede who spent all his off-duty hours sitting in an upright chair on the boat deck, reading *The Katzenjammer Kids* out loud, slowly and ponderously enunciating such phrases as 'und all of a sudden, bang, und anodder vun, bang, und Sir Reginald Wienerschnitzel rolled into der swamp und vas seen no more except vunce und dot vas der last time.'

Johann's closeted life was the subject of considerable Wall Street speculation. Some said that he was a business genius who was eventually going to tower over Morgan and Rockefeller and Vanderbilt. Others said he was an eccentric who ate dandelions for breakfast, slept in full evening dress, and would never amount to anything. J. Paul Getty probably came nearest to the truth when he remarked that with Cornelius rigs pumping up millions of barrels of oil each day at Sweetwater, Muskogee, Seal Beach, and Checotah; with Cornelius nitrate plants in Gary and Peoria and Normal churning out tons of fertilizers and explosives; and with Cornelius underwriters in New York and Baltimore bringing in thousands of dollars of daily premiums – that with all this headlong rush of expansion and investment and complex management, Johann Cornelius didn't have *time* to socialize.

Handling a multimillion-dollar business that was running away with him was certainly exhausting, particularly since Johann had an ingrained reluctance to delegate. He hunched over his desk almost eighteen hours every day, and still had to leave work undone, papers unsigned, and contracts unread. He went to bed in the grey tight hours of the morning and read business documents until he fell asleep, and each day he was haunted at dawn by his own face in the tortoiseshell shaving mirror – red-eyed, lined, and weary. He would soon be thirty-six, but he looked like a man of fifty.

There could have been something else, though, that kept him so much to himself. He would never speak about it, but the waiters on the *Galveston Bay* sometimes walked into his office and found him sitting back in his leather chair, biting thoughtfully at his thumb-nail and staring at the photograph on his desk. One of the waiters had once had the courage (after five straight bourbons and a six-dollar bet) to ask Johann who the lady was. But Johann had done nothing but look at him as if he was transparent, and whisper: 'Ask Lennox.' Since the waiter hadn't the slightest idea who Lennox was, the identity of the beautiful but wistful woman had remained a secret.

Johann liked to come up on deck once in a while and take the air, particularly when land was still in sight. It also gave him the opportunity to check out his fellow passengers, of whom there were usually very few. He rarely spoke to them, but liked to observe them: the wilted would-be carpetbaggers returning North after failing to make their mark on an increasingly industrialized South; the widows who had buried their husbands on unfamiliar Southern soil going back to the bosom of their families with their faces as stiff as writing paper: the odd-job men, the out-of-work sailors, and health-conscious people in shapeless clothes who felt for reasons best known to themselves that a trip up the coast might be salubrious.

Today, though, as Johann stood by the rail, he saw a young man who looked nothing at all like an unemployed sailor, nor an odd-job man of any description. The boy was tall and very wholesomely good-looking, as if life hadn't chipped him yet, nor any unhappiness scoured him. He had wavy chestnut hair, this boy; and a fashionable sack suit in grey worsted with a shadow check. His face in profile was fresh and sharp, and if he shaved more than twice a week, then he used better razors than most. There was something about the boy that interested Johann, and he stood for a while watching him, his hands deep in the pockets of his wool frieze overcoat, his eyes watering in the wind.

After a while the boy turned away from the rail and walked along the deck, crossing the shadow of the smoke-stack in which Johann was standing. As he passed, Johann said: 'I shouldn't worry. It won't be too rough.'

The young man reddened slightly, and raised his hat. 'I've travelled by sea before, sir,' he said politely. 'I don't think a few choppy waves will put me off.'

Johann looked at him for a while and then said: 'So you're not afraid of the sea?'

'No, sir.'

There was another silence. The sea breeze sang through the wires above Johann's head. Johann said: 'You'll forgive me saying so, but you look as if you've left something behind of great importance.'

'Do I look like that?' asked the boy.

'Well, yes. It was the way you were standing. I take these trips quite often, you see, and I know when someone's left something quite important behind.'

The young man brushed back his hair. 'It seems that you're a very sensitive person.'

Johann shrugged. 'There are plenty of people who wouldn't agree with you.'

The young man turned and looked back toward Charleston. 'Actually, I've left my fiancée behind. Just for a few days, while I take a trip to New England, and then New York.'

'You would have been back sooner by train.'

180

'Yes, sir But, for this trip, my future father-in-law believes trains are not to be trusted.'

Johann gazed out across the light turquoise sea. 'Your future father-'n-law is probably right. Trains, on the whole, are not to be trusted. A train came in once, and a train went out, and one took fortune while the other brought dismay.'

The young man obviously didn't understand a word of this, and gave a polite grimace. 'If you'll excuse me,' he said, 'I'm going below to my cabin.'

Johann touched his arm. 'There's plenty of time for that. Come and have a drink. If you're engaged to be married, then perhaps we ought to celebrate.'

The young man looked unhappy. 'I regret, sir, that I have no idea who you are.'

Johann smiled. 'That's probably all for the best. But my name is Johann Cornelius, and I dabble a little in oil.'

The young man extended his hand. His handshake was as firm and crisp as the rest of him. 'I believe I've heard of you, sir, and I'm pleased to make your acquaintance. My name's Jack Field, and I'm an attorney.'

Johann raised an eyebrow. 'I'm gratified to hear it. The Lord defends those who defend themselves. Come along, the bar's just here. You'll find that Errol can mix up the best New Orleans Sazerac you ever tasted. Not that I'm a drinker. I was simply told it was so.'

Jack smiled uncertainly as the bulky, Dutch-looking man in the dark blue frieze overcoat ushered him toward the varnished double doors that led inside to the restaurant and bar. It was only a small bar – six feet of polished red marble flanked by two huge Bordeaux lamps engraved with bunches of grapes. Behind it stood the sour-faced Errol in his starched white bartender's coat, his moustache waxed into rigid upright spikes. Errol was the pride of the small Galveston steamship line, although it was only because of an unmentionable incident at the Bank Exchange bar in San Francisco in 1904 that he wasn't still mixing drinks with the renowned Duncan Nicols, instead of tramping it up and down the coast shaking up cocktails for customers who usually disposed of them straight over the ship's rail at the first heaving of unsettled seas.

Jack Field and Johann sat on leather-topped stools, and

Errol immediately poured out a small brandy for Johann and passed it across the counter. Then he said to Jack: 'You're a bourbon man, sir, if I'm not mistaken.'

Jack glanced at Johann, but Johann's face remained uncommunicative and blotched by the wind.

'Well, yes,' said Jack. 'I'll take an old-fashioned.'

Errol mixed the drink so fast it looked as if he had eight pairs of hands. He set it on the bar, and said without any hint of expression in his voice: 'That's the best old-fashioned you'll ever taste, and that includes the Pendennis Club in Louisville, Kentucky, where they invented them. If you ever want another old-fashioned as good as that, come back here. You won't get one no place else.'

Johann grimaced. 'Every barman in the world believes he's the best barman in the world, and the only thing different about Errol here is that he probably is.'

Jack was tempted to ask 'Then what the hell is he doing here?' but he was sensitive to the feeling on the SS *Galveston Bay* that most of its regular passengers and crew had pasts they would rather forget and presents they weren't particularly keen to face, and so he contented himself with a grin, and raised his glass in a toast.

'To smooth sailing,' he said.

Errol polished his cocktail shaker with an immaculate cloth. 'There's the tail end of a hurricane suppose to be blowing itself out off Cape Hatteras, so don't bet on it.'

Johann lifted his brandy. 'In that case, I think it's worth drinking to. Smooth sailing.'

They sat in silence for a while, and then Jack said: 'You'll excuse me saying so, but it seems that you take this trip pretty often.'

Johann grunted. 'Too damned often. Two or three times a year If I didn't like to keep a personal eye on my business in Texas and my business in New York, I wouldn't go near this tin punt for money.'

Errol muttered: 'Me neither,' but when they turned to look at him, he was assiduously pouring chilled lemon juice into a flagon, and he didn't even raise his head.

'You're quite a famous name in oil these days,' said Jack

'That's right,' said Johann. 'Oil and chemicals.'

'I was trying to get into the oil business myself,' Jack explained. 'You know, the legal side of the oil business. It seems to me that it's wide open right now, and that a good sound attorney could make himself a lot of money'

Johann gazed at Jack with pale, unexpressive eyes Jack felt that he was being weighed and scrutinized like a sack of sugar. He said: 'Do you have many attorneys working for you, Mr Cornelius?'

'More than I'd like,' Johann replied. 'Up until now, I've used regular established law firms. McErrow and Johnson in Texas, a..d Orris and Nussbaum in New York.'

'I've heard of Orris and Nussbaum. They're pretty impressive people.'

'They seem to do their best,' remarked Johann. He was biding his time, waiting to see what this young man was going to say next. He had the interesting feeling that Jack Field was something special, that Jack had taken the SS *Galveston Bay* to New York because Johann's destiny had ordained it. Johann never doubted for a moment that fate ordered other people's lives around his own; and it was for that reason he had stopped Jack Field on the deck and introduced himself. He never usually felt inclined to speak to anyone on these trips, and he hardly ever spent time in the bar. But today seemed to be different, and so did Jack Field.

Jack said: 'Personally, I've always believed that an industry needs lawyers to match the way it does its business.'

'Oh?'

'Well, if I was representing an oil company, I'd get out to the oilfields and learn the business from the bottom up. I'd take a look at the major leasings for myself, and see what the problems of drilling and pumping and storing and refining really are, so that whenever I stood up in a court of law I'd know what the hell I was talking about. There are too many lawyers who represent their clients without the remotest understanding of their clients' business. Oil is a rough, tough, technical business, to my way of thinking, and I think it needs rough, tough, technical lawyers.'

Johann sipped his drink and ran the tip of his tongue across his thick lips.

'You seem to have very strong views about it,' he said.

'Well, that's the way an attorney has to be.'

Errol set a small dish of sesame cocktail cookies on the

bar, and Johann picked one out and bit into it carefully.
All the time, he kept his eyes on Jack.

He said: 'If you're so opinionated, and if you're so worked
up about the way an oil attorney ought to work, then what
are you doing about it? Have you talked to anyone? Shell?
Standard Oil? Why haven't you talked to me?'

Jack smiled. 'Well, it's a long story. But it's all to do
with my engagement.'

'Tell me.'

Jack didn't want to say anything about Ellie at first; nor
about Mr Jackson's stipulation that if he wanted to have
her hand in marriage he would have to stay in South
Carolina. Explaining something like that to a man as hard-
bitten and isolated as Johann Cornelius seemed to make
him sound as if he was all milk and water. But, on
reflection, Jack reckoned that if he'd made the decision,
then the decision must be defensible, and Johann would
probably understand his choice.

'I guess the problem is that I'm in love,' Jack said. 'Not
just infatuated, or swept away by romance. I'm in *love*. I
can feel my emotions as strong as if I could distill them
and bottle them and set them on the shelf. The way I see
it, a love like that only comes once in a lifetime, whereas
oil will always be there.'

Johann listened to this, and then ran his hand over his
thinning, pomaded hair. Errol said: 'Another brandy, sir?'
but Johann shook his head.

'Mr Field,' he said, 'you've made a poor decision.'

Jack coloured. 'I don't think marrying Ellie will prove to
be anything of the kind, sir. She's a beautiful and intelligent girl. And independent, too, which is rare enough.'

'I didn't mean that,' said Johann. 'Of course she's beautiful and intelligent, or you wouldn't have fallen in love.
I'm not denigrating your fiancée, Mr Field. I'm sure she's
lovely. But I *am* criticizing your decision. No woman, no
matter how exquisite, can give you back the business
opportunity that you are so gaily throwing away.'

Jack laid his glass on the table; and Errol, without being
asked, mixed him another old-fashioned. Jack said: 'I'm not
sure that I like the way you're saying that, Mr Cornelius.
You hardly know me.'

'I know you better than you think, my boy, because I

know myself. I also know about oil, and you are wrong about oil. Oil will not always be there. Or rather, the same opportunities to get into the oil business will not always be there. This is a tough, grabbing business and the big boys are going to have it sewn up in two or three years. That includes me. No, if you want to work in oil, then you must start right now, because if you don't, you'll be a South Carolina attorney for the rest of your days.'

Jack swallowed bourbon. 'Maybe you're right,' he said, 'but at least I'll be happy.'

'Come on,' said Johann impatiently, 'you know that I'm right, and you also know that you won't be happy for long. Her family may have pressured you into thinking that life is fine and genteel in Kingstree, South Carolina, but where's the challenge? Where's the money? What you just said to me about oil attorneys makes sense. If you worked that out for yourself, then you've got a good head and you can see a business opportunity when it's there. Do you seriously believe you're going to be content to mince up and down the sidewalks of Kingstree for the rest of your life, lifting your hat to elderly ladies and remarking on the way the dust from the lime trees spoils your velvet collars?'

Jack said fiercely: 'Do you know what it's like to love someone the way I love Ellie?'

There was a pause. Then Johann shook his head. 'I probably don't,' he said softly. 'But do you know what it's like to be rich?'

'I know what it's like to be comfortably off, yes.'

'Not comfortably off, *Rich*. When you're rich, you're never comfortably off. You're . . . you're . . .'

Johann raised his right hand, his fingers curled as if he were clutching a mass of banknotes. He could hardly articulate what he felt about wealth, especially to someone who had just turned down wealth in favour of marriage. He could see Jack watching him expectantly with those brown alert eyes, but he knew that if he described his desire for money the way it really was, the boy would not only fail to understand, he would probably be shocked as well. One day Jack might grasp what he was saying, but not today.

'You're addicted,' he finished baldly.

Jack watched him for a while. Johann couldn't make up

his mind if the boy was afraid of him or not; but when Jack eventually spoke, Johann decided that he wasn't. He liked that. The boy was young, and not ashamed to admit it. If there was one thing that Johann couldn't take, it was a green young smart aleck.

Jack said: 'In that case, I'm obviously not an addict. Well, not a complete addict, in any event.'

'There's no such thing as a halfhearted addict, Mr Field. Not where money's concerned.'

'Oh, I think there is, Mr Cornelius. In fact, I think there are many of us would go halfway for money, but not the whole way.'

Johann sipped the last of his brandy. 'What do you call "the whole way," Mr Field?'

'Giving up Ellie. That, as far as I'm concerned, would be the whole way. Then, I'd also say that giving up one's religion for the sake of money, that would be going the whole way. Or murdering for it.'

'Then it's wrong to kill for the sake of money, in your opinion?'

Jack frowned. 'Not just in my opinion, Mr Cornelius. I believe that it's also in the opinion of most civilized people.'

'Really.'

Behind the bar, Errol said, quite apropos of nothing: 'That Duncan Nicols, he could mix you one of his Pisco punches in 1880 A.D., and mix you another one of his Pisco punches in 1903 A.D., and you couldn't tell the damned difference.'

Johann commented: 'Errol, that's probably an indictment of the public palate, more than proof of Duncan Nicols' matchless barkeeping, and I'd be pleased if you'd keep your mouth shut.'

Jack said: 'I don't understand. How can you possibly justify murder for the sake of money?'

Johann rubbed his forehead. 'You can't understand that at all?'

'No, sir. I can't.'

'Well, let me put it this way. Supposing that I had committed murder for money. How would you defend me in a court of law?'

Jack shrugged. 'It's very hard to say, not knowing the circumstances.'

186

'Well, let's say that in my pursuit of money, I let a woman die by wilful neglect. What tack would you take with the jury? What philosophical points would you raise to convince them that what I'd done was in the best interests of America?'

Jack took his pipe out of his coat pocket and absentmindedly fingered the bowl. 'Personally, I wouldn't raise *any* philosophical points. I don't think that a court of law is the right place to make abstract appeals to notions of "greater good" or "best interests." You see, what really counts is winning the sympathy of the jury, and what a great many lawyers don't seem to understand is that juries are made up of ordinary people with a very limited grasp of what's going on.'

'Go on,' said Johann, his eyes narrowed.

Jack Field shrugged self-consciously. 'Of course, I'm only a junior attorney. I'm not even a partner yet. But this is the way it seems to me. I've been along to hear cases where a famous attorney makes a historic speech on a fine point of law, bringing in all kinds of obscure precedents and high-flown references, and you can see the jury sitting there with their mouths hanging open, for all the world like a pen full of pigs, and they plainly don't understand a word.'

'So what would you do?' Johann asked.

Jack Field stuck his pipe in his mouth while he found his tobacco. Then he took it out again, and said: 'I'd appeal to things that the jury could understand. I'd bring in old soldiers, and have them testify that you gave money to the veterans' hospital. I'd bring in the mayor, and have him say that you'd always served your community well. I'd bring in honest-looking workmen, to tell what a good boss you were, and how you lent them money when times were hard. And, of course, I'd bring in a widow whose husband had died in your service, and have her say that you'd looked after her ever since. Then, and only then, I'd have someone from your company explain why you had to neglect this woman in favour of making money.'

Johann half-smiled. 'You sound quite cynical for such a young man.'

'I'm not cynical at all,' said Jack, shaking his head. 'I wouldn't be trying to mislead the jury, or defend an action that couldn't be defended. All I'd be doing would be to show the jury why you'd behaved the way you had, but I'd be showing them in terms of real life, rather than terms of law. I believe in plain speaking, Mr Cornelius, that's all.'

'I see. And what would be your own views on such an offence? Could you think yourself, that letting someone die could be justified in the interests of industry?'

Jack, taking out his tobacco pouch, paused and looked worried. 'Do you mean, could I believe myself that making money for the good of the nation is a valid mitigation of fatal negligence?'

'Yes. I mean exactly that.'

Jack turned this one over in his mind. He stalled for time by slowly stoking his pipe, because he had a curious feeling that a lot more depended on his answer than the outcome of a hypothetical argument. He was not insensitive to personal auras; and Johann Cornelius had a gravitational attraction about him that drew lesser particles like Jack, and Errol and everyone and everything else that wasn't screwed to the floor, inexorably and inevitably toward him.

From the restaurant, while the ship swayed and tilted into the Atlantic, they heard the clatter of knives and forks, as the two black stewards laid the tables for lunch. The marine engines pulsed steadily through the red-carpeted floor beneath their feet, and Jack Field looked at Johann Cornelius and wondered what he ought to say. There was a smell of pea soup in the air.

Jack said: 'I think I would have to know you better before I answered you truthfully.'

'But surely you have an opinion?'

'What can I say? You might be a saint, Mr Cornelius, and the person in question might have brought her death upon herself. On the other hand – if you'll forgive my impertinence – you might be a terrible cad, and have driven her into an early grave by your own callousness.'

For a moment Jack thought that he might have annoyed his host. But then Johann gave a small nod, and turned to Errol and said: 'Fix me one more brandy, Errol. I think I might have something to celebrate, too.'

Jack could sense a subtle change in Johann's demeanour. It seemed that the questioning session was now finished, and that Johann was about to make some remark about Jack's performance. What Johann actually said, though, made Jack's hair prickle, and his white rubber collar feel uncomfortably tight.

'I think our meeting today was no lucky chance,' said Johann. 'In fact, I think it was one of those strokes of fate that make life stride forward in the way it does. You and I, Mr Field, are going to do great things together.'

'I beg your pardon?'

Johann laid a thick-fingered hand on Jack's shoulder. 'You came on board celebrating an engagement. Well, I think you will disembark at New York with a great deal more to celebrate. I would like you to work for me, in Texas and Oklahoma, on the oilfields.'

Jack stared. 'I'm afraid that I don't follow,' he said in a small, congested voice.

Johann took his brandy from the bar. 'I need a young attorney who can immerse himself in the oil business and turn out to be the best oil attorney there ever was. I want a man who knows about crude and cracking, salt domes and sand beds; and at the same time I want him to hold his own in a court of law. In other words, Mr Field, I want you.'

'Mr Cornelius, you've only known me five minutes.'

'If I couldn't judge a man's integrity in five minutes, then I'd never survive in the oil business.'

'But, Mr Cornelius, I'm afraid it's out of the question.'

'Isn't it just what you wanted?'

'Well, yes, but if I go to work in Texas, then I can't marry Ellie. I mean, that's the whole point of my staying in South Carolina.'

Johann looked at Jack over the curved rim of his glass. The ship rose and sank in the Atlantic swell. Across from the bar, the deck doors opened, and one or two passengers in mackinaw coats came in for their lunch. One of them said: 'Lamb cutlets, is it? What about a flank steak?'

Johann said: 'It's time you learned, Mr Field, that there is nothing in life that can't be fixed.'

'What are you saying? That you can fix it for me to marry Ellie *and* work in Texas?'

'Why not.'

'Because Mr Jackson expressly forbids it, that's why not.

189

He doesn't want Ellie starting her married life in an oil town, and that's all there is to it.'

Johann lowered his head and looked down at the brass bar rail, and the gleaming copper spittoon. 'Do you agree with Mr Jackson?'

Jack stared at Johann hard. 'I suppose so,' he said cautiously.

'Well, *do* you, or *don't* you? You seem clear enough in your mind about matters of law. *Do* you think it's right for this Mr Jackson to have such a hand in your career and your future fortune, or *don't* you?'

'You have to understand that I love Ellie, and I also respect her family. There's nothing amiss with Mr Jackson, I can assure you. We're already friends.'

'Friends? What kind of a friend won't let you go off and make your way in the world, just because he doesn't want his daughter to get downwind of a few roughnecks? Oil towns are tough, Mr Field, but you won't be spending all your waking days in oil towns, and most of the time you'll be sitting in an office that would make Mr Jackson's look about as dandy as a bench in the park.'

Jack got off his stool. He knew that Johann was deliberately provoking him, but at the same time he couldn't help himself from being provoked. He said, with as much control as he could manage: 'Sir, that's my future father-in-law you're talking about.'

Johann smiled. 'I know. And I admire the way you're defending him. But he's not right, is he, even though he's kind? If he's prepared to have you marry his daughter, then he's got to accept that you're going to become her husband and her master, and that if you want to take her to Texas, or Oklahoma, or even the moon, then that's your right and your privilege, and it has nothing to do with him.'

'Mr Cornelius, I don't want to fall out with my parents-in-law, and that's all I can say. I've given my word to Mr Jackson already.'

Johann raised his eyebrows as if to say: *Ah, well, it can't be helped,* and downed the remainder of his brandy. At that moment, Jerry Slobodien came in from the deck in a shiny grey jacket with a velvet collar, and a shoestring tie with a diamond stud. His black hair was grown long for 1909, and combed back in glossy wings of bear grease.

'This is my business manager, Mr Slobodien,' said Johann. 'Perhaps you'd like to have luncheon with us, and we can talk some more?'

Jack hesitated. He felt indecision stirring about inside him like a potful of greasy stew. If it hadn't have been for Ellie, he would have taken Johann Cornelius' offer there and then. But he believed in honour; and if he'd given his word of honour to stay in South Carolina, then stay in South Carolina he would.

He said: 'I'll eat with you, Mr Cornelius. But I must warn you that I won't change my mind.'

'That's all right,' said Johann. 'People who change their minds easily can change them back again just as quick, and what I prefer is dedication.'

They went through to the ship's dining room, a pale cream-painted salon with twelve circular tables covered with white cloths, where some of their fellow travellers were noisily sucking pea soup. Outside the windows, the grey sea rose and fell, and the last few seagulls swooped for scraps. One of the black stewards came forward and pulled back their chairs for them, and they sat facing each other with stiff smiles while the second steward brought the day's menu. It was pea soup, with lamb cutlets to follow, and persimmon pie.

'Generally, I take my lunch in my cabins,' Johann explained. 'The cook's a Chinaman, but he can sometimes be bribed to make a passable Welsh rabbit.'

'I think I'll skip the soup,' remarked Jerry Slobodien, glancing at the diners at the next table. 'It sounds like it's too damned loud.'

One of the diners, a mild-looking bespectacled man in a green tweed suit and a canary-yellow bowtie, dabbed his lips with his napkin and stared at Jerry Slobodien balefully. But the oil manager gave him a silent dark-chinned grimace in return, and the man returned to his soup like a startled turkey.

'Incidentally, Mr Cornelius,' said Slobodien, reaching into the breast pocket of his coat and producing a crumpled scrap of paper. 'We just had a message from Orris and Nussbaum. It seems that we have been legally restrained from breaking ground at Sapulpa Bluffs.'

'Restrained? Why? By whom?'

'Mr Spizak doesn't know yet. He only found out when he was trying to clear the final details of the lease. Some party acting on behalf of some other party has persuaded the district courts to hold up our drilling operations until the deed and title of the lease can be properly established.'

Johann's mouth tightened in annoyance. 'That's ridiculous. We leased those oil and mineral rights fair and square from the Baptist church.'

'Not according to this mysterious party who's taken out this restraining order. This mysterious party seems to think that all rights in the land at Sapulpa Bluffs are still owned by Seminole Indians, and this mysterious party has even produced a certain Chief Wewoka, from Boggy Depot, Oklahoma, whose rights we're allegedly infringing.'

The steward came up with his pad and his pencil and said: 'What'll it be, gentlemen? The cutlets is ecstasy itself.'

'Ecstasy itself? Where did you ever learn yourself a phrase like that?' demanded Jerry Slobodien.

'Mr Abraham Ruef, sir. He travelled on this steamer once, sir. A fine man, sir, but Jewish.'

'You're not exactly a white man yourself, Dudley. Just bring what you have, and we'll eat it.'

'Very good, sir.'

'And bring us a bottle of that red wine the captain drinks, and three glasses.'

'Two glasses,' said Johann. 'I've had enough for one day.'

'Yes, sir.'

Jack, who had been sitting very silently, unfolded his napkin and said: 'There is a way around it, you know.'

Johann looked up alertly. 'A way around what? You mean this snag at Sapulpa Bluffs?'

'Well, I think so. One of my subjects at Harvard was land registry and titles.'

'And?'

Jack coloured. 'I'm not entirely sure about this. I mean, I'd have to check it up in the law books. But the way I remember it, the Seminole Indians signed an agreement with the U.S. government in 1867, revoking all their mineral rights in the state of Oklahoma.'

Johann looked at Jerry Slobodien and raised a meaningful eyebrow.

Jack said: 'I don't like to guess at things without knowing

the facts, but it seems to me that this "Chief Wewoka" is probably a fraud, and that someone's obtained this restraining order just to delay your drilling.'

Johann thought about this, and then nodded. 'That could make sense. Colton and Moffat have both been interested in Sapulpa. But what can we do? This order's been granted in a district court.'

'That doesn't matter,' said Jack. 'Even if Chief Wewoka is genuine, he can't possibly have any claim on your oil rights. You could have that restraining order overturned by suppertime.'

Johann sat back in his dining chair with a grin.

'You know something, Mr Field. You're wasted in South Carolina. Wasted. You're a natural-born oil attorney if ever I came across one. What do you think, Jerry?'

Jerry Slobodien was lighting up a thin black cheroot. 'Whatever you say, Mr Cornelius. It all sounds like good news to me.'

'I'd have to check on my facts,' said Jack doubtfully. 'I'm only speaking from memory. It could be that the agreement with the Indians has been rescinded by now.'

'Not a chance.' Johann smiled. 'The day we give anything back to the Indians is the day we've scraped this country's resources down to the bare bone. Don't doubt your legal talents, Mr Field. You have just the kind of fighting spirit I like.'

Jack toyed with his knife. 'I'm very flattered by your comments, Mr Cornelius. I really am. But I've already explained the position I'm in, and there's nothing I can do, or want to do, to change it.'

Johann smoothed back his sparse blond hair. 'You think I'm trying to tempt you away from the straight-and-narrow path?'

'No, sir. I know that your offer is fair, and I believe that I could make a good oil attorney – and probably will, when the time is right. But the circumstances cannot be altered. I have given my word, and Ellie means more to me than any career possibly could

'Well,' said Johann, 'your love for your bride-to-be is admirable. If only your love for your work were equally strong'

'Ellie is the most beautiful creature on God's earth, Mr Cornelius.'

'In your opinion.'

'Love is always a matter of opinion, Mr Cornelius. Like honour.'

The black steward, Dudley, arrived with the pea soup. Johann picked up his spoon at once and began to drink it. Jack watched him in surprise; and Jerry Slobodien, his cheroot still dribbling smoke, watched Jack.

Jack licked his lips. Then he clasped his hands together and closed his eyes and said quietly: 'For the food and drink that we are about to receive, we thank Thee, O Lord, amen.'

He opened his eyes. Johann had paused, with his spoon dripping soup into his plate. There was an unfortunate hiatus, while the ship creaked and rolled, the engines vibrated through the deck, and the knives of the diners at the next table grated and squeaked on their dishes as they tried to dismember the tough little lamb cutlets that were ecstasy itself.

'Are you ready to eat now?' asked Johann, and there was a serrated edge on his voice.

Jack said: 'Quite, thank you, sir.'

Johann laid down his spoon, and wiped his mouth with his napkin. 'You mustn't think that I'm irreligious, Mr Field, but if there's one thing I cannot bring myself to do, it's to give thanks to a higher authority for what I eat. All the food that goes into my mouth gets there because of my own efforts, no matter how wonderful the Lord is for stocking the earth with abundant lunches.'

Jack said nothing for a moment. He found it almost impossible to work out what manner of man Johann Cornelius really was, and the feeling unnerved him. It wasn't only the deck that was rising and falling beneath his feet; it was his self-assurance as well.

'I think,' said Johann, 'that you and I are going to get along fine. What do you think, Jerry?'

Jerry Slobodien crushed out his cigar, and winked across the dining room at a prim young girl in a velour bonnet who had just come in from the deck. She looked like a governess on her way home to New York. Jerry Slobodien said: 'Oh, you'll get along all right. It's just a question of terms. Isn't that right, Mr Field? Terms.'

Jack, at that moment, felt more uncomfortable than he ever had before in his whole life. 'I beg to disagree,' he said quietly, and he couldn't understand why Johann Cornelius and Jerry Slobodien exchanged such self-satisfied smiles.

Just before dawn the next morning, the SS *Galveston Bay* began to run into rough seas. In South Carolina, the previous night, Ellie had heard rain on her bedroom window just before she fell asleep, but out here, six miles off Cape Hatteras, the rain came with the whiplashing tail of a hurricane. It had already shrieked its way across southern Florida, forcing the palm trees to lash and grovel, lifting off rooftops, and stirring up fishing boats so that they champed and foamed at their moorings like rabid dogs. Now, ailing and ill-tempered, it was twisting out eastward across the Atlantic, bannered with dirty skies, and it was still fierce enough to raise the ocean into thirty-foot peaks. It tilted the SS *Galveston Bay* across massive grey-green slopes, and drove the ship through tumbling buttes of spray, until the marine engines whined and rumbled and strained, and the bulkheads groaned like old men having bad dreams.

During the storm, Johann Cornelius remained at his desk under a dim green-shaded lamp, bent over a long report on the geological conditions of a new lease in California. Jerry Slobodien stayed with him for a while, but then went up to the observation saloon to smoke a cheroot and amuse himself at the discomfort of the other passengers. Most of the early-morning coffee and kippered herring had long since disappeared over the rail, and now the *Galveston Bay*'s guests sat with plaid rugs around their knees, their cheeks the colour of newspaper, silently praying to the gods of abdominal equilibrium, if there were any, to deliver them from nausea, and lead them not into regurgitation.

Jack Field, who hadn't eaten much breakfast, looked a little better. He was standing by the starboard window, watching the seas rise and plunge all around them, smoking his pipe Jerry Slobodien came over and leaned his back against the handrail next to him, casually puffing out smoke.

Jack said: 'Quite a blow.'

Jerry Slobodien nodded. 'Ass-end of a hurricane. Nothing to get excited about. We've been through worse than this.'

'I think I'm glad I said no to the bacon, all the same.'

Jerry Slobodien laughed.

The ship turned in the sea, paused, and then dropped twenty feet into a trough. Rain slashed against the saloon windows, and even through the thick glass Jack could hear the wind screaming in the masts and the wires. Deep beneath them, within the ship, he heard another sound, too, like a cartload of logs being delivered down a cellar chute. He glanced at Jerry Slobodien, but Slobodien either hadn't heard it, or had, and didn't care.

'Mr Cornelius is really regretful that you haven't changed your mind,' remarked Jerry Slobodien.

'Oh? I thought he was just playing games.'

Jerry Slobodien shook his head. 'Mr Cornelius never plays games. I've know him six, seven years; and I've never seen him play any games yet. He doesn't have that kind of humour.'

Jack gripped the rail tight to keep his balance on the heaving deck. He was beginning to wish that he hadn't started this pipe, but then, to knock it out in front of Jerry Slobodien and all the rest of the seasick passengers was an awful admission of landlubberliness. A suppressed burp that tasted of coffee and Balkan tobacco rose in his throat, but he managed to keep smiling.

'Does Mr Cornelius have *any* humour?' he asked.

'Oh, sure. But not the style that many people understand. He's amused by what-do-you-call-it.'

'I don't know,' said Jack. 'What *do* you call it?'

'Poetic what-do-you-call-it. Justice.'

Jack wedged his pipe in between the varnished rail and the saloon window. 'You mean that he likes to see people getting their just deserts?'

'That's correct.'

'Has he ever thought that he, too, might one day get his just deserts?'

Jerry Slobodien grinned wolfishly. 'Jack,' he said, 'I like you. But I'll tell you one thing. If Johann Cornelius ever gets his just deserts it'll be nothing more nor less than he runs out of people prepared to be bought.'

196

'But that will never happen. Most men have a price.'

Jerry Slobodien shrugged In that case, he won't get his just deserts.'

Jack, alerted by the oddity of this cónversation, and indeed by the oddity of the whole day's conversations, had half an inkling of what Jerry Slobodien was trying to say. But he wasn't at all sure whether Slobodien was trying to provoke him into changing his mind about working for Johann, or trying to warn him off altogether.

The SS *Galveston Bay* shuddered like a locomotive trying to get itself a grip on the rails. Jack said: 'Before I met Ellie, I would have considered working for Mr Cornelius as a great privilege. But I'm afraid that I can't be shaken. I respect Mr Cornelius, but I also respect my future father-in-law, and that's the way it has to be.'

Jerry Slobodien said: 'Well, it's your funeral.' But just as he said 'funeral,' the ship's engines stopped, and the deck of the saloon suddenly tilted their way, so that bottles and glasses rushed off the top of the bar and smashed against the mahogany panelling. Several of the passengers dropped their plaid rugs and shouted 'What's happening? Steward – what's happening?'

The ship rose and slid and wallowed, and for a few moments it was almost impossible to keep a footing on the deck. Jack felt himself thrown with a bang against the saloon window, then back again, and he saw his pipe sliding twenty feet away across the carpet. Outside, tall spires of foam rose above the deck, and as far as Jack could see, the ocean was a greenish landscape of restless mountains under a black sky.

An alarm bell started to ring. Jack said: 'We're sinking! My God, do you think we're sinking?'

Jerry Slobodien put a spindly leg out and stamped on his cheroot. 'No such luck, if you ask me. They're just trying to scare us into paying double fare.'

The alarm bell kept on ringing. The ship heaved around between the waves with a sickening aimlessness, and the girl in the velour bonnet vomited across the patterned carpet. Jerry Slobodien said: 'That's *her* off the list. I can't take a woman who can't hold her breakfast.'

Jack said: 'For God's sake! We ought to get to the lifeboats!'

'You think a lifeboat's going to do any better than this tub?'

'Dammit, Mr Slobodien, this ship's helpless!'

At that moment, one of the ship's officers, a fat Spanish-looking man in a gold-braided cap, gold-braided pants, and a woollen undervest, hurried erratically through the sloping saloon with a bullhorn. He wrapped an arm around one of the mahogany pillars and called out, in unnecessarily stentorian tones: 'Ladies and gentlemen! The captain says to regret the ship's cargo is shifted! We are therefore listing! Seriously! Therefore, we must make haste to the lifeboats! Ladies first!'

One man shouted: 'What about my belongings? All my papers?'

'Sorry, sir! No time!'

'But I've got thirteen thousand dollars down there! That's five years' work!'

'Sorry, sir! The captain says to make all haste! The cargo is shifting quick! Maybe the whole ship turn over!'

Jerry Slobodien said: 'Where's Carl? We have to warn Mr Cornelius.'

Jack gripped his shoulder. 'You find Carl. I'll go for Mr Cornelius. I have to go down there anyway. There's a box in my cabin I can't leave.'

'You heard what he said!' snapped Jerry Slobodien. 'There's no time! Just warn Mr Cornelius and get on up here!'

The SS *Galveston Bay* creaked and dipped alarmingly, and the lights dimmed to a faint unhealthy orange. Through the salt-crusted windows, Jack saw a grey glassy cliff that seemed to move toward them as if it was on rollers, and he felt the ship pause in a trough, preparing itself to receive the tons and tons of sea water that were towering over it.

He made his way across the crazily angled saloon to the ship's main stairs. Engravings of Lily Langtry in carved teak frames beamed at him beatifically on each side. Clinging on to the brass handrail, taking one tilted step at a time, he looked down and saw water coursing across the red floral carpet on the deck below. Behind him, he heard Jerry Slobodien shouting: 'Carl! *Carl*! We have to get out of here!'

The ship suddenly swayed, and Jack was thrown across

the staircase, tumbling over and over, bruising his back on the edge of the stairs, and he landed on all fours in the seething, gurgling waterfall that ran across the carpet. Coughing, hurt, he picked himself up and climbed toward the corridor where Johann Cornelius' first-class staterooms were. There was blood coursing from both his nostrils and mingling with the sea water that ran down his face, and a livid bruise on his forehead where his head had struck a brass lamp bracket. But he knew that he couldn't leave Johann Cornelius to drown, and neither could he lose Earle Jackson's family jewels. He managed to stagger ten or twelve feet down the corridor, with the rolling of the ship throwing him heavily from side to side. But then the *Galveston Bay* turned sidelong against the seas, and the howling force of the hurricane tilted her over so violently that Jack found he was skidding across the wet mahogany panelling of the corridor walls. He grabbed for a door handle, and held on to it tight, while the vessel shivered and shook all around him, and thousands of gallons of ocean collapsed through the doorways and hatchways all around him.

The ship rolled again, and Jack saw a door swing open a few yards farther down the corridor. It banged open and shut a few times, and then the bulky shape of Johann Cornelius emerged, pulling himself out of his cabin like a man rising out of his coffin. Johann made his way toward Jack on his hands and knees. The ship was heaving so desperately that there was no possibility of staying upright, no matter how rich you were.

'Mr Cornelius!' shrieked Jack. 'The ship's turning over! We have to get to the lifeboats!'

'Well, get on with it!' Johann shouted back. 'I'll follow!'

'I have to go to my cabin!'

'Don't be so goddamned foolish! This goddamned ship's going to fall apart in a moment!'

'But I can't leave the jewels! I have all of my fiancée's family's heirlooms in there!'

Johann had reached Jack now. The Dutchman was soaked through, and his face was cut from a toppling lampshade, but it was rigid with determination. He managed to heave himself up to his feet as the ship slopped uneasily into a trough, and he bent forward and offered his hand.

'*Come on, we'll get out of this together!*'

'*But the jewels!*' Jack protested frantically. '*I was entrusted with them! I can't leave them there!*'

Johann pulled Jack roughly upright, and Jack seized the brass rail that ran along the side of the corridor to steady himself.

'*I must!*' he shouted.

Johann pushed him savagely toward the stairs. '*Get going! Don't argue! If you're that worried about your damned family jewels, I'll pay for them! I'll give you whatever they're worth! Now, let's go before we damned well drown!*'

Two of the *Galveston*'s crew had come climbing and scrambling down the main staircase to look for them, and so they half-slid and half-crawled through the rushing shallows that poured across the deck, with Johann shoving Jack ahead of him, and reached out for the sailors' hands.

'Up on deck to your left!' ordered one of the crew. 'And make it quick as you like!'

Jack hesitated for one moment, and turned, but Johann pushed him again and said: 'I'll *pay!* Now, get up those stairs!'

Outside on deck, in the slanting rain and the shrieking wind, the lifeboat was already being winched up on its davits. The pale, frightened faces of the passengers and crew, of whom there were only twenty-three altogether, were swinging to and fro in the boat like a gallery of colourless portraits. Jack and Johann were helped up over the boat's slippery side, and they found seats next to Carl, Johann's manservant, who was holding a wet comic paper and looking alarmed and confused. The green seas that rose around them were so immense that Jack couldn't believe that they would possibly say afloat.

With pulleys clanging in the gale, the lifeboat was winched out and lowered down the rusty, leaning side of the steamship toward the ocean. Eventually, the waves slapped at its keel, and then caught it and tossed it away from the *Galveston Bay*, and then back again, and Jack clung on to the narrow seat, his eyes tight closed, hoping that Ellie would never have to be told that he was drowned.

The last crew members slid down the swaying winch lines and clambered on board. Then they pushed the boat away from the hull of the SS *Galveston Bay* with oars, and they were swept off into the canyons of green and grey, too scared for their lives to shout to each other, or sing, or do anything but grip their seats as hard as they could, and pray to God for the hurricane to blow itself out.

The last Jack saw of the steamship was her black-painted stern, streaked with rust and clustered with barnacles, her brass screws raised to the filthy skies, as she sank quickly beneath the Atlantic. Then there was nothing but sea, and wind, and grey clouds that rushed eastward over their heads.

They sat in the dark hotel drawing room under an old cracked oil painting of the frigate *Merrimack*, before she was turned into an ironclad. Through the gardens, lined with orderly plane trees, they could see the wide shining stretch of Hampton Roads, and the flags fluttering in the distance at Newport News. They had ordered brandies, and they sipped them with the quiet appreciation of men who know that the world is a man's world, and very regulated, and that life would remain as stable and as dignified as this even when the painting over the mantelpiece was twice as old as it was today. It was a light breezy afternoon, but the drawing-room windows were all closed, so that inside, where the two men sat, it was silent and still.

Earle Jackson said: 'I can't stay for too long, I'm afraid. We're taking the three-o'clock train back to Charleston.'

Johann, dressed in a borrowed and badly fitting grey suit, answered: 'That's all right. I'm leaving on the New York mail train myself at four. How's Jack?'

'The doctor said he was lucky not to have fractured his skull. But he's more cheerful this morning. I just thank God you're all safe. You should have seen my daughter's face when the intelligence reached us.'

'Jack's a fine fellow,' said Johann. 'Very shrewd for his age, but pleasant, too. Your daughter's a lucky girl.'

Earle Jackson gave a brief smile, but nothing else.

Johann said: 'I think this is going to put me off steamers for good. My manager's been spending the morning trying to persuade me to purchase a railroad car. I can't say that I'm entirely against the idea, either.'

Earle Jackson nodded. There was a silence that wasn't

altogether comfortable. Outside the window, out on the Roads, they could see a naval escort at anchor, and a flurry of yachts leaning into the wind.

Earle Jackson said: 'I really came here to thank you.'

Johann looked at him. 'Thank me? What for?'

'Well, for saving Jack. He says that you saved him. He was all for going to rescue my family heirlooms, but he says you pushed him back up on deck.'

Johann coughed. 'Anyone else would have done the same And, quite incidentally, I promised to pay for those heirlooms, whatever they were. You must give me some idea of how much they were worth.'

Earle Jackson shook his head. 'No, I won't hear of it. Jack's life is worth more to my family than any jewels or paintings that ever were. To me, too. Ellie was so relieved – well, I have to say it brought the tears to my eyes.'

'Ellie's your daughter? The one who's going to marry Jack?'

'He told you?'

'Oh, sure. We had quite a long talk on the boat, before the Lord God intervened and sank us. But listen, I did promise Jack that I'd pay for those jewels – really. If you fix a price, I'll have my bankers send you a certified cheque in the morning.'

Earle Jackson looked down at the Kashmir carpet. He said, in a low voice: 'I'd rather you didn't. It's really not necessary. It was just some jewellery that belonged to my mother.'

'Was it insured?'

'Of course. For less than its auction value, I suspect. But quite enough.'

'Well,' said Johann, 'it's up to you. If you want to be recompensed, I gave my word, and I'm willing to keep it.'

Earle Jackson said: 'What I had in mind was something different. I wanted to offer something to *you*. As a way of saying thanks for saving my daughter's happiness.'

Johann looked at Earle Jackson with pale, narrowed eyes for a while. For some reason that he couldn't pin down, Earle Jackson seemed unduly unsettled, almost *shifty*, especially for a man who had sought an audience with him in order to thank him for saving the life of his future son-in-law. Johann was intrigued by Earle Jackson's discomfort.

but at the same time he was quite prepared to take advantage of it without knowing its cause. He recalled forcing a Californian landowner down to a rock-bottom lease deal a couple of years back, simply because the man was betraying, for whatever private reason and however unconsciously, a deep anxiety to sell out.

Earle Jackson said: 'I was thinking of offering you a horse, as a matter of fact. My plantation, Fortuna, is also one of the finest stud farms in South Carolina. There was a particular chestnut I had in mind, a yearling. It's called Charleston Lightning.'

Johann sipped at his brandy without taking his eyes away from Earle Jackson's face. Then he got up from his seat and walked across to the fireplace, where he stood for a while and examined the painting of the *Merrimack*.

Finally he turned around. He said, with heavy kindness: 'I'm very flattered by your offer, Mr Jackson, and very gratified. But I'm afraid I don't really have any use for horses. I rarely have any time to myself, and when I do, I catch up on my sleep. I'm a businessman. Paper, ink, accounts, money. I couldn't know what to do with a horse.

Earle Jackson was a little put out. He said: 'Oh, I was hoping you'd kind of like it.'

Johann smiled. 'I would. Don't get me wrong. But I'd rather you kept the horse yourself, and made good use of it, than give it to me. I wouldn't like it to go to the glue factory for lack of use.'

'Well,' said Earle Jackson, taking a short breath, 'I'm afraid that I don't have anything else to offer. It's no use giving you money.'

'No,' said Johann, still smiling.

There was another awkward silence. Johann stood beaming down at Earle Jackson's bent head as if he were about to lay a blessing on him, or bestow a knighthood. Earle Jackson lifted his brandy glass and tipped back the last of his brandy.

'There is one thing,' said Johann.

'Yes?'

'I don't want you to misunderstand me. I'm not trying to interfere in your life, or in the way you run your family affairs. But right now you have the last word on something, on some*one*, rather, whose services could be more than useful to me.'

Earle Jackson stared at him, uneasy.

Johann sat down again, still smiling. 'What I'm saying is that young Jack seems to me to have the qualities that I've been looking for in an oil attorney. Apart from which, he has some very radical notions about oil, and the profits of the oil industry, and some even more interesting ideas about oil and law and business morals. He's young yet. Inexperienced. But oil's a hard business, and a young man can learn quick.'

Earle Jackson said faintly: 'Jack still has his training to finish. He's indentured to his father's firm in Kingstree.'

Johann looked poker-faced. 'Is that a handicap?'

'Well, no, but Jack's father thinks that – well, and I agree with him that Jack should stay for a while in his home state.'

'What does Jack think?'

'I presume that Jack agrees. Nobody's forced him to stay in Carolina.'

'And Ellie?'

Johann was watching Earle Jackson closely with every question, and when he asked about Ellie, he knew at once what Earle Jackson's sensitive spot was. Earle Jackson flinched, almost as if Johann had struck him a playful pat on the cheek. The muscles around his mouth tightened, and he couldn't smile for a hundred dollars.

'Ellie's place is in South Carolina society,' her father said quietly, 'growing up gracefully alongside of her mother and me. I know you've made your wealth in oil, Mr Cornelius, and I don't mean to speak offensively, but there is no place for Ellie in a boom town on the Western frontier, amongst wildcatters and suchlike.'

Johann remarked: 'You seem uncommonly fond of your Ellie. Most parents these days would give a chestnut yearling and a year's supply of feed just to see the back of their daughters.'

Earle Jackson looked away. He said quietly: 'Yes, Mr Cornelius, I am uncommonly fond of Ellie. But then, to me, Ellie is a very uncommon daughter. She – well, she reminds me of her mother, when she was young.'

Johann grinned. 'I see. But I don't think you have any

204

cause to worry. Boom towns are not all mud and whiskey, you know, and wildcatters can be quite human once you get to know them. Some of them have even been heard to pass the time of day.'

'I realize that, and I didn't mean to cause you offence. But I'm afraid that I had to stipulate that if Jack and Ellie were to marry, then Jack should stay in South Carolina and finish his training, with a view to taking up a partnership with his father.'

Johann lifted an eyebrow. 'So it's a chestnut yearling or nothing?'

'I'm afraid so. But you're still very welcome to that.'

Johann was silent for a short while. Then he put down his glass, and laced his big fingers together, and said: 'There was a time, years and years ago, when I wanted to own somebody too.'

'I don't follow.'

'She was a girl,' explained Johann. 'Younger than Ellie, but very beautiful. And just like you, I wanted to have that beauty, actually have it, all to myself. I bought that girl, because in those days and in that place you could still do things like that. I kept her in a case like a specimen of butterfly, or bird. I loved her in a way that I didn't believe anybody else could ever understand. But I believe *you* understand, Mr Jackson, because it appears to me that you love your Ellie in very much the same kind of way. Not profanely, but possessively.'

Earle Jackson tried to look fierce. 'You're not trying to suggest that—'

Johann raised his hand. 'I'm not trying to suggest anything, Mr Jackson. I'm just telling you that beautiful young girls can make a man behave in jealous and irrational ways that maybe he shouldn't. Even daughters. Maybe *especially* daughters.'

He lowered his eyes. 'Regrettably, I know from my own experience that beauty is infinitely fragile, and that it can't be put in a case and breathed over. You can sigh for it and you can ache for it, but you can't own it, not ever. I tried to, and I wound up crushing it.'

'What do you mean— *crushing* it?'

Johann shrugged. He could hardly believe it, but even after all this time, he still felt a lump in his chest for

Carina. He said, in a tighter voice than he'd meant to: 'She died, mostly because of me. I wasn't even there to see it happen.'

Earle Jackson blinked, but then he recovered himself a little and said: 'Well, I'm sorry. But I'm afraid that it's really nothing to do with me. I made my decision for Ellie's own protection, and for Jack's own protection, too.'

'Protection against what?' asked Johann. 'Protection against experience? Protection against smallpox, or bad food, or the timetables of the Southern Pacific? Protection against life? You can't protect people from their own talents, Mr Jackson.'

'I'm not attempting to. I simply believe it's wiser if Jack bides his time.'

Johann gave one sharp, decisive shake of his head. 'Then you're wrong. Jack is the right age, with the right talents, and he's keen as mustard to get into the right business. If you let me hire Jack Field as my oil attorney in Texas, without letting it stand in the way of his happy betrothal to your daughter, then you're doing Jack a favour, and you're doing Ellie a favour, too. Jack's going to be a wealthy man if he comes into oil right now, there's no two ways about it. But if he doesn't, then he's going to stay a South Carolina mouthpiece for the rest of his life, and Ellie's going to stay a South Carolina mouthpiece's lady.'

Earle Jackson looked exceedingly discomfited, as if he'd climbed into a pair of briar tweed pants without remembering to put his long johns on first. He said awkwardly: 'I don't really want to argue about it, Mr Cornelius. I came here to thank you, and I believe that I have. If you don't feel able to take my horse, then that's the way it is. But I can't offer you anything else.'

Johann said: 'That's all right. But let me ask you to think about what I've told you, just for a day or two. And do something else, too. Ask Jack what he really feels, and Ellie. And then think about yourself. Just how long can you keep Ellie cupped up in your hands, Mr Jackson? You're going to have to let her go someday. She's not a bird, and she's not a butterfly. She's a young woman, with a right to her own future.'

For a moment, Johann thought that Earle Jackson was going to lose his temper, and tell him to stop interfering.

But there were heavier pressures on Earle Jackson's conscience than Johann Cornelius – Ellie herself, for one – and he lifted himself from his club chair as if he were a carrier taking up his backpack after an unaccustomed rest.

'Very well, Mr Cornelius,' he said in a thin tone. 'I'll agree to think about it. When I've made up my mind, I'll have one of my friends in New York call around to give you my answer. Is that fair enough?'

'Fair enough.'

Out in the hotel garden, Johann could see Jack and Ellie promenading between the trees hand-in-hand; Ellie with her candy-striped parasol, and Jack in a brown suit as badly fitting as Johann's. On board the SS *Galveston Bay*, Jack had told Johann that he would never understand how much he loved Ellie; but then, the SS *Galveston Bay* was resting now on the bed of the Atlantic Ocean, alongside the wreck of the *Merrimack* and a dozen other ships; and declarations of love, unlike ships, are rarely commemorated in oils, or hung above the mantelpiece as souvenirs.

Johann smiled, and pointed out of the window at the happy couple. All that Earle Jackson could do was turn away, leaving his empty brandy glass on the table, and close the door behind him.

The girl was waiting for him in the foyer of the Plaza as he came back from a long and difficult meeting with Du Pont. An unexpected summer shower had slicked the sidewalks outside, and the hotel was crowded with wet umbrellas and chattering people hoping for taxis. Johann walked across the patterned carpet to the gold-painted gates of the elevator bank, and stood patiently while an elderly woman in furs was helped out of the car.

The girl was sitting in one of the two elegant little armchairs in the foyer, about ten feet from where Johann was standing, and she made no attempt to get up. She said clearly: 'Mr Cornelius?'

Johann turned. She smiled.

'Did you call me?' he asked.

'You *are* Mr Cornelius?'

'That's right.'

She lifted an arm. She was very petite and pretty, and she was dressed in an expensive summer coat of beige wool.

She couldn't have been older than eighteen or nineteen. Johann suddenly realized that she expected him to go across and take her hand.

He came over with a slow, even walk. Then he held her hand, in its matching beige glove, and kissed it.

'Well?' he said with a cool smile.

'I have a message for you,' she told him. 'My name is Hester Forbes, and my father is a friend of Mr Earle Jackson, of South Carolina.'

'I see.'

'Well, you don't, really. Father was going to bring this message himself, but he had to go to the doctor for his piles.'

'I beg your pardon?'

'Aren't they an occupational hazard for businessmen?'

Johann looked down at her seemingly innocent heart-shaped face. 'I suppose so,' he answered, amused.

'Anyway,' she said, 'I was going across town myself so I said that I'd deliver it. The message is – "Texas it is." Do you understand that?'

Johann nodded. 'I think so.'

'I'm pleased about that, because it's double-Dutch to me Do you want to buy me tea while I'm here?'

'I wish I had time, Miss Forbes. But I regret that I have a meeting in fifteen minutes' time.'

She pulled a face. 'Oh, well. Father did say that you made your money by sheer hard labour. It's been nice to meet you, all the same. Most millionaires are so small. You're very big for a millionaire, do you know that?'

Johann couldn't help grinning. 'I didn't know there was a national size-to-wealth ratio.'

'Of course there is. There's a ratio for everything. By the way, what religion are you? You're not Jewish, by any chance?'

'I'm Dutch Free Church. Why?'

Hester took a small notebook with mother-of-pearl covers from her bag, and pencilled a few words in it.

'Nothing,' she said. 'I'm just working out another ratio.'

'Not an eligibility-for-marriage ratio?'

She looked up, and went a little pink. 'How did you know?'

He took her beige-gloved hand and squeezed it Miss

Forbes, you're an eligible-looking girl yourself, and every eligible-looking girl in the USA is searching for an eligible-looking millionaire.'

'I wasn't going to propose,' she said. 'Leap year was last year.'

Johann held her hand for a moment longer, and then let it go. He raised his hat.

'Thank the Lord,' he said, 'for small mercies.'

It must have been a season when wheels turn, when doors open and close. When Johann came down to the desk the following morning, the receptionist handed him, among his usual mail, a long white envelope postmarked Boston, Massachusetts, and inscribed 'strictly private.' He tucked the rest of his letters into his inside pocket, and carried this one, unopened, into the dining room where he sat down at his accustomed table by the window, overlooking the park, and propped the letter against the salt and pepper.

He knew nobody in Boston that he could think of. He had done no business in Boston. The handwriting, an even blue-black copperplate, was unfamiliar. The letter remained untouched while the waiter brought him coffee, and while he ordered two poached eggs, with bacon and toast.

Eventually, he picked the letter up, and tore it open with his butter knife. There were two sheets of white bond, sharply folded, each filled with the same even handwriting. He sipped his coffee and began to read.

After the first three lines, he set his cup of coffee back in its saucer. He laid the letter on the table, and smoothed it out with his hand, as if he were trying to erase what was written in it. When the waiter came up with more coffee, he didn't even notice.

The letter read:

Dear Mr Cornelius,

It is six years since we last saw each other, although I have followed the progress of your career quite assiduously in the newspapers. I am afraid that I have to bring you intelligence that is both bitter and sad. I can only hope that you mourn when you hear it with just a fraction of the grief that you caused yourself by your own cruel actions.

On the last day of April, Mrs Beatrice Mulliner was found dead in the bathroom of her apartment in Roseland, Tangipahoa Parish, Louisiana. She had retreated to Roseland after the shame and dishonour you caused her in Edgar, Texas, hoping to find a fresh beginning, and to build again her broken hopes and self-esteem, but apparently this proved beyond her capacity. She took her own life by cutting her wrists and her throat with an open razor, and she bled to death within a very few minutes.

I am writing to you now because of what Mrs Mulliner said in the note which she left behind. She said that she was taking her life because the assault she suffered at the hands of oilmen from your own corporation was a greater pain and besmirchment than her soul could bear, although in a manner which she felt you could not understand, she loved you still. She had tried to form a liaison with an oculist who practised in Roseland, but when he proposed matrimony to her, the disgust she felt at her past was too great for her to bear, and she could not accept. It was then, despairing of her future, she decided to take her life.

She made one suggestion, sir, which I trust you will not take as an impertinence from me but as a last request from a lady who loved you and who died in the cause of that love. She asked that in her memory, and as a way of atoning for the agony you caused her, you should pay me a regular allowance, and to give me letters of introduction to whichever railroad officials might best help me to further my intended career in the railroads.

She said that I must not make such a request appear as a threat, but that you should consider your personal involvement with members of government, society, and business most carefully before coming to your decision, since I have in my possession her manuscript letter which describes in detail everything about your conduct in Edgar and elsewhere, with the names of corroborating witnesses.

I can be reached at any time at the above address. I hope that the Lord enables you to find peace of mind, and some respite from your guilt.

Yours,
Daniel Forster

Johann was shaking as he laid down the letter. He felt cold and queasy, and he seemed to find it impossible to rise from his chair. All these years he had lived with some kind of hope that Beatrice still loved him, that she was still alive and safe; and he could have counted in scores the dreams he had dreamed of meeting her in strange places, in ornamental gardens and at railroad stations. He could feel her body in his hands even now, a warm ghost. He could almost reach out and touch her hair. He could almost hold her.

The waiter, a white cloth over his arm, came up with his bacon and eggs, and stood waiting for Johann to remove the pages from the table.

'Sir?' he said, at length.

Johann looked up. He was very pale.

The waiter said: 'Are you all right, sir? Shall I bring your breakfast later?'

Johann found the strength somehow to sit up straight and give a tense, humourless smile.

'No, no,' he said. 'It's nothing. I think I've just discovered that one has to pay for one's past mistakes.'

'Very true, sir,' nodded the waiter. 'Would you like the pepper?'

1921

America's present need is not
heroics but healing; not nostrums
but normalcy; not revolution but
restoration; not surgery but serenity.

— Warren G. Harding, Boston, 1921

It was Jack Field's first free Saturday for nine weeks; and so he took Randy to Riverside Park, where they punted a ball around for twenty minutes, and then sat on a bench in their overcoats, sharing a paper poke of hot chestnuts, and watching the N.Y. Central freight trains as they clattered ceaselessly backward and forward in wreaths and curls of white smoke. Jack enjoyed the noise and the bustle. Most of the incoming trains sounded like travelling farmyards – cackling and bleating and lowing – as animals were brought in from the Western states for slaughter in Manhattan's abattoirs. And then there was the honking and parping of motor horns from the Dodges and Maxwells and Briscoes that teemed up and down Riverside Drive; and the echoing hoot of ferries from the 129th Street pier. It was a bright, snappy, blue-skied day in November, 1921 – the year that Jack Dempsey knocked down Georges Carpentier at Boyle's Thirty Acres in Jersey, the year that Babe Ruth raised his home-run record to fifty-nine, the year that a bathing belle scandalized spectators at Washington's Potomac Beach by rolling down her stockings past her knees, and most important of all for Jack Field, it was the year that Warren Gamaliel Harding was inaugurated President.

In a few days' time, on November 19, Jack Field would have been working for Cornelius Oil for twelve years. He owned a five-bedroom apartment on Central Park South, tastefully decorated in warm golds and browns by André Manche, and hung with paintings by Sisley and Degas; and a seven-bedroom colonial house in New Hampshire, with nearly two hundred acres of woodland and pasture. For Jack and Ellie Field, money had brought furs and servants and automobiles, but it had also brought calm and satisfaction, because they both enjoyed their small family and their leisure, and money had given them the opportunity to indulge their happiness in both. Ellie still liked to bake cookies and prepare dinners (her devilled turkey was

215

mouth-watering), and there were still plenty of times when Jack enjoyed taking Randy out on New Hampshire's lakes in early fall, when the leaves were rusting off the trees and the still waters mirrored the far peaks of the White Mountains, to fish and talk and munch cold chicken and fruity kolaches in the crisp fresh air, and never think about Johann Cornelius or oil or chemicals all day. Those days of freedom weren't so frequent now, especially since the slump in oil prices and Harding's inauguration in March. But Jack and Randy's closeness wasn't strained; and Jack could sit back now on this bench in Riverside Park and look at his nine-year-old son with a fatherly warmth and affection that reassured him he was human, even after nine straight weeks of exhausting legal negotiations in smoky hotels and offices.

Jack hadn't changed much in twelve years. He was broader, and looked better-fed. But he still had that sharp, Mount Rushmore profile, and that brown wavy hair that had first attracted Ellie. He wore a well-cut camelhair coat with a tie belt, and a dark brown suit from Savile Row, London, but he hadn't remembered to put his shoes out for cleaning last night, and he could never tie his necktie straight. Randy had inherited the wavy hair, but there was a softness in the boy's face that always reminded Jack of Ellie, and there were times when he could put his own hands around Randy's thin wrists and marvel at his son's half-elegant, half-awkward childishness.

He didn't know what Randy was going to be when he grew up, and right now he didn't much care. But he could look across at his own black touring car parked at the kerb, with his black-uniformed chauffeur, O'Hara, stretching over the mudguard to polish the hood, and he could only pray that Randy wouldn't get himself involved in the same business.

A ferry went by, strung with bunting, and blew its whistle. It reminded Jack disturbingly of that day on the SS *Galveston Bay* in 1909, as the ship had moved slowly out of Charleston harbour. Randy, who was peeling a chestnut with his thumbnails, said: 'You're not going to doze off, are you, sir?'

Jack blinked at the boy, and then smiled. 'No, no. I wasn't dozing off. I was just thinking.'

216

The boy brushed chestnut shell from his navy barathea coat. He wore grey knee socks and a grey tweed cap. He frowned at Jack in concern, and said: 'You weren't thinking anything awful, were you?'

'What makes you say that?'

'Well, sir, you had an awful face on.'

'Did I? I guess I've been working too hard.'

Randy bit into the soft amber flesh of his chestnut, and chewed it. A maroon-painted freight train from the P&P Railroad clanked past, carrying coal. Randy said: 'Will you *always* have to work so hard? We haven't been out to the lakes for weeks and weeks.'

Jack dry-washed his face with his hands. 'Things have changed,' he said tiredly. 'These days, the oil business is really getting to work, and when the oil business gets to work, *I* have to get to work, too. Did I ever show you an oil contract? They're as thick as a Webster's dictionary, some of them, and the only difference is that they don't explain what they mean.'

Randy said solemnly: 'Mother thinks you ought to take a vacation, sir.'

Jack grinned, and affectionately straightened the boy's cap. 'I know she does. And *I* think so, too. Just as soon as things settle down, we'll take a trip to the mountains and do some skiing. Now, how would you like some tea at the Claremont?'

'Oh, yes, please,' said Randy; but then he frowned again and said: 'Is it the President, sir?'

'Is what the President?'

'Well, I heard you talking to Mr Cornelius on the telephone. I didn't mean to listen but I couldn't help it. You said the President was as dumb as they come.'

Jack looked at his son in surprise. It was hard to believe that only a few years ago this serious-faced small boy had been lying in his crib in their house in Tulsa, sucking a red-rubber rabbit and watching the nursery curtains rise and fall in the morning breeze. He said: 'When did I say that?'

'I don't know, sir. Last week, I think. *Is* the President dumb?'

Jack leaned forward on the park bench. A long freight train with Pacific Fruit Express cars, and stock cars from

Chicago, and cars with the old Chesapeake & Ohio cat symbol, and Erie Lackawanna cars, came clanging and clattering by. When it had passed, he said: 'Well, the President's not dumb exactly. He was smart enough to get himself elected, and he knows how to make people like him. He's a good-looking man, you see, and he's sociable, and he talks plain English.'

'But he's dumb?'

Jack grinned. 'Let's put it this way. When Mr Cornelius and I went down to Washington that time to talk about the Navy oil reserves, we were invited around to the White House to meet Mr Harding, and we had a real pleasant chat. We talked about theatre, and sports, and all about Mr Harding's dog Laddie Boy. He cracked a few jokes, too. You couldn't help but like him.'

Randy said: 'So what was wrong with him?'

'Well,' answered Jack, 'he may be a very cheery kind of a fellow, but he's not much of a President. A President has to do more than look good and talk good and make people feel happy. It seems to me that he really doesn't know very much about anything at all, and when all the jokes are over, you can suddenly see that he's the kind of man who doesn't really have a mind of his own. In my opinion, all the thinking that's going on in Washington these days is being done by the President's old cronies from Marion, Ohio, and *they're* sharp, I can tell you. Mr Cornelius says they're sharp as corkscrews, and twice as twisted.'

Randy licked his lips against the cold. 'Does that mean they tell lies?' he asked his father.

Jack shook his head. 'Not in so many words. But they're always ready for what they call "a little deal," or a "business proposition" – and that usually means that some of the money that should have ended up in someone else's pockets winds up in theirs.'

'Then they're robbers! Are they robbers, sir?'

Jack took out his cigar case. After all the years he'd been working as chief attorney for Cornelius Oil, after all the conferences and caucuses and negotiations and understanding, after all his professional efforts to use shades of language that would make 'pressure' seem like 'persuasion,' and 'diversion of funds' appear to be 'legitimate outlay,' this was the first time that anyone had ever come out cold and

218

said what inwardly he had always felt. He was working, no bones about it, amid saw-toothed tigers in business suits.

He clipped his cigar, and fumbled in his coat pocket for his lighter. He still preferred a pipe, but when you worked as intensely as he did, there wasn't time for any of that leisurely stoking and lighting up and relighting.

He said: 'You can't really call them robbers, Randy. But I guess you could call them opportunists. They make the most of any chance they get, and once they've sunk their jaws into something, they won't ever let go. It's a tough world, and that's all there is to it.'

Randy looked up at him. He was feeling a desperate sympathy for his father that he didn't know how to express. He said: 'Sir? Are you sad, sir?'

'*Sad*?' said Jack. 'What do you mean by sad?'

Randy tried to think. But all he could say was: 'I don't know, sir. You just seem to be sad.'

'Well, I guess I'm tired, more than anything. I've just spent nine weeks solid talking oil business with the government, and believe me, *that* can make you feel sad.'

Randy swung his legs aimlessly. Then he pointed out across the Hudson and said: 'Look at that ferry! It's got flags and balloons!'

In spite of the cold wind, the boat was packed with people, and they could hear the faint strains of 'My Rambling Rose' wafting across the water. The ferry's black-and-white-striped funnel was pouring out twists of brownish smoke, and down on the open rear deck there was dancing and singing and laughter. Jack wouldn't have been at all surprised if there was beer on board, too, although a passing police launch did nothing but toot the ferry a greeting on its whistle.

Jack said: 'That looks fun, doesn't it? Maybe we should take the ferry across to the Palisades one day, and fry some bacon down on the beach.'

Randy nodded, without answering. He seemed to have gone quiet, as if he felt that some of the trust between them had been taken for granted. And maybe it had, thought Jack. His son had been sensitive enough to see that he was sad, and all he'd done was fob the boy off with the same kind of crocodile smile and meaningless words that he used for the people at work.

He said: 'Randy?'

'Yes, sir?'

Jack sat around on the bench, and looked at his son squarely. 'Randy, if I tell you something, can you promise to keep it to yourself? It's somethimg important – something to do with the reason I'm feeling sad. But it has to be a secret, and that's honest Injun.'

Randy looked up. When he saw the boy's face, Jack wondered how he'd even had the gall to ask him to keep it quiet. This is your son, he reminded himself caustically. Not Warren Harding or Johann Cornelius or Albert B. Fall. Your own son, Randy Field.

Randy said: 'Honest Injun, sir.'

Jack coughed. 'It's to do with these people who work for the government. These people you said were robbers. Well, over the past nine weeks, I've been working on one of these "little deals" of theirs for Mr Cornelius, and believe me, it's one of the trickiest pieces of work you've ever heard of. It's been my job to clear up the legal side of it, so that what we're doing is all legitimate, or at least *looks* that way.'

The ferry boat whistled loudly, and a shower of red balloons bobbed up off the deck and tangled with the afternoon wind. There was the sound of three cheers, almost swallowed by distance and traffic.

Jack said: 'When we wrap up this deal, a lot of people stand to make a great deal of money out of it, and that includes me. I could come home with sixty or seventy thousand dollars. But what I really have to ask myself is – do I deserve the money, and do they? Or are we really swindling it from someone else?'

Randy didn't say a word, but looked at his father and knew that he was unhappy. Unhappiness, up until now had been nothing more severe than a pedal car that had shed its wheel; or no more shoofly pie at suppertime; or perhaps the day that Mother had wept because grandfather had packed his trunk to go see God. But what Randy saw in his father today was a very different mood of unhappiness. It was (if only he could have recognized it) the distinctive pain of a man who realizes, after more than a decade of hard work, that he has probably made the wrong choice of career, and that he should have given all those years and months, all those sweltering summers and sharp winters, to some quite different occupation, something which would have brought him up to the threshold of middle age in one whole piece. Instead, Jack Field was just finding out that his loyalty and his integrity had been wrongly invested, and that the last man on earth with whom he should ever have associated himself, let alone devoted himself, was Johann Cornelius.

Jack lifted his son's chin with a gentle hand and looked at the bright eyes and the snub nose that was blanched by cold. Across the street, a flag snapped in the wind, and a motorcar indignantly hooted at a horse-drawn wagon.

'Randy,' he said, 'you're only nine years old, but I want you to try to follow what I tell you, because there are going to be times in your own life when you come across problems like this. Times when you have to make up your mind whether you're going to do the honest thing or the easiest thing. Times when you have to turn around and say, well, I'd like to be richer, but I'm not going to do what it takes to be that way.'

Randy nodded. Jack wasn't sure whether he'd really grasped what he was trying to say, but he went on anyway. Apart from Ellie, he had nobody else to tell, and right now Ellie was worried enough about Margaret, her mother, who was hospitalized in Charleston with chronic sciatica.

Jack said: 'Years ago, before you were born, and I was just started at Cornelius Oil, Mr Cornelius asked me to buy up oil rights in a piece of land in Oklahoma. Now, it was fine land, this – all forest and field – right by the Kiamichi River in Pushmataha County. Mr Cornelius had done a few surveys up there, and he reckoned there was good Oklahoma crude lying deep down at six thousand feet. So, I bought up the rights.'

He sucked at his cigar a couple of times to keep it alight, and then he said: 'The trouble was, when we came to set up drill rigs, the county authorities stepped in with a conservation order and wouldn't let us drill there. They said they wanted the land for a public park and a nature reserve, and when we appealed, the state supreme court upheld them. They said – and I guess they were partly right – that an oil town right slap in the middle of a beautiful place like that would've looked like an eyesore.

Rigs and pipes and storage tanks and raw pine huts aren't the prettiest scenery you can think of.'

'So what happened?' asked Randy. Jack could see that his son felt gravely honoured to have his father's confidence on such an important matter, and he was clasping his cold thin knees, like young Walter Raleigh listening to the wise old salt on the beach.

Jack said: 'Up until President Harding was sworn in, nothing happened at all. I tried almost every year to have that conservation order changed or overturned, but the county authorities kept on saying no, and besides them there were plenty of people in Washington under Woodrow Wilson's administration who didn't like Mr Cornelius one bit, and they made sure we were blocked off time after time.'

A 4-8-2 freight locomotive came wuffing and clanking by. It stopped for a moment to wait for a signal, and then slowly moved off, with a lot of dripping and steaming and hissing.

Jack lowered his eyes. 'Things certainly changed, though, when Mr Harding was sworn in. You see, Mr Wilson was always such a lonesome kind of a man. I only met him a few times, but he was sick, and he was tired, and he was still clinging to some kind of notion that we could all live in a peaceful perfect world, if only we worked ourselves hard enough. Because of that, he was always sticking his oar into business matters, and making business life harder than I guess it needed to be. But Warren Harding – well, Warren Harding is a different breed of biffalo-buffalo-bison altogether. He says he wants to help American businessmen go their own way, and all of a sudden it's all back-slapping and folksy talk, and the government is actually wheeling and dealing alongside of us.'

Randy took off his grey tweed cap and scratched his short wavy hair. 'Isn't that good?' he asked his father. 'Don't you want wheeling and dealing?'

'Well, some of us do,' answered Jack. 'But, just like I said before, it depends what that wheeling and dealing is going to cost us, as far as doing the right thing is concerned. Somebody once said that President Harding was the same size and smoothness all the way around, but the way I figure it, that's only because he always turns to face you,

222

no matter which quarter you come at him from. I've been talking to some of the men behind him for the past nine weeks, and believe me, there's nothing smooth about them.'

He stuck his hands in the pockets of his camelhair coat, and he remembered the smiling, persuasive expression of Albert B. Fall, the Secretary of the Interior, leaning over a walnut table so polished that his face was reflected upside-down, like the two theatrical masks of tragedy and comedy.

Jack said, in a thick voice: 'Quite soon after we met Mr Harding in May, the Secretary of the Interior called me up and suggested that we should open talks about the land at Kiamichi. Well, those talks are what I've been doing for the past nine weeks.'

'Are they going to let you drill there?' asked Randy.

'Yes, but only if we do something for *them*.'

'And is that what's making you sad?'

'In a way. What we have to do in return for drilling clearance is to pay Mr Fall, or lend him, a very large amount of money.'

Randy pulled his cap back on. He said: 'Is that wrong, sir? To lend him money?'

Jack nodded. 'A government official is supposed to represent the interests of all the people, and if he takes money to represent one person's interests against the rest, then that's wrong. Can you see that?'

'Even if it's you?'

'Yes. Especially if it's me. And that's because I ought to know better.'

Randy said: 'I *think* I see what you mean.'

Jack put his arm around him. 'It doesn't matter if you do or you don't. One day, you'll remember this, and you'll remember what kind of a choice I had to make.'

A hooter sounded from a construction site not far away, and Jack suddenly realized how chilly it was. The sun was settling into a low bank of mauve clouds over Weehawken, and the Hudson was purplish-grey now, and coldly restless. Jack stood up and held out his hand.' 'Come on, let's go get that tea. I could just fancy a hot raisin bun.'

Hand-in-hand, father and son walked across the grass toward the touring car. O'Hara, the chauffeur, saw them coming, gave a last *hah*! of breath to the gleaming bodywork, and tugged his tunic straight. Behind him, the fading sunlight had turned Grant's Tomb into a pale Grecian stage set, as pink and chalky as almond dragées.

'We're going to the Claremont for tea,' said Jack. 'Then we'll make our way home.'

O'Hara, his cap tucked under his arm, his carroty hair ruffled by the wind, opened the door for them; and they climbed into the leathery interior of the touring car. With his usual bland face, O'Hara remarked: 'It's passably fresh, sir,' and arranged a heavy plaid blanket over their knees. Then he closed the door and got up behind the wheel. It was a standing family joke that O'Hara never used a committal word when a noncommittal one would do. He had once amused Jack by describing a torrential downpour as 'moistness,' and even the most hilarious comedy show or song to him was only 'diverting.'

It wasn't more than a few yards to the Claremont, of course; but Randy had just gotten over the grippe, and Jack knew just how much displeasure he would have to face from Ellie if he brought the boy home with the snuffles. But as they settled back in their seats, Jack began to wonder what life would be like without chauffeured automobiles to keep them warm; without steam-heated apartments and furs and good food. Once you've shopped for your jewellery at Cartier and Van Cleef, once you've dined at the finest restaurants, once you've mixed with the most glittering names in New York society, how can you ever be satisfied with shopping at the neighbourhood markets, or looking for a cheap overcoat at Macy's, or taking the trolley car with everyone else?'

Jack said: 'Would you miss all this, if we didn't live this way? Having a man to drive you around? Having all the food you wanted, and always staying warm?'

Randy lifted his head and looked at him. The boy was genuinely puzzled. He didn't answer, but simply shook his head, and it was only then that Jack realized he couldn't answer, because the question to him was quite meaningless. For all Randy's grown-up ways, for all his seriousness, he was plainly unable to understand that life could be led without luxury, and that those ragged boys who danced and played kazoos outside the Carlton and the Rialto picture palaces on Broadway were real boys, actually living boys, like himself. As O'Hara stuck out an arm that was rigid as a signpost, and pulled smoothly away from the kerb, Jack sat back with the feeling that he was living a precarious charade, and that he was beginning to make his mimes too obvious to be mistaken. Sooner or later, Cornelius was going to turn around with that taciturn face, and challenge his loyalty; and he knew what he was going to have to say. And if Albert B. Fall pushed him any further on the Kiamichi lease, it was going to be very much sooner than later. There was a crucial meeting scheduled for November 17, at the Hotel Vanderbilt, and that was just days away. At that meeting, Fall had promised, 'all would be revealed,' and Jack Field was going to have to make up his mind whether he could swallow that 'all' or not.

Outside the Claremont, O'Hara opened the touring-car door for them, and they stepped out. They walked inside, and a waitress showed them a table by the window, where they could sit and look out over the river, which was twilit now, and strung with lights from the Jersey shore. A ferry went past in the half-darkness, leaving V-shaped rippling shadows on the water, and the lights of the automobiles on Riverside Drive rushed past like glowing beads.

Jack ordered a milk shake, a pot of tea, and two hot raisin buns. Then he sat there and smiled at his son, who was sitting opposite with such seriousness and gravity, and wished there was some way he could tell him how much he loved him without sounding sentimental or mawkish.

Instead, he said: 'It's just possible that we might have to leave New York. It depends on what happens over this oil business.'

Randy said: 'Will I have to leave school?'

'I'm afraid you will, if I lose my job.'

'You could always get another job, sir.'

'Oh, yes?'

'Well, you could drive a train.'

Jack sat back and laughed. 'Yes, I guess I could drive a train.'

The waitress arrived with the tea and the toasted buns, and they spread the butter on thick and sat for a while in silence while they ate. Then Jack said: 'In the next week, I'm going to have to make up my mind. Do I stick with my job, and Cornelius Oil, or do I stick with what's right? And

I can tell you, Randy, that's not an easy choice to make, because I love you and your mother, and I always want to give you the best.'

Randy said, in a matter-of-fact voice, with his mouth full of bun: 'You do, sir.'

'I do what?'

'You *do* always give us the best. It's like today. I've had the best day today that I've had for ages.'

Jack looked at his son, and hardly knew what to say. Instead, he buttered himself another bun, and ate it with a lump in his throat. He remembered what J. Paul Getty had once said to him, out in Oklahoma, when one of their wells ran prematurely dry. Getty had poured himself a drink, downed it, and then looked around with that lemon-drop face of his, and said: 'If there's one thing you shouldn't worry about, it's poverty. It's good for you, once in a while. Lord Byron once said that adversity is the first path to truth; and truth, Jack Field, is a whole sight more valuable than oil.'

Jack reached across the tablecloth and laid his hand on Randy's. He said softly: 'How would you like to go fishing tomorrow? Just you and me?'

And the way that Randy looked then made him take out his handkerchief, and wipe his eyes, and invent some story about hot buttered bun going down the wrong way.

Ellie was sitting with her feet up reading *This Side of Paradise* when the front door opened and Jack and Randy came noisily into the hallway, laughing and breathless from their obligatory race down the corridor, which the long-suffering Mrs Vandersteen from the opposite apartment called 'the elephants' Olympics.'

Ellie laid down her book on the reading table and went to meet them. Jack was trying to throw his hat across the hall so that it landed on the coat peg in one toss, and Randy was hopping around with his scarf over his face pretending to be the Masked Bandit. Ellie leaned against the doorway and watched them with a tolerant smile.

Jack said: 'Hi, darling. We've had a terrific time. Really terrific.'

Ellie shook her head. 'How you two can turn a simple

226

thing like hanging up your hats and coats into the *circus maximus*, I'll never know.'

She leaned forward and kissed Jack, and then helped Randy with his shoelaces. 'Would you like a cocktail, Jack?' she asked. 'And you, my freezing cold boy, what would you say to a hot malted?'

'Has Ethel gone home?' asked Jack.

'I let her go early. It's a long ride up to the Bronx.'

'Okay, then,' said Jack, rubbing the circulation back into his hands, and walking into the drawing room, 'in that case *I'll* make the malted. I make the best malted this side of the Rocky Mountains, don't I, pardner?'

'Yes, sir!' agreed Randy, stooping to pull up his long grey socks.

'And I'll have an old-fashioned,' Jack said, and he took Ellie's hand and kissed her again, more lingeringly this time, a kiss that finished up with a smile.

Their apartment was up on the ninth floor, fronting Fifty-ninth Street. Through the open drapes you could see the twinkling lights of automobiles and carriages, and the winter trees of Central Park standing in lamplit drifts of curled-up russet leaves. It was a warm apartment, with soft quiet carpets, and fine mid-Victorian antique furniture, upholstered in dark brown velvet. There was a sparkling chandelier, and velvet drapes the colour of clover honey, and around the walls, apart from the English and French impressionists they loved so much, were pencil-and-ink sketches by Kandinsky and Modigliani. In the corner overlooking Fifth Avenue and the Sherry-Netherland Hotel stood Ellie's grand piano, brought up from South Carolina when they first moved to New York.

Jack went down the corridor into the kitchen and took milk out of the icebox. The kitchen was decorated in a fashionable combination of cream and pale green, and they had an electric washing machine which their maid Ethel worshipped as if it was a South Sea island god.

'Albert Fall telephoned again,' said Ellie, as Jack poured the milk into a saucepan.

'Did he say what he wanted?'

'He said it wasn't urgent. He was just checking to see if you could make it on Monday. I think he wants to run over that Kiamichi contract again '

'Again? We just spent two months running over it.'

'Well, call him back if you like.'

Jack lit the gas flame. 'I'd rather not. I'm giving myself a weekend vacation, and Johann Cornelius himself couldn't get me to leave my family right now. Where's the sugar?'

'Where it always is. You talk about Johann as if he's your lord and master.'

'Well, you have to admit that he's got the right initials. What's that book like?'

Randy came in with his clockwork locomotive, and said: 'Excuse me, sir, but I think the spring on my train's broken.'

Jack hunkered down to take a look at Randy's bright blue tinplate engine. He wound it up with the key a couple of times, but each time there was a rasping noise, and the wheels refused to turn. Ellie said: 'Jack! The milk's boiling over!'

Jack rescued the saucepan and carried it across to their new electric blender. 'Don't worry, Randy. If we can't get the old loco to work, I'll buy you a new one.'

Randy glanced at his mother, and then back to Jack. 'Will we be able to afford it, do you think?' he said seriously.

Ellie looked at Jack in surprise. 'Afford it?' she said. 'A two-dollar train? Of course!'

'I won't have one if we can't afford one,' said Randy. 'I can always push the carriages along.'

Ellie ruffled his hair. 'You won't have to push the carriages, darling. We'll buy you a new train the minute the store opens up on Monday. Now, look, here's your malted. Take it along to your room and drink it there. Ethel left you some supper in the oven, and it'll be ready in a half hour.'

Jack switched off the kitchen light and they went back into the drawing room. Ellie went to the cocktail cabinet to fix him an old-fashioned, while Jack eased himself into a plump button-back chair and reached for his pipe and his matches.

'What's all this about not being able to afford things?' asked Ellie. 'What ideas have you been putting into Randy's head now?'

Jack shrugged. 'It's nothing.'

'Well, it must be something. He doesn't normally worry about the household budget.'

Jack rubbed a slice of tobacco between the palms of his hands. 'All I did was tell him that he shouldn't take wealth for granted.'

Ellie came over with his drink.

'Why shouldn't he take it for granted?' she asked. 'He's never going to have to eat stale bread and dripping, is he? There are some things you *have* to take for granted.'

'I didn't mean that. But this business with Fall is getting pretty parlous.'

'*Parlous*? What do you mean by that?'

Jack tried to smile. 'It's really nothing to worry about.'

Ellie said: 'Jack?' and frowned. She came and knelt beside him, and he knew then that he'd hidden his anxiety about as well as a bearded goat under the bed. Her face was as soft as always, with those wispy coppery curls and those eyes as grey as flaked slate; but she was looking cautious and concerned, and that meant she had sensed his awkward husbandly efforts to protect her from something harsh. He averted his eyes. He always felt embarrassed when he tried to keep things from her, and he made a fussy, fiddly performance of stuffing his pipe with Virginia Ellie was always open and fresh, and she tried daily and energetically to prove herself independent, no matter how much their men friends smiled in pained condescension, or her girl friends tittered in disapproval. So when he attempted to protect her, like now, he felt as if he was selling her out, instead of performing a virtuous and spousely duty. Now that she was over thirty, and now that women had had the vote for over a year, Ellie had become self-possessed to the point where she could argue with Johann Cornelius over dinner until he coughed and went red and thought up some excuse to leave early; and she had once told Grover Whalen, that dapper young man who devised so many of New York's extravagant welcoming ceremonies for visiting celebrities and returning heroes, that to be greeted the Whalen way must have made many famous men suspect that they had unwittingly drowned on their way across the Atlantic, and that they were being received in the front lobby of Pandemonium. But, in spite of her assertiveness, Ellie was still graceful and pretty, and as she sat beside him in her short

229

loose housedress of strawberry-coloured silk, Jack was as much stirred by her femininity as he was by her strength.

He confessed: 'It's too early to say anything, really. But I get the feeling they've manoeuvred me into an impossible situation. And this week Fall's going to lift the lid off his latest mess of stew, and expect me to dip in as hearty as the rest.'

'I don't understand,' she said.

He lifted his eyes. 'It's very simple. Albert Fall is going to push through permission for Cornelius Oil to start drilling operations at Kiamichi, provided Mr Fall himself isn't entirely unrewarded.'

'Then he wants a *bribe*?'

'Essentially, yes. But it's more complicated than that. He doesn't want to be paid out of company funds. He wants us to raise the money through some bright new scheme he's just worked out, which he's going to tell us about this week at the Hotel Vanderbilt. He wants us to run some kind of a racket that enables him to clear his money free of any suggestion of conspiracy or connivance, and pay it straight to him.'

Ellie listened to this, and then reached out and brushed her husband's forehead with her fingertips, as if she was touching something very precious and fragile.

'You know me,' said Jack. 'You know I'm not opposed to incentives. When you're in the business, you always have to drop a dollar here and a dollar there if you want people to do you any favours. But this is worse than bribery. This is beginning to look to me like deliberate and systematic swindling.'

Ellie brushed back her short copper curls, and looked worried. Alongside her diamond-and-sapphire engagement ring was a wide gold wedding band engraved with the intertwined initials 'J&E.' She said: 'What's going to happen if you say no? What if you won't bribe him?'

'Then we lose the Kiamichi lease and I lose my job.'

'Johann wouldn't sack you, surely. Not after all these years'

Jack tamped down his tobacco with his broad thumb. 'Johann sacked Jerry Slobodien remember? And Jerry was with him a darned sight longer than me'

'Jerry was drunk all the time

'That wasn't why Johann sacked him He sacked him

because he held up production at Sweetwater to rescue a trapped burro, and he lost us eight thousand barrels of oil. Johann doesn't give a nickel for your morals and scruples, you can have them or not have them and he doesn't care. But if they start losing him money, then that's the end of it. You're out.'

Ellie held Jack's hand, and looked up at him anxiously. 'Is that what's going to happen to you?'

Jack set down his drink. 'I don't know. It depends what Fall is going to ask us to do.'

'But you've gotten involved in some pretty greasy things before, haven't you? I thought they were part and parcel of the oil business. There was that awful Sinclair proxy business you set up in Washington, wasn't there? What makes this one so different?'

Jack pulled a face. 'I don't know. I guess what really shocks me is the way that the government is giving such barefaced encouragement to anybody who believes in making a fast buck, and the way they make damned sure that a good share of every fast buck ends up in their own pockets. I'm not an idealist, Ellie. You know that. And I'm not an innocent, either. I've done a few legal deals that would have made my father's hair fall out, especially when we were having all that trouble with Woodrow Wilson. But I believe in drawing a line somewhere, and I think I believe in government that's at least reasonably honest.'

He paused for a moment, and then he said quietly: 'I guess I've compromised myself just once too often, too. A time does eventually come when all the dollars in the world can't pay you back for your lost integrity.'

Ellie stood up. She was still his petite, pretty Ellie; although there was an over-thirty softening in her skin which reminded him of Margaret Jackson, her mother.

He said: 'I didn't want to tell you until I knew something for certain. But the way Fall's been working these past nine weeks . . . well, I'm pretty certain he's cooked up a dilly.'

'Jack,' she said gently, 'you could have told me.'

He rubbed his eyes. 'I could have, and I guess I should have. But what with your mother—'

'My mother's my mother. Nobody could ever replace her. But you're my husband.'

231

'How is your mother?' he asked.

'She's feeling much better, as a matter of fact. I had a telephone call from Dr Shura today.'

'Well, that's good news. At least something's going right.'

She said 'We won't have to leave the apartment, will we?'

He shrugged. 'I don't know. Not right away. But if I leave Cornelius Oil and strike out on my own, it's going to take a big chunk of capital and we're going to have to cut out the chauffeur-driven limousines and the big parties. I'm a rich man, Ellie. I guess I must be richer now than Johann Cornelius was when I first met him. But I'm only going to stay rich if I get my money working, and that means much more creative investment, and much more financial risk. The bank balance is going to take a heavy knock without that annual two hundred thousand coming in like clock-work.'

Ellie thought of Randy's tinplate locomotive. 'Clockwork breaks down sometimes, Jack, but the railroads keep on running.'

Jack smiled. 'Randy said I could always take a job as a railroad engineer.'

'Maybe that's not such a bad idea: I met that young Daniel Forster a couple of weeks ago. The shooting star of P&P Railroad. He said they were looking for good legal executives and management.'

Jack sighed. 'I feel like an out-of-work vagrant already.'

'You could always start a private practice, like you were going to do when you were younger.'

'It's too soon to think about that,' he said tiredly. 'If there's any way I can work around this problem, instead of meeting it head-on, then I will.'

'But you don't think you can, do you, my darling?'

He stared across the room for a moment, clenched in his armchair like a man on the Rocket-to-the-Moon ride at Coney Island. Then he said: 'No, I don't believe I can.'

She smiled, but she wasn't very happy. 'Well,' she said with a tight little breath, 'it looks like we'll have to start economizing.'

He said: 'Would you miss it very much? New York?'

She nodded. 'I'm very happy here Jack. I guess it's the kind of city where a woman can do things and be things

232

that nobody would tolerate anyplace else. And then there's all the parties and the dances and the dinners. I'd miss the theatres, too.'

He looked down at his knees. They seemed to belong to somebody else altogether, and he half-wondered if he still had the power to walk. He said in a throaty voice: 'I could always tell Albert Fall yes.'

She turned. 'And come back home without your honesty? Just for the sake of parties and dances? I wouldn't let you do it!'

Ellie came and perched herself lightly on his lap, and kissed his forehead with three kisses. Then she looked right in his eyes and said: 'I married you because you were straight as Abraham Lincoln, and good-looking as Rudolph Valentino, and a better lawyer than Arthur Garfield Hays and Clarence Darrow rolled into one. Don't you ever disappoint me by saying yes to a carpetbagger like Fall unless you know you're really doing the right thing.'

He lowered his eyes. 'You'd miss the jewellery, too, wouldn't you? And having your new fur coats every fall.'

She placed one finger across his lips and shushed him. 'I love you,' she whispered. 'That's all that counts.'

He felt tears in his eyes even though he didn't want to show how worried he was. She brushed them away for him, and hugged him close, and said: 'Don't you ever fret about money, my darling. If I have to live in a cabin in the Blue Ridge Mountains, and cook succotash every night but Sunday, when it's roast raccoon – then just as long as you're there, and Randy's there too, then I'll be happy. I might even learn to cook up white lightning.'

He couldn't help laughing through his tears. 'My wife, the bootlegger.'

She stroked his forehead, and kissed him again, and then said: 'You mustn't underestimate me, you know. I love you, and I think I can share your worries as well as your good times. If we end up with our pants hanging out at the back, well, that's too bad. At least people will know that we're honest.'

'I don't know. I'm beginning to wonder what's honest and what isn't.'

She shook her head. 'You know what's honest. *You're* honest. You always try to do the best thing and the fairest thing, and the only time I've really seen you act tricky is when it won't hurt anyone at all. Oh, and crosswords. You're always tricky when you fill in crosswords.'

He picked up his matches. 'Well, if I haven't acted tricky up until now, this could be my big chance, right?'

She plucked his pipe out of his mouth. 'Don't light it now. Come to bed.'

He said: 'What? What about Randy?'

She grinned and tugged at his arm. 'Randy's playing with his fort. He's going to be hours.'

'Ellie, I come home and tell you my whole career's on the line, and you want to go to bed?'

'Don't be so conventional! Don't you think it's the best tonic?'

'Why, sure, but—'

Ellie pulled him upright. 'Come on, then.'

They walked arm-in-arm through to the corridor, and peeked through the doorjamb into Randy's playroom. Randy was kneeling on the floor, his malted milk forming a crinkly skin, while he set out dozens of lead soldiers in ranks of four. Jack circled his arm around Ellie and whispered: 'Looks like Bull Run. That should take at least another half hour. He's pretty short on Yankees.'

Silently, with that slow hurry that only lovers know, they went to their own bedroom and locked the door behind them. It was a high-ceilinged room, and a wide four-poster bed hung with a figured cream silk canopy like a Moorish tent. The rugs were thick and white and soft, and all around there were mirrors in gilt ormolu frames in which their faces were reflected like a gallery of gentle portraits. Outside the window, they could hear the faint sounds of juddering taxicabs waiting for fares from the Savoy-Plaza, and the leisurely clopping of horse-drawn hansoms; and someone in another apartment was playing 'I'm Always Chasing Rainbows' on a Victrola. But Jack and Ellie were quiet within their love for each other, and they stood for a moment and kissed in the shaded light from the bedside lamps like a honeymoon couple at some grand hotel in Europe.

Jack kissed Ellie's forehead, and eyes, and lips, and he held her close, feeling her warm skin through the thin slippery silk of her dress, his eyes lowered, so that all he could see was a close-up of her pink moistened lips, her teeth just parted by the tip of her tongue.

He said: 'How come it's always like the first time with you?'

She butted him very gently and affectionately with her forehead. 'Because it always is. And because each time is always the best.'

'You think I'm crazy, don't you?'

'Why should I?'

'I don't know. For the first time, we've gotten ourselves a government that wants to bend over backwards to help us. And all I can do is throw myself off the edge of a cliff because I'm so damned burdened with principles.'

She outlined his lips with the tip of her finger. Her grey eyes were staring into the future, or maybe the past. She said: 'Would you be happy if you said yes to Fall?'

He shook his head.

For a moment she looked at him with her head on one side, and then she smiled and said: 'In that case, what the hell are you so worried about?'

The musical fanatic in the next apartment put on 'Smiles,' and Jack took Ellie's hand and foxtrotted around the bedroom with her, humming in an off-key tenor. He circled her around to the bed, and then plunged sideways onto the white brocade bedspread, like a man pitching himself into the surf, and he pulled her over with him. They bounced and laughed, and he lay chuckling on his back while she straddled him and kissed him all over his face.

'Freud says that everything we do has its roots in sex,' Ellie grinned. 'Perhaps you're acting so firm and upright at work because you're so firm and upright at home.'

They looked at each other for one half-serious moment, and then burst out laughing again. He wrapped his arms around her, and they kissed with an urgency that started off playful and grew more and more passionate. He felt her warm saliva slide from the side of his mouth onto the bedspread. Then he reached down and touched her thigh, where her thin dress had ridden high, and he caressed all around the firm rounded curve of her bottom, until she bent forward, and gasped in his ear.

They didn't even undress. In that elegant Central Park bedroom in 1921, in a dim unfocused light that transformed

235

them into soigné fantasy characters from the White Star poster for first-class travel aboard the *Majestic*, with the crackling strains of 'Dardanella' and 'Hindustan' faint in the next apartment, and the air delirious with perfume, they made love with an erotic grace that was rare even for them. She arched over him, her back curved, her Vaselined eyelids glistening, her mouth open; and beneath her he lay with his muscles tensed in the lamplight, and his face tightened into the expression of a man who hears or sees or touches something so close to perfection that he can hardly bear it. Sometimes they whispered or cried out when they made love, but this evening they were almost silent. Ellie moved up and down on Jack, and what she felt for him then didn't need sounds or words. What he had said tonight hadn't frightened her, as he had thought it might. Instead, it had given her fresh faith that he was a man of great honesty and self-discipline – qualities which she had begun to suspect might be slipping out of his grasp at Cornelius Oil. So the rigidity she felt inside her was more than physical. It was the hardness of a man who could act like a man, and she loved him for it. He held her waist tight in his strong hands as he began to approach his climax – so tight that he hurt her. But all she craved was oneness with him, closeness with him, and she forced herself down on him harder and harder until he was touching her sensitive womb with every thrust, and she winced with the strange painful pleasure of it.

They came so close, for just a few dark dazzling moments, that Ellie could feel the tears in her eyes. She didn't know where her own body ended and Jack's began. It seemed that he was her and she was him, and that she could blissfully spend the rest of her life with his penis sheathed inside her, and his hairy testicles hanging between her own thighs like odd proud jewellery. But then her mind blinked – like looking into the black back of a Kodak camera and pressing the shutter – and she knew that they were almost through, almost there, and she was still desperately trying to cling on to the closeness as Jack dug his fingernails into the soft flesh over her hips and said: 'Ellie, oh Ellie. Oh, Ellie,' and his warmth flowed into her in three quick pulses.

It was a long time before they opened their eyes, and when they did, they felt as if they'd just returned to their apartment from a three-month trip abroad. They lay side by side, kissing and stroking each other, and talking in whispers They talked about Randy, and about a winter vacation in Florida, and about Johann Cornelius. Ellie, lying back, said: 'Do you think Johann really loves Hester? I always get the impression they're pretty remote from each other. I mean, remoter than us.'

Jack twined her hair around his finger. 'It's impossible to say. In any case, it's none of my business.'

Ellie propped herself up on her elbow. 'You know what the Kubceks think, though, don't you?'

'No, I don't know what that Kubceks think. What do the Kubceks think?'

'Well, Mrs Kubcek at least is quite certain that Johann has another woman. A secret mistress tucked away someplace.'

Jack shook his head. 'There's no chance of that. He doesn't have the time. In any case, I don't think he loves anyone or anything except himself, and money.'

'Perhaps he had a passionate love affair when he was younger.'

'Sure. And perhaps you can run automobiles on peanut butter.'

Ellie picked up a pillow and playfully hit him with it. 'You never take anything seriously,' she said.

He held her tight, and kissed her. 'I take Johann Cornelius very seriously,' he told her. 'Because if I didn't, I'd wind up more than jobless, and more than broke.'

'What do you mean – more than jobless?'

'It's difficult to say. But Johann's one of these people who bring out the best in you and the worst in you, both. He can make you feel that you can do anything, make any amount of money, conquer the world in five minutes flat. But he also makes you feel as if you've got to sell yourself out to do it. I think he knows what morals are, although some people believe that he doesn't. But he seems to believe that if you're going to be rich, and stay rich, you have to change your idea of morality to suit your financial ambitions, if you see what I mean.'

Ellie sat up. The curve of her breasts, limned with light from the bedside lamp, held Jack's eye while he spoke.

He said: 'Johann makes you understand that nothing is

237

sacred and nothing is safe – that's if you *really* want to be rich. Maybe you're right, and he did have a passionate love when he was young. But if he did, he's buried it under ten tons of concrete and he's not letting it out. He's fond of Hester, sure. But I always get the feeling that he married her to bear his heirs and to run his household and to walk into official dinners on his arm, and not for much else.'

Ellie snuggled against his chest. 'And how do I know you didn't marry *me* to do that?'

Outside, in the study and the sitting room, their telephones began to ring in jangling chorus. Jack kissed her and answered: 'Simple. If that was all I'd married you for, I'd hop out of bed right this instant and pick up that phone. As it is . . .'

He pushed her gently back on the pillow, and lifted himself over her, breathing as he did so: 'Ellie . . .'

On the morning of November 17, 1921, Jack took a taxi down to Wall Street to have a talk with Johann Cornelius. He was due at the Hotel Vanderbilt later, for the oil meeting which Albert Fall had described as 'essential and crucial.' He wore a brown overcoat of marled tweed, and a brown hat with a wide band. He was still handsome, but he was pale, as if he needed to take a few weeks' vacation in the sun.

Johann was sitting behind his desk in his dark oak-panelled office looking morose. He had been trying to float a new bond issue in cooperation with the House of Morgan, but the financiers were proving picky about the terms of the issue and the total capitalization required. He greeted Jack with a snappy 'What time do you call this?' and shuffled papers around as if he was tired of the whole business.

Jack said: 'It's only eight. Did you expect me earlier?'

Johann didn't answer. He was wearing an unusually severe black suit and a white gates-ajar collar. Behind him, on the office wall, was a photograph of the Texan town of Amarero, now one of the most industrialized oil centres in the whole state, with rigs and storage tanks and a brand-new cracking plant. A leafy house plant languished on the window ledge.

'I'm pretty sure that Fall's going to come up with the big

one today,' remarked Jack. 'I have all the papers on Kiamichi here if you want to see them.'

Johann tapped his gold propelling pencil on the green leather of his desktop. 'I wish those Bolsheviks had blown up the whole damned building,' he said petulantly.

'You mean the Morgan Building?' asked Jack. 'Are they giving you trouble with the Seal Beach issue?'

'You name something they're *not* giving me trouble with.'

Jack sat down opposite in a comfortable brown club chair. He never understood why Johann didn't leave his stocks and bonds negotiations to himself and the rest of their legal and financial staff. Apart from the fact that Jack had several close friends at Morgan, he was on good terms with William H. Remick, the president of the Stock Exchange, and he could have handled the Seal Beach issue with a great deal more diplomacy and speed than Johann himself. It was a complicated ruse to whip up over seventy million dollars for a quick Cornelius expansion programme, and it needed both timing and subtlety. Maybe the only real difference was that Johann, despite his financial thuggery, would probably wind up with better investment perform- ances than any of his staff, but as Nathan Frank, Jack's young deputy, said: 'Being asked to buy bonds by Johann Cornelius is like being asked by your rabbi to buy tickets to the B'nai B'rith dance. You just don't say no.'

Jack said: 'They'll come around. They just need to feel they're being magnanimous.'

'It seems to me that there's too much damned magna- nimity around and not enough sound investment. I'm going to have another try at Western Banks while Morgan's are sitting on their hands.'

Jack shrugged. 'That's up to you. In any case, this meeting at the Vanderbilt is a little more urgent.'

'Who's attending?'

'Harry Sinclair, for certain, and James O'Neil. They've been thick with Fall since way back when.'

'Anybody from Standard?'

'Bob Stewart probably.'

Johann rubbed his eyes with his knuckles. 'It sounds to me like Albert's setting up some kind of mutual-benefit society. What does it sound like to you? All the old gang who dug deep in their pockets for Harding and Cox last year, paid back with interest.'

'I think it's a little more than that. Fall's been taking a pretty unnatural interest in oil.'

'There's nothing unnatural about an interest in oil.'

Jack picked out a sheaf of paper bound with red legal ribbon. 'It depends which oil it is, and what form your interest takes. Supposing, for instance, we were talking about oil which was being held in reserve for the U.S. Navy.'

'Supposing we were? There are three naval reserve fields, aren't there? Buena Vista, California, Elk Hills, California, and Teapot Dome, Wyoming. So what?'

Jack looked at his shoes and wished that he'd remembered to have them polished. 'Well, let me put it this way. Under whose jurisdiction would you expect these naval reserves to fall?'

'Are you playing games?'

'Not at all. You'd expect them to fall under the jurisdiction of the Secretary of the Navy, right?'

Johann said nothing. His hard, cautious expression was enough. It told Jack Field that what he was saying had better be good, or else. At forty-eight years old, Johann was probably at his most abrasive, at his most competitive, and he had the harsh maturity of granite. Jack, like everyone else in Cornelius Oil and its associated industries, had often skinned his hands against the granite, and he knew how uncompromising it was.

Jack said: 'During May, President Harding transferred custody of all these naval oilfields from the Secretary of the Navy to the Secretary of the Interior. No particularly cogent reason was given.'

Johann raised an eyebrow. 'So the oil is now at the disposal of Albert Fall – every oilman's friend?'

Jack pulled a wry face. '*Some* oilmen's friend. Not so much ours. I still think he bears a grudge about your campaign contribution, and what you said about Hughes being a sheep in sheep's clothing.'

'I like to be apolitical,' said Johann, pronouncing the word 'apolitical' with peculiar relish. 'I don't like my business to go in and out with the political tide. That's all.'

'Well,' said Jack, 'whatever Albert Fall felt about you in

the past, he's obviously going to forgive you now From all of our talks on Kiamichi, it's pretty clear that he's prepared to be nice to us if we're prepared to be nice to him. Just *how* nice, and what we have to do in return, remains to be seen.'

Johann got out of his chair and went to the window. Through the grimy rain-washed glass he could just see the corner of the Morgan Building, and the Corinthian pillars of the Stock Exchange. The Morgan Building was still pitted and scarred from the window-sash weights that had been blasted into it by last year's anarchist explosion.

He said: 'Albert's playing some kind of game. Now, what do you think it is?'

Jack lifted out a closely typewritten report. 'I had my people give me a rundown on these naval oil reserves. They were set aside in 1909 to give the Navy a protected supply of fuel oil in case of war. The trouble was, though, that several oil companies, including us, took up leases right on the edge of the government fields, Elk Hills in particular, and we've been pumping up oil that, very likely, comes from underneath Navy land.'

Johann turned around, his hands clasped behind his back. 'What was the trouble? They could have put offset wells along the boundary of their land to neutralize the drainage. That's what *we* do.'

'*They* did, too. But now something else has come up. The military are getting themselves all jittery about a war with Japan, and they don't just want their oil protected, they want it up out of the ground where they can lay their hands on it. That means that Fall is probably going to ask for competitive private bidders to pump up the oil, keeping some of it back as a royalty to meet the needs of the Navy.'

Johann thought about this, and then nodded. 'So Albert has at least three plum leases on his hands?' he asked.

'That's right.'

'And he's trying to set up some kind of back-scratching society of oil executives, with the probable prize of Elk Hills or Teapot Dome or Buena Vista to whichever executive scratches his back the best?'

'That's the way I see it.'

Johann tapped his pencil against his teeth. 'Well,' he said

at last, 'what line are you going to take when Albert puts this proposition in front of you?'

Jack took out his folded handkerchief and patted his forehead. It seemed desperately hot in Johann's office, and he would have done anything to take his coat off. He said uncertainly: 'That's why I came to see you. I need to know what line *you* want to take.'

Johann looked at him. 'You're my legal adviser,' he pointed out. 'You tell me.'

'I can't – not until I know what Fall's going to suggest. I just wanted to know how far you were prepared to go along with him.'

'You mean, would I like the Teapot Dome lease, or the Elk Hills lease?'

'Well, yes.'

Johann nodded. 'Of *course* I'd like them. They're choice tracts of oil-bearing land.'

'Even if we have to get involved in something less than strictly legal?'

Johann went back to his chair. 'Has Albert suggested anything illegal so far?'

'Not in so many words. He keeps talking about 'mutual interests,' but he hasn't made it plain what these really are.'

'Then he hasn't?'

'No.'

'In that case,' said Johann, 'I can only presume that he's not going to suggest anything illegal now. But it's up to you. You're the business lawyer, and this is one particular area where I bow to your judgment. You go along there today and work it out for yourself. Just make sure that whatever you decide, it's in the best possible interests of Cornelius Oil.

'Supposing he wants an immediate answer?'

'Then give him one. But make certain it's the right one.'

Jack took a shallow breath? 'That's what I wanted to know,' he said unhappily. 'What *is* the right one?'

Johann sat back and inspected Jack through slitted eyelids. 'The right answer,' he said dryly, 'is the answer that you can bring back here and have a raise for.'

'And the wrong answer?'

Johann shook his head, and gave a small smile. 'I don't

242

threaten people, as a rule,' he remarked. 'Threatening people lets them know where they stand, and that inhibits their performance.'

Jack looked down at the heap of paper on his knees. Slowly, thoughtfully, he began to collate it and tidy it up.

'All right,' he said at last. 'Shall I call you when it's over?'

Johann glanced at the clock above the door. 'No. I'm out of the office later this afternoon, talking to Fishman's. Meet me at the Gotham at five sharp.'

Jack stood up. He felt as if he'd been sent out with a rolled-up copy of *The Wall Street Journal* to do battle with mythical monsters. He cleared his throat, as if he was going to say something else, but he knew that he had nothing else to say, and he turned around and left the office with his head bent in thought. Johann's receptionist called after him: 'Your hat, Mr Field! Your hat!'

During the afternoon, pale sun penetrated through to Johann's office, and he laid down his pencil and went to the window again. For some reason that he couldn't quite put his finger on, he'd been feeling restless lately, out of sorts. It wasn't just that business was going through a difficult time, and that the market was alternately boisterous and suicidal. It was something to do with himself, a feeling that he had left some decision about his life undecided.

He had been married to Hester Forbes Cornelius for almost ten years now, and their anniversary was approaching. He thought he might buy her ten exceptional diamonds to mark the occasion. He was contented with his marriage, and proud of his three children, and yet he felt as if going home to Hester when business was through, dining with her, talking to her, even sleeping with her, was an oddly unimportant part of his life. She was there to soothe him, and there to run his household, and there to make sure that they attended the right parties with the right people. She knew about French impressionists, Mozart, and the care of opera hats. She had decorated the house lavishly and expensively and in taste that had aroused the admiration of *Ladies' Home Journal*. She knew diplomats and socialites and celebrities, and spoke with equal confidence on H. G. Wells's *Outline of History*, the best-selling book of the year, as she did on art or education or business. But, to Johann, it was like a shadow theatre, this marriage; an experience that comforted and entertained him, and yet which he never seemed to live in the round. Whenever he talked about himself and Hester, it always sounded as if he were talking about another couple whom he happened to know quite well. This wasn't because he didn't feel affection for Hester. She was pretty and self-assured, and she had a particular knack for making him feel both masculine and reasonably cultured, and less like a rough-cut robber baron. He was more confident in her company, and more likeable, than at almost any other time. But he still suspected that real life had come to a twilit close in 1903, when Carina had fallen from the sixth-storey window on Fifty-fifth Street and Beatrice had deserted him; and that every day of marriage and child-rearing and dinner parties that had happened since then had been acted out by a well-paid extra who looked and spoke exactly like Johann Cornelius, and who kept his outward life going while the genuine Johann Cornelius, still sat in the empty waiting room of 1903, with the magazines growing older and dustier on the table, hoping that time and fate would prove to be nothing more than dreams, or mistaken calendars, and that the door would open and there would stand Beatrice.

He could never explain, even to himself, how much he had adored Beatrice. He was prepared to admit that what he had loved, what he still loved, was a hazy and romantic picture of Beatrice which she had never actually lived up to. But if she had made him happy, what did it matter?

As he stared sadly out of his window, watching the sun behind the grey November clouds, he wondered if his relentless appetite for money and power had really been responsible for what had happened to Beatrice and Carina.

His desk telephone rang, and he went over to pick it up. His receptionist said: 'Mr Cornelius? Your wife's here. She wants to know if you have five minutes.'

He looked down at his desk. There were heaps of letters to sign, and two thick folders of stock assessments to go through. But he said: 'Okay. Show her in.'

Hester came through the door in a low-belted camelhair coat and a small cloche hat. She came over and kissed him, fragrant with Chanel, and put down her big red-and-black snakeskin bag on the chair.

'I've been shopping,' she said I thought I'd call by and ask you what you wanted for dinner. The Daughertys aren't coming over till nine.'

He said: 'Oh. Well, whatever you like. I seem to remember that Mal likes his lobster.'

Hester made a pencil note in a small diary. 'Lobster, that's right. And maybe some entrecôte steak. You look thoughtful.'

'What?'

'I said you look thoughtful.'

'Oh. Well, I have been.'

Hester gave him a funny look, and sat on the edge of his desk. Physically, Hester and Johann were an ill-matched couple. Where he was beefy and built on a large scale, she was small and detailed and very pretty. She had a heart-shaped face, a long and graceful neck, and her hair was shingled. Her eyes gave her most of her character, because they were round and brown and enormous, and her dinner guests would gaze into them mesmerized until she looked away, and then they'd wonder what on earth she'd been talking about.

She was the elder daughter of Mr and Mrs James Forbes, originally of Wakefield, Massachusetts, and in her day she had been the most eligible lady in New York. Her father, a humorous and inventive man of Scottish descent, had made an appreciable fortune out of royalties for his patents for colour-printing machinery, and although he lived in Manhattan, he still farmed in Wakefield as a profitable hobby. He had been well-heeled enough to send Hester to private college, as well as dispatching her to Zurich for a year to finish her off.

Her second (and romantically decisive) meeting with Johann had been quite accidental. Johann, against his will, had been dragged off by Latham T. Jolley, the Minnesota mineral billionaire, to join a weekend party at his 'hide-away,' as he called it, in Norwalk, Connecticut. If it hadn't been for an imminent contract signing worth eighteen million dollars, Johann wouldn't have even contemplated going. But, as it was, he spent Saturday and Sunday pacing the corridors and reception rooms of Jolley's distinctly unjolly mansion, trying to feel that he was doing his duty, and drinking too much brandy.

He had come across Hester in the library, sitting in a big leather armchair asleep. It had been a warm afternoon in 1910. The coincidence had intrigued him so much that he had sat himself opposite her, and watched her as she slept, and thought how pretty she was in her rose-coloured day dress, with her hair tightly braided and pinned up. The dusty sunlight had crossed the room from the skylight above them, and gradually she had woken up, and seen him sitting there, relaxed in his chair, his pale blue eyes regarding her fixedly from over the hand that he held in front of his face. He could even remember her first words to him. 'Oh,' she had said, 'it's you. Didn't you know that only married people should watch each other sleep?'

She was nineteen and he was rich. He wasn't like the New York boys, either. He was blunt and direct in business and he knew what he wanted, although he had a baffling evasiveness about him, too, which intrigued her. He never spoke about his background, nor his past loves, but she felt sure that she could winkle it all out of him in time.

Perhaps they had fallen in love. It appeared that way. There were visits to concerts, where Hester sat with eyes sparkling and Johann sat beside her so rigid that he could have been an advertisement for someone's patent starch. There were weekends at Wakefield, and these days Hester often leafed through the albums of sepia photographs, showing Johann in his shirtsleeves poling a punt, or Johann sitting cross-legged on the grass, squinting into the sun as he ate a sandwich.

That, in any event, was their courtship, and their marriage had seemed inevitable. There wasn't much passion, but it seemed right that culture should marry money, since by their union both could be enriched. They had a set-piece wedding in New York, with showers of confetti, and an organist who believed that sheer volume was the essence of good music. Afterward, as they were driven away by carriage, Johann had kissed Hester and said: 'You're going to make me a wonderful wife,' and he was right, she had. When they had come home, she had established herself as chatelaine of all his houses, particularly Lynwood's Island and with an extraordinary sense of realism for a girl so young, she had counted herself lucky that she was rich, and that Johann was fond of her, even if he wasn't a tiger.

Their sex life was proper, and quite polite, and involved the lifting up of nightshirts and nightdresses. It wasn't untypical of 1911, though, and it was quite enough to produce Roderick, and then John, and then Hope. Roderick was at private preparatory school now, seven years old with plump legs, and poor at games. John was four, and serious, and Hope was two, a wilful little girl in flounces and bows.

Johann said: 'I may be late this evening. I have a meeting with Fishman's.'

'Is that why you're thoughtful?'

'Not really. I was thinking about us.'

'Us?' asked Hester, raising an eyebrow. 'What do you mean by "us"?'

'Well, you and me.'

Hester took out another notebook and tried to decide what wines she should order up from the cellar that evening. 'I hope it was something flattering,' she said, ticking off a Pouilly Fuissé.

Johann shrugged. 'It wasn't anything much. I suppose I was just trying to work out if we'd had a good marriage or not.'

Hester put down her book. She gave a short, uncertain laugh.

'I don't know what you mean,' she told him. 'Of course we've had a good marriage. We still do.'

He came over and stood close to her. 'But you are happy?' he asked her. 'You don't feel I haven't been loving enough?'

'Of *course* not,' she said lightly. 'Why, what on earth brought this on?'

'I don't know. I was just beginning to wonder if I was neglecting you.'

'Of course you're not neglecting me. What woman could have half what I've got?'

He sat down in his chair. 'I didn't mean that kind of neglect. I meant as far as love was concerned. I sometimes feel that I haven't been paying enough attention to you. Not the right kind of attention.'

'My dear, if it's bed you're talking about—'

'No, no, I don't mean bed. I mean, don't you sometimes feel that there's something between us – like a window, or a closed blind – and that all we can see of each other is silhouettes?'

Hester looked quite mystified. Johann didn't often speak about his emotions, and the trouble was that whenever he did, she couldn't understand a word of what he was saying. She twisted her mouth into an odd little smile and said: 'Hmph.'

Johann rested his head against his hand. 'You're right, I guess. Maybe I've been cooped up in this office too long. I'm going stir crazy.'

'You could take a vacation.'

'Where? I don't fancy sailing. The last damned ship I went on sank right under me. The good ship *Galveston Bay*.'

Hester glanced at him archly. 'You could fly.'

'Fly? You're joking.'

'No, I'm not, actually. I've been thinking it's time you had your own airplane.'

Johann lifted his head. 'I beg your pardon?'

'I said, "I've been thinking it's time you had your own airplane."'

'What do I need an airplane for? What's wrong with trains?'

'They're slow, that what's wrong with them. Anyway, an airplane would suit you – suit us. You could fly on up to Lynwood's Island after work, and it would only take you a half hour.'

'Hester . . .'

She smiled, and fixed her big brown eyes on him. 'You know it makes sense, Johann. You could get around the country in a tenth of the time it takes you now.'

Johann pulled a face. 'Well,' he said, 'I'm not sure. I hear people get pretty airsick.'

She shook her head. 'Haven't I always been right?'

'Well, sure, but—'

'Wasn't I right about taking over Haymann Drugs after the additive scandal? And wasn't I right about buying the *Kronprinz* from the Navy? And wasn't I right about Knut Insurance?'

Johann couldn't help grinning. 'Very well,' he said quietly, 'I have a wife who's always right. Maybe I should retire and let my wife take over the business.'

Hester looked at him, and he wasn't sure whether she was serious or not. 'I don't have your strength,' she said plainly. 'And I don't have your determination.'

'Hester . . .' he interrupted.

Hester pecked him on the cheek, put her bag over her arm, and went to the door. But as she was about to leave, she said: 'Johann . . . there's nothing wrong is there?'

He shook his head. 'No. I guess I just need a break.'

'Well, I'll start finding out about your airplane. That will give you something to look forward to. Maybe Curtiss or Ford or one of those people. You can give it to yourself as an anniversary present.'

He said: 'Okay,' and then she left, waving to his receptionist on the way out. She took the elevator down to the street, and Johann's long black limousine was waiting for her, attended by their patient chauffeur, Carl, the same white-faced Carl who had escaped with Johann and Jack Field from the SS *Galveston Bay*. It was only when Carl had closed the door for her, and the car had moved away from the kerb, that she allowed herself to sigh and look out of the window at the crowded New York sidewalks with an expression that could have even been pain.

Jack Field walked from the Vanderbilt to the Gotham, in spite of the cold. It was dark now, and he turned the collar of his tweed overcoat up against the night wind. All around him, New York was busy with home-going traffic, and the sidewalks were crowded with young stenographers leaving their offices, most of them fashionably . dressed in short skirts and coats, with striped woollens and long scarves. Hot-chestnut and bagel vendors stood on the street corners, shuffling their feet and prodding their fumy coke. There was a sharp smell of winter in the air.

Jack reached Fifty-fifth Street, and went up the front steps of the Gotham. Only twenty feet away, in 1903, Carina had lain dying on the sidewalk, a Carina who would remain forever fourteen years old. Jack pushed his way through the engraved glass doors and crossed the lobby to the front desk. He said: 'Mr Cornelius here? Tell him it's Mr Jack Field.'

The desk clerk rang up to Johann's suite. Then he said to Jack: 'All right, sir. You can go on up.'

In the elevator, Jack watched his face in the small dim mirror. He had already decided what he was going to do, but it was curious to watch himself doing it. Reflected in store windows along the streets, glimpsed in the windows of passing taxis, and now in this elevator mirror at the Gotham, was the face of a man who had probably made up his mind years and years ago that business was not the divine mission that Dr Cadman was professing it to be, and that businessmen had no more right to consider themselves the chosen vessels of the Lord than anyone else, no matter how many jobs they created, or bonuses they gave, or babies they kissed.

Jack was not a Red, and never could be. But what he had heard today at the Vanderbilt Hotel was more than sufficient to persuade him that, if such corruption had to exist, then he would rather not be part of it. If that meant his resignation, he could make enough money as a criminal counsel, or as a family attorney, or as anything else at all. But even if there was no other way to make a living than to accept the proposals that Albert Fall had come out with during today's meeting, then Jack would have preferred to panhandle on the Bowery rather than say yes.

The elevator stopped. Jack stepped out and walked along the overheated corridor to Johann's suite. He pressed the bell.

Johann came to the door himself, in a bottle-green bathrobe. His legs were bare, and he smelled of soap. Jack said: 'I hope I haven't disturbed you.'

Johann closed the door behind him. 'Not at all. I just finished a meeting with Fishman's, and I felt like a bath. Do you want a drink? You look half-frozen.'

'An old-fashioned would go down well.'

'Help yourself. The bar's over there.'

Johann went and sat down on the wide velour settee while Jack took off his scarf and his overcoat and propped his briefcase against the side of a chair. The suite was dimly lit and hushed, with thick mushroom-coloured carpets and closed drapes. Two cigar butts were crushed out in a modern stainless-steel ashtray.

'Well, then,' said Johann, as Jack poured out his cocktail. 'How did it go?'

Jack shook Angostura in his drink, and stirred it. He

could see half of his own face in the mirror in front of him, and Johann's white, blond-haired leg. He said: 'I think you're probably going to ask me to quit.'

There was a short silence. Johann sat up and reached for his brandy. He said: 'I don't ask people to quit unless I have a good reason. You know that.'

'What about Jerry Slobodien?' asked Jack, knowing that he was reckless to ask.

Johann glanced at him sharply, then shrugged. 'Jerry was a special case. Jerry was cheating for years. And, besides, he didn't take it personal.'

Jack turned around. 'Well,' he said, 'that's as may be.'

Johann watched him. 'Why don't you just tell me what you did that makes it so probable that I'm going to sack you?'

Jack sat down in one of the wide, soft armchairs and loosened his tie.

'No, don't tell me,' put in Johann before Jack could speak. 'You said no to Albert. Albert put something up and you turned it down. He offered you Teapot Dome, and you turned it down.'

'Not quite,' said Jack, 'but nearly.'

Johann swallowed brandy. 'You'd better tell me, in that case.'

Jack nodded. 'I'd kind of guessed what was going to happen. The trouble was, Fall never trusted us as much as he trusted Sinclair and O'Neil and all of those others. 'We were too . . . well, non-political.'

Johann smiled when Jack said that, but he didn't interrupt.

Jack set down his drink. 'As far as I can make out, it's going to work this way,' he explained. 'Humphreys has agreed to sell out of his Mexia field thirty-three million three hundred and thirty-three thousand barrels of oil, at a dollar-fifty a barrel.'

Johann frowned. 'What's wrong with that?'

'Nothing. Except that he doesn't sell it to Sinclair Consolidated or Prairie. He sells it to the Continental Trading Company of Canada.'

'The what?'

'That's just what *I* was asking. But wait. The Continental Trading Company of Canada then resells the same oil to

Sinclair Consolidated and Prairie Oil, but at a dollar-seventy-five a barrel, and that makes a profit of twenty-five cents a barrel.'

Johann's face went rigid. 'Twenty-five cents multiplied by thirty-three million is what?'

'Albert Fall worked it out for us. Eight million dollars, plus. That's after commission and kickbacks.'

Johann nodded slowly. 'Eight million dollars. I see. And I don't suppose I can guess who the joint shareholders of the Continental Trading Company of Canada might be.'

Jack coughed. He felt as if he might have caught a cold on his way up from the Vanderbilt. He said: 'You're absolutely right. Bob Stewart, Harry Blackmer, Harry Sinclair, and Jimmy O'Neil. And us, if we're game. They're prepared to split the money five ways if we want to, and that's cash on the nail that doesn't get reported back to directors or stockholders. Pocket money. Or pocket *bonds*, actually. The money will all be paid off in Liberty bonds.'

'What does Fall stand to make out of it?'

Jack took out his handkerchief and wiped his nose 'That's the really tricky part. If any of us feel generous enough to part with any of these bonds in Mr Fall's direction, he might be favourably inclined toward us when it comes to allocating private leases for Teapot Dome and Elk Hills. He might look on us with even further favour if we lavished a few bonds on Will Hays. The Republican National Committee seem to have found themselves stuck with a campaign debt for Harding and Cox that won't go away.'

'They're going to pay off their campaign debt with Liberty bonds? *Those* Liberty bonds?'

Jack shook his head. 'Of course not. They'll persuade a few of their wealthier friends to contribute to the campaign fund, and slip them Sinclair's Liberty bonds in return. Hey presto, dirty bonds become clean bonds.'

'What about Kiamichi?' asked Johan gruffly.

Jack shrugged. 'Kiamichi gets cleared for drilling if we opt into Continental Trading. Otherwise, no.'

'And you've already opted out, on our behalf?'

Jack didn't answer. He felt flushed, as if his temperature was up above normal. Down in the streets below them, he heard the screaming of a police siren.

252

Johann sat silent for a long time. He toyed with his glass of brandy, swirling it around and around. Jack watched him closely, sipping his old-fashioned, and sweating.

Eventually Johann said: 'Do you want to leave Cornelius Oil?'

Jack looked puzzled. 'Of course not.'

'Tell me the truth.'

Jack paused, and then nodded. 'Well, if you want to know the truth, I guess I've been worried about it for quite a long time.'

'I know that.'

'You *know*?'

Johann looked at him fixedly. 'Of course I know. You're one of my top executives and I hate to delegate. Do you think I walk around with my eyes shut? I'm supposed to have a hide like a bull and a bite like an alligator, but don't you understand just how much of that is bluff? I'm God in that office, Jack, and just like God I have to know everything and everybody, and just how they feel.'

Jack said: 'If you *knew*, then—'

Johann waved him into silence. 'You're one of the best people I've ever had. You're a talented lawyer and a good businessman and you're also a nice guy. I wanted to get as many years out of you as I possibly could, and that's why I haven't asked you this question before. I knew you weren't happy, but I needed your skill. That's what we call intelligent use of available resources.'

He put down his drink, and added: 'As soon as I knew you were discontented, I put up your salary, remember? It wasn't a bribe to keep you, Jack, but I hoped it was some kind of recompense for doing a job you didn't really enjoy.'

Jack lifted his hands in surrender. 'This sounds like you're getting around to firing me.'

Johann gave him a sloping, half-humorous smile. 'I will if it makes you feel any better.'

Jack said: 'I told Fall and Sinclair no. I told him there was no possibility of Cornelius Oil getting involved. That's good enough reason for kicking me out of the door, isn't it?'

Johann stood up. Jack could hardly see his face against the soft shine of the lamps. Johann said: 'Did you think no was the right answer?'

'Well, yes. I did. I wouldn't have said it otherwise.'

253

'Why did you think it was right?'

'Because the profit doesn't add up in the long term. One-fifth of eight million dollars is only one million six hundred thousand, and *that's* only supposing the whole deal goes through. Apart from that, if we're expected to hand that out to Hays and Fall in the expectation of leases at Teapot Dome and Kiamichi, then the math just doesn't make sense. Not for us, anyway. We can raise money for bribes and backhanders with much less risk. This administration is too damned thick with wheelers and dealers and good old pals from way back. It's creaking with corruption and before long it's going to get itself found out, and if that's going to happen, the last place I want Cornelius Oil to be is damn slap in the middle of it.'

Johann listened to this, and then slowly nodded.

'I think Diogenes could stop here, if I understand my *Pocket University* correctly,' he said, in a gentler voice than Jack had ever heard him use in his whole time at Cornelius Oil.

Jack said nothing.

'You made the right decision for the right reasons,' Johann went on. 'I was worried this afternoon that you might muff it, because you thought that I wanted Teapot Dome and Elk Hills at any cost. But you didn't. You did right. This whole government is going to get itself in a deep and serious mess pretty soon, and it's going to count in our favour with the Senate if we made a point of keeping our hands clean. Apart from that, lost causes are never completely lost.'

'What do you mean?' asked Jack.

Johann grunted. 'Watch this,' he said, and picked up his telephone. There was a long silence, and then he said: 'Moira? Get me Albert Fall on the line. He's probably round at the Mellons'.'

For almost five minutes, neither of them said a word as Johann waited for his assistant to find him the Secretary of the Interior. At last Johann said: 'Albert? It's Johann. I thougnt I'd find you there.'

Jack could hear a tinny, diminutive voice on the other end of the line. Then Johann said: 'Albert, I've just been talking to Jack Field. Yes. Yes, that's right. Well, I know you're disappointed, but that's the way things work sometimes. No. I respect his decision. Well, I'm sorry.'

Johann traced a pattern on the telephone table with his fingertips while Fall answered him, and then he said: 'My real worry is Kiamichi. Yes, that's it. You see, the thing is, Albert, I'm pretty keen to get my people started out there. Well, I know all about give-and-take, Albert, and that's why I've called you. I know we're not taking part, but the point is that what you're all doing with Continental Trading Company – well, it's the kind of operation you'd like to keep hushed up, right? Top security, right?"

Johann glanced across at Jack and winked. Then he said: 'The way I see it, Albert, we can keep our mouths religiously sealed for you, but only if you do something for us in return. Something like clearing the problems on Kiamichi. No, Albert, don't say that. What do you mean? No, it's not like that at all. It's just a plain and simple deal. We make sure the Continental Trading Company stays a secret between us, and you give us a little help in Oklahoma. Now, what's so terrible about that? Okay. Yes, I know. But Senator Walsh might be interested, mightn't he? I mean, he's really hot on that kind of thing right now. Yes. Well, that's all I'm asking. Yes. Okay. Well, call me tomorrow. That's all right. But, Albert – make sure it's yes. All right. Good night.'

Johann set down the phone. He was obviously amused. He walked across to Jack with his hands in his bathrobe pockets, and he was smiling broadly.

Jack said: 'You've got quite a nerve.'

Johann nodded. 'It's the only way to get ahead.'

'Well,' said Jack, 'what do I do now? I came here expecting to get fired, and now it seems that I'm not.'

Johann rubbed his chin. 'No, you're not fired. But maybe this is as good a time as any for you to get out of this business. If you're not happy, then there's no point in kicking your heels around here for the rest of your life.'

Jack coughed. He didn't know what to say.

Johann sat on the edge of the table beside him, and rested a big hand on Jack's shoulder.

'What you did today was good work,' he said, 'and I appreciate good work. So let's say that I pay you for that work, and that I give you a small parting gift to help you get along in whatever kind of lawyering takes your fancy.'

He got up, and went over to the desk, which was littered with letters and papers and stock reports. He opened his chequebook, unscrewed his pen, and wrote out a cheque. Then, flapping it to dry the ink, he came back to Jack and handed it to him. Jack didn't mean to look at how much it was, not in front of Johann, but he couldn't help dropping his eyes and glancing at it.

'It's ten thousand dollars,' said Johann. 'It's not a fortune, but it's the same amount that somebody once gave me, to start me off. I couldn't let you leave with any less than that. Or any more, for that matter.'

Jack said softly: 'Thank you. Ten thousand is plenty. If you made a million out of it, I guess I can, too.'

Johann said: 'I'm going to miss you, you know. I want us to stay friends.'

Jack nodded. 'I'd like that. I guess it hasn't been too easy for us to get along together lately, the way things have been.'

'Well, let's talk about that later,' said Johann. 'Right now I suggest you get back home to Ellie. You look like you're coming down with a head cold.'

Jack stood up and gathered his coat and briefcase together. He still felt as if he had to say something else, even if it was only good-bye. He went over and offered his hand to Johann, and they shook.

'I won't forget any of this,' he said. There was a catch in his throat that might have been his oncoming cold.

Johann grunted. 'You'd better. Because if you ever tell anyone else what happened here tonight, I'm going to ram that oil rig up where it hurts the most.'

On the way home, Jack made two stops. He went to a Greek store on Third Avenue, which was the only store he could find open, and bought a red tinplate train. Then he stopped off at the next corner and bought himself a hot bagel, which he ate as he walked back across town to Central Park South. It was a freezing night in November, 1921, and the cold brought tears to his eyes.

1927

When Your Guests Are Gone — Are You Ever Sorry You Invited Them? Be Free From All Embarrassment! Let the Famous *Book of Etiquette* Tell You Exactly What to Do, Say, Write, or Wear on Every Occasion!

— Advertisement, 1927

Spring, in that small corner of Pennsylvania, always seemed to arrive early. You could have motored up from Johnstown or Altoona, and the trees there may still have been bare, but here in the valleys of Robinstown, the buds were already sticky and fresh, and the clouds seemed to roll warmly across a sky that was promising summer when everyplace else was still paying off the debts of winter.

That day in March, 1927, it had rained a while before dawn, but now the sun was out, and the puddles in the tracks were reflecting the sky like pieces of broken blue china. There was a fresh smell of wet grass and the dew clung on spiderwebs beneath the overhanging trees. The shadow of cumulus swam leisurely across the rounded hills that kept Robinstown safe from the bitterest northeasters, and secluded from strangers and travelling brush salesmen.

Down by the village store, Martin Levon, the storekeeper, was heaving barrels of beans and sacks of red potatoes from the back of his Ford pickup. A maroon flivver came chugging slowly down Main Street, its narrow tyres splashing in puddles and mud. It drew up alongside him and coughed to a stop.

"Morning, Martin,' said the driver.

Martin didn't turn around, but hefted the barrel up against the wooden store wall.

"Morning to you, Grover.'

The driver, Grover Bean, climbed carefully out of the car and limped across to the boardwalk. He was one of the most important men in town, since he owned most of the grazing land north of the Asquahanna River, and all the mineral rights besides, and his herd of dairy cattle had won prizes every year from 1922. He was lean and tall, with a wide-brimmed hat over a face as long and mournful as a bloodhound's.

Martin finished unloading his pickup, and chained up the tailboard. Grover sat down on one of the old kitchen chairs outside the store and lit himself a thin cheroot. The morning breeze blew the smoke away over his shoulder.

'It's going to be a fine spring day,' said Grover, leaning back. 'I reckon that we could do with such a day, too.'

Martin wiped his nose with the back of his shirtsleeve. 'Guess so, but I prefer to have her *wet* than to have her *dry*. Wet days, folks hang about the store longer, and gen'rally purchase more.'

The two men sat for a few minutes, smoking and appreciating the day. It wasn't considered proper in Robinstown to come out and state your business straightaway. The community (Pop.: 350) was too small for that. You discussed family matters first, and hemmed and hawed, and in the end you finally got around to saying what was on your mind.

Grover said: 'I was reading last night that they can send moving pictures through the airwaves like the wireless these days. Seems they're going to test it out soon, this year maybe. It's the television, they called it. Now, that sounds interesting, doesn't it?'

Martin sniffed. 'Don't see the use of it. It don't make no difference if you just hear a feller play a banjo, instead of seeing him, does it?'

'Oh, there's more to it than that,' said Grover. 'They reckon they can bring you sports, right into your own home, right the moment it happens. And you could see the President speak, clear as day, when he's in Washington and you're home.'

Martin scratched the back of his head. 'Now I *know* there ain't no use for it? It's bad enough having Coolidge in the White House, without having him setting in my own home, without as much as a please or thank you.'

Grover, who was a firm believer in Republican 'normalcy', and had once been invited to a charity buffet in Philadelphia which Calvin Coolidge was supposed to attend (he hadn't, because of flu), started to laugh.

'There isn't any turning *your* head, Martin. Not by wireless nor television, nor any gimcrackery or hokum going. You're a good man!'

Martin relit his dwindling cigarette and shook out the match He looked at Grover hard, as if he sensed that the farmer had something important to say.

'It ain't often you're free with the compliments, Grover.'

Grover's face abruptly went serious, like the creases dropping out of a tablecloth.

'No,' he agreed. 'It isn't. But then, it isn't often we get the chance to make anything out of ourselves.'

Martin said nothing but waited for Grover to continue. He had all day, and all tomorrow, and all the day after that, and so there wasn't any point in rushing it. Grover Bean had something important to say, and because he was a gentleman, he was going to say it in the way a gentleman should.

'Last month, I had myself a letter,' said Grover. 'It was written from Pittsburgh, from the Kruyper Dye Works. All official, headed notepaper and all. It seems they're planning on setting up a factory here, at Robinstown, and they want to use the Asquahanna River for the dye process. They'll bring in a railroad spur, and build houses for the workers, and expand the whole place like you'd never believe it.'

Martin stared at him. 'They want to build a *factory*? Here – in Robinstown?'

'They sure do. They made an offer for the Slope Meadow and the South Hill, and two or three of those old pastures we don't use anymore, and they say they're going to bring in work and money and make Robinstown into a boom city.'

Martin frowned. 'It sure sounds like something. But what about the farmers hereabouts? What's it going to do to them? They're my regular customers, Grover, and even if I get more customers, I don't care to see my old friends sold down no river, dye works or dammit.'

Grover shook his head. 'You don't understand. See there – along the river bend – that's where the factory goes. The workers' houses go up beyond the woods, and you'd never even see them. It's all on my land, and most of it's land I don't use no more, and woods, and the top of the Rabbit Ridge. Why, the Rabbit Ridge is so steep you can't get cattle up there unless you carry them up on your back. It isn't any use to me.'

Martin stood up and walked over to the edge of the boardwalk. He shaded his eyes against the sunlight, and looked out over the valley of the Asquahanna, at the soft valley with its blossomy trees and its little cluster of painted clapboard houses.

'I guess it would liven things up, as far as business goes,' said Martin slowly. 'I mean – think of all the folk who would live here regular, and come to buy at the store day by day.'

'That old cash register wouldn't stop ringing,' said Grover enthusiastically. 'You could be a wealthy man, Martin, if you worked hard and you played your hand right.'

'They wouldn't have no company store?'

'I could make them promise that, as a condition. I haven't signed any papers yet. I wanted to see what the town said first.'

Martin turned around, and he was emphatic. 'Well, you make 'em promise that. No company store, and then they can come in here and build themselves a hundred dye works! Even two hundred, if they've a mind to!'

Grover laughed. 'I'm glad you like the idea, Martin. There are going to be plenty who don't.'

Martin grinned. 'You get old-fashioned folks in every community. But I'd say this dye works calls for a celebration. I've got myself a couple of bottles of L. L. McKenzie's special out back, if you'd care to step inside.'

Grover shook his head, but smiled. 'I prefer to keep my brains where they belong at this time of the morning. Anyhow, it seems that the Kruyper people may be up here today, to talk over the land sale, and I wouldn't want them to think I was anything but temperate, would I?'

Martin nodded. 'I guess not.'

He coughed, and shuffled his feet for a while, and then he said: 'I guess they're giving a fair price.'

Grover shrugged. 'That's something that everybody in the whole of the county is going to want to know. How much did Kruyper's grease old man Bean's palm for the dye-works land? Well, I'm going to say it out straight, so there's no gossip and there's no exaggeration. What they've asked for here is a package of land taking in all that area like I said, and what they're paying is two hundred and fifty thousand dollars.'

Martin whistled. 'That's a quarter of a million bucks! They're going to pay you a quarter of a million bucks for the Rabbit Ridge and the Slope Meadow and a few bits of old scrub? They have to be nuts!'

'Hold on there,' said Grover, lifting his hand 'That's all

good land, with good rich soil, and what they don't want to build a dye works on, they could use for grazing, or growing, or whatever they wanted.'

'You just said yourself the Rabbit Ridge was no good for grazing. If *you* ain't ready to haul a cow up there on your back, do you think *they* will?'

Grover pulled a face. 'How should I know? They asked for it, so maybe they got ways and means.'

'A quarter of a million dollars,' said Martin huskily, and had to sit down on the bean barrel again. 'That's more money than I ever saw. You know something, Grover, I always said you was a gentleman, and I was absolutely right. If you won't take a small drink with me right now – well, I suggest you take a large one!'

Grover Bean, pleased with his news and his imminent wealth, at last relented. Martin went in to fetch the moonshine out of the long-case clock in the wall, and he called to his wife, Katherine, to fetch glasses, because this was celebration time, whether it was ten in the morning or not. They were going to have more customers in their store than a dog has fleas, and everyone around was going to be rich.

As the spring morning warmed up, they sat around a barrel on the porch, and Martin poured them stiff shots of L. L. McKenzie's home-brewed stuff, and they laughed and smoked some more, and anyone who passed by was told the news. As Grover had predicted, it wasn't every member of the Robinstown community who was pleased to hear that their houses were soon going to be overshadowed by a dye works, but most of them recognized that it was going to give them financial security at a time when financial security was getting a little thin on the ground.

It was just past eleven when they saw three large black sedans glittering in the sunlight as they came slowly up the rough Asquahanna road and through the ash grove farther down the valley. Almost silently, the cars drove toward them in the mud, and pulled to a halt beside the village store.

'Looks like a funeral t' me,' said Martin, and then cackled out loud.

Grover Bean looked more serious. 'Maybe it's the Kruyper people, come to talk about the works.'

Across the street, the gingham curtains of old man Johnson's house were obviously atwitch, and George Purvis, keeper of the peace, switchboard operator, and savings-bank manager, came trudging across the street in his plaid shirt and his suspenders with his ginger moustache awry and ready for anything.

The sedans had darkened windows, and it was impossible to see who was inside. For a moment they stayed there silent and unmoving, like sinister apparitions from another planet, but then the doors opened, and three chauffeurs stepped out to open the rear doors.

Out of the first car climbed a sharply dressed young man in grey with a briefcase and rimless spectacles. He had that smooth, wellfed look of successful junior attorneys, and the fact that he didn't care about stepping into the thick black mud of Robinstown's Main Street showed Martin that he must have enough money to own more than one pair of shoes. He came across to the store, and raised his hat to them, 'for all the whole world,' as Martin said later, 'as if he was going to sing us a song.'

'Is either of you two gentlemen Mr Grover Bean?'

Grover stood up hastily, almost knocking over his tumbler of moonshine. His long doggy face was purpler than usual, and he wiped his palm on his breeches before he shook hands.

That's me, sir. I'm Grover Bean. I'm honoured to make your acquaintance.'

'How do you do,' replied the young man in grey. He had a peculiarly tart way of smiling. 'My name's Oswald Stone, and I represent the Kruyper Dye Works. I suppose you received my letter about the final negotiations for the sale of your land?'

Grover said: 'Yes, I did, yes, thank you,' in a kowtowing kind of way that really disturbed Martin, who was unusually clear in his perceptions after two and a half glasses of L. L. McKenzie's special.

'We can go over the details later,' said Oswald Stone. 'In private.'

Grover said: 'Surely. By the way, this is Martin Levon, who runs the store here, and this is George Purvis, our law officer and manager of the Asquahanna Savings Bank.'

The Robinstown men said: 'How do,' a little suspiciously, and made no effort to shake hands.

Oswald Stone stepped up onto the boardwalk and scraped the mud from his feet. He noticed the half-empty hooch glasses on the barrelhead, but he didn't remark on them. Instead, he turned around and inspected the town and the valley as if he was planning on converting the whole place into a holiday camp.

'Nice township you have here,' he said briskly. 'Real nice.'

George Purvis put his big head on one side and said: 'That's the way *we* like it.'

Stone smiled. 'Of course you do. And we aim to help you keep it that way. If anything at all, what we plan to do here is going to be an improvement. It'll bring some life into the place, pep it up a bit.'

Purvis said: 'Happen we don't want it pepped up? Happen we prefer things the way they are?'

'Well' – Stone smirked – 'that's something that you and Mr Bean here are going to have to thrash out between you. Mr Bean has offered us the land, straight and legitimate, and nobody can blame him for doing that.'

Purvis looked steadily at Oswald Stone for a moment, and then turned around and looked with equal weight at Grover Bean. For some reason, Grover seemed embarrassed, and he couldn't hold George Purvis's stare for more than a couple of seconds.

'It seems to me,' said Purvis, 'that the sale of a man's land is a man's own business. But it also seems to me that if a man's land is going to be used for something that's going to make waves all over town, like this is, then I reckon it's the town's business, too.'

Martin Levon scratched his spiky hair. 'That's all well and good now, George,' he said gently, 'but you have to think of the trade. There ain't nobody round Robinstown who's done good for themselves since the war, and with all them dairy prices dropping every day – well, maybe we got to fix to do something. The future ain't in farming, and that's for sure.'

George Purvis spat onto the road. 'That's hogwash and *you* know it. As long as there's people who need feeding, there's going to be farmers. So there's surpluses of grain, and there's surpluses of butter, and there's more meat than Calvin Coolidge can stuff in his mouth at one go. But I heard there's a bill in front of Congress for selling surplus stuff abroad at low prices, and clearing the surplus, and *then* you'll see if the future's in farming or not. You'll sit here in Robinstown, with black smoke choking your cattle and dye poisoning your river, and you'll wish to the Lord Almighty that you never done what you done this day.'

Oswald Stone didn't seem to be the slightest bit perturbed by this speech, but he beckoned to one of the chauffeurs standing by the three limousines, and when the man came across to see what he wanted, he whispered something in his ear.

The chauffeur nodded, and walked back to the second car in the cortege, trying to avoid the puddles in his shiny brown boots.

Oswald Stone said to George Purvis: 'There's someone here that I'd like for you to meet. Maybe, when you've talked to him, you'll change your opinions.'

George Purvis shook his head. 'There's only one thing that's going to change my opinion, and that's the end of the world. When that day comes, you can put up dye works till you bust.'

The chauffeur opened the rear door of the second limousine, and a man climbed slowly out. When he stood up to his full height, Martin Levon realized, almost immediately, who it was. The man was broad-shouldered and heavily built, like a prize bull in a well-fitting vicuna coat, and he wore a grey hat over a broad, mature, but rather reddened face. He came walking toward them with his head lowered, touching the muddy road with the tip of a black cane, and it was only when he stepped up onto the boardwalk that he lifted his head and looked them all in the eye. Not one of them had spoken, and even now they didn't know what to say.

The man removed one grey kid glove and extended a chunky, stubby-fingered hand. George Purvis shook it first, and it made him wince, because the man had a hard grip and three heavily engraved gold rings.

'I'm Johann Cornelius,' said the man, looking from one to the other. 'I'm the owner, in a way, of the Kruyper Dye Works.'

Oswald Stone smoothed back his hair. 'Mr Cornelius will be pleased to answer any questions. You have some questions, don't you, Mr Purvis?'

George Purvis looked suddenly small and shabby next to Johann. His open-necked work shirt was faded and patched, compared with the white pristine gates-ajar collar of Johann's shirt, and Johann's impeccable necktie, and his hands were rough and scarred.

Still, he managed to find his voice. He looked defiantly at Johann and said: 'I don't have no questions, Mr Cornelius, no questions at all. All I have is objections. The way I see it, you've led Grover Bean here astray with money, and now he's prepared to sell you land for a purpose that won't suit this township. That's the way I see it.'

Johann nodded.

'What makes you think that a dye works won't suit this township, Mr Purvis?'

George Purvis coughed. 'I'm not a rich man, Mr Cornelius, not like you, but I've lived in this township most of my life and I know what suits it and what don't. When Congress passes that bill for selling farm surplus abroad, why, this place is going to start to come to life again, slowly, and that's why we don't want no factories here, poisoning our rivers and pushing us out of our rightful land.'

Johann's face was expressionless. 'Do you really think that Congress will get that bill past the President?'

George looked fierce. 'Why, he don't have no choice.'

Johann remained bland and unmoved. 'He does, I'm afraid, and I'll bet you five hundred dollars that he vetoes that bill straight out.'

'Aw, come on . . .' said George. 'He don't have no choice.'

Johann turned on him. 'No, my friend, it is *you* who have no choice. You don't have a choice at all. You're going to be pulled by your ears into the future of this nation whether you like it or not. You're going to be part of what makes America great, and what makes America great is nothing to do with squabbling farmers and antitrust laws and softheaded, softhearted meliorists.'

He reached out and seized George Purvis's shoulder. He pointed up the valley, toward the distant woods and the hazy curves of the Rabbit Ridge. 'What do you see there?'

he whispered loudly. 'When you look up that valley, what do you see?'

George was uncomfortable, but he didn't have the temerity to shake free from Johann Cornelius' grip

'I see trees,' he said awkwardly. 'Trees   and grazing land.'

'And what else?'

George squinted. 'I don't know. Clouds?'

Johann let him go. 'You see trees, and grazing land, and clouds?'

'I guess so,' said George, rubbing his shoulder.

Johann shook his head, like a fond uncle shaking his head at the ignorance of a dull nephew.

'I see those things, too, Mr Purvis, but I see something else besides. I see a river, and whenever I see a river I see power, and water for factory work. The power is free, and the water is free, and that means economy, and profit. I see something else, too, but that something else is a secret, because that something else is going to make this town rich and me richer. Come on, Mr Purvis, this is America. This is the land of opportunity. Didn't it ever occur to you to become rich?'

George Purvis opened his mouth and then closed it again. Martin Levon was looking at him, and so was that lawyer fellow, Oswald Stone, and he just didn't know what to say. Sure, he used to dream about riches, and buying himself a fancy automobile. But that was just foolishness, and as he grew older, it faded out of his mind. He knew that big money wasn't for him, and he grew to be satisfied with his small musty office, his black cylinder stove, and his blue pot of quietly simmering coffee.

'Well, now,' said Johann Cornelius with a thick-lipped smile. 'I think it's time we settled this property transaction for good. Would you care for a ride, Mr Bean? Maybe we can talk over the final details and get this show on the road.'

Grover Bean tugged his jacket straight, and nodded in acquiescence. But even as he walked toward the long black Cornelius cars, he turned back toward George Purvis, who was staring at the boardwalk with the stunned, hopeless look of a priest who wonders if his faith has somehow gotten itself entangled in selfish desires and worldly conundrums, and he felt he wanted to say something to George, just about anything at all, even if it was only 'Sorry.'

Inside the limousine, it smelled of deep-buttoned leather and brandy. The tinted windows made it gloomy, like a travelling sepulchre, and it was hard to distinguish the faces of all the men who were sitting there. Someone opened a briefcase, and there was a rustle of papers and deeds. The door was closed to exclude the breeze and the world outside.

'Sit down,' instructed Johann Cornelius, pulling out a jump seat for him. 'Make yourself at home.'

Grover sat, biting his lip with nervous concentration.

Johann quickly ruffled through the papers, refreshing his memory. Then he looked up and said: 'I trust there's nothing here that you object to, Mr Bean?'

Grover coughed. 'Well, sir, there's the question of fencing on the south, and I'm asked to make a couple of inclusions on behalf of the townsfolk.'

'What are they?'

'Well, I want it stipulated that all the dye-works people spend their money at the local store, and that you have no company store in competition; and I also want it made plain that the river is not to be poisoned by dye, since two herds of cattle drink out of it below the ash grove.'

Johann turned the pages of the contract until he came to the relevant pages. He read them carefully, and then looked up again at Grover.

'Those are your stipulations, are they?'

'Yes, sir, they are.'

Johann sighed, and rubbed his forehead. Oswald Stone, sitting next to him, recognized the signs of his impatience, and gave one of his bitter little smiles.

'Mr Bean,' said Johann in a weary voice. 'We are offering you two hundred and fifty thousand dollars for your land. Is that enough, or is it not enough?'

Grover looked at Oswald Stone, and then to another Cornelius aide sitting in the limousine's darkest corner.

'It's enough,' he said. 'We've agreed to that.'

'Well, then,' said Johann, 'if it's enough, take it. Just don't try to impose ridiculous sanctions and stipulations on me, because if I make a contract I make a contract, plain and simple, and there's to be no frills and exceptions and odd clauses to make it into a pig's dinner. Either sell me the land, or don't sell me the land. It's up to you.'

Grover swallowed. It hadn't occurred to him for one moment that Johann would face him with a choice like that. The truth was, he deperately needed the money, because his farm had been through three bad years, and he was seriously in debt. To allow the bank to foreclose on his outstanding loans was out of the question, especially to a gentleman, as he considered himself to be, and the only way he could raise the capital was to sell.

'Well . . .' said Grover uncertainly.

'Well, what?' retorted Johann. 'Are you going to sell me the land, or aren't you?'

Grover lifted his head. 'Yes, sir, I will,' he said clearly.

'That's what I wanted to hear,' said Johann. 'Oswald, pass Mr Bean a pen, and let's have his John Hancock down on the dotted line.'

The contract was unfolded and laid out for Grover on a small walnut table in the back of the limousine. Oswald Stone handed him a pen, and Grover held it poised for a while, pretending to examine the contract for one last time, although the words were unfocused and blurred. The men in the car waited patiently for him, and when he had signed his name in blue-black ink, there was no disturbing haste to take the contract back. When the writing was dry, Oswald reached out for it and said: 'Satisfied?'

Grover nodded, without looking up. 'Yes, sir, I am.'

'Then here's your cheque for two hundred and fifty thousand dollars, as agreed.'

Grover took the cheque without looking at it. He tucked it into the pocket of his jacket, and mumbled: 'Thank you.'

He was just about to open the limousine door when Johann Cornelius caught his arm.

'Mr Bean,' he said. 'I would rather you examined the cheque.'

Grover Bean said: 'I trust you. There's no need.'

'No, no, you must,' insisted Johann. 'I would hate you to think that you'd been tricked, or cheated. Just make sure that it's right'

Grover took out the cheque and peered at it closely. 'It seems fine to me, thank you,' he said.

'That's very good,' said Johann. 'I want to thank you for

270

your helpfulness, and I want you to remember me with good cheer, no matter what happens next. These days, there isn't enough good cheer.'

'No,' said Grover, uncertain and anxious as he stepped out of the car. 'I suppose there isn't.'

The limousines drove Johann back through the Pennsylvania hills as far as Altoona, where his Ford Tri-Motor airplane was waiting for him, at four o'clock in the afternoon, on a rough field strewn with daisies. As the engines coughed and droned into life, ruffling the grass back and scattering a flock of finches, Oswald Stone came aboard to give Johann a final briefing on the Robinstown deal.

The interior of the plain silver airplane had been built as a small office, with a cushioned basketwork chair for Johann, and four more basket chairs for his passengers. The inside of the fuselage was lined with walnut veneer, and there was a cocktail cabinet with engraved glass doors. Johann's desk was neat and almost bare, and everything on it – pens, ink, and paper – could be secured firmly into place with brass clips. On this flight back to Lynwood's Island, he was working on a complex transfer of preferred stock, and the papers had already been laid out for him by his secretary, Henry B. Keith, a sniffy young man who accompanied him in badly pressed linen suits wherever he went.

Henry Keith was up front talking to the pilot, while Johann's Negro travelling valet, Lester, was preparing a light salad at the back of the plane – opening up lunch baskets and porcelain jars, and laying out Nova Scotia smoked salmon, fresh cold asparagus, crisp Chinese lettuce, peaches, and white wine.

Oswald Stone checked his pocket watch and said: 'There's only one difficulty left.'

'What's that?' asked Johann. 'I thought you said the whole thing was ready to roll.'

'Well, it's not a *new* difficulty. It's the railroad.'

Johann didn't look up, but unclipped a gold propelling pencil from his coat. 'I thought I told you to settle that,' he said, almost as if he wasn't listening.

'I *tried* to settle it. I spent the whole of yesterday with McFarlane. But they still have reservations. I don't know

271

why and I've been trying to find out why. But all the way along, their board of directors has been extremely hostile, and they still won't give us any of the assurances we want.'

Johann said: 'I'm not moving one bucket of earth until we get those assurances, do you understand that?'

'Yes, sir, I do. But I can't say right at this moment that it's going to be easy.'

Johann was already giving most of his attention to the stock-option figures in front of him. Oswald had to speak very loudly to make himself heard over the rattling of loose plates and bottles of ink and pens and the overwhelming *grroowwrr* noise of the motors.

'Sir,' he said, 'I get the feeling that the railroad wouldn't lose any sleep if we didn't get this operation rolling at all.'

Johann sniffed, and wrote a question mark next to a list of oil holdings. 'What makes you think that?' he asked quietly.

'I beg your pardon, sir?'

'What makes you think that? *Why* wouldn't they lose any sleep? And why can't you handle a two-bit operation like the P&P Railroad without whining and moaning and making excuses?'

'I'm sorry, sir,' said Oswald, embarrassed. 'But it seems to me that they have a vested interest in keeping our Robinstown operation right under their thumb. They've been haggling for months over freight charges and quantities, and we still haven't been able to resolve an economic carrying structure.'

'Why don't you speak English?' said Johann roughly. 'You mean they want too much money for hauling our output.'

'Well, that's right. And they won't come down. They're still talking thirty dollars a short ton.'

'That's out of the question. What do they think we're running – a railroad benevolent fund?'

'I asked them that, sir, but they wouldn't give way. They say they want thirty dollars and that's final.'

Johann laid down his stock reports and thoughtfully pulled at his thick red lips. His thin hair was oiled to his scalp with brilliantine, and parted in the centre, like the sparse mane of a child's rocking horse.

'Thirty dollars, huh? Now, why should they want that much?'

'I don't know, sir,' said Oswald. 'It seems to me that they're pricing themselves right out of the market.'

Johann nodded. 'Yes, it does. But why should they? The only reason people do that is because they don't really want the work in the first place, or they only want it on very specific conditions. Why shouldn't the P&P Railroad want the work of carrying our product from Robinstown?'

'Maybe they don't want us to open up at Robinstown at all.'

'But why not? I thought we had everybody straight on that.'

Oswald stood up. Seeing people off in airplanes always made him afraid that he was going to be inadvertently trapped on board and flown to some place that he distinctly didn't want to go. His wife, Janina, was cooking Schnitz-und-Gnepp tonight, too, and it was one of his favourites.

'I was thinking, sir, that if I can't get P&P to cut their rates—'

'*Cut* them? I want them *halved*! And on the same guarantees, too!'

'Well, sir, yes,' said Oswald. 'But if they still won't come down, I was thinking that maybe we could discreetly call in a couple of private detectives. Everybody's supposed to be straight, but somebody's obviously holding out. We should find out who.'

Johann sat back in his creaky basketwork chair. 'Hmm. I don't usually care for that. How much stock do we hold in P&P?'

'A little less than nine percent, sir.'

'Who's the majority stockholder?'

'It's supposed to be a holding company based in New Jersey called . . . here we are . . . TransMechanic.'

Johann scribbled down the name. Then he said: 'Okay, leave that side of it to me. Meanwhile, keep pressing them. Give them twenty-four hours to make up their minds, and if they still can't halve their rates by then, call in a good detective and have him sniff around the board. I'm not having any half-raw bunch of Dutchmen make a monkey out of me, and that's all there is to it. Oh, and something else. Get a man up to Robinstown to watch that Purvis guy. See if he can't be persuaded to soften up some of his attitudes. When this thing takes shape, the last thing I want is a bad press. I'm not having another Ludlow massacre.'

'Sir, I don't really think—'

'*Do* it, Oswald, will you? Soften him up. We're going to have enough problems when they find out tnat the dye works isn't even a dye works, without Bolsheviks like him giving us a hard time.'

'Okay, sir, whatever you say. I'll try to cable you out at the island if I hear anything before the end of the week.'

Henry Keith came back from the cockpit in his rumpled suit and announced that they were ready for takeoff. Oswald tried to think of some parting words he could say to Johann to make him feel that he was doing a great job down here in Pennsylvania, but couldn't. He grabbed his papers and his briefcase and clambered down the little alloy ladder to the grass, holding his hat against the roaring draught from the propellers.

The Tri-Motor's door was closed, and the airplane bumped around into the wind. The pale afternoon sun turned the propellers into slanting curves of light, and there was a brief smell of kerosene in the air. Oswald stood in the field waving as the airplane gathered speed and began to trundle away from him, but he was quite sure that Johann wasn't waving back. Johann was such a sour, practical bastard that he wouldn't waste the energy. He was the first rich man that Oswald had ever worked for, and even though Oswald was elated by the prestige, and very much better off than he had ever been before, he was sometimes driven to such depths of servitude and humiliation by Johann's criticisms and demands that he went back to his suburban home in the better part of Pittsburgh and wept and shook on Janina's shoulder.

The plane picked up speed and its tail wheel lifted from the grass. Then, with a throttled roar, it tilted itself awkwardly into the air and began to climb toward the west with the ungainly look of a large goose trying to waddle up an icy slope in winter. Oswald watched it for a few moments more, until the sound of its engines had almost completely dwindled away, and then he turned back to his sedan.

Two and a half thousand feet in the air, Johann was drinking one frugal glass of chilled Meursault and cutting wafer-thin slices of well-peppered salmon. Opposite, Henry

274

Keith was making do with a quick cold beef sandwich – not because Johann objected to his sharing the salmon, but because he himself always felt so uncomfortable sitting at a luncheon table with his taciturn employer. These days, Johann talked business when he did talk, and he never saw the purpose of putting other people at their ease, with the result that many of his dinners and receptions were bristling with agonized silence. When Hester had once asked him why he didn't try to make more conversation, he grudgingly answered: 'The only word that's worth speaking is the word that makes a buck.'

Henry knew that Johann wasn't as totally insensitive as that remark made him out to be. For a man with so many employees, and with his finger in so many pies, flans, turnovers, and pasties, Johann was unusually introspective. John D. Rockefeller Jr. had called him 'that fellow with the hard heart and soft head,' and the very first time that Andrew Mellon had met him, at a reception held in 1925 by the Secretary of Commerce, Herbert Hoover, Mellon had been struck by the way that Johann wandered about as if he were the victim of an automobile accident, in a state of suppressed shock. Johann was, in 1927, as rich as Irénée Du Pont, and a powerful political figure. He owned banks and chemical plants and his opinions appeared regularly in the three Southern newspapers he controlled. He was beginning to buy into aviation, and his position as chairman of the Federal Commission on Foreign Trade Restrictions gave him a unique opportunity to influence foreign markets, particularly Germany, in favour of his own corporations. Yet – as an emotional being – there was something about Johann Cornelius that unsettled almost everybody who met him. A terrible wound-up tension, as if he was holding back some pain, or some fear, or some anger, and would never release it.

As the Ford Tri-Motor droned across the border into New York State, Johann paused from his work for a moment to look out of the little rectangular windows, and watch the sun settling smokily into the evening clouds. He enjoyed flying, because it gave him a sense of what he owned, and the potential which he still had to realize. He could look out over the endless fields and highways of America, fading into soft dusk in the western distance, and hear the chilly rush of the evening wind on the plane's wings.

Henry Keith, seeing him staring out of the window, had a look too. He coughed and said: 'It's a great sight, isn't it, Mr Cornelius?'

Johann didn't answer at first, but then he sat back and looked at this pale-faced young man with his creased suit, his polished brown hair, and his long bony nose, and he said flatly: 'Yes, it's a great sight.'

Henry sat back too. 'Are you through with the oil-stock papers, Mr Cornelius? Because if you are, I'll double-check them alongside the Daylong figures.'

'Nearly through,' said Johann absently. He was twiddling with his gold propelling pencil as if he had something on his mind. Henry Keith had never seen him quite so preoccupied.

'Mr Cornelius . . . is anything wrong?'

Johann continued to twiddle. 'I'm not sure,' he said slowly. 'I was just thinking about the Robinstown setup.'

'You mean the P&P Railroad? I'm sure that Oswald can handle it. I know he's kind of green, but he knows what you want.'

Johann shook his head. 'It's not that. I just want to know why they're being so goddamned awkward. Someone, somehow, is trying to throw a monkey wrench into this, and I wish to hell I knew who it was.'

'TransMechanic?'

'It could be. Do we know who TransMechanic are?'

'I've heard of them,' said Henry. 'They're a holding partnership for several different engineering and railroad interests, but I'd have to dig a little deeper to find out who the *éminence grise* might be.'

Johann nodded. They were flying into some broken cloud, and he had to reach out and steady his glass of wine.

'Henry,' he said after a while, 'what do you *think* about Robinstown?'

Henry, who had been shuffling papers together and clipping them into neat stacks, was taken by surprise. Johann hardly ever asked him his opinion of anything, and even when he offered it, he was usually ignored. Perhaps it was the Meursault, or perhaps Johann was tired, but he seemed to be in a dark brown, thoughtful mood. Henry sat up straight in his basket chair and tried to think of a sensible, moderately impressive answer.

'Well, sir, I think it's . . . it's *good sense*. It gets us into a new district in a new field of endeavour, and it . . . well, it's an exciting beginning . . . I mean, for all of us . . . and, well, it's . . . it's very exciting.'

Johann rubbed his eyes.

'I know it's exciting, Henry,' he said patiently. 'Profit, by definition, is exciting. But what I want to know is what you *think* of it. What your *entrails* say. Is it distasteful, for instance? Or immoral? Have you thought about that?'

Henry Keith frowned. He was a little nearsighted, but he thought eyeglasses made him look too much like Dwight Morrow and so he preferred to sit near things and squint at them.

'You're frowning,' said Johann in a critical voice. 'Don't you know what "immoral" means?'

'Well, sure I do,' said Henry. He tugged his crumpled jacket around himself and looked unhappy. 'I just don't really understand how "immoral" fits in with the Robinstown setup.'

Johann stared at him for almost a minute. Then he said: 'Henry, you are a pretty good secretary. You sharpen my pencils, you fill up my inkpots, you keep everything neat and tidy. You know how to pass on instructions, and you don't make mistakes.'

Henry said: 'Thank you, sir,' but very uncertainly.

Johann lowered his head. 'Your trouble, Henry, is that you will never understand power, and if you don't understand power, you will never understand money. The two are completely and irrevocably interlinked. If you have money, but you disregard the power that it brings you, then you will lose that money, as sure as the leaves fall off the trees in September. The exercise of power is the only safeguard against theft, swindle, takeover, inflation, and economic decay.'

Henry said: 'Mr Cornelius, I didn't know that you found my work to be unsatisfactory.'

'It's not your *work* that's unsatisfactory. It's your soul. You have an unsatisfactory *soul*. Maybe you're young, and you haven't even realized you have a soul yet. That could be it. But it's about time, because you're in the major leagues now, Henry, and there is no room for a man who doesn't have a satisfactory soul.'

'Sir?' said Henry. He was more baffled now than he could ever remember. He was beginning to sweat, in spite of the chilly air that was blowing through the airplane, and for a moment he seriously wondered if Johann was actually sacking him.

Johann sipped the last of his wine. He dabbed his lips with a clean Irish-linen napkin and signalled to Lester to clear away his dishes.

'Henry,' he said slowly, 'you can't deny that most people think I'm a tyrant.'

'Oh, sir, I wouldn't say—'

Johann waved a thick-fingered hand at him. 'Come on, Henry, don't be such a goddamned ass-licker. Everybody in the world thinks I'm a tyrant, including my wife, and that's the way it has to be. But what they don't know, what they never guess, is that I'm only half the tyrant I could be. The reason for that is that *power*, unless it's handled with great care and responsibility, is the kind of tool that can fly out of your hand and hit you straight in the eye. Nobody with great power uses all the power at their disposal. You think Junior does? Or Mellon? Power is only effective when it's used sparingly and with consideration for morals and principles; and the more sparingly you use it, and the greater consideration you show for morals and principles, then the more powerful you can become. If I used all the power I could muster against you – you personally – then I could break you. But what's the use of that? It's far more profitable if I use only a fraction of my power, and have you working for me.'

Henry scratched his head. 'I'm sorry, sir, but I still don't see how this applies to Robinstown. I'm sorry.'

Johann rubbed his forehead like an uncle trying to explain simple geography to a cretinous nephew.

'Henry,' he said, 'we have misguided Mr Bean into believing that he has sold us land for a dye works. A dye works won't go down too well in Robinstown, but at least it's on the margin of what the people will swallow. The question I'm asking you is concerned with the morality of buying land for a dye works, using borrowed federal funds for the purpose, when our real intention is to strip the whole place bare and dig up coal. You know as well as I do that if we strip the ridges and the pastures around there, the farmland will erode, and in five years you won't be able to feed a Colorado beetle around there, let alone a cow.'

Henry swallowed. 'I see,' he said, nodding at last. 'I see.'

'You *see*, Henry, but what do you *think*?'

Henry looked down at his lap. It was piled high with papers, and he stared at them as if they had dropped from nowhere.

'I think, sir, seriously, that morality doesn't come into this particular deal. I mean, morality is one thing, but what you're doing is for the good of the most people, and that's moral, surely? There'll be coal, and work for hundreds of men, and with the way that farm prices are going, a mine has to be worth much more than agricultural land. Apart from that, sir, you have to drag these people into America's future, by their ears if necessary.'

Johann listened to all this, and then closed his eyes. He was beginning to feel like fifty-four. His heart seemed to beat deeper and slower, like a heavy swimmer churning his way through tidal troughs. His blood seemed to run more tiredly, and his head was almost permanently aching with the strain of remembering the scale and the extent of his investments and his properties.

Henry wiped his nose with his handkerchief. The Ford was now vibrating and bucking between the clouds, and he was glancing nervously out of the windows to see what was happening, and where they were.

'I have ... well, I guess I have one question. If you don't mind my asking it.'

Johann said: 'Be my guest.'

'Well, sir, can I please ask what *you* think about Robinstown? Do *you* consider it moral? I'm sorry if that sounds kind of impertinent, but you did say that—'

Johann laughed, once, out loud. There was no humour in his face at all.

'Henry,' he said, 'you haven't understood a single word.'

'Sir?'

'Listen, Henry, I was born on a farm, the son of a dairy farmer, just the same as those people up in Robinstown. My father died of a stroke, and from working too hard. Farming is a tough, miserable, badly paid existence,

279

especially these days, and it's thankless, too. But look at mining! Miners might get paid more, but then mining's tough and miserable, too, and miners die young from dust on the lungs, and collapsing shafts, and floods. They never see the sun and it's grinding hard work.'

Henry said: 'You make one sound just as bad as the other.'

'They *are*, Henry, and that's the whole goddamned point! The only thing that isn't quite so bad is sitting here, comfortable and rich, and telling all those poor bastards what to do, and even *this* can be hell. Life is an accident, Henry. An accident! A serious accident in which people really die. The only morality of the Robinstown deal is that it's not as bad an accident as it could have been. And *that's* the point.'

The two men sat and stared at each other in the curious half-darkness of the cabin. Then the lights flickered on – a pair of bronze lamps in the shape of Olympic torches – and the pilot called back from the cockpit: 'Some pretty rough weather up ahead, sir! I suggest you stay in your seats!'

Johann leaned over and peered out of the airplane's windows. The sky outside was that odd green-black colour that gun barrels go when they've been rubbed too slowly with charcoal. Rain was rapping against the glass, and outside the motors sounded as if they were groaning and grating their way through a mixture of cornmeal and broken glass.

The Tri-Motor swayed, and dropped fifty or sixty feet to starboard. A bevy of pens rolled off Johann's desk and scattered on the floor. The motors strained and pulled, and the plane was buffeted from side to side by an angry, cross-tempered gale.

Johann gripped the arms of his chair firmly. '*Lester*!' he called.

The black man appeared from his seat at the back. He was obviously frightened, but he was doing his best not to show it. Nobody showed emotion in front of Johann, not even his own children.

'Yes, sir?'

'Lester, pull the drapes. I don't want to look out of the windows just now, and neither does Mr Keith.'

'Right away, sir.'

He went around the swaying cabin, holding on to the brass handrails on each side, and drew the small brown velvet curtains. Soon – except for the pitching and tossing and the grinding drone of the motors – they could have been sitting in a small office anyplace at all.

It took them twenty minutes to battle their way through the storm, and they only cleared the last of the heavy clouds as they made their descent toward Lynwood's Island. Henry Keith was very white, and hadn't said a single word during the whole experience. To him, it was oppressively claustrophobic to fly with the airplane's curtains closed, as if he was being forced to run blindfolded through a strange city, in the pouring rain. But Johann had simply bent over his desk and continued to check column after column of figures, until he was satisfied that the stock negotiations were ready.

The Ford Tri-Motor, with its marker lights blinking, moaned across a calm night sky, pale with clouds, toward the gleaming Hudson. Close in to the west shore, thickly forested, was the dark pear shape of Lynwood's Island, and as they circled around it, Henry Keith could make out the white square cottage and the ornamental gardens.

On the ground, a row of white lights was switched on to show the pilot where to land, and he turned into the wind again to bring the airplane down. They bumped hard onto the turf, bumped again, and then they were trundling quickly past the end of the long gardens and toward the trees. The motors popped once or twice, and then stopped.

Johann rose stiffly from his seat and stretched his back while Lester brought his hat and coat. Henry Keith was busy gathering up papers.

'Henry,' said Johann, as his secretary went forward to talk to the pilot.

'Yes, sir?'

'Henry, you must never confuse morality with fate. One has nothing to do with the other, and if you understand that, then you may stop being frightened when you fly.'

Henry blinked. Then, for the sake of settling the whole discussion, he said: 'Yes, sir. I see. I'll remember that,' and went through the curtains to check how much fuel the homeward trip had cost them. It was probably just as well he went quickly, because he didn't see Johann Cornelius grin.

Hester had heard the airplane circling around the island from the sewing room. She lifted her head for a moment to make sure it was Johann, and not a mail plane or one of those people on their way to Pocantico, but then she carried on with her embroidery with the small smile of a wealthy Protestant wife who knows that her husband is about his business as he should be, and that all is in domestic equilibrium.

Hester didn't particularly care for embroidery, but the fact that she didn't care for it made her needlecraft into a kind of decorative self-imposed penance. At the moment, she was sewing an elaborate pillow cover in a traditional pattern of roses and leaves and forget-me-nots. She spent very little time on her own, except for her hour of sewing in the white oval sewing room, and somehow she felt it was important to undertake some task that was both difficult and dislikeable.

Her age may have had something to do with it. She would be thirty-six in August, and she had been married to Johann for sixteen very uneven years.

As she heard the Ford Tri-Motor land, she laid down her embroidery and rang a small silver bell. Her personal maid, Marise, a quiet and rather sophisticated young French girl with a bun in her hair and lips that Johann always called 'cupid's cushions', came into the room. She was dressed in grey, like most of their staff, with white lace collar and cuffs.

Hester, sitting on her Sheraton sewing chair, said: 'You've been smoking.'

'*Pardonnez-moi, madame*?'

'You heard, Marise, quite clearly. You've been smoking and I can smell it from here. How many times do I have to tell you that young ladies do not smoke, and that I forbid it?'

Marise bustled across the room to help her mistress clear away the silks and the needles.

'I apologize, madame.'

'You will do more than apologize. You will promise me, upon your oath, never to do it again.'

282

Marise closed the sewing basket with its gilded clasps and put it away. 'Yes, madame, I promise upon my oath'

Hester stood up. Because she was only five-feet-two, she looked quite diminutive next to Marise, like a wind-up doll on a souvenir jewellery box. She was wearing a pale lemon afternoon dress, with long silk fringes, and strings of perfect Indonesian pearls. She said: 'You have probably heard the airplane.'

'Yes, madame.'

'I will say hello to Mr Cornelius in the morning room, and then I will dress for dinner. I shall wear my oyster dress, I expect, and I want the peacock brooch and the diamond bracelets I wore last month at Newport.'

'Very well, madame. I shall have them laid out.'

'Good. Is Stainer around?'

'I think he brings brandy for Mr Cornelius.'

'Oh. Well, when he's done that, tell him to set dinner in the garden room.'

'Very well, madame.'

Hester left the sewing room and walked across the square central hallway, her yellow shoes tapping on the polished mosaic, and went into the morning room. It was high and rectangular, this room, with a view from its tall ranks of windows down the long slope of the garden to the Hudson. At night, its rich russet drapes were drawn, and if it was cold, a log fire was built up in the formal steel Victorian fireplace, as it had been tonight. The walls were the colour of pale spring primroses, and the floor was polished herringbone parquet, with antique Indian rugs. There were Early American paintings of Iroquois settlements and Puritan villages around the walls, as well as two Cubist pictures of guitars by Georges Braque.

Hester sat by the fire in a small crinoline chair. The butler, Stainer, had left Johann's usual silver tray of Napoleon brandy ready for his arrival, along with ice and soda.

After a few minutes, she heard voices in the hall, and the door was opened. Johann came in, laughing about the storm they had flown through, and ribbing Henry Keith for his fright; and Henry himself followed afterward, looking bilious and ready for bed.

'How are you, my dear?' asked Johann. He came across,

leaned over like a toppling redwood, and kissed her. She kissed him politely back.

'We hit an electric storm just a while back, and poor Henry was getting himself ready to meet his Maker!'

Hester raised an eyebrow. 'I suppose we should all be ready to meet our Maker, at any time.'

'Henry isn't!' Johann laughed. 'Henry has a great deal to confess before he's ready for the pearly gates!'

'Johann,' admonished Hester. 'Remember that Henry is your secretary.'

Johann sat down. Suddenly the burst of humour and enthusiasm seemed to leave him, and he said nothing more for a while. Henry, embarrassed, sat himself down in the most uncomfortable chair in the room, and gave Hester a short series of weak smiles. She was used to it. Because she was very pretty, and because she was so much younger than Johann, the men who had to work for the Cornelius empire would often turn to Hester for sympathy and help. It was only when they had spilled out their hearts to her, as most of them eventually did, that they realized she was almost as hard-shelled, in her own way, as Johann was. She never betrayed their confidences, not even to Johann, but then she never betrayed her husband, either.

Johann unlaced his black Peal's oxfords. It was a habit of his that Hester deplored, but she allowed him to do it when he'd been working particularly hard. Stainer, the English butler, an infinitely mournful man with silver side whiskers and blotchy red cheeks, came squeaking in on evening pumps to pour his drink.

'I omitted to tell you, sir, that a Mr Lindbergh telephoned, and requested that you telephone him back.'

'What did he want?'

'I had the impression, sir, that he was seeking funds for some scheme of aviation, but further than that I could not say.'

Johann took his brandy and sipped it.

'I must say I think I've heard of Lindbergh,' he said. 'But I'm damned if I can remember why.'

Henry said: 'Do you want me to call him, sir?'

Johann shook his head. 'Right now I want to get this Robinstown deal sorted out. It worries me.'

Hester said: 'I thought Robinstown was all arranged

'It was supposed to be,' answered Johann, leaning back on the big velvet-covered Chesterfield. 'All the right pressures have been applied on all the right people. All the proper palms have been greased. But I get the feeling that somebody's being awkward, and I get the feeling that they're being awkward for their own personal reasons.'

Henry shrugged. 'We could easily find out who it is. All we have to do is check with Grossmith.'

Johann said: 'I don't want to do that unless I can help it. What I really want to know is the real truth about TransMechanic.'

'I could find out now for you, sir. It would only take a call to the office.'

Johann thought about that, and then nodded. 'All right, Henry, that's a good idea. Tell them to track every proxy as far back as they can. I don't particularly want to take any action until I know who I'm up against.'

'Very good, sir.'

Henry seemed to be glad of the opportunity to slip out and leave Johann and Hester alone.

'Did I tell you that John's at home?' asked Hester.

'He's *home*?' said Johann, surprised. 'What's he done now – played hooky from school?'

'They've had Spanish influenza. One junior boy has died of it, apparently, and they've sent the rest of them home for the term.'

Johann sipped some more brandy. 'But what's he going to do? He can't slope around here for six months. How about some private tutors?'

Hester said quietly: 'I thought you could handle that.'

'Handle what?'

'A little private tutoring. Take him around with you – show him how you work. He's got to see you in action someday. Why not now? I think it's a golden opportunity.'

'I think the school needs to be sued bankrupt.'

Hester stood up and walked across to the window. She parted the drapes and looked out at the dark garden and the distant glitter of the Hudson River Her own pale reflection was superimposed on the night like a ghost seeking admission to the real world.

'He'd adore it, you know,' she said coaxingly

Johann sipped brandy and pulled a face.

285

'You've no idea how much he respects you,' she added. 'He defends you to the death, even when they're teasing him at school.'

'Why should they tease him at school?'

'Well, of course they do. He's John Cornelius isn't he? He's rich and famous, and his father's well-known as a financial tyrant'

Johann smirked

Hester came across and sat beside him, perched on the edge of the Chesterfield. She thought that Johann was looking very tired and much older, but at the same time she wanted him to know the truth.

'You can't be a whole man, Jo, unless you take some time out for your children. Your business won't be a whole business, either, because when they're old enough they should come into Cornelius Oil and help you. If you don't have time for them now, if you don't show them the ropes, you'll have to spend three times as much time with them later.'

Johann fixed an eye on her. 'They're *my* sons,' he said. 'They've got *my* brains, and *my* strength. *I* managed to make a fortune without any help from my father. Why should *I* mollycoddle *them*?'

'Oh, Johann, I'm not talking about mollycoddling. But times have changed. Nobody can make big fortunes now the way that you did. There isn't the land, and there isn't the oil, and apart from that, there isn't the legal opportunity. You know that.'

Johann stared at the fire. 'I remember what happened the year we got married. The Supreme Court dissolved Standard Oil New Jersey. But I don't remember anyone saying then or ever that it was illegal to go on making money. John and Roderick will make money, don't you worry about that, and they won't need their father holding their hands, either.'

Hester said: 'You're wrong, Johann. Have you talked to them lately?'

'Of course not. They've been at school.'

'Well, it's about time you did,' said Hester. 'I mean it, Johann. You're assuming all kinds of things about them without even knowing what they're really like.'

Johann blinked in surprise. 'But they're like *me*!'

Hester shook her head. 'They're not entirely like you. Not as much as you seem to think they are. Roderick, for instance, doesn't have half of your strength, and he'll never be ruthless as long as he lives. John's got a bit more energy than Roderick, but he's not a business fanatic. He likes swimming and riding and things like that, and books, too. As for Hope – well, Hope's a handful. I can't imagine what she's going to be like when she's older.'

Johann said: 'Hester, why are you telling me this? It's going to be *years* before those children are ready to understand business.'

Hester twisted her pearls around, and said nothing.

Johann said: 'I come home, and suddenly everyone's accusing me of being a bad father. I mean – why?'

'Because it's got to be said sometime, and because I've been talking to John this afternoon. You just don't realize, do you? He wants to get to know his father, he wants to understand you, he wants to be close to you. You're so remote to him, Johann. You're a mysterious stranger who sometimes asks him how his schoolwork is going, and that's all.'

Johann thought for a moment. The clock above the steel fireplace chimed seven, very prettily.

Hester said: 'Go and talk to him, Johann. Now, before dinner. Just give him a chance to know that you care.'

Johann looked up. 'All right,' he said quietly. 'If you think it's necessary.' He drained his brandy glass and set it back on the tray, and then he silently and thoughtfully tied his shoelaces up again.

John was upstairs in the children's library, reading a book about famous automobile races. He was a short little boy of ten years old, with a brown corduroy buster suit and very close-cropped hair. When Johann walked in, he immediately jumped up and said: 'Oh! Good evening, sir!'

Johann said: 'Hello, John,' and spent a few moments pacing around the library and peering at some of the books on the shelves. John stood there rigidly, licking his lips in apprehension, while Johann picked up the illustrated volume he had just been reading.

'Automobiles, huh? You like automobiles?'

'Yes, sir. I do.'

287

'Hmm,' said Johann, 'I see.

Johann paced some more, and then he sat himself down on the edge of Hope's old school desk.

'Sit down, John.'

John, a little uncertainly, sat down.

Johann coughed. He gazed for a while at this odd little boy in his brown breeches, and he wondered what in the world he was going to say to him. The strangest thing of all was that Hester had assured him that this boy, his own son, wasn't even like him at all, but a completely new and individual person. In a funny kind of way, that struck him as rather ungrateful of John, and lacking in respect.

'Your mother and I thought we should have a talk together, you and I,' said Johann. His voice seemed to stick, and he cleared his throat. 'Your mother seems to think that you'd like to get to know me a little more, and maybe find out what it is that I do for my living.'

'Yes, sir,' answered John in a very small voice.

'What did you say?' asked Johann.

'Yes, sir. I would like to.'

Johann reached forward and awkwardly patted John on his bristly head.

'Do you like school?' he asked.

'Yes, sir.'

'And what's your best subject?'

'Singing, sir.'

Johann nodded, and then frowned. 'Singing?'

'Yes, sir. I came top.'

'You came top in singing?'

'Yes, sir.'

Johann blew out a loud brandy-flavoured breath. 'Well, John, I suppose that's something. But, tell me. What do you think is the *use* of singing?'

John lowered his eyes. Two crescents of dark eyelashes on two pale cheeks.

'I don't know, sir.'

'You don't know? You made the effort to come top in something, and you don't know what use it is?'

'Yes, sir.'

Johann got up from the school desk and paced about the library a little more. He hadn't been into this room for two or three years, and he felt uncomfortable, as if he had

288

trespassed. But this business with the children, what Hester had said, had irked him. He felt he had to carry out some fatherly commission, but he wasn't entirely sure what it was, and whatever it was, it was bound to be irritating. He scratched his scalp.

'John,' he said, in his gentlest voice, 'it's a big hard world out there.'

John bit his lip and nodded, glancing out of the darkened library window as if he expected to see actual fighting on the lawns.

'It's a big hard world and you have to be prepared for it. You have to be *strong*. You have to know your field. That's the only way you're going to survive. Do you understand me? You have to be tough!'

'Yes, sir.'

Johann stared at the boy for a while, and then he said 'How's your math? Is it good?'

John dropped his eyes again. 'Quite good, sir.'

'How good is quite good? What position in the class?'

'Tenth, sir.'

'And how many boys in the class?'

'Ten, sir.'

Johann didn't answer at first, but began to tap his foot on the floor. Why was this boy so dumb? He came from a clever mother, and a financial genius of a father, so why did he act so dumb? Johann recognized that he was beginning to grow angry, and he had to make an effort to parcel up his anger and put it aside, at least for the moment.

'Tenth out of ten isn't "quite good," John,' he said quietly. 'It's disastrous. Don't you think so?'

'Yes, sir.'

'Well, if you're no good at math, what are you good at? Apart from singing? There must be some talent in that thick little skull of yours, surely?'

'Composition, sir.'

'You mean writing? You're good at writing?'

'Yes, sir. I came second in composition with two gold stars.'

'Well, that's something. What kind of things do you write?'

'I wrote "My Father", sir. We all did.'

Johann bent his head toward the boy for the first time.
'You wrote a composition about me?'

'We all did, sir. It was "My Father." '

'Could I see it?'

John looked up at him.

'Please, John, could I see it?'

Without a word, John went over to a small brown leather suitcase and opened it up. He handed a sheet of lined paper to his father, and then stood there and watched his father's eyes flicker over the few lines of round, pencilled script.

It read:

My father is very rich and is the Cornelius Oil billionair. He is very old and does not have much hair. I like it when he goes away because my mother lets us have dinner in the garden room and sometimes eat squob. My father is stric and we have to do what he says. I would like to buy him a nice wig for his birthday because even though he is stric I do love him because he is my father. He has an airplan called the Ford Tri-Motor.

Johann read the composition twice. Then he laid it carefully on the edge of John's writing desk, and stared at it for several silent minutes. John stood with his hands behind his back, waiting expectantly for his father's comments. It seemed as if, somehow, time had arrested itself, and Johann was unable to move.

Johann swallowed, and then said stiffly: 'Did you mean this?'

John didn't quite understand him, but nodded.

Johann turned away. He didn't know why the composition made him feel so disturbed. He took out his handkerchief and blew his nose, and for the first time in years he felt as if he was going to cry.

John said: 'Do you like it, sir? When I wrote about not much hair, I didn't mean—'

Johann shook his head. In a hoarse voice he said: 'I like it. I want you to write some more, when you have the time. Get to be the best in your class.'

He ruffled his son's hair with his big hand, and then he

290

turned around without another word and closed the library door behind him.

Henry Keith was waiting for him in the hall.

He said: 'Mr Cornelius? It was easier than I thought it was going to be.'

Johann, still preoccupied with John's composition, stared at Henry as if he was a time-traveller who had suddenly materialized from another century.

'What? What was easier?'

'Tracing the stock proxies, sir. I got the office onto it right away, and they had a stroke of luck.'

'Well?'

Henry consulted a long list of names. 'A great many of the TransMechanic stockholders are small private concerns with excellent *bona fides*. But the controlling interest, and *ipso facto* the controlling influence in the P&P Railroad, is a corporation from Delaware called BM Industries.'

'Oh, yes?'

'BM Industries is under the personal control of a man called Daniel Forster.'

Johann stopped in mid-step, his hand poised to open the morning-room door handle, his mouth half-open as if to speak. It was like a spell, the name 'Daniel Forster' – a spell that could paralyse a man where he stood.

Johann turned around. His voice was very thick, like surf through gravel on the beach. 'Are you sure about that?'

Henry looked worried. 'Well, yes, sir Of course We've been through fifteen different . . .'

Johann's eyes dropped slowly toward the mosaic floor. He obviously wasn't listening to a single word.

Henry said: 'Mr Cornelius? Is there anything   ?'

Johann shook his head. 'No,' he said roughly 'There's nothing wrong. Why don't you go get yourself something to eat now? I want to speak to my wife.'

Three days later, in Robinstown, Grover Bean left his red-painted house soon after breakfast and decided to walk down the wide sloping meadow that fell toward the Asquahanna River and check on his young Freisian. The weather was a little colder now, and he wore a thick overcoat of green speckled tweed and a knitted scarf The sun was just up over the Rabbit Ridge, falling through the trees in long shafts of light, and Grover's breath smoked as he trudged through the grass.

There was a muddy track that curved up toward Grover's house from his main gate above Robinstown, and when Grover walked along the highest ground he could see most of it, and almost down to the Asquahanna besides. The birds were cheeping and chirping in the branches, and high above his head the cirrus clouds were lazily trailing their white hair in the sky. Grover whistled as he went, an off-key repetitive whistling that echoed from the ash groves.

It was quite by accident that he saw George Purvis's car. He was beginning to descend the slope now, and he might have missed seeing it altogether if a rabbit hadn't scampered out of the grass, and Grover Bean hadn't climbed onto the higher ground again to see where the rabbit might have sprung from. The rising sun glinted from the flat windshield of George Purvis's old Briscoe, and Grover paused and squinted downhill to where the car was parked – strangely askew and with its offside door hanging open.

He jogged as fast as he could through the tangled grass until he reached the track. He couldn't see inside the car because the sun was shining off the glass, but when he came close he realized that George Purvis was still in the driving seat. He stepped up nearer and said, 'George?'

The morning was very quiet and still. His feet crunched on the rough cinders that he'd put down in the winter to help his flivver through the mud. When he reached the car door he saw that there was blood on the cracked leather seats, and that it was dripping from the car and forming a rusty pool on the road.

He didn't want to look at George Purvis, even in death. He walked quickly and stiffly down to Martin Levon's store and telephoned the sheriff of Asquahanna County from there. Martin Levon stood by the phone while he made his call, wiping his floury hands on a cloth and staring at Grover Bean in silent stupefaction.

Eventually, Grover hung up.

'Is he coming up here?' said Martin, awed. 'The sheriff, I mean?'

'He has to,' said Grover. 'He said it would take him a

292

good hour, and we weren't to touch nothing at all in the meanwhile.'

'I wasn't planning to,' said Martin. 'I can't abide the sight of human blood.'

'Well, me neither.'

Grover stepped out onto the front boardwalk and took a deep breath of cold morning air. Martin followed him, still wiping his hands.

'Who d'you reckon could have done it?' asked Martin. 'You don't reckon it was them dye works people, do you? Just because he wouldn't say he liked it?'

Grover gripped the rail of the boardwalk and stared down at the muddy street.

'I don't know, Martin. I'm beginning to wish I never signed that land away. It seems to have brought more trouble than it was ever worth.'

Martin sniffed. 'Well, you can say that,' he said. 'And the trouble with trouble, as my old grandfather used to say, is that it begets more trouble.'

Grover looked across at him oddly. 'I remember your grandfather,' he said, as if it were suddenly and terribly significant.

Daniel Forster was washing his hands in the men's room of the Harvard Club on West Forty-fourth Street in New York City when Walter Grossmith, class of 1907, walked in. Grossmith took the next basin to Forster, and proceeded to hang up his coat and remove his cuff links. Their reflections faced each other side by side in the mirrors above the faucets, two smooth-faced and successful men who were approaching middle age with the assurance of comfortable incomes and society friends.

Grossmith filled up his basin and began to wash his hands. As he soaped them, he began to glance at Forster from time to time as if he recognized him. Then he said: 'Excuse me, sir, but don't I know you?'

Forster was dabbing his face with a towel. He paused, and looked at Grossmith with the usual cautious expression that people with hundreds of friends and acquaintances reserve for faces they can't quite place.

'I know,' said Grossmith, as if a divine light had illumi-

293

nated his memory. 'You're Dan Forster, the railroad man! Correct me if I'm not one hundred percent right!'

'Yes,' said Forster, still a little baffled. 'You're absolutely right.'

'I'm Walter Grossmith,' said Walter Grossmith. 'These days I work for the Department of Commerce. Excuse me if I don't shake hands.'

'Pleased to know you,' said Daniel Forster.

'You know something,' went on Grossmith conversationally, 'I never even realized what it took to run a railroad until I went on a tour of the Union Pacific sheds, and then I was absolutely amazed. I saw the whole shebang – the boilers cleaned out, the schedules made up. It was real interesting stuff.'

'Yes,' said Forster, as the washroom attendant helped him on with his coat. 'It's very interesting, isn't it?'

'Mind you,' continued Grossmith, 'I don't suppose you see much of that kind of thing in your job, do you? I guess you're mostly a desk driver, right?'

Forster brushed his hair, and then laid down the brushes.

'That's right,' he said. 'I have other interests as well.'

'My grandfather was a railroad man, way back in the seventies. He used to sit me right down on his knee and tell me about the times they had to slow down to hardly any speed at all, because the tracks were thick with buffalo.'

Forster was ready to leave now, and he looked impatiently at his pocket watch.

'Did you ever know that August Busch had Busch beer piped into every room of his private railroad car?' said Grossmith, lavishly rubbing suds between his fingers. 'Now, that's the kind of railroad style that seems to have died out these days, don't you think? Whatever happened to the old private railroad cars like they used to have in the nineties?'

Forster shrugged. 'There are still one or two of them around. And you can always rent a private car from Pullman.'

'That's very interesting,' said Grossmith. 'Now, what would a thing like that cost?'

'Well, that's very hard to say,' said Forster testily. 'You have to pay the rental plus eighteen first-class railroad fares. It depends on how far you want to go, and how you want to travel. Now, if you'll excuse me—'

'I wasn't thinking of travelling anyplace special,' interrupted Grossmith. 'I just wondered if such things were still possible.'

Daniel Forster looked at his watch again. 'Yes, quite possible,' he said. 'Now I really must go.'

Walter Grossmith, his hands rinsed and dripping, turned around to face him. For some reason, Forster paused again. There was some quality about Grossmith that caught his attention; something curiously unnatural, as if Grossmith was talking and working to some prearranged plan. Dan Forster had always been sensitive to atmosphere, and it had helped him more than once, like the time he had walked into a railroad board meeting and *known* instinctively that there was a heavy power play in the air. It was an instinct which had been sharpened by his constant awareness that Johann Cornelius was always some place behind him, and could always take back what he had once handed out, with interest.

Forster was thirty-three; a tall and cultured man with a tendency to leanness and the arch inflections of a Southern accent. He had a roundish, intelligent face, and clear blue eyes which reminded his wife, Betty, of Tom Mix. Despite his neat dark business suit and his crisp white turn-down collar, and despite the sheen of a barbershop shave, many of Dan Forster's friends felt that he would have looked better on a horse, in a tall white hat.

'Mr Grossmith,' he said, 'it's been a pleasure to meet you, but I have business associates here for luncheon, and I really have to leave. Maybe we can talk about railroads some other time, if you come here regular.'

Walter Grossmith dried his hands. He was a short, fortyish man with bright yellow suspenders and a bulky, big-nosed, funny-papers face like Huey Long's. He said: 'Okay,' quite affably, but then he said: 'Will you do me one favour?'

'What's that?'

'Will you just tell me what you think about railroad rebates for coal transportation?'

Daniel Forster looked confused. '*Coal* transportation? Any *particular* coal transportation? I mean, rebates are possible

295

for heavy freight users. That's been a regular deal with Standard Oil and other corporations for years. But you'd have to talk to one of our freight managers about that.'

Walter Grossmith put on his coat, brushed his short curly hair, and stepped out of the washroom into the club's lobby with his arm interlinked with Daniel Forster's like an old buddy. Forster was too polite to pull away, but he looked around him in embarrassment, particularly when he saw two or three of his friends coming in off the street.

'It's really the *principle* that concerns me more than anything,' said Grossmith. 'Why should some users be given preferential rates while others are squeezed out?'

'I don't know, without having the details in front of me,' said Forster, flustered. 'Listen, you really must—'

. 'Oh! Look who's here!' said Grossmith brightly, as a small man with a striped suit and a neat moustache came in through the door and crossed the dingy carpet. 'If it isn't my old friend!'

Walter Grossmith released Forster's arm and put out his hand. The small man twinkled his eyes and said: 'Hi, Walter,' and they shook hands. Then Walter said: 'This is Dan Forster. You know Dan Forster, the railroad man?' and the small man shook hands with Dan Forster.

At the moment Dan Forster gripped the small man's hands, and at the split second that his smile was at its widest and most welcoming, a man who had been standing in the darkest corner of the lobby, apparently waiting for a friend, lifted an Eastman camera out of the folds of his overcoat and took a flash picture. He then walked quickly out of the club and disappeared into the street.

'What the hell was that?' snapped Dan Forster. 'What the hell's going on here?'

Walter Grossmith stepped forward again. The small man seemed to have disappeared as magically as the cameraman. He took Forster's arm once more, and said in a low voice: 'We're very sorry about this, but it seems you've made a pretty silly kind of mistake.'

'Mistake? What mistake? Listen – what is this?'

'Calm down, Mr Forster. There's no point in losing your temper.'

'What the hell are you talking about? You can't come in

here and take pictures of people without their permission! I'll have you tossed out of here and blackballed!'

Walter Grossmith hushed him down. 'Mr Forster, please. It wasn't *me* who took the picture, now, was it? Just calm down.'

Daniel Forster gripped Grossmith's lapel and held him close. Several other members turned around to watch, and there was a disturbed murmur of conversation in the background.

Forster whispered: 'Unless you tell me what's going on here, I'll tear your head off. I mean that. Now, talk.'

Grossmith didn't even look up at him. 'It's very simple, Mr Forster. You've made a bad mistake. You remember the old Crédit Mobilier scandal on the Union Pacific? Well, it's at least as bad as that. I'd say it was almost twice as bad as that.'

Forster's round face was bright crimson with anger and confusion. He said: 'Who *was* that? That friend of yours? Who *was* it?'

'Friend of mine?' said Grossmith. 'I don't know what you're talking about. I never saw the fellow before in my whole life, except in the newspapers.'

'You shook his hand! That's the only reason *I* did!'

Grossmith gently eased Forster's fingers away from his lapel. 'No, Mr Forster, I think you're mistaken. *I* didn't shake his hand. Why should I shake the hand of a man like that? I'm an influential man. I have my reputation to think of. I can't be seen shaking the hands of men like that, particularly in a place like this. Why, what would people say?'

Forster took a deep breath. Then he said: 'Very well. It's all beginning to fit into place. Just tell me who it was so that I know what I'm up against.'

Grossmith took his arm again and led him toward the club room. A couple of friends passed by and said: 'Hi, there, Dan!' and Daniel Forster had to give them a tight smile and a nod.

'This can be very painless if you take it nice and gentle and see things real reasonable,' said Walter Grossmith.

'I'm listening,' Daniel Forster told him tersely.

'Well,' said Walter Grossmith, 'it appears that you've

been kicking up some dust with the P&P Railroad over the Kruyper Dye Works out at Robinstown, Pennsylvania.'

Forster stopped walking and stared at Grossmith with his intense blue eyes. He knew what was coming next; it was as plain and obvious as a P&P locomotive coming around a Pennsylvania curve, and there was nothing at all he could do to step out of the way.

Grossmith said: 'It would be kind of appreciated in some circles if you had a quiet word with the P&P freight people and told them to think about a rebate for Kruyper's product. After all, we don't want to hamper good old United States commerce, do we? And we don't want to stand in the path of progress.'

Forster said: 'Is that all?'

Grossmith grinned benignly. 'It would be pretty pleasant if it were, wouldn't it? But I'm afraid there's something else. All of a sudden, you feel like disposing of some TransMechanic stock, just because it makes sense these days to allot the right shares to the right trust, and you feel like doing it at giveaway prices.'

'And what if I *don't* feel like doing it?'

Grossmith chuckled. 'Mr Forster, you're a vulnerable man! The New York papers would have a real ball with that picture of you, particularly when they read the captions that go along with it.'

'What captions?'

'The captions that say: "Pennsylvania Railroad Owner in Cahoots with Mobster." '

Forster pulled out a club chair and sat down. A waiter came over and said: 'Would you like to order, sir?'

Forster said: 'I'll have a sidecar. This gentleman isn't staying.'

Grossmith waved his hand. 'Of course I'm staying. Make that two.'

Eventually Forster said: 'All right, Grossmith. What mobster?'

Walter Grossmith leaned back and reached in his pocket for a cigarette. He made a big fuss of lighting it and puffing out smoke before he answered.

'That little fellow you seemed to be so friendly with in the lobby was Jackie Morello, who is not a particularly enormous mobster in his own right, but is recognized by all and sundry, and particularly by the New York Police Department, as a close business associate of Frank Gizzi. Gizzi – as you're well aware – was unfortunately involved in that business of corrupting officials of the Baugh-Menominee Freight Corporation to transport illegal liquor across the state line.'

Forster, staring dully at the floor, said: 'Go on.'

Grossmith tapped his cigarette in the ashtray. 'There isn't much more to say, is there? Mr Cornelius recognizes that he is beholden to you from way back, but Mr Cornelius also feels that he has done you proud and given you everything you ever asked him for, and any further attempts on your part to interfere with his life or his business will not be taken particularly kindly. My personal advice to you is that you should go about your business, forget this has ever occurred, and live a long and happy life. Are you married?'

'Yes,' said Daniel Forster. 'Two children.'

'That's very nice,' said Grossmith. 'I'm always glad to do business with family men, because they're so amenable.'

'Is that a threat?' snapped Forster. 'By God, if you threaten me—'

Walter Grossmith laid a soothing hand on Forster's arm. 'You've been paid your price, Mr Forster. Don't think you're going to improve on it, because you're not. Everybody has their limit, and when you started playing coy with the P&P Railroad, that's when Mr Cornelius reached his. Now, please. Let's just talk about railroads, and forget about all this unpleasantness, shall we?'

Daniel Forster stood up. He tugged down his vest, and stared at Walter Grossmith as if he were the devil, or at least a fairly prominent demon.

'I'll be damned if I'll ever speak another word to you, Grossmith. And I'll be damned if I don't see that you get what you deserve, one day, whenever it is, and however it's done.'

Grossmith smiled, and shrugged. 'If nothing else,' he said, 'I think I deserve a medal for tact.'

1934

DAVID BOOKBINDER TO
CORNELIUS OIL AFTER
COLTON FURORE

Mr David Bookbinder, chief legal executive for Colton Oil up until the shareholders' meeting débâcle two weeks ago, has taken his Golden Smile to Cornelius Oil, where Mr Johann Cornelius is reported to be 'more than happy' with his new associate. Informed sources say that Bookbinder, 47, a onetime legal eagle for Cullings Maidment Sparks, has a substantial share of Cornelius stock, and a salary that should keep him in law books for at least three centuries.

–New York Daily Post,
August 17, 1934

Later that year, Dutch Schultz, who had been a fugitive from justice since January 25, 1933, was to walk into the office of United States Commissioner Lester T. Hubbard at Albany to surrender himself. It was not to be revealed in the publicity statements that he had been driven to Albany from Lynwood's Island in Johann Cornelius' own Rolls-Royce; nor was it revealed where Schultz had been hiding so successfully for almost two years.

It was the twilight of the Prohibition era and of all the gangsters and racketeers who had thrived on it. In less than a year, federal agents had shot to death John Dillinger, Pretty Boy Floyd, Homer van Meter, and half a dozen lesser public enemies; and on the day that Schultz surrendered, Lester M. Gillis (better known as Baby Face Nelson) was to be found lying dead in a ditch at Niles Center, Chicago, with seventeen bullet wounds sustained the previous night in what the newspapers called 'a sanguinary encounter.'

The changing mood was probably no better illustrated than by Commissioner Hubbard, who didn't recognize Schultz when he came to give himself up, and had to have his memory refreshed on Schultz's case by his attorney. Nineteen thirty-three had been more than a year away; it had been a whole era away. This was 1934.

It was a year that opened with Mae West in *I'm No Angel* and Katharine Hepburn in *Little Women*. It was a year when trolley cars gave way to motor buses on nine New York City lines, including Madison, Fourth, and Lex. Mrs Anna Antonio, a twenty-eight-year-old mother of three who had murdered her husband for his $5,000 insurance, was executed in the electric chair at Sing Sing. She said: 'I'm not afraid to die.' It was a year that began with a savage winter in New York, and then saw temperatures rise to 117 degrees in Oklahoma, with thousands left homeless and destitute in the blizzards of dust that swept the West. John Jacob Astor married Ellen French, fifty strikers were wounded by police bullets in Minneapolis, and President Roosevelt went looking for swordfish in Hawaii. In Louisiana, the Kingfish, Huey Long, was joking that he'd bought himself a silk shirt with a collar so high he had to stand on a stump to spit, and on Wednesday, May 23, a warm and fair day in that same verdant state, Texas Rangers and sheriff's deputies ambushed Clyde Barrow and Bonnie Parker outside of Gibsland and reduced them, according to eyewitnesses, to a 'smear of red, wet rags.'

That same day, forty or so miles to the west, in Shreveport, Johann Cornelius was standing in the burned-out ruins of the first Cornelius Oil gas station on Jewella Road. The ashes smudged his brown-and-white two-tone shoes, and dirtied the cuffs of his cream linen pants, but he stood there stolidly with his hands deep in his coat pockets, his eyes shaded by his panama hat, staring at the charred timbers and the twisted metal framework, and he looked immovable. Not too far away, on the black-streaked sidewalk, Henry Keith talked to the city fire marshal, but both of them treated Johann's grief as something personal, and made no move toward him until he called them.

The sky was almost cloudless, except for a few smoky puffs of cumulus over Cross Lake, and even though it was only half after eleven in the morning, everyone could tell that it was going to be another roastingly hot day. Leaves of a scorched ledger peeled away one by one from their burned binding and fluttered across the street.

After a while Johann said: 'Henry.'

He said it softly, but Henry heard him at once. He came across the smuts and the ashes on tippy-toes, and stood beside his employer, holding his pants legs a couple of inches off the ground.

'You wet yourself?' asked Johann.

Henry Keith blushed. 'No, sir.'

'Then don't stand there looking as though you have. If you need a quarter to have your pants cleaned afterward, I'll lend it to you.'

Henry Keith let the cuffs of his pants drop. 'Thank you, sir.'

Johann crunched a few paces over the wreckage.

'Well, Henry, who do you think it was?'

'*Who*, sir? I don't understand.'

Johann waved his hand impatiently. 'Who lit the torch, or threw the bomb, or whatever it was that razed this place to the ground?'

'You think it was arson, sir?'

'Well, don't you?'

Henry Keith looked uncomfortably around. 'I'm not sure, sir.'

Johann shook his head slowly. There was a sooty smudge on his cheek.

'This gas station burned because somebody wanted it to burn, Henry. It burned because there's somebody around who wants to see our retail gas sales go to the wall. Somebody who wants to keep the gas market to themselves.'

'You really think that, sir?'

'I wouldn't say it if I didn't really think it. Jesus Christ, Henry, if I was in their position I'd probably do the same thing.'

Henry Keith shook ashes from his foot and looked unhappy. 'I could always get some detectives onto it, sir.'

Johann eyed his aide from the shadow of his hat. 'Detectives won't help us. We need someone clever. Someone who knows the gas-station market better than us. I feel too much like an innocent in Paradise.'

'Oh, I wouldn't say that, sir.'

'Well, that's because you're prone to attacks of dumbness, that's why. The only way to get on top is to admit to yourself what you don't know, and I don't know this gas-station business any better than I know the length of a piece of string.'

At that moment, the city fire marshal came striding toward them in his big yellow rubbers. He had a scorched, weathered look to his face, and a bristly moustache.

'Mr Cornelius, sir?'

Johann nodded.

'We've, uh, sifted through most of the wreckage now, sir.'

'And what have you found?'

'Well, there ain't no evidence in favour of arson, sir, but on the other hand, there ain't no evidence against it, neither.'

'I see. Well, that's good enough for me.

'You mean you believe it was done deliberate?'

Johann prodded at the black ruins with his foot. 'The moment I heard what had happened, I knew it was done deliberately. The only question remaining in my mind is who did it.'

The fire marshal took off his helmet and wiped his forehead with the back of his hand. 'Can you think of anyone who don't like you too much?' he asked, trying to be helpful.

Johann almost laughed. 'Hundreds,' he said in a husky, amused voice.

The fire marshal stood there for a while longer, nodded and sniffed, and then went back to his new red-painted Plymouth PE DeLuxe, complete with shiny brass bell. Johann and Henry Keith trod gingerly over the ashes until they had reached the sidewalk, and then Johann said: 'I want you to put the word out.'

Henry Keith tugged down his rumpled coat and tried to look intense.

'The word, sir?'

'That's right. Put out the word that anyone who feels like helping us out, as far as gas stations are concerned, can expect a lifetime pension for their trouble.'

Henry Keith jotted that down. 'Right, sir. I'll do that right away, sir.'

Johann clapped him on the back, too hard for comfort. 'That's a clever boy, Henry. Let's make sure we get this bastard, whoever it is, and let's make sure we sew him up for good and all.'

Johann was dining in his hotel suite that evening, around eight o'clock, when the telephone rang. Henry Keith answered it while Johann sat there with a mouthful of duck terrine. The hotel room, the best they could find in Shreveport, was decorated with fading yellow flowers and various etchings of Shreve's Cutoff and Mack's Bayou, all rendered with a vaguely depressing dedication to reality.

Henry Keith said: 'Yes?' and Johann swallowed his terrine with a mouthful of Sauternes. He hated wines with any trace of sweetness, but this was the best and the driest the hotel stocked.

On the telephone, Henry Keith said: 'You're kidding.' Then: 'You're kidding.' Then: 'When did this happen?'

Johann said harshly: 'Who's kidding? What the hell's going on?'

Henry listened for a while longer, then put his hand over the mouthpiece.

'It's our office at Austin, sir. They just had reports from the Texas Rangers and the local police that three of our gas stations went up during the afternoon. At Tyler, Waco, and Temple, sir.'

Johann pushed away his wheeled table and stalked over to the telephone, wiping his mouth with his napkin. He snatched it from Henry's hands and said loudly: 'Who's that?'

'My name's Irving, sir,' said a nervous voice on the phone.

'Well, Irving, what the hell's going on?'

'I just got the news, sir. Three gas stations were burned down, and one of our staff killed. Two others got bad burns trying to put down the flames. The fire people say it's almost certainly arson, sir.'

'Jesus, Irving, that's four in two days!'

Irving didn't sound at all happy. 'Yes, sir, it is, sir. I'm afraid that it is.'

'Irving,' said Johann darkly, 'I want guards on every single gas station we've opened. I want them armed and I want them now. If anyone, anyone at all, tries anything funny, then they've got specific orders from me to shoot. Do you understand that?'

'Yes, sir. Right away, sir.'

Johann put down the phone. He rubbed his eyes for a moment, and then he said to Henry Keith: 'Fetch me the gas-station file.'

He pushed aside his dinner and laid out maps and lists. With his gold-nibbed Larkwood pen he marked with a cross all the four gas stations that had been attacked, and then he sat back in his chair and stared at them. Henry Keith said: 'Are you looking for some kind of pattern, sir?'

Johann shook his head. 'Whoever's got the nerve to go around bombing gas stations isn't going to worry abou' whether he's doing it systematically or not. Hell, I just want to know *who*.'

'I put the word out, sir. We may get an informant

Johann leaned forward glumly and peered at the maps. 'Don't count on it,' he said in a soft, almost reflective tone. 'Whoever's involved is pretty sure of himself, and pretty sure of us.'

'Do you think they'll go for more gas stations? Or do you think they're just trying to warn us off?'

Johann raised his eyes at Henry and there wasn't the slightest trace of humour on his face. He would be sixty-one this year, and that was exactly the age he looked. The creases around his eyelids were deeply scored, and his thin hair was a shade of yellowish grey. He had established himself as one of the fiercest and most autocratic oil billionaires in the country, and he was still spreading himself through petrochemicals, shipping, and any kind of business he could lay his hands on. He and his ever-more-complicated corporations were spinning denser and denser webs of influence through American life, taking advantage of a struggling economy and mid-Depression despair to invest everywhere at rock-bottom prices. Before 1929, and the Great Crash, he had amassed sufficient liquid funds to see Cornelius Oil over the worst. This was partly because of financial naïveté and partly because he believed more in himself than he did in other people. Whatever it was, he had remained rich, though less rich, while others went broke. Now he was reaching out to acquire himself food chains and gas stations and hotels and factories. He had put up twenty-four gas stations through Texas, Louisiana, Alabama, and Mississippi in twenty-two months. But now, quite obviously, someone had sat up and taken notice, and whoever that someone was, they didn't like what they saw.

Johann was mellowing with age. There was no doubt that he wasn't the same hard-faced tycoon who had wrestled against financial desperation and impossible pressures to build Cornelius Oil up from the ground. He wasn't even the self-controlled, philosophizing creature who had bought Robinstown from guileless and greedy men so that he could rip away the soil for coal. He still felt energetic, still felt expansionist; but he was also beginning to take into account the personal price that his business and private life had cost him. Sometimes he sat at his desk for hours on end, staring out at the rain that dribbled down his office windows, and he would shake his head and reflect, almost

308

with disbelief, on the way that everything, whether it was oil or money or love or hatred, had its own exact toll.

Now, at nearly sixty-one years, he was gradually beginning to appreciate what his self-suppression had done. It had rendered him almost incapable of offering affection to anyone else at all, even Hester. And yet now, for the first time since his days in Amarero, he was feeling the need to love. He could picture himself as a marble statue, against whose feet wreaths and offerings were laid, and against whose chilly lips kisses were often pressed. But he was incapable of returning any of this devotion, and he remained emotionless and petrified. Even for four hundred million dollars, it may have been too high a price to pay.

Henry Keith said: 'You're worried?'

Johann coughed, and shook his head. 'Not at the moment. But if this continues, I could be. So today it's gas stations. What's it going to be tomorrow? If they think they can run us out of the retail business, how long is it going to be before they try to run us out of the wholesale market? And how long before they start blowing our rigs up?'

Henry Keith tried to look as pessimistic as possible. Johann said: 'What are you looking so damned miserable for?'

'I thought the situation warranted it, sir.'

'The situation never warrants a face like that. Now, what the hell are we doing about finding out who did it?'

Abruptly the phone rang. Henry blinked and sat up straight, and Johann flicked a glance across at him that meant 'answer it – quick.' Henry picked up the earpiece and said: 'Yes?'

There was a long pause. Henry could tell that there was someone there, and yet this someone didn't seem to feel like answering straightaway.

Then the voice said: 'You're not Mr Cornelius, are you?'

'This is his secretary,' said Henry Keith. 'Mr Cornelius is busy right now.'

Again there was a quiet pause. Then the voice said: 'What's he busy doing? Throwing pails of water over his gas stations?'

Henry Keith frowned. 'Listen,' he snapped, 'who is this?'

The voice sounded placid. 'You'll find out. Do you want to find out? The word seems to be that you do.'

Henry Keith said crossly: 'Listen, whoever you are. If you have some information on those gas stations, I reckon you'd better come out with it.'

The voice was unworried. 'What if I don't?'

Henry Keith didn't quite know how to answer that. He covered the phone and hissed at Johann· 'It's some guy who knows something about the gas-station bombings.'

Johann raised an eyebrow. 'How much does he want?'

'I didn't ask him.'

'Well, *ask*. Why the hell do you think he's calling?'

Henry Keith uncovered the mouthpiece and said: 'What's your price, mister?'

There was another lengthy pause. Then the voice said: 'My price is negotiable. Ask Mr Cornelius, if he's there, whether he remembers a picture of Loch Lomond.'

Henry Keith said: 'What? What are you talking about? I can't ask him that.'

'Ask him.'

Henry laid the phone down again. He said: 'I'm sorry, sir, but he says to ask you if you remember a picture of Loch Lomond.'

Johann was in the middle of estimating what four new gas stations were going to cost him. He said: 'How the hell should I know?'

Henry Keith went back to the phone. 'I'm sorry, mister. He doesn't know. Now, why don't you just give me your name and your number and I'll—'

'Ask him if he remembers a railroad whistle. A boy, and a railroad whistle.'

Henry Keith said: 'Sir? He's crazy. Now he wants to know if you remember a railroad whistle. Look, shall I tell him to—'

Johann's face rose from his maps and his papers like a grey shroud coming out of a washing machine. He whispered: '*A railroad whistle*?'

Henry Keith didn't know what to do. He nodded dumbly. Johann got up from his chair, walked across the room, and took the phone out of Henry's hands. He said in an almost inaudible voice: '*Yes*?'

The voice at the other end of the line seemed to know at once it was him. It asked, with obvious satisfaction: 'Ah! So you *do* remember it!'

'What of it?' said Johann.

'Not a great deal. But enough to make it worthwhile we meet. I'll tell you where.'

'Here is okay. Suite 501, the Shreveport Inn.'

'There is *not* okay, I'm afraid. Those people who are giving you so much trouble know you're there. They know whom you meet, and they know where you go. Today you were out on Jewella Road, looking over that burned-out gas station of yours.'

Johann said: 'Of course I damn well was. Any lamebrain could have guessed that.'

The voice replied: 'It doesn't make any difference. I don't want to meet you at the Shreveport Inn. There's a seat on the south side of the main entrance to Querbes Park. I'll meet you there at a quarter of ten tomorrow morning, and I want you to come by yourself.'

Johann rubbed his forehead for a while, and then he said: 'How shall I know you?'

The voice almost seemed to smile. 'Oh, you'll know me. There's an old Latvian saying which says: "Friendship brings you close; marriage brings you closer; but a shared secret is a mingling of blood." '

The phone at the other end was laid down. Johann held the receiver in his hands for a few moments, and then put it back on the cheaply varnished side table as if it was a precious family heirloom.

Henry Keith asked: 'Are you all right, sir?'

Hester had remained at Lynwood's Island. It was Hope's fifteenth birthday party that weekend, and fifty or sixty of her friends from school were coming up to celebrate the occasion with champagne punch and dancing on the jetty. Roderick was away at college, but John had taken a week off school, and Stainer, the butler, who had an aged sister quite close to New Paltz, had driven him home in the maroon Rockne sedan which Johann had bought for the servants.

John was seventeen, and at the peak of his athleticism. He was doing better at school than when he was younger, but he was best at relay running and throwing the javelin. Whenever he came back to Lynwood's Island, he spent hours sculling, and on the day that Johann was inspecting his burned-out gas station in Shreveport, John was rowing up and down the river with long, systematic strokes, while Hester and Hope stood on the jetty and watched him, the way that women do. The bright bunting that had been strung from the jetty for Hope's birthday was popping and fluttering in the wind, and Hester had to place one hand lightly on her wide straw hat with its long blue chiffon band. The other hand rested equally lightly on Hope's shoulder.

'Doesn't he scull well?' said Hester. These days, at the age of forty-two, her prettiness was fading in the way that a pressed flower fades between the pages of a Bible, but she still had the style and self-possession with which Johann had first fallen in love. Her daughter was not half as pretty; but fifteen was the swollen age of hips and breasts and puppy fat, and hair that flopped lankly over her forehead no matter how frequently she washed it, and blushing too much, and the curse.

Hope said: 'I hope his friends at school don't think he's a showoff.'

Hester waved to John as he sculled past them. The surface of the river was glittering like hammered glass, and John's sculls worked their way across the reflected light in energetic angles. He couldn't wave back, of course, but he grinned.

'Boys have to show off,' said Hester. 'It's their nature.'

'Daddy doesn't show off.'

'He's a man, darling, not a boy. And in any case he doesn't have to.'

'Will he be back for my birthday?'

Hester said: 'I don't know. He's had a great deal of trouble down in the South. He called me this morning and said his gas station at Shreveport was completely burned down.'

'I hope he comes back. I've got a present for him, too. I made it myself.'

John was almost out of sight now, behind the overhanging trees that came down to the river's edge. It looked as if he was going to scull himself around to the boathouse and come ashore, so Hester gently guided Hope away from the jetty and back up the garden toward the house. It was warmer away from the river, and the old trees frothed and danced in the late-spring wind.

Hester said: 'Do you love your father, Hope?'

Hope stopped, and stared at her mother in surprise. 'Of course. He's my father. I've made him a foot-warmer to wear in his airplane. You can put both feet into it at once, and it's made of felt. I sewed his initials on it.'

Hester looked reflective and sad. The band around her hat rose and fell in the breeze.

'He never uses anything else you've ever made him,' she said. 'Why did you make him this?'

Hope pushed her hair back away from her forehead. 'I don't know. I suppose I keep on thinking that one day he will.'

'He's not a sentimental man, Hope. Not even with his family. That's what a lot of people don't understand.'

'But he loves us, surely?'

Hester smiled. 'Yes, of course. Well, yes, I suppose so.'

They carried on walking up the neatly raked gravel path As they climbed beyond the trees, they could look back toward the boathouse and see John dragging his scull up the duckboards.

'I sometimes think that Daddy's upset about something,' said Hope.

Hester didn't answer at first. She couldn't tell her daughter that the very same thought had occurred to her the night after she had married Johann, and that after twenty-three years of marriage she was still no nearer finding out why. She said: 'Oh, I'm sure he's not, darling,' and waved to John to hurry up and join them.

John was out of breath by the time he caught up. He was sweating, and he had to dab his face with his rowing towel to mop it up. Hester said: 'You were wonderful, John! I've never seen you scull so well!'

John looked pleased. 'I hope to make the team this season. They're pretty picky, though. Even Laurence didn't make it, and you know how good Laurence is.'

'I know how much money his father makes, if that's any criterion.'

John followed his mother and sister into the square central hallway of the house, with its mock-Roman mosaic

313

floor. His sports pumps squeaked as he walked. He said: 'Is Dad coming home tonight?'

'Not for a couple of days, dear. Maybe the weekend, if he can get away.'

John thoughtfully rubbed the back of his neck with his towel. 'Well, in that case, do you think you could spare me a half hour this evening? I guess I've got something I need to discuss.'

Hope glanced at her mother, but Hester's face showed only motherly calm. These days, it was rare for John to confide in his parents. He occasionally mentioned that he wanted to go into law, or that he was going to try for the swimming six at school; but the rest of the time he behaved as if the only things that ever entered his head were sports and jazz and racing cars. Hester had suspected for a long while that John's closest friends were probably his school-mates, and that he told his most personal thoughts only to them. She knew why, too. Ever since he was young, he had been brought up by his father to believe that the only way a man could survive in the world was to keep his most sensitive side turned away from other people. Whenever John had tried to be affectionate toward his father, he had been met with nothing but remote, lukewarm smiles, and as far as his family was concerned, he now thought that this was the only way to behave.

Hester said: 'I've got some spare time now. Why don't you come into the sewing room? Hope, I'll see you later. Are you going out to Lynwood tonight to see Sally? Or are you staying in? It's salmon for dinner, I think.'

Hope said: 'That's okay. I'll stay.' Then she went off to change, while Hester took her son's muscular arm and walked with him into the oval sewing room. She closed the door firmly behind them and pointed to one of the elegant balloon-back chairs.

John said: 'I'm kinda sweaty. Maybe I'll stand.'

Hester said: 'Whatever you wish,' and perched herself upright and precise on her favourite sewing chair. Beside her was an embroidery frame with an almost completed cushion cover of riotous rhododendrons.

She asked him: 'You're not in any kind of trouble?'

John didn't answer at once. He went over to the window and looked out over the back of the house. The peacocks

314

were sweeping the lawns with their tails, and a gardener was busy digging in plants.

He said: 'It's pretty hard to explain, really. I mean, it's pretty hard to find the right words.'

'Try me.'

'Well – I guess it's usually the kind of a thing a guy would bring up with his father.'

'Yes?'

'I mean, I would have . . . I *would* have talked to Dad about it – but he isn't here too often – and in any case he's not really the kind of . . . well, I don't want to sound as if I'm insulting him . . .'

Hester lowered her eyes. She picked at a stray thread on the embroidery frame. 'John,' she said, 'I know exactly what you're trying to say.'

John was embarrassed for a moment, and acted a little goofy. 'Yeah, well, if you know what I mean then it's okay . . .'

Hester said: 'Is it to do with sex?'

John went very red. He hadn't realized that his mother could use the word 'sex,' that she could actually let it pass her lips. He mumbled and muttered, and then at last he said: 'Well, kind of.'

Hester held out her hand. 'John, come here.'

John didn't want to come at first, but then he reluctantly stepped over and laid his young perspiring hand in the dry middle-aged palm of his small and elegant mother. On her fingers were emeralds and diamonds that, auctioned, would have bought half a block of Manhattan real estate.

'John,' she said, 'I love your father in my way, and my way is a way that nobody else can understand. I will never tell you that he is a cold man, or an inconsiderate man, or a cruel man. He has done cold, and cruel, and inconsiderate things. You know that for yourself. But I have been married to him for long enough to know that there is something else inside him, shut away, that in all his years he may never reveal. He is just as capable of love and happiness as the rest of us, but for some reason, perhaps lots of different reasons, he has declined to let love and happiness have much of a part in his life.'

John pulled up a chair and sat down. He hung his towel over the back of it, and looked at his mother with the kind of earnestness that only a seventeen-year-old with a sex problem could muster.

He said: 'I guess you love him pretty much, huh?'

Hester nodded. 'Yes,' she said. 'I do.'

'Well,' said John, 'I love Hazel pretty much as well.'

There was a small silence, during which the Delft porcelain clock on the sewing room's light walnut side table ticked with delicate patience.

Hester said warily: 'Hazel? I don't think you've mentioned any Hazel before.'

John grinned in embarrassment. 'No. I haven't, as a matter of fact. I kind of met her in Poughkeepsie. Me and Jim Walach went to the movies one night, and that's when I kind of met her.'

'You kind of met her?' asked Hester coolly. 'What does that mean?'

'Well, we went to see *Meet the Baron* with the Three Stooges, and then we went to a soda fountain, and that's where she works.'

Hester stared at her son as if she could hardly believe what he was saying. John shuffled his feet and said: 'She's real pretty, Mom. She comes from a real good family, too. Her pop sells insurance. I guess he probably sells some of Dad's insurance, too. I mean, I guess most insurance salesmen do.'

Hester said: 'Do I understand you correctly? Are you trying to tell me that you've fallen in love with a soda jerk?'

John protested: 'Hey, Mom, she's not exactly a soda jerk. You couldn't call her a soda jerk.'

'What else would you call her? And for goodness' sake stop using that awful language. I am not "Mom", and I never will be.'

'I'm sorry, Mother. But Hazel's a real nice girl. We went out together a couple of times on weekends, and you can take it from me she's bright and she's intelligent. She only works at the fountain to make a little extra cash to help her through school.'

Hestor rose from her chair as if by mystic levitation. Then she went across to the glass-fronted bookcase and peered into it like someone consulting an oracle. John could see her face dimly reflected in the glass, and somehow she looked like a young girl. The words she spoke, though, were far from young.

'I know what you think of us, sometimes, your father and me. I know that you choose to confide in others, rather than us. But don't you really think that the blame is as much yours as it is ours?'

Hester turned and faced him. He could see now that he had made her very angry.

'Your father worked his way up from nothing to build one of the greatest business empires this country has ever known. There is nobody in the whole of the continental United States who does not know your father's name and what it stands for. My own family was of high quality and breeding, and between us your father and I gave to our children the very finest elements of aristocracy and industry. You children – Roderick and Hope, and you, John – should be the elite of America.'

'Mom, the whole *thing* about America is that we're *equal*. That's how Dad made it, and that's how I'm going to make it. Hazel is equal to me and I'm equal to her, and what's more, Hazel is equal to you, too!'

Hester took one convulsive step forward and slapped her son's face.

'How dare you!' she breathed. 'How dare you speak of your mother in the same breath as a common working girl!'

John didn't answer. It hadn't been a hard slap, but it had taken him completely by surprise. He had never seen his mother so furious before, and he didn't know what to say or how to explain what he felt. Hester turned away from him and stood by her embroidery stand as if it was a lectern from which she was going to preach.

'I thought we had taught you well. I know that you have had trouble with your father, but I thought we had taught you well. I thought that you were the bright one, the one who was going to be clever and perceptive and friendly. Instead, you don't seem to have understood a single thing about your position, your responsibilities, or what you're going to have to do when you mature. Equal! How can you say such a thing? Do you really believe that gardener out there is equal to you, or that he's ever going to do more than grub in the soil for your appreciation?'

'But, Mom—'

317

Hester gave a brief shake of her head to show that she wasn't prepared to listen. 'We are all equal in the eyes of God,' she said, 'but we are none of us equal in the eyes of society Good Lord, John, you might just as well have dated a nigger!'

John wiped the sweat from his upper lip with the back of his hand. Then he said quietly: 'Well, that's it, Mom. I have.'

The silence was like cracked ice. Hester said: 'What?'

John coughed. 'Hazel is coloured, Mom. She's a coloured girl.'

There was one second of paralysing tension, and then Hester threw back her head and laughed. John could see her gold bridgework and he looked away.

'John, you *fool*!' Hester continued laughing. 'You and your practical jokes! I should have known as soon as you mentioned the Three Stooges! Oh, I'm so sorry I lost my temper! What an idiot you must think I am! The whole idea!'

John, embarrassed by his mother's laughter, couldn't help smirking as well, and Hester took that as a plain indication that he was making fun of her.

'But just remember,' she said, getting out her tray of silks in readiness for sewing, 'it's all very well to play a joke on me, but your father might think differently. He doesn't quite have the same sense of humour.'

In a small, congested voice, John said: 'Mother, it's true.'

Hester sat down and started to thread her needles with shining peacock blues and greens. 'Yes, dear. I'm quite sure that it is. Are you staying in for dinner tonight? Do you know something, you had me so *mad* for a moment . . .' She smiled indulgently, and put down her sewing to lay a hand on John's arm. 'You're a funny boy. You always have been. Do you remember the time you put those earthworms in poor Hope's rubbers . . .'

John found it impossible to speak. His throat was choked up, and he knew that if he didn't keep a tight rein on himself, he was probably going to cry.

'Mother,' he said, on the brink of tears, 'you have to understand that it's true. Hazel is coloured, and she's a real girl, and it isn't a joke. We're in love.'

Hester was still smiling, but the humour was leaking out

318

of her smile like ink spreading across a damp letter. 'You realize what you're saying, of course?' she asked John frigidly. 'If this really isn't a joke, you realize what you're saying?'

'Mother, I can't help it. I love her.'

'You can't love coloured people. It's ridiculous. Nobody does.'

'Mother, I love her! We want to get married!'

Hester let out a short, testy sigh. 'John, you are seventeen years old and you are the son of Johann Cornelius. Not only are you far too young to marry anybody at all, you are certainly never going to marry a nigger who works in a soda fountain! You must tell her that it's finished between you, and the sooner you do it, the better. I won't have it. The very idea!'

John's eyes were filled with tears now. He felt as if his insides were being torn down like layers of wallpaper. He said: 'Mother, you can't stop us! We've already made up our minds!'

'What do you mean, I can't stop you? Of course I can stop you! You're far too young to marry, and that's all there is to it. And in any event, I refuse to have a nigger for a daughter-in-law. Think of the embarrassment!'

John kicked his mother's embroidery frame, and it tipped over sideways in a confusion of threads and silks. '*Will you stop calling her a nigger!*' he shrieked.

Hester stood up. Her eyes were wide with fury. 'You pathetic boy!' she snapped. 'You silly, senseless boy! What in the world do you think you're trying to prove?'

John went down on his knees and gathered up the silks. He set the embroidery frame straight again. But he didn't look at his mother, and he didn't answer her question. He said, instead: 'I'm sorry. I didn't think you'd get so mad.'

'You didn't think I'd get so mad? What was I supposed to do? Give thanks to the Lord that my youngest son has been dating a coloured girl? I don't know how you can bear to kiss her! I suppose you've kissed her?'

'Yes.'

'The idea of it! It sends shivers down my spine! You must tell her at once that you're finished, do you understand me?'

'I can't, Mother.'

319

'You can and you will.'

'It isn't as easy as that.'

'Oh? And why not, pray?'

'She's having my baby. She's pregnant.'

Hester believed him this time. She looked at him, how young he was, in his sweat-stained sports shirt and his scuffy white rowing pumps, and she raised her hand and gently ran it through his tousled hair. John couldn't quite understand why she was being so gentle now, and he thought for a moment that she was going to give in, and let him marry Hazel and raise their child. He whispered: 'Mother . . . ?'

His mother slowly, slowly shook her head. 'My poor young boy,' she said, in a voice so soft he could scarcely hear her. Then she turned and walked over to the telephone and picked up the receiver. 'Stainer?' she said. 'Will you get me Dr Nash?'

John frowned. 'Dr Nash? What does Dr Nash have to do with it?'

'Sit down, John,' said Hester, and he sat. Then she brought her chair nearer and sat down, too.

'John,' she told him, 'you must tell me where Hazel is. What her address is. Does she live in Poughkeepsie? Or does she live someplace near?'

'She lives in Poughkeepsie, but—'

'Then you know the street, and the number?'

'Sure, but—'

'It's no use, John. Whatever you say, the best thing will have to be done. It's better for . . . Hazel . . . as well as yourself. I'm afraid that there's no getting away from it.'

John said: 'But Hazel's here, Mom. I mean, she's in Lynwood, staying at the Lakeshore Hotel. I told her to come up here, so that when I'd explained what had happened to you, or maybe Dad, then she could . . .'

'She could what?'

He smeared the tears away from his eyes with his hands. 'Well, she could meet you. You know?'

Hester gave a small deprecating laugh. 'No, my dear, I don't know. How could you think of it? Really, John, I would have thought better of you.'

John said: 'But she's there, Mom. She's waiting. Mom, she's having my baby.'

Hester raised her hands. 'It's completely out of the question. She is not to have your baby and that is why I have telephoned Dr Nash. Do you know her room number?'

John stared at his mother disbelievingly. 'Mother,' he said, 'it's my baby! It's a person! It's a person that Hazel and I *made!*'

'You're talking to a woman who has had three children,' replied Hester. 'A baby is not a person until it is born, and even then it can be less than a blessing. Your coloured friend is simply pregnant, and that is all there is to be said. Dr Nash will do everything he can to terminate her pregnancy as painlessly and as promptly as possible. There! That's the telephone! That will be Dr Nash now.'

John, frantic, said: 'Mother . . . you can't!'

Hester went over and picked up the receiver. 'I can,' she said firmly, 'and I certainly will.'

Then, as John listened in silent despair, she said: Dr Nash? It's Mrs Cornelius. I have a favour to ask you of the utmost discretion.'

She began to explain what had happened, but John didn't stay to hear the end of the conversation. He left the sewing room and went outside to the front steps, where he sat beside a stone lion and watched the May breeze ruffle the grass, and the sparkling waves of the endlessly flowing Hudson. He didn't cry any more. He was beyond crying. He simply sat there with his chin in his hands while the afternoon went by, and nobody, on Hester's explicit instructions, disturbed him.

She knew that he would get over it.

At ten o'clock the following morning, in Shreveport, Johann Cornelius and Henry Keith were seated side by side on the green-painted park bench at the south side of the main entrance to Querbes Park. Johann was dressed in a fawn spring suit with chalk stripes, and a fawn felt hat. Henry Keith, as usual, looked as though he had slept the night in the back of an Okie's pickup. The morning was overcast, although the sky was breaking up in the west, and Johann was growing increasingly annoyed and impatient.

'He said quarter of ten, didn't he?' he said, opening his gold half-hunter.

'That's what you told me, sir.'

'Well, if he said quarter of ten, why the hell can't he get here on time? What does he think I've got? Money to burn?'

They waited another ten minutes, and almost as Johann was about to give the rendezvous up and go back to the Shreveport Inn, the gates of the park swung open with a squeak and a plump middle-aged man in a dark suit and a fawn hat came in and walked over toward them. As he came closer, Johann saw that he was neat and smart, with a pink expressionless face, and glittering near-together eyes. He looked, in a way, rubbery, like a bothersome baby in a business suit. His nose, at first glance, could have been a large French snail having a rest on the slow journey up his face. His hands and feet were doll-like, and he smelled of cologne. He stopped right in the front of them, clicked his well-polished heels, and said: 'You must forgive me. It isn't easy to get away.'

Johann looked the man up and down without changing his disgruntled expression. 'I hope you know you've kept me waiting for nearly a half hour,' he said hoarsely.

'Please,' said the man, 'forgive me.'

Johann sniffed. 'Well, there's not much else I can do. Are you going to sit down?'

'I thought we'd walk. It's more difficult for people to overhear when one is walking. There's an old Polish saying which says: "The cuckoo that calls in the same nest every day is soon snared." '

Johann said: 'There's an old Texas saying which says: "If you've got something to tell me, you'd better spit it out." '

'Very well, then,' said the smooth-faced man. 'Let's walk.'

Side by side, the three of them strolled around the crisscross paths. They could have been nothing more than old friends discussing their schooldays. The morning grew hotter, and Johann had to stop to wipe his hatband with his handkerchief.

'I still don't know your credentials,' he told the pink-faced man. 'I don't even know your name, although you very obviously know mine.'

'I was coming to my credentials,' the stranger said calmly. 'I assure you that they're very good.'

'You said something on the telephone about a railroad whistle.'

'Of course,' said the man. 'That's my trump card.'

'You know Daniel Forster?'

'I met him by chance. He came to us for money when his railroad was low on funds. He told me how well you looked after him.'

Johann mopped the perspiration from his neck. 'Did he say why?'

The man, with his eyes slitted against the glare of the sun, looked around the park. 'Oh, yes,' he said. 'He told me all about that.'

'Why should he?'

'Because he wanted money. Everything has its price, you know.'

Johann said, with irritation: 'You're telling me that?'

'Not really. I don't need to. But if you want any further proof that I know just what I'm talking about, then think of people like Kyle Lennox and Carina.'

Johann stopped wiping his face and stood completely still Then he turned to the pink-faced stranger and said: 'What do you know about Carina?'

The man beamed. 'More to the point,' he said, as if he was very pleased with himself, 'what do I know about the Excelsior Hotel?'

Henry Keith was looking baffled. 'Excuse me, sir,' he broke in. 'I'm not entirely sure that I—'

Johann hushed him. 'You'll find out soon enough. That's if this gentleman has his way. Or perhaps this gentleman would like to tell us his name first, and why he's acting so smart?'

The man beamed even more. 'Of course. My name is David Bookbinder, and I run the legal department of Colton Oil. My master, if you can seriously call him that, is Percy F. Colton.'

'*Colton!*' barked Johann.

David Bookbinder raised an eyebrow. 'I thought you might be interested to hear that name again. Especially since you've been having such trouble with your gas stations.'

Henry Keith said: 'Are you trying to say that Percy Colton's behind these bombings?'

David Bookbinder prodded at some wastepaper with the tip of his cane. 'Not in so many words. But it would seem logical, wouldn't it? Colton has one of the largest chains of gas stations in the South and Southeast, although not all of them are openly trading as Colton Oil. There's Texas Star, Abilene, Golden Power – more than half a dozen – and they're all his. What would you do if some upstart billionaire like Mr Cornelius here started opening newer and better gas stations right in your own backyard?'

Johann stopped walking, and stood for a while in the shade of a tree, fanning himself with his hat.

'Very well,' he said, 'supposing it's Percy Colton. What's your price for stopping him?'

David Bookbinder smiled. 'It's not quite as easy as that. I want more than a price. I want to take over Cornelius Oil.'

Johann let out a sharp bark of obvious disbelief.

'Well, that's out of the question, of course.'

David Bookbinder didn't seem to have heard. He said: 'I want one percent of the equity, and a permanent position as chief executive.'

Johann said: 'You're crazy. That's completely out of the question. Do you realize how much one percent of the equity in Cornelius Oil works out at?'

David Bookbinder nodded. 'That's why I'm asking.'

Johann sat down on a sawn-off stump. 'All right,' he said quietly, 'what do I get in return?'

'You get a lot,' answered David Bookbinder. 'You pay a lot, but you get a lot.'

'Like what?'

'You get to take over Coltons and stop them once and for all. You also get to hear nothing but wonderful silence from that long-forgotten railroad whistle.'

Johann put his hat back on his head. 'You think I care about that?'

David Bookbinder started beaming again. 'Of course you care! Why else would young Daniel Forster find himself so handsomely set up in the railroad business at such a tender age, and why else would he find ten thousand dollars a year deposited in his bank by anonymous donors? Come on, Mr Cornelius, I've talked to Daniel Forster and I know just what happened in 1903. It was all very regrettable, and it was all very unfortunate, but it's better to let bygones stay that way, don't you think? Especially now you're handling so many government contracts, and sitting on the board of overseas trade. What would Eleanor say if she knew what one of her favourite NRA supporters had been up to?'

Henry Keith didn't understand any of this, and he looked at Johann worriedly, as if seeking tacit permission to kick this persistent busybody right out of the park. But Johann showed no signs of anything but thoughtfulness, and when he answered David Bookbinder, his voice was unusually subdued.

'I was thinking only the other day that everything in life has its price,' he said quietly.

David Bookbinder said: 'Yes.'

'How can we stop Colton?' asked Johann bluntly.

David Bookbinder took a cigar from his breast pocket, peeled off the band, and clipped a sharp V in the end of it with a gold cutter. Then he stuck it in his mouth and searched for his matches.

'I believe we're going to have to do it on two levels. One, we're going to have to hit back at *his* gas stations, so that he knows you're prepared to do battle. And two, we're going to have to creep up behind him and purchase ourselves a voting majority in Colton Oil. There's a Romanian folk saying which goes: "When you're fighting the cat, remember the claws." In other words, we're going to bite him in the front and claw him in the back.'

Johann said: 'You seem very confident that I'm going to agree to all this.'

'Naturally. That's because you have several motives to do so, any one of which is irresistible. First, you'd like to get your own back at Colton for trying to squeeze you out of Houston-West. Oh, yes, I know about that. It's all in company minutes. You have to read between the lines, of course, but I also talked to Arnie Styvers, and I have a fair idea of what they did.'

'Second?' asked Johann baldly.

'Second is simple. Second, you'd rather keep Daniel Forster quiet. After that Robinstown business—'

'What the hell do you know about that?'

David Bookbinder smirked. 'My dear fellow, I not only know about it, I did it. When poor old Oswald Stone was told to soften up some irksome fellow in the Asquahanna Valley, back in 1927, well ... there was only one person

325

they could go to. I don't want to sound as if I'm bragging, Mr Cornelius, but years ago I realized that big business could flourish quicker and more effectively if it had the strength to enforce its desires as well as express them.'

'Are you saying what I think you're saying?'

'Of course. Right from the early twenties, I've made a point of cultivating gang leaders and mobsters as personal friends. I know most of them intimately, and most of them know me. We work together hand-in-glove, and whenever we want something done, we get it done. Colton had a strike in November out at Greensboro, North Carolina. Well, we put some pressure on some of the strike leaders and their families, and it was all over in three days. That's what I call effective action.'

Johann stopped at the side gate of the park and looked at David Bookbinder for a while. The plump lawyer puffed at his cigar in the midmorning sunlight, and waited with complete equanimity for Johann's comments. Anyone with the young Riccione brothers as bosom friends could afford to.

Johann said: 'All right, what's the third irresistible motive?'

Bookbinder smiled. 'The third motive is that you need me. You're expanding faster than you know what to do with yourself. I agree with your expansion, but you're going to have to be careful. You need more care, more strategy, and more friends.'

Henry Keith said: 'Does that mean we have to get to know gangsters?'

David Bookbinder shook his head. 'Just leave that side of it to me. You'll meet them, of course, when the time's right. But first let's get Percy Colton out of the way before he does any more damage.'

'You mean bomb his gas stations?' asked Henry Keith nervously.

David Bookbinder looked pleased with himself. He sniffed the Shreveport air as if it was a place that he liked to be. 'You might think about hitting Colton first right where he hit you,' he said affably. 'He's got a Texas Star station out on Youree Drive.'

'And who's supposed to throw the bombs?' asked Henry Keith sarcastically. 'Us? In gift-wrapped parcels?'

David Bookbinder shook his head. 'I know a local Grand Dragon and a couple of Night Hawks who'd be pleased to assist.'

'The Klan? I thought you were Jewish.'

'I am. But friends in need are always friends indeed, no matter what their religious priorities. And in any case the Youree Drive station is operated by coloureds, which gives the KKK an added incentive. It will also make it look like a racist attack, rather than a spot of business, which will take some of the suspicion off you.'

Johann lowered his eyes. Even though it was early, he was feeling hot and exhausted, and he badly needed a brandy-and-soda. He leaned against the park's green railings and said: 'Mr Bookbinder, you'll have to give me time to consider this. One percent of Cornelius equity is worth at least five million dollars at today's prices, and I don't think even Rockefellers give that kind of money away to strangers. Not in Querbes Park, anyway.'

Bookbinder sucked his cigar. 'That's all right, Mr Cornelius. I'm not pushing. But just remember that every day that goes by is going to see another gas station go up, and that if you *do* finally refuse to accommodate me, the balloon goes up as well. Daniel Forster may be happy to keep his mouth shut for ten thousand dollars and a few threats against his job and his family, but I'm not. All right?'

Johann nodded. 'I understand,' he said quietly. Then he said: 'Blackmail's always an ugly thing, isn't it, on both sides?'

David Bookbinder carefully moulded the ash of his cigar against the point of the railings. 'Yes,' he answered, equally softly. 'But I have a feeling we'll be together long enough for you to say that again to me, several times.'

Henry Keith glanced at Johann, and Johann looked at David Bookbinder. Then David Bookbinder said: 'I'll call you,' and walked quickly out of the park and across the sidewalk to a fawn Buick club sedan, which had been waiting by the kerb with its engine ticking over.

The black girl had been sitting for most of the morning on a hard rush-seated chair which she had placed right in front of the hotel window. She had lifted the net curtains away from the glass so that she could see better, and she had draped them around her like a woman in a bridal veil. She was unaware of the irony; but then, she was still waiting for a telephone summons from John.

Her name was Hazel Seymour and she was the daughter of Charles Seymour, whose father had been a slave in Richmond, Virginia, when he was a boy. Charles Seymour's father, coincidentally, had belonged to the grandfather of Edward Secker, who was later to marry Hope Cornelius. It was almost as if some unfinished business had yet to be settled between the two families, one way or another.

Hazel was studying to be a mental nurse at Rockland State Hospital. She was financing her studies by working during the evenings at Zee's Creamy Sodas & Drugs in Poughkeepsie, which was where her folks lived, in a shabby-respectable house in the less elite part of town. She was sixteen years old.

Maybe it was the fixed idea that you just didn't love whites that had lulled Hazel into being so open and receptive to John. One evening, when she was tired and hot, and her candy-striped apron was sticky with syrup and ice creams, John had sloped into Zee's with another kid the same age and they had parked themselves on chrome stools at the counter. But it was only when John had handed over a twenty-dollar bill, which was the biggest bill that Hazel had been given all evening; and it was only when she caught him looking at her and smiling across the counter while she was pouring raspberry syrup for a raspberry milk shake, that she began to think that he was inter-*esting*, as her poppa used to say. She smiled back, uncertainly, and spent the rest of the evening wondering why in the world she had.

He had been waiting for her, alone, when she left the soda fountain that evening at half-past eight.

And he had followed Hazel four blocks, protesting the upright and innocent quality of his interest in her. He only wanted a *date*, and what was so all-fired awful about a *date*? In the end, flattered, she had agreed to go on a picnic with him on Saturday afternoon, which was her only free afternoon. She told her momma, of course, that she was going out walking with her friend from the neighbourhood, Leila Miller, and she had made sure that John picked her up from Zee's, and not from home. The whole idea of talking and having fun with white people made her feel peculiar inside, although when John arrived outside Zee's that Saturday in his own bright red Hupmobile convertible, the one that Hester had given him for his birthday, and when Hazel saw the basket packed with hams and pies and fresh fruit and wine, and particularly when John gave her a flowering corsage to match her dress, her feelings took a double dip and she didn't know whether to sit up in the car with her nose in the air like an African princess, or crouch down so far behind the dash that nobody could see it was her.

It was a day of strong blue skies and mountainous white clouds, and they drove the little red car into a field of yellow mustard, and talked and ate as if they were rich folk stranded in somebody's dream. Around four o'clock it grew chilly, and the clouds built up heavy and metallic, so John put up the car's canvas top, and they sat in green-and-yellow gloom while rain rhumbaed on the roof and dribbled tearfully down the windows. It was then that they first kissed, and having first kissed, there was no keeping them apart, and even after the fresh California peaches and the Kentucky ham, they almost devoured each other. Hazel went home that night to her parents' home with the dingy brown wallpaper and the sepia photographs of Charles Seymour in a rigid white collar and derby hat, and she quietly ate her supper of burgoo and cornbread as polite and tame as ever, but inside her emotions had gone completely wild, and she knew she had fallen in love.

Now she waited in her small room at the Lakeshore Hotel, patient and pregnant, expecting not only John's baby but his family's friendship as well. The management had been reluctant to provide accommodation for a darkie at first, but it was hard for them to resist the wishes of any Cornelius, no matter how junior. Anybody who did business at Lynwood's Island stayed at the Lakeshore at one time or another, and Johann and Hester occasionally ate there.

Just after two, when Hazel was beginning to feel hungry for lunch, a long silver car drew up outside the Lakeshore Hotel, its tyres inscribing semicircles in the white gravel. Hazel leaned forward, and saw one of the rear doors of the car being opened by the Lakeshore's porter, and John step out. He stood there for a moment, and it looked as if somebody inside the car was giving him last-minute instructions, for eventually he nodded, and walked up the steps and went inside the hotel.

Hazel found herself shaking. She pushed aside the net curtains and put the chair back in the corner of the room. She didn't want John to think that she had been staring out of the window all morning. That would make him feel anxious; and she didn't want to make the father of her baby anxious. She took off her shoes and sat down on the bed with a copy of *Vogue* that John had bought for her, and tried to look as if she was calm and relaxed, and as accustomed to wealthy living as he. On the first page she opened, she saw a long gold evening dress for one hundred and thirty-five dollars, which was almost exactly what her father managed to bring back after two months' work.

There was a subdued knock at the door. She said: 'Who is it?' She quickly patted her hair in case the net curtain had disturbed it.

John said: 'It's me. Can I come in?'

'The door's open.'

He walked in, and somehow he looked different. In Poughkeepsie, he had always been young and fun and fashionable. But now he was wearing an expensive grey double-breasted suit, and his hair was combed with unaccustomed neatness, and he had a fragrance about him too that she didn't recognize. He came over to the bed, leaned over, and kissed her. It was meant to be a lingering kiss, but somehow they didn't feel like lingering very long. John sat down on the edge of the bed.

'Well,' he said, 'how are you?'

She shrugged. 'I'm fine. I've missed you.'

'I've missed you too. I'm sorry you had to wait so long.'

'That's all right. Just so long as you fixed your folks.'

John nodded, and didn't answer.

'You did fix your folks okay, didn't you?' she asked him.

He let out a short laugh. 'I sure fixed 'em!'

'You don't sound very certain.'

He laughed again. 'Of course I am.'

'Well, what did they say? What did your momma say? When you told her? She must've said something.'

John took her hand between his, and smiled at her. She wished he wasn't smiling. He usually smiled only when he thought something was funny, and what was funny about any of this?

'Mother was . . . surprised, of course.'

'Surprised, or shocked?'

'Well, a little shocked. It's her first grandchild, after all, and she wasn't really expecting it!'

'I guess not. But I am.'

'Well, we all know that. But in any case, everything's going to be fine. We're going to take you right now to see Dr Nash, the family doctor. He's got a clinic here, and he can check you over and make sure everything's fine.'

Hazel said: 'Right now?'

John grinned. 'The sooner the better, huh?'

'John, that's real nice, but I'd appreciate some lunch. I haven't eaten since dinner last night. I'm real hungry. In fact, I'm so hungry, I could eat a white man.'

John laughed some more. Why was he laughing so goddamned much? It seemed like he was frightened of something, or embarrassed.

Hazel said: 'John . . . everything's all right, isn't it? There isn't anything wrong?'

John shook his head. 'Hazel, everything's perfect. All we have to do is get along to Dr Nash, and then we can go get ourselves something to eat.'

Hazel frowned. 'I don't want to see Dr Nash. I don't *need* to. I saw my own doctor in Poughkeepsie. He says it's six weeks gone and everything's fine.'

John bit his lip. Then he said: 'Dr Nash is the finest in the whole country. That's why we use him. He's a really nice guy. Wait till you meet him. I mean, he's the country's best.'

'John—'

John gripped her hands strangely tight. He said: 'Listen, Hazel, just for me. Go see Dr Nash just for me. Will you do that? Now, look, it's almost two, and I said we'd be round there at ten after.'

Hazel got up from the bed and walked across to the wardrobe. She could see herself in the mirror, dark and tall, and in the angle of light that fell behind her she could see John sitting, his head bent and his knees together, like a man waiting in a cell.

She said: 'You're worried about something. Why are you worried? Was your momma real mad?'

He looked up with artificial brightness. 'Mad? No, she settled down to the whole idea pretty well. She's a very understanding person.'

Hazel said: 'Do I get to meet her?'

'Oh, sure. Well, I guess so.'

'You only guess so? I'm going to marry her son, and you only guess so?'

'Well, Hazel, it's . . .'

Hazel turned around. Her voice was calm and sad, but there were no tears in her eyes. The way she was standing, one hand on her hip, her head bent slightly to one side, made her into a dark silhouette that was as soft and sorrowful as anything by Renoir. The room was lit only in greys and browns, with a rectangle of reflecting mirror from the wardrobe.

She said: 'There's something wrong, isn't there? Your momma didn't like this one little bit.'

John clenched his knuckles. 'Really, Hazel, everything's fine. Now, all we have to do is—'

Hazel slowly shook her head. 'Don't lie, John. I can take anything you've done to me, but not lies. Why don't you just tell me what truly happened, the truth, no matter how bad you think it's going to be?'

John said: 'You weren't supposed to know.'

She laughed, softly and forgivingly. 'No, I guess that I wasn't. What de darkies don't know cain't hurt 'em.'

'Hazel—'

'I'm sorry. I know you've never been like that. But it's your momma, isn't it? I should've known. If I'd've had any sense, I wouldn't't've even come this far. She doesn't want her dear young baby boy mixing with coloureds. What she especially doesn't want is a half-caste grandchild. She doesn't want to have to order up chitterlings for one while the rest of the family is having *pâté de foie gras*.'

John stood up. She could tell that, two or three hours ago, he had probably been crying. But between that time and now, he had made up his mind about something, and whatever it was, it wasn't in her favour, nor in favour of the baby that was growing inside her.

'I've let you down, haven't I?' said John.

Hazel went to the window, pulled back the net curtains, and looked down at the long silver car in the drive.

'Yes,' she said, 'you have. But I guess the pressure must be more than most people can stand.'

'What pressure?'

'Oh, the family, and the fortune. I can't expect a young boy like you to give up hundreds of millions of dollars just for love. And in any case, you don't really want to, do you? If you married me, and if we had this baby, you'd have to spend the rest of your life fighting the snobs who wouldn't invite you to dinner because you'd be bringing a black wife, and the kids who'd make this baby cry its little heart out because it wouldn't be black and it wouldn't be white and it wouldn't know *where* it belonged. You'd have to fight your family and your money and your own self, and I can't rightly ask you to do that. One coloured girl from Poughkeepsie is not worth that.'

John reached out and touched her arm.

'Hazel,' he said, 'I love you.'

She turned and smiled.

'You thought you did, once. Don't lie, John, it's not worth it. I can see by your eyes that you've made up your mind. I'm not going to force you.'

'Oh, Hazel, I'm so sorry. I don't know what to say. I thought if I talked to Mother she'd understand. I thought if I . . .'

Hazel let the curtain fall. She went over to the wardrobe, opened it, and took out her suitcase. It was a new brown leather suitcase that John had bought for her specially. They had taken care when they chose it, because John had said she could take it on her honeymoon, too. That was only two or three days ago, but now it was nothing more than a new suitcase that she almost wished she didn't have. She started to pack her few belongings, her dresses and her hairbrush and her red shoes.

John remained by the window, staring silently out at the grounds of the Lakeshore Hotel. He couldn't understand why he felt so little emotion. Perhaps he had already cried himself out for one day. It was in the night, that night, that it was going to start hurting.

Hazel clicked shut the suitcase locks and went to get her coat from the back of the door.

'John?' she said, as she put it on.

John didn't answer.

She came closer, and looked at him with such tenderness and regret on her face that, if he had turned toward her, he would have understood far more about her, and maybe something about himself, too. But he kept his eyes on the driveway outside, and on the impatient fingers he could just discern drumming on the silver car's steering wheel.

'John,' she said again, 'I can't say I won't be sad, and I can't say that I won't miss you, because I love you more than anyone I ever knew, and this wrench is going to hurt me so bad. I'm going to cry for you, John, when I'm in private, and by myself, but I'm not going to cry in front of you. If you don't want me, and you don't want the baby we made, then I'll just have to do the best I can.'

John said quietly: 'What are you going to do about the baby?'

'What do you *think* I'm going to do? I can't expect my momma and poppa to look after me while I sit around the house getting fat, can I?'

'If it's money . . .'

Hazel looked at him. He lowered his head in embarrassment.

'Well,' he said, 'if it's money . . .'

She almost smiled. 'You're ashamed of saying that, aren't you? Well, there's no need. I'm going to get rid of this baby, and since it's your baby as well as my baby, I'd appreciate some financial help.'

John turned around at last. 'I'm sure that Dr Nash—'

She shook her head emphatically. 'No white man is going to touch me. Not to take away my baby. And in any case, that was the way you planned it, wasn't it? You and your momma were going to take me to see your wonderful Dr Nash, and your wonderful Dr Nash was going to take a look, and all of a sudden, my *God*, what's *this*, an unexpected miscarriage! Oh, Miss Seymour, we *are* sorry. We *do* apologize. How clumsy, to give you an accidental D-and-C like that! Come on, John, I'm studying to be a nurse. I'm also a woman, and a pregnant mother. And I'm black. What you wanted to do was bad, and it was cruel, but I know why you planned to do it, and I know just how terrible your load must be.'

334

'Load? What are you talking about?'

'The load you have to bear on your shoulders, John. My cross is that I'm coloured, but your cross is heavier than mine. You're *rich*.'

John listened to this with a perplexed expression that showed he didn't grasp it at all. How could wealth be a burden? Money was the universal lightener of loads, the lifter of heavy weights. When you had money, you could afford to hire somebody to carry your cross for you. He turned back to the window, his mouth pursed as if he had sucked a candy and found it had a centre of liquid vinegar

Hazel said: 'Will you give me a ride to the railroad station?'

John glanced at her. 'I can't make you change your mind?'

'What choice do I have? To lose my baby in Lynwood, or to lose it in Poughkeepsie? They're not that far apart.'

'Maybe I can talk to Mother some more.'

Hazel smiled sadly. 'No, John. You know it's no use. I came up here with a crazy dream that couldn't ever come true. I guess I knew it couldn't happen, right from the start. One day you'll find yourself a nice white lady from a nice respectable family, and you and she will settle yourselves down together and live the way your momma always wanted.'

John lifted her suitcase off the bed. She opened the door for him, and as he passed her by on his way into the hall, she said: 'Besides . . .'

He stopped. 'What do you mean, "besides?"'

She leaned forward and kissed his forehead. It was a dry, chaste kiss. 'It doesn't matter,' she told him.

'No – tell me, please.'

She dropped her eyes. 'All I was going to say was that when I find a man to marry, and a man to give me children, I'll want a man who stands by me, no matter what, and a man who stands by his baby. That's all.'

They stood there in silence for almost a minute. Then John hefted the suitcase and went downstairs to the waiting car. Stainer opened the trunk for him, and he stowed it away. He wouldn't let anyone else carry it. He wanted to understand what a load was. Hazel came down, pulling on a pair of beige gloves, and Stainer opened the rear door of the car for her to get in.

Hester was sitting in the front seat. She looked severe and elegant in a dark grey suit, with a spray of diamonds on her left lapel. She turned and said to Hazel: 'I'm sorry, we haven't been introduced. But John has told me all about you.'

Stainer started the motor, and the car scrunched out of the hotel driveway. Hazel sat with her arms held tight around her, as if she was cold. The inside of the car was five degrees warmer than it needed to be, and it was fragrant with leather and perfume.

John said: 'Hazel just wants to go the train station, Mother. She doesn't want to see Dr Nash.'

Hester turned around in her seat to look at Hazel. 'Are you *sure*, my dear? Dr Nash is one of the finest in the country. We'll quite happily pay.'

Hazel was watching the trees flicker past. She shook her head without looking at the woman who was never going to be her mother-in-law.

'I just want to get home, thank you, ma'am.'

Hester said: 'Please yourself, my dear. We're only trying to help.'

John put in: 'You can still change your mind.'

Hazel turned her head and looked at them both. 'Help?' she said, with a taste of bitterness in her voice as sharp as the pith of a fresh-peeled lime. 'You wealthy white people have never helped anyone except yourselves, and you never will. Charity begins at home, doesn't it, Mrs Cornelius, and what's more, you make sure it stays there.'

Hester said airily: 'You can be as rude as you like, my dear. You'll be on that train in ten minutes.'

John said, as if he were reciting the label of a patent-medicine bottle: 'Did you know that this is a Pierce Arrow "Silver Arrow" saloon, and that it was one of only five made for the Chicago World's Fair last year? It has a V-12 engine that develops 175 horsepower and it cost upwards of ten thousand dollars

Hazel, who hadn't meant to, wept. John wept too, but only because he realized what he had actually been able to inflict on another human being without the benefit of money, and that within a few days his first baby would be

336

lying dead and bloody in a hospital trashcan, unable even to dream of wealth and Pierce Arrows and dull days like this on the banks of the Hudson River.

The Grand Dragon of the Shreveport Ku Klux Klan lived in a tidy white-painted suburban house with ranch-style fences and floral curtains drawn back and tied like the curtains of a doll's house. He was standing outside in his front yard when they arrived in David Bookbinder's fawn limousine, with a contented expression on his broad, sun-burned face that reminded Johann disturbingly of Kyle Lennox's face, thirty-one years and a dozen centuries ago. It was as if David Bookbinder had deliberately selected this man to nudge his memory and remind him of his buried trespasses.

The Grand Dragon came forward to meet them as they climbed out of the car. He was physically enormous, like a huge side of bacon from a prize-winning pig. He wore a very starched white sport shirt and very crisply pressed khaki pants, and sandals that revealed two rows of toes as pink and orderly as prawns.

'How do you do, David,' he said, and squeezed David Bookbinder's hand. 'And these are your friends, right?'

The day was glary and hot. Johann wore sunglasses and a straw hat, and Henry Keith had almost dissolved into perspiration and crumpled linen.

Johann said: 'Johann Cornelius,' and took the Grand Dragon's hand. Then he said: 'What do I call you? Your Dragonship?'

The Grand Dragon guffawed. 'Now, you don't have to do that. The name is Chesley Crowther. And in any event Johann, it ain't considered particularly diplomatic to men-tion the Klan names around here no more, on account of the official line against it. But come inside. There's some beer on ice, if that takes your fancy.'

They trooped inside. The house was small and furnished with cheap light-varnished chairs and tables in the Grand Rapids style, but it was kept conspicuously clean, and there was a new icebox humming and whirring in the kitchen. Chesley went to open the beer while Johann sat himself down and looked around. On one wall was an embroidered sampler which said 'God Is White', and on the opposite wall hung a photograph of Chesley Crowther and twenty other heavily built citizens of Shreveport on a fishing trip.

'Well, now' – Chesley grinned, handing out glasses of Old Milwaukee – 'it's a long time since you been down this way, David. Just as well, considering you ain't strictly one of us.'

He sat himself down, swallowed a long gulp of beer, and then fastidiously wiped the foam from his upper lip with a pressed white handkerchief.

'David is our one exception to the rule,' Chesley told Johann, leaning over with a confidential wink. 'And that's because David is a powerfully interesting and influential fellow, ain't you, David? He's our latter-day Judah Benjamin.'

David Bookbinder sipped his beer and then put it down on the table.

'It's a question of expedients,' he said calmly. 'There are times when business interests and political interests override racial feelings. Personally, I think Chesley here is an inexcusable bigot, but he knows I think that, and we've decided to share the same bed from time to time, no matter how uncomfortably.'

'I thought the Klan was pretty well broken down here,' remarked Henry Keith. 'At least, that's what they say in the North.'

Chesley Crowther laughed, and swallowed some more beer, and patted his upper lip, and laughed again.

'Saying the Klan is broken is akin to saying the church is broken,' he said. 'As long as folks believe in the supremacy of the white man, and so long as folks won't tolerate communism, and welfare, and mixing of the races, and letting the nigger despoil what we have in this pure country of ours, then the Klan will stand strong. We've got a heritage to protect, Henry, and we're going to protect it if it means shooting every nigger and every bleeding-heart liberal in the belly!'

Johann said dryly: 'What I really want to know, Mr Crowther, is whether you can mount an effective and confidential campaign against Colton gas stations. The racial politics really don't interest me.'

Chesley turned on him. 'They don't interest you, huh? Well, let me ask you something. If you found your son or

338

your daughter had been mixing and mingling with niggers, what would you feel about that?'

'I don't know. It's never happened, and I don't suppose it ever will.'

Chesley waved his meaty arm in a dramatic sweep. 'That's what you say now! But unless you fight all those who seek to prove that the Negro masses ain't biologically inferior, then the Negro masses are going to rise up against you, and they're going to mix and mingle with your sons and your daughters. How would you like a nigger for a son-in-law, or a daughter-in-law maybe? How would you like a half-breed mutt as your grandchild and your heir? I have pride in what I am, Johann, and I hope to God that you do too.'

David Bookbinder looked across at Johann for one brief moment, and in that moment Johann wondered just how much this quiet and curious man knew about his past. He felt almost as if his entire character were laid open for Bookbinder's inspection, like a soldier's kit.

He said to Chesley: 'Mr Crowther, I know where the Klan's sympathies lie. But there is no possibility that any of my children will fall in with blacks, and if they did I would do my level best to make sure that they pretty promptly fell out again. Now, do you think we can talk about business?'

Chesley raised his hands in a conciliatory gesture, and parked his big, well-laundered bottom back in his chair. 'What you're asking is whether I can cause some ruckus round at the Colton gas stations, and make it look like a regular Klan ride?'

Johann nodded. 'Mr Bookbinder here has given you most of the details, I think? We want the gas station on Youree Drive burned flat.'

Chesley scratched his ear. 'That sounds easy enough. But what happens if we get any trouble from Dan Gibbons?'

'Dan Gibbons is the local police chief,' explained David Bookbinder. 'We have him very tame, Chesley, don't worry. I paid him a visit at home last night, and he's looking forward to a new car. He won't come around until you're well away.'

'That sounds regular enough,' agreed Chesley. 'And what's the main fee for the night's work?'

'Ten thousand dollars,' said Johann. 'All in used bills, all paid immediately after the job's done.'

Chesley like the sound of that. These days, the Klan was divided, weak, and desperately short of funds, and when the time came for a new Grand Wizard to be elected to preside over the Invisible Empire, Chesley knew that cash in the bank would give him a fighting chance at the polls. He said: 'I'll drink to that,' and raised his glass.

They talked for a little while more, discussing the details of the night's raid, and then Chesley showed Johann the Klavern in the back room of the house, the dark and sacred room in which the Shreveport Klansmen met.

Johann rubbed his eyes tiredly. Perhaps the whole world was populated with endless variations of himself, and his own crippled emotions. He said to Chesley: 'Thank you, Mr Crowther. I'm sure you'll do us a fine job,' and pushed his way back into the daylight.'

That night, at midnight, the Klan rode again in Shreveport for the first time in almost nine years. They clattered up Youree Drive on horses, fifteen of them in white pointed hoods and fluttering white robes, yelling and screeching and waving fiery torches that roared and smoked. The streets were deserted as they rode into the forecourt of the Texas Star gas station, where one sleepy coloured attendant had been sitting with his feet up reading a comic book and listening to late-night country music on his radio.

The Klansmen dismounted and burst into the attendant's cabin. The boy's name was Charlie Wright, and he was so terrified by the Klansmen's spectral appearance that he wet himself. He dropped onto his knees, and one of the Klansmen hit him in the neck with the butt of a rifle. He fell against his chair, stunned.

They rifled the cash register and smashed every window in the room. They turned over filing cabinets and ripped open drawers, scattering papers and receipts. Then one of them brought a red tin can of gasoline over from the pumps, and they splashed it over the cabin, and all over Charlie Wright as well. Backing off, they tossed matches into the cabin, and it exploded into a funnelling blowtorch of orange fire.

While three Klansmen erected the traditional cross at

the side of the forecourt, the rest of them rampaged around on their horses, firing their rifles into the air and hooting like owls. At last the cross was up, and they set it alight and in the darkness of a night in 1934 the hair-raising symbol of racial purity blazed as bright as it had in years gone by.

Charlie Wright, awakened by agony, tried to stumble out of his burning cabin. The Klansmen whooped and hollered as they saw him staggering like a man of flames from the doorway. He made it as far as the gas pumps, with his hair and his clothes and his face alight. But then he dropped to the ground, and his body lay there blazing, while at his home five blocks away his mother looked up at the clock and decided it was time to put his supper on.

When the Texas Star gas station exploded, the *whump* of detonating gasoline fumes was heard four miles away, and it shattered windows a quarter of a mile in every direction A spinster who lived across the drive thought the end of the world had arrived, and so she promptly went upstairs and climbed into her lodger's bed for a grand finale. A dog was blown through the back of its kennel, hurled across fifty yards of garden, and ended up on the dining-room table of an elderly librarian who was eating alone. At the fire station, the fire chief waited for ten minutes, as required, and then sent the engines out.

Along Youree Drive, the Klansmen galloped in frenzy and elation, ghosts in bedsheets and wizards' hats. They split up at the corner of Ockley Drive, and rode off to their homes, still shouting and calling like wild banshees, while the tall cross burned by the wrecked gas station, and sirens wailed from the west.

In his hotel room, Johann drew back the drapes and listened to the clamorous noises of the night. David Bookbinder was sitting there, too, with a glass of whiskey and a last cigar. Henry Keith was in the next room, talking on the telephone to Cornelius managers and brokers in New York, preparing the plan of financial investment for the following day.

'Well,' said Johann, letting the drapes fall back. 'It seems we've lit ourselves quite a fire.'

David Bookbinder nodded placidly. 'Fire has to be fought

with fire. And men like Percy Colton have to be put in their place. He's an old bird, but he's a tough one.'

'Do you really believe he'll give in?'

'He has to. We already hold a seventh of Colton voting stock, and once it gets around that his gas stations are being systematically destroyed by the Klan, we'll quickly get our hands on a whole lot more.'

Johann said: 'You're a strange man, Mr Bookbinder. You have strange methods of working.'

David Bookbinder smiled. 'Does that mean you've decided to employ me?'

Johann lifted his eyes. 'I never really had much choice, did I? I made my bed in 1903, and now I've damned well got to lie in it.'

David Bookbinder shrugged. 'I'm pleased you can see it that way. It could have been pretty unpleasant otherwise. I hate blackmail, you know.'

Johann went over to the side table and poured himself a glass of brandy. He sipped it, and closed his eyes while it soaked down his throat.

'Yes,' he said, 'I can almost believe that you do.'

He sat down, hunched forward in his chair, with his glass held in both hands.

'Mind you,' he went on, as if David Bookbinder really needed any kind of explanation, 'it wasn't blackmail that finally decided me.'

David Bookbinder said nothing, but pursed his lips and blew a smoke ring up at the ceiling. It rose, spun, and then dissolved.

'What happened in 1903 was something that I've never quite understood. I sometimes look back on it, you know, and I wonder if I was quite mad. I took up with a girl of twelve or thirteen, and she gave me such friendship that I think of her now as a miracle. In a way, I suppose it was me who caused her to die. Then I lost the love of a woman who was more beautiful than you could imagine, and let her fall into the hands of men who destroyed her pride and her womanhood forever. And her life, too.'

David Bookbinder said: 'You talk of love very glibly.'

Johann pulled a face. 'When I say love, I mean devotion. I'm not sure that I know what love is.'

'Of course you do. Why do you think that you felt about

342

these unfortunate ladies the way you did? You have always been in love.'

'You mean with myself?'

David Bookbinder shook his head. 'You are in love with wealth. Of course, I haven't known you all your life, but you exhibit the symptoms of a longtime sufferer.'

'Wealth?'

David Bookbinder looked at him with what could almost have been kindness. 'That's right. It's a rare but serious disease. It's even worse than being in love with money.'

'You're talking nonsense.'

'No, I'm not. The love of money is a very specific love, and it is almost always found among those who will never be rich. If you adore the smell of ten-dollar bills, the feel of treasury paper between your fingers, then you are a financial sybarite, but you are not a lover of wealth. Real wealth is a cold and abstract goddess, Mr Cornelius. To love real wealth you must be elevated and inspired by the *concept* of riches. Have you noticed how the rich carry no money with them? The ecstasy comes from within their minds, not from within their wallets.'

Johann eased himself back in his chair like a man settling himself into a scalding bath. 'Does the love of wealth have to make me so dissatisfied?'

'*All* love makes you dissatisfied,' said David Bookbinder. 'That's the very definition of love.'

'But why did I let Beatrice slip out of my grasp? Why did I let her go? And Carina, I should have protected Carina night and day!'

David Bookbinder stood up and walked across to the ashtray, where he ground out the butt of his cigar.

'I'm not an alienist, Mr Cornelius. I'm not even a rabbi. But in my humble opinion, I'd say that you were doing exactly what any man does when he is trying to control an obsessive and unrequited love. You were seeking in women some substitute for your passion for wealth. How much easier to love a woman than to love wealth! To love wealth is like following a golden mirage that you can never quite grasp. But, unfortunately for you . . .'

Johann looked up.

'Unfortunately for you,' said David Bookbinder, 'your women, no matter how wondrous, were not enough. You

343

pushed them and yourself to the very limit of what you could take You thought you loved them, but they became grist for the mill which has ground out your fortune. No, Mr Cornelius, it was all very sad, and it was probably not your fault, but I suppose it was inevitable, or as the Russians say "the return of the summer birds is no surprise." You had to discover how little you loved women to realize how much you loved wealth.'

Johann did not answer for a long time. He sat sunk in his chair, endlessly rotating his brandy glass, his forehead furrowed and his mouth turned down.

Finally he said: 'I'm going to appoint you, Mr Bookbinder, as the chief executive of Cornelius Oil. This is on the strict understanding that none of what you know about my life in Texas is ever revealed to anyone. I will also make over one percent of Cornelius equity.'

He paused once more, and then he said: 'For our own personal working relationship, I want you to know that you have partly succeeded in blackmailing me, and partly failed. If I had been determined to resist you, I would have done so, and probably succeeded, no matter what scandal you dug up. But I feel that appointing you will do me some good, although quite what kind of good, I am not yet sure. I think you will probably be a permanent reminder to me of what I am, because we are not very different, you and I. Everyday I can look at you and see myself in my rawest form, and that is the only effective way I can think of to punish myself enough.'

David Bookbinder smiled. 'Believe me, Mr Cornelius, your choice is wise. Now, perhaps you can do me a favour?'

'What is it? Do you want me to put your appointment to music?'

'Nothing like that. I have a friend who has had some trouble with a federal grand jury, and he's looking for someplace quiet to stay. I wonder if you have a small room or two up at Lynwood's Island?'

'What's his name?'

'Oh, you know him well. Or you should. Dutch Schultz.'

Johann swirled his brandy around. He was not happy, but at the same time he felt as if some nagging tooth had been pulled, and that tomorrow he might actually wake up and feel no pain.

'So this is how it begins, is it?' he said softly.

David Bookbinder beamed. 'Beginnings are always bedevilled by uncertainties,' he said. 'Do you want to shake hands?'

Johann looked up at his new chief executive, and then shook his head. 'One day, perhaps. But not now.'

Outside, they heard the sound of an ambulance bell. It was all that was left of Charlie Wright, on his way to the city morgue.

Percy F. Colton was nearly ninety in 1934. *The New York Daily Post*, which didn't like him, frequently called him 'the Methuselah of Money.' But even though his rotund face had withered and collapsed, and even though he now attended all his business meetings with a uniformed nurse on either side of him, he still maintained a reputation for hard dealing and ruthless self-protection. It was a general assumption on Wall Street that he had something to do with the bombing of Cornelius gas stations, although nobody could quite agree on the degree of his involvement; and it was also a general assumption that Johann Cornelius had somehow inspired the Ku Klux Klan to strike back.

But what is was not known anywhere was that David Bookbinder, the head of Colton's business-law department, was already working against his boss's interests, and that he was laying complex and elaborate plans for kicking the supports out from under the Colton oil empire completely.

It happened on August 2, 1934, a warm and cloudy Thursday, the same day von Hindenburg died in Germany, and the morning that the first fourteen-passenger night flight arrived in Los Angeles after crossing the continent from Newark.

On the eighteenth floor of the Colton Building on Park Avenue South, hundreds of Colton shareholders assembled at a special meeting to discuss the effects on Texas Star and Golden Power retail sales because of three months' burning and bombing by the Ku Klux Klan. Things had gotten so serious that few automobilists would stop at Texas Star gas stations, for fear of retribution from the Night Hawks. Sales had dropped fifty-eight percent, and were still sliding.

Once the shareholders were assembled in the long, blue-carpeted gallery, Percy Colton himself arrived. He shuffled up to the board table on two sticks, with his white, bright, Colgate-polished nurses helping him along. Everyone stood as a mark of respect, and there was even some applause. David Bookbinder, on the far end of the board table, was clapping louder than anyone.

Percy Colton sat down, and handed his sticks to one of his nurses. There was a rustle of anticipation and excitement in the hall, and some of the directors looked around uneasily, as if they sensed that something unusual was up.

Percy Colton rapped his gavel. 'I call this meeting to order.'

There was a last buzz of conversation, then silence.

Percy Colton looked around with red-rimmed rheumy eyes. 'This extraordinary meeting of Colton Oil shareholders has been called to sound out your feelings about the little problems we've been having with our gas stations down South.'

Someone said: 'Little *problems*? You're *kidding*!'

The heckler was hushed up, and then Colton said: 'I want to tell you now that I believe we have this problem licked. Ostensibly, it looked as if the Ku Klux Klan was raiding our gas stations because of our policy of employing coloured attendants. But I've been doing some investigations of my own, and I believe that we have one of our major rivals in the petrochemical industry to thank for these wanton attacks.'

Another voice said: 'So what are you going to do about it.'

And someone else called: 'Who started the bombing in the first place? That's what I'd like to know!'

Colton banged his gavel. 'We're doing everything we possibly can! You have to understand that whenever one of our places is attacked, the local police and fire departments are bribed into looking the other way, and they've obviously been bribed enough to keep on looking the other way for quite some time yet. Now, the KKK doesn't have that kind of money to hush up a few local flatfoots, so that means someone with considerable financial resources is systematically destroying our gas stations.'

'And why?' shouted a woman from the back. 'Because *you* started destroying *their* gas stations first!'

346

There was a jumbled roar of approval, and a burst of applause. A man in a navy-blue suit and spectacles stood up from the second row and raised his hand.

'Mr Chairman, I want to propose a motion!'

Colton banged his gavel again. 'Sit down!' he snapped. 'You can propose motions when I've finished speaking!'

'Mr Chairman, I want to propose a motion right now! I want to propose that this corporation has no confidence in its chairman and board of directors, and demands their resignation as of now!'

Someone else jumped up and shouted: 'I second the motion!'

Again there was a roar of approval. Colton looked angrily around the hall, and then banged three times with his gavel, until the shareholders gradually settled down into silence.

'Very well,' he said caustically. 'It's out of order, but if you want to vote on that motion, then I'm agreeable. Let's get this childish yowling over with, and then we can get down to business. Mr Kharmann, will you be kind enough to count hands?'

'Yes, sir.'

Colton looked around him again, more slowly this time, identifying the faces he knew were friendly, and the faces he was more doubtful about. There were quite a few new faces, and many he didn't know at all. He said softly: 'All those in favour of the motion please show.'

At least half the hands in the hall went up. Mr Kharmann, peering at the crowded seats through bifocals, counted as quickly as he could. 'Thank you,' he said at last, and the hands went down.

Percy Colton said: 'All those against the motion please show.'

More hands went up. Mr Kharmann counted, and then sat down to figure out the results. The hall remained absolutely silent while he totted up share proportions and proxies.

After almost five minutes, he abruptly lifted his head. He was quite pale, and he took his spectacles off before he said anything.

Colton snapped: 'Well? Let's get on with it!'

Mr Kharmann shook his head. 'We can't, sir. The motion is carried.'

Colton snatched the figures from under Mr Kharmann's nose. 'Carried? Don't be so damned ridiculous!'

He looked down the list of voting shareholders, and then jabbed his finger at one of the most influential names of all – Carina Hydraulics.

'Who's this?' he said, his voice rigid with fury. 'Who's this Carina Hydraulics? I thought Carina Hydraulics was tied up with our Kansas operation! How come they voted against us?'

The directors on the board looked at each other, nonplussed. Then one of them said: 'David – you know Carina, don't you? Didn't you arrange that investment?'

Amid the hubbub and shouts, David Bookbinder stood up and faced the meeting. He raised one hand for silence, and at last got it.

'It appears,' he said, 'that I have made a terrible mistake.'

Again there was a confused babble of voices.

'Please . . .' he said, 'let me explain. I was under the impression when we sold our new share issue in June that Carina Hydraulics was a well-financed corporation that was eager to invest in Colton Oil and in whose integrity and dependability we could absolutely trust. We were going to let them use our storage and refining facilities, and in turn they were going to put several million dollars in our expansion.

'Regrettably—' he went on, but his next few words were drowned in shouts of dismay and surprise.

He lifted his hand. 'Regrettably, Carina Hydraulics, although it is a legitimate corporation of the highest standard, is not exactly what you might term friendly. It is owned for the most part by Kruyper Coal, which in turn is almost entirely owned by Cornelius Oil.'

There was a shout of amazement. Two reporters ran from the room at once, heading for the nearest telephones.

Colton rose from his seat as if he was a withered puppet being tugged up on a string.

'Cornelius?' he spat. 'Cornelius?'

David Bookbinder did his best to look abashed. 'I regret, sir, that this is indeed the case. And I'm afraid that Cornelius Oil also holds voting majorities in Hulbert Aviation Fuels, and Rockaway Properties, and Nash Lumber Corp., and Eastern Wave Insurance, all of which' – he lowered his voice respectfully – 'have voted against 'he board today.'

Percy Colton sank back in to his chair. One of his nurses held a cool red-fingernailed hand against his brow The other one shook out some tablets.

David Bookbinder said: 'I can only take the blame for this remarkable rout myself. It was because of my lack of thoroughness and my inattention to detail that so many voting shares fell into the hands of Colton Oil's major rival. I was remiss in that I failed to check back proxies with sufficient care, and I accept full responsibility for what has happened today. I would be pleased if you would accept not only my apologies, but my immediate resignation.'

Colton pushed away the proffered tablets. 'Just get me out of here,' he said harshly. 'Just let me get some air.'

Much later that evening, David Bookbinder arrived at Johann's brownstone mansion in Gramercy Park. He was admitted by Vucinzki, the butler, who took his homburg hat and showed him into the room where, years later, Roderick would sit and sift through the files of letters and memos that told the story of what Bookbinder was about to do. Johann was sitting in his favourite chair, with papers spread all around him, dictating replies into an Edison recorder.

'Sit down,' he said. 'I'm almost through.'

David Bookbinder sat. Eventually Johann scooped up his papers into an untidy stack, switched off the recorder, and rang the bell for Vucinzki to come collect them. Then he turned his attention to David Bookbinder and said: 'Well? That's that, isn't it?'

David Bookbinder took out a cigar. 'You're pleased?' he asked with a small, provocative smile.

'I don't know. I suppose Carina got her revenge at last.'

'I think we all did. In any event, it was time that old PFC went off to a nursing home and wove baskets.'

Johann nodded.

David Bookbinder said: 'I suppose you know that you're now the third-biggest oil producer in the United States?'

'Yes. Henry told me. He also asked me to make sure that you called off the Klan.'

'I have already. The Grand Dragon was quite disappointed. He said they haven't had themselves so much fun in years.'

'Some people have fun wringing chickens' necks,' said Johann.

The two men sat there for a while, saying nothing. They made strange uncomfortable partners.

Finally Johann said: 'I was thinking.'

David Bookbinder raised his eyes.

'I was thinking that, since this is a week for revenge, I ought to do the job properly.'

'What do you mean?'

Johann appeared to be focussing on something very far away. He said: 'There's a restaurant on Fifty-eighth street. The Carbonnade.'

'I know it. It used to be called Eduard's.'

'That's the one. Well, I want you to buy it. When you've bought it, I want you to fire everyone there and close it down.'

David Bookbinder looked at Johann narrowly. Then he said: 'My guess is that years and years ago, the staff of the Carbonnade insulted you. Am I right?'

Johann didn't answer.

David Bookbinder said: 'The best thing for you to do is leave well enough alone. I expect the manager and the waiters from 1903 are long gone. And anyway, I like eating there. They serve kosher beef.'

Johann thought about this, and eventually nodded. 'All right, if that's what you want. But if you want my opinion, Mr Bookbinder, I think that you'll be the death of me.'

David Bookbinder clipped his cigar, and in the silence of Johann's room, the cutter made a distinct *snip*, as if someone was cutting a film.

1937

CORNELIUS ANNOUNCES AVIATION PLANS

'WORLD'S GREATEST AIRPLANE' ALREADY UNDER WAY

Roderick Cornelius, elder son of oil billionaire Johann Cornelius, and leading Cornelius Oil executive, today revealed his plans for building and flying the world's largest and fastest passenger airplane.

'What we are setting out to do here today will shrink the world,' he told a conference of aviation specialists and news correspondents in Charleston, West Virginia.

—New York Times.

September, 1937

On dull days, the new Cornelius Oil Building on lower Broadway took on a sort of despairing magnificence, like a giant hunchback, fatuously gilded and decorated for the passing amusement of a decadent prince, squatting in a rainy palace yard. On Wall Street, it was popularly known as 'Groaning Grange.' Its architect was a graceless imitator of Cass Gilbert, the designer of the Woolworth Building; but where Gilbert could make a Gothic spire seem ethereal and weightless, this man could only pile one massive block on top of the other, the more titanic and overbearing the better, and then garnish his huge and heavy-shouldered creation with as many irrelevant embellishments as possible.

The building was tiresomely constructed in a muddy shade of brown granite, all thirty-five hideous storeys of it, and it was as depressing inside as it was out. Every office was panelled in South American mahogany and carpeted in brown, and every door handle and radiator was moulded with bronze vine leaves. There was even a rumour that the architect would have liked stained glass in the windows, but someone (probably Hester) had drawn the line at that. Lauder Greenway had called the building 'a monument to everything that money can buy – and I mean *everything*.' And when James Gamble Rogers visited the lobby, soon after the building opened in 1936, he took one look at the black-veined-marble walls (plagiarized from the Straus Building) and dubbed it 'the most expensive funeral parlour in American history.'

The Cornelius family were aware that their main office was architecturally aggressive, but 'The House,' as they usually called it, was the kind of bulky physical presence that they wanted their empire to have. It was a temple to their fortune and the way they had made it. As Johann said: 'I want every passing banker, every passing investor, every stray Rockefeller staring out of the Standard Oil

353

Building, to look at my building – to *have* to look at my building – and see that it stands for what we are. We're rich, solid, powerful, traditional, and arrogant. If it's ugly it's because we *want* it ugly, and there isn't a damned thing that anyone can do about it.'

David Bookbinder's office was on the thirty-fifth floor, a secluded eyrie among the uppermost spires. It was humid and cloudy in New York City on June 9, 1937, but during the afternoon a few scattered showers had helped to relieve the oppressive airlessness, and David Bookbinder had been sitting in his office with the windows wide open, so that a few spots of rain fell on the papers and files he had stacked on the sills. He enjoyed the sound of the showers on the buttresses outside, and the fresh smell that breezed into his room, and he thought wryly that when his accounts department received the bills for handling, they would look as though they were marked with tears.

Bookbinder was less settled than usual, because Johann was in the city. There was a strike of teamsters over pay and working hours. Hester was in town, too. She was visiting friends for afternoon tea, and then Roderick was taking her to see Maurice Evans in *King Richard II*. Roderick was twenty-three, and inclined to be pudgy, and he was increasingly nervous because Johann had given him orders to investigate the possibility of Atlantic flying-boat routes. The day of the airship had come to an abrupt and horrifying end on a wet evening last month, when the *Hindenburg* had exploded over New Jersey. Now it was rumoured in the trade that Pan American was testing out the intercontinental airplanes, and Johann wanted to make sure that Cornelius Oil had a share of whatever was going. Hester thought the idea of flying across the Atlantic was exciting, but Roderick disliked heights, and had even bet his friend Davina Beerenberg twenty-five dollars that Amelia Earhart wouldn't make it. Davina was nuts about airplanes, and had taken the bet enthusiastically.

John was on summer vacation with a friend from Harvard. They were spending some time in Florida, visiting some progressive young writers they knew on Key West, and then they were going to tour some of the Cornelius oilfields in Texas, as a filial duty to Johann. John had sent

David Bookbinder a cheeky picture postcard which said: 'Today I ate my first conch. I have to admit that it reminded me of you.'

As far as the Cornelius empire was concerned, business was reasonably brisk; but months ago David Bookbinder's sensitive nose had begun to make him uneasy about the stock market, particularly with copper prices the way they were, and he was doing everything he could to prepare the organization for a cutback and a possible recession. He had had a long telephone conversation with Daylong Oil that morning. Their vice-president, Al Foretto, had talked about car showrooms that were crowded with unsold cars, and a public that was finding luxuries increasingly expensive to buy.

'I can't get over the way the New Dealers are blaming *us*,' Foretto had said. 'All this talk of the "sixty families" pushing up prices. I had a deputation from the cracking plant only yesterday, asking if they could personally put their grievances to Mr J.'

'And what did you tell them?'

'I told them I'd pass the message on to you.'

'And what did they say to that?'

'I can't repeat it.'

'Repeat it,' David Bookbinder had said. 'I'm not a child.'

'Well,' Foretto had said unhappily, 'they said they wanted to talk to Edgar Bergen, not Charlie McCarthy.'

David Bookbinder had laughed. After all, he was in a strong enough position to find it funny. He rarely listened to the radio himself, except for weather and stock reports, but he knew about the *Chase and Sanborn Hour*'s newly famous ventriloquist act, and the idea that the Daylong workers regarded him as a wooden mouthpiece for Johann Cornelius made him chuckle.

His amusement hadn't done much to relieve his anxiety, though. He had already spoken to Henry Morgenthau, the Secretary of the Treasury, at a private reception at City Hall, and protested about the cutbacks in government spending In his usual storybook manner, he had taken Morgenthau to one side and said: 'When a man is balancing on a wire, Henry, he can only go forward, backward, or downward.'

Morgenthau had said roughly: 'What do you think I am? A circus act?'

Bookbinder had patted his back and said: 'Maybe so. Just think about it when the situation requires you to step sideways.'

At around half-past four that afternoon, it started to rain again and David Bookbinder left his desk and went to the window. He had an angled view of Bowling Green, thick with hurrying umbrellas, and when he turned uptown he could see the grey and spectral spire of the six-year-old Empire State Building, gleaming with a faint yellow wash of hidden sunlight. Traffic honked dolefully, and a light wind blew across from the Jersey shore. He took a cigar out of his thick leather case and carefully removed the band.

It had been David Bookbinder's fiftieth birthday last month, in mid-May, with a champagne party out at Lynwood's Island. At the same time, he had celebrated his third year with the Cornelius family, and Hester had given him a gold card case inlaid with lapis lazuli and studded in rubies with the number three. When he had the case valued for insurance, the broker had suggested a round $215,000.

Johann had grumbled that the gift was a waste of money, but he hadn't grumbled for long. After three years of working with David Bookbinder, he was beginning to admit to himself that, in spite of Querbes Park, and in spite of Beatrice and Carina, David Bookbinder had a way of manipulating stocks and bonds that was almost magical, and a special talent for exerting pressure on unwilling senators and congressmen. He almost wished that Bookbinder had been around in the days of Albert Fall and the Teapot Dome business, instead of Jack Field.

In three years, David Bookbinder had probably done better for himself than in the whole of the rest of his life put together, and that included his years at Colton Oil. Johann often remarked that, whatever else was wrong with David Bookbinder, at least he put his money where his mouth was.

From his undistinguished beginnings, David Bookbinder was now making well over $1.5 million a year, and paying less tax than a Pennsylvania coal miner. But he never forgot his origins, nor his luck.

The door of David Bookbinder's office opened without warning, and Johann stalked in. David Bookbinder didn't turn around. He knew it was Johann, because nobody else would dare to walk in like that without knocking. He took out his cigar cutter and clipped a V in the end of the rich closely packed Havana tobacco.

Johann flung his black homburg on to the desk and stood there in his grey summer overcoat, looking big and elderly and fierce. His jaw was working around as if he had something in his mouth that he couldn't decide whether to spit out or not.

'David,' said Johann huskily, stepping forward and finding a chair for himself. 'Do you think I'm getting old?'

David Bookbinder remained at the open window, with his pinstriped back to his employer. He said: 'There's a saying, I forget who said it.'

Johann, his arm resting on Bookbinder's desk, sighed and stared at the floor.

'The saying asks whether it is better to be rich, or better to be wise,' went on David Bookbinder, turning around as he spoke, and reaching in his tight vest pocket for his lighter.

Johann looked up. Bookbinder lit his cigar, and stood silhouetted in front of the window for a moment, in clouds of smoke, like Mephistopheles freshly arrived from hell.

'I suppose you have a cute answer,' said Johann.

Bookbinder smirked. 'The answer's not cute, it's true. The answer is that it's better to be rich, because the wise man spends his days at the rich man's door.'

Johann grunted. He wasn't in the mood for Bookbinder's folklore. He said bitterly: 'That may have been true whenever that saying was invented, but it certainly isn't true today. Maybe Roosevelt was right.'

'Roosevelt?' queried Bookbinder.

'Well, dammit,' said Johann. 'If the Supreme Court is supposed to be too old at seventy, what hope do the rest of us have at sixty-five? I'm old, David, I'm old and I'm worn out. I'm tired of business and I'm tired of oil, and most of all I'm tired of myself. I don't care if I'm rich or wise. I'm exhausted.'

David Bookbinder walked around his desk and sat down.

He laced his fat pink fingers together like a plateful of frankfurters and blinked at Johann seriously.

'Don't tell me,' he said. 'You had a bad day with the teamsters.'

'Bad?' snorted Johann. 'They're totally intractable! I was down there talking to the so-called boys from Local 818, and I got absolutely no place at all. They've been getting twenty-five bucks a week, which is more than almost anyone in the country, and now they want thirty-seven or nothing.'

Bookbinder said: 'Were the newspapers there?'

'Of course they were.'

'Maybe I should have gone down in your place. I'm not quite as quotable as you. I hope you didn't say anything colourful.'

Johann pulled his coat around him petulantly. 'I think I've been in this business long enough to say *what* I like to *whomsoever* I like, David. I did nothing worse than call the CIO an avaricious ratpack on the backs of honest capitalism, or something like that.'

Bookbinder sucked his cigar. 'I hope you're kidding,' he said in a placid voice.

'Of course I'm kidding. But I'm not taking any more of this. I want you to get Fred Durham up here first thing in the morning, and we'll start to talk about layoffs. I'm not going to be blackmailed, David, and that's final.'

Bookbinder could hardly resist a small, fat smile. 'Let's not forget why I'm here, Johann,' he said. 'And let's not be too free and easy with our aspersions. Okay?'

Johann didn't answer. He sat champing his expensive bridgework for a while, and then said: 'Do you have any coffee in this place?'

'Sure,' said Bookbinder. 'Like a bagel?'

'Yes, why not?' said Johann. 'I haven't eaten since breakfast. This must be the toughest day's work I've done in five years. The next thing we know, those teamsters are going to be sitting down like the General Motors boys.'

Bookbinder shook his head. 'Don't worry about it. For every General Motors there's a U.S. Steel. And for every man in work today, there are going to be two men out of work tomorrow. The way that the market's going, Johann, another recession is absolutely inevitable. There's no getting away from it. In two years' time, the CIO will be nothing more than a distant and rather unpleasant memory.'

Bookbinder leafed through his accounts. 'I won't say the next couple of years are going to be easy. But I've already cut way back on production, and I'm ready to unload labour if we have to. I've negotiated one or two new outlets abroad, and I think we should weather the storm without too much capital loss.'

'Did you sign that German contract?'

'Of course. We have two shiploads of heavy-duty tyres on their way to Hamburg right now. I'm still cool on the Mercedes-Benz contract, but it could work out okay.'

Johann turned around as Stephanie came in with a rattling tray of silver coffeepots and Spode cups, and a plateful of buttered bagels covered with a crisp white napkin. She poured their coffee out for them and kept glancing nervously at Johann as he began with difficulty to munch his bagel, as if it was amazing that a multimillionaire could actually be bothered to eat anything so mundane.

When she had gone, Johann said: 'It's good to see that you put profit before honour.'

'What do you mean?' asked David Bookbinder, knowing exactly what he meant.

'Let's put it this way,' said Johann, sipping his coffee. 'Your patron Mr Rothschild wouldn't exactly have kicked his heels in the air, would he, if he'd known you were going to do business with Herr Hitler?'

Bookbinder grunted. 'I'm not the only one, Johann. There are plenty of financial worthies out there on Wall Street today who are looking at their bank balances for guidance, rather than their racial consciences. Hitler's in the market for engineering goods and tyres and all kinds of stuff. He wants the commodities, we need the money. I think the Atlantic Ocean is a long enough spoon if we have to sup with the devil.'

'That's what *you* think,' said Johann. 'One of these days, Herr Hitler is going to fly over here in his Zeppelins and take potshots at you through your office window.'

'Not that the *Hindenburg* was anything to go by,' murmured David Bookbinder, pointedly raising his eyebrows.

They sat for a few minutes in silence, drinking their

coffee. There were no telephone calls, because David Bookbinder always left instructions that his meetings with the Almighty were sacrosanct, and that nobody was to call or interrupt. With the rain pattering against the windows, and the wind flapping the loose papers on Bookbinder's desk, they could have been shut away from the world in some timeless carpeted vessel, with no view outside but the clouds, and no sound but the faint barking of car horns as New York City came to the close of another showery summer day.

'You know something,' said Johann, rubbing his eyes, 'you and me ought to sit down someday and work out just what the hell we mean to each other.'

Bookbinder grinned faintly. 'It's a romance, Johann. Didn't you know?'

Johann snorted. 'Some romance!'

David Bookbinder said nothing for a while, but he puffed out smoke in small puffs, and looked as if he was thinking seriously. After a while he cleared his throat and said: 'Many great friendships start off the way that we started off together; many enduring friendships. They last because there are no illusions, and never have been.'

Johann said dryly: 'I could ruin you. You know that, don't you?'

Bookbinder nodded. 'Of course you could. But why should you? There are some dramatic gestures that are worth the price, but that wouldn't be. That's why I believe we have a romance of a kind. We are two souls who both believe in the intrinsic virtue of capital, floating together down a tunnel of love. We have to trust each other in the dark, like sweethearts do.'

Johann brushed bagel crumbs from his coat. 'Why do you always have to have your windows wide open?' he asked. 'Look what happened to Jean Harlow. Caught herself the winter influenza and was dead in a week.'

'Would you weep at my funeral?' said Bookbinder.

Johann said: 'Just about as much as you're going to weep at mine.'

There was a light rap at the door, and Stephanie showed Hester in. She was dressed in a smart dove-grey afternoon suit with chalk stripes, a floppy-collared cream silk blouse, and a black crocheted vest. Her dark hair was softly waved, and she wore a small grey turban with a veil and a diamond-studded plume. She didn't like the fashion for openwork hats and peaks because they didn't show her big eyes to their best advantage.

The two men stood up, and Johann offered Hester a chair. David Bookbinder went across and closed the window.

'How were the brotherhoods?' asked Hester, sitting down and opening her pocketbook. 'Tea, I can tell you, was *dreadful.*'

Johann coughed. 'If you insist on taking tea with those incredible old dragons, I think you have to accept the consequences. David and I have just spent the afternoon . . .'

'Romancing?' suggested David Bookbinder.

Johann squinted across at him with a narrow-eyed look that Hester missed. He licked his lips, and then nodded.

'That's right,' he said. 'Romancing.'

'Well,' said Hester briskly. 'If that's all you're doing, perhaps we ought to go up to Gramercy Park and get ourselves changed. Roddy's coming round at seven, and your dinner's at half past, isn't it?'

Johann nodded glumly. 'I'm addressing the Republican Finance Club on the long-term problems of relief cuts. Although after my fun and games this morning with the CIO, I'm beginning to wonder if welfare's worth it. The American worker needs a kick in the rear, not relief.'

'Is Hope back from Connecticut yet?' asked David Bookbinder.

'She certainly is,' said Johann. 'Haven't you noticed the haggard look on my face?'

David Bookbinder leaned forward on his desk. He coughed. He didn't look directly at either of them when he said: 'Are you still having . . . well, *difficulties*? With Hope?'

Hester obviously didn't know whether she wanted to tell David Bookbinder anything about Hope or not. Her relationship with her husband's chief executive was courteous, but in a very stilted way. You felt that if their financial destiny were not so tightly intertwined, they would both have gladly passed each other on Broad Street as though they had never met. Hester privately thought that David Bookbinder was little more than a Semitic mobster, and that his complexion was like some cheap candy that small boys bought at Coney Island. She had once said so, to Johann's irritation. Bookbinder, for his part, was quiet and wary in Hester's presence, and would never talk seriously about business. He wasn't entirely certain that Hester knew very much about the way in which he had taken over the management of Cornelius Oil, and he didn't intend to give anything away.

But in any case it was Johann who told Bookbinder about Hope, and so Hester didn't have to make the decision, although she sat there tight-lipped and wished that Jo would try to keep his private life private, especially from a man like this.

'I'm old for a father,' said Johann. 'I know that. Hope's eighteen and I'm almost sixty-four. Maybe I don't understand the younger generation, and maybe that's the trouble. But she's wild! How can you bring up a girl like that, in good homes, with plenty of everything she wants, and a good education, and discipline, too, but still she turns out wild!'

David Bookbinder took out a very large white handkerchief and tooted his nose. 'How wild is wild?' he asked in a muffled voice.

'Well,' interjected Hester, 'she used to go around with John Roosevelt and John Drayton during the Christmas vacation, and you know what sort of horseplay *they* get up to. But now it's worse.'

'Worse?' broke in Johann. 'She wears short skirts, she has her hair cut like Jean Arthur, and dammit, David, she *smokes*. I wouldn't be surprised if she kept a hip flask, and drank liquor.'

David Bookbinder said: 'Have you tried having it out with her?'

'I would if I could understand a word of what she says! She's always talking about "boogie-woogie" and "killer-diller" and everything "sends" her. She goes out every night and spends her allowance like it's going out of style. Four, five hundred dollars a week, sometimes more, on some dumb crowd of kids who spend all their spare time racing up and down the highway in sports cars, going to parties and getting up to God knows what else. I mean, do you happen to know what an "alligator" is?'

'An alligator,' put in Hester, 'is a young person who likes

swing music. I thought even *you* could have worked that out.'

'I don't *want* to work it out,' said Johann testily. 'I want to speak to my daughter in English, not some foreign language that nobody's heard of. She's a wild girl, David, and she's wilful, and as far as she's concerned, I'm just some antique old has-been from the older generation.'

David Bookbinder smiled. 'We could cut off her allowance if you wish,' he suggested. 'It's kind of hard to make whoopee without the wherewithal.'

'That wouldn't do any good,' said Hester. 'Most of her friends are wealthy. They'd just advance her the money – *give* her the money – until we gave in.'

'I see,' said David Bookbinder. He laid his cigar on the edge of his ashtray.

'She's wild and wilful, that's all,' repeated Johann. 'Thank God there hasn't been any gossip in the newspapers about her, but if she goes on the way she is, it's bound to happen sooner or later.'

David Bookbinder looked down at his desk for a while and then said quietly: 'Do you really mean she's wild and wilful, or do you mean she's the only person who's ever stood up to you and gotten away with it?'

Johann slowly turned his head when David Bookbinder said that, like a large and threatening beast looking around itself for the impudent monkey that has pulled its tail during feeding time.

'David,' he said softly. 'I'll pretend I haven't heard that.'

David Bookbinder kept smiling. 'That's all right, Johann. You pretend you haven't heard that, and I'll pretend that I haven't heard of the year 1903.'

There was a curious silence that Hester didn't understand at all. Outside the window, the rain had stopped now, and dark evening clouds were gathering gloomily from the west. Hester blinked uncertainly at both men and said: 'Nineteen-oh-three? What's so special about 1903?'

Johann didn't answer straightaway, but then he lifted himself laboriously out of his armchair and wrapped himself up, with slow dignity, in his overcoat.

'It's a joke,' he said in a hoarse and heavy voice. 'Nineteen-oh-three is a joke.'

And David Bookbinder smiled at Hester, and nodded, and

363

smiled again, as if to say that indeed it was, and a very good joke at that.

The three cars bounced and walloped over the rough country roads, their headlights jostling through the warm summer night. Even from quite a way away, you could hear the young people shrieking and laughing as they swerved from one side of the road to the other, and someone was trying to play 'Don't Be That Way' on a clarinet, but was obviously too drunk and out of breath.

By the time they reached the crossroads, the three cars were almost neck-and-neck, taking up the whole roadway, and the kids were yelling and shouting to each other as they raced faster and faster toward the junction with the main highway.

'Get off, Eddie! Yayyy!'

'Ohhh, this sends me! This really sends me down!'

For a moment, two of the sports cars bumped against each other – running board grinding against running board – but then they blared across the main road with their horns going *parpp-parrpp-parrpp!* and were swallowed up in the darkness on the other side.

They drove for another ten minutes, gradually losing speed, until they drew up at a small muddy turnoff, and killed their engines. All of the kids were laughing and joking, and someone was saying: 'I sat on my hat! Would you look at that? I sat on my goddamned hat!'

Still talking and shrieking, they climbed out of their cars and stood around while one of the boys, in evening pants and shirtsleeves, did his best to open a bottle of bourbon.

'Boy, if my mother could see me now!' One of the girls giggled. 'She'd go nuts! I mean really nuts!'

'If your mother's here I want to know about it,' said the boy with the bourbon. 'She's a fine woman!'

He gave a mock-lustful cackle, and everybody laughed.

After a while, the boy managed to open the bottle, and they all sat around in their dinner suits and evening dresses and made themselves comfortable on running boards or rugs, and lit up Old Golds and passed the bourbon around The sky was a dense blue through the rustling black fingerwork of trees and branches, and a damp breeze was blowing. Somewhere far away, toward Danbury, a motorcycle sawed its way monotonously through the early evening. Their cigarettes glowed orange in the dark, and the kid with the clarinet kept on tootling the opening bars of 'Begin the Beguine.'

'You know your trouble, Mel,' called one of the girls. 'All you can do is begin to begin "Begin the Beguine." Why don't you ever *finish* it?'

'Nuts to you, Virginia,' said Mel. 'One day I'll be up there on stage with Artie Shaw, and then you'll squawk out of the other side of your mug!'

'What are you going to do? Hold his coat?'

Sitting on the running board of Eddie Kaiser's red Chrysler convertible, Hope Cornelius listened and laughed. She was feeling full of sparks tonight – bright and smart and pretty. In her clinging white silk evening dress, with its deep décolletage and feathery plumes over her breasts, she knew she looked at least two years older than eighteen. The bourbon hadn't passed around to her yet, but she was puffing assiduously on her Old Gold, and holding her head up in a very sophisticated way. She wore red lipstick, heaps of mascara, and she had plucked and pencilled her eyebrows into thin curves. Her wavy brown hair was tucked into a white curved evening hat, and her only jewellery, apart from her rings, was a big butterfly brooch in rubies and amethysts.

Next to her, Eddie Kaiser was smoking his cigarette in an ostentatiously 'tough' way, taking deep drags and blowing the smoke out through his nostrils. He was a beefy young boy, and his overtight tuxedo and black-and-white shoes didn't make him any less noticeable.

He turned to Hope and grinned in the darkness. His hair was shaved short and prickly at the sides, with a brilliantined centre parting on top. He said: 'Some fun, huh?'

Hope took a little sip of smoke. 'It's okay,' she said carelessly. 'If you like sitting in the woods on a wet night, drinking whiskey out of the neck of a bottle.'

'Why, sure I do,' said Eddie Kaiser. He was seventeen, and in four years' time he was due to inherit something in excess of four million dollars from his father's patent-medicine business. His high school friends nicknamed him 'Pills.'

'I'd like to do something original for a change,' said Hope.

'We're always doing the same kind of thing. We have parties, we go dancing, we go to nightclubs. I mean, that's all we ever do. I want to do something *wild* that *means* something.'

'I'd like to do something *wild*,' put in John Deerman enthusiastically.

'Well, *this* is wild,' said Mel Herbert. Then he said uncertainly: 'Isn't it?'

Hope looked around at all the young, well-fed faces. Among them, these dozen or so children were worth more than the capital reserves of some small countries, and yet here they were, sitting in a soggy wood in New York State on a showery June night, drinking whiskey and wondering what to do with themselves.

'If you think this is wild,' said Hope, 'then I suggest you go home and play Mah-jong with your mother. With any luck, you might faint from the excitement.'

'Maybe we should go round to your dad's place at Lynwood's Island,' one of the girls suggested to Hope. 'We could play poker, and every time one of us loses a hand, we could make it a rule that they have to take off a piece of their clothing.'

'Aw, that's dumb,' said Eddie Kaiser.

'You only think it's dumb because you can't play poker.'

'I can too! I just think it's dumb. If I want to get a girl's clothes off, I don't have to sit down at some dumb card game and do it.'

Philip Strachan called out: 'Why don't you do it then, smartie? I don't recall you taking any girl's clothes off.'

'You button it,' snapped Eddie Kaiser. 'Just because you're the Casanova of the campus.'

'Hey,' said John Deerman, passing the bourbon bottle to Hope, 'I heard my father tell this real funny joke the other day. I mean, it's real dirty, but it's real funny.'

'I don't want to hear any jokes,' complained Virginia. 'You're the only person who can tell a joke and make me feel sad.'

Hope took a swig of bourbon from the bottle and passed it. She said quietly: 'That's because J. D. is exactly like his father, and J. D.'s father, just like *all* of our fathers, comes from a bankrupt generation.'

'My father's not bankrupt,' said Cicely Schweizmann.

'He's rich, and that's his whole trouble Cicely, a dark-haired girl with a camelhair jacket slung over her shoulders, was memorable for her enormous breasts. Philip Strachan used to say about her 'God thought that rich girls are always unhappy, so he gave her an extra helping to make up for it.'

Hope said: 'That's what I mean, Cicely. Our parents are all wealthy, but mentally they're bankrupt. They don't know anything. I mean, our whole country's been through eight years of poverty and hardship and sweat, and they still talk about brotherhoods and workers like they're some kind of rabid scum.'

'Hey, wait a minute,' said Eddie Kaiser. 'That's John L. Lewis talk, that is.'

'More like *Grapes of Wrath* talk,' commented Kenny Thursgood.

'I don't care what kind of talk it is,' said Hope. 'Why do you think we're sitting here in these stupid woods drinking whiskey? Because we don't want to be sitting at home listening to our pompous parents talking their usual unreal garbage about the world today and how they help to run it.'

'I don't think my father's unreal,' put in Mel Herbert. 'He's stuffy, I'll give you that. But I don't think he's unreal. You have to give our parents something. They sure know how to make money.'

'That's about *all* they know,' said Hope. 'And do you know what their money costs the people who work for them? Do you really understand what it costs, in *humanity*, for you to stick a forkful of *pâté de foie gras* into that fat face of yours? Don't you read the papers? Don't you read about the strikes and the Okies and the struggle th country's going through?'

'Oh, come on, Hope,' said Philip Strachan. 'The best thing that our parents can do for this country is make money. You know that as well as the rest of us. If your daddy didn't have those oil wells of his, pumping out that lovely liquid money, about five hundred thousand people would be out of work tomorrow. What's the cost of one forkful of *pâté de foie gras* compared with what your daddy's putting into this country, and what he's doing to keep the economy strong?'

'But the CIO—'

'Forget the CIO. The CIO is a communist subversive group, and they're doing everything they can to bring this nation to its knees. Well, they won't do it!'

'Hey, listen,' put in John Deerman. 'Are we here for a political discussion or are we going to have some fun? Hope, you said yourself you wanted to do something original.'

'Yes, come on, Hope,' said Cicely. 'We can't change the course of history sitting out here.'

Hope stood up and brushed the seat of her dress. 'Okay,' she said pertly. 'I have an idea.'

'We stick up a gas station?' asked Kenny Thursgood. 'I'm sure Philip would like to do that.'

'No,' said Hope. 'I'd like to do something that's wild, but at the same time it's wild for a *purpose*.'

'I know,' said John Deerman, 'we assassinate Roosevelt.'

'Not that purpose,' interrupted Hope. 'If we assassinate anybody, we ought to knock off Hearst, or someone like that.'

Eddie Kaiser said: 'For God's sake, Hope. How are we going to do *that*? And what *for*?'

'I don't really mean we ought to knock off Hearst,' said Hope. 'But we have to do something clever. It has to look like it's a practical joke – you know, just high-spirited kids horsing around. But at the same time we have to make sure that it blows a Bronx cheer at something that our parents believe in. Do you understand?'

'My father believes in eating lightly boiled eggs for breakfast,' said Kenny Thursgood. 'You want me to blow a Bronx cheer at lightly boiled eggs?'

'Don't be so childish. It has to be something that shakes their very foundations. Like the class structure.'

'The class structure? I don't understand.'

'Well, you wouldn't. But this is what we do. We go back to the highway and we cruise up and down until we find ourselves a hitchhiker. Or maybe we stop off at a diner and look for some truck driver, or any old down-and-out. It has to be someone who looks real awful, and poor. Then we pick him up, and take him with us to the Royale Country Club, and we treat him like an honoured guest. We get our usual table, and buy him a bang-up dinner, and make all the waiters bow and scrape to him, the same way they bow and scrape to us.'

'Go on,' said Philip Strachan. 'Then what happens?'

'Well, that's it,' said Hope. 'Can you imagine Hugo's face when we walk in? Can you imagine all those stuffed shirts who eat there, when they turn around and see some decrepit old bum drinking his soup straight out of the bowl? I mean, don't you think that's beautiful?'

In the darkness of the clearing, the kids looked at each other in bewilderment, and then back at Hope.

'Is that supposed to be a blow for socialism?' asked Philip Strachan.

'Can you think of anything better?' Hope said.

'Well, no, I can't. But it doesn't seem like much of a blow for socialism. I thought socialists sat down in factories and stuff like that. I can't see Richard Frankensteen telling his workers to go dine at the Royale Country Club, can you?'

Hope said: 'What *are* you? Don't you understand what something like this can *do*? Everybody who knows us – all our parents and everybody – they'll just think it's another practical joke. They won't get too sore about it, and they'll stay just as complacent as they always were. But the workers, the socialists, they'll see what we're doing for what it is. We're bringing down the system, a little at a time, and showing we're not made of the same rigid conservative stuff as our parents.'

John Deerman scratched his head. 'I think it's a funny idea,' he said. 'But I don't quite see where the socialism comes in. I mean, I'm willing to go along with it just because it's funny.'

'Well, as long as you go along with it, I don't mind,' said Hope. 'Maybe you'll understand it when you've gotten yourself some political sophistication.'

'I don't mind doing it,' agreed Kenny Thursgood. 'It's better than playing strip poker, and it's certainly better than standing around here.'

'Virginia?' asked Hope. 'How about you?'

Virginia shrugged. 'If we're all doing it, I guess I'm game.'

Cicely said huskily: 'I could be his escort. I could really wiggle in there, you know – like Jean Harlow.'

'You mean like Jean Harlow used to.'

369

'Come on,' said Philip Strachan, 'if we're going to do it, let's get it real well organized, so that we all know what we're doing. A practical joke is only funny if you do it well. Otherwise you're wasting your time. Eddie . . . do you still have that spare tuxedo in the trunk of your car?'

'I think so,' said Eddie Kaiser. 'It's probably kind of crumpled, but I guess that's all the better.'

After twenty minutes of arguing and giggling and elaborating Hope's idea, the kids agreed on a plan of action. They climbed noisily back into their three cars, with Hope and Cicely Schweizmann sitting in the rumble seat of Philip Strachan's convertible, and started up. Then they turned around on the narrow road and made their way back to the junction with the main Newburgh-Danbury highway. It was almost ten-thirty now, and the sky was lighter now that the clouds had cleared. The forecast for tomorrow, June 10, was warm and fair.

They turned upstate when they reached the highway, and after driving for only three or four minutes they found the perfect place. By the side of the road, set well back in its own cinder-strewn parking lot, was a small diner and gas station. It was a low wooden building with a green-spotted tarpaper roof and a zinc chimney that wafted the odour of bacon grease into the warm summer night. Through the lighted windows the kids could see the owner, a stocky man in a white undershirt, clearing up after the day's business. A feed truck had just pulled out of the parking lot, and its red tail-lights were disappearing in the direction of the Hudson Valley. At a table alone sat a gaunt-looking man in an old grey suit, with a cup of coffee and a doughnut.

The three cars drew up by the side of the highway, and Philip went back to confer with Eddie Kaiser. Then he came back to Hope and said: 'We're all set. Do you want to go in and do the honours?'

Hope climbed out of the car, and Philip helped her down to the side of the road. For a moment he held her hands and looked down at her, handsome and curly-haired, with a serious face.

'You're a girl in a million, Hope. Do you know that?'

She didn't answer. She didn't particularly like standing there with Philip, holding hands by the side of the road,

370

with all the other kids looking on, but Philip was almost compulsively boring, like the Ancient Mariner, and just like the wedding guest, she could not choose but stay.

'I know you think that our mothers and fathers are pretty old-fashioned,' he said. 'But you have to remember that we're all looking for a brighter future. *All* of us – not just socialists and workers. The rich have rights too, you know.'

Hope lowered her eyes. 'For someone as bright and as well-educated as you are,' she said, an octave higher than she'd wanted to, 'you really don't have much vision.'

Philip wasn't upset. He liked girls with spunk. 'You're a rare one,' he told her, smiling.

'Yes,' she said.

The night wind flapped the gleaming silk of her dress against her slim ankles. She said: 'I suppose I'd better get going. Just give me a couple of minutes to size everything up. I'll give you a wave from the window if I need any help. Eddie, did you find that tuxedo yet?'

'I'm just looking,' said Eddie in a muffled voice from the trunk of his Chrysler.

'Good luck, Hope,' said Philip, and climbed back into his car. He gave her an impossibly jaunty little wave, and then started up. Eddie found the tuxedo and clambered into his car. The three cars backed up out of sight by the trees at the edge of the parking lot, and then cut their engines and switched off their lights. Soon there was nothing but the rustle of the wind and the soft sound of the stirring trees.

Hope crunched across the cinders and climbed the three wooden steps to the door of the diner. Most of the lights inside had been turned off now, and she could see the owner wiping his hands and hanging up his apron. She opened the screen door and went inside.

The owner looked up, but the man in the grey suit, the down-and-out, kept his eyes on his tepid coffee and the last crumbs of his doughnut. Inside the diner it was uncomfortably warm, and there was a clinging smell of fat and bacon grease. A large pound cake lay under a smeary glass dome like an exhibit at the museum of fossils. An electric fan circled tirelessly and uselessly around on the ceiling, casting its flickering shadows over worn-out brown oilcloth upholstery, two rickety pinball machines and a Myrna Loy calendar.

371

'We're closed, lady,' said the owner abruptly. He was short and Slavic-looking, with cropped grey hair and a soiled plaid shirt. There was a row of blunt pencils in his breast pocket.

'I just wondered if I could get some help,' said Hope, trying to look as wide-eyed and helpless as possible.

'What kind help?' asked the owner. Behind him, on the wall, was a faded picture of the frozen Vistula at Bydgoszcz, and a yellow rosette saying '1st.'

'It's my car,' said Hope. 'I was just passing and it broke down. It made a noise like poopity-poopity poon-tang and just stopped.'

'Well,' said the owner, shaking his head. 'From cars I don't know.'

Hope said anxiously: 'I did think of calling a garage. You know, to come and tow it for me. But a garage will take hours. I have to be in Newburgh tonight, it's absolutely essential, because my poor dear uncle is desperately sick and supposing he dies while I'm waiting for a tow truck?'

The owner found this a little hard to digest. He shook his head again and said: 'From cars I don't know. One end, other end. From cars I don't know nothing.'

Hope said: 'Do you think maybe that gentleman sitting over there knows something about cars?'

The owner stared at her. Then he turned his head and stared at the down-and-out sipping the last dregs of his coffee under the Myrna Loy calendar.

'Him?' asked the owner.

'Yes, *him*,' said Hope. 'There's nobody else in here, is there?'

The owner shrugged. Then he called out: 'Hey, you!'

The down-and-out didn't realize that the owner was shouting to him at first. He continued to sip his coffee, peering into the cup as if he was making sure that there wasn't an extra mouthful hiding in there someplace.

'Hey, you!' called the owner again.

The man laid down his cup and looked up. He was haggard and prematurely grey, with the sharp pointed face and exhausted eyes that characterized all those who stood in line for soup, or hung around railroad yards, or sold bootlaces or wind-up dolls on the corners of countless city streets. His striped shirt was frayed, and his grey suit was

372

worn shapeless. He could have been fifty, but he was probably nearer to thirty-five. There was a desperate destroyed composure about him, like a once-fashionable steamship reduced to dredging estuaries. He could have been handsome once, in a bank-clerk kind of a way, but now his face was neutral with poverty.

He said: 'Are you talking to me?' and his voice was very soft and polite.

The owner said: 'You think I talk to myself?'

The man said: 'I'm sorry. No.'

For what was apparently the first time, the man looked across at Hope. His eyes didn't seem to register any kind of surprise at seeing a young girl in a shining white silk evening dress in a cheap roadside diner at ten-thirty at night, but he did say 'Good evening' to her and straightened his greasy tie.

'What you know from cars?' demanded the owner. 'This lady, she's broke down. What you know from cars?'

The down-and-out stood up. He was short, and very thin, and Hope noticed that he wore no socks. He came forward, trying to walk straight, and said: 'What appears to be the problem, miss?'

Hope looked at him warily. Now that her 'blow for socialism' was actually happening, she felt frightened as well as excited. She had thought about it for weeks – ever since the last row she had had with her mother. The idea had seemed silly at first, but the more she thought about it, the more she liked it. She wanted to do something that made pompous people look as shallow and mean as they were; and also she wanted poor and down-trodden men like this to know that she and her friends weren't all spoiled brats, idling their time away at sailing and dancing and skiing, but that the next generation of rich would be genuinely charitable, honestly helpful, and free of the grotesque rigidity that had led them all into 1929.

It was partly a blow at her father, too. Johann Cornelius had never wanted Hope to be anything more than his pretty little daughter: bright but obedient, spirited but ready to come to heel when required. She sometimes wondered if he was trying to prove something to himself by the way he treated her. She knew how influential her mother was in his life, and he had an unnaturally gruff, evasive way of dealing with strong and independent women All through her girlhood, Hope had tussled against his suffocating intolerance, like the time he had refused to let her join the Lynwood Girl Scouts because he was adamant that she should be a pretty girl, a feminine girl, and that she would hate fending for herself. He had shouted at her: 'Pampered? Of course you'll be pampered! I won't have it any other damned way! What do you think I made all my money for? Why do you think I struggled? Some girls would give their right arms to change places with you!' Hope remembered him saying that because her mind had conjured up a disturbing impression of a strange girl sitting in *her* chair, in *her* frilly frock, but with only one arm – the price this girl had paid to change places with Hope.

Now this emaciated down-and-out stood wearily in front of her, an unsuspecting champion for her rebellious cause. He gave a hoarse, hollow cough, and raised his hand in front of his mouth. She noticed now dirty his fingernails were. Crescents of cheesy black. He sniffed.

'My . . . my car's broken down,' she said quickly. 'I think it must be something quite simple. It isn't a flat or anything like that. Perhaps I flooded the engine. I sometimes do that. I wonder if you'd be kind enough to . . . take a look for me.'

Her voice seemed to dwindle away very small. The down-and-out looked at her with washed-out eyes, and she noticed for the first time that one was blue and the other hazel.

'Miss,' he said courteously, 'I am, or I *was*, an insurance man. I'm afraid automobiles are a mystery to me, just as they are to this gentleman here.'

The diner's owner nodded, as if that was the wisest remark he had heard in several years, and hung up his dishcloth

'From cars,' he said, 'is mystery.'

Hope was growing anxious. She said: 'Well, couldn't you just come out and see? It's only just outside. Maybe you can think of something to get it running.'

The down-and-out tugged at his nose. 'Well,' he said, 'I still think a tow truck is your best bet, but I'll come and have a look. How much do I owe you, Mr Leszno?'

'Ten cents.'

Hope opened her white jewelled pocketbook, reached

inside, and took out a ten-dollar bill. She said: 'Let me pay for that.'

The down-and-out eyed the bill suspiciously. He already had the dime ready in his hand, and he laid it carefully on top of the cash register with an audible click.

'That's all right,' he said quietly. 'I still pay my way.'

Hope flushed, and put the bill back in her purse. 'Well, please yourself,' she said. 'I didn't mean to suggest that—'

The man waved his hand as if to say that she should forget it. He said: 'Good night, Mr Leszno,' and walked with Hope to the screen door and opened it. The shadow of the electric fan windmilled over their backs as they stepped out into the night.

Hope said: 'It's just over there, by the trees. I was lucky to get it off the highway.'

As they walked across the parking lot, Hope said: 'By the way, my name is Hope Cornelius. Would you mind telling me yours?'

The man looked across at her. In the blue gloom of the evening he seemed almost spectral. The darkness clung in the hollows of his eyes, and his cheekbones were as narrow as a rat's. He said: 'Why do you want to know?'

'Well' – she shrugged – 'I like to find out what my Galahads are called, in case I ever need them again.'

The man coughed. 'Do you think it's ever likely that our paths will cross in the future?' he asked.

'You never know.'

'Well, I don't think so,' he said. 'Whoever you are, Miss Cornelius, you're obviously a very wealthy young lady, and I am nothing more than a vagrant who used to sell insurance. I don't spend a lot of time in Palm Springs, you know. In fact, I mostly work this area doing packing and odd jobs for the local stores. I earned two dollars yesterday, cutting cords of firewood from dawn until midnight.'

Hope frowned. 'Haven't you heard of the CIO?'

'Oh sure,' said the man, sticking his hands in his pockets. 'But it's no use belonging to a brotherhood of workers if you're not a worker to begin with. Besides, I don't agree with communism.'

'They're not communists. Their whole purpose is to protect people just like you.'

The man stopped walking and stared at her.

'You're pretty unexpected, you are,' he said. 'If you don't mind my saying so.'

'What do you mean?'

'You're wealthy. Is that your car there, under those trees? Wealthy people don't generally hold with brotherhoods.'

Hope said: 'The point is, I know what it's like to be rich. My father's rich, and because he's rich, he's lost all his humanity. That's why I hold with brotherhoods, because I want to see some humanity.'

The man coughed again. They reached Eddie Kaiser's red Chrysler, standing empty under the rustling trees. The man walked around it once, examining it, and then went around to the front.

'Well,' he said, 'I guess we'd better take a look under the hood.'

He peeled off his jacket, folded it in half, and laid it carefully on the ground. Then he rolled up the patched sleeves of his shirt and started to grope for the catches that held the hood.

'I hope it's nothing too serious, Mr . . .'

The man looked up. 'Bausor, if you must know. Lewis Bausor, from Yonkers originally.'

'That's a nice name,' said Hope. 'Do you mind if I call you Lewis?'

'Do whatever you want. You've got the money to.'

Hope leaned against the side of the car. 'Now, come on,' she said. 'You know that isn't true.'

'Isn't it?' asked Lewis. He lifted the Chrysler's hood and peered inside. The engine was highly polished and immaculate. The cylinder heads had been plated in chromium, and there was the soft gleam of brass and machined aluminium everywhere.

'This is some engine,' said Lewis. 'I'm not sure I know where to start looking.'

'Maybe there's nothing wrong with it,' said Hope.

Lewis wiped his hands on his pants. 'Well, if it won't start . . .'

Then he stood up straight, and looked at her across the raised hood.

'What do you mean?' he asked. ' "Maybe there's nothing wrong with it"?'

Hope twirled her pocketbook. 'Just that. Maybe there's

nothing wrong with it. Maybe I brought you out here for some different purpose altogether.'

'Like what?' said Lewis defensively.

There was a giggle, and a shuffling sound in the shadows of the trees. Out of the darkness stepped Philip Strachan and Eddie Kaiser and Virginia and Cicely and Mel and all the rest of the kids. They came and gathered around the car, while Lewis Bausor stood there in his neatly rolled-up shirtsleeves, looking from one to the other in complete bewilderment. Philip, all gleaming white dickey front and gleaming white teeth, came right up with his hand out in welcome and said: 'Hi.'

Lewis turned to Hope. He said: 'Who are these people? Would you mind telling me what's going on?'

'They're my friends,' said Hope with a smile. 'It's a surprise. Everybody . . . meet Lewis Bausor, from Yonkers!'

Philip Strachan shook Lewis' hand and said: 'How do you do, Lewis? I'm Philip, and this is Mel, and that there's John Deerman, and if you'd just like to come around here I'll introduce you to everyone else.'

Lewis lifted his hands as if to protect himself from this torrent of sociability.

'Now, hold on, please,' he said. 'Just a minute. Would someone mind telling me what this is all about?'

Philip Strachan put one arm around him. An immaculate black tuxedo sleeve and white laundered cuff against worn-out stripes.

'Lewis,' said Philip intimately, 'it happens every so often that our secret society of socialites meets in the rural reaches of New York State.'

Lewis frowned but didn't say anything.

'When we meet,' said Philip Strachan, 'we select for one evening a deserving member of the public, and we treat him to a night of feasting and merrymaking. Our philosophy is that even though the laws of wealth are immutable, which prevents us from distributing our property freely and without let across the entire nation, we can at the very least take single and individual Americans of lesser means and give them a fleeting taste of the joys of being rich.'

Lewis Bausor licked his lips. He looked as if his mouth had gone dry, and next to Philip's well-fed bulk, he appeared on a smaller scale altogether, like the villeins in medieval paintings who are always drawn tinier than their feudal lords.

'Mr Bausor,' explained Virginia, 'what Philip means is that we're going to take you out for a meal. As a kind of gesture.'

Lewis Bausor bent over and picked up his folded jacket. He turned to Philip, and said in his soft voice: 'I appreciate your thought, sir, but I'm afraid that I just ate.'

'A cup of coffee and a doughnut isn't *eating*,' put in Hope.

Lewis shrugged. 'Maybe not to you. But that was all I could afford.'

'That's precisely the point,' put in Eddie Kaiser. 'That was all *you* could afford, but *we* can afford more, and we want you to *have* more. We want you to have one real good six-course dinner that you can remember for the rest of your life.'

'Oh, say yes,' said Cicely Schweizmann. 'Please, Mr Bausor, *do* say yes!'

Lewis Bausor said: 'Six-course dinner?'

'That's right,' enthused Kenny Thursgood. 'With turtle soup, and prime steak, and fresh trout, and all the hot biscuits you can eat.'

Lewis lowered his head. He coughed. They waited and nudged each other and giggled while he made up his mind. After a while he looked up again and said: 'I suppose really you're doing this to ease your conscience?'

Philip Strachan pulled an exaggerated face of mock horror.

'Conscience, Lewis? How you misjudge us! I don't blame you, of course. Everybody misjudges the wealthy. But let me tell you that no man can have a conscience if he makes money in the service of his country. We have no conscience. All we want to do is to share some of our good fortune around.'

Lewis looked again at Hope, with a questioning expression, as if trying to check that it was all right to say yes. Hope nodded, and grinned at him; and, reassured, he grinned back. 'All right,' he said. 'If it's going to make you all happy, I accept. You know, I haven't had a good dinner like that in three years. The last good dinner I had was in 1934, on Thanksgiving night, when a man picked me up just outside of Poughkeepsie and took me back to his home. That was my last good dinner.'

Eddie Kaiser came forward with his spare tuxedo.

'You'll have to wear this, Mr Bausor. The place we're taking you, they don't allow business suits.'

One of the girls tittered at the idea that Lewis Bausor's worn-out grey outfit could be seriously regarded as a 'business suit.' Philip Strachan said: 'Quiet, please! This is going to be a very dignified occasion.' The girls all *shushed* each other, and giggled some more.

Eddie took Lewis Bausor around the back of his car to change into his tuxedo, while the rest of them got themselves ready to leave. Hope, for some reason she couldn't quite understand, felt subdued and quiet, and she waited by the side of the red Chrysler, staring out across the parking lot to the diner, where the lights at last went out, and Mr Leszno locked up for the night.

'*Tarantara!*' trumpeted Eddie Kaiser. They all turned around, and out of the shadows came Lewis Bausor, dressed in Eddie's tuxedo. He was smiling sheepishly, and tugging down the black coat to try to make it feel more comfortable. Considering that Eddie Kaiser was a tall and hefty young man, and that Lewis Bausor was undersized and scrawny, the fit wasn't too bad. The coat was a little dusty and crumpled from lying in the trunk of Eddie's car, the white dickey was already spotted with soup, and the pants were so long that they concertinaed over his shoes, but as Philip pointed out, he didn't have any socks on, and the long pants would help to hide that omission from the Royale's maitre d', who was pretty punctilious on matters of dress.

Lewis Bausor came toward Hope, pressing down his straggly grey hair with the flat of his hand.

'How do I look?' he said hoarsely.

Hope nodded, and gave him a half-smile. She felt something tightening her throat, almost as if she wanted to cry. She knew that crying was quite ridiculous, and she knew that what they were doing was a real blow for socialism, but all the same it was hard to keep her eyes from blurring, and when she spoke she sounded as hoarse as he did.

'Lewis,' she said, 'you look just fine.'

They climbed into their three cars. Lewis shared the rumble seat of Philip's car with Kenny Thursgood. They set off, with a roar of over-revved engines and a salvo of horns, for the Royale Country Club. Mel Herbert produced his clarinet once again, and serenaded them as they sped through the moth-laced night.

It took twenty minutes of chaotic driving to reach the Royale. They sped in through the impressive wrought-iron gates, and slewed their cars around on the circular gravel driveway. Although it was late, the club was still brightly lit and crowded, and there were Cadillacs and Packards and Chryslers glistening like schools of expensive fish in the parking lot.

'Well, old man,' said Kenny Thursgood cheerfully, helping Lewis Bausor out of his seat, 'what do you think of it?'

Lewis Bausor, in his crumpled tuxedo, stood on the perfectly raked gravel and lifted his eyes slowly upward – up from the semicircular sweep of marble steps, up to the massive open doors and the glittering hallway inside, up to the columns and porticoes and ranks of shining windows, up to the ledges and shutters and stone acanthus leaves.

Hope came around the car and took Lewis Bausor's arm. He was standing there with such a white face that he could have been dusted in flour. It was only in the light of the driveway that Hope began to see how worn-out and sick he looked, and how incongruously the tuxedo hung on his bony body. He should have been in the hospital – not making an entrance at the Royale Country Club. But she squeezed his thin arm through the thick folds of his coat and said: 'Come on, Lewis. This is going to be beautiful.'

As they reached the door, Philip Strachan, with Cicely Schweizmann on his arm, caught up.

'I'll go first,' he said. 'I'm sure I can soft-soap Hugo. Anyway, I don't think he'll dare.'

'Who's Hugo?' asked Lewis Bausor.

'Oh, he's the maitre d',' said Virginia. 'A very particular man, if I might say so. So make sure you hide your ankles.'

They went through the doors into the lofty, brightly lit hallway. The floor was a dark mirror of highly polished Italian marble, and there were yew shrubs in decorative green-and-yellow ceramic pots all around. Ahead of them rose a maroon-carpeted staircase, and the foyer above that led to the principal restaurant. Even from the hall, they could hear the lilting sounds of the orchestra and the low murmuring of conversation.

'Better than Joe's greasy spoon,' said Kenny Thursgood. 'In fact, better than *anybody*'s greasy spoon.'

They trod upward through thick carpet, and crossed the foyer. Above them, floating in pastel clouds across a cupola dome, were nymphs and goddesses and overweight cherubim. With Hope clutching Lewis' arm tighter and tighter, they approached the tall doors of mahogany and engraved glass that led into the Royale's restaurant. Hope could already see Hugo, the small, dark-haired, ruthlessly particular maitre d', and her heart beat in irregular bounds. She didn't dare to look at Lewis Bausor, who was shuffling along beside her with his pants trailing on the carpet.

Inside, the restaurant was decorated in red velvet and plush, with a hundred gilt tables all crisply laid with white linen, solid silver cutlery, and rococo candelabra. At one side, the orchestra played on their rostrum, fiddling their way through endless elegant chamber music. At the other side, double doors opened into the kitchen, and dinner-jacketed waiters hurried in and out of these like bees flying in and out of their hive, carrying silver trays of salmon and pâté and oysters and the *pigeonneaux royaux, sauce paradis* for which the Royale was renowned. Not only was there an aromatic mingling of sauces and fruits and liqueurs and *filet de boeuf*, but there was an equally aromatic mingling of conversation, with the well-bred vowels of New England spicing the broad, flat, languid language of sunbelt profiteering. The restaurant, as usual, was crowded.

Hugo spun on his patent-leather shoes as they walked in, and gave his customary unsubservient bow.

'Monsieur Strachan,' he said. But his eyes flicked over Philip's shoulder, and checked out everyone else like a gunfighter checking his chances of survival.

'Good evening, Hugo,' said Philip. 'Crowded tonight?'

Hugo's round French face twitched in something like a smile. 'As always, Monsieur Strachan.'

'Well,' said Philip, 'I want a table for fourteen.'

'All members, Monsieur Strachan?'

'That's right.'

'And the gentleman with Mademoiselle Cornelius?'

381

'Oh, I forgot him. Yes, he's a guest.'

Hugo produced the guest book as if he had been hiding it under his dickey. 'You will, of course, sign for him, Monsieur Strachan?'

Philip blushed slightly, and hesitated. 'Well, actually,' he said, 'he *is* a guest of Miss Cornelius.'

Hugo didn't budge. 'Lady members, sir, cannot sign the register on behalf of gentlemen visitors.' All this time, he was keeping his eyes on Lewis Bausor, and taking in with meticulous observation the lopsided dickey, the hurriedly tied bow, the sagging jacket, and the trailing trousers. Lewis Bausor leaned on Hope's arm with the dispirited collapse of total pessimism, and she felt as if she were taking the Scarecrow in to see the Wizard of Oz. He coughed once or twice, but suppressed it as much as he could

Philip Strachan shrugged, and held out his hand for a pen. Hugo had it uncapped and poised as instantly as if he had plucked it out of the air. Philip signed, and turned back as he did so to give Hope a humourless and well-boiled smile.

Conversation in the restaurant subsided as Hugo led them all between the tables to a long banquette by the window. Most of the diners were friends of their parents, and they waved and smiled as they went. 'Good evening, Mrs Vanderhaugh.' 'Good evening, Mr Sharp.' 'Good evening, Miss Gaylord.'

As Hope passed one table, she heard Mrs Vanderhaugh, the lubrication widow, say in her usual piercing whisper: 'Who on earth, my dear, is *that*? Has he come off a *raft*?'

Hugo seated them all at the long table. Lewis Bausor sat uncomfortably next to Hope, and gave her a nervous grin. Kenny Thursgood and Virginia sat opposite, and Philip Strachan sat at the head of the table on Hope's left. The orchestra began to play a rather inaccurate version of the Trout quintet, and the surrounding conversation began to rise again. Only once or twice did diners at nearby tables cast worried looks at Lewis Bausor, but Hope was too happy to care, and Lewis Bausor was far too anxious to notice.

The wine waiter came and asked them if they would care for an aperitif or a cocktail. Lewis Bausor looked around him, biting his lips, as everyone ordered. Then the wine waiter said to him: 'Sir? Your pleasure?' and he almost shouted: 'A dry martini!' Hope thought to herself: He's done well, he's coping, and she tried not to think about his sockless feet.

They sipped their aperitifs in awkward silence. On his second martini, growing flushed, Lewis Bausor began to talk more, and gain some confidence, and they listened to him with a mixture of indulgence and disquiet. Hope could sense the tension all around her, and she kept glancing over to the velvet rope where Hugo stood, in case she caught him telephoning her father.

'I can tell you,' said Lewis Bausor, picking up his fish knife and buttering his bread roll with it, 'that I've seen things on park benches that would make your hair curl. You think you've seen life? You wait until you see the bums that hang around the Bowery, the way they live. Stinking drunk on wood varnish, crawling with lice. And some of them respectable men at one time, bankers and the like! And women, too! I remember in thirty-five, when I was in the Midwest, I saw women who would do anything a man cared to for fifty cents, except they were usually so filthy that you would have given them fifty cents to go away. I was on the Chicago elevated railroad, and I saw a woman, no doubt a respectable housewife before the Depression, raise her skirts and administer a pessary, clear in front of the whole car!'

At the next table, Mrs Edwin Daumier, wife of the New York investment chief, raised her hand to her brow as if she had a headache. She was a porky little woman with a hooked nose, in a low-cut black dress, and Hope was aware of her reputation as one of the Royale's most snobbish and most tiresome members. She had obviously heard every word that Lewis Bausor was saying, and it wasn't doing much to improve her enjoyment of her *suprême de volaille Jeannette*.

Hope touched Lewis' arm and said: 'Please, Lewis, you mustn't talk so loud. They're kind of sensitive here about the raw side of life.'

Lewis turned to her. His eyes were pink and watery, and Hope suddenly realized that on two martinis he was already drunk. His stomach had been empty, except for a cup of coffee and a doughnut, and he probably hadn't touched gin in years.

'Sensitive?' he asked. 'Of course they're sensitive! That's why you kidnapped me, isn't it, and brought me along? You wanted to show all these stuffed pigeons in here that you were liberal and free-thinking, isn't that right? I knew that all along. *I* came for the six-course dinner, but *you* invited me here for the sheer pleasure of shocking all these old turkeys, didn't you?'

'Lewis, *please*,' said Philip Strachan in an urgent whisper. 'Keep it down, will you?'

Lewis coughed, and wiped his mouth with his folded napkin.

'I don't understand you kids,' he said, shaking his head. 'You're not made of much, are you, except sugar and spice and all things nice?'

Hope said: 'I don't know what you mean. Don't you realize what a first this is, bringing you in here? Don't you see that you've just broken through the whole barrier of wealth and snobbery?'

Lewis Bausor almost laughed. 'I haven't broken through anything! The only reason they let me in here was because I was with you. I couldn't have gotten in here by myself in an ice age.'

'But you're here, all the same,' said Kenny Thursgood.

'Oh, sure, I'm here, but you're making damned sure that nobody knows about it. Keep your voice down, Lewis! Don't make a mess with your bread roll, Lewis! What's the point of dragging me in here if nobody knows?'

Hope said hotly: 'The papers are going to know, tomorrow, because we're going to tell them!'

The waiters were bringing the hors d'oeuvres. On Hope's recommendation, Lewis was having chilled Mediterranean prawns and plover's eggs. It was laid in front of him by a waiter who could scarcely suppress his disapproval of serving a man who looked, and smelled, like a hobo in borrowed finery, and it didn't help when Lewis picked up his fork and prodded the elaborately arranged dish so hard that one of the little eggs rolled off his plate and halfway across the tablecloth.

Hope was having turbot soufflé, and Philip Strachan was making do with Parma ham. They all started eating, but

384

it was apparent that, all of a sudden, they didn't have much appetite. The wine waiter brought a crisp and fruity German Moselle, and Lewis swallowed glassful after glassful. Across the table, Kenny Thursgood gave Hope an unsteady grimace, as if he was definitely beginning to regret the whole thing.

'Well,' said Lewis, cramming prawns and plover's eggs into his mouth and tearing off some more bread, 'what are these papers going to say? "Down-and-outs get hungry like the rest of us, and need to eat"? Is that what the great breakthrough is? Discovering that losers are human beings too, and that people with no money need to eat just as much as people with lots of money? Is that it?'

'Of course not,' put in Mel Herbert. 'Everybody knows that a down-and-out is a human being. That's not the point of the joke.'

Lewis Bausor stopped chewing. A prawn tail hung from one side of his mouth. He said softly: 'Joke? What joke?'

'Well,' said Mel, 'you have to admit that the whole idea is kind of amusing. I mean, you coming in here, and all. I mean, it's pretty wild. You have to admit that.'

John Deerman said: 'Every practical joke makes a serious point, Lewis. Behind every laugh, there's a cry of pain. Behind his smiling makeup, every clown cries.'

Lewis Bausor stared at him with his thin, ratlike face, his eyes glittering with drink. He said: 'Is *that* what this is all about? It's a *joke*? Hope . . . is that right?'

Hope felt confused. She said: 'It's not *exactly* a joke, Lewis. I mean it's not a joke on you. It's more a kind of charade. Can you see what I mean? What we're trying to say by bringing you here is that rich people live like that all the time. In charades. But it's not *you* that looks absurd. It's all these people here. By having you sit down here, eating their food, drinking their wine, sharing their restaurant, you're showing just how selfish and inhumanitarian they are.'

The waiters were clearing away the hors d'oeuvres plates and bringing the fish. Trout, delicately steamed in herbs. Philip Strachan said. 'Try the fish, Lewis, the fish is terrific,' but Lewis Bausor was too wound up now to turn his attention to food

385

'You don't know anything, do you?' he said loudly and incredulously 'None of you kids know shit!'

At the next table, Mrs Daumier raised her hands to her ears, and her escort, Señor Perova from the Spanish embassy, signalled with a wave to Hugo that something was wrong. Hugo began to weave toward them through the white tables like a little speedboat making its way through the sea.

Lewis Bausor said: 'How the hell can *I* make *anyone* here look ridiculous? You expect *me* to make *her* look stupid?' He pointed wildly toward Mrs Daumier. 'She looks stupid already, but I will always – *always* – look more stupid than her, because I'm poor and she's rich! You can't touch anyone who's rich! Don't you understand that? You're rich yourselves and you don't even know the simple facts of money! You may be fools, but nobody's a bigger fool than us bums and us down-and-outs, because we worship what you've got, and because of that we worship *you*, more than saints, and that's the whole truth!'

Señor Perova, a heavy-shouldered man with a frilly white evening shirt and a drooping moustache, came over and tapped Lewis Bausor on the shoulder.

'Sir, I suggest you apologize!' he said thickly.

Lewis Bausor looked up at him with unfocused eyes and said: 'Go suck yourself. I was leaving anyway.'

Señor Perova, without any further argument, hit him on the side of the head. There was a general gasp. Lewis Bausor tipped backward off his chair and fell against the window, cracking one of the panes. Philip Strachan leaped up and held Señor Perova's arm.

'Please . . . señor! It's not his fault! I'm terribly sorry! Mrs Daumier . . . please accept my personal apologies! This man is my guest, and I take full responsibility. I'm afraid it's the drink, he's not used to it! Kenny, will you give me a hand to get him out of here!'

Hope was kneeling down beside Lewis Bausor. There was a raging red bruise on his cheek, and he kept putting his hand to his mouth as if he thought his teeth might have been broken. Hope looked up and said: 'No, Philip! He's my guest and he's staying! That's the whole point of it! They only have to see someone like him, and they turn into wild beasts!'

386

' 'What do you mean, "they"?' snapped Philip. 'These people aren't "they"! They're *us*! It's this guy who's "they"! Now, let's get him out of here before he causes any more trouble!'

Hope was crying. 'It wasn't his fault, Philip. He just didn't know what he was supposed to do. He just didn't know how important it was!'

Hugo had reached them by now, and he was clucking and fussing around, and straightening the cutlery and rubbing his hands.

'You must leave!' he said. 'Please . . . you must all leave! This is most distressing!'

'I'm not leaving,' said John Deerman. 'I haven't finished my dinner yet.'

'Well, this person must leave,' insisted Hugo, gesturing toward Lewis Bausor, who was now sitting up on one elbow. 'He must leave absolutely at once.'

'For what reason?' challenged Hope, her eyes blinking with tears. 'There's been an argument, it's over, everybody's satisfied. Why does he have to leave? He's my guest and I want him to stay.'

Hugo rolled his eyes upward, and looked away as if his mortal dignity had been mortally offended. '*Immm*-properly dressed,' he said curtly. 'That is all. *Immm*-properly dressed.'

'He has a tux,' pointed out Kenny Thursgood, who had returned to eating his trout. 'You can't deny he has a tux.'

Hugo pointed a rigid finger toward Lewis Bausor's ankles. His pants had ridden up in the scuffle, and there, in plain view, were his grey naked shins.

'No hosiery,' said Hugo. 'There is, in existence on his feet, no hosiery, and the rule is plain. Without hosiery, dinner is refused.'

Lewis Bausor painfully climbed to his feet. The restaurant was silent now, and everybody in the room was staring at him with hostile curiosity. He whispered to Hugo: 'Help me out, please, will you? I don't feel so good.'

Hugo turned away. 'You must help yourself out. I decline to touch you for reasons of hygiene. I have my diners to consider.'

Hope said: 'Come on, Lewis, I'll help you,' and she lifted his arm across her shoulder. She looked at Philip Strachan, but Philip Strachan stood with his arms by his sides and still didn't move. Slowly, jerkily, they made their way back across the restaurant, back toward the tall glass doors, and as they passed each table, it seemed that their passing stirred up conversation again, and by the time they had reached the velvet rope, where Hugo watched them imperiously as they left, the restaurant was lively with chatter and laughter, and the orchestra was playing Rimsky-Korsakov, and out of the kitchen doors came a fiery silver tray of crabmeat *crêpes louise*.

'Miss Cornelius,' called a sombre voice as she helped Lewis through the swing doors. It was Gordon Eames, the Royale's secretary, a big glossy man who looked as if he polished himself all over every morning with beeswax. He had small pince-nez, and he was peering at her through them with an expression of considerable pain.

'Good evening, Mr Eames.' She was out of breath. She didn't look up, because she knew that her mascara had run.

'Miss Cornelius, it has come to my attention that you were responsible for introducing this person into the club.'

'Yes, Mr Eames.'

'In that event, I shall, of course, be obliged to inform your father. I am sure that we, the committee, can be lenient; but I am not at all certain how your father will consider your conduct.'

Mr Eames signalled to two of the green-jacketed footmen who stood by the side of the foyer, and they came forward and took Lewis Bausor by the wrists. Lewis himself did not resist, or even stir, but leaned against the wall with his face pale and his whole body stringless and slack.

'You may return to your party, Miss Cornelius,' said Mr Eames. 'I will see that this person is expelled.'

For a moment, Hope hesitated. She turned to Lewis Bausor and reached out her hand to him, but he wouldn't or couldn't lift his head, and when she said, 'Lewis . . . I'm sorry,' he didn't even appear to have heard her. She left him there and went back into the restaurant, where Hugo had considerately ordered that her trout should be kept warm on a chafing dish. It wasn't until weeks later that she realized how predictable a girl she must be, for nobody more perceptive than a restaurant waiter to know, infallibly, that she would return to her meal

The two footmen took Lewis Bausor out into the night.

388

They marched him silently between them up to the end of the gravelled driveway, to the decorated gates which stood at the country club's entrance. Once they were off country-club property, in the shadows of the highway, they proceeded systematically to beat him up, punching his face and chest and kicking him savagely in the groin and legs. He lay there on the road for most of the night, with a broken jaw and four fractured ribs, his face resting in half-digested prawns and plover's eggs.

A week later, on an afternoon of deep blue sky and idle clouds, they sat in a sloping pasture of oxeye daisies and long grass a few miles outside of Charleston, West Virginia. They were visiting Roderick's new orange-brick Queen Anne mansion to join him for a birthday picnic, and also, discreetly, to scrutinize Roderick's new girl friend, Celia Lulworth, whom he had met just two weeks before at one of Davina Beerenberg's parties, and about whose charm and beauty and '*wit*, mother!' he had been enthusing ever since. Hester had found it quite a bore to go to the theatre with Roderick in New York, because he talked about nothing else except the wonderful Celia, and how rippingly well they got on together.

A warm breeze was blowing from the southwest, a soft and sleepy wind that some of the local folks called 'the used-up breath of Kentucky.' The daisies nodded, and butterflies flickered through the grass all around them. Lester, Johann's travelling valet, had laid out a cream-coloured damask cloth on the ground under the shade of some old Virginia oaks, and the Cornelius party sat there in their pretty and decorative summer clothes, sipping tulip glasses of Dom Perignon, and nibbling at upland plover, soft-shell crabs, steak-and-truffle pies, as well as ripe English cheeses and small crystal dishes of *soufflés glacés*.

Johann, whose white-painted twin-engined flying boat was moored on the placid blue lake only half a mile from the house, had flown down from Lynwood's Island with Hester that morning, and he was sitting in a folding chair with his feet in the sun and his face plunged in shadow, munching his pie as if he had something on his mind. He wore a white barathea suit that seemed incongruously *sportif* for him; he was tanned, and grizzled by oncoming age, but he still looked like a man who had spent most of his adult life in smoke-filled offices.

Hester, in a lemon-yellow dress with a ruffled collar and a print of pale pink flowers, was wearing a wide yellow hat with a soft chiffon veil, which she had tucked up while she ate her soufflé. She was speaking in unusually guarded tones, mainly because she wanted to see what Celia had to say for herself. She knew that her son's new friend was the only daughter of Henry Lulworth, the adding-machine millionaire, but she had also heard stories about the Lulworth's family's sanity. There were tales that William Lulworth, the second son, was able to work out applied calculus in his head, as long as he kept his eyes shut, and that he spent entire weeks solving such obscure problems as the very hour when the residents of Butte, Montana, would next see an eclipse of the moon, for fun.

But Hester had to admit that, on first sight, Celia was proving almost more than suitable. She was a tall, pretty girl, with china-blue eyes and lips that were so full and red that they didn't need lipstick. Her blonde hair was fashionably waved, but her style of dress was formal enough to meet with Hester's approval. She wore a pale pink pleated summer skirt, and a soft silk top in white, with strings and strings of pearls around her neck. She spoke brightly and wittily, but never too precociously, and she managed to converse and eat simultaneously without the usual difficulty that Roderick had.

Hester could sense that Celia, though sparkling, was also very strong, and although she herself was always antagonistic to other women as confident and capable as herself, she knew how important it was going to be for Roderick to have a woman with both elegance and steel. Johann, she thought (as she gently stroked the leg of his white ducks), was growing old. It wouldn't be long before Roderick had to take over his fortune and his problems, and she had seen too much of Johann's agonizing struggles with the government, the unions, the price of raw materials, and the price of working with David Bookbinder to think that Roderick had the stamina to carry such a weight on his own.

Roderick, looking plump and hot, his hair stuck down with pomade, was sitting cross-legged at the far corner of the tablecloth. He had taken off his garish red-and-green-striped blazer and was hacking away at a piece of cold poached salmon. Hope, who was in an unsociable mood these days, had taken her glass of champagne and was sitting a little way away on the crooked arm of a tree, swinging her legs and staring out over the gently falling grassland toward the lake.

Lester came around with more pies, warm and crusty from his portable straw-lined hotbox, and the warm afternoon seemed to roll softly around them like all the summer days that ever were.

'Don't you think Roddy's house is coming on well?' asked Hester, looking down toward the square orange-brick mansion. The sun lit it up as she spoke, and then faded again.

Celia smiled. 'I do rather,' she said. 'I'm so looking forward to seeing it finished. I must say, though, it's difficult to say what the *hallway* is going to turn out like, with all those blue drapes all around.'

Hester smiled back, without really smiling at all. 'They do make the hallway cooler, you know. It gets intolerably hot here in summer.'

'It's a very unusual blue,' remarked Celia. 'It reminds me of mackerel, when they're not too fresh.'

Hester's mouth pursed. 'I chose it myself,' she said. 'If you knew anything about it at all, you would know that it's called Skagerrak blue, and that it was used by the royal house of Sweden to decorate many of the rooms at Drottningholm, the queen's summer palace.'

'Skagerrak blue?' said Celia with an interested nod.

'It *cools*,' explained Hester. 'It is an icy blue, a Scandinavian blue, and that is why it has such a cooling effect.'

Roderick had a mouthful of salmon. He said: 'If you ask me, the whole place would've looked better in red. Now, there's a colour to cheer you up. Red.'

'Nobody *did* ask you, Roddy,' said Hester, buttering herself a small crumbly cracker.

'It's my house,' pointed out Roderick.

'Well, that's as may be, but it's going to be decorated in *my* taste. If I let you have your way, the whole place would look like a mixture between a bordello and a garage'

Celia couldn't help laughing. 'Your mother's quite right, Roddy,' she said. 'I mean . . . just look at your blazer. Red and green! I didn't know whether I was going out with the heir to the Cornelius fortune or a downtown traffic signal.'

Hester raised her head. She looked piercingly calm, an expression which Celia found disturbing but also impressive.

'I assure you,' said Hester, 'that you are going out with the heir to the Cornelius fortune, and it would probably be just as well if you did not forget it.'

Johann was wiping his mouth with his napkin. 'I'm stuffed to bursting,' he said. 'That was a good spread, Lester. Remind me to have those steak-and-truffle pies again sometime.'

'Thank you, Mr C.,' said Lester. He was grey-haired and stooped now, but he had been serving Johann Cornelius on planes and boats for almost sixteen years, and he wasn't planning on immediate retirement. Lester was the only man around that Johann seemed to treat with any degree of kindness and consideration. Everybody else was expected to anticipate Johann's whims and instructions at least an hour in advance, and have everything he wanted tied up and settled by the time it first crossed his mind.

'Well, Roderick,' said Johann, sitting back in his folding chair and lacing his big fingers together, 'how's the airplane side of things?'

Roderick glanced at Celia, and gave a grin. 'That's how we kind of met, really, Celia and me. You know Dee Beerenberg has learned to fly solo? Well, she gave a big party up at her parents' place, and that's where we first bumped into each other.'

Johann glanced at Hester and nodded. Hester said: 'I think your father was really inquiring about the transatlantic routes you were working on.'

'Oh, them! Oh, they're all in pretty good shape now. But I think we may have to do some kind of cooperative deal with Pan American to begin with. It's a question of available know-how, and available engineering. There are so few people around who can give you a feasible estimate on transatlantic routes that everything you do is pretty much a shot in the dark.'

Johann, concealed in shadows, didn't raise his head. Sitting as he was in the bright afternoon sunlight, Roderick found it difficult to see his father's face beneath the trees, and he had to squint.

Johann said: 'Did I ever tell you the story of how I started Cornelius Oil?'

'Well, sure, sir, lots of times.'

Johann nodded again. 'Of course I did. And what did I tell you? What did I say was the one most important thing that kept me going – the one most important thing that made me rich instead of poor? Why am I rich, Roderick? Can you tell me that? Why am I rich when poor old Joe Schmoe in the street doesn't have two red pennies to rub together?'

Roderick looked uncertain, but Celia took his hand to reassure him. The gesture didn't escape Hester's attention, and she noted it down as a plus in Celia's favour. She knew the girl had deliberately teased her over the decoration of Roddy's house, but she was mature enough to understand that they had simply been going through the time-honoured ritual of son's girl friend challenging son's mother. In a matriarchal society – which, as far as she could see, *every* civilized society was – it was a necessary stage in a young man's journey through life. He was passed on from mother to wife like a Christmas parcel, quite oblivious of the complex and wary examinations that went on between them.

Roderick said: 'One of the things you told us, sir, was that you should always be bold. Always grab hold of the chance when it comes, because good chances never come twice.'

There was a long silence. Far away, by the lake, a reed warbler started whistling, and the breeze riffled the grass and the flowers like a mother passing her hand over the hair of her favourite child.

'And?' said Johann at last.

'. . . and, well, that's about it,' stammered Roderick. 'I mean it's all a question of chances. And of seizing those chances. Quickly, you know, and not letting them go.'

Johann sniffed. Then he said: 'Don't you think that the transatlantic air business is something that we ought to seize right now? While the chance is still here? Can we *beat* Pan American, instead of cooperating with them? Can we build our own airplanes? Can we become the first corporation to fly a scheduled weekly airplane service to Europe? Is *that* a chance worth seizing?'

'Why, sure it is!' said Roderick overenthusiastically. 'We could get in there straightaway. That's if it's something you really want to do.'

Johann rose from his chair and stood for a while under the tree, his hands in his pockets and his back bent with age.

'Roderick,' he said, 'it's not a question of whether *I* want to do it or not. This is *your* project. It's up to *you* to decide if you want us to invest in airplanes for transatlantic flying. I will always have to give final approval to your budget, and so will David, but unless you learn to stand or fall by yourself, then what am I going to do when it's time to hand all this huge corporation over?'

Roderick was deeply embarrassed, especially in front of Celia. He said thickly: 'I'm sorry, sir, I didn't mean that. I just meant that if the corporation's overall policy—'

'There *is* no overall policy, not on air flight! I gave you carte blanche to *create* a policy. Now it's up to you to tell me what you want to do!'

'Johann,' admonished Hester. 'This is Roddy's *birthday*. Do we have to talk about business? I'm sure you're boring Celia to death.'

Johann turned around. For the first time that afternoon, the sun fell across his face, and Celia saw his pale glistening eyes, his thick nose, and his sagging jowls. His white collar looked too tight for him, but he stood in such a way that it appeared to be the only thing that was holding him up. He was a heavy, old, ugly man, but he had a sense of suppressed energy that held Celia's attention completely.

'This young lady isn't bored,' said Johann. 'I've been watching her, and I know she's not bored. She's a young lady who understands wealth, and young ladies who understand wealth are always interested in finance, with some exceptions.'

He raised his eyes momentarily and looked over at Hope, who was now lying on her back in the grass twenty yards away, making daisy chains, and swinging her bare feet.

'I'd like to hear your opinion, Miss Lulworth,' said Johann. 'You know about flying, don't you? You've been

394

around with the Beerenbergs and the Earharts. What do you think we ought to do about transatlantic flight?'

Celia lowered her eyes and smiled modestly. 'I'm afraid I'm not an expert, like Roddy.'

'All the same,' insisted Johann, 'tell me what you think.

'Well,' she said. 'I think it's probably wiser to play it safe.'

'What do you mean by that?'

'I mean that flying itself, actually running your own air fleet, seems so uncertain. Look at the Zeppelins! Up until last month, everybody thought we were going to go back and forth over the Atlantic by airship, but now you wouldn't get most people up in one of those things if you offered them a free flight and a thousand dollars spending money.'

'Well, you're probably right,' said Johann. 'But what's your suggestion? I'd like to get *some* money invested in aviation.'

'I think you ought to place your money in all the services that people who fly are going to need, no matter *how* they fly. Things like carrying cargoes, and catering for passengers while they wait for suitable weather to fly. People always eat and drink when they travel! And what about things like filling up airplanes with fuel? It must take hundreds of gallons to fly the Atlantic. If you can monopolize all the services on the ground, you can let the air fleets take all the risks with airplanes and crashes and explosions, and you can sit there taking in a steady profit without any of the dangers.'

Johann listened to this, and then chuckled. 'You have a wise head, Miss Lulworth. I've a good mind to kick out David Bookbinder and hire you instead.'

'There speaks the voice of an optimist,' said Hester, a little bitterly.

Johann ignored her. He turned to his son Roderick and said: 'Well, Roddy, you've heard what Celia has to say about flying. Now what about you?'

Roderick stood up and walked around to the shade of the oaks, shaking his head.

'I have to admit it's a very sound theory,' he said, 'but it's not exactly the stuff that Cornelius fortunes are made of, is it? I mean, you can't call air freight the gold mine of the future, can you? How much freight can any airplane carry? Only a few hundred pounds, at the most And the cost! Who's going to pay a thousand dollars to send a couple of tyres to Europe when for eighty dollars they can send a whole car by sea? No, if there's any money in the air it's in passenger airplanes, and I'd like to see the Cornelius name on our own machines.'

'Our own machines?' said Johann. 'You mean ... build our own airplane?'

'Well, that's right.'

'You seriously want to do that?'

'Sure. In my opinion, it's the only way. If you have your own airplane you control all the ancillary things, like freight and so forth, and you can name your own prices for them.'

Johann took out his handkerchief and slowly dabbed his forehead. The wind had dropped, and it was ninety-five degrees in the sun. The reed warbler called again down by the lake, and Lester was collecting the plates.

'Roddy,' said Johann slowly, so that only Roderick could hear. 'When did all of this come to you? It wasn't just this minute, was it? Because of what Celia said?'

'Of course not! I've been working a couple of weeks on this.'

'And you really believe that it would be a good idea for Cornelius Oil to go into aviation?'

'Absolutely. I mean, one hundred percent.'

'Well,' said Johann, 'the best thing you can do is write me a report. Include all the figures, all the finance, and make sure it's sitting on my desk at Lynwood's Island by Friday next.'

Roderick blinked in unexpected pleasure. He lifted his hands as if he were going to clasp his father's arms, but Johann simply grunted and turned away.

'Sir, I—'

Johann coughed. 'Don't say a word, Roddy, not one word. This is your test, and if you say any more, you might make me change my mind. Sooner or later this business is going to be in your hands, and I want to make sure that if you have two or three or more million dollars to invest, that you do it properly. If you want to build an airplane – well, I'll give you the money and you can build it. But, by God, it had better be the best damned airplane that ever was.'

Roderick glanced at his mother. She reached up a hand to him, and he held her fingers for a moment, and then let go.

He said to his father: 'I won't let you down, sir. I promise.'

Johann beckoned to Lester to fetch him his stick. He said: 'No, Roddy, you won't.'

Roderick went back to Celia with a grin. He didn't notice the look that passed between Celia and Hester, the look of shared understanding about the true implications of what had just happened. It was, in fact, the first look in a series of looks that were the negotiations and the discussions in the gradual handover of Roderick from one woman to another; a look that he himself was too involved with his new airplane project even to notice, let alone comprehend.

Later that evening, when Hope sat in her bedroom overlooking the woods that curved around one side of the house, there was a rap at the door. She said: 'Come in,' and Hester came in, still dressed in the formal blue evening gown she had worn for dinner, but with her hair let down ready for bed. Hope was sitting in a large green wing chair by the window, her bare toes on the sill, reading *Veil of Iron*. She said: 'Hullo, Mother.'

Hester sat down on the end of Hope's mahogany bed and put her hands together in the way she always did before she made a serious announcement.

'I suppose you're going to tell me off for sitting on a tree all day, instead of talking about boring old airplanes with you and father?' said Hope.

Hester said: 'I hope we're not that severe a family.'

'It depends on your mood, Mother, if you must know.'

'Well,' said Hester, 'it isn't that.'

'Oh, I thought it was. Well, what is it? What other neinous crimes have I committed?'

Hester said: 'Look at me.'

Hope sat up and looked at her. She said: 'It must be serious. Who am I supposed to have murdered?'

Hester said quietly: 'You haven't quite murdered anyone, you'll be pleased to hear, but this morning your father had a telephone call from the newspapers Apparently a vagrant was picked up by you and some of your friends a week ago and taken to the Royale Country Club, where his behaviour caused grave offence to many of the members. He had to be ejected from the club, this vagrant, and while he was being ejected, he became violent, and it was necessary for the club's footmen to use physical force against him.'

Hope said quietly: 'Go on. What happened?'

'He ran away, apparently,' said Hester in a toneless voice. 'He ran away and disappeared into the night.'

'I don't understand.'

'That isn't all. He was found two days later in a field not far from the club. He had obviously dragged himself there. He was dead from hunger and exposure.'

Hope stared at her mother, and tears dropped from her eyes and onto her open book.

'Not Lewis,' she said. 'Not Lewis Bausor. Please.'

'You know his *name*?'

Hope covered her face with her hands. 'Oh, God,' she wept. 'Oh, God, I feel so awful.'

Hester said: 'Hope . . . you must listen to me. Do you mean to say that you actually *knew* the man? You were consorting with a down-and-out?'

Hope tried to answer, but couldn't. Her mother handed her a small lace handkerchief, and she dabbed her eyes and blew her nose. Her mother said: 'It's all right, I don't want it back.'

At last Hope lifted her head, wiping away the last tears with the side of her hand. She said: 'I only knew his name. I think he came from Yonkers. I never knew him before. Oh, God, Mother, I feel so guilty. I feel like I killed him myself.'

Hester said coldly: 'Perhaps, in a way, you did.'

Hope sat there biting her lip and staring at her mother with reddened eyes. She knew that Hester would always do whatever mothers were supposed to do, and more. She said all the right words, at all the right moments. She never forgot birthdays or special treats. She always attended school events, and she dressed as every girl hoped her mother might dress. But somehow it was impossible to penetrate Hester's motherliness any deeper than that. It was seamless and beyond criticism, and yet because of that it seemed like an act. Real mothers are occasionally imperfect, but Hester never was.

'I'm not going to ask you to explain yourself until you want to,' said Hester. 'That is *not* because I wish to spare your feelings, but because I want you to dwell on what has happened, and consider your part in it, and then come to your father and myself and tell us the truth in the spirit of contrition which you should.'

'Mother,' said Hope. 'I am *not* contrite! I did it for a reason!'

'What reason could there possibly be? You dragged an unfortunate man of no social standing into the Royale, and you not only humiliated him but you made a fool of yourself. I understand from Mr Eames that Philip tried several times to dissuade you, but you insisted on carrying on with your idiocy. You couldn't even listen to your friends!'

'Mother,' said Hope, 'it wasn't *like* that! I took Lewis Bausor to the Royale because I wanted to show that even rich people can have compassion. Or don't you understand what compassion is?'

Hester remained still and upright. A shuddering crescent of light, reflected from a gilt Louis XV mirror on Hope's bedroom wall, shone on her right cheek. Outside, the gardeners clattered their barrows and lawnmowers back to the stables. Someone was whistling 'Stormy Weather.'

'My dear,' said Hester, 'I may not be up-to-the-moment, as you are. But I do know that holding a vagrant up to ridicule in one of the most select country clubs in the nation is not, by anybody's standards, a compassionate act.'

'Mother, I—'

'Don't interrupt! *Think*, instead of interrupting! Think of how selfish you were! You wanted to prove that you weren't rich and spoiled? What a way to do it! Did you once consider this unfortunate man's feelings when you took him into the Royale? Did you once consider that he might have his own dignity and pride, no matter how mean and poor he looked to you? By what right did you treat him as your plaything? Or were you so blinded by the glory of your little crusade that such things didn't enter your mind?'

Hope couldn't answer. Two more tears ran down her cheeks, and she felt a deep, choking pain in her throat.

'This man's death isn't the only tragedy you've caused,' continued Hester. 'If you'd taken any interest in your father's affairs, you would have known that he is engaged in delicate negotiations with the Brotherhood of Teamsters A great deal of money and many jobs depend on the outcome of these negotiations, and if he cannot persuade the union to compromise, he may have to throw hundreds of men out of work.'

Hester reached forward and raised Hope's chin. 'Look at me,' she said. 'How is your father going to negotiate with workingmen if his daughter has treated one of their number with such contempt that he has died?'

There was a long silence. Hester eventually stood up and went to the door. She looked across at her daughter for several minutes without speaking, and for the first time in her life, Hope found it impossible to read what her mother was thinking at all. Hester's expression was remote, and yet touched with something that might almost have been pity.

'In the morning,' said Hester, 'you will have Nora pack your case. Your father is going to fly you to Connecticut, and you will stay there with the Landseers for as long as your father and I wish you to. The Landseers have already been telegraphed, and they have agreed to have you. While you are there, you will see none of your usual friends. Neither will you smoke cigarettes or drink liquor. I want you to understand that this is a punishment.'

'The Landseers?' said Hope. 'Oh, Mother, please—'

'It could have been worse,' said Hester. 'It was all I could do to persuade your father not to disinherit you altogether. He is very angry, Hope, and it will take him some time to get over it. He said . . .'

There was a pause. Hope looked up, and for some reason her mother looked suddenly confused.

'He said that *all* life, especially innocent life, is sacred, and that you must never abuse the power over life that money gives you. Do you understand?'

Hope whispered. 'Yes, Mother. In a way.'

Hester took a light breath. 'I hope, for your own sake, that you do.'

1938

COSTER REVEALED AS SCHULTZ ALLY

McKesson & Robbins Head and
Gangster Were Partners in
Bootleg Operations

Arthur (Dutch Schultz) Flegenheimer was not only aware that F. Donald Coster was an ex-convict named Philip Musica, but was associated with him in illegal liquor dealings from 1927 until the gangster's murder eight years later, it was revealed yesterday. Federal investigators are still uncertain, however, how Musica could have remained undiscovered for so long, and are continuing their search for an unknown ally or allies in the legitimate world of corporate business.

—*New York Times,*
December, 1938

It had just stopped raining when Celia arrived at the airfield in her cherry-red Bentley and parked outside the office door. She stepped out of the car in her French-styled linen suit and tugged at her gloves as she walked across the puddly concrete apron toward the main hangar. There was a fresh breeze blowing from the east, and the clouds were tumbling away to leave the sky blue and clear.

She went into the open doors of the hangar, and was surprised at the silence. For once, the huge half-finished airplane that stretched from one end of the gloomy building to the other was resting in peace, unattended by fitters, riggers, welders, and electricians.

She called: 'Roderick?'

There was a cough from the far end of the hangar. Roderick appeared from the tail of the airplane, dressed in greasy white coveralls, with a cheese sandwich in his hand.

'*Roderick*,' said Celia. 'What *are* you doing?'

He came over. 'Sorry, my darling. I was having lunch with the boys.'

'You promised to take me over to the Hunting Lodge for lunch or had it slipped your mind?'

'Oh,' he said, surprised. 'I thought that was tomorrow.'

'I can't possibly go tomorrow. You know that. I have a planning meeting with Denis Mulligan tomorrow at the Bureau of Air Commerce.'

Roderick looked sheepishly at his cheese sandwich

'Well, it's too late, now,' said Celia. 'You might as well finish it now you've started it.'

'It won't take me long to wash up,' said Roderick. 'We can be there by two.'

'I don't *want* to be there by two. I don't *like* lunching late. I like to have time for a cocktail, and anyway, I can't spend the rest of the afternoon sitting over lunch.'

'Well, I'm sorry,' said Roderick. 'I guess I got involved in the C-1 again. You know something, we've really licked those engine-mounting problems now. This baby is going to fly like an angel.'

Some of the fitters came out now, wiping their mouths after their impromptu lunch, and picking up their wrenches and screwdrivers to carry on with their work. They had been assembling the C-1 for three months now, and Roderick planned for a first proving flight in the middle of September.

'I just wish you'd spend a little less time messing around with oil and wrenches and a little more time on the business of selling airplanes,' complained Celia. 'You don't seem to understand that you're wasting your own money doing all this yourself. You're *far* more valuable in the boardroom. As it is, I've had to see the British by myself, and Pan American, and after I've seen Mulligan tomorrow I'm going to have to talk to the Hughes people.'

Roderick had a mouthful of sandwich. 'I'm sorry, darling I just think that you're the best person for the job.'

'Of *course* I'm the best person for the job. But it shouldn't *be* that way. *You* should be doing all this. These airline people hardly know you, except from what they've read in the papers. You ought to make personal contacts. It's all very well having a wonderful airplane to sell, but if you haven't prepared the groundwork, you'll find that Curtiss or Boeing or one of those other people have gotten in before you.'

'Darling,' said Roderick, 'I know you mean well, but there is no point at all in trying to market something which I don't yet have.'

'Of course there is! You're not thinking ahead! An airline has only so much money to spend on planes, and if they've already committed it to someone else while you've been fiddling around with the final screw-tightening and propeller-polishing, then you're sunk, aren't you? You've committed Cornelius Holdings to twelve million dollars on this project, and if you don't sell it, then you're twelve million dollars down.'

Roderick slapped his hand against the C-1's aluminium nose.

'This airplane is going to speak for itself. And I wish for once that you'd let me do things my way '

Celia sighed and turned away. Sometimes she despaired

404

of Roderick. He was so well-meaning and gentle, and he always remembered to bring her flowers and jewellery, but his mind was like layers of kapok. It took so long for any intuitive ideas to penetrate that she usually gave up and put them into action herself. It was simpler, and saved hours of futile argument. Besides, ever since their unsuccessful wedding night, when too much Dom Perignon had left Roderick floundering and flaccid, she had promised herself (and him) that she would give him all the direction and courage that he usually lacked.

'I would really like you to come tomorrow,' she said 'Denis tells me that he has a very good test pilot in mind.'

'A test pilot? For the C-1?'

'What else?'

Roderick wiped his hands on a piece of rag. 'I was thinking we might persuade Corrigan to do it.'

'Oh, forget about Corrigan. He's too worked up about this transatlantic flight he wants to make.'

'He sounds like a good pilot, though,' asserted Roderick.

A tall young man with a small moustache and a droopy tweed suit that hung around him in billowing folds came walking across the hangar with an armful of blueprints. This was Lem Cosnett, the chief designer of the C-1, and Roderick's closest adviser on aviation. Roderick had chosen him because he had barnstormed through Indiana and Ohio for six years, and knew more about the quirks of civil airplanes than most engineers would learn in a lifetime of sitting at a drawing board.

'I'm still worried about the stalling speed,' he said to Roderick in his twangy voice. He caught sight of Celia, and said: 'Hallo, Mrs Cornelius. How are you?'

'Busy,' said Celia. 'How are you?'

'Well, I'm worried about the stalling speed,' he repeated. 'If this bird takes off with a full payload, and if we can't get those engines to build up power a little quicker, then we're going to end up flat on our tail.'

'I thought they'd beefed the engines up,' said Roderick.

'Well, they did,' replied Lem. 'But you have to realize this is a big airplane. I mean, it's bigger than I really wanted to build it.'

Celia said: 'It's big that's going to pay. There's no commercial point in building anything smaller.'

Lem glanced at Roderick, but Roderick simply shrugged.

'Maybe I can get Rolls Royce to quote for engines,' suggested Lem. 'Oppenheimer tells me they're building a first-class rigout for Vickers That could give us some more horsepower.'

Roderick shook his head. 'I'm sorry, Lem. There isn't time. Mrs Cornelius needs a February delivery date at the latest. She's already had three pencilled orders from the Pentagon, and tomorrow we're going to see the director.'

Lem took out an Old Gold and lit it.

'Well,' he mused, 'if you're prepared to take the risk . . .'

Celia said: 'What risk?'

Lem opened out his plans and held them against the nose of the plane. 'When you build any new airplane,' he told her, 'you come up against certain imponderables. You find that the plane behaves different in the sky than you thought it was going to. It's a question of design, and balance, and the whole relationship between your power plants and your airframe. I can only calculate up to a certain point how the C-1 is going to behave, and the rest is guesswork. Well, my guess is that we may have trouble on takeoff because of the unusual weight of this baby. The motors may not be able to develop sufficient power quickly enough to take it up.'

'You mean it would crash?'

'Not necessarily. But it might mean that it's limited to certain airfields which have very long runways. That cuts out short-haul freight work from local airfields around the U.S.'

Celia looked testily from Roderick to Lem, and back again.

'Why didn't we know this before?'

'Well, Mrs Cornelius, it's a brand-new airplane, and we just couldn't foresee what was going to happen.'

'I don't think that's any excuse at all,' snapped Celia. 'Do you have any idea how much money we've already invested in this machine?'

'Yes, but—'

'It's not a question of "but"! We're not in business to build airplanes for our own amusement. We're in business to make this airplane pay. And if it's going to pay, it's got to be capable of flying out of every airfield in the continental United States, as well as half the airfields of Europe.'

Roderick coughed, embarrassed. 'Celia,' he said gently, 'I really think we ought to wait until the C-1's completed, and then we can test it and see for ourselves.'

'Don't you realize how *expensive* that would be?' asked Celia. 'I'd rather abandon it now if it's not going to pay its way, and cut our losses.'

Roderick was about to say something, but stopped himself. He said to Lem: 'I'll be back in a moment,' and then he took Celia's arm and led her out of the hangar into the fresh July sunlight. Celia waited until they had reached her parked Bentley, glittering with raindrops, and then she turned around and said: 'I suppose you're going to go into one of your wounded-bull-elephant routines now.'

Roderick was angry. He looked like his father when he was angry – big and liver-lipped and fierce. He said: 'If you talk to me like that again, in front of the staff—'

'Don't be ridiculous,' she said. 'The staff have as much responsibility as you do. You shouldn't even be down here, anyway, dressed up like a monkey on a stick. If you behave like a labourer, you'll find you get treated like one.'

'By *you*? My *wife*?'

'Of course not. But you really must sort your ideas out. We're not playing games anymore. Your father gave you this money to invest in a plane, and if it doesn't work, you're in real trouble. I'm only trying to help you out of a fix.'

Roderick walked moodily around to the front of the car and laid his hand on the solid-silver mascot of a flying Mercury. In the distance, across the scrubby airfield, a V-shaped flock of ducks rose from the Ashland marshes and wheeled into the wind.

'You've changed, you know, since we married,' he said almost truculently.

Celia looked at him. 'Yes,' she replied. 'I suppose I have.'

'You have to realize,' he said, without turning around, 'that a man has certain drives – certain ambitions. My ambition is to build a plane that's better and more exciting than any plane that's ever been built before.'

'You know what your father always says. Making a profit, by definition, is exciting.'

'But it's not everything,' protested Roderick. 'There's more to life than making a profit.'

Celia sighed. 'I wish you wouldn't persist in being so incorrigibly naïve. Of *course* there's more to life than making a profit. But making a profit is the essence of business, and that's what this airplane is. It's not an Erector set, it's a piece of commercial speculation.'

Roderick stared at his bride across the reflecting hood of the car. She *looked* the same as the laughing young girl he had taken down the aisle three months ago in New York. The wedding cars, Lincolns and Hispano-Suizas, had stretched for eleven blocks, and it had taken a whole city refuse truck to clear up the confetti. But she didn't talk like a pampered young girl anymore. She had turned out to be a hard-bitten businesswoman – impatient, ruthless, and unwilling to admit that anything was more important than the right percentage. What he failed to understand was that she was protecting her position in the Cornelius family hierarchy by protecting Roderick, and that she was keenly aware that her own influence and success were inextricably enmeshed with his. It wasn't that she didn't love him. She didn't, as a matter of fact – not wholly and passionately. But she had never looked for love in the men she knew. What she really wanted was *command*.

Roderick saw none of this. He just saw a pretty young girl with a peekaboo hat, her blonde wavy hair blown by the afternoon wind, and he was perplexed and hurt that she was being so intolerant toward him. He wondered vaguely if he was giving her enough presents.

'You never wanted me to build this plane, did you?' he asked her. He sounded like a small boy. 'That day at the picnic, you made that pretty clear to all concerned.'

'Don't be so ridiculous, darling. I was just saying that there's more financial risk in the airplane industry than there is in freight shipment and servicing.'

'Oh, God. You talk like J. P. Morgan on a wet Tuesday.'

'Roddy!' she said in a shocked voice. 'How *can* you say that? After all I've been doing to help this project along!'

Roderick was confused. He came around the car and held out his arms apologetically, but he was still wearing his greasy coveralls, and she held her arms up to protect her pale linen suit like a mother protecting her infant from a leering stranger.

'Celia,' he said. '*Please*. We seem to be arguing all the time these days.'

'*I'm* not arguing,' she said haughtily. 'It's *you*.'

He sighed. 'All right, it's me. I'm sorry. Maybe I should leave the fitters for a while and get back to my desk. Maybe I'm working too hard.'

'It doesn't seem to me that you've been working hard at all. You seem to spend most of your time tinkering with oily bits and pieces and eating sandwiches.'

Roderick pointed toward one of the motor housings on the wing of the C-1. 'You see that?' he said abruptly. 'I made that. I actually made it. With my own two hands.'

Celia looked briefly and nearsightedly toward the hangar. 'Did you, darling?'

'Yes.'

'Well, that's nice. Now, if you take off your dirty things, I can give you a ride back to the house. If you're actually going to make the effort to come see Denis Mulligan with me tomorrow, then you'd better do your homework on the flight schedules and the operating costs. And, *please*, don't let anyone start spreading rumours that the plane can't lift itself off the ground. That would be disastrous.'

Roderick looked at his wife for a moment, and then thoughtfully smacked the fist of his right hand into the palm of his left.

'Give me five minutes,' he said in a voice that sounded more than a little defeated. 'I have to tell Lem what I was doing this morning. Just for the progress chart.'

As he walked back to the hangar, she said: 'Was it a worthwhile morning's work?'

He stopped. He said. 'Yes. I put in the rudder.' And then he disappeared under the shadow of the C-1's wing to go tell Lem.

Johann was sitting in a cushioned basketwork chair by the swimming pool when David Bookbinder and his dark-suited young companion arrived at Lynwood's Island. The pool was enclosed by glass, with a dome that on hot days could be opened up like the leaves of a transparent water lily, allowing the summer breeze to circulate inside. There were rare plants growing in pots all around, many of them flowering and scented, and some of them trailing right down to the water's edge.

Johann was wearing a large red-striped bathing suit, and was sitting back reading the paper. There was a gold-trimmed telephone on the bamboo table next to him, and a silver tray with brandy-and-soda. Birds flittered and chirruped in and out of the dome, and a quiet fountain played among the leaves.

The pool was one of Johann's favourite haunts in the summer, when the pressure of business eased off. He didn't swim much, but he liked to feel that he might take a dip if the mood took him. There was a view through the windows across the wide back lawns of the house, toward the woodland and the rhododendron garden, and the sprinklers were making glittering rainbows across the grass. He wasn't a gardener, but he was relaxed and eased by gardens, and he'd once told Roderick's business tutor that 'no garden, however small, should be without a swimming pool and a couple of acres of woods.'

David Bookbinder came around the edge of the pool, followed closely by the man in the dark suit. Their footsteps echoed inside the greenhouse, and their reflections dipped and wavered in the water. Johann put down his paper and watched them approach.

David Bookbinder said: 'This is Merrett Kale.'

Johann reached out his hand without getting up. 'How do you do, Mr Kale. You'll forgive my casual apparel.'

'It's a pleasure to meet you, Mr Cornelius. I've heard a great deal about you.'

'Who hasn't?'

Merrett Kale grinned, and sat down uncertainly on an upright basketwork chair opposite Johann, while David Bookbinder dragged over a daybed and lay back with his hands folded over his potbelly like Buddha on his summer vacation.

Johann reached over for his brandy-and-soda and inspected Merrett Kale without saying a word. Kale was one of the smart young breed of new Navy Department executives, with a crispness about him that made you think he even starched his underwear. His face was lean and fit in a Buster Crabbe way, and he wore a prickly little moustache

410

that didn't suit him. His hair was cropped short, except for a sandy curl at the front that he obviously considered dashing. His shoes were polished like black glass, and he wore a blue polka-dot necktie with a tiny knot.

'Well, Mr Kale,' said Johann slowly. 'I hope you had a pleasant flight up.'

'Yes, sir! That's an impressive airplane you have there. I don't think I've ever flown in anything quite like it.'

'No, you haven't. It's the only one there is.'

David Bookbinder said comfortably: 'I hear John Livingston's in trouble. Dewey's trying to tie him in with Hines.'

Johann said: 'I heard. Our friend on the grand jury had a word in my ear the other day. What does Walter say?'

Bookbinder unwrapped a large Havana cigar. 'He's not sure. Cooper told him they may be making arrests in a couple of days.'

'Arrests? I don't know what's the matter with these people. They see rackets behind every bush.'

Bookbinder flicked his lighter and fed his cigar to the flame 'You have to admit the electrical business was getting a little out of hand,' he said, puffing smoke.

Johann shrugged. He'd known for some time that Thomas Dewey was going to try to corner Livingston. After all, it was one of the largest electric companies in the country, and with the grand jury investigating collusive bids between electrical contractors for private and municipal work in New York City, a confrontation had been trembling in the air for months. Johann's own electrical division, Allen Voltage Corp., was lying particularly low at the moment, with all the books in the hands of his certified accountants.

Johann turned to Merrett Kale. 'You look like an ambitious kind of a fellow,' he said in a toneless voice

Kale flapped his hands like two pale puppets. 'Well, yes, sir . . . I guess I am.'

David Bookbinder said, without taking his cigar out of his mouth: 'Mr Cornelius wants to know *how* ambitious.'

Kale coughed, 'Well, sir, I believe I'm *very* ambitious.'

'In other words, you want to get to the top?'

'Yes, sir!'

'The top of what? The Navy Department?'

Kale smirked. 'Actually, sir, I'm more interested in politics.'

'I see,' grunted Johann. 'So you'd like to be President?'

'Not quite, sir. But I'd like to find myself someplace where I can have some real influence.'

'You don't think you have influence now?'

'In some respects.'

'In what respects?'

'Well, sir, I'm involved in the contract department. Contract evaluation is my line.'

'You mean when someone puts in a bid to build something for the Navy, it's your job to evaluate how cost-effective it is, and whether it's the right kind of tender?'

'That's correct, sir. I don't have the last word, of course, but my comments are always taken seriously. I was an honours graduate in marine engineering, sir. Best of 1931. I'm kind of a blue-eyed boy in blue.'

Johann sipped his brandy. His eyes never left Kale's face, and after a while the young engineer found himself looking at the mosaic floor of the swimming pool, involuntarily avoiding the relentless stare of a man who had a dollar for every minute that Merrett Kale had lived.

A peacock, shining like a blue enamel brooch, strutted through the iridescent spray of the lawn sprinklers, and a warm summer draught blew in through the open windows of the greenhouse. In the distance, there was the silly, conspiratorial warbling of doves.

Johann said: 'You've come here because you have something to offer. I presume that what you have to offer bears some relation to your tasks at the Navy Department.'

Merrett Kale took out his handkerchief and patted perspiration from his neck. His starched collar was cutting into his skin and making him sore.

'Well, sir,' he said, 'I've always felt that industry and government should cooperate more closely. I know that the law requires defence contracts to be put out to tender, but quite often it's obvious who the best contractor for the work is going to be, right from the start. Unfortunately, because of the red tape and the committees, the best contractor isn't always selected. Maybe his price is a little high, or maybe the secretary doesn't like his face.'

'I think you can spare me the explanatory prologue,'

remarked Johann. 'Would you please just explain what you have to sell?'

Merrett. Kale blushed. 'It's not as easy as all that, sir. But it so happens that the last session of Congress provided for four 35,000-ton warships for the Navy. The same basic type as the *Washington* and the *North Carolina*. That's a twenty-eight knot ship with nine sixteen-inch rifles in three turrets, and an armoured belt about fifteen inches thick.'

'And?'

'Well, sir, they're coming up for offers.'

Johann nodded thoughtfully.

Merrett Kale said: 'They could be very profitable contracts, Mr Cornelius. Very profitable indeed.'

Johann looked at him.

'There's talk of Congress giving the go-ahead on 45,000-tonners, too,' added Kale. 'We have plans in preparation already.'

Johann said dryly: 'The President is talking about disarmament. He says that war contracts are only of passing value to the economy.'

Kale shook his head vigorously. 'That's just what he says for public consumption, sir. At the Navy Department we don't have any doubts. One way or another, this country has got to get itself ready for war.'

'You think so?' asked Johann.

'I'm sure of it, sir. And in any case, the President isn't going to be *that* reluctant to start placing war contracts. Passing value is better than no value at all.'

David Bookbinder tapped a chunk of ash on to the floor. He said: 'Tell Mr Cornelius your offer, Mr Kale. He likes things blunt.'

'Well, sir,' explained Kale, 'it so happens that if your shipping people want to bid for these four warships, my department will be involved in vetting your tenders.'

Johann almost smiled. Then he said: 'How much do you want?'

'If your bids are accepted, a quarter of a million dollars.'

Johann glanced across at David Bookbinder. Bookbinder simply shrugged, as if to say that any decision was entirely up to Johann.

Johann couldn't quite make up his mind. He'd seen hundreds of men like Merrett Kale – men who'd done well in their chosen profession and then found that their chosen profession wasn't as glamorous or as lucrative as they'd hoped when they were milk-fed college graduates. They'd approached him from every major corporation he could think of – from Tide Water and Standard, from Chrysler and Du Pont – and the story was always the same. They'd been wrestling for months, sometimes years, with the fantasy of selling their souls for what they considered was real wealth, and when the moment actually came, they invariably sold themselves more than cheap.

Thoughtfully Johann said: 'How do I know I can trust you, Mr Kale? For all I know, you could be an agent for the grand jury.'

'You can check my credentials if you like,' said Merrett Kale. 'I'm sure you have the means to do it.'

'We do,' put in David Bookbinder. 'And you can bet your life that we will.'

Johann said: 'It's too much.'

'You mean a quarter of a million.'

'That's right.'

Merrett Kale bit his lip. 'I'm sorry, that's the price.'

'I'll give you half that.'

'I'm sorry, I can't risk it for less than two-hundred-fifty thousand.'

'I'll give you half that, with ten thousand dollars cash in advance, nonreturnable.'

Merrett looked up. 'Nonreturnable? Whether you get the contracts or not?'

'That's what I said. You can have it right now, cash in your hand.'

Merrett Kale hesitated. He knew that $125,000 was too cheap a price for helping Cornelius Shipping win the warship contracts, but at the same time ten thousand dollars, to him, was a great deal of money, and if it was nonreturnable he could walk out of here and keep it without even having to compromise himself. If the contracts were fortuitously awarded to Cornelius, he could take the credit and collect the rest of the money, and if they weren't, it was too bad. He would still be ten thousand better off, and he wouldn't have risked anything.

He looked at David Bookbinder, and then at Johann

All right,' he said emphatically. 'It's a deal.'

Johann picked up his telephone and said: 'Henry? Yes, it's me. I want you to take ten thousand dollars in cash out of the safe and bring it out to the pool. . . . Yes, right now.'

The three of them waited in silence for several minutes. Now that the deal was concluded, Merrett Kale couldn't think what to say. He was embarrassed at having accepted a lower offer, but at the same time he was quite pleased with himself for having out-manoeuvred the great Johann Cornelius into giving him ten thousand dollars for nothing. It was money for old rope. Money for jam. He felt like smiling, but obviously couldn't.

'Do you swim, Mr Kale?' asked Johann.

Merrett Kale said: 'I'm a sailor.'

'I know that, Mr Kale,' said Johann. 'What I meant was, "do you swim?" as opposed to "do you sink?" '

Merrett Kale didn't know what to make of that remark, and said, instead of answering: 'I admire your pool, sir. It's very fine.'

'Yes,' said Johann. 'It's the only one there is.'

Henry Keith came out of the house in his shirtsleeves, carrying a manila envelope. His hair was thinning on top, and he had dark mulberry-coloured circles under his eyes, but he had survived twelve years of Johann Cornelius remarkably well. It was probably because he had never been ambitious. Johann always said that he liked his employees to set their sights high, but Henry Keith knew that meant setting their sights slightly below Johann or any of his family. He had seen too many aggressive young executives come and go to have any illusions about that.

Henry nodded to David Bookbinder, and then passed the envelope to Johann. Johann opened it up and riffled through the bills.

'The usual procedure on these?' he asked Henry.

'That's right, sir. The usual.'

'Here you are, then, Mr Kale,' said Johann, and passed him the money. Merrett Kale took it, and flicked through it himself.

'You don't trust me?' Johann smiled.

Merrett Kale coloured. 'It's just a habit, sir. I didn't mean to suggest—'

'It's a good habit,' said Johann. 'Always look your gift

415

horses right in the mouth. You'd be surprised at how much bridgework is missing.'

Merrett Kale stood up. 'Well, sir,' he said. 'I'd better be leaving. I don't want anyone asking questions.'

Johann nodded. 'One of my chauffeurs will take you out to the railroad station. I believe there's a train for the city every half hour.'

'Thank you, sir. It's been a real pleasure to do business.'

'Anytime, Mr Kale. Let's keep our fingers crossed for those ships, shall we?'

'I'll be in touch with Mr Bookbinder, sir, and I'll keep him informed.'

'I'm sure.'

Henry led Merrett Kale out of the swimming pool and back to the house. After they had gone, David Bookbinder sat there with his fingers laced together, puffing placidly at his cigar and enjoying the sunshine.

'You know something?' he said.

'What's that?'

'I believe I've finally converted you.'

Johann took a long swallow of brandy-and-soda. 'Converted me to what? Systematic skulduggery?'

Bookbinder laughed. 'There's an old saying, you know, which sums this occasion up perfectly.'

Johann said: 'I was afraid there might be. What is it?'

'It's Polish. The market gardeners used to use it, in Lwow. They used to say, "Even the largest apple on the tree, no matter what it promises the woodcutter, will fall when the branch is snapped off." '

Johann thought about that. Then he said: 'I think I see what you mean. You're ahead of me, aren't you?'

'I think I'm paid to be ahead of you.'

Johann picked up his telephone again and said: 'Henry? Has that gentleman left now? . . . Good. What train did he hope to catch? The three-thirty-two . . . That's excellent. What time does it get into Grand Central? . . . All right. That's fine. Now put me through to Eddie Corcoran, will you? . . . That's correct, in Norfolk.'

He laid the phone back, and sat there for a moment with his eyes closed, listening to the soft slopping of the water in the pool, and the squittering birds.

The telephone jangled and Johann reached over and picked it up.

'Eddie? This is Johann Cornelius . I'm fine, how are you? ... Listen, Eddie, I have a little problem here, and it's causing me some embarrassment I thought you could maybe help me out. ... Yes, that's right Well, it's one of your Navy Department people. I don't like to tell tales out of school, but there's a lot of money involved, and I don't like to see people take advantage. No, quite right. Yes. His name's ... What's his name, David?'

'Merrett Kale.'

'Eddie? His name's Merrett Kale. I believe he works in your contract division. Young guy, quite bright. That's it. Well, he came around here this afternoon and all but promised me the work on four 35,000-ton warships. Cornelius Shipping, that is. All I had to do was pay him a quarter of a million bucks, and the contracts were in the bag. ... Well, that's right. I know you can't believe it, Eddie, but that's the way it was. I stalled for time, and paid him ten thousand in advance. My secretary has the serial numbers. Yes, in cash. He's carrying it with him now, on the three-thirty-two from Lynwood, gets into Grand Central at five-seventeen.'

David Bookbinder listened to Johann talking, and thoughtfully sucked at his cigar. A ragged cloud was moving across the sun outside, and the lawns went suddenly dull. All the sparkle went out of the sprinklers, and he wondered if it was going to rain.

'There's one thing more,' said Johann, on the telephone. 'Well, I'm afraid that's right. The mood that the government's in right now regarding rackets, you can't be too careful. We don't want rackets in the Navy Department, do we? But what I *do* want to do is put in for these ships all the same. Maybe not the whole four. But two. If I can wrap up two of them, then there's no need for any disappointment, is there? ... Come on, Eddie, you know what I mean by disappointment! *I* don't want to be disappointed by missing out on some patriotic defence work, and *you* don't want to be disappointed by having this treacherous bum Kale blot your record. Now, isn't that a fair definition of disappointment? .. Good. I knew you'd understand. ... All right, call me back. But don't forget, that's five-seventeen at Grand Central. All you have to do is ask him where he got it, and see what he says. . . , Terrific. Good-bye, Eddie.'

'Short and sweet,' remarked David Bookbinder as Johann put the phone down.

'We've got him by the balls and he knows it,' said Johann gruffly.

Bookbinder said: 'Yes, I guess we have,' and eased his bulky body up from the daybed. He sat there watching the pool for a while, and then he stood up and brushed down his jacket.

Johann said: 'You're going straight back to the city?'

'I guess so. We have a meeting of Kruyper Coal at eight.'

'I was hoping you might stay for dinner. Hester's away in Vermont for a couple of days, and I wanted to talk.'

Bookbinder put away his watch. 'Was it urgent? What you wanted to talk about?'

'It could be. It's just that I'm kind of concerned about our involvement in rackets.'

'You're scared of Dewey?'

'Aren't you?'

'Why should I be?' asked Bookbinder. 'Tom's a good friend of mine. And any involvement we have with organized rackets is entirely for our own protection. We've been through this before. Any business on the scale of Cornelius Industries needs to keep complete control of all of its manufacturing and distribution, right down to the last truck. And let's not kid ourselves the police can protect us. I worked out that by cutting in Gizzi on the railroad contract, we saved ourselves almost three-quarters of a million last year from the decrease in pilferage and hijacks.'

'Suppose someone decides to unburden their soul? Someone like our good friend Merrett Kale?'

'Oh, come on, Johann, you're getting chicken-livered in your old age. We can always have Walden Farrow to lunch.'

Johann rubbed his face tiredly with both hands. 'I suppose so. It just seems to me that wining and dining the Justice Department isn't much of a substitute for keeping our hands clean.'

Bookbinder stared at Johann with a beady, riveting look that could have been surprise but was probably disgust

'Don't you get holy with me,' he said in a soft voice

Johann turned away. Sometimes he felt such a bristling

dislike for David Bookbinder that he could hardly bear to look at him. Bookbinder was like some goading younger brother who followed him around all day, worrying him and nagging him and enmeshing him in hopeless complications. He could see himself in David Bookbinder, and that's what made it worse. All the less pleasant traits of his own personality, which he normally kept firmly repressed, were openly buzzing around David Bookbinder like a swarm of blowflies.

Johann said: 'Have a swim before you go.'

'A swim?'

'I find it refreshing. It washes off the contamination.'

Bookbinder looked at Johann in silence for a minute or two, and then grunted a small, fat laugh. He said: 'I might at that.'

The Landseers were holding a garden party at their place in Connecticut, and John awarded himself the weekend off from his summer school at Worcester and drove down there in his green Buick convertible. He hadn't seen Hope since her banishment from Lynwood's Island, although they'd spoken on the telephone a couple of times, and he was looking forward to chewing the fat. The prospect of a Landseer garden party wouldn't usually have been sufficiently compelling on its own to bring him all the way down to Hartford, but apart from Hope, he knew that Susan Grainger Steadman was going to be there, and there was quite a lot about Susan Grainger Steadman that tickled his fancy. She was dark and vivacious, and he understood from Philip Strachan that she was not averse to 'third base.'

The Landseers were such tedious people that John often used to think that they held special family meetings to decide how they could make themselves even more boring than they already were. They lived in a large ugly half-timbered mock-Tudor house on a nine-acre estate outside of Hartford, most of which was lawns but some of which was neatly cultivated woodland. Mr Landseer was a senior partner in the old Connecticut law firm of Higgs Chandler Askew, and he was renowned for his thoroughness but not his haste; he had managed to prolong one complicated claim for damages for eleven years, and the way the case was proceeding it looked as though it would take another eleven years to settle it The defence had several times protested to the bench that Landseer was trying to bore them out of court and the bench had yawned and openly agreed.

Martin Landseer, their only son, was the model of his father. He was twenty-three now, and he was studying corporation law with the promise of a good position at General Motors. He was a sloping-shouldered young man with fair hedgehog hair, steel-rimmed spectacles, and a protuberant Adam's apple. His white ducks always seemed to be mangy, and his shirt collars curled up like stale sandwiches. He was a well-known jerk.

A shower had just passed over when John drove through the brick arch at the head of the Landseer's driveway and sped down toward the house. It always rained when the Landseers held a garden party, and the servants spent more time rushing in and out with tarpaulins to cover the tables than they did serving drinks. There was a marquee, with bedraggled bunting, and a brick barbecue that was smoking heavily. Everyone was clustered on the veranda of the house, talking and laughing loudly, and some of them waved as John tooted his horn.

As he climbed out of his car, a rather stuffy sun was coming out from behind the clouds, and people began to wander back onto the lawn. A seven-piece band was there, in red-and-white-striped blazers and straw skimmers, and they were busy wiping off their kitchen chairs with their handkerchiefs. John straightened his tie and walked across to the veranda to say hello to Mr and Mrs Landseer, and see if he could find Hope.

'Well, how are you?' said Mr Landseer, squeezing John's hand and forgetting to let go. 'You sure look top-notch, if I can say such a thing.'

'Is Hope here?' asked John.

'She certainly is. As a matter of fact, this party is really being given for her.'

'That's kind of you. I'm sure she's thrilled.'

'Not so thrilled as we are, I can tell you.'

John said: 'I don't quite understand.'

Mr Landseer winked, and his monocle dropped out. 'It's supposed to be a secret, really. They're going to announce it later.'

420

John managed to retrieve his hand. Behind them, the band started to play 'Tiger Rag.' 'Announce what?' he asked.

'Well, I really shouldn't say it, but I must tell you that I'm real proud, and happy as a boy's father could be.'

At that moment young Martin Landseer came up and said: 'Father, I think Harris wants to know when he can start serving the cold lobster.'

'Hi, Martin,' said John.

'Oh, hi, John. Glad you could make it. How's the summer school?'

'Pretty tough. Is Hope around?'

'Sure. Has father told you the news?'

Mr Landseer said: 'Not me, son. I've kept my lips sealed as tight as a jar of pickles.'

'Did you get the job?' asked John. 'The legal thing at General Motors?'

Martin nodded his head. 'I guess you're related, so you ought to know first. Hope and I are middle-aisling it. This is our engagement party.'

John blinked at Martin Landseer in total surprise. Of all the jerks that walked the northeast United States, Martin Landseer had to be the jerkiest. Hope knew that. Hope had even said so herself. She had once seen Martin Landseer in his bathing costume on Long Island, and called him 'a kipper in a brown woolly bag.' How could she think of marrying him? He was boring, like all the Landseers, but one could forgive him an inherited defect. It was his whining, smarmy, ineffectual personality that annoyed John, let alone the fact that he rooted for Yale and thought that Max Schmeling should have won his rematch with Joe Louis. John couldn't understand what Hope could possibly see in him. Perhaps he had hidden talents, like a very long thing, but he couldn't see Hope giving up fun and parties and social adventure for a *thing*, no matter how magnificent.

'Well' – Martin Landseer grinned – 'aren't you going to congratulate me?'

John held out his hand. Shaking hands with Martin Landseer was like wringing out a wet dishcloth. How could Hope actually let hands like that fondle her body?

'Have you   fixed a date?' asked John, hot and cross.

'Sure.' Martin winked. 'We're aiming for next spring. I can tell you, your sister has made me a really happy man.'

'She's made *all* of us happy,' put in Mr Landseer, dropping his monocle. 'Mrs Landseer calls her an angel, and I think that's about the right word for a girl as charming and composed as your sister, Hope.'

John said: 'You're very kind.'

Martin Landseer slapped him awkwardly on the back. 'We'll be brothers-in-law! Don't you think that's something!'

John gave a wan little smile. 'How are your sausages?' he asked.

Martin Landseer said: 'Fine!' but then realized he didn't understand what John was saying, and said: 'I beg your pardon?'

'Your sausages. They look like they're getting pretty well grilled out there.'

The Landseers' cook, a painfully thin woman in a tall white hat, was trying to prod cutlets and wieners on the brick barbecue. Smoke was billowing out across the lawn, as thick and foul-smelling as last month's Quackenbush fire out in Paterson, New Jersey.

Instead of going to help his future brother-in-law to bring the barbecue under control, John dodged off around the back of the house to see if he could find Hope. The first thing he wanted to know was what this nonsense about marrying Martin Landseer was all about. She could have had her pick! He knew for a solid gold fact that Philip Strachan was gaga about her, and even Eddie Kaiser said she was a doll. So why had she chosen Martin? Out of perversity? To punish Mother and Father for sending her away? Or had she really been smitten?

He walked around the back of the house and found Hope on her own, sitting at the far end of the veranda, eating strawberries and whipped cream with a spoon. The spoon flashed in the smoky sunlight. Her head, in a white feathery hat, was bent down over her crystal bowl, and she didn't see him at first; she was gently rocking herself in a swing seat and tapping the veranda rail with the tip of her toe every time she rocked. As he came toward her, he thought she somehow looked like a photograph of herself; and when she turned and saw him, and smiled, he was convinced that he would never forget seeing her like that, across the clipped lawn and jostling marigolds, behind the white-painted veranda rail, in her white hat and her loose white embroidered summer dress.

He came up the three steps onto the veranda's wooden floor and said: 'Hi.'

Hope reached out a hand. There was a sparkling engagement ring on her finger, but he pretended he hadn't noticed it.

'Do you like it?' she asked.

He nodded. 'Sure. It's a nice ring.'

'Nice? It almost broke the Landseer family for the next hundred years. Eighty thousand, if it's a dime.'

'Since when did you count the cost of things?'

Hope was licking her spoon clean. She stopped licking and looked up at John with a clouded face.

'You don't sound like you're very enthusiastic,' she said carefully.

'Well, to tell you the truth, I'm not.'

'You don't like me counting the cost of things?'

'That's part of it. Have you counted the cost of marrying Martin?'

Hope put down her strawberry dish. 'I don't know what you mean.'

'Sure you do. What happened to the kipper in the brown woolly bag?'

Hope shrugged noncommittally.

'You don't love him, do you? I can't believe that. What about you and Philip?'

Hope looked away. 'Philip's just a dumb preppie, that's all.'

'Oh, that's ridiculous!' said John. 'Philip's very fond of you, and what's more, Philip's a bright guy. At least he doesn't look like a refugee from a thrift store!'

Hope stared at him fiercely, and he saw something in her face – something hard and decided but also self-destructive – that he had never seen in her before. He sat down on the veranda rail and folded his arms and said: 'I just don't see what you're trying to prove. Martin won't make you a husband – not in a million years.'

'Martin's very sensitive.'

'Oh, sure. Like a marshmallow.'

'You don't understand. He's kind and he's gentle and I

423

feel sorry for him. He'd do absolutely anything I asked him to.'

John frowned. 'And that's what you want in a husband?'

'I just want it in somebody. There's never been anyone like that in my life. It's either been Father, who's totally dedicated to his business; or Mother, who's so goddamned relentless; or Roddy, who's spending all his time crawling around Father; or you.'

'And what's my trouble?'

Hope tapped at the rail with the toe of her shoe. 'Your trouble is that you're too damned honest.'

'You think that's a fault?'

'It is in our family.'

John sighed, and reached into his pocket for a tin of Balkan Sobranie cigarettes. He offered one to Hope, and they lit up. The smoke from the barbecue was now hanging thickly around the side of the house, and the sunlight was falling through it in shifting spokes. They could hear the band playing, and the shouts and laughter from the rest of the guests.

Hope said: 'I have this desire to look after people weaker than myself.'

'Don't you think Father has that?'

'Yes, I do. But he's buried it someplace inside of him. I sometimes think that he cares very much. I think I inherited this feeling from him. But because of the business, and because of what we are, we're not allowed to show it.'

John said: 'Is that why you're marrying Martin? Just because you want to be kind to someone less fortunate than yourself?'

Hope watched some small boys in white knickerbockers running around and around in the smoke; and heard their nurse calling to them from somewhere out of sight. The nurse said: 'Montmorency! Montmorency!' in a high piping voice.

Hope said: 'Is it wrong to be kind?'

John tapped his ash into the flowerbed. 'Of course not. But you have a duty to be kind to yourself, as well. I'm not trying to tell you how to run your life, Hope, but consider what you're doing before you do it. I mean, think about it Martin Landseer isn't exactly Clark Gable.'

'He's not Johann Cornelius, either, thank God.'

John looked at her acutely. 'You don't dislike Father that much, do you?'

Hope kicked at the veranda. 'You bet I do!' she snapped. But then she let the momentum of her kick squeak her backward and forward on the swing, and die away, and then she said: 'No, I don't really.'

John said: 'Whatever Father says – I know he's kind of gruff sometimes – but whatever he says, he loves you.'

'I don't know whether he loves anybody. Least of all me.'

'Hope,' insisted John, 'you don't have to marry Martin Landseer just to prove something to Father. That's the wrong reason completely.'

Hope gave the garden swing one last push and then stood up. She reached over and kissed John on the cheek, almost absentmindedly, the way a distracted mother kisses her son on his way to a college football game.

'I want to marry Martin Landseer because I want to see what it's like to be charitable and kind. I want to see what it's like to devote your whole life to someone weak, and give them strength. It didn't work with Lewis Bausor – you know, that poor man who died. But I know that I *could* do it if I really tried.'

John said: 'You're more like Father than you even know.'

Hope smiled as though she didn't believe him. But she didn't say any more, because Martin Landseer came cantering around the back of the house in his yellow suspenders, his white ducks smudged with smoke, and a black smut on the end of his nose. He was calling: 'John! John! It's getting out of control, John! You'll have to come and help!'

While John and Hope had been talking, they hadn't noticed that the rolling smoke from the barbecue had grown even darker and thicker, and that it was now almost impossible to see down to the end of the garden. From the lawn at the side of the house they heard coughing and shouting and the band trying to strike up another tune with the ragged uncertainty of men who don't know whether to play or run.

John stripped off his coat and followed Martin back through the smoke to the brick barbecue. It looked like a cocktail party on the battlefield at Gettysburg, with elegant young things standing around with martinis while the clouds of war rolled past in dense and choking billows. From the veranda Mr Landseer was shouting apopletic directions to his servants, who stood at a hesitant distance from the blazing barbecue, holding pails of water and looking miserable.

'Don't drench it, or there's no lunch!' he was shouting. 'And don't throw water on the meat! Watch the meat, will you, for God's sake!'

'John! What can we do?' panted Martin. 'You're good at this kind of thing! What can we do?'

John looked at this flapping, useless young man with the smut on his nose and felt almost sorry for him. But he didn't feel *that* sorry. A jerk like Martin Landseer needed teaching a lesson, especially when he came sniffing around John Cornelius' sister. He put his arm around Martin's shoulder and said confidingly: 'I'll tell you what to do. Impress your friends. Do what they used to do out on the Cornelius oilfields when they had a gusher that caught fire.'

'What was that?' asked Martin anxiously.

'They snuffed it out with dynamite. Just snuffed it out. You won't need water, and you won't spoil the meat.'

'But we don't have dynamite. At least, I don't think we have.'

'You have some kerosene, don't you? There's a can of kerosene right there.'

Martin looked worried. 'Yes . . .'

'Here's what to do. Screw the lid on tight, and thrown the can of kerosene into the barbecue. One bang, and you'll snuff that fire right out, and save your party.'

'Do you think it'll work?'

'Of course! They used to do it on the Cornelius oilfields all the time. They had roustabouts who did it for a living!'

Martin Landseer took off his spectacles and wiped the soot off them on the tail of his shirt. 'Well, okay, if you think it's going to work.'

John said: 'You go ahead. I'll just wait here and make sure everything's all right.'

'Okay.' Martin nodded and skirted around the thickening smoke of the barbecue to the far side, where the can of kerosene stood on the small pavement patio along with the charcoal and the skewers and all the rest of the cook's paraphernalia.

He called out: 'It's okay, Father! I'm going to try something! Just keep your distance!'

The servants looked relieved that they weren't going to be called on to throw their pails of water. Mr Landseer shouted: 'You be careful, there, Martin! That's two hundred dollars' worth of good meat there!'

Hope came around from the veranda with her handkerchief over her nose and mouth. John saw her and ushered her back again. 'I should stand well away if I were you. Martin's doing something with kerosene. I'm not quite sure what.'

Nobody could quite believe it when Martin Landseer picked up the can of kerosene, tightened the lid, and scuttled up to the brick barbecue with it, shielding his face from the guttering flames with his upraised arm. The band had been playing 'Ah, Sweet Mystery of Life,' but as the cornet player and the banjo plucker saw Martin with his can, their music dwindled away like water down a bathtub drain, and they scattered from their chairs.

Martin awkwardly heaved the can straight into the fire, and then, only five or six yards away, turned around and clapped his hands over his ears. Mr Landseer bawled: *Martin! What the devil are you doing?*' but neither he nor anyone else had the time or inclination to rush into the smoky epicentre and rescue his reckless son.

There was a sound like warping tin, and then immediately afterward an immense bellowing bang. Wieners and chops and T-bones sprayed through the guests in a greasy hailstorm, and the brick barbecue itself was thrown straight up into the air like a handful of jacks. There was a lot of screaming from the girls, and hoarse exclamations from the men, and above all of the hubbub you could hear Mr Landseer shouting: 'Martin! Martin! Are you all right?'

John ran around through the rubble and scattered meat, worriedly trying to locate Martin. My God, he'd had no idea that the fool would be dumb enough to *stand* there! Supposing he was dead, or terribly hurt? Supposing he was lying among the sausage links with his head blown off

He found Martin standing a little way away. The Landseer boy was smiling shakily. His hair was standing on end, and his spectacles were hanging from one ear. He had no clothes on at all except for his shoes and his socks.

When he saw John, he reached out his hands and mouthed: 'John . . . I can't hear! I can't hear very well! I can't hear!'

John shouted: 'I'd better find you a pair of pants!'

'I can't hear you!'

Martin nodded, and John went running back toward the house, through milling and babbling guests, his face set as tight as he could manage, to stop himself from laughing.

Mr Landseer caught his arm as he reached the veranda. 'Where's Martin? Is he alive? Where is he?'

'He's okay, Mr Landseer. He's kind of shocked. Look, he's over there. Can you tell me where his room is, and I'll get him some pants.'

Mr Landseer seemed to be as deaf as his son. He hurried across the wrecked and smoky lawn, one hand raised like a father in a Greek tragedy, muttering as he went: 'My God, the meat. My son, the meat. My God.'

It was only when John glanced along the shaded veranda to the back of the house and saw Hope standing there with her face pale and her eyes wide with anxiety that he thought he might have played the wrong sort of joke altogether. He began to wish he'd kept out of it and gone looking for Susan Grainger Steadman instead.

Roderick wasn't altogether happy about the test pilot that Denis Mulligan had suggested for the C-1, but today was too late to do anything about it. It was the last weekend in September, 1938, rainy and stormy for the most part, and Roderick had been obliged to divide his time between the last-minute preparations for the C-1's maiden flight, struggling in the small hours of the morning with landing-gear pistons that stuck and four Pratt & Whitney motors that refused to cough in unison, and his office desk. In New York, the Republican State Convention had predictably selected Thomas Dewey as candidate for governor, and David Bookbinder had been rearranging and redistributing Cornelius interests with a bad-tempered feverishness. He was forever calling Roderick on the telephone and asking if he could warehouse canned meats and liquor in Charleston, or whether he could move his tobaccos to Ashland, or if it was possible to reregister Cornelius corporations in other states.

The test pilot's name was R. S. Fairbanks, and he used to fly coast-to-coast sleepers in the early days of the Douglas DC-3, in 1936. He was a bony, taciturn man from Harrisburg, Pennsylvania, with weary-looking eyes and a thin moustache. He habitually wore a brown leather flying helmet with the strap undone, a dusty black cavalry jacket, and riding breeches. He spoke in dry and oblique sentences, and had told Roderick that he thought the C-1 was 'no better and no worse than a Sikorsky Clipper, and that ain't saying nothing.'

Just before dawn on Saturday morning, October 1, Roderick drove down to the Ashland airfield in his laurel-green Pierce Arrow, one of the last Pierce Arrows to be built before the company went bankrupt. He parked outside the main hangar and stepped inside the building through the small access door in the huge sliding portals which protected the C-1 from the rain and the salt-marsh winds. All the lights were blazing and the hangar was noisy with stammering drills and shouting men and the whine of compressors. Lem Cosnett, sweaty and tired in a fawn pullover with unravelling sleeves, came over and shook Roderick by the hand.

'Is she fit?' asked Roderick. He tried to sound as matter-of-fact as possible. A doctor inquiring after a young girl's health. But they both knew how much this date meant. They'd been working frantically for weeks to make sure the C-1 was ready on time, and on Monday night Roderick had even driven all the way to Cincinnati and back to pick up a set of instruments for the start of Tuesday morning's construction. What's more, instead of his laundered blue coveralls, he was dressed today in a dark wool double-breasted suit and a crimson silk tie, and even though it was only five-thirty, he had already shaved. He was prepared, psychologically and sartorially, for the C-1's first triumph.

Lem Cosnett leafed through his clipboard. 'I guess we're all fixed except for a couple of checks on the landing gear.'

Roderick reached out and touched the airplane's plain aluminium elevator. 'You know something, Lem, she's beautiful

Lem had been checking off his last-minute list of procedures. He looked up at Roderick and wiped his forehead with the back of his hand.

'As far as I'm concerned, sir, she doesn't get beautiful until she flies.'

'Flies?' asked Roderick. 'Oh, she'll fly, all right! She'll fly like a bird.'

Lem lowered his eyes again. 'Jack's still not sure about the motors. He's done what he can, but he's still not sure.'

Roderick took his hand off the elevator. His fingertips had made dabs of condensation, which gradually melted away.

Lem said: 'It's kind of a short runway, after all.'

Roderick thought about that, and then shrugged. 'You know what Mrs Cornelius said. If we can't lift her off from short runways, then she's not a commercial proposition.'

Lem nodded, not particularly joyfully. 'Yes, sir, I know that.'

Roderick stared at him hard. 'What you're saying is that you know that, but you're still not sure about the motors.'

'It's forty-one tons of airplane, sir. It's as big as a Clipper, and it's going to take a lot of runway.'

'That's Mr Fairbanks' job, isn't it? It's up to him to get her into the air.'

'He can't do it without the power, sir.'

Roderick turned away and walked around the tail of the airplane, inspecting the panelling and the control surfaces. 'What you don't seem to understand, Lem, is that Mr Fairbanks is the finest pilot in the world, according to Mrs Cornelius, and also according to Mr Denis Mulligan. He's such a fine pilot, in fact, that he could get the C-1 off the ground if it had no motors at all.'

Lem said: 'Yes, sir.'

Roderick looked back at him across the reflecting tail-plane, so that he seemed like a man standing chest-high in the sea. 'I don't believe that, and I'm sure you don't believe it, either, but it's the official line, and since Father appears to subscribe to the Fairbanks fan club too, we're stuck with things the way they are.'

'Yes, sir.'

'Okay, Lem. Let's get around this baby and see what the boys think of her chances.'

Together, Roderick and Lem went on a short tour of the C-1's hangar, talking to riggers and aero engineers and mechanics. To each, Roderick put the same question: 'How do you think she's going to fly?' Most of them thought good. Some of them said: 'Okay, I guess.' But he still kept on asking, until he was satisfied that every man in the hangar believed that the C-1 was going to climb up into the rainy skies this very morning, and wheel over West Virginia like a silver albatross.

They drank coffee out of enamel mugs, and waited around for R. S. Fairbanks. The test pilot arrived at eight, wearing his accustomed flying helmet and black jacket, but this time he was sporting his medals as well. He came straight up to Roderick and said: 'I gather we're ready.'

Roderick cleared his throat. 'We believe so. I want to take off at nine.'

Fairbanks blinked his noncommittal assent, and then turned abruptly on one heel. 'Is there any coffee left? I'm as parched as a possum's ass.'

Roderick looked down at his shiny black Alan McAfee shoes with their almond-pointed toes and punched decorations. He said: 'You know what to do if you run out of airfield and you're still short of power.'

'I know the orders, yes,' answered Fairbanks, spooning four sugars into his coffee and stirring it.

'You'll throttle back?'

'If necessary.'

'This is a small field. Remember that. It's probably going to be close.'

Fairbanks swallowed his coffee in three big mouthfuls, put down his mug, and wiped his mouth with a folded handkerchief. 'Ready when you are, Mr Cosnett.'

With R. S. Fairbanks in the cockpit, they went through the final routine of checking every flap and trim tab on the whole airplane. Rudders and ailerons opened and shut like the lids of magician's boxes. Then, at eight-thirty the hangar lights were switched off, one by one, and two mechanics rolled back the sliding hangar doors, allowing the grey grimy light of an overcast day to filter over the polished metallic skin of the C-1 A Ford pickup was backed into the hangar and linked to the airplane's tail wheel.

431

Slowly the giant machine was towed out of the hangar backwards, a huge glistening salmon caught by the tail.

Roderick stood in the chilly wind with his hands in his pockets watching the airplane drawn out onto the airfield. He checked his Cartier wristwatch. It was a quarter of nine now, and he hoped his father and mother would arrive in time for the first takeoff. Even if they didn't, he could have Fairbanks fly his baby over and over and over again, for his father's benefit, or to show off to his mother, or for anyone who still needed proof that he wasn't the dogged and obedient elder son any longer, strong on devotion but lacking in flair. He wasn't the awkward asthmatic who couldn't keep his pencils sharp. He was the airplane maker, the man who was going to take America into the stream-lined future, the dapper confidant of Howard Hughes and Charles Lindbergh and Bennett Griffin. This year, almost 200,000 people would fly by air, and next year, thousands more. Roderick had a dream that scores of Americans, rich and poor, would soon be girdling the globe by Cornelius Airways. He could picture it clear in his mind – a world teeming with airplanes, all winging their way hither and thither, with smiling families peeping from every porthole – mothers and fathers and uncles and aunts – happily travelling through clouds and sunshine in a miraculous aerial future which he, in his beneficent industrial genius, had created for them.

It started to rain. Celia's cherry-red Bentley appeared around the corner of the hangar and stopped. Their English chauffeur, Wilkinson, opened the door for her and held an umbrella over her head as she walked across toward Roderick, severe but faultlessly elegant in a grey cape and turban hat, and holding her toy silver-haired poodle, For-tescue. Fortescue had just had a permanent wave, and Roderick thought that he looked like Harpo Marx's toupee on legs

Celia offered her cheek to be kissed. She didn't look at the airplane She said: 'Are we ready to start, darling? You know we have the general coming down this afternoon for the Army Air Force, and at three there's Commander Armbruster You haven't forgotten, have you?'

'No, I haven't forgotten. Where's Father?'

'Oh, he'll be here. Your mother couldn't quite decide on

432

the mink or the silver sable. Personally, I think they're both much of a muchness.'

'I suppose you've had another row.'

'Of course not. More of a *contretemps*.'

'What was it this time?'

'Oh, Roddy, it's too boring. Your father wanted David Bookbinder to come, but your mother said she detested him, and *no*. So then your father made his usual speech that if it wasn't for David Bookbinder, the world would have long ago collapsed into economic ruin. That's when I told both of them to stop bickering and finish their breakfast, and of course your mother said she wouldn't have *anyone* speak to her like that, and so on and so on. But they'll be here later, don't fret. Your father won't let you squander twelve million dollars on an airplane that won't fly, and he won't believe it can fly until he sees it for himself.'

Roderick said doggedly: 'Of course it's going to fly. What the hell does he expect?'

Celia tickled Fortescue under his curly chin. 'That's what we're here to find out, isn't it? Whether it flies or not?'

Roderick didn't answer. He was watching Lem Cosnett taking a last prowl around the C-1, his clipboard on his arm, checking the tyres and the landing gear. Now the plane was out in the open air, it appeared deceptively small, even though its wings spanned 151 feet, and it was 160 feet from its streamlined nose to its tall tail. Roderick actually found himself wondering whether it *was* going to fly, or whether he was guilty of absurd delusions and self-aggrandizement. He looked up and the frayed yellow clouds were hanging very low, with only a faint dirty-yellow light seeping through them from the early-morning sun. A piece of newspaper tumbled across the grass and caught itself on the wheel of the C-1, flapping and damp, until a mechanic hurried over and fastidiously removed it.

Celia remarked: 'You seem depressed, Roddy. Are you?'

Roderick looked at her. He sometimes wished she wasn't so pristine and beautiful. She wasn't pretty; no one could call her that. But she had a cold perfection to every part of her face that had once made him believe she was a goddess. Perhaps she still was. But he knew now that it was less

433

than easy for a mere mortal to cohabit with a goddess, especially one as relentlessly devoted to success as Celia.

'I'm not depressed,' he said flatly. 'I'm a little anxious, that's all.'

'I thought you would have been magnificently pleased. Full of your own achievements. There it is, Roddy. A big, beautiful airplane, and you built it yourself.'

'Yes,' he said. He didn't sound very convinced.

Celia laid Fortescue down on the grass, and the toy poodle stood at the end of its slender studded leash, quaking like a powder puff with chronic pneumonia.

'Have you heard any more about Hope?' asked Celia. She was deliberately changing the subject, but Roderick didn't altogether mind. He was too nervous about the C-1 to talk about it, or whether it was going to fly. It was enough that it was actually *there*, parked on the grass a few yards away, a dull silver torpedo with looming wings. It was enough that he could smell the oily odour of airplane fuel, mingled with the salt tang of the marshes. It was enough that he could hear the dry bark of R. S. Fairbanks from the cockpit window, calling: 'Oil pressure normal, flaps normal, fuel normal, landing-gear indicator normal, hydraulics normal.'

A small flock of birds flurried overhead in the slanting wind. Roderick took out his clean handkerchief and blew his nose.

'Hope?' he asked, absentmindedly. 'She's still planning on marriage, as far as I know. John sees more of her than I do. It's still a sensitive subject around here.'

'What does your mother think?'

'I don't think she's particularly pleased. But Martin Landseer's an honest wight.'

'A what?'

'It's medieval for "guy". I guess it's the only word you can use for someone like Martin. Slow but well-meaning. If there was still hay to be forked in the world, Martin would be the kind of fellow forking it.'

'I see,' said Celia a trifle coldly.

'Well, *you* may,' Roderick told her, 'but Mother certainly doesn't. Nor does Father They both believe she'd marry the first person available to spite them for all that fuss last year '

434

'You mean the man who died?'

'That's right.'

'I don't see the connection.'

'Neither do I, frankly, but John believes that she's obsessed with the idea of looking after the world's lame ducks. She didn't succeed with that vagrant in New York, so now she's turned her attention to Martin Landseer.'

'Is he that much of a lame duck?'

Roderick coughed. 'Let's put it this way. When he was at college, the frat told him to steal a lady's drawers as an initiation. He came back a couple of hours later with the drawers out of a dressing table.'

Celia didn't allow herself to smile. She said: 'There's nothing we can do, is there? I mean, she's not stupid. She must know what she's getting herself into.'

'I don't know.'

'Well, I know, even if she doesn't. You would have thought that the man who died would have taught her a lesson. When the wealthy mix with the not-so-wealthy, no matter how benevolent their intentions, they usually wind up destroying them. She'll end up doing the same thing to Martin Landseer, you mark my words.'

A midnight-blue Rolls-Royce limousine, with whitewall tyres, its bodywork polished like a starry sky, appeared around the corner of the hangar. The chauffeur opened the door and Johann and Hester stepped out, regal and slow, and stood for a moment to make quite sure that everyone was aware of their arrival. Roderick went over to greet them, but Celia kept her distance and made an unnecessary fuss over the wretched Fortescue.

Hester was looking pale, and was wearing an ankle-length black fur coat. She extended a limp arm to Roderick, and he grasped her hand and briefly kissed it. Johann appeared tired, too, and he was masked like a bandit in a plaid scarf. On the lapel of his long vicuna overcoat, he wore a carnation with a sprig of fern.

'I'm so glad you could make it,' said Roderick, taking his mother's arm. 'This is going to be the most terrific day of my life.'

Johann said: 'So that's the airplane, is it? Is it ready to go?'

'Almost, sir. We're just making the last checks now.'

'What are you going to call her?' asked Hester. 'Not just the C-1, I hope?'

'I'm going to wait until she flies first,' said Roderick.

Hester said: 'I think you ought to call her Eastward Ho! That sounds so romantic, doesn't it?'

Roderick smiled uncomfortably. 'Yes, I suppose it does.'

Lem Cosnett came over and inclined his head respectfully to Johann and Hester. Then he murmured in Roderick's ear: 'It's no use.'

Roderick frowned. 'What do you mean?'

Lem Cosnett said 'Excuse me' to Johann and Hester and led Roderick aside by the arm. He said quietly: 'There was too much rain last night. The airfield's sodden. If I was sure of the power, I'd say okay, but I'm not. If the plane runs into the marshes, it's going to take days to get her out.'

Roderick bit at his fingernail. He looked irked.

'I'm sorry,' said Lem, 'but that's the way I feel about it I'd rather wait until the weather dries out.'

Roderick said: 'When's that going to be? What's the forecast?' He knew what the forecast was.

'Stormy.'

'Then it's going to get worse, isn't it, not better? Are you seriously suggesting we've got to hold this twelve-million-dollar airplane all winter, just because the grass is wet?'

Lem Cosnett looked unhappy. 'I have to give you my opinion.'

'All right,' said Roderick. 'you've given it. Now let's talk to Fairbanks, and see what *his* opinion is.'

He walked across the grass toward the C-1, ducking under the fuselage and rapping on the hull just below the cockpit. The window slid back and R. S. Fairbanks stuck his head out. 'Yes, sir?'

Roderick said: 'Mr Cosnett here believes the ground is too wet for a takeoff. How do you feel about it?'

R. S. Fairbanks pulled a face and thought about it. Then he called back: 'I once took off from Casper, Wyoming, in a force-eight gale, with lightning striking all around, and the soil was flooded six inches deep with rain. What's worse, my wheels caught a fence on the way up, and I flew all the way to Scottsbluff, Nebraska, with fifty yards of barbed wire, three fence posts, and a wooden feed trough flying behind me.'

Roderick still wanted to make sure. 'So you believe you can fly today?'

'Mr Cornelius, I'm ready for off.'

Roderick turned to Lem Cosnett. 'There's your answer,' he said quietly. 'He can do it, and that's good enough for me.'

Lem Cosnett held his clipboard to his chest. He didn't agree, but he knew that he was going to have to give in. He nodded and said: 'All right, if that's what you want to do. I'll get myself aboard.'

Roderick went back to Johann and Hester. Johann said: 'Is everything all right? It's cold out here. I don't want your mother catching pneumonia.'

'Everything's fine, sir. They're ready to roll.'

They stood in the soggy and persistent wind as one by one the motors spluttered and the propellers turned over. Lem Cosnett climbed into the plane and closed the main door. Roderick held Celia's arm, but she seemed more interested in Fortescue than she was in him and after a while he let go. Johann and Hester both appeared preoccupied and quiet, and Roderick began to wonder if any of his family were really interested in him or what he did at all. The motors were revved up faster and faster until the airplane was shuddering and all conversation was sawn away in a droning torrent of noise. Hester held her hands over her ears and Roderick felt almost embarrassed that he was causing his mother so much discomfort.

In the distance, the windsock stood stiffly toward the northeast. The huge plane began to roll slowly across the grass, and then turn its nose into the breeze. From where they were standing, they could see R. S. Fairbanks lowering his goggles. He was a pilot of the old school. He liked to fly with the windows open.

The grumbling roar of the motors grew louder still, and then R. S. Fairbanks released the wheel brakes and the airplane began to move off along the bumpy grass. Hester clapped her hands, excited now, and cried: 'It's off! Look, darling, it's off!'

Trundling away from them faster and faster, the C-1 gathered speed until its tail wheel lifted from the grass, and it was running on its two main wheels. Roderick found he was digging his fingernails into the palm of his hand, and that his face felt as rigid as a plaster mask. He could hear Fairbanks gunning the motors until they were screeching, and held his breath as one main wheel lifted off the ground momentarily and then sank back again.

None of them spoke as the airplane ran on and on over the grassy airfield. Roderick was tensely aware that if Fairbanks didn't get it off the ground in the next three or four seconds, then he was going to have to throttle back and call the flight off. He heard the motors rise to a throaty howl that he had never heard from them before, not even during their weeks of punishment testing, and he knew that Fairbanks was giving his takeoff every ounce of power possible.

'Oh, God, fly,' he whispered. Only Celia heard him, and she touched his shoulder with her hand; not comfortingly, but as if to reassure him that, yes, the world was very hard.

Even when he saw spray rising in clouds from the airplane's wheels, and knew that Fairbanks had run it into the marshes, Roderick still believed that it would rise miraculously off the ground. Fly, you bastard, fly! But then he saw showers of mud, and the sound of the motors suddenly dropped off with a sinking, complaining whine.

'He's botched it!' cried Roderick in an oddly effeminate voice. 'He's run it into the mud! For God's sake, did you see that? He's run it straight into the mud!'

Roderick, heavily, began to run across the airfield in the direction of the marsh. The airplane still hadn't come to rest, and he looked like a man chasing a plane that he had just missed by a minute or two. Johann and Hester and Celia stayed where they were, watching him gallop awkwardly through the wet grass in his celebration suit.

The airplane appeared to sink sideways, with its tail in the air and one wing broken. Then, without warning, one of the motors made a flat walloping sound and burst into flames. The wallop echoed back to Roderick from the hangar behind him.

He stopped where he was. Panting, he turned around and began to run back to the buildings. He shouted to Celia: 'The car! It's quicker! Get in the car!'

The riggers and mechanics were already running past him with fire extinguishers. He climbed clumsily into the Pierce Arrow and started it up, driving erratically across the muddy ground. One of the riggers saw him coming and jumped onto the running board as he passed, and climbed in beside him.

One wing of the airplane was blazing fiercely. Already a dark spiral of smoke was staining the grey sky, and marsh birds were wheeling and turning all around it. Everything was unnaturally quiet, except for the engine of the Pierce Arrow and the sound of tyres slithering in the mud. It was only now that Roderick appreciated how heavy and wet the airfield really was.

They reached the edge of the marshes and the car refused to go any farther. They climbed out into the shallow water and ran in long splashing strides toward the burning plane. It had run almost a hundred yards into the marsh before its wheels had sunk into the soft ground and its undercarriage had collapsed. The bright orange flames were reflected in the wind-ribbed waters, and there was a strong aroma of airplane fuel.

Roderick splattered around the burning wing to the nose. He could see R. S. Fairbanks sitting there, apparently unconscious. He called to the rigger: 'Can you get the door open? It looks like they were knocked out!'

The rigger, shielding his face from the heat of the fire, tried to locate the main door. He called: 'I got it! But it's too hot to touch!'

Roderick ran back around the wing to the side of the plane. The fire was out of control now, peeling back polished aluminium from blackened spars and ribs, and charring the sleek motors into dark carcasses. The main door was within reach, but the rigger was right. Roderick tried to touch it and the tips of his fingers were seared into blisters.

He yelled: '*Lem! Can you hear me? Lem!*'

He listened, but there was no response from inside the plane.

The rest of the mechanics and riggers were now splashing toward them across the marsh, and they had fire extinguishers and crowbars.

'The main door's red-hot already!' shouted Roderick 'Get it open – fast!'

The fire began to twist and lick at the fuselage, making a soft funnely roar as it fed on wood and upholstery and airplane fuel. The riggers banged at the main door with their crowbars, and tried to prise it open, but one by one they had to step back, their faces bright red from the heat, and their best shirts scorched brown.

'Can we get in through the cockpit?' yelled Roderick. He was panicking now. The flames were spitting and crackling all along the fuselage, and at any moment the gallons of aviation fuel in the starboard wing could explode and burn all of them.

They circled around the charred wreckage of the port wing to the cockpit. They knew they were too late. The fire was already so far advanced that a man would have to be suicidal to try to rescue Lem Cosnett from the airplane's roasting shell. Once inside, he would probably never get out.

The windows of the cockpit were as brown and smoky as the mica door of a household furnace. Roderick shouted to two mechanics: 'Give me a lift up here! Maybe I can get the pilot out!'

The mechanics gripped their hands together to form a step, and lifted Roderick up against the hot curved aluminium of the airplane's nose. He peered inside the open window, and he could see R. S. Fairbanks sitting almost peacefully in his seat. He shouted out: 'Fairbanks! Fairbanks! You have to get out!'

He shouted again and again, but then the airplane's skin grew too hot to touch, and the mechanics had to let Roderick down onto the marshy ground again.

'I think Fairbanks is dead already,' he said, his face white. 'At least I hope so. I can't get him out of there. There isn't a chance.'

One of the mechanics, a stocky man with wavy white hair and bright blue eyes, said: 'I think we'd better move back now, Mr Cornelius. The whole shebang's going to blow herself up in a moment.'

Reluctantly Roderick said: 'Okay.' They splashed their way through the muddy waters and tufted grass, feeling the heat of the fire on their backs, and then they stood fifty or sixty yards away to watch twelve million dollars of airplane and two lives burn into ashes The smoke piled heavily into the sky, and the plane's framework steamed and crackled as it steadily sank into the marsh.

Almost a minute had passed when they heard what sounded at first like a bird whistling. Then they suddenly realized it was a very high-pitched human scream. Roderick felt as if he was being frozen, or as if he was numbed by whiskey. He didn't seem to be real at all. The flames were mirrored in the waters of the marsh, and someone inside the airplane was still alive!

'It's Fairbanks!' said the white-haired mechanic hoarsely. 'I'll swear that's Fairbanks!'

None of them moved. They were airplane builders and they knew that there was nothing on earth they could do. The open window of the cockpit was far too small to extricate the burning pilot, and the main door of the airplane was now buckled and twisted and impossible to open. Two of the riggers actually knelt down in the waters of the marsh and prayed, and the rest of them stood with their heads bowed, hoping that R. S. Fairbanks wouldn't scream for too long.

'That fuel's going any second,' warned the white-haired mechanic. 'Watch it now! It's going any second!'

Through the rippling heat, Roderick could see something moving. He thought it was a fragment of burning fuselage. But then he saw it waggling up and down, and he understood – coldly and in total fear – what it actually was. By some superhuman effort, R. S. Fairbanks had actually forced his head and his shoulders out of the tiny cockpit window, and was trying to escape from the agonizing heat of the blazing plane. He had torn his scalp and his face as he pushed through the sharp aluminium frame, and one of his ears was almost severed. All the time, he was shrieking, in a voice of such desperation and pain that Roderick started to shake with terror. The fire must already be burning Fairbanks' legs, and yet his blind will to survive was so compulsive that he didn't consider that he was turning himself into a bloodied and mutilated cripple in order to escape it.

One of the riggers started to run toward the plane, but Roderick bellowed: '*No!*' and just as the man hesitated, the fuel in the starboard wing exploded, and chunks of fiery aluminium sprayed into the air. Roderick felt a flying

441

fragment of hot metal graze his face, and he clapped his hands over his eyes to protect his sight. There didn't seem to be any noise – just a compression of the surrounding air, which tightened and then released itself.

Roderick walked back to his abandoned Pierce Arrow. He sat himself in the front seat and started to cry. He clutched his arms and swayed backward and forward like a child, with tears streaming down his face, and his lips curled down in a blubbering howl. He called for his mother, over and over, and after a while his mother came, driven across the grass in state in her midnight-blue Rolls-Royce. She held his blistered and smutty hand with her own cool fingers, and let him rest his pomaded hair against her black fur coat as he twisted his necktie around and wept. 'Oh, Mother, oh, Mother, oh, Mother . . .'

Johann stood a little way off, regarding with a solemn face the last few fires that flickered across the marsh. Celia stood a pace or two behind him, stroking Fortescue. At the moment, she preferred to leave her husband in the tender care of the womb that had borne him.

Johann said, without turning around: 'You suspected this would happen, didn't you? It's a tragedy.'

Celia stopped her stroking and raised a beautifully plucked eyebrow. 'I'm not sure that I know what you mean.'

Johann shrugged. 'It's no use pretending. I knew what you were the day I first met you. A strong lady. I've met them before, you know. I'm even married to one. You wanted to put money into air freight and ground services, and Roderick wanted to fly planes. You were right and he was wrong. And now two innocent men have died.'

'It might have flown,' said Celia. Johann looked back at her over his shoulder and was both satisfied and disturbed to see that her face was quite deadpan. He grunted.

Celia stepped forward, until she and her father-in-law were side by side. 'It might even have been a *success*,' she said softly.

Johann shook his head. 'Success comes from getting things right. From getting everything right. The motors were wrong, the decision to fly on this field was wrong, the leadership was wrong. Sooner or later, something like this was inevitable. This airplane would have died a quiet death even if it hadn't died a noisy one. I'm sorry it was so noisy.'

Celia said: 'It was well-insured. Overinsured, in fact, with Lloyd's.'

Johann nodded. He poked his cane into the soft soil and watched muddy water fill the hole he had made.

'I'm interested in everything that happens within the Cornelius business,' he said. 'I took the trouble to have your order books examined. I saw, to my surprise, that you hadn't been selling airplanes at all.'

Celia gave a faint smile. 'I wondered when you'd notice.'

Johann looked at her. 'It's my business to notice.'

'And are you angry?'

'Why should I be? At least you've salvaged something out of this fiasco.'

'I thought you might be angry,' said Celia. 'I thought you might think that I wasn't giving Roderick a fair chance.'

Johann took out a handkerchief. The wind and smoke had made his eyes water, and he dabbed at them carefully. 'There are no fair chances in business,' he said calmly. 'This was Roderick's test, this airplane. It was a test of his commercial perception, but it was also a test of his ability to survive.'

'He hasn't come out of it very well, has he?'

Johann pulled a face. 'That depends on how you look at it. According to your books, Cornelius Airways has air-freight orders for – how much is it? – something over a million dollars. That's a twelfth of my capital investment defrayed already, apart from insurance.'

Celia said: 'It just seemed like a terrible risk, putting all of your investment on one airplane. That's why I went around selling air-freight services, whether we were going to ship on our own planes or someone else's.'

'You're a smart lady.'

Celia stroked Fortescue in a slow, almost bemused way. 'I don't quite know how I'm going to break it to Roderick. But I suppose I'll manage.'

'He should be pleased,' said Johann.

'No, he won't be. Not at first. He'll think I didn't believe in him. He might even try to make out that it was my fault the plane didn't fly.'

Johann tapped his cane against the ground. A fire wagon was jouncing across the grass, but it wasn't hurrying, and the firemen weren't even sounding the siren. Most of the fragments of the C-1 could be stamped out underfoot.

Celia said: 'Does this leave Roddy stranded?'

'In what way?'

'Are you going to pass control of the business to John?'

'Why should I? He didn't come out of it very well, but *you* did. Because of you, I don't see why Roddy shouldn't take over the business when the time comes. I just want you to understand that when he does, David Bookbinder and all the senior staff will know that every decision he makes has to be discreetly vetted by you. Roddy will never know about that proviso himself. He is my son, after all, and he has little enough left to be proud of.'

'Doesn't that make you feel . . . I don't know, *deceptive*?'

'Does it make *you* feel deceptive?'

Celia turned away. She didn't want to answer that question. Johann gave a short, humourless laugh and said: 'There are times in all of our lives when we are deluded by others for our own good. Don't you agree?'

Celia said: 'I suppose so.'

Over in the Pierce Arrow, Roderick was still sobbing Johann heard him and grimaced. Celia laid her hand on his arm and said gently: 'Don't be too hard on him. It's not his fault entirely. He was trying very hard to impress you.'

Johann nodded. 'You're a good girl, Celia. I wish I were free to give you more.'

'Free?'

Johann lowered his head. 'You'll understand one day.'

Celia was about to ask him when, and how, but he turned away and walked over to her car. Roderick was now patting his reddened eyes with his handkerchief and trying to tidy himself up. Hester said: 'I think he'd better go home.' It's been a dreadful shock. Those poor men.'

Johann stared down at his son for a long moment. Then he said: 'Roderick?'

Roderick kept his eyes averted and didn't answer. When Johann spoke again, his voice was a harsh, slow baritone.

'A long time ago, Roderick, I wept tears like you are doing now. But I wept them because someone had sacrificed something for me which they valued beyond price. You must never weep for yourself again. It is a luxury that not even people as rich as we are can afford.'

Johann didn't wait for his son to reply. Roderick couldn't possibly have anything to say which would interest him, in any case. He walked back to his mud-splattered Rolls-Royce and disappeared inside. Hester kissed Roderick briefly on the forehead and followed him. The chauffeur closed the door. It was like a door that had closed in 1903. As they backed up, turned, and drove away, the smoke from the burning C-1 dirtied the skies behind them, and the last few fires glowed on the marshes like the fires of a primitive settlement. It rained again, harder this time, a faceful of wire rods, and Celia had to drive the Pierce Arrow back toward the hangar, with Roderick sitting numbly beside her in the front seat. Raindrops hung on the tip of his nose and the lobes of his ears like three diamond pendants.

On the first day of April, 1939, in the same week that President Roosevelt approved the plans for two 45,000-ton battleships, Hope was married in Hartford, Connecticut, to Martin Landseer. After the ceremony, thirty-five cars took two hundred and fifty guests back to the Landseer house, where they danced on the lawn to most of Benny Goodman's orchestra, which had been dressed for the occasion in yellow blazers and white ducks, which they had to give back later. Hope appeared to be joyously happy, although Philip Strachan did say that perhaps she was hysterically happy. She twirled her way from guest to guest, laughing and chattering and drinking too much champagne. Martin trailed around after her with a bashful smile, and he was asked by one bitchy young thing with kiss-curls and an off-the-shoulder dress: 'Haven't I seen you in *Snow White*?'

Hope wore a fashionable crinoline dress with flounces and bows, and as she circled the lawn, her head thrown back and her eyes alight, she looked as if she was starring in a glamorous movie of her own life.

Johann was testy and irritable that day. He disliked weddings intensely, and he particularly disliked the Landseers. It was only because his own daughter was getting married and because Mrs Landseer was a long-standing friend of Hester's that he came at all. When he stood in church and gave Hope away he looked as miserable as Robert Taylor when Greta Garbo died in *Camille*, and afterward, when a fussy fat woman told him that he hadn't

445

lost a daughter but gained a son, ne said: Madam, I would rather have contracted hepatitis.'

There was a five-tier cake, with silver horseshoes and silver bells, and photographers with Kodak plate cameras popped off flashbulbs like Chinese firecrackers. A cub reporter from the Hartford papers asked Hope how she was going to spend her time now she was Mrs. Hope Cornelius Landseer, and she answered with a voice as pealing and gentle as a nunnery bell: 'I'm going to look after my husband, in every way.'

There was a curious feeling in the air. The clouds were as thick and high as cliffs. Johann and Hester had flown over Flushing Meadow in their private DC-3 on their way to Connecticut, and had looked out over the glittering sprawl of the New York World's Fair, all ready for opening in three weeks' time. The Trylon had cast its seven-hundred-foot shadow like the pointer of a sundial. Now Johann was standing on the veranda of the Landseer house in a grey top hat and morning suit, masticating a slice of wedding cake as if it was baked from dust. Beside him Mr Landseer was pink around the ears and telling Johann endlessly and tediously that they were both fathers-in-law together, correct, and how they ought to play regular rounds of golf out at Hurstview Golf Course, because Mr Landseer was a member, and it was a fine course. Johann said he knew it was a fine course because he owned it. He then asked Mr Landseer why he didn't buy himself a monocle that didn't keep dropping out. The band played 'In the Mood.' One of the young men at the reception had fought in Spain and was telling a butterfly crowd of girls how he had ridden horseback through the bombs and shrapnel at Caldetas and just reached the harbour in time to catch the *Omaha* as it steamed away with American evacuees. Hope went around in her crinoline dress like the clockwork doll on the top of a jewellery box. The sun went in and out behind the clouds, so that the afternoon was sometimes as flat as a newspaper picture, and sometimes bright and sparkling with flags and trumpets and bottles of champagne In spite of the sunshine, Johann knew that America was preparing to lay down two of the world's biggest battleships, at a cost of ninety million dollars each, and that there was probably going to be war.

United States Attorney Godfrey K. Prescott was in his long steamy greenhouse when his wife came to the door and called him. He was a dahlia fanatic, and he grew the best blooms that New Rochelle had ever seen. He regularly won prizes, and his red-brick chimneypiece was clustered with rosettes and honourable mentions.

'Can't it wait?' he said irritably. 'Can't you get the fellow to call back?'

'Dear, he said it was quite urgent. It's to do with McKesson & Robbins.'

Prescott sighed and peeled off his rubber gardening gloves. He walked back to the house in his striped apron and went into the sitting room through the French doors. Sunlight fell in bright trapeziums across the velvet-covered antique furniture, and the silver presentation cigarette box winked at him from the table. He picked up the telephone and said: 'Yes?'

There was a crackly silence. Then a low, hoarse voice said: 'Is this Mr Prescott, the U.S. attorney?'

'That's right.'

'Well, I have some information for you. I guarantee it's good stuff. I'd like to meet you someplace and talk it over.'

Prescott ran his hand through his black wavy hair. 'Can't you tell me now?' he asked his informant. 'Are you calling from home?'

'I'm calling from a bar in New York City. I can't tell you too much right now.'

'Give me a general idea.'

The man coughed. Somewhere in the background, Prescott could hear the sounds of music and laughter.

'Just a rough outline,' insisted Prescott.

'Well, it's about Phil Musica. You've been asking what his outside connections were.'

'That's right.'

'I can name his main connection. I can prove it, too.'

'What else?'

'I can definitely tie Musica in with Dutch Schultz, and I can tie Dutch in with Musica's main connection.'

Prescott reached across to the cigarette box and took out a Lucky Strike. He lit it awkwardly with the Regency-style lighter, and puffed blue smoke across the slanting shafts of sun.

447

'What kind of evidence do you have there?'

The man said: 'Wait one.' Then, after a pause he said: 'I got letters and papers and contracts. But it's worth something.'

'How much is something?' asked Prescott.

'Five g's.'

Prescott sucked at his cigarette. 'That's a lot of lettuce for one name.'

The man said: 'It's a big name, Mr Prescott. It's worth every penny.'

Prescott thought for a moment. Then he said: 'All right. Where can we meet? Can you get yourself out of the city without attracting attention?'

'I think so.'

'Get up here right away, then,' said Prescott.

'You'll have the money?'

'Not right away, but if the information's good, I'll give you a personal cheque and a signed guarantee.'

The informant didn't say any more, but promptly replaced his receiver. Prescott held his telephone in front of him for a moment, as if he expected it to say something else, but then he laid it back on its cradle and went back outside. His wife, reclining on a striped deck chair, said: 'Anything interesting, dear?'

He shook his head. 'I don't know. The fellow's coming here later, and then I'll see.'

His wife said in mild exasperation: 'Not another gangster? I don't think the neighbourhood's gotten over that awful Gizzi man yet.'

Prescott smoked his cigarette. 'It's to do with Philip Musica. It could be a break.'

'I see, dear. Well, I just hope the man's not too rough, or too flashy, or something.'

Prescott went back to his greenhouse. He had been working on the Musica case ever since the McKesson & Robbins scandal had broken, and he was still convinced that Musica had had secret connections in big business. Masquerading under the name of F. Donald Coster, the onetime gangster Musica had used the reputable drug house of McKesson & Robbins as a front for embezzlement and the export of airplanes, armaments, food, and blankets to foreign countries. At one time Coster-Musica had tried to export two million rifles.

In spite of the scale of his rackets, the seemingly respectable head of McKesson & Robbins had fooled bankers, investors, and accountants for years: and Prescott was convinced that somewhere along the line he had taken expert guidance from some *éminence grise* with a genius for swindles. Musica was undeniably a major-league embezzler, and during the early 1930's he had close connections with Dutch Schultz, but it took style and imagination and limitless resources of ready money to do what Musica had done, and Prescott knew that Musica had none of those assets at his disposal. There had to be a contact in Wall Street.

Musica's own version would never be heard. When police had arrived to arrest him in January at his stately house in Fairfield, Connecticut, he had promptly committed suicide. Godfrey Prescott often considered that Musica might have felt it more prudent to silence himself painlessly than to have his big business contact do it the hard way.

During the length of the afternoon, he potted fresh plants, and the sun dropped down behind the gabled roofs of his house. At five o'clock he checked his watch and began to tidy up for the day. As it turned out, his informant never arrived in New Rochelle, and Prescott never heard from him again. During the days and weeks that followed, Prescott often sat at his desk and wondered what the man might have had to say; but like all officers of justice, he was patient and calm and inured to the casual and constant presence of sudden death.

1940

President Roosevelt tells us that there is always give-and-take when it comes to allocating military contracts. Well, let me ask him this: Who's doing the giving, and who's doing the taking?

—Senator H. K. Hubslager,
April 12, 1940

A warm spring wind was ruffling the palms along the driveway as the long white Cadillac Imperial sedan swept silently toward the house. It circled the ornamental fountains, watched with hushed anticipation by the assembled staff of thirty footmen, maids, cooks, and cleaners, their white jackets and overalls starched as crisp as cuttlefish shells, their hair combed and gleaming, and their eyes screwed up against the morning sun. The sedan came to a stop in front of them, and they stood as stiff and straight as they could while the fawn-uniformed chauffeur smartly opened the door and lowered the carriage step.

Johann, the leg of his light grey suit raised far enough to reveal the oddly endearing sight of his summer combinations tucked into the top of his silk socks, stepped heavily and carefully down from the car, and then supported himself on his cane while the chauffeur helped Hester. He was looking sallow and tired, and hunched, and he put on his hat with the slow care of an old man.

Hester took Johann's arm, and turned to face the staff with a bright smile. She had reached the age of forty-eight with energy, strength, and that radiant dignity that is peculiar to the wealthy and the self-assured in middle age. She wore a simple spring coat in primrose-coloured wild silk, and a wide-brimmed hat to match. Her eyes were hidden behind dark sunglasses, but only because she found it impossible to sleep on airplanes, and they were red from eyestrain.

They looked, as they stood there on the raked brown gravel, like a proud and happy old couple, and the staff spontaneously greeted them with a spatter of applause.

Radec, their butler, came forward in his swallowtail coat and bow tie, and dipped his big round head respectfully.

'Nice to see you, Radec,' said Johann in a thick, warm voice. 'How's the chilli today?'

'I hope, better than ever,' answered Radec, displaying two

453

ranks of glittering white dentures. 'Miguel has been fussing here, fussing there, meat, chillies, vegetables, ever since he heard sir was coming. And madam, too, forgive me. You are looking as beautiful as ever, madam.'

'I could use a brandy-and-soda,' said Johann, and he leaned on Hester to help him toward the house. 'I feel as dry as a hole in the desert.'

Behind them, Max Wemmer, the vice-president of Cornelius Oil California, was waltzing about in his red-and-white blazer and white golf cap like an animated barber pole, directing the removal of Johann and Hester's sealskin luggage from the trunk of the Cadillac. A visit from the Almighty himself was an exciting and nerve-wracking rarity these days for the Cornelius staff out on the Coast, especially since Johann had been kept busy in New York for over a year by the worsening of Hitler's war and all the complicated business problems that went with it. There was sunken shipping to worry about, trade embargoes to worry about, requisitioned warehouses and goods to worry about, and it was only now that Johann had allowed Hester and his doctors to persuade him to take a short vacation at Carina Mia, his secluded twenty-five-bedroom Spanish palace outside of Pasadena.

Inside the house, it was cool and dark. Their footsteps echoed on the polished marble floors. There was a soft rustle of palms from the gardens, and the plashing of waterfalls. The staff were chosen, and well-paid, for their quietness and their discretion, and they hurried here and there in a busy hush.

'I'll take my drink on the balcony,' said Johann, handing Radec his hat. 'Are you going to freshen up, my dear?'

Hester took off her dark glasses. 'I want to take a bath and lie down for a while, unless you need me. Radec . . . can you get Maria to open the green bedroom? It won't be so hot there.'

Johann leaned forward and kissed Hester on the forehead. He clutched her hand and squeezed it. 'I'm going to do what you asked,' he told her. 'I'm going to sit down and have myself a good peaceful vacation. I guess I deserve it.'

'You're not the only one.' Hester smiled. She had spent the last six months feverishly fund-raising for one of Eleanor Roosevelt's welfare committees, and the prospect of

⌐relaxing at Carina Mia, with its Turkish baths and pools and restful rooms, seemed like bliss.

Max Wemmer came in, his heels clicking on the floor, his vacation smile tacked firmly into place.

'Okay, sir, that's everything. If you need me, I'll be downstairs in the office. I'm just going to sort out the day's trading figures for you, and then get those oil estimates you asked for.'

Hester looked at Johann rather sadly. 'You asked for oil estimates?' she said.

Johann coughed and tapped his cane on the floor, abashed. 'I need to know what the rest of the fellows are doing, even if I don't do anything myself.'

'Well, you take care,' chided Hester, and kissed him. Maria, her red-haired and elegant Italian secretary, had arrived now, a divine Botticelli in a pale green linen suit, and curtsied a greeting, and so Hester said: 'I'll see you later, when I feel less like a stranded lobster.'

Johann, fastidiously escorted by Radec, walked across the wide hall to the elevator, and he stood patiently still while they rose to the second floor.

'It's been more than a year now, hasn't it?' asked Johann, as Radec rattled back the gold-painted trellis gates.

Radec nodded. 'We understand, sir. We don't feel abandoned. All the staff were very pleased with their Christmas gifts, sir.'

'I gave you a gold Larkwood pen, didn't I? Do you like it?'

Radec bowed his head in pleasure. 'It's very fine, sir, but it's even finer that you remember what you gave me.'

Johann smiled without answering. Every head butler in every one of his houses had received a gold Larkwood pen; but winning the confidence of his personal staff, the people who actually cared for his clothes and his food and his ageing body, was becoming an increasingly pertinent pursuit. He would be sixty-seven this year, and he was beginning to feel increasingly weary and increasingly short of breath.

'We have a print of *Ninotchka* in the house, sir, if you want to watch it sometime,' said Radec.

'Yes, I might,' said Johann. 'Isn't that the picture with Garbo laughing?'

Radec walked with him along the marble-flagged upper corridor, in which was hung one of the largest private collections of Goya sketches in the world. Through the yellow-tinted Spanish glass, Johann could see the distorted outlines of the San Gabriel mountains, and the deep blue sky was turned to watery green. He had always liked this house in Pasadena; it was spacious and secluded and almost monastic. It would be easy to spend the rest of his life in its cool rooms, meditating and sleeping, and listening at night to the soft katabatic winds from the mountains.

The butler opened the double carved doors that gave out onto the balcony room. This was one of Johann's favourite retreats, one of the few places where he could sit and relax and relish being rich. It was decorated in rich Mexican colours – reds and greens and golds – with a dark blue mosaic floor that had been taken piece by piece from the sixteenth-century Church of San Carlos del Rincón in Oaxaca and reconstructed here. Along one wall was a deceptively simple oak table, waxed to such depths that Johann always felt he could drown in it, set with white ceramic dishes of guava, papaya, and pineapple. The story went that the table had been sawn from the deck boards of one of Sir Francis Drake's galleons, and that it was stained in English sailors' blood.

It was the view from the balcony itself, though, that made the room so serene. It looked out over the subtropical gardens that surrounded Carina Mia, an eighty-acre paradise of roses and orchids and magnolia, with glades and waterfalls and winding pathways. In the distance were the tiled rooftops of La Canada, and the sandy-coloured mountains, and the haze of a California morning.

Johann walked to the edge of the balcony and propped his stick against the pierced-stone balustrade. He took a deep breath of mountain air and closed his eyes.

'You're tired, sir?' asked Radec solicitously. 'Your drink is coming up right away.'

Johann opened his eyes and looked out over the gardens. A sprinkler was twirling around and around, shedding diamonds all over the closely shaved lawns. He gave a small, wry smile.

'Tiredness is only relative to how much work you have to do,' he said in a husky voice.

'You can rest here, sir, surely? For a week or so?'

'Well, I'm supposed to. But this war is keeping us pretty busy. We're caught between the government on one hand pushing for all the nitrates we can produce and all the oil we can pump up and all the ships and airplanes we can build, and the Germans on the other hand, confiscating our goods in Europe and sinking half our consignments and blowing up what they don't steal. I just heard this morning that the Luftwaffe bombed the Savage Hotel in London last night – bombed it flat. Apart from the fact that it was the only hotel in London worth staying in, I happened to own sixty-six percent of it.'

Radec went across the balcony and brought up Johann's chair, a big rattan peacock chair with its seat upholstered in Mexican tapestry. Johann eased himself into it, and sat there for a while in silence, a small reflective smile on his face, listening to the gentle sounds of the garden. One of the footmen came in with a glass of brandy-and-soda for him on a silver tray and set it down beside him with a dish of salted black olives.

'It's just like I remembered,' Johann said quietly.

Radec nodded. 'It's yours, sir, and it always springs to life when you come back here.'

Johann said: 'Did I ever tell you why I called it Carina Mia?'

Radec coughed politely behind his fist. He had started his career as a waiter at the Hotel Tarnow, in Warsaw, where Polish aristocracy had once eaten, in one evening, four hundred quail in black-currant sauce, and danced polkas on the tables, and he knew how to cope with the oblique conversation of the rich.

'Yes, sir. I remember it was a touching story.'

'It wasn't completely true, the way I told it.'

'No, sir?'

Johann picked up his glass. He paused for a while, his eyes staring blankly at the bubbles that rose to the rim. Then he said: 'I don't suppose it matters, though, what's true and what isn't. Not after thirty-seven years.'

Radec waited, immaculately posed, for Johann to say something else, but when he didn't, and it was plain that he wasn't going to, the butler softly clicked his heels and prepared to withdraw. He had almost reached the door when the telephone rang. He diverted himself toward it like a deflected torpedo, and lifted it out of its gilded cradle.

'Mr Cornelius' residence.'

He listened for a moment, and then placed his hand over the receiver.

'It's a call for you, sir. Said to be personal.'

Johann shook his head. 'I'm not taking calls now. Take a message and give it to Max Wemmer.'

Radec spoke into the phone again, and then said: 'It's Mr Jack Field, sir. Apparently he's calling from the front gatehouse.'

'Jack Field? I don't believe it! Give me that phone!'

Radec brought the telephone over and set it on Johann's table. He tugged a clean linen square out of his breast pocket and quickly buffed up the receiver before handing it over.

Johann said: 'Jack? Is that you?'

There was a crackle, and then a familiar voice said: 'Hi, Johann. I just dropped by to pass the time of day. Can I come on up?'

'You came to Pasadena to pass the time of day? I thought you were based in Washington now.'

'Well, that's right. But your office told me you were here, and I was kind of anxious to see you.'

Johann smiled. 'The way I hear it, you don't have *anything* to be anxious about these days. They tell me you're doing pretty good.'

Jack laughed. 'No complaints. But listen, if this is a bad moment, I can come back in the morning. I didn't realize you'd only just arrived.'

Johann shook his head. 'No, Jack, you come on up. I'll have the guard open the gate, then what you do is drive around to the left side of the house, around by the fountain, and park there. It's about a half-mile. What do you feel like drinking?'

'My throat tells me a collins.'

'I'll see you in five minutes.'

Johann set down the phone, and then dialled the house switchboard to put him through to Hester. She was soaking in the tub, but every bathroom at Carina Mia had a telephone.

'What's so urgent?' she asked him.

458

'Guess who just arrived, unexpected?'

'Don't tell me David Bookbinder. I couldn't bear it.'

'No, no, nobody like that. Jack Field.'

'Jack Field? But that's wonderful! I must come on down. Did he say why he called?'

'Just a passing visit, as far as I can tell.'

'Is Ellie with him?'

'I didn't ask.'

'Oh, Johann. That's typical of you. You're quite useless.'

Johann grunted. 'Maybe I am. But you're the only person in the world who's allowed to say so.'

In a while Johann heard a short, discreet knock at the door. Radec went to answer it, while Johann reached for his cane and lifted himself strenuously to his feet, his brandy-and-soda in one hand, his back as straight as he could manage. Jack Field, in a snappy double-breasted white suit and a black-and-white-striped tie, came breezing in with a wide smile.

'Johann!' He grinned and took Johann's arm in a firm, friendly grip. 'It's real good to see you. Real good.'

Jack Field, in his early fifties, was fit and tanned as a yachting instructor, although his wavy brown hair was greying now, and his cheeks were engraved with the lines of a man who had fought very hard and very bitterly to get what he wanted. Johann saw the struggles of Jack's career marked on his face, but he also recognized that tensile bearing that comes with great confidence and great success. From an awkward and muddled beginning in 1921, through near-bankruptcy in 1929, Jack had built up one of the finest law practices on the eastern seaboard, Field-Babson-Field, with Oliver Babson, the eccentric genius of tax law, and his own son, Randy Field. Jack Field's personal fees for a business brief were now so high that *Fortune* remarked laconically that 'it is probably the greater economy to defend your own case and lose than have Jack Field as your advocate and win.'

The footman brought in drinks and nuts, and Jack and Johann settled themselves down on the balcony, smiling at each other with the kind of shy pleasure that comes from meeting an old friend. They hadn't seen each other for over three years, although they still exchanged Christmas cards and Hester occasionally met Ellie at charity committees.

459

'Is Ellie not with you?' asked Johann.

'No, no. She's spending a month in South Carolina, looking up relatives. She's just as lovely as ever, I'm pleased to say.'

'And Randy?'

'He's okay. He's doing pretty well. In fact, he's thinking of moving out here to California. Either Los Angeles or San Francisco.'

'You still look as if leaving Cornelius Oil was the best thing that ever happened to you.'

Jack stirred the ice in his drink. 'I don't regret it, Johann. Any of it.'

Johann coughed. 'I'm glad of that. They tell me you're a very high-powered fellow these days. What's next? The Supreme Court?'

'Not for me. I'd rather argue than decide.'

Johann raised his glass. 'I'll drink to that.'

There was a small silence. They smiled at each other. Then Johann said: 'I suppose I ought to be using your services, seeing as how you're the best damned lawyer around. Do you give discounts to friends?'

Jack laughed. 'Do *you*?'

'Certainly. Anytime you need a few thousand barrels of crude, just let me know.'

Jack smiled at that, but the smile didn't stay on his face for very long. He took a taste of his drink, and then he looked at Johann seriously and worriedly. A breeze made the palms in the garden rustle and hiss, and the flowers nodded in crimson agitation.

Johann said: 'You've got something on your mind.'

Jack pulled an apologetic face.

'Well,' said Johann expansively, 'I guess it's kind of hard to visit your friends these days for the sake of friendship alone. We're all too busy.'

Jack said: 'What I've come for . . . well, I hope you'll see that it *is* friendship.'

Johann didn't look at him. Instead, he narrowed his eyes and peered across the valley at the mountains, as if he was expecting a smoke signal or a heliograph message from distant peaks.

'The truth is that the government is looking for some kind of scapegoat right now,' said Jack.

'Scapegoat? What for?'

'It's the war, I guess. There's been a lot of pressure from the left about kickbacks and racketeering on military contracts. It's public money, after all. And there's a pretty determined group of senators who want to make a name for themselves by catching some big corporation paying out bribes to Army and Navy and Air Force officials.'

Johann nodded reflectively. 'I think David Bookbinder mentioned something about that. Senator Hubslager was one. David calls him the Whining Example.'

'That's the man. Well, he's determined to make a public circus out of prosecuting half the Pentagon and any big business concerns he can catch with egg on their face. He says we can't criticize the Germans and the Japanese until we put our own morals in order.'

'Who does he think he is? Saint Peter?'

Jack shrugged. 'It doesn't matter if he thinks he's God. He's chosen the right moment to kick up about corruption, and Roosevelt would rather toss him a small fish to keep him quiet than stir up a lot of mucky water trying to deny that defence contracts have occasionally been awarded on the basis of golf-club memberships and vacations in Bermuda, instead of by open tender.'

Johann frowned. Jack, looking at him, thought how tired and old he was these days. The balcony was so quiet that he could hear his watch ticking.

Jack said uncomfortably: 'Last week – at the end of last week – I was approached by Senator Jorkins. He and Hubslager have been crusading together for years. Jorkins asked me to put together a draft prosecution case against two leading corporations, so that they could assess which case they could most effectively proceed with. One of those corporations was Rehoboth Engineering.'

Johann looked up. Rehoboth Engineering was building six motor torpedo boats for the U.S. Navy and over thirty landing craft for the U.S. Marines. It was owned jointly by Cornelius Shipping and Kosket Finance, both of which were major Cornelius companies.

'What's the other corporation?' asked Johann.

Jack shook his head. 'I'm sorry, but that's confidential.'

'You're not proceeding with the cases, are you?'

'Of course not. I had to declare my interest in Cornelius

corporations and turn the whole thing down. It's gone to Usher-Oppenheim-Clark, as far as I know.'

'Did Jorkins tell you what kind of angle they're going for?'

Jack nodded. 'That's why I flew here today. I think you're in for a rough ride. They know about your deals with Eddie Corcoran in the Navy Department over the 35,000-tonners, and they also know about Admiral Messenger.'

'What about him?'

'Well, I expect you recall what he said to the Navy specifications people. "I'd rather face the Germans with one motor torpedo boat built by Rehoboth than fifty built by Norfolk." '

Johann couldn't help smiling. 'Yeah, that *was* pretty exaggerated, wasn't it? But everybody knows that Admiral Messenger has his own way of putting things. He's a national hero, and if you're a national hero, you're allowed to be eccentric.'

'Eccentric, yes – corrupt, no.'

'What do you mean?'

'I mean that Hubslager knows that you paid the admiral twenty thousand dollars to build a new vacation home at Narragansett.'

Johann thought about this, and then spread his hands as if to say: Well, what's twenty thousand dollars between friends? 'If a big corporation happens to build a home for a great and respected American, what's wrong about that?' he asked rhetorically.

Jack sat up and fixed his eyes on Johann with all the intentness that Johann could still remember from the day he had quit Cornelius Oil.

'It's not the house, Johann. You could have gotten away with that. You could have come clean, and said you made a genuine mistake, and contritely given the house to some needy old widow instead.'

Johann smiled. 'You're still the same old Jack, aren't you?'

'Not quite,' said Jack. 'Because I don't have any ideas at all about how you're going to explain away the boys.'

Johann didn't move, didn't speak, as if he was expecting Jack to say something more. Then he raised his eyes and said dryly: 'What boys?'

Jack stared at Johann blankly, trying to work out if he was joking, or lying, or playing some kind of elaborate game.

'You really don't know?' he said, and his disbelief was plain.

Johann shook his head. 'If I knew, Jack, I wouldn't ask you. We've known each other too long for hedging. Besides, I have to say that you're the only man alive to whom it is no pleasure at all to lie.'

Jack stood up and walked to the balustrade of the balcony. As he did so, two ground doves flew up from the bushes, their wings flickering red in the clear sunlight. He sat on the balustrade and reached into his inside pocket for a brown envelope, which he carefully opened.

'If you really don't know about this,' he said quietly, 'I'm afraid that you're due for a bad surprise.'

'Not much surprises me these days,' retorted Johann, and held out his hand for the envelope.

He took out a dozen black-and-white photographs, obviously taken under difficult lighting conditions. They showed a shadowy bedroom with a wide four-poster bed, on which lay an elderly man and three young boys, none of whom could have been older than fifteen. They were all naked, like plucked guinea fowl, and the photographs showed them in one sexual pose after another. The most graphic picture of all showed the elderly man lying on his back, deeply penetrating a young boy who lay on top of him with his legs held up in the air by his friends. The elderly man was clearly recognizable as Admiral Messenger.

Johann numbly returned the photographs to their envelope and handed them back. He said in a tight voice: 'You'd better explain.'

Jack tucked the pictures back in his pocket. 'It's very simple,' he said. 'In return for his help in securing the motor-torpedo-boat contract for Rehoboth Engineering, Admiral Messenger was not only given a house by his good friends at Cornelius Shipping. He was given some house-guests as well. These three boys were procured by one of your executives and driven around to Narragansett one weekend for your great and eccentric national hero to play with. The only problem was that Senator Hubslager had your executive tailed by private detectives, who took these pictures. Worse than that, two of the boys have been traced, and are quite willing to say in court that they were forcibly abducted, that they were forcibly seduced, and that it was a Cornelius Shipping man who arranged it.'

Johann swallowed as if he had a cactus in his throat. He said: 'I didn't know about this, Jack. I didn't have any idea.'

'Would it have made any difference if you had?'

Johann glanced up sharply. 'Do you want an honest answer to that, or a moral one?'

'You don't have to answer at all. It's not my place to judge what you do. I've probably done worse myself, morally speaking.'

Johann ran his hand tiredly through his hair. 'The honest answer is that I might have considered it. But I can't believe those boys were anything else than just what they looked like. Young whores. I don't believe anybody got themselves abducted or seduced, forcibly or otherwise. Those boys went because they were paid, and they probably enjoyed themselves as much as Admiral Messenger. That doesn't mean to say that it doesn't sicken me, or that it doesn't disgust me, because it does. It makes my flesh creep to think that we had anything to do with it. But how the hell can Hubslager expect to make an example of Cornelius Shipping if all he has to show is dirty pictures and two male whores?'

Jack slowly shook his head from side to side. 'You're wrong, Johann, and you know it. By the time those two male whores get put up in front of a court of law, they're going to have their hair perked up and their Eton collars on, and if they tell the judge that the dirtiest thing they ever did before meeting your wily Cornelius Shipping man was trip over their hoops and muddy their knickerbockers, then he's going to believe them. And so is every decent Christian parent from Narragansett, Rhode Island, to Gravity, Iowa. This prosecution isn't just a case of business corruption. That's nothing to get the public worked up about It's to do with morals, and scandal, and it's been a long time since the public had a good meaty scandal to get their virtuous teeth into. This is going to be very bad news for you, Johann, and that's why I came to warn you.'

Johann took a deep breath. 'Well,' he said gently, 'I appreciate it.'

'I'm just returning a great many old favours.'

Johann called: 'Radec!'

'Yes, sir?'

'Get Mr Bookbinder on the telephone, right away.'

Jack said: 'I don't want you to do anything rash, Johann. They haven't made up their minds if they're going to go ahead yet.'

'What do you mean by rash?'

'Well, nothing. But I've heard that ˋDavid Bookbinder tends to take . . . well, overdecisive action.'

'Overdecisive?'

'Oh, come on, Johann, you know what I mean. There are one or two stories around about what happens to people who get in his way.'

Johann finished his drink and then swirled the ice around in his glass. 'Yes, I suppose there are. But you needn't worry. If anyone is going to take overdecisive action in this particular instance, it's going to be me.'

'Why don't you call Hubslager direct? Maybe you can mark out some middle ground.'

'Middle ground? The only ground I'm going to mark out with him is the ground I'm going to bury him in. Politically speaking, of course. If he has the goddamned self-righteousness to—'

'Johann,' interrupted Jack. 'This is serious. Really serious. You could find yourself out of Washington, out of society, out of all your committees, out of shipping, out of government contracts, you name it. This country will turn any number of blind eyes to bribery, and extortion, and graft, but it won't tolerate anything to do with sex. Even if those boys are shown up for the male whores they very probably are, you still can't win! They'll say that you corrupted a grand old sailor for the sake of your own grubby profits, that you buy and sell children for sex, that you're a pimp and a pervert! You can't take that kind of publicity, Johann; nor can your business reputation. You can beat up strikers, you can even have business rivals assassinated. But if you get the mark of sexual corruption on you, it's going to take years and years to wash it clean.'

Johann said nothing. His chin was lowered on his stiff

465

white collar, and his mouth was creased downward in serious thought.

Jack said: 'If nothing else, Johann, think of Hester. Think of Roddy and John and Hope. If you don't come to some kind of compromise with Hubslager, if you don't give him some kind of concession, he's going to make sure that he drags all of you down. How could Hester walk into a charity-committee meeting with the papers full of that kind of stuff?'

Johann raised an eyebrow. 'Hester's a strong woman,' he said simply.

'I know that,' said Jack kindly. 'But she doesn't have to go through something like this. I'm thinking of all of you, Johann. I really am.'

Johann toyed with an olive. 'What kind of concessions do you think Hubslager would find attractive?'

'I'm not sure. But he might be persuaded to look more favourably on Cornelius Shipping if he's promised some kind of future support.'

'What kind of future support?'

'Campaign contributions might do it. Or it might be enough if you promise to ease off your political opposition to organized labour.'

Johann's eyes widened. 'And he's trying to take *us* to the cleaners for corruption?'

Jack said: 'That's the way of the world, Johann. Corruption is only what the other fellow does.'

'Have you talked to Hubslager personally? You're not mixed up in this, are you?'

Jack shook his head. 'As far as I'm concerned, the whole thing stinks like a dead catfish. But we're friends, Johann, you and I. You got me started, you paid me well, and you never stood in my way when I really wanted out. You're much more appreciative of people, and much kinder, and much more sensitive, than most of your staff or your friends will ever realize. And I guess that's why I'm here today, saying what I'm saying now.'

Johann lifted his head. Then, slowly, he held out his hand, and Jack took it. For a long time they clasped hands together, looking into each other's eyes, partly with comradeship, partly with mystification at their own selves and their friendship, and partly as a recognition that they could only hold hands for a brief moment before each of them would have to face the consequences, bitter or happy, of his own life.

'Okay,' said Johann. 'But I'm still going to bury Hubslager. Deeper than a goddamned sugar-pine root.'

Just then the door opened and Hester came in, wearing a long silk robe and a red-and-yellow head scarf.

'Jack,' she said, holding out her arms. 'Such a pleasure to see you!'

After dinner that evening, Johann retired to bed early and left Hester and Jack in the drawing room. They sat on the rich leather Chesterfield in the shaded light of Mexican brass lamps, finishing their coffee and liqueurs and talking quietly. Around them, on the shadowy walls, hung dark portraits of Spanish heroes, bewhiskered and cuirassed, and plants in hanging baskets. Through the half-open doors they could hear the soft hesitant sound of a plectrum-plucked guitar, as one of the trio who had entertained them during dinner played a gentle romantic melody.

'It's almost too restful for comfort,' said Jack. 'I bet you wish you could stay here forever.'

'Sometimes.' Hester smiled, pouring him another cup of coffee. 'But I think I'd miss the cut-and-thrust of New York society, wouldn't you? You have no idea how keenly it sharpens the mind, all that social skulduggery.'

Jack, looking handsome and oddly boyish in his tuxedo and black tie, said: 'You never seem like the kind of woman to bother with etiquette and pecking orders and bringing out your daughter.'

'On the contrary, I adore it. My mother gave dozens of parties when I was a child, and she always used to keep me up-to-date on who was acceptable, and who wasn't, and why. Johann wasn't at all acceptable when I first met him, but I suppose that was part of the attraction. I was a very forward young girl, you know, and the idea of having a very rich husband with the manners of a sodbuster rather appealed to me.'

She smiled at the memory. 'He seemed very masculine after all those Harvard lounge lizards, and I suppose I thought I could tame him. I did, in a way. But I never wanted him to get *too* civilized. Hope says that I must have had a Fay Wray complex, whatever that is. I suppose she means that I preferred King Kong to King George.'

Jack laughed. 'You'd better not let Johann hear you say that.'

She brushed back her hair. 'He wouldn't mind. He does have a sense of humour, you know, even if it is a bit biblical.'

'He seems tired.'

Hester nodded. 'It's the war. He's been working too hard. I wish he'd delegate more, but he won't. Roderick's been pleading to take over the chemicals side, but I don't think Johann really trusts him. He's on the airplane and boat side now, Roderick, and I'm sure he's underemployed. Compared with Johann, anyway.'

'Does Roderick run Rehoboth Engineering?'

'I believe so, yes. Yes, he does.'

'Since when?'

'A year or so, maybe longer. Why?'

Jack rubbed at his cheek thoughtfully. This was going to be difficult to put into words, and he wasn't even sure that he ought to try. But he was already worried that Johann was going to be far too inflexible with Senator Hubslager, in a situation that could be solved only by compromise and crocodile tears. He said a little uncertainly: 'How much notice does Johann take of what you say?'

'*Notice?*' said Hester. She looked at him curiously. Her diamond pendant earrings caught the lamplight for a second, two sparkling showers of brilliant gemstones. She was wearing a fashionably wasp-waisted evening dress in pale lavender satin, and there was a fragrance about her that made Jack realize how much he missed Ellie.

'I didn't mean to be rude,' Jack said hastily. 'What I meant was, if there was a difficult problem that needed very special handling, do you think you could persuade Johann to treat it with a little less than his usual zeal?'

Hester put her coffee cup back on the silver bird-cage tray. She had suspected that Jack's visit wasn't entirely social, and now she knew she was right. Very quietly she said: 'You'd better tell me what's gone wrong.'

'Well, it's early days yet,' said Jack. 'But it looks like Senator Hubslager is putting together a bribery-and-corruption case against Rehoboth Engineering and Cornelius Shipping.'

'Bribery and corruption? But what are they supposed to have done?'

'I can't tell you all of it. It's too damned nasty. But it's a lot to do with kickbacks and rigged tenders for military contracts. All I *can* say is that it's potentially dynamite, and that's why I had to come and talk to Johann personally. I wanted him to understand that lowering his head and charging straight for Senator Hubslager's solar plexus is the worst possible thing he could do.'

Hester's eyes darkened a little. They were very brown, very intense. She said: 'How nasty is too damned nasty?'

'Nasty enough to make the name of Cornelius take on the social odour of soiled laundry.'

'Well, *what*? I'm not a child, Jack. I do know something of the world's less savoury side.'

Jack coloured. 'I know that, Hester. It's just that if Roderick's running Rehoboth, then he's ultimately responsible for what happened, and it's kind of hard for anyone to tell a mother that her son has been ultimately responsible for something as bad as this.'

Hester was sitting very upright. In the next room, the guitar was picking out the sad melody of 'Aguascalientes,' and a spidery shadow revolved across the whitewashed wall as a soft draught turned one of the plants in its basket. She said in a measured voice: 'I would never say this to anyone else, Jack, but Roddy is not ultimately responsible, in any real sense, for very many of his own decisions. Roddy's a builder, you know. A dreamer. But he's not a decision-maker. Most of his really important policy comes from Celia. She's a very hard, capable girl, and I'm afraid that she often takes the place of Roddy's spine.'

Jack was embarrassed. He hadn't wanted to force Hester into having to say anything like that, either about Johann or any of her children. He liked Roderick, although he was quite aware of how soft he was, and Ellie got on well with Celia. But even if Roderick hadn't been personally responsible for sending those boy whores to Admiral Messenger, his weakness had enmeshed his mother and his father in what could turn out to be the worst big business scandal in years.

Jack said: 'Whoever was actually responsible, the whole Cornelius organization is going to have to carry the can back, and that means Johann. Someone bribed Admiral Messenger into supporting Rehoboth's tender for motor torpedo boats by procuring three young boy prostitutes for him. Senator Hubslager has full details – even photographs – to prove it.'

'And of course Johann wants to tear Senator Hubslager's head off,' said Hester.

'You're not shocked?' asked Jack.

Hester held her hands demurely in her lap. 'No, Jack, I'm not shocked. I might have been ten years ago. But times have changed. I remember the first time I found out that Cornelius Oil had provided a young lady-of the night for some French customer's personal entertainment. I was horrified. But different people have different prices, Jack, and I suppose that when you're running a successful business, you have to be aware of what those prices are.'

'I just wish the press and the public shared the same view.'

Hester brushed her dress straight. 'I'm not saying that I'm not revolted, Jack, because I am. But I'm not shocked. What did Johann say?'

'He was outraged, of course. He hadn't known anything about it. But what concerns me is that he's going to challenge Hubslager to bring it out in the open, and Hubslager has so much evidence he can't possibly fail to wipe the floor with all of you. Unless you can get Johann to ease off, Hester, you've got big trouble.'

'Well,' breathed Hester, 'I'll try my best. It's just that Johann is a little funny about sex.'

She lowered her blue-shaded eyelids. 'I don't know why, and it has never been any good asking him, but Johann seems to feel that sex is for the reproduction of children and the occasional release of temper. There, I shouldn't be telling you that, either. But we've been friends a long time, Jack.'

'Hester . . .'

She shook her head. 'You don't have to say you're sorry. I wouldn't tell you if I didn't want to.'

She stood up and walked across the polished parquet floor, her lavender dress mirrored in the dark wood so that she looked like an ice skater on a mysterious pool. She crossed her arms across her breasts as if she was trying to keep warm.

She said simply: 'Being married to Johann has been a very strange experience. He can be so spontaneously generous he can almost make you cry. He can be affectionate, in a gruff kind of way. But I don't think that he has ever actually loved me, or, come to that, anyone. Perhaps there *was* someone, once. I didn't meet him until he was thirty-six so I suppose he must have known some young ladies. There was a very old photograph among his belongings when we moved to Lynwood's Island – a girl in a feather boa. But I only glimpsed it once, and I think he must have hidden it or thrown it away.'

Jack sat still and alert, his fingers tautly laced together, hoping that Hester would spare him the most deadening details of her twenty-nine years of marriage. He didn't want to be put in the position where he would have to make a choice between them, because he loved them both. He said: 'All I really need to know is how much you can persuade him to hold off on Hubslager. An investigation of all this Admiral Messenger business can wait until later, when we're sure we're out of the woods.'

Hester looked across at him a little sadly. 'Yes,' she said. 'I think I can persuade him to keep his temper.'

They were silent for a few minutes, while the guitar played an old Mexican love song that was almost absurdly romantic. Then Hester said: 'I should have married a man like you, really. Younger, and less complicated.'

Jack didn't say anything. He lowered his eyes and looked down at the floor, and wished that life wasn't so damned involved. Hester walked back to the settee, her skirts rustling, and stood beside him. She hesitated for a moment, and then she laid cool fingers on the back of his neck, and massaged him with strong, sensitive strokes.

'I sometimes feel that I threw my womanhood away. Not my intelligence, or my personality, because Johann has never abused either of those. But he never makes me feel like a woman and nothing else. It makes me so frustrated sometimes, because he's so masculine and so physically attractive. He may have had the capacity to love when he

471

was younger, you know, but if he did, he lost most of it on the way.'

She knelt down on the rug in front of him and clasped her hands around his neck, so that he was looking straight into her wide brown eyes. Even at forty-eight, she was still pretty, and her dress was cut low enough to show the cleavage of her small, rounded breasts. The laugh lines around her eyes, those that hadn't been smoothed away by Dr Carlsson and Dr Michael, only softened the pertness of her heart-shaped face.

'Do you know what the words of this song mean?' she said, as the guitar music strung its Spanish passion through the rooms.

Jack cleared his throat and whispered: 'No.'

Hester's tongue moistened her lips. 'They talk of a young girl from Cuatro Ciénegas who hears that her lover has died in the war, and gives him up for lost. In fact, he was only wounded, but when he returns to find her, she has already married someone else, a merchant she secretly despises. She sings this song standing on the veranda of her house as she watches her lover walk down the street arm-in-arm with her younger sister. The chorus says, "I sold my adoration for a thousand thousand pesetas, but all the tears in Coahuila cannot buy it back." '

Jack looked at her carefully. He said: 'You're lying. This song is "The Flowers of Tulancingo." Ellie has a record of it.'

Hester smiled, and then bent forward and kissed him warmly on the lips. 'If I were Ellie,' she whispered, 'I'd be proud of you for saying that.'

By the time they had bicycled through the long grass and down to the edge of the lake, they were thoroughly out of breath and laughing at their own unfitness. Hope got there first, but then Philip had the picnic hamper on his handlebars, and he was red in the face and sweating when he finally dismounted.

'At least you won't have to carry it all back.' She laughed. 'We'll have eaten it all.'

'Just because it's going to be *inside* me instead of *outside* me, that doesn't mean it's going to weigh any the less,' protested Philip.

They propped their bicycles up against a shady shell-bark hickory, and Philip unstrapped the hamper and laid it down on the long grass. He spread out the plaid blanket that had been neatly folded on top of the food, and then turned the hamper around so that Hope could take out the cold roast chickens and fruit.

She passed him the chilled champagne, wrapped in paper to keep it cool. 'That's your department,' she said. 'And I think I could do with some now. That is absolutely the last time I take up any suggestion of yours. "A gentle cycle down to the lake." My God! It was more like the Tour de France.'

'We made it, didn't we?' retorted Philip. 'A fainter heart would have given up on Taghkonic Hill.'

'It's not my heart I'm worried about,' said Hope, 'it's my legs. I'm going to have calf muscles like a Russian ballet dancer.'

Philip untwisted the wire from the champagne bottle. '*One* of you has to have muscles,' he teased her, 'and Martin doesn't seem to be playing his part.'

'Oh, Philip!' she said, and tossed a peach at him. He ducked, laughing.

'I'm not trying to be rude,' he told her. 'It's just that the last time I called around at Gracie Square, I accidentally hung my skimmer on Martin's nose instead of the hat stand.'

Hope pursed her lips, but didn't answer this time. She set out the fruit and busied herself with arranging the picnic plates. Philip looked around the raised lid of the hamper and said: 'Hope?'

Again she didn't answer. He said: 'You're not cross, are you? Come on, I was only joking.'

She glanced up, and he could see by her eyes that she wasn't really annoyed.

'Just remember this,' she said, opening the pickle jar and forking out a warty green pickle, 'there's only one person around here who's allowed to criticize Martin, and that's me. He's my husband, and I'm his wife, and whatever I think about him in private is my business. Apart from that, he doesn't *mean* to be skinny and stupid.'

Philip twisted off the champagne cork and lifted two long-stemmed glasses in his left hand so that he could fill them up to the brim with *brut*. 'Martin's not *that* stupid,' he remarked, waiting for the fizz to settle. 'He's eastern sales ·VP for Chrysler, he's found himself an apartment on the river, and he's married to you. There's a million guys a hell of a lot smarter than Martin who would have given their front teeth for all of that.'

He passed one of the glasses to Hope. 'Mind you,' he added with a grin, 'I have to agree that he's skinny.'

They ate their chicken and fruit, and drank their champagne, and then sat back against the trunk of the hickory, feeling sleepy and contented. It was a hot, hazy day in New York State, not far from Kent, Connecticut, where Philip Strachan's father had a small summer retreat. It was only a half-hour's drive from the diner where, just three years ago, Hope had picked up Lewis Bausor; but everything that had happened that night now seemed like nothing more than a movie they had once gone to see, so long ago that they could scarcely remember who was in it.

Three years hadn't done much to mature Philip Strachan's wit or deflate his pomposity, but they had certainly improved his looks. His face had lost that precocious rich-kid look, and his hair was shorter and less cherubically curly. By the time he was thirty, he was probably going to look just as rugged and heroic as his father, Senator William Strachan, and undoubtedly bore the pants off people twice as readily. He was finishing his studies in banking and accountancy before entering the family brokerage firm as a junior partner. He could be very boring when he talked about the market.

But Hope, sitting by the lake in a gauzy print dress and white shoes, her broad-brimmed straw hat lying beside her on the grass, was not particularly interested in conversation. She was lonely for the companionship of a man who didn't always remember to bring her flowers, who didn't always agree to do whatever she wanted, visit whichever restaurants or theatres she wanted, buy her whatever gifts she pined for. She was lonely for a man whose body felt hard like a man's, who smelled like a man, who acted as roughly and impulsively as a man could. She drank champagne and orange juice too early in the morning, flirted with too many husbands at too many soirees and dances, drove her De Soto coupé through so many stop lights that her glove compartment was crammed with unpaid tickets, and twice already, when Martin was away on business in Detroit, had made love in the back of automobiles to men she had tipsily picked up at dinner parties.

Martin was in Boston this weekend, planning a special sales boost for the new $895 Chrysler Royal. To begin with, Hope had considered that it might be dutiful to visit his parents in Connecticut, but on Friday evening Philip Strachan had called and asked if she wanted to join him upstate for a picnic the following day. She remembered, quite out of the blue, what he had said to her that night they had taken Lewis Bausor out. '*You're a rare one.*' So – perhaps to see if he really meant it – she said yes.

Leaning on his elbow in the grass, Philip took out a cigarette and lit it. Across the glittering surface of the lake, a tight flock of white-winged scoter ducks flapped and flurried. Philip said: 'Are you really as unhappy as all that?'

Hope rested her chin on her knees and gazed wistfully out at the water. 'I don't think I really know what happiness is.'

'Well, neither do I. It's a state of mind, right? But I know what *un*happiness is.'

She sighed. 'Do you have a cigarette?' she asked him. He passed her his, and she took a long drag and then passed it back. She puffed out the smoke in an impatient narrow stream.

'To tell you the truth, Hope, I don't know why you married Martin in the first place. You knew that you wouldn't get along.'

'Oh, we get along all right. He's really quite friendly, in a doglike way.'

'But don't tell me you want to stay married to a *dog*. I could have let you have King. He's a thoroughbred, and what's more he's handsome, and I bet he would have made a damned sight more interesting husband that Martin.'

'Philip, don't insult him. I don't want to hear it. I don't even want to discuss it.'

Philip shrugged. 'It seems crazy to me.'

'What does?'

'Well, why stay married when divorce is so easy? You could get yourself free in six weeks with a good lawyer.

Tell the judge that Martin's been cruel to you. Going off on business trips and leaving you to fend for yourself. All that kind of stuff. The courts love it. And if you sob into your hankie a couple of times, they'll award you the whole apartment in Gracie Square and fifteen grand a year.'

Hope took the cigarette from him and inhaled the smoke deeply. 'I don't need money, Phil. And I don't particularly care if I never see the inside of that pokey little apartment ever again.'

Philip said: 'More champagne?'

She held out her glass. 'I only married Martin to show Father that I was independent. A big act of defiance. If you send me off to the Landseers as a punishment, then I'll damned well make it look as if I loved every minute of it. My God, what a price to pay. Do you know something, I can look at Martin standing there in his pyjamas, all ready for bed, and I can think to myself, look at you, you awkward little worm. I wish a huge great bird would come swooping down and carry you off in its beak.'

Philip loosened his tie. 'It could be arranged. I'll have a word with the Audubon Society.'

Hope smiled, and shook her head. 'I have a terrible feeling that I'm never going to get rid of Martin Landseer as long as I live. Maybe that's my punishment for Lewis Bausor. I can't conceive of God doing anything worse to me, can you?'

Philip said: 'Cheer up, this is supposed to be a picnic.'

'You should have brought a gramophone,' she told him. 'At least we could have had some music.'

'A gramophone? By bicycle? And I suppose I could have balanced the records on my head?'

Hope stood up and took a few steps down toward the rushy brink of the lake. 'You're not like Martin,' she said. 'Martin would have carried a five-piece jazz band on his shoulders if I wanted him to.'

She kicked off her shoes. 'It's so hot,' she said. 'It's like being in Africa.'

'We could go for a swim,' suggested Philip.

'We haven't brought towels.'

'We could lie on the grass and let the sun dry us off. That's what they must have done before towels were invented.'

476

'Nobody invented towels. How can you invent a towel?'

Philip stood up, too, and began to unbutton his white shirt. 'Somebody must have. You don't think that Neanderthal men came down to the waterhole with Turkish towels over their arms and back brushes, do you?'

Hope turned around. The sun reflected off the water that lapped in between the rushes and lit up her face with curves of light. Her eyes were clear and pale. She said: 'All right, then. Let's swim.'

She bent her head forward, and Philip unbuttoned her dress down to the waist. As he loosened the last button, he leaned toward her and kissed the back of her neck, just where her wavy brown hair came to a fine downy point. Out on the lake, two or three of the scoter ducks flustered up from the water, but then settled back down again.

Hope's dress fell to the grass, around her ankles, and she stood in her short oyster-coloured satin slip, her head still lowered, her arms down by her side. Philip came up even closer behind her, and nuzzled at her hair, and held her around her waist with his lean, muscular arm. He whispered: 'If only you'd taken more notice of me before.'

She let her head fall back against him, and he kissed her forehead. 'If only *you'd* taken more notice of *me*.'

His hand reached and cupped her soft breast through the thin slippery fabric of her slip. He gently rubbed her nipple between his finger and thumb, until it was crinkled and stiffened. She said, even more softly: 'We ought to swim.'

He didn't answer, but lifted her slip over her head, while she raised her arms to help him like a surrendering Victorian nymph. The slip fell to the grass, and was caught by the warm summer breeze, and blew over and over.

She turned around, wearing nothing now but her French step-ins and her gold bangles. She put her arms around him, and he squeezed and fondled her breasts with his strong fingers until she shivered, and bit at the muscles of his chest with her teeth. They kissed, so deeply that she felt as if she was being swallowed alive, and the only times she opened her eyes she saw his tanned cheek, his lashes, his curly hair, and the spangled green sunlight that danced through the leaves of the hickory tree.

He reached his hand inside the loose leg of her French step-ins and touched her. She knew that she was moist, like a ripe peach that someone has just bitten into. His fingers parted her, and then worked deeper and deeper inside, until his hand was slippery enough to force his index finger, right up to the knuckle, in her tightest place, and he could slide his thumb in front. She gasped and shivered, but he tugged at her, gently and sensuously and insistently, his finger caressing the ball of his own thumb through the sensitive membrane that divided them, until all she could do was plead with him to stop, to go on, to pull her into thousands of tingling fragments. He was so close that she could hear his breath roaring in her ear, and feel his hardness against her leg. But a moment came when it seemed like the whole day was giving way beneath her, and she buried her face in his chest, her eyes tight shut, and she could feel his fingers inside her like fingers of buzzing electricity, touching every nerve in her thighs and her stomach, and she held him tight, tight, tight and gasped: '*Ah*!'

He stroked her, caressed her, and said: 'Hope. My own darling Hope.'

She stayed close, shuddering, weak. But then the feeling began to ebb away gradually, and she raised her head to look into his eyes. 'No,' she said in a wobbly voice. 'Not *your* darling Hope.'

He touched her forehead. 'Do you think it could be? Ever?'

She smiled, glancing away toward the grass where her slip lay discarded. 'I shouldn't think so. But you never know. The future always leaps out at us by surprise.'

Without saying anything else, she unbuttoned his white summer pants and helped him to take them off. His thin knee-length cotton undershorts clung to his hardened penis like the sheet around an unveiled statue. She tugged them down, and held his rearing erection in one of her small, well-manicured hands, her diamond and topaz rings glittering against the dark red of his swollen flesh. She stroked him once or twice, up and down, and he gripped her shoulders and murmured something which she couldn't hear but could easily understand.

From across the lake, even through the haze of midday heat, they could be seen quite clearly. Hope, naked, clinging to the scaly trunk of the hickory tree, while Philip stood behind her and pushed himself into her. You could even have heard them gasping and laughing, and Hope's high-pitched squeal when Philip at last reached his climax. Then, bare and brown as two children, they splashed through the rushes into the cool water, and swam for almost twenty minutes, their heads bobbing on the still surface. Philip could be heard singing 'The Yellow Rose of Texas,' and Hope joined in the chorus with an exaggerated trill.

Afterward they lay on the grass until the sun was nibbled by the tops of the water oaks around the lake, and the breeze began to blow cool, and then they dressed and gathered up their blanket and their picnic hamper and mounted their bicycles to go home.

The late sun fell orange through the turning spokes of their bicycle wheels. Hope had given her French step-ins to Philip as a lighthearted memento, and he had tied them to his handlebars so that they fluttered as he rode. There was a warm scent of early-summer evening. Hope was so happy, and yet so unhappy, that her eyelashes were sparkling with tears.

They said very little else. They stopped once, before they reached the driveway up to the Strachan house, and Philip touched her hair and her lips with gentle fingertips.

'Do you think that it might be any use?' he asked her in a throaty, uncertain tone.

'I don't know,' she told him.

'Can we meet again?'

'Not like this. It would have to be secretly. Martin would never suspect, but his parents would, and so would mine.'

He looked down at her thin wrist, with its heavy gold bangle.

'You wouldn't mind if I called you? Maybe soon?'

'Philip, I don't know. You mustn't stampede me.'

He swallowed. 'I know. But I love you.'

She reached out and stroked his cheek. 'No, you don't. You just imagine you do.'

He shrugged. 'Maybe you're right. But you know what they say about imagination. It can move mountains.'

'Not imagination. Faith.'

'Doesn't Faith go with Hope?'

She kissed him, quickly and affectionately, and then

479

mounted her bicycle again. 'So does Charity,' she called back, and she was halfway down the driveway before Philip could catch up.

Jack met Ellie off the Carolina train at Union Station, and helped her carry her parcels and hatboxes to where their navy-blue Buick Phaeton convertible was parked outside in the sun. It was a sweltering day, but Ellie looked fresh and cool in a green lawn dress and a white hat with green ribbons. Jack opened the car door for her, gave the porter a quarter for stowing her suitcases away in the trunk, and then climbed into the driving seat.

'No chauffeur?' she asked.

He started the motor. 'What's the matter with *me*?'

'Nothing. I just hoped Lloyd wasn't sick.'

'I gave him the day off. I felt like collecting you myself.'

He pulled away from the station concourse and steered the Buick out through the congested, glittering traffic. The sun beat down on the back of his neck, and he put his hat on.

'How was California?' she asked him, searching in her pocketbook for her powder compact.

'Hot. How was South Carolina?'

'Hot, too. But it was so nice to see everybody, I didn't care. You should see Rose's children now. It was only last year they seemed like babies. Now they're all in grade school, and Billy has no front teeth at all.'

'Umh-humh.'

Ellie raised her compact and quickly powdered her nose. Jack turned down Louisiana Avenue toward Constitution Avenue, and the dome of the Capitol flickered into view behind the trees.

'How's Randy?' she asked him.

'Randy? Oh, well, he's fine. Just fine. He's working on a case for the Department of Agriculture right now. Could be a good step forward, if he wins it, and I think he will.'

Ellie closed her pocketbook and smiled. 'Do you remember when he wanted you both to be railroad engineers?'

'What brought that up?'

She looked across the car at him. 'I don't know. Maybe I was just thinking of way back when.'

480

'You sound like you're still nostalgic for South Carolina,' he told her, without turning his head.

'Maybe.'

They drove in silence along Constitution Avenue, past the Ellipse and the White House, and out toward Theodore Roosevelt Bridge. It was breezier once they were out over the Potomac, and Ellie took off her hat and fluffed out her hair. In middle age, much of her prettiness had been erased, and she was plumper now, and there were faint crisscrossing crow's-feet around her eyes. When she wore sunglasses, she looked like Bette Davis would in twenty years' time.

'Are you tired?' Jack asked her.

'Only slightly. Why?'

'I'd like to drop by Senator Karlbeck's house to pick up some information he promised me.'

Ellie shrugged. 'As long as I don't have to socialize. Is it important?'

He checked his mirror and pulled out to overtake a huge diesel truck with 'Manassas Transport' emblazoned in dirty red letters down its flanks. He said: 'It's to do with Cornelius Shipping.'

'You mean the corruption prosecutions you were telling me about?'

Jack nodded.

'Is it serious?' she asked.

'So-so.'

'Well, how serious is so-so?'

Jack glanced at her, and pulled a face. 'Disastrous, if you must know. There was a chance that Senator Hubslager would go for Brookline Industries instead of Cornelius Shipping. But this business with Admiral Messenger was too juicy for him to resist. They've dropped their intended action against Brookline, apparently, and now they've got three law firms working on files for the Senate committee on government contracts and the New York district courts.'

Ellie reached across the seat and laid a gentle hand on his knee. 'Do you really have to get involved?' she asked him. 'It won't do you much good if it comes out that you've been supporting Johann – especially if he's found guilty of corruption.'

'He saved my life once.'

481

'I know that, Jack, but you can't go on repaying someone for saving your life forever.'

Jack gave her hand a quick, affectionate squeeze. 'He saved my life and I was able to spend my life with you, and that's why I'm quite ready to do whatever he needs me to do whenever he needs it.'

He signalled right, and turned down the quiet, wide tree-lined stretch of Patuxent Drive, where Senator Karlbeck lived.

Ellie said: 'Do you know how much you flattered me by saying that?'

Jack smiled. 'I wasn't flattering you, my darling. It's the truth. It's the way I feel.'

They pulled up beside a scrupulously neat brick-and-weatherboard house with lawns of unnatural emerald brightness and rows of umbrella magnolias that stood as stiff as terrified children. Outside the white-painted front porch, a tall elderly man with a grey flat-topped crew cut, heavy spectacles, and a baggy brown cardigan was trimming creepers to grow in severely parallel rows.

Jack let Ellie out of the automobile, and they walked up the swept flagstone path. Jack called: 'Good morning, Senator! How's the garden?'

The old man hung up his clippers on the creeper trellis and peeled off his gardening gloves. 'Good to see you, Jack! How are you, Ellie?'

'We can't stay long,' explained Jack. 'Ellie just arrived from South Carolina, and she's looking forward to resting up. She did the grand tour of the aunts and the cousins and the nephews back home.'

Senator Karlbeck scratched the back of his prickly neck. 'Fanny's been threatening to drag me off on a tour like that for years, back to Montana. I was almost delighted when war broke out, because that meant I was too busy, and couldn't go.'

'Now, then, Senator,' said Ellie.

Senator Karlbeck grunted in amusement. 'It won't make no difference when the time comes. Fanny always outvotes me, no matter what. I'll tell you something – if my pals in the Senate could see the way that she badgers me and bullies me about, why, they'd pass a National Henpeck Act in sympathy.'

Jack smiled guardedly. 'Did you get the information?' he asked.

Senator Karlbeck threw a questioning glance at Ellie, but Jack said: 'Don't worry about it, Ellie knows. I told her all about it when Hubslager first approached me.'

'Well, as long as you both realize that this is top-security stuff,' advised Senator Karlbeck. 'If it ever came out that I'd told you, I'd have to deny it most strenuously, and you'd be the one who'd wind up holding the baby.'

'I know that, Senator,' said Jack.

'Well, then,' said Karlbeck, pushing his hands into his pants pockets, 'I can tell you for starters that Hubslager is dead set on prosecuting Cornelius Shipping and all of its responsible executives. But he's not going to move until late September or early October, when the election is just cooking up nicely. Then he's going to blast the trumpets, bring up the curtains, and hope to catch as many people as possible with their pants down.'

Ellie inquired quietly: 'Does the President know?'

Senator Karlbeck shrugged. 'It's hard to say for sure. But Hubslager had a half-hour meeting with FDR two weeks ago, and I can't think of anything else which a no-hoper like Hubslager could discuss with the President, can you?'

'So what's his angle?' asked Jack, gently touching one of the white, cup-shaped flowers of the magnolia.

Senator Karlbeck rubbed his chin. 'There are several possible angles. But you might be interested to know that some Communist group was hawking a list around Washington a few months back, and that list contained the names of all those major corporations which were secretly paying substantial campaign contributions to the GOP. And when I say substantial, I mean millions.'

'One was Cornelius Shipping?' asked Ellie.

'You guessed it,' said Senator Karlbeck. 'And my guess is that Hubslager got hold of that list, and only brought his bribery-and-corruption investigation to bear on those particular corporations that were marked on it. He isn't so much interested in industrial morals as he is in getting FDR elected for a third term. If he can prove that the GOP candidate has been financed by profits from sexual corruption, why, that's as damning as saying that the man's a pimp. Roosevelt couldn't lose.'

483

'What's Hubslager's motive?' Jack wanted to know. 'Apart from being a Democratic senator?'

Senator Karlbeck looked glum. 'What's the motive that makes any of us do anything? Personal ambition. Hubslager's forty-six now, but he's never held a government post more important than fish-and-fowl protection. If he can show that the GOP and Cornelius Shipping are as queer as a three-dollar bill, then FDR is obviously going to be grateful, come inauguration time.'

'I thought Johann got along fine with the President,' interrupted Ellie.

'Sure,' said Jack, 'and Hester's like Eleanor's favourite sister. But that's only because Johann doesn't take political sides in public, and if he does make any contributions, he does it in secret. If you ask me, most of Cornelius Shipping's contributions were okayed by David Bookbinder, anyway. Bookbinder's pretty anxious to keep on the right side of Dewey.'

'What a mess,' said Ellie.

'Sure it's a mess,' agreed Senator Karlbeck, 'but then, politics always is. And apart from that, you may – just may – have a lever.'

'What's that?'

'It's not going to be easy, and you're going to have to find your own way of working it. But there's one thing that could silence Hubslager, and that was his own involvement in 1938 with the Welfare Investment Plan.'

Jack raised an eyebrow. 'I remember that. But he got good publicity out of it, didn't he? He raised millions of dollars for old folks, and everybody said what a great charitable guy he was. Mr Charity, they called him, didn't they? At least for a month or so.'

'One of my colleagues in the Senate has some pretty solid information that shows Hubslager and Jorkins diverted nearly three hundred thousand dollars of the Welfare Investment Plan into their own pockets.'

'You're kidding! Who?'

Senator Karlbeck pulled a wry face. 'I can tell you, but it may not do you much good. It's Senator Strachan, and Senator Strachan is ambitious and far-sighted enough to have his eye on the forty-four elections.'

'What does that mean?'

'It means that he's still gathering witnesses and affidavits and facts. He's taking his time over it, you see, because he's counting on Jorkins running for President in forty-four, and he wants to make sure that he's got a real humdinger of a scandal to drop right down Jorkins' chimney when the forty-four primaries start.'

'You mean he won't release the information now?'

'Not for all the whiskey in Paradise. And especially not for something as petty as discrediting Hubslager. As far as Senator Strachan is concerned, Hubslager is the nearest thing that a human being ever got to a chitterling, and he certainly doesn't want to waste his prize scandal on a creature like that.'

'Have you asked him?' said Jack.

Senator Karlbeck nodded. 'Oh, yes. We had lunch last week at the club. But he's keeping it close to his chest. The only reason I found out about it myself was because he needed my affidavit on a whole lot of investment transactions.'

Jack looked thoughtful. A dusty wind rustled through the magnolias and set the blossoms bobbing. Across the street, a chauffeur was buffing up a black Cadillac Sixty Special, watched by a solemn small boy in a striped T-shirt. The blue summer sky was streaked with high cirrus.

'Do you need some money?' Jack asked Senator Karlbeck. 'Did you have to pay anyone off?'

The senator shook his head. 'Just take it as a favour. It won't do you much good in any case if you can't persuade Strachan to give you what he's got.'

Ellie said: 'Is it really worth pursuing? I don't want Jack to get himself tied up with something that's going to damage his reputation.'

Senator Karlbeck laid an affectionate arm around her shoulders. 'I'll tell you something, Ellie. If the day came when I didn't put my reputation on the line at least once, then I'd pack my bag and take myself back to where I came from. Risking your reputation is what your reputation is all about.'

'It still worries me,' she said. 'I mean ... it could be a terrible scandal, couldn't it?'

Senator Karlbeck shrugged, and started to put his gardening gloves back on. 'I guess it could be. But remember that the only difference between a political scandal and a normal piece of day-to-day Washington business is that the newspapers got to hear about it.'

'You're an old cynic.' Ellie grinned and kissed the senator's cheek.

They talked for a while about the forthcoming elections, and then they said their good-byes. On the way back to the car, Ellie said: 'What on earth are you going to do now? We've never met Senator Strachan, have we? Isn't he supposed to be incredibly hard-baked?'

Jack opened the door for her. 'Hard-baked or not,' he said, 'he must be open to some kind of persuasion. It looks like the only chance we've got.'

Ellie said: 'You don't have to do this, Jack. You could drop it right now and nobody would mind. Not even Johann. He'd understand.'

Jack closed the car door and sorted out his ignition key. 'I know that,' he told her quietly. 'But I guess I've committed myself. And you know what you once told me. You said that if I ever gave in to thieves and carpetbaggers, then I'd really disappoint you; and I don't ever want to do that.'

Ellie was about to say something else, but Jack said: 'The senator's waving good-bye,' and they both turned to wave back. Then they pulled away from the kerb and drove back down Patuxent Drive to the main highway. It was dusty and glaring hot now, and Ellie untied her thin silk scarf.

'I love you,' she said. 'Just as much as ever. Even more than ever.'

Jack looked at her. 'I love you, too.'

She reached across the back of the seat and gently touched his greying hair.

'You're worried about something, aren't you? Something you're not telling me.'

He shrugged, as if it was nothing.

'You're not just doing this to pay Johann back for saving your life, are you? You haven't even thought about that shipwreck for years.'

He turned the Buick south, and they drove into a blur of golden sunlight and bright concrete highway. 'It's one of those things. Suddenly you feel like settling old debts.'

'Not you, Jack. And not this way. You know Johann's

guilty, don't you? Even if he didn't know about Admiral Messenger personally, his corporation knew and that makes him morally responsible. And I'm sure he knows about every other bit of bribery and chicanery that goes on. Come on, Jack, you don't even *like* him particularly.'

'I don't *dis*like him.'

'You said yourself only two or three months ago that he looked dignified and elderly and respectable, but that was only skin-deep.'

'Well, that's true.'

'Then why are you getting yourself involved in all this? I don't understand it. I know that it's dog eat dog and cat eat mouse, and Senator Hubslager's no more honest than Johann or anyone else, and I know that you feel you owe Johann something, but not this much, surely?'

Jack said: 'I owe Randy something. I owe Randy some kind of commitment. Something to say that I understand.'

'Randy? What does Randy have to do with it?'

Jack drove in silence for a while. Ellie said: 'Jack?'

He turned and looked at her with a face made tired by sadness. 'There's a roadhouse just along here,' he told her quietly. 'I think we'd better talk about this over a drink.'

They pulled off the road and parked in the parking lot. The roadhouse was mock-Tyrolean timber, with a hedge of dusty firs, and a neon sign that said 'GO D EATS.' A fat man in a tiny panama hat was sitting in a pale green Hudson Eight, devouring a whole poloney and listening to the baseball scores. A truck flashed past with a mournful doppler sound.

It wasn't the best place to talk about anything so sensitive or dear. They sat at a small smeary table by the window, where blowflies buzzed and rattled against the glass, and a hostess in a red velour jacket and a pillbox hat brought them two tasteless collinses. Behind the bar, the bartender was carrying on a long nasal harangue against anyone who felt we ought to stay out of the war, but of course *he* couldn't go fight the Germans personally since his grandfather came from Dresden.

Ellie whispered: 'What's wrong, Jack? You've been talking so strange today. What's happened?'

Jack couldn't speak at first, couldn't get the words to rise past his larynx. He looked down at his drink, and then he

487

said: 'It's Randy. He took me out to lunch a couple of days after you left for Carolina.'

'He's all right, isn't he? I mean, he's not ill?'

'No, no, he's fine. It's nothing like that.'

'Then what did he say?'

Jack raised his head. Ellie was amazed and disturbed to see that his eyes were glistening with tears. Tenderly she reached out and touched them, and they sparkled on her fingertips.

'I don't know what kind of a parent I've been, not to have noticed,' Jack said miserably. 'I don't know how I could have let him suffer like that. He tried to tell me before a couple of times, but somehow he didn't think I was listening, or he got scared.'

'*Jack,*' said Ellie. The tears were sliding down his cheeks now, and a red-haired woman sitting opposite them turned and stared.

'He said that when he was young, it didn't matter so much. He thought it was some kind of a phase that everybody went through. But by the time he was seventeen, he knew for certain. He was very unhappy round about then, do you remember? Very confused and argumentative. Didn't seem to know what he was or what he wanted out of life.'

Ellie breathed: 'Yes. Yes, he was.'

'Well,' said Jack, taking out his handkerchief and wiping his eyes, 'he managed to come to terms with it, in a way. Managed to work hard, play hard, and keep his mind off it. He still went through agonies, trying to keep it from me. From us. But he managed.'

There was a terrible silence between them. Outside in the parking lot, they could hear the fat man's car radio faintly playing 'A Tisket, a Tasket.'

Then Jack said, with such pain that Ellie had to take his hand across the table: 'This time he couldn't hold it back any longer. He's fallen in love, and he says that his love is returned. It's Maurice Ritchie, his clerk.'

Ellie stared at him. She had guessed what he was going to say, almost as soon as he had started to tell her, but she had tried to believe that it was something else, anything else, but that. She said: 'Oh, my God,' and put her hand to her mouth in overwhelming grief.

'He wants to go away,' Jack continued quietly. 'Someplace where people don't know who he is, or who he belongs to. He wants to set up house with Maurice and then start his own law firm. He talked about Los Angeles or San Francisco. He said he was sorry.'

'Sorry?' wept Ellie. 'Oh, my God, *he* doesn't have to be sorry. It's us! The perfect parents, weren't we? Or we thought we were. And we didn't even guess. Oh, Jack . . . oh, my God.'

Jack sipped his drink. 'That was part of the reason I got involved with this Hubslager business. I suppose it was dumb, but I felt that if maybe I showed that I could understand people like that, maybe protect them, then Randy would see that I . . .'

He rested his head in his hands.

'I don't know what Randy *would* see,' he said in a desperately unhappy voice. 'But he's my son, and I don't know what else I can do.'

Ellie said: 'Please, Jack. Let's go home.'

Jack nodded. The bartender was saying: 'Mind you, if I could afford to dress like Robert Donat, I would.' And outside, in the lot, the radio played 'When the Moon Comes Over the Mountain.'

Senator William Strachan's secretary, Florence, who was known throughout Washington as the girl whose eyes said 'bed' and whose legs said 'piano,' opened the varnished door of his office and announced: 'Mr Henry Keith, sir. You're expecting him.'

Senator Strachan didn't take his well-polished Alan McAfee shoes off the desk. Instead, he looked up at Henry over his horn-rimmed half-glasses and shouted harshly: 'How are you, Henry? Take a seat.'

Henry tugged up the pants of his creased blue suit and then perched himself awkwardly on a small chair next to an overweening rubber plant. 'I'm real pleased you could fit me in, Senator,' he said with an uncertain grin 'I'm sure you must be pretty busy these days, what with November and everything.'

'That's right,' growled Senator Strachan. He was a hand-some, large-headed man with closely cropped grey hair and a Harvard tie. He was one of those uncompromising and

489

slightly unhinged Republicans from whom Johann usually tried to stay away. Extreme views may have been fine for winning elections, but they caused nothing but ructions in industry, and apart from that, Johann preferred quiet company these days, and that was why he surrounded himself with moderate men.

'I don't know how much Mrs Cornelius told you on the telephone,' said Henry.

'Nothing. She simply said it was urgent and important. And I can tell you now that it had better be.'

'Oh, it is.'

Senator Strachan stood up and paced stiffly around his desk. His office was panelled in light oak, and hung with half a dozen amateurish oil paintings that his wife had given him for Christmas. On his desk was a photograph of Philip on his graduation day, a saintly smile on his lips; a family crest with the motto 'Brains & Brawn' beneath it; and a scale model of the U.S. submarine *Squalus*. He kept the *Squalus* there to remind himself that out of the worst disasters, something good could always be salvaged.

Outside the window, there was a scrubby lawn and a view of the back of the Justice Department. It was another hot, hazy day.

Senator Strachan said: 'I can't say that I've ever had the opportunity to talk to Mrs Cornelius for long.'

Henry Keith opened his briefcase and gave a little hiccuping cough like a sick chipmunk. 'She's a very pleasant lady, sir. She knows her own mind. But most pleasant.'

'So I believe,' replied Senator Strachan flatly.

Henry sorted out an untidy heap of papers, dropped a lot of them, then fished in his pocket for a handkerchief. He blew his nose loudly, then collected up his papers again. 'Summer cold,' he explained.

Senator Strachan sat on the edge of his desk and waited impatiently.

'Right, now, here we are,' said Henry. 'There's a long report from the Greenbaum Detective Agency, and something from Pinkerton, and one or two random bits and pieces from Judd.'

Senator Strachan put his magnificent head to one side and looked down at Henry with a sour, gritty expression.

'*Judd?*' he asked, as if he had a sudden mouthful of bile. '*Greenbaum?*'

'Yes, sir. They're both pretty reputable private-detective agencies up in the New York–Connecticut area. They weren't hired by us, I hasten to tell you, but by Mr Martin Landseer.'

'Landseer? That was the fellow that Hope Cornelius married, wasn't it? Bit of a milksop, if my memory serves me.'

'Well, sir,' sniffed Henry, 'you could say that.'

'All right, then. So Mr Martin Landseer hired some private detectives. What does that have to do with me?'

Henry wiped his nose again. 'Well, what Mr Martin Landseer wanted to find out was whether his wife, that is, Mrs Hope Cornelius Landseer, was being entirely, well, loyal.'

'Isn't that why *any* man hires a private detective?' put in Senator Strachan gruffly.

'I guess so. It varies. In this case, though, we have some pretty clear evidence of adultery. It seems, I'm sorry to say, that Mrs Hope Cornelius Landseer has been having a pretty constructive relationship with your son, Philip.'

Senator Strachan folded his arms. 'Where did you dredge up this so-called evidence?' he demanded.

'Mr Landseer supplied it. He's considering divorce.'

'And that means he's going to cite Philip?'

'Well, that's right.'

There was a silence. Senator Strachan walked back around his desk, sat himself down, and stared at Henry from under his bushy grey eyebrows. Henry smiled back, a little nervously, and wiped his nose again.

'What's the alternative?' asked Senator Strachan at last, resting his chin on his square fist.

'Well, sir—'

'I gather there *is* an alternative. I mean, you haven't flown here from California just to tell me that Martin Landseer is citing Philip.'

Henry put his papers away untidily. 'Mrs Cornelius doesn't want you to feel that you're being pressed, sir. But she does have a suggestion.'

'Go on.'

'Mrs Cornelius said that she could dissuade Martin

Landseer from citing Philip by agreeing to pay the Landseers a substantial divorce settlement.'

'And what would I have to do to ensure that *that* happened?'

Henry rustled and bustled in his briefcase again, and brought out more paper. 'Well, sir, Mrs Cornelius understands that you have some information relating to the Welfare Investment Plan of 1938, in which Senator Jorkins and Senator Hubslager were pretty substantially involved.'

Senator Strachan raised an eyebrow. 'Word gets around, doesn't it?'

Henry smiled. 'It sure does, sir. Even walls have ears.'

'Well,' said Senator Strachan, 'even if I did possess such information, what about it?'

'Nothing at all, Senator. Except that Mrs Cornelius would really care for a copy of everything you have on the matter, on the understanding that she could use it or release it whenever she wanted.'

Senator Strachan stared at Henry Keith balefully for a long time without saying a word. Then, abruptly, he shouted: '*Hah!*'

Henry Keith blinked, and sniffed.

Senator Strachan rose from behind his desk like a rhinoceros topping the crest of a hill. In a voice that was powerful, deep, and almost steady, he said: 'Mrs Cornelius wants information on Senator Jorkins and Senator Hubslager? Mrs Cornelius does, does she? Well, you can go back to California and you can tell Mrs Cornelius that if she wants information on anything she can get it the way that I got it. The *hard* way.'

Henry Keith looked abashed. 'You don't want to cooperate?'

'Cooperate? This is extortion! The usual grinning, oily, Cornelius extortion! I'm supposed to save my son from public scandal by giving Mrs Cornelius valuable political information? Just imagine if the whole damned country were run that way! No, sir, Henry, I'm telling you that if Philip has been misbehaving himself with Hope Cornelius Landseer, then Philip has got to take what's coming, no matter how much it hurts him or his family, because nobody in the world, and especially not Hester Cornelius, is going to blackmail me for anything. Not for *anything*, do you understand?'

Henry Keith sat tight and silent. It was only when Senator Strachan had thumped his fist on his desk and sat down again that he ventured to speak.

'Is that what you want me to say?' he asked meekly. 'That you don't care what happens to Philip?'

'Does Mrs Cornelius care what happens to Hope? Can she really exploit her daughter's sexual adventures for the sake of business? What kind of a mother can do that?'

Henry coughed and looked down at his scruffy brown shoes. 'Well, sir, I have to tell you that the consequences of this are going to be pretty serious. If we don't solve this problem with Senator Hubslager one way, we're going to have to solve it another.'

'Well, you just damned well *solve* it another way,' grated Senator Strachan. 'Because this information is mine, and it's going to stay mine, and I wouldn't help you or Hester Cornelius if you were hanging on my window ledge by the tips of your fingers.'

Henry Keith shrugged. 'Okay, sir. But just remember that you *are* on the first floor.'

Senator Strachan pushed a button on his desk, and Florence appeared at the door like a wooden woman out of a weather house.

'Mr Keith is just leaving us,' the senator said harshly.

Henry Keith closed his briefcase and stood up, getting himself entangled in the rubber plant. 'You sure you won't spend some time reconsidering?' he asked quietly

Senator Strachan shook his head, tautly and almost imperceptibly; and so Henry shrugged, and said 'Okay,' and winked at Florence as he ambled out.

They met in Morningside Park, under the shadow of the Cathedral of St John the Divine. It was so hot that Philip had to take off his coat and fold it over the back of the bench. Hope, in a light grey pleated skirt and a pale yellow silk blouse with padded shoulders, kept fanning herself with a *Ladies' Home Journal*. The forsythia bushes looked brown and dusty in the unnatural heat

'I suppose your mother told you what happened,' said

493

Philip, unfolding his handkerchief and patting the sweat from his forehead.

Hope kept her hands demurely in her lap. She said: 'Yes.'

'I'm proud of Father, anyway,' said Philip. 'At least he wouldn't be swayed.'

'That doesn't make any difference to us, does it?' put in Hope.

Philip shrugged. 'Was there ever any "us," really?'

'You said there was. Perhaps I misheard you.'

Philip leaned over toward her. 'No, when I said "us," I meant . . .'

Hope turned away. 'It doesn't matter. Whatever you meant then, if you don't mean the same thing now, then it doesn't matter. You're not my husband.'

Philip said: 'Well . . .' and looked embarrassed. Across the park, an old man was scattering bread to the pigeons as he walked, like a sower of seed in a biblical picture.

Hope said: 'This has to be the last time, you know. We can't meet anymore.'

'Don't you *want* a divorce?'

'It looks as though I'm going to get one, whether I like it or not.'

'But surely your mother wouldn't—'

'Wouldn't she?' interjected Hope. 'You don't know Mother.'

Philip looked glum. 'I've never been cited before. I suppose it's going to appear in all the worst newspapers.'

'And the best,' said Hope.

Philip gave a queasy little smile and nodded. 'I guess you're right.'

Hope sat quietly for a few minutes, nervously twisting her diamond rings around and around. Then she said: 'Did you try persuading your father?'

'Oh, yes. Of course I did. But he said that America always comes first, which, being translated, means Senator William Strachan's political career always comes first. He won't give your mother anything on Hubslager – not a single sausage – not even if she tells him that my grandmother's been sleeping with half of Congress.'

'But *why* won't he?' asked Hope.

Philip pulled a face. 'Because he's impossibly stubborn, being Irish, and because he won't have a woman telling him what to do, not even Hester Cornelius, and because if he lets your mother have this information on Hubslager now, he's throwing away one of his best weapons against Jorkins in forty-four.'

'Surely the Welfare Investment Plan is going to be stale news in forty-four. That's even if Jorkins is nominated. Personally, I'd rather nominate a warthog.'

Philip sighed and brushed back his hair with his hand. 'I agree. But just try telling Father.'

There was another long pause. High up in the vivid blue sky, a silvery transatlantic Clipper droned by, its wings catching the sunlight. It was almost lunchtime, and the first few office workers were venturing into the park with sandwiches and flasks.

'I wonder what that detective said?' said Hope.

Philip frowned at her.

'According to Mother, Martin's had me followed for *months*,' Hope went on. 'Ever since we went to the Manuccis for Twelfth Night, and he came out into the conservatory and caught me kissing Robert Scheinhorn. I think it's repulsive. Exactly the kind of repulsive thing that Martin would do. I mean, if your own husband can't trust you . . .'

Philip said: 'Yes,' in a flat, disinterested voice.

'Thousands of people do it these days,' insisted Hope. 'It's nothing to get divorced about. Nothing to send private detectives out about. Martin's so damned old-fashioned.'

Philip leaned back on the bench and closed his eyes. 'It's your mother I can't get over. What an opportunist! When Martin came creeping around with that stuff about you and me, she must have thought the gods were smiling on her. Just what she needed to squeeze my father – "Give me the dope on Hubslager or else I'll make sure your son gets publicly cited in my daughter's divorce." She doesn't give a damn about anyone, does she? Not you, not anyone.'

'Not me especially,' said Hope with gentle bitterness. 'She's always considered that I'm too much competition, and that's why she's always made sure that she keeps me out of the way. Don't worry, Philip, I'm used to it.'

'How can you ever get used to a mother like that?'

'People have worse mothers. People have mothers who beat them, or flirt with their boyfriends, or get drunk.'

Philip nodded, and then said: 'What are we going to do now?'

'I don't know,' admitted Hope. 'I guess it's up to Martin. He's gone to stay with his parents for the time being, and I suppose they'll work out whether he's going to divorce me or not.'

'You don't care?'

'Of course I care. My God! My mother's tried to use my own body to buy my father out of a prosecution. What's even worse, she's failed God knows what's going to happen now.'

Philip took her hand. He looked into her eyes with a serious if slightly preppie expression.

'Hope,' he said gently, 'I want you to know that I'm very fond of you.'

She put her head on one side and smiled. 'Fond? That's not even worth a divorce, really, is it?'

'I don't know. I wasn't trying to hurt you.'

She lifted her face to him and kissed him. 'Oh, Philip.'

He smiled. 'I guess I'll see you in court. I don't suppose it'll be that painful.'

Hope, quite unexpectedly, began to cry.

'Being rich is always painful,' she told him.

At Carina Mia, at evening time, Johann was sitting on the balcony with a last brandy-and-soda. The air was warm and soft, and from time to time he almost fell asleep.

Hester came in from the bedroom, wearing a long dressing gown of black silk that swept noiselessly over the mosaic floor. She bent over and kissed him on the forehead, and whispered: 'Johann?'

He opened his eyes. 'I was thinking,' he said gruffly. 'I wasn't asleep.'

She pulled over a small rush chair and sat down beside him. 'I just talked to Senator Strachan again,' she said quietly. In the dusk, Johann could see her elegant profile as a soft silhouette.

'Well?'

'He won't change his mind. He said that if Martin wants to cite Philip as correspondent, then that's tough on Philip. Can you believe it? He said he can't mollycoddle Philip, any more than *his* father mollycoddled *him*.'

'Have you spoken to Hope?' asked Johann.

'Well, briefly. She knows what's going on.'

'And she's not concerned about it?'

'I don't know. She can't stand Martin, so I don't suppose she particularly cares.'

'She didn't tell you?'

Hester stroked his forehead. 'I don't think she wanted to.'

'Well,' said Johann, 'it looks as if we're going to have to deal with Hubslager the difficult way.'

'Do you think I ought to speak to David Bookbinder?'

'You?'

Hester shrugged. 'I may dislike him, but I have to live with him. And even the worst people can be useful sometimes.'

Johann rubbed his watering eyes. 'I sometimes wonder what we're trying so desperately to protect around here. Our reputation? Who cares what anybody thinks about us? Maybe our souls? Don't ask me, Hester. I think I'm too tired to worry.'

Hester said: 'It's all right. I'll call David tonight. He's in Jersey, isn't he?'

'That's right. But tell him to think about it first, before he gets anything done. I don't want anything ill-considered.'

She kissed him again. 'Nothing ill-considered,' she promised, and left the balcony room to make her call.

On the night of July 9, 1940, a black Plymouth sedan carrying four passengers was involved in a collision with a gasoline truck at the junction of Ditmas Avenue and Flatbush Avenue, in Flatbush, New York. The gasoline truck exploded and all four passengers were trapped in the blazing Plymouth, out of reach of passersby and firemen. They died, according to the local fire department, 'horribly.'

The passengers were later identified as Lieutenant E. N. Scargas, of the New York police; Mr Gorton Tighe, a New York attorney; and two boys of fourteen and thirteen, Antonio Carlo and Francisco Delray, both of Brooklyn. The truck driver was never found. *The New York Times* suggested that the boys were vital witnesses in a rumoured corruption prosecution, and that they were on their way to be interviewed by New York investigators about their involvement in what may have been 'an important scandal.'

A spokesman for the New York district attorney's office refused to confirm or deny these suggestions, but agreed that the boys had been involved in a forthcoming case as 'quite important witnesses' and that the case would now almost certainly have to be dropped.

Five weeks later, on August 14, 1940, Admiral Peary Messenger went for an early-morning swim in the ocean off Narragansett, Rhode Island, and disappeared. An intensive search by the Coast Guard during the afternoon had to be called off because of the failing light.

1945

We are having our little troubles now — a few of them.
They are not serious. Just a blowup after a letdown
from war.

— Harry S. Truman,
Gilbertsville, Kentucky, 1945

Those days, in the first fall after the Second World War, in those strange breezy times of demobilization and peace, in the beginning of the Truman era, with the boys coming home from Europe and the baseball fans looking forward to a season when games would be played without war cripples and 4-Fs; in those times of Toots and Caspar and Thimble Theater and Ginger Rogers in *I'll Be Seeing You*, the Cornelius family rarely visited the House at all. The only consistent exception was Roderick. He had always fancied himself as a Wall Street man, and even though he had very little to do except mooch around the offices and set everybody's teeth on edge, he enjoyed the suppressed bustle of financial paperwork and the endless tapping of ticker-tape machines.

He was there, at the House, on a rainy Thursday in October, 1945. He was sitting in a creaky leather armchair in the gloomy penthouse office on the thirty-fifth floor, where David Bookbinder sat behind his enormous desk the size of an aircraft carrier and directed the day-to-day flows and transactions of Cornelius money.

Bookbinder had been busy all morning. It was one of those curious days when the market still showed signs of depression psychosis, but was just beginning to catch the light-headed fever of boom times. He was rearranging some of the Cornelius holdings in war-related industries, but he was reluctant to turn too much over to peacetime production, particularly with the news from Europe of 'Soviet encirclement.' While he talked endlessly on the telephone, Roderick had been drinking his Scotch.

As lunchtime neared, there were fewer phone calls and more paperwork. Bored, Roderick stirred his Scotch whisky with his forefinger, and then absentmindedly sucked it.

'You shouldn't do that,' said David Bookbinder, without looking up from his papers. 'It reminds me of Foster.'

Roderick blinked, vaguely surprised. 'Does Dulles do that?'

Bookbinder nodded.

'I thought you liked him,' said Roderick a little suspiciously.

Bookbinder methodically ticked off stocks and holdings, and then tossed the papers into his pending tray. 'I do,' he said, screwing the top on his Waterman pen. 'But you couldn't say that style was Foster's strong suit, could you? Even Janet's sick of his socks.'

'I never noticed his socks.'

Bookbinder clipped his pen into his vest pocket and stood up. 'I knew Foster when Bill Cromwell was paying him fifty dollars a month, and that was fifty dollars better than most law clerks used to get in those days. Foster was such a hick we used to call him the Kansas Kid. He could put on a Brooks Brothers suit, and in five minutes flat, he could make it look like one of Charlie Chaplin's castoffs.'

Roderick said reflectively: 'I don't mind what he does with his suits. I just wish he'd play the game a little more *our* way and a little less *their* way.' He nodded in the vague direction of the Standard Oil Building.

'It's all a question of connections,' said Bookbinder. 'As it happens, they've put far more money into their connections than we have.'

'Is that *your* decision?'

'Not entirely. Personally, I'd much rather have Foster as an ally than an enemy. He's going to wind up Secretary of State one of these fine days, and if we're not buddies by then . . . well, you can use your imagination.'

'Father says he's a saboteur in saviour's clothing,' said Roderick.

'What makes him say that?'

'I don't know. Maybe he's just prejudiced. Father never liked what Dulles did with American Oil, and I guess we've all been biased against him ever since.'

'American Oil was centuries ago.'

'Sure. But Father has his favourite hates, and Dulles is one of them. He says he's gotten too spiritual, and I don't think Father believes in spiritual economics. He says there's only one thing worse than an idealistic Communist, and that's an idealistic Republican. As far as Wall Street goes, they're a total frost.'

'Wall Street,' sniffed Bookbinder, 'is suffering from terminal mediocrity. And *now*, of all times!'

Roderick shrugged. He took a clean white handkerchief out of his dark blue double-breasted suit and patted a few clear drops of perspiration away from his neatly clipped sideburns.

'Well, sure, it's mediocre,' he said, 'but I don't think that's necessarily bad. Maybe we *need* to be mediocre. Father says that the whole secret of managing a complicated corporate budget is to have a highly developed sense of the wishy-washy.'

Bookbinder laughed roughly. 'Don't you worry what your father says. Your father used to prod cows for a living.'

'And now you're upset because he prods you?'

'Your father's growing old,' replied Bookbinder flatly. 'Sometimes, for old times' sake, he tries to provoke me. I used to be a boxer at law school – did you know that? I was very athletic. Your father used to enjoy riling me up at important meetings, just to watch me clench up my fists. He used to say: "David, what I'm waiting for is the day when you punch Howard Pew straight in the nose!" '

Bookbinder walked over to the window and looked down thirty-five floors into the rainy streets of lower Broadway. The sidewalks were beetled with shiny black umbrellas, and a tangle of Checker cabs and limousines were honking at each other dolefully.

'I sometimes believe, Roddy, that your father made his fortune as a kind of revenge.'

This sort of conversation was too mystical for Roderick. He opened his gold half-hunter and checked the time. 'Are you coming for lunch?' he asked. 'I promised to meet Celia at the Plaza.'

'You had lunch there yesterday.'

'I know. But Victor likes to ride in the hansom. And apart from that, Celia has this ... *thirst* for Gouron's cream-of-chicken soup. She says she gets it every year, as soon as the weather turns cold. If I didn't believe that lightning can only strike in the same place once, I'd swear she was, well, expecting.'

'Pregnant?' said Bookbinder, raising an eyebrow.

Roderick frowned. '*Expecting*,' he corrected carefully. 'But she's not, of course. It's just the soup.'

David Bookbinder went over to the coat stand and took down his dark grey pinstripe coat. There was a fresh pink carnation in the buttonhole, wilting a little in the office's seventy-degree heat, and he sniffed it ostentatiously before he put the jacket on.

'You should wear a carnation, too,' he said to Roderick. 'Your father's garden produces the finest carnations in the whole state. A mark of pride.'

'I can't stand carnations,' replied Roderick distastefully, swallowing the last of his Scotch. 'They remind me of funerals.'

Bookbinder looked at him. 'That's why you should wear one,' he said.

Roderick, for some reason that he couldn't understand, found that remark distasteful. He said: 'You're a pretty morbid bird today.'

Bookbinder tugged his vest down over his plump stomach. 'Better to be a morbid bird than a plucked duck,' he remarked enigmatically.

'If you trust my driving, we'll go in the car,' suggested Roderick, shaking himself into his dark Chesterfield coat.

Bookbinder was lighting a cigar. 'You drive *yourself*? Is this the new democracy? Is this why we fought the Japs?'

'I like driving,' said Roderick. 'I brought the Lincoln down this morning, and she's a real dream. V-12 L-head engine, and a Liquamatic gearshift. I parked her downstairs.'

Bookbinder grunted. 'If you knew as much about finance as you know about those damned automobiles of yours, I could die a happy man.'

Roderick went red. He usually went red when he was put out, or embarrassed. At thirty-one, he was a big, heavy-boned young man, with a wispy blond moustache that he had started to grow when Celia was away in the hospital giving birth to Victor. He looked more like his father than ever these days, and his expensive clothes never seemed to sit on him comfortably. His hats always looked too small, and his overcoats billowed around him in copious folds. His big feet were laced up in shoes like black polished barges.

The two men walked side by side through the outer office.

'I'm going for lunch, Miss Kaminsky,' said Bookbinder.

They reached the high black marble lobby and stepped across its echoing oval floor to the garage entrance. Several passing employees raised their hats or said 'Good afternoon, sir.' Roderick acknowledged them with a hasty, embarrassed smile, but David Bookbinder didn't even turn his head.

The Lincoln, a white 26H coupé, was parked at the foot of the stairs. Roderick unlocked the doors, and they climbed in. It smelled of rich new hide upholstery and Celia's perfume. A large yellow teddy bear with a wide leer on its face was propped up in the back, along with Victor's teething ring and rattles. Roderick started the engine, and the car bounced on soft suspension up the garage ramp and into the street.

It was October, and it was chilly and wet. Impatient business executives stood at street corners waving their umbrellas at passing taxis, and stenographers and office boys crowded the sidewalks. Burned-smelling smoke drifted across Broadway from bagel stands, and there was still the odd postwar feeling in the air. It was regretful, as if a dream were over, and now we had to forget about fantasies of glory and struggle and our boys overseas, but it was also elated, in a peculiarly practical kind of way, because now we could think about housing, and new cars, and jobs, and television sets, and front-runners at Aqueduct. James Thurber would be fifty-one in two months' time and he had just published *The White Deer* – the story of a prince who had to find a thousand jewels in ninety-nine hours.

Roderick, steering the Lincoln uptown, said: 'I give up.'

'You give up what?' said Bookbinder.

Roderick looked at him. 'I give up on the plucked ducks.'

'Well, forget about the plucked ducks. Think about the carnations.'

Roderick pulled up at a red light. A young veteran in Army uniform, with one empty sleeve safety-pinned up, came across and tapped at the window.

'Our glorious fighting forces,' remarked Bookbinder sarcastically

Roderick wound the handle down. 'Yes?'

The vet was only about twenty-one or twenty-two. He was thin and scraggy, with an unshaven chin and eyes that were red from sleeping on Broadway doorsteps. He said, very politely: 'Is it possible that you might have the price of a bowl of soup?'

Roderick turned to David Bookbinder. 'Do you have any change? I'm penniless.'

David Bookbinder patted his pockets, and then shook his head. 'I'm sorry. I haven't carried a billfold in six years.'

Roderick searched his own coat again, but he had nothing at all. He said to the veteran: 'I'm sorry. We'd like to help, but we don't have any money.'

The veteran stared at them. He had rain on his eyelashes. He stared at Roderick's expensive Chesterfield, and Bookbinder's fragrant cigar. He said: 'You don't have any *money*?'

Roderick was embarrassed.

The veteran said: 'How can you sit there and tell me you don't have any *money*?'

Roderick said: 'Well—'

'I don't want any, not now,' said the boy. 'I just want to *know*.'

'Well,' said Roderick lamely. 'It's just that ... we don't have any use for it.'

The veteran was still staring at them when the light changed and Roderick thankfully pulled away. He said to Bookbinder: 'Remind me to carry some change with me in the future. I don't want that to happen again. Better still – you carry some.'

Bookbinder reached into his coat and took out a wad of bills. He ruffled through them and said: 'My dear Roddy, I always do.'

Roderick glanced over at the bills. Then he stepped hard on his brakes and pulled into the kerb. A taxi blasted its horn at him, and the driver yelled: 'Ya brainless bastard!'

David Bookbinder pretended to look surprised. 'What's the matter? Why have we stopped?'

Roderick said: 'Just give me the money!'

'What do you mean? *All* of it? There must be four hundred dollars here.'

'Just give me a twenty. Come on, quick.'

David Bookbinder said: 'You're making a mistake, Roddy!'

'I don't think so. Now, give me the twenty.'

David Bookbinder sighed, and peeled off the bill. Roderick

snatched the money, climbed out of the car, and ran back along the sidewalk in the rain. He bumped into women with bags, men with briefcases, umbrellas, and strollers. He reached the traffic light, and the young soldier was there, waiting for the red. Roderick ran across the street and tapped him on the shoulder.

The boy turned. He was so much shorter and thinner than Roderick that he made Roderick feel like a huge overfed giant. Roderick held out the twenty-dollar bill.

The vet stared at it. 'What's that for?' he said.

'My friend found it in his coat. I wanted to give it to you.'

The boy stared at the trembling bill in Roderick's hand, and then he looked up into Roderick's eyes.

'Please,' said Roderick, 'take it.'

The vet looked down at the money again.

'Take it,' urged Roderick.

The boy said carefully: 'I don't have change.'

'Change? What change?'

'A bowl of soup, with bread, is five cents. I don't have change for a twenty.'

'Well, take all of it. Have a hundred bowls of soup.'

The boy lowered his head. 'Mister,' he said, 'I've lost my right arm, and I've lost my job, but I don't think I've lost my pride.'

'You can't eat pride,' said Roderick. It was raining hard now, and he was getting wet.

'No,' said the vet. 'And you can't buy pride, either.'

Roderick impatiently pushed the bill into the boy's top pocket.

'Pride or no pride, take it anyway. Take it as a favour to me.'

The boy took the twenty out of his pocket with his good left hand. Then he put it up to his mouth and tore it into shreds with his teeth. In the rain, the fragments stuck to his lips.

Roderick looked at him. For some reason, he felt alarmed. He said to the boy quietly: 'Are they all like you? All the boys who came back?'

The vet brushed dollar confetti from his mouth and turned away. Roderick reached his hand out to touch the boy's shoulder again, but then changed his mind. He was being elbowed and buffeted by passing shoppers and he was getting soaked. He went slowly back to the Lincoln, opened the door, and climbed in.

David Bookbinder was waiting for him patiently.

'Well?' he said, sucking his cigar. 'Did he take it?'

Roderick didn't look across at him. He started the engine and pulled the car out into the lunchtime traffic.

'What makes you think he didn't?'

David Bookbinder chuckled, and tapped his forehead with his forefinger. 'Psychology, Roddy, that's what. The psychology of money.'

'I didn't know money had a psychology. I thought psychology was all about dirty dreams.'

'And you your father's son? Tch-tch!'

Roderick shrugged. 'I guess I'm a disappointment, huh? Just tell me how you put a share certificate on a couch, and then maybe I'll understand.'

'It's very easy,' said Bookbinder, sticking down a wayward leaf of tobacco with spit. 'You just demonstrated the psychology of money in its purest form with that one-armed bandit at the street corner.'

'Goddamned jaywalkers! How's that?'

'You offered the kid too much. A twenty-dollar bill was too abstract for him. He's probably never had one before in his whole life. To him, it was just so much paper – Monopoly money. The same goes for most of the people out there. The reason they're never going to get rich is because they don't want to. No – it's true. As soon as you start talking money in zeros – as soon as you start talking about bonds and stocks and options – most people go glassy-eyed with boredom.'

'Maybe that's just as well,' said Roderick, slowing down for another red light.

'It is,' agreed Bookbinder. 'All most people want are *things* – like a house and a shiny car – and *prestige* – like a fancy executive title and a key to the first-class washroom. You don't have to offer them money. If you give a guy a name like "corporate vice-president," he won't even worry that you're paying him five thousand dollars a year less than you could be. Give him a company car instead of a raise. He'll love you for it.'

Roderick nodded. 'In other words, don't offer a man the

508

price of a case of champagne when all he wants is a bowl of soup.'

'Exactly,' said Bookbinder.

They crossed West Eighth Street and continued uptown on Broadway. The windshield wipers purred backward and forward like two nodding cats, and the rain pattered onto the Lincoln's convertible roof. On a street corner two cops stood next to a soggy poster for Hitchcock's *Spellbound*, with rain dripping from their caps.

'I'm beginning to wonder what all this is about,' said Roderick. 'First of all it's ducks, then it's carnations, now it's psychology and management.'

David Bookbinder puffed his cigar quietly. 'I did want you to be properly prepared. I didn't mean to be devious.'

Roderick grunted. 'I don't think you can *help* being devious. Father says that . . .'

Roderick suddenly stopped. In Bookbinder's eyes he detected the faintest flicker of emotion. It was the telltale widening of the pupils when the stud-poker player spreads out a winning hand – the nervous telegraph that gives away boxers before they strike.

'It's Father,' said Roderick. 'You're setting me up to say something about Father.'

David Bookbinder nodded.

'Is he all right? I mean . . . there's nothing *wrong*, is there? His health's okay?'

David Bookbinder said: 'I tried to keep this for later. This isn't exactly the time and the place to tell you.'

Roderick said anxiously: 'David – please. I have to know.'

'Well,' said David Bookbinder, 'your father's been having tests.'

'I know that. He was up at the sanatorium last month. He told me that everything was fine, and Dr Clarke said he was one hundred and five percent.'

David Bookbinder looked out of the car window. Droplets of rain clung to the glass and dribbled shakily downward.

'Your father was trying to protect you from distress. He was also trying to protect the whole of Cornelius Oil. The last thing we wanted to happen was a run on shares, particularly now. But the truth is, Roddy, that your father is a sick man.'

'Sick? How sick?'

'It's his heart. It's weak, and it's diseased. Dr Clarke diagnosed it last Thursday, and Dr Scheiner gave a second opinion, and agreed.'

David Bookbinder was silent for a moment. When he spoke his voice was steady and flat, but there was something regretful in it, too – the kind of grey nostalgia that blew through New York for a war that had just finished, and a dream that had just faded away.

'He's been feeling breathless and suffering pain for almost two years now. For everybody's sake, he's kept it quiet. Your mother knows, but nobody else. If he takes life easy, he could survive for a while, but there's no real chance of curing it.'

Roderick was driving slowly and mechanically, and almost ran a red light.

'I don't know what to . . .'

'I know,' said David Bookbinder. 'It's a tough break.'

'Isn't there some way of . . . I mean, David, the family can afford to give him the best treatment in the world! Surely *someone* can help? Some specialist? What about that Swiss doctor that mother went to? The one in Basle.'

Bookbinder dropped his cigar out of the window, and shook his head.

'They've given him six months at the outside. The treatment just doesn't exist. Even if your father was twice as rich as he is now, he couldn't do anything about it. You can't buy what doesn't exist.'

'But, Jesus, can't we   ?'

David Bookbinder shook his head again. 'The best thing we can do is keep it under wraps. I didn't want to tell you about it just yet, but I guess you had to know. John doesn't know, though, and neither does Hope. I advised your father against telling them.'

Roderick was very pale, and he didn't answer.

'The thing is, Roddy,' said Bookbinder, 'that I'm worried about what's going to happen next. You father's illness is very tragic and it's very sad, but we must make calm arrangements for the future. Unless we're very careful, we're going to find ourselves in a sticky situation, particularly with the market the way it is.'

'Don't you think that John and Hope have a right to know?' asked Roderick flatly.

510

Bookbinder coughed. 'Well, of course they do. Watch that truck, Roddy. Of course they have a right to know. But the reason I suggested that they didn't find out just yet was because of all the problems over inheritance.'

Roderick said: 'We don't have any problems. All three of us have enough trust accounts to sink the *Missouri*.'

David Bookbinder took out his handkerchief and coughed into it.

'That's quite true, Roddy. But what we have to think about now is whether those trust accounts are in the most profitable posture.'

'What's that supposed to mean?'

Bookbinder was obviously searching for the most delicate way to phrase his next remark. He said slowly, with his tiny hands coming together to form a protective cup: 'Every fortune, when it's passed from father to son, is at risk. Inheritance tax is one risk, sure. The Fords found that out. Until they set up the Ford Foundation, they were faced with 91 percent inheritance tax on Henry Ford's 58½-percent holding, and 91 percent of nearly $700 million isn't two slices of lemon Danish.

'But there are other problems as well. If you disperse your fortune to avoid inheritance taxes, you run the risk of that fortune never coming together again as a single political and financial force. Too much stray money goes into many odd foundations and trusts, like it did with the Rockefellers, and that kind of thing has a debilitating effect on the power of the central fortune. I don't think we'd like that to happen with the Cornelius fortune, would we?'

'I still don't see what you're getting at.'

Bookbinder smiled distantly. 'Not yet you don't. It does require a little explaining, and it also requires some gentle rearrangement of funds. But let me put it this way for now. Wouldn't you rather see all the Cornelius trust accounts and stock holdings legally and bindingly arranged so that all came under one controlling force – instead of being split up into fragments?'

Roderick's forehead furrowed, and he didn't reply.

David Bookbinder leaned over toward him. 'Wouldn't you rather have your hands on the reins of the whole team, for instance, instead of allowing John and Hope to gallop some of the best horses into any old mire they felt like? Don't you think that's wiser? Don't you think that's safer for all of us?'

Roderick looked across at Bookbinder and tried to read what was happening behind those small, intent eyes.

'I guess the principle's right,' he said uncertainly. 'But what about the technicalities? And what would John and Hope have to say? The money's theirs, after all. Maybe they're younger, but they're not stupid.'

Bookbinder sat back. 'I didn't say they were. But I do believe, Roddy, that if anyone has the guts and the go to manage this fortune, it's you. Look at you – you're the spitting image of your father. Do you think he worked all his life, created this empire with his bare hands, just to have it dissipated?'

They were driving east along Fifty-ninth Street to the Plaza. The sky over Central Park was thundery grey, and the trees rolled and rustled like frothing horses in the rainy wind. Roderick drew into the carpeted sidewalk and pulled on the Lincoln's hand brake.

'I don't know, David,' he said. 'Let me think about it, huh?'

David Bookbinder buttoned up his coat. 'That's okay. Give it a couple of days. But remember your father's condition, Roddy. You can't leave it forever. There just isn't that much time.'

That same rainy afternoon, in a small and quiet apartment in the East Fifties, John Cornelius was lying on the blue silk quilt of a double bed smoking a Turkish cigarette. He could hear the rain pattering against the glass of the window, and the echoing sound of car horns and traffic, but he seemed almost completely at peace, watching the thin ribbon of smoke rise to the apartment's decorative plaster ceiling.

He was naked. He was short and stocky for twenty-eight, with a darker complexion than his brother Roderick, and a sharp, muscular face, like a football player from Notre Dame. His body was yellow with fading suntan, and patterned with whorls and eddies of black hair. There was a coarseness about his appearance that wasn't unattractive – a heavy shadow on his chin, and stubby, hairy fingers. But there was refinement as well. He was relaxed like a

512

swimmer floating on the ocean at an expensive resort, and he had grace and accuracy in every movement.

Around him, the apartment was bijou but luxuriously furnished. Thick brown carpets, walls covered in pale shot silk. A rose-period Picasso hung by the bedroom door, showing a sad-faced *saltimbanque* on a horse. The bed was French, made of carved mahogany, with elegant wooden flowers and petals twining around the headboard. There was a persistent fragrance of Guerlain perfume and exotic tobacco, mingled with that well-heated smell that pervades the apartments of the wealthy all over the world.

A girl's voice called from outside the bedroom: 'John! Where are you now?'

John reached over to the silver art-nouveau ashtray beside the bed and crushed out his cigarette. 'I'm at Getty's. Right this very minute, I'm putting a very interesting proposition to J. K. Carter about refining facilities at Port Arthur. He's looking at me with his well-known puzzled expression, and he's nodding his head like the jackass he is.'

There was the sound of someone walking unevenly in wood-soled mules. The girl appeared at the bedroom door, a small Slavic-looking creature with dark curly hair, slanting brown eyes, and a finely defined jaw. She was wearing an embroidered silk négligé in shiny pink, and she carried a highball glass in each hand, clinking with ice and cold gin. Her name was Mara Malinsky, and this was her third week on the East Side. Her small breasts wobbled under the silk as she walked toward the bed.

'Does J. K. Carter *accept* the proposition?' asked Mara, sitting down beside him with the two frosty drinks in her hands. 'Or does he say, "John Cornelius, get back to your love nest, and treat Mara Malinsky to everything she deserves, and a few things she doesn't"?'

John rubbed his chin, mock-thoughtful. 'No,' he said at last. 'He accepts the proposition.'

In gleeful retaliation Mara pressed both highballs firmly against John's hairy nipples. He yelped, and rolled over, splashing cold martini all over himself. Mara set the glasses down on the marble-topped bedside table and threw herself on top of him, laughing and struggling. They tussled and kissed and fought, and then John suddenly found himself with his hands around her bare bottom, her négligé raised up around her waist, and he was looking up into those eyes the colour of unskinned almonds, and her lips were almost parted, moistened, as if ready to kiss him. Gently he lifted his head and touched his mouth against her. She ran her hand through his thick dark hair. Then she kissed him back, licking his teeth like a child after rock candy.

He stared at her for a long time. There was a strange photographic light in the room which made the whole afternoon seem like a long romantic movie. The scene where the lovers tangle in the sheets. Lips touch and tongues softly click. The scene where the young mistress walks naked across the room, thin and delicate, with wrists and ankles slender enough for the smallest bangles. The sound of the bidet running as she squats to douche away his semen.

'Shall I play some music?' she asked. 'Are you in the mood for music?'

John grinned and touched the tip of her nose with his finger.

She got up from the bed, straightening her négligé. She was not yet used to being wanton. This was, after all, only the fifth time they had 'been' together, and she was still uncertain of herself. She walked across the bedroom to the polished mahogany Victrola and opened the lid. He watched her through half-closed eyes, idly stroking his own hairy belly.

'You know what you remind me of?' he said.

She looked up. The dim October light caught one of her eyes, and made it transparent like a carnelian.

'No,' she almost whispered. 'What?'

'You remind me of a woman I once saw when I was visiting France with my mother. I was only ten years old. Ten or eleven. We went to the beach at Arromanches. It was quite cold and grey, and you couldn't see very far out to sea. There was a woman sitting in the sand dunes with a scarf around her head. She had a husband in a striped blazer and a very yappy dachshund. She was eating strawberry cakes and drinking wine from a plain tumbler. I fell in love with her straightaway, and it's only just occurred to me that you look exactly like her.'

Mara lowered her head to read the label of the record she was putting on.

'Have you fallen in love with me?' she asked. She wound the handle round and round, and raised the heavy pick-up arm to check that the needle was still sharp. She didn't look around.

John sat up on his elbow. 'Would you believe me if I said I had?'

She thought about that. Then she said: 'No. I don't think I would, really.'

'Would you *like* me to fall in love with you?'

She shrugged. 'What I would *like* and what I can *get* are two different things, aren't they? But, anyway, I don't think you would. You're very *different* for a trillionaire, but you are a trillionaire, aren't you? You talk romantic, but you do some very trillionairish things.'

'Like what? What have I done lately that's trillionairish?'

Duke Ellington crackled into the room, playing 'Ev'ry Hour on the Hour I Fall in Love with You.' Mara twirled around the bed, lifting her négligé so that its long sleeves floated through the air.

'You've ensconced me,' she said, 'in this dreamy apartment. You've bought me a car. And you've made sure that my slightest whim is attended to, and always pronto! I only have to say fried baby clams, and I get them!'

John laughed. 'That's not trillionairish. Listen, come here, and I'll tell you what trillionaires do. You really want to know?'

She swooped onto the bed beside him. 'I bet it's boring,' she said, blinking at him cheekily. 'I bet that being a trillionaire is such a yawn that you have to hire special people to put their hands in front of your mouth for you.'

'If you're talking about my brother, Roddy, then you're absolutely right. Roddy is the staunchest, most conservative trillionaire that ever breathed. He's stingy, too. He steals stationery from cheap hotels, and towels from bus stations. He's the only trillionaire who's got "Property of U.S. Treasury" printed on his toilet paper. He collected a few rolls on his last visit.'

'You're kidding again,' said Mara. She reached for her highball and took a long drink. Then she turned over on her back and stared at the ceiling. 'I'll bet your brother,

Roddy, is the kindest, most generous guy in the whole world.'

John sniffed. 'You're right, as a matter of fact. He is. He'd give his last doughnut to Earle McAusland.'

'I get the feeling you resent him.'

'No, no,' said John, swallowing cold gin. 'I don't resent him. Why should I? He's the kind of older brother that some younger brothers would give their left legs for. What you have to understand, *ma chère* Mara, is that when you're an heir and an executive in a corporate entity like Cornelius, you support your family no matter what. You can't tell where blood ends and money begins.'

She turned over and examined him from close up, as if he was an unusual sculpture.

'Don't you ever get lonesome?' she asked.

He shook his head. 'That's one of the great fallacies that people with thin wallets like to believe about people with fat wallets. It isn't lonesome, being rich. Not unless you're a real recluse. I mean, I guess my father isn't very sociable these days, but he used to be, when he was younger. When you have bottomless reserves of money, you can meet whoever you want, you can have parties and dinners whenever you want, and you can fly hither and thither whenever you want. Did you know that I have my own plane?'

'Your own? You mean it belongs to you personally?'

'It sure does. But that's nothing. Roddy has five. He has them all parked in a big shed down at his place in Virginia, and whenever he's down there, he goes and ogles them. He's kind of an airplane nut.'

She sat up. 'Would you like to hear another record?'

'Sure. Anything you like.'

She padded over to the Victrola again. As she was sorting out what she wanted to play, she said: 'I really find it frightening.'

'Frightening? What?'

'All your money. It scares me.'

'I don't wave it at you, do I?'

'You can t '

He didn't answer that. Instead, he reached over for his gold cigarette case and carefully removed an oval Turkish cigarette. He lit it with his glittering lighter, puffed out blue smoke.

Mara laid the steel needle into the groove of 'I Can't Put My Arms Around a Memory.' There was a small smile on her lips when she turned back and looked at John – half-wistful and half-resigned.

'I knew when you picked me up that you couldn't take me around. But it all seems so strange. You must be rich, because you're John Cornelius. Yet I can't experience any part of your life, and I can't see what it is that makes you rich, or why you enjoy it. I have to sit up here in this ... ivory tower, and the only time I see you is when you're stark naked.'

John blew out smoke. 'In that case, you see me at my best.'

She pretended to be exasperated. 'You're so conceited. I'm sure that you look quite presentable when you're dressed.'

He smoked thoughtfully for a while. Then he said: 'You're a strange girl, Mara.'

She didn't look up. She was watching the record label go around and around as the needle hissed its way through the faint strains of trumpets and trombones.

He got off the bed and walked across to where she stood. Naked and hairy, he kissed the back of her neck. They were momentarily knotted together by thin strands of curling cigarette smoke, like printed lovers on a Valentine's Day card.

'I promise,' he said. 'I promise that when Irene and the girls go south, I'll take you out. First stop – the Starlight Roof at the Waldorf. Now, how about that?'

She turned around, pouting. 'You're mocking me,' she said. 'You never go there.'

'I do too. I was there last week, and I cut a rug with Hedy Lamarr.'

'You're a liar.'

He grinned. 'Well, maybe I am. But there are plenty of places we can go, and not be recognized. I'm not a movie star, you know. The common rabble in the street don't know me from Adam.'

'Nor do I,' she said 'You're always as naked as Adam when you're with me '

She stroked his shoulder, her fingertips circling softly

517

around. She was gazing sadly across the bedroom as if she could already detect the shadows of a heartbroken future. She sighed.

'I guess I came too late,' she said. 'I can borrow your body, but that's about all. I can never be part of your life.'

'You don't have to be jealous of Irene,' he said, frowning.

'But I am. She can share your life, and your home, and your children. She can stand by your side at parties, and go riding with you, and what can I do?'

John went across to the ashtray and tapped his cigarette. The afternoon light was growing dimmer, as if it was being filtered through layer after layer of white muslin. At almost the same moment he tapped the cigarette, Roderick was drawing into the kerb outside the Plaza, and pulling on his hand brake.

John said: 'When Irene goes south, there's no reason why we couldn't hold a dinner party. I have a place on East Eighty-second Street, and a cottage out at the Hamptons.'

'You mean a discreet dinner party?' asked Mara. 'A few well-trusted friends?'

'Who do you think I meant? The editor of the *New York Post*?'

Mara said: 'John, don't treat me like a child. I'm twenty-one. I'm a woman and I have the instincts of a woman. You can't shut me up here for the rest of my life, and just use me when you want me. I have to be able to participate in what you're doing. You have to give me the chance to give you something back. I can't do that when you hide me here.'

'Well,' he said uncertainly, 'I'm sure we can work something out.'

She looked perplexed. 'Don't any of your other friends have mistresses? Kept women? Surely it wouldn't shock them that much?'

'Mara, it's not a question of shocking people.'

'Then what? If it's not a question of shocking people, why can't we have a dinner party with your usual friends? Just wait until Irene's gone south, and have a dinner as normal. You can always say I'm your long-lost cousin from Holland, or something like that

John sat on the edge of the bed. He ran his hand tiredly

518

through his hair. 'Mara,' he said, 'do you have any idea who my usual friends are?'

She put her head on one side. She wanted him to look up at her, to give her a clue, but he didn't.

'Rich people, I guess,' she said lamely. 'Du Ponts, and people like that.'

John nodded. 'Last week,' he told her, 'I had a small informal dinner for eighteen people. The Duke and Duchess of Windsor were there, and so were Clara Bell Walsh, Harvey Firestone Jr., Sir James Dunn and Lady Dunn, and a sprinkling of other people you might recognize. Howard Hughes, for instance. Those are my usual friends.'

Mara stared at him. 'The Duke and Duchess of Windsor? You know them?'

John at last looked up. 'I met them through Roddy. The duke's very partial to Scottish haddock, and Roddy knows an airline pilot who can fly them in special.'

'Haddock?' said Mara unbelievingly.

'That's right. And broiled woodcock, if you're interested.'

'You're mocking me again. You're avoiding the issue.'

John said: 'There is no issue. I'm very fond of you, Mara, and I want to keep you around. But I can't stroll around town with you hanging on my arm, because I have responsibilities to my family and my stockholders and everybody else who's associated with me because I'm known to be respectable.'

She rubbed at the soft carpet with her mules. 'You make it sound . . . very heartless, somehow.'

She could see he was annoyed. He was sensitive, and he hadn't wanted to say what he had, but she had cornered him into it. They both knew that his money and his reputation were inescapable facts of life, and that everything they did – every laugh, every kiss, every act of love – would have to be conditioned by them. She reached over and kissed him gently on the side of the face. 'I'm sorry,' she whispered.

He smiled wryly and took her hand. 'It's not your fault. You feel that way because you're generous, not because you're mean. You're a lovely girl, Mara, and however long I can hold on to you, I shall.'

'Am I that different from Irene?'

The record was finished, and it was circling around with

a breathless *click-hisss-click-hisss-click-hissss*. The way that the early-afternoon darkness was crowding into the room made John feel like switching on the lamps, but for some reason he was reluctant to. It was almost as if, once he did that, he was admitting that their hours together were nearly over A small Swiss carriage clock chimed lightly from the drawing-room mantelpiece, and he knew it was half-past two. Rain pattered against the window like some one throwing a handful of raisins.

'I thought Irene was so beautiful,' said Mara. 'I've seen her photograph so many times. She looks so serene.'

John nodded. 'Yes, she is serene. But you can carry serenity too far. If you carry serenity to its ultimate limits, you wind up mummified.'

'Isn't she very . . . relaxed?'

John stood up and walked over to the Victrola. He watched the record scratching around without making any move to turn it off.

'She believes in recreation,' he said. 'She swims, she rides, she plays tennis. She does all the right strokes with all the right folks. She's a bright hostess, and everybody says how wonderful her taste in wallpaper is. She's a good mother, too. She dresses the twins beautifully, and if they were old enough to speak, they'd ask to go play with the Vanderbilts.'

Mara's slanted eyes dropped.

'Then why me?' she said.

There was a soft silence. John said: 'I know what *you're* thinking.'

'What am I thinking?'

'You're thinking I'm a frustrated husband who's been temporarily displaced by his newborn babies, looking for a little entertainment after hours.'

She couldn't help smiling. He came over and knelt down in front of her, his penis hanging between his hairy thighs like a curious species of fruit.

'You're thinking that I don't really love you at all, and that as soon as I've gotten tired of you, I'll toss you by the wayside and go on to some other floozy. You're thinking that I'm specious, caddish, and villainous, not to mention sex-starved.'

She leaned forward and they rested their foreheads

together, gazing in close-up at each other's eyes. She touched his ear.

'That's right,' she said. 'That's just what I'm thinking.'

They stayed like that for a while, face to face, and then John stood up.

'If you'd like to change the record,' he said, 'I'll fix the celebration drink.'

'What's to celebrate?'

'I don't know. You and me, I guess. The weather. President Truman's new hat. Anything that takes your fancy.'

She held out her hands for John to help her up from the floor. He lifted her, and embraced her closely in his arms. She had a thin, almost childlike body, but there was something intensely erotic about her as well. There was a contrast between her slightness and her fierce appetite for lovemaking that aroused him. It was as if a child had just discovered sex, and was overindulging herself without any qualms of conscience or morality. To John, brought up under Johann's regime of regular churchgoing and Hester's dislike of any song or story that was remotely suggestive, this was something to make his nerves tingle and jump alert, and his hair rise up on the back of his neck.

'You do things to me,' he said, quiet and amused.

She kissed him. 'You do thing to me, too.'

He patted her small behind as she went to change the record. 'This drink I'm going to mix you is the ultimate drink of all time,' he said, reaching for his green silken bathrobe and wrapping it around himself. 'It was invented by His Majesty King Alfonso of Spain, at the men's bar of the Paris Ritz.'

He disappeared briefly into the kitchenette, and returned with a silver tray. On the tray was a Georgian silver wine cooler crammed with crushed ice and containing a dark green bottle of Moët & Chandon's Dom Perignon Cuvée 1934. Beside the cooler were two half-litre goblets of chilled and misted silver, and a bottle of Remy Martin vintage cognac.

Mara, choosing a record, said: 'Champagne? Where in the world have you been hiding that?'

John laid the tray ceremoniously down on a small Bauhaus table and grinned. 'I hid this in the saucepan cupboard when I came in. All the time we've been spooning and crooning, this beauty has been steadily chilling.'

He took the champagne out of the ice, unwrapped the foil, and popped the cork out. The foam, as dry and astringent as a mouthful of prairie dust, surged into the silver goblets, and when they were brimful, John added three good-sized measures of cognac to each.

'Wait . . .' he said. 'I nearly forgot the strawberries!'

Mara laughed with sheer pleasure. 'Strawberries? And champagne? You have to admit that *this* is trillionairish!'

John came out of the kitchen with a woven basket tied with pink ribbons and crammed with fresh strawberries.

'This isn't trillionairish,' he said. 'This is what we rich folk call *piggish*.'

They sat on the bed while slow, treacly jazz hissed out of the Victrola. John handed Mara her goblet and picked up his own. She looked down into it, and the reflections of silver and champagne made flickering patterns on her face.

'It smells absolutely beautiful,' she whispered. 'Like liquid money.'

'It's called the King's Death,' said John. 'You're supposed to drink it in three or four swallows, and then gorge yourself on strawberries.'

She giggled. 'Shall we try?'

'We have to. It's the only way to drink it.'

'Is there anything you have to say before you drink?'

John shook his head. 'The drink speaks for itself. You can say "I love you," if you like.'

Mara swirled the goblet gently around, and watched the scintillating bubbles rise from the surface.

'I think perhaps instead I'll make a wish.'

'Okay. What will you wish?'

'It's a secret. But I expect you know what it is.'

He drank. The champagne was cold, and foamed in his mouth as if his teeth were turning to froth. Then the cognac warmed its way down his throat, and smoothed away the dryness.

'Yes,' he told her. 'I know what it is.'

By the time Roderick had finished his lunch at the Plaza, and Celia had persuaded him to take young Victor around the park in Pat Rafferty's hansom, John and Mara were wet-eyed with drink and seized by a lewd and unreal

522

passion that led them to make love over and over, sometimes collapsing on each other breathless when they were
only halfway through, sometimes teetering on the very
brink of it – but kissing with wide-open mouths and
salacious tongues, and clawing at each other as if they
wanted to scratch and bruise their flesh, and finishing up
slower, slower, with the pace of the Twentieth Century
Limited coming to rest, with a long bout of self-inflicted
cruelty which left Mara facedown on the shiny blue quilt,
weeping out loud from pleasure and agony, and John
panting against the cold glass of the window, his cigarette
burning away untouched in its ashtray.

Hope, as usual, was feeling brittle and annoyed. She had
come in and out of the morning room five times, and each
time Edward was sitting in his big brown brocade armchair,
The Wall Street Journal raised in front of him like the sail
of an old schooner, reading his slow and considered way
through the market digest.

Finally, huffing in temper, she banged at the paper with
her fist.

'Is there anyone in?' she snapped. 'Or have you all gone
to sleep in there?'

Edward, unperturbed, shook his newspaper back into
shape. 'We are not asleep in here, Hope. We are reading.'

Hope clucked her tongue. 'I suppose the fortunes of the
Ohio Oil Company are far more interesting than what
we're going to eat for dinner tonight.'

Edward didn't stir.

Hope snapped: 'I suppose the closing prices of Sears,
Roebuck are more attractive than your own wife.'

Edward folded down one corner of his paper and looked
at her. 'I'm catching up with the news. Is that such a
crime? A man can't catch up with the news in his own
house?'

Hope tossed her head impatiently. 'Well, that's just
dandy,' she said. 'That's just wonderful to know. At least
you've made it clear where I stand.'

'And where do you think that is?' asked Edward.

'I damned well *know* where it is! I have to organize the
whole of this evening's dinner, and all the entertainment,

523

and all you can do is sit on your rump and read yesterday's paper. That's where I stand, Edward the Second!'

Edward shrugged, and went back to his reading. But Hope stood over him, tapping her foot on the parquet floor, her arms folded and her eyes sharp with anger.

Eventually Edward couldn't ignore her any longer, and he dropped the corner of his paper down again.

'Did you want something?' he asked courteously.

'Oh!' she said. 'You've noticed I'm here!'

'Yes,' he said slowly, 'I *have* noticed you're there. In fact, I'd have to be deaf, dumb, blind, and paralyzed not to notice you're there. Now, what is it you want?'

'God,' she said, spreading her hands in a histrionic appeal to the ceiling. 'You're impossible!'

Edward put down his paper altogether. 'I'm not impossible, Hope, I'm just trying to have ten minutes' reading. Is that too much to ask?'

'Edward,' said Hope, 'how long have we been married?'

'Why – do you think it's too long?'

'It's four months,' said Hope sharply. 'Four months last Thursday.'

'And?'

'And you're sitting here reading the paper when you could be helping me! That's not young love, is it?'

Edward carefully scratched one eyebrow. 'It could be,' he said. 'It depends how closely you equate love with money.'

'I don't equate them at all!'

'No, well, maybe you don't. But then you've never had to worry about money, like I have.'

'What's that supposed to mean? I just don't think that love equals money, or money equals love, that's all. And I think I have enough experience of both to speak with some authority, don't you?'

'I wouldn't deny it.'

'So what do you mean? What does young love have to do with dollars and cents? Or is that the way you usually measure it? Are you a man, Edward Secker, or are you an adding machine?'

Edward picked up the paper again. 'There's some interesting news in here about Daylong Oil, of Ohio.'

Hope stared at him as if she could hardly believe he was

real. She blew out her cheeks in exasperation and clapped her hands to the side of her head.

'I knew it!' she said. 'I married a financial maniac!'

Edward smiled, but without much humour. 'If you'd *listen* for a change, instead of jumping to uncomplimentary conclusions, you might understand what I'm trying to tell you.'

'I don't have *time* to listen,' rapped Hope. 'I have to organize the terrapin. I have to make sure the partridge has arrived, and I have to demonstrate to that dummy of a cook the simplest possible stuffing for mongrel goose. Not that you care.'

Edward shrugged. 'Okay, if you have to go, you have to go. I'd hate to think we had disorganized terrapin in the house. I'll be down later, just as soon as I'm through with the paper, and I'll sort out the wine.'

A pale-faced girl in a long white apron appeared in the morning-room doorway. She knocked shyly and said: 'Excuse me, Mrs Secker. There's a telephone call from your mother.'

Hope gave Edward one last hot-and-bothered look and stalked off to the phone. Edward watched her go, half-amused and half-affectionate, and shook his head like a fond father.

His marriage to Hope had been one of those tangential and unexpected matches that seem to work because of their very unlikeliness. Hope was still in hiding when he first met her, isolated from society by her parents and friends until the last sickly memory of her scandalous divorce from Martin Landseer faded away. Hope had spent most of her exile at Lynwood's Island and in Boston, dressing whenever she went out in severe black and navy-blue suits, and almost always veiled. Like many women who have fallen from social grace, she attempted to make public atonement by working for charity; and it was while she was chairing a meeting of the Veterans' Aid Society out at Lynwood that she had met Edward Secker.

Edward was thirty-six; a tall, large-boned man with a slight stoop and a dry way of talking. When he wore his reading glasses he reminded people of FDR, because he had that same big face, placid forehead, and those same small, intense eyes. Hope used to say, when she first met him, that he was so lengthy and angular that he had to fold himself up when he sat down, like a carpenter's rule.

He came from a reasonable, hardworking family – the Seckers of Virginia, specialists in fine tobaccos. His father, a one-legged planter with huge grey moustaches, had sent him through Harvard Law School, and he was now a junior partner in Donleavy, Settle, the Wall Street lawyers. Edward was conscientious and businesslike, but he had a kind of clean-cut gusto that had appealed to Hope in those suffocating and funereal days after her divorce – an enthusiasm for sailing and swimming and golf that had blown through her life with refreshing ingenuousness.

The refreshment was wearing off a little, but the marriage had done more for Hope than she realized herself. She had been twenty-six in May, and was a classically tempestuous Gemini. She was petite and still very pretty, just like her mother had been, and the only obvious Cornelius characteristic she possessed was her awkward temper. But there were dark smudges under her wide brown eyes, and her triangular face seemed to have a haunted quality about it – a worried shadow that passed over it in photographs and at odd, unguarded moments.

Hope always dressed beautifully. This morning, as she made the arrangements for tonight's family dinner party, she wore a dark green woollen dress with a V neck, square shoulders, and short sleeves. Her chestnut hair was swept up and held with green combs, and around her neck she wore a simple emerald choker. She usually spent two or three hours every morning getting ready for the day, and at Marchings, their twenty-bedroom house on Long Island, they always changed for dinner. Edward was boisterous, but he was also traditional, and insisted on what he called 'manners.'

They had an unusual social life. It was alternately busy and remote. Some weeks they had guests every day, and glittering dinner parties for lawyers, business contacts, movie people, publishers, artists, and visiting acquaintances from Europe, and they always made the society pages, even when Hope was doing something as mundane as shopping for hats on Fifth Avenue.

At other times, though, they lapsed into isolation, and Hope would go for long walks in the grounds with their two red spaniels, treading through the wet leaves and brushing her way through overhanging trees and bushes. The grey fall skies hung very low over their white L-shaped mansion, and there was a sad smell of winter in the air. Those were the times when Hope began to wonder what marriage to Edward was really going to be like. His humour and his energy might have helped her to put the Landseer scandal behind her, and soothed her emotional fears, but what would happen when she was completely cured? Would she turn around and look Edward in the face and realize that it was nothing but overwhelming weariness and frailty that had caused her to marry him, and that their relationship was really nothing more than the affectionate bond between a doctor and his patient?

As once she confided in her friend Faith Schickman, the opera singer: 'I don't want to spend the rest of my life in a hospital for broken hearts. Once I'm healed, I want out.'

Edward was friendly and affectionate enough, though. He liked making love, although he wouldn't take off his wide-striped pyjamas; and he would often kiss Hope very demonstratively in front of other people. He liked riding and he enjoyed cigars, and he was planning on taking her south to Virginia for their first vacation. There had been no honeymoon because of the pressure of Edward's work, but he was always talking about taking her to Europe – 'and I'll make love to you under the Vienna moon.'

Right now, on this wet October day, he seemed more preoccupied with business than usual. He had chosen to stay at home and finish up his backlog of paperwork rather than go into the city. He had already spent several hours on the telephone, and Hope had never seen him scrutinize the paper so thoroughly. She didn't care for business very much. To her, money was money regardless of its origin, and you spent it on clothes and houses and parties. It smothered you in fine jewellery, and sometimes it protected you from great harm.

She was in the big, high-ceilinged kitchen, going over the dinner arrangements with the cook, Mrs Polanski, when Edward eventually came down. There were heaps of vegetables all over the solid pinewood table: broccoli and earthy potatoes, pale rooty parsnips and speckled squashes. Already the polished copper saucepans and decorative moulds were assembled, and the black kitchen maid, a pretty, cheerful girl with the unlikely name of Yolande, was scraping and slicing potatoes and grinding herbs. The old sink and range had been replaced by the Seckers with an up-to-date stove and dishwasher from Westinghouse, but the kitchen hadn't lost its antique charm.

'Well,' said Hope sharply, 'have you finished the funny papers?'

Edward nodded, and stole a red currant from a white enamel bowl.

'I've finished all right. Unfortunately, they're not so funny.'

'What's that mean? That's okay, Mrs Polanski, the nuts can wait until later. What's that mean, Edward?'

Edward stuck his hands in his pockets and looked around the kitchen.

'Can we go someplace else? Just for a minute? I think there's something you ought to know.'

'Is it really that urgent?'

'It's . . . essential.'

Hope sighed. 'All right. Can you cope with that, Mrs Polanski? I won't be too long.'

Mrs Polanski, a puffy-faced woman with great red forearms like Popeye, squinted at Edward suspiciously and nodded.

'I cope,' she said thickly. 'You just tell me the hows and the why-fors, and I cope good.'

They went upstairs, and Edward opened the door of his study – a small book-lined room just off the main hallway. There were Harvard pennants on the wall, and an oar from Edward's sculling days. On the desk, which was littered with open books and heaps of paper, was a silver statuette of an athlete in rather long drawers. Edward said: 'Sit down,' and pointed to a fat ugly chair with a brown cushion on it. Hope, quite stiffly, sat.

Edward shuffled through the papers.

Hope said: 'I feel as if you're about to tell me something awful. Something I don't want to hear.'

Edward said: 'Uh-huh. I am.'

She sighed impatiently as he went on shuffling paper. 'You're not a bigamist, are you? Or is that too much to hope for?'

Edward ignored her. He pulled out a long scribbled list

of names, crisscrossed with arrows and figures and percentages, and said: 'Here we are!'

Hope sat back and crossed her legs. She was always elegant, but there was often a nagging tension and impatience about her, and her friends frequently felt she was bored, or tired, or anxious to get on to her next appointment. Only Edward was impervious to it, because Edward was linear in his thinking and dogged in his progress, and if he knew that there was no logical reason why Hope should be bored, tired, or anxious, then he presumed that she wasn't, and didn't concern himself about her twitchiness at all.

Edward held the list up and waved it slowly back and forth, like a doubtful small boy waving at a Shriners' parade.

'I don't have proof yet,' he said emphatically, 'but I do have a pretty clear suspicion.'

'You have a pretty clear suspicion of what? I wish you'd make sense.'

He made a steeple of his hands. The dull daylight reflected from one lens of his spectacles, turning it blind.

'It's very hard to explain,' he said, 'and if I wasn't me, and if I didn't happen to be married to you, then I don't think I ever would have noticed it at all. But when you look at what's been happening from our particular point of view, it all starts to smell pretty unusual.'

'*Edward*,' said Hope testily.

'No, no,' put in Edward. 'Just let me tell you. It's important to both of us, and it's especially important to you. After all, it's *your* money. If someone tried to pick your pocket, you wouldn't let them get away with it, would you? So don't let them pick your inheritance.'

'I beg your pardon?' said Hope. She had been idly fondling the long-drawered athlete, but now she turned around.

'Your inheritance, Hope. I know it sounds absurd. But someone is trying to squeeze you out of your inheritance.'

Hope put her hand to her mouth and let out a small affected laugh.

'Edward! What a ridiculous idea!'

Edward wasn't abashed. 'It is ridiculous, I agree. But you take a look at these papers. Whether it's ridiculous or not, it's happening, and it's happening right under your nose. Daylong Oil is a particular instance.'

'Daylong? But I control that company, don't I? I'm the largest stockholder, anyway. You know that as well as I do.'

'Well,' said Edward, 'you *think* you're the largest stock holder.'

'What's that supposed to mean?'

'Look here. You own 23.2 percent of Daylong stock. The remaining 76.8 percent of stock is divided among fifteen other stockholders, and the largest individual share that any of those stockholders owns is nine percent.'

'So what's the probem?'

Edward took off his reading glasses and rubbed them with his handkerchief. He looked big-faced and nearsighted without them – like a large carp staring out of a bowl on the sideboard.

'The problem is that one of the minority stockholders has just sold four percent of stock to the Williamsburg Associated Bank.'

Hope shook her head, uncomprehending. 'What does that mean? Four percent isn't much.'

'No, it isn't. Except that seven of those fifteen other stockholding companies are controlled, in their turn, by banks or trusts or oil corporations which, in *their* turn, are controlled by Cornelius Oil – and specifically by the Cleveland division.'

Hope frowned. 'That's Roddy's division, isn't it? I mean – Roderick manages Cleveland?'

'He certainly does. Now let me tell you something else. Up until this Williamsburg bank transfer, Roderick's holding companies owned 19.1 percent of Daylong common. But it so happens that the Williamsburg Associated Bank is controlled 63.5 percent by Schuster Mills of Chicago, and Schuster Mills of Chicago, apart from reciprocally owning 2.05 percent of Daylong stock, is itself controlled by Cornelius Oil Cleveland.'

Hope stared at Edward in disbelief. 'Edward, are you telling me that Roddy actually controls my company? The company that Father gave to me?'

'It certainly looks that way,' said Edward. 'But I'm afraid that isn't the worst of it.'

'What could be worse than that? I mean, what on earth is he trying to do?'

'Let me tell you During the past month, there have been dozens of subtle sales of small percentages of stock in almost every corporation and fund in which you have an interest. Each time, no matter how many deceptive holding companies and banks are involved, the result is the same. Roderick takes control.'

Hope was silent. Then she said: 'Give me a cigarette.'

Edward passed her an inlaid wooden box with a brass tennis racket for a handle. He lit the cigarette for her with a silver lighter, and she blew out an unsteady stream of smoke.

'Edward,' she said, 'if this is some kind of a prank . . .'

Edward looked at her and said nothing. He simply shook his head, and she knew that he was speaking the truth. Edward liked to boast about the shark he once caught off Florida, but he never exaggerated about money. His law firm was known for its dryness.

'All right,' said Hope. 'What about David Bookbinder? He's supposed to manage the family money and protect us from things like this. Surely he knows what's going on.'

'I'm sure he does,' said Edward. 'In fact, he's probably instigating the whole operation. I don't like to be rude about your brother, but can you really see Roderick working out a deal like this, and carrying it off without a hitch? It's only a fluke that *I* found out.'

'But what about Father?'

Edward put his glasses back on and squinted at Hope with a serious, sympathetic face.

'I don't believe your father knows. But I do believe that your father has something to do with it.'

'I just don't understand,' said Hope. The cigarette burned between her long, emerald-painted nails, and she felt unsafe and uncertain. She hadn't felt as bad as this since her divorce. This morning, everything had been reasonably secure and composed, but now she felt that familiar dropping sensation beneath her feet, like discovering that your best friend really hates you, or that a love affair has suddenly and inexplicably gone sour.

'It took me a long time to work it out,' said Edward. 'There were several possibilities – several reasons *why* Roderick should suddenly want to take control of all your interests – but only one fitted the bill.'

He looked down at Hope's high-heeled crocodile shoes. He seemed to be searching around inside of himself for words, like someone in a bookstore who can't make up his mind which book to buy. Then, looking up again, he said: 'Your father isn't a well man.'

Hope's cigarette paused an inch away from her parted lips.

'He's been up to Lynwood Sanatorium to have a checkup,' said Edward. 'Apparently he's been feeling bad for a long time. I happen to know one of the specialists up there. His brother went to Harvard Law School with me, and I was kind of friendly with the whole family. They owed me a favour, so they did something a little unethical and told me what your father's test results were.'

'Go on,' said Hope hoarsely.

'I know your father told the family he had a clean bill of health, but the truth is that he's suffering from heart disease. They expect him, the doctors that is, they expect him to be dead in about six months. Maybe sooner.'

Hope didn't move.

Edward said: 'I'm sorry I had to break it to you like this, but it seems that nobody else was going to tell you. David Bookbinder's known about it for days, and so has your mother. For some reason, they didn't want you to find out.'

'Does Roddy know?'

'Well,' said Edward, 'I expect so. That's why we're having this quiet game of proxies. He and Bookbinder are obviously trying to get their hands on the whole fortune before your father actually passes away.'

Hope said: 'It doesn't seem real. Father's been around for*ever*. What's it going to be like when he's not there anymore? I can't imagine it.'

Edward reached for a cigarette himself. He didn't often smoke cigarettes, but right now he felt he could do with one. It had been hard enough keeping his discoveries quiet, but now he knew he was going to be locked in a vicious and unequal battle between Hope's family and her own financia protection. For an outsider, that wasn't going to be all flowers and candy. He knew what the Cornelius family had done to Hope's first husband, Martin Landseer, and the story of Johann Cornelius and Daniel Forster was one of the great Wall Street mysteries. As the saying went:

'Never cross a Cornelius.' He lit up, watching Hope's worried face and wondering if he ought to be equally worried himself.

'What about John's interests?' asked Hope. 'Have you found out anything about those? Are they trying to do the same to him?'

'I don't know yet,' said Edward. 'I don't have complete lists of stock proxies yet. But, logically, I'd say that they were. In some cases you and John hold stock in the same corporations, and they'd obviously want to stop you two from joining forces and outvoting them. It's been a very sneaky, very cleverly managed operation, and the reason they're doing it now is so that they can take full advantage of your father's condition. They want his seal of approval on the whole thing.'

'He'd never give it! He'd burst a blood vessel if he even knew about it!'

'Not necessarily. It depends how they told him. Listen, Hope, your father's seventy-two years old and he's not the businessman he used to be. He's old, and he's staid, and he forgets things. He's put far too much trust in David Bookbinder lately because he can't remember what's happening from one day to the next. If you ask me, Roderick and Bookbinder are going to wrap up the whole thing by persuading your father to sign over his controlling interest in Cornelius Oil Cleveland to Roderick personally, which will mean that directly or indirectly Roderick will own or control eighty percent of the family's oil and chemical and shipping interests. He's already a heavy stockholder in Cornelius Oil itself and Cornelius Oil New Jersey. That doesn't include Hester's slice of it, but then I presume that Roderick is Hester's favourite baby.'

Hope nodded. Her cigarette was burning her fingers, and she crushed it out in an ashtray with 'Gleneagles Golf 1937' engraved on it.

'There's something even more sinister,' continued Edward, 'but I don't know whether I'm letting my imagination run away with me.'

Hope said baldly: 'You'd better tell me, whatever it is.'

'It's a question of trust funds,' said Edward. 'As far as I can make out, there are dozens of trust funds set up for you and John and Roderick, right? Now, I don't know the

533

conditions placed on all of these funds, but I get the impression that most of them are subject to the arrangement that you can draw interest from them for the rest of your life, but you can't touch the capital.'

Hope said: 'Yes, that's right.'

'Well,' said Edward, 'if you can't touch the capital, then the capital presumably passes to your children, and to John's children and Roderick's children.'

'Yes,' whispered Hope.

'But what happens if you don't have children? I mean, here's hoping, but supposing you don't? Or what happens if you have children and they die before they reach the age of maturity?'

Hope frowned. 'In that case, the capital continues to be held as a trust fund by the central Cornelius Fund, and the interest is payable to the Fund.'

'Which is managed by David Bookbinder?'

'Yes, but—'

'But *nothing*, Hope! Those are the facts!'

'Are you seriously suggesting that—?'

'I'm not suggesting anything, but I do think that the situation is potentially dangerous. If Roderick and Bookbinder can put the squeeze on all your inherited common stock, and if they can make sure that they hold the whole of Cornelius Oil in the palm of their hand, then you don't think they're going to balk at taking over the trust funds, do you? How much are those trust funds worth? Two hundred million? Three hundred million?'

Hope touched the emeralds around her neck. 'But they *can't* take them over,' she said. 'Not unless ... well, not unless they ...'

Edward raised one meaningful finger. 'Not unless you and I remain childless, and the twins don't live long enough to collect.'

Hope was silent for a moment, but then she said: 'Oh, that's ridiculous! I know Roddy's a bit weak when it comes to finance, but ... well, that's *absurd*! He'd never do anything to hurt anyone!'

Edward puffed his cigarette awkwardly. He didn't inhale, and he let out the smoke in little round clouds, like the cartoon train in *Dumbo*.

'I don't think that Roderick's anything to worry about.

534

He's your brother. If you ask me, he doesn't really under stand what's going on. But David Bookbinder disturbs me a lot.'

'David's a big fat Jewish teddy bear! He's been looking after Cornelius money for years!'

Edward shook his head. 'Don't let his jolly fat looks fool you. I saw Lucky Luciano once, and he was the most ordinary and respectable-looking guy you could hope to meet.'

Hope stood up and walked over to the window. The rain was still sliding slowly down the glass, and the trees and bushes of their small estate were clinging with mist.

'I don't know what to say,' she said. 'You've knocked the bottom out of everything I've ever believed.'

Edward stared at the floor. 'I can't prove it yet. You know that. But I had to warn you.'

'Yes, I suppose you did. But what can I do now? They're all coming to dinner tonight. Even David.'

'Well, for the moment you'll have to make out that you don't suspect them at all. But we must get your father aside and see if we can break it to him. Once he signs over that Cornelius Oil Cleveland stock, we don't stand a chance.'

Hope traced a pattern on the window with her fingertip. 'Do you think he'll believe you?'

Edward rubbed the back of his neck tiredly. 'No, I don't. But he'll believe *you*.'

She turned. 'You don't expect *me* to tell him?'

'Someone has to.'

There was a long silence. Then, from outside, there was a hesitant rap at the door. Edward said: 'Come in!'

It was the pale-faced maid. She said: 'Mrs Secker, there's been an accident.'

Hope glanced at Edward and then snapped: 'Accident? What accident?'

The maid was confused. 'It's Mrs Polanski. She let the terrapins out by mistake, and they've crawled under the Frigidaire!'

Hope stared at the maid for a moment, and then gave a loud burst of nervous laughter 'Oh, my God,' she said in her most overdramatic voice 'They'll mate!'

It happened so quickly that, years afterward, Irene could never remember whether it was Ally who had cried out first, or whether it was Clara. She couldn't even recall if it had been raining or not (it was), or where her mother-in-law had been standing when she first ran out into the street.

They were spending the day at Johann's heavy brownstone house overlooking Gramercy Park. John was downtown, negotiating refinery facilities with Getty Oil, but later in the evening they were all going to drive out to Hope's place on Long Island for dinner. Johann and Hester would continue in the evening to Lynwood's Island, while David Bookbinder's chauffeur was going to drive everybody else back to the city.

Irene didn't much care for Cornelius family gatherings, but she liked Hope and Edward, and nobody expected her to participate much. Even John these days seemed to have eased off his earlier pressure to 'get yourself involved' and to 'think Cornelius.' Life seemed to be settling down again, and because John was away so frequently on business, she could recultivate some of her old friends, and spend hours of play and leisure with the twins.

That afternoon – the same afternoon that John was having his 'Getty Oil meeting' with Mara – Irene was sitting in the library at Gramercy Park, embroidering herself a flowery dressing-table mat. The sky outside was brown and gloomy – the sky from an early newsreel – and she had to wear her spectacles to see what she was doing. She didn't like to switch on the light, because Johann was snoring softly in his library armchair, almost buried in the shadows of his bookshelves and in the gathering darkness of an October day, and Willkie, his black Labrador, was sleeping around his feet like a fitful puddle of Indian ink.

Irene was a beautiful woman even if she wasn't a sensual woman. She was tall, and she carried herself with such poise and inbred dignity that bell captains never questioned her carefully measured tips, and strange men in the street raised their hats to her. She had a perfect oval face, with precise little lips, and immaculately arched eyebrows. Her eyes had once been described by Fiorello La Guardia, who quite often came to dinner at Gramercy Park, as 'visionary.'

In fact, they were very pale grey, and only looked visionary because she was marginally nearsighted.

She had met John Cornelius three years ago, when he was twenty-five and she was twenty-three. It was 1942, and New York was still in a guilty, frustrated flummox about the war. John had wanted to go to Europe and save Holland single-handed from the Nazis, but Hester had insisted that her two sons were 'captains of commerce' and shouldn't go. Johann, in a surprisingly surly mood, had grumbled that if they went, the government would commandeer his oil and his ships and his chemical plants, and if that happened, they needn't bother to come back. So the boys had half-reluctantly remained in the States to keep the pumps pumping and the factories turning out airplanes, ammunition, canned foods, and waterproof capes, not to mention record profits.

Irene, brought up in a repressive Bostonian atmosphere, where she had always been required to dress in sober colours and walk two steps behind her mother, had only begun to open her petals after a year at finishing school in Switzerland, and even then she was one of the palest flowers in the garden. It wasn't surprising that John, in 1942, had impressed her deeply. He was active, stylish, energetic, and good-looking. He always drove open convertibles, even when it rained, and he swam and rode and played terrific golf. They had met one summer night at a party at Grosse Pointe Shores, Michigan, and because he was drunk and she was happy, and the orchestra was playing 'I Found a Million Dollar Baby in a Five and Ten Cent Store,' they had sworn undying love.

The twins, Ally and Clara, were now eleven months old, and nearly walking. Right now, at half-past three in the afternoon in October, 1945, they were upstairs at Gramercy Park, sleeping. They would soon wake up and want their supper (soft-scrambled eggs and milk).

Johann, old and dry in his library chair, began to stir. From where she was sitting, Irene could only see his stubby-fingered hand with its brown liver spots, and the glisten of his old eyes somewhere in the shadow. He cleared his throat thickly and leaned forward.

'You still sewing, Irene?' he called. He like Irene. She

was one of his favourites; and he always spoke to her gently. Irene looked up.

'It's growing too dark now, Father,' she called back. 'I think I'll have to stop.'

Johann took out his handkerchief and dabbed his mouth. 'Am I going to see my babies before you tuck them in for the night?'

'We're taking them out to Long Island with us, Father. You can see them at Marchings.'

'Well, I always like to see them when I can. The way I feel these days, I wonder if each time I see them isn't maybe the last.'

'Father! That's no way to speak!'

Johann reached across with stiff fingers and switched on the table lamp next to his chair. A circle of electric light illuminated his age. He was a big man who had collapsed and shrunk with the passing years. There seemed to be nothing inside his green cardigan and his grey flannel trousers but the loosely assembled parts of an old bedstead. He was bald except for a few untidy white wisps around his ears, and his skin was tanned into that pale parchmenty colour that passes for health among the very old and the very sick. His blue Dutch eyes had been rinsed of colour, and his cheeks were like wrinkled beets that had been left to dry in the sun.

He cleared his throat again and sniffed.

'Oh, I shall be around for a little while yet.' He smiled. 'I didn't make my pile just to please my children. I want to enjoy some of it myself.'

'I always knew you were a playboy at heart,' teased Irene. She stuck her needle through her embroidery, laid it aside, reached over, and kissed his softly withered cheek.

Johann held her hand for just a moment, and ran his thumb over the sapphire and diamond rings.

'It's a strange thing about wealth,' he said, watching the diamonds sparkle and the sapphires wink.

'What is? You can't blame yourself for being wealthy.'

'I don't. But it's strange all the same. No matter where you get your money from – even if you lie and you cheat and you steal – it doesn't matter at all once you've got it. A gangster can rub elbows with anyone he likes if he's rich

538

enough, and everybody will say how virtuous he is, and how temperate.'

'But you're not a gangster, are you? How can you say that!'

Johann stared across the room at the sepia shadows of the passing clouds.

'No,' he said quietly. 'I'm not a gangster. But I'm not a holy saint, either. Some of the money I made wasn't as clean as it might have been, and some of it, the making of it, caused other people great pain.'

Irene, still bent over him, frowned at the freckles and blotches on his bald head.

'Father . . .' she said. 'Is anything wrong?'

He looked up. 'Should there be?' he said.

'No, no. I didn't mean that. It's just that you seem to be . . . well, you're very reflective. You're not usually as thoughtful as this.'

Johann shook his head. 'No, there's nothing wrong. I'm just exercising an old man's prerogative, and rambling on.'

'You're not worried about anything?'

'Worried? When you get to my age, you don't worry about a thing. It isn't worth the effort, whatever it is. No . . . I'm just thinking about the things I've done and the things I haven't done . . . and wondering whether they were good or bad . . . or whether I should have done better.'

Irene looked at him for a while, and then quite spontaneously brushed her fingertips across his forehead.

'You won't think I'm impertinent, will you, if I say something?' she asked him.

He shook his head. 'When you and I get together, Irene, we're best buddies, and best buddies can never be impertinent. You tell me what you've got to say, and I'll do my best to answer.'

She said: 'Well . . . I just wanted to ask you if you were lonesome.'

There was a silence. Johann didn't answer and he didn't stir, but his eyes seemed to lose their perception of the present, and stare back year by year, over decades and quarter-centuries and long-lost times when things were different, and carriages rattled in the sunlit streets of Broughton, Texas – streets that were now busy with automobiles, and crowded with stores. Irene, for one moment, thought she had gone too far and asked him a question that went too deep, but when the moment had passed, he looked up, and smiled at her, and stroked her wrist.

'Everyone gets lonesome sometimes,' he told her. 'But with you, and with Hester, and with those babies of mine, those twins, I could never stay lonesome for long.'

What she didn't know, though, was that inside his mind as he spoke he was firmly closing a front-parlour door. Click. And sealing away the old mahogany furniture, and the decorated drapes, and a night that he had thought about many times in forty-two years.

'All right, Father,' she said. 'I'd better go and get the twins ready. Hope expects us out there by eight.'

She left him, even though she had to pause at the door and look back to make sure he was all right. She had a feeling he might be crying, but he wasn't. She wasn't to know that he never cried. She closed the library door and went quietly upstairs on the plush green carpet, up to the nursery room that Johann and Hester kept for the twins.

Ally was already awake. She was lying on her back, cycling her legs in the air and chatting seriously to herself. Clara was still fast asleep, a bubble between her lips, one chubby hand tucked under her cheek. Both twins had cornsilk hair and big blue eyes, and an odd look about them that was one hundred percent Cornelius. Their nursery was wallpapered with flowers, and they slept in two identical cribs, hand-painted in France with tiny roses and cupids. Today they both wore long cream nightdresses of Brussels lace, underlaid with coffee-coloured silk linings. Their nanny, Miss Bendizzi, was already with them, laying out their travelling clothes for the evening. They were going to wear their brown tweed velvet-collared coats, their brown corduroy button-up leggings, and their dark brown berets.

Miss Bendizzi was a madonna, too, in her own way, but a Modigliani madonna, all olive skin and green eyes and big breasts. She wore a crisp white uniform and a white cap, and she spoke appalling English with almost religious sincerity.

'I give them eggs for just a moment,' she said as Irene came in.

'That's all right,' said Irene. 'We're leaving at around six-thirty; so there's no need to rush. And how are my little angels? How's my beautiful little Ally?'

Ally lifted her hands and smiled with pleasure. Clara, in her crib, began to open her eyes and stir.

'This one does pooh-pooh,' said Miss Bendizzi. 'If you can leave yourself outside, I make everything clean.'

'Thank you, Miss Bendizzi,' said Irene. 'Just give me a call when they've finished their supper, and then bring them down to the day room. Their grandfather wants to see them while they're still awake.'

Clara was crying now. Her face was red, and she clenched and unclenched her fists. Miss Bendizzi clucked over the crib, and lifted her out.

'You don't cry! You be happy! Everything for you is wonderful!'

Irene kissed her twins and went downstairs to her own bedroom. It was just a little after five now. Hester was already bathing for the evening, and the faintest smell of gardenia bath oil wafted down the upper landings. Johann had gone to be shaved, and Jack, his valet, was pressing his dinner suit. As Irene sat at her wide mirrored dressing table, taking off her makeup and waiting for the coloured maid Suzie to finish drawing off her bath, she thought about Johann, and hoped that John wouldn't be too late back from his meeting. He had promised to catch up with them if he was delayed, but she knew how involved and endless oil negotiations were.

She bathed, using glycerine soap for her sensitive skin. On the fourteen-carat gold faucets, elaborately designed by German goldsmiths in the 1890's, drops of condensation formed, and ran cool down her bare toes. She sang psalms under her breath (it still embarrassed her to sing out loud) and wallowed back in the warm soft water and thought how lucky she was.

'Consider the lilies, how they grow . . .' she recited to herself as she soaped her little breasts.

Her own maid, Letty, a dark-skinned Andalusian girl with nails like Count Borgia's unwashed daggers, had laid out Irene's evening gown. It was a new creation from Gerard Watkins, her favourite designer, and it had just the kind of haughty simplicity she wanted. It was made of shimmering white watered silk, with a deep but narrow

541

neckline that was framed in V-shaped pleats, like the leaves of a book folded back. The shoulders were fashionably padded and square, and the skirt fell with perfect simplicity.

In front of the mirror she gave herself silvery Betty Grable eyes, a bright red rosebud mouth, and subtly rouged her cheeks. For jewellery, she wore a brilliant star-shaped diamond pendant that Hester had given her on their first anniversary, and a whole cluster of diamond rings, including the $555,000 Newport Stone.

By six-fifteen, almost everybody was ready. They assembled in the day room while the servants brought their hats and coats and wraps. Hester was still upstairs, changing her mind about her green shoes, but the twins were there, and Johann had Ally on one knee and Clara on the other, and he was singing an old Dutch farm song to them, about how the rooster lost his temper with the silly hens, and crowed and crowed all night, and the little girls giggled with every cracked crow.

Vucinzki, the butler, came in to announce that the cars were outside, and that he had umbrellas for everyone, because it was raining hard. Just then, Roderick and Celia arrived, and there were kisses and greetings and loud helloes. Roderick was looking flushed after drinking too much whiskey at lunchtime, and Celia was icy and charming as usual, particularly when David Bookbinder came in, dripping wet from the rain, like a pink porpoise that had just flopped in from Marineland.

In the early-evening darkness outside, the cortege of black shiny Cadillac limousines, jewelled with raindrops, was waiting. There were lots of laughter as the servants held umbrellas over their heads, and car doors slammed and lights lit up and V-12 motors purred politely into life.

It happened, like all tragedies, with absurd quickness and at a time when hardly anybody was actually looking. Hester had arrived in the hallway, and everybody had turned in her direction to say 'Good evening' and 'How are you, Mother?' Irene was carrying Ally, and was about to hand her to Letty, so that Letty and Miss Bendizzi could sit in the back of the last limousine together and care for the twins. Miss Bendizzi was carrying Clara, and because there were no spare umbrellas, she had stepped out into the road, covering Clara with her coat. The chauffeur was holding the door open for Letty on the kerb side, and so Miss Bendizzi had to open the street-side passenger door herself.

A dull grey Buick sedan, splashing through the puddles of Gramercy Park, skidded almost gracefully toward the line of parked limousines and struck the door of the last Cadillac just as Miss Bendizzi was placing Clara carefully inside. Everyone turned at the sudden *bosshhh!* of colliding metal and the curious silence that followed. Then Miss Bendizzi wailed, with pain and with hideous shock, and they rushed around to see what had happened. As they did so, the Buick reversed, pulled away from the wreck, and skewed off into the night with a howl of tyres.

Irene, in her white silk dress, fell on the road in complete collapse. There was blood everywhere, and glass. The Buick had struck the limousine's half-open door and crushed Clara between the door itself and the door frame, as well as smashing four of Miss Bendizzi's fingers. Little Clara's body, in its brown tweed coat and its button-up leggings, was almost torn in half.

They carried and dragged Irene back into the house. She lay on the settee in the day room, shivering and almost unconscious with shock. She had lost one of her white satin slippers in the street, and the police cars and ambulances that arrived later ran over it several times. Roderick rang the Getty Oil People to try to find John, and discovered that he was not at Getty at all and that there was no meeting about refining facilities at Port Arthur, and never had been.

Almost unnoticed in the confusion and horror, Johann, in his black dinner suit, carefully and slowly climbed the stairs. He was tall, but he was bent and old, and his face was suddenly blue. As he climbed each step, his hand clutched for the banister rail, and he heaved himself higher and higher without knowing why he was doing it or where he was going. He just had the feeling that if he made it to the top of the stairs, he would survive.

He looked upward toward the bright French chandelier hanging over the first landing. It sparkled and glittered in front of his eyes. It was like a Holy Grail, floating and twinkling above the peak of a holy mountain. Behind him, he heard sirens, and slamming doors, and the sound of someone crying.

He knew he could never make the top. He thought he would stop to rest. It was so difficult to breathe, and nothing seemed to be clear or comprehensible.

He said: 'Oh, Clara,' and fell sideways. His face was pressed against the soft stair carpet. He could see every detail of it, it was so close. Every scratch on the brass stair rod, every mark on the nails that had fastened it into place. It seemed quite amusing to him that a man rich enough to have a view of the whole world should end his life with a view so completely restricted.

He said: 'Oh, my little Clara.'

He only wished it were possible to shed tears.

Four days later, while Johann was still deep in a coma in his private rooms at Lynwood Sanatorium, Edward Secker met David Bookbinder, by prior appointment, at the front bar of the Colony on Sixty-first Street. Edward had to wait half an hour for Bookbinder to arrive, and he sat tense and unhappy with his dry martini, reading a folded-up copy of *The New Yorker*. Outside, the day was crisp and cold and bright, and the Colony's lunchtime trade came in with heavy overcoats and red cheeks.

Eventually Bookbinder arrived. He shook Edward's hand with his own cold, plump fingers. Marco, the barman, took his order for a Scotch on the rocks, and Bookbinder sat himself down, breathless and overweight, and said: 'I'm sorry I'm late. They're digging up the streets again, and it's murder.'

Edward, lean and lanky in his dark pinstripe business suit, raised his eyebrows at that.

'Is it?' he said. He was wearing a black armband and a black necktie. David Bookbinder wore a dark club tie with a gold crest on it.

'Have you seen Irene?' asked Bookbinder. 'John's thinking of sending her away for a while, maybe down to Roderick's place in West Virginia.'

'I saw her briefly,' said Edward. 'She seemed all right, but I don't even know if the shock has really sunk in yet.'

David Bookbinder sipped his drink and nodded. 'It does usually take a few weeks,' he said heavily. His beady eyes were looking around the bar for anyone he knew. He seemed uninterested and bland to the point of boredom, and Edward was beginning to wonder if he'd made the right decision, bringing him here.

'I ... er ... I don't suppose you know how Johann is?' asked Edward.

Bookbinder didn't look at him. 'All right,' he said. 'The last I heard.'

'They think he'll pull through?'

'They don't know yet. He needs a lot of rest. It was only a minor seizure, but when you're that age ... well ...'

Edward said: 'I suppose you're right. And he does have a history, doesn't he, of heart disease?'

Bookbinder didn't blink, but he still kept his eyes away.

Edward said: 'You knew that, of course, didn't you? About the disease? You knew how little time he had left?'

Bookbinder swirled his glass around so that the ice clinked against the sides. The bar was filled with the mingled murmur of wealthy New Yorkers in the process of sharpening their lunchtime appetites. The rich smell of roasted meat mingled with the bouquet of dry sherry and gin, and someone said: 'Come on, Jerry, let's eat.'

Edward leaned forward. 'Aren't you going to answer me?' he whispered to David Bookbinder. 'Or are you thinking up an alibi?'

Bookbinder at last looked him in the face. 'I don't have to answer anything that *you* say,' he said with a small, puckered smile. 'I'm only answerable to Johann Cornelius.'

'Wrong,' contradicted Edward. 'You're also answerable to Hope, and to John. You manage their money, and that makes you very answerable.'

David Bookbinder's smile was slowly drained of its satisfaction, but it still clung to his face, like a price tag on a cheap suit.

'You're being very irregular,' he told Edward, his eyes following the laughing, chattering people who were going in to eat.

'I don't think *you* can speak to *me* about irregularity,' Edward answered quietly and tersely.

'Oh, no?'

'Not when you're shifting stocks around like cattle on the Chisholm Trail.'

David Bookbinder grunted in amusement.

'Not when you're trying to take control of the funds and corporations that are my wife's rightful inheritance,' persisted Edward.

Bookbinder reached into his pocket for a fat hide cigar case and took out a long Havana. He offered one to Edward, but Edward said: 'No, thanks.'

'Please yourself,' said Bookbinder. He clipped the end of the cigar, and lit up. He was wreathed for a moment in clouds of blue smoke – a financial Caesar in rapidly vaporizing laurels.

'It's my opinion,' said Edward, 'that you are trying to use Roderick as your stooge. You're working through Roderick's stock and Roderick's corporations to put the squeeze on every block of stock that John and Hope inherit, so that the only person who will ever have any say in the way the Cornelius fortune is organized is *you*. Well, you're found out.'

Bookbinder sucked his cigar thoughtfully. Then he said: 'Edward . . . you must think I'm unusually naïve.'

'I don't think so at all. I think you've done this whole thing very well.'

'Of course I have. I didn't mean that. What I meant was that you must think I'm naïve if you suppose that your finding out is going to make the slightest difference.'

Edward looked at Bookbinder sharply. 'What do you mean by that?'

'Precisely what I say. You've laid your cards on the table – very good, then I'll do the same.'

'What cards?'

'*What* cards? My dear Edward, I always have cards. You don't survive on Wall Street for as long as I have without keeping something in reserve.'

Edward raised his glass to the barman for another martini. Bookbinder's Scotch was still half-full.

'You've made it plain to me that you disagree with my financial policy,' said Bookbinder. 'You've also placed me in an awkward position as far as the market's concerned, because I'm still in the process of negotiating for stock, and if the word gets around that I'm buying, then most of the prices will go up by a great deal more than I particularly wish to pay.'

'So?' said Edward. 'Give me ten minutes, and I'll give the story to *The Wall Street Journal*.'

Bookbinder laughed. 'Oh, you wouldn't do that. Because one story deserves another, and if you give my story to *The Wall Street Journal*, I'll make sure that Hope's real story goes to the *New York Post*.'

Bookbinder said this in such a jocular way that for a few moments Edward didn't even realize how much he was being threatened. Then he turned around and stared at Bookbinder in total disgust.

'You'd really do it, wouldn't you?' he said. 'You'd really, actually do it!'

'Yes,' said David Bookbinder. 'I would.'

Edward, when Bookbinder had first walked into the bar, had decided not to raise the subject of trust funds. But when Bookbinder said that, he was so furious that he couldn't hold it back any longer. He leaned forward and hissed right in Bookbinder's smooth pink face: 'What about Clara?'

Bookbinder drew back.

'Clara?' he said, unsure.

'Yes – what about Clara? And what about Clara's trust funds? And what about Ally's trust funds, if Ally accidentally happens to wind up the same way?'

Bookbinder screwed up his little eyes. 'Are you seriously accusing me of what I think you're accusing me of?' he said unsteadily.

Edward nodded fiercely. 'That's lousy grammar, but yes.'

Bookbinder scratched a small fragment of cigar leaf from his golden front teeth.

'In that case,' he remarked, 'you're a bigger fool than I thought you were.'

He reached into his briefcase and took out a copy of the afternoon paper. He laid it on the bar, and pointed with his pudgy finger to a news item at the foot of the front page. It said: 'Cornelius Baby Heiress Death: Hit-and-Run Driver Charged.'

Edward read through it quickly. A construction worker from East 169th Street had been arrested in the Bronx after his grey Buick sedan was seen by a traffic cop to be damaged. He was accused of driving while drunk and

547

failing to report an accident. His name was William Peebles, and he was forty-eight.

'Does that sound like a hit to you?' asked Bookbinder, his voice tight but controlled. 'Do you honestly believe that anyone could be *that* callous, and *that* avaricious? Even me?'

The telephone behind the bar rang twice. Marco picked it up and talked into it for a while. Then he passed it over to David Bookbinder and said: 'Call for you, Mr Bookbinder. Your office.'

Edward watched David Bookbinder's face as a tiny, tinny voice spoke to him on the other end of the line. For the first time ever, he felt he was in the wrong financial division. David Bookbinder had too much money and too much power, and all Edward could do was hop and scream and protest. He was quite ready to believe that Bookbinder was capable of systematically wiping out the next Cornelius generation, but he knew that belief and suspicion were useless. Even facts, even evidence, might not be enough. To force David Bookbinder's hand, he was going to need to work carefully, subtly, and with months of proper preparation.

David Boodbinder laid down the phone. He was perspiring, and he wiped his plump neck with his handkerchief.

'That was the House,' he said in a low voice. 'Johann's bad. They don't expect him to last the day.'

'Do they want us up there? At Lynwood?'

'Right away. My car's outside. We can go in that.'

Edward swallowed his drink, stood up, and buttoned up his coat.

'David . . .' he said, before he signed the check.

'Yes?' said Bookbinder.

'I want to forget this for now. But I have to say, I have to warn you, that I'm not going to let it rest. You can't lean on Hope's inheritance, and that's all there is to it.'

David Bookbinder reached for his overcoat and his homburg. With his cigar in his mouth, he reminded Edward of an old-style racketeer. As he buttoned up his coat with his tiny pink hands, he stared across the bar as if he were thinking of something else altogether, like what he was going to eat for dinner, or the halcyon days of the gold standard.

'Well,' he said absently 'that's your privilege.'

A little way apart, they walked into the front lobby. Next to the glittering Van Cleef & Arpels showcase, David Bookbinder stopped for a moment and faced Edward squarely for the first time. The reflected glitter of diamonds was all around him, as if he had suddenly become celestial.

'I myself am like a species of sea urchin,' said Bookbinder. 'I may be soft inside, but you have to chew your way through a mouthful of prickles before you'll ever find that out.'

Edward didn't say anything. A woman in a grey square-shouldered suit, fragrant with Chanel, raised her eyebrow at him as she passed. He turned away.

'That,' added Bookbinder, taking his arm, 'is a word to the wise.'

The slanting sunlight caught them as they stepped out onto Sixty-first Street, and across town they could hear the roompity-boompity sound of a marching military band playing 'Anchors Aweigh' as yet another division of marines was welcomed home from the war. The sound echoed flatly against the buildings as the band paraded slowly up Fifth Avenue, passing the smoking bagel stands, the ghostly plumes of steam, and the throngs of shoppers who were looking forward to their first Christmas at peace.

1954

BOOKBINDER QUITS CORNELIUS

'Reasons of health,' says oil exec

Wall Street Reporter

David Bookbinder, the 67-year-old supremo of Cornelius Oil, has announced his retirement 'as of now.' Known for his three decades in the oil business as the man with the golden smile, Bookbinder denied suggestions that he had been ousted by pressure from the Justice Department because of his involvement in big business graft in the 1920's.

—New York Daily News,
September, 1954

It was the year that TV dinners were invented – turkey, sweet potatoes and peas on the same compartmented tray. It was the year that Bill Haley released 'Rock Around the Clock.' It was also the year that Lucille Ball appeared pregnant in *I Love Lucy*, the year that necklines plunged to daring new depths, and the year that Nash and Hudson combined to form the American Motors Corporation. The Comics Code Authority banned horror comics and demanded that 'all lurid, unsavoury, and gruesome illustrations be eliminated.' At the movies, Rock Hudson starred in *Magnificent Obsession*. Two million Americans were out of work, and during the early summer, children ran around the streets crowing 'Point of order, point of order,' in imitation of Senator Joseph McCarthy.

It was 1954. Cadillacs began to sprout tiny fins, Dwight D. Eisenhower was President, and David Bookbinder resigned as chief executive of Cornelius Industries.

Bookbinder was carefully packing away framed letters in a brass-bound trunk, along with his gold cigar box and his pigskin memo pad, when Roderick rapped loosely at the half-open door and walked in. David Bookbinder didn't look up. Cornelius executives had been shuffling in and out of his office all morning, picking over the remnants of twenty years with the company. He reached over and took a small ivory statuette from his desk and packed that alongside his memo pad.

Roderick parked himself on the arm of Bookbinder's leather chair. He said: 'How are you doing?' in a concentratedly offhand way. Bookbinder said: 'Okay,' and stowed away some blue-backed law books.

Roderick hummed a tuneless tune and folded his arms. He was trying not to show how relieved he was that David Bookbinder had actually decided to surrender without a fuss, but at the same time he was still anxious that he might change his mind at the very last moment and stay. It was impossible for Roderick to imagine what Cornelius Industries was going to be like without David Bookbinder, and until that bald head had actually disappeared down the corridor for the last time, he wasn't going to let himself believe it.

He said: 'Do you have any plans yet? Vacation, maybe?'

Bookbinder grunted. 'Maybe.'

Roderick nodded. 'I hear that Hawaii's pretty nice this time of year. Have you ever thought of Hawaii?'

Bookbinder paused in his packing and stood straight. He glanced across at Roderick as if he were someone who had momentarily caught his attention in the street. 'No,' he said tiredly. 'I have never thought of Hawaii. Right now, I'm too busy thinking about Washington, D.C.'

Roderick said: 'I thought we could take a ride.'

'A ride? That sounds like a James Cagney picture.'

Roderick blushed. 'I didn't mean it to. There's a restaurant out in Connecticut I'd like to try. It's only an hour's drive. I thought we could maybe go over some of the final details there.'

Bookbinder said: 'I don't usually go for business lunches.'

'Well, I know that,' said Roderick. 'But it's a fine day, and I guess the circumstances are kind of . . . well . . .'

Bookbinder thought for a while, with his pudgy hands on his hips. Then he said: 'Okay. When do you want to go?'

It was September. The sky was a crisp pottery blue, and the leaves in Connecticut were beginning to turn. They drove in Roderick's green-and-white Oldsmobile Ninety-Eight, with the top down. David Bookbinder wore a black homburg hat and sat with his hands crossed in his lap. Roderick was dressed in plaid tweed, with a jaunty Tyrolean hat with fishing flies on it.

As they drove, Roderick said   There are one or two things I'm going to have to know.'

'Yes,' answered David Bookbinder flatly. 'I guess you'd better.'

'I have to know some of the names, and what the connections are.'

'Of course. The connections are aware of that, too.'

'You mean, they're ready to discuss some kind of settlement? I presume they'll want some kind of settlement.'

David Bookbinder took out a cigar. The Oldsmobile Rocket engine swept them across deserted intersections, past peeling country stores, through curves of wooded highway. Behind the flickering trees, stretches of lake water gleamed like half-hidden mirrors.

Bookbinder said: 'You're going to have to be sensible, you know.'

'What do you mean by that?'

'Well,' explained Bookbinder, reaching out and pressing the car's cigarette lighter, 'you're not dealing with high-school societies. You're dealing with wealthy and organized businessmen who have helped Cornelius Industries for over twenty years. Most of that help was perfectly legitimate. Some of it was less so. But you have to understand that in two decades, a nation's interpretation of what is legitimate and what isn't inevitably alters. There was a time when organized labour was the filthiest phrase in the book. It didn't matter if you leaned on the CIO. These days, you have to be careful. *More* careful, anyway.'

Roderick stared through the curved windshield at the sun-flecked highway ahead. A new white Corvette zipped past them, its radio blaring 'Shake, Rattle and Roll,' and disappeared up ahead.

He said slowly: 'What about the killings?'

Bookbinder peeled the label off his cigar. 'Well,' he said, unperturbed, 'we don't exactly call them that.'

'It's still the same, though, isn't it, whatever you call it?'

Bookbinder smiled reflectively. 'I guess it is. But your father could always see it my way.'

'What way's that?'

'He could always see that any business of the size of Cornelius Industries, as it moves through the years, has to come up against opposition, and eliminate that opposition as it arises.'

'Is that a fancy way of saying that you knock off anybody who gets in your way?'

'Of course not.'

'Well, explain it to me.'

Bookbinder held the cigarette lighter against the end of his cigar and sucked in smoke. When he was lit up, he said: 'I can't stand smoking in the fresh air. It makes a good cigar taste like Christmas wrapping paper.'

Roderick didn't answer. If David Bookbinder didn't want to discuss his disreputable past in detail, then that was his privilege. But it was desperately important for Roderick to know what had been committed in the name of Cornelius Industries over the years, and what underworld connections the business still had. He couldn't pretend that he wasn't alarmed; but he genuinely felt that once Bookbinder was gone, he could ease the Cornelius corporations out of most of their criminal connections, and return them to legitimate working.

He asked: 'Was it true what he said, that old man from Pennsylvania?'

Bookbinder smiled. 'That was a long time ago, what happened in Pennsylvania. That was in 1927, before I started to work for your father. I'd only met your father once. A strange man, your father, that's what I thought when I first met him. That was in 1925.'

'I didn't ask for a history lesson. I just wanted to know if what the old man said was true.'

Bookbinder shrugged. 'It was true in a way. He was setting up the Robinstown open-cast mine in those days, up in the Asquahanna Valley. Some of the folks there were ready to sell out right away, because they were hard times then, for farmers, in 1927. But there was a little local opposition, and your father wanted it painlessly removed. It was a risky operation, you see. Everyone thought he was setting up a dye works, including the county authorities. They didn't know he was set on stripping every square inch of turf for ten square miles.'

Roderick took a right fork, and the Olds bounced its way down a small dusty side road. Branches tapped and squeaked against the car's bodywork, and birds fluttered and jumped in the trees.

Roderick said: 'It bucked up the town's economy, though, didn't it? That's a prosperous place even today, Robinstown, last time I checked the figures.'

'Sure,' remarked David Bookbinder. 'It's kind of changed, of course. In 1927 it was all grass and cows.'

'So what about this local opposition? How did you "painlessly remove" it?'

Bookbinder sighed. 'It was all pretty roundabout. I had a call from a friend of mine in Pittsburgh. His name was Joey Divine and he distributed bootleg liquor. He said that some young character had approached him with a contract on behalf of someone named Johann Cornelius, and did I know who Johann Cornelius was. As it happened, I did. As I said, I'd met him first in 1925, at some reception or other. I told Joey to leave the contract to me, and I had a word with Arthur.'

'Arthur?'

'Arthur Flegenheimer. Dutch Schultz to you. He was a friend of mine in a manner of speaking. There's an old Turkish saying which talks about "the two pebbles which roll down the same dry watercourse, and knock each other along." It's a way of describing occasional help from someone you don't see too often. That was how Arthur and I used to work.'

Roderick slowed the car down for a tight tree-lined bend. They emerged by a sparkling river, where a white-painted Colonial-style restaurant stood between the rusting autumn trees and the reddish-brown rocks of the creek bed. There were several other cars already there, and Roderick parked alongside them.

Before he opened his door, he turned to David Bookbinder and said: 'Dutch Schultz was murdered, wasn't he?'

Bookbinder nodded. 'That's right. The year after I joined Cornelius Industries. They caught him in a chop house in Newark. He was in a coma for hours, but all he spoke was babble, and he never told the cops who did it. It was a cheap hoodlum called Charlie Workman, as a matter of fact.'

Roderick said: 'Did you—?'

But David Bookbinder raised his finger to his lips and closed his eyes. 'Don't ever ask it,' he said gently. 'It's one of those answers that won't ever do you anything but harm.'

They climbed out of the car and went up the rustic wooden steps that led to the restaurant's entrance. A toothy girl in a red plaid suit showed them to a small table by the window, where they could watch the river rushing over the stones. Farther upstream, Roderick could see an old cottage with smoke trailing idly from its chimney. He ordered clams and entrecote steak.

As they drank their cocktails, Roderick said: 'So what the old man said was right? Someone from Cornelius Oil really did kill the Robinstown sheriff?'

Bookbinder's eyes were hooded. 'In a manner of speaking.'

Roderick let out a deep breath. 'No wonder Walter was so insistent you resign.'

'He was, yes. He's been a good friend, Walter has. But I guess that fate put him in an awkward spot. I don't blame him. At least he's kept it out of the papers, and away from the FBI.'

Roderick said: 'Who else?'

'Who else what?'

557

'Who else has died in the same way? Did you "painlessly remove" anyone else?'

Bookbinder looked slowly around the restaurant to make sure that they were not overheard. He could see the waitress coming with their clams, and he paused until she'd set them down. He tucked his napkin into his collar, and squeezed lemon over the greyish shellfish with complete equanimity.

'There were one or two.'

Roderick frowned. 'One or two? When? What do you mean, one or two?'

David Bookbinder stared up at him. 'Before you start getting too excited, don't forget that pilot of yours, Fairbanks, and that Cosnett fellow. If Walter hadn't had a word with the Bureau, you might have found yourself in considerably more embarrassing trouble than me.'

Roderick said tensely: 'I'm not trying to sound off. I just want to know the facts. You mean you actually took out contracts on people who opposed you?'

Bookbinder swallowed a clam. 'We're not the only corporation with a record of physical enforcement,' he reminded Roderick mildly. 'I think you might remember the Baldwin-Felts men at Ludlow, and you might remember Harry Bennett at Ford, with his six hundred armed thugs, and you might remember Frank Costello and Joe Adonis and Ben Siegel.'

Roderick sat back. 'Christ, David, I knew we had some protection on a small scale. I mean, you have to look after your trucks and your warehouses. But what you're talking about is organized crime!'

Bookbinder took a sip of water. 'Don't be naïve. You know damned well that every major business in the entire country has to have some connections with gangsters. A billion-dollar enterprise without its own enforcement arrangements is no safer than a whale stranded on a beach. Obviously we've kept our major connections as quiet as possible. Most of them were made through me. We've kept you well out of it so far, but now you have to know.'

They sat in silence while the waitress took away their empty clam dishes and brought their steaks.

Roderick said: 'You mean to say that my father knew all about this? Every detail?'

'Not every detail. But he knew. Your father and I and Dutch

558

Schultz went to see *She Done Him Wrong* together, did you know that?'

'I never saw it,' said Roderick.

Bookbinder wiped his mouth. 'Arthur loved it. Your father didn't. He said that Mae West was too mature. That was the word he used. "Mature." '

Roderick didn't seem very interested in his steak. 'David,' he said quietly, 'I want to know how many people have died.'

'It's not too many,' answered Bookbinder, munching. 'Do you think we could have some wine?'

When he returned to the house at Gramercy Park that evening, he was withdrawn and thoughtful. After his lunch with David Bookbinder in Connecticut, he had spent most of the afternoon combing through the company's files and lists of connections, with Bookbinder sitting a little way away in his leather armchair, placidly smoking his cigar and filling in Roderick's background knowledge with pertinent comments and explanations.

'You knew Philip Musica?' Roderick had asked, with eyebrows raised, as he held up a sheaf of correspondence from McKesson & Robbins, dated 1935. Bookbinder had nodded. 'Sure. In its way, it was a very useful arrangement,' he explained. 'The only trouble was, Philip wasn't smart enough to keep himself out of the limelight. Sad, that. You know he committed suicide?'

Roderick, tight-lipped, had answered: 'Yes.'

Now, in the quiet drawing room of his own home, he called for old Vucinzki, the butler, to bring him a whiskey, and he sat down in a high-back Jacobean tapestry armchair, his father's favourite, and opened up a buff file in which he had brought home all the most pertinent letters and documents relating to David Bookbinder's cooperation with racketeers and Cosa Nostra. There were letters from the 1920's, soft with age and typed in purple ink, from men like Lucky Luciano and Big Jim Colosimo. There was a complicated correspondence with Michael Ahern, one of Al Capone's attorneys, on legal matters relating to tax. Throughout all the years that David Bookbinder had controlled Cornelius Oil, and its sister industries of shipping, insurance, coal mining, air freight, and foods, its negotiations with almost every union had been characterized by threats of violence, its prices had been fixed by payments to government officials, its trading monopolies had been protected by skilful bribery, and its occasional legal errors wallpapered over by policemen, judges, and attorneys who were prepared to be lenient in return for a brand-new set of fancy golf clubs. There was no question that David Bookbinder had been clever, conscientious, and thorough. Everything he had done had been undertaken in the best interests of Cornelius Oil. Roderick, feeling a small twinge of embarrassment, even recognized that Bookbinder's attempt to corner a voting majority of Cornelius Oil stock for himself and Roderick in 1945 had probably been the most efficient and practical step to take. As it was, his father's death had forestalled any further transfer of stock, and Hope's husband, Edward, had made quite certain that the remainder of Hope's inheritance remained intact. John, too, although he had chosen exile in Washington, had kept a close eye on his Cornelius shares, and there was no chance that either of them could ever be dispossessed again.

What Roderick found unsettling was that almost every letter and document in the file he had brought home was, from a business owner's point of view, both realistic and sensible. If your corporation was in danger of Senate investigation for breaking antitrust laws, didn't it make sense to treat a couple of leading senators to free vacations in the Bahamas, and a Cadillac Biarritz apiece? If the CIO was threatening to shut down your chemical plants, wasn't it good business to send a few persuasive pugilists around to encourage the workers to change their minds? And if there were profitable contracts to be had, like warships or airplanes or fuel supplies, where was the harm in making sure that the men who awarded the contracts were in no position to give them out anyplace else? This, surely, was what free enterprise was all about. It was the name of the game. And although Roderick didn't approve of Bookbinder's connections with racketeers, he had to admit that they had been used sparingly and shrewdly, too, and that they had never dominated the essential business of discovering and refining oil, building ships, and carrying cargo. Cornelius Industries, as far as Roderick could make out, had never trafficked in bootleg liquor or drugs, or been party to fraud or embezzlement. But with an elaborate but discreet network of bribed officials and sympathetic gangsters, David Bookbinder had simply ensured that Cornelius corporations had burgeoned and spread over twenty years without any hindrance from government, law, tax men, or petty extortionists.

The only thing that mystified Roderick was why his father had allowed David Bookbinder such extensive control for so long. Maybe it made good sense to have underworld connections, but from what Roderick could remember of his father, the old man had been quite capable of forming his own. Roderick sat in Johann's chair for two or three hours, while the sky grew grainy and dark outside in Gramercy Park, and he still couldn't work out why David Bookbinder had ever worked for Cornelius Oil at all. Even now, at the very end, with the threat of the Robinstown murder hanging over his head, Bookbinder had only resigned because Walter Grossmith, their most influential government connection, had insisted. There had been too much pressure from the Justice Department for him to do otherwise.

Roderick was still sitting there when Celia came back from her afternoon appointment with Trans World Airlines. She laid her pocketbook on one of the antique occasional tables, peeled off her fawn gloves, and said: '*You* look morose.'

Roderick stretched. Some of the papers fell off his lap. 'I'm worried,' he said. 'And I'm baffled.'

Celia tinkled the bell for the butler. 'In that case,' she said, 'it's business as usual.'

Roderick ignored her. He collected up the fallen papers and said: 'I was talking to David today. We had lunch at the Waterside Inn.'

'How nice.'

'We went over this Robinstown business. You know, the homicide disclosures, all that.'

'Did he squeal?'

'David doesn't squeal. He's not the type. But he did give me a pretty thorough rundown on every connection he's had for the past twenty years. It's all here. I was staggered when I read it. Did you know that Cornelius Oil actually paid twenty-five thousand dollars to Enzo Torino to protect their meat-packing interests in Chicago? Did you know that?'

Celia took out her long cigarette holder and lit a cigarette. 'When was that? Eighteen years ago? What does it matter?'

'It matters because Enzo Torino is still alive. He might be locked up, but he hasn't lost the power of speech. And that isn't all. We have business arrangements and shipping deals with people like Frank Gizzi and the Riccione brothers and every gangster you can think of. Not thirty years ago. Not thirty days ago. Today.'

Celia didn't appear at all disconcerted.

'You know that George O'Hare protects our air freight. You can't call him a shining angel of purity, can you?'

'Celia, George O'Hare is a minor thug. These men are known public enemies. Major-league mobsters.'

Celia said: 'Where on earth is Vucinzki? I'm dying for a martini.'

'Celia, listen!' snapped Roderick. 'Gizzi and the Ricciones and Albert Hagermeyer are gangsters. Organized criminals! How can we possibly justify having a concern like Cornelius Industries tied up with people like that? Not just tied up! We use their outlets, their couriers, their finance systems, their muscle, everything. We use them to bribe State Department officials to fix foreign contracts. We threaten unions and newspapers, and we even paid a TV company to forget a programme on Anastasia. Celia, we're up to the neck in cahoots with some of the worst gangsters in the whole United States!'

Celia tapped her ash placidly. 'I don't know what you're flapping about. They're on our side, aren't they? The time to flap is when they're not.'

Roderick stared at her. He was about to say something, but at that moment Vucinzki came creaking in and asked her what she would care to drink. They waited in silence until the old butler had considered her request for a very dry martini with his usual deep, pondering sighs, and shuffled off to get it. Then Roderick said: 'I think you *knew*.'

'Knew what, my dear?'

'You know damned well what! You've known all along!'

Celia turned away, irritated. 'There's really no need to shout. I'm not deaf.'

'You're not blind, either, or stupid.'

'Well, what's that supposed to mean?'

'It's supposed to mean that you've been doing most of the practical day-to-day business, while I've been nodding and waving and generally behaving like a dumb figurehead; and that if you've been doing most of the practical day-to-day business, then you must have known about these people all along! Christ, Celia, you must have *met* them!'

Celia sat upright, her eyes as cold as pebbles. 'Are you that

562

pathetic?' she asked him. 'Are you that . . . *numb* to what goes on around you?'

'I've been trying to run a multinational corporation!' yelled Roderick. 'I've been trying to run one of the country's largest oil producers, and one of the country's largest wholesale-food chains, and the country's third-biggest shipbuilder, and one of the country's major air-freight corporations, as well as chemical companies and pharmaceutical companies and insurance companies, and so many goddamned enterprises I don't know what they all are! I found out yesterday we've owned the Larkwood Pen Company since 1931, and all my life I've been *buying* the damned things!'

Celia stood up. She was dressed in a brown-and-red Dior day dress, clinging around her hips and elegantly split up each side. Her modern diamond brooch, in the stylized shape of a flying hawk, winked at Roderick in the last fading light of the day.

'Roddy,' she said, 'you're forty years old this year. Don't you think it's time to grow up?'

He stared at her. 'Time to grow *up*?'

Celia lowered her eyes, but not in humility. She was reciting something that she had known for years she would eventually have to recite, and she was trying to recall those careful words she had been putting together for just such a moment as this.

'On the day that the C-1 crashed, your father explained what he was going to do,' Celia enunciated quietly.

'Explained? Explained to whom?'

She glanced up. 'Explained to me.'

'*You*? What do you mean?'

She sighed. 'Oh, Roddy, it's so damned obvious. Your father gave you one big expensive opportunity to prove what you were made of. He invested millions of dollars in testing your mettle, because there were billions more at stake. You couldn't expect him to give you control of Cornelius Industries if he thought you were too weak to manage it.'

Roddy was pasty, and his jowls were shaking like a frustrated dog's.

'Weak?' he said hoarsely. '*Weak*?'

He turned on his heel and then turned back again.

'*Weak*?' he repeated, as if he wasn't at all sure what the word meant.

Celia looked away. If there was one spectacle which displeased her more than Roderick when he was being affectionate, it was Roderick when he was trying to make a histrionic scene.

'If I'm . . . weak . . .' snapped Roderick. 'If I'm *weak*

'Oh, don't stutter, Roddy, for goodness' sake.'

'Listen!' bellowed Roderick. 'If I'm weak, then why did he hand it all over to me when he did? Why did he put me in charge? Why does it say on my door "Roderick Cornelius, President"? Why does it say that? That's what I'd like to know!'

Celia raised her neck up and up as if it were on an endless crank.

'Of course you're president,' she whispered. 'But even presidents can be puppets.'

She lowered her eyes again, but she still had that stiff, arched posture that frightened Roderick so much. He felt sometimes that Celia was not a real woman at all, but a brand of sarcastic robot. He watched her in genuine horror and fascination as she explained what for sixteen years he had never suspected.

'Every single decision of major policy which has affected every single branch of Cornelius Industries since Johann died has been taken jointly between David Bookbinder and myself,' said Celia precisely.

'You have not written one memorandum, one report, one suggestion, one instruction, or even one cheque that has not been vetted by one of us or both of us. That was your father's explicit instructions to both David Bookbinder and myself, and that was exactly what happened.'

Roderick opened his mouth, said nothing, and then closed it again.

Celia stood up. 'Your father loved you, in his way, and he wanted to maintain the pride of the family name. But he was not a believer in dynastic rule for its own sake. He didn't believe that a son necessarily inherits his father's abilities. That's why he tested you with the C-1, and that's why he made sure you never really laid your hands on any power or money at all.'

Roderick went over to the window. He seemed to have aged fifteen years in fifteen minutes. The strained light made his face look haggard and ancient.

Celia said: 'Perhaps you think it was wrong of me to agree to do this behind your back. Well, perhaps it was. But I did it because I wanted money and power for myself, and I wanted the same for you, and if this was the only way to get it, then that was the way it was going to have to be.'

Roderick said softly: 'You and David Bookbinder. What a combination.'

Vucinzki rapped on the door, and then came in with Celia's martini. She took it off the silver tray and dismissed the old butler with a wave of her hand.

'There was no love lost between me and David Bookbinder,' she said. 'But at least he was the kind of twisted personality I could trust.'

She sipped her freezing martini, and then walked over and laid a cool hand on her husband's shoulder. He looked at it; at the sapphires and diamonds on every finger; and then he turned back to the night.

'I knew all about David Bookbinder's little plan to corner John and Hope's inheritance,' she said evenly. 'He didn't do it to protect you, or even in the best interests of Cornelius Industries. He did it entirely to keep me out of things, so that when Johann died there would be only one puppet-master instead of two. He wasn't only buying out John and Hope; he was tying up their shares in a holding company that would have made it impossible for me to exercise any influence over them.'

Roderick said dully: 'Then poor little Clara didn't die in vain.'

Celia held Roderick's shoulder for a moment longer, and then released it. 'No,' she said almost inaudibly.

Roderick turned. 'I don't suppose you know whether it was an *accident* or not,' he said in a curiously bland tone of voice. 'You seem to know everything else.'

Celia frowned. 'Roddy, you're not suggesting . . .'

Roderick walked tiredly over to his chair and sat down. He rubbed his face with his hands. 'I don't know. You seem to know enough gangsters.'

She pursed her lips. 'I don't know *why* Clara died,' she said coldly. 'I believe it was an accident, a genuine accident. It only seemed suspicious afterward because David Bookbinder turned it to his own advantage. I suppose you can say that was immoral in itself. But he loved the twins, in his own rather repulsive way. He wouldn't have harmed them.'

'But once Clara was dead, it was all right to use her death

565

to make himself a little more money? Is that what you're saying? My God, he may not have killed her, but he certainly
acted like a gangster once she was gone.'

Celia sipped her martini.

'Well, that's the whole point of this conversation, isn't it?'
she said. 'Your . . . moral compunctions about employing the
mob.'

'Is it so strange to have moral compunctions about consorting with criminals?' asked Roderick. 'Or is it acceptable
behaviour these days? Maybe you should explain it to me. I've
been a puppet for so long, I think I've lost the facility to think
for myself.'

'Roddy, please!'

'No, Celia, tell me! Tell me about these people! Tell me who
they are, and what they do, and how often you see them! Are
they fun? Are they witty? Do they make jokes about beating
people's brains out and crushing little girls in automobile
doors? What do they like for supper? Can they dance well? Do
they buy their jewellery or do they steal it?'

Celia took three stiff paces across the room, swung her arm,
and smacked Roderick across the face. He jerked back in his
chair, but he didn't attempt to retaliate. He didn't even raise
his hand to the three lacerations on his cheek where nearly
two and half million dollars' worth of gemstones had cut his
skin.

'I see . . .' he said slowly. 'You've learned their techniques
as well as their names.'

Celia turned away, furious, clutching her crossed arms.

'God, Roddy, you're such a fool! What do you think America
is? The heavenly land of opportunity? There is one rule that
keeps a big business alive in this country today and that is
the rule of suppressing your competitors. The market for oil
is only so big. If we want a bigger share, we have to take it
from someone else. And that someone else certainly isn't going
to stand by and let us do it without a fight. Yes, of course we're
in league with gangsters. Some of them are ugly and vicious
and stupid, but most of them are extremely cultured, extremely
sophisticated, and know more about this business than you
do. They know the realities of life, Roddy, and they're set up
to deal with them.'

Roderick reached down to where his papers were untidily

stacked on the floor. He lifted one up at random and read from it.

'In 1952,' he said, 'we were indirectly responsible for the bombing and closure of seventeen rival gas stations in Louisiana, Texas, and Arizona.'

He picked up another sheet, turned it the right way up, and squinted at it.

•'In 1950 we paid the Ricciones one thousand dollars to send a man to burgle the offices of the Department of the Interior, so that we could acquire vital papers which would enable us to bid successfully for development land.'

He shuffled for another one, but Celia said: 'That's enough.'

Roderick looked up. 'Enough for what? Enough to make you feel guilty?'

Celia shook her head. 'It's enough, that's all. You've made your point. Now I think you'd better face the truth.'

'Face the truth?' asked Roderick. 'What the hell do you think I'm doing?'

Celia turned around. 'I mean *really* face the truth. Face to face. I want you to meet Ricardo Riccione, in person.'

Roderick lowered the sheet of paper he was reading, and their eyes met over the top of it with the strange caution of two people meeting for the very first time.

David Bookbinder's retirement was not a long one. He never made it to Hawaii, although he did get as far as Key West, where he rented a shady wooden house three doors down from the house which Ernest Hemingway made famous, and he walked along the quiet streets, through the fingery shadows of palms, wearing a wide straw hat with a blue band around it, and long khaki shorts. They make leather sandals on Key West, and he bought himself a pair of those, as well as a big straw bag to take picnics of cold lobster and chicken around the island. Some days his stout crimson figure was seen on the flat white beach by the airfield, staring out at the flat blue ocean. Other days, he sat on Conch Quay, wearing black sunglasses that didn't suit him, and read back issues of *The Wall Street Journal*. Or he'd stand at the corner of Wadell and Vernon, stock-still, in his droopy shorts and flowery red-and-yellow shirt, as if he was receiving a message from God, and had to stop to hear it through.

Two weeks after he had left New York, on a windy Thursday

afternoon with a hint of hurricane in the air, he returned to his rented house to find the front door open.

He paused for a long while at the front gate. The garden was lush and green and overgrown, with palms that nodded and fragrant tangles of wild orchids. A flurry of tiny parakeets shrilled and twittered over his head.

David Bookbinder turned slowly and looked down the placid street. His nose was red and peeling because he had spent the morning on the white sands of West Beach. Under his arm was a folded copy of *Metallurgical Review*. He took off his sunglasses and bit his lip. Across the road, a black man slept at the wheel of a two-tone Packard Patrician. The palms rustled and dipped.

He could have, and probably should have, walked away. But instead he went through the gate and stood for a moment on the path, peering into the darkness of the old, elegant house. He could see the blue-black shine of the floorboards, and the shadow of an ugly little Chinese table that stood in the hall. He called the name of his cleaning woman: 'Cristobel?'

There was no reply. He climbed the steps of the veranda. He waited at the doorway for a moment or two, and then went inside. He laid his creased magazine on the hall table.

They were waiting for him in the drawing room. They seemed to have no doubt at all that he would come; or that when he saw them, he would make no attempt to escape. They were relaxing in two of his wicker armchairs, smoking hand-rolled cigarettes in black paper, and when he appeared at the door one of them simply said: 'Come on in.'

The room was cool and civilized, with large dark paintings behind reflecting glass, and small brass tables from Kashmir. The two men didn't seem to belong there at all; like two helmeted football players at a croquet tournament. One of them was tall and heavy with a blond crew cut and horn-rim spectacles with one cracked lens. He wore crumpled light grey slacks and a yellow short-sleeved shirt. The other man was younger, hipper, with curly black hair and a big greasy nose. He wore a loose-fitting T-shirt and patched denim pants. His faded sneakers shifted and shuffled on the floor, tapping out the beat to some unheard rock-'n'-roll song that was playing in his head.

David Bookbinder stood there in his leather sandals and his shorts and said: 'Who are you? Who sent you?'

The crew-cut man didn't even look up. He sucked at his cigarette, and kept his eyes on the floor as the smoke leaked out of the side of his mouth. He asked solemnly: 'Are you Mr Bookbinder?'

David Bookbinder stayed where he was. He said: 'You'd better get out of here, quick.'

The young hip hoodlum glanced at his crew-cut friend, and his feet kept dancing. The crew-cut friend said: 'We ain't going no place.' Then he took one last drag at his cigarette, and nipped it out between his finger and his thumb before tucking it thriftily back into his shirt pocket. He stood up.

David Bookbinder felt a surge of fright in his stomach, but he was too experienced to run. If you ran, they hit you straight-away. If you stayed where you were, there was always a chance that whatever irrational processes went on in their distorted, deprived minds, they might consider it more amusing to have mercy than to kill. The crew-cut man came around him and gripped his wrist with such viciousness that he said: 'Ah!' but that was all.

Conversation was pointless. These men had no idea why they were here, and they probably had no idea who they were working for. They led him down the passageway, past foxed and fly-specked prints of privateers at anchor, and out of the back door with its green-and-yellow stained-glass panels to the garden.

They descended the wrought-iron steps into the luminous emerald shade of palms and acacias. A lizard ran across the path in front of David Bookbinder's feet. Somewhere in the trees, a bird sang a repetitive and complicated song that sounded like 'Here we go again, boys, here we go again.' It was sultry and stifling in the garden, and sweat ran down David Bookbinder's neck.

The three of them walked around the back of the house until they reached the dilapidated, peeling shed where the garden tools used to be kept. A tangle of gourds, speckled and warty, grew down one side of the wooden roof.

The young man with the curly hair forced the shed door open Inside it was musty and dark, with that pervasive smell of tropical mildew The man with the crew-cut ushered David Bookbinder inside, and they stood there for a while, as their eyes grew gradually accustomed to the dim light, amid broken seedling pots and rusted shears, and a roller with a cast-iron handle that must have dated from seventy years ago. The young man closed the door behind them and bolted it.

'What are you going to do?' asked David Bookbinder.

The crew-cut man coughed. He said: 'I guessed you kind of *knew.*'

David Bookbinder was an old man. He said: 'Can you make it quick?'

The crew-cut man shrugged. 'That depends on you. We gotta do it the way we was told.'

There was silence. The young man with the curly hair was rummaging around with something that sounded metallic, but he was out of David Bookbinder's line of sight. David Bookbinder said: 'Can I have a cigar?'

The crew-cut man said: 'It's too late for that. What do you think this is?'

David Bookbinder said nothing. Then the crew-cut man said: 'Anyway, cigars is bad for your health.'

The young man with the curly hair heard this remark and laughed. The crew-cut man said: 'Shaddup.'

David Bookbinder kept thinking that those who live by the sword must die by the sword, but all the same he wondered whether he really deserved *this* kind of death. He had always exercised violence with the utmost discretion and tact, and his own hit was the first that he had ever experienced first hand. He hoped and prayed that it would be abrupt and not bloody.

Those who had paid the two men, however, had not specified abruptness. They had specified a sort of homicidal joke. To carry it out, the young man with the curly hair dragged an old wooden seed box across to the door of the shed, and the crew-cut man made David Bookbinder walk over and stand on it, with his back to the door. When David Bookbinder saw the young man take up a handful of six-inch nails and a heavy carpenter's hammer, he realized, with terrified fascination, what they were actually going to do.

They forced a rag into his mouth so that he couldn't scream. Then the crew-cut man pinned him against the door with the weight of his body while the young hoodlum with the curly hair seized his left hand, dug the point of a nail into the flesh

570

of his palm, and hammered the nail right through into the wood with four hefty blows.

David Bookbinder tried to struggle, but then they grabbed his other hand and nailed that to the door, too. His eyes were bulging with pain and fear but he couldn't speak. They knelt down and unbuckled his new leather sandals, and then they crossed his feet over each other, and drove a third nail straight through his plump arches and into the door. The young man with the curly hair kicked the box away and admired his handiwork.

The crew-cut man said: 'It looks like he's too heavy. It looks like those nails are going to tear out of his hands.'

The other young man nodded, and picked up more nails from where they were scattered on the shed floor. With a couple in his mouth, he banged two more into each of David Bookbinder's arms, one through the muscle of the forearm and the other straight through the flinching bicep. By the time he had finished, David Bookbinder was almost unconscious.

The crew-cut man said: 'Don't forget to bring that hammer along. Wipe it clean and throw it off the quay.'

'Okay, Jackie.'

The crew-cut man sniffed, and reached in his shirt pocket for the cigarette butt. 'Okay, let's go.'

They swung the door open and for a brief moment David Bookbinder saw sunlight again. Then they closed up the shed, and locked it, and he was left with arms and feet of fire, hanging in the musty twilight.

He went through fifteen hours of agony. He wept, and sometimes he prayed. It never ended. He prayed that he would die. He tried to spit out the rag so that he could call for help, but he couldn't. The pain was so great that he slept, and then dreamed about it, and then woke up to find that it was real. He didn't dare move in case the nails tore through his sinews and hurt him even more.

Just after dawn on Friday morning, his bald head dropped between his shoulders and he died. The birds outside sang 'Here we go again, boys, here we go again.' The roller with the cast-iron handle, coincidentally, had been purchased on the same day that David Bookbinder was born.

His body was discovered eight days later by a Martinique-born handyman who was clearing out the house in preparation for new tenants. The police already knew what had happened, and had been well-paid to deal with it quietly. The coroner declared that he had died from a seizure, not at all uncommon in a man his age. Then he was cremated without publicity and his ashes were thrown, at night, into the dark and fluorescent waters of the Gulf of Mexico.

In 1954 the water commissioner of Toledo, puzzled for months by dramatic drops in the level of his reservoirs at unexplained times of the evening, suddenly realized what was going on. The citizens of Toledo were rushing to their toilets during TV commercials, and flushing their cisterns in simultaneous three-minute Niagaras.

Something else happened in 1954. John Cornelius, the president of Cornelius Armaments, came home early one evening from work and saw a red-and-white Chevrolet Bel Air parked in his hedge-lined driveway in Georgetown, and the white lace curtains of his upstairs bedroom drawn. The advertisements said about the Chevrolet Bel Air that it wrung more power out of every gallon, and that it was a long way from 'full' to 'empty.' A recent *Washington Post* feature on John Cornelius had called him 'that individualistic and pugnacious arms supremo.'

Tonight he wasn't pugnacious. As soon as he saw the red car on his sloping driveway, he glanced in the mirror of his own white Cadillac convertible and pulled out into the traffic. The evening sun was falling across the street in crisscross patterns of telephone wires and trees. He checked his rearview mirror just once more, and glimpsed his home, a stately Colonial six-bedroom house of dark brick and white pilasters, disappearing behind a passing moving van.

John didn't know whether he suddenly suspected Irene of having a lover or not. He had had a mistress himself, of course, but his relationship with Mara Malinsky was so unique, and so oblique, that he couldn't see how Irene could possibly get herself involved in anything similar. Still, he had to admit that she had a tacit licence to take another man to bed. All the gossip and the scandal about Mara must have been hard for her to take.

He took the folded handkerchief out of his breast pocket and dabbed his forehead. It was quite warm this evening. He was dressed in a light grey double-breasted suit and a white shirt with a polka-dot tie. If it hadn't been for the luxurious white Cadillac, you could have mistaken him for any one of the conformist and conservative middle-management men who poured out of Washington evenings and made their way home. In 1952, he had grown a small bristly moustache, which made him look five years older than his thirty-seven years. It was a kind of protection against the scandal and disapproval that he had faced from his family and his friends. Irene didn't like it much and called it his 'infernal Fuller.'

It was a half hour before the scarlet-and-chrome tail of the Bel Air began to back out of his driveway and into the street. John had been listening to a quiz show on the radio, and the Chevrolet appeared just as the quizmaster asked: 'And do you, Ed, know just what brand of hosiery your wife wears?' John switched the radio off and reached over to start the Cadillac's motor.

As the Bel Air passed him by, he raised his hand against his face so that the driver wouldn't recognize him. But he peeped through his fingers and caught a half-second glimpse of the man who may or may not have been his wife's lover. He was prepared for almost anything – prepared to identify a business friend or a golfing partner or a dinner guest. After all, lovers were rarely strangers. But what he wasn't prepared for was the man's colour. The driver of the Bel Air was black. A heavily built West Indian with dark sunglasses and an expensive lightweight suit.

Maybe he had thought of tailing the Chevrolet and confronting the driver with what he knew. But his hand stayed numbly on the gearshift, and he didn't move. The evening street seemed suddenly too windy and public and cold for a convertible, especially when a middle-aged woman in a print frock stopped beside him with a bulging A&P bag and said: 'Do you mind if I rest this on your automobile for just a moment?'

He told the woman: 'I'm just leaving.' He checked his mirror and saw his worried eyes. Then he released the parking brake and swung the Cadillac out across the street in a wide U-turn.

When he turned the corner and arrived outside his house again, the bedroom curtains were open He nosed the Cadillac down the driveway, tugged the brake, and climbed out He pushed his way past the dusty box hedge that lined the drive, and took out his key to open the blue Georgian front door.

Irene opened it for him. She was wearing a loose Japanese robe of pale green silk, loosely tied around the waist, and she looked even taller and saintlier than ever. On appearances alone, accusing Irene of adultery was like casting grubby aspersions about the private life of Saint Agnes. John paused in mid-step, his brass doorkey poised on the end of a gold chain that came from his pants pocket. He looked like a life-size ornamental lamp that was trying to plug itself in.

Irene said: 'Hello. You're back early.'

John looked at her. 'That's right.'

She stepped back, and he entered the house. He laid his papers and briefcase on the hall table. There was a hush inside the house that gave a curious theatrical quality to any sound or talking. Irene's silk robe, as she walked behind John toward the living room, was rustling like sad trees.

John looked around. The television was on, without any volume. The room had rows of windows that faced north over the garden. It had always been a chill, shadowy garden. Stone people stood around outside with mossy and petrified patience. The living room itself was neutral and tasteful, with large chesterfields in pecan-coloured hide, and Victorian armchairs covered in brown velvet. It was, of course, very Boston.

'You seem rather quiet,' said Irene. 'Would you like a drink?'

John shook his head.

'I've had another boring day,' Irene continued. 'But then, I don't really suppose you're interested.'

John walked over to the marble mantelpiece and opened a silver cigarette box. He took out a cigarette and lit it thoughtfully.

'Of course I'm interested.' He kept his eyes on the television, where a woman was doing something complicated with two boxes of soap powder.

'You don't seem to be.'

'Don't I? I'm thinking.'

Irene picked at the back of one of the chesterfields with her long pearlized nails. 'You still haven't said whether you want a drink yet.'

'I'm sorry. No, I don't, thank you.'

'I'm having one.'

John glanced at her, but shook his head again, and said nothing. Irene went over to the cabinet, took down a heavy Waterford crystal glass, and poured herself a large gin-and-tonic. It was Lewis' day off today. Usually she tinkled the little silver bell. She cupped the glass like a child with a mug of milk, and walked slowly back toward him. He puffed unsteadily at his cigarette.

'You're, un . . . not dressed,' said John.

Irene blinked at him, and then gave a funny little laugh. 'No,' she said in a high voice.

He felt as if he were sinking in an elevator. He despised himself for what he was thinking, and what he was about to suggest, but at the same time he knew that what remained of their marriage was not going to survive for very long unless he knew. Perhaps his guilt needed bathing with the cool knowledge that he wasn't alone in his need for someone outside their relationship to support and console him.

'Is this how you usually look when you have visitors?' he asked her. 'Is this how you usually . . . dress?'

There was a silence. Then Irene said: 'What do you mean? I don't have visitors.'

'No,' said John. 'But you did.'

There was another silence, longer and colder. Irene took a deep, wavering breath.

'I came back a half hour ago,' John said dully. 'There was a car in the driveway, and the bedroom curtains were drawn. I waited down the street and watched the car when it left.'

Irene said: 'You've been *spying* on me?'

'I don't think so. I don't think satisfying my curiosity about a strange male visitor who for some reason causes you to draw your bedroom drapes at four-thirty in the afternoon is spying. I think it's husbandly interest.'

Irene went to the window and pulled back the net curtain. A few yards away, an encrusted, bird-spattered statue of the Venus de Milo stared armlessly back at her.

'Your husbandly interest isn't usually as noticeable as this.' she said, without any attempt to conceal her bitterness. 'In fact, you're hardly ever here to display it.'

John lowered his eyes. 'I'm not trying to condemn you, Irene. I just think I've a right to know the truth.'

'What truth?'

'What truth do you think? The truth about you and this man.'

Irene shrugged. 'What do you want me to say?'

575

'You could start with his name. I think I'd like to know who I'm sharing my bed with.'

Irene turned around. 'Oh, I see. You automatically assume that he's my lover.'

'As a matter of fact, I do. What else am I supposed to think?'

'Why don't you try thinking nothing for a change, instead of squalid little suspicions?'

'Squalid!' snapped John. 'The man's black, and you call me squalid!'

Irene's pale eyes widened in shock. When she spoke, her voice was quavering with suppressed outrage.

'So that's it! You object because he's *black*! My *God*! John Cornelius, the fun-loving energetic liberal! The only good guy out of the whole rotten family! You don't mind strange men seducing your wife as long as they're the right colour! My God!'

She stared at him for a moment longer, and then she said: 'You disgust me. You make me squirm.'

John threw his cigarette into the empty grate. 'You make me feel the same way. It was your choice to stay after you found out about Mara. You could have divorced me. You could have walked straight out of the door. I told you what the terms were, and you were prepared to take them. You wanted to be a Cornelius wife, and a Cornelius wife you stayed.'

Irene came across the tapestry rug toward him. 'I didn't know there were *rules*,' she said. 'I didn't know that I was only permitted to take a certain variety of lover. Perhaps you'd better tell me what other objections you have. Is it all right if they're ginger? What about profession? Do you object to dentists, or tightrope walkers? Any religious scruples? No Jews? Come on, John, you'd better tell me so that I know! I'm sure there must be something else that sets your teeth on edge apart from darkies!'

John seized a leather cushion from the chesterfield and hurled it across the room. It knocked a small Staffordshire figure of a miserable shepherd off a mahogany sidetable, and shattered it.

'You whore!' yelled John. 'You stuck-up Back Bay whore! You played around with a black man in my bed, and you have the brass face to turn around and mock me?'

Irene looked at him with an odd smile. It was like the smile of a simple-minded child, or someone who is suffering from extreme shock. But she was neither simple nor shocked; it was a smile which meant that however much John insulted her, however much he bellowed and shouted, he was only doing what she wanted him to do at all times, and at any cost, and that was to take notice of her.

'I didn't take him to bed,' she said in her immaculate and aristocratic tones. 'He came to look at the air-conditioning.'

'In a mohair suit? Who are you trying to kid?'

Irene kept on smiling. 'He came, first of all, this morning, and when he came he wore coveralls. I took a fancy to him, and I asked him to call back this afternoon, when the maid had left. When he returned at three, he had taken a bath and put on a clean shirt. He picked me up in his arms as if I was a child, and he penetrated me standing up in the kitchen doorway.'

She loosened the tie of her robe. 'If you like, I can show you his semen.'

John turned back to the mantelpiece and took out another cigarette. As he lit it, he glanced up, and saw Irene's reflection in the gilded French mirror above him. Her robe was open, and he could see her small breasts and her pale body. He looked down at the grate, and didn't look up again.

'I think we had better revise our agreement,' he said quietly. 'I think that if we are going to stay together we had better protect ourselves from the wild animals that we are capable of turning ourselves into. From now on, I will tell you nothing about what I do, and I want to hear nothing about any of your sexual escapades, either. For Ally's sake, I am prepared to live with you as long as you like, but don't ever expect to be touched by me again.'

He turned and faced Irene, and his expression was grim and grey. She smiled at him benevolently.

'Oh, don't worry.' She smiled. 'I'll make you touch me. Whatever you say, I'll make you touch me.'

John didn't answer. He felt overwhelmed by frustration and fears. He was feeling jealousies that had never troubled him before. His affair with Mara had finished, for all practical purposes, nine years ago. But he was still haunted by guilt and he could never quite work out why. Was it guilt for the emotional injuries that Irene had sustained in the family row that had followed, and their self-imposed exile in Washington? Was it guilt for Clara's death? Or was it guilt for Mara

577

and for Ally? Whatever it was, it made him feel numb and chloroformed from reality; as if he would only be allowed to return to normal happy life when he had paid a long but unspecified penance. He was a naturally honest and sensitive man, but in the company of a woman like Irene, whose weakness was her greatest strength, he was almost powerless.

Perhaps his deepest guilt was that, for his own sake, he should have left her years ago.

He said: 'I think I'll have that drink now.'

Irene didn't move. She said: 'In that case you'd better get it yourself.'

He stayed where he was for a moment. Then he went over to the drinks cabinet and poured himself a small glass of Jim Beam bourbon. He drank it where he stood, the way that people stand at their bedroom washbasins and drink water.

'Quite frankly,' he said, 'I don't know whether you're making this up or not.'

'Making it up? Why should I do that?'

'I don't know. Perhaps you want to punish me.'

Irene pouted in mock sympathy. 'Oh, darling . . . how could I ever punish you?'

'Very easily. You punish me every time you throw my love for you back in my face.'

Irene sat down on the chesterfield and spread her Japanese robe around her so that she looked like a big pale pear-shaped bee sitting on a shiny flower. She said: 'To tell you the truth, John, I think you stopped loving me a long time ago. I don't think you've loved me since the war.'

'And that's your answer, is it? To fornicate with Negro handymen in the kitchen doorway?'

'Handy*man*, darling. There was only one.'

'You're making it up.'

'Am I?'

'Of course you're damned well making it up! It just doesn't happen!And in any event, what the hell is a black air-conditioning mechanic going to see in a Boston bluestocking like you? A man like that wants somebody sensual. He doesn't want a prim white wife in Bergdorf Goodman underwear!'

Irene raised an eyebrow. He couldn't tell if he had hurt her or not. She sipped her drink and said: 'Prim, am I?'

There was a moment's pause, and then she said: 'I don't know why you married me if you thought I was prim.'

I don't know either.'

'Do you really regret it that much?'

'Oh, Christ, Irene, I don't regret it. I just regret the damage I did, and I regret Clara's death, and I regret the way we've been limping along for nine years with nothing between us but mistrust and bickering.'

Irene lowered her eyes. Her eyelids were made up in a rather unpleasant shade of pale blue. 'Well,' she said, 'it wasn't my fault.'

'Does it really matter, now, whose fault it was?'

She looked up. 'You can say that because it was you – you and that Polish woman who didn't even have the decency to stay away from another woman's husband. It wasn't *my* fault and you know that it wasn't my fault, and now you're trying to say that it was.'

'I'm not saying anything of the kind. I'm saying that after nine years, it doesn't matter anymore.'

Irene's eyes began to get crowded with tears. 'If it doesn't matter, why do I still feel like this?'

'Like what?'

'Like being *horrible* to you. I can't help it. I love you, John, but I have to be horrible to you to make sure you still love me. I think that if I hurt you, but you still love me, then your love must be real.'

John stared at her. She was as saintly as ever, but now she was older, her saintliness was less visionary and magical and more like the pious rigidity of those painted plaster figures that Mexican women keep on their dressing tables next to the shell-backed hairbrushes.

He said huskily: 'You didn't do it, did you? That thing with the black man?'

She wept, and the tears dripped steadily onto her Japanese silk. John felt that he ought to put his arm around her, but for some reason he was disinclined to. He was probably put off by what she had said about *making* him touch her. And apart from that, crying did nothing to transform her into a soft and gentle wife who was desperately in need of his protection. She remained stiff. He felt it would have been like putting his arms around an effigy.

'I'm going out,' he announced quietly. 'If anybody wants me, I'll be down at the Republican Club.'

She nodded, and sniffed. She said: 'I'm sorry, John. I didn't mean to.'

He stood by the door trying to think of something to say; something that would make her understand that they were probably lucky to be able to live together without too much friction; and that passionate love was the last thing he wanted from her. He would have been quite happy to be left alone. But she sat there with her sad face, wet and weeping, and all he could do was turn away, and close the door behind him, and hope that while he was out she wouldn't do anything absurd, like swallow too many pills or bake him a chocolate angelfood cake.

As they reached the gates of Nineveh, Ricardo Riccione's estate out at Thornwood, New York, the last ragged clouds of a summer shower has just passed toward the Kensico Reservoir, and the fresh sun made the roads steam. Roderick, looking paler than usual, was driving his green-and-white Olds Ninety-Eight and wearing a charcoal-grey suit and a grey homburg hat. Beside him, Celia was as calm and cool as ever, in an ice-blue suit and a veiled hat to match.

Nineveh's gateheads were built from dressed granite, with black-painted gates of decorative iron with gilded leaves. Through the ironwork Roderick could see nothing but mature oaks, with an immaculate asphalt drive leading away behind them. As he drew up to the gates, a tall man in a well-fitting dark blue uniform appeared from a green-painted sentry box and walked over toward them.

'Mrs Cornelius,' said the guard, leaning across the car. 'It's good to see you.'

Roderick's expression tightened. Celia said: 'This is my husband, Mr Roderick Cornelius. I expect you'll be seeing some more of him soon.'

The guard nodded. He looked very Italian, with long sideburns and dark eyes. Although he was friendly, he could break a man's neck with a single violent twist of his hands. He said: 'Pleased to know you, Mr Cornelius. I've read your name a lot My name's Contini.'

Roderick grunted. 'Can we go in now?' he asked impatien..'

The guard wasn't at all fazed. 'Sure. Mr Riccione's expecting you. Take the car down to the end of the driveway, as far as the rose gardens, and someone will park it for you. Mr Riccione's in the gazebo right now.'

Celia waved and said: 'Thank you, Contini,' but Roderick remained annoyed and unsmiling. Contini saluted and went over to pull the switch that opened the high black gates.

They drove down between rustling leaves that irradiated them in lemons and greens. Roderick said nothing. The drive seemed to wind along for miles, and they smelled the rose gardens before they actually reached them: a dense and almost delirious scent of Sutter's Gold and President Herbert Hoover. Then they turned the corner and it seemed as if the grounds had effervesced with thousands and thousands of flowers.

He parked the car and climbed out. When he walked around and opened the door for Celia, she said: 'Isn't it divine? This really is the divinest place.'

Roderick helped her out. 'What is he? Some kind of horticultural maniac?'

Celia said: 'Ssh, don't be so provocative. The gazebo's this way.'

'Oh, so you've been there before?'

Celia linked her arm through his, and together they walked with guarded aplomb between the snow-showers of roses. Roderick was sweating, and he would have done anything to take a breath that didn't hang heavy with the scent of floribunda.

'You can see the gazebo from the house,' Celia remarked, almost like a professional guide, as they mounted a small slope between rhododendron bushes and bergamot. 'I've never actually *been* there, but I've *seen* it.'

As they came around the bushes, the gazebo came into view. It was built of white stone, with a cupola roof, and decorative stone balustrades all around. Behind it were the untamed woods of Riccione's estate, shady and cool. But in front, and below, all his ornamental gardens were stretched out with privet hedges and winding paths, and fountains that glittered and sprayed in the afternoon sun. His house itself was a severely classical twenty-bedroom house of pinkish Italian stucco.

The man himself was sitting in the gazebo painting in oils at a small easel. He was physically diminutive and very dapper, and he wore tiny gold-rimmed sunglasses. He could have been Al Capone's cousin, although several of his more politically minded friends remarked on a flattering resemblance to the Little Flower. Ricardo would have been delighted to have been christened Fiorello. He had an extraordinary sense of humour which relished the contrast between the sensitive culture and the total ruthlessness of crime.

Riccione, of course, was not alone. Twenty yards away, sitting mournfully on a small marble seat, a man in a pale blue suit and a fedora hat kept a restless eye on the surrounding woods and trees, and drummed his fingers on the high-powered rifle that lay across his lap. There were probably other guards around, too, concealed behind the rhododendrons, but you wouldn't find that out unless you were rash enough to reach suddenly inside your jacket for a cigarette

As Roderick and Celia approached the gazebo, Riccione laid down his brushes and stood up. He raised his hat and held out one small plump hand to assist Celia up the gazebo steps.

'My dear,' he said, kissing her. Then he turned to Roderick and smiled with a row of little white teeth, like a baby's milk teeth. 'And you, Mr Cornelius. How glad I am to know you.'

Roderick shook hands. He felt extremely nervous. When Riccione dragged over two white-painted garden chairs for them to sit on, the squeak of the metal feet against the stone floor of the gazebo made him feel depressed and alarmed.

'What are you painting?' asked Celia. 'It looks like a sort of rose.'

Ricardo nodded. It was impossible to see his eyes behind those maliciously small sunglasses.

He walked over to his little painting where it glistened wet on its easel. 'I think I have a talent for this, you know. If only I had more time. I am a great admirer of Beatrix Potter, the English lady. She painted flowers, and they came alive.'

Celia said: 'My husband has a talent for shipping things by air. He was an air pioneer, you know. He has a great talent for that.'

Roderick looked uncomfortable. He said: 'I'm a businessman, Mr Riccione. A businessman, plain and simple.'

Ricardo raised one eyebrow from beneath his dark glasses. It was like a black crow taking off from a black lake.

Roderick told him: 'It was a complete surprise, as a matter of fact, finding out that we did business with you. For one reason or another, mainly to do with my family and the way it works, I didn't know until now that your world and mine were so closely linked.'

The mobster nodded. He was so mild and courteous that Roderick found it increasingly difficult to sustain his annoyance. Ricardo Riccione was the kind of man to whom children came in distress, and around whose feet birds and squirrels clustered in the hope of crumbs. It was easy to suspend one's mistrust, and to forget that he and his late brother, Giorgio, were reputed to be responsible for more than eight-five violent murders. He said quietly: 'And what did you feel, Mr Cornelius, when you did find out? Were you anxious?'

Roderick looked up slowly. 'Well, I don't think "anxious" really describes it. It was more like finding out that your mother has been having an affair with the local rat catcher.'

Ricardo obviously liked that analogy, and smiled.

'Yes,' he said.

Together they watched the servant scale the last few yards of the slope with his silver tray. When he reached the gazebo, he spread a crisp linen tablecloth with a practised snap, and laid out silver knives and forks and condiments. There was a chilled bottle of Chablis Grand Cru in a silver cooler, and under fresh linen napkins were small salads in the shape of flowers, with tomatoes, anchovies, blanched capsicums, and a concoction of smoke trout and cream.

Roderick watched with a severe face as these appetizers were laid out. After the servant had uncorked the wine, poured each of them a glassful, and retired to a respectful distance, he said: 'What's this?'

Ricardo seemed surprised. 'You won't eat with me?'

Celia glanced at Roderick in displeasure.

'Mr Riccione,' said Roderick tersely, 'I came here to argue, not to eat.'

'Does one preclude the other?'

Roderick was mopping his neck with his handkerchief. 'What I'm saying, Mr Riccione, is that I find it difficult to break bread with people I don't admire.'

There was a pause of some moments. Riccione puffed out his little cheeks and tapped his little fingers on the arm of his garden chair, as if he were trying to think of a way to deal with a nephew who had expressly been told not to crawl under the strawberry nets.

'Well, Mr Cornelius,' he said at length, 'you don't have to eat. I cannot sit you on my knee like an infant and spoon it into you.'

Celia said 'Roddy, please, there's no need to make this more difficult than it really is.'

'It's difficult, all right,' said Roderick. 'And accepting Mr Riccione's hospitality isn't going to make it any easier.'

Riccione stood up. He walked to the rail of the gazebo, and then he turned around and spread his hands appealingly.

'You do not like me?' he asked. 'Is that it?'

'Don't be ridiculous,' snapped Roderick. 'I hardly know you. But I know your reputation, and it's your reputation that we've got to talk about today.'

'You mean you want to talk about roses?'

'You can stick your roses up your ass. I want to talk about mobs.'

Celia said: 'Roddy!'

But Riccione waved her into silence. He shook his head and walked back toward Roderick with an expression that may have been one of regret and consolation if it had been possible to see what his eyes were doing behind his sunglasses.

'I'm sorry, Mr Cornelius, but you're quite right. We should get down to brass tacks at once. Obviously we cannot be pleasant until each of us knows where he stands.'

He sat down, and sipped at his glass of wine. Then he said: 'I think it regretful that we did not meet earlier. You seem like a man who could have contributed much to our relationship with Cornelius Industries. But I know how it was with your father, and I also know that a series of unfortunate events led your father to pass the business to your wife and Mr Bookbinder, God rest Mr Bookbinder's soul.'

Roderick frowned. 'That's a little premature, isn't it? David Bookbinder's in Florida, on a long vacation. He may have retired, Mr Riccione, but I don't think he's counting on dying just yet.'

Ricardo Riccione shrugged. 'None of us ever do.'

'Are you speaking as an expert?'

'I am speaking as a man who enjoys his life and all the gifts of God to the fullest.'

'It seems you've also enjoyed extorting most of our clients to the fullest.'

Ricardo laid down his glass. 'Well,' he said equably, 'you can call it extortion if you want to. But terminology is not reality. The words of crime, and of business, and of politics, are all interchangeable. I do not see the distinction myself.

We are all of us concerned with the quality of life, and that is all.'

'What kind of quality does your life have?'

Riccione smiled. 'A very pleasing one, I like to think.'

'And what quality of life can a trucking corporation boast if it refuses to handle Cornelius goods before any other? Or a longshoreman who doesn't make a point of ripping open a few sacks of Du Pont fertilizers, or short-weighting Kaiser Cement in favour of Cornelius Cement? What quality of life does an insurance salesman enjoy when he doesn't return ten percent more Cornelius business in any six-month period than any other? Or a wholesaler who won't push Cornelius foods in front of all the rest? Can you tell me that?'

Ricardo wasn't at all troubled by what Roderick had said. 'Mr Cornelius' – he smiled – 'what quality of life would one of your secretaries enjoy if you paid her to take letters and she never did?'

'She'd get the sack.'

'Of course. Now, these people I look after for you – all these truckers and dockers and wholesalers and salesmen – they are being paid by you, too. But supposing one of them fails to perform his tasks, what can we do then? We cannot sack him. We have no legal hold over him because his very usefulness to us is that he works for someone else. The only hold we have is what I call the *forceful suggestion*.'

Roderick flicked a quick look at Riccione and then looked away. 'I can guess what that little sugar-coated expression means,' he said dryly.

'Perhaps you can,' said Riccione, 'but you probably imagine torture and beating up and bricks thrown through the window at night. That is what most people outside of this business imagine. I had a very famous young movie star for dinner last week, and she persistently asked me to show her my revolver. Well, Mr Cornelius, I haven't owned a revolver since 1922.'

Celia said: 'Ricardo isn't a hoodlum, Roddy. He's not like Dutch Schultz or any of those.'

'That's right.' Riccione nodded. 'When my people apply forceful suggestion, they simply make a character evaluation of the transgressor in question, and they apply psychological pressure to his weakest point. If he's been doing badly at work, for instance, they will suggest that it will be much safer for the man's job security if his boss doesn't know just how bad he's been. If he has a sick relative in the South Bronx, we might suggest that life would be easier all round if this relative wasn't evicted. We rarely have to take these steps. We have found that the fear inside a man's mind is a far more potent weapon that a blackjack.'

Roderick licked his lips. 'The reports I read from you and your brother mentioned that four men had been killed in 1950 for holding back shipments of Haymann Drugs, which are ours, in favour of someone else's. They also mention Jimmy Hoffa, and a few other choice names. Now, did these men die for real, or did you just make a forceful suggestion that was more forceful than suggestive?'

For the first time, Ricardo Riccione removed his dark glasses. His eyes were wet and myopic, and he appeared to be staring at something that was hovering over Roderick's head, although Roderick was quite sure that he was really focusing straight at him.

Riccione said softly: 'I do not understand what you are trying to impute.'

Roderick said: 'Isn't it obvious? I'm putting it as plain as I can. I want to find out exactly what sins you've committed in my name, with my money, and I want to put a stop to it.'

Celia was about to say something, but Ricardo raised his hand to show her that he was fully in control of the situation and that she needn't take sides against Roderick just for the moment.

'You are a strange man, Mr Cornelius. For a businessman, you're really most unusual.'

'I happen to have morals, if that's what you're suggesting.'

'Oh, it is not so much that you have morals. All of us have morals, of one variety or another. It is just that you fail to perceive what morals really are.'

He restored his tiny dark glasses to his nose, and sat back to look at Roderick with disconcerting interest.

Roderick blustered: 'If you've got something to say in your own defence, you'd better say it. Otherwise, I think we can say that the whole Cornelius-Riccione arrangement is off. And I mean o-f-f.'

Ricardo laughed 'Why should I defend myself? This is what you fail to understand about morals. We are both in the same business, you and I. We are both in the business of making as much money as possible with the minimum amount of effort.

Quite often this means that we have to exert pressure on people, and sometimes it means that we have to kill them. Although you were evidently not aware of it, there were many times in the past nine years when you asked for things to be done that could only economically be achieved by violence or assassination. Those four men who died in 1950 died because you – *you*, personally – insisted that Haymann Drugs speed up their distribution in the Midwest. That was what you wanted done, and although we had been reasonably content to let the situation ride in the past, that was what we did.'

Roderick turned to Celia. 'What's he saying? You told me that all my instructions were vetted by David and you!'

'That's right, darling. In this case, we happened to agree with you. It was a good idea.'

'But, Christ, Celia, you knew that they'd have to—'

'Yes.'

Roderick stared at his wife, but in her ice-blue suit she was as composed and perfect as ever. The Madonna of the Dollars. He blinked, and there were drops of perspiration on his eyelashes. The salt of it stung his eyes. He reached over and picked up a glass of white wine and drank some. It was crisp and fruity, and probably cost eighty dollars a bottle, but he might just as well have been drinking water.

He said: 'I asked David Bookbinder how many people had died, and he wouldn't tell me.'

Ricardo Riccione shook his head. 'It is better that you don't know.'

'But what the hell am I going to do? What happens if the same situation comes up again?'

Riccione got up from his chair and came to sit on the balustrade right next to Roderick, and he laid his hand on Roderick's shoulder. Roderick glanced uncomfortably at the pale pink fingers, and wondered, not for the first time, why everybody talked down to him, as if they were party to some secret knowledge that he was incapable of understanding.

'Mr Cornelius,' explained Riccione gently, 'we are simply working in two different departments of the same store. You are the big chief upstairs, and I am running your dispatch department. I cannot work without you, but neither can you work without me If what I am doing is a crime, then what you are doing is also a crime, because you cannot survive unless I help you.'

What do you mean?' asked Roderick, trying to turn his head around. 'Are you trying to suggest that I'm a criminal?'

'I am just demonstrating the unalterable truth. You can certainly run your business any way you please. You can run it on Quaker lines if you wish. Some corporations do, although I would be interested to see how Quaker their tax returns are.

'You can be as upright and as decent as a saint, but if you are, you must be prepared to pay the price for it. You will be penally taxed by a revenue service that never gives a sucker an even break. You will be undercut and cheated by your competitors and your own dealers. Your trucks will mysteriously find themselves with flat tyres on crucial delivery dates. Your factories will burn down. Your goods will be stolen. Your books will be juggled. In fact' – and here Riccione leaned forward and almost whispered in Roderick's ear – 'you will be eaten alive.'

Roderick sat for a long, long time in silence. Ricardo Riccione went back to his own seat, tucked a napkin into his collar, and began to fork up salad, watching Roderick all the time. Celia started nibbling, too, and sipping wine, but she obviously didn't have much appetite.

Roderick sighed. Then he said: 'I came here today knowing that everything you've told me was true. Maybe I just didn't want it to be true. Maybe I had a dream.'

Riccione munched, and nodded. 'We all have dreams, Mr Cornelius. What we must *not* do is allow other people to prevent us from fulfilling them.'

Roderick kept his eyes on the ground. His annoyance had abated altogether, and now he felt nothing but depressed. Perhaps he had known all along that he could never extricate Cornelius Industries from their involvement with men like Riccione, but it was more than painful to face up to the reality of his own weakness. He finished his wine, and when he looked up, the servant was standing at his side to pour some more. He lifted his glass.

'I will tell you a last something,' said Riccione. 'It may sound grandiose to your ears, but it is quite true. There is not a single person living in this continent who is safe from us. That shows you how much power your money can buy, Mr Cornelius. We can exert pressure on anyone you like; or, if it is unfortunately necessary, kill anyone you like. And I mean *anyone*.'

Roderick gave Riccione a lengthy, assessing look. He said: 'I presume when you say *anyone* you're excluding the President.'

Riccione looked surprised. 'Of course not! Who knows, we may be called upon to remove a President one day. Not that there is any chance of a Democratic President for a few years yet. But, yes, it could happen, if enough men like yourself got together and decided they disliked the President enough to pay the sort of prices I would have to ask.'

Roderick grunted mirthlessly. 'And what's the asking price on a President?'

Ricardo Riccione swallowed wine and smiled. 'Ask me when the time comes, Mr Cornelius. I am sure we can work something out.'

Celia said brightly: 'Are you going to show Roddy your new roses?'

They walked around the gardens and the house until a gong summoned them for lunch. Riccione showed them his personal mutations of Peace, and a new rose that he was trying to grow in memory of his late brother, Giorgio. Giorgio had died of leukemia seven months ago, at the height of an investigation into his connections with the Justice Department. Ricardo sniffed the new rose sadly, and had to turn away for a while to blow his nose. Roderick looked at Celia impatiently during this small display of fraternal emotion, but Celia's expression was inscrutable.

The dining room was white, with a floor of polished red Mexican tiles, and an indoor fountain that bubbled and gurgled and made it necessary for Roderick to excuse himself from the table at least twice. The house was more like someplace in Italy or Los Angeles than New York State. Ricardo joked that if he had a mortar he could fire shells from his front steps and straight into the Rockefellers' $200,000 playhouse at Pocantico. 'And wouldn't that be a harsh reminder that crime is always at the rich man's door.'

Five servants brought them fresh crabmeat frosted with avocado; quails roasted in bourbon; stuffed flounder; quenelles of veal and rosemary with asparagus; and strawberries. Beside them, rose petals floated in gold finger bowls, and the reflected light from their glasses of Bollinger champagne wobbled in curved patterns on the high ceiling.

Roderick ate very little. He felt as if he were being initiated into criminal society without any consideration for his own feelings. But if Cornelius Industries were going to survive intact, what else could he possibly do? For the first time in his life, he began to understand the price of money, something which his father had known from the very beginning.

'Ricardo,' he said, as he laid down his gold fruit spoon, 'I want us to come to an understanding.'

'I am very pleased.' Ricardo beamed. 'Understandings are the stuff of happiness.'

'I want an understanding about murder. There's nothing very happy about that.'

'Murder? My dear Roderick.'

Roderick laid his crumpled napkin on the table. 'It's important, Ricardo. It's important to me, and it's important to the whole future of myself and my family and all the thousands of people who work for us. I want it clearly understood that nobody is to be murdered to implement any Cornelius policy.'

Ricardo pulled a thoughtful face.

Roderick went on: 'I also want it understood that if any forceful suggestion is going to be necessary, then I want to know about it in advance, and I want to know exactly what it's going to be.'

Celia's eyes went from Ricardo to Roderick and back again.

Ricardo smoothed down his silver pomaded hair with the flat of his hand and said: 'You must see that we are not exactly employer and employee. What I am trying to say is that I do not work for you in the sense that I am your hireling. Your business is in partnership with mine, and is inextricably linked with mine. Many of the trucks you use belong to me, and most of the wholesale outlets you utilize on the East Coast are completely under my influence, even when they are not actually mine.'

There was a silence. Ricardo smiled, almost shyly. Then he said: 'If I deem it necessary, for the good of our joint interests, to eliminate some persistent opposition, then I shall do so. You are in no position to protest.'

'But—'

Ricardo raised a hand. 'No buts, Roderick. You do business your way, and I will do business in my way.'

'You're making me – and Celia – and everybody at Cornelius Industries accessories before the fact. Do you realize that?'

'Of course. You are also accessories *after* the fact. You knew what David Bookbinder had been involved in, and yet you made sure that he was protected from arrest and scandal. Isn't that, ordinarily, a criminal action?'

'It's no use trying to blackmail me, Ricardo.'

'But of course it is. What else can you possibly do? Are you going to allow an industry the size of Cornelius Oil to collapse like a poorly cooked soufflé, just to salve your own conscience? They would put you in prison – not because you were involved in homicide, but because you renounced the capitalist way in favour of some namby-pamby social idealism. Anyway, you are not that sort of man at all. You are not a suicide.'

Roderick pushed away his plate ferociously. 'Dammit, Ricardo, I don't want any more people to die! I don't want to be tied up with murder and extortion!'

Ricardo began to lose his patience. He took off his little dark spectacles again, and his eyes, though myopic, were anything but kind. 'Now you're being ridiculous,' he snapped. 'You have been tied up with murder and extortion all your life. The whole of Cornelius Oil was founded on murder and extortion, just like every other so-called respectable big business in the United States.'

Roderick didn't answer. He didn't really have anything to say. He knew, to his own discredit, that his protests were as hollow as papier-mâché puppets. He was frightened by killing, and the criminal underworld unnerved him. But he also knew that the strength of spirit he would need to cast off Riccione and all his kind was beyond him. As Riccione had said, he was not a suicide.

He said at last: 'I think you must give me some time.'

'How much time?' asked Ricardo.

'A day or two. I need to turn this over in my mind.'

'Of course.'

Celia said: 'Don't worry, Ricardo. Roddy will come around, won't you, Roddy? He's not as impetuous as he first appears.'

Roderick shook his head. 'I just want to think, that's all.'

'Of course,' repeated Ricardo, like a psychiatrist telling his patient that *of course* there were vultures perching on the end of the couch.

After lunch Riccione showed them his business suite. It was an endless room of thick carpets and deep leather chairs, with paintings by Stubbs and Gainsborough along the walls, and

591

a group of Italian bronzes. Roderick was thoughtful and worried for the rest of their visit, and when a small Italian chauffeur brought their green-and-white car to the front of the house for them to leave, he said nothing at all to Ricardo Riccione except: 'Thank you.'

On their way back to New York, as they drove through the late dusty sunlight toward the shining spires of Manhattan, Celia said: 'Don't you think he's perfect?'

Roderick glanced at her. 'Perfect? You mean Riccione?'

A warm wind was blowing off the East River. They cruised southward down FDR Drive amid shoals of Kaiser Manhattans, Dodge Firedomes, and Checker cabs. Taxi fares were twenty cents for the first quarter-mile and five cents for every succeeding quarter-mile. The sky was very pale and high. Roderick said nothing more until they got back to Gramercy Park, but on that summer day in 1954 he felt quite sorely that he had lost something of himself, and when he went upstairs and saw all the files and papers that David Bookbinder had given him, he no longer felt inclined to open them, and he knew that he would probably leave them fading and undisturbed for the rest of his life.

There was a family barbecue at Hope and Edward's place on Long Island that weekend. Roderick hadn't seen Hope for weeks, and he was surprised how pale she looked, even though it was late summer. She wore a grey cotton dress that made her look greyer still. Edward was a little worried about her, but said that it was probably tiredness. They were due to fly to Europe in a week for a vacation in Venice, Florence, Switzerland, and the Rhineland.

Roderick and Celia brought Victor with them. Victor was eleven now, and Roderick didn't like him a great deal. He was a plump, precocious boy with a particularly irritating line in sneering, uninformed conversation. Roderick sometimes watched his son talking to friends, or playing tennis with his big flat feet and his big fat thighs, and he wondered sorrowfully if *he* looked like that to other people, or whether it was something that Victor had inherited from Celia's side of the family.

Freddie and Tess were playing with the new German rocking horses that Edward had bought them. Freddie was seven, and all arms and legs and gappy teeth. Tess was five, and losing her little-girl prettiness. Despite the big candy-pink bow in her hair, she looked exactly like Edward. The rocking horses were glossy and grey and almost life-size, and the children rocked endlessly backward and forward on the grass, while Victor stood a little way away and pretended that he didn't want a turn, because rocking horses were for kids.

John and Irene were supposed to have brought Ally up from Washington, but Hope had gotten the impression from Irene that they had quarrelled over something, and they had called at the last minute to cancel. None of the rest of the family minded all that much, because John had a talent for making them feel awkward. They sat around the lawn on white-painted benches, while the servants brought them tasty little hibachi snacks, and the birds warbled and rustled in the overhanging trees. It was the kind of hot summer day when you could lie back in a hammock, close your eyes, and the world would change around you without you even noticing.

Later, when it was cooler, Roderick took a walk with Hope around the grounds. Hope was smoking, and lighting one cigarette from the butt of the other.

They stopped at a small grove of trees where a stream ran down into a goldfish pool. The water was dark green, and the bright orange fish stirred through shafts of green sunlight. Water boatmen sculled their way across the pool's meniscus.

Hope sat down on a mossy stone.

Roderick said: 'You'll spoil your dress.'

Hope said: 'It doesn't matter.'

Roderick coughed. 'I don't like to seem nosy,' he said.

Hope looked at him and blew cigarette smoke into the shifting rails of sun.

'Well,' she said, 'you're my brother, after all.'

Roderick said: 'You don't seem happy.'

'Does it show that much?'

'Well . . . Celia noticed it.'

'Celia's very sharp. I mean, she's very perceptive.'

'I guess.'

Hope dipped the tip of her cigarette in the pool and it fizzled out. There were mauve smudges under her eyes as if she hadn't been sleeping well.

'It's not Edward, is it?' asked Roderick uncomfortably.

'Edward?'

'He's not making you unhappy or anything? I don't want to pry, but you know how it was . . . well, with Martin.'

Hope gave a wan smile. 'Yes, I know how it was with Martin.'

'I've never seen you like this. Are you ill?'

Hope said: 'It's not altogether Edward. I don't love Edward, you know. I never have. I suppose when I married him I was trying to find something that Martin could never give me. You know what they say. If you marry wrong once, you'll marry wrong twice. You should never marry anyone to correct the mistakes you made before. If it hadn't been for Lewis Bausor, you know, this never would have happened.'

'Lewis Bausor? Who the hell is Lewis Bausor?'

Hope smiled sadly and reflectively. 'He's the workingman getting his revenge on the rich. It's very ironic, really.'

'Hope, I don't understand a word you're saying.'

Hope took out another cigarette and lit it.

'It doesn't matter. It's just a silly idea of mine.'

'But what the hell is this all about? Did Lewis Bausor do something to you? Is he blackmailing you? Listen, if he's blackmailing you, I can . . .'

Roderick stopped in mid-sentence. He suddenly thought of Ricardo Riccione. *'We can exert pressure on anyone you like; or, if it is unfortunately necessary, kill anyone you like.'* He looked at Hope behind the shafts of sunlight as if she were a vision in a holy grotto. She didn't seem quite real anymore; as if part of her soul had already decided to fade into the ground.

There was a silence. Hope said: 'Lewis Bausor died years ago. What I did to Lewis Bausor led to Father sending me off to the Landseers'. That was all.'

Roderick said: 'You're ill, aren't you? There's something wrong.'

'Yes.'

'Don't you want to tell me what it is?'

Hope smoked and watched the insects on the pond. 'Can you face the truth?' she asked him.

He frowned.

'Well,' she said, 'the truth is that I have cancer. In four or five months from now, I shall be dead.'

Roderick couldn't believe what he was hearing. He reached out a hand and laid it on Hope's shoulder, but through the

594

grey cotton of her dress she seemed to be as unsubstantial as a vision wrought out of steam or clouds. '*Hope*,' he said with a croak in his voice.

She blew out some more smoke. 'I haven't told Edward yet. Edward thinks I'm just overworked or under the weather. I didn't want to tell him until we'd come back from our vacation. I guess I should, in a way, but then, I didn't want our last vacation together to turn into a wake.'

Roderick said: 'Are you sure?'

Hope looked up at him quizzically.

'Are you sure it's cancer?' asked Roderick. 'Have you been to a specialist? I mean, you could have radiation treatment.'

'I've been to eleven specialists,' answered Hope. 'And that includes Dr Ray Parkwin and Dr Kulpeper. I've been to London and I've been to Ontario. I'm afraid the answer is always the same. I have cancer of the liver that has advanced so far that it would be hopeless to try to eradicate it. It's painful now, but an operation would be even more painful, and it wouldn't do any good at all.'

Roderick stood there numbly. Then, quite unexpectedly, he found himself crying. He shook and trembled, and the tears rolled out of his eyes and almost blinded him.

'I can't understand it,' he sobbed. 'You must be wrong. They must have made a mistake. Surely they can do *something*?'

Hope lit another cigarette and smiled. 'No, Roddy, they can't. It's all over, and I just have to accept it. I'm doing my best to enjoy what's left.'

'Oh, Hope, I'm so sorry. Hope, I can't tell you.'

She looked at him with a gentle, sisterly expression. 'You don't have to be sorry, Roddy. Out of everybody, you've always been the kindest. I mean that.'

He took out his pocket handkerchief and blew his nose.

'I've always been the softest. That's what you mean.'

'Well,' she said quietly, 'is that always such a bad thing? Softness?'

He mopped his eyes and then blew his nose one more time. He still had a lump in his throat, but Hope's total calmness was helping him to pull himself together. 'I don't know,' he said unhappily. 'I guess it is when being soft means that people might die.'

'You mean me? Don't be so silly.'

595

'No, no. I didn't mean you. I mean the whole Cornelius thing with gangsters and Mafia and people like that.'

Hope raised her eyebrows. 'So,' she said, 'you've found out about it. I was wondering when you would.'

'You knew too?'

'Not for sure. But Edward always suspected it. He knows some people in Arizona.'

Roderick said: 'David Bookbinder told me. It was David's connections with some murder in 1927 that forced him to leave. We had a lot of flak from the Justice Department, and they said they'd only cover up if David quit. I guess I was pretty naïve, but I didn't even suspect. I just gave out the orders and didn't question how they were carried out. Celia knew. I'm not sure how I feel about that even now. But I suppose she was only trying to protect me. The less I knew, the less likely I was to jeopardize the family. I guess I can accept that. Father knew what he was doing. But I still find it hard to swallow this whole thing of killing people, actually killing people, for the sake of business. I still find that very hard to swallow.'

Hope stood up and walked around the pool. He followed her, and together they made their way out of the grove of trees, up a small slope, and across a long meadow with a view of the silvery-grey strip of Moriches Bay and the distant dark Atlantic. The air was fresher here, and Hope stood with her face to the wind, her hair blown back and her eyes narrowed.

'What are you going to do?' she asked him.

He kicked at a divot of grass. 'I've been thinking. Celia and I went to talk to Ricardo Riccione the other day, out at Thornwood.'

'Riccione? Is he involved?'

'He's a mainstay, on the East Coast at least. But Albert Hagermeyer and Frank Gizzi are tied up in the whole thing too. I don't know how to tell you. The whole of Cornelius Industries has been run by racketeers for twenty years.'

'And they've killed people? People who've gotten in the way?'

Roderick nodded.

They walked in silence down through long swaying grass and flickering flowers There was a smell of the sea in the air, and for the first time Hope tossed away her cigarette and breathed in as if she really enjoyed it.

'Well,' she said, 'whatever you decide to do, you can always think that all those poor people who died got themselves one of us in return.'

Roderick stared at her in disbelief. 'You don't mean that.'

'Yes, I do. Do you really think our family could have expected to survive with impunity after everything we've done? One of us had to lay down her life as a punishment. And as it turned out, it was me.'

'Hope, you're talking crazy.'

She turned on him. Her face was streaked with windblown tears. 'I wish to hell I was. Don't you believe in fate? Don't you believe in the meek inheriting the earth, and the wicked being punished in hell? Or have you forgotten yourself as much as Father did, and David Bookbinder, and Celia? Oh, Roderick, we deserved to be punished, and we were!'

Roderick started weeping again, too. The two of them stood in the meadow, and Roderick held his sister close, his thirty-five-year-old dying sister, and he realized as he held her just how little he knew her.

'Hope,' he said, as he stroked her hair. 'What can I do to help you?'

She looked up at him. Her eyelashes were stuck with tears. She shook her head and said: 'Nothing, darling, nothing.'

They stayed that way for a long time, but then Roderick heard a rustling in the grass. and when he looked up, he saw Victor.

'Victor?'

The boy looked guilty. Roderick suddenly realized he must have been hiding in the long grass not far away. He gave Hope's hand a quick squeeze, and then walked over to where Victor was standing. Victor wouldn't look at him but put his hands in his pockets and tried to whistle.

'Why are you whistling?' asked Roderick.

'I don't know, sir.'

'You don't know?'

'No, sir.'

'Were you hiding in the long grass?'

'Me, sir?'

'Well, who else? Who do you think I meant?'

'I don't know, sir.'

Roderick snapped: 'Don't you know anything? And take your hands out of your pockets when you talk to me'

Victor did so, and stood there, plump and sulky He was

about to go to school in England, and he knew that there he would be able to do whatever he liked; because he was American, because he was rich, and because his stupid father wouldn't keep nagging him. He thought of his father as a kind of tiresome pet who never seemed to grow up, but which one keeps around out of a sense of duty. Even at the age of eleven, Victor had a sense of duty.

'I want to know what you heard,' demanded Roderick.

'Heard, sir?'

'Yes, heard, dammit! How many times have I told you not to eavesdrop? You've got ears like a damned rabbit! You're a damned rabbit, do you understand?'

Hope came over and touched Roddy's arm.

'It's all right, Roddy. Victor won't tell.'

Victor turned to her with his big crimson face and said: 'I will tell, so there.'

'Tell what?' Roderick wanted to know.

Victor was silent.

'Tell what?' bellowed Roderick.

'I'll tell Uncle Edward that Auntie Hope is going to die, and then you'll both be sorry!'

Roderick smacked Victor's face with a sweep of his arm that knocked the boy flat on his back on the grass. When he sat up again, Victor had a nosebleed, and he was gasping for breath.

'You vermin!' yelled Roderick. 'Don't you dare talk to me like that! You little rat! You disgusting little vermin!'

He pulled Victor onto his feet again by his collar. The boy was blubbering and trying to catch the blood from his nose in his hand.

'You will apologize to Aunt Hope!' Roderick shouted. He was almost screaming with rage. 'Go on – apologize!'

Victor stood there for a moment sobbing, but then he pulled himself free from Roderick's grip and ran back across the meadow and disappeared into the grove of trees in the direction of the house. Roderick watched him go, and then, panting, he sank to his knees and squatted down on the grass. Hope stayed beside him, her hand lightly touching his shoulder.

'I sometimes wonder how I ever conceived such a repulsive child,' Roderick said in a hoarse voice. 'There are times when I could drown him.'

'The child is the mirror of its parents,' said Hope, not unkindly, but pointedly.

Roderick shook his head. 'Well, he may be a mirror of Celia but I don't see what *I've* done to make him like that. I'll tell you something, Hope. When Cornelius Oil passes to Victor, it will be as crooked, and as devious, and as twisted as it was under David Bookbinder.'

Hope was silent for a while. Then she said: 'I expect you're right. It's sad, isn't it? But in some ways I've always preferred an out-and-out crook to a hypocritical angel, haven't you?'

She bent over and kissed the top of his head. Then she walked away in the direction where Victor had gone. Roderick stayed there for two or three minutes, but soon moved when he realized he was kneeling on an ant's nest.

1967

HELICOPTER CRASH KILLS CORNELIUS HEIR

A private helicopter carrying Cornelius Armaments tycoon John Cornelius, younger son of the late oil billionaire Johann Cornelius, crashed at Casper, Wyoming, late last night, after reportedly striking power lines. Cornelius and his three companions, one of whom remains unidentified, were killed instantly.

—The New York Times,
March, 1967

He was standing on the corner of Howard Street in a beautifully pressed lightweight suit of pale blue nylon jersey. He was tall, and slim for his age, and his grey hair was cut as crisp as a carpet. He was smoking a cigarette in an amber holder, and his hand was resting in an unconsciously self-revealing pose on his hip.

He was feeling in one of his beatific moods today. It was one of those days in San Francisco when the morning sun has a golden haze to it, as if it's shining through milky glass, and the city becomes strangely transfigured, like a ship of carefree friends floating off into the foggy Pacific.

He was pleased about his newly acquired house, a Gothic-style mansion off Mission, which he was having restored and redecorated. He was pleased about the outcome of his latest and longest lawsuit, in which he had defended the Sausalito Artists' Workshop after an obscenity bust at their last exhibition. But perhaps he was mostly pleased that he was meeting Irene's daughter, Ally, after so many months. The older members of the Cornelius family had been uncomfortably diffident about him for years, but it seemed that the younger generation were far more forgiving.

He recognized Ally from a long way off, through the colourful crowds on the sidewalk. She was walking toward him with her Indian-braid bag slung over her shoulder, and the fringe of her poncho swinging, and as she reached the opposite corner of the street, she had to screw up her eyes, because the light was so bright and diffuse and photographic.

A friend of his had called Ally the Cornflower Kid. He could see what his friend had meant. She looked clean and precious and shining. She had straight blonde hair, a pretty, almost Victorian face, and sky-coloured eyes that could have been cold if they hadn't been so expressive and alive. She wore a poncho that looked fresh and clean, and well-fitting jeans that were bleached and blotchy but quite new. On her feet were

Moroccan-leather sandals, all thongs and straps, with little silver bells on.

He raised his arm and waved to her. She waved back, and came running through the traffic. She took his hand in both of hers, and held it, and said: 'Look at you. Just look at you.'

He pretended to be put out. He pulled a face, and looked down at his immaculate suit, and said: 'What's wrong? Did I leave my fly open?'

Ally laughed, and squeezed his hand, and kissed his cheek. 'I can see why Mother disapproves of you,' she said, linking arms. 'In her book, flies are those things that buzz around horses' ears.'

He smiled. 'I promise you, my darling, I have never let *my* flies buzz around *any* horse's ears. But that's Irene all over. A charming lady, Irene, but very literal. Back Bay, Boston, all over.'

'You haven't changed a bit,' said Ally, almost dancing beside him as they walked along Howard to Fourth. 'You don't even look older.'

'I wish Douglas agreed.'

'Are you still with Douglas? I used to adore Douglas when I was a little girl. Did you know that Douglas can cut out pieces of newspaper and make those lines of dolls, all strung together?'

He raised his eyes upward in mock exasperation. 'Don't I, just. It's the only intelligent human response that anybody has ever been able to get out of him.'

'Are you happy, still?' she asked.

He looked down at her, and patted her hand in an oddly fatherly way.

'Yes,' he said, 'I'm happy. I'm doing what I want to do, the work I like, and I'm doing it with all the people I like. That, to me, is very close to paradise.'

She brushed back her long blonde hair. 'I'm glad,' she said in a soft voice. 'I just wish I could say the same.'

He nodded. 'It's going to take some time, isn't it, getting used to the fact that he's not around anymore.'

'It was all so silly. I can't bear it, thinking he died in such a silly way.'

'Nobody's death is silly,' he told her Especially not your father's. He was doing what he enjoyed doing, and apart from that, he died honest. He always held out for what he believed

604

'I don't think Mother always thought so.'

They stopped at the kerb, waiting for the walk signal. Beside them, a black-haired girl in a purple T-shirt was standing with a transistor pressed against her ear, listening to the distorted tinny sounds of 'She Loves You'. He said: 'You have to make some allowances for Irene. I think she tries her best to cope with being a Cornelius, but I don't think she always manages.'

Ally's eyes dropped. 'I guess that's right. She's gone off to Europe now, with her cousin, to mourn. That's what she says, anyway. If you ask me, she's gone in search of some ravishing Italian count, now she's free.'

He said: 'You mustn't be cynical. Whether she really loved your father or not, that wasn't her fault, any more than his. None of us are free to choose the people we love.'

He pointed toward an office building a few hundred feet farther up the street. It was a shabby eight-storey building with peeling pink paint and faded 1930's embellishments around the windows. 'I'm on the sixth,' he told her. 'Let's go up.'

As they stepped into the Lysol-smelling shade of the lobby, she saw his name neatly lettered on the office directory, between *Farrer Yorty (Holdings)* and *Fogarty Waste Oil*. It read *Field, Randolph K., Attorney-at-Law*.

His office was neat and fussy, with crowds of potted plants on the windowsill, shelves of leather-bound law books, and a reproduction of Seurat's grey, impressionistic view of the sea off Gravelines. He sat down at his tidy, leather-topped desk and opened up a silver cigarette box.

'Smoke?'

Ally took one, and he leaned forward to light it for her. She perched herself on the edge of his desk, one leg swinging, and blew out smoke. He sat back and watched her for a while as he fitted a new crystal filter into his cigarette holder.

'I guess nobody else could tell you this and get away with it, but you're looking prettier and sexier every time I see you,' said Randy.

She turned to him and smiled. 'Why, thank you, kind attorney.'

'I guess you didn't just call me up for the compliments,

though,' he said, fitting a cigarette into his holder and reaching for his matches.

'I wish I had, Randy. I wish I could say that I remembered how long it was since we last got together, and called you up because I wanted to see you.'

'You don't have to feel guilty,' he said, leaning back in his chair and crossing his hands over his trim stomach.

'I do. I can't help it.'

'But I'm an attorney. If it's an attorney you need, then I'd be very offended if you didn't come to me.'

She glanced at him with affection. 'You always know the right things to say.'

'That's what makes me a *brilliant* attorney.'

She stood up and walked across the quiet carpet to look at his painting of Gravelines. It was a sad, misty picture; the English Channel on a cold day of watery sunlight and edgy wind. She said softly: 'It's a friend of mine, a boy. I've only known him a couple of weeks, but we've had such an incredible time together. He's in terrible trouble. I just didn't know what to do.'

'Police trouble?' asked Randy. He took a sharp HB pencil out a blue glass jar and opened up the first page of a fresh notepad.

Ally nodded. 'They stopped him three days ago on Market. They searched him, and found a lid. He's been locked up in a cell ever since, and the public defender who came to see him was just awful. He's already been in prison once, for six months, and he thinks they're out to get him this time. You know, really put him away. I'm so frightened, Randy.'

Randy wrote a few careful notes, while Ally watched him seriously. He still looked like his father, except for a softer and more sensitive mouth, but he had a tired gentleness about him that Jack Field had never had. Jack Field had died in 1956 after three years of kidney failure; and Ellie, grieving, had died the following year. Ally, as a girl of eleven, had first met Randy at Jack's funeral, and she was so struck by the way that he had stood on his own in the dry brown grass of the cemetery, carefully avoided by both Cornelius relatives and Field relatives, that she had walked over and introduced herself, helplessly watched by a wincing Irene. From that day, Randy and Ally had been irregular but close friends, in the way that an uncle is close friends with his niece, and she had often written to him, telling him what she was doing at Vassar, and he had sent her colourful postcards of San Francisco in return.

Now, she was older, and she had decided on the course that her life was going to take; but that eleven-year-old girl in the expensive summer coat who had befriended a middle-aged man who was burying his father in ostracized silence was still within her.

Randy looked up from his notepad. He said, gently: 'Can you tell me the boy's name?'

'He calls himself Destry. Everybody does. I don't know whether that's his real name or not.'

'Does he know who you are?'

Ally shook her head. 'I'm incognito.'

'Incognito? What for?'

She lowered her eyes. 'Do I have to tell you? I mean, can't you just fix Destry's bail?'

Randy put down his pencil. He looked amused, but concerned as well. 'My darling, you don't have to tell me anything. I'm just interested in everything you do, that's all. You're my favourite Cornelius, remember. Don't tell me you're thinking of doing a Rockefeller, and opting out of your riches.'

'Would that be so terrible?'

'I don't know. What do you feel?'

She tapped her foot against the side of his desk, and the silver bells on her sandals softly jangled.

'I don't know,' she said. 'But I've done it. That's the reason I'm here, in San Francisco. I'm not just here visiting. I'm here for keeps.'

Randy sat up straight. 'You mean you're serious? You've really given it all up?'

'I haven't given it up. I've just left it behind,' she said, folding her arms under her breasts. Her blue eyes were empty of regret, but still sad, and Randy couldn't help noticing. He had given up himself one of the most treasured experiences of his whole life, a successful law partnership with his father, and he knew what it was to leave your family and your friends and your very self behind you.

'Do you want to talk about it?' he asked her.

She shook her head. 'Not now.'

'Well, would you like to have dinner tomorrow, and talk

607

about it then? Come round to my house. It's a real Gothic pile. I could cook you some tamale pie. It's my speciality.'

'I'd like that.'

There was quiet between them, and down in the street they could hear the wailing of sirens. Then Randy said: 'If you've really left it all behind, then I think the best thing you can do is stay right out of Destry's problems.'

'You mean you won't help him?'

'Of course I'll help him. But without involving you. All we need is for some eagle-eyed crime reporter to spot you in court, and your whole new life is going to be blown wide open. Apart from the distress that *you'll* suffer, my darling, it'll be bad news for the whole Cornelius family, and I do think you have to consider their feelings, too.'

She twisted the ends of her hair around her fingers. 'I suppose so,' she said reluctantly.

Randy stood up and came around his desk to sit down beside her. He asked her softly: 'Does your family know where you are?'

'Not exactly. Mother doesn't care anyway. She's too busy spending her inheritance on Flemish painting and feeling pleased that she kept Mara Malinsky's family out of the will.'

'Come on, Ally. You love your mother, don't you?'

Ally shrugged. 'I guess so. I just don't think she ever got over Dad not loving her. After she found out about Mara, she didn't seem to want to love anyone or *be* loved by anyone. That's what grandmother told me, anyway.'

'Ally,' said Randy comfortingly, and he put his arm around her thin shoulders. She could feel the tears starting, even though she didn't want them to. She hadn't imagined how beautiful it could be, to be anonymous and free; to meet people and talk to them on doorsteps and beaches without impatient chauffeurs waiting in the middle distance, or maids hovering with clean towels and fresh makeup; to stay up all night listening to records and drinking cheap wine and listening to the delighted squeals and squeaks of people making love, without parents or butlers or security staff eavesdropping at the doors Her first month in San Francisco had been hard, and sometimes painfully lonesome; but the very hardness of it, the mundane daily tasks of taking her clothes to the Laundromat, of wandering around supermarkets with a wire basket looking for cans of tomatoes and detergent, of making her bed and ironing her jeans, had for Ally a magical pleasure that she had never experienced before, because she had never touched a washing machine in her life, nor stepped into a supermarket. Going out and gathering the basic ingredients for a meal had, for her, been some strange brightly coloured ritual, distinguished by *oohs* and *aahs* of suprise and wonder, that she had seen only in television commercials. It was mainly Irene's fault. Constantly and neurotically aware that Clara had been killed by a construction worker, Irene believed unshakeably that the poor were conspiring against the rich, and she had made sure that Ally had grown up in hot drawing rooms and closeted limousines, served by carefully selected maids and valets and schooled by private tutors.

It was this claustrophobic existence, far more than her third share in the Cornelius oil and airplane fortune, that Ally had wanted to escape. All those stiff-necked dinners and social quadrilles; all those airless boardrooms and soundless apartments; all the suffocating, coddled attention of being rich. She had left because she desperately needed to breathe some real, smoggy, fresh, unfiltered air.

She had left, too, because her father had been instantly killed in March in a helicopter accident at Casper, Wyoming; and when that happened the Cornelius family had breathed a sigh that could have been sorrow but sounded suspiciously like relief. Cornelius Armaments, his personal division of Cornelius Industries, had been absorbed back into the family amoeba, and Irene, who had been living with him for the past twenty years in a hostile tizzy of doubts and hysteria and endless surrealistic fears, had at last been granted the release which she had pined for so long, and yet had longed for so little. Fulfilled in her role as a martyr, she had taken herself off to Europe to get over the mitigated tragedy of his passing, and to be photographed in black hats with veils on the Appian Way by Norman Parkinson.

For Ally, the tragedy had meant something quite different. Ally and her father had had something special between them; something which was encapsulated for Ally for all time in a memory of the hard winter of 1950, when he had taken her out secretly, buttoning her leggings himself with his stubby fatherly hands, doing up her coat, and carefully brushing her hair, and then slipping out on exaggerated tippy-toes by the servants' door, so that they could run with frosty breath to the pond out by the highway and skate, bumping and jostling with ordinary folk in cheap coats and woollen mufflers, and then sitting on a park bench afterward eating hot chestnuts from a paper poke, while a man in a frayed overcoat patted his own skinny daughter's head and told John Cornelius that if *he* had a million dollars, he'd buy himself a hog-raising business, and that was the way to make money, and John Cornelius, net worth 150 million dollars, had nodded and listened with an expression on his face that Ally had never once seen on any other Cornelius face, and which she realized years later was respect.

Now, in 1967, in San Francisco, she was trying to find that expression again, so that she could wear it on her own face. Being nothing more than herself, renouncing her money and her connections, was essential to her quest.

Randy took out a pristine white handkerchief and gave it to Ally to wipe her eyes. 'Would you like some coffee?' he asked her.

Ally nodded.

'Do you want to tell me some more about this boy? Destry?'

Ally blew her nose, and then shrugged. 'There's not much to tell. I met him at the Pizza Kingdom, of all places. I made such a mess of my Mexican omelette one night that I went out to buy some fast food instead. And there he was, standing in line. He's young, and he's really good-looking. Kind of thin, you know, with one of those faces like a tragic Norse god. Curly hair. Brown. Really wiry. What can I say? I almost fell in love with him at first sight.'

Randy gave a small, private smile. '*That* doesn't surprise me.'

Ally took out another cigarette and lit it. 'We got talking,' she said, 'and then we shared a pepperoni pizza.'

'Greater romances have sprung up around lesser things,' said Randy poetically.

'Randy, if any romance has ever been greater than this one, it certainly wasn't one of mine,' Ally told him. 'I mean, we hit it off together right from the start. He *values* things, you know? He has a box made out of tiny seashells that somebody gave him ir prison and he really takes care of this box. I can see him respect his belongings like that, and then I remember some of the boys that Mother tried to get me hitched up to, and you're not talking about the same kind of human being.'

Randy's intercom buzzed, and he asked his secretary for two cups of black coffee. Then he leaned forward thoughtfully and said: 'I have to ask you this. It's not squealing, or anything like that. But I have to know if you were aware of his possession of drugs.'

'Of course I was. We smoke a couple of joints every evening. More, if there's a party.'

'Did he actually buy and sell drugs, or was everything he got hold of kept for his own consumption?'

Ally brushed back her hair. 'He used to deal, in a kind of amateur way. Mainly to friends. Grass, hashish, speed, that kind of thing. But I don't think he does it now. He's not a *criminal*, Randy, any more than ten thousand other people out there are criminals.'

'Have they charged him?'

'I guess so.'

'Do you know for sure? If they haven't, we can have him out of there in two minutes flat. *Habeas Corpus*.'

'Well, I don't know. You'd have to check with the police.'

Randy scribbled a note. 'I intend to do that.'

Ally laid her hand on the desk. Randy glanced up and saw it resting there – five short fingernails, unlike any other Cornelius fingernails, and three Indian silver rings.

'Randy . . .' said Ally.

There was a pause. Randy was pretty sure what Ally was going to say. He found himself hoping, really hoping, that it was true.

'I love him, Randy. He's the best thing that ever happened to me. Please help him, won't you?'

Randy reached across his desk, and took her hand, and nodded. 'I'll get right on it,' he told her warmly. 'Perry Mason won't have nothing on me. I promise.'

She went reluctantly back to her apartment on Brannan Street to wait for news. Randy was understanding, consoling, but firm. Until Destry was out of jail and onto the streets, he didn't want Ally anywhere near. If the newspapers got wind that a Cornelius heiress was trying to rescue her hippie lover from prison, a simple matter of arranging bail would turn into a nightmare of television cameras, reporters, crowds, and public inquiries. Even when Ally insisted she could face up to anything, Randy still ushered her out of his office, kissed her forehead, and told her to go.

'Remember what you've decided to be,' he told her gently. 'If you've given up the Cornelius family, then you've given up all your Cornelius influence, too. You can't have it both ways. Not if you want to stay sane.'

She walked slowly up the narrow, uncarpeted stairs of the old rundown three-storey house where she lived. Her own apartment was on the top landing. As she took out her key, she looked out of the smeary window at the buildings and rooftops outside, and at the high stately clouds that sailed in from the ocean.

She opened the door into her bed-living room and slung her braid bag down on the floor. The room smelled of waxed pine and coffee. There was a high brass bed with appalling springs and a patchwork cover, a marble-topped washstand with a blotchy mirror, and a sadly collapsed settee. On the walls were dozens of psychedelic posters for the Grateful Dead and Bob Dylan and Jefferson Airplane, and in the thick of those posters, poignantly small amid the golds and greens and the luminous pinks, was pinned a black-and-white Polaroid of a thin-faced young man with curly hair and a frown.

She walked through into the kitchen and put the chipped enamel pot on the gas stove for coffee. The sun was beaming through the thin flowery-patterned drapes, and the kitchen was lazily warm. There were jars of wooden spoons and butter moulds, flaky strings of garlic, colanders and spice jars, and three old-fashioned copper saucepans that she'd picked up at a garage sale in Mill Valley. She sat down at the rough-scrubbed wooden table and took off her poncho. She shook out her last cigarette.

She was only beginning to realize how difficult it had been to ask Randy for help. It was something that had required more strength than she could have imagined possible. As Ally Cornelius, she could have spoken to any heavyweight West Coast lawyer she liked, and had Destry out in half hour by sheer legal and political bludgeoning.

The coffee began to bubble and she turned down the gas. There was a knock at her door, and she went to answer it. It was Galina, the Czech girl who rented the room across the landing. Galina took Ally for what she said she was, and never questioned her unnerving innocence about pressing her clothes shopping for food, or cooking even the most rudimentary meals From the day she was seventeen, when Irene had first allowed her to wear cosmetics, up until the week she booked her flight to freedom in San Francisco, Ally had never made up her own face. After she'd appeared four or five times with shakily drawn eye pencil and smudged lips, it was Galina who had patiently showed her how to do it.

'Any news of Destry?' asked Galina.

Ally shook her head. 'I haven't heard yet. I went to see the lawyer this morning, and he said the best thing I could do was to stay home and wait.'

'*Wait*? Did Lenin wait?'

'I don't know,' Ally confessed. 'Did he?'

'I don't know, either. You'll never meet a Czech who knows anything about Lenin.'

Ally smiled. 'You'd better come in and have some coffee. I hate to talk in doorways.'

Galina came in.

'Does he think he's going to get Destry out, this lawyer?' she asked, pulling out a kitchen chair and sitting down with her legs crossed like a cossack.

'He's ninety percent sure. It's a pretty minor kind of a bust, and he doesn't even know if they've booked him. He's down there now, trying to fix bail.'

Galina took out a cigarette and lit it by striking a match against the sole of her boot. She tossed the pack across to Ally.

'These narcs are unbelievable. They're picking up kids with half an ounce of grass, and all the time there are guys selling horse on the street corners like it was sticks of rock candy.'

Ally took down two pottery mugs and poured out coffee. The sun had gone in now, and it was oddly dark.

'I've been feeling so helpless,' she said quietly.

Galina shrugged. 'That's the way the fuzz want you to feel. That's the way the whole of straight-up America wants you to feel.'

'It just seems so unfair. If you knew what went on when some of these big corporations . . .'

She stopped herself. Galina looked up at her.

'When some of these big corporations what?' asked Galina.

Ally looked away. 'Well, who knows for sure? But I guess there are people stealing a hell of a lot more money and doing

613

a hell of a lot more harm in the name of legitimate business than there are on the streets.'

'Well, right.'

Ally lit her cigarette and took two or three long, steadying drags before she spoke again.

'I know that Destry's been in prison before,' she said in a soft voice. 'But he said he was straight. He said he wanted to stay straight. I mean, where's the harm in smoking grass? He wasn't selling it. He just wanted to feel good, and do good, and be good. But just because they remembered his face, they busted him. It seems insane. It seems like they actually want to drag people down.'

Galina sipped her coffee. She grimaced.

'What did you make this with? Ground tarpaper?'

'I'm sorry. I've got some cream here, if you want it.'

Galina poured half a carton of cream into her mug, and two spoonfuls of brown sugar, and stirred it vigorously.

'At least it'll taste like tarpaper with cream and sugar.'

Ally said: 'It's really thrown me off, this bust. It was so beautiful this last week, Destry and me. It was only Wednesday we went down to the ocean. We spent the whole day swimming like a couple of kids. I can't tell you. He's so . . . *natural*. He doesn't demand anything. He doesn't keep laying some heavy number on you. He just sits there and smiles and makes you feel good.'

Galina nodded. 'I know. It's hard. But if this lawyer's any use, he'll have him out in a couple hours.'

'Oh, God. I hope so.'

Galina watched Ally for a while, smoking, and then she said: 'Did you ever get involved with someone as much as this before? A boy?'

Ally cast her eyes down, and picked at her nails.

'Just a few. Not like Destry.'

'That goes without saying. There aren't any like Destry.'

Ally glanced up. 'They were all boys my mother wanted me to marry. Short hair and tapered pants. If they didn't look like Alfred E. Neuman, they had bad breath and played golf.'

Galina pulled an understanding smile. 'Six kids and a Country Squire before you could say "suburb". I know the score. My mother was a little crazier than that, but believe me, it was equally urrgh. More like a goddamned nightmare.'

614

The telephone rang out in the hall. Ally jumped nervously, and then put down her coffee mug and ran out to answer it.

'Well?' said Galina when she came back.

'Wrong number. Guy wanted the Imperial Dragon Restaurant.'

Galina sniffed. 'I don't recommend he comes here, unless your chow mein's improved.'

Ally sat down again and held her mug cupped in the palms of her hands. She was silent for a while, and then she said: 'Galina?'

'Umh-humh?'

'What's going to happen when . . . well, if . . . ?'

'When, if, what?'

'Well, what happens if Destry and I stay together for a long time? What happens then?'

Galina frowned. 'What do you mean, what happens then? What do you think happens then?'

Ally bit her knuckle uncertainly. 'It's just that . . . well, what happens if I want to get married?'

'Married?' asked Galina, surprised. 'You've only known the poor guy a couple of weeks, and apart from that, he's still locked up in the slammer.'

'I know. I know that. But I can't help thinking about it.'

Galina crushed out her cigarette. 'I don't understand you. I mean . . . why do you feel the need? You can live together for as long as you like, no complications, you're both free.'

She pulled her chair in closer to the table and leaned forward confidentially. 'Look,' she said, 'I know that the whole parent-society bit still weighs down on you. It does that to everybody when they first leave home. You feel guilty because you rejected what your parents have got, you feel guilty because you disobeyed them, you feel guilty because you hurt them. But you got *free*, and that's what's really important. Don't you think that? You did actually get free. And no matter what guilt you feel, what hang-ups you have, you owe it to yourself, and to Destry, and to everybody your own age who feels shut up and trapped and depressed, you owe it to them to stay loose. I mean, what are you really leaving behind? A small house in New Jersey, a family car, church on Sundays, boys who look like Alfred E. Neuman, and twenty dollars a week allowance. It's not exactly paradise, is it?'

Ally thought for a while about what she had really left

615

behind. Houses like vast châteaux, fleets of glossy limousines, parties and dances and banquets, and glib boyfriends drawn from the most eligible ranks of Harvard and Yale. She whispered: 'Yes.'

They stayed together, Galina and Ally, while the day drew on. They smoked a joint, and played the new Beatles album over and over, and once or twice friends dropped by to ask how Destry was. The phone remained silent.

At around three, they heard footsteps on the stairs outside, and a sharp knock. Ally went to the door, her head light with pot, humming 'Strawberry Fields Forever', and opened it. There, on the landing, in a black summer overcoat and black hat, in a strange and striking replay of another time, another era, when someone else had arrived at a door in black, and irrevocably disturbed the life of another Cornelius, stood Victor.

Ally said: '*Victor*? Is that you?'

Victor planted one black glossy foot across the threshold. 'Well,' he said loudly with a big pink grin, 'it looks like we've tracked down our dropout at last.'

Ally retreated as Victor came into the room. He smelled strongly of 4711 cologne. She hadn't seen him for six months, but he didn't change. He was *overinflated* rather than heavily built, swollen with wealth and drink, and there was an orchid pinned to his lapel. He himself was so bulbous and big, and the orchid was so delicate, that it looked as if someone had pinned it on him for a joke. He walked uninvited into the kitchen, red-faced and perspiring, and dabbed at his face with a white handkerchief. Galina stared first at him, and then Ally, with her cigarette dangling from her lower lip in complete surprise.

'Who's this?' she wanted to know. 'Mr Magoo?'

Ally was white. She demanded: 'What do you want? How did you find me?'

But Victor was fatly unabashed, and he pulled out one of the kitchen chairs and sat himself down. One of his pants legs was pulled up, revealing a pale chubby calf and black silk socks. He said: 'Aren't you going to introduce me?'

Ally felt her whole life sinking away like water down a washbasin. If there had been some way to vaporize Victor where he sat, melt him away like a carton of butter on a hot day, she would have given six months of her life to have it.

The past, fat-bottomed and overbearing, had suddenly come and sat itself down on the rare and delicate future.

Galina raised her eyebrows.

'I'm Galina,' she said, sticking out a hand. 'I'm Czechoslovakian.'

'Pleased to know you,' said Victor. 'They make some pretty good ball bearings in Czechoslovakia.'

'Oh, I don't come from there. I come from De Kalb, Illinois.'

Victor looked a little confused. 'De Kalb? Can't say that I know it.'

'Really?' inquired Galina. 'It's the seat of Northern Illinois U, among other delights too numerous to mention.'

Victor glanced up at Ally. 'I think she's putting me on,' he said with a knowing smile. 'De Kalb, Illinois? That's rich.'

Galina was about to say something, but then she sat up straight and shook her head. She could hardly belive that this apparition from Wall Street, with its short prickly Eisenhower-generation haircut and its excruciatingly narrow lapels, was actually living and breathing. She stared at Ally, then back to Victor, as if she was trying to grasp how and why Ally could possibly be involved with such a waxwork.

Ally said: 'Is it something important? Well, it must be, mustn't it, if you have to come pushing right into my life like this.'

Victor reached into his inside pocket and took out a gold-and-alligator cheroot case. 'Oh, sure, it's important. And I have to tell you that it was the devil's own job to find you.'

'Then you were suited to it,' said Ally coldly, and went to stand by the window with her arms folded and her face hard with disappointment and anger. She felt used and unpleasant, as if her hair was dirty.

Victor lit a cheroot and puffed out blue smoke. He said to Galina, with an intimate wink: 'Mother doesn't like these, you know. But since we're going hippie . . .'

Galina looked amazed. 'Oh, sure,' she said, unsettled.

Ally didn't turn around from the window. She said: 'I left a box number. Why didn't you write? You didn't have to track me down.'

'Well, we do like to keep tabs on the family,' said Victor. 'It's just a question of insurance.'

'Insurance?' asked Galina.

Victor nodded 'That's right. The insurance people get a

little edgy if anyone of us drops out of sight altogether. So does the stock market, of course. And understandably. There's a great deal of money at stake.'

Galina smiled without humour. She glanced at Ally again, but Ally was keeping her head turned away, wishing that Victor would say what he had to say and disappear.

'I kind of guessed why you left,' said Victor, turning to Ally. 'I mean, I can sympathize. But I think you have to understand that you can't dump all of your responsibilities overnight like that, no matter how much you feel you want to be free. Your name's on a whole lot of stock, Ally, and we can't transfer that stock or convert it or do a single goddamned thing with it unless we have your signature.'

'I appointed a proxy. Rick Heller has power of attorney.'

'Not now. We had to let him go.'

'You fired Rick? What right did you have to do that?'

'We didn't have any choice. He was dragging his heels over the Asquahanna deal, and when it came to foreign trading, he was in over his ears.'

'You fired him because he was voting on my behalf, and that made him almost as powerful as you. That's why you fired him.'

Victor peeled a fragment of cheroot leaf from the tip of his tongue, where it had stuck.

'Well, you're entitled to your opinion,' he said blandly. 'But the truth is that you can't just walk off and leave forty-seven million dollars' worth of stock lying around unattended.'

Galina's eyes widened, and she looked from Ally to Victor in disbelief.

'Forty-seven million dollars' worth of stock?' she said, her lip curled in jokey disbelief. 'You're saying that Ally owns *forty-seven million dollars' worth of stock?*'

Victor took out his pocket watch and checked the time. He looked at Galina as if he couldn't quite understand why she was asking such a mundane question, as if he'd asked Ally about nothing more than change for a dollar. 'That's right,' he said matter-of-factly. 'Give or take a few million. Oil's fluctuating these days.'

Galina took a long and shaky drag on her cigarette. 'Well, if Ally owns forty-seven million dollars' worth of stock,' she said, 'what's she doing here?'

Ally rubbed her eyes tiredly. 'She's trying to escape,' she

said softly. 'She's tired of servants and limousines and board meetings. She wants to get some clean air and meet some real people.'

Victor turned his head to look at her. There was a patronizing expression on his face, as if he was thinking: Ah, well, they all go through this stage, but it'll pass. They soon come to realize that money is what makes America live and breathe

Galina said: 'You walked out on forty-seven million dollars? You mean that? Were you *crazy*?'

Ally shook her head. 'I would have been crazy to stay. I had about as much freedom as a rat down a well.'

'Oh, come on now,' Victor joshed her. 'It wasn't as bad as all that. Look, I'm having your house at Corona del Mar redecorated, so you can spend a few weeks there before you go back to Washington. Or you can stay at White Point if you like. Freddie's away in Europe.'

'White Point?' said Galina. 'White Point is that fucking great palace out at . . .'

She stopped herself. She looked at Ally as if something magical was happening, as if Ally was gradually changing into a sparkling statue of solid gold and platinum in front of her eyes. The cigarette smoke drifted in blue rags across the table. Ally's eyes had caught the sinking afternoon light, and they were paler and sadder than Galina had ever seen them before.

In the second-floor apartment below, a record player was playing Country Joe and the Fish.

Ally pushed her hair back away from her face. 'You might as well know it,' she said. 'You would have guessed it someday, anyhow. My real name is Ally Cornelius.'

Galina nodded slowly and understandingly. 'I knew it,' she said. 'I knew it had to be something as bad as that. The whole way you've been talking. Jesus Christ. And this is Victor Cornelius, right? One of the richest young men in the whole wide world. Jesus, I don't believe it. Ally, you're a zillionaire.'

'Yes,' whispered Ally. She felt the tears prickling her eyes.

In the silence that followed, Ally could sense the walls closing in again. The soundless gulf between Galina's poorness and Ally's wealth was already blurring and disfiguring the way they saw each other and talked to each other, as if they were trying to speak over hundreds of miles on fading Marconi sets. Now, when Galina looked at Ally, she saw *rich*. Ally was pretty, and friendly, and thoughtful, but all of these qualities were obscured by a glittering unscalable mountain of money.

Victor said: 'Are we going to talk business or not?'

'What do you want to talk about?' said Ally in a dull voice.

'Well, everything. We need to know what you're going to do. Are you going to stay here forever? It took six detectives to find you. You know that? Six! You can't carry on this way. Apart from the fact that it's unfair on me, because I have to manage most of your investments, we need to know what you're doing and where you're living so that we can administer the trust funds properly. Then there's your dividends. We have to make sure they're held in escrow under the correct terms until finally you get tired of this hippie farrago and come on home.'

Ally turned to Victor and looked him full in the face. 'Victor,' she said, 'I don't want the money held in escrow. I don't *want* it. You can do what you like with it. This is not an illness I'm going through, that's going to pass. I've made a lifetime choice that this is the way I want to be. You can do whatever you like with the money.'

Victor's cheroot had gone out and he relit it. 'You're really being very selfish,' he told her placidly. 'Your inheritance is arranged the way it is to save the whole family tax. If you're going to continue to take this attitude, which I'm sure you won't, but if you *do*, then you're going to make it necessary for Dick Marini and me to transfer your stock, and that could cost us a fortune, as you're obviously aware. Anyway,' he said, looking pointedly at Galina, 'don't you think we ought to talk this over in private?'

Galina lifted her head aggressively. 'I don't think I want to leave, *signor*, unless Ally asks me.'

Victor rubbed the back of his neck. 'This is pretty confidential stuff, Ally.'

'Oh, dammit, Victor, I don't care,' Ally snapped back. 'As far as I'm concerned, this is ancient history. I've renounced it. If you've got something to say, then say it. If you don't want to, then get out.'

Victor spread his plump hands innocently. 'You don't have to be so aggressive. I'm only asking for your approval on a contract.'

'Well, then, ask for it. You don't think Galina's a covert agent for Dow Chemical, do you?'

Victor shrugged. 'Okay. But I'll have to ask Alex in. He's waiting on the landing with all the papers.'

'How very servile of him.'

Victor went to the outside door and whispered something. He returned with a tall, blue-chinned man in a dark suit and radiantly white button-down shirt. Victor sat down at the kitchen table again, and the blue-chinned man opened a brown leather briefcase for him and stood patiently by while he sorted out the papers he needed. Victor spread heaps of letters and draft contracts all over the tabletop, and then nodded to Alex to leave them. Ally recognized the man from the San Francisco offices of Daylong Oil, and it was as remote and unreal as recognizing a stock actor from a 1950's movie.

'What do you want me to do?' asked Ally.

'I just want you to countersign a couple of these contracts, that's all.'

Galina looked from Victor to Ally and back again like a solitary spectator at a practice tennis tournament. Ally took one of her cigarettes, lit it, and said: 'What's it for? Napalm? Guided missiles? I'm not signing for any of those.'

'Funding, that's all,' said Victor. He pushed the contracts across the table. 'There, and there, and there at the back

Ally, in the golden light from the window, her elbow crooked and her cigarette held high, her hair shining in blonde filaments, didn't answer at first, didn't even move. But then she took the pen resignedly, nudged the contracts nearer with the heel of her hand, and quickly signed.

'Is that all?' she asked flatly.

Victor smiled, and shucked the pages straight. 'That's about it. Oh . . . except that we would like to know what your plans are. Are you going to stay here for a few months, or what?'

Ally lowered her long eyelashes. 'I don't know,' she said quietly. 'I haven't made any plans.'

'Well, would you let me know if you decide to move? It's just a formality. Insurance, mainly. You know how it is.'

'Yes, I know how it is,' said Ally. 'That's why I'm here.'

Victor stood up and tugged down his creased coat at the back. 'There is one other thing,' he said, licking his lips.

'What's that?'

'Well, it's a question of discretion. If you're going to live here, we would like to suggest that you try to stay away from anything that might prove publicly embarrassing.'

'You mean she shouldn't stroll down the Embarcadero with her tits hanging out?' inquired Galina.

Victor frowned at Galina uncomfortably. 'I mean drugs, and alcohol, and things of that kind.'

Ally said: 'Victor . . . why don't you please just leave?'

Victor sighed. 'I'm not trying to tell you how to lead your life, Ally. I'm just trying to protect you.'

'Forget it, will you?' said Ally.

'I know why you're acting this way,' Victor told her. 'You think that I'm unsympathetic, don't you? You think because I'm always up to my ears in accounts and contracts that I don't see what goes on.'

'I didn't say that. Did I ever say that?'

'Maybe you didn't, but it shows in your attitude.'

'Come on, *signor*,' said Galina, getting up from her chair. 'Why don't you leave the lady alone?'

Victor ignored her. He said to Ally: 'Listen. I know what it's like to feel this thing's getting on top of you. We all feel it from time to time. It's a terrific burden, a terrific responsibility. But you don't get rid of the responsibility just by walking out of the door. The thing to do is make sure you relax from time to time, take a few days off, and then you can get back to it fresh.'

'Victor, I don't *want* to get back to it.'

'Look at me,' said Victor, as if he hadn't heard her. 'I come out to the Coast now and again. I even have a couple of girl friends out here Did you ever see Sheila, from the Westwood Club?'

'The Westwood Club?' said Galina. 'I thought only geriatrics went there. Geriatrics and rednecks.'

'You can mock all you like,' said Victor. 'But at least I get away from work for a while and then come back to it feeling good. Maybe all you needed was a break, Ally. But you can't live like this for the rest of your life.'

'Why not?' asked Ally.

Victor looked around at the two tiny rooms, the sagging settee, and the clusters of posters. 'Well . . .' He chuckled. 'What can I say?'

Ally moved over, and took Galina's arm. ' "Goodbye" would be nice,' she told Victor softly.

Victor stood and looked at her for a long time. What made her behaviour even more irritating to him, quite apart from the trouble she had caused over contracts and stock, was that she was so damned pretty, and he could have fancied a kissin cousins relationship without any extra encouragement at all. He dropped his eyes, and found himself looking at the way the nipple of her big, heavy breast was outlined by her cheesecloth blouse.

'Okay, then,' he said, with phlegm in his throat. 'But I'll have to keep tabs on you.'

Ally showed him to the door. Alex from Daylong Oil was sulking out on the landing. Victor gave Ally a little fat-fingered wave, and then said: 'Let's get out of here, Alex, before the goddamned rodents get us,' and they disappeared noisily downstairs.

Galina was standing in the kitchen with her hands on her hips. 'Well,' she said, 'how about you?'

'How *about* me?' asked Ally wryly. 'Do you want some more coffee?'

'Do you have some wine? I think I could use it.'

'Surely.'

They sat at the table without talking for a while, sipping the sweet red California burgundy. Than Galina said: 'What are you going to do? Go back?'

Ally shook her head.

'But how can you go on living here, when you've got all that money? I mean, it makes no sense. Why eat out of a can when you can afford the best restaurants?'

'Galina, that isn't the point.'

'Well, maybe not, honey, but it's part of it. You left the money behind, but you didn't dump it. What are you going to do – commute between a penthouse office and a cold-water walkup?'

Ally drank her wine and looked sad.

'I'm not trying to bring you down, Ally,' said Galina, holding her hand. 'But I don't want to see you pulled this way and then that way, like you were just now. You're going to find it hard enough to discover where you're at as it is.'

Ally picked at a knothole on the table with her fingernails. 'I guess you're right,' she said disconsolately. 'But I don't know what else I can do.'

'Can't you sign your holdings over to someone else in the family?'

'Not without upsetting years of trust-fund arrangements

and charity foundations. It wouldn't be fair on the charities, apart from anything else.'

'Well, can't you just spend all the money you've got? Jesus, if you have any trouble doing it, I don't mind helping!'

'Oh, Galina, you're beautiful.' Ally smiled. 'But you don't even realize how rich I really am. If I bought twenty Cadillacs a day, every day of my life, I wouldn't even use up one-half of one percent of my capital. I can't spend it, or even give it away, fast enough to use up the accumulating dividends and interest. And all these trust funds and foundations are so complex, and they're so interdependent, that it would take me years to sign over everything I've got altogether, and by that time it would have accumulated even more. Today, right this minute, I am probably worth a hundred million dollars.'

Galina sat back in her chair, shaking her head in amazement and amusement. 'It doesn't seem real. It just doesn't seem real '

'It's real all right. And it's like being born with a hunchback

Galina was going to say something else– that it didn't make any difference, that she still liked Ally in spite of her money, that she'd never feel tempted to ask her for a handout or a loan but somehow the words didn't want to come. The rich are only different because they can have all the things they want but that difference alone is a chasm that is almost impossible to bridge.

The sun fell across a yellowed reproduction of John Heade's *Orchids, Passion Flowers and Hummingbird*, from the Whitney Museum Out on the landing, the telephone started to ring

They were almost shy when they spoke, like children.

She said: 'Destry?'

His voice was very soft. She held the telephone close against her ear as if it could warm her whole mind.

'Ally?' he said. 'Ally, they let me out.'

She stood on the landing, silhouetted by the last light of the day, with Galina watching expectantly from the half-open doorway, and she sobbed with relief. Galina came over and held her tight, and wiped away the tears with her Czechoslovakian scarf.

'Did they treat you bad?' she asked him. 'Are you okay?'

'I'm fine. There was just some kind of mix-up down here. It seems that one of the detectives on duty last week had special instructions to hold me. Some mix-up, God knows why Anyway, I'm out.'

'Oh, Destry, I love you. I can't wait to see you.'

'I love you too, baby. I've missed you.'

Ally wiped her eyes again, on her sleeve, and said 'Did they grant you bail? Did Randy fix it for you?'

'They dropped the charges. It seems like the fuzz know this lawyer friend of yours from way back. I heard him tell them that if they didn't have sufficient evidence, he'd kick their asses all the way to hell and back again.'

'I'm so happy. I can't tell you how happy I am. Oh, Destry.'

'Listen,' he said, 'come around to my place. I have to wait here a half hour, then I can go. They want me to sign some paper or something. Come around at eight, maybe eight-fifteen, and we'll cook some food and smoke some grass and—'

'Yes,' she said. 'Yes.'

There was a crackly silence; then Randy came on the phone. He said: 'Feeling better now, my darling?'

'Randy, you're wonderful. I don't know how to thank you.'

'You can pay my usual fee, if you like.'

'Oh, Randy, more than that.'

'Okay. You can come to lunch next week at the St Francis Yacht Club, so long as you don't wear your Levi's.'

She smiled. 'That's a deal. Thank you, Randy. Really, thank you.'

In a voice that she wouldn't have recognized as sounding exactly like his father, Randy said: 'Ally, for you it's a pleasure.'

She hung up the phone. Galina was standing by the window. 'Destry's out?' she asked. Ally nodded.

'Oh, I'm real pleased,' said Galina.

Ally hugged her. 'I'm so excited! I'm going to see him at eight.'

'Are you going to tell him?'

'Tell him what?'

'Well, that you're not who he thinks you are. That you're really Ally Cornelius, instead of Ally Pocznicz.'

Ally looked at her strangely. 'I don't know,' she said in a low voice. 'Do you think it makes any difference?'

'Do you?'

'I'm not sure. But I'm still the same person, no matter what my name is – aren't I?'

Galina leaned back against the landing window. 'Unh-hunh. You may still feel the same, but will Destry still feel the same toward you? I mean, apart from anything else, he's suddenly going to find out that you could buy him and sell him fifty times over in the same street, and how's he going to feel then? It doesn't do much for a man's, you know, ego.'

'Destry doesn't have that kind of ego.'

Galina shrugged. 'Don't count on it. Where I come from, every man has an ego.'

Ally thought for a moment, biting her nail. Then she said: 'In De Kalb, Illinois?'

She caught a taxi up to Destry's place – the first taxi she had used since she first arrived in San Francisco. She felt oddly guilty about it in one way, as if it was selling out, but on the other hand she knew she was trying to prove something to herself. If she was honest about what she was, if she faced up to her problem, then maybe she'd be able to discover herself. She was rich – impossibly and unavoidably rich – and perhaps she had to admit it.

Destry's room was in a yellow-painted wooden house on a steeply angled corner of Telegraph Hill. There were geraniums in pots, and a marmalade cat slept on the wall outside with its paws tucked in. The fading sunlight was still warm but somehow regretful. She paid off the taxi driver, and then climbed the three white steps at the side of the house and pressed Destry's bell. The card under the bell read 'J. Di Maggio.'

He came down the stairs three at a time, and she saw his lean outline through the hammered-glass window. He opened up the door, and there he was, lean and narrow and brown, with that Panlike curly hair and that sharp chiselled face, and Ally felt her breath tightening and all the happiness she had never believed she could ever have come bubbling up.

They hugged each other on the doorstep, and Ally shed tears against his thin bare suntanned chest, and a black woman walking down Telegraph Hill with her shopping basket stopped at the kerb to stare at them.

Destry held her away from him, so that he could look at her. He had a friendly, foxy smile that made her feel so wanted and so loved that she wished he could smile all the time, day and night. He was wearing nothing but his faded worn-out jeans, with a hefty brass-buckled belt. He kissed her, and he tasted like Chinese food and marijuana.

'You're an angel in disguise,' he whispered. 'Or maybe you're not.'

'Maybe I'm not what?'

'Maybe you're not in disguise.'

They climbed the rickety, burlap-carpeted stairs to the landing, and then stepped into his room. He had a wooden crate upended by the window, and a hammer and nails on the floor.

'I was trying to fix up some wind chimes,' said Destry. 'I kind of like wind chimes. They make me feel like I'm some kind of Tibetan monk.'

Ally kissed him and fondly fingered his small brown nipples. 'Do you *want* to feel like a Tibetan monk?' she asked him.

He shrugged. 'I don't know. I picked up the chimes in a store next to the police station, when I was buying food for this evening. They just seemed like a good idea.'

Destry's room was plain and spare compared with Ally's. The walls were whitewashed, and the floor was carpeted with sisal matting. He slept on a mattress covered by a plain white quilt, and cooked on a gas ring on a plain black-painted table. There were some rainbow-dragon trees in earthenware pots, and a rice-paper painting of the gate to the Temple of Confucius at Ching-hai. The room was always serene and welcoming, though, and Ally and Destry had spent hours there, talking or making love or just sitting in silence, listening to the sounds of San Francisco at night. Faint rock music, distant ships, clanging streetcars, laughter.

Ally stood in the centre of the room. Her hair was brushed and shining, and she was wearing a mini-dress of pale blue crochet. She said, very simply: 'I love you. You know that, don't you?'

He grinned, and didn't answer.

'I hardly even realized what I felt about you, until this happened,' she told him. 'But I can't hide it.'

He was still grinning. She suddenly realized he was bashful, and that he was so pleased by what she was saying that he didn't know how to act. She knelt down beside him, and touched his curly hair, and kissed his lean brown cheek.

'There's something else I can't hide,' she said softly.

He raised his eyes.

'It's something important. Something I should have told you before.'

He shrugged. 'You don't have to tell me anything, if you don't want to. You know that. It's today that matters, not yesterday.'

She bit her lip. 'I know. But this affects today.'

'Badly or gladly?'

'I don't know. I guess it's up to you.'

He got up from the floor and climbed onto the upturned crate with a mouthful of nails. 'Is that in the centre?' he asked her, holding up the wind chimes over the window.

She stood up and nodded. He levelled up a nail, and started to bang.

'Destry,' she said, 'you have to know that I'm rich.'

Destry bent the nail, and then hammered his thumb.

'Christ!' he swore, sucking it, and then waving it around in the air.

Ally watched him, looking worried.

'Destry,' she said. 'I'm *rich*.'

He got down off his crate, hugging his thumb in his armpit. 'Do you think Tibetan monks have this much trouble?'

'I don't think so. I guess they just think of Buddha, and the pain goes.'

'Okay, I'm thinking of Buddha. Buddha, Buddha, Buddha. It still hurts. Maybe I need more training.'

She took his wrists. He looked at her, saw that she was serious, and quieted down. 'Did you say something?' he asked her.

She nodded. 'I said that I was rich. You think I'm just ordinary, but I'm not. I'm very, very rich,'

He stared at her with a half-smile, unsure if he ought to believe her or not. Then he said: 'Okay, you're rich. That's okay.'

'Destry,' she said, 'you don't understand.'

'Sure I do. You have rich parents. You left it all behind. It's the old, old story. I don't mind. Ally, honey, I want you because of what you are, not what your old man's got stashed away in the bank.'

She brushed back her hair. 'It's not my old man. It's me. I'm not really Ally Pocznicz at all. I'm Ally Cornelius, of Cornelius Oil.'

He frowned, but then his frown faded, and he laughed. 'You're putting me on. Come on, you're putting me on. *Cornelius Oil?*'

She squeezed his wrists tighter. 'Destry, I'm a multimillionairess. I have houses, cars, airplanes, boats, racehorses, and furs. I have a thirty-percent share in the Pacific International Building on the waterfront. I may even own this house, for all I know.'

'For all you know?' he said light-headedly. 'You mean, you could own a house and *not know*? Ally,' he said seriously, 'is this a true fact? You're not kidding?'

She shook her head. 'I couldn't lie to you. I went through a bad enough time getting you out of jail. I'm Ally Cornelius. I can't help it. I was born that way.'

He whistled under his breath. Then he walked up the room, and walked back down again. 'You're really Ally Cornelius? *Really?*'

She nodded. 'You want to see some ID? Here's my driver's license.'

Grinning, he took it, and looked at it. 'You're right,' he said, as if he had just discovered it was Christmas tomorrow. 'You really are.'

He walked around the room again, and then he said: 'Shit. How about that. You really are. You're actually Ally Cornelius.'

She said hesitantly: 'Is it . . . ?'

He looked at her, still smiling. 'Is it what? Is it *okay*?'

She nodded.

He came over and he put his arm around her and kissed her hair. 'Are you different than you were this morning?' he asked very gently, in her ear.

She said 'No' in a small voice. She was on the edge of crying.

'Well, neither am I,' he said. 'And if you're Ally Cornelius, that only makes me feel proud. Me – with a multimillionairess! Don't you think that's something?'

'I've . . . well, I've kind of renounced my money,' she said awkwardly.

'Renounced it? What for?'

'I guess it was too much for me. It was taking up too much of my life, too much of what I was. I mean, I still own what I

629

owned before. I still have the same income. But I left it behind when I came to San Francisco.'

Destry sat down on the crate. 'I don't know what to say,' he told her. 'I don't know whether to ask you for a hundred bucks for a new hi-fi, or whether to say that I just love you.'

Ally wiped a tear from her cheek with the back of her knuckle. 'Do you think you still could?' she asked him.

He laughed. 'You're kidding! You're a good-looking multi-millionairess, and I can't say that I love you?'

There was an edgy pause. Then Destry said: 'I'm sorry. I didn't mean it to sound bad. I mean that I love you whether you're poor or wealthy. I sometimes wish I was rich myself, but wishing isn't going to make any difference, any more than wishing is going to make you poor.'

'It's going to change things, this,' she whispered.

He got up, and hefted his hammer. 'Sure it is. You can't expect it not to. But it doesn't have to change things for the worse, does it?'

'I don't know.'

'Well, hand me those wind chimes, and let's get them up.'

Destry stood on the box, and finally managed to bang a nail in straight. Ally passed up the wind chimes, and she couldn't resist touching his leg with her hand as if Destry standing on this upended orange crate were a priceless Praxiteles marble that she couldn't resist stroking.

Destry said: 'It hasn't even sunk in yet. I've fallen in love with a girl, and she turns out to be someone else. I mean, you can't rush me. Listen, how many houses do you own?'

'Eight. Not including my place at Corona del Mar.'

'Eight houses! Shit!'

He climbed down from the orange box. He put his thin arms around her waist and kissed her on the forehead. 'I guess I'm still suffering from shock,' he said tenderly. 'Right now, I don't know whether I'm pleased that you're Ally Cornelius, or whether I'm scared. But it doesn't matter. I'd like to stick around to find out.'

Ally kissed him back. 'So would I,' she murmured.

They kissed deeper, and his tongue probed into her mouth. 'I think I'm going to put on some music,' he said quietly. 'I got the new Love album today, and I think it's going to put me in the mood.'

He walked across the room, unselfconsciously unbuckling

his jeans. He dropped them, and kicked them away with one leg. His body was all skinny and hard and muscular, tanned as a gypsy all over, and his long penis with its smooth purple head was already half-erect.

Ally pulled her dress over her head and unlaced her sandals, but she didn't take her eyes off Destry. He was squatting by the record player like some brown faun that had trotted in curiously from the magic forest.

She took off her panties and then sat down on the floor under the tinkling wind chimes, and Destry turned around and grinned at her. 'You look like that calendar that Marilyn Monroe did. You know the one? You have those same big soft tits. In fact, I think yours are even bigger.'

He knelt down beside her and kissed her hair and face.

'Does bigness matter?' she asked him.

He pulled a mock-lustful face. 'Does bigness matter? That's like asking if french fries come with the hamburger.'

She giggled and rolled over the floor. He caught her legs, and held her, and nibbled and kissed at her knees and her thighs. Then he looked up at her, and his eyes were gentle but serious.

'Did any man ever go down on you before?'

She blushed. She didn't know what he meant.

'Go down?'

He parted her legs with his hands. 'Down here,' he said.

She said: 'I don't . . .'

He grinned. His front teeth were square and white. He stuck out his pointed tongue, and then dipped his head forward. She felt something warm and wet drawing a line upward from her anus, and flickering like a cat at her clitoris. It made her shudder, and she reached down and gripped his curly hair as if to make him stop, but also to make him stay.

'Destry,' she whispered, 'you mustn't.'

He took no notice. He licked again, and then again, and again. She felt a growing sensation of tension and warmth between her legs, and after a few moments, she put her hands down there and opened herself even wider for him, so that the tip of his electrifying tongue could thrum on the tip of her clitoris, and then slide between the glistening folds of skin to dip itself into the wet darkness of her vagina.

Above her, the wind chimes spun and spangled and turned,

631

and the brown curls of Destry's head bobbed between ner thighs. Love was singing.

Her orgasm came like a steel trap in her back. She was tensed and panting, her head back against the floor, her eyes tight shut and her face in a reddened grimace. She clutched her breasts in her hand, her nails digging into the soft skin, and her thumbs rapidly rubbing her nipples. It was the slowest orgasm she had ever had. Destry was licking and licking and each time she thought she was on the verge of making it, the steel trap would relax a little, and she'd have to brace her muscles again. But then the trap snapped, and she shrieked out loud, kicking and struggling to keep him away, and yet smother his face even deeper in her juices.

She lay there for a long time. San Francisco spun around her, slower and slower. In the kitchenette, she heard Destry pottering around, and the clink of glasses. The album was still playing, although she could have sworn that they had already been making love for hours.

He came back in, and sat down on the floor beside her. He laid out his lid of grass, and while she fondly watched him, he separated stalks and seeds, and prepared his joints.

'You always seem so composed,' she told him.

He was licking the paper. 'I wasn't always like that.'

'You're open, but you're self-contained. You seem to know exactly what you want.'

Destry leaned over and kissed her. 'It took me four horrible years to discover how to do it. The secret is, you give whatever you can, and you don't ask anything of anybody. You don't even ask people to love you.'

'Do you like it that I love you?

'Of course. I love you, too.'

'Do you mean that?'.

'Yes. I wouldn't say it if I didn't.'

Ally was so pleased that she practically cried. She rolled over and kissed his bare foot.

'You shouldn't do that, you know,' he told her.

'Why not? I love you.'

'Well, you're a rich young lady and I'm just a bum Rich young ladies shouldn't kiss the feet of bums.'

He finished rolling the first joint, and reached over for his matches to light it up.

'Were you always a bum?' she asked him.

* He took a deep drag of grass smoke and closed his eyes. 'I was born a bum,' he told her. 'My father was a railroad engineer and my mother was an office cleaner. I don't think they ever meant to have me. They were both about a hundred when I was born.'

'Did you ever want to be anything? I mean, did you ever have a dream?'

Destry passed her the joint. 'Oh, sure. When I was five I wanted to an insurance salesman. I didn't know what they did, but I knew they had fancy cars, and that's what I wanted. Then when I was ten I wanted to be an ace reporter, but my schoolwork was too bad, and my father died, and in the end I was a delivery boy for a grocery store.'

'Destry,' said Ally softly, 'what about us?'

'What about us?'

'Well, what are we going to do?'

He rubbed his thin cheek thoughtfully. 'I don't know. I guess we'll just have to work out each day as it comes around. I mean, I can't pretend that I still feel exactly the same about you. Your money impresses me. It's impressive. I can't help it. It's a natural response.'

'I don't want to impress you. Not with my money, anyway. I just want to make you love me.'

'Can't you do both? I mean, Ally there's nothing *wrong* with money.'

She sat up, her hands on her thighs, and looked at him close. 'Oh, there is,' she told him. 'Money is so corrupting. Money is so damned corrupting.'

Destry took back the joint, sucked at it hard, held the smoke, and then let it all out, and shrugged. 'Corruption like that I could stand,' he told her.

She laughed. She was getting a little high, and her laugh sounded metallic and ringing. She kissed him, and whispered: 'You're beautiful. You're beautiful and I love you.'

Destry folded his arms around her neck and held her close. 'In a minute,' he murmured, 'I'm going to do things to you that you won't even believe.'

'Like what?' she whispered back.

'Just you wait and see.'

He got up to turn the record over. Ally lay back on the floor again, listening to the wind chimes, and watching the reflections of automobile taillights streaming across the window, like red blood cells coursing through some darkened artery.

There was a ring at the downstairs bell. Destry said: 'I'll get it! Where did I leave my pants?'

'On the floor,' called Ally. She heard him rooting around for them, and then the rustle of denim and the sharp zizz of his zipper. Her mind seemed very far away and relaxed. His footsteps, bare feet, went out into the hallway. The apartment door clicked.

Somebody had already come up the stairs and was standing on the landing. She could hear gruff voices. She listened for a few moments, but she couldn't catch what they were saying. They seemed to go on and on for such a long time that eventually she sat up and reached over for one of the Mexican blankets to wrap around her. Then she padded out to the door to see what Destry was doing.

The glare of a naked bulb didn't seem to light the landing at all. There were two men there, and Destry was standing against the crumble-plastered wall with his hands up in the air. Ally said: 'Destry?'

The men turned around. They were heavy and their faces looked as if they'd been roughly hewn out of rocks. One of them lifted a badge and said: 'San Francisco Police Department.'

'What's he done? What's he supposed to have done?'

'Don't you worry, Miss Cornelius. The best thing you can do is get yourself dressed.'

Ally clutched the Mexican blanket tighter around her neck. 'But I don't understand. He hasn't done anything.'

'Ally,' said Destry in an oddly hollow voice. 'Just do what he says.'

There was a uniformed cop at the foot of the stairs. A red flashing light from the patrol car outside lit him with a scarlet theatrical glare.

'Are you bringing him down, Lieutenant?' called the cop.

'Sure. Just wait till we've searched his apartment.'

Ally said in a high-pitched voice: 'I suppose you have a warrant?'

The detective held out his fist toward her and opened it. Lying there, crushed and damp, was Destry's joint. 'This joker is up for illegal possession of a dangerous narcotic. Don't talk to me about warrants.'

634

Destry said again: 'Ally . . . just do it. Just go inside and get dressed.'

One of the detectives said: 'Shut up, Carlsson.'

Ally said: 'Carlsson?'

'George Carlsson,' said the detective. 'Also known as Curly, also known as Destry. We've been pulling him in for years. You name a goddamned low-life we haven't. Goddamned hippies.'

Ally said: 'I'm going to call my attorney. He's down on Fourth Street. Destry . . . don't say anything till then.'

The detective said: 'Miss Cornelius, I advise you to stay out of this. You have to understand that we're doing this for your own protection.'

'I won't stay out. Now, give me a couple of minutes to get dressed and then I'm coming down to the station with you.'

'Miss Cornelius—'

'I'm not going to argue. Just remember who I am.'

She turned to go back into the apartment, but then she heard a scuffling noise. In the dim light of the landing, it seemed that Destry was holding a knife. She saw the blade of it flash as one of the detectives wrestled to get it free.

'Watch yourself!' yelled one of the detectives hoarsely. 'Watch yourself!'

The knife clattered and spun on the worn linoleum. Then, in three long gelatinous seconds, the detectives stepped back, and Ally saw they were holding guns. Maybe the grass was affecting her sense of time, but she was sure that the knife fell *before* they raised their guns, and she wasn't convinced that Destry himself had even been holding the knife.

They fired once and the noise was so deafening that all her senses were blotted with sound. Two wide red splashes marked Destry's chest, and then the patrolman fired from the foot of the stairs and blew half of Destry's head away. The boy turned and collapsed, and the detectives holstered their Specials and looked down at him.

Ally tried to scream, but it came out as nothing but a squeaky, airless gasp. She found herself bending over in shock and then she was on her knees, her head against the open door, so shaken by Destry's sudden death that she felt as if every nerve that gave her body motion and meaning had been stripped and disassembled like a torn-apart television.

'You see that?' said one of the detectives. 'Did you see him pull that knife?'

'They're all the goddamned same,' answered the other one. To Ally's ears, he seemed to be talking from the bottom of a deep, echoing well. 'Goddamned low-life.'

The patrolman came up the stairs and peered at the crumpled body. There were pink lumps on the wall, and Ally realized with a kind of detached disgust that they were pieces of Destry's brain. The patrolman said: 'Did you see that knife? The way he pulled that knife out? It was either him or Phil.'

Ally got up from the floor and walked across the landing pale and trembling. She tugged at the sleeve of the detective named Phil. He turned around and frowned at her, as if he had never seen her before in his life.

'You've shot him,' she whispered.

The detective didn't answer. Ally pushed past him, and knelt down beside Destry's body. His face was against the floor, and his eyes were open in what looked like a studious inspection of the floorboards. She wanted to close them, but somehow she couldn't bear to touch him.

'I'm sorry, Miss Cornelius,' said the detective gruffly. He had near-together eyes, and a scarlet sport coat with coffee stains on it. 'I really am sorry, but you saw the knife for yourself. He pulled a knife.'

'He shouldn't have pulled it,' explained the patrolman. 'When you see something like that, you have to respond. You know what I mean?'

Ally stood up again. She said: 'He had no knife. He didn't even own one.'

The detectives glanced at each other. 'He must have,' said the one called Phil. 'Maybe he kept it hid.'

Ally paused for a moment, but then she turned away from the boy who had just been her living lover, and nodded. 'Yes,' she whispered. 'Maybe he did.'

The cop said: 'Lady, I really suggest you get your things together and leave this place to us. We're going to have to search it for dope, and it's better if you ain't here.'

Ally lifted her head. 'What about me? Aren't you going to arrest me too?'

The othere detective said: 'What for?'

'For possession. For smoking. I was smoking too, you know.'

The detective laughed. 'You were? It was his stuff, though, wasn't it?'

'Maybe it was,' insisted Ally, 'but you'd arrest me under normal circumstances, wouldn't you?'

The detective shook his head. 'You ain't done nothing. My advice to you is to get your things and go.'

The detective called Phil said: 'Your cousin's waiting for you outside. He'll take you home.'

It was then that Ally felt a freezing sick sensation that seemed to break everything she had ever understood about life into chips of ice. She looked from one detective to the other and said: 'My cousin's outside? You mean, he came *with* you?'

'He, uh, tipped us off. He was worried about you. We've had you followed right from Brannan Street. With a hoodlum like this, I think you ought to go over and tell him thanks.'

'This guy's a known hoodlum,' said the other detective.

Ally opened her mouth, and then closed it again. There was nothing at all to say. She pulled the Mexican blanket tighter around herself and then went back into the apartment to dress. All the time she was putting her clothes on, she kept her eyes fixed on a blank place on the wall, and tried to close her ears to the bangling sound of the wind chimes.

She took only one souvenir. It was a piece of paper on which Destry had been writing a poem the night they had first made love. His ball-point pen was still resting on it, and she lifted the paper without touching the pen.

It said:

The day's in disguise;
It's wearing a face I don't recognize
It has rings on its fingers & silken roads in its eyes
& body & blood both speaking as old friends at a secret
  lunch

She crossed the street and Victor's black limousine was waiting there. Victor himself was sitting in the back, behind tinted glass, his legs crossed, reading *Business Week* with his horn-rimmed half-glasses on the end of his protuberant nose. The chauffeur who had been hovering around the car having a discreet smoke, beetled over at once when he saw Ally and opened the door for her.

Victor looked up Inside the car, it was cool and air-conditioned and it smelled of nothing but Victor's after-shave and hide upholstery. The chauffeur closed the door and sealed the two of them away.

Victor said: 'Is it all over? Have they arrested him?'

Ally's lower lip was shaking and she found it difficult to speak. But she was determined not to cry. To cry for Destry in front of Victor was not what her tears were for. She swallowed hard, and then she said, 'You know what happened. You set it up, and you paid for it yourself.'

Victor took off his spectacles and stared at her. Then he noisily folded up his newspaper and said: 'Now, wait a minute. You think I had anything to do with this?'

'The police told me. They told me you tipped them off.'

'Yes, I did tip them off. But that was only because this person you were seeing was—'.

'Was what? Was a human being who's lying dead up there? He's dead, Victor, as if you didn't know! He's lying up there on the landing with his brains halfway up the wall!'

Victor said: 'You're kidding! Is this some kind of a joke? What are you trying to do?'

She turned on him, and now she couldn't stop crying, no matter what. But they were tears of anger, tears of desperation, and maybe more than anything else, they were tears for what she was – and no lover, nor flowers, nor beads, nor bells, could ever change that.

'I don't know *what* you did! I don't *have* to know! Everything this family touches turns out the same! As soon as we find something beautiful, something worth loving, we turn it rotten, or we kill it! You're a murderer, Victor, just like I am for loving him, and just like those stupid detectives are for believing what you said!'

Victor was sweating. He forced Ally roughly back against the seat and said: 'Now, hold on a goddamned minute. Will you hold on for one minute?'

Ally turned away, her face wet with tears. 'I don't want to listen, Victor. I don't want to hear. It's not going to make any difference.'

Victor said: 'Well, you're going to hear whether you like it or not. I've put up with you and Freddie and Tess for long enough. Oh, it's terrific for you! Oh, sure! You can come and go as you please and collect your dividends whenever you feel like it. But who the hell do you think is keeping this whole thing going? Who the hell stays up until four in the morning working out the financial policy and the tax structure and the investment planning?'

Ally whispered: 'I'm sure you're doing a wonderful job. Do you want that in writing?'

'Come on, Ally, don't be smart. The truth is that one of my six private detectives tracked down this boyfriend of yours, and found out that he was a known pusher. He did a stretch in the penitentiary in Vancouver for dope peddling, and then he came down here.'

Ally said: 'My God, Victor, I knew all that. But he wasn't a murderer. He didn't have to pay for what he did by dying.'

'No,' said Victor, 'he didn't. But when you're on the wrong side of law and order, you have to accept the risks. Apart from that, he was doing more damage than he ever realized by dating you.'

The ambulance arrived, lights flashing and siren whooping, and bounced to a halt across the street. The rear doors opened, and two white-jacketed attendants hurried out with a stretcher. A curious crowd had gathered at the corner, and two cops were holding them back.

Ally said tiredly: 'He didn't even know who I was until today.'

'And he still wanted to see you?'

'Of course he wanted to see me. What do you think?'

Victor reached into his inside pocket for his cheroot case. He took one out and put it between his lips. He looked thoughtful.

'I just thought that if he knew who you were, he'd lay off. He'd understand his responsibilities. It's his own fault, you know. If you're a known criminal, you can't expect to . . . well, you know, get involved, hobnob with people like us.'

Ally turned and stared at him. 'People like us?'

'Sure,' said Victor. 'Can you imagine what the newpapers would have said if it had gotten out that you were dating a convicted pusher? Can you imagine what that would have done to the public-relations image of our pharmaceutical division? Ally, you own eleven percent of Haymann Drugs. Don't you understand what it would do to their business if it got out?'

Ally brushed back her soft blonde hair. The street lights caught it, and touched it with filaments of pale gold. She said softly: 'Victor, it's *my* life. What I do with my own life is nothing to do with Haymann Drugs or Cornelius Oil or anyone else.'

'That's where you're absolutely wrong,' said Victor, lighting his cheroot.

'What do you mean? You mean I can't go to bed with a man because some dreary drug company in Indiana doesn't like the idea of it? Or because *you* disapprove?'

Victor nodded. His head was so wreathed in smoke that for a moment it looked as if he had no head at all. Then the limousine's air-conditioning drew it away, and revealed him serious and pink and sweaty.

'You're a very rich young lady, Ally. You didn't get rich through working, but through being born. You didn't have to do anything, and you don't have to do anything now. But nobody gets anything for nothing, and in return for your wealth you have to behave with a sense of prudence toward everyone whose livelihood depends on it. When you decided to go to bed with that drug pusher, you put the job of every man at Haymann Drugs at risk. You put millions of dollars in jeopardy. And you could have had your name, and *my* name, and your *father's* name, too, dragged through print as if it was offal.'

Ally sat back in the deep, comfortable seat of the car. She said: 'I suppose it doesn't matter to you that Destry is dead.'

'Of course it matters. I don't want to see you hurt.'

Ally turned her eyes toward him. 'You shouldn't say things like that unless you can sound as though you mean them.'

'I do mean it.'

'But you knew that the police were going to go after him. You tipped them off.'

'I've told you why. I just had to act in everyone's best interests.'

'You didn't act in Destry's best interests.'

'Of course not. He was the rotten apple.'

'Is that what you think he was?'

'Well, sure. I know that you can't see him that way, but—'

'You're damned right I can't see him that way! Whatever he was, whatever you thought he was, you had no right to judge him! How you can sit here and decide if a man's going to live or die without feeling disgusted with yourself, I can't imagine.'

Ally's voice was catching, and she was crying again. 'Oh,

Victor,' she said, 'you're such a stupid pig. You're such a blind and stupid pig.'

Victor was embarrassed by her tears, and didn't answer. After a while he said: 'Can I take you anywhere?'

She turned to him, her eyes red, and said: 'When I see you now, sitting here, I really understand why all these hippies have come to San Francisco. You're twenty-four, Victor, and you're an old man already. You've lived your whole life in twenty-four years, and now there's nothing left for you to do. At least the hippies have come in search of some hope.'

Victor took out his handkerchief and mopped his forehead. Then he pressed the intercom button and said to his chauffeur: 'Mark Hopkins, please, George. I have an appointment with Goldberg.'

The chauffeur started the motor. Ally said: 'You can take me to Brannan Street first, and then to the airport.'

Victor looked at his gold-and-platinum watch. 'It's after nine. My appointment's at nine-thirty.'

Ally said: 'Victor, you killed my lover today. Don't you think you could at least summon the humanity to give me a ride to the airport?'

'I don't understand.'

'You don't understand?'

'You said I killed your lover. I mean – yes, Ally, I tipped off the cops, but you can't possibly say that—'

Ally said quietly: 'I don't mean that you killed him personally, with your bare hands. I'm grieving, Victor. Will you please just take me home?'

Victor pressed his lips together in barely controlled exasperation, and looked at his watch once more. But then he pressed the intercom button again and said: 'George, make that Brannan Street, and then the airport.'

The limousine made an awkward three-point turn across the street. Although Ally didn't want to look, she couldn't help seeing the attendants bringing down the stretcher through the hammered-glass door, past the wall from where the sleeping cat had now disappeared. The body was covered with a blue sheet, the colour of tears on Tarot cards.

Victor said: 'Are you all right for money?'

With Galina standing numbly beside her, she telephoned Randy. His secretary kept her waiting for almost five minutes, out then she got through. He said: 'Ally?' in an odd, strained voice that immediately unsettled her.

'Randy,' she said, 'it's Destry.'

There was an embarrassed silence. Then Randy said: 'I know. I had a·call from the captain of detectives just ten minutes ago.'

'Randy, it was murder! He didn't *do* anything! He just opened the door, and they started hassling him, and then they shot him down!'

Randy didn't answer. Ally said: 'I swear it, Randy. He didn't even threaten them! They were trying to make out that he pulled a knife, but it wasn't his. Randy, I can swear to that in court!'

Again there was silence.

Ally said: 'Randy?'

'I'm still here.'

'Is there anything wrong? You're not saying anything.'

He sighed. 'No, there's nothing wrong.'

'But can't we *do* something? Can't we take those detectives to court?'

Randy sounded hesitant. 'I guess we could, under normal circumstances. Maybe you can do it on your own. But I'm afraid that you're going to have to count me out.'

Ally frowned. She could scarcely believe what he was saying. 'Count you out? I don't understand. What do you mean, count you out?'

'It's really very simple,' said Randy. 'I had a call from someone else, too, apart from the cops. A man called Lupino, which is a name that you'd better forget. He said some pretty threatening things about Douglas.'

'Randy . . .' said Ally.

Randy's voice was hoarse with anxiety and humiliation. 'Ally, I'm sorry. I don't know what other course to take. I'm not going to tell you anything but the truth; and the truth is that I'm scared.'

Ally ran her hands through her hair in resignation and sadness.

'Oh, Randy,' she said with tears in her eyes.

'Forgive me, my darling,' he asked her.·'I love you, but you know what Douglas means. We've been together a long time, Douglas and me, and if anything happened, I don't really think I'd have very much left to live for.'

'Randy,' she wept 'You know I love you. You know that you don't have to ask me that. I could always forgive you. Always.'

There was a silence, and then he said: 'You should see another attorney, if you can. See if you can get some justice done. But, please, try not to bring me into it.'

She said, crying: 'I don't know. I'm not sure.'

'But *try*,' he insisted.

She shook her head. She was too upset to speak. She kept seeing that last slow-motion moment when Destry spun and fell against the wall, over and over, as if he would forever spin and fall, spin and fall, for the rest of her life.

At last she said: 'Take care, Randy. Please take care. Goodbye.' And the last time that a Cornelius would ever speak to a Field, fifty-eight years after Jack Field stepped aboard the SS *Galveston Bay*, passed by.

Galina held Ally close to her and whispered: 'Don't cry. Come on. Rich girls don't cry.'

It was early the following morning when she arrived in Washington D.C., on the businessman's red-eye special. As the 707's shadow fled over the gleaming Potomac on its way toward Dulles, she sat by the window trying to repair her makeup in the mirror of the compact, and saw how vacant and expressionless she looked. *I wonder who I am now*, she thought to herself, *and what I'm doing here*.

She had only hand luggage, and she was out of the airport terminal in fifteen minutes. It was going to be a hot day. A blue-grey haze was gradually being dissolved by the mounting sun, and the taxi driver's radio announced that temperatures up to ninety-six degrees were anticipated.

Tired, drained, she sat in the back of the taxi as it carried her across the river and past the white reflecting spire of the Washington Monument. The taxi driver, a black man with horn-rimmed eyeglasses, said, 'That's the White House there, on your left.'

She nodded and said: 'Thank you.' She had been there for lunch once at a time when Lyndon Johnson had been trying to be nice to some of the richer and more influential Republicans. LBJ had called her 'the prettiest-looking Cornelius ever.' Ally had joked: 'You can pick me up by the ears if you like.'

The taxi driver said: 'This is it, lady,' and pulled up outside the Madison hotel at Fifteenth and M. Ally paid him and stepped out The sidewalk was crowded and the nine o'clock sunlight fell across it like pieces of mirror. The doorman tipped his cap and said· 'Good morning, Miss Cornelius. I hope you're well '

She nodded almost imperceptibly and went through the doors into the foyer. A cluster of Japanese businessmen was standing around in light blue raincoats, holding brand-new brief-cases and looking confused. Ally went up to the desk and signed in. The desk clerk said: 'I was sorry to hear about your father, Miss Cornelius. Real sorry.'

Escorted by the bell captain, she went silently up to her suite. She knew that she couldn't keep herself composed for very much longer, and when the bell captain started to demonstrate the bedside lamps and the television and the drinks cabinet, she gave him a twenty and said: 'Please go. I'm very tired.' He nodded and bowed and vanished like a conjurer.

In a kind of emotional slow motion she fell face forward on the bed. She cried bitterly, in deep painful sobs, for almost fifteen minutes. Then gradually she felt the shock and the distress subsiding, and she lay there in the brilliant sunshine that crossed the bed, trying to restore her mind and relax her body. Even now she understood that she couldn't mourn Destry for very long. Whether she could ever discover herself again, though, was another question. Yesterday, on that landing in San Francisco, she had lost more than a lover.

She slept for three hours and the day passed her by. At five-thirty, when the sunlight was beginning to climb the opposite wall, she had a long bath and washed her hair. Then, sitting on the edge of the bed with one towel wrapped around her head and another for a sarong, she picked up the phone and called Clyde.

'Hallo?'

'Clyde . . . is that you?'

'Sure. Who is this?'

'It's Ally. I'm in Washington.'

'Ally! I didn't recognize your voice. What are you doing here? I heard from Freddie and Tess you were in San Francisco.'

'I was, until this morning.'

'What's wrong? You sound funny '

Ally bit her lip. She didn't want to cry on the telephone. She said: 'Something bad has happened. I can't tell you now. Can you meet me here for dinner?'

'The Madison?'

'That's right. I'll book a table at the restaurant.'

'That's fine. Make it seven-thirty. Are you sure you're all right?'

Ally said: 'I'm okay now. I had a rest today, and I'm feeling a little bit better.'

'Okay. I'll see you later on. Look after yourself.'

Ally laid down the phone. Across the room, in the large mirror, she could see herself sitting on the bed in her yellow towels, pale and peaky like a painting on the wall of a woman whom nobody loves.

Clyde was probably the only person who could give her any help. That was ironic, really, because if the Cornelius family had had its way, she never would have known of Clyde's existence. They spoke of him, whenever they had to, as if he was some variety of unpleasant grippe, or a stray dog that none of them could ever quite manage to put out of the way. What made it even more irritating for them was that he was successful; he had inherited the best of his father's qualities for making money, and even though he was nowhere near the multimillion-dollar league, he was a brisk and efficient young manager, and at the age of twenty-one he was an equal partner with a young wheeler-dealer called Ulrik Schroeder in Sorensen's Fast Foods.

Ally hadn't known that she had a half-brother until she was sixteen. Then, by chance, she had seen her father in the restaurant of the Ritz-Carlton Hotel in Boston with a strange young boy – a boy with dark curly hair and a rather Slavic-looking face – and they had been talking to each other intently over lunch. Ally had been shopping with a girl friend of hers from Cambridge, and since she and her friend were both dieting, they had decided on oysters, salad, and broiled scrod. When they were ushered into the Ritz's restaurant, there was John Cornelius, her father, looking unexpectedly flushed and happy, and there was this curious boy.

She remembered walking straight over to her father's table, and the expression on her father's face when she had said: 'Hello, Daddy. Is this someone I ought to know?'

John Cornelius had stood up, laid a hand on the boy's shoulder, and said seriously: 'Ally, this is your brother.'

It had hurt and shocked her at first, but two days later her father had spent an afternoon with her in New York, and given her tea, and explained all about Clyde and why he had kept him a secret. Somehow, whenever she thought about Clyde from then on, she remembered the taste of Lapsang-souchong and lemon, and Scottish scones, and her father's crisp white cuff with its ruby links.

'I once loved a girl named Mara,' her father had said. 'She was very beautiful, and we had an affair. It didn't mean that I loved your mother any the less, or that I don't love your mother now, but as you grow older you will discover for yourself that love takes many different shapes, and that it is possible to love more than one person at the same time, though not always in the same way.

'I finished my affair with Mara when Clara died. There was no question then of it being able to continue. Your mother suspected what had happened, and I myself felt guilty, because I was in Mara's arms when Clara was killed. It took me many years to get over that. But Mara was pregnant with my baby, and when the boy was born she wrote to me and told me what had happened. I sent her money, and supported the boy, and now he's grown up. I see him from time to time, and he's a boy to be proud of. He's like you in many ways.'

'But why did you keep him such a secret?' Ally had asked.

Her father had looked dejected. 'Your mother insisted that you never know. I had to agree. But now you've found out for yourself, and I'd like you to get to know him. He knows all about you.'

Ally's first formal meeting with Clyde had been arranged by their father. They had lunch in New York. It had been snowing that day, and there was a sense of unreality about the entire occasion. Ally could hardly believe that for sixteen years she had had a brother and that she had never known. At first she had felt angry with her father, but as she talked to Clyde more and more, and found that he was enthusiastic and stable and actually happy, she came to understand that if anyone was to blame for the absurdity of their relationship, it was her mother. Ally had developed a crush on Clyde which she had never quite gotten over.

She hadn't seen Clyde for six months, and when he walked into the bar of the Madison in his sharply pressed grey suit, with a white flower in his buttonhole, she was pleased to see that he hadn't changed much. He was tanned a darker brown, and he had put on a little weight, but apart from that he was still the same Clyde Malinsky who had sat opposite her that day in New York, with the snowflakes tumbling against the restaurant window, and explained to her that he wanted to be rich, like their father, but on his own terms

'Clyde,' she said, and he leaned over and kissed her. 'Oh, Clyde, it's so good to see you.'

He sat down, and admired her. She had plaited her hair up the way he liked it, and she was wearing a blue-and-pink chiffon evening dress with a low-cut front that showed her breasts. Around her neck was a three-strand golden choker, and on one wrist she wore a set of eight gold bangles, all different, that had been commissioned from Cartier.

'You get prettier every day.' He smiled. 'Would you like another drink?'

'I'm all right for now. I don't really want to start drinking.'

'Are you afraid you'll never stop?'

'I'm afraid I might cry.'

He reached into his inside pocket and took out his cigarette case.

'You said something awful had happened. Are you going to tell me what it is?'

'I'd like a cigarette.'

When he had reached over and given her a light from his Chinese-red lacquered Hermès lighter, she blew smoke and started to explain. He watched her seriously with his dark, upslanted eyes as she told him about her experiences with the hippies in San Francisco, and about the fleeting love affair with Destry that had ended with his shooting. She didn't cry, but when she had finished telling him what had happened she raised her hands to her face for a moment as if she were trying to convince herself that it really was Destry, and not her, who had died on Telegraph Hill.

Clyde said: 'Did you love him very much?'

Ally said: 'It wasn't so much that I loved him. I did love him, I think. I could have loved him even more. It was just the way that he was killed. He was killed as if he was an irritation to Victor, and I suppose to society as well. Even if they hadn't shot him, he would have gone to the penitentiary for possessing drugs, and I wouldn't have seen him again.'

Clyde was drinking a Bloody Mary. He took a long swallow

and then said: 'That really reminds me of what Dad used to say.'

Ally frowned: 'What does?'

'This whole thing. The way your boyfriend was killed. Dad always used to say that it was dangerous to cross the Cornelius family.'

'But Dad was a Cornelius, too.'

'He was to begin with. But after that affair with Mother, and after *me*, he was pretty well ostracized. Well, you know that. He used to say that he never quite made it to the inner sanctum. They allowed him to run Cornelius Armaments, but all the major decisions were made by Roddy and Grandpa and David Bookbinder. Dad was always out in the cold.'

Ally said: 'But they weren't *dangerous*, were they? I mean, they were very powerful men. But they wouldn't have killed anybody.'

Clyde reached for his drink. 'Wouldn't they? I don't know – not entirely. But Dad always used to say that it was real strange that all throughout the family's history, anyone who's ever been any kind of embarrassment has wound up dead or ruined. I even wonder about Dad sometimes.'

'Oh, Clyde, you can't think that . . .'

'Well, I don't know. I don't have any evidence. But I guess a helicopter accident is a pretty easy thing to arrange, if you have the right contacts.'

Ally bit at her knuckle. 'I can't believe that. It seems like some kind of detective story.'

Clyde said: 'I know. It's absurd. Well, it *seems* absurd on the face of it. But Dad was always saying that Grandpa and David Bookbinder were the kind of people it paid to say yes to.'

'But Dad had something to be sore about. I mean, the way they treated him after Clara died – the way that Mother treated him . . .'

'Sure. Some of what he said must have been sour grapes and nothing else. But he was always going on about Bookbinder, and why Bookbinder had to resign, and he always used to say that if he could only find out the facts, he could give Book-binder a taste of his own medicine.'

The maitre d' came through the doors from the restaurant and informed them that their table was ready. They went through and took their seats and Clyde ordered a half-bottle of champagne to start the meal off. The Montpellier was crowded as usual, and candles sparkled on every table.

When they'd ordered, Clyde said: 'I don't have any proof about this, and I could be completely off the track. But when Bookbinder resigned in 1954, it wasn't just because of old age, like everyone thought.'

'Why not? He must have been near seventy.'

'He was. But he was still active, and he was perfectly fit. What's more, he resigned just before an important oil deal in the neutral zone with the Kuwaitis, and the whole thing ended up in Getty's lap instead. Dad said that what happened was that someone tied Bookbinder's name up with a murder that had been committed about thirty years before. Apparently it was a complete fluke. One of these writers who goes around interviewing old-timers had gone to the backwoods of Pennsylvania and talked to some ancient old guy, and lo and behold the ancient old guy had said he was going to break his silence after all this time and tell who'd done a famous unsolved local murder.'

Ally finished her champagne. 'Clyde,' she said, 'this all seems so farfetched.'

'It is,' insisted Clyde. 'It *is* farfetched. Dad said that, too, but that's why he believed it. He said it was so farfetched you could never have made it up. It just had to be true.'

'And the murderer was David Bookbinder? Is that it?'

Clyde shook his head. 'Oh, it wasn't as obvious as that. The book writer managed to track down the murderer's sister, who lived in Pittsburgh or someplace like that, and even though the murderer was long since dead, she remembered who had called him up that day in 1920-something and given him the hit job. So the writer tracked down the guy who had commissioned the killing, and as far as Dad knew, he spilled the beans.'

'What are you saying?' asked Ally with a quizzical look. 'That David Bookbinder was a hired gun?'

Clyde shook his head. 'Not in a thousand years. But in some way, Dad used to think that he was connected with people who were. I don't know how, or who, or why. All I know is that Dad used to say that if you added up all the people who had got in Grandpa's way, you'd be surprised how many of them had died from unnatural causes.'

'But David Bookbinder's *dead* now,' said Ally. 'How could this have anything to do with Destry?'

'Because I *feel* it,' answered Clyde. 'Because I feel that what happens to ordinary common murderers happens to organizations as well. Once they've established the criterion that wealth and power are worth more than human life, they'll continue to eradicate anyone who threatens or even provokes them.'

'Clyde,' said Ally gently, 'you're not getting paranoid about this, are you?'

Clyde forked up some lobster. 'Well, maybe you think I am. But let me tell you some other people who irritated Cornelius Oil, or its associated corporations. Andrew Bailey, of Incorporated Electrics, and he died in a shooting in 1936. Dutch Schultz, the numbers racketeer, and he died in a shooting in Newark in 1935. And the latest one I can find is Henry F. Preston, who was the man who tried to sue Cornelius Oil for offshore pollution in 1961. He died in an "accidental" shooting at his home in Jacksonville.'

Ally said: 'I don't know why you don't tell someone about this.'

Clyde grunted. 'Who? The government? The police? Maybe I'm on the wrong track, and I'm just chasing shadows. But supposing I'm right? How long does it take before the eradication squad gets after me?'

Ally finished her lamb and laid down her fork. 'Clyde,' she said, 'I don't want to sound patronizing, but are you sure that it's not just your feelings about the Cornelius family that's making you think all this? I mean, maybe it's nothing more than a coincidence.'

Clyde chewed his food in silence for a moment. Then he looked up and said: 'Are you convinced that Victor had nothing at all to do with your boyfriend's death? Are you absolutely sure that he didn't pay those cops a few hundred bucks to finish him off?'

Ally stared at Clyde for a moment, and then lowered her eyes.

'Well?' said Clyde.

'No,' answered Ally in a husky voice. 'I'm not sure at all.'

Clyde reached across the table and held her hand. 'That's exactly the way I feel about it,' he told her. 'I don't have any evidence, only guessing and hearsay, but from what I know of Grandpa and Roderick and Victor – well, I wouldn't put it past them. That's all.'

'Do you think we ought to tell Freddie and Tess?'

'I don't know. I don't think so. Tess is okay, but Freddie has his feet in both camps. Even Tess is kind of flippant. I don't think she'd take it too seriously.'

'So what are we going to do?' asked Ally. 'How can we find out more?'

Clyde said: 'I don't know. I don't know what to do. Sometimes I think the whole idea is totally stupid, but the more I think about it, the more it makes sense.'

Ally said: 'Have you tried talking to Emma?'

He shook his head. 'I don't see Emma anymore. We split up about a month ago.'

'I'm sorry.'

'Oh, it was bound to happen. Mutual disregard.'

The waiter brought a plate of iced chestnut soufflé for Clyde, and he started to spoon it up. Ally had nothing but black coffee.

'No wonder you're putting on weight,' she told him.

'It's not the food,' he said. 'It's lack of exercise. I'm chained to my desk fourteen hours a day. Sorensen is growing all the time. Did you know we're now the second largest distributors of hamburger meat in the whole region?'

She grinned. 'No, I didn't. But I'm impressed.'

He said: 'You know, I always thought it was a pity that you and me were related.'

She didn't say anything, but waited to hear what he was going to say next.

'What I mean is,' Clyde explained, 'we always get along so well. You know, you're the first person I've been able to speak to about this David Bookbinder thing. It's been bottled up inside me, and when you can't speak your mind, you wonder if you're going crazy.'

'You're not crazy. You may be wrong, but you're not crazy.'

'That's what I think.'

He scraped up the last few traces of his soufflé and then sat back in his chair. 'Are you going back home?' he asked her.

'Home?'

'Well, back to New York.'

'Mother's still in Europe. There's no point.'

'And you've given up San Francisco for good?'

'I'm not sure. I think so. I had a dream when I went there, of why I was, and what I could be. But it was only a dream. Victor came along and woke me up.'

'I think Victor's an unmitigated worm,' said Clyde. 'He's been crawling around ever since he was old enough to talk, and he's never had the guts to stand on his own two feet.'

Ally shrugged. 'Perhaps we shouldn't be too hard on him. After all, he's the only one who keeps the business together, as he keeps on reminding us.'

'That's untrue,' said Clyde. 'If anybody keeps that business together, it's Celia. Did Dad ever tell you about Roderick and the aeroplane?'

'I don't think so.'

'Remind me to tell you sometime. It's a painful story. Now, listen . . . do you want a brandy?'

Ally reached out her hand and touched the back of Clyde's tanned wrist. 'Do you think we could have one upstairs? I'm feeling kind of tired now.'

He looked at her narrowly.

'Upstairs?'

She nodded. Her eyes were misty, and the flickering white candle in the centre of the table made them shine like moonstones under water.

'Ally . . .' he said.

She grasped his wrist tighter.

'If you don't want to come,' she said softly, 'then all you have to do is say no.'

He said: 'Are you sure you really want me to?'

She nodded again.

Clyde took his hand away and reached for his cigarettes. He gave one to Ally and lit them. She puffed nervously for a few moments and then said: 'I suppose I shouldn't think of things like that. I suppose you think I'm still in shock.'

He shook his head. 'No, I don't think that.'

'You seem to disapprove.'

'I'm not disapproving. If you must know I'm very moved.'

'Moved?'

He leaned forward across the table. 'I fell in love with you the day I first met you. I never thought that you might feel the same way about me.'

'You didn't guess?'

He took his cigarette out of his mouth. 'How could I? I hardly ever see you.'

'Well,' she told him unsteadily, 'it looks like we're the two misfits. The two odd-feathered birds who stuck together.'

'You're not a misfit.'

'I had a twin who died. You don't know how much of a misfit that makes me feel.'

Ally signed the check and they left the Montpellier and walked out into the hotel lobby. A bus was parked on M Street outside, and more Japanese tourists were arriving in the lounge. A woman in a mink wrap was holding her toy dog and complaining to her bald bespectacled husband about the heat. Finally he snarled: 'Mildred, I'm not God, dammit. If you want it to freeze, ask Him.'

Ally and Clyde went up in the elevator. They were accompanied by a man in a loud plaid jacket who sniffed continually. They didn't hold hands or even look at each other.

Ally unlocked the door of her suite and they went inside. The drapes were drawn and the chambermaid had turned down the corner of the bed. Ally shucked off her shoes and went across to switch on the television. 'Would you like a drink?' she asked him. 'It's all in the cabinet there. The key's in the drawer.'

While Clyde poured them brandies, she walked over to the window and looked out at the night. The faint honking of motor horns was mingled with the monotonous sound of the air-conditioning. She felt light-headed and excited, as if something good was going to happen to her.

The ten-o'clock news was on television. There was a protest about discrimination in Maryland schools, and a county official was trying to explain his policy to a group of disgruntled parents. One of the parents said: 'It ain't natural. It just ain't natural.'

Ally turned from the window and lifted her evening dress over her head. It settled on the floor like a pink-and-blue cloud. Clyde was sitting on the end of the bed with his glass of brandy, and she went up to him in bra and panties and turned her back.

He looked at her curving back, and the spread of her hips. She said 'Please unhook it for me.'

He reached up and unhooked the catch of her bra. Her breasts came free, and he put his hands around and felt the soft weight

653

of them in his fingers. The tips of his index fingers touched at her nipples and they knurled and hardened.

She turned around and put her hands on his shoulders. He kissed her breasts, softly and lightly at first, but then he took the stiffened nipples between his lips, and sucked them against the roof of his mouth. Then he nipped her with his teeth, and she closed her eyes and sighed. She held one of her breasts in both hands, and offered it up to his kisses and his bites until she could hardly take any more.

She pulled off his coat almost violently, and then stripped off his tie and his shirt. The sleeve of the shirt tore, but neither of them cared. Then she pushed off his shoes, and tugged at the belt of his pants. She was whining with excitement when his pants were around his knees, and she gripped his rigid hardness through his white shorts.

They were both panting hard when she climbed astride him and reached down to guide his erection up between her legs. Then she arched herself backward and almost lifted her knees clear of the bedcovers, so that she sank down on him with her full weight. It went up so far that she cried out, but she wanted it that way. She wanted it to be so beautiful that it hurt, and so painful that it was beautiful.

Clyde said: '*Ally . . . Ally . . .*' but after that it was nothing but ferocious kisses and the feverish strenuous coupling of two people who had to blot out the meaning of the act with the passions of the act itself.

At the moment of orgasm, Ally bit her own hand so hard that she almost wept. Then it was all over, and they were lying side by side, sweating and gasping for breath, elated and terrified by what they had done.

Ally rolled over, winding herself in the bedcovers. Clyde stayed where he was, wiping the perspiration from his face with his hand.

She said: 'I suppose you know we've condemned ourselves to hell?'

He coughed. 'Do you really believe that?'

'Why not? I like to think there's a reward in heaven for being good. So there must be a punishment for being sinful.'

'Is that what they told you in San Francisco?'

'They don't preach anything but love and forgiveness in San Francisco. That's apart from how to roll joints and steal paperback books.'

'They didn't tell you how to cope with incest?'

Ally sat up. She looked at Clyde for a long time. 'Don't use that word,' she said. 'It doesn't describe it at all.'

'That's what it's called, isn't it?'

'No. It's love, not incest.'

He got up off the bed and rescued his coat from the floor. 'Do you want a cigarette?' he asked her.

She watched him take two out of the pack and light them. 'I wish you wouldn't call it that,' she said. 'We're only half-related. We don't even look alike.'

'Celia thinks we do.'

'I don't care what Celia thinks. Celia's a domineering old bitch, in any case.'

Clyde sat down on the bed and gave one of the cigarettes to Ally. 'It's not even so much what Celia thinks,' he said gently. 'It's what the law thinks, as well. We could be arrested for this.'

She lay back and watched the smoke rise to the ceiling. 'I get the feeling you're trying to make me feel guilty,' she said.

'I just want you to understand the problems.'

'If I love you, is that a problem?'

'Not in itself.'

'But it's a problem if anybody else finds out?'

He nodded. 'Perhaps we ought to agree to stay away from each other.'

She said: 'Could you?'

'Could I what?'

'Stay away? After this.'

He shrugged. 'It doesn't have any future, does it?'

'That's not what I asked.'

He stood up again and walked naked to the window. She looked at his broad back and his muscular buttocks. He had the body of a man who hasn't quite reached maturity – still lean and well-proportioned, but gradually broadening and thickening across the shoulders and hips.

'I could quite easily love you so much that I would never be able to let you go,' he said simply. 'I told you that I fell in love with you the day I first saw you. In a way, I've loved you ever since. It's always seemed to me that we have so many secrets to share, and that we're so much alike. After I met you, I had fantasies about you. Some of them were really sexual. Now we've actually made it all come true, and it was a hundred times better than any of the fantasies. But that's the trouble. It's like everything else, isn't it? It's too good to be true. It can't happen and we both know that it can't.'

There was a long silence. Then Clyde came back to the bed and sat down beside her again. She reached over between his broad thighs and held his soft penis in one hand, gently squeezing it and caressing it.

'Yes,' she said, without letting go. 'Yes, you're right.'

They went to the cemetery where their father was buried. He had asked in his will to be buried in Washington, the city he had made his home after Clara's death in 1945. The cemetery was on a tree-shaded slope not far from the parkway, and when they arrived early in the morning the wrought-iron gates had just been opened. It was still fresh, and the lawns were damp with dew, but it was going to be another hot and humid day.

Ally wore a simple black dress and a black hat with a veil. Clyde wore a dark suit with a black tie. They didn't speak as they walked up the meticulously rolled gravel path to the top of the hill where their father lay.

It was a simple white marble gravestone, and all it said was: *John F. Cornelius. 1917–1967. Beloved Husband of Irene.*

They stopped in the shade of the rustling trees. Ally knelt and laid a spray of white chrysanthemums on the grave, among the earlier flowers that had already wilted.

Clyde said: 'I guess I still can't get used to it. I just can't believe it's him.'

Ally didn't answer. Her eyes were filled with tears. For one fleeting moment she remembered that day on the skating pond, going around and around on the ice, with her father laughing and the sun like a dull orange bulb in the wintry sky.

Clyde turned away and looked down the slopes of petrified gravestones to the bluish haze that came up from the Potomac. He had felt desperately lonely since his father died, and coming up here did nothing to make him feel any better. His mother had suffered a debilitating stroke three years ago, and had been in a nursing home ever since. He saw her once a month, but as time went by he found he was making excuses not to go tnere It was too depressing, arriving with flowers and books to find her pale and paralyzed in her blankets, unable even to smile at him in the coffee-coloured sunlight of her medicated room. His father had been his strength and his courage ever since he was small; and the thought of that warm and active man lying here in this cemetery was more than he could stand.

Ally said: 'You don't think we've let him down, do you?'

Clyde shrugged. 'No. We haven't let him down. He understood love, didn't he? I mean, he understood the kind of love that other people don't understand. He's probably here today because he loved someone else, instead of the person he was meant to.'

'I wish I could talk to him now, about Destry.'

'He'd probably say the same as me.'

'What's that?'

'He'd say that it was always bad luck to cross a Cornelius, and then he'd tell you to leave the whole thing well enough alone.'

Ally lowered her head. 'I was thinking of going to the newspapers. Perhaps to *Time* magazine.'

'What would you say? "My drug-addict lover was shot dead in a police raid and I suspect my cousin"? You don't have any evidence.'

'We know about David Bookbinder.'

'We know what Dad told me about David Bookbinder. But Dad's dead. And even if we could prove it, there's no *prima facie* connection between what David Bookbinder did forty years ago and what Victor's doing now.'

Ally said: 'Isn't there *any* justice?'

Clyde laid his hand on her shoulder. 'Against the rich, no. Especially not against Victor.'

Ally looked down at her father's grave. She had wanted to come because she needed to reassure herself that he had once actually existed and apart from his letters and photographs, this was now the only tangible evidence. But she didn't believe that he was really there, lying in his gold-handled coffin under the dry soil. It seemed such a strange place for him to be.

Clyde said: 'I think I have to go now. Ulrik's expecting me at ten.'

Ally didn't turn around. She said: 'I'll wait here for a little while. I don't know when I'll be able to come again.'

'You're leaving?'

'I think so. I think it's better. I'll go and stay with Freddie and Tess in L.A.'

Clyde stood there for a little while, saying nothing. 'I do love you, you know,' he said at last.

'I know,' answered Ally. 'I love you, too.'

He didn't seem able to leave. He walked a short way down the path, but then he turned around and she was staring at him so sadly that he stopped. He came back again and he put his arms around her and brought her forehead close to his. Through the veil of her hat, her face was like a face in a shadowy looking-glass. He could see the tears on her cheeks, and he was so upset that he could hardly speak.

'Ally, I love you, but we can't.'

She nodded, and swallowed.

'Please, Ally, just tell me that you understand. It isn't because I don't love you.'

She lifted her head and looked at him.

'I'll find somebody else,' she said with a lopsided smile. She reached into her pocketbook and took out a handkerchief. 'I'm sure I'll find somebody else.'

He took hold of her arm. 'Don't make me feel that it's my fault,' he said quietly. 'Just say that you understand.'

She dropped her gaze to the ground. The tears were clinging to her lashes. She whispered: 'I understand, Clyde. I know that we can't go on.'

'And you'll find somebody else?'

She smiled sadly. 'I expect so. Nobody like you, but somebody to love.'

He nodded. 'Well, me too.'

'You'd better go now,' she urged him. 'You don't want to be late for Ulrik. Not when you're doing so well.'

He lifted the black veil of her hat and kissed her. Her lips were warm and soft and salty with tears. Then he lowered her veil again and without saying another word, he turned and walked off down the cemetery path.

Ally stood watching him go, her hands and feet neatly together as if she was standing in church. He gradually disappeared behind the rows of trees, until all she could see was the top of his head, and then that was gone too. She thought: How small people shrink, and how quickly, when they walk away. They dwindle away as if by some extraordinary and uncanny magic, leaving me life-sized and alone.

Farther down the cemetery, she saw an old bent woman in black, a posy of hothouse violets in her hand, making her way painfully and slowly toward a tombstone where a gleaming white angel stood, its arm uplifted, one finger pointing upward to the hazy sky.

1976

I stand for something that this country needs now more than at any other time in its history. Integrity in government . . .

— John T. Russell,
Los Angeles, 1976

Halfway through dinner, Victor pushed away his mutilated plateful of fish, picked up his champagne glass, and rose unsteadily from his seat. Ariadne, who was smoking nervously at the other end of the table, said: 'Have you finished?'

Victor nodded. 'I don't usually eat dinner,' he explained slurrily. 'This was all for your benefit, anyway. I put o⁻ weight very promptly, if I eat dinner.'

'Victor . . .' she said.

'Bring your glass,' he told her. 'I want to sit down in the library.'

She looked quickly at the three servants, standing silent and attentive in the pale green dining room, waiting to clear away the wreckage of their uncomfortable meal. Then she stubbed out her cigarette and followed Victor through the carved double doors into the dim shaded light of the library.

He closed the doors, coughing. He didn't look at her. He said: 'You really shouldn't have come, you know. At the moment, I'm very busy. I have a lot to do. I told you I'd get in touch.'

She attempted a smile. 'Victor, I came because I *love* you! I wanted to give you a surprise.'

'You did that all right,' he muttered ungraciously, but it was so low that she didn't catch what he said. He looked sweatily around the room for his half-finished glass of champagne.

Victor had been drinking almost all day. His big red perspiring head lay on his starched white collar like a boiled New England ham on a platter and it was almost surprising not to see carrots and potatoes arranged around his ears. He had taken a tumbler of Calvados with his scrambled eggs at breakfast, and since then he had attended a full-scale business luncheon with a Pennsylvania coal company; a society wedding reception for the daughter of a Jewish textile importer he didn't like; and the launching of a friend's new yacht down at Sandy Bars. If there was any advantage in owning your airplane, it was the way you could be flown from one alcoholic event to another, with little unnecessary interruption.

Now he was back at Spiermont, his pillared white Colonial mansion on Cape Cod, feeling freshly drunk on top of a pounding hangover, and wanting nothing more than to be rid of Ariadne. His mother was arriving in the morning, and he had fifteen sets of investment accounts to prepare.

When Victor was drunk, which was often, he became brutally argumentative, and as he argued, his arms flailed around like windmill sails. He had a broad, bovine face, like his father's, with a fleshy nose that was cleft at the tip into two prominent bulges.

Awkwardly propped on the big red leather chesterfield, in his formal black dinner jacket and his white dress shirt, he looked like a Wisconsin spinach farmer at his uncle's funeral. In fact, the only instantly appealing point about Victor was that according to a recent issue of *Fortune*, he was the seventeenth richest man in the United States of America.

Ariadne wouldn't sit down. She paced around Victor in a possessive circle. She was not rich. She wasn't even moderately wealthy. She had flown from Los Angeles that same day on a ticket she couldn't afford, and this dinner, which was such an irritation to Victor, meant, in her eyes, the difference between a life of beautiful dreams and a permanent state of gravelly reality.

She tried to be coaxing. 'You're like a *child* sometimes,' she said. 'Like a little boy who can't make up his mind. You need people to make up your mind for you. Can't you see that's why I've come?'

Victor shrugged.

Ariadne felt unsteady and woozy with drink, but she stayed alert. She was a tall, supremely groomed young girl of twenty-one, whose glittering earrings flashed to match her teeth and her dark, acquisitive eyes. You might have guessed she was wealthy the first time you saw her, but every spare cent she earned was invested in looks – in clothes, in hair, in cosmetics. Her tension gave her away. The rich may be a great many things, but they are rarely tense. Tension is for those who have to struggle to survive.

The mahogany doors of the library had eased slightly ajar, and as the servants cleared away the assaulted remains of the poached turbot, they listened discreetly to the blurting of

Victor and the anxious coaxing of Ariadne like a radio serial they didn't want to miss. They kept their eyes on the Sèvres porcelain plates and the Georgian silver cutlery, never permitting themselves anything more than a trace of a smile, even when Victor slapped the arm of the leather chesterfield and shouted: 'But that's Los Angeles! Los Angeles is a completely different fettle of kish!'

Ariadne had her back to him. She was picking at the spine of a leather-bound book with a long red fingernail.

'Is it your family?' she asked him quietly.

'It's nothing to do with my family. My family doesn't come into it. Don't pick at that book, it's a first edition.'

She turned. She was fraught with fear, but she tried to sound as calm as she could. This unfamiliar, offhand version of Victor, so different from the Victor she had known on the Coast, needed careful and sensitive handling.

'I just thought it might be. Your family, I mean. Maybe your mother. You told me she was very . . . well, protective.'

Victor didn't answer. He wouldn't even raise his eyes. His finger went round and round the rim of his glass, making a low screeching sound.

'Victor,' she said. 'You're so strong when it comes to business, and everything else. People admire you, and respect you. They do what you tell them to do, and they don't feel anything but admiration. I've seen it.'

He swallowed champagne. 'So?'

'So why do you let your family rule your heart? Can't you make up your own mind who you want to fall in love with? Can't you do what you want to do?'

'I am doing what I want to do,' growled Victor pettishly. 'I'm getting drunk.'

He reached behind him, knocking over a decorated glass table lighter, and lifted across a half-empty bottle of Moët champagne. He felt awkward and inflated and big, a clumsy giant from Jack and the Beanstalk. He wished to God that Ariadne would go away, but he didn't know how to tell her. He thought she was terrific-looking and arousing, and sexy as hell; but her bluntness and her West Coast manners alarmed him. He knew that he could no more introduce Ariadne to his Mama than turn up at a badminton tournament in black leather pumps. Victor was a man who believed in subtlty and safety. He avoided out-and-out confrontations whenever possible and at all costs. At the age of eight, from the safety of his treehouse, he had sent his younger cousin Freddie to negotiate with his nurse over the ticklish question of some stolen fruitcake. He really wished that Freddie were here now. Ariadne had been stimulating company out on the Coast, but back here, in the quiet cultured circles of Eastern wealth, she looked to him exactly what she was. An ambitious, open-minded, acquisitive hostess from a topless lounge.

He splashed champagne unsteadily into his glass. He felt frustrated and embarrassed enough to crush the glass in his fist, to squeeze it and snap it like Ariadne's mawkish, misguided sense of romance. But he controlled himself, like a trainer tugging the chain of a flea-ridden dancing bear; and he banged the bottle back on the table.

'Victor,' persisted Ariadne. 'Why do you think I came here? I thought you wanted me. You said you wanted me, and when I didn't hear anything, I came.'

'You *shouldn't* have come,' he mumbled. 'I told you what I was going to do. I said I would call you, remember? I said I would call you, and then we'd see about your coming East.'

'Victor, that was three weeks ago. You didn't call.'

'But I was going to,' he said.

She gave a twitchy little smile of desperation. 'Victor, darling, you said you wanted to marry me. I thought if you wanted to marry me, you wouldn't mind. Victor, we were practically *engaged*. You said you wanted to marry me, didn't you?'

He slurped his champagne noisily. He almost shrugged a denial, but even Victor didn't have the nerve to do that.

'Let's say we discussed it,' he said. 'As a possibility.'

Ariadne bit her lip. 'A possibility? Is that all? Just a possibility?'

'Well,' he conceded, trying to make her feel better. 'Let's say it was a little more than a possibility. But it was just a discussion – now, wasn't it?'

'I don't know,' she said simply. 'I suppose I'm all right when I'm out on the Coast, but when I come here, I'm not quite the kind of girl your family likes to have around. Is that it?'

Victor didn't look up. He watched the bubbles rise to the rim of his glass. He wondered, not for the first time, where the bubbles came from. He peered underneath his glass, but as far as he could make out, they seemed to materialize from nowhere at all.

Ariadne shook her head. 'Christ,' she said. 'You're twelve years older than me, and you're five hundred times richer, and you're just like a little kid.'

She didn't know whether she felt like crying or not. All the time, on the flight across to Boston, she had known deep inside her, that he didn't really want her. But it's not easy to give up a dream, particularly when you've just had one tempting taste of it to whet your appetite. She had even told her mother and father she was going East to get married and that when she came back they'd have a wonderful surprise. What was worse, when she'd opened her pocketbook on the plane to find her hairbrush, there was the faded lace garter that her mother had worn at her own wedding, and fifty dollars in creased bills. The money was a gift from her father. He was Greek, and wouldn't send his daughter away without a dowry. Standing in Victor's lavish library, surrounded by leather-bound first editions and volumes of rare prints, she felt the painful absurdity of what she was trying to do. With the whole of her dowry, she couldn't have afforded one book from one shelf.

Victor cleared his throat. 'What you have to understand, Ariadne . . .' he said blurrily. 'What you have to understand is that I have to think about more people than just myself. I am a man of . . . responsibility. I am an heir, you see, and heirs must give very careful consideration to the people they marry.'

Ariadne took a deep breath. 'In other words, you don't think I'm good enough?'

Victor rubbed his eyes. 'For God's sake, Ariadne. You always oversimplify everything. Don't you see that—'

'I don't see anything. All I see is, I thought you wanted me, and now I think you don't.'

Victor drank, and spilled champagne down his chin. He wiped it clumsily with his handkerchief, and then mopped his sweating pink forehead. He sniffed.

'Ariadne, you're being blunt with me, so I'm going to be blunt with you.'

She said softly: 'Go on, be blunt.' But at the same time, she came across and sat down next to him on the leather sofa, very close, with her breast against his arm, and her knee touching his. She took the crumpled handkerchief out of his breast pocket and wiped champagne from his black satin lapel.

'Well,' said Victor, 'our family, the Cornelius family, has been part of American life for seventy years.' He was trying to sound businesslike and pragmatic, like a man explaining the workings of his new lawnmower to his next-door neighbour.

'I see,' said Ariadne. She caressed his knee, which twitched.

'We have interests in oil, in engineering, in airlines . . . thousands upon thousands of people depend on us for their livelihoods . . .'

'Victor,' she said, leaning forward, so that her lips were almost touching his cheek.

He looked at her sideways, without moving his face. If he moved his face toward her, their lips would touch, and that was just what he didn't want.

'What? I'm explaining it to you.'

She stroked his leg. 'You've explained it over and over. You don't understand. I don't want you for oil, or engineering. I don't want you for any other reason except you're Victor.'

He frowned. 'Look,' he said. 'I want you to know that I don't think you're gold-digging.'

She drew back a little. She stared at him – his pink Dutch face. There was something about him – something clumsy and foolish and gauche – that made her feel frustrated and deeply affectionate at the same time. How could a man be so rich and so competent, and yet so ham-fisted in love?

Her fingers traced patterns around the heavy gold rings on his hands. The question is: Can you separate a man from his money? His money represents what he is, what he's made of himself, his background and his character. If wealth is part of Victor's character, is it immoral to want the wealth as well as the man?

'Victor,' she said gently, 'remember those nights in California?'

'Sure,' he said uncomfortably. He was sweating like a ton of pink wax.

'Remember that time we went swimming in the moonlight? That was real beautiful, wasn't it? And remember how we went back to the room, and I dried you, and pampered you, and we made love?'

'Yes. I remember that.'

'Victor,' she said, curling his fine blonde hair around her finger 'wouldn't you like me to do that for you always? Wouldn't you like me to do that for you *now*?'

He tried to reach past her for the champagne bottle. She pressed up against him, and kissed him, little kisses, all over his face. He screwed up his nose.

She's turning me on, he thought to himself. She's turning me on and I refuse to be turned on. She's too brash and she's too cheap, and I wish to God she'd stayed where she was. What's going to happen if Mama turns up? What's she going to say if she sees me sitting in the library with a topless dancer from L.A.? Doesn't this girl realize I have responsibilities? Look at the size of her goddamned breasts! How could I introduce a girl with breasts like that to the British ambassador, or the Parke Stanfields, or anyone? He felt like an adolescent boy caught playing with himself over a copy of *Playboy*.

'Ariadne . . .' he said, trying to fight off her kisses.

'I *know* you've got problems,' she said. 'I know it, darling, I know it. You've got problems with your family and problems with your life and everything. But, Victor, just answer me one question. Don't you think I'd make you a terrific wife?'

Victor felt cornered. 'It's difficult to say,' he said blindly.

Ariadne pressed closer. 'Victor, what are you *talking* about? You told me you loved me. Didn't we have the best two weeks in the whole world? You said you loved me, Victor. You *promised* you did.'

He stood up very abruptly. His white shirt-tail was hanging out of his dinner jacket at the back.

'What are you going to do?' she asked him.

Victor said nothing. He rang the long brocade bell pull for the servants. After a while, his neat little butler, Eustace, appeared, looking like the diminutive Italian barber he had once been. Eustace conscientiously avoided looking in Ariadne's direction, and gave his usual little bow.

'Eustace,' said Victor thickly, 'I want some more Moët.'

'Yes, sir.'

'I also want you to tell Rosen to get a car out. Miss Skouros is staying in Hyannis tonight. Book her a room at Dunfey's.'

'Very good, sir.'

Eustace turned and left. Neither of them noticed that he

669

left the library doors marginally ajar. Victor was too busy simmering in his own inadequacies, and Ariadne was searching in her pocketbook.

'There,' she said, holding up a crumpled handful of dollars.

Victor focused his eyes on the money like a man on the beach trying to see which one of a hundred swimmers is his drowning aunt.

'What's that?' he said.

'Money. You might as well have it. It's my dowry, from my father. It was all that he could afford.'

Victor lurched. He couldn't keep his balance, and he had to sit down.

'Money? What do you mean?'

Ariadne was starting to cry. She wished she wouldn't. She didn't feel like crying. But somehow the tears wouldn't stop pouring out of her eyes.

'I thought I was going to marry you. It was what you said, and I believed you. I'm sorry. But you can have the dowry. You deserve it, I suppose. You've got so many responsibilities, after all. Every little bit helps, doesn't it?'

Victor's eyes bulged. 'What the hell am I going to do with that? How much is it?'

'Fifty dollars.'

He stared at her as if he couldn't believe that sums of money actually came that small.

'Fifty dollars? What the hell am I going to do with fifty dollars?'

Ariadne was weeping openly now. The tears were impossible to stop. They left dark streaks of makeup down her cheeks, and her eyes were blotted like a letter left in the rain.

'It's all . . . my father . . . could afford . . .' she sobbed.

Victor heaved himself to his feet again. He was almost glad she was crying, because that made her look ugly, and when she was ugly, she was defenceless. He could lose his temper with her, the way he lost his temper with inefficient tax lawyers and fumbling accountants.

'For God's sake!' he shouted coarsely.

She lowered her head. Her shoulders shook with intermittent sobs. She had no handkerchief, and she had to wipe her eyes on the backs of her hands.

'I don't understand what you want,' he said impatiently.

Look at that necklace, how many girls do you know with necklaces like that?'

She dumbly put her hands behind her neck and tried to unfasten the necklace, but the clasp wouldn't open.

'I don't care about it,' she wept. 'If you want it back, you can have it. I'm sorry I cost you so much money.'

'I don't want it back!' shouted Victor. 'What's the matter with you? Just because we have a two-week affair, does that mean we have to stay together for the rest of our lives? You'd hate this life! You'd hate it!'

'And what about you?' she sniffed, looking up with a tear-blotched face. 'Would you hate me, too?'

'It's not *possible*,' he said impatiently.

'Why?' she said in a shaky voice. 'You haven't even told me *why* it's not possible.'

He spread his arms. He had an expression of testy resignation on his face. 'You don't grasp what I'm saying,' he told her. 'It's not up to me. I have to think if the destiny of the entire family.'

'Destiny? Don't you ever think about love?'

He didn't answer.

'Don't you ever think that I love you, Victor, and that you might even love me? I saw feelings inside you during that two-week affair that I haven't seen once tonight. Victor, you're a stong, emotional, loving man, but you're letting your family and your money and your own fears stand in your way.'

Victor looked at her. 'You don't know anything about me,' he said, trying to sound cold.

Ariadne's eyes widened. The light from the heavy-shaded library lamps gleamed down her silvery skin-tight dress, as if shiny orange liquid had been poured down her body.

'I know a lot about you,' she said huskily. 'I know that you're sensitive when you allow yourself to be. I know that you're full of affection, when you allow yourself to let it out. I know that you're rich. I know that you don't know anything about real life at all, or real feelings, and that you're terrified that somebody's going to show you. It's very easy to be brave when you're rich, Victor. But it's only when you're poor that bravery really means anything. You're scared of me, aren't you? And you're even more scared of your family.'

Victor reddened 'I think you d better get out of here,' he said. 'I think you've said enough for one night.'

She shook her head You don't even know how much I love you, do you?'

'Look, Ariadne . . .'

She stood up and walked across the shiny parquet flooring. She put her arms around his neck and she tried to draw herself in close to him. He stood sagging and motionless like a pile of pillows about to collapse on the floor.

'Wouldn't you like to give it just one more try?' she whispered. 'All we have to do is leave everything and go upstairs. Even if we don't get married, we could remember this one last night. Wouldn't you like to do that? Wouldn't you like to feel me again, the way you used to, back in California?'

Victor swayed. He couldn't see properly, and he felt nauseous. I want her. I want that soft silvery body of hers, and I want to hear her moan and whimper because I'm giving her everything she craves for. But if I do that she'll still be around tomorrow, and the family are coming around for their meeting tomorrow, and what's Mama going to say about a two-bit topless dancer in a wrinkled evening dress?

He raised his arms, the same way that she had raised her arms to unfasten the necklace, and he pulled her hands away from his neck.

'Ariadne, you have to understand—'

'Victor,' she said, soft and hurt.

'It can't work, Ariadne.'

'You haven't even said why. You haven't even told me why. I spent all of my savings coming here, Victor, because I thought you wanted me. You haven't even said why, or anything.'

He looked at her, standing there, with her smeary makeup and her huge great breasts, and he didn't even pity her.

'It's a question of fitting in,' he said in a bald voice.

She didn't understand. 'What do you mean, fitting in? What kind of fitting in?'

He swallowed. 'Socially. It's a question of fitting in socially.'

She let out a long breath. It hurt her, when he said that, but it also gave her an irrational surge of hope. He was so unsure of himself with women that he thought it would crush her, saying that. He didn't even realize that insults would

672

only stir up her optimism. If he insults me. he must feel *something* for me. At least he's not totally indifferent. If he despises me – well, hatred is supposed to be the next thing to love, and perhaps I can do something about it

All that was wrong with that equation was that Victor knew nothing about soap-opera psychology, and even less about sentimental love. Ariadne, on the other hand, watched, and believed, *The Waltons*.

'Victor,' said Ariadne gently, 'you don't even know what your own feelings are, do you, Victor? Victor, love, you don't.'

Victor stood stiff and uncertain, like President Nixon in the last days of his resignation.

'It has,' he said, 'to be a political, family, and financial decision. I can't take it right away. It has to be thought about.'

She shook her head, almost lovingly. 'Oh, God, Victor, you're such a little baby.'

'Look,' he said awkwardly, 'if you need anything to tide you over . . .'

She stared. 'What do you mean?'

He stuck his hands in his pockets and looked embarrassed 'I mean, if you need any money. If you're in a bind.'

He might just as well have come straight out and called her a cheap West Coast whore. She kept on staring at him, trembling, and she stared at him so long that he had to turn away from her and gaze nervously at the rows of leather-bound books.

'You're paying me off,' she said in a hushed voice.

'Ariadne, it's nothing of the kind. You know what I have to contend with. How could we ever think about *any* kind of future together without thinking about it in a wider context? It has to be analysed in a wider context than just a personal relationship.'

'I won't take your money, Victor.'

He turned, impatient. 'It's not a *question* of taking my money. You just said yourself that you spent your savings coming here. Ariadne, I appreciate what you did. I appreciate it, from the bottom of my heart. I just want to make sure that you're not out of pocket, that's all.'

'Out of pocket?' she said disbelievingly. 'Victor, I love you '

'I *know* that. Ariadne, I *know* that. But, right this minute, I have to confess that I don't know what to say to you.'

'Will you ever know?'

'Ariadne . .

'You just said we had a future together.'

'That was an "if".'

'Well, what does that mean? Does that mean you're really still thinking about it? You have to tell me, Victor. You can't just leave me like this.'

Victor closed his eyes. Through the waves of his hangover, Ariadne's voice sounded like someone speaking through a tin funnel, across a windblown baseball diamond.

'I think you'd better leave,' he said quietly. 'Rosen will drive you to Dunfey's.'

'Victor, I can't go until you tell me.'

He opened his eyes again. She was still there.

'Victor,' she said. 'Please . . .'

'Ariadne,' he said carefully. 'It's going to be very difficult. Look . . if you want to . . .'

'What?'

'Look, you can keep the necklace.'

They stood there facing each other. The big-boned millionaire in the dinner jacket with his shirt-tail hanging out, and the tall curvy dancer in the too-tight silver dress. They faced each other, and for a long while it seemed as if they didn't understand, either of them, why they were there or what they were doing. They looked at each other like two strangers on the Staten Island ferry.

Ariadne, stunned, reached up to touch the emerald pendant, as if it were something she had been carrying about with her all along, and which she had only now discovered to be the real cause of all her misfortunes.

She felt panic; real, sickening panic. If he really meant it, if he really made her go, then she had nothing to go back to at all. For the first time in her life, with Victor, she had walked on handmade Persian carpets, eaten off antique French porcelain with solid silver knives and forks, sipped château-bottled wines and real champagne, dressed in silk and sat on velvet. It was a world that had seemed before like a fantasy, but she had discovered that it really existed. Going back meant her deadend job in the Starlight Lounge, an emerald necklace that would just about pay for the whole trip, and two mystified and oversympathetic parents. She would turn up at her father's tool shop, alone and miserable, and they'd make a fuss over her, feed her with garlic soup

674

and hot rolls, and in the evening she'd bury herself in her mother's arms and cry until it was too painful to cry any longer.

She stepped uncertainly toward Victor, her hands out in front of her, a newly blind woman reaching for the safety of a handrail she couldn't see. Victor gripped her wrists and held her so that she couldn't touch him. She made a funny little noise like a cat mewing.

'Ariadne,' he said. 'You mustn't take this thing the wrong way.'

His words were tightly leashed, but his mind wasn't. He didn't know what he was going to do now. His irritation and his anxiety, aggravated by his drunkenness, were making him act like a crude man-sized puppet made of logs. He wanted to get rid of her. She excited him physically, but he preferred to feel pain at losing her, to wallow in self-pity and talk about 'the terrible lonesomeness of great wealth', than to have to cope with Ariadne's passions and Ariadne's appetite for crude emotion. What she didn't realize – and what he only half-understood himself – was that he was not a whole man. He was already the victim of a crushing disaster, with terminal injuries. He had been buried, at birth, under a mountain of money.

'Victor,' she pleaded. 'Want me, Victor.'

He mouthed 'No' practically silently.

'Victor, you don't know how much I need you. Victor, what am I going to do without you?'

He let go of her arms, pushing her away from him like casting off a rowboat.

'Get a good night's sleep,' he said hoarsely. 'We both need a good night's sleep. I'll call you in the morning and then we'll see.'

'I can't wait, Victor. I won't be able to sleep unless you tell me now.'

She was crying again. Head down in deep, noisy sobs.

'Ariadne . . . I can't tell you now. What do you want me to say? For Christ's sake, let's just call it a day!'

She stood in front of him, clutching herself in her own arms, sobbing like a goose. Victor knew what you had to do in cases of hysteria. He stepped forward, quiet abruptly, and slapped her face.

He didn't expect her to hit back. That was the last thing he

675

thought would happen. But Victor had never hit a woman before; it was something he had seen in movies and read about in magazines. And he had never before provoked a girl who had spent three years of her working life in a topless lounge. Perhaps the fact that she hit him back was the most convincing reason not to marry her.

He had half-turned away in the split second after slapping her, and he didn't even see it coming. The first thing he knew, she had smacked him hard across his right ear, and pushed him violently in the hip. He stumbled clumsily over the big green library chair, and fell with a painful jolt on his right knee. A whole swarm of fear and hopelessness and rejection came flying out of her, and she scratched and pummelled and smacked him, and he had to raise his arm to protect his face.

'*God!*' she shrieked. '*You bastard! You total bastard!*'

'*Get the hell off!*' he roared, but she fell on top of him, breasts swinging, and they sprawled across the parquet floor, kicking and wrestling and struggling. Victor managed to seize one of her wrists, but she reached down with her other hand and squeezed him between the legs, so agonizingly hard that he screamed out loud. Enraged, he flung her over on her back and held her against the polished boards with his own weight.

'Ariadne!' he gasped. 'For Christ's sake . . . *Ariadne!*'

She jerked her face to one side. She wouldn't look at him. She didn't want to hear anything but the words for which she'd flown three thousand miles.

'Ariadne,' slurred Victor, pressing on her even more heavily. 'Listen, Ariadne. I'm talking and I want you to listen. We had a great time together on the Coast. I'm not denying it. Don't let it ever be said that we didn't have a great time together on the Coast. But you have to see my side of the story. Can you see my side of the story, Ariadne?'

She wouldn't answer, and she still wouldn't look at him.

'Ariadne!' he snapped. 'Can you hear me, Ariadne?'

In response, she simply twisted her body underneath him.

Victor was an adolescent when it came to sex. When girls came close to him, and he could feel their warmth, he responded with a directness that both excited and embarrassed him. Now Ariadne was shifting between his thighs, and the effect was immediate. He was shaking and trembling, and he could feel knots tightening up in his muscles like twisted trees. How could she be so tantalizing and so dumb at

676

the same time? How could she lie there wriggling between his legs, being so blind and nagging and ridiculous? He couldn't marry her. Couldn't she see that? Couldn't she understand? Why the hell did she keep on nagging and nagging and nagging? Couldn't she understand English?

He despised her, and at the same time he felt a rush of lust that made him grimace with frustration. He wanted to hurt her, and rape her, and see her jump and jolt and beg for mercy and beg for more. He felt heated urges that made him almost incoherent.

'*Ariadne*!' he shouted again.

She kept her face away. He raised his arm and smacked her across the cheek – such a cracking blow that her head jerked. Her cheek was blotted with a wide scarlet mark, and tears ran out of her eyes, mingled with black eye makeup.

'*I'll hit you*!' he bellowed. '*I'll hit you again*!'

Ariadne saw sheets of red in front of her eyes, and all she felt was pain. She twisted herself around underneath him, breaking free, and tried to wriggle away like a slippery silver snake. She nearly made it, scrabbling on hands and knees on the shiny parquet floor. But Victor clawed out and caught her ankle, and he wrenched her toward him, panting and gasping.

He was shrieking, himself, with rage. They were both kneeling, and he hit her straight in the face with his fist. She felt her nose burst inside, and she banged back on the floor like a falling chair. Blood sprayed over her lips and splattered her breasts.

Victor fell clumsily on top of her. He seized hold of her silver evening dress at the back, and he tugged it with his big red hands. She whimpered and cried and hit back at him, but he tore the dress halfway up, baring her naked bottom and her curved waist. He bear-hugged her around the body, and pulled open his own trousers with one hand.

Her blood dripped quickly onto the floor in front of her. She twisted again, and tried to pull herself away, but Victor held on to her with a bitter, unremitting, clamplike grip.

'Victor,' she bubbled. 'Please . . .'

He pushed himself against her. He was coughing with the effort. He pushed and rubbed himself against her again and again. Ariadne, with her eyes almost closed with bruises, watched the blood splash onto her hand, and realized that

677

Victor was trying to rape her, but couldn't. He loved her so little that he couldn't even rape her. After a few seconds, without a word he let her go. She heard him fall back onto the library floor. On hands and knees she crawled over to the table and unwound the napkin from the bottle of champagne to bathe her nose.

Victor himself felt winded and numb. He lay on the floor with his fly open, staring up at the library ceiling, a man knocked down in the accident of his own destiny. The chandelier sparkled in his eyes and reminded him of birthdays. He knew what he had done to Ariadne, but he had no idea of what he might have done to himself. Right now, right at this moment, he didn't want to think.

Ariadne managed to stand up. The napkin was dark red, but she could feel a clot forming in her nose, and the worst of the bleeding seemed to have stopped. Her head pounded, and her eyes were misty with pain. She felt like the survivor of a senseless accident, nothing else. She was shocked and quivering and a long way past tears. The greatest shock of all was not the punch, nor any of the violence. It was the final, total rejection. The millionaire was lying like a bundle of washing on the floor of his library, and he really didn't want her. She sat down on the chesterfield, feeling faint and giddy, and then she was sick. Some of it was fish, but most of it was champagne.

Now there was no alternative – she had to stay the night. Victor called Dr Weywood up from Hyannis, a fussy and tiresome old man with very chilly hands, and Dr Weywood examined her face, and gave her a cold compress, and told her she was lucky she hadn't broken her nose. Before he let the doctor into the room, Victor gave Ariadne a confused speech on why she had to say that she had taken a fall from a horse. Ariadne lay in her white nylon nightie in the large French walnut bed, unmoving and still shocked, and didn't say anything at all.

Victor left her. He took a long shower, sudsing his plump body over and over with coconut-oil soap. Then, in a dragon-patterned bathrobe of ultramarine silk, he went into his office and called his personal lawyer, Dick Marini, on the telephone. Eustace brought him a tray of black coffee, which he drank in quick, scalding mouthfuls. He checked his watch and it was two-thirty in the morning.

He leaned back in his own reclining chair, swivelling around so that he could look out over the night-time gloom of his grounds, and waited while the phone rang and rang and rang. Eventually it was picked up. A weary voice said: 'Who is this?'

'Dick? It's Victor.'

'Oh, hi, Victor. Do you know what time it is? Don't you whiz kids every sleep?'

'Dick, I think I have a little problem here.'

'Can it wait till the morning?'

Victor drummed his fingers on the brown leather top of his desk. 'If it could wait until morning, I wouldn't have called you now.'

Dick sighed. 'Okay. What's wrong?'

'Well . . .' said Victor. He suddenly realized he was embarrassed. He could hardly find the words to describe what had happened; but he knew, for his own protection, that he had to. 'Well, Dick, it's a girl.'

'A girl?' Dick managed to keep most of the surprise out of his voice. 'What kind of a girl?'

Victor blurted it all out. 'She's a girl I . . . uh, met in Los Angeles. You remember that West Coast business trip I did three or four weeks ago, in April? That was the time. I just met her, you know, in a club. She wasn't anything special, but, you know, we kind of got along. She stayed around for the whole two weeks and we kind of got along pretty well.'

'I see,' said Dick. He was evidently taking notes. 'Did you sleep with her?'

'Well, I guess a couple of times. But that's not the problem.'

'What is the problem?'

Victor poured himself some more coffee. The silver spout rattled unsteadily against the cup, and he just couldn't keep it still.

'She, uh, came up here. I mean, she flew up here today. She was here when I got home, and she seemed to have the idea fixed in her mind that I had promised to marry her. I mean, Dick . . . don't ask me where she got the idea, because you know how careful I am. But that was what she was saying. She said she loved me, and she wanted to marry me, and that

679

out on the Coast I was supposed to have suggested that I marry her.'

Dick Marini sniffed. 'What kind of a dame is she?'

'Er, well, she's not exactly a Bouvier.'

'A hooker?'

'No, no, nothing like that. She works in one of those lounges, you know? The topless lounges. Kind of a hostess.'

'In other words, a hooker.'

'Well, I don't know.'

Dick made more notes. Then he said: 'Did she threaten you?'

'Not exactly.'

'What do you mean, not exactly?'

'Well, this is the problem. She went on and on at me, and in the end I asked her to stay for dinner – I mean, just for the sake of courtesy. She flew all the way from L.A. just because she had this kind of stupid idea that I was in love with her – you know? I hardly even remembered the girl, but the least I could do was feed her. Anyway, we both got drunker than we should, and we had a kind of an argument.'

Dick sounded suspicious. 'What kind of an argument?'

'Well,' said Victor uneasily, 'she got hysterical, so I hit her.'

There was a lengthy silence. Then Dick said: 'Go on. You hit her, and what then?'

'She hit me back. So I punched her in the face. And that's just about it.'

'You punched her in the face?'

Victor coughed. 'That's about the size of it, yes.'

'Where is she now?'

'She's right here, asleep I guess. I called Dr Weywood, and I told her to say that she'd taken a dive off a horse.'

'She did what?'

Victor frowned. 'She fell off a horse. I told her to say she fell off a horse.'

Dick Marini tried not to sound too exasperated. But his voice was tightly under control when he said: 'Victor, you just did the worst thing you could have possibly done.'

'How's that? What do you mean?'

'I mean that, as your guest, that girl was your responsibility, and you want to tell a court that you let her ride one of your horses, after a boozy dinner, in the dark?'

Victor swivelled around and leaned heavily on his desk. 'What court? What are you talking about?'

'The court that every right-minded citizen goes to when someone very rich does them the slightest injury, that's what I'm talking about. So what's it to be? She fell off a horse, which makes you negligent, and liable for damages; or you punched her in the face, which makes you a sitting duck for assault charges. Either way, you're going to drop a bundle of money, and worse than that, you're going to cop some very bad press.'

Victor chewed at his thick raspberry-coloured lips and said nothing. He didn't blame himself for what had happened. It had been a nasty snag devised by fate and misfortune especially to trap and confuse him. He didn't even blame Ariadne. Victor had been brought up to believe that destiny and the lives of the Cornelius family were the woof and the warp of American history, and that other people were simply incidental flecks of coloured wool. He thought nothing at all of Ariadne, except that she had been picked by fate to arouse his lust, and that his lust had made things go wrong. His own failings were far more important to him than any of Ariadne's strengths.

'Dick,' he said carefully, 'we have the election November.'

There was no reply.

'Did you hear me, Dick?' he repeated.

'I heard you. I'm thinking.'

'Dick, we have to keep any mention of this out of the papers. And away from Mama, too.'

Dick mulled over that. 'Don't you think you have a duty to tell her?' he suggested. 'She wouldn't thank you if it came out later.'

'I don't know. I don't know what to do. Christ, Dick, that's why I'm calling you. Give me some creative suggestions.'

'Well,' said Dick, 'do you think she's susceptible to money?'

Victor coughed. 'I'm not sure. I offered her something before – kind of expenses – but she didn't seem too interested. She comes from a pretty run-down background, though. Her father runs a garage, or a handyman store, something like that. I guess I could try waving a few conciliatory dollars under her nose.'

Dick said: 'Wait till I get there. I think you've done enough

681

already. Meanwhile, don't admit to anything. Were there any witnesses? Did anyone see you hit her?'

'There was nobody else in the house.'

'How about servants?'

'I don't understand.'

'Victor, in court, a servant's evidence is just as valid as anyone else's. Did any of the servants see you do it?'

Victor tried to think. 'Well, there was Eustace and one of the others. They helped clear up afterward. The girl had a nosebleed. But they didn't actually see me hit her. No, I mean nobody saw that.'

Dick let out a short, tight sigh of relief. 'Thank heaven for small mercies. Listen, go to bed now. Keep that girl around at your place. I'll come round first thing in the morning and talk to both of you. I don't want her to think that she has any grounds for complaint against you. But on the other hand, I also want her to know that if she tries to get smart, it's going to be the worse for her.'

Victor swallowed tepid coffee. 'I could tell her that myself.'

'Victor,' warned Dick, 'that is not your line of country. Leave it to me. You pay me enough to do it, and I'll do it well. Meanwhile, don't talk to the girl at all, except to state simple facts like "this is your breakfast" or "oh, what a beautiful morning." You got it?'

'Okay, I got it. But listen, Mama and the family are coming around tomorrow.'

'All right. I'll make it early. Thanks for your call.'

'Okay,' said Victor, and laid the receiver down. He sat motionless, hunched, for a long while. He was beginning to feel bruised and sick and desperately tired. He still had all his investment figures to go through, and it was a quarter of three in the morning. The biweekly family meeting – once every alternate Thursday – was scheduled to start at nine-thirty, and Victor was expected to have his statistics ready. He dragged a heavy file across the desk toward him, and opened it up. The first page said: 'Lubricant Equity (Panama).' He unscrewed his pen.

About an hour later, when all the servants had gone to bed, and the corridors of Spiermont were silent and dark, Victor thought he heard a car engine start. He looked up from the pool of light in which he was working, with his horn-rimmed half-glasses perched on the end of his bulbous nose, and listened. There was a kind of rustling noise from somewhere outside, but it may have been nothing more than an early-morning wind rising up in the trees. He checked his watch, shrugged, and went back to work.

By half-past five, he had finished. A grey, haggard light was beginning to strain through the office windows, and outside he could make out the shadowy shapes of the trees and the sloping lawn. He stretched, rubbed his eyes, and then reached over and switched off his desk lamp. He was tired, but he liked to work at night. He like the idea of staying up late while the rest of America slept, toiling through figures that would keep thousands of slumbering men in employment. When the sun rose, they wouldn't even know what Victor had done to protect their jobs in the still small hours.

He stood up and walked to the window. Somehow, when the sun came up, problems didn't seem so bad. The problem of Ariadne, once Dick Marini had sorted it out, would be tidied up, parcelled into a legal file, and that would be the last of it. He remembered the heated nights that he and Ariadne had spent in California, and he had a dark small twinge of regret; but as Ariadne had made her bed, so she would damn well have to lie in it. Girls from topless lounges don't marry responsible chief executives, and that was an indisputable rule of American life. Out of his top drawer Victor took a small cheroot and lit it. He didn't smoke very often, but this morning he felt he deserved it. The lighter on his desk, in the shape of an oil derrick, was a gift from his mother.

He opened the French windows and stepped out onto the wide Italian-marble patio. There were round, well-trimmed rosemary bushes in cerise marble pots, and wrought-iron tables and chairs. There was an early-morning chill in the air, and the grassy slopes were white with dew, but Victor felt he needed refreshing. He discarded his leather slippers and in his blue bathrobe walked on pudgy bare feet across the patio, down three steps, and into the grass

A few birds chipped and cheeped in the trees, but otherwise the estate was silent, and the house was dark.

He made his way around the back of the house, where tall Doric pillars supported a stark and elegant arch. There was a wider patio at the back, with a long, hedge-lined swimming pool. The pool was entered by wide, semicircular steps, at the top of which stood a white marble statue of a naked nymph riding a giant sea horse. Victor liked the statue, because it was sexy, and fashioned with an exquisite eye for detail, but his Mama considered it 'unnecessary'.

The pool looked cold and silvery this morning, like a breathed-over mirror, and the hedges alongside it were sparkling dully with dew. Victor approached the pool from the slope above the back of the house, down a series of grassy steps, and admired, as he approached, the symmetry of the house's reflection in the still water.

It was only when he reached the marble patio around the pool itself that he realized the surface of the water was covered in oil. It was streaked with iridescent, curving rainbows of scum. Frowning, not understanding what had happened, he looked around the pool for signs of vandalism or oil cans. There was nothing. The white naked nymph, with her frozen erotic smile, rode her sea horse down the far end of the pool, and mocked him to say it was she.

'Eustace!' he called, even though he knew that Eustace couldn't possibly hear him. His voice sounded flat and weak. 'Eustace!'

He stepped right up to the edge of the pool and peered through the oil into the water. Then, there was no mistaking what had occurred. Dark, flat, and distorted, the outline he saw was of a Cadillac limousine, drowned in the deep end of the pool, leaking oil and gasoline in misty clouds.

His heart thumped, and he felt desperately short of breath. He still didn't know what this meant. He went down on his hands and knees, shading his eyes against the white reflections from the house, trying to make out the shape of the submerged car. It was one of his own, one of three Cadillac Broughams he kept at Spiermont, and someone had evidently driven it across the grass, across the patio, down the steps, and into the water. He could even see the tyre marks on the edges of the steps.

Victor had to lean right over the water before he could see clearly enough to discover who had done it. Wallowing against the driver's window, stirred by the faint currents in the water, was a pale human arm, and the shine of a body that was silver as a herring.

684

He clambered to his feet, panting, and this time he really didn't know what to do

Celia Cornelius, with an uncanny sense of occasion, had arrived in a large black hat, with black plumes. She was a tall, elegant woman of sixty, her striking face still beautiful, with a thin distinctive nose, china-blue eyes, and full, naturally red lips. Her hair was shining platinum white, tinted with an aura of pink, and her sapphire-and-diamond earrings tinkled from ears that were as soft as a young child's. In her superbly tailored black suit of watered silk, with her lean gold-knobbed cane, she looked like a wealthy raven, or the matriarchal proprietor of a fashionable funeral parlour. She spoke in high, dry tones, and lifted her hand toward people when she addressed them, as if waiting for them to click their heels and kiss it.

'The question is,' she said imperiously, 'why did the unfortunate girl do it? *That* is the question.'

Dick Marini sniffed. He was leafing back through his notebook, trying to read his squiggles of the previous night.

'That's just one of the questions,' he said bluntly. 'The whole thing is a mass of imponderables. I think the best thing we can do is find out just how much we can get away with, and just how much we can't.'

Celia frowned. 'I don't think the Cornelius family has ever had to *get away* with things, Mr Marini. Victor is not exactly a hardened criminal, to say the least. The poor boy has asthma.'

'So did Al Capone,' said Dick. 'I don't remember it did *him* a lot of good.'

The family had gathered. Unusually, they sat in the south drawing room, a spacious, coffee-and-white room decorated in French rococo style. There were tall windows on three sides, and the morning sun slanted through hand-worked curtains of Brussels lace, casting decorative patterns over the polished maplewood floor. Between each of the windows stood small gilded tables with curved and decorated legs, topped with Dresden vases. Above them was a series of richly coloured eighteenth-century Dutch oils depicting views of Amersfoort at different seasons in the year.

The family themselves sat around the carved and gilded fireplace on an antique Indian carpet of subtle reds and blues

685

A rare and fascinating Fabergé clock, decorated in gold and enamels, chimed softly on the mantelpiece. In the elaborate mirror behind it, like another painting, you could see Celia Cornelius, rigid and upright in a tall-backed chair of old gold plush; Dick Marini, plump and worried, sitting next to her on a French dining-room chair; on a long rust-coloured settee, quiet and casual, Victor's cousin Freddie, Freddie's sister Tess, and his other cousin Ally; and Victor himself, in a pea-green jacket that made him look even more washed-out than he really was, slumped in an awkward rococo chair eating chocolate mints.

'Sounds to me like Victor's done it again,' said Freddie. He was a lean, laconic-looking young man of twenty-nine. His hair was light brown, long, and brushed back. There was something about his face that reminded people of a thin Dustin Hoffman. He wore a red-and-blue-striped blazer and white Humphrey Bogart pants.

Celia looked at him with disapproval. She always had disapproved of Hope's children, particularly when she remembered how often they had ganged up against Victor. They ought to remember that Victor had dedicated the whole of his life to the Cornelius family, from his childhood days, when he counted her garden-party guests on a nursery abacus, to the present time, without once denying his parentage, or his responsibilities, or giving up his duties. A sense of duty may be unexciting, but all of their wealth depended upon it, and through their wealth, the men and women they employed. A sense of duty was more than *Hope's* children had ever had.

'Victor has not "done it again," ' said Celia dryly. 'Victor has always assumed his full burden of duty and obligation, and that has made Victor consistently more open to pressures from outside. Which is more than we can say for some.'

'I propose the first move we make is inform the police,' said Dick Marini. 'It's four hours now since Victor discovered the car, but we can easily say that he discovered it much later, and there won't be any material evidence to dispute that. Apart from that, it wouldn't have made any difference to Miss . . .'

'Skouros,' said Victor.

'To Miss Skouros. She was dead, must've been dead, as soon as the car filled up.'

'Do we *have* to call the police?' asked Celia. 'Isn't it possible that we can deal with this matter in another way? I'm not talking about anything *illegal*, but I do think the family must come first. We do, after all, have the facilities to take responsible action.'

Freddie snorted. 'What do you call responsible action? Paying the girl's parents to swear she was drowned on the *Lusitania*?'

Dick Marini lifted one pudgy hand. 'We've got a problem here that's got some kind of precedent. What we don't need, especially with Victor's election involvement, is another Chappaquiddick. I know this is different, before you all start shouting me down, but in the eyes of the public the whole thing's going to look remarkably similar. Maybe Victor isn't the candidate himself, but his name is closely linked with John Russell's, and if there's any suggestion of scandal or negligence, we're going to find ourselves up to our necks in political mud. So what I'm saying is, the first thing we do is call the cops. That's just what Teddy Kennedy *didn't* do, and that's just what he found so tough to explain.'

Victor was about to say something, but he closed his mouth. His mother, in any case, had lifted her hand regally in Dick Marini's direction, and was giving her own opinion.

'I believe we ought to discuss it a little longer. The trouble with calling in the police is that the whole thing is immediately taken out of our hands. The girl is dead, and there's no bringing her back.'

'Jesus,' said Freddie, 'I hope not. The topless dancer from two fathoms!'

'Freddie!' snapped Victor. 'If you think this is some kind of a joke, then I suggest you get out of here and laugh up your sleeve someplace else. The girl happens to be dead, and the whole family's involved.'

Ally, so far, had said nothing. She rarely had much to contribute at family gatherings. She wore a plain, carefully cut dark blue dress and there were dark circles under her eyes. She didn't smoke, and she sat with her hands in her lap, listening to the random conversation of her cousins with solemn intentness.

Dick Marini made a few notes and then turned around to Ally and said: 'What do you think Ally? Do you have any views?'

Ally didn't look up. She was picking at the clasp of her gold

687

bracelet in a way that reminded Victor disturbingly of Ariadne picking at the spines of his leather-bound books.

'I think the first consideration we have is toward the parents of the dead girl,' she said quietly. 'I also agree we should call the police. There seems to be a lot of talk about saving Victor's political reputation, but I seem to remember that this family was supposed to live by the principle of doing right by other people.'

Celia raised one elegant eyebrow. 'Ally, dear, I don't recall that anyone suggested anything different.'

Ally shook her head. 'I think,' she said firmly, 'that your suggestion of responsible action was another way of saying that we ought to find some way to shirk our responsibilities.'

Celia pursed her lips, and she rapped the gold ferrule of her walking cane on the floor, *tap-tap-tap*, as if casting an impatient spell.

'Mr Marini,' Celia said tautly, 'I think you'd better explain to Ally what will happen if the press gets hold of this.'

Dick Marini pulled a face. 'There's no doubt that they'll call it Chappaquiddick II. This is supposed to be a real clean election, and on our side we've done everything we can to make sure that our candidate and our campaign staff are gleaming white and straight as arrows. This thing, this accident, this could mean the whole difference between victory and failure.'

Ally, now, did look up. Her blue eyes were slightly myopic, and they were always disturbing and bright.

'Is that it?' she asked. 'Is that the price of telling the truth? A seat in the White House?'

Freddie blew smoke. 'Aw, come on now, Ally. You're being a little melodramatic here. The real point is, what are we going to do to save Victor's bacon?'

Ally flushed. 'I thought you were on my side,' she said. 'I thought you believed in this family's ideals.'

'Of course I believe in the family's ideals. But what's the good of having ideals if it doesn't make any difference whether you have them or not? We're talking about a dead girl here, and as Celia says, we can't really do much to bring her back to life. I think Victor's behaved like a complete screwball, but what's done is done, and what we have to do now is see if we can minimize the problem.'

Victor reddened, but Celia raised her hand to silence him.

She liked the way the tone of the argument was going, and she didn't want Victor antagonizing Freddie at such a sensitive moment.

Tess said· 'I still think we ought to call the police. The longer we leave it, the worse it's going to get.'

Ally shrugged. 'I don't mind what you do, as long as you tell the truth. I just don't see how we can continue to support a political career if we've got something like this to hide. All right, it may not make any difference to anyone else if we don't have ideals, but it will make a terrible difference to *us*.'

Celia gave Ally a frosty little smile. 'I do think you're jumping to conclusions, Ally, dear. When I talked about responsible action, I was very *insistent* on the word "responsible". What is *not* responsible is to call the police without being quite clear what we are going to say to them. I am not talking about lies. I am not talking about distortion. There will be no cover-ups in this family. We bear too much of an obligation toward the people of America for that. But it is irresponsible to inform the police and the press and the public about this incident without first weighing what its historical implications might be.'

Victor nodded. He, too, believed that the Cornelius family held the reins of American history in their hands; and that if a Cornelius sneezed, the whole of Wall Street was likely to catch a cold. It was far easier for him to accept what had happened with Ariadne as a historical event rather than as a mean and embarrassing personal failure.

'Victor is not a malicious character,' said Celia, appealing to the family in her dry, gin-and-tonic voice. 'He is honest and hardworking, and he has dedicated more to this family than anyone since Johann himself. But while *we* know that what he did was nothing more than give way to a spate of rage, history will judge him very differently, and with very much colder eyes. It is hardly dishonest, hardly irresponsible, if we simply make sure that the public sees him as we do, for what he really is.'

Freddie squashed out his cigarette in a small French porcelain ashtray. He didn't like Victor; he never had, and never would. He disliked Victor's fat crimson face, and his clumsy behaviour, and above all he disliked his incongruous little-boy obedience to Mama, which gave Freddie the complete creeps. Many of their past differences had been grudgingly papered over, but Freddie still *physiologically* felt repelled by his older cousin. Unlike Victor, Freddie was not particularly fond of thankless, masochistic toil. He did not see himself, like Victor, as a kind of Carl Sandburg figure of finance, adding up 357 columns of credits and 589 columns of debits before daybreak. Freddie lost money faster than Victor, especially when he gambled on fringe stock issues and stud poker; but he also created money faster, and more ingeniously.

Despite their mutual dislike, Freddie now made up his mind to stand behind Victor and offer his practical support. It was a matter of family loyalty and financial common sense. If social and economic boats were not to be rocked, then Victor must appear blameless. Freddie didn't dismiss the political considerations, either. A Cornelius man in the White House – John Russell – would be the family's greatest coup in years. It would mean fresh opportunities for adventurous investment, and enough government contracts to underpin some of the less stable Cornelius enterprises, such as Woodward Tires. Victor was a stupid ox as far as Freddie was concerned, but right at this moment, the ox needed all the encouragement he could get.

'Celia,' said Freddie, 'I think it's time we stopped talking about history and started talking about practicalities.'

'Very well,' said Celia a little icily. She was waxing eloquent on the dutiful virtues of her only son, and she did not really care to be interrupted by one of Hope's young people. But she waved her hand and said: 'Tell us, then. What practicalities?'

'The police, for a start,' interrupted Dick Marini. 'They're a practicality. Are we going to call them or not? I vote we do. We have to.'

'Wait a minute,' said Freddie. 'Of course we call the police. But what we have to consider is – *to what*?'

Tess frowned at him. 'What do you mean, Fred – *to what*?'

Victor inspected his cousin morosely, but said nothing.

'I mean this,' explained Freddie. 'As things stand, Victor will be considered to blame for this girl's action. Not legally, perhaps, but morally, in the eyes of the voting public What we have to do is change the *appearance* of what happened, so that the voting public has a positive and sympathetic reaction to Victor, instead of a negative and hostile reaction.'

690

Ally sighed and sat back. 'Go on,' she said. 'Let's hear the dastardly plot.'

'It's not a plot and it's not dastardly It's a simple adjustment of focus. At the moment, it looks as though this girl killed herself in Victor's pool because he wouldn't marry her. Public sympathy goes out to the girl, because she's been rejected by a plutocratic meathead—'

'*Freddie*,' said Celia coldly.

'It's no good saying "*Freddie*" like that,' said Freddie. 'We have to look at it the way the public is going to look at it. As far as the public is concerned, Victor has denied this girl her inalienable right. The inalienable right of every small-town American girl to marry a millionaire.

'The point is . . .' said Freddie, taking out another cigarette and lighting it. 'The point is that *what actually happened* is not relevant. It's not a question of telling the truth, or of not telling the truth. None of us really *knows* what occurred. Maybe it's important to find out why she did it. Maybe it isn't. I mean, it could have been a complete accident. But, at the moment, we have no way of knowing. So the only known fact, the only possible truth we can tell, is that the girl is dead.'

Dick Marini checked his watch. All the time they were talking, the pool water was seeping into Ariadne's tissues, giving forensic scientists clearer and clearer information on the time of her death. If they didn't make up their minds soon, then Ariadne's corpse was going to make up their minds for them. He made a few quick notes, and some rough calculations.

'What I propose we do,' said Freddie, 'is stop acting like a bunch of frightened hit-and-run drivers and start acting like a family with influence and resources. We have the resources – let's use them. If we all agree that our responsibilities only stretch as far as announcing the girl's death and taking care of the girl's parents, then I believe we can work out a watertight story.'

Celia lifted her beautiful elderly head. 'I think "watertight" is a rather unfortunate word, in the circumstances. But I believe you're right. This family has a far greater obligation to the nation than it does to one single person, and I don't think that the unfortunate girl herself would have wanted us to abdicate our mission simply for the sake of admitting something that, in the final analysis, was not our fault.'

She did not notice how quickly she had absorbed Victor's personal problem into the family's collective conscience. Ariadne's death was no longer Victor's difficulty alone; it was a guilt that had to be borne by all of them, and absolved by all of them, for the sake of the family name. A family linked by finance is far more inextricably entangled than a family linked by love. Love ties, but wealth welds.

Dick Marini said: 'I'd like to know what you mean by "refocusing" this problem, Freddie. I'd also like to remind you that we don't have a great deal of time. A police autopsy will pinpoint the moment of death to the nearest couple of hours, particularly in a case of drowning.'

Ally said: *'I'd* like to know how this family manages to have a far greater obligation to America than it does to Americans. This girl might have been a topless dancer, and not very bright, but she was a living person, wasn't she? And a voter.'

Celia tried to smile. 'Ally, dear, let's leave the ethical issues aside until we find out what Freddie has to suggest.'

'How *can* we leave the ethical issues aside?' said Ally hotly. 'This whole thing is an ethical issue! We're *talking* about ethics, and about accepting our responsibilities! Just because we're rich, does that make us divine?'

There was a difficult pause. Victor coughed. Freddie finally leaned forward on the settee and said: 'Money doesn't place anyone above their obligations, Ally. But it can make it easier to get around certain restrictions. You know that. You learned it the same way as I did,'

'Yes,' said Ally. 'I do know that. And sometimes I wish to God that it weren't true.'

Tess said: 'I agree with Ally about the ethics. But I also think we ought to listen to Freddie's suggestion. There's no point in arguing about what we *are*; it's what we decide to *do* that counts.'

Dick Marini said: 'I second that. And I suggest you make it quick. If we don't decide on something within the next thirty minutes or so, we're going to have to call the cops anyway.'

'All right,' agreed Freddie. 'Here's the idea. As I said, it doesn't involve anything more than altering the framework

692

of what happened. We just want people to view it in the right light. Victor, you'd better butt in and tell me if anything doesn't ring true, or can't be supported by what actually occurred. All we're doing here is a public-relations job on recent history.'

From time to time, while Freddie spoke, Dick Marini checked his watch. But after a while he relaxed and listened instead, and when Eustace came in with coffee and *petits fours*, he hardly noticed.

Around lunchtime two of the ground staff started to drain the pool. The oily water gradually inched down the sides, leaving a ring of smeary grey grime, and the two men smoked and didn't say much at all. They had their eyes on the watery shape of the submerged Cadillac resting under the surface with its dead driver.

One of the men said: 'Would you kill yourself like that? I wouldn't kill myself like that.' The other man shrugged. He didn't look like the type who would attempt to kill himself in any way at all.

Inside the house, Dick Marini and Freddie were both in Victor's study making a long series of phone calls. Victor himself was excluded, on the grounds that the less he knew about the cover-up, the better it would be for him. Victor wasn't glib when it came to public relations, and the financial press treated most of his handouts with healthy scepticism. He only managed to keep his widespread image as a millionaire good guy through his lavish parties and receptions for newspaper reporters and (more shrewdly) their editors. Victor had learned that a well-placed crate of champagne was worth any persuasion in the world – at least any persuasion of which *he* was capable.

Celia had retired to the conservatory, and sat among the green frondy palms and ferns talking to Victor's father, Roderick Cornelius, on the long-distance phone. She had taken off her black plumed hat and it lay on a white wrought-iron chair like an exotic pet cat that was suffering from the heat. The midday sun glimmered through the green-tinted glass of the conservatory, shining on the blue-and-yellow Turkish-tiled floor, and Celia sat amid this tropical scenery, her back upright, with a small glass of very dry sherry on the table beside her. She could have been an exiled Italian widow living in North Africa, or a countess in Victorian England.

Roderick sounded impatient and tired on the phone. He had spent six days in Strasbourg tying up a complicated airline deal with Flugwerk GmBh. He was embroiled in a heavy set-piece business battle, and he was attempting to bring the whole deal to its grinding climax within six or seven hours. Apart from that, it was seven o'clock in the evening in Strasbourg, and he'd been working since five A.M. It wasn't hard to see how Victor inherited his doggedness.

'I don't like the sound of this *at all*,' he was saying. 'Can't you have a word with Santana at the FBI? I've known him for years, and he owes us a favour.'

Celia said: 'Darling, I don't think so. Victor brought it up, the same suggestion, but Freddie says the FBI is very sensitive about scandal these days.'

'Well, I don't know. I don't like the sound of it *at all*.'

'Darling,' said Celia, 'it does seem the best way. We've been over it in detail, and even Dick Marini agrees it's foolproof.'

'What does Dick Marini know? The last time we did anything that Dick Marini suggested, we ended up with a 250,000-dollar settlement. Isn't there any other way? This sounds crazy.'

'There must be plenty of other ways,' said Celia, brushing a hand over her pink-tinted hair. 'But we don't have any more time to think of them. It's either this or going straight to the police and telling them what really happened. It's not the family reputation I'm worried about, Roddy, it's the whole election, and everything. If people find out that Victor's been having trouble with girls from strip clubs, what kind of confidence are they going to have in John Russell?'

Thousands of miles away, Roderick gave an angry little grunt. 'You wait till I get back there,' he snapped. 'I'll tan Victor's ass so he can't sit down for a month.'

'Roddy, he's not a little boy anymore.'

'Then why the hell does he behave like one? Topless dancers! What the hell's the matter with him?'

Celia sipped her drink. 'Hester once told me that in 1932 you went out with a girl from a burlesque show in Denver, Colorado.'

'That's ancient history. What I'm worried about is *now*. How long is this thing going to take?'

694

Celia glanced at her Piaget watch. 'Freddie says it should all be over by six this evening. Give or take ten minutes.'

'Freddie's an overconfident smartass.'

'And you're tired, darling. Why don't you have a nice drink and put your feet up for half an hour? You'll feel much better.'

'Better? How the hell can I feel better? I've just found out my son is a negligent womanizer and my nephew is a certifiable lunatic! Apart from that, my own wife's helping them out. What am I supposed to feel better about?'

Celia sighed. 'Roddy, darling, just get some rest. I'll call you later when I know some more.'

'I don't like one bit of this, and if I was over there, I'd put a stop to the whole thing. You're all as dumb as each other.'

'Roddy, you don't have to be rude.'

Roderick Cornelius let out a thin, exhausted sigh.

'I'll call you later,' said Celia. 'I promise I will. Just don't worry about it. I can't say I like Freddie myself, but he knows what he's doing.'

'All right,' said Roderick. 'I surrender, as usual. But don't forget to tell me what's going on. Don't worry what time it is. If you have some news, call. I should be at Flugwerk most of the night anyway.'

'Very well, darling. Now, remember I love you. Good-bye.'

Celia laid the phone down and took another sip of sherry. The taste was dry and crisp, and it warmed her. She had telephoned Roddy out of political courtesy, but she really didn't take too much notice of what he said. He was too engrossed in his freight and his airplanes and his containerization policy. He was just like Victor. They were men out of the same mould; men who stumbled around directionless until they were guided and powered by a strong woman. She sometimes considered that the true genius of the Cornelius family was to marry the kind of women who could urge them into ambitious and constructive moneymaking.

She opened up her black crocodile pocketbook and took out her diary. With a small pencil of figured gold and silver, topped with a single ruby, she wrote herself a reminder to telephone Roddy when she had some news for him.

Victor, his father's lesser shadow, now paced the lawn outside of Spiermont, like a man waiting for the birth of his first child. He wanted to smoke a cheroot, but decided against it, in case Mama saw him and disapproved. Today Victor

695

urgently needed encouragement and approval, and he admitted, even to himself, that he was prepared to do almost anything to get it.

In the distance, he saw the two brown-overalled groundsmen draining the pool, but he didn't go near. Instead, he restricted his pacing to the velvety surface of the croquet green, whistling tunelessly and trying to look nonchalant, as if he was on vacation.

Freddie, watching him from the study, remarked to Dick Marini: 'What do you think Victor's up to? He looks like a racing steward trying to make up his mind whether the going's too soft.'

Marini was in the middle of a complicated call. 'Don't ask me,' he said. 'That guy's got problems.'

It was an hour before the surface of the pool had dropped low enough for the tail end of the Cadillac to emerge. By then Freddie and Dick had finished their arrangements, and they came out to watch. Celia, Tess, and Ally stayed indoors, occasionally glancing out from the sitting-room windows to see how the work was progressing, but keeping well away from the prospect of dead dancers.

One of the groundsmen lit a cigarette and offered one to Freddie. Freddie took it, and the groundsman made a shield with his hands to protect the flame from his lighter.

'You know something,' said the groundsman. 'When you're dead, it don't matter a damn how much money you got.'

Freddie smiled at his impertinence. 'No, it doesn't,' he said quietly. 'But it matters to the people you leave behind.'

Inch by inch, the oily water fell away from the car. Soon the whole rear end was clear, and water was gushing from the trunk. Freddie could see the huddled shape of Ariadne in the front seat, her hair in sodden rat tails, her white cheek pressed against the window. He felt his breakfast rising up inside him like a mangy dog turning over in its sleep.

'Is the tow truck ready?' he asked Dick Marini, and Dick Marini nodded.

'They brought it up the driveway ten minutes ago. They're keeping it out of the way until we get the chance to sort things out. Not a pleasant sight, is it?'

Freddie dragged deep on his cigarette and said nothing.

Soon the pool was empty, except for streaks of oil along the bottom and the water that ran out of the drowned car. One of the groundsmen put on a pair of rubbers and stepped tenta tively down the greasy slope to the car's side.

'She's dead, all right,' he called. It was an absurd thing to say, but he was nervous and nauseous, and it was all he could think of. Nobody answered anyway.

The other groundsman joined him, and together they opened the car's door and dragged Ariadne out. Her silver evening dress shone like crumpled cooking foil. They carried her laboriously up the slope of the pool, up the steps, and laid her on a stretcher. One of them covered her up with a neatly folded white sheet.

Freddie, smoking, walked over to the stretcher and looked down at the crisp, well-ironed shroud. Then he bent forward, and with two fingers lifted the edge of it. The girl had her eyes closed. She was a startling shade of bluish-white, like Stilton cheese, and her cheeks were puffy and swollen. There was a dark brown bruise on her nose.

'So you're Ariadne,' he said. He almost expected her to open her eyes and answer. But she stayed dead, and he dropped the sheet back and stood erect. Dick Marini was standing right behind him.

'Okay,' said Freddie. 'Let's get this thing moving.'

Dick Marini waved his hand, and there was the sound of a heavy diesel starting up. A large orange-painted tow truck backed slowly around the side of the house and across the lawn. It was driven by Walther, Victor's heavyset chauffeur, and, alongside him, the owner of the Hyannis Circle garage. They manoeuvred it up to the edge of the swimming-pool steps and halted. The garage man, a short stocky Pole in red overalls and a red baseball cap, unfastened the two hooks from the back of the truck and slithered down toward the Cadillac to fix them on. He had been paid a great deal of money, and he did just what they told him to do, and didn't even look around. They wanted this car out of the pool, they were going to get this car out of the pool. For five grand, you didn't ask how the hell it got here, or nothing.

The hooks were secured. The Pole shouted to Walther, and Walther gunned the truck's diesel. Slowly, link by link, the winding gear tightened the tow chains, and the Cadillac began to shift. Soon, wet tyres squealing, the long navy-blue limousine was dragged up the tiled bottom of the swimming pool, bounced up the semicircular steps, and hoisted into position behind the orange tow truck. The diesel burbled, and Walther drove slowly away, the Cadillac swaying behind him, until he was out of sight around the house and disappearing down the long wooded drive.

Freddie ran his hand through his long brown hair and turned to Dick Marini with a grimace. 'Well, that's the car. Now let's see what we can do with the late Ariadne.'

They were still talking when Victor approached, looking tall and queasy in his light green jacket.

'How are you feeling?' asked Freddie. 'It won't be long, and we'll have the whole thing wrapped up.'

Victor nodded. 'Is that her?' he asked, pointing to the clean white sheet.

'That's right,' said Freddie. 'If she meant anything to you at all, I wouldn't look.'

Victor lowered his head and scuffed at the grass with his pointed Gucci shoe. 'I wasn't planning to,' he said indistinctly. 'But I don't think she meant much.'

Dick Marini and Freddie exchanged glances as Victor turned around and mooned off in the direction of the house. Then Freddie shrugged and said: 'Okay, this is what we do . . .'

By five-thirty that evening a fresh wind had sprung up, and the windsock at Hyannis Airport was stiffening and rolling. The sky was still clear, except for a low bank of faded creamy clouds in the southwest, and there was a smell of newly mown grass in the air.

The Lear jet was waiting on the concrete runway, its twin engines whistling in high-pitched harmony. Not far away, a long black Cadillac limousine was parked. A small group of men in pale summer jackets were talking together, while their buff-uniformed chauffeur polished imaginary smudges from their gleaming car.

'You have the route marked out here,' said Freddie, pointing to his windblown chart of the northeast coast. He was wearing dark polarized glasses, and it was impossible to see his eyes. 'When you reach this point, you will radio a routine weather report. If we respond in the affirmative, you carry on flying until you reach here. Then you send a Mayday. You got that?'

The pilot, a lean sad-eyed Belgian with a sandy little toothbrush moustache, nodded agreement. He stood hunched up, with his hands jammed deep in his windbreaker pockets, shuffling his feet in a complicated waltz of his own invention.

'Right,' said Freddie. 'Fifteen seconds after you send the first Mayday, you begin your dive. Send two or three more Maydays, but don't forget to bail out here. Don't forget to activate the pressure switch, either, or the plane won't explode. We'll alert the Coast Guard, and you should be picked up within five or ten minutes. You got all that?'

'Sure,' said the pilot. 'I done this kind of thing before.'

Freddie checked his watch, and looked across at Victor and Dick Marini.

'It's five-thirty-two. Anyone got any doubts, any reservations? Because now is the time to say so.'

Dick Marini shook his head. 'Let's just get it over with.'

Victor nodded ambiguously. He was red-faced and nervous, even in his elegant pale blue mohair suit by Themy of Paris. His thin hair rose and frayed in the afternoon breeze.

Freddie touched the pilot's arm. 'All right, then. Get going. And don't forget to signal in the right places at the right time, otherwise this whole thing's dead as the dodo.'

The pilot gave a lopsided grin. 'Dead? I think that's what you want, huh?'

Dick Marini was blowing his nose. 'No wisecracks, thanks,' he mumbled. 'We just want a job well done. I guess we'll see you later on.'

The pilot gave a mocking little salute and began to stroll toward the jet. Victor whispered worriedly: 'How much do you think we can trust a fellow like that? Supposing he flies straight to Boston and calls the police?'

'We can trust him,' said Freddie coldly. 'He knows damned well who we are, and he knows damned well that if anything goes wrong, he's never going to work again, not on any airline, anywhere. Apart from that, he was recommended by Boaz.'

'That's not a bad recommendation,' agreed Dick Marini. 'I just hope he's got good luck, as well as a good reference. You know something, this allergy's going to kill me one day.'

'It's the hay-fever season,' said Victor.

The Belgian pilot climbed into the Lear jet and they saw the door close. He didn't even wave. After a few minutes the plane's engines began to whine louder and higher, and it moved away from its parking place with a slight shudder and a bounce of its wheels. Victor, Freddie, and Dick Marini, their hands over their ears, watched it move away like a white shark into the wind.

'I hope this works,' shouted Dick Marini. 'That jet cost the best part of half a million.'

Freddie leaned over and yelled back: 'If this works, it'll be cheap at twice the price.'

Victor – as he had all day – remained obstinately silent. It was humiliating enough to have messed up his handling of Ariadne without having his cousin sort out the situation for him. To him, Freddie was unreliable, changeable, and feckless, and the idea of being in Freddie's debt gave him a lumpy pain like indigestion.

At 5:45 the Lear jet received clearance for takeoff. It whistled off down the runway and, quite abruptly, climbed into the sky. They shaded their eyes against the late sun as they watched it turn in a wide circle and then head toward the southwest.

'Okay,' said Freddie when the sound of its jets had dwindled away in the distance. 'I think it's time we got ourselves back to the house. In about an hour from now, those phones are going to start ringing.'

Walther opened the limousine's doors for them, and they climbed in, like mourners leaving a funeral. Victor cleared his throat and said: 'Home, Walther.'

Victor's private secretary, Douglas Schuman, was waiting for them when they got back. He was a young, round-faced business graduate from Yale, with a shiny Captain Marvel forelock and an inexhaustible wardrobe of dark suits with narrow lapels and tapered pants. He had been working on Victor's tax assessments with the IRS in Chicago, and he had flown into Boston at a moment's notice. As Victor's limousine crunched to a halt on the gravel drive outside Spiermont's imposing pillared portico, he came forward with a wide grin and his hand held out.

'Victor!' he called. 'Hi!'

Victor, slightly dazed, shook Schuman's hand and said: 'Hello, Douglas.'

Douglas beamed. 'It's great news, sir. It really took me by surprise. I can't tell you how thrilled everyone is. Terrific news.'

Victor looked at him. Nothing had been great or terrific or thrilling all day as far as Victor was concerned, and it took a full thirty seconds before understanding began to sink into his mind. Freddie, when summoning Douglas from Chicago, must have told him the cover-up story. Douglas only knew the 'refocused' side of things.

'Yes,' said Victor baldly. 'It's great news, isn't it? I'm very happy.'

'I can't tell you how thrilled everyone is,' said Schuman. 'Everyone is really thrilled. Mrs Kabotnik tried to get you some flowers, but she didn't have the time. It's wonderful news.'

Victor, as they walked into the house, turned to Freddie and raised his blond eyebrows in questioning worry. Freddie, hidden behind his dark glasses, simply wiggled his fingers in a discreet wave.

'Is Mama still here?' Victor asked.

'She's dressing for the evening,' said Schuman. 'I guess she'll be down in an hour. Miss Tess and Miss Ally are still here. They're in the music room.'

Dick Marini said: 'I guess I'll freshen up too. Am I staying for dinner?'

Victor didn't answer. Freddie nodded to Dick and said: 'Sure. Stay. We're going to need you.'

Victor walked through the high-pillared hallway, his footsteps echoing on the red-streaked marble floor, past the curve of the magnificent white staircase, and into the music room. It was a pale eggshell blue, this room, with a highly polished parquet floor and a glorious French chandelier. A dark Steinway piano stood near to the white-curtained windows, and there were matching chaise longues, covered in dark blue velvet. Tess was sitting at the piano, playing Debussy, her cigarette holder held between her teeth. Ally was relaxing on a chaise longue with her shoes off, her eyes closed.

Victor said: 'Well, that's taken care of that.'

Ally opened one eye. She didn't reply. At this moment, she didn't know whether to feel pity or disgust for Victor, and she didn't want to say anything that would reveal either one. The family had decided to gather round and solve Victor's problem together, and that was all that mattered for the time being. She didn't like Freddie's plan, but she had agreed to go along with it for the sake of their business and political interests.

Reluctantly, Ally had to admit that the family's interests were her own, regardless of the ethics, and regardless of Victor's guilt. Ally had been through enough pain and heart-searching on her own account to know that social morality is one thing and survival is something else.

Tess stopped playing and flicked her ash into a small porcelain saucer.

'Are you frightened?' she asked him, turning around on her stool.

Victor frowned. 'Frightened? Why should I be?' He walked heavily over to the window, parted the white lace curtains, and looked out.

'Well,' said Tess, 'there's always the chance of getting caught.'

Victor shrugged.

'And there are always ghosts,' said Tess. 'You know, invisible shades that clank their chains in the night.'

Victor turned around. 'You and Freddie, you both came out of the same cookie jar, didn't you? You don't know the difference between serious and sick. The way you talk, you'd think I did this on purpose.'

Tess made a moue. 'Right now, it doesn't really matter whether you did it on purpose or not. Right now, you're being pulled out of the mud by your nearest and dearest.'

Victor coughed. He reached in his pockets for a handkerchief, couldn't find one, and rang for Eustace.

'The trouble with you and Freddie is that you don't have any sense of proportion,' he said. 'Where do you think money comes from? You think I go out every morning and pick greenbacks off the trees? You've lost sight of real life, that's your trouble.'

'Real life?' Tess laughed. 'That's rich. If you think you've been living real life all these years, you're in deeper trouble than I thought. If you want to see real life, Victor, you ought to try doing what we did – Ally, Freddie, and me. Get out there, out on the streets, and meet people in the raw.'

Victor didn't look at her. 'You came back, didn't you?' he said. 'You met people in the raw, but you came back.'

Ally lifted her head. 'Better to have come back than never to have been at all,' she said quietly.

'That's bull,' said Victor. 'There's just as much reality in a column of figures as there is in a crowd of people. People and

702

figures, they're the same thing. The whole of society, the whole reason we're here, is based on the making of money. The desire for money is the constant motivating force behind great art, great literature, great works. Kindness is money. Generosity is money.'

'Love is money?' said Tess.

Victor didn't answer. Instead he said: 'This family has got together and this family has helped me out. The situation wasn't my fault, but I was man enough to tell the truth about what happened and take the responsibility for it. I want you to understand that, Tess. And you, Ally. If I'm going to be hounded by this for the rest of my life . . . well, you'd better tell me now. I made an honest mistake. I got myself mixed up with a girl that I shouldn't have, and it went sour. I admit that. Now stop preaching about it, and gloating over it, and let's get things back to what they were.'

Freddie, Dick Marini and Douglas Schuman came in, followed by two of the staff in white jackets, with four bottles of Moët in silver coolers. As the corks popped and the crystal tulip glasses were filled with effervescent wine, Celia came down, dressed in a flowing Dior dress in a mixture of violets and dusty pinks.

'What's the celebration?' she said, looking alarmed. 'Victor, darling, what's happened?'

Douglas Schuman intervened. 'This is my idea, Mrs Cornelius. I thought we ought to break out some champagne to toast the happy news. Does everyone have a glass? Don't you think this is the most thrilling thing that's happened all year?'

Victor, biting his lips, said: 'Douglas—'

'It's wonderful,' interrupted Douglas. 'The whole staff in Chicago knows about it already, and they're wonderfully, wonderfully pleased. This is a great day '

Freddie ran his fingers carefully through his long brown hair. He looked across at Celia and gave an imperceptible shrug that meant 'What can I do about it?' Celia returned the shrug, and then turned away. Freddie may have helped Victor out of a spot, but that didn't mean that she had to like him.

'Come on, now,' said Douglas. 'Let's drink a toast. Let me propose this. Lift your glasses, please. Come on, lift your glasses. I want to propose a toast to Victor, and to the lovely girl he's going to marry. What's her name, Victor?'

Victor couldn't speak. Dick Marini whispered: 'Ariadne.'

'That's beautiful,' said Douglas. 'To Victor, and to Ariadne. May they have all the happiness that a long life can bring them.'

There was an excruciating silence. Then Freddie raised his glass and said loudly: 'To Victor and Ariadne,' and everyone else muttered 'Victor and Ariadne' and drank.

At a little after six, the captain of the tanker *Esterbrook*, making its way down the coast of Long Island, heard a noise like material ripping. He looked up from his paperback book just in time to see a small white aeroplane tumbling through the blue summer sky, and then a dark puff of smoke. There was a bang no louder than someone slamming a door.

Immediately the captain ordered the tanker turned. The engines slowed, and it began to circle to port in a wide, foamy arc. Churning through the glassy blue sea, it took the *Esterbrook* eleven minutes to reach the oily debris of the little white jet. Pieces of wing and spar rose and dipped in the calm water, but there was no sign of life at all.

They circled the wreckage for nearly fifteen minutes more before they saw the orange smoke from a signal flare, about half a mile away. Nosing through the fragments of jet, they came up alongside a man in a life jacket, his watery parachute floating beside him like a silky squid. The man kept calling out: 'The girl! Did you see the girl?'

The captain leaned from the rail as rescue nets were lowered down the side, and two seamen clambered down to lift the pilot out of the sea. 'No girl!' he called back. 'No sign of any girl!'

Victor wore a black suit and a black tie. Dick Marini, sitting next to him, wore a grey suit with a black armband. Victor's pale face looked even whiter in the glare of the television lights.

The press conference was hushed and subdued. It was held in the billiards room at Spiermont, and CBS technicians had helped the staff arrange purple drapes across the room to serve as a suitably sombre backdrop Victor and Dick Marini sat at a long polished table, with microphones in front of them, while the twenty or thirty press people sat facing them on dining-room chairs.

'Mr Cornelius,' asked a sympathetic woman reporter with upswept glasses and a husky voice, 'did you have a wedding date planned?'

Victor shook his head. 'No, not yet.'

'Mr Cornelius,' said another reporter. 'Is this the greatest personal tragedy that has ever happened to you?'

Victor swallowed. 'I can't think of anything worse. All I can say is, it must be God's will, but I'm heartbroken.'

'I understand you've donated ten thousand dollars to the dead lady's parents.'

'Yes, I have. I never met them, but they're sharing my grief.'

The woman reporter said: 'Mr Cornelius, do you have any idea what happened yet?'

Victor shook his head. 'She left Hyannis Airport just before six. I went there myself to say good-bye. She was flying back to Los Angeles to tell her parents the good news. Then about an hour later, when I was celebrating my engagement with my family . . . well, I heard the news.'

One reporter stood up. 'Mr Cornelius,' he said, 'on behalf of the *Massachusetts Post-Dispatch*, and I guess on behalf of everyone here, I want to offer you our sincere condolences.'

Victor lowered his head. 'Thank you,' he said quietly. 'You've all been very kind.'

Dick Marini, on the corner of his notepad, was doodling, like an illuminated manuscript, the word 'refocus.'

The day after, Victor received his first letters of sorrow from a grieving public, and a misspelled cable from Mr Theodoros Skouros, thanking him 'from the deeps of my hearts' for the ten-thousand-dollar token of condolence. The same day, the last pieces of his Cadillac limousine were cut up by the Hyannis Circle garage, and sent, jumbled up with the rusted parts of dozens of other cars, to the Cohen Scrap Foundry in Boston. Douglas Schuman, puzzled but obedient, sent out several large cheques, drawn on West Virginia Investments, Inc., to the proprietor of the garage, to the pilot of the Lear jet, to several members of the staff at Spiermont, including Eustace and Walther, and to Dick Marini. He also sent a cable to Roderick Cornelius in Strasbourg, on Celia's instructions, saying, 'All tidied up. Love, C.'

Victor that night ate dinner alone, chewing at his lamb like a horse, and wondering what he could possibly say at the funeral, if and when Ariadne's body was ever washed ashore.

1976

RUSSELL WITHDRAWS CANDIDACY
CITES HEART COMPLICATION
By Gerry Simons

In a shock announcement last night, Republican candidate John T. Russell said that he was dropping out
of the race for nomination for President because of
heart complications. He said he was 'deeply grieved'
that he was unable to continue his campaign, but said
'it's better to be a live nonentity than a dead President.'

—*Washington Post*,
1976

Victor was just blotting his monthly stock-assessment book when the telephone rang. It was two or three in the morning, and he was sitting alone in his oak-panelled office, his desk heaped with papers and folded IBM readouts. He picked up the phone and said: 'Yes?'

'Victor? This is Dick Marini.'

'Morning, Dick. You're up early. Or late, whatever it is.'

'Victor, we've got ourselves a problem.'

Victor tucked the receiver under his chin and continued to tot up figures. 'Okay . . . shoot.'

'They found Ariadne Skouros. Her body was washed ashore at Fire Island, the Pines or thereabouts, and two gay skinny dippers rushed off and told the Coast Guard.'

'When was this?'

'Well, this was yesterday morning.'

'Yesterday *morning*? How come we didn't find out until now?'

'I guess the police didn't realize who she was at first. But they traced her pendant. You know, the emerald pendant you gave her? They traced it back to Cartier, and Cartier told them you bought it.'

Victor sniffed, and sat back in his leather swivel chair. Outside his windows, the night was still impenetrably dark. He could see a reflection of himself sitting out on the patio.

'All right, so they found her. What's the problem?'

'The problem is that they've handed the investigation to homicide.'

Victor picked at a stray thread on his shiny blue mohair pants. He said: 'Have you talked to Henry?'

'I can't get hold of him. I only just heard myself.'

'Well, will Henry fix it?'

'I don't know.'

Victor sniffed again. He felt he had a head cold coming on. 'What do you mean you don't know?' he demanded. 'He's always been helpful up till now

709

'Sure, but it's election time, isn't it? And I know for a fact that he doesn't like John Russell too much.'

'What am I supposed to deduce from that?'

Dick Marini was doing his best to sound optimistic but at the same time he was anxious not to let Victor feel that Ariadne's discovery was just another situation that he could buy his way out of. There was a chilly draught blowing under the door in Washington, and Dick was growing worried that Victor's blatant financial and moral support for the West Coast Republican clique was going to leave him politically isolated in the upcoming elections. Ever since the days of the New Deal, the Cornelius family had managed to perform a curious but effective political quadrille which involved supporting the Republicans but courting the Democrats; but Victor had either refused to understand the subtlty of the family's political posture or had simply closed his eyes to the reality of Jimmy Carter and the Southern left.

Dick Marini said: 'If Henry doesn't fix it, you could be implicated in a homicide inquiry, and if you're implicated in a homicide inquiry, then it's Chappaquiddick times ten, and John Russell doesn't stand a dog's chance.'

Victor sat up rigidly in his chair. 'Are you trying to tell me that Henry Chapman would do that deliberately?'

'I'm sure of it.'

'Well, how about the local police? What do they have to say about it?'

'There's a captain of detectives named Styles. He's a pretty awkward customer. We checked him through on the FBI computer, and he's a staunch Democrat. What's more, he originally came from De Soto, Georgia, which is in Sumter County, just like Plains, where Carter comes from.'

'That's all I need. Can't you buy them off? How much will they take?'

'Victor,' said Dick Marini patiently, 'they won't be bought.'

'Don't give me that,' snarled Victor. His cold felt worse. 'Find out the price, and I'll write you a cheque.'

'Victor, it won't work.'

'What the hell do you mean it won't work! It's always worked! From time immemorial it's always worked! What's so goddamned holy about this present generation of cops that they can't be bought?'

Dick Marini was silent. Victor was sweating and red in the

710

face, and he felt that he could do with a drink. He rang the bell for Eustace.

Dick Marini said: 'I'm telling you, Victor, as honest as I know how, that you may have to come clean on this.'

Victor was silent for a moment. Then he said: 'Dick, I want to tell you something in return. I paid three-quarters of a million dollars to fix this situation. I don't expect it to get fouled up now. That's three-quarters of a million dollars, Dick.'

'Yes, Victor, I know. But it wasn't the cover-up that went wrong. Least, I don't think so. The whole deal with the Lear jet and the crash and everything was perfect.'

Eustace still hadn't arrived, and Victor pressed his bell impatiently again.

'Perfect, was it?' he snapped to Dick Marini. 'Then why are they calling it homicide?'

Dick Marini sighed. 'It seems like someone called them up.'

Victor frowned. 'Someone called *who* up?'

'The homicide squad. Someone called the homicide squad and told them it could have been murder.'

'Well, who the hell did that?'

'We don't know. But I was talking to Jack Manners from the Massachusetts paper, and he said that they were just about to break a story on the homicide squad's secret informant.'

Victor banged his fist on his desk. 'But I didn't *kill* her, for Christ's sake!'

Dick Marini sounded resigned. 'I know you didn't, Victor. But that's not the point, is it? Any breath of scandal and John Russell is sunk. I'm sorry, Victor, but there's nothing I can do.'

Victor rubbed his face with his hand. He felt exhausted and anxious, but he was still determined that he wasn't going to be licked. His grandfather would never have given in. Well, neither would he. He would fight the bastards until he dropped. That was what being a Cornelius was all about.

'Dick,' he said quietly, 'I want you to think about this, and I want you to think good. I want you to call up Dino Riccione at Thornwood, and I want you to ask him for a quick hit.'

Dick Marini didn't answer at first. Victor said: 'Dick? Did you hear that?'

'Sure,' said Dick Marini. 'I heard it.'

'Well, what's wrong?'

Dick's voice was dispirited. 'Oh, come on, Victor, it's no use. You might just as well come straight out with the whole thing. You can't go hitting people these days, not like you could when your father was young. If you hit people, you get reporters swarming all over you like goddamned flies. Every reporter in the whole of the continental United States wants to be Woodward and Bernstein, and you don't stand a chance. In any case, who the hell are you going to hit? Captain Styles?'

'No. Henry Chapman.'

'Victor, you want to assassinate an assistant attorney general? You're out of your mind!'

Victor, in a sudden burst of temper, shouted: 'I'll get rid of anyone I damned well choose!'

'Victor—'

'I can buy and sell Henry Chapman seven times in the same street! What's more, I can buy a better attorney than you, so I suggest you get off the phone and consider yourself out of work!'

'Victor, for Christ's sake!'

Victor was boiling with fury. His voice was almost incomprehensible with sudden rage, and one of the maids upstairs thought that someone was screaming with pain. She was well-trained, though, and she turned over and went back to sleep. What the rich did was none of their domestics' business.

'*Dick*!' shrieked Victor. 'I will not have you stand in my way! If the way to get out of this is to hit Henry Chapman, then so help me I'll hit Henry Chapman. And the President, too, if that makes any difference!'

There was a long silence. Victor held the phone as if he was trying to crush it in his hand. His head was bent, and he was panting with emotional exertion. Finally Dick Marini said: 'If that's what you want, Victor, then I quit.'

'What do you mean, you quit? You're under contract! You can't quit!'

'You can stuff your contract.'

Victor was about to answer, but then he changed his mind. Instead, he banged the phone back on its cradle, and stood there for several minutes with his face working in suppressed temper. His cheeks were suffused red like boiling wax. He pressed the button for Eustace again, and then picked up the phone and dialled his mother's private number. It rang and rang twenty or thirty times before he gave up and laid the phone down again.

It was only then that he realized why Eustace was not answering his calls.

The gold-coloured Cadillac Seville drew up outside Golden Gardens Park, in Seattle, and the chauffeur turned off the windscreen wipers. It was a heavily overcast day, and curtains of rain were washing across the city from Puget Sound. Inside the car, concealed by tinted glass and trickling raindrops, insulated by thick carpet and Tchaikovsky in quad stereo, sat Ally Cornelius. She wore a severe grey suit that made her look older than she was, and her hair was drawn back from her face. Her only jewellery was her diamond earrings – two clusters of finest De Beers stones that sent rainbows of light through the dull rainy day.

The chauffeur sat still and said nothing. Ally had asked him to be as quiet and as discreet as he knew how. He had a blue shine on his chin and a black shine on his shoes, and there wasn't a single speck of dust on his cap. His hands rested in his lap in grey kid gloves.

After a few minutes, a black Buick Riviera drew up behind the Cadillac and stopped. A young man climbed out of the driver's seat, ran quickly through the rain to the gold-coloured car, and tapped on the door. The chauffeur immediately got out and opened the door for him.

The young man sat down, breathing hard, and brushed the rain from his hair. Ally kept away from him to begin with, but when he raised his eyes and they really looked at each other for the first time in nine years, she let out a small and painful sob, and reached out for him with both hands, and with devouring kisses, and with tears.

'Ally,' he whispered. 'Oh, my God, Ally.'

She couldn't speak for a few moments. She was too choked up. But then she sat back and held his arms, and took in his tanned face and his English suit and everything about him, and she was laughing and crying both at the same time.

'Oh, Clyde, it's been so long.'

He had to take his handkerchief out and blow his nose. They both laughed at the noise he made.

'You haven't changed,' he told her. 'You haven't changed one little bit.'

She shook her head. She was hardly listening. She could hardly believe that it was actually him, and that he was actually sitting beside her

'Even if I have changed, it doesn't matter. I still love you just as much.'

He lowered his eyes.

'Don't you still love me?' she asked him.

He nodded. He managed to say: 'I can't talk,' and then the tears ran down his cheeks and he had to turn his head away and cover his mouth with his hand. She gently touched his face, and stroked his hair, while his shoulders shook and he did whatever he could to control his emotions.

'That's ridiculous,' he said at last, in a voice that sounded as if he had a bad cold. He blew his nose again. 'I don't think I've cried like that in years.'

Ally kissed his lips. 'It doesn't matter. You're beautiful. It's nothing to be ashamed of.'

He said: 'How long are you here in Seattle?'

She shook her head. 'Just as long as you are.'

'You mean you don't have a schedule?'

Ally reached out and touched the Cadillac's window, and traced the path of a dribbling raindrop with the tip of her finger.

'I've given up schedules,' she said. 'I've made up my mind that I want to be happy.'

'You're staying?' he said.

She nodded. 'If you'll have me.'

He sat back and took out his cigarettes.

'I can't believe it,' he said. 'I know you're real, but I can't believe it.'

The rain blew across Shilshole Bay, and across the trees of Golden Gardens, and washed their car. Ally said: 'I guess I knew all the time that I'd come back and find you. I guess there are some things you just can't forget.'

Clyde looked at her gently. 'It's been a long time, Ally. I mean, nine years is a long time.'

She said. 'In a strange way, it was Victor who decided me.'

'Victor?'

She smiled. 'It's strange, isn't it, how you can accept a

714

situation for years and years, and then all of a sudden you see it for what it is. Like, the scales fall from your eyes.'

'Victor did that?'

'Oh, he didn't do it deliberately. But you know this business with him and this girl who died? The girl in the plane crash?'

'Sure. It was on TV.'

'Well, I was there at Spiermont when the family decided what they were going to do about it.'

Clyde blew out smoke. 'What do you mean, "what they were going to do about it"? What *could* they do?'

Ally said: 'The girl didn't die in the plane crash at all. She died the night before, at Spiermont.'

Clyde stared at her in complete surprise.

'You're kidding! You mean that Victor *killed* her? Is that what you mean? Come on, Ally, Victor couldn't kill an ant!'

Ally said: 'He may not be able to kill one, but he could certainly rough one up. Apparently this girl was some topless dancer he'd been messing around with in L.A., and she flew to Cape Cod and tried to persuade him to marry her. They had a fight, and the next morning he found her sitting in one of his limousines, right down in the deep end of his swimming pool.'

Clyde was amazed. 'You mean they fished her out of there . . . out of the pool, and then they took the body . . . and they . . . Jesus Christ!'

He stared at her. 'You mean they crashed that plane on *purpose*?'

Ally nodded. 'Spendthrift, isn't it? But Freddie thought that nobody would ever suspect that anyone would throw away a half-million-dollar airplane, just to get rid of a Greek girl that nobody knew. Not even Victor Cornelius.'

'Well, Freddie was damned right.'

'He was right, but he must have forgotten to spread enough hush money around. As it was, the whole thing was a waste of money. Someone talked.'

'Do they know who it was? Hey, how about that? The Deep Throat of Spiermont!'

Ally shrugged. 'It could have been anybody. Do you mind if I have one of your cigarettes?'

'Of course not. Here.'

He clicked his gold Dunhill lighter and she fed her cigarette from the flame. Then she took a deep breath, blew out smoke, and relaxed.

'What I learned from Victor,' she said, 'was what Dad nearly learned years and years ago.'

'And what was that?' asked Clyde.

'I learned that no matter what I did – no matter how much the Cornelius family might frown on me – I couldn't ever do anything as fundamentally immoral as any of them.'

Clyde watched her in silence. She said: 'Our love, the love that I feel for you and the love that you feel for me, is purity itself compared with them.'

Clyde said: 'You found out more about David Bookbinder, and all those killings? Is that it?'

She shook her head. 'I don't think anybody will ever find out. There are too many important people implicated. But if those killings were done in the way that this business was done, then all I can say is that this family is rotten to the core, and always has been.'

'Do you think that's what Dad nearly got to understand?'

'Oh, I think he always knew they were rotten. But he was like the rest of us. Well, like Victor and Freddie and Tess and me, anyway. It was always easier to be rotten than to be poor.'

She watched her cigarette smoke unfurling upward. Then she said: 'What he almost saw, but not quite, was what Victor showed me in San Francisco with that boy Destry, and what he clearly showed me at Spiermont. In his way, Victor killed them both – Destry *and* Ariadne Skouros. And he did it simply because to him, and to the rest of the family, money is more important than human life itself.'

Clyde said: 'You're a Cornelius yourself, Ally, and you're not poor.'

Ally gave him a smile like bitter chocolate. 'I know. I tried to shuck it all off once, and I found that I couldn't. It's a curse I've got to live with. I won't pretend that it isn't a benefit, too. There are times when I thank God that I'm wealthy, although I daren't think about the people who died to help me stay that way. But the best I can do is try to be happy, and try to stay away from Victor and Celia, and use my money the best way I can.'

She reached out and touched his face. 'I've wasted nine years, Clyde, because I believed I had a duty. I don't want to waste any more. People can think and say what they damned well like '

Clyde crushed out his cigarette. He said: 'How did you know I was in Seattle?'

Ally smiled. 'I have my sources.'

'Did they tell you how I was doing, these sources?'

Ally shook her head. 'They just told me your telephone number, that was all. And *that* cost me five hundred dollars.'

Clyde nodded. He took out another cigarette and lit it. Ally felt warm and happy all over, and she knew that they could make it now. After nine years of missing Clyde, after nine years of trying to deny how she felt about him, she had come to her decision, and now he was here, as good-looking and beautiful as he was that day she first met him, the son of her father and her father's mistress, Mara Malinsky.

'Clyde . . .' she said. 'You're doing okay, aren't you?'

He looked at her. 'Oh, yes. I'm doing well. It's Malinsky Fast Foods these days. One-point-five-million-dollar turn-over. We supply the whole of King, Pierce, and Snohomish counties, and that includes the city, too.'

She touched his hand. 'I'm so glad to see you,' she said. 'I don't know how to tell you how glad I am to see you.'

Clyde nodded. The rain drummed on the Cadillac's roof, and they sat at the kerb by Golden Gardens Park, three thousand miles away from Cape Cod, Massachusetts, and it seemed to Ally that nine years had elided into nine hours. But even nine hours, of course, could always be nine hours too long.

She noticed the sparkle of tears in Clyde's eyes. She knew then that there was something wrong, although her tenderness toward him was so strong that she couldn't guess what. She touched his wet eyes and said: 'Clyde . . . what's the matter?'

He let his chin drop on his chest and he wouldn't look up. He said: 'I was hoping they might have told you.'

'Who?'

'Your private detectives. The ones you hired to find my telephone number.'

'I don't know what you mean. What *should* they have told me?'

He sucked at his cigarette. 'Maybe they should have said that I was married, with two young daughters.'

717

Ally raised her head. She found herself looking at the Cadillac's roof. She seemed to stay that way for a long time. Then she lowered her head, but she didn't cry. She said: 'I didn't know. I just didn't even guess.'

'How could you? I'm not a celebrity. And, let's face it, we've been keeping ourselves apart.'

Ally turned to Clyde, and when she spoke there was a slight shake in her voice, but not much. She said: 'Your daughters, they must be beautiful.'

Clyde said: 'Yes.'

'And you're happy? Please say you're happy.'

Clyde tried to smile through his tears.

'What are their names?' asked Ally. 'Do you realize . . . I'm an aunt, and I didn't even know it!'

Clyde said: 'There's Janie, she's six; and Elizabeth, and she's two. They're both a couple of tomboys. We live out east of the city near Clyde Hill, if you can believe it.'

Ally said gently: 'With you, I could believe anything. Do you remember the day we first met in New York?'

'Sure. The snow. The waiter with the gimpy leg.'

'And that evening in Washington, at the Madison?'

'The good old Madison. Yes.'

Ally was silent for a while. Then she started to cry – silently but unstoppably, her mouth clenched tight. Clyde tried to touch her, but she waved him away and said: 'Go.'

'Ally, I—'

'Go,' she wept. 'Please, my darling, go. I love you so much. Please go. Please!'

Clyde waited for a minute or two, but Ally couldn't stop crying, and so he leaned forward and gently kissed her forehead. Then he opened the Cadillac's door, and stepped out into the lancing rain, and ran back to his Buick.

The last he ever saw of Ally Cornelius was her pale face at the rear window of her car, tinted blue, and streaked with rain from Puget Sound that fell and fell and fell on Golden Gardens.

On the golf course at Kenwood, as the amber evening light touched the distant trees, and the shadows of the golfers strode long and narrow across the grass, Roderick Cornelius stood for a moment and sniffed the air like an old hunter sniffing a trail. Beside him, the assistant attorney general,

Henry Chapman, adjusted his red peaked golfing cap and swung his club in preparation for an awkward shot around the rough.

'This course doesn't get any easier,' Chapman remarked in his deep, gravelly voice. He was a stocky little man with a bristling white moustache and a face that looked as if someone had sandpapered it. 'Either that, or I'm sore out of practice.'

Roderick said absentmindedly: 'I haven't played here for years.'

Chapman took a couple of swings. 'It's okay if you're concentrating, and you think. It's one of those courses you need to *think* your way around.'

Roderick said: 'Umm.'

There was a moment's silence, then Chapman called '*Fore!*' and clipped the ball badly into the tufty grass. His black caddie took off his hat, wiped his forehead, and looked as if he wished he'd been a riverboat minstrel instead. Chapman handed over his club, and they started to walk.

Roderick said: 'I guess you must know that I'm not just here for the golf.'

'Well, I know you wanted to talk.'

'And I guess you know what I wanted to talk *about*.'

Chapman said nothing. He was one of those lawyers who preferred his clients to come out and say what they meant. In his court days, he was rarely guilty of leading his witnesses, and rival attorneys often claimed that it was what he judiciously omitted, rather than what he actually said, that gave him most of his legal successes. One disgruntled opponent had dubbed him 'The Angry Silence.'

Roderick said: 'I've been talking to Victor about what happened.'

'Oh, yes?'

'He's assured me that there's no question of homicide, and certainly no foul play.'

Chapman thought about this. Then he said: 'Someone must have believed there was. Otherwise they wouldn't have tipped off the police.'

'I'm sure it's just an old employee with a grudge. You know how servants are.'

Chapman stopped walking, and stared at Roderick with rheumy eyes. 'I don't want to know how servants are,' he said

719

harshly. 'What I want to know is what their masters think they're doing.'

'Well . . .' said Roderick, embarrassed. 'It was all a mistake.'

'A mistake? *The Massachusetts Post-Dispatch* is suggesting that Miss Skouros was dead before the plane hit the water. In fact, they're even implying that she was dead before it took off.'

'Henry, that's absurd. Do you seriously think that we'd crash a five-hundred-thousand-dollar airplane just to dispose of a cadaver?'

Henry Chapman rubbed his moustache. Then he said: 'Yes.'

Roderick looked away. The sky was fading into a pale violet colour and in the distance a few clouds idled away the later afternoon like curdled thick cream. He said heavily: 'You're right.'

Chapman grimaced. 'I thought I was. I've known you Corneliuses longer than most. You're rich with a capital R. An airplane like that grows on trees as far as you're concerned.'

Roderick said: 'But it still wasn't homicide.'

Chapman raised a bristly eyebrow. 'What was it, then? A sudden fatal attack of indigestion?'

'Henry, it isn't funny.'

'At five hundred thousand a shot, I should say not.'

Roderick said: 'The girl killed herself. She drowned herself in the swimming pool at Spiermont. She was upset with Victor, and it seems like they'd had a fight the night before. Victor . . . well, Victor confessed that he punched her. Almost broke her nose.'

Henry Chapman sighed. 'Why didn't he come out with this in the first place? Why didn't he tell the truth? It's the easiest way, you know. I've had confirmed killers let off the hook because they told the truth.'

'Come on, Henry, use your common sense. Victor is John Russell's biggest supporter. If any of this gets out, Russell is absolutely dead.'

Henry Chapman pulled a face. 'That's no skin off of my nose

'Maybe it isn't. Maybe it's no skin of *any* of our noses. The way things are going right now, we'll be lucky to get anyplace at all.'

'You mean Carter can swing it?'

'I don't know. But things a damned sight stranger than that have happened.'

'In that case, Roddy, what are you worried about?'

Roderick sighed, and ran his hand over his balding head. These days he seemed to have trouble getting through to people, making them understand what he was saying. He didn't look like a man on the wrong side of sixty; but then he didn't look young, either. There was a stiffness about him, a haphazardness about his thinking, and a way of lifting his head and attending to some distant, long-forgotten time, all of which gave him away. His life had almost gone by, and he was still trying to remember what he'd done, and why, and whether there was anything important still to be achieved.

He said: 'Henry, we've always been friends, you and I.'

'That's correct.'

'You know what Victor means to me.'

Henry Chapman had arrived at the clump of grass where his ball was buried. He knelt down and inspected the lie of the land.

'Actually, Roddy, I don't know, no. You've never told me. In fact, as a matter of honesty, I've always gotten the impression you don't care for Victor too much.'

'Henry, I'm asking a favour.'

Henry Chapman slowly stood up. He looked Roderick square in the face.

'Roddy,' he said, 'you can ask me a great many things, a great many favours, and I'd do my best to oblige. But don't ask me to cover up your son's involvement in whatever this business is, because I won't.'

'Henry, it's vital. If there's a single breath of scandal right now, John Russell's candidacy is totally washed up. Jesus, Henry, it's bad enough with the *Post-Dispatch* spreading rumours. This thing has to be contained.'

Henry Chapman grunted, and smiled. 'Someone else said that, not too long ago, and look what *he's* doing today.'

'Henry, this isn't Watergate.'

'No,' said Henry Chapman, 'but it still amounts to a conspiracy to obstruct justice. A criminal offence has been committed, and you're asking a member of the administration to use his influence to prevent due process of law.'

Roderick stared at Henry Chapman for a moment, chewing at his lip. Then he said: 'Henry, you've got to help me '

'Why?'

'Because I'm asking, Henry. And because of what you've done in the past.'

Henry Chapman smiled at Roderick mildly. 'Is this blackmail?'

'Oh, come on, Henry, of course it's not. But you've helped us out before, and we've paid you off, and you've got to admit that gives us a certain amount of leverage.'

'Does it? I wonder. I think you're in a worse position than me. In fact, I think you're in a terrible position. If I don't help you, Victor's in for trouble; and what are you going to do about it? Tell the press that you've been paying me off? Not in a thousand years. If John Russell ever stood a chance before, he certainly won't stand one then.'

Roderick sighed. He was conscious that the caddies were waiting, and that the light was failing fast. In a half hour it would be too dark to play any more. A flock of birds rose up from the distant trees like coal dust shaken from a mat.

He said: 'Henry, I'm asking you for help. No pressure, no blackmail, no nothing. As your friend, I'm just standing here and asking you.'

Henry Chapman beckoned his caddie. He said: 'Niblick.'

Roderick waited patiently for Chapman's answer. The light seemed to sink even deeper, and a cool breeze rustled across the grass from the direction of Wood Acres. It was on evenings like this that he became aware of just how vast a continent he was standing on, and how tiny a thing he was in the whole of America. He felt like a speck on an endless map, speaking in a tinny transistorized voice.

Henry Chapman hefted his golf club. Then he put it down and turned to Roderick with a friendly but regretful face.

'Roddy,' he said, 'I'm as guilty as hell of taking your money, and I've done some bad, unethical things in my time. But I think maybe that a reckoning's due, not just for me but for all of us, and that's why I'm going to say no.'

Roderick was silent for a long time. Then he said: 'I see.'

Henry Chapman said: 'If you want to scratch this game, I'll quite understand.'

Roderick gave a faint, quick smile. 'No, Henry. Let's go on.

The least you can do is give me the chance to lick the hell out of you.'

Henry Chapman nodded. 'Okay, if that's what you want, I guess you might as well. After all, Celia's going to lick the hell out of *you*, ain't she?'

The morning she came around to say she was sorry there was a feeling of unsettled weather, and rain. The towers of the World Trade Center were dissolved in cloud, and across in Jersey the showers were falling in ragged grey sheets.

His intercom buzzed, and Freddie said: 'Yes?'

'Mr Secker, sir? There's a visitor.'

'What kind of a visitor?'

'It's Mrs Marini, sir. She says it's important.'

'Mrs Marini?'

The secretary's voice was apologetic. 'I tried to tell her you were busy, sir, but she wouldn't take no for an answer.'

Freddie bit at his thumbnail. Then he said: 'Okay, Jeannie. Just have her wait for a couple of minutes.'

He switched the intercom to hold. On the six silent television screens banked on the opposite wall of his office, Jimmy Carter was alternately frowning and grinning, Olive Oyl was sleepwalking along a high-rise girder, a black housewife dressed up as a hula dancer was frantically trying to guess the price of a yellow Pinto, and a posse of cowboys rushed hell-for-leather toward Sesame Street and a Wrigley's Spearmint commercial.

He tiredly rubbed at his eyes. He had been trying to work all morning on a new oil-storage system. The company's supertankers were delivering crude and processed oil in such gargantuan quantities these days that many of their smaller customers were unable to cope. But he hadn't been able to concentrate on oil. He'd been feeling restless and edgy, as if people had been walking on his grave. He took out a cigarette and went to the window to look out over Wall Street.

This was the same thirty-fifth floor eyrie from which David Bookbinder had looked out during his days with Cornelius Oil. The decorations were more artistic now, with Flemish tapestries hanging on the walls, and a Louis Quinze commode that had cost as much as the combined annual telephone accounts of every citizen and office in Granite City, Illinois. But the atmosphere hadn't changed. There was still that heavy charge of wealth and influence; and an almost medieval sensation that, from here, a whole empire of oil and shipping and airplanes, a whole army of secretaries and vice-presidents and pilots and roustabouts, a whole torrent of dollars and share certificates and fiscal notes, were all directed and orchestrated to rise up in the morning, to busy themselves all day, and carry on their profitable whirl and flurry far into the night. David Bookbinder used to remark that it wasn't the view of the Hudson that attracted company presidents to penthouse offices, nor the idea that they might be marginally closer to God. On the upper floors, it was easier for them to picture the world below them as a map which stretched from horizon to horizon, and over whose colourful and many-textured surface their staff and their customers flowed industriously and obediently to and fro.

Freddie stood by the window, the cigarette dangling from his lip, his eyes narrowed against the smoke. Although he couldn't have known it, he looked almost uncannily like his mother had looked on the day she had stood in the wind overlooking Moriches Bay on Long Island and told her brother that she was dying. Freddie was too thin for his height, and his white silk shirt and well-pressed 1950's-style pants made him seem strangely frail. One of his girl friends, a moist-eyed romantic with bushy pre-Raphaelite hair and a muscular father in waste mercury, had told him he looked just like Byron would have looked if Byron had been Michael Douglas' brother.

He checked his wafer-thin gold wristwatch. He couldn't keep Helen waiting too long. He hoped she didn't have much to say, wouldn't scrape at the scabs of their recently closed wounds. He was going to have to leave the office in a half hour anyway and take his helicopter up to Lynwood's Island. The whole family was due to gather this afternoon at three, to celebrate Hester's award from the American Women's League for her outstanding services to American womanhood. For lots of reasons, he wasn't going to miss it

Eventually he pressed the intercom buzzer and said: 'Jeannie?'

'Yes, Mr Secker?'

'Send Mrs Marini through, please.'

He walked across the soundless carpet to the far side of the room, where it was darker. Beside him, the television screens jumped and flickered. He kept his eyes on the office door, waiting for it to open. He was trying to keep his heart from beating too hard, his respiration from quickening. But her quiet knock surprised him anyway, and when she stepped in through the door, he couldn't think of anything to say but: 'Hello, Helen. How are you?'

She stayed by the half-open door. She was the same Helen, but different – the way that lovers always are when you meet them again after weeks of parting. He had remembered her hair the way it was two months ago, in a beautifully cut bell that had just covered her ears. Now her hair was curly and wavy, and her eye makeup was darker. He had remembered the navy-blue suit she had worn the last time he saw her. But now she was dressed in a pink summer coat, and she smelled of some fragrance that was unfamiliar. She was small, and still just as pretty, with those high cheekbones and those wide sad eyes; but no matter how often he had once kissed those cheeks, and no matter how often his lovemaking had caused those eyes to close, they had never been his.

'Come on in,' Freddie told her. 'Close the door.'

She smiled at him. 'You're not afraid of being compromised?'

'No more than I ever was.'

She pushed the door to, but didn't quite close it. Then she walked across to the French chaise longue and sat down carefully on the edge of it. The light from the television screens moved across her face like a Siamese shadow play. Freddie opened the French stained-glass cigarette box on the table and held it out to her.

'Thank you,' she said, and took a cigarette.

There was an uncomfortable pause. Freddie went to his desk and brought over a table lighter. He flicked it alight for her, and she leaned forward to feed from the flame.

'I didn't expect to see you again,' he said quietly. 'At least, not in private.'

She blew out smoke, and looked up at him with her wide brown eyes. 'I guess I didn't either.'

He sat down opposite her, in a revolving leather and hickory-wood chair, and watched her smoke. He said: 'It's hard to believe how far apart two people can get, after they've been so close.'

'Do you think we're far apart?'

He nodded. 'I used to share your bed, Helen. But now I

725

couldn't even touch you, any more than I could touch Jeannie, or any other woman who didn't love me.'

Helen frowned. 'I never said I didn't love you'

'You said you didn't want to see me again. Don't you think that's good enough?'

She looked at him sadly through the trailing smoke of her cigarette. 'I guess it is,' she admitted, 'if you want to look at it that way.'

'Well, Helen,' said Freddie, 'I don't think I had much of a choice.'

She stood up and walked across to the row of television screens. Brutus was stomping on Popeye, and *Gilligan's Island* was just starting. She said: 'Don't you ever switch these off?'

Freddie took out another cigarette. 'They're a guide to popular taste, and popular taste is something the Cornelius family seems to have lost sight of.'

'How about the Marini family?'

'How should I know? I'm not Mr Marini, and I've been given the brush-off by Mrs Marini.'

She turned and looked at him, and the regret and concern on her face was so plain that he found himself turning away and searching for his lighter.

'It couldn't have worked, Freddie, could it?'

'Well, I don't know about that. I was never given the opportunity to find out. Maybe it couldn't, maybe it could. But listen, what are we talking about it for, anyway? It's over, right? We've wrapped it up. We put it all down to experience and faced the future with a happy though tears-tained smile.'

'Freddie . . .'

He clicked the lighter but he couldn't get it to catch. He said: 'Helen, it's no damned use. If you don't love me, I can't force you.'

'But, Freddie . . .'

He gave an exasperated sigh. 'But Freddie, what? But, Freddie, I want to start all over? But, Freddie, I think we had a good thing going? Come on, Helen, you told me it was through. You couldn't take the strain of deceiving Dick any longer. You couldn't stand lying to your children. You couldn't face your friends in case any of them secretly knew. Helen, you just weren't cut out for illicit affairs, and neither was I So let's leave it like that.'

She pressed the back of her hand against her forehead.

'Freddie,' she said softly, so softly that her words fell like dead birds during a heat wave, 'I came to say that I was sorry.'

He left his cigarette, unlit, on the edge of the desk. He came across and held her shoulder, and looked at her in silence for a long time. In the shadows his lean, angular face looked tired. He said: 'Sorry? What for?'

'Sorry for everything. I never should have let it happen in the first place.'

'Oh, come on,' he chided her. 'You didn't *let* it happen. It just happened. These things are always happening. It's what you decide to do about them that makes for all the heartache.'

'All the same, I was wrong. I didn't want to hurt you. And I'm sorry.'

'That was all you came to say?'

'I came to say that I still love you,' she said, raising her chin in a slight but unmistakable challenge.

He didn't answer, except to turn away and shrug.

'I came to say that if you want to go on, if you think you could stand the strain of going on, then I'd rather go on than quit. It can't work, but that isn't what's important. I know that now.'

She crossed her arms over her breasts, and sucked at her cigarette as if it was oxygen. Her left hand, with her thin gold wedding band, was clutching nervously at her pink linen sleeve.

'I couldn't leave Dick,' she told him. 'I couldn't stand a divorce. But I've had a chance to see it all in perspective. I've had a chance to rest. And I miss you, Freddie. I miss you desperately.'

There was a silence on which their lives turned. There were tears in Helen's eyes, but she refused to cry. She wasn't going to win him by weeping, she had already made up her mind about that. If he still loved her, if he still wanted her, then she was prepared to make love with him whenever and however she could. But she didn't expect his pity, or his guilt, to make up his mind for him.

She thought of the moment – the very instant when he had first grasped her hand at a summer party on the jetty of Lynwood's Island, and how they had danced across the boards, with an eighteen-piece band playing a schmaltzy version of 'I've Been Loving You Too Long to Stop Now,' while coloured lights reflected and dipped in the dark water of the Hudson like drowned Christmas trees. Dick had been tied up for hours in a tedious caucus with Victor, and so Freddie and Helen had danced together until the band stopped for a beer and a smoke, and then Freddie had led her down to the side of the river, among the overhanging trees that rustled and whispered in the dark. They had sat on a sawed-up log, sipping champagne and listening to the laughing and chattering of guests on the jetty and up among the fairy-lighted trees and bushes.

She had never really spoken much to Freddie before. She had always thought him cold and a little arrogant. But when he talked about his mother, and how he had tried to grow up within the Cornelius family without being crushed by the insensitive ambitions of Victor and the overweening matriarchy of Celia, she began to understand this remoteness was only a device to protect his unconventional beliefs about business and money and the management of other people's lives. Freddie was quick and perceptive, and when it came to money he was prepared to take hair-raising risks. But he was also unfailingly considerate to the men and women who worked for him, which was the strongest characteristic that he had inherited from his father, Edward. Helen had sensed that sympathy on the first night they had been together, and it had drawn her compulsively.

They had slept together one Thursday night when Dick was away with Victor on a business trip. She remembered that, just before dawn, Freddie had said: 'Is this the way you fall in love with people?'

And she had said, stroking his hair: 'We mustn't.'

Now, in the gloom of Freddie's office, she stood waiting for him to say that they must.

The intercom buzzed. Freddie leaned across the desk, flipped up the switch, and said: 'Yes?'

'Your helicopter's ready, Mr Secker. So whenever you're ready . . .'

'Thanks, Jeannie.'

Helen said: 'You're leaving?'

He nodded. 'I have to go up to the island. Grandmother's being decorated.'

'What with? Candles?'

He smiled. 'You don't change, do you? Too sharp to love, too soft to lose.'

She looked a little sad. 'I guess I have to protect myself, like everybody else.'

Freddie sat on the edge of the desk. 'Maybe you should come up and join in the celebrations. It's the American Women's League. They're presenting Grandmother with some kind of a plaque, in grateful acknowledgment of everything she's done for American womanhood.'

Helen didn't say anything, just stood cradling herself as if she was feeling the cold.

'Of course, most of what she's done for American womanhood has been financial,' said Freddie, trying to be breezy. 'Part of a long-term tax-reduction scheme that Victor worked out. Like the Hester Cornelius Institute of Domestic Craft, and the Hester Cornelius Day Schools, and the Hester Cornelius Memorial Library.'

He finally got his lighter to work, and he lit up his cigarette. 'But it's more than just money, you know. She's eighty-four, and she's managed to make herself into a figurehead. The grand old lady who dismisses women's liberation as Communist subversion, and upholds the right of the suburban housewife to whiten her laundry, bake her tollhouse cookies, bring up her kids with clean faces and short hair, and kiss her husband before he leaves for work.'

'Is that so bad?' Helen smiled.

'I didn't say it was. John Wayne said that Hester Cornelius was the only heroine that America has left. Mind you, Frank Zappa said she was the Empress of Shake'n'Bake.'

Helen came over and rested her hand on his. 'What are we going to do?' she asked him. There was no resentment in her voice, only plain and simple needing to know.

He looked at her. The soft grey morning light made her look almost magical. He knew that he loved her. He had loved her right from the very beginning, with a love that had stayed with him day and night, a tune that wouldn't fade, a fragrance that wouldn't die away. But whether he could go through all the uncertainty again, and all the pain of parting, he didn't know.

He said gently: 'If I asked you to leave Dick, would you come?'

She stroked the back of his hand in ar absentminded way. 'You know what would happen if I did that Dick would refuse to confide in you anymore, but Victor would refuse to sack Dick, and even if he did, it would look as if the Cornelius family were deliberately axing him because Freddie Secker had happened to fancy his wife.'

'Let them think what they damned well like.'

'You know you couldn't let it happen, Freddie, not that way. Think of the harm it would do.'

He watched her fingertips tracing patterns along the veins of his hand. He said: 'It's a grown-up world, Helen. Dick's got to face up to it sometime. If it isn't me, it's going to be somebody else.'

She shook her head. 'It could never be anybody else. Not for me.'

'Then leave him.'

There was a pause, but then she whispered 'No,' and he knew that she meant it. 'I'll be your mistress, Freddie, for as long as you want me and as long as we can. But I can't leave Dick, not now.'

He thought of the way she used to smell, in the early mornings, when they were both lying naked on the wide curtained bed at his house in Charleston. It was a mingling of Gucci and drying sexual juices, of grass from the west wind and flowers from the gardens. He could almost picture her breasts, with their wide nipples roused by the cool that came off the lake, and the feel of her hair against his cheek. He remembered that one morning he had woken up to find her gone from the bed beside him, and he had walked through into the music room to see her sitting nude at his white Steinway piano, her back straight, her face silhouetted against the fuzzy light of the rising sun, playing Mozart.

He crushed out his half-finished cigarette and stood up. 'Okay.' He shrugged. 'If you can't leave Dick, then you can't leave Dick.'

She looked at him anxiously. 'Then you won't . . . ?'

He touched her cheek, and then ran his long fingers into her hair 'I couldn't resist you,' he told her, his eyes steady and dark. 'Whether it's wrong or right, whether you can leave him or not.'

She could hardly believe what she was hearing. 'You mean you'll forgive me?' she asked him.

He held her hands tight between his, and nodded. 'There's nothing to forgive. You don't ever have to forgive anyone for loving you.'

'Freddie,' she said, and the tears slid suddenly down her cheeks. Freddie held her tight, and even though her perfume was strange, and her curly hair was unfamiliar, she was still the same Helen Marini he had held just as tight in New York and Washington and Charleston, during nights that always had mornings, and afternoons that always grew dark too soon. He kissed her, and she tasted of salty tears, and he could feel the wet on his own eyelashes as well.

'Why don't you come up to Lynwood's Island?' he asked her. 'I could have the helicopter take you back to your home by two.'

'I couldn't. I told Dick I was shopping.'

'So what? Say you had lunch at the Pierre. It takes about as long to get served as a helicopter round trip up the Hudson.'

She smiled at him through her tears. 'You never change. You're always so damned impetuous.'

'Better to be impetuous than moribund.'

She kissed his cheek very softly and said: 'All right, then. When do we leave?'

He checked his watch. 'Two and a half minutes flat. I never like to be late for any Cornelius function. Not since Victor paid off Isaac Hayes just before a party we had at Carina Mia, in Pasadena, because he said he didn't like rock 'n' roll. Can you believe that?'

'Of Victor, yes.'

They kissed again, slowly, with the relish of people who haven't kissed for a long time. Then he said: 'Helen, I'm glad you came. I don't know what the hell's going to happen now. But I'm glad you came.'

'I'm glad, too. As long as it doesn't hurt too much.'

He shrugged. 'It might. It probably will. But I guess there isn't much that's worth having that comes easy.'

Freddie's intercom buzzed again, and Jeannie said: 'I don't want to rush you, Mr Secker, but the helicopter's waiting. If you want to get up to the island by one-thirty . . .'

'Okay, Jeannie,' he told her, smiling at Helen. 'And please inform Captain Kroscek we'll have one extra passenger.'

There was a silence. Then Jeannie said: 'Mrs Marini, sir?'

'That's right.'

He switched off the intercom and looked at Helen wryly.

'Jeannie's very protective.' He smiled. 'Almost motherly.'

'Do you need a mother?' asked Helen.

He lifted his black Yves St Laurent blazer from the back of his chair. 'I had one once,' he said. 'I guess I didn't ever get to know her too well, but I certainly had one.'

He brushed back his hair, straightened his tie, and opened his desk drawer to take out a bottle of Balenciaga after-shave. 'I can remember her funeral more than anything,' he went on. 'It was very simple, one of the simplest funerals I guess this family ever had. I stood there and it was such a beautiful day, I could just imagine her spirit fluttering out of the grave and flying off into the sky, like a dove or something. I was glad, in a way, she was free. She was always so frustrated, and sad. She was like someone who got on the wrong train, and wound up at some strange terminus, and wandered around the streets of this strange place and never found out where she was really supposed to go.'

Helen turned her face away. 'That happens to more women than you'd even imagine.'

He touched her arm. 'Did it happen to you?'

She looked wistful. 'I was one of those unfortunate people who discover that life is like that joke about the Polish concert. Admission is free, but they charge ten dollars to get out.'

Freddie said: 'Helen, you can still go back home. I don't want to mess up your life.'

She shook her head. 'Life isn't worth living unless it's nicely messed up. I tried to get over you, Freddie. I think I even tried to make you hate me. But I guess I couldn't bear it if you did. Just think about it. I'm the wife of a prosperous and hardworking young attorney who may just get to the top of the heap one day. What happens when I meet a man like you? You're handsome, and you're young, and you're sympathetic, and you're sitting on more money than Dick will ever see in ten lifetimes. If I said that I preferred a staid, safe marriage to an affair with you, I'd be ready for the funny farm.'

Freddie reached for another cigarette, lit it, and blew out smoke.

'Your mother died of cancer,' said Helen.

Freddie nodded.

She took the cigarette out of his mouth and crushed it in the ashtray.

'I love you,' she said, putting her arms around him. 'And that's all I can say.'

The door opened, and Jeannie came in with Freddie's briefcase, packed with carefully arranged work for the next twenty-four hours. She was a short girl from Pittsburgh with wiry auburn hair that flew up from her scalp as if she had just stuck her fingers in an electric socket. She wore clashing turtlenecks of pink and red, and she treated Freddie as if he were precious porcelain. She gave Helen a quick, cautious glance and said: 'Everything's here, Mr Secker. You won't forget the insurance assessments for Daylong, will you?'

Freddie said: 'I won't,' and as Jeannie turned to go, he called: 'Jeannie?'

She paused. 'Yes, Mr Secker?'

He gave her a gentle grin. 'Thanks, Jeannie. You're very good to me.'

Jeannie coloured. She said: 'Enjoy your flight, won't you?' and then bustled quickly out of the office as if she had an urgent appointment.

Helen said: 'She's in love with you. Can't you see that?'

Freddie looked embarrassed. 'She's a terrific secretary, I know that much.'

They left the office and took Freddie's private elevator, decorated inside with rococo gilt mirrors, to the uppermost floor. Then it was a short climb up plush-carpeted stairs to the roof exit and the helicopter pad. As they stepped out of the elevator car and mounted the stairs, they could already hear the roaring of the helicopter motor and the whistle and drone of its downdraught.

'Hold on to your hairstyle,' cautioned Freddie as he opened the door onto the pad.

Amid a deafening whine of turbines and the flack-flack-flack of idly turning rotors, the huge white-painted Sikorsky helicopter was waiting for them, a glistening albino dragon in the grey cloud of a humid Wall Street afternoon. The top of the Cornelius Oil Building roof had supported a radio tower in the 1930's, but Roderick had ordered it removed in 1955 to allow helicopters to land there, although it had taken three years of tussles in the district courts and eleven special legal dispensations before the pad had first come into use.

A staff member in an orange fluorescent helmet and green coveralls ushered them quickly across the pad and into the open door of the helicopter. Then he closed the door behind them, gave the thumbs-up to the pilot, and the twin-rotored monster rose from the roof and tilted away toward the northwest.

Inside, the helicopter was warm and extravagantly decorated. The main cabin was carpeted with a thick shag-pile rug in rich burgundy, and the walls were padded and lined with white moiré silk. There were deep-buttoned leather chairs, a wide leather-topped desk, and a divan draped with long-haired furs.

From the rear of the helicopter, balancing himself against the turbulence, came Freddie's flight director, Eric Peterson, a stocky Vietnam veteran with a peppery crop and a face as chunky as Barre granite. He was dressed in a smart light grey suit, but he looked as if he would have greatly preferred to be kitted out in khaki fatigues. Behind Freddie's back, he referred to the white Sikorsky as 'the hovering whorehouse.'

They shook hands. Freddie said: 'Mrs Marini is just along for the ride. I'd like you to take her back to Manhattan as soon as you've dropped me off at the island.'

'She's not staying for the celebrations, sir?'

'She has to get home to Mr Marini, don't you, Helen?'

Helen felt uncomfortable, but she nodded briefly. Beneath their feet, the helicopter angled and sloped as it turned away from Manhattan and began to beat its way northward past Englewood Cliffs, and up the foggy Hudson.

Eric Peterson scratched the back of his ear with his silver pencil. 'Beg your pardon, Mr Secker, but Mr Marini's up at Lynwood's Island, too. He flew up this morning with Mr Victor Cornelius.'

Helen said: 'What?'

'They left about ten. I don't think Mr Marini was planning on going up there, Mrs Marini, but it seemed like Mr Cornelius and him had a lot to talk over, and they decided to carry on with their meeting on the way.'

Helen glanced at Freddie anxiously. But Freddie simply laid a comforting hand on her shoulder and said: 'Well, that's fine. A nice cozy family gathering, huh? Now, how about some cocktails, Eric? Then Mrs Marini and I have a few problems to talk over in private.'

Eric looked at Freddie and then at Helen, and back again. His eyes closed no more than a snake's do, and he nodded. 'Very good, sir. Tell me what you want and I'll have Zim bring them through.'

They ordered a screwdriver and a Scotch on the rocks, and then sat in armchairs by the window, looking out at the fragments of cloud and the shadowy outline of the river beneath them. Freddie held Helen's hand, but she was so nervous now that she had to take it away.

'Do you have a cigarette?' she asked him.

He went over to the desk and brought across the gold-and-enamel cigarette box.

'There's no reason for Dick to find out you're here, you know,' said Freddie. 'When we land, all you have to do is sit away from the window, and they'll take this thing up and off again the moment I've climbed out.'

She puffed smoke. 'It's just beginning to remind me of what it was like before. All that lying, and all those nasty little deceptions.'

'If you like, you don't have to come up to Lynwood's Island at all. I could have us turn around and deliver you straight back home.'

'That would be silly. And in any case, you'd be late. I don't want to make you late.'

'Helen . . .'

She shook her head. 'It's all right. I'll hide. I'm used to hiding.'

'Is that what you really want to do?'

'I don't know what I want to do. But as long as Dick doesn't find out, it doesn't really make any difference, does it?'

Freddie frowned. 'But Dick doesn't suspect anything, does he? What does it matter if I give you a ride up to the island? Suppose you just dropped by the office, and I was my usual impetuous self and offered you a trip for the hell of it?'

She stood up, and paced across to the other side of the cabin. 'There's the Tappan Zee Bridge,' she remarked.

Freddie said: 'Helen . . .'

She turned.

More quietly he said: 'Helen, does Dick *know* about us?'

She came back and sat down beside him. Her eyes were misted and her expression was sad. The smoke poured from her cigarette in an endless dribble. She said: 'Yes, he does.

735

I'm sorry. He asked me point-blank one day. I was so surprised that I told him the truth.'

'And that was when you broke it off?'

She nodded. 'He said that if I didn't promise to stop seeing you there and then, he'd make sure we had the most muckraking divorce since . . .'

Freddie glanced up. 'Since my mother?'

'Yes,' she whispered.

Freddie let out a long, taut breath. For a minute or two he didn't know what to say, and he gazed down at the dim shores of the Hudson with a feeling of dull resignation.

Helen reached out and stroked the back of his hair. 'I knew that I shouldn't have told him. But I didn't know what else to do. And he said that as long as I kept away from you, he wouldn't say a word to anyone, and that he'd go on working with you as if nothing had happened.'

'It takes a pretty tough man to make a promise like that.'

'Dick isn't only tough, Freddie. He's forgiving, too. And you can't say that he hasn't kept to his word. He's been quite normal when he's talked to you, hasn't he?'

'Oh, sure,' agreed Freddie with a hint of bitterness. 'Very magnanimous, considering that I've been screwing his wife.'

'Freddie, please.'

'Oh, for Christ's sake!' snapped Freddie. But then he turned away, lowered his head, and said: 'I don't know, Helen. What's the damned use of it all?'

She looked at him wistfully. 'The use is that we love each other, don't we?'

He raised his head. 'I guess so. But you're right. We haven't been together for more than a couple of hours, and it's started all over. Cheating, and lying, and playing hide-and-go-seek. If you're going to have to hide, Helen, I'm not sure that I can go through with any more of this. It has to be out in the open or nothing.'

'Freddie, I *can't* leave Dick. Not now.'

He turned and looked at her steadily and strongly. 'Helen, you're going to have to make up your mind. This is too much of a strain for both of us. For *all* of us. Maybe it wouldn't be so bad if I didn't love you so much. We could meet now and again, and fuck, and leave it at that. But I *do* love you, and I don't want to go on pretending that I don't. Sooner or later,

736

it has to be me or it has to be Dick. You know that as well as I do.'

'I thought we could carry on for just a little longer,' she said quietly. 'It isn't easy to pluck up the courage to tell someone like Dick that you're walking out for good.'

'But it has to be done, Helen,' insisted Freddie. 'It has to.'

'Even if he rakes up a terrible scandal?'

'I can survive scandal, and so can you. Maybe Hester won't like it, and I'm sure that Roderick won't, but they've all had their share of dirty linen aired in public, and it's never done *them* any lasting harm.'

Helen gave a quick, uneven smile.

Freddie said: 'I'm not asking you to leave him if you really can't. You know that, don't you? I can drop you off home right now, and we can forget that today ever happened. But I can only say that because I really love you. I want all of you, Helen. Not just a part.'

She turned and looked down the length of the cabin. 'Does that door lock?' she asked him.

He frowned. 'Sure.'

'Then, if we made love, nobody could come in to interrupt us?'

Freddie paused, and then nodded.

She said: 'I've never made love in a helicopter before.'

'Helen . . .' he said.

But she held out her hands for him and whispered: 'Please, Freddie. It's been two months.'

He stood up and held her in his arms. She looked up at him, and there were tears in her eyes. He peeled back her pink summer coat, and it fell softly on the thick-carpeted floor. Underneath she was wearing a simple grey lawn dress with a loose bodice and a thin cord around the waist. The overcast lunchtime light that strained through the helicopter's windows cast a faint shadow of her bare breast beneath the thin material.

He kissed her for a long, silent time. His right hand caressed and squeezed her left breast until she let out a small sharp breath. Then she kissed him again, almost savagely, and bit at his ear. His pants did nothing to hide the rearing hardness he felt for her, and he quickly tore away from her and went to lock the cabin door, stripping off his shirt as he went.

737

He came back to her, and unzipped her dress. They were both panting, like runners reaching their stride in a cross-country race. The dress slipped off her, and underneath she was wearing only her panty hose. Her breasts were small and pointed, with nipples as tight as puckered lips, and between her thighs the seam of her tights clung deep between the plump labia which she always kept shaved and childlike.

They seemed to fall back on the fur-covered divan a thousand times, a blur of arms and legs, an action replay over and over. The divan bounced under their weight with bionic slowness, and the fur rippled and shook itself. Freddie felt the soft bearskins enfold his naked back, silky and ineffably sensual, and then Helen was on top of him, her warm weight naked except for the golden crucifix that dangled between her breasts. She kissed him and licked him, and then he rolled over on top of her, and pushed himself into her with a hard, impatient thrust. She snuffled, and her fingernails bit into his shoulder. He pushed harder, his head bent down so that he could see where they joined, his rigid dark-red flesh immersed in her pink bare glistening flesh. He thrust quicker and harder, harder and quicker, and she lifted her bottom and thrust against him. He felt so stiff that he could hardly believe he wasn't touching her womb, her stomach, even her throat. For her part, underneath him, she felt smothered in fur, pressed down by his muscular body, and filled up, completely filled up, but she wanted to be stretched wider and wider, stretched by one man or two men or three. She could fantasize six men at once, their erections tied together like fat red asparagus, forcing their way inside her.

All the time, the Sikorsky helicopter bucked and swayed and tilted underneath them as they flew, oblivious, over Highland Falls and West Point, into a misty summer afternoon.

Freddie came much too soon. He pulled back too far, and slipped out, and white warm translucent droplets smothered her thigh.

Helen, in a high-pitched voice, said: 'No! No, Freddie, no! Oh, no!' and tried desperately to smear the fluid between her legs. She was so frantic that she was trembling.

Freddie, ecstatic one second and shocked the next, sat up on his haunches and stared at her.

738

'Helen?' he said, a haunted query, almost unheard in the thrumming vibration of the helicopter's cabin

Her hand was still cupped between her thighs. She looked up at him, her eyes wide with alarm.

'Helen?' he demanded, louder this time.

She was tense for a second, her face drawn and electrified. Then she clamped one hand over her mouth, and turned away so that she was buried in the fur. Freddie saw her ribs convulse under her soft skin, and heard her sob.

He leaned forward and said softly: 'Helen?'

She lay still, the tears squeezing out of the corner of her eyes and forming a clear pool against the bridge of her nose.

'It's something else, Helen, isn't it? It's not just Dick and me.'

She nodded miserably.

He stayed there for a moment, and then he got up off the divan and went to pull on his pants. Over the RT, Captain Kroscek announced: *Six minutes to Lynwood's Island, Mr Secker.*

Freddie went back to the divan. He lit two cigarettes, and offered one to Helen. She didn't move at first, but then she sat up, pushed her hand through her wavy hair, and took it.

'You're going to have to get dressed in a moment,' he told her gently. 'We'll be landing in a few minutes.'

She closed her eyes and nodded. 'I know. I'm sorry.'

'You don't have to be sorry.'

'Don't I? I came to say I was sorry this morning, but all I seem to have done is make everything worse.'

Outside the window, there were dark green forests and silver rivers and fragments of cloud. The helicopter began to bank around, and Freddie knew that Lynwood's Island was probably in sight.

'Get dressed now,' Freddie advised. 'Then I'll have Eric fly you home.'

Helen nodded dumbly, and got up off the divan to find her dress and her panty hose. There was a polite knocking at the cabin door, and Freddie called: 'Just a moment, Eric!'

Helen, buttoning her dress, said: 'I suppose you've guessed.'

'I don't know,' answered Freddie. 'Perhaps you'd better tell me.'

'Well,' she said, 'I guess it had to come to this one day Desperation has its own reward.'

He looked at her and didn't reply.

Helen said simply: 'They shared a taxi home, you know, Dick and one of your office gossips. That's how he found out about you and me. Well, I just thank God I was only two months pregnant then, and it didn't even show.'

'*Pregnant?*' said Freddie. He knew it, and yet it still came at him like a Greyhound bus.

Helen put on her sandal. 'I got rid of it, of course,' she said. 'It was very easy, and it didn't even hurt. I cried for a week, but that wasn't difficult to explain. Tears of joy, you see, to be back from my walk on the wild side. I don't know whether Dick believed me, but I suppose he had to. At least I wasn't seeing you anymore and that was enough.'

Freddie licked his lips. He felt as if he needed a drink.

'You were *pregnant?*' he asked hoarsely. 'You had my child, and you got rid of it?'

She took a long drag from her cigarette and set it down on the ashtray. 'You mustn't think that I don't love you,' she said, so unhappy that she could barely keep from crying. 'I love you more than you'll probably give me credit for.'

'But *why?*' he wanted to know. 'If you want to stay with Dick, why do you want *me* to make you pregnant?'

She lifted her chin as proudly as she could. 'Dick's my husband,' she told him. 'I love you, and I mean that. But what I have with Dick is very deep and very special, and I know that I'll never leave him. The only trouble is, he can't . . .'

There was a long pause. The helicopter was coming down now, and they both felt pressure on their ears. When Helen spoke again, her voice was flat and distant, like someone speaking into a kapok mattress.

'We both had tests two years ago. I'm ovulating perfectly well, but Dick has what they call a low sperm count. It's *possible* for him to father a child. That's what they told us. But not very likely.'

Freddie felt an emotional pain like washing himself all over with ground glass. It was almost as if he couldn't breathe, or think, or talk.

'So you looked for a suitable father?' he asked her unsteadily and he didn't even sound like himself.

She shook her head. 'I didn't have to look. I was head over heels about you already. If there was anybody in the whole world I wanted to give me a baby, apart from Dick, it was you.'

Freddie took a deep breath. He said harshly: 'I don't know whether to be flattered or nauseous.'

Helen rested her head on her hand and started to weep Silently, but with obvious agony.

'So today was a second try, was it?' asked Freddie. 'When Dick found out about us the first time, and you had to abort my foetus, you decided you'd have another go? Say you were sorry about last time, and string me along for a couple of months so that you could get yourself knocked up?'

Helen couldn't answer. Over the RT, Captain Kroscek announced: *'Landing in one minute, sir. Please take your seats.'*

Out of the windows, Freddie could see Lynwood's Island and the stately symmetrical house. He sat down in one of the armchairs and smashed out his cigarette in the ashtray.

'You'd thought you'd acquire some good stock in your family, did you?' he yelled, over the sudden roar of the helicopter's turbines. 'A good strain of millionaires?'

Helen lifted her head and looked at him, her eyelashes spiky with tears. 'Oh, Freddie,' she wept. 'Oh, Freddie.'

The helicopter pivoted slowly, and settled on its wheels. Captain Kroscek cut the turbines, and then there was no sound but the mournful whistling of the rotors as they spun slower and slower and slower. Eric Peterson emerged from the rear cabin, and without even an inquisitive glance at Helen, operated the door-opening lever and put down the steps. He stood, silent and attentive, while Freddie sat with Helen, and Helen cried. A faint warm breeze blew in from outside.

'I want you to do one thing,' said Freddie quietly. 'I want you to fly back to Manhattan, and then take a taxi home, and I want you to forget that you ever thought anything about me except that I'm one of the men who employ your husband.'

He stayed for a few more moments. Then he collected his briefcase and climbed out of the helicopter without a word. Helen called: *'Freddie!'* but he didn't turn around.

'What if I'm pregnant?' she asked him bitterly. 'What happens if I'm pregnant?'

Freddie paused. The summer wind blew in his hair, and she thought he looked so beautiful that to let him go was like losing days out of her life. He said in a clear voice: 'Tell Dick. He'll be happy.'

As he walked toward the house, he saw Dick Marini standing close to Victor among the yew shrubs on the terrace. He saw Celia and Roderick, Ally and Tess. And behind him, the white helicopter rose into the grey summer skies and lifted Helen away, pregnant or not, its rotors flick-flacking along the Hudson Valley until their sound was nothing but echoes, and then even the echoes themselves were lost.

Celia was feeling particularly bitchy, and Freddie's punctual arrival did little to mollify her. She had considered herself the grande dame of the Cornelius family for years, and when any attention was lavished on Hester, she became shrill and argumentative, sending the servants on awkward errands (today she wanted a bottle of Swiss eyedrops that were almost impossible to find in Lynwood), and tying up the switchboard with endless calls to Germany and South America. She was dressed in a flouncy scarlet dress that did very little for her but emphasize her age, and when Freddie arrived on the terrace she was sitting on an upright gilt chair like a bright, exotic, but decidedly elderly bird, a dry sherry on a garden table beside her, her cane tapping impatiently on the stone flags.

Victor stood behind her, as sullen as a raincloud; and for the first time in months Freddie noticed Dick Marini, plump and beady-eyed, and he thought how remarkably Dick resembled a young, though much duller, Mario Lanza. He tried not to think about Dick Marini's sperm count, but it did fleetingly strike him as unaccountable that a woman like Helen should find such a depth and love in him. Well, no, perhaps it didn't. He was being unfair.

Tess came over and took Freddie's hand. She was wearing a loose filmy dress of printed cotton, and dozens of gold bangles. She kissed him as a sister kisses a brother, and a little bit more besides. Ally, wearing dark glasses and looking pale, kept her distance.

'Good flight?' asked Victor disinterestedly.

'I've had worse.'

One of the footmen came out of the open French doors and asked Freddie what he wanted to drink. He ordered a Jack

Daniel's, straight up, and Tess raised an amused and inquisitive eyebrow.

'I'm feeling tired, that's all,' said Freddie. 'Is the old lady down yet?'

'She's having her *medication*,' put in Celia archly, as if she didn't start each day herself with two handfuls of vitamins and tranquillizers and natural health tablets.

'What time are the guests arriving?'

'Most of them by Lear jet at two-thirty,' said Victor. 'One or two by train and car. The usual gaggle of hysterical women, I suppose. Just like the year that Mama won the award.'

Freddie's drink arrived, and he raised it up, as if he were about to propose a toast. But then he said: 'I didn't know you won an award from the American Women's League, Celia. What was it for?'

Celia turned her sharp profile away impatiently. 'Services to our country's womanhood,' she replied as coldly as she possibly could.

Freddie felt oddly reckless. He looked Dick Marini straight in the eye and said sharply: 'That's very good. I'll drink to that. The servicing of American womanhood.'

Celia said in tones of infinite distaste: 'You're just like your father. *And* your mother.'

Freddie laughed, a brittle laugh that didn't have very much to do with humour, and he kept his eyes on Dick Marini. 'That's more than some people can say,' he observed, although he wished almost immediately that he hadn't. It wasn't Dick Marini's fault. The man was trying to hold on to his career and his wife, both, and you couldn't take him to task for that. It was just that, emotionally and physically at least, he seemed so vulnerable, like an upturned turtle on a hot beach.

Ally, who was sipping a dry martini, said: 'I would go up and see Hester quite soon if I were you. She knows all about the Skouros thing. I don't think she's particularly amused.'

'She's eighty-four,' said Tess, taking out a cigarette. 'What does it matter if she's not particularly amused?'

Victor, who was dressed in a bottle-green velvet suit that made him look like a pale fat Las Vegas croupier, paced across to the stone balustrade of the terrace and looked out over the sloping lawns.

'She may be eighty-four,' he said with exaggerated patience. 'She may not even be *compos mentis*. But legally and financially she holds you and me and everyone else in this family by the throat. Until God in His infinite wisdom decides that He wants her back, then we're stuck with her, and don't you forget it.'

'Spoken with your usual grace,' said Freddie artlessly.

'Oh, for goodness' sake,' Celia interrupted.

Freddie knocked back his drink and set the empty glass down on the balustrade. Then he went into the drawing room through the French doors, and walked through to the elegant oval hallway. A squat man in a three-hundred-dollar pin-stripe suit and a black beard was just coming down the stairs.

'Dr Nathan, isn't it?' asked Freddie.

The doctor came down to the bottom stair, clicked his heels, and gave a small bow. 'Mr Secker. I'm pleased to see you again.'

'How's Grandmother? I was thinking of going up to say hello.'

'Yes, you can do that,' Nathan told him. 'She's not as sharp as she used to be. She has trouble remembering small things, you know. But she's in excellent health for a woman of her age. Really excellent health.'

'This won't be too much for her, this presentation this afternoon?'

Dr Nathan shook his head. 'When you get to that age, the only things that are worth avoiding are repeats on television and radishes. I like to advise my patients to lead a full life. Dr Pellen and Dr Weiss are of the same opinion.'

'Will you come with me?' asked Freddie.

'Surely,' assented Dr Nathan. 'She's up in the gallery.'

They climbed the curving staircase, with soft turquoise carpet underfoot. Then they walked along gloomy corridors flanked by oil paintings as dark and glossy as tabletops. They passed long-case clocks that ticked and chimed. Through the windows, they occasionally caught glimpses of the gardens, green and mysterious, like gardens seen in dreams or through the keyholes of doors with no keys.

Eventually they climbed another wide flight of stairs and walked along a marble-floored gallery which ran the length of one entire wing. The gallery was glazed with yellow-tinted windows, and looked out over a bare lawn with croquet wickets, where Freddie and Tess and Ally used to play when they were children. Freddie hadn't come up to Lynwood's

744

Island in a long while, and he was disturbed by the sense of wealthy neglect. Everything was clean and orderly and polished and in good repair; yet everything was untouched and unused, and the only sound these corridors heard was the footsteps of nurses and doctors, quietly and discreetly protecting the frail existence of the richest woman in America. The yellow glass gave the whole place a curious effect of the light, so that he felt as if they had arrived in an old photograph.

At the extreme far end of the gallery, sitting in an elaborate wicker chair, her legs covered by a wool blanket, was a white-haired old woman in a white dress. As they came nearer, they could see that her face was the colour of laundry, and that her hair, although it had been plaited into a white ring, was sparse. But her dress was embroidered with white silk and edged with Nottingham lace, and on her withered fingers were white diamond rings that had cost millions of dollars. Beside the old woman was a small marquetry table, on which rested *The New York Times*, *The Wall Street Journal*, a copy of Shakespeare's *King Henry V* bound in white kidskin, a hand bell, and a glass of water.

Dr Nathan approached the old woman first. She didn't look up at him to begin with. Her eyes were the colour of pale pebbles, and seemed to be almost blind. Dr Nathan said: 'Freddie's here. He's come to see you.'

The old woman nodded. 'Come a little closer, Freddie,' she asked in a thin voice like the rustling of tissue paper.

Freddie coughed and stepped forward. He bent down and kissed the old woman lightly on the forehead.

'Hello, Grandmother.'

The old woman reached up and tugged at his sleeve. 'You're a bad boy, Freddie. You must come to see your grandmother more often.'

Freddie said: 'I'll try. I've been pretty tied up.'

'Try to untie yourself then,' she said with a faint smile. 'I'd rather see you than anyone.'

Freddie grinned, and nodded. 'Okay. That's a promise.'

'We could play a game of backgammon,' said Hester. 'I'm hot stuff at backgammon, aren't I, doctor?'

Dr Nathan grinned. 'Your grandmother pastes me at backgammon every Thursday without fail.'

Freddie said: 'You're looking pretty well. Are they kind to you?'

Hester shrugged. 'They're as kind as they can be.'

Dr Nathan said: 'She's had three transfusions this month, to try to restore the balance of her corpuscles. It hasn't been easy for her.'

Hester smiled. 'I really sometimes wonder if it's all worth it. If it wasn't for these industrious gentlemen, I would have been lying in my grave years ago.'

Freddie hunkered down beside her chair. 'But you're happy, aren't you? You've got all this Women's League work. I mean, you're not *un*happy?'

Hester said: 'I have a reason to live, if that's what you're trying to say.'

Freddie picked up the white kidskin Shakespeare. 'I see you're reading *Henry V*.'

Hester nodded. 'You can learn a lot from Shakespeare. You ought to persuade Victor to read it, as a daily task.'

'I can't get Victor to read anything. I lent him *The Great Gatsby* four years ago, and he hasn't gotten past the title page.'

'It doesn't surprise me. But there's a phrase in *King Henry V* that sums up Victor rather aptly.'

'Grandmother,' said Freddie, although he couldn't help smiling, 'you shouldn't upset yourself.'

'I'm not upset. You mean I shouldn't rock the family boat. Shouldn't take sides.'

'Well, I don't know. But I guess if you have something you want to say to Victor, you ought to tell him straight to his face.'

Hester ignored him. 'Fluellen says it,' she remarked brightly. 'He says of Captain Macmorris: "By Cheshu, he is an ass, as in the world: he has no more directions in the true disciplines of the wars, look you, than is a puppy-dog." '

Freddie said: 'Victor can't help the way he is.'

Hester looked serious. 'But *you* can.'

There was an uncomfortable silence. Freddie licked his lips.

After a while Hester touched Freddie's shoulder and said: 'I have arranged my estate so that, when I die, you will be the principal beneficiary You will have more control over Cornelius Industries than anyone. But I must admit that I nearly

746

cancelled my will when I heard how you handled this ridiculous business of Ariadne Skouros. It was a silly scandal that could have been forgotten in a day. Instead, you've blown it out of all proportion. You've amplified it and advertised it, and you've lost John Russell his chance of election.'

'There's still time,' insisted Freddie.

'No,' said Hester. 'Victor was destructive and stupid, but *you* allowed yourself to be panicked; and if there is one luxury you can never allow yourself in this kind of business, it's panic. There is too much at stake.'

'If Victor's butler hadn't gone to the police, nobody would have ever found out.'

'That's precisely the kind of half-baked thinking I'm talking about,' retorted Hester. 'If Victor had been an employer who treated his staff as they were supposed to have been treated; if Victor had been the kind of man who inspired loyalty and trust, then this butler of his would never have tattletaled behind his back. And if *you'd* known what you were doing, you would have realized that one of Victor's servants was bound to talk. It was the first thing that I thought of, and I'm eighty-four.'

Freddie said: 'We're still waiting for an autopsy on the Skouros girl. If there's no indication that she died in a swimming pool, we might still get away with it.'

Hester pursed her lined lips. 'I've spoken to Dr Weiss. He says that if the police examiners are any good at all, they'll undoubtedly find traces of chlorinated water in her body tissues.'

Freddie bit his lip and glanced across at Dr Nathan, standing patiently and quietly by.

'It's still not entirely certain,' he said. 'I guess we're still in there with half a chance.'

Hester closed her eyes for a moment and then opened them again. 'It's about time you realized that your money does not make you divine,' she told him. 'Your grandfather began to understand that – perhaps too late – but he understood it all the same. It is the combination of great wealth and great personal humility that makes a rich man great.'

Freddie didn't answer. A bay-breasted warbler perched on the branch of a tree outside the tinted window, and he could hear it singing a thin, slurred song.

'I know what you're thinking,' said Hester. 'You're thinking that I'm senile, and that I've been sitting here in my chair devising all kinds of heresies to irritate you and make your life difficult. But I know what's going on, Freddie. I know that you keep in touch with public opinion, but I read everything, watch everything, and I talk to more people in a day than you talk to in six weeks. You can't get away with cover-ups like this anymore. John Russell can't put himself up for election with this business unresolved, because as sure as the wrath of God, Ariadne Skouros will rise right out of her watery grave and drag him down. One day, if not now.'

'Grandmother,' said Freddie, 'if men like John Russell don't lead the country, then who will? I believe he's honest, and he's bright, and what are we going to do? Throw him on the scrap heap just because of some damned fool mistake of Victor's?'

Hester looked at him coolly. 'The President is elected to look after the least of the American people,' she said. 'If John Russell gets to the White House on money donated by Cornelius Industries, and if he appoints Victor to some government office or other, which he surely will, then where is the sanctity of the least of the American people?'

'The least?' asked Freddie. 'What about the greatest?'

'You think that *you're* the greatest?' the old lady retorted. Freddie said quietly: 'No.'

'Well, I'm glad you said that,' Hester told him. 'Because whatever Victor and Celia think, your grandfather didn't think it, and I'll show you why.'

Freddie looked up. 'I don't understand you.'

Hester tinkled the bell on her marquetry table. 'You'll see. You may not understand still. But at least you'll see.'

Dr Nathan said: 'I don't want you to get yourself excited, Mrs Cornelius. You've got a hectic afternoon ahead of you.'

'Dr Nathan,' said Hester with heavy patience, 'nothing has excited me since Victor Mature came to visit in 1954.'

A door at the side of the gallery opened, and two nurses came through, in white uniforms and starched headpieces. One of them was as plain as a small rowboat, but the other was busty and blonde, and she gave Freddie a coy glance as she walked in

'I wish to take Mr Secker through to Mr Cornelius' *special* room, announced Hester. 'I will take Mr Secker's arm, but you will accompany us along the corridor in case I feel faint.'

Dr Nathan said: 'Do you need me any longer? I have to go check on that new plasma centrifuge.'

'No, no, you run along,' said Hester. 'Freddie will look after me.'

Freddie helped her rise from her chair and grip onto his arm. He was amazed to feel how light she was, as if her bones had all dried up to paper and her skin had been mummified. But she stood quite erect, and although she walked with careful, pedantic steps, she was just as feminine as she had been when she first sat in the foyer of the Plaza and said to Johann Cornelius: 'Texas it is.'

They went along the gallery, and then turned a corner to the north side of the house. Through the window, Freddie could see an angled corner of the glass-covered conservatory pool, where Johann had talked to Merrett Kale. Then they passed through a shadowy part of the corridor, lit by teardrop chandeliers and hung with Early American paintings, including three original artnoveau poster designs by Louis Rheade that Freddie had never seen before.

'Here is the room,' said Hester, steadying herself. 'Now, wait a moment while I find my key.'

The door looked like any other door on the upper floors of the house. It was polished beaded mahogany with brass doorplates, with a gilt number painted discreetly in one corner. But the two nurses stood well back from it, as if Hester were opening up a chapel, and it was obvious that Room 347 had a significance and an atmosphere that was almost religious, at least in the Cornelius canon.

Hester produced the key and gave it to Freddie. She rested her dry, withered hand on his and said: 'You are the only member of the family who has seen this room, apart from me I want you to understand that you must regard it as a privilege. Now, open the door.'

Freddie inserted the key and turned it. Then he pushed the door a little ajar, and stood back for Hester to precede him into the room. There was a vague smell of mothballs and must.

'No, no,' insisted Hester. 'You go first. Just walk in. I'll wait here. The nurses will look after me.'

Freddie gave an uncertain smile. Then he pushed the door wide open and stepped inside.

It was gloomy, this room, because the windows were so

heavily draped; and in any case it was foggy outside. But as he walked into it, he was aware of more than gloom; there was the shadowy presence of years and years of memory as well. He looked around it, taking it all in, but he couldn't understand what it was or what on earth it meant. Hester had called it Mr Cornelius' *special* room, but what was special about it, except that it was so musty and antique and unlived-in?

There was an odd lingering smell of stale potpourri which pervaded everything. It seemed to hang in the wine-coloured drapes, cling in the lace curtains, which were embroidered with baskets of roses, and saturate the grotesque Gothic furniture.

The room was impossibly crowded with turn-of-the-century American furniture: wine tables, china planters, china cabinets, cake stands, and standard lamps. The mantelshelf was draped in bottle-green velour, and crammed with knick-knacks: cheap pottery statuettes, clocks, sepia photographs, brass souvenirs. On the brown-wallpapered walls were dozens of watercolours, etchings, and silhouettes.

One photograph caught his attention immediately. It was standing in a small oval black-enamel frame on a table by itself. It was a portrait of a wistful-looking woman in a feather boa, a woman who, even by modern standards, was remarkably beautiful. Freddie picked it up and peered at it, and as he did so, he became conscious that Hester was standing in the doorway.

'Is this you?' he asked, lifting the photograph up so that she could see it.

She shook her head. 'No. It isn't me.'

Freddie set the photograph back on the table again. 'I don't really understand what this is all about. The room looks like something out of an old-time western.'

Hester sat herself carefully down on one of the ugly carved-oak armchairs. 'It is,' she said.

'But what does it mean? What's it all about?'

Hester's pale face was like one of the watery portraits on the wall. She couldn't even begin to explain to Freddie how much this room haunted her; how long she had tried to grasp what it was and why it was here. In a faint, faded voice she said: 'I always knew this room existed, all through my marriage. But Johann told me it was somewhere to keep some

750

particularly special antiques, and he never encouraged me to come up here. Sometimes he disappeared for hours on end, and I suppose he sat here and meditated and relived whatever this room meant to him.'

'You have no idea? He never told you?'

Hester shrugged. 'It was only after his death that I began to understand it was a shrine. In his will, he asked for the whole room to be destroyed, but I managed to have that overruled. I wanted to know why he wanted to have it destroyed, and I can only imagine that he felt it might cause me distress. The only possible clue is that photograph. It has written on the back, "J. from B." But I don't have any notion who B. might be.'

Freddie walked around the room and then stood by the window.

'Does it matter?' he asked. 'He loved you, didn't he? Does it really matter if he had some lingering memory of some other woman?'

Hester smiled. 'No, of course it doesn't matter. I don't think now that Johann loved me with all his heart, but we were happy enough. He was a passionate man, your grandfather, and fierce, but he was easily influenced, too, as many rich people are.'

'Grandmother, why did you show me this room?' asked Freddie. He was beginning to feel claustrophobic, as if his dead grandfather's life was pressing in on him from all sides.

Hester looked up. 'I wanted to show you that Johann eventually grew to understand something that Victor will never understand, and that Roderick and Celia have only accepted with such impatience and intolerance that they will never be able to tell him about it. Our wealth gives us power over other people, but if we use that power without consideration, then we are repaid for our trespasses against others a hundred times more painfully than the pain we have actually inflicted.'

She closed her eyes and sighed.

'It always amuses me that Communists and liberals want to punish the rich. The rich are already punished. Roderick was punished very young, I'm sorry to say, when his airplane crashed and killed his friends Your mother, Hope, was punished, mostly by her own conscience. Poor John was punished hundreds of times over, and I suppose you might

751

say that he died a rich man's death. Irene was punished, and Ally was punished, and so was Tess. I don't know whether anyone has punished you yet, Freddie, but they will. As for Victor, he is storing up for himself the greatest retribution of all. But who knows? He might come out of it human.'

Freddie said huskily: 'This room? Was this Grandfather's punishment?'

Hester nodded. 'I think so. For some reason, long before I met him, a room like this was vitally important. Something must have happened in it that he regretted for the rest of his life. Maybe it was something to do with "B." I shall never know. But all I can say is that I want you to grow up intelligently and wisely, and I want you to behave like a human being, no matter how superior or wealthy you are; because otherwise you'll leave a room like this yourself when you die, or something very much like it.'

Freddie looked around. There was nothing more to say. The room was silent and dead and inexplicable. He said quietly: 'All right, Grandmother. Let's go join the others. They must be starting the presentation soon.'

Hester smiled tiredly. 'You're quite right, Freddie. I must try to enjoy myself. That's what Sir James Charles said to me once, when we had dinner on the *Aquitania*. He was a tremendous eater, you know, and a bon vivant. He said that if you didn't drink as much as you could, and eat as much as you could, and laugh as much as you could, then you might just as well suck cough drops and live in Cleveland. I'm not *quite* sure what he meant, but I think I caught the gist of it.'

There was a polite knock at the door. It was Mrs Dubuque, Hester's lady's maid, a practical, bustling woman with a well-groomed silvery-grey bun and an infallible eye for dressing old ladies with style and dignity.

'Your gown is laid out, Mrs Cornelius,' she said. 'And Mr Roderick says the presentation is due to start in forty-five minutes

'Freddie, said Hester, 'I'll have to hurry. Now, be a good boy and see if you can have a word with Roderick and Celia before the guests arrive. Particularly before John Russell arrives. I want him to announce his retirement from the presidential race this evening.'

'Grandmother . . .'

Hester, rising from her chair, paused and looked at him.

'You've got troubles of your own, haven't you boy?' she asked him.

He lowered his eyes. 'Nothing serious.'

She held his arm. 'All problems are serious, but you're going to have more, particularly when the medical examiners find out that Miss Skouros drowned in a swimming pool. So do your best, my dear, and I'll see you later.'

Freddie watched Hester walk slowly off toward her dressing room, accompanied by Mrs Dubuque and her two nurses. The blonde nurse with the big breasts turned shyly around as the small procession turned around the corner, and Freddie gave her a quick grin. Perhaps he could find some consolation there for Helen.

He went downstairs, and found the rest of the family assembled in the small ballroom. It was decorated in gold and grey, with a glossy maplewood floor, and tall windows that overlooked the south rose gardens. The fog had begun to disperse, and sunlight fell in triangles through the glass onto the parquet, glittering with specks of dust. The far wall was clad entirely in mirrors, and so a looking-glass family, uneasy and strange, was standing in the middle distance, occasionally casting surreptitious glances at the real family. A buffet lunch of cold Kentucky hams, cold turkey, artichokes, asparagus, fruit, and cheeses was laid out for the expected guests. The cutlery shone like shoals of sardines.

'Well,' said Roderick as Freddie came in, 'how's she feeling?'

'Very spry,' answered Freddie.

Celia pursed her lips in irritation. 'She's been feeling spry for the past forty years.'

'She's also determined,' added Freddie.

Victor caught the tone of his voice and turned away from the buffet table, where he'd been spreading a small cracker with a huge blob of Beluga caviar. His mouth was still full from the last one.

'Determined? Determined about what?'

'About you, mainly,' Freddie told him. 'But about all of us.'

'You're not in *league* with her, are you?' asked Celia.

'*Celia*,' protested Roderick ineffectually.

Freddie put his hand in his pocket and looked relaxed. 'Don't worry, uncle. I'm not particularly ashamed of being in league with my own grandmother, who also happens to be the conglomerate's largest single stockholder.'

753

'You have to admit that she's getting pretty senile, darling,' said Tess.

Freddie shook his head. 'She's old, that's all. A lot of the time that makes her wiser, not dumber.'

Victor brushed cracker crumbs from his green lapels. 'So what particular sparkling gem of wisdom has she come up with now?'

Freddie looked across at Ally, who was standing by one of the windows in a grey suit with a pleated skirt, smoking and staring out over the gardens. He said: 'She's decided that John Russell should withdraw. She wants it announced this evening.'

Celia went white. '*She's* decided? *She's* decided?'

Dick Marini said: 'It's out of the question. If John Russell quits now, that's tantamount to admitting Victor's guilty of homicide. You might just as well wire him up to the chandelier and have done with it. I think we all agree that he *may* have to, but—'

'It's impossible,' put in Roderick. 'I won't agree to it. I'm not having Victor made into a scapegoat. Not for you, not for her, not for anyone. Who the hell does she think she is?'

'She's your mother,' remarked Ally quietly, without turning around. Roderick, stung, ignored her.

'It does seem kind of premature,' said Tess. 'I mean, they haven't even finished the forensic tests yet, not properly.'

Freddie stood his ground. 'It's what she said.'

Celia gave him a look like a snap of ice. 'And I suppose you agree with her, like you always do, in the ever-improving hope of reaping the profits of her bequest? It may surprise you to learn that business and politics aren't *all* opportunism, my child. There are occasional moments when we have to lay the lust for personal gain aside.'

Dick Marini said: 'It's going to look so bad in the courts.'

'Courts?' snapped Victor. 'It won't even get to the courts There isn't any reason at all why we can't clear this up with the police, and why John Russell can't get into the White House the way we planned. I've already laid out six million dollars for this, and I'm not about to give up now.'

'I'm not so worried about the money,' said Roderick guardedly. He remembered his fruitless, evasive conversation with Henry Chapman. 'But I *am* worried about putting Victor's neck on the block.'

'Maybe it would do Victor good,' said Ally.

Celia shook her scarlet flounces and lifted her profile like an irritated turkey. 'If you have nothing more to contribute than common insults, Ally, I suggest you leave. We're discussing a mature problem here, in a mature fashion.'

'You're discussing how to save your spoiled brat's hide,' Ally retorted, turning away from the window. Her eyes were still concealed by dark glasses.

'Come on, now, Ally,' said Tess.

'No, I won't "come on." It's true. It's no longer a question of preserving the family's integrity, of upholding our so-called historic role. We tried to do that before, tried to convince ourselves that we could alter the appearance of what had happened so that we would all appear to be the aggrieved instead of the aggressors. I'm disgusted with myself for being a party to that airplane crash. I'm disgusted with myself for believing that my position in life set me above the law.'

'Now, look here,' interrupted Dick Marini, 'nothing illegal's happened here. Well, not *prima facie* illegal. Victor could well have been flying Miss Skouros' body home to her parents, in which event he's only guilty of failing to report her death to the authorities. There's no evidence of foul play.'

'No evidence of foul play?' said Ally scornfully. 'You're deceiving yourselves more than the police and the public put together.'

Freddie lit a cigarette and put away his lighter. 'I'm afraid I agree with Ally. I know that the airplane crash was my idea. I know that I'm just as responsible for what happened as any of you. But we have to stop the whole thing right here before it gets out of hand. In my opinion, John Russell has to withdraw, for whatever pretext, and then we have to sit down with the police and the district attorney and see what we can do to get Victor out of a hole.'

Victor banged the table so hard that the cutlery jangled.

'Freddie, it's my damned money, and John Russell is my damned candidate! You would have chipped in quick enough for your share of the goodies if they'd elected him, right? You wouldn't have preached about the law if you'd come in for some nice fat government contracts, right? So don't you, or you, Ally, or anyone else stand there and damned well pontificate at me. John Russell doesn't withdraw, and that's it!'

Celia looked with acid satisfaction from Freddie to Ally and back again. There was an awkward silence.

Freddie calmly smoked his cigarette. 'I think you're forgetting something, Victor,' he said in a quiet voice.

'I don't think so,' said Victor irritably.

Freddie smiled. 'I think you're forgetting that while you have a majority shareholding in one or two of your corporations, over sixty percent of them are subsidiaries of Cornelius Oil or Cornelius Shipping.'

Roderick rubbed his cheek nervously. He could see what was coming.

'Any major donations to political candidates from any of those corporations can be vetoed by the stockholders of the parent companies,' said Freddie. 'Article seventy-six of the corporations' charters, if you feel like looking it up.'

Celia rapped her cane on the floor. 'So what do you propose?' she said frigidly. 'A show of hands?'

'That isn't a bad idea at that,' said Freddie. 'All those in favour of John Russell withdrawing his candidacy say "aye." '

'Aye,' said Freddie and Ally together.

Victor laughed. 'It's preposterous. Even with Grandmama on your side, we still outvote you.'

Tess said: 'Aye.'

Roderick coughed. 'I hope you're not serious, Freddie. You know what this could mean.'

'I'm extremely serious,' said Freddie. 'I want us to come slap-bang face to face with what we are, don't you? Face the fact that we're all Corneliuses. Even if it splits us up.'

'You're out of your mind,' said Victor. 'That's the most half-assed thing I've ever heard. Who the hell do you think keeps this business running? What the hell good am I going to be in Attica?'

'They won't send you to prison,' said Freddie. 'You let a poor dumb girl drown herself in your swimming pool. That's not exactly a five-to-ten.'

Outside, they heard the high, distinctive whistle of an approaching Lear jet. Roderick looked at his watch and said: 'That must be the first of the guests. I think we'd better adjourn this impromptu board meeting and finish it later.'

'No,' said Celia sharply, raising her hand. 'I want to know where we stand. I want to know if you'd really vote against us, you three. I want to know if we're friends or enemies.'

'I stand with Victor,' said Dick Marini, looking at Freddie. There was a bitter wealth of meaning in the way he spoke.

'And we stand against,' responded Ally. 'We're serious, Celia. We own too much of America, we have control over too many people's lives. There's too much of our own money at risk, too. If this cover-up is discovered in three or four years' time, who on earth is ever going to trust us again?'

She took off her dark glasses. There were circles under her eyes, from lost nights of sleep over Clyde, and maybe over Destry, too, and Clara.

'I think it's time this family came clean,' she said simply.

There were footsteps outside, and a burst of laughter. A footman came into the ballroom, leading an excited party of women from the American Women's League, all dressed up in their summer finery. As if they were all worked by the same switch, the Cornelius family turned toward the ladies, and their frowns of anger, of determination, of opposition, of resentment, were all magically replaced by welcoming smiles.

That evening, when a soft summer darkness was clotting in the branches of the trees, and the warblers were calling across the lawns, Freddie went upstairs to see Hester. The old lady was sitting at her dressing table, and Mrs Dubuque was brushing out her hair.

Freddie looked at her wan reflection in the dressing-table mirror.

'You were magnificent,' he told her. 'The ladies all loved you.'

'Oh, I didn't do anything much,' said Hester. 'I just gave them a great deal of money.'

Freddie raised his eyes and gazed out toward the river. All he could see was a silver patch of light. He looked back at her dressing table, crowded with jars of night cream and skin restorer and expensive perfumes.

'You know that John Russell has declined to withdraw,' he told her.

'Yes,' she nodded. 'But he will.'

'Are we going to make him?'

Hester shrugged. 'That means putting pressure on Victor, doesn't it?'

'Sure.'

'Do you want to put that much pressure on Victor?'

Freddie rubbed his eyes. 'I don't want to . But I don't think we have much choice.'

'It'll split the family,' she cautioned him.

'Yes. But hasn't it always been split? It seems to me that Johann was two kinds of personality, you know, and that he sired two kinds of people.'

Hester smiled. She didn't say whether she thought he was right or wrong.

'Which kind are you?' she asked him.

He looked at her, and shook his head. 'I don't know.'

She opened a side drawer of her dressing table and took out a crumpled piece of ruled paper. She opened it out and read it carefully to herself, although she had obviously read it hundreds of times before. Then she passed it to Freddie.

'It's something your uncle John did, years and years ago. I want you to have it.'

Freddie took it, and saw a few lines of childish handwriting. They read:

My father is very rich and is the Cornelius Oil billionair. He is very old and does not have much hair. I like it when he goes away because my mother lets us have dinner in the garden room and sometimes eat squob. My father is stric and we have to do what he says. I would like to buy him a nice wig for his birthday because even though he is stric I do love him because he is my father. He has an airplan called the Ford Tri-Motor.

Freddie read it twice, and then gently folded it up.

'Johann adored that,' said Hester. There were tears in her eyes. 'He used to say that it was the nicest thing that anyone ever wrote about him. He was, you know, a very sensitive man.'

Freddie nodded. He bent forward and kissed her. Then he said: 'Sleep well,' and left the room. He walked along the gallery in the dim yellow-tinted light, feeling as if Johann, and John, and everyone the Cornelius family had ever known, or loved, or hated, or done business with, were all beside him.

He heard the rumble of a Lear jet leaving the island's runway. That would be Victor, leaving for Spiermont. Roderick and Celia had already gone, closeted in their long black Fleetwood, without even a wave. Tess was leaving for California in the morning, and Ally was spending a few days with friends in Lynwood before going back to her house and her business in Washington.

He went downstairs, and across the drawing room, and out of the French doors. He stood on the twilit terrace for a while, smoking a cigarette and listening to the whistling of saw-whet owls. Then he turned and went inside for a cold supper of ham and potato salad.

Pieces of what happened were everywhere. They were scattered across America, dusty and forgotten, and they are still there today. The school composition that Hester gave to Freddie was only one small piece out of thousands; and there are many which have long since disappeared.

In a railroad collectors' store in Milwaukee, Wisconsin, lies the real railroad whistle that the Broughton stationmaster gave to Daniel Forster, and which Daniel Forster blew like crazy. Outside a suburban house in Cleburne, Texas, hangs one of the lamps from Johann Cornelius' New Orleans motorcar, and when they have cookouts the owners light it up. There are still fragments of the aluminium skin of the C-1 airplane keeping the rain out of a backyard toolshed in West Virginia; and a chicken farmer from Muskogee drives Celia's cherry-red Bentley on special occasions.

Some of the mementos are fine, while others are nondescript. Ariadne's emerald pendant was eventually sent back to her parents, who sold it after four months to raise the down payment on a new house. It now belongs to the wife of a supermarket manager in South Pasadena. The faucets from the bath in which Beatrice Mulliner committed suicide were fitted to the side wall of a gas station in Galveston, and are still used today for filling radiators. The Pierce Arrow 'Silver Arrow' in which Hazel Seymour was driven to Lynwood railroad station is now a collector's item, and stands in a private motor museum in Waco, Texas.

Elsewhere, if you looked hard enough, you could find jewellery and automobiles and airplanes and moth-eaten furs. You could probably find John's Duke Ellington records, cracked and dusty, on a Greenwich Village stall; or the picture of Loch Lomond that hung in Carina's turret room in Edgar. You could find Edward Secker's Gleneagles ashtray, or David Bookbinder's leather-bound law books. Every family, every story, has its debris.

About the people, though, it would be pointless to ask questions. About Roderick, Celia, Victor, Freddie, Tess, and Ally; even about Hester, and her long-dead husband. Because you could never say that they were happy or unhappy, that they were proud or that they were ashamed. You could never say that they were satisfied, or sad, or racked with guilt. You could only say that they were rich.

Solitaire

Prologue

His mother had always been able to surprise him. It had been her way. But she had never surprised him as much as this. He lifted the huge diamond out of the dark blue velvet socket of her jewellery box, and held it up in the curtained dimness of her bedroom with a sensation of sudden vertigo. It was a brilliant, fiery, rectangular-cut stone, larger than a man could comfortably swallow, and it was still unmounted; untouched and untampered-with since the brilliandeer had buffed it up to its final dazzling polish.

He had no exact idea of how much diamonds were worth, although he had heard that if they were monstrously large, as this one was, they could no longer be valued carat for carat: that would put them beyond the reach of even the world's richest men. But even at auction, this diamond would have to be valued at hundreds of thousands of pounds, perhaps millions.

'I'm a millionaire,' he thought to himself. It was like emerging from a wine-cellar into the open air and discovering that he was drunk.

He had no doubt at all that the stone was real. He remembered as he turned it around and around in his fingers what his mother had whispered to him only five weekends ago on the wisteria-wrapped verandah of the Reverend Ponsford's house at Herne Hill, when everybody else had been playing croquet on the sun-blinded lawns.

'Your father made sure you were taken care of,' she had said. 'Your real father, that is. He provided for you, and for your children, but secretly; so that when I go, you shall never want.'

'You're not going to *go*,' he had smiled at her, and taken her hand between his. In its white summer glove, it had felt like a dead starling, all bones and feathers.

I

But whether she had experienced a premonition or not, a kind of Tarot-reading from the weather, and the clouds, and the postures of the reverend gentlemen who were playing croquet, she *had* gone, within three weeks of the croquet party, of a summer cold that turned to pneumonia. At the age of thirty-three, Peter Ransome found himself to be an orphan.

The effect had caught him off-balance. He had not been prepared for the abrupt loneliness of it; nor for the pain that he would suffer as he tidied up his mother's affairs with Messrs Winchell & Golightly, Solicitors and Commissioners for Oaths, of Croydon; and as he cleared up his mother's house in Kennington, in South London, not far from the Oval cricket ground. As he came across photographs and memorabilia from his mother's past: a sepia print of his stepfather with the Bishop of Woolwich, another of his mother arm-in-arm in some scrubby landscape with Cecil Rhodes, a lion's-tooth necklet, a silver snuffbox with an embossed view of Victoria Falls, he began to feel as if he no longer knew who he was, or why he was here. He had inherited all of these fragments from other people's lives, but there was no longer anybody in the whole world to whom he was directly related.

His stepfather, the Reverend Hugh Ransome, had died of a seizure the day before Queen Victoria's Jubilee celebrations, on 21 June 1897. The excitement of arranging a party for Kennington's children and old folks had been too much for him: that, and the heat.

His real father had died a year before that, drowned, after a well-publicised incident on the cruise liner, *Andromeda*, off Madagascar. One witness had insisted that Mr Blitz had 'recklessly and with aforethought' hurled himself over the rail of the quoits deck into the Indian Ocean, and had swallowed enough water to sink himself before the ship could be brought about. But Mrs Blitz had strenuously denied any suggestions of suicide. Her husband had been 'in bustling health', she had told the coroner, prettily, and he had been eager to start up a new property business in Cape Town.

But now Peter was here, in the big redbrick house in Montacute Road, overlooking a tired triangle of grass and plane trees, with his mother's jewellery case open in front of him, and a

2

diamond between his fingers that was bigger than he would have thought possible. It *had* to be real, he was convinced of it, even though he had no expertise in diamonds, and no means of testing the stone, apart from using it to scratch his name on the bedroom window, which somehow did not seem like a very reverent idea. In the five years since his stepfather had died, Peter had gradually become aware that the love between his mother and his real father had been something intense, and very special, and that even their eventual separation had not been able to extinguish it.

If the love between his mother and his real father had been only half as fierce as his mother had described it (and being a modest woman, a vicar's widow, it had probably been twice as passionate, and twice as jealous as she had told him), then this diamond which symbolised it just *had* to be authentic, and flawless, too.

His mother's maid, Olive, came into the bedroom, with a japanned carpet sweeper, her hair a chaos of henna-stained curls and tortoise-shell combs. 'It wouldn't be disrespectful to open the curtains, do you think, sir?' she suggested. 'I would hate to think of you straining your eyes. My 'enry strained his eyes, fighting in the dark at Nicholson's Nek.'

Peter clasped the diamond protectively in both hands, and turned around in a way that was stiffer and more mannered than he would have liked. 'By all means draw them,' he said. 'I don't think Mother would have wanted to see the house so gloomy in any case, do you?'

Olive drew back the thick brocade drapes with a rattle of brass rings. The London sunlight fell across the patterned rug, and on to the white-covered bed on which only a fortnight ago his mother had closed her eyes for the last time, as if asleep. On the wall beside the bed hung a plain wooden crucifix: his mother used to tell Peter that she had been given it by a missionary in South Africa, when she was still a young girl – before she could even speak English.

'You'd like some tea, sir?' enquired Olive.

Peter kept his hands clasped tight together. 'Yes, tea,' he said. 'I shall be down directly.'

'Very good, sir.'

When Olive had gone, he left the dressing-table and walked across to the oval cheval-glass by the window. In it, he saw a dark, shy-looking young man in a plainly-tailored grey suit; a young man whose complexion was too dusky to be English, and yet whose short straight nose and sharply-defined forehead were too European to be those of a pure-blooded African. Racially, he was a thrice-cut cake: a third Dutch, a third Hottentot, and a third German-Jewish.

He was used to the difficulties of having tinted skin. He was an automobile mechanic, working for the Vulcan motor car company in Southport, Cheshire, but he knew that for all of his talent with a spanner he would never make chief engineer. He raced, too, a little, whenever there was a spare 10-hp car and enough ethyl. But he would never be allowed to make the grade as a first-class driver. This was an England which tolerated half-castes as the inevitable outcome of a far-flung colonial empire, but which scarcely ever admitted a 'fuzzy-wuzzy' to the inner circles of society.

It had helped Peter that his stepfather had been the Reverend Hugh Ransome, much respected for his work amongst the poor of south London, and amongst the heathen in South Africa. His stepfather had taught him manners, and proper dress, and all the niceties of small conversation. But none of these graces had really been enough to whiten his face, and he had known ever since he was at school that only an Act of God could win him admission to the prizewinner's enclosure of Edwardian society.

Perhaps this diamond was it. The one miracle which could change everything. He opened his hand, and the huge stone was warm, already infused with his own heat. The sun caught it, just the tip of it, and it flared up with brilliant rainbows and shatteringly bright triangles of reflected and re-reflected light, a spangled hall-of-mirrors in miniature.

'Your father made sure you were taken care of,' his mother had whispered, and the words fell on his memory like sheets of soft tissue paper.

He recalled sitting by his mother's knee almost twenty years ago on a winter's night in the old vicarage, toasting muffins on the end of a fork, his cheeks hot as baked apples, and he remembered his mother saying, 'Did I ever tell you the story

4

of the man who gave up everything he had, all his possessions, even the estates that he adored so much, just to buy his secret love the most precious stone in the whole world?'

He had said no, tell me. But she had simply smiled in an absent-minded sort of way, and tousled his hair, and told him to be careful not to drop his muffin into the coals. Now, however, he knew what she had meant.

He looked through the drawers of his mother's dressing-table until he found a silk drawstring sachet that had been used for carrying a gold powder compact. He dropped the diamond into the sachet, tightened the string, and slipped it into his pocket. Then he straightened his necktie in the looking-glass, and went downstairs to the front parlour, where Olive was setting out the tea things. There was a large Rockingham pot of fragrant Ceylon, and a small plate of rather stale rock cakes.

'You're looking pale, sir, if you don't mind my saying,' said Olive. 'You're not considering going down with the fever?'

'I didn't have it in mind,' said Peter. 'Would you pour?'

Olive poured, and the steam from the cup twisted up into the sunlight like the Indian rope-trick. 'I keep dwelling on your mother, sir,' said Olive, sadly. 'Such a lovely woman, you know; and even lovelier when she was younger.'

'Yes,' said Peter, sipping his scalding tea. He didn't really want to share his memories with Olive. 'I miss her very much.'

He finished his tea alone. He tried one of the buns, but they were too dry and somehow they tasted of death. At last, at three o'clock, he left the house and walked down to the end of the road, to wait for the horse-drawn omnibus to take him over the river into London. Across the street, as he waited, two barefoot street Arabs were trying to shin up the gas-lamp on the corner, watched in awe by another boy in a boater hat and a sailor suit, whose nanny had paused to gossip on the pavement with a postman.

The omnibus arrived late. Because it was a fine summer's day, Peter sat up on the roof, and smoked a cigarette. There was a traffic jam on Blackfriars Bridge, and the omnibus had to wait there for almost ten minutes, while a cool breeze blew up the Thames from the docks, fragrant with spices and

5

peppers from unloading ships and warehouses. Peter took out another cigarette, but tossed it half-smoked on to the road.

He arrived at a small jeweller's shop just opposite Holborn Circus a few minutes before five o'clock. The late afternoon was crowded with carriages and cabs and horse-drawn drays, and the noise of horseshoes and iron-bound wheels grinding on the wooden road-blocks was almost deafening. A bell jangled as he stepped into the door, and then there was silence as he closed it behind him.

The shop was very small. There were mahogany-and-glass showcases on all sides, crammed with rings and pendants and silver perfume-holders – lower middle-class jewellery, the kind of jewellery that a jobbing clerk might give to his lady-love at Christmas, or a shopkeeper buy for his wife on their wedding anniversary. There was a smell of dust and silver polish and jeweller's rouge.

From a door at the back of the shop came a man as lanky as a tailor, with blond hair which flopped over his right eye. 'My dear fellow!' he said, as soon as he saw it was Peter. 'What a complete surprise!'

Peter held out his hand. 'How are you, Samuel? You're not getting any plumper.'

'Not for want of eating, though,' said Samuel. 'Business has never been so brisk. Have you come down for anything special, or just for a jaw?'

Samuel Kellogg had been a schoolfriend of Peter's in Kennington, although when Samuel's father had died of consumption he had moved to Bloomsbury to live with his Uncle Max, and help in the family jewellery business. Still, the friends had kept in touch from time to time, even when Peter went to Southport, and only last summer they had met for supper in Oxford Street, at Runcorn's Chop House.

'My mother passed away,' said Peter. 'I've been down in Kennington clearing up the house.'

'My dear chap,' said Samuel, sympathetically.

'She was frailer than I thought,' Peter told him. 'I suppose she never really was cut out for the British climate. She always used to suffer from colds, and the influenza.'

'All the same, I'm very sorry,' said Samuel.

'Thanks,' said Peter, trying to brighten up.

'Won't you come through to the back?' asked Samuel. 'I have some tea left in the pot, and some capital veal pie.'

He lifted the mahogany flap of the counter, and Peter followed him through into a dark back room, where there was a badly dilapidated sofa, a fireplace still clogged with last winter's ashes, and a jeweller's workbench, cluttered with silver wire and forceps and soldering irons. On the wall was a saucy calendar of a naked theatre girl with plumes of ostrich feathers in her hair and strings of pearls around her ankles.

'I don't suppose you've seen anything of Walter,' said Samuel, taking the lid off the teapot and peering into it suspiciously.

'Not a peek. I heard he went off to Malaya to plant rubber.'

'He always did have the look of a rubber-planter, I must admit.'

Peter moved four or five tattered copies of *The London Illustrated News* from the sofa, and sat down. 'I don't know. What does a rubber-planter look like?'

Samuel shrugged. '*Rubbery*, I suppose. Shall I brew some fresh?'

'Don't bother. What I really came about was more in the line of business.'

'I see,' said Samuel, sitting down. He cut a piece of veal pie off a twenty-one pound slab, and pushed it into his mouth. 'I suppose your poor mama left you quite a bit of disposable jewellery?'

'I haven't been through it all yet,' Peter told him. 'But I was mainly concerned about *this*,' and he produced from his pocket the small drawstring purse, which he loosened, and then turned upside-down over Samuel's workbench.

The diamond rolled out on to the bench, and lay on its side, sparkling in the gaslight. Samuel, his mouth still stuffed with pie, stared at it as if God had just dropped a third tablet of commandments from the heavens above.

'What on earth . . .?' he asked. 'You're not telling me that's a real stone?'

Peter nodded. 'I'm pretty well convinced of it.'

'But that's a *diamond*,' said Samuel. 'You don't find dia-

7

monds in that sort of size. That's as big as the Regent. Bigger. It can't be real. Where on earth did you get it?'

'My mother's jewellery box.'

'Not even in a safe? It can't be real. My dear chap, if that were a real diamond, it would be worth ... a million pounds. Maybe more. You wouldn't keep it in a jewellery box. You'd have it locked up, in Coutts.'

'Maybe you would, and maybe you wouldn't. What burglar would ever suspect that a vicar's wife would have a million-pound diamond in her jewellery box? A couple of rings, maybe; a pinchbeck pendant. But not a million-pound diamond.'

Samuel picked the diamond up and frowned at it. Then he reached for his jeweller's loupe, his 10 × magnifying lens, and peered at it even more closely.

'It's difficult to tell in gaslight,' he said. 'But if it *is* a real diamond, it's magnificent. A slight pinkish tinge to it, don't you see? Very slight, but enough to make it a "fancy" diamond, and increase its value four to five times over, if you can find anyone to pay that sort of money.'

'Then you think it's genuine?'

'My dear chap, I couldn't tell you for certain. This is the whole illusion of the diamond business. Not even quite reputable dealers are capable of telling whether some diamonds are real diamonds or not. There are plenty of very capable fakes around these days: and if they're mounted, they're even harder to detect. Some tricksters set inferior diamonds in a fine gold or silver setting, you see, and paint the back of the gems so that they reflect more light. There was the famous rainbow necklace of the Romanoffs, for instance. George Kunz, an American gemologist, and a very sceptical fellow, discovered by scratching the backs of the diamonds with his finger-nail that they were nothing but second-rate stones with paint on them.'

'But this stone isn't mounted,' said Peter.

'No,' replied Samuel. 'But it could be topaz, or strass, which is high-density lead glass, or even quartz; although I doubt that it's quartz, because it appears too brilliant.'

Peter was silent for a moment, watching his friend examine the stone through his loupe, but then he said, 'I have to tell you something which may make you change your opinion.'

'Well, do,' said Samuel, 'because if this is a real diamond, then you're in the money for the rest of your life, and I'm not joking.'

'The Reverend Ransome wasn't my real father,' said Peter. 'I know that I always pretended he was, when I was at school, but that was only because I was embarrassed about it. My real father was Barney Blitz.'

Samuel put down the diamond and looked at his schoolfriend in astonishment. 'Now, you're really having me on toast. This is just a practical joke, isn't it? You're going to go back to all the fellows at Kennington and tell them how Samuel Kellogg thought a piece of glass from a Christmas cracker was worth millions of pounds.'

'Samuel, I'm telling you the truth. I swear it. When my mother was in South Africa, she lived with Barney Blitz for years. He was my real father.'

'Well, you could knock me down with a feather,' said Samuel.

Peter pointed to the diamond. 'That's why I'm quite sure that the diamond is real. And that's why I have to know where I can take it to sell it. I don't want to be sold short. My father gave that stone to my mother so that my future would be secure. I wouldn't want to let him down by giving it to the first diamond dealer I meet for only a quarter of what it's worth.'

Samuel looked at the stone for a long time. 'You'll excuse me,' he said, 'but I've never seen a diamond like this before, and I never will again. I want to make sure that I remember this moment. So, Barney Blitz was your father, was he? You could knock me down with a feather.'

'The point is,' said Peter, 'where can I go with such a diamond?'

Samuel laid the diamond carefully back on his workbench. 'There's only one man that I know of. Garth Steinman. I don't know whether you've ever heard of him or not, but he's a dealer in unusual and speciality jewels only. Quite an eccentric, but a very rich eccentric. He acquired the Montfort emeralds for the late Queen. He's a friend of the Rothschilds, and of J. P. Morgan. He has a house in St John's Wood, although he may not be there now. He winters in Italy, and spends his summers in Switzeriand.'

Peter took back the diamond and slipped it into the draw-string sachet. 'I can only try. Do you think you can find me his address?'

'My dear chap,' said Samuel, 'for the sake of a diamond like that, I'll even *take* you there.'

Samuel closed the jeweller's shop early, and the two of them hailed a hansom from the corner of Gray's Inn Road. The rush-hour traffic was easing off now, and the early evening sunlight filled the interior of the cab with gilded motes of dust. Neither of the friends spoke very much as they turned westwards towards Euston station. Peter felt as if the whole of his world had altered, as if he were now involved in a theatrical per-formance of his own life, rather than the real thing.

It took them a little over twenty minutes to reach the quiet sidestreet in St John's Wood where Garth Steinman's resi-dence stood. The Steinman house was only one of a whole row of huge, expensive mansions, each with a high wall and hedges. In those days, St John's Wood, although it was only a mile or so north of Marylebone, was a quiet secluded village of its own, and the air was noticeably fresher than it had been in Holborn. Peter and Samuel alighted from the cab and paid the cabbie 1s 3d, with 3d tip.

Samuel rang at the bell-pull on the gate. But it was almost five minutes before a gardener, who was trundling a wheel-barrow of dug-up daffodil bulbs, came past the front of the house and noticed them. A little while later, a footman in a green coat and stockings came out to enquire what they wanted.

'Mr Steinman, if he's at home,' said Peter.

'You have an appointment, sir?'

'I have something better than an appointment.'

'Sir?'

'I have the largest diamond he's ever seen in his life.'

The footman said, 'I'm afraid Mr Steinman is seeing nobody today. He has a headache.'

Peter took the diamond out of his pocket, and held it up. It flashed in the sunshine as brilliantly as if it had actually caught fire. The footman could not keep his eyes off it.

10

'Tell Mr Steinman that you've seen the diamond for your-self,' said Peter, quietly. 'Tell him that it will be more than worth his while to forget his headache for five minutes.'

'Yes, sir,' said the footman, and retreated towards the house. Peter glanced at Samuel and gave him a teeth-gritted grin, half optimistic and half fearful.

Another five minutes passed before the footman returned. Without a word, he unlocked the gates, and beckoned them inside. He locked the gates behind them as they walked up the sloping gravelled driveway towards the pillared portico of the house. The flowerbeds all the way along the drive were clustered with white and yellow roses, and the fragrance was almost nauseating. Peter was reminded that he had not eaten anything all day, except for one desultory nibble at his rock cake.

The footman opened the black-painted front doors, and led the friends into a wide, high-ceilinged hallway which had been decorated in a style which Peter could only think of as over-extravagant Byzantine. There were arches everywhere, decorated with gold and peacock-blue mosaics, and a fountain of nude entwined mermaids splashed water into the cool echoing silence.

'You'll come through to the afternoon room, sir?' asked the footman, and ushered them into a sunny yellow-carpeted library at the far side of the hall.

At a wide leather-topped desk, smoking a Turkish cigarette in a long holder, sat a small rotund man with shiny brushed-back hair, and a monocle. He was wearing a yellow silk dressing-gown which matched the colour of the carpet, and yellow silk slippers.

On a chaise-longue at the opposite end of the room, next to a wall of gilded and leather-bound books, lay a very pretty girl who looked no more than sixteen or seventeen years old, with an embroidered silk headband around her blonde, upswept hair, and dressed in a multi-layered negligée of such fine laon and lace that Peter could distinguish the rosy pink of her nipples.

'You'd better introduce yourselves,' said the fat man behind the desk.

'My name's Peter Ransome,' said Peter. 'And this is Mr Samuel Kellogg, my friend. Mr Kellogg is a jeweller.'

'I see,' said Garth Steinman. 'And what are you?'

'I am an automobile mechanic,' said Peter.

Garth Steinman jotted a few notes on to the diary that was open in front of him. Then he closed it up, and said, 'What is an automobile mechanic doing with a large diamond, that's what I ask myself.'

'I came by it legitimately, Mr Steinman. It was a bequest from my late mother. My ... *recently* late mother.'

'My condolences,' said Garth Steinman. 'Your mother was a wealthy woman? Should I know her name?'

'She was not wealthy in any other respect, save this diamond,' Peter told him, quietly.

Garth Steinman looked up, one eye closed, the other eye staring through his monocle like a freshly opened clam. 'I see. Well, a diamond's provenance is not too difficult to check, if you know the right people to ask. My man told me that the stone was exceptional, by all appearances.'

Peter took the diamond out of his pocket again and set it precisely in the centre of Garth Steinman's closed diary. Garth Steinman kept his eyes on Peter for more than ten seconds before he turned his attention to the stone.

'Well, then,' he said. On the other side of the room, the pretty blonde girl had sat up and taken notice.

While Peter and Samuel stood and watched him in silence, Garth Steinman laid the diamond on a sheet of white paper, and examined it closely. His cigarette now burned unnoticed in the ashtray, and the only sound in the room, apart from the faint splashing of the fountain in the hallway, was Steinmen's hoarse breathing, in and out of his open mouth.

Now Steinman took out a 20 × loupe, and scrutinised the diamond for brilliance and fire, and also to check whether it contained any 'clouds', which are small clusters of bubbles; and 'butterflies', which are cleavage cracks; or 'naats', which are the knotty flaws that sometimes appear at the interface between twinned crystals.

After long minutes of study, he eventually put the diamond down again, and tucked his loupe into the breast pocket of his dressing-gown.

'I am very seldom taken by surprise,' he said, thickly. 'I

know the value and the whereabouts of almost every major gemstone in the world. I have friends in the Russian court; in Vienna; and in Berlin. I was a close friend of Cecil Rhodes before he died last year, and Mr Ernest Oppenheimer regularly sends me cables from De Beers, and dines with me whenever he comes to London, or to Berne.'

Garth Steinman paused, and then lifted up the diamond in his right hand. 'This, however, has taken me by surprise. It is genuine, I can assure you of that. No paste diamond could be made to this size without its falsity being immediately obvious. And who would attempt to fake a stone of this immensity? It would be absurd. Mr Ransome – that is your name? – this diamond I believe to be the famous Rio Diamond, which was sold at auction in 1888 to a New York diamond dealer called Greenberg. I don't remember how much it fetched, about two millions, I think. But its size, and its cut, and its colour – all correspond with what I know of the Rio.'

The blonde girl had now got up from the chaise-longue and crossed the room, the lacy train of her negligée dragging across the canary-yellow carpet. She stood a little way away from Garth Steinman's desk, and stared at the diamond as if it were a hypnotic eye. Peter gave her a quick, friendly smile, but she did not return it.

'How much do you think the diamond is worth now?' asked Samuel.

Garth Steinman puffed out his cheeks. 'It depends on its history. If Mr Ransome here can establish that it is rightfully his, then we can make some enquiries right away, of dealers and collectors, and of royal courts, and we may be lucky enough to be able to close a private sale, which usually fetches more than an open auction. The market price is quite steady at the moment – so we may get three to four millions, if we play things right. I'd expect a commission, of course, of thirty per cent.'

'That seems excessive,' said Peter.

Garth Steinman smiled tightly. 'Seventy per cent of three millions, which is what you'll be left with, is rather more than seventy per cent of nothing. There aren't many men on earth who can sell this diamond for you, I assure you. Well – you must know that, or you wouldn't have brought it here to begin with.'

'He's right, Peter,' said Samuel.

Peter thought for a moment, and then nodded. 'Very well, Mr Steinman, I'll leave the sale to you. I shall require a receipt, of course, to the effect that you're holding the diamond. And I shall also require you to seek my approval before you close the sale.'

'Naturally,' said Garth Steinman. 'Can I offer you a brandy?'

It was more than a month before Peter heard from Garth Steinman again. Then, when he was back at the Vulcan motor works at Southport, on a sullen August day, he received a telegram saying, *Entrain for London at once. I have a sale –* Steinman.' He told his chief engineer that he was feeling sick, and took an omnibus back to his small walk-up flat on the outskirts of Southport to pack, hurriedly, a portmanteau. By tea-time, his train was pulling out of Northampton on its way to London, and the first flickers of lightning were lighting up the eastern horizon, over towards the flatlands of East Anglia. He arrived in St John's Wood at six.

Garth Steinman met him at the door. This time, Steinman was dressed in a consummately-tailored afternoon suit, with a wing collar, which gave his head the appearance of a pale Christmas pudding on a white dish.

'You've been remarkably prompt,' he said, and showed Peter inside. 'Do you like nudes?' he asked, as they passed the fountain in the hallway.

Peter glanced at him. 'In moderation,' he replied. 'There's a time and a place for everything.'

Garth Steinman cackled out loud. 'I like your style, Mr Ransome. But then a man of your potential wealth can afford to have style.'

They went through to the library. There was no sign of the blonde girl who had been there before. Instead, by the window, smoking a cigar, stood a broad-shouldered man of about fifty, wearing a black tailcoat and striped trousers. He had a permanently amused expression on his ape-like face, and a very bushy moustache.

'Mr Ransome,' said Garth Steinman, 'I'd like you to meet Herr Albert Ballin. You might have heard of Herr Ballin – he is the managing director of the Hamburg-Amerika Line. He is also a close personal friend of the Kaiser, and that is why he has come here today.'

Herr Ballin stepped forward, one hand thrust into the pocket of his trousers, the other around his cigar. He looked at Peter for a while, his eyes half-closed against the smoke, and then he said, 'I have inspected your diamond, Mr Ransome, and I have made Mr Steinman an offer. My intention is to present it to the Kaiser as a gift on his next birthday.'

'Well, I'm sure the Kaiser will like it,' said Peter, hesitantly. 'Is the offer fair, Mr Steinman?'

'Three millions, seven hundred and fifty thousand,' smiled Garth Steinman. 'Three millions to be paid in two instalments in cash, in a London bank. The remainder in Hamburg-Amerika securities.'

Albert Ballin sat down in a small armchair, and crossed his podgy legs. 'You will not refuse me, Mr Ransome? I have a reputation for getting everything I want. My enemies call it *ballinismus*.'

'I can recommend that you accept the offer,' said Steinman. 'I doubt if anybody else is in a position to be more generous than Herr Ballin.'

Peter thought for a moment, and then shrugged. 'The arrangement seems fair to me. As long as Herr Ballin is satisfied.'

Albert Ballin nodded. 'I am *more* than satisfied. This is one of the great treasures of the earth.'

'You want to have it tested first?' asked Steinman.

Ballin laughed. 'I think I trust you. Mind you, I could always drop it into a glass of clear crème-de-menthe, couldn't I? That's supposed to be an infallible test for diamonds.'

Garth Steinman said, 'You can drop it into whatever you want. But I should warn you that the old crème-de-menthe test is something of a romantic fallacy. The theory behind it is that, in crème-de-menthe, a diamond will show up clearly, because of its high refractive qualities, whereas a synthetic stone will disappear. The trouble is, plenty of up-to-date synthetics have high refractive indices, too. I would hate you to fool yourself.'

'Very well,' said Herr Ballin. 'I will forego the test. If you are content with the price, Mr Ransome, I will talk to my bankers in the morning.'

'The price is fine,' said Peter. 'I'm just wondering if the destiny is right.'

'The *destiny*?' asked Herr Ballin.

'I'm wondering if this diamond was really meant to be the personal property of the Kaiser, and to be inherited by the German monarchy.'

Garth Steinman walked across to his desk, where the diamond was lying on a small cushion of white velvet, and picked it up. 'You should understand, Mr Ransome, that diamonds, even more than people, have their own destiny. Whatever their owners do, they will always find their place in history. If this diamond is not happy with the Kaiser, then it will not stay with the Kaiser. In any case, why should you worry? You are a rich man now, and you can do whatever you wish. Racing those motor cars of yours, I shouldn't be surprised?'

Peter said, slowly, 'Yes.' But he found himself looking at the diamond, and the way it sparkled, and he was suddenly reluctant to lose it. Garth Steinman recognised the expression on his face, however, and heartily grasped his shoulder. 'You will never get a better price, old fellow. And, believe me, diamonds are better off in the hands of those who can really afford them. To everyone else, they bring nothing but grief and despair.'

'*Sehr philosophisch*,' smiled Herr Ballin.

Peter took the diamond in his hand one last time. It meant so much more than Herr Ballin or Garth Steinman could ever understand. It was the crystallisation of the love between his mother and his father, the last adamant reminder of the passion that had created him, and of private fears and ambitions that he could only guess at.

'Very well,' he said, at last, and laid the diamond down again. He shook hands with Herr Ballin, and with Garth Steinman, and left the house quickly, without saying another word.

Later that day, he stood by the Thames at Chelsea embankment, as the sun sank behind the cluttered rooftops of World's

End. He tossed pennies into the river because now he could afford to; and each penny that splashed into the water created for one split second a sun-glittered diamond of its own.

He had never felt so lonely in his life.

ONE

From inside the apartment, as he reached the top of the stairs, Barney could hear his mother arguing, and sobbing, and banging her ladle. It was the same as always. A jumble of rage, entreaty, tears, and stunning absurdities. Enough to turn a good son's loyalty head-over-heels. 'If your father should walk in now! What would he say?' 'Why didn't I have sons like other women – sons who respect their mother?' 'Don't you know how much I suffered, giving birth to two *schlimazels* like you?' 'Is this the reward I get?'

Barney took the brass latchkey out of his dark vest pocket, on its long fine chain, and held it up for a moment. Then, with resignation, he unlocked the door. At the far end of the landing, rain still spattered against the frosted-glass window, like a pessimistic Romeo throwing up occasional handfuls of gravel. Barney hesitated, and then pushed the door wide. The scorched-tomato smell of burned goulash blew out of the apartment on the damp evening draught. He touched the *mezuzah* which hung on the doorframe, and stepped inside.

On the wall, beside the peg where he hung up his coat, there was a steel engraving of Drensteinfürt, in Westfalen, Germany. The picture was grimy and foxed. Barney touched that too, the same way his father used to.

Mrs Blitz was in the kitchen, a one-woman band, racketing her ladle against the sink, the cupboards, against the iron pans that hung above the range. Her hair was wiry and wild, as if she had just come in out of a hurricane. The goulash pot was smoking furiously on the hotplate, and there were half-chopped vegetables strewn everywhere.

'You wait!' she was screeching. 'You wait until you run out of friends, and out of money, and out of love!' And she beat against the colander, and the door, and the tin bowl in the sink. 'You talk of gratitude! Duty, you talk of! Is this gratitude? Is this what you call duty? *Riboyne Shel O'lem!*'

Barney closed the apartment door behind him. And even though his mother was screaming, 'Don't come crawling back to me! Don't you ever come crying for money!' She stopped in mid-sentence at the almost inaudible click of the lock – silent, aghast, frozen, in case it was actually *him*, *Tateh* himself, Barney's father, returned from the cemetery with his smile and his moustache and his best broadcloth suit.

'Mama,' said Barney, gently.

Slowly, like a woman in a theatrical production of her own personal tragedy, Mrs Blitz came towards him, her arms out-stretched, and she clutched him so tight around the chest that he could feel her bony ribs through the thick fabric of his vest, her terrible scarecrow thinness, and it was all he could do to embrace her like a son, and consolingly stroke her frayed black hair, and whisper, 'Mama . . . another *tarrarom*? . . . now what for?'

Joel, his older brother, appeared at the far end of the kitchen. Joel was slighter than Barney, with his mother's dark hair and his mother's thin, intense face. His shirtsleeves were rolled up tight, and there was a purple marking-pencil behind his ear. He looked at Barney, and then across at the range, and then he walked over and took off the burning goulash pot.

'Well, it's a good think the neighbourhood wasn't hungry tonight,' he remarked, fanning away the smoke with his hand. 'Mama just burned enough goulash to feed everyone from here to Cherry Street.'

'What's wrong?' asked Barney, still holding his mother close, but more stiffly now.

His mother raised her head. It was difficult for Barney to believe that she was the same bright, fierce woman who had brought up the Blitz family – the same woman who had fed them with meatballs and clothed them in flannels and sung them songs of Münster, in 'the good old days'. It was even harder to associate her with the pretty girl who laughed from the pinchbeck photograph frame in the parlour, the girl who clung with pride and delight to the arm of that smiling, puff-chested man who stood beside her, all top hat and well-brushed moustaches.

But four years ago, on the seventh day of Tishri, that man had died of consumption in his upstairs bedroom; and while she waited outside his door, listening to the mumbling of the rabbi and the doctor, Feigel Blitz had slowly come apart, not just mentally, but physically as well, so that her eyes no longer seemed to fit her face, and her mouth appeared to speak without her forehead realising what she was saying. She could look elated, and say something moody and odd. She could look unhappy, and say something cheerful. The woman who stared up at Barney now was a scrambled jigsaw of the mother he had once loved dearly. The neighbours upstairs called her a *meshuggeneh*, a crazy woman. The rabbi, when he visited, would always take Barney's hand, and squeeze it, as if to say, I understand your problems, but, *nu–nu*, she's your mother, after all.

Barney repeated, 'What's wrong, Joel? What's happening here?'

Joel shrugged. Mrs Blitz said, 'He's leaving. He's packing his trunks.'

'You're *leaving*?' asked Barney.

'That's right,' said Joel. 'And if it hadn't been for the Great Fire of '45 here, and all this shouting and screaming, I would have had the chance to tell you decently.'

'I don't believe it,' said Barney. 'You mean you're packing now?'

'He's packing now,' put in Mrs Blitz. 'Shirts, shoes, even his pants!'

'You want I should leave my pants behind?' retorted Joel.

'Barney, you tell him,' wept Mrs Blitz. But, just as abruptly, she turned around and screamed at Joel, 'You're just like your father! That's what your father did – he left me! He went! Right when I needed him most of all!'

Barney held his mother's shoulders tight. 'Mama,' he said, 'yelling isn't going to get us any place at all.'

'No more is whispering!' cried Mrs Blitz. 'Yell, cry, what's the difference? Maybe I should sing him a song! *Ein Knabchen sah' ein Röselein steh'n ... Röselein auf der Heide ...* You remember that? But what's the difference? He's still going to walk out ... a first son walking out on his own mother, on his own brother! God should bring down a curse on you, Joel!'

'God already did!' Joel shouted, and banged the door so hard that dry plaster showered down from the laths around the frame.

Feigel Blitz clutched Barney's wrist. She did not say anything, but her face twitched as if she could feel something crawling up her back. Then she released him, and suddenly turned away.

'You're hungry?' she asked Barney. She picked the goulash pot out of the sink, lifted the lid, and inspected its charred contents.

'I can eat out,' said Barney.

'No, no ... I can easily make you meatballs ... maybe some sauerkraut?'

'Mama –'

'Well,' she said, replacing the lid on the pot. 'I know what you're thinking. He's a big boy now, he has a right to do whatever he chooses. But he has a family. Now his father's gone, he's the head of the table. You don't think that's a responsibility?'

Barney took a breath. He said, 'Yes, Mama, that's part of it.' Beside him, on the kitchen wall, was a calendar for 1868, a gift from Mrs Jana across the landing. There was a Polish quotation from the Bible for today's date: '*Badźcie nasladowcami moini, tak jak ja jestem naśladowca Chrystusa*'.

'I have herring, too,' suggested Barney's mother.

Barney stood in the kitchen for a moment, watching his mother dither from the scratched deal table to the sink, and back again, and smile at him with that infectious, dotty, frighteningly vacant smile. 'You'd like a herring?' she asked.

'I have to talk to Joel,' Barney told her. 'Now, please – promise you'll wait here, and make me some supper – and don't start yelling again. Will you, please?' He was very conscious, in his mother's home, of how American he sounded.

'Well, what do you think?' she asked him, in that ambiguous way that always infuriated him.

He opened the door at the far end of the kitchen, and walked along the dark narrow corridor to Joel's bedroom. The door to his mother's room was open, and he glimpsed as he passed the high sawn-oak bed, the stolid dressing-table, the pictures of the old country. There was the smell, too, of stale violets and powder, of a middle-aged woman sleeping on her own. He felt a wince of pain. *She's your mother, after all.*

Joel had the larger of the two other bedrooms. Its grimy window looked out over Clinton Street, where the gaslamps were already lit, although it was only seven o'clock, and late in April; and the rain was rattling in the gutters. Joel's two trunks were laid open on his iron-frame bed, and he had almost finished packing. His striped nightshirts, his books on geology and sailing, his best brown boots.

Barney stood in the doorway and watched him. Barney was tall for his age, nineteen, and meaty across the shoulders. Everybody in the family said he took after his *elter zayde*, his great-grandfather, Yussel Blitz. It had been Yussel who had first started the coat-cutting business by making winter jackets for the farmers and butchers in his home village of Drenstein-fürt, near Münster, on the grey Westphalian plain. Not that Yussel had looked much like a tailor: he had been strong, and husky, from a poor but respected *mishpocheh*. Barney had been told over and over again that he had inherited Yussel's brown curly hair, and wedge-shaped forehead, and that nose of Yussel's which looked more like the nose of a prize-fighter than a Jewish *schnoz*.

All Barney had inherited from his mother were his eyes – deep-set, and bright, and brown, as shiny as the toes of Joel's best boots.

'You didn't warn me,' Barney told Joel, quietly.

'Well – it was sudden,' Joel replied, rolling up a last pair of hand-knitted socks. 'I didn't even decide myself until last night. I was having tea with Moishe last night ... and I just suddenly decided. But what's the difference? You know the business as well as I do. Now, it's yours.'

'What's the *difference*?' Barney demanded. 'The difference is that you've left me stuck with the whole thing, and nobody to help me. That's the difference!'

'Moishe will help.'

23

Barney rubbed his eyes. He was exhausted after a long day over his desk, and walking around the stores. 'Why didn't you tell me you wanted out?' he asked. 'We could have talked about it, found some kind of solution.'

'There wasn't anything to talk about, and the solution is that I'm going,' said Joel, flatly. 'Barney, I'm sorry. If you don't want to carry on with the business, then sell it. Buy Mama a home uptown. Let the *kuzinehs* look after her.'

'Ruchel and Rivke? Those two old crows? They'd kill her in six months. And, besides, what about everybody who works for us? Ten people, including David. What are *they* going to do if I sell?'

Joel closed the lids of his trunks, and began to buckle up the leather straps. 'Barney,' he said, controlling his voice, 'the simple truth is that I don't care. I know how it sounds. I know you think I'm letting everybody down, you included. But I've been choking for years, and if I don't get out now, then I'm going to end up like Father before I'm thirty. I'm *choking*, Barney. On chalk, on barathea, on thread. I'm choking on Clinton Street. And more than anything else, I'm choking on Mama's –'

He paused, ashamed of what he was going to say. 'I'm choking on Mama's love, and Mama's temper. I can't be a stand-in for *tateh* for the rest of my life. I can't measure up. I don't even want to measure up.'

Joel stood silent, his hands on top of one of his trunks as if it were a piano, and he was going to pick out some lost, sentimental tune.

Barney said, 'What are you going to do?'

'I've signed on to a passenger steamer, the *Stockdale*. She sails tonight, from the Cunard Liverpool Steamship Wharf, in Jersey. She's bound for England, and then for South Africa.'

Barney walked across the green and yellow linoleum floor to the window. There was hardly anybody around now. It was supper-time, and still raining hard, one of those wet New York nights when it seems as if the whole city is out at sea. Across the street, on the opposite sidewalk, a bagel-seller stood by his smoking cart, his shoulders hunched, water cascading from the brim of his hat.

'I'm going to miss you,' Barney told Joel. '*Soixow*, I always thought we were going to stay together for the rest of our lives. You know, partners.'

Joel attempted a smile. 'I'm not going away for ever,' he said. 'I just want to breathe for a while, that's all. I've had ten years of vests and linings and lapels. Come on, Barney, you know what it's like.'

'Sure,' said Barney, without turning away from the window. 'It's all sweat and toil and not much money. It's Moishe, and David. It's trying to cope with Mama's tantrums, trying to eat your way through a meal that was cooked for six people, just so you won't upset her. But what would *Tateh* think, if he knew?'

'*Tateh*'s dead,' said Joel, emphatically. He looked up at Barney, and then he reached out his arms for him, and the two brothers gripped each other close, cheek against cheek. Barney, in spite of his disappointment in Joel, or maybe because of it, found that his eyes were sticky with tears.

'Joel,' he said hoarsely.

'I have to go, Barney,' said Joel. 'I'm going to miss you ... I'm even going to miss Mama ... but I have to.'

Barney stood up straight. He wiped his eyes with his handkerchief, and blew his nose. 'Sure,' he said. 'I know.'

Joel said: 'Hey ... you remember the time we sewed up the cuffs of *Tateh*'s best pants?'

'I remember,' said Barney. 'He got straight out of bed, pulled them on, and fell flat on his face. Laugh?'

Joel gripped his younger brother's shoulder. 'He belted us, remember? "A *shtik* like that you should try on your father!"'

They didn't know what else to say to each other. Barney knew Joel well enough to realise that, whatever he said, Joel was going to leave. Joel had always been that way. Quiet, determined, and stubborn. Maybe he had too much of his mother in him.

'South Africa, huh?' he said. He tried to sound conversational. 'The land of the *schwarzers*?'

Joel smiled, and then laughed. 'You'll manage without me. When I'm sitting in a grass hut, stuffing myself with elephant-flavoured *bialys*, you'll be turning out broadcloth pants by the dozen!'

25

Barney said, 'Yes. I guess so.' He felt sadder than he could possibly explain.

Mrs Blitz appeared in the bedroom doorway, clutching her hands together. Barney glanced at Joel, and then said, 'Mama?'

'It's ready,' she nodded. Her eyes darted from side to side like tropical fish.

'Okay, then, we're coming,' said Barney. 'Joel – you're going to join us at the table?'

Joel looked at his strapped-up trunks. 'I can't be too late. The ship leaves at ten.'

'You've got time for a last meal,' said Barney.

They went into the kitchen, still smoky, where bread and meatballs and cold gefilte fish were laid out for them on heaped-up plates, enough to feed ten ravenous men. Joel pulled out Mrs Blitz's chair for her, and she sat down primly at the end of the table.

'Well,' she said, serving out meatballs, 'have you decided what you're going to do?'

Joel picked up his fork and eyed his mother carefully. 'I'm leaving, Mama. I told you.'

'Didn't you listen to what Barney told you?'

'Barney didn't tell me anything. Barney knows what I feel. Anyway, it's a chance for Barney to run the business. It's good experience.'

Feigel Blitz looked from one of her sons to the other. 'I hope you're not trying to tell me you're both in this together?'

Barney, chewing meatball, said, 'I can't persuade him to stay, Mama. He's my older brother. He wants to go, and that's it.'

'You're really leaving?' snapped Mrs Blitz.

Joel put down his fork again, and pushed away his plate. 'I told you, Mama. I'm going. And I really think it's better if I do it right now.'

'Sit down,' ordered his mother, coldly. Her face was white, and set.

'Mama, I'm going. There's nothing in this whole world that can –'

'*Shah!*' shrieked Mrs Blitz. 'You think I made you this supper for nothing – that you should eat it, and then leave me?

What kind of son are you? What's your father going to say? Are you crazy, leaving the business? Blitz, Tailors? How can you turn your back on it?'

'Mama, please,' pleaded Barney. 'He's going to leave, whatever you say. Can't we just eat and say *Shema* and let him go with a blessing? Mama?'

Mrs Blitz swept her arm across the table, hurtling plates and meatballs and gefilte fish all over the kitchen floor. Then she seized the long sharp knife she used for slicing bread, and stabbed wildly at Joel's hands. Joel jumped back, lost his footing, and stumbled over his chair. Mrs Blitz got up from the table and went for him, the knife held over her head in both hands.

Barney was quicker. He overturned the deal table with one hefty thrust, so that it fell on top of his sprawling brother. Then he lunged for the knife in his mother's hands, yelling, 'Mama! What are you doing? *Mama!*'

He was too late to stop her first downward stab. The black-bladed knife, worn thin and keen from years of constant whetting, sliced right through the skin between Barney's thumb and index finger, and into the raw muscle. Blood spattered everywhere, scarlet exclamation points. Barney gripped his wrist in pain, and sank sideways on to his knees.

There was a hideous silence. Mrs Blitz stared at her sons in shock. Joel eased the overturned table off his legs, and stood up, brushing egg and fish and breadcrumbs from his trousers. Barney, bleeding, crouched on the floor amongst the chairs and the meatballs, his teeth gritted and his face grey like newspaper.

From another apartment, they could hear an unsteady violin playing a *mazel tov* dance. Young Leib Ginzberg, practising for his sister's wedding. It sounded ludicrously jolly.

Joel, without a word, tore a long strip from the tablecloth, knelt down beside Barney, and wrapped it around his thumb. Mrs Blitz stayed where she was, swaying slightly, as if she were on the deck of a ferry, the knife still clutched in her hand.

'I'll get you round to the doctor,' Joel told Barney. 'That's going to need stitching.'

Barney shook his head. 'You'll miss your ship. It's eight o'clock already.'

'You're my brother,' argued Joel.

Barney shook his head even more decisively. 'I can go to the doctor by myself. I want you to catch that ship. If you don't leave now, you never will.'

Joel looked towards his mother.

'*Leave,*' insisted Barney. 'Isn't this exactly why you're going, this kind of scene? Isn't this exactly what you want to leave behind?'

Joel stood up. He was flustered now, undecided. He wiped sweat from his forehead with the back of his hand. His mother looked at him with an expression that could have been resignation, or regret, or just plain contempt for everything and everyone, including herself.

Joel said, 'Mama –?'

But Mrs Blitz simply turned away, and walked off towards her bedroom. They heard her close the door behind her, and turn the key in the lock. The brothers looked at each other in silence.

'If you're not careful, she'll kill you one of these days, *chas vesholem,*' said Joel.

Barney said, 'No. She'll kill herself first.'

'I'd better say goodbye,' Joel told him, without any enthusiasm at all.

He went to his mother's bedroom door, and knocked. There was no answer. He made a face at Barney, shrugged, and shouted: 'Goodbye, Mama!'

'Go!' Mrs Blitz screeched back at him. 'And a *choleria* on you!'

Joel hesitated, then sighed. 'I'd better go fetch my trunks,' he said to Barney. 'I'll take them down to the street, and call a cab. You go straight round to the doctor. Don't wait.'

The two brothers stood in the shadowy hallway. 'This is goodbye, then,' said Joel.

'You're not going to touch the *mezuzah*?' asked Barney.

Joel smiled, and shook his head. 'It was never anything more than superstition, as far as I was concerned. I only did it because Father did it. And, remember, this isn't my home any more.'

28

They embraced tightly. 'I love you,' said Joel. 'I'm sorry I've left you with everything, the whole burden.'

'I'll manage,' Barney told him.

'I guess you will,' said Joel. 'But you wait – one day, when I'm rich, I'll come back. That's a promise. And I'll make *you* rich, too.'

Barney held his injured hand close against his chest. The tablecloth bandage was already dark crimson.

'Goodbye, Joel,' he said. 'God bless you.' Then he walked off quickly along the landing, and down the stiars.

They had snow early that year, in the third week of October. Barney was walking back from a long sales meeting with the men's-wear buyer of B. Meyberg & Co., on Broadway, and the afternoon streets were suddenly furious with white flakes. He tugged up the collar of his black wool coat, and straightened his hat, and hurried along Hester Street with his hands deep in his pockets. The snow did not settle. It was soon trodden into slush by the horsedrawn cabs and streetcars, and swept up by the rascally, emaciated men who had appeared with brooms at every intersection, tipping their caps and holding out their grimy mittens for nickels. But, as Barney trudged up the staircase of Blitz, Tailors, brushing the snow from his shoulders, and knocking it off the top of his hat, he felt as if the year which had only just begun was already half over, and he wondered how many more times he would climb this narrow wooden flight, brushing the snow from his coat, growing older and greyer with each successive climb.

He stopped on the landing and looked back towards the street, where the soft snow still pattered on to the sidewalk. He frowned.

In the little glazed cubicle by the tailor's shop door, David was warming his feet by a smoky oil fire, and sewing a silk braid edging to a detached sleeve. Barney opened the door, stepped in, and hung up his hat on the bentwood stand.

'Is Moishe back yet?' he asked.

David nodded. 'Ten minutes. Is it snowing? Itzik said it might snow.'

'It's snowing. Did you sweep up yet? It's getting late. I don't want this place looking like a rubbish-dump all through *Shabbes*.'

'Moishe asked me to finish the braid. It's the Military Academy order.'

Barney, picking up a sheaf of bills and invoices from the upright desk in the corner, said, 'Okay. If Moishe says so.'

David went on sewing. He started to hum, a monotonous tune without a beginning and without an end. Barney glanced at him in irritation as he read through the bills, but he did not say anything. David was a simpleton, a *golem*, and if Barney had told him to shut up he would not have understood. He might even have burst into tears.

It had been Barney's father who had taken David into the business, as a favour to one of the *kuzinehs*. Tall, big-nosed, with a pear-shaped body and soft dangling hands, David was the third child of Rivke's eminent and illustrious stepbrother, Dr Abraham Stein, the gynaecologist. Dr Stein, who lived on Fifth Avenue, albeit in one of the more modest mansions, had fathered three big-nosed daughters, and eventually David. For all his parents' early pride, David's mind had suddenly stopped developing at the age of thirteen, and after three grotesque incidents of exposing himself to the downstairs maids, and to one of Dr Stein's most genteel lady patients, Dr Stein had uncomfortably asked Rivke to persuade Barney's father to find the boy a place at Blitz's. To keep him out of harm's way, you understand? To keep his mind off – well, *things*.

That Rivke woman, with her barbed-wire hair and her ostentatious garnets – that Rivke woman could talk anyone into doing anything. Barney's father used to say that she could crawl into your bones. 'She crawls into my bones,' he used to say, gritting his teeth, and crunching up his face.

So David went on humming, with his simple future assured; and Barney, tired, tugged at the curls around his ears and tried to work out whether today's mail had brought him a profit or a loss. Usually, these days, it was a small profit, but it was hard, running the business without Joel. Moishe was a help when it came to rushing out orders, or to estimating how much broadcloth to buy; but Moishe did not want responsibility. He did not want to worry himself with cash flows, with profit margins, with rates of interest. He thought – and maybe quite rightly – that only the Lord had control over such things, and who was he to interfere in the works of the Lord?

Through the dusty glass of the cubicle where he was standing, Barney could see part of the cluttered, low-ceilinged workroom, lit with so many gas jets that it looked almost like a holy place during *Chanukah*, the Festival of Light, illuminated with dozens of *menorahs*. Under the lights, their heads bent over their work, his cutters and basters and seamstresses toiled away at the last few military coats for the academy; and although the sky outside their window was as dark as corroded copper, and still whirling with snow, they never raised their eyes once. They had an order to finish before the Sabbath.

Barney glanced back at David. 'Are you going back to your parents' house for *Shabbes*?' he asked him. 'Back to Fifth Avenue?'

David, still humming, shrugged.

'Maybe you'd like to come spend *Shabbes* with me, and my mother?' suggested Barney.

He didn't try to sound too encouraging. In fact, to his own restless shame, he was praying that David had already promised to spend the Sabbath with his own family. He tried not to think how often his father had brought home an *oyrech auf Shabbes*, even a filthy street musician once, with an oboe; and, one *Shabbes*, an extraordinary and eccentric prize-fighter, who had insisted on bending spoons and straightening them out again. 'At least he straightened them out again,' Barney's father had told his mother. But somehow, because of his own sparkling character, Barney's father had always been able to transform awkwardness into joy, embarrassment into laughter, and every one of those Sabbath days had been glowing with family love, and devotion, and affection for their guests. At least, they had always seemed that way.

Barney knew that he was different from his father. Warier, quicker to lose his temper, and more critical of weakness. Maybe it was New York that had made him harder, and less tolerant of those whining *shlemiels* who lived off their friends. More likely, he had been soured by the difficulty of running Blitz, Tailors, all by himself, and the violently changeable

31

moods of his mother. Since Joel had left, Mrs Blitz's mind seemed to have tilted even further askew, and one morning last week he had caught her ripping at Joel's mattress with a knife, panting, convinced that Joel was hiding inside it just to tease her, just to play a malicious joke on his dear mad mother.

David finished sewing his braid, bit the thread between the teeth, and then looked up at Barney almost primly. 'Yes,' he said. 'I'd like that.'

'Fine,' said Barney, unenthusiastically, in his most American voice. 'I just have to talk to Moishe, find out what's going on, and then we can go.'

He stepped out of the cubicle into the workroom, and walked along between the benches to the far end. Usually, the loft was noisy with laughter and conversation. Blitz's was not a sweatshop. But this afternoon, with only two hours to go to sundown, and the room still heaped with work, it was almost silent, except for the crisp cutting of scissors through cloth, and the hiss of gas.

Over in the corner, where dozens of bolts of worsted and tweed and broadcloth were stacked, Irving and Hyman were cutting out the last of the uniform pockets; and beside them, on a stool, thin and studious, young Benjamin was busy threading needles. Irving and Hyman, both silver-haired, were Blitz's two best cutters. 'Cut!' Barney's father used to say. 'Those two could cut tarpaper, and make you a coat to be proud of.' They looked like brothers, Irving and Hyman, although they were not. Irving, with magnifying spectacles perched on the end of his nose, and a concentrated expression like a barn-owl, had immigrated from Munich. Hyman, whose black vest was always forested with glittering needles, had brought his family to New York from Zamosc, in Poland. But they were inseparable. They spent feast days together, and went fishing together off the Stanton Street pier, and shared a ridiculous sense of humour which had Barney laughing for hours at a time.

'You sold Meyberg's those overcoats?' called Irving, without looking up, as Barney approached them.

'They're taking half a dozen on trial.'

'On *trial*?' put in Hyman. 'The cloth we used for those, a

shmatte! They should know those coats are guilty, without a trial.'

Barney grinned. One of his seamstresses glanced up, the soft and docile Sarah Feinberg, and he touched her on the shoulder as he passed.

He found Moishe by the window, folding up tunics and inspecting them closely for uneven stitching or loose buttons. He was short, Moishe, and hugely fat, with hanging jowls, and a bald pate that lay in the chaotic nest of his gingery hair like a speckled roc's egg. His belly, swollen by years of gorging himself with *matzo* dumplings and bread pudding, had a bouncing animated life of its own; and on several occasions, Irving had peered down the front of Moishe's bottle-green vest, and called, 'How are you doing in there, *bubeleh*?'

'Well, Barney,' said Moishe, spreading a fresh sheet of tissue-paper over another folded tunic. He wiped a finger under his left eye, a sign of tiredness.

'You're almost through?' asked Barney. 'I want to close up in twenty minutes.'

'An hour maybe should do it,' Moishe told him, reaching past him to take another completed tunic from Benjamin.

Barney looked beyond Moishe, out of the window, where the snow had suddenly dwindled into thin, spiralling flakes, and the clouds that had banked themselves over the Jersey shore were dramatically brightening up, like the *Ecstasy of St Theresa*, by Bernini. Sunlight glistened briefly on the rooftops across the street, and the rattling of horse-drawn carriages began to grow busier and louder.

'Listen, you don't have to finish this order today,' Barney said, looking around at all the uncompleted tunics. 'Monday morning's going to be fine. You can send the uniforms out by carrier.'

Moishe, almost imperceptibly, shook his head, and folded the tunic's sleeve.

'Moishe,' insisted Barney, 'it won't *matter*. By the time you've packed up this order, everybody at the Military Academy will have gone home for the weekend anyway. They may be *goyim*, but they've got families, just like us. You think they're going to wait around, biting their nails, for tunics?'

'We told them we'd deliver,' said Moishe, dogmatically. He fixed Barney with tiny, uncompromising eyes, beady as raisins in a loaf. 'At Blitz's, when we say today, we mean today. Not tomorrow, nor the seventeenth day of Tammuz next year. *Today!*'

Barney, suppressing a smile, watched with proprietorial interest as Moishe folded one more sleeve, and brushed away a speck of lint with an exaggerated sweep of his podgy hand. Then he said, 'I seem to remember, Moishe, that your name is Teitelbaum, not Blitz. I'm Blitz, and what we say at Blitz's, that's my *medina*, not yours. Now, in twenty minutes, we close, whether you've finished this order, or not.'

Moishe reared his head up, like a surfacing walrus. 'You think your father would have let a two-hundred-dollar order go out two days late?' he demanded. 'Your father would have taken off his coat, and rolled up his sleeves, and helped me to pack – not stood there like a *fonfer* and told me to finish up! We have pride here, at Blitz's! A reputation! Even your brother Joel would have helped, and what Joel knew from tailoring you could have written on the head of a pin!'

Barney grinned, and appreciatively threw his arm around Moishe's fat shoulders. 'Just wrap it up for the day, Moishe. I appreciate your loyalty to Blitz's. I love your hard work. I love you. But it really won't make any difference at all, whether you finish this today, or Monday. Come on, Moishe, it's almost *Shabbes.*'

Moishe dragged a handkerchief from his pants pocket, and dabbed at his jowls. 'Your father should have seen you,' he said. 'You're an American now, you know that? All talk, all big ideas, and no work. A *shlepper.*'

'Sure, sure,' said Barney. 'So much of a *shlepper* I've persuaded Meyberg's to take six of those tweed overcoats on approval, and give me ten firm orders for shooting-jackets. You know the ones with the leather patches?'

Moishe looked down at the tunic he had been folding, and then at Barney. 'Ten, huh? Well, they could have taken fifteen.'

Barney raised his hands in mock-surrender. 'Moishe, with you, I'll never win. But meanwhile, we're not doing so bad, are we? Turnover's good, profits are steady. Maybe in a month

34

or two we can think about paying everybody a little more.'

Moishe sniffed. 'We're doing all right, I suppose. I guess I remember the old days too clearly, when your father was here.'

'Well, of course you do. How can I blame you for that? I'm young, and I'm different. But I'm not too young to understand how you feel.'

Moishe laid his hand on Barney's shoulder. 'Barney, let me ask you something. Something personal, serious.'

'Sure,' said Barney. He turned his head around, and called, 'Irving, Hyman – you want to clear up now? We're closing the shop in twenty minutes.'

'Listen to me,' said Moishe, gently. 'I'm not being critical. Simply truthful. I've been watching you for six months, ever since Joel left, and working with you. You don't like this business, do you? This tailoring. You're doing your best – as far as profit's concerned, you're doing good. But your heart's not in it, is it?'

Barney frowned at Moishe warily. 'What makes you say that?'

'Oh, come on, Barney, I'm not a blind man. Look how you've changed everything here since Joel left. All this ready-to-wear stuff we're making, for stores, and colleges, even for postal catalogues. Thirty tunics for the New York Military Academy? We never had an order like that in the whole of our fifteen years.'

Barney did not say anything. While Moishe had been talking, Irving had come across the room, and now he was standing two or three feet behind them, listening.

'Moishe's right, Barney,' Irving said. There was tenderness in his voice, understanding, but also regret. 'Blitz's was always bespoke before. High quality suits, made to measure. Some of the best in New York. We've still got the regulars, sure, the customers who know what they want, and won't change their tailor for anything. But these days, when you say Blitz's, most people think of ready-made. The trade does, for sure, and it won't be long before the customers do, too.'

'Another thing,' put in Hyman. 'David tells me you've been turning customers away.'

Barney let out a breath, took out his pocket-watch, and checked the time. 'Well,' he said, 'I can't deny it.'

'Deny what?' asked Irving.

'Any of it,' said Barney. 'I can't deny that my heart isn't really in tailoring. Nor can I deny that I've been trying to change Blitz's from a gentleman's personal tailors into a house with a good name for ready-mades. I can't even deny that I've been turning personal customers away. The truth is, it's a business, as far as I'm concerned, and that's it. And how can it make any business sense at all for Irving to spend two days cutting out one suit, for which we're going to change ten dollars forty-three cents the piece, when he could be cutting out *six* suits, for which we're going to charge six dollars and twenty-two cents the piece? It seems like it's to *your* advantage, and to *my* advantage, and especially to the advantage of the families and children who depend on us.'

Moishe looked uncomfortable. 'You're right, Barney, in a kind of a fashion. But Irving here, and Hyman ... they're artists. They can make a suit like it's magic, the way the coat hangs on the shoulders, the way the lapels roll over.'

'I know,' said Barney. 'Moishe, I *know*. But that's why the stores like their ready-mades so much. As far as ready-mades go, they're superb.'

'But, Barney. Understand me. You're asking Michaelangelo to put up wallpaper.'

Barney was about to snap back at Moishe, but then he stopped himself. These men were family, old friends of his father, and what was more, craftsmen. He was sensitive enough to know what Moishe was talking about and to know that if he didn't check himself, he'd be liable to let his anger and his impatience go hurtling off like a pair of ill-trained dogs. Whatever his father had given him – humour, and warmth, and balance – he still had his mother's hair-trigger temper. He lifted his hands, as if to show Moishe and Irving that he had understood them, as if he was suing them for peace.

'Listen,' he said, softly. 'I know that I've been asking you to undertake work that's way beneath your skills. But try to see it from my point of view, too. I've been building up some capital so that Blitz's can grow, and strengthen itself. Maybe

I've been overhasty. I'm young, I know that. Maybe I've been overdoing the profit motive, and not paying enough attention to the heart of the business. But, if the profits improve, everything's going to change. When we're solidly back into credit, we can set up a real quality tailoring department like you've never seen. Better than ever. All I'm asking you to realise is that we can't go from *peklech* to Lord & Taylor in six days. Not even in six months.'

Hyman slowly nodded. 'Spoken like an American,' he said, turning away, and his intonation was as bland as only a Yiddisher could make it – so bland that Barney could not tell if it was an insult or a compliment, or simply a resigned and accurate comment.

Moishe went to find his coat, and everybody else began to pack up, folding bolts of fabric, sticking pins and needles back in their pin-cushions, clearing away paper patterns, sweeping up scraps of basting and snarls of thread. One by one, the gas jets were turned down low, until the twilit workroom was beaded with scores of tiny blue flames.

'I expect you're looking forward to going home tonight,' said Moishe, brushing his hat.

Barney, who was helping to scoop up buttons, said, 'No more than usual. Why?'

'Such an *oyrech auf Shabbes* you've got,' winked Moishe.

'You mean David?' asked Barney, hefting up a bolt of navy blue union cassimere.

'David?' said Moishe. 'I don't mean David, I mean Leah Ginzburg. You didn't know she was coming? Her *bubbe's* sick, and so her mother's had to go to Front Street to take care of her, and her father's still in Jersey, so she's spending the Sabbath with you. Maybe Sunday, too.'

'Who told you?'

'Your mama. Who else? She came up here this afternoon while you were round at Meyberg's.'

'Leah Ginzburg?' Barney demanded, throwing down the cloth. 'How come you wait until *now* to tell me? *Oy gevalt*! If I'd known, I would never have invited David. David I asked, with Leah coming! Why didn't *David* tell me, for the love of God? He must have known!'

Moishe, buttoning up his coat, gave Barney a fat, sympathetic grin. 'Maybe David likes Leah as much as you do. Maybe he likes your mother's *knaydel*. Maybe he forgot.'

'Forgot? That *nebech* never forgets anything.'

'Well, you should be grateful,' said Moishe. 'It isn't every *Shabbes* you get the opportunity to do such a good deed. You should thank the Lord.'

Barney looked at him fiercely for a moment, and then relaxed, and laughed. 'I guess you're right. Thank you, Lord, for giving me this opportunity to show charity to my fellow man! But with Leah Ginzburg around, I should have David Stein, too?'

Irving came over, wrapping his long grey woollen scarf around his neck like a failed snake-charmer taking home his exhausted python. His wife always made him wear a scarf, even in summer, in case of what she called 'wind stiffness'. 'Listen, Barney,' he said, hoarsely, 'I don't want you to think that I'm *kvetching*. But we're family here, right? We can say what's on our minds. No secrets. Maybe next week we should talk over the whole business, all this ready-made work you've been asking Hyman and me to do. It's not our kind of work. I'm unhappy, for one; and I know that Hyman's unhappy. And, worst of all, Sussman knows we're unhappy, too.'

Barney said: 'Sussman?' The amusement faded from his face as rapidly as sensitised silver darkening in sunlight. 'They've made you an offer at Sussman?'

'I can't tell a lie,' said Irving.

'Well, then,' said Barney. 'If Sussman's made you an offer, and you're not happy here, you'd better leave. I wouldn't want to keep you here against your will. And the same goes for Hyman. Him, neither.'

Moishe looked at both of them uneasily. 'Come on, Barney,' he said, 'we're all tired. Let's leave it till Monday.'

Barney, without taking his eyes off Irving, nodded slowly. 'Sure,' he said. 'And maybe, during the Sabbath, we can all read what the *Talmud* has to say about loyalty.'

There was an embarrassed silence. Then Irving went off without a word, closely followed by Hyman. Barney watched the two of them walk between the glowing blue spots of light, their heads bowed; and then he turned to Moishe and said, 'Well?'

Moishe shrugged. 'They'll come around. But they're old men, remember, set in their ways. Joel they could accept. He knew how to cut, he knew how to make up, he was his father's elder boy. He didn't try to turn the business on its head. You, they're not sure of.'

Barney stood with his hands on his hips. The door of the workroom closed behind Irving and Hyman with a vivid squeal, and then a shudder of badly fitting wood. He saw their silhouettes through the glass of the cubicle as they went slowly downstairs.

'All right,' he said, 'let's leave it till Monday. But don't let's forget who's the *baleboss* at Blitz's, huh?'

Moishe put his arm around Barney's waist. 'Take some advice, will you? Rest, pray, and remember that everybody's got one love in their life, outside of their family. Yours may be money. Irving and Hyman's, it's cutting a perfect suit.'

David was waiting for Barney in the cubicle, wrapped up in a bright brown coat that Irving had once caustically described as 'the camel's feedbag'. His near-together eyes were bright with anticipation. 'Are you ready?' asked Barney, testily, and David waggled his head up and down with enthusiasm. What a lunatic, thought Barney. And what an *oyrech*.

'You go ahead, I'll lock everything up,' said Moishe, producing a fat jangling ring of keys. 'You have your guests to take care of.'

'Sure,' said Barney, and clattered quickly down the stairs to the wet street, without looking back to see if David was following. Of course David was following – so closely that when Barney reached the sidewalk, which was jostling with last-minute shoppers and tailors and trimmers on their way to the Turkish baths, and creaking pushcarts, and scampering children, David was right behind him, and bumped into him.

'*Shalom aleichem*, Moishe!' Barney called back, up the stairs, although his eyes were on David.

'*Aleichem shalom*,' came down the echoing response.

Barney took David's arm as unwillingly and impatiently as if it were the handle of a valise crammed with filthy laundry, and tugged him through the evening crowds of Clinton Street to the flat-fronted tenement on the corner of Monroe Street, No. 121, where his mother would already be laying out his clean clothes for the synagogue.

It began to snow again, in wet, fitful whirls.

The neighbourhood was quiet when they returned home from the synagogue; enchanted with the particular stillness, that deep sense of rest, that always used to fall over the crowded homes of New York's Lower East Side at sundown on Fridays. In almost every house and tenement, even in basements where damp marked the walls and the cupboards rustled with rats, wives and mothers and daughters were dressed in the finest clothes they owned, and were lighting up the *Shabbes* candles.

'Blessed art Thou, O Lord our God, King of the Universe, Who has sanctified us by Thy commandments, and has commanded us to kindle the Sabbath lights.'

The sky above Clinton Street was smudged with clouds; umber ink on wet cartridge paper. It was too warm for snow now, but a thin drizzle slanted between the row houses and the shuttered stores, and the sidewalks shone with wet. In the windows all around, candles flickered; and through the streets the husbands and fathers walked silently home from the synagogue, each of them invisibly accompanied by the hosts of Sabbath angels they had brought back from their prayers. Their footsteps echoed all about them.

This was slumland, dirty and broken and uncompromising. The garbage from the day's trading lay sodden in the gutters – cabbage leaves, screwed-up wrapping paper, scraps of bloody meat, fish guts. Even a plateful of noodles, trodden into the filthy slush. Barney stopped on the corner of Monroe Street, opposite the old Rutgers mansion, and for a moment or two he looked around at the rain and the trash and the lighted windows, and he felt a coldness that brought him close to tears.

David said, 'What are you waiting for?'

Barney dabbed at his eye with the handkerchief pinned to his lapel. 'You wouldn't understand. Let's go.'

David kept pace with him as he crossed the street. 'You could try me,' he said.

'Try you?' asked Barney.

'Well, you're sad, aren't you?' David remarked.

'Isn't everybody? Tell me what there is to be happy about.'

'Most of the time, you seem like you're happy,' said David.

'Most of the time isn't *Shabbes*. Most of the time I'm too busy trying to keep the business afloat, too busy arguing with buyers in dry goods stores and department houses, too busy fighting with Irving and Hyman and everybody else. I don't have a moment to myself; and it's only when you have a moment to yourself that you feel anything at all. Tonight, it's sad. So what?'

'So why are you sad?' David wanted to know. Barney was striding along so quickly now that he was panting to keep up.

'I don't know,' Barney told him. 'If I knew, I don't suppose I'd tell *you* about it, anyway.'

David clutched at his sleeve, slowing him down. 'Do you really hate me that much?' he asked.

'I don't hate you. Why should I hate you?'

'You hate me because I'm dumb.'

'Listen, David, I don't hate you.'

'Then why don't you tell me why you're sad?'

'Because –' Barney hesitated, and stopped. They were standing outside his tenement building now. All along the street, the drizzle had turned the gaslamps into sow-thistles. Barney looked down at the six steps which led up to the black-painted front door, and across at the wet iron railings. David waited beside him, shivering, as if he had travelled a thousand miles to hear the secret of the universe from a renowned rabbi.

'I'm sad because I can never be what my father was,' said Barney, more to himself than to David. 'My father came here to New York when he was fifteen, with my grandfather. He brought some of the old ways along with him, he remembers what the old country was like. But I'm an American. I can't *help* being an American. But I can't carry on the old traditions the way my father did. Do you understand what I'm saying? I know what the old ways are. I study whenever I can, even

41

on the streetcar. But they're not part of me, and I'm not really part of them.'

He wiped rain from his eyelashes with the back of his hand. 'I feel like I don't belong. I'm not really one of the *Deutsche Jehudim* any more, and I'm not really an American. I feel, I don't know, shut out.'

David silently chewed his lips. It was impossible to tell if he understood any of what Barney was saying or not.

Eventually, in a curiously childish lisp, he said, 'Remember thou wast a prisoner in the land of Egypt.' And without explaining himself any further, he climbed the steps to the front door. Barney stayed where he was for a while, feeling the drizzle on his face as if it were some kind of uncomfortable penance for doubting his Orthodox beliefs. Then he took out his keys and followed David inside.

Leah Ginzburg was standing in the hallway when Barney opened the door of the apartment. There was a rich aroma of roasted chicken and soup, mingled with the musty, penetrating smell of spices. 'You're soaked,' she said gently.

David grinned at her. 'It's God's tears,' he said, and then turned back towards Barney and grinned at him, too. Barney gave him a quick, embarrassed smile.

'Your mama was afraid you were going to be late,' Leah told Barney.

Barney did not say anything. He did not want to be uncharitable to his mother on the Sabbath, and tell Leah that his mama's usual terror was that he was not going to come home at all.

'She's in the parlour?'

Leah nodded. Barney had known Leah, and had a crush on her, ever since he was seven years old. The Ginzburgs used to live across the street, on the third floor of No. 129. In the dusty summers of his childhood, Barney had played with Leah on the front stoop, or round the wheels of the pushcarts where Polish and Armenian Jews with their beards and their kaftans sold fish, and sewing notions, and fruit. Those had been hot crowded days, those early days on Clinton Street and Hester Street, and all that had mattered in Barney's world had been his parents' doting affection, and a whipping-top that hummed, and a six-year-old girl with a pretty, heart-shaped face, and curls that strayed out from under her scarf.

Leah's father had started out with a pushcart, selling second-hand clothes. Then he had rented a small store on Hester Street, and started a dry goods business. Because of the poverty of his customers, the dry goods business had soon expanded into a pawnbroker's business; and before long, Mr Ginzburg had invested enough money to be able to move out of Clinton Street and buy a modest house further uptown. These days, he was a senior partner in Loeb & Landis, the finance company. But he had never forgotten his friends from the Tenth Ward; Moishe Teitelbaum, and Irving Finkelstein, and – while he was still alive – Barney's father, his old *chevra* who had helped him when he was freshly bewildered off the boat, the fellow Jews who had fed him with soup and given him places to sleep when he first arrived.

Barney's mother did not know it, and Barney himself had only discovered it when he had gone through Blitz's books after Joel had left, but Nathan Ginzburg had lent Blitz's over a thousand dollars, interest-free, just to keep going through the slump of 1857. The money had never been paid back.

But here was Leah, a guest for the Sabbath, in a simple white dress with a white lace overlay, and a white silk scarf over her head, dark-skinned and beautiful, with those brown eyes that looked like the eyes of an Eastern European gypsy. There was something wild about Leah. Barney had always been able to imagine her mouth stained in berry-juice, and gold rings on her toes; and, on some nights, in dreams, he had imagined her naked – small, only an inch over five feet, but big-breasted for her height, with skin so soft that it electrified his fingertips – and on those nights he had woken up sweaty and confused and ashamed.

'This is David Stein,' said Barney. Leah had been dressing when they had first come home to wash and to change their clothes. Barney's mother, fidgety but reasonably friendly, had not wanted to disturb her.

Leah curtsied to David, and David grinned again. Barney

43

expected that his mother had already told Leah that David was retarded. Or maybe she had not. She was so abstracted these days, so unpredictable; her mind was like a smashed mirror.

Mrs Blitz came out of the parlour. 'What's happening?' she asked. 'You're saying your prayers in the hallway?'

Barney said, 'I'm sorry, we're coming.' But the sight of his mother had given him a sharp, unpleasant thrill. For the first time in years, she was wearing her wedding-dress. It was yellowed, and part of the hem had come loose, but it was the same extravagant white dress of silk and Dresden lace which she had worn in Germany on the day that she had married Barney's father. It looked dated and almost macabre. It was tight as a sausage-skin around her waist, and under the armpits it was already stained with nervous perspiration. Barney could feel something off-key, something unpleasant, in the way his mother waved him into the parlour. *Her wedding-dress? Why?*

The parlour was small, but it was their best room. The walls were papered with flower baskets on a dark red background, and the drapes were best red velour. There was a cheap rose-wood chiffonier on which the *Shabbes* candles burned, and a dining-table which Barney's father had brought all the way from the Pig-Market on his back. It smelled stale, as if every Sabbath past had been celebrated here and breathed here and the window had never been opened – as if Barney's mother had tried to entrap in this room all the ghosts of her vanished happiness.

Barney took his place at the head of the table. Leah, sitting on his right, smiled at him shyly. He did not want to look at David, whose lacquered, toy-soldier grin had not left his face since he had walked into the apartment. Nor could he look for long at his mother.

With a dry throat, he said, 'Thus the heavens and the earth were finished, and all the host of them. And on the seventh day God ended his work which he had made; and he rested on the seventh day from all his work which he had made. And God blessed the seventh day, and sanctified it...'

He blessed the wine, and made the *broche* for the Creation of the Sabbath, and for the departure out of Egypt. He had already silently said a *broche* to himself when he had seen Leah in her Sabbath dress; that special *broche* reserved for seeing beautiful people. He sipped the wine from the Kiddush cup, and he was aware when he lifted his eyes that Leah was watching him carefully. In a whisper, she sang the prayer to welcome the ministering angels which had returned home with him from the synagogue.

'May your coming be in peace, may you bless us with peace, and may you depart in peace ...'

Barney's mother, even before Leah had finished, began to spoon chopped chicken livers and olives on to their plates. Leah's voice faltered, but Barney raised his eyes to her in encouragement, and she finished the prayer just as Barney's mother pushed in front of her a mounded plateful of liver that would have stopped Moishe Teitelbaum in his tracks.

'Sabbath feasts are not what they were,' complained Feigel Blitz. 'When your father was alive, Barney, he made it holy! The whole family gathered round the table, Joel and Barney, and whichever *oyrech* Barney's father had brought home with him from the gutter! Holy, that's what they were! And a family! So where's my family now?'

Leah reached across the white linen tablecloth and held Mrs Blitz's hand. 'Mrs Blitz,' she said softly, 'we're your family now. Nobody's forgotten you.'

David was staring down at his plate of liver in bewilderment, as if he could not work out where it had come from. Then, fastidiously, he picked up his fork and began to nibble away at the edges of it.

'All the reverence, that's gone,' Feigel Blitz was saying loudly, to nobody in particular. 'Father would sit where Barney's sitting now, and describe his prayers in the synagogue. What he'd felt in his heart! The nearness to God! But now, what do these young Americans know of caring for their tortured mother? What do they care of the *mitzvoth*? Leah! Tell me, what do they care?'

Leah glanced at Barney, and blushed. The gentle grip she

45

had on Mrs Blitz's wrist was abruptly reversed, as Mrs Blitz seized her arm and stared at her in indignation. 'You think of marrying such a *gonif* ? You think of taking him away? Oh, no, he has duties! Duties to his mother! You'll see! That young man is wedded already to his faith! Tonight, that young man is going to be married! Not to you, my fine young lady! Oh, no. To his duties! To *me*!'

Ribóyne Shel O'lem, thought Barney. *That's why she's wearing the wedding-dress.*

'Mama,' said Barney. 'Can we just eat the dinner, and leave the talk until later?'

Leah said, 'This chopped chicken liver, it's delicious. Do you think I could take the recipe home to Mother?'

Feigel Blitz touched her forehead with her fingertips, as if she were blessing herself. 'Maybe it's your father's fault,' she muttered. 'He was devout, yes, but he cut off the *payess*, tried to make himself American. Americans don't wear *payess*, he said! Have you ever seen an American with side-curls? Two days after we came here, two days off Ellis Island, and he cut them off, and later his beard, too. But the day he cut off the *payess*, I cried all day. Your poor father.'

David put down his fork. 'I *know* you,' he said to Leah, with childish abruptness. 'I met you before.'

Leah looked at Barney. Barney, very slowly, shook his head.

The *Shabbes* feast went on, punctuated only by occasional skirmishes of quirky anger from Feigel Blitz, and empty, tangential comments from David. By the time it was over, Barney was trembling, wound up as tight as a hundred feet of silk lining, too tense to say anything sensible, or even devotional. He left the table, and went straight to his room, where he stood in the darkness with his fists clenched, and his teeth clamped together, and prayed for strength more ardently than he had ever prayed before.

Oh God, King of Heaven, give me strength to survive my mother. Give me faith so that I can be what she wants me to be. Give me peace.

And more than anything else, O Lord, let me know, deep within myself, that I am a real Jew. Let me feel in my bones and my blood that I have inherited my father's beliefs, and the beliefs of his fathers, and of their fathers.

There was a light tapping at the door. Barney opened his eyes, and turned around. The tapping came again. 'Barney? It's me, Leah.'

He opened the door. He was sweating. In the dim light that fell along the corridor, he could see her eyes glistening, the shine on her lips. He said, with more gentleness than he had ever spoken to anybody before, 'Leah? What is it?'

'I wanted you to know that it's not your fault,' she whispered. 'The dinner, what your mother said. I know that she's not –'

'The neighbours call her a *meshuggeneh*,' said Barney, baldly. After the performance his mother had given during dinner, he no longer felt so loyal. But he still found it difficult to hold back an unexpected prickling of tears.

Leah touched his hand. 'I understand. That's why I came to say that . . . well, I don't hold it against you. I'm fond of you, Barney. We've always been friends.'

'Yes,' he said, in a hoarse voice.

They stood watching each other in silence for almost a minute. Barney, for one vivid second, could remember sitting beside her under a pushcart on the corner of Hester and Clinton, concealed from the street by the drapes and folds of fabric that hung down from the cart on every side. It had been shady in there, their own private house, and grown-ups had been nothing more than a shuffling parade of disembodied boots and shoes. Leah must have been seven then, or maybe eight. The summer of 1858, when Barney's father, unknown to his family, was being kept alive by Leah's father. Leah had worn an emerald-green dress, and she had smelled of warm child, and perfume. If Barney could ever think of a moment when he had fallen in love with her, it was then.

Leah reached up and touched Barney's cheek. 'Don't let her make you too unhappy,' she said.

He shook his head.

They paused for one more instant, and for the rest of his life Barney never forgot the way she looked then, her head slightly tilted to one side, her lips touched by a smile.

'I love you,' he told her, not so much as a lover would, not trying to tell her anything except that he loved her for being Leah, and for being a friend when he needed one.

47

She smiled a little more widely, and then she went off down the corridor towards the kitchen. Barney could see his mother in there, clearing dishes. He could also see David, leaning awkwardly against the door-frame, munching on a dill pickle. What a Sabbath, he thought, and closed his bedroom door again. In the dark, he cupped his hands over his face, so that it was even darker.

He knew he had friends. He knew he had *meshpocheh* who would help him. But that wasn't really enough. He was only nineteen years old, and to have to keep the tailor's business going, especially with such cranky opposition from Irving and Hyman, and to have to cope with his mother's incessant tantrums, that was almost too much. What was even more distressing was that he had not heard from Joel in six months, not a single letter. He felt as if he were carrying the whole of Blitz's and the whole of his mother's madness by himself, like a sackful of wriggling goats.

Later, in the parlour, by the light of the Sabbath candles, he read aloud from the book of Deuteronomy. 'Thou shalt not sacrifice unto the Lord thy God any bullock, or sheep, wherein is blemish, or any evil-favouredness: for that is an abomination unto the Lord thy God.'

His mother sat opposite, her hands folded in her lap, her eyes peculiarly half-closed, so that Barney could just see them glittering under the lids. David did not even seem to be listening. He was fiddling with the tassels that hung down from the tablecloth and grinning from time to time at Leah. Leah herself was attentive, but obviously uncomfortable. Sometimes, as Barney read, she whispered the words of the *Torah* along with him.

'If there be found among you . . . man or woman . . . who hath gone and served other gods, and worshipped them, either the sun or the moon, or any of the host of heaven, which I have not commanded; then thou shalt bring forth that man or that woman, and shalt stone them with stones, till they die.'

At last, early, they retired to bed. Barney's mother went without a word, without even a blessing. Leah was to sleep in Joel's old room, and David was going to spend the night in a makeshift bed on the sofa. That sofa, sagging and shiny with wear, had been a bed of refuge for more *oyrechs* than Barney could remember. He and Joel used to help their father lug it down the stairs to the back yard to fumigate it with Persian Insect Powder, guaranteed to kill bedbugs, croton bugs, and fleas.

Barney, in his nightshirt, stood by the rain-freckled window of his bedroom and looked out at the back yard, and at the mean tenements all around. Washing-lines were suspended from every kitchen window, and on some of them, heavy with damp, hung sheets and bedcovers. Up above the washing-lines was the night sky, pale with cloud.

He climbed into bed. Beside him, on a small wooden shelf he had put up himself, was the leather-bound *Torah* that his father had given him, along with his prayer-shawl, his *tallis*, on the day of his *Bar Mitzva*. There was also a dim, out-of-focus daguerreotype of Joel, already faded by the sunlight which fell through Barney's bedroom window for only an hour each day.

Quietly, his head on the pillow, he said a prayer. He blessed his mother and hoped that the Lord would see fit, in his mercy, to make her well. He prayed for Joel, wherever he was; and he prayed for himself, for patience, and for wisdom, and for enough strength to carry him through the coming years.

He slept, and dreamed almost straight away of Leah. He dreamed he was running after her along Hester Street, in the direction of the Bowery, shouting at her in a strangely strangled voice to stop. But she kept on running ahead of him, not turning around, mingling with the crowds of midday shoppers, her white dress lost in a kaleidoscope of light and shade. It was a stifling day, the Lower East Side in August. He could hardly breathe, and his body seemed to be drained of energy. He felt as if he were going to collapse into the gutter from sheer weakness.

Then, abruptly, he woke up. His eyes wide, his ears alert. He could hear Leah gasping in the next bedroom – odd, choking gasps, as if she were suffering from asthma, or throwing a fit. But then she moaned, 'No – *no*, David – no!'

Barney ripped back his bedcovers, rolled out of bed, and tugged open his bedroom door. Leah's door was already wide open, and her bedside lamp was still lit, although the wick was

49

guttering so low that Barney couldn't see anything at first but harlequin shadows. Then Leah cried out again, and wrestled around on the bed, and he understood what was happening.

It was David. Childish, ridiculous David. He had flung himself on to Leah's bed, right beside her, one leg across her hips. His borrowed nightshirt had ridden right up, and Barney could see his fat bottom, and a glimpse of his stiff purple penis. He was wrenching at Leah's nightdress with the jerky, insistent movements of a vicious marionette, a rabid Pinocchio. Leah's arms were twisted above her head, caught up in her bodice and lacy sleeves, and she was struggling to break free. Barney saw, with aroused horror, her wide-brimmed nipples, the curve of her thighs.

He caught David by the scruff of his nightshirt, tearing it loudly. Leah screamed, and tried to wriggle out of the way, but David shoved Barney away from him with lunatic strength, and dropped back on top of her, hugging her possessively close. Barney grabbed him again, and managed to heave him off the side of the bed on to the floor.

'You're crazy!' yelled Barney, so harshly that he hurt his throat. 'You're crazy!'

David scrambled crabwise across the rug, his big white bottom up in the air. Barney kicked him, and knocked him against the green-painted bureau. David yipped, clutching his head.

Barney felt a rage so fierce that it filled his lungs like a wind at sea. He dragged David on to his feet, throwing him against the bureau so that he struck his back, and fell to the floor again in a clattering shower of hairbrushes, combs, and hair-pins.

'You're filthy!' Barney screeched at him. 'Filthy and crazy and sick!'

David groped for the bedside table to lift himself up again. His face was white, and there was phlegm swinging from the end of his nose. Barney seized him again, and tried to raise him up on his feet, but the soft worn cotton of his nightshirt tore right down the front, and David collapsed inside it like a conjuring trick.

Barney reached inside the nightshirt and snatched David's

hair, pulling his head clear, and tearing out a whole bloody lump of scalp. There was nothing that could reach Barney now, no control, no reasoning, no sanity. He punched David in the side of the face with his fist, and then right between the eyes. He shook him, and kicked him, and pummelled at him, while David flopped heavily from one side of the floor to the other, squeaking and crying with every punch.

At last, his teeth chattering with shock, Barney stood over David, exhausted. Leah was kneeling up on her bed, her blanket clutched around her, her face as familiar but as ghost-like as the face that appears when you bend over the water of a washbasin.

'Barney –' she said, desperately. '*Barney –*'

Barney heard her, but did not want to answer. He was still bursting with his own anger. 'As if everything else isn't enough,' he breathed at David. 'As if the business isn't enough, as if Irving and Hyman aren't enough. And now you! What am I supposed to do? I'm supposed to look after *you* for the rest of your life? I'm supposed to hold your hand, you foul-minded *golem*? I can't do it! I don't want to do it! You're crazy, you're nothing but a crazy lunatic!'

He leaned against the bureau, breathing in short, frustrated gasps. David was still hunched up on the floor, dabbling at the blood that dripped from his nose, and mewling.

'That lousy business is lousy enough without you!' Barney shouted at him. 'A whole stinking roomful of bad-tempered old men and stupid women! All cloth, and gas, and struggling to keep the whole thing going! My God in Heaven, David, if it wasn't for that madwoman who calls herself my mother, I would have left it years ago! Joel had the right idea, he got out! Well, that's what I should do, and leave the whole whining, crazy, *kvetching* lot of you to choke on your own problems!'

There was that kind of total silence when you feel that someone, somewhere in the world, must have died. David crept blindly over to the bed, coughing, his torn nightshirt decorated with splatters of blood. Leah was crying, her tears shining in the dim light of the burned-down oil lamp, her fingertips pressed against her lips.

'*Madwoman?*' asked a soft, disturbing voice.

Barney looked towards the door. In the corridor, still wearing her wedding-dress, stood his mother. Her hands were demurely held together as if she were posing for a wedding-picture. Her hair was dishevelled, and she wore no shoes, but she was smiling.

'Mama?' said Barney. 'Mama, I'm sorry. I didn't mean it. I lost my temper. This – David here was attacking Leah. I saw red. Mama?'

'You'd leave me?' said Mrs Blitz. 'You'd go, like your father went, like Joel went? You'd leave me all alone? Is that what you've wanted to do all along?'

'Mrs Blitz,' put in Leah, her words crowded with tears. 'Mrs Blitz, he didn't mean it.'

David mumbled bloodily, 'Thou wast a prisoner in the land of Egypt.'

'Well, now I know the truth,' said Feigel Blitz. 'Now I know everything. A madwoman he calls me. Mad! And after all our years of marriage! Did you think I was mad the day you married me? Did you look at me when we were dancing together, and think, this girl is crazy? Did you think that all those years ago? What? Jacob – I'm asking you a question!'

The sound of his father's name gave Barney a sensation like being prickled with needles all over. It was scarcely ever mentioned, either by Feigel or by Barney, and even their family friends had grown to learn that the name of Jacob was almost a holy word in the Blitz household, a name that Mrs Blitz did not like to hear mentioned lightly.

'Mama?' Barney said, stepping slowly towards her. 'Mama, it's *me*, Barney.'

'You won't leave me,' she told him, shaking her head with a cramped, sideways motion. 'You won't ever leave me. Not any more.'

She turned, and walked unevenly along the corridor to the kitchen. She closed the door behind her, and turned the key.

Barney let out a breath. 'You'd better go clean up,' he said to David. 'There's a jug of water and a bowl on my dresser.'

David edged out of the room, keeping as far away from Barney as he could. Barney ignored him, and looked instead towards Leah.

'It wouldn't surprise me if you wanted me to take you someplace else,' he said. 'Maybe to Mr and Mrs Feinbaum.'

She said, 'No. I'll be all right. I'm upset, more than anything. He didn't hurt me.' There were still tears in her eyes, and her shoulders were shaking.

'I don't know what to say,' Barney told her. 'I don't know how I can ever make amends.'

'It wasn't your fault, Barney. You weren't to know.'

'That's twice tonight you've had to forgive me.'

'Don't you *want* to be forgiven?' she asked him.

He rubbed slowly at his knuckles. There was a chip of skin flapping up from his fist where he had hit David in the teeth. 'I just wish I was anyplace else but here,' he said. 'Anyplace at all but here.'

'I think I'd like some tea,' said Leah. 'Do you think it would be breaking the Sabbath to make some?'

Barney said, 'No. Not after this. I'll go put the kettle on the range.'

He went back to his room and shrugged on the worn-out maroon robe that had once been his father's. David was over in the corner, carefully bathing his swollen lips with cold water. He did not say anything when Barney came in, but he stopped dabbling in the washbasin, and he waited tensely until Barney had left the room again.

Barney went to the kitchen and tried the door. It was still locked, so he tapped at it. 'Mama? Open up, it's Barney.'

There was no answer. He rapped once more, and called louder, 'Mama! You have to open the door!'

He wondered if maybe she had locked the door behind her and gone out. If so, he and David and Leah were shut in, because ever since their old friend Daniel Lipschitz had enlarged the kitchen for them by bricking up part of the corridor, the only way to the bedrooms was by passing through the kitchen. He pounded on the door again.

'Mama! Listen – I'm not going to leave you! I promise! Just open the door!'

He heard a shuffling noise inside the kitchen. Then a pillowy thump – as if his mother had fallen against the door.

'Mama? Are you okay? Do you hear what I'm telling you?'

53

'*You promise?*' his mother asked, in an indistinct whisper.

'Mama, I promise. I was mad, that was all. David was messing with Leah and I went off my head. Can you understand that, Mama? Mama?'

He waited. He rattled the doorknob impatiently. 'Mama,' he said, 'you're going to have to open this door. I mean it.'

At last, he heard the key slowly turn, and the cheap lock levers click back. He pushed the door, and it opened a few inches, but his mother seemed to be leaning against it.

'Mama, can you step back?' he said. 'What are you doing, Mama? You're leaning on the door. Can you step back?'

His mother made a gargling noise. He realised then that something terrible had taken place, that his mother had done something hideous. He shoved hard against the door, and squeezed himself through. It slammed shut behind him, swung by the listless weight of her body. She stared at him, and laughed at his horror.

She had attacked herself with the kitchen knife. Her forehead was speckled with small triangular wounds where she had attempted to dig the point of the knife into her head. Her cheeks were in bloody slices, and there were ribbons of blood running down her neck. The front of her wedding-dress was a chaos of lace and gore, where she had furiously mutilated her breasts. All around the kitchen there were bloody handprints and bright red splatters.

Barney felt dizzy. The whole kitchen seemed to tilt like a weighing-scale around the fulcrum of his mother's leering face. Then, with an incongruous chuckling sound, she slid sideways to the floor.

'Leah!' called Barney. His voice echoed inside his head. 'Leah, help me!'

David put his head around the door, his chin red with bruises. He blinked at Mrs Blitz, and the splashes of blood, and he said, with the desperation of a child, 'What's happened? Barney, what's happened?'

Barney knelt down beside his mother. Her eyes, masked in blood, turned towards him. She whispered, 'Jacob?'

Barney took her hand. It was sticky with congealing gore, as if it had been painted. 'Feigel ...' he said. He had never called her by her name before. 'Birdy.'

'You love me, don't you?' she pleaded. 'You won't leave me?'

'No,' he told her. He was crying now. 'No, Feigel, I won't leave you.'

'It's been so long,' she said. Blood was welling out of the side of her mouth now, and on to the linoleum. 'Don't leave me any more. Please, Jacob.'

Her eyes stayed open, but they lost their life. Her arm fell to the floor. Barney looked up, his mouth pursed with grief, and saw Leah standing in the doorway, stiff with fright.

'I've killed her,' said Barney. 'My own mother.'

Leah backed away from the kitchen, her hands raised to her cheeks. She accidentally bumped into David, who was standing in the corridor distraught, biting his nails. She stared at him as if she did not know who he was.

Barney stood up. He wiped the tears away from his eyes, and marked his face with his mother's blood. When Dr Seligman finally arrived, an hour later, he was standing by the kitchen range, his head in his hands, waiting for the kettle to boil.

'Tea?' he asked Dr Seligman. Dr Seligman took off his pince-nez, looked around at the blood, and quickly shook his head.

He found Joel's letters after the funeral. He was sitting on his mother's bed, sorting through her jewellery and her papers, and there they were – three of them, carefully folded away in a scarf.

The first was from Liverpool, England. The Atlantic crossing had been rough, and Joel had been seasick for three days; but now the weather had cleared and he was enjoying himself. He still loved her, and he sent his love to Barney. The Liverpudlians were a curious race of people, who never spoke of walking anywhere, but always 'legging it'.

The next letter was from Capetown. 'Mama, you must be sure to tell Barney what a place this is! What opportunities!' The third letter, more stained and crumpled than the other two, had arrived only two weeks ago from Oranjerivier, South Africa. Joel had invested his seaman's wages in a small farm, and he was working the land. 'Please let Barney come out to join me – I need the help badly, and I know Barney would love it. Don't keep him in the tailor's shop – Moishe can manage just as well. Mama, we'll make our fortune if we can work together out here. This is the real *goldeneh medina!*'

Barney folded up the letters and tucked them back in their envelopes. He sat on the bed for a long time, looking at them, not moving. Outside in the corridor, he heard Leah's mother say, 'Such a *levaya* I wouldn't have given a dog! Did you hear what the rabbi said?'

He had not understood until now how much his mother must have suffered. She had loved his father so much that she had seen his death as deliberate desertion. The Lord would not have made her suffer so much. It must have been Jacob's fault. And so when Joel had left, too, her suspicions had been confirmed. There was some hereditary quirk in the Blitz family which made their young men footloose, and disloyal. Soon, she was going to be left all on her own, useless and unloved.

Barney looked down at his right hand, at the crooked white scar which ran an inch between his thumb and his index finger. Dr Seligman had said nothing at all when Barney had asked him to sew it up, but maybe Dr Seligman had known what was inevitably going to happen. Maybe he should have seen it himself.

There was a hesitant knock at the bedroom door. He said, 'Come in.'

It was Irving and Hyman, embarrassed and dithery. Irving said, 'I guess we've come to say how sorry we are. Such a shock, you know, and your mother such a fine woman. A saint.'

'A saint?' said Barney. There was an embarrassed pause. Hyman, nervous and apologetic, shrugged.

'You're going to keep on the business?' asked Irving. 'Blitz, Tailors?'

'Any reason why I shouldn't?'

'No, not at all. Just asking.'

'That's okay then,' said Barney. 'As long as you're happy. You've always got Sussman's to go to, if you're not.'

'Sussman's,' said Hyman. 'I should *cholilleh* go to Sussman's?'

'Maybe,' said Barney. 'I'm selling my share of the business to Moishe. I'm pulling out.'

56

Irving frowned. 'You can't do that. This is your father's business.'

'My father's dead, in case you've forgotten. Now my mother's dead, too, and that leaves me with no responsibility to keep the business going whatsoever. I've had enough, Irving. I'm sorry.'

'But you were doing so good.'

'You didn't seem to think so a few days ago. Bespoke, you wanted, not ready-to-wear. Come on, Irving, you mustn't let sentimentality cloud your better judgement. You've been in the tailoring business for forty years. A young upstart like me should tell you what suits to make?'

'We delivered the tunics to the Academy,' said Hyman. 'They said the workmanship was excellent. They'll order again.'

Barney gathered up the letters and the papers on the bed – his mother's identity papers, her birth certificate, the letters from friends and relatives left behind in north Germany.

'That's good news,' he said, without lifting his eyes. 'Too bad you'll be going back to private orders only.'

There was another knock, and Leah looked around the door. Barney stood up, and offered his hand to Irving in the confident manner of a man who wants friendship, but not forgiveness. Irving took it, and gave him a regretful smile.

'I'm sorry to see you go. Blitz's won't be the same, with no Blitz.'

'It'll probably be better,' said Barney.

Irving and Hyman left, and Leah stepped into the room. She stood staring at Barney for a long time before she spoke.

'Moishe Teitelbaum told me you're going to sell up,' she said, gently.

He nodded.

'You're not – well, you're not acting too quickly, because of what happened on Friday night?'

'No,' he said flatly. 'I've been wanting to go for a long time. Ever since Joel left.'

'Are you going to stay here, in New York?'

'For what? For this rundown apartment on Clinton Street? For the sake of my mother's memory?'

'For me?' suggested Leah.

Barney laid his hand on the cold brass bedrail. The bedroom seemed suddenly very confined, and stuffy, and stale. His mother's silver-backed hairbrush lay on the dressing-table, still clotted with her own wiry hair. Unlike many Ashkenazic Jews, Feigel's family had not held with shaving their daughters' hair when they were married. There was nothing in the Bible which decreed that a woman had to wear a *shaytl*, a wig, Feigel's mother had protested, and a scarf was far more becoming.

'I have to go,' said Barney. 'There's nothing to keep me here but bad memories.'

'I love you,' said Leah, boldly.

Barney took her hands. They were small, and cold.

'You think you love me,' he said. 'But who else have you met? All those prissy boys your mother invites around for tea? Anybody would look lovable, compared to them.'

'But,' she said, more firmly, 'I love *you*.'

He kissed her forehead. 'I'm going to have to go. I want to be rich, Leah. I want to be able to come back to New York and buy a mansion on Third Avenue. Give me two years, that's all, and I'll come back and deck you out with gold. That's if you still want me.'

She stroked his cheek with the back of her fingers. 'Mother always says you look like one of those toughs from the Bowery.'

He gripped her wrist. Then he lifted her fingers against his lips, and kissed them. Her eyes glistened with tears.

'You won't forget to come back, will you?' she asked him.

He shook his head.

There was another knock at the door. It was Rabbi Levitz, stocky and fussy, with his thick ginger beard, and his tiny spectacles.

'Come in, rabbi,' said Barney. 'We were only talking about the funeral.'

The rabbi lifted his hands. 'Bless you,' he nodded. 'You make a fine couple.'

Leah turned to go. 'One day, maybe,' she said, softly.

Rabbi Levitz smiled at her as she walked out of the room. 'That was just what I wanted to talk to you about,' he told

Barney. 'Isn't it time you were thinking of marriage? You could certainly do worse than Leah Ginzburg.'

Barney rubbed his eyes. 'I'm tired, rabbi. I've just buried my mother. I don't want to talk about marriage.'

'But you're going away, aren't you? So Moishe tells me.'

'That's right. I was thinking of going to California. But there's a letter here from Joel, from South Africa. He says he's bought a farm there, and he wants me to help him. So, well – I guess I'll go.'

The rabbi held his arm. 'You should take a Jewish bride out with you. Maybe a girl like Leah. You never know what kind of woman you're going to meet in Africa. Maybe a *schwartzeh*.'

Barney couldn't help smiling. 'They have Jewish girls in South Africa, too, rabbi.'

Rabbi Levitz made a deprecatory face. 'Dutch, maybe. But no *landsleit*. No Germans.'

They stood side by side for a while in silence.

'Well,' said Rabbi Levitz. 'I shouldn't take up your time. I just wanted to tell you how sorry I am about your mother. I remember Feigel when she was such a pretty, gay girl. She and your father were my favourite young couple.'

'My mother's in Heaven?' asked Barney. 'Despite ...?'

The rabbi nodded. 'She was possessed by a devil, a *dybbuk*, and she exorcised it the only way she knew how. She pierced her flesh to let it out. Your mother is in Heaven, Barney, with your father. She led a good life.'

'And me?' asked Barney. 'Is there a place in Heaven for me?'

'There shouldn't be?' frowned the rabbi.

'I don't know. Sometimes I feel as if I can't keep a grasp on my faith. Sometimes I feel more like an American than a Jew.'

'You can't be both?'

Barney looked away. 'I've tried. But when I think of my father, and my grandfather, and my great-grandfather ... I feel like I don't belong any more.'

The rabbi grasped Barney's shoulder. 'You belong,' he said, simply. 'You're not the only young man I've talked to who feels the way you do. Your father used to feel it. He cut off his *payess* to make it easier for him to do business with Gentiles, and because he wanted to show that he'd left the past behind him.

59

It happens with every generation – questioning, doubt, who am I? A German, or a Jew? An American, or a Jew?'

Barney said, 'What, then? What's the answer?'

'The answer is to study the *Torah*, to seek enlightenment in the word of God, and to perform your sacred obligations with a happy heart. That is all.'

'That's enough?'

The rabbi smiled. 'Some of the greatest men in Ashkenazic history have devoted their entire lives to those three tasks, and have still died unsatisfied.'

The small funeral party began to disperse after an hour. Mr and Mrs Ginzburg came into the bedroom to offer Barney their condolences – Mr Ginzburg mournfully shaking Barney's hand, and Mrs Ginzburg tightening her lips and looking scornfully around the shabby apartment like an inquisitive chicken. When all the guests had left, Mrs Kowalski came down from her apartment upstairs to clean up. Mrs Blitz had always looked down on Mrs Kowalski – that ignorant *Poylish opstairsikeh* – but Mrs Kowalski washed up the wine glasses carefully, and swept the kitchen floor, and asked Barney in a motherly way as she wiped her hands on her apron if he wanted 'a bite supper'.

Barney, sitting alone at the kitchen table with a last glass of wine, said, 'No, no thank you. I have to get used to doing things for myself now.'

Mrs Kowalski hung up her apron behind the door. 'You should get a wife,' she told him, with a wide grin. 'What's a man, with no wife?'

Moishe bought out Barney's share in Blitz, Tailors, for $2123, although he was only able to raise $750 of that in cash. The rest was pledged as a mortgage on Moishe's brownstone-fronted house on Suffolk Street, which he owned, and by Moishe's cousin Avrum, who was part-owner of a kosher butcher's in Brooklyn. Barney took $150 straight away to the Inman steamship office on Broadway and bought himself a ticket to Liverpool on the *City of Paris*. Afterwards, he went to Lord & Taylor and kitted himself out with a new lightweight suit, in khaki; two pairs of stout canvas walking boots; shirts; underwear; and thick socks. He also purchased a Colt Shopkeeper's revolver, since Joel had described Cape Colony as 'very wild'.

The evening before he was due to sail, he climbed the stairs to the workroom of Blitz's for the last time. Everybody had gone home, but as he stood in the centre aisle between the workbenches he could imagine them all there, and hear the chatter of the girls, the slicing sound of the scissors, and the thump-thump-thump as Hyman rolled over a bolt of broadcloth. He ran his hand along the worn woodwork, and tried to remember how his father had looked, bent over a pattern, with his black business vest and his dangling gold watch chain, in those days when Barney had been sent along the street by his mother to take him a tray covered by a white napkin. *Latkes*, usually, or cold gefilte fish. His father would sit Barney on his knee while he ate, and say, 'One day, you and me, we're going to be working here side by side.'

The workroom door squeaked open. It was Moishe. He came puffing along to the end of the benches, and handed Barney a small package, wrapped up in brown paper.

'I went round to your apartment,' he said, mopping his forehead. 'Mrs Kowalski told me you'd probably be here.'

'What's this?' asked Barney, holding up the package.

'Open it and see.'

Barney slowly tore open the paper. Inside was a flat cardboard box, and inside that, neatly folded, a new prayer shawl. Barney lifted it out, and laid it carefully over his arm.

'I'm touched,' he said. 'Thank you.'

'It's from all of us. Irving and Hyman too. We want to wish you good luck, but not to forget us.'

'I couldn't forget you. I'm sorry I've let you down.'

'Let us down? How's that? You're young, you have yourself to think about. You have to follow the voice inside of your own head. Your father came to America to seek his fortune. You have to go someplace else.'

Barney wrapped the prayer shawl up again. 'I'm going to miss Clinton Street,' he said, 'for all of its problems.'

Moishe gripped his shoulder affectionately. 'Clinton Street is going to miss you.'

61

It was cold, dry, and windy the next morning, when Barney closed the apartment door behind him and stepped out into the street. He hefted his worn brown leather valise, and walked the length of Clinton Street to the intersection with Hester Street with his head bent, not looking at the sad landscape of his past. On the corner of Hester Street, the wind was so piercing that he had to turn his coat-collar up.

The *City of Paris*, one of the first screw-driven Atlantic steamers, held the blue riband for the fastest crossing from Liverpool to New York, at thirteen and a half knots. But during Barney's voyage, in the first two weeks of November 1868, the ocean was so tumultuous, like a vast encampment of grey army tents which were constantly being raised and then struck, and then raised again, that the steamship rolled and wallowed for six days at less than eight knots. Barney, huddled on the second-class deck in oilskins, had never felt so sick or so battered-about in his whole life, and by the end of the first week he began to believe that he had spent years on this tilting deck, under this barr granite sky, and that he was doomed to churn across the Atlantic for ever. To pass the time, he read magazines, or played cards with an earnest seven-year-old English boy who was never sea-sick and won three games out of four. He prayed, in the cabin he shared with a tall Scotsman, who was all tweed and elbows; and sometimes he and the Scotsman would struggle their way around the deck together, gripping the rails and the ropes, and scurrying in a hilarious *pas-de-deux* from one side of the promenade to the other when the ship heeled over in the waves. The second-class steward cheerfully described their progress as 'labouring, pitching, lurching, and spraying all over'.

It was drizzling when they docked at Liverpool. The *City of Paris* was two days late, and Barney had missed by six hours the sailing of the White Star steamer *Rubric* to Lisbon, and then down the coast of Africa to Cape Colony. In a noisy shed with a corrugated iron roof, he bought himself a ticket instead for the German ship *Weser*, due to sail in four days. Then, lugging his valise, he walked through the wet cobbled streets of Liverpool looking for somewhere to stay.

He felt utterly alone during those four days. He stayed at a small bed-and-breakfast house, run by a massive woman with a blaring laugh and a taste for topping up her cups of cheap bright tea with straight gin. Her husband was away in South America, she told Barney, and she was always glad of comfort. He took 'comfort' at first to mean liquor, but when on the second night she came tapping at his door to ask if he cared to come along to her room and share a nightcap, he was left in little doubt that she was looking for what a coarse friend of his father used to call 'a *yentz*'. For one unbalanced moment, he was almost tempted. It was still raining, he was thousands of miles away from home, and to lie in *anybody's* arms would have been reassuring. But he told himself that God was with him, and so were the best wishes of his friends, and he turned over in his narrow horsehair bed and tried to get to sleep. A steamship's siren blew him a mournful and echoing goodnight.

On the third afternoon, he walked along by the Mersey, watching the gulls swoop over the grey, rain-speckled water. Behind him were the docks, the funnels of coasters and packet ships and Atlantic steamers; and a stolid Victorian skyline of prosperous stone office buildings. Ahead of him was the dismal stretch of the estuary, and, on the far side, the wet green hills of Cheshire.

He thought of his mother, and for some odd reason he began to imagine that she was walking beside him, just one or two paces back, out of his line of sight. He stopped, and turned around, but there was nothing. Only the reflecting cobbles of the quay, and the rainy sky. He said a prayer for her. He wanted to think about her the way she had been before his father died – gentle and smiling. The bloody leer in the kitchen was a picture he would have to discipline himself to forget.

He took his meals at a small Jewish delicatessen close to the docks, Weinmans, where he sat at a sticky marble-topped table surrounded by steamed-up mirrors, and ate fatty salt beef. The proprietor was bustling and unfriendly: Barney could scarcely understand his Liverpudlian Yiddish at all. But on the morning that Barney was due to leave, the proprietor waved him away when he came up to the counter to pay 9d for his breakfast. 'Wherever you're going, you'll need the money,' he said, dismissively. 'Go on, before I change my mind, and good luck.'

The *Weser* was a paddle-steamer of the Bremerhaven

line, and almost twenty years old. Barney was allocated an awkwardly-shaped cabin close to the port paddlewheel housing, which he was to share with a Portuguese wine salesman, who sweated profusely, and gibbered in his sleep, and spent every day staring morosely at the ocean and picking his teeth with a quill. But after a choppy crossing of the Bay of Biscay, and a day's delay at Corunna to repair a broken paddle, the *Weser* began to make a steady seven knots southwards on a calm sea, and each day that dawned through the porthole of Barney's cabin was sunnier, and warmer, and more gilded with promise.

As the paddle-steamer rounded the dim coastline of Sierra Leone, and then followed the Ivory Coast, the Gold Coast, and the Slave Coast, Barney stayed for hours on deck, even during mealtimes, to watch the misty green reaches of West Africa slide slowly past. The sky was streaked with cirrus, but the yellowy-coloured sea, stained with silt from the Niger delta, still sparkled with reflected sunlight.

Off Cape Coast Castle, the *Weser* anchored for a day to take on fresh supplies of water and fruit. There was no harbour here, and everything had to be rowed through huge foaming breakers by native oarsmen. Barney leaned on the *Weser*'s rail and watched for almost the whole afternoon as surfboats came up alongside, and fruit was swung aboard in nets. Up above the scattered rooftops of the town, on the ramparts of a squat, hybrid building that was half castle and half country house, a huge Union Jack flapped idly in the wind. Barney could just catch the mildewed smell of jungle on the air, and the sweetness of overripe fruit.

'Now, *this* is an interesting place,' remarked an Englishman called Hunt, who had joined the *Weser* in Lisbon. Hunt was immaculately smart, quite handsome, but only four feet eleven, so that he looked like a ten-year-old boy in a false beard and a white tropical suit. He had taken to passing occasional remarks to Barney when they were out on deck, and to nodding courteously to him over the dinner table. 'That castle there, Elmina Castle, used to be a great slave emporium. Thousands upon thousands of slaves were sent off to America from there – caught by the Ashanti and brought to the coast with chains round their necks. So you could say that this is where your Civil

War started, couldn't you, if you were to take a long view of things?'

'I guess so,' said Barney, cautiously.

'You *are* an American, aren't you?' Hunt asked him.

'Yes. An American. And a Jew.'

Hunt drew back the lapels of his coat and tucked his thumbs into his neat white vest. 'Well,' he said, with a sharp little laugh that Barney did not really understand. 'I'm sure you're going to play *that* down.'

'Why should I?'

Hunt leaned his elbow on the ship's rail. Behind him, another surf boat was being rowed up to the *Weser's* side, with a cargo of lemons. 'My dear chap, *I* don't mind so much who my chums are, but there are plenty of fellows in Cape Colony who do. You're not English, so they won't worry so much about your school; but they'll certainly give you something of a cold shoulder if they know you're one of the Chosen. They won't treat you as bad as a kaffir, but almost. So if I were you – word of advice – I'd play that side of things down.'

'Why are you telling me this?' asked Barney. He could hardly believe what he was hearing.

'I like you, that's all. You look like a decent sort.'

'Well, maybe I am, but I can't deny my forefathers, just for the sake of socialising with a few bigoted Englishmen.'

Hunt lifted his eyebrows, and let out a stagey little sigh. 'The trouble is, old chap, that those few bigoted Englishmen are the only people out there, apart from the Boers, and *they* talk like ducks, and eat nothing but ham and cheese. There's the blackies, of course, but you wouldn't have much sport if you had nobody but *them* for company.'

'My brother's out there. He says it's a land of great opportunity.'

'So it is! But it all depends on your point of view. Opportunity, certainly. But opportunity for what? I work for the Governor, Sir Philip Woodhouse, and I can tell you on unshakeable authority that Cape Colony is more than a million pounds in debt. There's no wealth there. Oranges, oxen, a few farms, and that's precisely all. Everybody's scratching a living. Why you're going there at all, I can't imagine.'

Barney took out his handkerchief, folded it into a padded square, and wiped the sweat from his face and neck. The green canvas canopy over the second-class promenade deck was supposed to keep it cool, but instead if only served to trap whatever breeze there was, and make it five times hotter. It looked as if the *Weser* was almost ready to leave now. The surfboats had all pulled away, and there was a shudder through the length of the ship as steam was built up.

'I'm looking for a fresh start,' said Barney. 'That's the only reason I came.'

'You'll get *that* all right,' said Hunt. 'But you have to know people. Listen, I can help you, you know. Get you out to Oranjerivier with someone reliable – introduce you to Mr Pelling at the bank. You don't drink, do you, you Jewish chaps?'

'Why?'

'No reason. I was just wondering if you'd like to come down to my cabin for a spot of brandy. Excellent stuff, French. Bought it in Lisbon.'

'Thank you, no,' said Barney.

'Well, how about a game of rummy? Not for money, of course, just for the fun of it.'

'I don't –' Barney hesitated. He didn't like to be rude. Then he said, 'All right. For a half-hour, maybe.'

Hunt stood up straight, and fluffed up his beard with waggling fingers. 'That's excellent. I'm pleased. Why don't you come down in ten minutes or so? It's 23C, starboard side. Knock like this.' He demonstrated a postman's knock on the ship's rail. *Rat-tata-rat-tat – rat-tat*!

Barney watched Hunt strut off along the deck, and then turned back to the ship's rail. The *Weser*'s paddlewheels were beginning to turn over, churning up the sea into a brown froth, and she let out a piercing whistle that echoed flatly from the shoreline. He was thinking deeply, as the *Weser* began to beat her way out to sea, through the Gulf of Guinea, towards her next port-of-call, Port-Gentil, less than one degree south of the Equator, in Gabon. He touched the *yarmulka* on top of his brown curly hair as if he were discovering it for the first time.

After ten minutes, he left the rail and went down through

the varnished doors of the front hatch to C deck, where the second-class passengers were berthed. All the portholes were open, and the ventilators were open, but the humidity down there was suffocating. He rubbed perspiration from his forehead as he walked along the starboard side of the ship, looking for 23C.

He reached it at last, and knocked. Hunt called, 'Come!' and he hesitantly opened the door.

The green canvas blind was drawn across the porthole, so that the tiny cabin was irradiated with a curiously submarine light. The table had been folded down from the wall, and a deck of cards was laid out, as well as a cut-glass decanter of brandy, a carafe of water, and two glasses. Hunt was in the corner, wearing a dark blue bathrobe. He was inspecting himself in the mirror by the porthole, and patting lavender-water on to his cheeks.

'I feel quite faint,' he said, without turning around. 'It's no wonder they call West Africa the White Man's Grave. The heat! And you can get anything here. Portuguese itch, malaria, smallpox, Guinea worm, kraw kraw. You hardly have time to say you hope to God you won't get it, before you've got it.'

He suddenly turned around. His hair was combed flat, and he appeared to have smeared rouge on his cheeks. 'Well, my Chosen friend,' he said. 'What do you think?'

Barney stared at Hunt in disbelief. He had seen effeminate-looking men parading along Broadway, and soon after his Bar Mitzva his father had talked about some of the extraordinary sins of the flesh. But Hunt had transformed himself from a dapper little Englishman into something quite different altogether. A small and sinister clown, with a powdered beard.

'Do you think I look debonair?' demanded Hunt. 'I was a Winchester boy, you know. It wasn't Eton, but it wasn't bad. The flower of pretty youth, innocent and hopeful. The bloom of the British Empire.'

Barney stayed where he was, in the doorway. 'I'm sorry,' he said. 'But I don't think I'd better come in.'

'But you must! The cards are all ready! And I'm sure I can persuade you to try some of my brandy.'

Barney gave a gritty little grin. He was over the shock of

seeing Hunt in his make-up and his robe, and now, in a way that he could not quite understand, he felt sympathy for Hunt, and even warmth; but he knew that nothing would persuade him to enter that green-lit cabin. It would not be fair on Hunt, for one thing; and Hunt was certainly more than Barney was capable of handling – at least, without hurting the man's feelings.

'I don't feel too well,' said Barney. 'I think it must be the heat. Or maybe the fish we had for luncheon.'

'My dear chap, if you don't feel well you ought to lie down. Here – please – you can take my berth.'

Barney raised a hand. 'I'd really rather go back to my own cabin. Thank you all the same.'

Hunt came forward, frowning like a wife who is beginning to suspect that her husband's late business meetings might have been taking place behind the drawn drapes of the St Nicholas Hotel. 'It's very *difficult* out here, you know,' he said, in a sensitive voice. 'One's superiors aren't always very understanding of one's ...'

He hesitated, and then said, 'Predicament,' as if it were the answer to a puzzle which he had been trying to solve all day.

Barney said, 'I think I know what you mean.'

'Yes?' asked Hunt, brightening.

'Well ... maybe not entirely,' said Barney. 'But you have to understand that I'm in a predicament, too. My predicament is that I don't want to upset you, but I can't accept your invitation. I'm sorry.'

Hunt's mouth tightened. His face flickered through a dozen emotions, like a moving-picture machine on a seaside board-walk. Then, with a flourish, he opened his bathrobe, baring his flat white chest, with a scraggy plume of dark hair on his breastbone, and his soft crimson penis. He stared at Barney with bijou defiance, challenging him to say that he was not impressed and aroused – or at the very least impressed.

Barney could not think of anything else to do but bow his head, and say, 'Excuse me,' and turn away. Hunt said quickly, '*My dear friend* –!' But Barney began walking at a fast pace back along the second-class corridor until he reached the companion-way. He climbed up to the promenade deck, and stood for a few minutes in the shade of the awning to collect himself, watching the ochre-coloured sea slide by, and listening to the endless slosh-slosh-slosh of the paddles.

A steward in a tight, sweat-stained tropical jacket came up and asked him almost ferociously if he cared for a glass of lime juice and seltzer. He said, 'No thank you,' and went along to his stuffy little cabin to lie down for an hour or two, and read.

The *Weser* steamed into Table Bay on Thursday, 3 December 1868, just as the sun was nibbling at the edge of Table Mountain. It was summer in the Southern Hemisphere, and even though it was only eight o'clock, the day was already windy and warm. Barney, along with most of the other second-class passengers, was crowded against the rail.

The *Weser* gave a long whistle as she beat her way slowly into the shadow of the massive flat-topped mountain. There were already six or seven ships riding at anchor offshore, including two stately tea-clippers on their way back to England from Bombay. The crew of one of them, with clay pipes and pigtails, watched the *Weser* with casual interest from the foredeck, and whistled shrilly at a pretty young wife who was blushing under her parasol on the first-class promenade.

Once the ship's anchor had plunged into the sea, most of the passengers, chattering and shuffling, filed back to their cabins to finish their packing. Barney, who had already closed his single leather valise, stayed by the rail and took a long, unobstructed look at Capetown.

Under the sheer sandstone ramparts of Table Mountain, which were already shining gold as the sun rose higher in the sky, the houses and churches and offices were clustered amongst glittering green oaks and mulberries. Most of the buildings looked Dutch – flat-fronted and painted white, with neat brown thatched roofs – although Barney could see several new buildings in the heavy, prosperous style of British imperialism, and a seventeenth-century sandstone castle. Two distinctive spires rose above the town – one like a slender wedding-cake, and the other with the plain sharpness of a Dutch Reformed church.

Even though there was a strong smell of salt on the wind, Barney caught an aroma of flowers.

'Well, home again,' said a voice beside him. It was Hunt, in a formal grey suit, smelling of lavender-water.

Barney nodded. He did not really know what to say. He reached into the pocket of his summer suit, freshly-pressed for his arrival by the *Weser*'s Chinese laundryman, and took out a pair of wire-rimmed sunglasses, with tiny black lenses, which he carefully hooked around his ears.

Hunt chuckled nervously, 'You look rather sinister in those. Like a chap I used to know in Kaffraria, who used to shoot Bantus for the sport of it.'

Barney took the sunglasses off.

'You know,' said Hunt, 'I really want to say how sorry I am for what happened the other day. You were frightfully sensitive about it. I mean – quite a few other chaps might have reported me to the captain, or even to the Governor. You were very decent about it.'

Barney looked towards the shore. Already, four or five lighters were being rowed towards the *Weser* through the surf.

'It's nothing,' he said.

'Well, it was appreciated all the same,' said Hunt. 'And if you can ever forgive me for what I did, I really would like to help you. I can arrange for a guide to take you out to Oranjerivier, with a bearer, of course; and I'll introduce you to Mr Hutton at the Standard Bank. It's the very least I can do, considering.'

Barney looked at Hunt for a moment. Then he held out his hand. For the first time since Joel had left him in charge of Blitz's – or maybe as far back as the day when his father had died – he began to feel confident, and self-possessed. He was not quite sure why. Perhaps it was because he had managed to deal with Hunt in a way that he had never been able to deal with his mother, or with Moishe, or with David Stein.

'It says in Genesis, Forgive the trespass of thy brethren,' he told Hunt, simply.

Hunt shok his hand, and then stepped back to show that he did not intend to try any further intimacies without being asked.

'That's excellent, then,' he said. 'I'll find you somewhere to stay tonight, and then tomorrow I'll look for a guide.'

They were rowed ashore within the hour. On the rock-strewn beaches, knee-deep in the foam, black porters were waiting to lift their bags and their trunks out of the lighters and on to a motley assembly of ox-carts, horse-drawn omnibuses, and waggons. A rather shabby brougham from Government House was waiting to collect Hunt, and he enthusiastically offered Barney a ride into the town centre.

'After Portugal, the Cape always strikes me as so *civilised*,' said Hunt, neatly crossing his legs as the brougham jolted them over dry rutted roads. 'It may not have Lisbon's restaurants, or Lisbon's opera, or Lisbon's commercial life. But, by God, you know where you are with people. The order of life is clear-cut, and immutable.'

'I thought you said Cape Colony was very poor,' said Barney.

'Oh, it is,' nodded Hunt. 'And that's what gives life its clarity. No rich Latins of dubious parentage, trying to aspire to white society. No blackies to whom one has to be even the remotest bit polite. There are a few quarrelsome Boers, of course, but most of the really disagreeable ones have trekked out to the Transvaal and the Orange Free State.'

'No Jews?' asked Barney.

Hunt gave him a brief, uncomfortable grimace.

'Not many,' he agreed. 'Not many.'

They rattled their way into Townhall Square, a broad dusty plaza flanked by stately white Dutch façades, some of them supported by Ionic pillars and decorated with festoons of carved fruit and flowers. The square was thronged with people and animals in almost equal proportions, and an old man with a monkey on a chain was standing not far away from Barney's coach with a Dutch hurdy-gurdy, so that the jostling of oxen and the fluttering of chickens and the constant to-ing and fro-ing of the crowds was set to a strange, droning score.

There were dozens of British soldiers around, in caps and blouson tunics, with their fashionable waxed moustaches and goatee beards; and nearly as many Jack Tars, with muttonchop side-whiskers and wide-brimmed boater hats. Around them, eager for their shillings, swarmed street-sellers with high-pointed straw hats and shoulder-poles laden with everything from sweets to live poultry. And across the square, walking with that swaying dignity that few American Negroes of Barney's acquaintance seemed to have been able to preserve through generations of slavery, Bantu women made their way in their bright headscarves and their flowery Mission-school dresses that may have clothed them from neck to ground in Victorian modesty, but could never suppress the jubilant roll of their hips and the complicated jiggle of their breasts. Almost all of these women seemed to be carrying under their arms a huge bundle of assorted necessities, such as oranges, figs, fish, bunches of greens, and a bored child.

The brougham drew up outside a thatched Dutch building called The Thatch Inn, and the black coachman climbed down to open the door for Barney and extend the steps. Hunt said, 'You find yourself a room here for tonight. Talk to Mr Shearer, he's the proprietor, and tell him you're a guest of Government House. Then tomorrow, at noon, I'll meet you at Clark's Eating House on Adderley Street.'

The coachman carried Barney's valise into the Inn's front doorway, and across the cool black and white tiles of a wide entrance-hall. Then he scurried away. Barney walked up to the mahogany reception desk, above which an array of ill-matched clocks told the time in London, in Moscow, in New York, and The Hague. He stared up at the grimy ormolu clock which told him it was only five o'clock in the morning in New York, and he tried to imagine Clinton Street as it must be now – dark, and freezing, and thick with snow.

The clerk behind the counter was watching him with a composed, monkey-life face. Then, without impatience, he asked Barney: 'Yes?'

'Oh, I'm sorry,' said Barney. 'I wanted a room for the night. Just a single room, that's all.'

'That's all your luggage?' asked the clerk, peering over the counter at Barney's valise as if it were a small and unwelcome dog.

Barney shrugged his assent. The clerk scratched his ear with the end of his pen and noisily turned the pages of the hotel register.

'I have an upstairs back. Bit cramped, I'm afraid. Bit hot too, being right under the roof.'

'I *am* a guest of Government House,' ventured Barney.

The clerk stopped scratching and looked at him with an expression that was on the pitying side of sympathy. 'Oh,' he said. 'In that case, I'm going to have to ask you to pay in advance, too.'

'Is Mr Shearer here? The proprietor?'

'Good God, no. Mr Shearer wouldn't stay in Capetown in high summer. He's gone up to Wellington, for his health.'

Reluctantly, Barney paid for his room, and a grinning Bantu in voluminous white trousers showed him up the winding stairs to the upper landing, and along the corridor. Halfway along the corridor hung a colour lithograph of Queen Victoria and Prince Albert, which the Bantu cheerily saluted.

The clerk had been right. Barney's room was tiny, and so hot that he began to sweat as soon as he stepped into it. But it was clean, with whitewashed walls, a wide-boarded yellowwood floor, an iron bed, and a single riempie-thonged chair. He went straight to the window, and opened it, and found he was looking out over a small fenced garden, dense with bougainvillaea, and overshadowed by a tree which he later learned to call a *Huil Boerboonboom*.

Behind the garden, and beyond a scattering of old Cape-Dutch houses, rose the foothills of Table Mountain, and then the mountain itself. Over the clear-cut edge of the mountain, huge white puffy cumulus clouds hung in a sharp blue sky.

Barney sat on the edge of his bed. He said a *broche* for the vivid scenery of Capetown, and a *broche* for his room, and a *broche* for his safe arrival. Then he raised his head, and closed his eyes, and breathed in the scent of flowers and fruit and warmth. He felt as if he had arrived, prematurely, in Paradise.

That evening, he ate alone, in the garden, under the rustling leaves of the *Huil Boerboonboom*, his meal lit by a candle. He was served a curious fried fish which the waiter told him was *snoek*. He drank a fruity Cape wine, and finished his meal with slices of bread spread with *moskonfyt*, a thick grape syrup. From the tables all around him came the scissorlike accents of British farmers, talking about apricot growing, and cattle farming, and

73

the shaky condition of the Colony's economy. A skeletal Scotsman with a brambly red beard was leaning back in his Zandevelt chair and declaring in a loud voice, 'Well – it's my opinion that Sir Philip ought to trek out and find himself another diamond. A few more like the Eureka, and he could at least afford to give Government House a fresh lick of paint.'

One of his companions swallowed a large mouthful of whiskey and shook his head. 'No such luck, McFee. You remember that James Gregory fellow – the one they sent out from Emanuel's in London? Well, he's written a report in this month's *Geological Magazine*, and he says there isn't a single chance of finding diamonds out on the Orange River, or anywhere around. An imposture, he calls it. A South African Bubble.'

'There was the one diamond, though,' pointed out the man called McFee. 'And if there was the one, why shouldn't there be others?'

'It was a fluke,' put in another farmer, dogmatically. 'If you found a sovereign in Riebeeck Square, you wouldn't start digging up the road, would you, to look for more? Gregory says the Eureka was probably dropped by an ostrich.'

'Och, where's your optimism?' said McFee. 'Just think about it. A fellow would only have to find himself one respectable diamond, and he'd be rich for the rest of his life.'

'Are *you* going to trek out to the Orange River and start scrabbling around for one, then?' asked his friend.

McFee raised his glass. 'Not I, Bernard. Too much sweat. And, besides, I wouldn't know what a diamond looked like if I tripped over one.'

Barney lay on his twisted sheet that night, under the shadows of his mosquito net, and thought about what McFee had said. *One respectable diamond. Just one respectable diamond.* Outside, in the hot fragrant darkness, a few of the guests were still drinking and laughing. Someone played an impromptu air on the fiddle for a while. Barney slept, and dreamed of meeting Joel. For some reason, Joel would not look at him, and Barney woke in the small hours of the morning feeling a hair-raising sense of fright.

*

Clark's Eating House was the favourite lunchtime meeting-place for the young shipping agents and bank tellers who worked in the stately white stone buildings of Adderley Street. Clark's did a tolerable beef pie and mashed potatoes, as well as antelope steak, and curried *snoek*. Barney was there ten minutes before Hunt, and he took a table by the window, and asked for a carafe of white wine. All around him sat loud young men with British public-school voices and faces the colour of corned beef. A woven fan flapped steadily overhead, stirring the sweltering air, and vaguely irritating the aspidistras which stood around the eating-house in hideous blue jardinières.

At last Hunt came through the door, wearing a smart white suit and a straw boater. He was tugging along behind him a mournful Boer, whose faded grey linen jacket and worn-out *veld* boots accredited him at a glance as a professional *trekker*.

'Well, you found your way here all right,' smiled Hunt, shaking hands. 'This is your guide, Simon de Koker. Mr de Koker – this is Mr Barney Blitz, from New York.'

Simon de Koker took off his floppy hat and studiously wiped around the sweatband with his table-napkin. He had one of those long, lantern-jawed Boer faces, fringed with whiskers, with tiny sun-bleached eyes, and a mouth that was permanently downturned – whether out of pessimism, or pain, or Calvinist disapproval, it was impossible for Barney to tell. Barney later used to say that when the Lord was fixing on the babies' smiles, He accidentally stuck Simon de Koker's smile on upside-down.

'You want to trek to Oranjerivier?' asked Simon de Koker, in that snipping accent of the Cape Dutch.

'My brother's there. He has a farm.'

'A Jewish fellow, in Oranjerivier, with a farm?'

Barney was pouring Hunt a glass of wine, He paused. 'That's right. His name's Joel Blitz.'

Simon de Koker took a long drink of wine. Then he slowly shook his head. 'I know every farm in Oranjerivier. There's nobody farming out there by the name of Blitz. And no Jews, for sure.'

Barney reached into the pocket of his suit and took out Joel's letter. 'He wrote me and told me. Here it is, look – a sketchmap of how to get there from Oranjerivier itself.'

The Boer took the letter and studied it. His nose was beaded with perspiration. Eventually, he handed the letter back and said, 'I know the farm you mean. Derdeheuwel, it's called – third hill. It used to belong to a voortrekker called van Diedrich. Then van Diedrich died, and his daughter sold it. I don't know to whom. But now it's owned by a Portuguese fellow. No question about that. A man called Monsaraz.'

Barney sat back. He felt suddenly, and peculiarly, alone. He had imagined all kinds of difficulties in making a new life for himself in Cape Colony. Joel had written in graphic detail about the heat in the summer and the frosts in the winter, and the thieving Hottentots. But Barney had never thought for a moment that he might not be able to find Joel at all.

'Listen,' said Hunt, 'we ought to order lunch. What will you have, Barney? I can recommend the *snoek*.'

'I had *snoek* for dinner last night,' Barney told him. 'I'll try the antelope steak.'

'Is it *kosher* for Jews to eat antelope?' asked Simon de Koker.

Barney nodded. 'Antelope have cloven hoofs, and chew the cud. I learned that from school. The cooks here may not prepare it according to strict dietary law, but when there's no option, we are allowed to eat some things that are *trayf*. Otherwise the whole world would be populated by starving Jews.'

A Malay waiter came up and took their order. Hunt called for another carafe of wine, and some bread. He sat drinking and chewing for a while, and frowning hard.

'Do you still want to go out to Oranjerivier?' he asked Barney. 'It's all of 700 miles, you know, by horseback or ox-waggon, and that's going to take you the better part of five weeks, maybe longer. It could take you two months. And then, supposing your brother isn't anywhere to be found?'

'What else can I do?' asked Barney. 'I won't be able to find any work here. I'm a tailor. And not even a very good tailor, at that.'

'How much money do you have?' asked Simon de Koker.

'About ninety pounds,' said Barney.

'Well,' said Simon de Koker, dolefully, 'that should last you six or seven months, allowing for the cost of your trip out to

76

Oranjerivier, and your lodging when you get there. I know a farmer who might rent you a *solder*, a loft.'

'But how do I find my brother?'

Simon de Koker shrugged. 'He's either dead, from malaria, in which case you won't have much trouble finding his grave. Or else he's drunk, and you'll find him at Maloney's Bar, near Dutoitspan, more than likely. Or else he's sold up whatever he's got left, and moved on, in which event you may never see him again. It all depends.'

Barney took a piece of bread, tore it, and began to eat it unbuttered. 'I have to *try* to find him,' he said. 'You can understand that.'

'Of course,' said Hunt. 'But what will you do if he's dead, or gone off without a trace? It's not very hospitable out there, you know. Those that malaria doesn't dispose of, the blackies will.'

'What about diamonds?' asked Barney. 'I heard some fellow yesterday say that if you could find yourself a decent-sized diamond up by the Orange River, you'd be made for life.'

Simon de Koker laughed, although his mouth remained bitterly downturned. Listening to the noise he made was about as pleasant as closing your finger in a doorjamb. 'Diamonds?' he said. 'There was one diamond, the Eureka, and that was found by the Orange River a couple of years ago by a fellow called Schalts van Niekirk. But that was an accident. A twist of fate. It probably came from hundreds of miles away, that diamond, in some animal's paw; or maybe in the crop of an ostrich. They showed it at the Paris Exhibition last year. But you won't find any more, and you'd be a damned fool to try.'

'How much will you charge to take me out to Oranjerivier?' asked Barney.

The food arrived – Hunt's grilled *snoek*, and Simon de Koker's pie. The waiter set Barney's antelope steak in front of him, and asked him if he wanted *moskonfyt* with it. Barney shook his head.

Simon de Koker said, 'I'll take you to Oranjerivier; and find you lodging, for ten pounds, plus feed for the oxen, water at threepence a bucket, and thirty shillings for the bearer.'

'You're a fool to go,' said Hunt, cutting up his fish. 'I could

77

easily get you a job here, with the Cape Bank, or even at Government House.'

Barney sniffed the rare, aromatic smell of antelope meat. In those days, the Great Karoo was thick with antelope.

'Well,' he said, 'I was a fool to give up my business in New York and come all this way to meet my brother. But I think I'd be a greater fool if I didn't make an effort to find him. If you'll guide me, Mr de Koker, I'll go.'

'Oh, I'll guide you,' said Simon de Koker, as he cut up his pie-crust.

Simon de Koker, despite the permanent misery of his expression, turned out to be far more amiable than he had first appeared. He was waiting for Barney outside The Thatch Inn on the morning they were due to leave for Oranjerivier, clad in a red-checked shirt and a huge white hat, and smoking a meerschaum pipe. In the back of his waggon, drawn by a single disconsolate ox, was his own rhinoceros-hide travelling trunk, and a bulging canvas gunny-sack which looked as if it had been stuffed with five small boys.

'No bearer?' asked Barney, as he lifted his valise on to the back of the waggon, and climbed up.

'Not yet,' de Koker told him. 'Just for the sake of convenience, we're travelling as far as Paarl by train.'

The railroad that climbed inland from Capetown to Wellington, a winding distance of sixty-three miles, was Cape Colony's only line, apart from a seven-mile spur which connected Durban, the principal town of Natal, with the coast of the Indian Ocean. No telegraph lines penetrated inland, and all mail and provisions had to be hauled out to the Transvaal and the Orange Free State by ox-waggon. Simon de Koker's gunny-sack was crammed with letters and packages for British and Boer farmers. Some of the letters had been franked over a year ago.

'Those Boer farmers are made of nails,' said Simon de Koker, as he turned the ox-waggon around in the rutted yard of Capetown's Dutch-fronted railroad station. 'Most of them trekked a thousand miles or more, and what they had to endure across those mountains and deserts, well, God only knows. It's going to be bad enough for us, I warn you, but thirty years ago it must have been hell. Even now they're barely scraping a living. But, they're free from the British, and that's their main concern.'

The small steam locomotive laboured up through the sandstone mountains, away from the ocean, under a glaring sky. Simon de Koker sat with his arms tight-folded and his legs crossed, looking out at the trees and brightly-coloured shrubs and rocky *krantzes*, and placidly smoking his pipe. The only other occupants of the carriage were a Dutch girl with huge pale forearms and a blue summer hat the size of a small cartwheel, and an agitated Englishman of about twenty-five, who perspired furiously, and kept fiddling with a selection of large butterfly nets.

Barney asked Simon de Koker, 'Do *you* think I'm a fool, trying to find my brother?'

De Koker shrugged, without taking his pipe out of his mouth. 'If your brother's alive, and you find him, then who can say that you're a fool? But if he's dead, and all his money's gone, and you don't find anything but a gravestone ...'

'I dreamed about him the first night I was here,' said Barney. 'I dreamed he was alive.'

'Well, man,' said de Koker, his face still a study in sadness, 'that might increase his chances.'

Paarl was little more than a small collection of Cape-Dutch cottages and farms in a flowery, upland setting. The air was fresher here, and the scent of summer blooms was carried on a wind that was dry and bracing. It was only a few miles from here, at Wellington, that the proprietor of The Thatch Inn was spending his summer vacation. Barney and Simon de Koker climbed down from the train, and crossed the yard to where an ox-waggon was waiting, tied up to a rail under the shade of a row of mulberry trees. A blackman was asleep in the back of the waggon, his frayed straw hat over his eyes, his long bare legs clustered with flies.

'They've given me Donald again, the bastards,' said Simon de Koker, without any apparent emotion. 'Donald, wake up, you idle Kaffir! Do you know why they call him Donald? His name's Simkwe, really. But some bloody Scotchman paid him to take him across the Great Karoo, and always called him Donald. Whenever Simkwe said, "Me Simkwe," that bloody Scotchman said, "You're Donald, Donald, and don't forget it, Donald."'

Donald jerked awake. 'I'm awake, sir!' he shouted.

'I'm pleased to hear it,' said Simon de Koker. 'Go get our bags from the train, and be quick about it.'

'Yes, sir!' Donald exclaimed, and hurried off towards the depot. He was thickset for a blackman, and his skin was the colour of treacle toffee, instead of the intense black of the Bushmen or the Zulus.

'He's a Griqua,' Simon de Koker explained. 'Half Hottentot, and half Boer, and more than half stupid. It's the sun, if you ask me. It's *braaied* his brains.'

'What are we going to do for water, and provisions?' asked Barney.

'That's just where we're going now,' Simon de Koker told him. 'This waggon, and Donald, both belong to a fruit farmer friend of mine, Henk Jeppe. I sent word we were coming a couple of days back, by train. He should have everything ready for us, six pounds the lot.'

Donald came back across the square with Simon de Koker's rhinoceros bag on his head, and the other two pieces of luggage under his arms. 'Mr Henk says you going to Oranjerivier, Mr Simon.'

'That's right, Donald.'

'That's good, Mr Simon. My sister live in Oranjerivier.'

'I thought your sister lived in Hope Town.'

'That's my *other* sister, Mr Simon.'

Donald climbed up on to the waggon, and clicked a loud Xhosa-like click to the oxen. Slowly, their angular haunches going up and down like the bobbins of a sewing-machine, the oxen turned out of the square and along the street.

'Donald has sisters everywhere,' remarked Simon de Koker. 'They're not really sisters, if you know what I mean. But he was brought up by a British missionary, and he learned the art of hypocrisy at an early age. Decorum before truth, you understand.'

Without being asked, Donald drew the waggon up outside

a large *strooidak* church, with an elegant white Dutch façade and a graveyard surrounded by a low whitewashed wall. Simon de Koker eased himself down from the seat, and entered the churchyard through the wrought-iron gates at the front. Barney watched him standing silently amongst the cypress trees, his hat in his hand. After a while, he came back, and climbed up on to the waggon again.

'I used to have a wife,' Simon de Koker said, as the waggon clattered downhill between rows of young cultivated pear trees. 'Seven years ago, that was. I was going to settle down, and start farming. I married her here, in Paarl. That's where she used to live – see that loft house across by the wall there?'

Barney waited for Simon de Koker to tell him more, but the guide seemed to be finished with his explanation. They jiggled around on the ox-waggon's seat in silence until they turned at last into the gateway of a tidy little fruit farm, where chickens clustered in the front yard, and a big blonde woman was hanging up sheets on a washing-line. The hillside all around was planted with rows of apricots and oranges, their leaves rustling in the wind like hushed applause.

Simon de Koker stepped down. 'It was a bird snake,' he said. 'Adaleen's first trip out to the bushveld. We were collecting sticks for the campfire, and she picked it up. Bird snakes look like dried-out branches, you see. Well, it bit her, and there wasn't anything I could do to save her. I brought her back to Paarl only two weeks after we'd left.'

'I'm sorry,' said Barney.

Simon de Koker looked at him expressionlessly. 'You can't be sorry, man. If the people of this country ever stopped to be sorry, then it would never survive, and neither would they.'

Henk Jeppe came up to greet them, a short scarlet-faced man with cropped prickly hair and a handshake that was solid meat. 'How are you keeping, Sy?' he asked Simon de Koker. 'And what's this, a Jewish fellow?'

'Barney Blitz,' said Simon de Koker. 'He's off to Oranjerivier to find his brother.'

'If I were you, man, I'd be careful,' advised Henk Jeppe. 'There's plenty of hard-cooked customers out by the Orange

River who don't take kindly to Jews, or even Catholics, for that matter.'

'I'm an American, Mr Jeppe,' Barney told him. 'And my parents travelled just as far as any of your Boer farmers to get away from persecution. The Boers and the Jews seem to me to have a great deal in common.'

'Well, have it your way, man,' said Henk Jeppe. 'But that's just a friendly word. A hard country breeds hard people. Do you know where your brother is?'

Barney shook his head. 'I'm just going to have to ask around until I find somebody who knows where he went.'

Henk Jeppe glanced at Simon de Koker and said, *'Dit is een krankzinnig idee.'*

'Misschien,' shrugged Simon de Koker. *'Dat weten we pas wanneer we het proberen.'*

Barney said to Henk Jeppe, 'You're asking Mr de Koker if I'm crazy?'

Henk Jeppe, embarrassed, raised his hands in a gesture that seemed to mean, 'What can you expect?'

Their waggon was waiting for them in the back yard of Henk Jeppe's farm. It was covered with a hooped canvas top, like a Conestoga waggon, and packed with six barrels of water, two cases of *biltong*, dried apricots, fresh oranges, bacon, cheese, and gunpowder. The four oxen which Henk Jeppe was going to hire them to draw the waggon were lazily swishing at the midday flies in a nearby *kraal*.

'Another word of advice,' Henk Jeppe said to Barney, his beefy hands propped up on his hips. 'Get yourself a decent hat. One with a wide brim. Otherwise you *will* go *krank*.'

That night, Barney and Simon de Koker were guests at the Jeppes' supper table. There was casseroled beef with fresh vegetables, sugar-roasted ham (which Barney politely refused), and little pastry envelopes of cheese and peppers which reminded Barney of his mother's *kreplach*. Under the light of the oil lamps, the long table was lined by Henk Jeppe's three big, ruddy-faced sons, his two well-built daughters, his nephew, his wife's white-haired father, and his taciturn, wrinkle-faced foreman. An 'at-home' lantern burned in the dining-room window, to show passers-by that the Jeppes were willing to receive guests.

After dinner, Henk Jeppe read from the Bible, while his family sat around him in respectful silence. Simon de Koker yawned.

'We're off at dawn tomorrow, Barney,' he said, at the foot of the spiral yellowwood staircase, as Barney went up to bed. 'In a couple of days, you're going to get your first look at the Great Karoo.'

Their lonely trek across the Great Karoo had a profound effect on Barney that eventually brought him closer to God, but detached him from his Orthodox background like the silky seed of a South African *stapeliae* flower, which floats away on the wind as soon as the sun opens the seed pod.

The landscape was arid, dusty and endless, with pale broken hill formations on either side of them – the Swartberge to the south-east and the Nieuweveldberge to the north-west – and nothing ahead of them but a flat, heat-misted horizon. The ox-waggon creaked and jolted across the baking plains of silt and volcanic ash for hour after hour, its wheels flattening the scrub and the Bushman grass, and Barney sat under the shade of the canvas cover sleeping or reading or simply staring at the barrels on the other side of the stifling interior. Simon de Koker smoked his pipe and said very little. The pungent smoke was blown away by the wind.

Barney thought about his mother, and his father, and about the words of the *Torah*. The Children of Israel had trekked across the desert like this, seeking the fulfilment of a promise, and they had doubted God again and again. Faced with such limitless tracts of desolate land, whipped by whirlwinds, scorched by the sun, it was natural to doubt. Yet the un-certainty that Barney felt as he crossed the Great Karoo was not that the Lord did not exist. The evidence of His existence was everywhere – in every range of hills, and every mile of scrub – and if anything, Barney felt nearer to the reality of the Lord out here in the bush than he had in the synagogue on Clinton Street.

What he was beginning to question were the dogmas of his Orthodox upbringing. His childhood studies had prepared him well for a life in the Jewish ghetto of New York's Lower East

Side. But it had left him open and unprepared for the hugeness and drama of the Lord's earthly creation when it was confronted in the raw. The shimmering landscape of the Great Karoo was far more convincing proof to Barney of God's eternal plan than a whole snowstorm of pages out of the *Teitsh-Chumash*. He began to feel that if he learned to live in this country, and to adapt himself to the ways of the people who lived here, he was far more likely to understand God's purpose than if he slavishly recited *schachris*, *mincha*, and *mairev* every day, and kept his nose in the *Talmud*.

Years later, he wrote, 'I was brought up in the ways of a religion that was preoccupied with struggle and survival. Yet, in New York, where was the struggle? We were poor, yes. We had to work hard. But your mother's oven going out on the Sabbath, and spoiling the *kugel*, that's a struggle? For that you have to learn to survive, life or death? In Cape Colony, I saw for the first time what struggle and survival actually meant – and, at that age, the struggle and the survival themselves meant more to me than any religion I had ever been taught.'

On the third day out of Paarl, as their wagon bumped across the *hooyvlakte*, the hay flats which grew from the rich silt around the Ganka River, Barney climbed out on to the waggon's wooden seat wearing a wide buff bush hat. Simon de Koker glanced at him, but did not remark on it.

'There are sheep here,' said Barney. 'Are we close to a township?' He pointed across the flats towards the distant grey dots of a grazing flock.

Simon de Koker knocked his pipe on the waggon's stinkwood brake handle. He had been driving for the past two hours, while Donald slept in the back, his long spidery legs dangling over the tailgate. The desert felt ancient and vast, which it was. Under its layers of deep volcanic ash were compressed the fossils of thousands of prehistoric creatures, 270 million years old; and the previous night, as they gathered sticks for the campfire, Barney had picked up a stone scraper that dated from the times when primitive Bushmen had lived on the Great Karoo.

'We're coming close to Beaufort West,' explained Simon de Koker, in a matter-of-fact voice. 'Those sheep over there are part of Arthur Kinnear's merino flock. You'll see more, as we get closer to town. They make their living from wool around here. Wool, wool, and more wool.'

'It looks too dry for sheep,' commented Barney.

'Oh, you'd be surprised,' Simon de Koker told him. 'There are plenty of underground springs around here. I've come here after a heavy rainstorm, and the green grass has been springing up, and the cosmos flowers, and it looked just like the land of milk and honey. The Hottentot call this land "the Koup", which if you translate it literally means "sheep tail fat". That's how they describe prosperity.'

They travelled on for an hour or two, until they reached a low promontory overlooking the town of Beaufort West. Simon de Koker reined back the oxen, who turned their heads and stared back at him with brown rolling eyes, and let out a chorus of frustrated *meeerrrms*. Through the thorn bushes, at the foot of the rise on which Simon de Koker had drawn the waggon to a stop, the red and brown rooftops of Beaufort West were spread out in a wide valley. Barney could see the lantern-shaped belltower of the town hall, and the grandiose grey stone frontage of the municipal buildings. But he could also make out the modest, well-kept farmhouses and homes amongst the almond, acacia, and cypress trees. Beyond, to the north-east, in the direction of Three Sisters and Victoria West, there was nothing but a hazy skyline.

From where they stood, they could hear faintly the fussing of chickens and the laughter of two men who were thatching a roof nearby. Someone was banging a hammer, and the echo fell flat across the veld, as flat as the shadows of late afternoon.

'You took off your little cap,' said Simon de Koker.

'My *yarmulka*? It wasn't really practical.'

Simon de Koker nodded, as if he understood everything. 'The only practical equipment on the Great Karoo is a good wide hat, a team of healthy oxen, plenty of water, and a good rifle. There are still quite a few lion and leopard around.'

'You don't think that a Bible is necessary equipment?' asked Barney.

Simon de Koker pulled a face. 'If you go in winter, sure. It can get frosty at night, and you can't always find enough wood.

A friend of mine burned his Bible page by page, just to keep warm out on Kompasberg one night. The pastor forgave him, because he started at Revelations and worked backwards.'

They spent the night at the home of a sheep farmer called Alf Loubser, who lived in a T-shaped hand-built cottage with a riempie-thonged ceiling. Loubser and Simon de Koker sat outside together on the verandah and drank oily Dutch gin, washed down with lager, while a pressure-lamp hissed on the table, and the last light of the day glowered grudgingly behind the peaks of the Nieuweveldberge. Barney sat a little way away, feeling grimy and exhausted. Loubster's daughter Louise, a shy blonde seventeen-year-old in blue gingham and wooden clogs, kept bringing him glasses of sweet white wine and little home-made zwiebacken.

'You're not happy?' she asked Barney, as she sat cross-legged on a cushion and watched him eat.

'Happy?' he asked her. 'Why shouldn't I be?'

'I don't know. You haven't smiled, or laughed.'

He looked at her. She was pretty, in a *milchedig* Dutch way, with blue eyes and an upturned nose. The pressure-lamp, just behind her, crowned her with glowing, dancing moths.

'I guess I feel a little strange here,' Barney told her. 'A little homesick. It's winter in New York, where I come from. There should be snow.'

It was dark now, and up above the Koup the southern stars were glittering. A dry, hot evening wind was blowing from the north-west, from the Kalahari.

'Do you have a wife?' asked Loubser's daughter.

Barney shook his head.

'I often dream about a husband,' the girl told him.

He reached out and held her hand. She wore a thin silver ring on her third finger, set with an opal.

'Nils Groenewald gave me this ring,' she said. 'He said it should be a keepsake, until he came back. He went to Bloemfontein to work on a cattle farm. One day, he said, he will have a farm of his own. Then he will come back and marry me.'

Barney said gently, 'You're in love with Nils Groenewald?'

'He's very upright. Very stiff. My friend Attie says he's a real Boer with an upper-case "B". But, I like him, yes.'

Mevrouw Loubser came to the screen door of the farmhouse and called, 'Louise! Come and help me wash the plates! Then you must go to bed!'

Louise stood up, brushed her apron, and then, spontaneously, bent forward and kissed Barney on the forehead.

'Goodnight,' she whispered. Her breath smelled of cloves, from her mother's apple cookies.

Simon de Koker looked around at Barney over his shoulder. His expression gave nothing away, but Barney could guess what he was thinking. On the other side of the table, Alf Loubser was finishing off a mug of his home-brewed pils. He was ruddy and squat, Alf Loubser, and handsome as a well-bred pony. He sensed that something had passed between Simon de Koker and Barney, but he missed the meaning.

'Well,' he said, 'we'd better turn in. I'm up at five tomorrow.'

Barney had been given a small whitewashed room at the side of the house, next to the wood-store, where aromatic cords of pearwood and yellowwood were stacked in readiness for autumn. There was a plain Dutch bed in there, as well as an upturned fruit-box which served as a side-table, a jug of water and a bowl. Barney stripped off his shirt and his trousers and slowly began to lather his body with green household soap.

Outside his shuttered window, a wide-spreading coral-tree flickered in the moonlight.

There was a hesitant knock at his door. He frowned, and said, 'Wait a moment, please,' and reached for his towel. The door opened straight away, and it was Louise. She quickly closed the latch behind her, and stood in the candlelight with her eyes sparkling and her hand held breathlessly on her chest.

'Louise,' said Barney. 'You can't come in here.'

'Why not? I often sleep here, in the summer. Especially when we have guests in the house.'

Barney tugged his towel a little tighter around his waist. 'Come on, Louise – supposing your father finds out you're here?'

'Why should he? You wouldn't tell him, would you? Nils Groenewald never did.'

Barney glanced towards the bed. 'You and Nils . . .?'

'I love Nils. I love you, too. Won't you kiss me?'

87

'Louise, I hardly know you,' Barney protested, but softly.

She came closer and put her arms around his neck. 'Then I shall have to introduce myself to you. My name is Louise Stella Loubser. I am seventeen years old. I live with my mother and my father in the middle of nowhere at all. I used to pretend that I wasn't lonely, when I was younger. I had my dolls to talk to. But now dolls aren't enough.'

Barney whispered, 'I have to move on tomorrow. I may not ever see you again.'

Louise kissed him on the lips. Close to, she felt very soft and arousing. 'That's *why*,' she told him.

She unfastened the top button of her blue gingham dress. Barney looked at her, and felt as if he were drunk or dreaming. He had kissed Naomi Bernstein in a furious collision of closed mouths when he was fifteen; and at the age of seventeen he had walked out with a tall pretty girl from Cherry Street until she had given him up for a *goyish* messenger-boy with a wave of blonde hair like a cockatoo's crest. But he was still a virgin; and even though his father had carefully explained to him the facts that a young man should know and the sacred duty that a young man should remember in his relationships with young ladies, this encounter with Louise was making him feel hot and inexperienced and giddy with need.

She took his wrist and placed his hand gently on her breast. He stared at her, at the half-moons of candlelight that shone under her eyes. Her eyelashes were so fair that they seemed to be sparkling. He leaned forward, slowly, and kissed her.

'Sometimes I ask my dolls to tell me how to be happy,' Louise murmured. 'They never answer me. They never tell me what I should do.'

The second button of her dress, Barney twisted undone himself. Then the third, and the fourth. Louise, open-mouthed, watched Barney's expression with childish but proprietary interest as he slipped his hand under her bodice and cupped her bare breast in his palm. He felt her nipple rise.

'You look so serious,' she said. 'But you're very beautiful. I love your curly hair. You're such a beautiful stranger.'

Barney retreated towards the bed, tugging Louise after him,

and sat down. He wrestled the towel away from his waist, so that it dropped on to the earthenware tiles on the floor. Louise stood over him and bunched up her gingham skirts, raising them high, revealing to Barney the sturdy curves of her white thighs, and the albino blondeness of her pubic hair. His chest tight with anticipation, his mind locked fast with lust, Barney ran his fingers down the sides of her bare legs, and whispered, 'Louise Stella Loubster . . .'

She climbed on him, coughing once or twice, her dress tucked under her elbows. Then straight away she started bouncing up and down on him, as if she were churning butter. Her small white fingers clutched the short curly hair at the back of his neck, and she pressed his face forward into the folds of her gingham bodice. Her nipple was pushed right into his eye. She bounced harder and harder, and he felt as if he were being forced to run 500 metres down a dark drainpipe in a crouching position.

'*In Godsnaam*,' Louise panted.

Barney didn't know whether to throw her off his lap or push her down harder. But at last – at last – he was gripped by a spasm that swamped his discomfort, and flodded his guilt and his inexperience, empty kegs on an ebb tide, and in the last shaking moments he gripped Louise Stella Loubser so tight that she cried out, 'Ah! Ah!' for air.

They lay side by side on the bed until the candle was almost burned down. Through the shutters, Barney saw the slotted sky begin to lighten, and he heard the dawn birds twittering on the coral-tree outside. It was morning on the Great Karoo.

Without a word, Louise kissed him, and buttoned up her dress, and left, holding her wooden clogs in her hand as she tiptoed along the duckboards which connected the woodshed with the house. Barney stood by the half-open door and watched her go. One of the geese said, '*monnk*'.

Barney and Simon de Koker set out at six, after a breakfast of cheese and brown bread in mevrouw Loubser's black and white tiled kitchen. Already, Alf Loubser's lunch of boiled mutton and dumplings was simmering on the iron range, fragrant with bay-leaves and rosemary. There was no sign of Louise.

'You'll give my regards to your daughter,' said Barney, as he climbed up on to the ox-waggon. Simon de Koker and Donald were already seated, and Simon de Koker was tamping shag tobacco into his pipe.

Mevrouw Loubser's eyes slanted sideways. She wore a white bonnet, like a woman in a Vermeer painting. Her hands were rough from digging vegetables and bleaching linen and plucking geese.

Simon de Koker snapped his whip in the morning air. Donald grinned widely at nothing in particular. The oxen plodded out of the Loubser's yard and out along Donkin Street, where young pear trees lined the route from Oudtshoorn and the south. The sky was already deep blue, and rich with cumulus clouds.

'How did you find Louise?' asked Simon de Koker, after twenty minutes or so, when they were on the outskirts of town.

'Louise?' asked Barney.

Simon de Koker let out an unexpected giggle. 'She's simple, you know. Touched in the head. Poor old Loubser's been dying for someone to give her a baby so that he can marry her off.'

There was a long silence. Then Barney said, crossly, 'I though she was going to marry someone called Nils Groenewald.'

'Ah, well, that's the story, man,' said Simon de Koker. 'She *was*. But Nils Groenewald trekked up to the Transvaal to make his fortune in cattle farming, and in a week he was killed by a Zulu. Degutted, so they say. And ever since then ...'

Barney stared at Simon de Koker, but said nothing. As they trundled out north-eastwards across the wind-ruffled *hooyvlakte*, they saw Alf Loubser and some of his boys in the distance, gathering in a flock of merino sheep. Simon de Koker waved, and Alf Loubser waved back. Barney tugged the brim of his veld hat further down over his eyes and looked the other way.

In later months, Barney remembered the trek across the veld to Oranjerivier as if it had happened to somebody else. This somebody else had spent six weeks of his life jostling from side to side on the hard wooden seat of the ox-waggon, surrounded by blinding curtains of dust. This somebody else had gone out every evening into the darkness gathering sticks, and then sat exhausted by a popping, crackling campfire, while Donald stirred up a pot of beans and biltong – or, if they'd been lucky with the guns that day – fresh antelope steaks, steaming with blood.

One night, for hour after hideous hour, this somebody else had lain awake under a baobob tree listening to lions roaring – a ravenous, echoing sound like tons of coal being dropped down an empty well. And every day, as the morning winds stirred the Karoo, this somebody else had prayed to arrive in Oranjerivier safely, undevoured by beasts and unbitten by snakes, please God; and to find his brother alive.

They reached Oranjerivier quite suddenly; and for Barney, unexpectedly. One minute they were crossing the veld, their waggon jolting and shaking across stretches of dried grass and windblown sand. The next they were rolling along a grassy track beside a muddy and easy-flowing river.

'There,' said Simon de Koker, nodding along the riverbank. 'That's Oranjerivier.'

Barney stood up on the brakeboard. He had not known what to expect. But here it was – a clustered settlement of twenty or thirty houses and cottages, surrounded by tents, flags, storehouses, *kraals*, and makeshift huts.

'You can take me straight to Derdeheuwel?' asked Barney.

'Whatever you like,' said Simon de Koker.

They drove through an avenue of gossiping willows, and then out past the main settlement of Oranjerivier to a small farm spread across the side of a hill. The farm was fenced around with split rails, and the track which led up to the house was lined with blue poplars and sausage trees. It was past four o'clock, and the shadows of the trees crossed the hard-baked ground like the spokes of a wheel.

Donald drew the ox-waggon up in the farmyard. The place looked dilapidated and deserted. On top of the thatched roof of the house, a rusted weathervane groaned and shuddered in the north-west wind. The white paint was flaking from the stucco façade, and most of the window frames were rotted and grey. A stray cockerel strutted across the yard, stared at them indignantly, and strutted off again.

'There's nobody here,' said Barney.

Simon de Koker jumped down from the waggon and tethered the oxen up to the verandah rail outside the farmhouse. The four dusty beasts stood patiently in the late sunshine, occasionally twirling their tails at the flies. 'You don't know Monsaraz,' Simon de Koker remarked.

While Donald knocked a crust of mouldy meal out of a bucket so that he could bring water for the oxen, Simon de Koker gripped Barney's sleeve and led him along the verandah to the front door. The door was wide open, and the tall Boer dragged Barney straight inside without knocking or shouting or tugging at the tarnished brass bellpull.

The inside of the farmhouse was spectacularly filthy. There was dust and rubbish all over the floors and the rugs, and the hallway was cluttered with pieces of rusty dismantled ploughing machinery, a broken wall clock, two backless chairs, dozens of empty paint-pots, torn-up Portuguese newspapers, a banjo with no strings, two bales of Bushman grass, more wine bottles than Barney could count, and a dim cheval mirror in which both Barney and Simon de Koker found themselves reflected like phantoms of the old voortrekkers, brown and sweaty and smothered in dust. On the veld, their only mirror had been a tiny metal disc which they had used for shaving, and so this was the first time Barney had seen himself properly for over six weeks. He looked thinner and yellower in the face than he had imagined himself, but he looked like an Afrikaner.

There was a clatter from one of the side parlours, and a tall black woman appeared, her hair twisted around in red and blue beads, her eyes bloodshot with gin. She wore a simple white cotton dress which was ragged around the hem and soiled with dirt. She could not have been more than twenty years old, and yet she leaned against the wall scratching at her elbow like an old woman. She sniffed. She did not seem to be able to focus on them.

'Where's Monsaraz?' demanded Simon de Koker. 'Bossman in?'

The woman made a vague gesture and then lurched past

them, disappearing through a door which Barney supposed must lead to the kitchen.

'I hope you're not shocked, man,' said Simon de Koker. 'You'll see plenty worse examples of what civilisation can do to the native races. Mind you, the natives have always been pretty gruesome around here. If a woman had twins, they always used to kill one of them at birth, by stuffing mud in its mouth. And I could tell you some stories about the Zulu.'

Barney glanced at him, and then, without a word, pushed his way into the room from which the black woman had just appeared.

Inside, it was dark. The shutters were closed tight, so that only a few chinks of sunlight penetrated the suffocating heat and the shadows. There was a ripe, overwhelming smell of sweat, sex, and dead flowers. On a brass bed in the corner, fully dressed in a grubby white suit and a Panama hat, with his limp penis hanging from his open fly, lay a sallow young man with a pointed beard.

'You're Monsaraz?' asked Barney. 'You own this place?'

The young man on the bed did not answer.

'I'm looking for my brother,' said Barney. 'Derdeheuwel used to be his. His name's Joel Blitz. Mr de Koker here says you may have bought it from him.'

Monsaraz scratched his face noisily. 'Blitz, was it?' he asked, in a voice that was refined, but slurred by drink. 'I knew his name had to be something Jewish. He told me Barker.'

'Do you know where he is?' asked Barney.

Monsaraz sat up, frowned, and then stood up, tucking himself back in his trousers but not bothering to fasten the buttons. He walked with dragging feet across to a tall mahogany bureau, and poured himself a large gin from the stone bottle which stood beside the mirror on top of it. As he drank, he watched himself, as if for signs of rapid decay.

'Well,' he said, wiping his mouth, 'the truth is that I have no idea. No idea whatsoever. I paid him the money, exchanged the deeds, and off he went. He tried, you know, but he couldn't make the farm pay.'

'It doesn't look like you're doing much better,' remarked Simon de Koker.

'No,' Monsaraz agreed, 'but then I'm not trying.'

Barney said, 'Joel didn't give you any idea where he might be going at all?'

Monsaraz belched. 'He wasn't that kind of a man. Very ... taciturn, he was.'

'That doesn't sound like Joel,' said Barney.

'People change when they live out here,' Monsaraz told him. 'Look at me. I used to be one of my bank's most promising young overseas agents. Now I'm a sod farmer. Well, I'm not even that.'

Simon de Koker said, 'This place stinks.'

Monsaraz poured himself another gin. 'Yes,' he said. 'It stinks of self-pity. Do you want a drink?'

Barney shook his head. 'I want to find my brother, that's all.'

'I wish I could help you,' said Monsaraz. 'But men disappear out here. Sometimes because they want to, sometimes because they don't want to. It's just a little worse than hell.'

'Listen,' said Barney, 'what would you say if I stayed here for a while? Maybe worked the farm for you.'

Monsaraz peered at him. 'What would you want to do that for?'

'I need the work, and I need a place to stay. You have money, don't you?'

Monsaraz looked suspicious, and then waved his arm. 'A little,' he said. 'Do you mean to say you'd want paying as well?'

'If this farm was straightened out, it could make a reasonable living for both of us. You could pay me out of the profits.'

'Well, listen to you,' said Monsaraz, coming up closer. 'The young businessman.'

Simon de Koker pulled a face. 'What do you want to stay here for?' he asked Barney. 'If you want to look for your brother, I could find you a room with the Reitz's. Good and clean. This place is a muckheap.'

'It needn't be for long,' said Barney. 'If other farmers can make a living around here, then so can Mr Monsaraz.'

'I don't know,' said Monsaraz, uncertainly. 'Your brother couldn't make a go of it.'

'I'm not my brother,' Barney told him.

Monsaraz swayed, and shrugged. 'All right, then. If you want to. But don't expect any help from me.'

Barney turned to Simon de Koker. 'I'll pay you now, for bringing me here,' he said. He felt suddenly self-assured, although he was not completely clear what he wanted to do, or why he wanted to stay. 'If it's possible, I'll take Donald off your hands for a while, too, so that he can help me hire some workers. We can afford workers, can we, Mr Monsaraz?'

'As long as their wages don't encroach on the gin budget,' said Monsaraz. He looked pale and rather unsteady, as if he were going to be sick. 'That woman was like a spider,' he added, in a mutter. 'A great black spider.'

Outside, in the yard, Barney gave Simon de Koker seventeen pounds. Simon de Koker beckoned Donald over, and laid his arm around the black man's shoulders.

'You stay here with Mr Blitz, help him find kaffirs to work on this farm,' he said. 'You take care of Mr Blitz, or else next time I come by I chop off your sausage. You got me?'

'Yes, sir,' nodded Donald, grinning widely. 'I like to stay here in Oranjerivier. Very good sisters here, very kind. I stay here long time.'

Barney smiled, and took Simon de Koker's hand. 'Thank you, Mr de Koker. I think you showed me more than the way here. I think you showed me that Cape Colony is a country that you have to fight to live in, or not live in at all.'

Simon de Koker wiped the sweatband of his hat. 'You came here because of a tragedy, didn't you? Someone died? Someone you want to forget?'

Barney nodded.

'Well,' said Simon de Koker, 'don't forget them completely. I never forget my Adaleen. This country should be their memorial.'

He lowered his head, and then raised it again, looking Barney clearly in the eye. His downturned mouth was almost twisted into a smile.

During the autumn, when the wild syringa trees on the bush-veld began to turn to the colour of fresh-minted pennies, the first rumours began to fly around that more diamonds had been found on the Orange River. Barney did not pay them much attention at first. Through January and February of 1869, with

95

Donald fussing and strutting around behind him, he was working from first light until way after dark on the farm at Derdeheuwel.

They employed a dozen kaffirs now, and two half-educated Griquas. One of the Griquas was a second cousin of Nicholas Waterboer, chief of the most numerous of the Griqua tribes, and Barney appointed him foreman. The other Griqua, whose name was Adam Hoovstraten, was tall and lanky like a giraffe, but handy with a saw; and Barney set him to repairing the farmhouse and the stables.

Derdeheuwel had been neglected for years. Barney could see the marks of Joel's first efforts to clear it – a half-tilled field at the back of the farmhouse, and a new chicken-run. But it looked as if Joel had quickly lost heart and given up. There was even a new windmill lying on its side in the barn, still waiting for a well to be bored and for someone to erect it. The second week he was there, Barney borrowed drilling equipment from the farmer across the hill, a hard Englishman called Stubbs with a face like crumpled brown paper, and within five days he had his windmill up and working.

Monsaraz took hardly any interest in the proceedings at all, except occasionally to lean on the verandah with a drink in his hand, watching Barney repairing the cattlesheds. If Barney looked his way, he would raise his glass and call, '*Salut!*' Then he would wander back into the house and lie down in his darkened room with one of his black girls. There were two of them – one he christened Prudence and the other '*A Moça da Fazenda*', which simply meant 'The Village Girl'. He seemed to fornicate with them on and off all day and half of the night, although he never took off his white suit.

Barney was convinced that Monsaraz had thousands of pounds hidden on the farm somewhere. Monsaraz never worked, and never ran short of liquor; and whenever Barney asked for money to buy livestock, he would push an envelope filled with five-pound notes under Barney's bedroom door after dark. By early March, Derdeheuwel was fresh-painted, and stocked with over a hundred head of hardy Scottish cattle, all at Monsaraz' expense. But Barney never asked him where the money came from, or why anyone with what appeared to be bottomless funds should choose to live in near-exile on the Orange River.

Every night, after the cattle had been brought in, Barney would sit in his parlour by the light of an oil-lamp and write letters. He wrote a tender note to Leah, back in New York, and to Moishe. But he also wrote regularly to post-offices and attorneys' offices and local divisional councillors all over north Cape Colony and Griqualand, asking for news of his brother. Not many of his letters were answered. None of them held out any hope that Joel could be found. 'This is a vast and dangerous domain,' wrote an official from the Crown Agents in Hopetown, with Imperial pomposity. 'It is quite conceivable that your brother could have been devoured by a lion.'

In March of 1869, Cape Colony caught diamond fever. Schalk van Niekerk, who had discovered the Eureka diamond four years earlier, came across another stone that had been picked up by a Griqua shepherd boy on a farm near the Orange River. It had come into the possession of a Kaffir witchdoctor, who used it as a magic charm; and van Niekirk had been obliged to pay the man 500 sheep, ten cattle, and a horse for it. But when he sent it down to Capetown for evaluation, it turned out to be a superb white diamond of eighty-five carats, the Star of South Africa, and it was eventually bought by the Earl of Dudley for £25,000. Laying the diamond on the table in front of the Cape Parliament, the Colonial Secretary Sir Robert Southey announced, 'This is the stone, gentlemen, upon which the future of South Africa will be built.'

A correspondent in the *Colesberg Advertiser* asked sarcastically, 'I wonder what that fellow Gregory would say now, if he were here. Perhaps in this instance it was also dropped by an ostrich (?)'

Within weeks, more diamonds were picked up along the banks of the Vaal River a little further north, inside the boundaries of the Orange Free State. The *Cape Argus* carried headlines that screamed *Diamonds! Diamonds! Diamonds!* and by April the tracks from Capetown were crowded with diggers of all nationalities.

The Great Karoo was as dust-blown and as pitiless as ever, and several diggers died on the way, but one reporter said that 'they saw in their lively imaginings diamond fields glittering with diamonds like dewdrops in the waving grass or branches of trees along the Vaal River, and covering the highways and by-ways like hoar frost.'

So – regardless of the political independence of the Orange Free State, which had been so bitterly won by the Boers after the Great Trek of 1834, its territory was rapidly invaded by swarms of avaricious prospectors, whose one determination, when they woke up each day, was to be rich before lunch. Soon, every likely stretch of riverbank along the Vaal and the Orange had been staked out as a claim; and latecomers to the diamond fields had to start 'dry diggings' further inland. The Boer farmers around Hopetown and Klipdrift and Pniel found their fences torn down and their trees uprooted, and one by one they gave up the struggle to farm on land that was ravaged again and again by illegal prospecting, and they sold out.

In the early months of the diamond rush, Barney walked along the banks of the Orange River near Derdeheuwel a few times; and occasionally crouched down to sift the gravel through his fingers. But he found nothing that looked remotely like a diamond, and not long after, the tree-lined river banks where he took his evening walks were staked out by diamond diggers. Once or twice, out of curiosity, he went down to watch them sieving mud through kitchen sieves, and separating pebbles with their wooden scrapers. They hardly ever talked to him, though, these bearded men in their cheap work shirts and their clay-stained trousers, except for a suspicious 'good day'. They sat over their wooden rocker-tables for hour after hour, winnowing out the tiniest of diamonds from the huge heaps of mud and gravel which their Kaffir labourers dug out for them. Barney thought that diamond prospecting looked like some kind of fairytale punishment, like spinning a haystack into golden twine.

Soon the pink and white cosmos flowers were blooming on the grasslands, the heralds of winter. It rained mercilessly hard for two weeks, which was good for the farmers. The Afrikaners always said cheerfully, 'The weather looks fine', when the stormclouds started to gather. But the rain was miserable for the diggers, especially when it grew colder, and the tracks and the excavations became rutted and rimed with frost, while the sun shone weak as an opal through the clouds. Still, diggers continued to arrive from Capetown and Durban, in their hundreds, in jolting waggons or on tired horses, and they were always ready to toss up their hats and cheer when they reached the willow-shaded banks of the Vaal, and always ready to pitch their makeshift tents wherever they imagined they could find diamonds.

Some struck it rich almost immediately. One young digger was kneeling in a church to pray, and he found a diamond pressed into the earth floor. One English digger gave up his claim in disgust, having hacked away at it for weeks and found nothing; but the man who took his claim over only had to dig down six inches before he came across a diamond of nearly thirty carats, which he sold for £2500.

Barney found that business at Derdeheuwel farm picked up. Oranjerivier was not so close to the first diamond diggings that its fields were invaded by would-be millionaires, or its fences and barns torn down for firewood. But it was close enough for Barney to be able to send one of his Griquas along each day with a waggonload of milk, eggs, and fresh water, and sell them to the prospectors at prices which improved Derdeheuwel's balance-books dramatically. Milk, 1s 6d the bucket; water, 5d the bucket; eggs, 2d each. Expensive – but where else could the diggers go? Barney even set up a kind of employment agency for kaffir labour, using Donald as a translator and a go-between with the local *dikgôrô*, or native communities; and although he charged £3 5s 3½d the month for each kaffir, which was a good deal more than anybody else, many of the diggers preferred Barney's labourers to the usual scallywags who hung around the diggings, simply because they were reasonably honest. If any of Barney's kaffirs were tempted to take revenge on their masters for beatings or bad treatment by pocketing or swallowing any of the diamonds they came across, Donald would make sure they were given a first-class thrashing. 'A few teaching smites,' he called it, rather biblically.

'Shortly, the diamonds will all be gone,' said Monsaraz one night, as they sat at the dining-table, eating Donald's *bobotie*. 'Then all these human earthworms will leave us alone.'

Barney looked at Monsaraz over the leaning flames of the candelabrum. Monsaraz' face was white from Dutch gin and lack of sun, and there was a sharp muscular spasm beneath his left eye.

'I'd rather they stayed,' said Barney carefully, reaching for his wine. 'They've been very good for the farm. We made fifty-eight pounds profit this month.'

Monsaraz pushed his plate away. 'Why does he always cook this Malayan muck?' he asked, under his breath. He poured himself a tumbler of gin, which he swallowed in three steady gulps.

Barney said, 'Life is going to change around here, Mr Monsaraz. You have to accept it. They found a seven-and-a-half-carat diamond along by the river this morning. Give them a couple of years, these prospectors, and they'll have built themselves a whole city at Oranjerivier, with a townhall, and a courthouse, and a –'

'A courthouse?' bristled Monsaraz. 'You think that's amusing? A courthouse??'

'I simply said that –'

'I suppose that's your Jewish sense of humour? A courthouse? I suppose you think that's funny, to torment me like that?'

'What are you talking about?' asked Barney. 'All I said was that –'

'You know damned well what I'm talking about!' Monsaraz shouted. 'You know *damned well* what I'm talking about!'

He stood up, staggering twice to find his balance. 'You know damned well what I'm talking about,' he repeated. 'Damned well.' Then, with his mouth stretched open and his throat swelling and contracting like a bullfrog, he vomited half-chewed meat and vegetables all the way down the front of his white suit. Barney closed his eyes, and said a prayer.

There were many times during the following two years when Barney felt like leaving Derdeheuwel altogether. But Monsaraz was rarely so offensive again, and the simple fact was that, short of sailing all the way back to New York, Barney had nowhere else to go. He still believed that Joel must be living in Cape Colony or the Orange Free State somewhere, and he took to leaving Donald in charge of the farm and riding in a small horse-drawn surrey as far as Hopetown, Jagersfontein, and even up to Klipdrift. He often loaded the back of the waggon with dried meat, cheese, and dried fruit, which he sold to the diggers he met along the way. Sometimes the diggers paid him in colonial pounds, but more frequently they paid him in small diamonds. As winter flourished into spring, and spring gave way to a harsh, hot summer, Barney got to know the diggers well, and how they worked, and which were the most profitable claims. He also made the acquaintance of some of the diamond buyers who had followed the prospectors out to the diggings.

His favourite buyer was Harold Feinberg, whose office was a small wood and corrugated iron shack not far from the Vaal River at Klipdrift. Feinberg had come out to South Africa from London's East End, leaving his father's cigar-making business because of his health. He was thirty-six years old, round and asthmatic, and always wore a white pith helmet, even indoors. Whenever Barney came by to see him, he would invite him in to the fierce heat of his little back room, and they would sit in riempie armchairs and drink black tea, while Harold Feinberg pushed diamond after diamond across his desk and explained to Barney what the qualities of each one were, and what kind of a price he expected it to fetch.

'This one here, for instance ... seven and three-quarter carats, perfect, but glassy. This one here ... twenty-one carats, but flawed ... you just have to learn what to look for.'

From Harold Feinberg, Barney learned all about illicit diamond buyers ... the men who camped out on the edge of the diamond fields and paid spot cash for diamonds regardless of where they came from, or who brought them in. It was to these unlicensed buyers that most thieving kaffirs brought the diamonds they had pilfered from their masters' claims, and on whom dishonest diggers would offload the stones they had omitted to tell their partners about. But, on the whole, the diamond diggings were quite lawful and orderly. A stern-faced Englishman called Stafford Parker had appointed himself *landdrost* and local governor of the Klipdrift area, and president of the Diggers Protection Association. Drawing on his hair-raising experiences of the violence of the California gold-rush,

Parker made every incoming digger read, sign, and obey a long list of rules and regulations, and he appointed 'magistrates' on daily duty to hear any complaints or disputes. Thieves were punished by flogging, or by being dragged backwards and forwards across the stony bed of the Vaal River a few times behind a galloping horse.

In 1870, Stafford Parker even went as far as declaring the diamond fields to be a Diggers' Republic, of which he was the first president. Barney met him twice – the first time outside Dan Evans' tent at Gong Gong. The local Griqua chief Jan Bloem was there, too, sitting by the campfire on a small folding stool, in the loudest yellow-checked suit that Barney had ever seen. Bloem's umbrella, tightly-rolled, had been stuck into the soft earth beside him.

Stafford Parker turned out to be white-bearded, small, and tanned to the colour of a roasted chicken. He shook Barney fiercely by the hand, and said, 'Digger, are you? No, you can't be. Hands aren't callused enough.'

'I'm a farmer, sir, at Oranjerivier.'

'You don't look like a farmer. You don't *sound* like a farmer.'

'I was in business in New York, originally,' said Barney. 'A tailor.'

Stafford Parker eyed him sharply. 'Tailor, hey? Jewish?'

'Yes, sir.'

'Hmm. Well, make sure you don't get yourself into the diamond-buying business. There are too many kikes in that already.'

Barney coloured. 'Too many what, sir?'

'Kikes,' replied Stafford Parker, in a crisp voice. 'That's what they call you fellows, isn't it?'

'Some people who are too ignorant and abusive to do otherwise call us kikes, yes, sir.'

'That's what I thought,' replied Stafford Parker. 'And I'm afraid to say that by a loyal Englishman's lights, being ignorant of those fellows who crucified Our Lord, or being abusive towards their descendants – well, those failings hardly count as anything but justifiable.'

Stafford Parker had sauntered off, stiff-legged, and Barney had been left taking deep, angry breaths. From across the other side of the campfire, Jan Bloem had been watching the exchange with an interested smile.

'The English have a way of upsetting everybody they meet,' he said, after a moment or two. 'They've been practising it for generations. Henry the Fifth, Sir Walter Raleigh, George the Third, and now Stafford Parker. You must let it roll off you, like the rain off your umbrella.'

Barney had looked at him. The voice that had come from the black man's savage-looking face, with its flat glistening cheeks and its tight-curled beard, had been extraordinarily civilised. Two hooped earrings shone gold under the black man's tall stovepipe hat.

'You must come to my village sometime, and talk about Judaism,' the Griqua went on. 'We Griquas have very strong Christian beliefs, and a great love of religious music. I would be most interested to hear about your points of view on the Bible.'

'Yes,' said Barney. He did not know what else to add. For the first time in over eighteen months, he had been obliged to defend his Jewishness, and it was a disturbing experience, particularly since he had let so much of his observance slide, apart from saying *schachris*, *mincha*, and *mairev* every day, and resting over *Shabbes*. Now, an odd-looking halfcaste actually wanted to discuss the *Talmud*.

'I'll – I'll, er – be back this way in a month or so –' Barney had told him. 'I'll ask my foreman to show me how to get to your village.'

'Well, I'll look forward to that,' said Jan Bloem, and lifted his hat.

Back at Derdeheuwel, as the cosmos flowers flourished again to greet the oncoming winter of 1871, Monsaraz grew steadily gloomier, and drunker, and more introspective. Since Barney had first met him, he appeared to have aged five years, and his hair was already wild with white. He started shouting in the night, long unintelligible tirades; and sometimes he would lock himself in his room for days on end. Other times, though, he would seem quite himself, and he would take dinner with Barney on the verandah if it was warm enough, and restrict himself to a few glasses of pinot chardonnay.

Once, just once, he sent Barney one of his girls. She knocked at his parlour door one evening in June 1871, when Barney was sitting at his desk in the long white cotton robe that Donald had found for him at the kaffir market. It had wide sleeves, this robe, and was printed all around the hem with red shapes like *springbok* horns.

'Master?' said the girl, opening the door. She was small, and handsome, and very black. Her hair was twisted into small pigtails, each of which was decorated with a circle of beads. She wore a simple toga of brown–dyed cotton, under which her big firm breasts swayed with obvious nakedness.

Barney looked up from his writing. He laid down his pen. His eyes were beginning to feel strained these days and he had been thinking of sending to Durban for some spectacles.

'Yes?' he asked her. 'What do you want?'

'Master Mont-harry tell me come.'

Barney stood up. 'I see. Did he give you a message?'

'He say you all alone, master. I come to make you not alone.'

'You mean he sent you to come share my bed?'

The girl nodded.

Barney examined the letter he had been writing. 'Dear Sir, I have for some years been attempting to trace my brother Joel Blitz or Barker, and I wonder ...' He picked up his pen, and snapped it sharply in half, tossing the pieces back on the table.

The black girl stared at him in wonder. '*Efidile*,' she said.

Barney knew what the word meant. 'It has died.' The Bantu believed that household articles were possessed of spirits, and if they broke a plate or a cup, they always said '*efidile*', just as if a man had died.

The next morning, over breakfast, he and Monsarez had a fierce argument. Monsaraz was still drunk from the previous evening, and he kept coughing up blood-streaked phlegm.

'I don't want you to send me any more of your black girls!' Barney shouted at him.

'I was doing you a service!' Monsaraz retaliated. 'God, you're a priggish, ungrateful bastard! I thought you were human enough to want a woman, that's all, and so I sent you one!'

'I'm human,' said Barney. 'But when I find a woman, it will

be a woman of my own choosing. Not one of your disease-ridden rejects!'

'That wasn't a disease-ridden reject!' retorted Monsaraz. He had to stop for almost a minute while he coughed and coughed and coughed. Eventually, he took a mouthful of gin, gargled with it, and spat it on the floor, and he was able to continue. 'That was the girl I call Zanza. She's a Tswana. I call her Zanza because she plays like a musical instrument. One of those xylophone things they make out of iron.'

'I didn't want her,' said Barney as steadily as he could manage.

'Well, that's all right by me,' Monsaraz told him. 'But it just makes me wonder how you can keep your head screwed on straight. All work and no women. Do you Jews have saints? No? Well, you ought to, because you'll qualify, for sure.'

The same afternoon, Barney rode out to the north-east corner of Derdeheuwel on one of the five horses he had bought in Hopetown. He enjoyed riding, although he did not ride well. Monsaraz said he looked like a side of beef being bounced in a blanket. He reined in his horse on top of a small kopje and looked out over the sloping fields which led back to the white-painted farmhouse. It was a cool, windy day, and he wore a tweed jacket which he had cut down from an overcoat.

Monsaraz, however coarsely he had put it, had been right. He needed a woman. More than that, he needed a wife. Someone who could live with him as a lover, and a friend, and a sharer of secrets and responsibilities. He realised, not for the first time, how painfully lonely he was. He was twenty-two years old, and yet apart from his casual acquaintances among diggers and farmers and diamond-buyers, he was almost completely friendless. He went fishing with Donald sometimes, but Donald's garrulous bursts of that half-Afrikaans dialect that the Griquas spoke, were usually incomprehensible to Barney, and in the end Donald's company became childish and irritating.

He felt inside him enormous warmth towards people, even Monsaraz, and deep reserves of emotional strength. He knew he was good at business, and at organising the farm. Yet there was some greater ambition on the edges of his consciousness which he unable to grasp – an ambition that was as dark and tense as the hour before a summer storm. Only when he clearly understood what this ambition was, would he be able to express his feelings out loud – because until he understood what he wanted out of his life, he would not know who he was or what he was, or what destiny had brought him here.

Most of the local farmers quite liked him, although not many of them could understand his Jewish gentleness, or the comparative sophistication of his New York manners. The Boers were direct people, frank to the point of rudeness; and having trekked 700 miles to escape British domination, they had every right to be. Some called him 'Yid', right to his face; but then genially slapped him on the back until he was winded, and invited him to take a look at their new-born calves. They knew that his farm was neat, and the black fellows seemed to enjoy working for him, and as far as anybody could tell, he was turning a profit. What was more, he was an American Jew, not British.

None of them knew what he felt when he went to bed at night in the narrow yellowwood bed with the carved fruit-and-flowers headboard, exhausted from a day on the farm. None of them knew how often his dreams were visited by his dead father, sorrowful, hard-working, but ultimately ineffectual in that he had never taught his wife or boys to live without him. None of them knew how often he squeezed his hands into fists, and then slowly opened them again, expecting to find his mother's blood in the creases of his palms.

Those who liked him a lot called him 'the Jewish Boer', and he was often invited around to their homesteads for dinner. Pik Du Plooy, whose farm bordered Derdeheuwel to the east was a special friend, a real bread-and cheese Boer with a fiery face and white-blond hair. So was Simon de Klerk, a square little man whose farm on the opposite bank of the Orange River was called *Paddagang*, which meant Frog's Walk. All the same, as much as they liked his company, Barney was still an *Uitlander*, a foreigner, and a Jew; and whenever one of their daughters showed too much obvious admiration of his boxer's good looks, there would be testy silences, or loud and pointed remarks about how tough he was going to find it, poor fellow, to meet a nice Jewish girl all the way out here on the Orange River.

And quite apart from his Jewishness, Barney lived with Monsaraz, and Monsaraz was generally considered to be a devil.

One night, after he had shared a supper of beef dumplings with the Du Plooys, and was driving back to Derdeheuwel in his surrey, he stopped the ponies by the banks of the river, where the willows grew dark, and the fires of the diamond diggers glowed in the night like the encampment of some strange crusade. He sat with his eyes closed, praying for a bolt of lightning from the Lord – not to strike him down, but to illuminate his life, to show him clearly and emphatically what he had to do.

Nothing happened. The Orange River rattled over its rocks; the night breeze blew through the willows like the breathing of sleeping lovers; and the insects sang their monotonous *ihubo*, a song for a thousand voices.

But there were sparkling reflections on the surface of the water from the hidden moon, and Barney thought how much they looked like diamonds.

In the winter and spring of 1871, three completely unrelated events changed Barney's life for ever.

The first was that diamonds were discovered on Vooruitzigt, the estate belonging to two sour-faced Boer brothers, Johannes and Diedrich de Beer, about a mile away from Bultfontein. To begin with, the stones were picked up in the fields, sparsely scattered about. But after two months of only moderately profitable prospecting, a group of diggers, whose distinctive hats had earned them the nickname of the Red Cap Party had the good fortune to throw their black servant Damon out of their camp one night for drunkenness. The following morning, after wandering erratically up and down a small hill nearby known as Colesberg Kopje, Damon came back to them with his hands crammed with rough diamonds – more diamonds of better quality than any of them had ever seen in one place before. The rush was on. Within hours of the news getting out, scores of diggers swarmed to Vooruitzigt, and set about excavating the yellowish diamond-bearing soil with the fury of ants. Colesberg Kopje was promptly renamed 'De Beers New Rush', and a cluster of sheds and tents were erected around the hillock in double-quick time to house the prospectors, the diamond buyers, the gamblers, the attorneys, the tricksters, and the prostitutes. Even Harold Feinberg left his shack at Klipdrift and went up there, too – setting up a fresh office just opposite the London & South African Exploration Company on the muddy stretch of track that served as De Beers New Rush's main street.

Barney recalled afterwards that 'the whole of the countryside was humming with excitement, and there were dozens of stories of incredible fortunes being made overnight.' The De Beer brothers, who had bought their farm ten years previously for fifty pounds, sold out for six thousand, and went to farm elsewhere. They later said, ruefully, that a fairer price might have been six million pounds.

The second event that changed Barney's life was that an English attorney-at-law, Brian Knight, came to De Beers New Rush to set up in business, and brought with him his wife Clemmie and his two daughters, Agnes and Faith.

The third event was that Barney found Joel.

Barney trekked up to see Harold Feinberg at De Beers New Rush in October 1871. He was carrying with him a small leather pouch of uncut diamonds which had been given to him in exchange for fresh milk and eggs by the diggers along the Orange River, and he knew that Harold Feinberg would give him a reasonable price. Apart from that, he needed to get away from Monsaraz for a while. His Portuguese employer was becoming daily more drunken and less rational – breaking windows, collapsing over his meals, and beating the Bantu women who came around to 'jigajig' with him. Only the night before he had left Derdeheuwel, Monsaraz had regaled Barney with a long, sour-breathed story about the time he had locked himself in his room for three days with two Venda girls, aged nine and twelve, and what he had done to them.

Barney took Donald with him to Colesberg Kopje, and left the lanky Adam Hoovstraten in charge of the Kaffirs. Donald relished trips around the countryside, and he would sit self-importantly beside Barney on the wooden seat of their surrey, singing psalms at the top of his voice. Barney had not heard such quavering, off-key singing since Cantor Mittelman in New York. Donald regarded himself these days as Barney's permanent *major-domo* and gentleman's gentleman, and never talked about going back to Paarl.

'Maybe we find you a nice girl in Colesberg,' he said to Barney, as they sat by their evening campfire a few miles north of Ritchie, where the Modder River runs into the Riet. It was a cool, quiet night, and the sky was prickled with stars.

'What makes you think I'm looking for a girl?' asked Barney. He had hung his bush jacket and his riding breeches on a nearby bush, and now he was intently stitching his *veldschoen*, where the upper had come away from the sole.

Donald drew his long frogged coat around his shoulders. He was smoking a pipe, and the aroma of the tobacco mingled with the smells of the night. 'Mr Monsaraz says you look for a girl. But, a fine girl. Not black. Not whore, neither.'

'It's none of Mr Monsaraz's business. Nor yours, for that matter.'

Donald shrugged. 'You say so. But I help you find sister, if you want. I have five good sisters in Oranjerivier, maybe two in Bultfontein.'

'I've seen some of your sisters, Donald. Each one looks uglier than the last.'

'Ugly, maybe,' nodded Donald. 'Yes, ugly! But good for hours! Never get tired!'

Barney reached over for his enamel mug of strong Dutch coffee, and swallowed a mouthful. Tomorrow morning, they would arrive in De Beers New Rush, or 'Kimberley', as it had now been officially named. The British Colonial Secretary had protested that he could neither spell nor pronounce 'Vooruitzigt' or 'Colesberg Kopje', and he was not even going to try. Moreover, he thought it undignified for Her Majesty's Empire to include any community known as 'De Beers New Rush'. He had therefore taken it upon himself to rechristen the diamond diggings after his favourite foreign administrator, himself.

Barney said, 'What do you make of Monsaraz, Donald. I mean, really?'

Donald's glittering eyes looked back at Barney through the

firelight. 'The Bible says, "Judge not, that ye be not judged."'

'Monsaraz has already judged himself,' replied Barney. 'Whatever he's done, the memory of it is strangling him just as surely as a rope.'

'Well, then,' said Donald, noncommittally, 'if Mr Monsaraz judge himself, we do not have to. Already done.'

'It's the farm that worries me – my own livelihood,' said Barney. 'I've worked for two years of my life straightening that place out. What's going to happen if Monsaraz dies, or decides to sell out to the diggers?'

Donald took a glowing twig from the fire to relight his pipe. 'Mr Monsaraz will not sell. He say to me once – Donald, I come here to Oranjerivier because it is the end of the earth. A secret place. You say to anyone in Portugal, where is Oranjerivier? And they say, no, I don't know that place. Never hear of it, man.'

'People have heard of it now. The diamond rush is world-famous.'

'There you are,' agreed Donald. 'Because of that, Mr Monsaraz is a frightened person. But, he will not try to escape any more. He says he will die on his own *kleinplasie*, his own little farm.'

'I'm glad he's so sentimental about the place that *I've* licked into shape for him.'

Donald did not answer. He had never owned anything himself, and had never aspired to. White acquisitiveness was one of those mysteries of nature, like the extraordinary whims of Rhubega, the weather-god.

Barney lay back on his bedroll. A warm wind began to steal through the grass from the direction of the Modder. North Cape Colony on a spring night was one of the driest, most musical places on the Lord's earth. Dry music through dry grass, like the whistling of Venda herdboys, who could talk to each other over miles of veld by imitating speech patterns as they whistled.

Harold Feinberg was pleased to see him, although depressed about the world price of diamonds. He did not like his office much, either; it was nothing more than a stuffy lean-to with a corrugated iron roof, and a red-haired Irishwoman was annoying him by doing brisk business next door as a prostitute – 'so every ten minutes, the whole place shakes like an earthquake.' Harold offered Barney hot rum and milk, and while Donald went off to find himself a sister, the two of them sat on the step outside the office and talked.

'This diamond mine's even richer than anybody can believe,' said Harold. 'As a matter of fact, I'm doing princely – especially when you consider the world slump in the market. The diggers are bringing me first-quality diamonds out by the bucketful. I mean, literally, by the bucketful. In buckets! I can pick and choose what I want to buy.'

'So how come your office is so seedy?' asked Barney, with a smile.

'I'm supposed to build myself a Gothic building, five stories high, out of mud and straw and corrugated iron?' Harold wanted to know. 'They're sending out bricks and cast-iron balconies and all that kind of thing from Cape Town and Durban. But they won't arrive for a couple of weeks yet. Anyway, the office doesn't matter so much. The most important thing about diamonds is to be where they are. Whether you set up business in a hovel or a palace, that's not important. Be where the diamonds are dug, and you can't fail.'

Barney stirred his rum and milk with a spoon, and drained it down. 'I've been surrounded by diamond mines ever since I came here, but I'm still as poor as I ever was.'

'You're doing well out of the farm, aren't you?'

'Not too bad. But I'm not rich. And what do I get at the end of it? The farm belongs to Monsaraz, not me.'

'Maybe you should buy a holding at the mine.'

'Have you seen the prices they're asking? Well, obviously you have. Three or four thousand pounds. I don't have more than seventy or eighty pounds saved up.'

Harold, under his pith helmet, pulled a deprecatory face. 'You should try to go into partnership. Find someone who wants to dig with you. I mean it, Barney. This mine is once-in-a-lifetime, and when they've dug out all the yellow ground, that's going to be the finish.'

At that moment, a brusque man with a thick moustache and a pointed sun-topi came strutting along the boardwalk, tapping the boards as he came with the ferrule of his cane. Despite the heat, he was dressed in a dark suit, buttoned right up, with a starched white collar and a necktie. As he approached, Barney could see that his eyelashes were as white and spiky as a pig's.

Harold eased himself to his feet, still holding his empty mug. 'Mr Knight, sir. How are you this morning?'

'Offish,' delcared Mr Knight. He took out a handkerchief and loudly blew his nose.

Harold looked suitably sympathetic. 'I can't say that I envy you attorneys, in this scramble.'

'Well, it's not Lincoln's Inn,' replied Mr Knight, his cold eyes staring past Barney across the street. Barney turned and looked in the same direction, and caught sight of two girls in plain ecru sun-dresses standing on the opposite corner, twirling their parasols and talking to a tall young digger in a wide floppy hat.

'This is a young friend of mine from Oranjerivier,' said Harold. 'An American, from New York.'

'Really?' asked Mr Knight, but his attention was patently fixed on the girls across the street. At last, in a sharp voice that carried high above the clatter of a passing ox-cart and the general bustle of a mining town at mid-morning, he called, 'Agnes! Faith!'

The girls turned at once; and when they caught sight of Mr Knight they waved flustered farewells to the digger and came hurrying across the rutted road, their skirts held up out of the dust. They arrived pink-cheeked and breathless and obviously anticipating a telling-off.

'You'll forgive me for one moment, sir,' said Mr Knight, giving Barney the briefest of glances. 'But I have specifically required my daughters not to hob-nob with the diggers and riff-raff of this encampment; and, lo and behold, here they are flaunting my authority right in front of my eyes.'

Barney looked at Mr Knight's daughters first with curiosity and then with undisguised interest. Both of them were very pretty and trim; although the one he took to be Agnes was just a little more petite than her sister, and her fair ringlets were just a little curlier. Both girls had bright china-blue eyes, short straight noses, and squarish jaws. They could have been Swedes rather than Britons. But Agnes had the soft, slightly asymmetric smile that Barney would later have dreams about: the kind of smile that seems to be knowing and innocent both at the same time.

'This is Mr – er –,' said Mr Knight to his mischievous daughters, waving his hand at Barney.

'Barney,' said Barney. Harold Feinberg looked at him in mild surprise, but Barney remembered what Hunt had told him on the deck of the *Weser*. *If I were you, old chap, I'd play that side of things down.*

'Mr Barney, from New York,' said Mr Knight. 'I'm ashamed that his first sight of you should be in the company of a ruffian like that fellow across the street.'

Agnes and Faith both obediently curtseyed in Barney's direction. Barney, who had already taken off his hat, gave them an appreciative nod of his head. He caught Agnes's eye for a second that was as brief as a memory that he could not quite place – a snatch of music, or the sound of bells, or a familiar aroma.

'As a matter of fact, Mr Knight,' Barney said boldly, and somewhat to his own surprise, 'as a matter of fact I can vouch for the good breeding of that fellow across the street. I've done business with him several times – in Capetown, and here. He doesn't usually spread it around, but he's related to British nobility. The Earl of Liverpool, I think.'

Mr Knight squinted back across the street, but the digger had gone. 'Well,' he puffed, confused. 'Nobility, is he? It's surprising what a pass some of these blue-blooded gentlemen have come to.'

'These days, Mr Knight, everybody has to make a living,' put in Harold, gently. He gave Barney an exaggerated wink.

'Yes,' said Mr Knight. 'I suppose you're right. I suppose you are. And since he's nobility, Agnes, I think I can overlook your talking to him, on this occasion at least. But next time, remember to ask my permission; or to mention it to your dear mother.'

'Yes, Papa,' said Agnes, contritely.

'Good, then,' said Mr Knight. He tapped on the boardwalk with his cane as if he were trying to remember something that had escaped him, and brushed at his moustache with the side of his hand.

'Business good, Mr Feinberg?' he asked.

'Tolerable,' nodded Harold.

'So it should be,' said Mr Knight. 'And how about you, Mr –?'

'Barney,' said Barney.

'Well, yes. What's *your* line?'

'I'm a farmer.'

'Farmer, hey? Business good?'

'Tolerable,' said Barney.

Mr Knight fidgeted and puckered his lips. 'Yes. Well, how about joining us for dinner this evening? Is that a distinct possibility? Or is it not?'

Agnes, from the becoming shade of her sun-bonnet, smiled at Barney in obvious entreaty. Faith, seeing what her sister was doing, gave her a dig with her elbow.

'Yes,' said Barney. 'Dinner would be a distinct possibility. I'd be pleased to.'

'Good,' said Mr Knight. 'Eight then, at my place. Mr Feinberg here will tell you where to find us.'

Harold nodded, and smiled, playing the part of the obliging East End Jew. *Anything you say, my boy. Anything you say.* Mr Knight grimaced at him, and then continued his staccato promenade along the boardwalk.

'Well,' said Faith, giving Barney another little curtsey, 'you saved our lives! It seems that we owe you a favour!'

'You were very gallant,' smiled Agnes. 'You know who that *really* is, don't you?'

Barney shook his head. 'I haven't a notion.'

'His name's Jack Westbury. He's a digger, that's all; and not a very successful one so far. He spent all his inheritance on two claims at the Kopje, but so far they haven't turned up anything more than a few small stones that aren't worth anything much at all. But, he's very handsome,' she added, looking at Barney with her head slightly tilted to one side in a way that suggested *he* was handsome, too.

Mr Knight had stopped a few yards along the boardwalk, and had turned on his heel to glare at his daughters again with his piggy little eyes.

'We'd better hurry along,' said Faith, and took her sister's arm. 'But we'll look forward to seeing you at dinner tonight, Mr Barney. Good afternoon.'

Barney raised his hand as the girls hurried along the board-walk after their father, a wave that lingered like a photographic pose. Agnes, he thought. The lamb. A meek name for a very provocative young lady. He watched with amusement as the two sisters bustled past three half-drunken diggers, splendid in their unkept whiskers, their clay-caked trousers, and their hundred-pound velveteen jackets. The diggers stopped, colliding with each other like the boxcars of a shunted train, and stared after the Knight girls as they flounced along, obviously transfixed by every arousing glimpse of their narrow ankles. One of the diggers said something crude in Spanish, and the other two cackled high and silly, like geese.

'What's this "Mr Barney"?' Harold Feinberg asked Barney, gently, as Mr Knight took a daughter on each arm and marched them out of sight round the corner of the ramshackle Dutch Reformed Church.

Barney replaced his hat. 'Sometimes, it doesn't help to be a Jew.'

'Sometimes, in the Orange Free State, it doesn't help to be British. But you wouldn't catch Mr Knight calling himself some damned Boer name like Mr Botha, just for the sake of a dinner invitation.'

'You're misjudging me,' said Barney.

'All right,' shrugged Harold.

Barney turned on him. 'Listen, Harold. I was brought up to be a tailor. Measuring and cutting and delivering bespoke overcoats. That was considered to be a suitable vocation for a Jewish boy. That, or being a rabbi. Well, maybe I'm wrong, and maybe it's terrible of me to deny my background. But since I've left the Lower East Side, I've realised slowly that there's a whole world out here. A world of money, and influence, and class. A world where you can do a whole lot more than take orders for overcoats until you're a hundred years old. It's taken me a long time to build up the courage to say that I'm going to take what this world has to offer me. I've been guilty about my father's memory, and what I did to my mother. But now it's time for me to make something out of myself. To get some respect. And if I have to deny my Jewishness to do it, then I will. Because the day will come when I can stand up and say I'm Jewish, and I'm proud of it, and I'll be too rich and too powerful for anybody to be able to do a damned thing about it.'

Harold Feinberg sat on the stoop, swinging his empty mug by the handle. 'Barney,' he said, 'it makes me sorry to hear you talk like that.'

'I should spend the rest of my life second-class? Is that what you're asking me to do?'

'No!' said Harold Feinberg, fiercely. 'Because to be a Jew, no matter how poor, that's never second-class. We were delivered by the Lord our God out of Egypt. Do you know what that *means*? And you can stand there and tell me you're going to forget about that, forget about your duty to the Lord, at least until you're wealthy enough, and famous enough for them to let you in to all the right *goyish* clubs.'

'You never talked this way before,' said Barney.

'I never had occasion to,' Harold replied.

A man in a white apron walked the length of the dusty street with a wooden tray of honey-cakes on his head, clanging a bell. In the floury white light of noon, he looked like the spectre of a leper.

'I should go, then,' said Barney.

'You be careful of Mr Knight,' warned Harold. 'You may think he's posh, and worth getting to know, but no lawyer brings his wife and his daughters out to a place like this unless he's got a reason. That man practised in London first, until they struck him off. Then he tried to start up a law firm in Capetown, and they soon got wind of his little conjuring-tricks there, and that's why he's *here*. You watch him. He's a lawyer of ill-repute.'

Barney leaned his shoulder against the ironwood upright of Harold's office verandah. 'One day,' he said, 'you'll understand that I'm right.'

Harold looked up at him, and smiled. 'Yes,' he said. 'That's what I'm afraid of.'

In the musty gloom of his corrugated-iron office, with the walls rattling to the commercial ecstasies of the Irishwoman next door, Harold gave Barney £212 for his bag of tiny rough diamonds. Barney knew that £175 of this money had already been spent on new livestock, and on repairing the north wall of the cattle kraal. Monsaraz would take £30 for drink, and women, and laundry, Donald would have to be paid £2, and that would leave Barney with just £5 of his own. He appreciated that this was quite a respectable wage for a month's work: a private soldier in the British Army was still getting only £1 8s od a month, with deductions for extra food. But it was not enough to pay for a diamond-digging claim at Kimberley, or to build the footings of any kind of fortune.

He shook hands with Harold with unusual solemnity, and then walked out into the glare of the street. He wondered for a moment just what Monsaraz would do if he failed to return from Kimberley – if he kept the whole £212 for himself. But Monsaraz was an object lesson in the various ways in which a man could be gradually disassembled, morally and bodily, by self-imposed guilt, and Barney was quite aware that if he walked off with Monsaraz's money, he would be haunted for the rest of his life by memories of that filthy wretched man in his soiled white suit, and that he would hear his whispered obscenities in his ears until he died.

'That little Venda girl cried out only once ... but I hit her with my *sjambok* and she was quiet ... wet all over, shivering, naked, but quiet.'

Harold came to the door just as Barney left – fat-bellied, sad, with his pith helmet pulled down over his ears. 'Listen,' he told Barney. 'I meant what I said.'

'I know,' said Barney, and went back to embrace him. A passing digger paused unsteadily in the street and tried to focus on them through the blurring effects of two bottles of cheap London gin.

'I want you to know that you can always count on me,' said Harold, a little throatily. 'Whatever I've said, I'm always around to help a brother Jew. And, well, whatever you do ... don't stay on that farm too long. You'll never be a Boer.'

Barney was off to find Donald now, so that he could tell him there was no need to pack the trunks nor make the surrey ready until morning. Donald had discovered that Jan Bloem, the Griqua chief, was in Kimberley, to see for himself what riches lay within the boundaries of Griqua territory, and that Bloem had set up camp a little to the west of Colesberg Kopje with his two brothers, his pipe-smoking mother, his servants, and a number of cooks and washerwomen whom Donald regarded as extremely likely candidates for sisterhood.

Barney walked along Kimberley's main street with his hands in the pockets of his riding breeches and his hat pulled low over his eyes. He passed makeshift gambling dens, attorneys' offices, whorehouses, and general merchants. A half-caste girl in a tattered blue dress was leaning in the doorway of one of the shacks, and winked at him as he went by. He smiled back at her, and shook his head.

The Kimberley Mine itself was only a few hundred yards away, across the rough rock-strewn ground. Hundreds of men were digging at a wide, shallow crater with picks, their backs bent under the dusty sky. The sound of all those scores of picks hacking away at the soil was like an extraordinary percussive chorus. For one moment, most of them would seem to be tapping away in unison, but then the chorus would spatter into disarray. There were dozens of tents all around the mine, most of them screened from the wind and the dust by fences of woven grass, and there was a crowd of ox-waggons, too, all loaded up with timber. In the first few weeks of prospecting, the diggers only had to walk across the ground and start excavating where they stood, but some diggers had already sunk their claims ten or twenty feet into the ground, and they needed balks of wood to shore up the sides.

Barney stood for a while and watched the diggers and the kaffirs at work. Wheelbarrows of yellow soil were being propelled to the edge of the mine along the pathways between the claims until they could be emptied out in a heap by a digger's tent, and sorted through for gems. It was hot, strenuous work, but the rewards were worth it. One Dutchman named Smuts had bought a claim in the first two weeks of digging for fifty pounds, and gathered up £20,000 worth of diamonds in less than two months. And only a few feet from the place where Damon had scooped up the first rough diamonds, another digger had picked up a single stone of 175 carats, which had sold for £33,000.

While he was watching, a tall, sad-looking man in a droopy

felt hat and a loose bush-jacket approached Barney from the direction of the mine. He stood a few feet away, his hands on his hips, and grimaced from time to time as if he disapproved of what he saw. Barney glanced at him once or twice, and then said, 'You don't seem impressed.'

The man stared at him. He had a breaky nose and eyebrows as tangled as a bush. 'No,' he said, in a northern British accent which reminded Barney of the people he had met in Liverpool. 'In fact, I think the whole damn mine's a complete bog-up.'

'Excuse me?' asked Barney.

'A bog-up. A pig's dinner. Don't you understand English? They're hacking away there like idiots. Some of them digging five feet down. Some of them twenty. There's no organisation. No co-operation. What's going to happen when they get down a hundred feet?'

'They won't, will they? I mean, the yellow soil will give out way before they get down that far.'

The tall man stared at Barney in exasperation. 'You think the yellow soil is the end of it?'

'I don't know,' said Barney. 'But that's what the diggers say. They only found diamonds in the yellow soil along the Vaal and the Orange. Nowhere else.'

'Well, they're wrong,' said the man. 'Listen, why don't you buy me a drink, and I'll tell you how wrong they are.'

'Is this a touch?' asked Barney. 'I don't mind buying you a drink, but I'd like to know.'

'Not at all,' said the tall man, indignantly. He came closer, and Barney could smell the brandy on his breath. 'My name's Edward Nork. N - o - r - k, as in York. Or fork. I'm a geologist, late of Durham University. I once published a paper in the *Geological Magazine* on extinct volcanoes, and that's precisely why I'm here.'

'Volcanoes?' asked Barney, confused.

Nork took his elbow, and led him back to the main street, and along to a shed whose shingle announced that it was The Paradise Saloon. They went inside, where the atmosphere was thick to within two or three inches of the mud-packed floor with negrohead tobacco smoke, and where diggers in wide straw hats took their midday ease with clay pipes and whiskey.

'What would you like?' Barney asked Nork.

'A half-bottle will be sufficient,' said Nork, sitting himself down on a small keg. 'I've already been treated once this morning, and I do like to be modest in my intake.'

Barney called the saloon-keeper over – an Irishman with a filthy apron and smeary spectacles – and asked for a half-bottle of Jamieson's. When the bottle was brought, Nork carefully poured two or three fingers into his glass, and then proceeded to drink straight from the neck of the bottle itself.

'I like to save a little for when the bottle's empty,' he explained, quite unashamed. Barney shrugged. Nork's alcoholism was not his business.

'Now listen,' said Nork, 'the theory which the diggers hold dear is that only the yellow ground contains diamonds. But, geologically, that doesn't really make sense. If this shallow stratum of yellow ground is the only soil that contains diamonds, how did the diamonds get there, and where did they come from?'

Barney coughed, to clear the tobacco-smoke from his throat, and shook his head.

'Diamonds, my dear fellow, are nothing more nor less than a form of natural carbon, which is one of the world's most common and inexpensive elements,' said Nork. 'But the reason they are so hard, and so bright, and so adamant, is that they are made of carbon which has been subjected to tremendous heat, and tremendous pressure.'

'I see,' said Barney, trying to be affable.

'You *don't* see,' insisted Nork. 'Because there is only one place in the structure of the earth where carbon could have undergone such a conversion, and that is in the throat of a volcano. In the very pipe of volcanic material which rises from the depths of the earth to the surface.'

'Yes?' Barney asked him. He still was not sure what Nork was driving at.

'Don't you *understand*?' Nork said, in exasperation. 'Colesberg Kopje is nothing more nor less than the top of a pipe of volcanic soil which has risen up from the subterranean depths. The soil at the top is yellow simply because it has weathered; and you will find this yellow diamond bearing soil along the

Vaal and the Orange River simply because the river waters have washed it away from the tops of the volcanic pipes and borne it away downstream.'

'You mean that the diamond-bearing soil goes deeper than the yellow ground?' Barney asked Nork, keeping his voice down to a hoarse whisper. 'You're trying to suggest that it just goes down and down and down, and that we may never come to the end of it?'

Nork raised a significant finger. 'Not until you reach the very liquid core of the planet, my boy.'

'But I've seen diggers give up claims after they've got down to the blue bedrock.'

'That's their folly, the result of their ignorance,' smiled Nork. He took a swig from the bottle, and wiped the neck on his sleeve. 'The blue ground lies only sixty or eighty feet down. I know that it *looks* like bedrock; but I can assure you that it isn't. It's diamond-bearing soil, exactly the same as the yellow ground, only it hasn't yet been weathered. I've already christened it Norkite.'

'Norkite?' said Barney. 'I never heard anybody else call it that.'

'Well, you wouldn't have done,' said Nork, petulantly. 'They're all disbelievers, and fools. But you listen to what I've told you. One of these days, when they've dug the Kimberley mine down to the blue ground, and everybody believes they're exhausted, you'll be able to pick up claims for a tenth of what they're really worth – and *then* you'll be able to make a killing.'

Barney narrowed his eyes. 'If you're so sure of this, why are you telling me? Why aren't you keeping it to yourself, and buying up whatever claims you can lay your hands on?'

Nork thought about that, and then sneezed very loudly. 'You don't have a handkerchief, by any chance?' he asked Barney. Barney tossed him over a red rag that he had used earlier that morning for buffing up his shoes. 'I'm sorry, that's all I've got. But you can keep it.'

'It's the dust,' said Nork, 'and I'm not a healthy man. In fact, I'm a drunk, and I'm poor as all hell, and I couldn't even raise one hundredth of the price of a claim, even if I knew that I wasn't going to spend it on whiskey as soon as I'd saved it. Oh – you don't have to look so sorry for me. I don't need sympathy. We – imbibers – know just how deep we have dug our own graves.'

'But why did you tell me?' asked Barney.

Nork pulled a face. 'You remind me of someone I used to know,' he said. 'I don't suppose that sounds like a very convincing motive. But there you were – standing by the mine – and you looked so much like him that I immediately felt warm towards you. Friendly.'

'I *remind* you of someone?' Barney asked him. 'Who?'

Nork waved a dismissive hand. 'A digger. He's here now, at Kimberley. A splendid fellow. Very earnest, very good-humoured. But, well, you know, we fell out. People usually fall out with me after a while. It's Madame Alcohol that does it. I drink too much and say things that I don't mean. I once told him that he was a stingy as a Jew, and he tried to strike me with his pick. And, well ...'

Barney licked his lips. 'This digger ... his name wasn't by any chance Barker, was it? Joel Barker?'

Nork sniffed. 'Barker, no. His name was Havemann. But Joel, yes. Joel Havemann. He has a claim across on the other side of the mine. Number 172.'

Barney stood up at once. He felt breathless, short of oxygen, and the dense tobacco smoke in the saloon did not help. He said to Nork, 'Where can I find you again, if I need you?'

'Find me? Why would you wish to do that?'

'Maybe I want to talk to you some more about diamonds. But right now, I'm going over to 172. I think this man Havemann could be somebody I know.'

'Well ... you could always leave a message for me here,' said Nork. 'Or at any saloon in Kimberley. Or down at Mrs Sperring's whore-emporium. I can't afford the girls, you know, but sometimes Mrs Sperring gives me a bed to sleep on. We're both natives of Leeds, you know. We sit over a bottle of that awful South African cabernet franc and talk about the old times on Crown Street.'

'Okay,' said Barney. He shook Nork's hand, and said, 'Thanks. You may have helped me more than you know.'

'I hope I've helped you more than *you* know,' said Nork. He held up the half-bottle of whiskey, already more than three-quarters empty. 'You wouldn't consider ... before you go ...?'

Barney laid a pound on the barrel-top table. Nork raised his eyebrows at it, and said, 'Whoever you are, sir, you're a gentleman.'

Outside the saloon, Barney walked quickly through the dust and confusion of ox-waggons and donkey-carts around the rim of the mine. As he crossed the pathways through the diggings themselves, he heard German voices, Irish voices, Australians, and Greeks. As the historian James Anthony Froude had remarked on a visit to the diggings, there were 'diggers from America and Australia, German speculators, Fenians, traders, saloon-keepers, professional gamblers, barristers, ex-officers of the Army and Navy, younger sons of good family who have not taken a profession or have been obliged to leave; a marvellous motley assemblage, among whom money flows like water from the amazing productiveness of the mine.'

The mine was almost a mile across, and it was parcelled into more than 1600 claims. Under the determined rule of Stafford Parker, the Diggers' Union had agreed that each claim could be no more than thirty-one feet square – ten times the size of a man's grave – and that no individual digger could own more than two claims. That meant that the chaos of each tiny digging – with kaffirs heaving up buckets of dirt and trundling wheelbarrows around and bringing down great tumbling slides of rock with their picks – was multiplied under the hot afternoon sun more than a thousand times.

Barney heard a cheer a little way away. A kaffir driving a mule-cart had tried to steer his load along the narrow ridge between two deep claims, and the cart and mules had overturned, rolling down a twenty-foot slope and crushing the kaffir underneath one of the wheels and half a ton of rock. Two or three of the diggers were laughing loudly. Accidents were becoming so frequent that they were regarded these days as part of the general amusements.

Barney stopped for a moment, shielding his eyes against the glare. Two other kaffirs were trying to lift the capsized waggon off the man's pelvis, and the man was starting to screech. A gingery-haired digger was storming up and down beside them and shouting, 'Get that damned cart off my claim! Get the damned thing off!'

With another cheer, the cart was rolled further down the slope, dragging the mules with it. A splashy fountain of bright red blood golloped out of the kaffir's mouth.

It took Barney another twenty minutes to reach Claim 172, next to the claim owned by the British Diamond Mining Coy. It was dug down to a depth of about ten feet, and one of its ends was shored up against rockslides with sandbags. But there was nobody working there: only a kaffir in a brown hat and a loincloth sitting on a rock and sorting idly through a heap of dry soil.

'Hey!' called Barney.

The kaffir squinted up at him.

'Where's your bossman?' demanded Barney.

The kaffir shrugged.

'Mr Havemann, your boss. Where is he? He come back?'

The kaffir shook his head again, and went on sorting through the dirt.

Barney waited for a moment – then stroke impatiently down the slope and pushed the kaffir hard on the shoulder.

'I'm talking to you,' he snapped. 'I'm looking for Mr Havemann and I want to know where he is.'

Again, the kaffir looked blank.

'You speak English?' said Barney. 'Afrikaans? What? You speak Bantu?'

'You're wasting your time,' put in a dry voice, from behind him.

Barney turned around. At the top of the ridge which divided Claim 172 from Claim 173 stood a grey-haired suntanned man in a striped shirt and tinted eyeglasses. He came down, his feet sliding sidewise on the loose yellowish soil, and held out his hand.

'My name's Stewart,' he said. 'Have you had trouble with Havemann, too?'

'Barney,' said Barney, introducing himself. 'What do you mean by trouble?'

Stewart looked around the claim. 'Whatever he is, or *was*, Havemann was not what you might call your natural-born digger. They caught him yesterday, at last, and well deserved it was too.'

'They caught him? What was he doing?'

'I'm surprised you didn't hear,' said Stewart, still casting his eyes around. 'He'd bribed two or three of the kaffirs from the British Mining Company's claim, next door. Whenever they found a reasonable stone, they were passing it secretly to him, and he was giving them half of whatever he got paid by the IDB boys outside of town. Well, *you* can call it IDB. *I* always call it thieving.'

'He was stealing diamonds?' asked Barney.

Stewart rubbed grit from his eye, and examined it on the end of his finger. 'It's common enough. Stealing's easier than digging. And you can't trust these damned blackies an inch. They swallow more diamonds than they hand over. Last year, in Klipdrift, I caught one of my fellows with two thousand pounds' worth of diamonds pushed up his arse. At least I let him give them back to me the natural way. There was a Dutch digger on the Vaal who caught one of his kaffirs doing that, and he was so wild that he thrust his hand up the fellow's backside and dragged down three feet of intestine. All blood and diamonds. I saw it.'

Barney took off his hat and wiped the sweat from his forehead. 'What's happened to Havemann?' he said.

'Stafford Parker was here, so he dealt with it himself. Questioned the witnesses, everything. Three kaffirs said that Havemann had bribed them, so Stafford Parker ordered him to be staked out.'

'You're joking.'

'Why should I be joking? The man's a thief. What else do you think we ought to do with thieves? Shake them by the hand and buy them a springbok steak dinner at Groot's?'

Riboyne Shel O'lem, thought Barney, with real terror. He knew what staking-out meant. It was the worst of the rough-and-ready punishments that Stafford Parker and his unofficial magistrates meted out on diggers who jumped claims or tried to sell diamonds illegally. Worse than flogging, even worse than being dragged over the bed of the Vaal. Staking-out meant that a man was pegged to the ground without food and water, naked or half-naked, at the mercy of the sun and the wind and the ants.

Staking-out was almost always fatal. And if Joel Havemann was really Joel Blitz, that could mean that Barney's brother was already dead.

Barney tried to swallow, but his throat was constricted and dry. 'I, er, where did they do it?' he asked Stewart.

'Where did they do what?'

'Stake him out. Do you know where they did it?'

Stewart looked at him curiously. 'You want to go and see him? He must have taken *you* for something of a ride.'

'Well, yes, he – he walked out on me once. A long time ago.'

Stewart pointed out towards the south-east corner of the mine. 'They took him out there, as far as I know. About a quarter-mile south of Haarhoff's claim. Ask Haarhoff when you see him, he'll know. He shares part of 190 with a man called Marais.'

'Thank you,' said Barney, in a unsteady voice. 'Can you tell me what's going to happen to this claim?'

'They'll resell it. There won't be any shortage of takers.'

'I see. All right. Thank you again.'

He climbed out of the claim and began to toil his way southwards in the oppressive afternoon heat. He was painfully thirsty now, his tongue sore and swollen, and he stopped by one claim to beg a for a drink. A prickly-headed German digger with a face the colour of raw pork sold him a tin mug of warm brown water for 1s 3d. Barney did not blame him: out here in the middle of the Kimberley Mine, a bucket of water was fetching anything up to 5s 6d. The German watched him drink with fat-embedded eyes, and said, 'I dream of cold beer, myself.'

At the edge of the mine, where the wild scrub still grew, the man called Marais paused in his shovelling for a moment to give Barney directions to the place where he believed Havemann was staked out. He was mournful, and French, and through a mouthful of sausage he told Barney gratuitously that he had once served in the French Foreign Legion. 'It was the same as this, the Legion. All digging.'

Barney reached the place as if he were arriving in one of those small stagey clearings of which the set-designers for grand operas are so fond.

Siegmund: 'A drink! A drink!'
Sieglinde: 'Lo, the water
Thy thirsting lips longed for.'

The clearing was screened from the diamond mine by a thicket of thorns, and from the wider horizons of the veld by a row of stubby monkey-orange trees. A solitary Guiqua was standing nearby in a baggy white shirt and home-made cotton breeches, with a Bible under his arm. He raised his head as Barney came stumbling through the thicket, but he turned back almost immediately to the man who was pegged out naked on the ground, as if he were praying for him.

The man on the ground was silent, but not asleep. His wrists and ankles were bound tightly with thongs, and he had been stretched out in the shape of an X. His chest and his legs were already crimson with sunburn, and he was blotched and swollen with hundreds of insect bites. He was full-bearded, and his black hair was grown long, but bearded and disfigured as he was, Barney knew at once that it was his brother.

He stepped closer, treading for some reason with respectful softness through the grass. Now he could see the orange ants which teemed over the man's body in thousands – over his bruised thighs, over his penis, which was already swollen and distorted with bites; over his stomach; and even over his lips. He knelt as close as he could, and whispered, 'Joel?'

Joel, his face alive with ants, stared back at him. He tried to say something, but the ants wriggled into his mouth, and he had to try to spit them out. Barney turned around to the Griqua and asked, 'How long has he been here?'

'One night,' said the Griqua, in a careful Afrikaans accent. He raised the Bible which he had been carrying under his arm. 'I was reading to him. It says in the Bible to comfort the afflicted.'

'You can read?'

'I was schooled by the British missionaries, the same way Jan Bloem was.'

Barney reached into his pocket and took out his clasp-knife. Without a word, he began to cut Joel free. The Griqua stood and watched him for a while and made no effort to help; but when all the thongs were cut, he laid down his Bible in the grass, and assisted Barney in tugging Joel on to his feet. While the Griqua held him steady, Barney slapped the ants from Joel's body, and raked them, jerking and wriggling, out of his hair.

'Where can we take him?' asked Barney. 'None of the people in Kimberley will have him. Not even my friends.'

'This was Mr Stafford Parker's justice, you know,' said the Griqua solemnly. 'He will not let you escape him.'

'The name of Stafford Parker doesn't impress me at all,' retorted Barney. 'And, besides, this happens to be my brother.'

'*Water*,' pleaded Joel, in a thick whisper.

'I'll get you water,' Barney comforted him. 'Let's just get you out of this place first. Do you have any kind of transport?' he asked the Griqua.

'A donkey-cart. It's tied up by the monkey-orange trees.'

'Come on, then,' Barney told him.

Together, Barney and the Griqua half-carried Joel through the grass to the stunted monkey-orange trees, heavy with green and blotchy-orange fruit. The Griqua's cart was small, and the donkey looked at the three of them with misgiving as they approached; but they were able to lift Joel into the back, and cover him with a frayed plaid blanket.

'All right, let's go,' said Barney; and as quickly as they could, they bumped and wheeled their way across the rocky ground towards the north side of Kimberley's collection of shacks. Hardly anybody gave them a second glance, although Joel began to groan loudly for water again when they were passing the end of the main street.

The Griqua encampment was a mile or so beyond Kimberley, a small gathering of neat British Army tents on the long slope of a grassy hillside. The afternoon was already taking on the smoky gold of a north Cape Colony evening as Barney and his Griqua friend rolled through the lines of cooking-fires to the grandest tent of all, a one-time military band marquee which was now the travelling palace of Jan Bloem.

'Wait here,' said the Griqua, reining back the donkey, and

swinging himself down from the cart. 'I must first of all tell the chief what has happened. It is his decision whether you can stay here or not.'

Barney climbed down from the cart himself as the Griqua strode over to Jan Bloem's marquee. He lifted the blanket from Joel, and folded it up to make a pillow. Then he walked across to one of the Griqua women who was standing in a plain grey Dutch farmhouse dress, cradling a baby in her arms, and he asked her for water.

The woman called to a girl who sat stirring the black iron cooking pot over the fire. The girl nodded, and stood up, and went to a keg beside the tent. She came up to Barney with a dipper brimming with clear water, and followed him back to the cart.

'Joel, I've brought you water,' said Barney, gently. He raised his brother's head while the Griqua girl held the dipper to his dry, swollen lips. Joel sipped as much as he could, and then sank back on the blanket.

The Griqua girl looked at Barney with wide, dark-brown eyes. Some of the half-caste Dutch-Hottentots were remarkably ugly; but this girl had soft curly hair, the colour of brown chimney-soot, and a pretty, oval face. She wore the same plain grey dress as the woman with the baby; but her body had a natural grace which gave it a simple attractiveness and charm.

'This is your friend?' she asked, in halting English.

'No, my brother. *Broeder*,' Barney explained.

The girl said, 'He should ... get down. Sleep.'

'Is there any place for him to lie? A bed?'

The girl pointed to her tent. 'There ... is good.'

At that moment, in a black opera hat, a monocle, a brown striped racing suit and spats, Jan Bloem appeared from his marquee, with Barney's Griqua friend and two other Griquas behind him.

'Well, well,' he declared. 'It's you again. The kike.'

'I found my brother,' said Barney, with simplicity.

Jan Bloem peered at Joel. 'Yes,' he said. 'Piet Steyn here told me all about it.'

'Can we get him to a bed?' asked Barney. 'He's in real bad shape.'

'He's a thief,' said Jan Bloem, trying to screw his monocle into his left eye.

'Stafford Parker says so,' replied Barney. 'But I know Joel better than Stafford Parker. My brother never stole anything.'

'They were prepared to stake him out. To let him die,' commented Jan Bloem. His monocle dropped out again. 'He must have done something to warrant that kind of punishment. Or don't you think so?'

'I don't know. I just want to get him to bed.'

Jan Bloem linked his arms behind his back and walked around Barney as if he were inspecting a piece of garden statuary. Joel, on the back of the cart, let out a breathy groan. But Bloem ignored him, and continued to pace around Barney with his eyes fixed on him unwaveringly. The smoke from the cooking fires drifted between the tents.

'If I take your brother in – give him succour, as they call it, then in British colonial law I'll be an accessory to his crime. They might try staking me out, too.'

'This is your land. They wouldn't dare. If the British upset you, you might take up with the Boers; and if you did that, they'd lose all these diamond mines to the Orange Free State. No, Mr Bloem. There's no risk of that.'

Jan Bloem abruptly stopped pacing. 'The British are unpredictable,' he said. 'You never know what they're going to do next. Their politics are almost entirely dependent on the opinions of their newspaper readers.'

'My brother may be dying, Mr Bloem. If you won't take him in, then I'll just have to take him elsewhere.'

Donald emerged just then from a tent nearby, followed by a fat middle-aged Griqua woman who was pinning up her hair.

'Mr Blitz!' he called, and came over. 'What happen here, Mr Blitz?'

Barney explained, keeping his gaze steadily and cynically on Jan Bloem. 'The situation is that Joel's dying, but our Griqua chum here is more worried about politics, and the British Colonial Office, and the niceties of law.'

Donald bent over the donkey-cart and examined Joel closely. Then he pointed at Joel with a long finger and asked, 'This is he? This is really your brother?'

Barney nodded.

Donald turned on Jan Bloem, still pointing rigidly at Joel, and let fly with a fierce, guttural burst of Griqua. Jan Bloem flushed, and stamped his foot, and shouted back. But then Donald lifted one finger, and pointed upwards, and barked out a whole litany of expletives, until Jan Bloem waved his hand at him to stop.

'I give in,' he told Barney. 'Just tell this mad dog of yours to stop snapping at my ankles.'

'Donald,' cautioned Barney, and Donald felt silent, although he was still twitching with temper.

'This girl here will take care of your brother for you,' said Jan Bloem. 'Her name is Natalia Marneweck. She's a good girl.'

'What about Stafford Parker?' asked Barney. 'And the British authorities?'

'Well, I'll think about them when the time comes,' Jan Bloem told him, although with very little grace. Then he marched back to his tent with his followers in tow, clearing his throat every now and then as if he was on his way to do something extremely important.

'Natalia?' said Barney, turning to the Griqua girl. The girl smiled, and came forward to help Barney and Donald lift Joel down from the back of the cart. Another Griqua man walked across and took the weight of Joel's legs, and between them they carried Joel past the cooking fire and into the tent, where they laid him gently on a pallet of woven grass, covered with a blanket. Joel opened his eyes momentarily in the dim light inside the tent, and gave Barney a small, swollen smile.

Barney stood up. Apart from the pallet, the tent was furnished with nothing more than a brass-bound military chest, which had been spread with a white lace-edged cloth. There was a plain wooden cross standing on it, and a brush and comb.

The girl Natalia said, 'I will help ... your brother. Go now. Please. It is good he sleeps.'

Barney stayed where he was for a moment, looking down at Joel. For the first time since he had found his brother, he had time to think about New York, and Blitz the tailors, and the long years he had been searching since he had come to South

Africa. He held the back of his hand across his mouth, and the tears ran down his cheeks. Donald hesitated by the tent-flap, and the girl Natalia looked up at him with an expression of such gentleness and sympathy that he could do nothing else but smile at her.

'I'll come back in an hour,' he said, wiping his eyes with his sleeve.

Outside the tent, in the cooler breeze of the early evening, he asked Donald, 'What did you say to Jan Bloem? What made him change his mind?'

Donald shrugged, and turned the other way, across the warm shadowy reaches of the valley. The sun was glowering behind the wild syringa trees, and there was a smell of dry grass in the air.

'Oh, not much. I tell him to remember that Jew people and Griqua people are just one people under the Lord. I tell him to remember his Christian vows. I tell him also a great chief like himself has no dignity if he show fear for the British, or for white-beard Stafford Parker.'

'Is that all?' asked Barney.

Donald still did not turn around. 'Well, maybe I tell him I know of one time when he is not faithful to his wife. Maybe I say that if he does not take in your brother, his wife will find out all about his hanky-panky doublequick.'

Barney said, 'Blackmail?'

'Oh, no sir. Friendly reminder.'

Barney stood for a while with his hands on his hips, admiring the valley. 'You know something, Donald,' he said warmly, 'I think I'm beginning to understand the basic ethics of Christianity.'

Barney considered cancelling his dinner engagement with the Knight family that evening, but by seven o'clock Joel was still immersed in the deepest of sleeps, his eyes as red and swollen as ripe wild figs, and Natalia thought it unlikely that he would wake before morning.

'He won't die, though, will he?' asked Barney, standing over his bruised and slumbering brother.

Natalia shook her head vigorously, so that her curls flew. 'He not die. I promise.'

Barney held her arm for a moment. 'You've been good to him. Thank you.'

Natalia said, 'All Griqua good people.'

'I'm beginning to find that out,' said Barney.

Donald was waiting for him outside, holding the reins of the horses, and idly twitching the carriage-whip at the furry insects which flew aimlessly around him in the evening air. Not far away, beside one of the cooking fires, one of the Griqua men was playing an instrument which sounded as plangent as a Jew's harp, while a sturdy woman in a red wrap-around dress sang loud sallies from the Psalms.

Silently, Barney and Donald sat side by side in the surrey as the horses pulled them over the uneven grassland towards Kimberley. As they crested the rise, they could see out over the diamond mine, where a thousand tiny fires sparkled. There was an aroma of woodsmoke and cooking on the wind.

At last, on the outskirts of the main street, they came to the Knights' house. It was one of the better buildings in town – a white-painted frame bungalow with a long verandah and a shingled roof. There was a small picket fence around its neatly-planted front garden, and the path to the front door had been marked out with white pebbles. Through the open curtains, Barney could see Agnes setting the table, and Faith lighting the oil-lamps.

Donald said, 'What time I come back?'

Barney looked at his watch. 'Make it eleven o'clock. That should be just about right.'

'Just about right for you maybe.'

Barney raised an eyebrow. 'Why, what are you planning on doing?'

Donald gave a wide, checkered grin. 'Jan Bloem tells me new sister arrive today, good fat Hottentot. Jan Bloem says her name is Heavy Mary.'

'I might have known. Well, you can make it eleven-thirty. But no later.'

'You are a good fellow, Mr Blitz.'

As Donald clicked at the horses and drove the surrey away,

Barney walked up the Knights' front path, stepped up on to the verandah, and knocked at the black-painted door. He pretended not to notice the way the lace curtain covering the small window beside the door was hurriedly brushed back into place.

Mr Knight himself opened the front door, although it must have been quite a recent experience for him to have to admit his own guests. He was dressed, as before, in a buttoned-up black coat, and a gates-ajar collar.

'You're very punctual,' he said, in a tone of voice that made Barney wonder whether he considered punctuality a virtue or a slightly shameful peccadillo. 'The girls have been looking forward to seeing you.'

Barney stepped into the living-room. It was furnished with an incongruous collection of expensive mahogany tables, inlaid kingwood tallboys, and atrocious varnished armchairs and sofas. It was the sort of clutter you might expect to see on a refugee's pushcart, a mixture of valuable heirlooms and utter rubbish.

Agnes and Faith were both standing by the green-painted upright boiler, and they curtseyed, with a giggly sparkle in their eyes, as Barney came in.

'I think that I've been looking forward to seeing you two again just as much,' Barney told them. He took off his hat, and his gloves, and Mr Knight relieved him of them, only to juggle with them in embarrassment because there was no hallstand on which they could hang.

'It's been very difficult for us, moving out here to Kimberley,' said Mr Knight. 'We had to leave some of our most precious possessions behind. Apart from our friends, that is, and our social life.' He gave a harsh, high-pitched chuckle. 'And you can't exactly describe the social life out here as scintillating, can you? Not scintillating, by any means.'

'You've enough business here, though?' asked Barney.

Mr Knight at last found a place for Barney's hat, on the left-hand antler of a very sorry-looking stuffed springbok's head. His gloves, he fitted over the right-hand antler. 'Business?' he asked, drawing back his coat tails, and planting his fists on his hips. 'Oh yes, plenty of business. Squabbles over claims, squabbles over diamonds And quite a few squabbles over women, too.'

A small, pale lady with a face the shape and colour of a blanched almond appeared from the interior of the bungalow. She wore a drab dress of pale green cotton, and dangling earrings of amber cornelian, and when Barney took her hand he felt as if he were trying to save someone with greasy palms from falling over a small cliff.

'M'good woman,' mumbled Mr Knight, abruptly.

'Please to know you,' said Barney.

'Charmed,' said Mrs Knight, in a vague, bright voice. 'The dinner is almost ready.'

Agnes giggled. She was dressed very prettily tonight, in a pink dress of polished cotton with lacy frills at the neck and the cuffs and hem. Faith appeared a little more severe, in grey, with a cameo brooch at her neck, and her hair scraped back from her forehead.

'Mummy's had a very difficult time with the new cook, haven't you, Mummy?' said Agnes.

Mr Knight frowned, but Mrs Knight flapped her hands in amusement and desperation, and said, 'These Malays ... they can't understand plain English, that's the trouble. I told him to sauté the potatoes, and when I came back, he had simply placed all the *small* potatoes on one side of the drainer, and all the *large* potatoes on the other. "There, missis," he said. "I sort out all the potatoes, just like you say." Isn't it *impossible*?'

'She misses Capetown,' remarked Mr Knight, unnecessarily, as his wife returned to the kitchen to rescue the meal.

They sat down to dinner at last, at an oval table with a wobbly leg. Halfway through the soup, which was thin split-pea with enough pepper in it to make Barney feel as if he were going to sneeze the whole bowlful clear across the cloth, Mr Knight had to get up and wedge a copy of *Good and Great Churchmen* under the offending castor to keep the table level. He was red in the face when he emerged from under the cloth.

'It wasn't always this way,' he intoned, to the world in general. 'There was a time when we owned the finest mahogany dining-table in the entire Colony.'

'Never mind, dear,' his wife soothed him.

Faith said, 'Will you be staying until Sunday, Mr Barney?'

Barney was glad of a chance to lay down his spoon and dab at his mouth with his napkin. The napkin was real Irish linen, although rather tired. 'I'm sure I will,' he said. 'I have quite a few days' business in Kimberley.'

'Then you could accompany us to church?' said Faith.

'Faith,' protested her father, gruffly. But Barney could see that the idea did not altogether displease him. It may not have been appropriate for a young woman in England or in Capetown to seek a young man to escort her to church on Sunday, so that they might recite their devotions together, but here in Kimberley it was almost respectable. Better than chattering in the street with diggers, like a common whore. And certainly better than secret liaisons behind the assay office, which he would be unable to inspect either for quality or for moral content.

Mr Knight was sure that both his flirtatious daughters were still virgins, but only just. Another six months in this primitive hurly-burly of miners and prostitutes and thieves, and he would no longer be quite so certain. A daughter's virtue was so fragile, like a protea flower. And he knew, with a kind of quiet desperation, how very attractive to men his daughters were.

'You enjoyed your soup?' asked Mrs Knight, as Agnes got up to clear away the plates. The Knights were obviously very hard up, or else they had servant trouble. But performing the duties of a parlourmaid gave Agnes the opportunity to bend over Barney as she took his bowl, so that he could smell her perfume, and so that he could feel for a moment the young resilience of her breast against his shoulder.

'The soup was delicious,' said Barney. 'I haven't tasted soup like that since I was in New York.'

'I pity New York,' murmured Agnes, as she passed on to collect her father's dish. And she glanced back at Barney and gave him a twinkling smile that was both merry and provocative. Barney found himself blushing, and paying more attention to his breadroll than most people would have considered usual. Faith noticed what had happened, but Mr Knight was too busy propounding a legalistic theory for dividing up the diamond claims, and Mrs Knight was biting her lip and frowning at her husband in a hopeless attempt to follow what he was saying.

'You're a *gentleman* farmer, I suppose?' Mr Knight asked Barney, as Agnes brought to the table a large white tureen brimming with a brown and indiscriminate stew.

Barney gave him a sloping smile. 'I guess so, whatever that's worth in the middle of nowhere at all.'

'Well, it's worth a very great deal, old chap,' said Mr Knight. 'A gentleman farmer can be nominated for membership of the Kimberley Club; whereas any other kind of farmer may not.'

'Is the Kimberley Club so important?'

Mrs Knight tittered abstractedly as she served up the stew, and Mr Knight glared at her. 'Yes,' he said, turning back to Barney. 'It's a little rudimentary at the moment, but then the new building's complete, it'll look like what it was founded to be. A club for gentlemen of social standing; a place where business can be discussed among the select few; an *enclave*, if you like, for those of breeding.'

'You're a member yourself?' asked Barney.

Mr Knight folded his chins into his stiff collar with self-satisfaction. 'Billiards secretary, as a matter of fact.'

'And you're thinking that I might ...?'

'It would be of considerable advantage to you if you did. It's a question of those *within* the circle, if you see what I mean, and those *without*. And those *without*, well ... those *without* will never know what it means to be *within*.'

Mrs Knight tittered again, and passed Barney a plate crowded with unlikely-looking pieces of meat. Either she was serving up some completely unknown animal, or else her new cook had no idea of how to cut a brisket up into palatable pieces.

Agnes, her hands prettily clasped in front of her, said, 'Are there really Red Indians in America, Mr Barney? And bears?'

'Both,' nodded Barney, 'but not in New York.'

'So you've never seen any?' Agnes asked. Barney was suddenly conscious of her knee pressing against his under the tablecloth. He looked down at his plate, at the awkward lumps of meat and bone swimming in their pool of greasy gravy, and he wished he had not.

'I saw a Red Indian once,' he said. 'When I was a boy, a Comanche called Eagle Feathers visited New York, and was driven around the streets in a carriage. I was pretty disappointed, though. He wore a top hat and a morning coat, and carried a cane. Not very savage, I'm afraid.'

Mr Knight, sniffed loudly, said, 'Apropos of that – of savages, I mean – I defended a very interesting court-martial once, in Capetown. A chap charged with the theft of silver from the officers' mess at Cape Castle. He was said to have run up some pretty hefty gambling debts which he couldn't pay back. Chatsworth, his name was. Old Harrovian.'

'But not a savage, dear, surely?' asked Mrs Knight, vaguely.

Mr Knight fixed his wife with a look that went beyond mere exasperation. It almost seemed as if he were trying to melt her down by the force of concentrated eyesight.

'This chap,' he went on, still staring at his wife, 'this chap denied the charges completely. And the interesting thing was that the only witness to his alleged theft was a Kaffir cleaner. So after all the evidence had been heard, I stood up before the court-martial and asked them if they considered that kaffirs were more important in the Lord's scheme of things than, say, polo ponies – or *less*. And if they believed, as I did, that a thoroughbred polo pony was more important in the Lord's scheme of things than a Cape Coast blackie, then they would have to come to the conclusion that the only eye-witness in this trial was less than human, and that his so-called testimony was therefore inadmissible. I have to tell you, of course, that we were sitting in front of old Clough-Parker, who used to be an absolute fanatic for polo.'

Barney was stunned. 'And they let him off? Chatsworth, I mean?'

'Of course. Acquitted without hesitation. It shouldn't have come to a hearing, of course, except the colonel in charge of the mess on the night of the alleged theft absolutely hated Chatsworth's guts. Think he believed Chatsworth had been messing around with his wife, something like that. But – and this is the most important thing – old Clough-Parker's decision created something of an interesting precedent ... and the plea that kaffirs can't give admissible evidence in a court of law because they aren't human is still used today, although not as often as it was. It's known as the Polo Pony Precedent.'

Agnes's thigh was now pressing close and warm against Barney's knee, and when he looked at her, she gave him a smile of unmistakable desire. Barney felt excited and confused at the same time. He liked Agnes a great deal; she was pretty, and she stirred up in him the kind of tingling sensations that stayed with him in the morning after an erotic dream. But his experience with girls was limited to his childhood friendship with Leah, and his strenuous defloration by Louise Loubser. He had often stared covertly at the bare breasts of black girls around Oranjerivier, and thought about inviting one of them back to the farm. But in the end he had always been too shy, or too concerned about disease, or too worried that he might end up like Monsaraz, copulating like a fancy-dressed dog.

Faith must have sensed what was going on beneath the table, because she suddenly hissed, '*Agnes,*' as if to reprimand her sister and remind her who had invited Barney to church first.

But quite apart from the Knight girls' coquettish behaviour, Barney had something else on his mind – the possibility of getting Joel acquitted by Stafford Parker's magistrates. If Mr Knight could plead on Joel's behalf, and if the magistrate was prepared to accept the Polo Pony Precedent, then Joel could go free.

'I'll tell you what, Mr Barney,' said Mr Knight, 'if you're interested in becoming a member of the Kimberley Club, I could put your name up. It would stand you in excellent stead, you know.'

'*Billiards,*' said Mrs Knight, scathingly, for no particular reason at all. Barney glanced at her in alarm, but Mr Knight shook his hand to indicate that he should not take any notice.

'We could do with some more gentlemen,' said Mr Knight. 'And gentlemen, of course, includes American gentlemen. We're not xenophobes.' He let out another high, grating laugh, as if he were amazed at his own good humour and tolerance.

Barney reached under the table and held Agnes's knee to keep it still. He was feeling hot and flushed, and inside his best black trousers he had half an erection. 'You don't admit ... half-castes, I suppose?' he asked.

'Half-castes! My dear chap! We don't even admit Wyke-hamists! No, my dear fellow, there isn't a half-caste to be seen. Nor anyone of any of the inferior breeds. No Arabs, no Chinese, no Malays, and no bloody Frenchmen!'

'Jews?' asked Barney.

Mr Knight, with his mouth full of stew, stared at Barney as if he were mad.

'The day they admit a Jew to the Kimberley Club – that'll be the day that I drink five bottles of brandy one after the other and go to seek my place beside the Lord my God. Jews! Mercenary, money-grubbing Jews! What are you thinking about?'

'Actually ...' said Barney, in a dry voice, 'not all Jews are as grasping as they're made out to be. In fact, one of my very best friends turned out to be a Jew.' The words came out like toads, but he knew he had to say them. 'Jews can be very ... well, sensitive.'

'Oh, don't misunderstand me,' Mr Knight put in. He chewed for a while, with obvious distaste, and then removed from his mouth a large piece of fawn gristle, corrugated by teethmarks, which he parked prominently on the side of his plate. 'The Jew is a human being, no doubt of it; unlike your kaffir. He has his religion, no matter how perverse many of its tenets may be, and he has his family life. And I've heard people like yourself say that your occasional Jew can be most obliging. No, no, you mustn't get me wrong.'

Barney found it almost impossible to stop himself from pushing back his chair and walking out of Mr Knight's bungalow at once. His brains felt as if they were boiling. But the way that Agnes held his hand close to the warmth of her thigh was somehow soothing as well as erotic, and even more sobering was the thought that Joel's life was still at risk from the magistrates. Mr Knight, with his bristly quiver of well-sharpened bigotry, might well be the only person who could save him.

He had to admit to himself, too, that the idea of becoming a member of the Kimberley Club was something of an attrac-tion. It would establish him as a *bona fide* businessman, and give him the social credentials to start making his way to the top.

Where 'the top' actually was in the hugger-mugger of De Beers New Rush, he was not quite sure. But it had to be better than working Monsaraz's farm for him; and it had to be better than living like the Knights, on thin pulse soup and faded dreams.

'Perhaps you'd consider helping this Jewish friend of mine out of a difficult legal spot,' said Barney.

Mr Knight swallowed wine, and then looked at Barney with great care. 'A difficult legal spot, you say.'

'He's been accused, wrongfully, of theft.'

'Aha! Like our friend Chatsworth.'

'Well, that's right,' said Barney. 'And the similarity doesn't end there. As far as I know, the only witnesses were kaffirs.'

'What was he accused of stealing?' asked Mr Knight. 'Not diamonds, I hope.'

Barney nodded. 'It was said that he bribed kaffirs from the British Diamond Mining Company, whose claim was next to his, to bring him the best of their finds. He then sold them on the IDB market.'

'You're talking about Mr Havemann, aren't you?' put in Faith, in surprise. 'I thought he'd been sentenced, and staked out.'

Barney felt hot. 'You knew him?' he asked.

'Everybody knew him,' said Faith. 'But then, everybody here knows everybody. A very morose man, but quite handsome.'

'That's enough, Faith,' interrupted her father. He put down his knife and said to Barney, 'Is Havemann not dead then?'

'He's alive,' said Barney. 'He's not particularly well, but he's alive.'

'Stafford Parker will have him hunted down like a rogue lion, I promise you that, and probably shot.'

'Stafford Parker is not the law,' retorted Barney.

'No, he isn't, not technically speaking. But he has sufficient power and influence to keep the diamond fields under his own control. And you can't say that his control has been unwelcome. There is very little violence here, everything considered.'

'Nonetheless, he should consider an appeal on Mr Havemann's behalf.'

Mr Knight made a face. 'He may do, if the mood takes him.'

'And will you represent him?'

There was a lengthy pause, during which Mr Knight pursued a few rags of meat around the circumference of his plate with determined abstraction.

'There are many crimes committed around Kimberley, almost daily, which are tolerated by most of the diggers because they do not challenge their fundamental reason for being here. They are here for the diamonds, Mr Barney, and most of them have suffered much, and given up much, and travelled far, all for the sake of diamonds. There is blasphemy here, and prostitution, and drunkenness, and gambling. There is sodomy and there is incest. But all of these are considered to be little more than misdemeanours – diversions, if you like, for men of rough character, and forgivable. The stealing of diamonds, however, is *never* forgiven. To steal diamonds, you see, is to steal a man's life.'

'But will you represent him? Will you try? I have nobody else to turn to.'

'A Jew, and a diamond thief? You're asking a great deal, Mr Barney.'

Barney took a shallow breath. 'I know. And I know that you don't have much of a chance of success. But if you *were* to succeed – think of it. You'd be famous throughout the colony.'

'That's as may be,' replied Mr Knight, unimpressed. 'No – you'll have to give me time to consider it. And of course I'll have to talk to Mr Havemann to get his side of the story. Funny, though – I met him once or twice and I never realised he was Jewish. No side-curls, or anything like that.'

'Jews don't *all* look like Shylock,' said Barney, turning his attention first to Mrs Knight, surprising her in the middle of trying to pick a shred of beef from between her teeth; and then to Agnes, and to Faith. It seemed almost incredible to him that none of them had realised he was Jewish himself, although Agnes had probably mistaken his trembling and his heat for sexual arousal, and partly, of course, it was. His trousers felt tight and crowded, and he could feel the moistness of male juice on his cotton combinations. He had never known a dinner like it. Law, prejudice, desire, and indigestion.

142

After they had out-stared a mountainous blancmange of goat's milk, flavoured with strong vanilla, they left the table, with a great deal of chair-scraping, and sat around the green-painted upright stove. Mr Knight lit an oval Turkish cigarette, and reclined in his chair with his ankles crossed, twiddling his feet as he spoke. Barney sat on the end of the sofa, and Agnes perched herself on the arm right next to him, so that he could breathe in her perfume, and so that she could wind the curls of his hair around her fingers without her father seeing. She hummed under her breath, a repetitive and melancholy air which would always remind Barney of this evening as long as he lived.

'I'll give you one word of advice,' said Mr Knight, as the clock, on the wall struck eleven. 'Be careful with whom you associate; because in Kimberley you're known by the company you keep. Everybody's allowed their little entertainments – their black women, and so forth. That's natural. But, socially, you should keep yourself beyond reproach. Now, will you have a glass of tonic wine?'

Donald arrived at eleven-thirty, and looked distinctly white around the mouth. Barney bowed to Mrs Knight, and thanked her for dinner, while Mrs Knight giggled and blushed, and Agnes and Faith clutched each other tight and tried not to laugh. Mr Knight stood by with his 'heavens preserve us' expression.

Barney mounted the surrey and waved to the Knight family, who stood in the lighted doorway of their bungalow like a group posing for a Christmas photograph, waving furiously back at him.

'Enough waving?' asked Donald, raising his whip. But just as Barney was about to say 'more than enough – let's go', Agnes came bustling along the pathway towards him, her skirts held high, flapping something frantically in her hand.

'Your gloves, Mr Barney! You forgot your gloves!'

Barney climbed down from the surrey again. 'I'm grateful,' he told Agnes, as she came up close.

'I hid them,' she whispered. 'I wanted to say goodbye to you alone.'

Barney stared into her wide, glistening eyes. She was very

pretty, and she excited him like no girl he had ever met before. Not even Leah had made him feel this way. This girl was all wispy hair and spicy fragrances and moist, tantalising lips. She was well-mannered, but forward too, and the way she had drawn his hand up the length of her thigh during dinner had been electrifying.

Agnes held out her hand, and Barney sandwiched it between his own hands.

'I don't know what to say to you,' he said.

'I know,' she whispered. 'But it doesn't matter. I was in love with a lieutenant when we lived in Capetown . . . I had to leave him because of Papa's business. But he taught me what it takes to please a man.'

'I want to meet you again,' said Barney.

'Then come to church on Sunday. Be kind to Faith – but make sure you sit close to me.'

Barney was suddenly conscious of how hot the night was; of the tireless chirping of the insects in the bush. He was also conscious that Mr Knight was frowning from the verandah; and that his conversation with Agnes had overrun the time that any normal person would have taken to discuss the matter of mislaid gloves.

'You must go,' he said.

Agnes twinkled her eyes at him. 'I know. But won't Faith be jealous?'

She ran back down the path, and Barney stood watching her for a moment before he climbed back up on to the surrey.

'That woman knows you're Jewish?' asked Donald, flicking the whip, and clicking to the horses.

'What difference does it make?' Barney demanded, loosening his necktie.

Donald grinned at him. 'She not know? You not tell her?'

'No. There was no reason to.'

'You don't think God be angry?'

'Why should He be?'

'God doesn't like to be denied.'

'I wasn't denying God. Listen, Donald, to survive in this country, to make it rich, you have to be white, and Christian, and a gentleman. As it happens, I'm only one of those three things. But if I have to let people assume that I'm the other two – only *assume*, mind you, without barefaced lying – then I'll do it.'

'Very good,' said Donald.

'Very good? What's very good?'

'Excuse,' said Donald. 'Very good excuse.'

Joel was awake when he returned to the Griqua encampment on the hillside. Natalia was crouched by the side of his cot, feeding him with meat broth. When Barney came into the tent, Joel held Natalia's wrist, and said, 'That's enough soup, thank you. Really, that's enough.'

'You must get strength,' said Natalia, lifting the spoon again.

Barney sat down on the end of the bed. 'Do what your nurse tells you.' He smiled at Joel.

Joel was unshaved, red-eyed, and battered. Each cheekbone was shiny with purple bruises. 'What's the point in fattening myself up?' he asked Barney. 'Stafford Parker's going to set the dogs on me when he finds out that I've escaped.'

'Did they really leave you out there to die?'

Joel lay back. 'The punishment was three days staked out. If you don't die, it's a goddamned miracle.'

Barney said, 'I only heard what had happened to you by chance. Nork told me.'

'Nork? That buffoon?'

'He didn't seem like a buffoon to me.'

'He's the laughing-stock of the mine. Him and his theories about volcanoes. You get *shlimazls* like Nork around every mine, though. The thieves, and the clingers-on, and the so-called professors.'

Natalia stood up, and carried the bowl of broth out of the tent. Barney, brimming with affection, said, 'Joel, it's wonderful to see you. I've been searching for you ever since I got here. Three years, and here you are.'

'Well, you're a few months too late, little brother,' said Joel. 'If you'd come along earlier, you might have been able to help me dig my claim, and then maybe I would have come up with something.'

'Your claim didn't yield any diamonds?'

'A handful. Enough to keep me in food and water and precious little else. While everybody around me was digging up rocks the size of pigeons' eggs, and making a fortune, I was scarcely scratching a living. Why the hell do you think I bribed those *schwarzers* to give me the best stones they found?'

Barney stared at him. 'You mean you really did that?'

'How else was I supposed to live? You haven't dug a claim out there, you don't know what the hell it's like. It's so damned hot you feel like you're frying, and it's nothing but rock and mudslides and breaking your damned back.'

'How did they catch you?' asked Barney.

'One of the kaffirs got too smart. I was paying all of them half of what I got from the IDB boys, but this particular one said he wanted two-thirds, or else he'd go tell his bossman at British Diamonds what I was up to. Well, I should have paid him what he wanted, but I got mad at him, and told him to go to the devil. That's where he went – straight to Stafford Parker. And that's why Stafford Parker staked me out.'

'Listen,' said Barney, 'whether you actually stole those diamonds or not, I've found someone who might be able to help you. A lawyer, by the name of Knight. I told him you were a friend of mine, not my brother, because he's prejudiced against Jews. Yes, I know – but he's not the only one. And he got someone acquitted in Capetown once because the only prosecution witness was a kaffir.'

'Are you serious?' asked Joel. 'If I do so much as poke my nose out of that tent-flap, the Diggers' Association will tear me to tiny pieces. The best thing I can do is wait here until I've got my strength back, and then make a run for the coast.'

'Joel, you can't. What about your diamond claim?'

'They'll confiscate it anyway, and sell it off to the next bidder.'

'But it must have cost you everything you had!'

'It did,' nodded Joel. 'I bought the farm at Derdeheuwel out of the wages I'd saved at sea. Then I sold Derdeheuwel off to that damned Portugee for twice what I paid for it. He was desperate for a place, and rich, too, and I was bored with farming by then. That's when I bought a claim at Klipdrift, and

I did well, there. A good steady supply of diamonds that kept me well-dressed and drunk for over a year. Don't get me wrong, though. I saved a little money, too. So by May this year I had three thousand pounds for a single claim here at Kimberley.'

'Joel,' said Barney, sorrowfully, shaking his head.

'I hope you're not thinking to judge me,' retorted Joel, edgily.

'I should judge you?'

'You sound like it, *schmendrick*.'

'What's happened to you, Joel? You're so bitter.'

Joel rubbed the back of his hand across his unshaven chin. 'Bitter? You think I'm bitter?' He turned his face away. 'Yes,' he said, and his voice was less confident now, less aggressive. 'Yes, well I am bitter.'

'You want to talk about it?'

Joel sniffed. Although he was keeping his face hidden by the blanket, Barney could tell that he was upset.

'I'm such a damned waster,' he said. 'I had hundreds of pounds – thousands – when I was at Klipdrift, and I wasted it all. On drink, on gambling, on horses, on women. I was like a ridiculous child. I saved some, sure. But three thousand out of fifteen thousand isn't much to boast about, is it? Particularly when I gave most of it away to a woman.'

'A woman? What woman?'

Joel looked at Barney, and there were tears running down his blistered cheeks. 'She was a whore, Barney. A common whore. I didn't want to go with whores when I first came here. I tried to think of Mama. Somehow ... in some ridiculous way ... I still thought of myself as Mama's property. Almost her husband. If I went with whores, I'd be letting her down. But one night in Klipdrift I got drunk and I went to a whorehouse, and that's where I met Meg. She was Irish. She had hair like fire. And the first night we spent together, it was like a dream. In the morning, I paid her in diamonds for a whole week; and for that whole week we lay in bed and made love. Or fornicated. Call it whatever you like.'

Natalia came back into the tent with a copper basin filled with warm water, and a rough towel. She knelt down again beside Joel and started to dab his face.

'This *Meg* ...' said Barney. 'You gave her everything?'

'Almost everything,' Joel told him. 'I had three thousand pounds tied up at the bank, and so I couldn't lay my hands on it, thank God. But I bought her clothes, and jewellery, and whatever she wanted. I was crazy for love. Then one day I came back to my cabin a couple of hours early and found her naked with some German. That was the end of it. For a while, I was mad. I still think of her, and it still hurts me to remember what she did to me.'

There was a moment's silence between them. It had been a long time, and they were almost strangers.

But then Joel said, 'How was Mama, when you left her? Have you kept in touch since you've been out here?'

Barney said, 'You didn't get my letter?'

'Letter?'

'I sent you a letter just before I left New York. It was addressed to you at Derdeheuwel.'

Joel frowned. 'Mama's okay, isn't she? She's not sick?'

Barney took his brother's hand. He wanted to say, she's dead, she's been lying in the Jewish cemetery for years now – all those years in which you've been assuming that she's still alive. All those years in which you've been imagining her in her kitchen on Clinton Street, cooking ghostly meals which she never cooked, lighting every Friday evening those *Shabbes* candles which she never lit.

He wanted to say, she's dead, but the words would not leave his mouth.

Joel said, 'What's wrong? What's the matter? You've heard from her, haven't you? She's written?'

'Joel,' said Barney, in a hoarse voice, 'the reason I left New York was because Mama died.'

'She *died*? You're telling me that Mama *died*?'

Barney nodded.

'*Zeeser Gottenyu*,' whispered Joel. He held his hands together and covered his mouth.

'She, er ... we had one of those crazy arguments. She killed herself in the kitchen. She was going out of her mind, Joel. There was nothing that anybody could do to help her. Ever since *Tateh* died ...'

'Yes,' whispered Joel. 'Ever since *Tateh* died.'

'It wasn't your fault,' said Barney. 'It wasn't mine, either, although sometimes I have bad dreams about it. Sometimes I wake up and I can feel her blood on the palms of my hands. Wet, and sticky. But it's only a dream.'

'How did she do it?' asked Joel. The pupils of his eyes dilated, and he kept glancing sideways, as if he found it difficult to concentrate.

'Knife,' Barney told him, in one single strangulated word.

Joel closed his eyes. 'Knife,' he repeated, sadly. 'Poor Mama.'

They talked, in odd fragmented sentences, for another hour, until Joel began to tire. Barney told Joel everything that had happened to him since he left New York – about Hunt, and Monsaraz, and Stafford Parker, and about his evening with the Knight family. Joel seemed intent on making an immediate break for the Orange Free State, but Barney managed to persuade him that it might be worth talking to Mr Knight about his case, and about the possibility of lodging an appeal.

At two o'clock in the morning, Joel's eyes began to close, and Barney covered his brother with the blanket, and turned to leave the tent.

'Barney?' murmured Joel, sleepily.

'What is it?'

'She never haunted you, did she? I mean Mama?'

Barney said, 'All sons are haunted by their mothers, Joel. It's what motherhood and sonhood are all about. And maybe you and I are more haunted than most.'

Outside, in the grass, Natalia Marneweck was standing with a shawl around her shoulders. The sky above her was thick with showers of stars, as if all the thousands of diamonds from the Kimberley mine had been spilled across the darkness. She turned around as Barney came out of the tent, and walked towards him.

'Your brother is good now?'

'Much better, thank you, thanks to you.'

'I have blankets here, if you want sleep.'

Barney saw that two or three red and white woven blankets had been spread out on the grass to form a bed. He looked around the encampment, and all the tents were in darkness, apart from one or two dying cooking-fires, and a flickering torch outside Jan Bloem's marquee. The wind blew stealthily across the hillside, and raised the hairs on the back of Barney's neck.

Without a word, Barney went across to the blankets, and sat down. He eased off his boots, and set them side by side in the grass. Then he struggled out of his black coat, and folded it up.

'I go stay with my cousin now,' said Natalia. 'That tent, by the fire!'

Barney, unfastening his cufflinks, looked at her. In her white woollen shawl, with her curls blowing across her face, she appeared in the darkness like a heroine from a Victorian story-book, her face and her clasped hands impossibly sweet and pretty.

'Don't go,' he said. He was surprised by his own directness. He smoothed out the blanket beside him and said, 'Stay here with me.'

There was a silence. Natalia stayed where she was, making no move towards him, but making no move away from him, either.

'You think I lie with every man?' she asked him.

'I don't think that at all. I just want you to lie with me.'

She came across, hesitated, and then squatted down beside him. She touched his forehead with the cool fingers of her left hand. 'One day I find another man to lie with,' she said. 'But the Bible says he must be my husband.'

'You think I wouldn't consider marrying you? You're beautiful.'

She leaned forward and kissed his cheek. 'You, too, are beautiful. But I must not.'

She started to get up, but Barney gripped her wrist. 'I want you to stay with me,' he insisted.

Natalia tried to tug herself away, but Barney twisted her arm around and pulled her back on to the blanket. Then he scrambled on top of her, and gripped her between his thighs.

She stared up at him, panting. 'I shall cry out,' she warned.

Barney bent his head, and kissed her. First, she turned her face away, so that he could only kiss her neck and her cheek. But then she turned back again, with a gasp, and he kissed her full on the mouth. She bit his lips, and he tasted the sharp taste of blood, but he kissed her again, and again. She let out a stifled gasp, and pushed up against his chest.

Barney was too strong for her. His wide-shouldered boxer's body was too hard with muscle, too wiry with sinew, and all those months of working on Monsaraz's farm, all those days of chopping down trees and hammering fences, all those sweaty hours of hefting animal feedbags and heaving balks of timber, all gave his passion the physical power it needed to break its way loose.

His inhibitions gave way like an earth dam collapsing in front of a winter flood. His religious ethics fell like drowned fences. His respect for his father and his guilt for his mother were both swirled away. There was nothing inside his head but a thundering torrent of released repressions, of lust and anger and love that had never found any expression. His penis was almost painfully rigid, and already quaked with spasms that blinded him to anything but taking Natalia, and to letting go that tension that Agnes Knight had been tightening up inside him all evening.

He pulled Natalia's shawl away from her shoulders, and wrenched at the bodice of her mission-school dress. The cotton tore away with a noise that reminded him for one jigsaw-puzzled second of the tailor's shop on Clinton Street; but then her heavy brown breast was bared, and he clutched it in his hand, a whole handful of softness, with a hard nipple that protruded between his fingers.

'No,' whispered Natalia, as he squeezed and caressed her bare breast, rolling the nipple between his thumb and his finger. 'No, I must not.'

She fought him, but she fought him silently, digging her fingernails into his shoulder, and wrestling her body between his tight-clenched thighs. Yet every twist of her hips aroused him more, and by the time he had gripped her tight enough to be able to pull at his own buttons; the front of his underwear was already wet with his repeated ejaculations of sperm. He said something inside his mind that approached a prayer.

Frantically, he untangled himself from his combinations, half-standing, half-hopping, to step out of his trousers. Then, naked, he forced himself down on Natalia, and snatched at the hem of her dress.

She rolled over on to her stomach, kicking at him with her heels; but Barney rolled over with her and pulled up her dress at the back, exposing her bottom.

'Natalia,' he panted, through clenched teeth. 'Natalia, please, Natalia . . .'

With a muted mewling sound, Natalia tried to wriggle forward on her elbows through the grass. But now Barney seized her thighs, and dragged her back towards him. Forcefully, he parted the cheeks of her bottom with his thumbs, as if he were opening up the twin dusky-coloured halves of a large fruit. Inside the fruit, Natalia's flesh was glistening and pink, and her pungency aroused Barney even more.

He wrestled with her, and jabbed at her with his penis. Twice he struck her thigh, and twice she managed to twist herself away. But then he clutched her shoulders, and grabbed at her curls, and pulled her downwards and backwards so that she was forced to sit in his lap, and so that his hardened penis slipped inside her, deep and urgent and swollen with lust that had been confined too long.

At first, with her back arched, and her muscles as taut and dimpled as a marble by Michaelangelo, Natalia struggled against him. Then, as he thrust into her again and again, his hands grasping her breasts, one breast bare and one breast clothed, she began to struggle *with* him, until he realised by her trembling and gasps and her little birdlike cries that she wanted him, and that she had probably wanted him right from the beginning. This had not been a rape, but a demand from Natalia to show her just how strong he was prepared to be.

Towards the end, crouched together in the grass under that diamond-encrusted sky, they were thrusting together, faster and faster, like runners, or racing horses, and Barney's thighs were anointed with Natalia's slippery juices. They shuddered together, winced together in ecstatic anguish, grappled with each other for one last moment. Then it was over and they fell away from each other and lay apart on the blankets, each of them seeking breath and balance; each of them re-mapping their lives to take account of the cataclysmic landmark that both of them had just reached.

In one violent act of love, two destinies had been irrevocably altered. In five minutes, Barney had realised both his strength and his weakness, and what essential tasks now lay before him.

He grasped Natalia's wrist, and turned to stare at her. Her face glistened with sweat, and she was holding her one bare breast in her hand, absently fondling the nipple with her fingers, touching it lightly, teasing it. Her thighs were still parted, her sex sparkling in the light like diamonds, like some freshly cut-open eatable at a magical picnic under the clouds of the night.

'Do you hate me now?' Barney asked her.

Natalia stared back at him for a moment, and then shook her head.

'I shouldn't have done that,' said Barney. He sat up, and raked his fingers through his hair. 'My God, I shouldn't have done that.'

He started to look around for his discarded underwear, but Natalia sat up, too, and wrapped her arms round him, holding him close, burying her head in the middle of his naked back.

'I am already married,' she said. 'Last year, my husband die. I am so sad without him. I always say – I can never find another man – not like my husband. But you have that same look.'

Barney could feel her soft curls against his bare back, and the feeling was feminine, and reassuring, and warm. He reached one hand behind him, and touched her head gently. 'I could love you, Natalia,' he said, in a tone that almost made it a question, as if he were asking her to tell him that she could love him, too.

'You must call me Mooi Klip,' she said. 'That is what my husband always calls me.'

'Mooi Klip?'

'In Afrikaans, it means "pretty stone". It is what they call the first big diamond.'

He turned around, and kissed her smooth forehead. She

smelled of musky perfume, and Pears soap, and sweat. 'All right, Mooi Klip,' he told her. 'You shall be my pretty stone from now on.'

They slept together in the blankets until the first wan light of dawn, when the birds began to call across the valley, and the grass rustled in the wind. Then, when Barney was still half-asleep, the girl called Mooi Klip folded back her bed and went to light up a cooking-fire, so that by the time the sun came over the eastern horizon, she was able to bring Barney an enamel mug of hot tea and some warm, doughy bread.

Barney sat up on his elbow, sipping the tea and munching the bread, while Mooi Klip knelt beside him and watched him with the pleased, proprietorial interest of a new bride.

Stafford Parker arrived in the Griqua camp at noon, red-faced and white-bearded, and accompanied by his usual entourage of magistrates and diggers and Griqua interpreters. He had not come unheralded: a Griqua boy had run in through the lines of tents about half an hour before, and warned Jan Bloem that he should expect an important visitor. Accordingly, Jan Bloem was standing outside his marquee dressed in his best Sunday suit, while his mother sat not far away in a red plush drawing-room chair which had been a gift from Sir Philip Woodhouse, dressed in an emerald-green promenading gown with a prominent bustle, and smoking a clay pipe.

Barney had spent most of the morning with Joel, who had developed a slight fever, and was thrashing around on his cot in a chilly sweat. But when he heard two or three lookout rifles crackle on the ridge, he knew that Stafford Parker was coming, and he left Joel with Mooi Klip while he opened the tent flap and went outside.

'Well, then, how do you do,' said Stafford Parker, planting himself in front of Jan Bloem with his fists on his hips. It was an aggressive, confident pose, and it reminded Barney of Mr Knight. Barney came closer, so that he was standing only a few feet away from Mrs Bloem's parlour chair, and close enough to smell her Navy Cut tobacco.

'I do very well,' smiled Jan Bloem. 'How do *you* do?'

Stafford Parker reached behind him with a peremptory wiggle of his fingers; and one of his magistrates, a thin man with a particularly knobbly nose and a particularly blue chin, handed him a Bible. Parker held it up. and Barney recognised it at once as the Bible from which his Griqua friend Piet Steyn had been giving Joel 'comfort to the afflicted'. They must have accidentally left it behind on the ground when they cut Joel free from his bonds.

'This *Bible*,' said Stafford Parker, with enunciation so clear that it echoed, like the sound of two housebricks being clapped together, 'this *Bible* was found in an incriminating place.'

'Ah,' smiled Jan Bloem. 'And where would that be?'

'That would be a few hundred yards south of the mine,' Stafford Parker told him. 'At the very spot where a convicted diamond-thief was staked out for a sentence of three days, or death, whichever came the sooner.'

'I see,' Jan Bloem replied, unhelpfully.

'Well, apparently you *don't* see,' snapped Stafford Parker, shaking the Bible as if it were a box of sugar. 'Because the convicted diamond-thief was illegally released, and given refuge, and this Bible was left behind by whoever it was who let him go.'

'You have proof of that,' said Jan Bloem, expressionlessly. He turned to smile at his mother, who was relighting her pipe with a great deal of puffing and sucking and waving of matches.

'What proof do I require?' Stafford Parker demanded. 'Here is the Bible. The Bible is proof in itself.'

'It may have been dropped on another occasion,' Jan Bloem suggested. 'It may have been stolen from its owner, and dropped there as a deliberate red-herring.'

'I don't care for your mission-school English,' growled Stafford Parker. 'And I don't care for your excuses, either. It says in the flyleaf of this Bible that it belongs to Piet Steyn, and Piet Steyn, as everybody in Griqualand is quite aware, is a second cousin of yours. So if the convicted man is anywhere at all, he is here, with you, and with your mother, and all the rest of your cronies.'

'And what if he is?' asked Jan Bloem.

Stafford Parker stared at him with a grim, set, colonial

expression. 'If he is here, my good Mr Bloem, then I shall have the right to cause you more trouble than you have ever had to cope with before. I shall have the right to arrest you personally, and your second cousin, and everybody else in this encampment who has given the fugitive any assistance.'

Barney came forward now, and rested his hand on the cresting-rail of Mrs Bloem's chair. The old woman looked up at him curiously, with the face of a benign orang-utan, and nodded with every word he spoke, although she understood no English whatsoever.

'Your fugitive *is* here, Mr Parker,' he said. 'But he is under my care, not Mr Bloem's, and his release was entirely my responsibility. Nobody here is to blame.'

Stafford Parker turned and glared at Barney, and then said loudly, 'I know you. I know your face. I've met you before.'

'My name is Barney Blitz. We met at Gong Gong once. You called me a kike.'

'Aha,' said Stafford Parker brusquely, although Barney could tell that he was embarrassed.

Barney said, 'Your diamond-thief, as you call him, was not far away from death. I rescued him as an act of humanity. I also rescued him because I want to challenge your sentence against him – properly and fairly, in a court of law, and in front of a jury of twelve men.'

'That's absurd,' retorted Stafford Parker, waving his hand dismissively. 'He's already been convicted. His sentence has already been passed. If everybody challenged every sentence I handed down, this place would be chaos.'

'We should arrest you too, you know,' put in the blue-chinned magistrate, in a sharp Lancashire accent.

'Yes, we should,' huffed Stafford Parker, although it was clear that he was not going to try it. The everyday needs of law and order in Kimberley were generally satisfied by the trial and punishment of murder, claim-jumping, and diamond smuggling, those three. Any other offences such as rape, or harbouring a fugitive, or public drunkenness, were usually too complicated and confusing to be worth pursuing.

'You can arrest me if you like,' Barney challenged. 'But that will only make your miscarriage of justice more serious. I have a lawyer who is willing to make representations on Mr Havemann's behalf, and I think for the sake of your own reputation you should pay us some heed.'

'A lawyer? What lawyer?'

'A lawyer of considerable reputation, and that's all I'm going to say.'

'You're bluffing,' said Stafford Parker. 'You're doing nothing more than playing for time, while Havemann recovers his strength. If I let you appeal, and set a date for a hearing, he'll be scuttling off to the border as soon as he's well enough.'

Barney reached into the pocket of his coat and took out the £212 which Harold Feinberg had paid him for his diamonds. He held the money up, and said, 'There are more than two hundred pounds here. You can keep them as a bond.'

Stafford Parker frowned, while his magistrate leaned forward and whispered something in his ear. Then Parker replied, 'If I take that money, who's to say that you didn't bribe me? And why should I hear an appeal anyway? If I agree to hear an appeal, that would only be admitting that I might have been wrong in the first place.'

'Perhaps you were, through no fault of your own,' said Barney. 'But could you bear to live for the rest of your life with the death of an innocent man on your hands, all because you were too stubborn to listen to an appeal?'

Stafford Parker conferred with his magistrate again. 'I want a good sound jury,' he said. 'No Griquas, or foreigners. And no Americans, either.'

'Very well,' agreed Barney.

Parker was silent for a moment, pouting, while he thought about Barney's suggestion. His magistrate waited with obvious unease. Eventually, he said. 'All right. If you really believe you have a case to be heard, I'll hear it.'

'Do you want the money?' asked Barney.

Stafford Parker shook his head. 'You can keep your bond. I'm a man of my word, and I hope for your sake that you are, too.' He raised one rigid finger. 'Because if you prove to be playing me false, Mr Blitz, I'll have my dogs on you, and my dogs will chase you through thick and thin, through every part of this colony, just to get at your miserable Jewish guts.'

'*Kishkehs*, we call them,' grinned Barney.

Stafford Parker, however, had already turned on his heel and started to march away up the hillside. Only his followers looked over their shoulders at Barney, and Jan Bloem, and the old orang-utan woman sitting amidst the tents in her red drawing-room chair.

Jan Bloem thrust his hands into the pockets of his black Sunday suit, and regarded Barney with interest.

'You're strong today,' he said, pointedly. 'How come you're suddenly so strong?'

Barney shrugged. 'Joel's my brother. I think I've found a purpose at last, a purpose that I didn't have before.'

'Are you in love with somebody?' asked Jan Bloem.

Mrs Bloem cackled, and spat tobacco-coloured saliva into the grass. Barney did not answer, but found it impossible to suppress a smile.

Jan Bloem turned his head and focused his eyes on Natalia Marneweck's tent. 'Rik Marneweck was a close, special friend to me,' he said. 'I swore to him when he died that I would watch out for his widow.'

'I won't hurt her,' said Barney.

Jan Bloem made a face. 'You can't make promises like that. Even Jesus didn't make promises like that.'

Late on Saturday evening, a boy came with a message that a re-trial had been set for Monday afternoon, at three o'clock, and that Stafford Parker had already selected a jury.

'He'll have chosen nothing but Protestant bigots,' protested Joel, sitting up in bed with a blue china bowl of *sosatie* that Mooi Klip had made for him. His eyes were circled with dark shadows, and he was still unshaven, but he was much brighter than before, and he was already talking about ways in which he and Barney could make their fortunes in Zanzibar, growing cloves, or in Madagascar.

'That's precisely what I'd hoped for,' said Barney. He glanced up at Joel and smiled.

'You'd *hoped* for Protestants? One of the most damning points Stafford Parker made against me in my first trial was that I was a Jew. A thief by heritage, he said. I'd tried to hide it, of course. You know what they're like around here. But one of the diggers remembered me from the ship I used to work on; and that was that. Being a Jew was almost enough to have me staked out on its own.'

'Nonetheless,' said Barney, quietly, 'I was hoping for a Protestant jury. They'll have a choice, you see, between believing the evidence of a kaffir, a mere black, and giving some credit to a white man, whether he's Jewish or not. What I'm trying to do here, quite frankly, is play a greater prejudice off against a lesser prejudice.'

Joel scooped up the last of his *sosatie* and set the bowl down beside his cot. 'I always thought you had a good head for business,' he told Barney. There was admiration in his voice, but also a slight seasoning of jealousy. 'Maybe I should have insisted that you came along with me from the start.'

'There was Mama,' said Barney.

Joel rubbed at his eyebrow with his fingertips, as if he were trying to erase a smut of persistent guilt. 'Yes,' he said. 'I hadn't forgotten.'

'You shouldn't blame yourself,' said Barney. 'It wasn't your fault any more than it was my fault.'

'Maybe it wasn't. But you still dreamed about her blood on your hands, didn't you? And *I* still dream about the way she looked that night I walked out on you.'

Mooi Klip came into the tent and picked up the lantern to lower the wick. 'Joel,' she admonished him, 'it's time you sleep.'

'Who needs a mother?' asked Joel, with an ironic smile. 'This girl tells me when to wake up, when to go to sleep, when to wash my teeth. She feeds me and bathes me and treats me like her own.'

Barney stood up. 'You'll be better tomorrow. And by Monday you'll be fighting fit. Fit enough to fight the Diggers' Association, anyway.'

'When are you seeing that lawyer friend of yours?'

'Tomorrow, after church.'

'Church? They let Jews into church?'

'Mr Barney they let into church. Mr Blitz they don't.'

Joel raked his fingers through the stubble of his beard. 'I

hope for your sake they don't find out. They'll kick your backside all the way to Capetown.'

Mooi Klip straightened Joel's blankets, and then joined Barney outside the tent. Barney took her hand, and drew her close to him. He kissed her, and she closed her eyes and kissed him in return, softly, quickly, as if she were tasting *moskonfyt* on his lips.

She said, 'In two days, we go back to Klipdrift.'

'Who's going back to Klipdrift?'

'Jan Bloem, his mother, all of us. He speaks already to the British, and the diggers. Now he goes home.'

Barney touched her cheek with his fingertips. 'And what will you do? Will you go back to Klipdrift along with him?'

'My family is there. My mother, my father, and my brothers.'

'I know. But will you go back?'

Mooi Klip lowered her head. 'Do you want me to?' she asked him.

Barney licked his lips in uncertainty. When he had taken Mooi Klip in the grass, when he had first made love to her, he had not thought for a single second about the complications of starting a liaison with a coloured girl. She was pretty, and she had a gentle way about her that fascinated him, and made him feel like holding her close and protecting her. But this was Cape Colony, and she was a half-caste.

Mooi Klip whispered, 'The Griquas say that anything you know in your heart in the first minute you meet – that knowing will stay good for a whole lifetime.'

Barney looked at her, and then smiled. 'I know. That was one of the little mottoes that Jan Bloem gave me when he realised we were lovers – that, and a few paragraphs out of the Bible.'

'But something is wrong? You smile, but your eyes look hurting.'

She was right. Barney was already feeling pain. It was close to the pain that he had felt for his mother; and to the pain he still felt whenever he renounced his Jewishness; but this time it was more stifling, like the first pangs of a heart seizure. And, in a way, that was exactly what it was.

No matter how delicate and erotic Mooi Klip was, no matter how fine a wife she would make, she was a Griqua, and if he were to marry her, or even have her living in, then he knew that he would be sacrificing any chances he might ever have of making a name and a fortune for himself in Cape Colony business. He had already meet three or four of those unhappy men who had married or shacked up with blacks, and they were invariably disillusioned, defeated, and scraping their living from the fringes of white society. Storekeepers, grooms, or servants. White, but not socially acceptable.

If Barney could court and marry a girl like Agnes Knight, however, and make a friend of her father, then his future would start to look far more promising. A girl like Agnes would give him immediate credentials. It did not matter what legal trickery her father had been involved in when he was practising in Capetown; here in Kimberley he was white, well-spoken, and the billiards secretary of the Kimberley Club. Barney was smitten by Mooi Klip, but he had not been blinded to the fierce reality of Cape Colony's social stratification. Mooi Klip could only bring him poverty and humiliation; Agnes Knight could bring him wealth.

Barney had his mother's passion, but his father's sanity. In him, his parents' differences would rail against each other in perpetuity, even though both of them were dead.

'I shall go, then,' said Mooi Klip, in response to Barney's silence.

'I think I love you,' Barney told her.

'No,' she said.

'Listen – we've only been together for a couple of days,' said Barney. 'It's too sudden for you to ask me to take you along. I don't live a particularly easy life. And now I've got Joel to take care of, too – at least until we've sorted out his legal problems.'

Mooi Klip touched a finger to his lips, indicating that he should not say anything more. But he held her finger in his fist, and moved it away.

'Those aren't excuses. I don't need to make excuses for anything. What I'm trying to tell you is that I think I love you, but I have other things to do. When they're done, I'll come to Klipdrift and find you.'

She searched his face for reassurance that he was telling her the truth. Her eyes were myopic with tears.

'Don't tell me you love me if you don't,' she said. 'I only give myself in all my life to three men. One, a young lover. Then my husband. And now you. You look beautiful when I first see you. Now, I love you – more than you love me. Don't play with me. Don't tell me you love me if you don't.'

'Natalia ...'

'Mooi Klip.'

Barney held her tight. He lifted his head towards the clouds. 'Mooi Klip,' he repeated, in his gentlest voice. 'I love you, and one day soon I'm going to come to Klipdrift and find you.'

His destiny was shaping itself. He felt as if great and shadowy forces were moving themselves into place, in preparation for his future. And the dreams he had dreamed when he was crossing the Great Karoo began to solidify, and take on flesh.

Kimberley's Anglican church was a little white-painted building of dry timber and corrugated iron at the end of the main street, conveniently located for those who liked to pray for forgiveness as soon as possible after committing their sins right next door to Aunt Olive's Pleasure House, and opposite the Kimberley Bar.

On Sunday mornings, the white Christian élite of the diamond-digging community would assemble in the dusty churchyard in their finest clothes, to parade themselves, and exchange dignified words of greeting to each other, and re-assure themselves that God, and England, were both on their side. Although they rarely admitted it, not to themselves and especially not to the Germans and the Boers and the coloureds, it was often difficult out here amongst the flies and sicknesses of a Cape Colony summer to remember that the chapel bells were still pealing across the frost-silvered lawns of Oxford, and that crumpets were still being toasted in front of a hundred thousand British coal fires.

Barney, nervous, arrived early. He stood by the picket fence in his best black suit and a clean dinner shirt which he had borrowed from a reluctant Harold Feinberg. The single church bell was clanking dolefully across the street, and huge cumulus clouds were already mounting the morning sky like castles of thickened cream. It was hot, and Barney felt as if his coat were too tight under the arms.

At last, promenading along the boardwalk at the exact moment which Mr Knight had judged would be late enough to turn everybody's heads and yet not too late to be considered vulgar, came Agnes and Faith, both in severe but well-styled Sunday dresses, followed by Mr and Mrs Knight, arm in arm, with benign and superior smiles.

Barney took off his hat as the two girls entered the churchyard.

'Good morning,' he said, with a small bow. 'You both look charming.'

Mr Knight imperiously turned his head this way and that, to make sure that everybody had an opportunity to notice that he had arrived, and that he had clipped his whiskers. Mrs Knight's smile came in and out like the sun behind the clouds, whenever she remembered where she was, and what her firm instructions were.

'Not such a good turnout this morning,' remarked Mr Knight. 'Where are the Maymans? Bad form, you know, not turning out for communion. It's the one thing that keeps us together, keeps us civilised.'

'I guess you're right,' said Barney. 'Listen, I've seen my Jewish friend again. The one whose case I want you take?'

'Later, dear chap, later,' Mr Knight told him, with a dismissive wave. 'I'm not so sure it's the kind of case I want to have anything to do with.'

'Stafford Parker's agreed to a re-trial, tomorrow afternoon. He's picking a jury.'

'Is he now?' said Mr Knight, suddenly interested. 'Well, that should be an event-and-a-half.'

'That's what I thought,' said Barney, coaxingly. 'And if you were to defend my friend, and win ... well, then, think what a legal feather in your cap that would be. They'd report it in all the newspapers, and it would probably be heard of in London.'

'Ah, London ...' mused Mr Knight, lifting his chin at the

very thought of it. 'Well, my dear fellow, we'll see. Come back to the house after church, and we'll talk it over. It doesn't allow us much time, though, does it? Monday afternoon.'

'It won't be a case of evidence and fact,' Barney told him. 'It'll be a case of prejudice and fear. That's what you're good at, though, aren't you?'

Mr Knight gave a tight grimace. 'It is one of my specialties, yes, I suppose.'

Faith, impatient to take Barney's arm, said, 'Shall we go in, Papa?' Agnes, who was obviously sulking, stood a few feet away in the shade of a scraggly thornbush, her grey reticule twisted in her hands as if she were surreptitiously choking a chicken. Barney took Faith's arm, and then drew her across to where Agnes was standing, and held out his hand for Agnes's arm as well.

'Neither of you will object if I escort you *both* into church, will you?' he grinned.

Faith stiffened. Barney could feel her arm, which at first had wrapped around his so responsively, become as rigid as a wooden Indian's. But Agnes came forward, all smiles and little curtseys, and whispered, 'Obliged, Mr Barney. Obliged.'

As the last leaden clank of the church bell summoned them inside, the congregation crowded in through the door and took their places on their allotted pews. Inside the church, it was as hot and airless as a Dutch oven. There was an altar, spread with a crochet tablecloth, in front of which stood the Anglican priest, a pimply young curate from Wimbledon who had felt the call to undertake missionary work after a sad and sorry courtship. Beside him at an upright piano sat an elderly English woman with spectacles and a feathery hat.

The pews themselves were fine – solid carved mahogany from St David's in Capetown – dragged across the desert by ox-cart. The Knights sat close to the front, amongst the more illustrious members of the Kimberley Club, and two or three of the richer English prospectors. Between them, they gave off a powerful smell of lavenderwater and mothballs. Barney wedged himself in between Agnes and Faith and hoped that God would forgive him for worshipping Him in such surroundings, and in such unfamiliar words.

They sang hymns – and Barney had never in his life before heard such ragged, mournful singing. Mr Knight was in strong voice, and his quavering baritone held on to the last note of every verse long after the rest of the congregation had fallen silent. Then, they took communion, and like the rest of the assembly Barney shuffled forward to kneel before the altar and partake of the body and blood of Jesus Christ.

He closed his eyes as the communion wafer dissolved on his tongue, but there was no earthquake, nor was his brain vaporised inside his skull. He returned to his seat, and Agnes for one moment laid her small white-gloved hand on his thigh, and smiled to herself.

After communion, the young curate stood before the lectern and gave, in an odd barking voice, like an outraged chow, a mercifully short sermon about the price of redemption. As Barney sat with his leg pressed close to the warmth of Agnes's thigh, some of the words came through to him like an accusation.

'We all know the sad history of man's sin, and its penalty. Sin and death were somehow bound up with each other. It was said of the forbidden fruit, "In the day that thou eatest thereof thou shalt surely die." Man did eat thereof. God loved him still; and yet God was perfectly just, and therefore He must keep to His word, and exact and due penalty!'

Agnes, in her pale grey dress, with its tiny lace collar and its grey silk sash, kept her eyes on her hymnbook. Faith bustled around in her seat as if she were sitting on nettles, and came out from time to time with small explosive sighs. Only Mr Knight's attention was fixed exclusively on the sermon; or at least it appeared to be. Perhaps he was considering his own sins, as well as the sins of the people he had defended. Perhaps he was simply criticising the young curate's staccato delivery.

Back in the sunshine, and the dust, Mr Knight tugged on his gloves and said, 'Sin? You wonder what a raw carrot of a curate can possibly know about sin,' and that was all. He took his wife's bewildered arm and led her out of the churchyard and back along the street. Barney, with Faith huffing alone on one side of him, and Agnes pressing close to him on the other, followed a few yards behind.

At home, over glasses of paralysingly dry sherry, Mr Knight invited Barney to tell him more about Joel's offence, and what had happened out at Jan Bloem's camp. In the end, Mr Knight tented his fingers in front of his face, so that Barney could only see one of his eyes, and regarded him very thoughtfully.

'Jewish, you say, this Havemann? And not called Havemann at all, but Blitz? Well, we'd better keep that quiet. Juries don't care much for aliases. If a man has an alias, it means he has something to hide, and that in itself is an admission of guilt. Not the guilt in question, perhaps; but you know how illogical people can be. Especially diggers. If they were logical, they wouldn't be out here scrabbling in the dirt for diamonds.'

Barney took a sip of his sherry and then set the glass back on the rickety wine table beside him. 'Do you think you can get him off, that's the question?'

'He admits that he actually stole the diamonds, you say?'

Barney nodded.

'Well, of course, he mustn't admit that before a jury,' said Mr Knight. 'In fact, he must be outraged that anyone could suggest such a thing. He must be bursting with righteous indignation. He must look his accusers in the eye and tell them they're liars. But on no account must he call them *Gentile* liars; and on no account must he use any Yiddish expression which might remind the jury that he is a Jew. He must talk of the kaffirs as unreliable mongrels, and the whites as equals. Well – *nearly* equals. He must show that he knows his place in the world, too. He must conduct himself with the manner of, say, a wrongfully accused moneylender.'

Barney looked up. Agnes was coming into the room with a tray of cutlery, ready to lay the table for Sunday lunch. There was an unpleasant smell of boiling vegetables coming from the kitchen. Agnes polished the soup spoons on her apron, and pretended to admire herself in their curved reflections. Barney found himself thinking of her pale thighs, and whether the curls beneath her petticoats were blonde or brown. She was a tease, Agnes, and she stirred him.

'What do you think of that, then?' asked Mr Knight.

'I'm sorry – what do I think of what?' Barney flustered.

'What do you think of declaring a mis-trial on the grounds that nobody can produce any evidence? Nobody white, that is, or even coloured. You could find out for me, if you would, if any of Mr Havemann's accusers are converts to Christianity. Better if they're not. Better if they believe in Unkulunkulu, or Mdali. That's the odd question, of course. Is it possible to save a kaffir's soul if he doesn't have one? Does he acquire a soul, once he's been converted? Very interesting argument altogether. So what do you say, old chap?'

'It sounds fine to me,' said Barney, watching Agnes prancing out of the room.

'Good,' said Mr Knight, and stood up. 'I think we're going to pull this one off, by a short margin. It won't be easy, but I think we're going to pull it off. Oh – and one thing more. I've arranged for you to come round to the club on Wednesday evening, so that you can see what you think of it. See what the members think of you, too. Some of them don't like your Yankees, I'll admit, but you may be lucky.'

'I shall look forward to it,' said Barney.

'Course you will,' nodded Mr Knight. 'And there's something else, too. I can't help noticing that you and Agnes seem to get along rather well.'

Barney felt himself flush. 'We . . . well, I believe we like each other.'

'Good. I'm pleased. There's precious little a girl of Agnes's age can do, out in a God-deserted place like this. I'd be pleased to see her courted by a reasonable chap like yourself. Why don't you come round after the trial tomorrow, and take some dinner? We can play some music, perhaps, and you two can get to know each other better.'

'I'd like that,' Barney assured him.

'Course you would. Now, I'm sorry I can't invite you to stay right now, but the Wilberforces are coming round. You know Kenneth Wilberforce, do you? Well, he's very dull, between you and me, but he's membership secretary, and I have to humour the silly ass from time to time.'

'Father,' said Faith, putting her head around the kitchen door and pointedly ignoring Barney. 'Mama asks if you're ready to carve the meat.'

167

Mr Knight clapped his hands together. 'Meat!' he exclaimed. 'Something for a man to sink his teeth into! I'll see you tomorrow morning, my dear chap, along with Mr Havemann, and we'll make ourselves ready for the trial. Meat! That's what it is, to a fellow like me. Meat and drink!'

Later that Sunday, Joel and Barney and Mooi Klip went for a short walk down the slope of the Griqua encampment. Joel limped along with the help of a roughtly-carved walking-stick which a cousin of Piet Steyn's had made for him. He had shaved, and dressed in a blue checked workshirt and canvas trousers; and although he was still in pain, and short of breath, he was plainly very much better.

They reached a small sandstone outcropping, where Joel eased himself down with his back against the rock, and Barney and Mooi Klip sat beside him.

'You wouldn't think such a beautiful country could turn out so goddamned hard, would you?' said Joel.

'It can be licked,' replied Barney. 'There's nothing on earth that can't be licked, if you tackle it the right way.'

'What have you been doing? Farming!' Joel retorted. 'You don't know what it's like when you're scrabbling in the dirt looking for diamonds. It's hell on earth.'

'I shall soon find out.'

'What are you talking about?'

Barney ran his hand through his brown curls. 'Tomorrow, after the trial, we're going to set up in business together, you and I. Blitz and Blitz, diamond diggers.'

'I shouldn't count on it.'

'Why not? You've got one of the best lawyers in Kimberley.'

'I'm a Jew, Barney, and I'm well known around here. You don't seriously think they're going to let me go? You don't seriously think that Stafford Parker's going to undermine his own prestige by reversing his decision?'

Barney nodded. 'I believe he will. In any case, you'd better hope that he will.'

'This is against my better judgement, you know,' said Joel. 'I should have made a run for Wesselstroom as soon as I was able to move one leg in front of the other.'

'You'll get off,' said Barney, confidently.

Joel looked out across the blue misted valley. 'If I do,' he said, 'then Blitz and Blitz it's going to be. Fifty-fifty, down the middle. Partners. But I don't believe for one single moment that I will.'

After half an hour, Barney and Mooi Klip helped Joel back to the tent. Then they went together to the tent of Mooi Klip's second cousin, who was spending the evening with Jan Bloem, singing hymns and carols and some of the old Hottentot songs from long ago.

Inside, the tent smelled of incense and cooking. There was a wide straw pallet, wrapped in blankets, and a large wicker hamper in which Mooi Klip's cousin carried her belongings. On the blue poplar tent support hung a sad framed portrait of Jesus, surrounded by His cherubim.

Barney stripped off his shirt, and pulled down his trousers. He was already erect with anticipation. Mooi Klip turned her back and unbuttoned her dress with modesty, silhouetted by the small storm lantern which her second cousin had left burning for them.

She stepped out of her dress, and turned. Her shy nakedness made Barney quiver. She was brown-skinned, heavy-breasted, and her stomach had a sensual roundness which reminded Barney of an old French painting he had once seen, as a boy, on a pushcart in New York.

He buried his fingers in her hair, and kissed her. He said, 'You know that I'll come back for you as soon as I can.'

'No,' she said. 'I don't know that. But tonight I do not want to think about it.'

They lay down on the straw pallet side by side and stared closely into each other's eyes, as though each were concealing a cosmic mystery somewhere behind the darkness of their pupils. Barney kissed Mooi Klip's shoulder and it tasted slightly salty and perfumey, and it was like no other taste he had ever come across before.

They made love with the slowness and rhythm of a brass clock, and there were moments when Barney seemed to forget where he was, and what was happening, as if he were sleeping and waking and sleeping again. He could not tell how much time passed. But he remembered opening his eyes again and again to see Mooi Klip with her eyes closed, or looking at him intently, or sleeping, and all the while the storm lantern flickered like a signal from a forgotten past.

Toward midnight, they reached together a peak of almost unbearable sexual intensity, a moment when Barney looked downwards at the curves of their bodies, and saw how deeply he was penetrating her. Then there was a stillness between them, an unquiet peace, that same feeling that all lovers know when their lovemaking is ended. Why did it have to end, and will we ever make love again?

The music from Jan Bloem's marquee abruptly ended. Barney raised himself on his elbow and looked down at Mooi Klip with love and pain and a little fear. He touched her face with his hand, and then he said, 'I guess I'd better go.'

They assembled in the open air, diggers and gamblers and whiskery dignitaries and whores, and for most of that afternoon the clattering and shovelling and shouting of De Beers New Rush was silenced. This was a serious matter: the re-trial of a convicted diamond thief. And whatever the outcome of it, whatever Stafford Parker finally decided, that decision would affect the diamond diggers for years to come.

It was a hot day, intensely still. The horizons rippled and shifted, and heat flowed off the corrugated-iron rooftops like clear syrup. Up above the gathering of diggers, in the cloudless sky, hawks circled and circled as if they were too idle to swoop down on their natural prey, and the moon hung over the western horizon, pale-faced and friendless, an uninvited reminder of the night to come.

A leather-topped desk had been dragged out into the dust for Stafford Parker and his magistrates, and two fumbling kaffirs had propped up over it a wonky canvas shade, with fringes. The body of the court was made up of fifty or sixty chairs, of all shapes and sizes – Windsor chairs, wheelbacks, ladderbacks, and riempie-thong chairs – and Joel and Barney and Mr Knight sat at the side of Stafford Parker's desk on a broken chapel pew. Joel had heavily bandanged his left leg on Mr Knight's specific instructions ('make it appear as if you have suffered enough already') and his stick was propped against the seat.

At two o'clock, everybody was gathered, and Stafford Parker took his place in a high-backed chair to hear Joel's appeal. He tucked his thumbs into the pockets of his light grey vest, and raised his chin so that his white beard was lifted like an oriole's tail, and said, 'This court of the Digger's Republic is now in session.'

There was a murmur throughout the crowd, and Stafford Parker banged a gavel on his desk in protest. 'Let us have order. The Diggers' Protection Association and the Diggers' Republic were founded on the notion of order. Let it prevail today.'

Stafford Parker's blue-chinned magistrate stood up, and said, 'We are considering today an appeal by Mr Joel Havemann, of Claim 172, here at Kimberley Mine, against his sentence last week of staking-out, which was occasioned by his conviction for diamond thieving. Mr Havemann was released from his staking-out by friends – quite illegally – but he is represented here today by Mr Knight – who assures us that Mr Havemann can justify his escape, and also that he can justify his crime.'

There was another flurry of argument and scuffling, and Stafford Parker beat at his desk as if he were trying to flatten a sheet of gold. 'I have decided that this case should be heard,' he cried out, in a strained voice, 'and heard it will be!'

Gradually, the assembly came to order. The jury, who were sitting opposite Joel and Barney on two more pews, were as noisy and disorderly as everybody else, and when Barney looked them over, he could see why. Stafford Parker may have been playing at judicial fairness by allowing Joel's appeal to be heard in public, but he certainly was not taking any chances on the outcome. The twelve good men and true were crimson-faced Anglo-Saxons, all of them – the ill-mannered graduates of some of England's less honoured public schools – the kind of men who became planters and traders and Crown Agents. If Barney had not actually been depending on a jury that was bigoted at heart and crass in intellect, he would have despaired. They sat on their benches as if they were posing for a school photograph – plump with drink, fat-thighed, and smug, and with as little experience of law or life as the First XI of some redbrick boys' academy in Leicester.

'Mr Knight,' said Stafford Parker, donnishly, 'perhaps you would like to make your representations on behalf of your client?'

Mr Knight turned to Barney, smiled like an acid-drop, then gathered his notes and stood up. This morning's briefing had not been particularly successful. Joel had admitted his guilt to Mr Knight straight away, almost aggressively, and when Mr Knight had tried to cajole him into believing that he might have been mistaken, and that the whole affair might have been, well, *imaginary*, old chap – the inevitable result of too much heat and too much cheap whiskey – Joel had called him a *shtunk*, which Mr Knight had not understood, not literally, but which had offended him deeply.

'A *shtunk*,' he had repeated, in his sharp British accent. 'A *shtunk*. So that's what you think of me.'

Barney had taken Joel aside and talked to him earnestly for five minutes, trying to convince him that Mr Knight was his only hope for his release, the only man who could help him to get his diamond claim back from the Diggers' Association, and eventually, grudgingly, Joel had agreed to co-operate. He had made it clear, though, that he did not particularly care for little brother meddling in his life. 'I'm a grown man, Barney. I can manage my own affairs. I got myself into this mess, I should be able to get myself out.'

'So it's your pride that's bothering you?' Barney had asked him.

'Maybe,' Joel had admitted. Then he had spat on the grass. Barney had never seen him spit before.

Now, Mr Knight stepped forward in front of Stafford Parker's desk, his hand tucked behind him so that his coat-tails stuck out like the black plumes of a cockerel. He paused for effect, just like he had in the Kimberley churchyard, and Barney could imagine him stepping in front of juries in England and Capetown with the same theatrical strut. In the High Court in London, his pose may not have seemed particularly original, or impressive; but out here, in front of a motley crowd of diamond diggers, it was magnificent.

'There appears before you now a man who was rescued from out of the very maw of death ... a man who had looked into the eyes of His Maker and then been snatched away. Joel Havemann, a Jew, admittedly – but a very honest and straight-forward member of his race, who was convicted by the Diggers' Republic of the theft of several diamonds from the Kimberley Mine. It was said that he bribed kaffirs of the British Diamond Mining Company to pass him stones that he might illegally sell to the shadier buyers who have gathered around the fringes of this rush ... it was said that his own claim was proving barren of diamonds, and that instead he was attempting to make a fortune out of stolen stones...

'But let me ask you these questions!' exclaimed Mr Knight, swivelling around on one heel, and raising a rigid finger. 'Let me ask you if any of you knew Joel Havemann to be rich, to be the kind of man who lavished money on himself and his friends as if it were water! Let me ask you if you knew of any act of dishonesty that Joel Havemann ever committed! Joel Havemann worked a claim, and any of you need only to walk out to that claim to see how deep Joel Havemann has dug, how much strenuous effort he has expended. Does a dishonest man ever bother to work at all? If he intended to make his living by stealing, by dealing with the IDB buyers, then why did he bother to lift a single finger to excavate his claim? Why didn't he just waylay the kaffirs of the British Diamond Company on their way back to their shelters, and relieve them of their ill-gotten diamonds then?'

Now Mr Knight let his chins settle in his collar, and he pouted with offended righteousness. 'Far be it from me to suggest that the British Diamond Mining Company had a covetous eye on Mr Havemann's claim, which was contiguous with theirs, and which barred their way to the acquisition of a whole block of claims. Far be it! And far be it from me to suggest that those kaffirs who gave evidence against my client at his so-called trial last week were guilty of distorting reality. Yet – if you examine a map of the claims on the Kimberley Mine – it does strike you, doesn't it, that Mr Havemann's claim could have been quite an irritation to the British Diamond Mining Company; and it does strike you, doesn't it, that if those

173

kaffirs who were said to have supplied Mr Havemann with diamonds could be bribed by Mr Havemann, then equally they could have been bribed by the British Diamond Mining Company to perjure themselves in the interests of the company's financial expansion.

'Money talks,' said Mr Knight, narrowing his eyes towards the jury. 'And the more money, the less truth.'

Barney, sitting back on his pew, could see that the jury were interested but not totally convinced. One or two of them had folded their arms and clenched their jaws as if to show that no amount of clever argument and cajolery could swerve them from their opinion that Jews were dishonest, and that Joel, being a Jew, was therefore a liar and a thief. It was nearly three o'clock now, and the heat was roaring away like a furnace. In the second and third rows of chairs, the ladies began to wave their fans as furiously as a gathering of clipped pigeons. Barney saw Agnes, and caught her eye, and Agnes smiled at him coyly from the shade of her parasol.

Mr Knight said, 'I am sure that a representative of the British Diamond Mining Company will shortly get to his feet and tell you that my suggestions are utterly unfounded; that the British Diamond Mining Company looked upon Mr Havemann as nothing more than an industrious neighbour, and that even if his claim were standing in their way, they would have accepted the economic and practical problems with equilibrium and stiff upper lips. This representative may not tell you that the British Diamond Mining Company was the first to enter an offer for claim No. 176 upon Mr Havemann's conviction last week – but then, we could not possibly expect him to, could we?'

There was an expostulation of protest from a gentleman in muttonchop sidewhiskers and a tall beige hat who was sitting on the opposite side of the court, but Stafford Parker rapped his gavel again, and the gentleman subsided, and contented himself with industriously wiping his hatband.

'I wish to say one thing more,' said Mr Knight, in a quiet but distinct voice. 'The evidence that was brought against my client was the evidence of kaffirs alone. Ignorant, uneducated, and bewildered servants of the British Diamond Mining Company. Now, when this court first made its decision to convict

Mr Havemann, it may understandably have been incensed with what it heard. It may have been in a mood of righteousness and vengeance, which – when you consider how vital the discovery of diamonds is to all of our livelihoods – can be seen to have been fully justified.

'However, because of his ignorance, because of his want of enlightenment, because he was born to be a servant and a subordinate, the kaffir cannot justifiably be held to be a human being ... not in the same Biblical sense as a white man. Does it not say in Psalm 49 that regardless of a man's honour, *if he understandeth not*, then he shall perish like the beasts. Well, the kaffir understandeth not, and therefore, sad for him, he can only be regarded as a beast. A good, obedient beast, maybe, but a beast all the same.

'And there is no court of law in the world, Mr Parker, and gentlemen – there is no court of law in the whole world which can rightly convict a man on the evidence of beasts.'

Mr Knight, with solemn windbaggery, quoted the precedent of the Polo Pony; and Barney could see that Stafford Parker was suitably impressed. Then Mr Knight sat down, and invited anyone in the court to cross-question his client 'to their heart's, and their curiosity's, contentment.'

But Stafford Parker stood up, and banged his gavel, and looked around the assembly with a stare that silenced everyone, and certainly forestalled any questioning.

'Mr Knight,' he said, 'has spoken most eloquently on his client's behalf. He has raised doubts about his client's guilt which, in my opinion, have made the imposition of a sentence of staking-out questionable, to say the least. He is right: your unconverted kaffir is not an intelligent being in the accepted sense of the words. And, therefore, although I am reversing my own decision, and publicly accepting that my earlier judgement may have been incorrect, I direct that this jury find the Jew Joel Havemann to be not guilty of diamond trafficking, and that his claim should be returned to him.'

There was a babbling uproar for a moment, but then Stafford Parker banged everybody into silence again.

'I must set one condition on Joel Havemann's release, however; and that is that he remains under the supervision of his lawyer, or of some other responsible person. Obviously, he strayed from the accepted code of behaviour. How seriously, I am not now prepared to say; or to condemn him for it. He has been sufficiently punished already. But I must require that he is supervised.'

Mr Knight bobbed up from his seat, and said, 'I regret that Mr Havemann is no more than a client of mine, Mr Parker. I don't really think that I can accept responsibility for his future behaviour.'

'Is there anyone who can?' asked Stafford Parker.

Barney hesitated. He had been trying to avoid Stafford Parker's eye since the trial had begun, since Stafford Parker knew him for a Jew. Now, if he stood up and accepted responsibility for his brother, Mr Knight would know him for a Jew, too. And if Mr Knight knew him for a Jew, that would mean the finish of his courtship of Agnes, and the finish of his chances at the Kimberley Club.

'If nobody will vouch for Mr Havemann's future, I can always change my mind,' said Stafford Parker. 'I can always have him flogged, and his claim confiscated.'

Barney raised his eyes. Stafford Parker was smiling straight at him, and now Barney realised what the price of Joel's freedom was going to be. Stafford Parker had not become president of the Diggers' Republic through pomposity or blindness. He had known who Joel was, and why Barney had released him, and now he was demanding that Barney should stand up in front of everybody in Kimberley and declare that he was a Jew.

In the fifth or sixth row, Barney could see Harold Feinberg, in his sun-helmet, and Harold was deliberately looking elsewhere. Maybe Harold had always been right. Maybe he should never have renounced his faith, and his heritage. Maybe the essence of being Jewish was that your destiny was inescapable.

Then, unexpectedly, at the very edge of the crowd, Barney caught sight of Mooi Klip. She was dressed in red, with a red plumed hat, and she was standing next to one of her Griqua cousins, a tall and serious half-caste in a dark funeral suit, and a black floppy necktie. She did not wave to Barney, or give any indication that she had seen him, but appeared to be waiting with great patience for the outcome of the trial.

Barney raised his hand, and then stood up. 'I will vouch for Mr Havemann,' he said.

'I can't hear you,' replied Stafford Parker. 'You'll have to speak up a little.'

'I said, I will vouch for Mr Havemann.'

'You? And who are you? Will you introduce yourself to this court?'

'You know who I am, Mr Parker. We met at Gong Gong.'

'Ah, yes,' said Stafford Parker, 'but this *court* didn't meet you at Gong Gong. Only myself, in my personal capacity.'

Barney took a breath. The sweat was clinging in his eyebrows and running down the back of his shirt. All around him was a confusion of bright pink faces and staring eyes, like a bucket of freshly-caught shrimps. 'I come from Oranjerivier, where I work a dairy farm. Dairy and beef, that is. I've known Mr Havemann for some years. In fact, I knew him in the United States, before either of us came out to the Cape.'

'Aha,' said Stafford Parker. 'So you're fellow Americans?'

'Correct, sir.'

'Do you know anything of Mr Havemann's business reputation in the United States? Was he fair? Honest, was he?'

'Oh yes, sir,' said Barney, wiping sweat away from his mouth.

'And how about his personal life. Reputable, was he? And religious?'

'Very devout, Mr Parker.'

'Well, I accept your opinion,' said Stafford Parker, 'and I'm sure that you'd make a most reliable watchdog. But what guarantee does the court have that you would maintain a continuing interest in Mr Havemann? Can we be sure that you would be willing to maintain your duties as keeper for any reasonable length of time?'

'You have my word,' said Barney, simply.

'Aha,' said Stafford Parker. 'Your word.'

'You don't trust my word?'

'I have no reason not to trust it. On the other hand, I have no reason to trust it, either. There are plenty of men in Kimberley who live their lives very fast and loose.'

'You're trying to corner me, Mr Parker,' said Barney.

Stafford Parker tugged at his beard in satisfaction. 'I'm simply trying to establish your credentials, Mr –'

There was a pause, as suspenseful and heavy in the afternoon heat as a glob of honey on the brink of dripping from a honeycomb. Everybody turned to Barney, including Mr Knight, and waited for him to finish Stafford Parker's sentence for him.

Barney closed his eyes. The salt perspiration stung the pupils, like tears. Then he opened them again, and said, 'Blitz. My real name is Blitz. Mr Havemann's real name is Blitz, also. We are brothers. That, I would have thought, would be enough to quell any doubts about my continuing interest in his welfare.'

There was another burble of conversation, but Stafford Parker quickly brought the court to order.

'Well, then,' he said, 'I believe that I'm happy that Mr Havemann, or Mr Blitz, as we now know him to be, cannot be proved guilty of illicit dealing in diamonds. And I am also happy that he will be supervised in his future prospecting by a close and interested relative of the same religious and ethnological strain. Mr foreman, does the jury have any other opinion on the matter?'

A tall blond Englishman with a noticeable speech impediment stood up and said, 'We, we, we, we're happy to abide by that decision, Mr Parker. We, we, we, we thank Mr Knight for his excellent appeal.'

Stafford Parker walloped his gavel one more time. 'This court is dismissed. Thank you, gentlemen.'

Joel shook Barney by the hand. His face was glittering with sweat. 'My God, Barney, you've actually done it. And you, Mr Knight, thank you. I don't know what I can say.'

Mr Knight stood straight, and replaced his hat on his head with exaggerated care. 'It appears that the result of the appeal was a foregone conclusion,' he said, coldly. 'Mr Parker seemed already to have made up his mind.'

'I don't think so,' said Barney. 'He was very impressed by what you said.'

Mr Knight stared at Barney with disdain. 'I regret that I can't say that the admiration is mutual.'

'Mr Knight –' began Barney, but Mr Knight lifted a hand to silence him.

'I can understand why you deceived me,' he snapped. 'You are a Jew, and I am quite aware that many Jews feel envy and frustration which leads them to attempt to break into Christian society. But, the facts remain that you lied to me; that you made improper advances to my daughters while leading them to believe that you were eligible; and that you are a Jew. I do not mix with Jews, my family do not mix with Jews, and I can assure you here and now that there will never ever be a Jewish member of the Kimberley Club.'

Barney said, 'Agnes is fond of me. You can't deny that.'

'You can be fond of a dog until it bites you,' retorted Mr Knight.

'I would like to continue courting her,' Barney insisted.

Mr Knight pulled a sour face. 'It's quite out of the question. Courting? What on earth is the point?'

'Don't you think love is the point?'

'Love? Piffle! Agnes doesn't love you. And neither do you love Agnes. In any case, I forbid it. Now – I must go. I think I've made quite enough of an ass of myself for one day, without compounding the embarrassment.'

'Your fee?' Barney shouted at him, furious, as Mr Knight stalked off.

Without turning round, Mr Knight waved his hand dismissively. 'I want no fee. What I have had to endure from you this afternoon cannot be paid for. Not in money.'

'But you've won!'

Mr Knight stopped, and then walked back a few paces. 'I haven't won, you ninny. Stafford Parker has won. At my expense, and especially at yours.'

Barney watched Mr Knight take Agnes's arm, and tug her away from the court at a brisk march. Agnes did not turn around even once to look at Barney, and there was something about the way in which she held her head that communicated disdain, and rejection. Agnes had rubbed thighs under the dining-table with a Jew; she was not likely to be quick in forgiving herself, nor him.

At last, there was nothing but a disarray of chairs, and a

collapsed awning, and a few kaffirs sweeping up. Barney stood in the descending light of the sun, and took off his hat.

'I'm sorry,' said Joel.

'Hm,' said Barney, shaking his head. 'You've no need to be. It was my choice, to tell them that you were my brother. I'm proud of you, Joel, we'll make our fortune together, in spite of these Christians.'

From the other side of the court, walking slowly and demurely in her red dress, her hands clasped together, came Mooi Klip. She stood a little way away from Barney, her face concealed by the shadow of her hat, and waited.

'Mooi Klip,' said Barney, so quietly that she could scarcely hear him.

She came to him slowly, her hands still clasped in front of her, and then stood in front of him with tears running down her cheeks.

'I understand now,' she said, with such sympathy that Barney had to raise his eyes away from her, up to the blue and empty sky. 'I understand now everything. I'm sorry.'

Barney spent two more days in Kimberley after Joel's acquittal. Then, while Joel re-registered his claim as a fifty-fifty partnership, and cleared the site ready for further digging, Barney took Donald and Mooi Klip back down to Oranjerivier, to deliver Monsaraz his money and tell him that he was quitting Derdeheuwel for good.

There were heavy electric storms in the sky when they drove in their surrey along the banks of the Orange River, and the bush grass rippled like a fractious sea. At last they reached the avenue of poplars which led up to the farm, and Donald relaxed his hold on the reins so that the horses could trot home at their own pace.

'I feel bad things,' said Donald, as they reached the courtyard. Barney stepped down from the surrey and stretched himself, and he had to agree. The farm looked as broken-down and deserted as the first day he and Donald and Simon de Koker had driven up here. There were no horses in the stables; the krall gate was hanging loose; and it looked as if part of the feed store had been damaged by fire.

'I feel ghost,' said Mooi Klip anxiously, staying where she was on the seat of the surrey. She wore a grey travelling-coat, and a feathered hat which Barney had bought her in Kimberley, at Madame Francesca's. Strangely, she looked duskier and more Hottentot when she dressed in very severe European clothes.

Donald led the horses to a hitching-rail beside the stable, and then walked with Barney towards the house. The front door was hanging open, and the screen was lying flat on the boards of the verandah.

'Where are the kaffirs?' Barney wanted to know. 'Where's Adam Hoovstraten?'

Donald inserted two fingers in his mouth and let out a weird, carrying whistle. He waited for a while, but there was no reply. Beyond the farm buildings, on the curve of the nearby hills, the trees stood as if they had been planted on the very brink of the world. Barney said, 'Maybe Monsaraz decided to quit.'

Cautiously, Barney stepped up on to the verandah, and peered in at the front door. Dust and straw had blown into the hallway, and there were dozens of empty wine bottles lying on the carpet. 'Monsaraz?' he called. His voice sounded as flat as somebody calling into a linen cupboard.

With Donald a few steps behind him, he walked along the corridor as far as Monsaraz's bedroom. It was then that the smell first reached him; the stomach-turning odour of death, and it was all that he could do to stay where he was, and not retreat from the farmhouse as fast as possible.

'You smell that?' he asked Donald.

Donald, grey-faced, gave a nod of sickened assent.

Picking up a walking-cane from the floor, Barney pushed the door of Monsaraz's bedroom open a little wider. He did not need to go inside to see what had happened: the blinds that Monsaraz had usually kept drawn tight had been broken away from the window-frame, so that a geometric pattern of daylight fell across the bed.

Monsaraz had been hacked to pieces where he lay. There was blackened blood halfway up the wall behind the bed, and his white bearded face had fallen back at a ridiculous angle from his chest, where his assailant had half-severed his neck. His white suit was stiff with dried gore, and his waistcoat had been slit open so that he could be spectacularly disembowelled. He had been castrated, too – probably first, before any of the other injuries, so that the rutting dog of Derdeheuwel should suffer the greatest agony of all.

'Jealous husband,' remarked Donald, laconically. 'I tell him two or three times to take care.'

'My God,' whispered Barney.

They went outside again, into the breeze. Barney felt as unsteady as if he had been drinking. He grasped the verandah rail for support, and from the seat of the surrey Mooi Klip frowned at him in anxiety.

He walked across the yard. 'He's dead. Murdered. Somebody's cut him into pieces.'

Mooi Klip stared. 'What will you do?'

'I don't know what I can do. I don't know who his relatives are, or anything. I don't even know where he kept his money.'

'But the farm ... is the farm yours now?'

'I'm not sure. We're going to have to go through his papers to see if he left a will.'

Donald came over, stripping off his coat and then rolling up the sleeves of his shirt. 'I will bury him,' he said, firmly.

'You're sure? I don't know whether I could even go back in the house.'

'I was a guide, remember, Mr Blitz. Many times travellers die, and I bury them. I see worse.'

While Donald dragged Monsaraz's remains out of the bedroom, wrapped up in a brown blanket, Barney and Mooi Klip went into the drawing-room where Monsaraz had kept his disorderly array of papers and bills. Mooi Klip picked up a picture of a pretty French actress, torn roughly from a magazine, and said, 'This Monsaraz was lonely?'

'He had plenty of women – but, yes, I guess you could say he was lonely, *alav ha-sholom*.'

They were both silent as they heard the soft bumping sound of Monsaraz's bare feet being pulled along the corridor outside. Then Barney said, 'Why don't you make us some tea? The kitchen's through there.'

He sat down at Monsaraz's desk and began to sort out some of the documents. There were scores of credit and debit notes from the Credit Bank of La Coruna, as well as a heap of scrawly letters and half-finished diary entries in Portuguese. There were some dog-eared copies of a German illustrated magazine showing buxom Black Forest maidens with plaited hair, copulating with donkeys; and a small black book with a silk moiré cover which was thicketed with accounts.

Mooi Klip came back into the room just as Barney was trying to tug open the bottom left-hand drawer, which seemed to be jammed with waste paper. She said, 'Barney,' in a voice which made him look up straight away. Her hand was pressed over her mouth and her eyes were watering as if she felt sick.

She sat down shakily on the dusty sofa while Barney went into the kitchen. She had left three cups and a teapot on the table, and a tipped-over caddy of Lapsang Souchong. Barney looked around, frowning, unable to make out at first what it was that had upset her. Then he peered into the shadows of the scullery, and saw the bloody handle of a machete protruding from the sink.

He walked across the kitchen, quickly at first, but then he slowed, and stopped. Apart from the machete, the sink contained the sloppy remains of Monsaraz's genitals.

Barney went back into the drawing-room. 'I'm sorry,' he told Mooi Klip, tightly. 'I didn't know. I'm really sorry. Do you want a drink? There's bound to be some whiskey around.'

Mooi Klip shook her head. 'I feel better now. It was a shock. I don't know what it is till I look close.'

Outside, they could hear the echoing sound of a pick, as Donald dug a grave for Monsaraz in the hard-baked soil. Barney sat down again, and pulled at the bottom drawer of the desk as hard as he could. At last, with a ripping of paper, it came open, and banged on to the threadbare rug.

'My God,' said Barney, picking up crumpled handfuls of paper.

'What is it?' asked Mooi Klip. 'Is it money?'

'Is it money? British five-pound notes, hundreds of them! Just stuffed into this desk like rubbish. There must be thousands of pounds in here!'

Mooi Klip came over and stood beside him, resting a hand on his shoulder. 'You're rich, then,' she said.

Barney burrowed through the drawer, digging out more and more money. He held some of the notes up to the window, and as far as he could see they all bore watermarks from the Royal Mint, and they were all genuine.

'There must be nine or ten thousand pounds here. Maybe more. It's unbelievable.'

'What will you do with it?' asked Mooi Klip.

Barney smoothed one of the crumpled notes on his knee. He thought for a moment, and then he lowered his head. 'Nothing,' he said. 'It isn't mine.'

'But it *is* yours! Whose can it be, if it isn't yours? Monsaraz is dead!'

'Monsaraz stole it in the first place, or embezzled it. It didn't belong to him any more than it belongs to me. Why do you think a bright young man like that was rotting away in Oranjerivier? He was hiding from the people he robbed.'

'But who will ever know?' asked Mooi Klip. 'Nobody knows this money is here. If they did, they would come to take it. But even the man who killed Monsaraz did not take it.'

Barney let the smoothed-out note flutter down on to the rest of the heap. 'The man who killed Monsaraz was nothing more than a jealous kaffir. And kaffirs aren't even human, remember? The poor man had probably never seen a five-pound note in his whole life before. Apart from that – I expect he ran off as soon as he'd done what he came to do. He wanted blood, not money.'

Mooi Klip frowned. 'You will leave the money here, for somebody else?'

Barney reached up and touched her hand. 'I've found something out this week,' he told her. 'I've found out that it's no use pretending that I'm anything else but a Jew.'

She shook her head. 'I don't understand you.'

'I don't understand myself. When I was crossing the Great Karoo, on my way here to Oranjerivier, I made up my mind that I was going to put my religion behind me. I didn't think my beliefs were enough to help me survive in this place. I didn't think the rabbis in New York could possibly know what it was like to think of making your fortune in a country as wild as this one.'

He nudged the drawerful of five-pound notes with his foot. 'I didn't think, either, that anyone could get rich here unless they were a Gentile. How could I make friends with men like Stafford Parker, being a Jew? How could I become a member of the Kimberley Club? How could I court a girl like Agnes Knight?'

Mooi Klip caressed his fingers. She said nothing.

'Well, pretending to be a Gentile doesn't work,' said Barney. 'There isn't any disguise that can hide the fact that you're a Jew. Not masks, not names, not lies. So all I can do now is make the most of it. Make *more* than the most of it. All I can do is make sure that I'm the richest Jew in the colony.'

'But what about the money?' asked Mooi Klip.

Barney sighed. 'I've probably gone too far away from God to make my way back,' he said, 'but this is as far as I go.'

Mooi Klip waited outside while Barney finished going through Monsaraz's desk. At last, at the very bottom of one of the drawers, Barney found the deeds to Derdeheuwel farm and its surrounding acres. He tucked the deeds into his coat, dusted his hands off, and came out to join Mooi Klip and Donald in the courtyard.

'I've found the deeds,' he told them. 'After everything I've done here, I think I'm entitled to keep the farm. I'll rent it out, most likely.'

Donald said, 'If you're willing to wait for your first six months' rent, Mr Blitz, I'll rent it from you. If I can find Adam Hoovstraten again, he and me could work this place well.'

'You mean you want to stay?'

Donald gave a wide, ugly grin. 'I think it's time I stopped all this travelling, Mr Blitz. Travelling makes the soul restless. And I've got some good sisters in Oranjerivier.'

'Make sure they don't have jealous husbands.'

Donald turned around. 'I've laid Mr Monsaraz to rest in back of the kraal, Mr Blitz. You want to say a prayer?'

Barney shook his head. 'Just go bring that drawerful of paper money out of the drawing-room, carry it out here.'

Donald glanced at Mooi Klip. 'Whatever you say, Mr Blitz.'

Together, Barney and Mooi Klip walked slowly around to Monsaraz's grave – a narrow mound of dry earth, with neither cross nor marker to show that the son of Sgr and Sgra Monsaraz had been laid to rest here after a life of fear and misery and drink. Barney took off his hat and stood beside it, while Mooi Klip murmured a short mission-school prayer.

At last, Donald came out with the desk drawer. Five-pound notes fluttered in the wind, and some of them were tumbled away across the farmyard. He set it down at the head of the grave, and then stood back.

Barney knelt down, took out his matches, and struck one. The thin paper money caught alight straight away, and in a few moments the whole drawerful was blazing. One by one, the five-pound notes curled up and charred, and their fiery ashes were carried away on the breeze.

'Let's hope he rests now,' said Barney quietly; and without waiting for Mooi Klip, he walked slowly back to the surrey.

Barney still had the £212 which Harold Feinberg had given him for his diamonds, however, and that money he kept. When he and Mooi Klip arrived back in Kimberley, he spent almost all of it on a two-bedroom wooden shack not far away from the mine, on the eastern side of main street, and on picks and shovels and winching gear, which he bought from the Kimberley Mining Equipment Company. He had seen how deep some of the claims had already been dug, and he reckoned that within four or five weeks, he and Joel were going to have to wind the yellow soil out of their diggings with a rope and a bucket.

He employed six new kaffir labourers, and guaranteed to pay them bonuses for every diamond they found over five karats. They were an odd collection, the kaffirs. One of them had only one hand, but he could flick the handle of his shovel with his stump of a wrist so that each load of dirt landed precisely in his barrow, ten feet away. Another sang all day, in an octave of only five barely distinguishable tones, and on hot afternoons the sound of his droning voice drove Barney almost mad. The leader of the kaffir working-party was the smallest of all of them – a smiling, energetic imp whom Joel called his *shmeck tabac*, his little pinch of snuff.

Harold Feinberg came out to Claim 172 a week after Barney

and Joel had started digging together. He sat on an upturned wheel barrow and gave himself a thorough mopping with a white handkerchief.

'How's it going?' Harold asked, loudly, above the monotonous singing of the kaffir.

Barney, dressed in a loose sweat-stained shirt, baggy trousers and a broad-brimmed panama hat, stood up straight and held the small of his back. He had only been digging for a few days, but he felt as if he had already worked his way halfway through a life-sentence of hard labour.

'You've forgiven me, have you, Harold?' he asked.

'I should forgive you?'

'You made sure you turned the other way whenever I tried to catch your eye during Joel's appeal.'

'Hm,' said Harold, replacing his hat. 'That was when you were a Gentile. Nowadays, I hear that you've behaving like one of our own again, we should be so fortunate.'

'He's in love,' called Joel, from the other side of the claim, where he was directing his *shmeck tabac*'s efforts to pull down an overhang of crumbling rock.

'Ah, yes, I heard about that, too,' said Harold. 'I met Edward Nork two or three days ago, and he told me you'd set up house with that pretty young Griqua girl.'

'She's just housekeeping for us, that's all,' said Barney.

'I should doubt it?' asked Harold.

'You should *hok nit kain tchynik*,' said Joel, making his way across the claim in long, scrambling strides, and wiping his hands on a rag.

'These Blitz brothers,' Harold complained, with an expression of mock-despair. 'But tell me, how's business?'

Barney reached into the pocket of his work shirt and produced a handful of small rough diamonds. Harold Feinberg took them carefully into the sweaty folds of his palm, and then lifted the magnifying loupe around his neck so that he could examine them.

'What do you think?' asked Joel.

'Well . . . they're not bad,' said Harold. 'They won't earn you much of a fortune, but they're not bad.'

Barney pointed around to the sides of the claim, which was

already dug down to twenty feet. 'I reckon Joel was unlucky here. The upper debris had collapsed over the edge of the yellow soil, so that the first ten feet he dug didn't contain any diamonds at all. But now we're getting into the real business.'

'Well, I wish you luck,' said Harold. He grimaced at the sound of the kaffirs, singing as they dug. 'You and your *klezmer* both.'

Later that same afternoon, when the shadows from the rim of the mine had already filled their claim with darkness, Joel's impish kaffir came up with a stone of nearly ten karats. He dropped it into Joel's palm as calmly as if it were a large berry he had picked from a tree. Joel prodded it, scratched it with his thumbnail, and then said to Barney in a hoarse voice, 'Look at this, Barney. Come take a look at this.'

Barney laid down his pick. He held the diamond between his finger and his thumb, and he could not help grinning. 'Joel,' he said, 'I do believe the Blitz Brothers Diamond Company is going to show a profit today.'

Every day, they dug at their claim from the first reddish hints of dawn until it was too dark for them to see what they were doing. In August, it rained solidly for a week, and claim after claim collapsed in a series of mudslides, bringing sandbags and shovels and mule-carts down from one level to the next. Three Australians were buried alive, and a German digger was so badly crushed that his partner shot him to put him out of his agony. Some of the early diggers, satisfied with the few thousand pounds' worth of diamonds they had been able to dig out of the yellow ground, gave up, and sold their claims to the highest and most enthusiastic bidder.

By spring, most of the claims had been excavated so deep that the intervening roadways had collapsed, and the yellow soil had to be winched out to the rim of the mine in a series of hide buckets, suspended from never-ending steel cables. Each of these cables was wound around a series of pulleys, which was fixed to one of scores of rickety and elaborate wooden towers, clustering around the mine like pagan fortifications. The soil was offloaded at the towers, and then shovelled on to mule and ox-carts, to be taken away and sorted.

Mooi Klip became an expert at sorting diamonds. She spent

most of her days in a makeshift shelter not far from the edge of the mine, and there she supervised the kaffirs who tipped the broken ground into a heap in front of her, and pounded it with their shovels until it was broken down into manageable pieces. She watched them as they turned the soil in a rotary sieve called a *trommel*, which was Dutch for 'drum', and then banged away at the finer pieces which were left, before sieving them in fine-mesh hand sieves. Finally, she sat over the sorting table, picking through the stones with her delicate fingers. She wore small wire-rimmed spectacles for this close work, and Barney loved to surprise her as she sat working, because he thought she looked so pretty and vulnerable in eyeglasses.

At night, Barney and Joel and Mooi Klip returned to their shack, which they had now extended to include a large parlour and a verandah, and they would eat a supper of beef and beans before sitting around the fireplace, drinking rum and cocoa, and feeling the tension and pains of the day gradually leaving their muscles. Over the fireplace was a melodramatic litho-graph of the wreck of the steamship *San Francisco*, which Joel considered 'sobering'. He said it would always remind him of how nearly his own fortunes had foundered, and how close he had been to death.

But although Joel seemed more cheerful than he had when Barney had first rescued him, he was still visited from time to time by terrible doubts about what he was doing, and by nagging spells of furious dissatisfaction with himself, and with his surroundings, and especially with Barney.

'We should be living in a palace, the money we're making,' he said one evening in September. Barney was bent over the table, examining a heap of rough diamonds under the bright light of a pressure-lamp. Mooi Klip, her curly hair fresh-washed and brushed, was sitting by the fireplace hemming a red flowery dress. Because of the intense white light, the inside of the room looked like a stage-setting for amateur theatricals.

Barney said, 'I'm more interested in investing our money in another claim. By the end of the month, we should be able to put in a bid for Stuart's patch. Harold told me that Stuart was grumbling about the climate, and that he was planning on selling up and going back to Capetown.'

'You want *another* claim?' Joel demanded. 'Don't you think we have enough work to do with one?'

'We can employ more kaffirs.'

'Oh, sure. More kaffirs! But more kaffirs are going to mean more management, and more management is going to mean even harder work. Aren't you ever satisfied?'

Barney laid down his tweezers. 'What's the point of getting involved in any business of any kind if you don't expand? Right now, the Diggers' Committee only allow two claims per man – but that restriction can't last long. And then what do you think is going to happen here at Kimberley? The big companies will gradually swallow up the individual diggers, one by one; and in a year or two, you mark my words, there won't be any one-man outfits left. It won't be economic to dig one claim only. It won't be worth the effort of shoring up the sides, or of moving the soil to the edge of the mine, or of sorting out the gems. The big companies will undercut us, just because they're operating in bulk.'

'So what are we struggling for?' asked Joel. 'Why don't we sell up while the price is still good, and move out of this godforsaken place before we die out of boredom, or frustration, or some unheard-of disease?'

'Joel, we're just beginning. If we can buy up another claim then we can start to build up a big company of our own. The quicker we do it, the better. For God's sake – instead of being swallowed we could do some swallowing ourselves. Hasn't it occurred to you that you and I together could own the whole of that mine out there? The Blitz Brothers?'

'You're crazy. The heat's got to your brain.'

Barney tilted his chair back and looked at Joel steadily. 'Joel,' he said, 'if we don't work in the diamond business, then what business *are* we going to work in? You want to go back to tailoring? Or farming? You want to go back to sea?'

Joel snapped, 'Don't be so damned patronising.'

'I'm not being patronising. I'm simply trying to find out what you want out of life.'

'What the hell for? You're not my father, are you? You're my younger brother, my little Barnabas, my little son of consolation. Well, aren't you? And who followed whom out to South

Africa? Who bought this claim in the first place? So don't sit there raking through my diamonds and try to tell me what I should be doing with my life.'

'Joel, peace,' said Barney, alarmed by his brother's outburst. But Joel was not in the mood for reconciliation. He stood up, came over to the table, and seized a whole handful of rough, glittering diamonds.

'If it hadn't been for me, you never would have laid your hands on one of these stones. Not one! Now you sit there sorting them out like you're the diamond king of Kimberley. And all your plans! Your big dreams about buying more claims! We could own the whole goddamned mine, could we? Just remember who bought this claim in the first place!'

'I didn't ask you to give me a share,' said Barney, trying to curb his temper. 'Now, will you please put those diamonds down. I'm half way through sorting them.'

'Sorting them, shit!' Joel snarled, and threw the diamonds in a sparkling spray all over the room. 'You've dug yourself into my life pretty good, haven't you? Made me a laughing-stock in front of the whole town – the poor stupid kike who couldn't even save himself from being pegged out on the ground. Then you took half of my diamonds. Now I'm living like a lodger in my own home, and working like a kaffir in my own diamond mine, while you spend your time sorting gems and planning your high-faluting plans and fornicating with that *schwartzeh* like some ass-jerking dog.'

Barney punched Joel very hard in the mouth. The crack of Joel's front tooth breaking was so loud that Barney thought for a moment that he had broken his own knuckle. Joel staggered backwards, collided with a wheelback chair, stumbled, and then fell heavily on to the floor. He crouched there, spitting blood, and shaking his head.

Mooi Klip, without a word, quickly put down her sewing and knelt down among the scattered diamonds to hold Joel's head, and offer him her handkerchief for his bleeding lips. Barney felt as if he were bursting with some uncontrollable effervescence, a shaken-up bottle of beer, and he stood with both fists clenched, trembling, trying to hold back his anger, trying to tell himself that Joel was still sick, and still suffering the after-effects of his trial and his appeal, and that he should not have hit him.

Mooi Klip turned to Barney and said, 'Water. His tooth is broken.'

'He shouldn't have said that,' said Barney. 'I don't care what he feels about me, and I don't care what he says. We're brothers, after all. But he should never have said that about you.'

Mooi Klip simply repeated, '*Water*.'

Barney went to the scullery and came back with a blue enamel basin. Mooi Klip soaked her handkerchief, and gently dabbed Joel's mouth. After a while, Joel seemed to recover from the first concussion, and he pushed Mooi Klip's hand away.

Barney squatted down beside Joel and laid a hand on his shoulder. 'Joel, I'm sorry. Are you okay?'

'Never felt better,' mumbled Joel. He tried to pull himself up on to his feet by holding on to the overturned chair, but he lost his balance and fell forward.

'I don't need your help, thanks,' he told Barney, fiercely, as Barney grasped his arm.

'Joel, I've said I'm sorry. We're partners, aren't we? But you can't say things like that about Mooi Klip.'

'She's not a *schwartzeh*, is that what you're trying to tell me?' said Joel, tentatively touching his mouth with his fingertips. 'You're not living in sin, and exhibiting that sin in front of the whole of Kimberley?'

'I don't care about the whole of Kimberley, Joel. The whole of Kimberley can go to hell. And anyway, what's so high and mighty and moral about Kimberley? There are more whores to the acre in Kimberley than anywhere else in the world.'

'So she's a whore, too? Your *schwartzeh*? Is that what you think of her?'

'I didn't say that,' protested Barney.

'You never say anything, you hypocrite,' said Joel, pulling himself on to his feet. 'You just take what you feel belongs to you, and you take it by any means at your disposal. If your mama could see you now.'

'She can't see me, Joel. She's dead. And besides, I'm not

doing anything I'm ashamed of. I love Mooi Klip, and I love you, and if you'd just stop picking on me so often you'd understand just how much.'

Joel sniffed blood. 'You sanctimonious *pisher*.'

Joel went to his bedroom, and slammed the door so hard behind him that it opened again, and he had to close it more quietly and more firmly. Barney stared at the door for a moment or two, and then went down on his knees and gathered up the diamonds, one by one. Mooi Klip sat on the edge of her chair and watched him.

'He is so angry,' she said.

'You're not fooling. The trouble is, I don't know why.'

'Of course you know why,' said Mooi Klip. 'You have hurt his pride. You saved him from trouble, when he couldn't save himself. Now you are making his business work well, when all he could do was steal. You have bought us a house to live in, and you have a woman, too. What does he have? What has he done? You make him feel like a child.'

'I don't mean to,' said Barney, and it was true. He did not. He loved Joel and he looked up to him, too – whether Joel had made a success of his life or not. Had not Joel shown him how to make bows and arrows out of tailor's elastic, during those hot summers on Clinton Street, when they were boys? Had not Joel shown him how to cut a lining, and how to baste a lapel? Had not Joel protected him against those Armenian bullies along Hester Street, on his way to school? And had not Joel, one night in bed, with the rain tapping on the windows, explained in whispery and reverent detail the mysterious anatomy of girls?

But now Joel was so sour and stand-offish that Barney found it almost impossible to explain that just because *he* had a knack for business, and Joel had not, that did not mean that he loved Joel any the less, or that Joel was not making an equal contribution to their success and to their happiness. Barney wanted them all very much to be a family – himself and Joel and Mooi Klip – but Joel was far too jealous of Barney to play.

Barney felt as if every time he tried to keep the Blitz family together, it fell apart in his hands, like the crumbling clay of the Kimberley mine. The family seemed to be plagued by envy, or madness, or sheer bad temper.

He gathered up as many of the scattered diamonds as he could, and then he went back to the table. He did not say anything to Mooi Klip, but smiled at her briefly, to show her that he loved and appreciated her. He had not mentioned Agnes Knight to her again, not since that day in Oranjerivier when they had found Monsaraz dead. He had seen Agnes two weeks ago, though, in the main street in Kimberley, with her nose tilted to the sky, and her parasol twirling, and her pretty little shoes click-clicking along the dusty boardwalk. He had raised his hat to her from across the street, and said, 'Agnes?' in a rather discouraged voice; but she had flounced on, without looking his way, and he had not had the effrontery to follow her.

Agnes represented a lost dream. Agnes was a prickly reminder that he was *persona non grata* in the Kimberley Club, and that Jews were not particularly welcome in any of those dim rooms where billiards were played, and gin slings drunk, and reminiscences shared between chaps called Biffy and Charles about those dear summer days at Harrow, and those long autumn afternoons in Kent.

Mooi Klip, sewing, said, 'Perhaps Joel would be better if he found a wife.'

Barney spread the rough diamonds out on the dark brown velvet tablecloth in front of him. 'I don't know. He used to be so talkative, so friendly. Everything you'd expect from an older brother. But now ...'

Painstakingly, he began to sort out the diamonds again. First, they had to be divided according to colour and clarity. Most of the diamonds, over eighty per cent, were only fit for industrial use, for glass-cutting and engraving tools, and drillbits. These crystals Barney would sell by the sackful to the Capetown Industrial Diamond Company, or to Mr Schultz of Lippert and Company, from Hamburg, who always paid good prices for industrials.

Then, Barney picked through the stones of gem quality – sorting them by size first. The 'smalls' – anything under one carat – went to one side. The larger gems he categorised according to their shapes. Stones, which were unbroken crystals; cleavages, which were fractured crystals; flats, which were thin crystals like fragments of a broken window; and macles, which were twinned stones, and triangular in shape.

Few diggers could sort diamonds as well as Barney – but then he had listened well to what Harold Feinberg had told him – and in turn he had passed on what he knew to Mooi Klip. He had offered several times to teach Joel to sort diamonds, but Joel had waved him away and said that he would leave the 'fiddly business' to those who had the patience for it.

But sorting paid off. It meant that Barney knew exactly what he had to sell, and almost exactly what price he could expect for it, down to the last gold franc. It also meant that he learned to tell the difference between a good stone and an excellent stone, between a very spotted crystal and a slightly spotted crystal. Under his magnifying lens, he could detect the kind of flaws or inclusions which could easily be bruted off a stone when it was cut, and which would only reduce the value of a gem by a very small amount; and the flaws which lay nearer the centre of a stone, and which would give a cutter real difficulty.

Sorting by colour was simpler. Most of the browns and the yellows were unpopular, and so they were set aside as industrials, unless they were unusually large, or clear. But greens, or blues, or pinks were much rarer, and could fetch well above the regular price. Reds were so unusual that Barney had never even seen one.

The whites were more difficult to grade. The finest whites were often called 'blue-whites', and when he had first started sorting, Barney had spent hours trying to detect a slight trace of blue in his better gemstones. But he had learned from experience, and from a cynical Harold Feinberg, that 'blue-white' was a romantic diamond-salesman's fiction, rather than an accurate colour grading; and that most of the stones sold to a starry-eyed public as 'blue-white' were not even top grade whites.

Almost all of the whites that Barney and Joel were digging out of claim No. 172 were very faintly yellowish, which meant that as far as colour was concerned, they could only be classified as fourth- or fifth-grade stones. Occasionally, they came up with a fine clear white, but not enough to satisfy Barney that their claim was a good one. And they had yet to find a gem crystal of more than 12·8 carats.

'Have you finished?' asked Mooi Klip, standing behind Barney and gently stroking his cheek.

Barney laid down his loupe and pinched the bridge of his nose. He had been working since dawn, and his eyes were blurring. All he could see in front of him on the dark brown tablecloth was a rainbow jumble of sparkling light.

'Almost,' he told her. 'Do you want to go to bed?'

'I want to talk, too.'

He opened a notebook, and carefully scratched down the number and estimated value of the crystals on the table. 'Seven hundred pounds, if we're lucky. We should clear £2000 this week.'

'All this money,' said Mooi Klip. 'What are you going to do with it?'

Barney stood up, and closed his notebook. 'I'm going to put it into the bank, like I always do. And then, when he's ready, and when *I'm* ready, I'm going to buy up Stuart's claim next door.'

'I heard a kaffir say Stuart's claim is no good. They're down to bedrock.'

'That's what I hear, too, although Stuart says he's selling because of the climate.'

'But why should you want to buy Stuart's claim, if it's worked out?' asked Mooi Klip.

'Because I believe a man called Nork.'

'Nork?' queried Mooi Klip.

'He used to work with Joel. He's a little strange. A little eccentric. But he thinks the bedrock isn't bedrock at all, but something called Norkite. He thinks we'll find as many diamonds in the Norkite as we're finding in the yellow ground.'

'Is that true?'

'I think it's true. I'll lose a lot of money if it isn't.'

Joel's bedroom door opened. Joel stood there, dressed in nothing but his cotton combinations, his dark hair tousled, watching Barney and Mooi Klip with his mouth turned down in a disapproving curve.

'Nork,' he said, 'is a maniac.'

'Well, he's a little over-enthusiastic,' said Barney. 'He drinks a lot, too. But there's nothing wrong with his theory.'

'You're going to throw good money away on a crackpot geological theory? We're living in a two-bedroomed hovel, dressed in dime-store cottons, eating dried beef and beans, and you're going to throw money away on a theory?'

'I'm going to invest money in something that sounds like a pretty good gamble,' said Barney. 'Now, please, don't let's argue again. If you want to discuss it some more, let's talk about it in the morning.'

'Let's talk about it now.'

'Joel — I'm tired — so are you — and so is Mooi Klip.'

'Barney, my little son of consolation, I'm never too tired to talk about my future. Or what you're going to do with our money. Seventeen thousand pounds we've got now, festering away in the London & South African Bank. Seventeen thousand inert, useless, pounds. So we can buy out Stuart's barren claim. How much is that going to cost us? Eight thousand, nine? All right, that leaves us eight or nine thousand spare. What are we going to do with that?'

Barney put his arm around Mooi Klip's shoulders. 'We'll buy more claims, of course, when we can.'

Joel, his eyebrows drawing together like black iron filings drawn by a magnet, said, '*More* barren claims? *More* worked-out land?'

'It's not worked out. Maybe some diggers think it is, but it isn't.'

'Because Edward Nork says it isn't? *Riboyne Shel O'lem*, Barney, the man's crazy in the head! I knew him months before you did. Years! I even believed him myself for a time. But he's a lunatic. They should lock him up.'

'They haven't so far. And I believe him.'

Joel raked his fingers through his greasy, unkempt hair. With his mouth so bruised and swollen he looked like a prize-fighter. 'You won't take my advice, I suppose?' he asked Barney. 'You don't give me credit for knowing these diamonds fields better than you do?'

Barney tied up the last of the gemstones in a washleather bag. He did not answer.

'All right,' said Joel. 'But let me warn you of one thing. If we hit blue ground, and the blue ground turns out to be barren, then I'm going to take my money out of the bank, whatever's left of it, and I'm also going to insist that you buy me out of whatever claims we own at today's price.'

Barney looked at his brother with nothing but regret. He could not stand to see Joel acting this way: it reminded him so much of his mother. 'Very well,' he said hoarsely.

'*Mazel un b'rachah*,' said Joel, his voice sharp with irony. Because to speak these words, 'good luck and blessings,' were the time-honoured way in which diamond dealers sealed their business arrangements. They never drew up written contracts: a man's word was binding enough.

After Joel had gone back to bed, Barney went over to the wooden hutch where they kept their plates and their cutlery, and poured himself a small glass of brandy. He drank it in one mouthful, without looking round once at Mooi Klip, who was standing in their bedroom doorway watching him.

'Come to bed,' she said, quietly. 'This is not the right time for fighting.'

Barney turned down the pressure-lamp and extinguished it. He crossed the room by the shadowy illumination of the candle in their bedroom, and held Mooi Klip's hand.

'I don't want to fight anyway,' he said.

With the door closed behind them, and held by a hasp, Barney unbuttoned Mooi Klip's dress, and pulled it down from her shoulders. Her nipples showed dark through the fine white cotton of her embroidered bodice. He kissed her, and held her cheek close to his, and felt her curly hair between his fingers.

He was tired, and so he made love to her slowly, with his eyes closed. It was warm, between the percale sheets, under their patchwork comforter, and he held her hips up close to him with hands that were calloused now, and strong with work. Each time he slid into her he felt it was like sliding into an affectionate dream.

Afterwards, they lay side-by-side in the flickering candle-light with the covers thrown back. Mooi Klip's lips touched Barney's shoulder again and again in the lightest of kisses, and her hand cupped him between his muscular thighs.

'How do you think of me?' she asked him.

'What do you mean?' he grunted. He had nearly fallen asleep.

'I mean how do you *think* of me.'

Barney turned his head. 'I love you. You know that.'

'You don't think of me as your whore.'

'Of course not.'

'But we live together, and we make love, and we are not married.'

'That bothers you?' asked Barney. He sat up and leaned his head on the sawn-oak bedhead. On the opposite side of the room, on a small table, stood Mooi Klip's crucifix. Its shadow dipped and danced in the light of the candle.

'If my family knew, they would be very unhappy,' said Mooi Klip. 'And I think that I am unhappy myself.'

'You're unhappy? You've never said so.'

She looked away, picking at a stray thread at the edge of the comforter. 'It has never been the right time, before. But now I think you have to decide. You cannot live with me, and expect so much of me, and still nurse your dreams of Agnes Knight.'

Barney said shortly, 'You've learned a lot since we've been together, haven't you? And not just fancy English.'

'I've learned that you have a dream, and that your dream is sometimes stronger than you are.'

'Have you learned that I love you?'

'In your way, you do.'

'In my *way*? And what way is that? Don't you realise that one day I'm going to drape you in diamonds?'

Mooi Klip slowly shook her head. 'No,' she said. Her eyes sparkled in the candlelight. 'No, you will never do that.'

'But you want me to marry you?'

'Yes.'

'Would Jan Bloem give us his blessing?'

'I expect so. He does like you, although he finds it hard to admit it.'

Barney swung his legs out of bed, and sat up. 'What I don't understand is why you suddenly want me to marry you now. Is it what Joel said tonight? Is that what made up your mind?'

'A little,' she said. 'But there is something else, more important.'

'What's that?'

She ran her fingers down his back, and the feeling made him shiver. 'I think I'm going to have your baby,' she said.

He met Agnes a week later, by accident. It was one of those dark afternoons when low cloud hung over the veld like soft grey rags; when the horses were restless, and the noise of the picks and the winches from the Big Hole sounded oddly muffled, like grave-robbers working in a country churchyard.

The Knights had ignored Barney and Joel every time they came across them in the street. Kimberley was such a small place that it was impossible to avoid them altogether; but Mr Knight in particular was an expert in the social art of 'cutting', and he had obviously instructed Faith and Agnes to tilt their noses into the air in exactly the same way. The three of them would bustle past like excited guinea-fowl, all upraised beaks and flustering skirts and contemptuous petticoats.

But early on that Friday afternoon, when Barney walked into town to find a replacement diaphragm for one of their pumps, he found Agnes alone. She was standing on the boarded sidewalk in a cream linen dress and a wide cream sunhat with a brown silk *puggaree* tied around it. She looked as if she were thinking, or dreaming; but in any case she did not notice Barney until he was standing beside her, in his wide hat and his shirt with its sleeves tightly rolled up, and his suspenders.

'Agnes,' he said.

She turned, and stared at him wide-eyed.

'Barney!' she said, but then she remembered herself, and stuck her nose up, and closed her eyes.

Barney couldn't help smiling. 'I may be Jewish, Agnes, but I'm not going to bite your ankle.'

'Papa said I mustn't even look at you. Neither must Faith. We're under strict instructions, he said.'

Barney tilted back his hat. 'Do you really hold it against me so much? That I'm Jewish?'

She opened one eye.

'If you cut me, do I not bleed?' Barney quoted.

Agnes said, 'You don't believe in Jesus, do you?'

'Of course I believe in Jesus.'

'Papa said that Jews were almost heathens. Not quite. But almost.'

Barney looked away, across the dusty street. In the far distance, way beyond the trees on the horizon, lightning flickered like the tongue of an asp. 'We could have loved each other,' he said. 'You know that, don't you?'

She twisted the brown silk cord of her parasol around its *faux*-bamboo handle, but said nothing. The dim light gave her face the soft pastel colours of a portrait by Sir Joshua Reynolds; full of fancy and sentimentality and gentle allegory. A dust-devil stirred the chaff in the street, and far off to the north-west the lightning forked again. Unsettled times.

Barney said, 'I shall always hold you dear, you know. I suppose that's all I can say.'

Agnes said, 'I was supposed to buy Mother some ribbon.'

'Well, you'd better go then,' Barney told her. 'But it would be nice if you could at least say goodbye.'

Agnes turned. To Barney's surprise, there was a faint sparkle in the corner of her eye, where a tear had formed. She said, 'I don't even know why Father is so furious, that you're a Jew. You don't even *look* like a Jew; although he says you do, and that he should have guessed all along. "I invited him to eat at my very table!" he keeps shouting. I tried to argue with him, Barney, I promise you that I tried my best. But he won't let me see you. He won't! And Mother can't understand.'

Barney took a step forward, and held her hand. Her tiny fawn glove was decorated with fine Brussels lace. Her hand inside it was as warm as a small animal. He took off his hat, leaned forward, and kissed her cheek, unshaved and sweaty as he was, with dust in the curls of his hair, and grit around his mouth.

She whispered something indistinct, and Barney said, 'What?'

'I love you,' she said. 'Didn't you hear me? I love you. I've dreamed about you, ever since I first met you. Perhaps it's wrong of me, and I ought to feel guilty. But how can anyone feel guilty, when they feel passions as strong as these? Barney, I love you.'

Barney squeezed her hand. 'It's impossible,' he said. 'You know it is.'

Her face collapsed with grief. 'I've tried so hard,' she told him. 'I've tried to do everything that Father thought was best. Faith believes that I should stand up to him, and tell him that I'm going to walk out with you, no matter what. But I can't, Barney. All I can do is keep my love for you alive, inside my heart, and hope that one day everything will change.'

She took her hand away, and found her handkerchief, and wiped her eyes; but somehow that only made her sob even more. Barney gently put his arm around her, and led her to an iron bench outside a grocery store, where he sat her down, and sat beside her.

'I don't know what to say,' he told her. He was telling her the truth. How could he explain that he had given her up for lost on the day of Joel's trial, simply because the prejudice of her father and of all of the British colonial *goyim* seemed utterly impregnable? How could he tell her about Mooi Klip? He knew that his ambitions had deceived him: he had first been attracted to Agnes because she was the right sort of girl for a colonist to marry, pretty and presentable and radiantly Christian. But he was deeply infatuated with her, too; with her face and her figure and the childish wilfulness of her character; and now that he realised that she still wanted him, and still loved him, in spite of his Jewishness, the intense pain of losing her for ever – and it would have to be for ever – was like an amputation. He would think of that word later, for different reasons, but it would always remind him of losing Agnes.

Agnes said, 'I'd better go. Mother will be wondering where I am.'

He said, 'You won't do anything foolish?'

'Foolish? There's nothing foolish that I can do, not here in Kimberley.'

'I'm sorry,' he said, quietly. 'It should all have been different.'

'It wasn't your fault. You had to stand up for your brother. At lease you had the strength to do that.'

He replaced his hat, and tugged the brim straight. 'I'm beginning to wonder whether that was such a good idea.'

Agnes reached out and held his wrist. 'Listen, Barney,' she told him, 'I know you won't believe this, and there will probably be many times in the future when I will give you good reason not to. But I shall always keep a place in my heart for you. You will always be precious to me. Don't forget that, please.'

'I won't be able to forget it,' said Barney.

They parted on the corner of the street, while thunder began to bang in the distance, and the wind got up. As Agnes was about to walk away, Barney held her arm, and kissed her again, on the lips. She was elegant and small, and her mouth tasted of rosewater.

'Barney,' she said. 'I can't. If my father found out . . .'

Barney reluctantly let her go. 'Yes,' he said. 'I know. I didn't mean to compromise you.'

Quickly, she was gone. No matter how many times he met her now, he knew that he would never be able to talk to her again the way he had today. Each of them had a new life to seek out; new obligations to fulfil; and they would have to carry them out apart.

She reached the door of the notions store, and opened the door. For a moment she was silhouetted against the patterned glass. A mule stirred its hoofs at the tying-up post not far away, as if it was frightened of what was to come, but powerless to escape.

In October, the short-lived reign of President Stafford Parker of the Diggers' Republic came to an end. Parker abdicated graciously, though, because the diamond fields were now to come under British rule. At the beginning of November, two days before Barney and Mooi Klip were due to be married, the Union Jack was run up over the Big Hole, and the diggers stood around it and gave three cheers, and waved their hats.

The annexation of the richest diamond diggings in the entire world, with a production of £50,000 worth of diamonds a week, had been a masterpiece of British colonial burglary. Although the mines were well within the territory claimed by the Orange Free State, the Boers had neither the money nor the military strength to resist that particular combination of bullying and guile which had won for Britain some of the wealthiest geographic prizes that the globe could offer.

During the years in which the Orange Free State and the Transvaal had been poor, eking their living from the soil, the British had been content to leave them alone. But the discovery of diamonds on such an extraordinary scale could quickly have made the Boers a formidable enemy, and the British Colonial Secretary, Sir Richard Southey, had been growing increasingly worried about the prospect of two wealthy and hostile republics barring British access from the Cape to Central Africa.

'By definition,' he remarked at a dinner party, 'the only safe Boer is a poor Boer.'

The answer to Sir Richard's problems came when he discovered that all of the new diamond mines lay on land that was inhabited by Griquas. Because it had never mattered before now, nobody had ever satisfactorily decided whether the Boers had any right to claim 'Griqualand' as theirs. So, with great pomp and ceremony, it was announced that the Lieutenant-Governor of Natal, Robert Keate, would head a commission to arbitrate on the Griqua's territorial rights.

President Jan Brand, the Boer leader of the Orange Free State, protested in vain that a disinterested foreign country should decide the issue. It was a British matter, said Keate, dismissively, and the British could not possibly tolerate foreigners meddling in their affairs.

Keate's final ruling came as no surprise to the unhappy Boers. The Orange Free State, he concluded, had no jurisdiction over 'Griqualand', nor the diamond mines within its boundaries. And within days, the Griqua chieftains Nicholas Waterboer and Jan Bloem had been persuaded by Keate to ask the British to annex 'Griqualand' into Cape Colony. Up went the Union Jack over Kimberley, and into the British economy came an influx of diamonds more than six times greater than the annual production of South Africa's nearest rival, Brazil.

Enraged, President Brand sent a small commando force to Kimberley to try to recapture the diamond fields. But Sir Henry Barkly, the new Governor of the Cape, immediately responded by rushing up a thousand uniformed British soldiers. Angry, bitter, millions of pounds poorer, the Boers were forced to retreat. They had sustained an injury which would fester now for almost thirty years.

Barney and Joel and Mooi Klip went to see the flag being raised. On the far side of the crowd, Barney could make out the tall stovepipe hat of Mr Knight, surrounded by the feathery bonnets of his daughters. He linked arms with Mooi Klip, over-possessively, and led her through the jostling diggers to a small hillock, where she could stand on an overturned wheelbarrow and watch what was happening.

Joel remarked, 'At least we'll get some law and order around here now.'

'*You* talk of law and order?' smiled Mooi Klip.

'Proper law and order. Not barrelhead justice,' retorted Joel.

The flag was jerkily raised to the head of the staff, and a small military band, in white topis and bright red tunics, played *God Save The Queen*, and *Another Little Patch of Red*. Then there were more cheering, and more hat-waving, and most of the diggers streamed off to Dodd's Bar for a stiff drink. Barney lifted Mooi Klip down from her wheelbarrow.

It was then that Edward Nork appeared, walking like a long-bladed pair of scissors, and dragging behind him a diffident but very well-built young man with a round face, prominent ears, and the sort of well-combed wavy hair that always reminded Barney of British public schoolboys.

'These are the chaps!' Nork announced to his new charge. 'These are just the chaps I've been looking for!'

The young man flushed pink. He was wearing white cricket flannels with very baggy knees, and cricketing boots. He nodded to Barney and Joel and Mooi Klip, and said, 'I hope I'm not imposing. I met Mr Nork here by accident, and he insisted on taking me in tow, like a lifeboat.'

'I knew his father!' Nork exclaimed. 'I used to visit Bishop's Stortford on a bicycle, to visit a very clever young lady I once knew, and his father was the local vicar. We used to discuss the geology of the Holy Land together, his father and I.'

'My name's Cecil Rhodes,' said the young man, in a high-pitched, upper-class English accent. 'My father is the Reverend F. W.'

'I'm Barney Blitz,' replied Barney. 'This is my brother Joel, and this is Mrs Blitz-to-be.'

'Well, congratulations,' smiled Cecil Rhodes. 'My father always said that marriage is the closest estate to heaven that a man can enjoy.'

'You have an Anglican motto for every occasion?' asked Joel.

'I was brought up religiously, if that's what you mean,' Cecil Rhodes replied, cautiously, but not apologetically.

'Well, I think we all were,' said Joel. 'But it doesn't take long for the diamond diggings to drum that nonsense out of you. You'd better come and have some lunch. Do you like *frikkadeller*?'

'Do you mind if I bring my things along?' asked Cecil Rhodes. 'I have an ox-waggon tied up over there.'

'Nobody will steal it,' said Joel. 'What's on it? A shovel or two? A bedroll? You can pick diamonds up off the ground around here, so nobody's going to bother with stuff like that. Water, that's the only expensive commodity out here. Water, and women.'

They walked back to the house, where Mooi Klip stoked up the woodburning range and put the meatballs on to fry. Barney offered to help her, especially since she was pregnant, but she waved him away. At the kitchen door, though, she called him back, and gave him a long and lingering kiss.

'This day next week, I will be Mrs Blitz,' she said, warmly.

'And I will be your husband,' Barney grinned. 'So there.'

Joel was pouring out drinks. He was talking even more loudly than usual, and more abrasively. He did not enjoy having guests at the house at the best of times, and Edward Nork was a particular hatred of his, especially since Sir Joshua Field, another British geologist, had declared that the blue flaky 'bedrock' beneath the yellow ground might actually bear even more diamonds than the topsoil. Joel did not take to Cecil Rhodes, either. Rhodes had that brassy English self-assurance that made Joel feel like grinding his teeth. 'They think they own the whole damned world,' he used to complain to Barney.

'That's probably because they do,' Barney had replied, absent-mindedly.

Cecil Rhodes said, 'I'm joing my brother Herbert, as a

matter of fact, at the De Beers mine. Herbert used to farm cotton in Natal, and I took the business over when he left to go diamond-digging. I brought in a fine crop, too, and I would probably have been doing it still if the prices hadn't been so ridiculously low. You could never get rich by growing cotton.'

'Diamond-digging isn't as easy as it looks,' said Joel, handing round glasses of sherry. 'And it's certainly not for children.'

'Well, I'm eighteen,' said Cecil Rhodes, with a smile. 'I expect that's old enough.'

'Can we call you Cecil?' asked Barney, sitting down in his large woven armchair.

'I'd rather you called me Rhodes, if you don't mind. It's what a fellow gets used to at school.'

'You think you're going to strike it rich?' Barney asked him.

'Rich *and* powerful, I rather hope,' said Rhodes, artlessly. 'You see, it's my belief that the British are the first race in the world – with no offence at all to present company – and that the more of the world we inhabit, the better it is for the human race. The absorption of the greater part of the world under British influence would simply mean an end to all wars.'

'I hope you're not including the United States in your would-be empire,' said Joel. He finished his sherry in two or three gulps, and then poured himself another glassful.

'I don't see why not,' said Rhodes. 'We English-speaking peoples should stand together as closely as possible. If there be a God, I think what He would like me to do is paint as much of the world as possible in British red. Including America.'

'I always knew there was more than one God,' said Joel.

Rhodes made a face which indicated that if *that* was going to be the tone of the conversation, then it would be better if they changed the subject altogether.

'But if you're right, there must be more than one God,' Joel persisted. 'Because *we* were chosen of Adoshem, the true God, not the British. You can mock us for being chosen. You always have. But isn't mockery the last resort of the hopelessly envious? We were chosen, and you weren't; and no matter how many soldiers you send scurrying around the world, you can never alter that fact because it is historical and unalterable.'

'I really think you're missing the point,' said Rhodes. 'These days, it is a combination of wealth, power, and benign intention that makes Britain the chosen instrument of the Lord.'

'Benign intention? The Boers think you're the devil, personified.'

Barney put in, more quietly, trying to divert the conversation from religion and race, 'What do you really plan to do here, Rhodes? You sound as if you have something in mind.'

Rhodes looked him right in the eye, sitting up straight in his basketwork armchair as if he were being interviewed by his housemaster. 'What I really plan to do here, Mr Blitz, is make my fortune. From the little I've already seen of the mines, they're utterly chaotic. They need order, and system. They need to be managed on a large-scale, businesslike basis. If I can achieve that, then I'll have achieved what I came here to do.'

'Magnificent words for an eighteen-year-old,' said Joel, sarcastically.

'Sensible, though,' put in Barney. 'I'd better keep my eye on you, young Rhodes, or you'll be playing me at my own game.'

'Regrettably for both of your empire-building ideas, the Board for the Protection of the Diamond Industries still won't allow one man to own more than two claims,' put in Joel. 'And, by God, two is enough for anybody.'

Rhodes stood up, and tugged his cricket-flannels straight. 'I think we'll just have to see about that,' he said. 'And now I believe I've changed my mind about lunching with you, thanks all the same.'

'You're welcome to stay,' said Barney, amused by Rhodes' abruptness.

'Thank you, but I don't believe I will. I think your brother and I may have something of a clash, and I don't want to spoil your *frikkadeller* for you. You'll give my apologies to your charming fiancée.'

'Running off with your tail tucked between your legs?' smiled Joel. 'That isn't the spirit that got the map of Africa painted red.'

'We'll see,' said Rhodes. He nodded with courtesy to Edward Nork, who returned his nod with a waggle of his fingers; and then to Barney. But Barney had suddenly become aware that this seemingly equable young man was gripping the flannel of his trousers to sightly that he had torn the seam. He must have been within a hair's-breadth of completely losing his self-control.

Barney showed Rhodes out on to the verandah. It was a cool, windy day, and plumes of dust were blowing up from the Big Hole.

'Well, it seems that we may find ourselves in competition one day,' said Rhodes, in a rather metallic tone. He held out his hand to show that, between him and Barney at least, there were no awkward feelings.

'Yes – we may,' said Barney. 'In fact, I hope we do.' There was something about Rhodes' directness that unbalanced him. Rhodes seemed to understand the real implications of the wealth of Kimberley without any effort at all, whereas Barney had taken several months to grasp that these mines were so fabulously rich that anyone who managed to control them could control practically the whole of Africa. Barney felt as if he were up against a dedicated opponent at last, and the prospect both excited and scared him.

'If we do find ourselves competing,' Rhodes replied, 'then I can assure you that you're in for one devil of a scrap.' Then he began to walk back towards Kimberley with his trouser-legs flapping in the wind. A little distance away, with Barney still watching him, he stopped, and produced from one of his pockets a tin of cough-lozenges. He popped one into his mouth, and then continued walking, as steadily and confidently as if the whole diamond mine already belonged to him.

The night before Barney's wedding was the most catastrophic night he had ever lived through. The crisis came without any warning at all. All the arrangements had been made with the pimply young curate from Wimbledon to perform the ceremony at Kimberley's Anglican Church, and the banns had been read. Jan Bloem and his mother were expected to arrive from Klipdrift early in the morning, bringing Mooi Klip's family with him. Mooi Klip herself had butchered half an ox to be roasted, and with the help of a young Yorkshirewoman who lived with her husband in the shack next door, she had made dozens of biscuits and candies.

The inside of the house looked as if it had been decorated for Christmas, with plumes of dried grass and flowers, paper streamers, and stars cut from biscuit-tin lids. There were two barrels of wine, a cluster of borrowed mugs and glasses, and a barrel of sherry. The table was carefully set with plates, and Barney had made a special trip down to Walker's Lunch Rooms to borrow twenty knives and twenty forks. Joel, grudgingly, had torn two dozen napkins from a large dust-sheet – not because they could not afford to buy any, but simply because there were none to be had.

Mooi Klip, already glowing with the first stages of pregnancy, her hair shining, her eyes bright, and her breasts tightening the bodices of her dresses, took on an extra glow. A glow of pride, and rediscovered dignity, and plain love.

Just before noon on the day before the wedding, Barney and Joel went into Kimberley to meet a German salesman about pumping equipment. The weather had been wet and unsettled lately, and most of the claims in the Big Hole were so deep now that whenever it rained, they flooded with bright yellow water, and prospecting could sometimes be held up for days. Even pumps did not help much, although they were better than nothing. If the digger in the next claim did not have a pump, the water from his flooded workings would simply gush over into yours. There were 3600 individual claims in the Big Hole, and the British writer Anthony Trollope had said that it looked as if 'some diabolically ingenious architect had contrived a house with 500 rooms, not one of which should be on the same floor, and to and from none of which there should be a pair of stairs or a door or a window.'

The German pump salesman was stout, with hands like *haxe*, the Bavarian pork-knuckles. He sat in a stained-oak booth at Marshall's Restaurant with a large plate of chops and mashed potatoes in front of him, drinking whiskey and entertaining a succession of anxious diggers. By the time Barney and Joel arrived, he had sold all of the six steam-pumps that he had brought with him from Capetown, and was taking orders for six months ahead.

'But, I will buy you a beer as a consolation,' he told them, gaily waving a chop.

Out in the street again, Joel said, 'What do we do now? We've already lost six days through flooding.'

'Maybe I should go over to the De Beers mine, and see if anybody there can lend us a pump,' said Barney. 'Why don't you go back to the claim, and see what you can do to bale it out with buckets?'

'Okay,' said Joel. He hesistated for a moment.

'Is there something wrong?' asked Barney.

Joel took off his hat, dusted it, and then knocked it back into shape. 'I think I ought to say that I'm sorry,' he said.

'Sorry? What for?'

'Sorry for behaving like a mad dog. Sorry for being so vicious to you when you've done nothing but help me. Just – sorry.'

Barney put his arm around his brother's shoulders and held him very close. 'You don't think I understand how you've been feeling? You've been such a *farbissener*! But it doesn't matter. We love you, both of us. Mooi Klip and I. And that's the way it's always going to be.'

Joel sniffed, and wiped tears away from his face. 'I wanted so much to be strong,' he said. 'But I couldn't carry Mama, and I couldn't carry the tailor's business. When I was at sea, I couldn't take that, either. You know what work it is, on a merchant steamer? Two hours sleep, and twenty-two hours' shifting cargo. Then I bought the farm, and I didn't know how the hell to cope with that, either. It was all weeds, and dereliction! I couldn't even scratch the surface. Now, it's the mine. And it's still Mama, too. I can still see the way she looked. I can still hear her voice. Why in God's name wasn't I born to some other woman?'

Barney stood straight, and held Joel's shoulders with both hands. 'How can you talk this way, when you haven't failed at all? You haven't let anybody down – you've done nothing but succeed. You have a share in one of the richest diamond mines in the whole world. You have a brother who loves you, and a sister-in-law who's going to love you, too.'

'Your Mooi Klip thinks I'm crazy and cantankerous.'

'Don't be so crazy and cantankerous. Or course she doesn't.'

Joel smiled, and then took hold of Barney's curls and affectionately shook his head. 'You're right. I've been acting like a fool. Miserable, sour, and mean, for no reason. And that's why I'm saying sorry.'

'All right,' said Barney, gently. 'You're sorry. Now, don't let's anything more about it. It's my wedding tomorrow.'

They shook hands, and gripped each other tightly for a moment. Then Joel said quietly, 'I'll see you later. On your wedding-eve,' and walked off along Kimberley's main street towards the Big Hole. Barney climbed aboard their ox-waggon, snapped the whip, and steered their two oxen slowly out towards the De Beers mine.

It was an unusually chilly and windy afternoon. Dust and dry weeds tumbled across the veld, and Barney had to cover his mouth with his necktie. In the distance, he could see wind-devils dancing, and trees waving at him with wild helplessness, like drowning bathers. The sky to the west, from the Vaal River and the distant Kuruman Heuwells, was devastatingly black.

Despite the wind, he made the De Beers mine in good time. It was at this location that diamonds had first been discovered on Vooruitzigt, and the one-time arable fields were now deeply pitted with trenches and craters. Work had almost been abandoned here for a while when diamonds had been discovered on Colesberg Kopje, but not a bizarre selection of gallows-like winches were swinging the yellow ground out of the deep-dug claims as fast as they were at the Big Hole.

Barney tethered his ox-waggon, and walked to the rim of the mine. He could see that several of the claims, like his own, were deep in vivid yellow water, and that many of the diggers were doing nothing but sitting around, smoking and drinking and waiting for a couple of days of dry windy weather to evaporate the worst of their floods. But one claim, only a few hundred yards from where he was standing, was being diligently emptied by a noisy clattering steam-pump, and the kaffirs there, although they were ankledeep in water, were at least able to continue shovelling the yellow gravel into their buckets.

Barney skirted the edge of the diggings until he reached the tent where the owner of this claim was sitting. As soon as he saw him, Barney knew that he should have saved himself a walk.

It was Rhodes, sitting on a camp-stool in his cricket clothes, reading Plutarch's *Lives* while his kaffirs heaped mountains of sloshy yellow soil all around him.

'Barney Blitz,' said Rhodes, putting down his book. 'This is a great pleasure.'

'How are you doing?' asked Barney, nodding towards Rhodes' claim.

'Well, quite capital so far,' said Rhodes, in his high-pitched voice. 'I average about twenty pounds a day. Do you know I found a diamond of seventeen carats on Saturday, right outside the door of my tent? Just lying there!'

'You should get at least £100 for it,' said Barney.

'Well, that's what I thought,' nodded Rhodes.

'You must be one of the chosen, after all,' said Barney, with a wry smile.

Rhodes held up his book. 'It's all a question of education, you know. A good education, properly applied, is more compelling than a dozen howitzers. Do you what Pliny the Elder once said?'

'Pliny the who?'

'Pliny the Elder. Born, AD 23, died AD 79. And what he said was, "*ex Africa semper aliquid novi*", which means "there is always something new coming out of Africa." Now, I learned that at school when I was ten, and when my family doctor said I had to go somewhere dry, to help my tuberculosis, I remembered it. So I thought the very best thing I could do was join Herbert in Natal, and aren't I glad that I did?'

'You must be,' said Barney. 'Could I borrow your pump?'

Rhodes laughed, and kicked his heels like a small boy. 'I was wondering when you were going to ask me that.'

'Oh, yes?' said Barney, rather put out.

'Well, you're not the first,' smiled Rhodes. 'About every half-hour, one disconsolate digger or another comes up and asks me if he can borrow my pump.'

'I see.'

'You don't see,' said Rhodes, slipping a grubby white cricket sock between the pages of his book, to mark the place. 'I can't lend you my pump, because I need it. But I can *hire* you a pump.'

'You have a pump to rent?'

'I have two. They're inside the tent. Take your pick. Two pounds a day, if you're interested.'

'Where the hell did you get them?'

Rhodes was terribly pleased with himself, and kept rubbing the back of his neck with glee. 'I bought them from a frightful German, who was on his way to Kimberley. I used the last of the money I had left over from my cotton harvest. Eight cylinder pumps, eighty pounds. Not bad, eh?'

Barney slowly shook his head. 'I thought you said that nobody could make a fortune from growing cotton.'

'Do you want a pump?' asked Rhodes. 'You'd better make up your mind quickly.'

'All right,' said Barney, and took his brown leather wallet out of his crumpled bush-jacket. 'Here's eight pounds, for four days' pumping. But let me tell you this – these eight pounds are the first and last money that I'm ever going to pay you.'

'Quite right too,' said Rhodes, and smiled even more broadly.

Barney and Rhodes lifted the pump between them on to the back of the ox-waggon, and Barney rode back to Kimberley with the pump's discharge pipe rattling monotonously against the waggon's tailgate as a constant nagging reminder of what he had just been compelled to do. He felt relieved that he had found a pump, but depressed that he had been obliged to hire it from Rhodes. He should have had the foresight to buy up pumps himself. Eight pumps, rented at two pounds a day, would have meant sixteen pounds a day, which meant that Rhodes could cover his eighty pounds outlay in a single week.

There were plenty of fierce competitors at Kimberley – men whom Barney had already picked out of the milling mob of diggers as potential empirebuilders. Francis Baring Gould was one. Severe, haughty, he had excellent financial connections in London, and Barney knew that he was pressuring the Board to relax their old rule that one man could own only two claims. Another was Joseph B. Robinson, an unpleasant and gratuitously argumentative man whose nickname, even among his friends, was 'The Buccaneer'. But Barney felt able to cope with men like Gould and Robinson without too much difficulty. He understood what they were seeking out of the diamond mines – wealth and luxury and petty power – and how they intended to get it. Only Rhodes baffled him. Rhodes, for all of his humour, was almost impossible to puzzle out. And yet only Rhodes seemed likely to stand between Barney and his ultimate ambition.

Because now – with a clarity that fired him up like the finest of diamonds – Barney knew what his ambition was. His dream had taken shape, a bright and scintillating mirage rising from the African desert, and it had revealed itself as nothing less than the kingship of the Kimberley diamond mine. He wanted to stand on the North Reef of the Big Hole and look out across that burrowing chaos of intense human industry and know that it was all his.

He wanted to sink his hands into a bucket of diamonds, a whole bucket, and know that they all belonged to him.

The shadows were already sloping across the veld as he reached Kimberley again, and reined in the ox-waggon outside his bungalow. Most of the heavy cloud seemed to have passed over, and the western sky was like a lake of stirred magnolia honey.

Inside the bungalow, all the lamps were lit, and Barney expected that Mooi Klip was making last-minute alterations to the wedding decorations, and fussing over the range. He loved her the way she was at the moment: very feminine and flustered, and quite unlike the capable Griqua girl who had taken charge of Joel so calmly, on the day that Barney had released him. She had not lost her directness or her common-sense, but she had gained a new vulnerability, a new dependence on him, which Barney secretly enjoyed.

He released the oxen from their yoke, and led them around to the small kraal at the back of the house, where he watered them and fed them. Then, tying the kraal gate, he went around to the front door, and tried to push it open.

To his surprise, it was locked. He tried the handle again, but there was no question about it. He could not get in.

'Natalia!' he called. Then he banged at the door with the flat of his hand. 'Natalia, are you there?'

He thought he heard someone inside the bungalow banging at the floor boards, and then there was the clatter of a chair being knocked over. He listened, his ear pressed against the door. There was nothing for a while, until Mooi Klip's voice was suddenly raised in a scream.

'*Natalia!*' yelled Barney, hoarsely, and slammed at the door with his shoulder. It would not budge. It was built of solid imported wood, and it was held on with double brass hinges. '*Natalia!*' he bellowed again, and gripped the sides of the door-frame so that he could kick at it with his veld boots. One of the panels cracked, but the door still refused to give way.

Exploding with fear and adrenalin, Barney ran around to the toolshed at the side of the house, wrenched open the door, and seized a long-handled axe. Then he ran back to the front, and walloped the axe into the side of the doorframe once, twice, and once again. Splinters flew all around him, and each blow jarred the muscles of his arms.

He kicked at the door again, and again, and at last it racketed open. What he saw made him stop where he was, his axe gripped in both hands, his eyes dense with disbelief and fury.

Mooi Klip lay crouched on the rug, her red dress pulled up over her hips, her petticoat torn into shreds. Her naked thighs were criss-crossed with scratches, and patterned with bright crimson bruises. She was covering her face with her hands, and sobbing in a high, breathless pitch that scarcely sounded human.

Joel stood stiff and still in the corner of the living-room, his plaid workshirt open to the waist, baring his dark hairy belly, and his canvas trousers unbuttoned. His face was as grave and as odd as Barney had ever seen it. In his hand, upraised, he held the Shopkeeper's revolver which Barney had bought in New York as part of his supplies for the wilds of South Africa. The muzzle was aimed at the ceiling, but the way in which Joel was holding his arm up left Barney in no doubt that he was threatening him with his life.

Scattered across the floor and ground underfoot were cakes and pastries and baskets of plums. Even the three-tiered white wedding cake, a gift from Scheinman's the bakers, had been smashed sideways.

Barney, his brain as tight as an overwound clock, slowly laid down his axe. Then without keeping his eyes off Joel, he moved across the room and knelt down beside Mooi Klip, lifting her head on to his knee. She was shaking and crying, and she would not take her hands away from her face. Barney smoothed down her dress and held her close to him, gently rocking her, and stroking her hair.

'Are you all right?' he asked her. 'Are you hurt bad?'

Joel waved the pistol around carelessly as if he really had not meant to threaten Barney at all. But he did not put it down. He could see by the expression on Barney's face what would happen to him if he did.

'This isn't what it seems,' he said, lightly. He pulled at his left eyelid with his fingertip, as if he were rubbing sleep out of it.

'Isn't it?' asked Barney, in a deadened voice.

'It's, er – well, it started off as fun. That's all it was. Just fun.'

'Did you touch her?' asked Barney. He felt so cold that he couldn't move.

'We didn't do anything. We were just joking. Horseplay. That's all.'

'Did you touch her?' Barney repeated, more loudly.

Joel grinned. He wiped his nose with the back of his gun-hand. 'She was only arranging the table, that's all, and I thought that – if I –'

'*Did you touch her?*' screamed Barney.

Joel shrugged, and glanced sideways across the wreckage of the room as if he were looking for something special. 'Touch? Well, it depends what you mean by touch.'

'Did you assault her is what I mean.'

Joel's eyes darted back towards Barney, and he frowned.

Barney said, 'I'm going to kill you for this. I mean it. I'm going to kill you.'

He laid Mooi Klip carefully on the rug, and stood up. Mooi Klip lay on her side, bunched up self-protectively tight, her hands clasped in front of her mouth and her eyes wide open. She stared at nothing but the broken cakes and the trodden fruit, and she did not stop shaking.

'You said you were sorry, and I believed you,' Barney told Joel, circling around the table. 'I believed you!'

'I *was* sorry,' said Joel, swallowing hard, unable to look Barney in the face. 'I'm sorry now.'

'You're *sorry*?'

Joel's lips tightened, and then he burst out, 'What do you think it's like, living here with you two? Didn't you think of that, when you set up this cozy little household of yours?'

'What the hell are you talking about?'

'I'm talking about *her*!' said Joel, desperately. 'What do you think it's like, living here with her! Seeing her washing and cooking and cleaning everything up. Seeing her kiss you. Don't you think I'm just as capable of falling in love as you are? Or hasn't that ever occurred to you, that your brother Joel could fall in love? Maybe you can't bring yourself to believe that anybody else apart from the great Barney Blitz has any kind of real existence?'

Barney said, in a low-key, unsteady voice, 'She's my bride, Joel. You knew that. You *knew* that! And yet you could still attack her.'

'Attack her?' protested Joel, in an unexpectedly squeaky tone. 'You don't think that I'd stoop so low, do you? She attacked me! Tore her petticoats, begged me to take her before she was married to you. Begged me! Come on, Barney, she's nothing but a *schwartzeh*, and you know what they're like, even the educated ones! They've got morals like monkeys!'

Barney pushed aside the table, with a scraping of wooden feet, and advanced towards Joel with his fists raised. Joel stumbled back two or three paces, coughing, but then he gripped the revolver in both hands and pointed it directly at Barney's face.

'You'd kill me, would you?' Barney said shakily. 'Your own brother?'

'You're angry,' said Joel. 'You don't know what you're doing. I just want you to stay back.'

He edged around the room, keeping the revolver out in front of him. 'I've *told* you I'm sorry,' he repeated. There was a terrible monotony in his voice, like a deaf and backward child. 'I've told you I'm sorry, and I *am* sorry. But it's one of those things. Who can help it? Anyway, it's all over now. I can't turn the clock back. Even if I could, well, what good what it do? I haven't hurt her. She's pregnant already, so I haven't given her a baby. I wouldn't want to. My own brother's bride?'

Barney hesitated, and lowered his fists. Joel began to lower the gun, too, but when Barney made another move towards him, he quickly lifted it again.

'I think you'd better get out of here,' said Barney. 'Because I'm liable to go for you, whether you've got yourself a gun or not.'

'Oh,' said Joel. 'You're forgiving me, are you?'

'Just get out.'

Joel stared at Barney down the barrel of the Shopkeeper's revolver with eyes that seemed as impenetrable as stones. Barney could hardly believe that this wild and frenzied man was actually his own brother. He felt as if he had suddenly found himself in a petrifying nightmare of mirrors and anguish and broken cake.

There was a clattering sound. A few splatters of wet appeared on the floor around Joel's left foot. Joel wavered, but did not look down. His canvas trousers steamed with urine.

The brothers did not speak another word. Joel slowly retreated out of the doorway, almost tripping over Barney's long-handled axe. He crossed the vehandah, groping behind him for the rail, and then disappeared quickly into the evening shadows.

Barney stood motionless for almost a minute. Then he knelt down and gathered Mooi Klip in his arms, and carried her like a new bride into the bedroom, where he laid her carefully down on the patchwork comforter.

'I'm going to heat water for a bath,' he whispered, close to her ear, close to her sooty-brown curls. 'You can wash, and soak yourself, and then we'll clear everything up.'

'Barney,' she said, her chin crumpled with grief.

'Don't cry,' he told her.

'I can't help it. I can't help crying. How can you marry me now?'

Barney kissed her eyelashes, and the tears that clung to them like the raindrops that clung to the silverleaf.

'You're going to have my baby. How can I not marry you?'

She touched his face in the twilight. 'I don't know what happened. He was all right for most of the day. He went to the claim, and came back again. We talked about the wedding. Then he started teasing me, and trying to put his arms around me.'

Barney laid his fingers on her lips, to try to stop her talking, but she wanted to talk, and she took his hand away.

'I said no. I told him no. But he followed me around the room, and around the house, and he kept grabbing me and pulling at my dress. I called out for Janet next door, but she wasn't there, or else she didn't hear me. He wouldn't stop. He wouldn't leave me alone.'

'Mooi Klip,' said Barney, gently.

'Oh, Barney,' she sobbed, and clung to him tight. 'How can I marry you now?'

Barney couldn't speak for a long time. His chest and his throat felt congested with anguish and grief.

'You can marry me,' he managed to say, at last. 'I'll never forgive you if you don't.'

She turned her head away, and he looked down at her dark profile on the white pillow. Her eyes, and the pretty curve of her nose. He wished he were an artist, or a daguerreotypist, because he wanted to remember the way she looked, framed by the pillow, for ever. Mooi Klip, on Tuesday, 14 November 1871, a day of hopes and joys and indescribable pain.

'My mother and father will be here tomorrow,' said Mooi Klip. 'I will go back to Klipdrift with them.'

'Don't be ridiculous. Tomorrow, we're going to be married.'

'We can't. How can we? You have to stay with Joel. Half of the claim is yours. You can't give it up, just for me.'

'I still have the farm.'

Mooi Klip shook her head. 'You want to make your fortune. The claim is the only way. If you give it up because of me, you would never forget and you would never really forgive.'

Barney kissed her. 'You've crazy,' he told her. 'Do you know that? You're absolutely crazy.' But at the same time, the thought of what he and Joel were going to do about their thirty-one square feet of diamond-bearing ground had already passed across the back of his mind like a ghost seen momentarily at the end of a long corridor.

Mooi Klip closed her eyes. Barney said, 'He didn't hurt you, did he? He didn't hurt you inside? I mean, the baby's going to be all right?'

She gave a slight shake of her head. 'He didn't get properly inside me. I fought him all the time. I'm just tired now.'

'I'll heat the water,' Barney told her. He felt compelled to do something ordinary, something that required no thinking at all. Every thought in his head seemed to have been blasted out of him. He stood up and smiled at Mooi Klip with a smile that was meaningless, because it was neither loving nor reassuring. It was the smile of a man who is still suffering from shock, after an accident that has almost proved fatal.

She bathed in the zinc tub in the living-room, amidst the wreckage of her ruined wedding-breakfast. She wanted the water so hot that Barney could scarcely dip his hand in it; and she sat upright, her face expressionless, her hair tied up with a yellow ribbon. She said hardly anything at all, except to ask him to bring her another piece of soap.

Without looking at him, she knelt up in the tub and lathered herself between her legs over and over again, in a monotonous circular motion, until he felt like shouting out, 'It's over – it's all over – you're clean.' But she went on, and after a few minutes he hung the rough towel which he had been holding for her over the back of his chair, and went to the hutch to pour himself a drink.

Later, he made her some tea. She sat up in bed, wrapped in a blanket, and cupped the mug in both hands, like a child. Barney sat beside the bed with a fixed smile on his face until he realised that she was not even looking at him, and then his smile grew even more false, although he could not think of anything else to do. Should he frown? Or scowl? Should he shout at her to pull herself together? It was supposed to be her wedding-day tomorrow, the day that she going to be happy again, forever.

He held her hand, and although she did not take away, it lay in his grasp like a glove. He said, 'Mooi Klip?' but she did not answer. Her eyes and her thoughts, were somewhere else.

Sometime after one o'clock in the morning, after wedging the broken front door with a chair, Barney wearily undressed and slipped into bed. Mooi Klip was still awake, still sitting up with her eyes open. He put his arm around her but she was so unresponsive that after a few minutes, uncomfortable and embarrassed, he took it away again.

'We're still going to get married tomorrow,' he told her. 'We planned to get married tomorrow, and we will.'

Mooi Klip stared down at her hands lying on the patchwork comforter as if she could not work out whose hands they were.

Barney said, 'You are going to marry me, aren't you?'

'Someday,' she said, and nodded. 'Perhaps someday.'

They were woken up at dawn by someone shouting and banging at the front of the house. Barney threw back the comforter, and staggered naked to the bedroom door, where his cotton nightshirt hung on a cuphook.

'Barney!' a voice called loudly. 'Barney, come quick!'

He negotiated his way across the cake-strewn living-room, and tugged the chair away from the front door. It was bright outside, and still chilly with the dew that settled in the early hours of the night like imaginary diamonds. On the verandah stood Edward Nork, in grubby twill trousers and puttees, and a jacket that looked as if it had once belonged to the fattest man in Cape Colony. Behind him, two kaffirs were waiting with grins as orange as slices of sausage fruit, bearing a woven litter, on which was huddled the body of a man, smothered in blood and yellow mud.

Edward Nork said, 'You're going to have to be calm, now, Barney. It's Joel. There's been rather a bad accident.'

'Joel?' asked Barney. He could not understand what Edward Nork was trying to tell him. Then he looked again at the gory body on the litter, and saw a hand that was unmistakably Joel's hanging from one side. The shirt, although it was torn and basted with mud, was also unmistakably Joel's. Barney crossed the verandah as if he were still asleep, and one of the kaffirs said, 'He not dead, boss. He was screaming out just a while back. Screaming like blue murder.'

'Take him inside,' Barney instructed. But he looked up, and

there in the doorway in her nightgown was Mooi Klip, her face pale, her hands crossed over her breasts.

'Natalia,' said Barney, and she could hear the question in his voice. 'Natalia, it's Joel.'

She did not move, did not speak, but stood in the doorway waiting for Barney to make up his mind what he was going to do.

'He's hurt,' said Barney. 'He could be dying.'

Mooi Klip raised her chin defiantly. 'A funeral?' she asked him.

'I don't know what you mean. Look at him. He needs help.'

'You can have a funeral or a wedding,' said Mooi Klip. 'Not both.'

Edward Nork wound his loose jacket around him in discomfort. He was a geologist, and a drinker. He was always ill-at-ease in family arguments. 'Dwyka tillite does not answer back, nor put one into embarrassing corners,' he had told Barney over dinner, the night that Rhodes had first arrived. 'Neither does whiskey. But wives and children unfortunately do.'

Mooi Klip said, 'I don't care if he's dying or not, Barney. I don't want him here. And if you go to his funeral, I won't ever speak to you again. You won't get anything out of me but silence, for the rest of my life.'

Joel whimpered. Barney looked down at his battered, mud-crusted face, and saw that his lips were blue and that his eyes were rolled up so that the whites were exposed.

'What happened?' Barney asked Edward Nork.

Edward shrugged, as if to say that he knew, but he did not want to talk about it in front of Mooi Klip.

'All right,' said Barney. 'Get him inside.'

Mooi Klip retreated back into the house, and into the bedroom. She closed the door, and as Barney stepped in after her to clear the floor of cake and fruit, he heard her click the hasp into place.

'Down here,' he told the kaffirs. 'And gently, for God's sake.'

The kaffirs laid Joel down on the floor, and then ran off. Edward Nork, pacing around the living-room in embarrassment, said, 'Your wedding today? Looks like the food got a bit of a bashing.'

'It was *supposed* to have been my wedding today,' said Barney.

Edward nodded his head towards the bedroom door. 'Bit of trouble? I've heard some of those Griquas are rather hot-tempered.'

Barney knelt down beside Joel and unbuttoned his shirt. From the lumpy bruises that protruded from Joel's chest, it looked as if four or five of his ribs were broken. Joel groaned, and licked his muddy lips.

'Edward — will you do me a favour?' asked Barney. 'Stoke up the range. There's plenty of fresh firewood in the kitchen. I need some hot water to clean him up.'

'Don't you want to hear what happened?'

'Just get the fire going, please. I've had enough grief for one night.'

'Anything you say,' said Edward, and disappeared into the kitchen.

It took over half an hour to get Joel undressed and cleaned up, and laid on his bed. He whimpered and cried constantly, and Barney could feel that apart from his ribs, his left leg was badly smashed. His arms and legs were raw with cuts and abrasions, and the middle finger on his right hand was pulped almost flat.

Between them, with Edward holding his head and Barney tilting up the bottle, they managed to force Joel to drink almost a quarter of a bottle of brandy. He brought up a couple of mouthfuls of vomit, half-digested meat pie, and whiskey, but he kept enough of the brandy down to send him to sleep for a while.

'All right then, what happened?' asked Barney, closing Joel's door behind him. He glanced at Mooi Klip's door, but then looked away again. Edward noticed, though, and gave a wry schoolboy grin.

'We were all at Dodd's Bar,' said Edward. 'None of us were doing very much. Getting drunk, playing billiards, you know. Another entertaining evening in Kimberley. But then Joel came in, and I must say he looked rather mad. Mad in the English sense, if you know what I mean.'

'You mean he was acting crazy.'

'Well, quite so. He had a pistol, which he was waving around,

224

until Harry Munt took it away from him, and locked it in his safe. And I must say that Joel *smelled*, rather. Not too fussy about cleanliness, myself. You can't be, out here, with water so scarce. But he definitely *smelled*.'

Barney lowered his head and stood with his hands clasped at the back of his neck. 'Go on,' he said. 'Do you want a drink?'

'That's rather like asking an ostrich if it wants to fly.'

Barney drained the last of the sherry bottle, and then topped it up with sherry from the cask which had been intended for the wedding. He paused for a moment and stared at the cake, a broken litter of almond paste and white frosting, and crushed silver horseshoes.

'That looks a bit wonky,' said Edward, trying to be conversational.

'Yes,' said Barney, picking up one of the horseshoes and then dropping it again, 'I think that's the word. Wonky.'

Edward took his sherry, and drank half of it straight away. Then, wiping his mouth, he said, 'The trouble really started when that lady from Capetown came in. Well, *lady* isn't quite the word. Whore, is what she was. She was drunk as any of us, but the trouble was that she'd been waiting all night at Madame Lavinia's, and nobody had given her a try. It really wasn't surprising, to tell you the truth. Rather unfortunate boat race. Oh, I'm sorry. That's Cockney rhyming slang for "face"; it always amused me, don't know why. I didn't even go to Oxford or Cambridge. But anyway, there she was – drunk, and red-haired, and very much in the mood for mischief – and she decided to auction herself to the highest bidder.'

Barney poured another drink for himself, but right now his stomach felt too tight for him to swallow it. 'Go on,' he said, dryly.

'Well, this is the ticklish bit,' said Edward. 'There was a Dutch diamond buyer there, and he bid £25, and then £30, and then £100. He was quite out of his mind with Geneva gin, of course. I mean, almost insensible. But Joel seemed determined to bust him. And, in the end, he bid his claim.'

'He did *what*?'

'He bid his claim. All thirty-one square feet of it, in return for a night with madame from down the road.'

'But Joel doesn't *own* the whole claim. We're equal partners, fifty-fifty. He can't sell out without offering me the option to buy his half, any more than I can sell out without offering him the option to buy mine. He can't dispose of the whole claim on his own, and especially not in Dodd's Bar, for some flea-bitten prostitute.'

'That's what I thought,' said Edward. 'And, merry as I was, I told him so.'

'But?' demanded Barney.

'But, old fellow, I'm afraid that Joel has rather outsmarted you. If you can call it smart, of course, to hand over a £5000 diamond claim to a common prostitute, in return for a night of passion that you never had. Joel told me that he had never actually re-registered the claim in your favour at all. The claim is entirely his. So when he put in his bid for this drunken red-haired lady, he was entirely within his rights. And she will be entirely within *her* rights if she tries to enforce her ownership. Which, knowing her, at least from one night at Dodd's Bar, she most certainly will.'

Barney stared at Edward for a long time in silence.

'I'm sorry,' said Edward. 'If only I'd known, I would have told you sooner. But, well –'

'What happened?' asked Barney, harshly and soft. 'How did he get so hurt?'

'There was rather an argument,' said Edward. 'Do you have some more of that excellent sherry, incidentally? Thank you. Good. Anyway, the Dutch diamond buyer declared that he was in love with this lady from Madame Lavinia's, regardless of Joel's winning bid, and hauled her off with him. I must say there was a great deal of amusement at this ... you know the kind of thing. Laughing, and throwing bottles. So Joel led a whole gang of diggers out of Dodd's Bar, and they followed the poor little Dutch fellow all the way to his tent ... and when he was just about to stake his claim, if you understand what I mean ... just as he was settling down with this lady from Madame Lavinia's ... the whole lot of them heaved out his tent-pegs, and whisked away his tent, and there the poor fellow was, caught in the act!'

Barney looked away. He felt tired, and unreal, and Edward's story fell on his consciousness like dead leaves.

'There was something of a fight,' said Edward, almost apologetically. 'The Dutch diamond buyer wasn't much of a pug, but of course Joel was incapably drunk. There was a lot of scuffling, and then Joel fell down the side of the mine, into somebody's claim; and the ground being so wet, it collapsed on top of him. Rocks, winching-gear, everything. It took ten men to dig him out.'

'What about a doctor?' asked Barney.

'We tried Tuter. We sent somebody round to his home.'

'And?'

'He wouldn't come. He *couldn't* come, actually. He was drunk.'

'So my brother's going to die. Is that it?'

Edward had been holding up his empty glass, but now he set it down again, abashed. 'An awful lot of diggers die out here, Barney. It's one of the natural hazards of diamond-mining. There's malaria, dysentery, and cholera. There's women and there's drink. Your brother's quite lucky he won't linger.'

'Lucky?' said Barney. 'Such a *miesse meshina*, and he's lucky?'

'*Comparatively* lucky,' Edward corrected himself.

Barney crossed the room and looked in at Joel's door. Joel was lying just where they had left him, his face the colour of dirty canvas. His teeth were softly and endlessly chattering, and he twitched from time to time in pain. Barney knew only too well what would happen to him if he did not receive professional medical attention right away. Since they had started mining their claim, they had both seen scores of diggers and kaffirs poisoned by gangrene, or felled by blood clots to the brain. He remembered the time an Australian digger had crushed his left hand in the winding gear of his steel cable, and had tried to carry on working with his fingers bandaged up. He had died within two weeks of the foulest infection that Barney had ever seen. There were dozens of graves outside Kimberley, on the veld, and most of the men who lay in them had died for the want of a surgeon.

'There's nothing I can do, then?' asked Barney. 'I just have to wait here and watch him suffer?'

Edward had been helping himself to more sherry. 'I hear that

Sir Thomas Sutter is in Durban at the moment, visiting his nephew.'

'Sir Thomas Sutter? Who's he?'

'Only the most eminent surgeon and bonesetter in England, old chap. Barring the Queen's physician, of course. Don't tell me you've never heard of Sutter the Cutter?'

'No, I haven't. But he's no use to Joel, is he, if he's in Durban?'

Edward sighed. 'You could try to get him there. I mean, there's no guarantee that he'd arrive alive, or even in an operable condition. There isn't even any kind of guarantee that Sir Thomas would consent to operate. He's frightfully particular about who he cuts up, and frightfully pricey, too. But ... it may be worth a try.'

Barney closed his eyes. This was supposed to have been the happiest day he had ever woken up to. Now, like his wedding-cake, it lay in pieces. He wished to God that he had been born somewhere else, to someone else, in another day and another age. It would have been better never to have met Mooi Klip at all, rather than meet her and love her and lose her this way. And all because of his ridiculous brother.

'I suppose I should try to get there,' said Barney. 'As long as Joel doesn't suffer too much.'

Edward sat forward in his chair. 'If he does suffer ... well, Harry Munt's still got your gun.'

Shortly after nine o'clock, there was the sharp rapping of a cane on the front door. Barney had been bathing Joel's forehead with a wet cloth, while Edward had gone over to Dr Tuter's place to persuade him to prescribe some painkillers for the journey to Durban. Barney carefully propped Joel's head with a pillow, and went out to see who it was.

Silhouetted against the dazzle of the day, formally dressed in black, his hat straight and his walking-cane tucked under his arm, was Mr Knight.

Barney wiped his hands on a towel. 'Yes?' he asked. 'And what can I do for you?'

'Not much,' said Mr Knight, sharply. 'It's your brother Joel Blitz I've come to see.'

'My brother's seriously ill.'

'Well, I knew that. But all the same I have to serve notice on him. Laws of the land, and all that.'

'Whatever it is, you can tell me.'

'I really have to serve it on your brother.'

Barney rolled down his sleeves with two or three aggressive tugs at his cuffs. 'Either tell me, or get the hell out of here.'

'Very well. I suppose you could be considered to be standing in for him as his legal proxy. The fact of the matter is,' and here he cleared his throat, 'the fact of the matter is that I represent a young lady named Dorothy Evans, or "Dottie", as she is known to her friends. She came to me very early this morning in order to press her ownership of claim No. 172 at the Kimberley Mine which previously belonged in whole to Mr Joel Blitz.'

'I think the young lady must be making a mistake,' said Barney. 'Claim No. 172 belongs to my brother and that's it.'

'Well, you're wrong, I'm afraid. Miss Evans has written proof – written and witnessed – that your brother handed the claim over to her, complete with all mining equipment, at Dodd's Bar at approximately eleven o'clock last night.'

Barney looked at Mr Knight steadily. There was no doubt at all that Mr Knight was enjoying every moment of this. A sweet and legalistic revenge for the way in which Barney had tricked and humiliated himself and his family. 'There is no better situation for a Jew,' Mr Knight had told Dottie Evans that morning, 'than to be wriggling like an insect on the end of a very sharp stick.'

Barney said, 'What written proof? Show me.'

Mr Knight produced a crumpled piece of paper from the breast pocket of his coat, like a children's conjuror. 'A humble piece of paper,' he smiled. 'The label from a bottle of patent bitters, if I'm not mistaken. But the writing on it has all the weight of English law.'

Barney took the paper and read it. In a sloping scrawl, Joel had written the words, 'I Joel Blitz hereby pass all title in my claim No. 172 at Colesberg Kop to Dottie Evans, and all my mining equpt.' That was all. Joel must have been so drunk that he had even stipulated what favours Miss Dottie Evans was supposed to give him in return.

'This is worthless,' said Barney. 'Joel was totally drunk at the time. I have witnesses.'

'Witnesses? A collection of lechers and confirmed alcoholics?'

'Miss Dottie Evans herself is a whore,' Barney reminded him.

Mr Knight raised a beatific hand. 'She *was* a whore. She was, indeed, a whore. But now she has seen the error of her ways, and raised herself from the mire.'

'She can afford to, I suppose, now she has a free diamond mine.'

'Don't be so sour,' grinned Mr Knight, snatching the bitters label back between two grey-gloved fingers.

'I'm not,' said Barney. 'Right now, I haven't time to be sour. My brother is badly hurt and I have to get him to a doctor.'

'Well, I'm sorry,' said Mr Knight. 'I truly am. But – the law is the law.'

He looked around the living-room. 'Wasn't today supposed to be the day you were going to marry that little black girl?' he asked. 'I heard the banns read in church, and I must tell you that I stood up for you when one or two of the congregation started expressing objections. "Why should we allow a Jew and a blackie to get married in an Anglican church?" they asked. But I said, "Is that your spirit of Christian charity? The Griquas are just as much Christians as we are, and with any luck the Jewish fellow will learn the error of his ways."'

'You're right,' said Barney. 'I have learned the error of my ways. And it was you who taught me the lesson. You *momzer*.'

Mr Knight widened his eyes interrogatively.

'It's a name we give to anybody who's clever,' Barney told him. 'You know the type. Wily, smart, that type of person.'

'Well,' said Mr Knight, 'I'm glad you've taken the whole thing so well.'

'*Monzer* also means bastard,' Barney added.

Mr Knight pressed his tongue thoughtfully inside his cheek. Then he said coldly, 'I have to warn you that any attempt by you or your kaffirs to dig in claim No. 172 will be regarded as claim-jumping, and theft, and that if you are caught trespassing on claim No. 172 my client will consider your action as a most serious breach of her digging rights.'

'Get out of my house before I hit you,' said Barney.

Edward came back just as Mr Knight was leaving. He raised his hat to him, and was mildly surprised when the laywer brushed past him without even saying, 'Good day.'

'That was your legal chap, wasn't it?' he asked, emptying his coat pockets of dozens of glass vials of white powder. 'He didn't seem very jolly did he?'

'What are these?' asked Barney, picking up one of the vials and examining it. 'Are these painkillers?'

'Dover's powder, old chap. Ten per cent of opium, to be given in doses of five grains to begin with, up to ten if the pain gets worse. And I'm afraid you owe me eleven pounds for this little lot. Four pounds for the medicine itself, and seven to persuade Dr Tuter to give them to me. Mind you, he's quite addicted to the stuff himself.'

At that moment, the bedroom door opened. Barney turned around, and there stood Mooi Klip, in her pale blue overdress and hat, her gloves held tightly in her hand, her eyes swollen from crying.

Edward said quickly, 'I'll just go and give Joel his first dose. Dr Tuter said to start as soon as possible.'

'Thank you, Edward,' said Barney, his eyes on Mooi Klip.

Mooi Klip stepped out into the living-room. The sun from the open doorway sparkled on the $2\frac{1}{2}$-carat diamond betrothal ring that Harry Feinberg had ordered for Barney from Cape-town, and which Barney had slipped on to Mooi Klip's finger one warm evening when they had been sitting on the verandah outside, under a moon like a tiger's-eye.

She raised her hand and twisted the ring around and around, the way that women do when they feel anxious. She would not look at Barney, but stared sadly at their wedding-breakfast instead.

'I've packed my clothes,' she said.

'You're really going?'

She nodded.

'You know how much I love you, don't you?'

She nodded again.

He bit his lip. 'What can I say that will make you stay? Can I say anything?'

'Not now,' she said. 'Right now, you have to look after your brother.'

'I had to bring him in. You understand that, don't you? He's – well, he's probably going to die anyway.'

'I'm sorry,' said Mooi Klip. 'What I said outside, about never speaking to you again – I didn't mean it. I was just –'

'If you didn't mean it, then stay. Please. What do you think I'm going to do without you?'

Mooi Klip slowly shook her head. 'You don't need me now. I won't be anything but a burden. And everything that's happened ... it's spoiled this day for us, and we'd be foolish if we tried to patch it up. I don't want to be married with a broken wedding-cake. I don't want to be married while we're arguing. I want to be married to your properly, in peace, and in love; and to know that we can have nothing but happiness.'

'We *will* be happy.'

She smiled at him. A smile of such sadness and regret; but also a smile of determination. 'Not yet,' she said. 'We're not ready for each other yet, even if we ever were. I love you, Barney. I don't think you even understand how much. You've taught me about the world, and about all kinds of things. But I'm not really what you want, or what you need, am I?'

'You're going back to Klipdrift?' he asked her.

'As soon as my mother and father arrive.'

'And what are you going to tell them? And Jan Bloem?'

'I shall tell them the truth. That's all. The truth isn't difficult to tell. I still love you, and I'm not ashamed of that.'

'What about the baby?' asked Barney.

She laid her hand on her stomach. 'I shall cherish the baby. And when she's born, if we're still not together by then, I shall send someone with a message to you, so that you can come and see her.'

Barney felt as if a dry ball of desert weed had caught in his throat. 'You're so sure it's going to be a girl,' he said, trying hard not to cry.

'Wouldn't you like a pretty little daughter, just like me?'

Barney nodded. Mooi Klip came over to him, and put her arms around his waist, and held him very tight. He could smell that familiar smell of hers, like flowers and spices, and he wound her curls around his fingers the way he had always done, ever since their first night together under the stars at Jan Bloem's encampment. He could not believe that she was going. He could not believe that he might never hold her again. Her hard stomach, still high under her breasts, was pressed between them like the most precious possession they had ever owned. Brighter, and more valuable, than diamonds.

She whispered against his shirt, 'I heard everything that Edward said, about your losing the claim.'

'And Mr Knight?'

She said, 'Yes. I'm so sorry.'

'I guess I can start again.'

'You'll need money for Joel's operation,' she said.

'I've got enough in the bank.'

'You'll need the money in the bank, to buy another claim.'

'I've got the farm, too, at Derdeheuwel. I can always sell that, if I have to.'

Mooi Klip stood away from him, and opened her purse. 'I've been meaning to give you this, anyway. It wasn't really right that I should keep it.'

'What are you talking about?'

Tied tightly in a roll, and tucked into the small pocket at the side of Mooi Klip's purse, were scores of English five-pound notes. Mooi Klip pushed the roll into Barney's shirt pocket, and then kissed him on the lips, quickly, so that he could not make the kiss linger.

He took the money out again. 'Where did you get all this?'

'From Derdeheuwel, the day we buried Monsaraz. I admired your gesture, burning the money, but sometimes I think that women are more practical than men, even if their gestures aren't so admirable.'

'There must be six or seven hundred pounds here.'

'Six hundred and twenty. I've counted it.'

'I should burn it,' said Barney.

'You have your brother to look after.'

'What are *you* going to do for money?'

233

She smiled. 'My people will look after me now.'

'Aren't I your people?'

She came close again, and touched the unshaved bristles on his cheek. 'You will always be my people,' she told him. 'Oh, Barney, I love you so much.'

Edward coughed politely at the bedroom door. 'He's sleeping again,' he announced. 'But he's only going to get worse, not better. Do you want me to help you make up a bed on the waggon?'

'Yes, please,' said Barney, and turned away from Jooi Klip feeling as if there were nothing inside of him but tears that could not be cried.

Mooi Klip's mother and father arrived at eleven o'clock, all dressed up in their wedding outfits. Jan Bloem was there, too, and two of his favourite cronies, and Piet Steyn. Their shoes were all brightly polished, their hats were brushed, and in their morning-coats and striped trousers they looked, in the sarcastic words of Harry Munt, who had watched them pass from the boardwalk outside of Dodd's Bar, 'like the guests of honour at a gorilla's ball.'

Mooi Klip's mother was small as her daughter, but plump, and she was dressed up in a lemon-yellow day frock with a grey-piped bolero, and a hat that was dancing with huge white ostrich feathers. Her father was tall, handsome, and very black. Neither of them spoke English – only the curious Afrikaans of the Griquas.

There were tears and arguments and explanations as soon as they arrived. It had been enough for Mooi Klip's father that she should live with a man outside of wedlock, and be carrying his child. Now, using a confused Jan Bloem as an occasional interpreter, he started to shout in a loud demanding voice at everybody, including his wife. Barney sat tiredly on the verandah steps, his head in his hands, and waited until everybody had finished squabbling. The waggon had been made ready to carry Joel to Durban, with blankets and pillows and leather straps to keep his broken leg straight, and all Barney wanted to do now was go.

At last, Mooi Klip's father came marching over to Barney, with Jan Bloem beside him, and let out a burst of guttural Afrikaans. There were diamonds of sweat on his shiny black upper lip, and he was as indignant and upright as any father that Barney had ever seen. There was a fresh white orchid in his buttonhole.

Barney understood only one or two words of what he was saying, but the strain of the tirade was inescapable. Jan Bloem said dryly, 'You hear what he's saying, my friend? He's saying you took everything from his daughter, and gave nothing back. He's saying you should be ashamed of what you and your brother have done, and that if it wasn't flying in the face of the Lord, he would turn you inside-out, and use your insides to feed his dogs.'

'Tell him he's quite justified in being so angry,' said Barney.

Jan Bloem translated. Mooi Klip's father listened, and then lifted one quivering finger, and came out with another interminable salvo of explosive rhetoric.

'He's very upset,' explained Jan Bloem. 'He wants to know what you're going to do.'

'I'm going to take my brother to Durban to try to save his life,' said Barney, flatly. 'Then I'm going to come back here to marry his daughter.'

'He doesn't believe you,' said Jan Bloem. 'He says you're a scallywag.'

'Tell him I love Natalia.'

'He says if you love her, how could you treat her so wrongly?'

'Tell him it was all a series of tragic mistakes, and that he doesn't have to keep shouting at me because I think I've suffered enough already. I love his daughter, and for the time being I'm losing her. I love my brother, and he's hurt the only woman I love. Just tell him to look at my face and see what's there.'

There was a long frowning pause from Mooi Klip's father when Jan Bloem had translated these words. Then he leaned forward, his hands on his knees, and stared at Barney's face from only five or six inches away, his jet-black eyes searching Barney's expression as narrowly and as painstakingly as Barney himself ever inspected a rough stone from the mine. At last,

Mooi Klip's father stood straight, and self-importantly brushed a little fluff from the cuff of his coat.

'Well?' asked Barney. 'I'm going to have to go soon, if I'm going to make any distance before dark.'

'He says he still thinks you're a scallywag,' smiled Jan Bloem. 'However, he believes what you say, that you love his daughter. When your brother is well, he says, you must come to speak to him again. But he says he will not easily let you marry her, unless you have proved your good intentions.'

'I see,' said Barney, and attempted a friendly nod towards Mooi Klip's father. The Griqua's face remained impassive, and Barney found himself converting the nod into a stiff-jointed twist of his neck, as if he had been sleeping all night at an odd angle.

'He says one thing more,' said Jan Bloem. 'He says he has brought you a gift, and that he wants you to accept his gift regardless of what has happened today. He says he is not a rich man, but this is a good gift; and he hopes you will accept it.'

'Tell him I'll be delighted,' said Barney, cautiously.

Mooi Klip's father went off to get his gift, and Jan Bloem screwed his monocle into his eye and watched Barney with mischievous anticipation.

'You know why he's insisting that you accept this gift?' he asked Barney.

'Not entirely,' said Barney.

'Well, then, you're not as bright as I thought,' said Jan Bloem. 'He wants you to accept this gift so that you'll feel bound to come back and marry his daughter. And you can't blame him, can you?'

'I don't,' said Barney. 'If I had any control over events, I'd marry his daughter today.'

Jan Bloem gave him a sympathetic smile. 'I spoke to Natalia,' he said. 'You mustn't blame her.'

'I blame myself.'

'That's just as ridiculous. Learn to attribute blame where blame should be attributed. Don't be a martyr. That's my motto.'

'You're full of mottoes.'

'It's better than being wise.'

Mooi Klip's father came around the side of the bungalow, leading behind him on a frayed rope a swaybacked, moth-eaten horse. Barney took one look at the animal and glanced at Jan Bloem in quick, furtive desperation. Jan Bloem kept up his friendly grin, but his monocle dropped out of his eye and swung on its black silk cord. Barney could tell that he was only a sixteenth of an inch away from laughing.

'This is for you,' translated Jan Bloem, while Mooi Klip's father watched him expectantly. 'His name is Alsjeblieft.'

'Alsjeblieft?' asked Barney. 'That means *please*, doesn't it?'

'That's right,' grinned Jan Bloem. 'Every time you want this horse to do anything for you, you have to say Alsjeblieft.'

Mooi Klip's father held out the rope. Barney hesistated for a moment, and then took it. The horse snuffled and whinnied, and swung its head around.

Barney said, 'Please tell Mooi Klip's father that I am delighted by his gift, and that if I had the time I would invite him to have a drink with me. But he obviously understands that I have to go.'

'He understands,' said Jan Bloem. 'He says that this horse used to belong to an old *kopje walloper*, one of the fellows who went around buying up diamonds from the small diggings around Klipdrift and Dutoitspan. It was a good horse, in its day.'

Barney nodded and smiled to Mooi Klip's father. Mooi Klip's father nodded, unsmiling, in return. Then he let out a short, sharp volley of Afrikaans, which he ended up with an emphatic, '*huh!*' as if to say '*so there!*'

'What did he say?' Barney asked Jan Bloem.

'He says you can think what you like about the horse, but he paid £27 10s for it.'

Barney, wearily, smiled again. 'Tell him I'm eternally grateful.'

At last, Mooi Klip's parents were ready to leave, taking their daughter home with them. Mooi Klip sat between her mother and her father, her carpet-bag stowed in the back of the ox-waggon, and she looked as stiff and as pale as marble. Her mother give Barney a small, understanding wave, and Barney guessed what Mooi Klip must have said to her.

'One word,' said Jan Bloem, before he climbed up on to his own waggon.

Barney said, 'What's that? Don't count chickens before the eggs are laid?'

'No, it's not a motto,' said Jan Bloem. He held Barney's arm with one black, well-manicured hand. 'I just want to say that if you care for Natalia, come back as quickly as you can and marry her. But, if you don't, then leave her alone. She's pretty, she'll find someone else in time. One of our own people, more than likely; and whoever it is, they'll look after your baby for you. But don't hurt her any more.'

Barney laid his hand on top of Jan Bloem's. 'Thanks for your advice,' he said, 'but only Natalia and I can decide what we're going to do next. Not you, not her parents. Not anybody.'

'Well,' Jan Bloem told him, 'I wish you the best of luck in any case. What do you say? *Mazel tov!*'

'Say *mazel tov* when I get back from Durban with a healthy brother,' said Barney. The horse Alsjeblieft snorted and tugged at his rope. He could sense that Jan Bloem and Mooi Klip's family were about to set off, and he was feeling anxious about being left behind.

Mooi Klip turned around only once as her father drove their ox-waggon away through the midday dust, and steered around the rim of the Kimberley Mine. Barney thought he saw her mouth the word 'goodbye' but he could not quite be sure. Edward Nork came up and said, 'It'll work out all right, you know. It really must. Do you want me to take care of this dreadful horse while you're gone?'

'I suppose so,' said Barney, eyeing the creature's fraying mane and speckled, fly-bitten hide. 'If you can ride it, by all means ride it. If you can't, then probably the best thing you can do is to eat it.'

Edward looked at the horse reflectively, as if he could imagine it on a dinner-plate, with roasted potatoes and fresh peas. The horse snuffled nervously, and backed away from him on clicking hooves.

*

Not even Barney's voyage out to South Africa and his attempts to find Joel among the mines and settlements of north Cape Colony had been as harsh and as hopeless as his six-week journey to Durban. With Joel strapped in as comfortably as possible on a bed of blankets and pillows, Barney travelled day after day across the vast plains of the Orange Free State, under skies that were dark with sunshine, amidst dust that was as blinding as flour. The odds were almost overwhelming that Joel would die of infection within a matter of days, but when each morning broke across the grasslands and Joel was still alive, still murmuring and whispering and crying with the pain of his injuries, Barney would mount the waggon's seat and snap his whip at the oxen, and they would plod eastwards again, towards a blue hazy horizon which they never seemed to reach.

Joel had hours of lucidity, when he would lie amongst his pillows, his face set in a grimace, talking to Barney in short, agonised sentences about what had happened. Barney kept his back to his brother most of the time, rarely turning around. The Blitz family burden, at this stage in his life, was more than he could bear. He was driving Joel to Durban because he had to drive Joel to Durban, because it was the best hope for Joel's survival, and because Joel was his brother. There were no other reasons.

One Thursday morning, they saw for the first time the distant blue outline of the Drakensberg Mountains, which they would have to cross before descending into Natal, and then making their way down through Colenso and Pieter Maritzburg to Durban. Joel, propped up on his pillows, said, 'We shouldn't go back you know.'

'Because you've lost us our claim?' said Barney.

'Because there's nothing to go back for,' said Joel. 'It's a fool's game, diamond mining. What the hell's the point of it? You dig all day, you break your back, and for what?'

'We could have been rich,' said Barney.

'We could have been old before our time,' retorted Joel.

Barney wiped the back of his neck with a handkerchief. Ahead of him, the oxen plodded steadily foward, their heads down, their thin-bladed haunches rising and falling with every step. 'You can stay in Durban if you want to,' he told Joel. 'But I'm going back. There's all of our money in the London and South African Bank, for one thing.'

Joel brushed a fly away from his face. 'To tell you the truth,' he said, 'we have a little problem with that.'

Barney lowered the reins. 'Problem? What are you talking about? We have seventeen thousand pounds in that bank. What problems?'

Joel looked towards the horizon. 'We owe the bank two thousand pounds'.

Gradually, Barney drew the oxen to a halt. Then he turned on his seat and said, '*What?*'

Joel's face was ghastly with pain. Pursing his lips, he said, 'It doesn't matter. For God's sake, just carry on.'

'I want to know, Joel. What problem? How in God's name can we owe the bank two thousand pounds?'

Joel said, 'I gambled a little. At Dodd's.'

'You gambled? But you didn't gamble seventeen thousand pounds!'

Joel nodded. 'Just get this waggon going, will you? The sooner we get this trip over, the better.'

But Barney was wide-eyed, paralysed. 'You gambled all of those seventeen thousand pounds at Dodd's Bar? All of them? And two thousand more?'

Joel raised a hand beseechingly. 'Barney – will you please get going. I can't take any more of this.'

'*You* can't take any more?' screamed Barney. He jumped down from the driving seat, and advanced on Joel with his face crimson. 'How can you say that? Everything I've worked for, everything I've been counting on! You've wasted everything! All that talk about saving our money, about sticking to one claim only! God, you're crazy! God, you're as crazy as Mama was!'

Joel lay back on his pillows. He eas exhausted with heat and agony. 'All right, so I'm crazy. You got your gun back from Harry Munt. So shoot. Save yourself a journey.'

Barney stood beside the ox-waggon for over a minute, in the relentless heat of the afternoon. The oxen flicked their tails at the flies, and the insects chirruped on the veld, and there was nobody and nothing around for mile upon mile, as far as the settlement of Paul Roux.

He could have taken out his Shopkeeper's pistol and shot Joel in the head, and nobody would ever have known. He could have buried the body in the dust, and returned to Kimberley and told Edward Nork and everybody else at the mine that Joel had died of his injuries. Joel had gambled away all his money, raped his wife-to-be, ruined his wedding, and cheated him out of his claim. What else did he deserve, but death?

Yet Barney remembered his father, sitting by the pale light of the upstairs window at Clinton Street, and the way his father's fingers had turned the first thin page of the Bible, and read, 'What hast thou done? the voice of thy brother's blood crieth unto me from the ground. And now art thou cursed from the earth, which hath opened her mouth to receive thy brother's blood from thy hand. A fugitive and a vagabond shalt thou be in the earth.'

Barney turned his face in the direction of the wind, narrowing his eyes against the grit and the heat. Then he climbed back up on to the waggon, and clicked at the oxen, the same Xhosa click that Donald had taught him, and they continued their trek across the plains of the Orange Free State.

Each night was the same, huddled under blankets by a flickering fire, after a meal of dried meat, dried fruit, and warm water. Each night Barney had to let down the side of the waggon and help Joel to roll off on to the ground, so that he could lie on the dust on his back to empty his bowels. Most nights, Joel screamed out loud as he forced shit through his shattered pelvis; and then he would whimper incessantly as Barney cleaned him up. After that, there would be a gagged-down meal, a heavy dose of ipecacuanha, and a few hours of restless sleep. In the morning, the process would have to be repeated all over again.

Miraculously, though, Joel's crushed leg remained free of serious infection. It began to knit together in an odd crooked shape, and it gave him excruciating pain, so much so that whenever the waggon lurched down a rough slope, he would shriek out to Barney to shoot him at once. But the skin had not been broken, and most of the lacerations had now healed up, and as they approached the Golden Gate, Barney's hopes at last began to rise a little.

The Golden Gate was utterly silent and eerie as Barney's ox-waggon passed through. It was a towering formation of weird and brooding sandstone crags, rising out of the scrub like massive totems. Above the crags, the sky was as dark and unforgiving as always, and the lamb-catching eagles, the *lammargayers*, circled and circled on wings as wide as sailboats. As he wended his way upwards through the mountains, past Mushroom Rock and Brandwag Rock, with their dazzling golden faces, Barney could hear the distant grinding echo of his ox-waggon wheels like a ghostly reminder of voortrekkers from forty years ago. There were other echoes in these mountains, too: of the Bushmen who had lived here in prehistoric times, and had painted the sandstone caves with pictures of plants and bird and long-forgotten rituals. Of the cannibals who had once roamed the valley of the Caledon River, and who had slaughtered and eaten more than 30,000 people.

In breezy silence, Barney passed a dark and distant amphitheatre of basalt cliffs; and then climbed even further through the Drakensberg to Mont-aux-Sources, where the rivers divided, and where he crossed at last into Natal. From Mont-aux-Sources, on that vividly clear afternoon, he could see back into the Orange Free State, and Basutoland, and as far as Utrecht in the Transvaal, hazy miles of dust and trees and patches of greenery. Ahead of him, off to his right, he could make out the mountain they called Giant's Castle, where dark clouds gathered, even on a fine day, and lightning flickered incessantly. The black people had named this mountain N'Tabayi Konjwa, the mountain at which you may not point without terrible consequences.

Joel by now was delirious. He sweated and raved and screamed, and sometimes in the night he would let out a hideous inhuman shriek that had Barney sitting up in his blankets, scrabbling for his revolver, his body cold with fright.

But they descended the mountains at last into Natal, following the deep imprints in the rocks that the iron-shod wheels of the huge Boer waggons had left, when they had deserted their newly-established Republic of Natalia in 1842. Jan Bloem had told Barney all about those days, and it was easy for Barney to understand how bitter the Boers felt about the British. Their four-year-old republic had been annexed by the British by force, and the Volksraad, the Boer Parliament, had grimly voted to accept the annexation without fighting back. Almost immediately, the Boer farmers had packed their ox-waggons and trekked back west over the Drakensberg, to the Orange Free State, and the Transvaal.

Five weeks after he had set out from Kimberley, Barney steered his ox-waggon between the shalestone and yellow-wood cottages of Boom Street, in Pieter-Maritzburg, the capital of Natal. It was here, on the banks of the river that the Zulus had called the Mzunduzi, that the Boers had first found what they had believed to be their promised land. Pieter-Maritzburg, named after two voortrekkers called Pieter Retief and Gerrit Maritz, had been established on the floor of a broad, lush valley, over which the shadows of the afternoon clouds passed like memories.

Barney and Joel stayed the night with an elderly Dutch couple who ran a small dairy on the outskirts of town; and while Joel shivered in a cot in an upstairs bedroom, Barney sat wearily at the kitchen table and ate cheese and ham and drank home-made lager. The old Dutchman watched him through tiny spectacles, an unread copy of the *Natal Witness* lying in the table in front of him; but he only spoke when Barney had quite finished, and pushed aside the wooden board from which he had eaten his meal.

'You brought your brother all the way from the diamond fields?'

Barney nodded. 'I didn't have any choice. We don't have any surgeons out there – none that are worth a damn, anyway.'

'He must have suffered, your brother.'

Barney said, 'Yes. He's suffered. and he'll suffer some more before he's through.'

'Is it worth it?' the old Dutchman asked.

Barney looked him straight in the eye. 'Your people fought and died to build this town, and to stay free, and you're asking me if it's worth it?'

The old Dutchman picked up his paper. 'You're right, I

suppose. Do you know that I was there, under the acacia tree, when the Volksraad voted to let the British take over Natalia without recourse to arms. I was standing as near to Andries Pretorius as you're sitting now. I could have reached out and touched him.'

'Yes,' said Barney, tiredly. 'Now, I think I'd better get some sleep. I want to get to Durban tomorrow, if I can.'

'You might make Pinetown. But Durban? It's ninety miles, easily.'

'My brother's dying. I'll make it to Durban.'

After supper, Barney sat in an old rocking-chair on the tiled living-room floor, and dozed. The tiles were patterned with blue flowers, and first he dreamed of fire lilies and watsonia. Then he was riding again across miles of desert, with the oxen hunched doggedly in front of him. He dreamed of the strange pinnacles of sandstone that stood silent guard over the passes between the Orange Free State and Basutoland; and of the wild herds of red hartebeest and Burchell's zebra which fled across the grasslands.

He was woken by a cough. He had half-dreamed that it was a baboon barking in some far-off kloof. But it was the old Dutchman, bending over him with an expression of wrinkled concern. 'Your brother's worse,' he said. 'Do you want us to send for the priest?'

Barney had to stay for two days and two nights in Pieter-Maritzburg, while Joel twisted and shook and babbled in his whitewashed upstairs bedroom. It was December now, and the humidity was exhausting. For the first day, Barney did nothing but sit in the house, resting; but on the second morning he went down to the banks of the Umzinduzi to feel the early breeze blowing off the ruffled water.

The old Dutchman called the local doctor, a whiskery Englishman who rolled up his sleeves to reveal the hairiest arms that Barney had ever come across. But the doctor could do nothing better than to prescribe more Dover's powder to keep Joel's temperature down, and to express the opinion, as he was leaving, that Joel would soon by lying in a casket in Church Street.

On the third morning, however, when Barney went up to Joel's room, Joel was lying on his cot with his eyes open, and a hint of colour in his cheeks, and he managed to raise his hand in a half-mocking greeting.

'How are you feeling?' Barney asked him, drawing up a chair.

'I'm not dead yet, whatever that doctor thinks.'

'You heard him?'

'I couldn't help it. The window was open, and the man had a voice like a French horn.'

'Do you think you're up to travelling on?'

Joel apprehensively rubbed his left thigh. 'How far is it? This leg seems to have stiffened.'

'About eighty, ninety miles. The roads are better, though. So they tell me.'

Joel closed his eyes. 'Just fill me up with that specific, and make me comfortable, and let's go.'

The last few miles of the journey were gruelling. Under his broadbrimmed hat, Barney's face was streaked with dust and sweat, and Joel lay back on his grimy pillows with a face as ghastly as a waxwork. They could not reach Durban by night-fall, even though their waggon was light and almost empty of supplies, since Barney had to keep stopping by the side of the rutted road to bathe Joel's face with water, and dose him up with painkillers. They slept outside Pinetown, under their canvas shelter amidst the racketing noise of cicadas.

It was Saturday, 23 December, when they eventually arrived on the outskirts of Durban, like two exhausted survivors from some lost pioneering expedition, and passers-by stared at them in open curiosity as they slowly plodded towards the centre of town.

In spite of the heat, Christmas decorations were everywhere. There were flags flying outside the stores along West Street, and the ironwork uprights of the horse-drawn omnibuses were wound with tinsel. Durban lay under the deep blue lunchtime sky like a small, prosperous British town, with wide streets and smart carriages and buildings as solid as any in Croydon.

Barney asked directions of a red-faced English grocer who was standing outside his store in his striped apron, taking a mid-morning smoke. The grocer pointed out the Natalia Hotel with the stem of his pipe; but had certainly never heard of

245

anyone called Sir Thomas Sutter, or anyone related to anyone called Sir Thomas Sutter. 'Not unless you mean – but no,' he added, looking at Barney's clothes.

'That fellow in the back looks a bit dicky,' he remarked, gratuitously, as Barney whipped the oxen and turned the waggon across the street.

Barney guessed that it was suitably sad and ironic that he should stay with Joel at an hotel called the Natalia. The manager was reluctant at first to admit Joel; but when Barney paid for a suite in advance in English fivepound notes, he whistled sharply to four Kaffirs in white shorts to carry Joel on the hotel stretcher to his room upstairs.

'As long as he doesn't pass away,' the manager explained, noisily rubbing his hands as he watched Barney sign the register. 'It does disturb the guests, you know ... expiry.'

Barney looked around the green marble hotel foyer, with its drawn blinds and its leather armchairs and its obligatory elephant's-foot umbrella stand. After weeks in the mountains, he felt so tired that none of these staid Victorian surroundings seemed real; and the way in which straight-backed women in their long summer skirts came and went across the reflecting floor was like a silent ballet remembered from a dream.

'You don't happen to know a family called Sutter, by any chance?' Barney asked the manager. The manager had finished rubbing his hands and was now smoothing down his black, brilliantined hair.

'Sutter? Not *the* Sutters, presumably?'

'I don't know. Who are *the* Sutters?'

'Well, *the* Sutters own Sutters the shipping line. Second largest shipping line in Port Natal. And certainly the first people you'd think of if you ever wanted to send something up the east coast of Africa, no matter what it was. A parcel, or a parrot, or a piano.'

'Where do they live?' asked Barney.

The manager swivelled the register around and peered at Barney's signature. 'You can't possibly miss it. It's about a mile to the south, towards Umlazi. A large, lemon-coloured place, in its own palm grove. But you'll never get in without an appointment. Or even at *all*, dressed like that.'

Barney said, 'You can have your porter empty the Bible box on my waggon. There are two suits in there, and some shirts, and I'd like them sponged down, and pressed. Then you can send a plate of beefsteak and a bottle of mineral waters up to my room.'

'Anything else, Mr Blitz?'

'Yes. Is there a synagogue in Durban?'

The manager stared at him humourlessly for a long time. 'I'll enquire,' he said, and closed the register with a loud snap.

After a bath in a high enamelled bathtub on lion's-claw feet, with hissing hot water supplied by an arrangement of brass pipes like a church organ, Barney towelled himself down, and came back into his bedroom to find his wedding-suit neatly laid out on his bed, and his shirt ironed with so much starch that he had to push his hands down the sleeves with all the force of a Navy icebreaker cutting through Antarctic glaciers.

Under a silver cover, a rather tough beefsteak waited for him, along with a bottle of Ashbourne water, on ice. He sat down on the end of the bed and ate the steak quickly and hungrily. Then he went to the basin to wash his hands, tie up his necktie, and brush his wet hair.

Before he left, he went into the second bedroom to look at Joel. Joel was sleeping now, murmuring as he slept, but quietly, as if he were dreaming complicated and subtle dreams, rather than nightmares of pain and fear and sudden death.

Severe and smart in his dark grey suit, with grey gloves and a grey hat, Barney crossed the foyer of the Natalia Hotel with clicking heels. The half-caste doorman hailed him a hansom cab, and remarked on the closeness of the heat. Two kaffirs were sitting in the street outside, playing jacks in the dust. Barney tipped the doorman a shilling, and mounted the black-and-maroon hansom with the confidence of a man who is perfectly familiar with riding in carriages. The black cab-driver had only taken him to the corner, however, before he was dry-mouthed and sweating, and his hurriedly-chewed steak was sitting on his stomach like chunks of sodden wood.

They drove out of town and up the tree-lined road towards Umlazi. On his left, through the dense undergrowth, Barney could make out the glittering reaches of the Indian Ocean, with two mail steamers making their way towards Port Natal. The air was sickly-sweet with the smell of flowers and decaying sub-tropical greenery, and the sound of the carriage wheels was swallowed up by the chirruping of insects and the querulous cry of birds.

At last, they came to a small hill, almost unnaturally round, and vividly green. It was fringed with palm trees, and laid out with lawns and pathways that were so neat they were irritating to look at. The lower slopes of the hill were surrounded by black-painted iron railings, each one cast in the shape of a Zulu assegai, and admittance to the estate was only by way of a pair of iron gates, decorated with iron replicas of Zulu shields.

On the crown of the hill stood a fine symmetrical mansion, painted, as the manager of the Natalia Hotel had told Barney, in the palest of lemon yellows. There were small fruiting orange trees in green tubs all the way around the house at precise intervals, and accurately-clipped hedges beneath every window. Peacocks swept their tails around the gardens like clockwork toys.

'This is where you want?' asked the cab driver, turning in his wornout leather seat. 'Khotso?'

Barney sat upright. 'Is that what the house is called?'

'Yes, boss. Everybody know that. This is where you want?'

'I believe so,' said Barney. 'But wait here for me, will you?'

The cab driver reigned his carriage in under the shade of a coral-tree and lit up a clay pipe. Barney climbed down, crossed the road, and approached the gates of Khotso with appre-hension. The beefsteak had given him a griping pain in his stomach, and he would much rather have been lying on his bed in the Natalia Hotel, nursing his tiredness and his indigestion, than out here looking for Sir Thomas Sutter.

There was nobody at the gate; but there was a mechanical bell-pull, and Barney tugged at it twice. Then he waited, his back sticky with sweat, to see what would happen.

After a full minute, a small black man appeared, in peach-coloured trousers and a white sash, with a white turban on his head. He walked at an even pace along the precise perspective

248

of the front path, his arms swinging beside him military-style, and Barney could have timed almost to the second the moment when he was due to arrive at the gate.

'Good afternoon, sir,' the black man said at last. 'You wish to leave your card?'

'I wish to see Sir Thomas Sutter, if he's still here.'

'Sir Thomas? Well, sir, he's still here. But I'm afraid it's lunchtime. If you wish to leave your card.'

'Can you please tell him that I'm here, and that it's urgent? I've come all the way from the diamond fields at Kimberley.'

The black man raised his hands. 'With respect, sir, Mrs Sutter doesn't like to have luncheon interrupted. Not for anything. The Zulus attacked the Sutters once, sir, when they were on a picnic, and Mrs Sutter handed round meat sandwiches while the menfolk fought the Zulus off with pistols. So goes the story, sir.'

'I'm prepared to wait. It's a question of life or death.'

'Well, sir,' said the black man, rather regretfully. 'Life or death is one thing. Lunch is another.'

'I'll wait! My brother's dying, and I want Sir Thomas to see him!'

Just then, a girl appeared on the steps by the house – a tall girl, with dark brown ringlets, wearing a rust-coloured satin dress that was richly trimmed with Brussels lace. She hesitated for a moment, her pale hands held up like doves, trying to see what was happening down at the gate; and then she came rustling down the path with her skirts discreetly held above the patterned brick, and her head raised with aloof curiosity.

As she came closer, Barney could see that she was a very tall girl – almost as tall as him, even in her satin slippers. But her figure was in beautiful proportion, with wide shoulders, large breasts, and a narrow waist. Her face was square and strong, with vivid, wide-apart eyes; and if Barney had been asked to guess her nationality he would have said German or Polish rather than British. British women were almost invariably pear-shaped, with sloping shoulders and hips like gun-carriages.

Her voice, though, was as sharp and brittle as any girl from England's southern counties. And when she came up and said, 'What's the mattah, William? What's going on heah?' the black man touched his turban and stepped back as if he had been stung by a sjambok.

'Hello,' said the girl, looking Barney straight in the eye. 'I'm Sara Sutter.'

'I'm pleased to make your acquaintance,' said Barney. 'I'm Barney Blitz.'

'Well, well! Ess-ess and bee-bee! That must be a coincidence! Do you care for palmistry, at all?'

'I'm sorry?'

'Don't be. I'm an enthusiast, myself. Did you want to see Papa?'

'It was Sir Thomas I was looking for, as a matter of fact.'

'Great-Uncle Tee! What on earth do you want with him? He's getting ready for his afternoon nap, I believe! But come in! We can't have you standing outside looking like a lost soul, can we?'

William unlocked the gates, and swung both of them open, although Barney could easily have stepped through one. Sara Sutter looked him up and down, and said, 'You look very *hot*. Perhaps you'd care for a glass of lime-juice? Or perhaps tea?'

They walked up to the house together. Inside the railings of the house called Khotso, everything looked even more precise than it had from the road. Barney had the feeling that even if a snail were to be bold enough to silver the pathway, a black servant would have to come out and scrub the stones until the trail was gone.

'You're an American, I suppose, by your accent?' asked Sara Sutter. 'I can always tell an accent.'

'That's right. From New York, originally. But I live in Kimberley these days. I'm a diamond digger.'

'Are you *rea*-leh? How frightfully exciting! Father will be most interested to meet you, if only I can find him! And so will Great-Uncle Tee. Oh, look! What luck! There he is now!'

As they turned round a corner of the lemon-yellow house, they saw a tall white-bearded man with a belly as magnificent as a pregnant hippopotamus, sitting outside a pair of open French windows on a gilded sofa, smoking a cigar. He was wrapped in a blue and gold Chinese dressing-gown, and on his feet were a pair of white canvas polo boots. A copy of *The*

Times had been dumped in an untidy heap beside him, and was gradually being blown across the lawn by the afternoon wind.

'Great-Uncle Tee!' said Sara Sutter, gripping Barney's arm. 'I've someone to see you! Mr Blitz, from Kimberley!'

Sir Thomas Sutter looked Barney up and down with a single protuberant eye, his other eye closed against the smoke from his cigar. 'Mr Blitz? Well, how do you do! Pardon me if I don't get up, but it's taken me a good twenty minutes to get myself sat down. A heavy lunch, don't you know.'

Barney took off his hat. 'I'm real sorry to intrude like this,' he said. 'But a friend of mine in Kimberley told me that you were taking a vacation here, and I came on the chance that you would still be here when I arrived, and that you might agree to help me.'

Sir Thomas rubbed his beard. 'Jewish, is it, Blitz?'

Barney blinked at him. 'I'm sorry?'

'The name "Blitz". Jewish, is it?'

'Yes, sir. It is. We came from north Germany originally. Then we moved to New York. We used to be tailors, until we sold out and moved here.'

'I see. Well, I admire the Jews. They make excellent doctors. And they make excellent money, too. The Rothschilds are particular friends of mine.'

Barney did not know what to say. He simply shrugged, and lifted his hat slightly, as if he were pleased to hear it, which he was.

'Well,' said Sir Thomas, 'if you've come all the way from Kimberley on the chance that I might still be here, then obviously you want something. Some medical advice, perhaps? Some suggestions about starting a field hospital?'

Barney said, 'I want something, yes. But I'm afraid it's not that philanthropic.'

'You don't want surgery, I hope? I'm on holiday. I've left all my scalpels in London.'

'I'm afraid that's exactly what I do want.'

Sir Thomas puffed at his cigar. 'It's not for you, is it? You look as fit as a fiddle.'

'No, sir. It's my brother Joel. He was involved in a mining

accident out at the Big Hole at Kimberley. His left leg's crushed, and I think his pelvis has been smashed. He broke three, maybe four ribs.'

'I'm sorry to hear it. When did it happen?'

'Around six weeks ago.'

'Six *weeks* ago?'

'It's more than five hundred miles from Kimberley to Durban, sir. I got him here as fast as I could.'

Sir Thomas blew out his cheeks. 'Yes ... I can see that you did. You managed it in remarkable time, too. But by now I expect that your brother's fractures have knit themselves together again, and I doubt if there is very much that I can do.'

'His hips are still giving him pain, Sir Thomas, and his left leg is twisted right out of shape.'

'The skin isn't broken anywhere? There are no protruding bones?'

'No, sir. There were some cuts and bruises, but they've all healed up now.'

'Well,' said Sir Thomas, 'they sound like simple fractures. And if he's still alive after six weeks of bumping all the way from Kimberley to Durban, then he's probably going to stay alive. Can he walk?'

'No, sir.'

'His leg is distorted, I suppose? That's only to be expected. When the bone is broken, you see, a large clot of blood forms between the broken ends, and this clot gradually turns into what we call a soft callus. After a while, the soft callus attracts lime salts from the system, and these lime salts harden to form a thick ring of bone. Should the broken limbs not be properly reduced and set, however, an even thicker ring of bone than normal can form; and thus an awkward healing is more difficult to rectify.'

Barney said, 'I don't think his pelvis has even set properly. He keeps complaining that it's grating, and that it hurts.'

'That's what we call *crepitus*,' said Sir Thomas. 'If your brother is still feeling that sensation, then his pelvis may have been so badly damaged that it has healed and then re-broken. I couldn't tell without examining him.'

'Will you do it?' asked Barney.

Sir Thomas stared at him. In the gardens, the peacocks let out a long, sad whoop.

'My dear chap,' he said, 'I'm on holiday.'

'I can pay you.'

'I'm sure you can. But there are plenty of other good surgeons in Durban. There's Pieter Botha at the Durban Calvinish Hospital. There's Humphrey Young, in Port Natal. I don't even have the staff, or the facilities.'

'But you're the best,' insisted Barney.

Sara Sutter said, 'I don't know what you're arguing about, Great-Uncle Tee. You've been chafing to get back to work ever since you got here. You'd love to do it, wouldn't you?'

'But it's out of the question,' protested Sir Thomas.

Right then, a tall, straight-backed man in a white dinner-jacket came round the corner and confronted them with surprise.

'What's out of the question?' he said, sharply.

'This is Gerald Sutter, my nephew,' explained Sir Thomas. 'Gerald – this gentleman has simply called by to seek my medical opinion.'

'How do you do,' said Gerald Sutter, tightly, without offering his hand. 'I'm afraid my uncle is on holiday at the moment, and we really prefer it if patients leave him in peace. He's going to have enough of that when he sails back to London.'

'Mr Blitz has impressed me, though,' put in Sir Thomas. 'His brother was hurt in an accident at Kimberley, and he has brought him five hundred miles just to be treated by me.'

'I'm afraid Mr Blitz was being rather over-optimistic,' said Gerald Sutter. 'A man may travel six months to London to ask the Queen for a knighthood, but that doesn't mean that he deserves one.'

'Oh, Papa, you're being pompous,' said Sara. 'This is Natal, not London! And his brother may die!'

'All the same,' Gerald Sutter said, turning with a cold smile to Barney and making a following gesture with his hands that Barney should consider leaving.

'No, no,' put in Sir Thomas. 'The whole thing rather appeals to me. It has a what-might-you-call-it, a *drama* about it. I could give some useful lectures to my students when I get back, particularly on the subject of perseverance. If you can get me a theatre at the Dalitary Hospital, Gerald, I'll do it.'

'Uncle, really,' protested Gerald. Then he turned to Barney. 'My uncle was supposed to be resting. I can't say I'm keen on this at all.'

'I had to try,' Barney told him, simply.

Sara Sutter clapped her hands. 'Great-Uncle Tee is absolutely right! It is dramatic, isn't it? Just like a play! Mr Blitz, you must take some tea. I'm sure Great-Uncle Tee must want to ask you lots of questions.'

Gerald Sutter sighed testily. 'Are you sure this is what you want, Uncle? I can't persuade you to change your mind?'

'Gerald, my dear chap, you've given me the finest holiday of my entire life. Seven months of blissful solitude and contemplative study. I have enjoyed myself no end, and your house is aptly named. But here we have an interesting case of fractures that must be re-broken, and re-reduced, and re-set, in the most colonial of circumstances, and I must say that I would very much like to get my hands on it.'

At last, Gerald Sutter allowed himself a nod of acceptance. 'Very well, Uncle, if it makes you happy. Sara – would you call Umzinto and ask him to bring tea?'

Two black servants brought decorative garden chairs around, and set a table with a pale damask cloth. Then they poured out fragile white cups of tea, with neither cream nor sugar.

'This is the most expensive of the Formosa Oolongs,' remarked Gerald Sutter. 'It's called Peach Blossom, and in London it can fetch anything up to £8 the pound. Her Majesty drinks it, when she can get it. I have it every afternoon, at four.'

'It's excellent,' said Barney. 'I'm afraid we don't have such delicacies out at Kimberley, even those of us who can afford them.'

The next hour passed with such calm and civilisation that Barney began to feel at peace for the first time for months. The sun fell slowly behind the palms, so that their frondy shadows lay across the lawns, and the peacocks gathered round for any crumbs that might be left from the teatable. Sir Thomas talked about the difficulties of good bonesetting, and Gerald talked about fast steamers, and how he could have a packet sent from Port Natal to Delagoa Bay, a distance of 295 miles, in less than forty-one hours.

'All that concerns us now is the Zulus,' said Gerald, crossing his well-creased ducks. 'Mpande is not a well man, and if Mpande dies, we shall be left with Cetewayo, and Cetewayo is one of those black gentlemen who believes in the glorious days of Shaka.'

'And I'm afraid the days of Shaka weren't all that glorious,' added Sir Thomas. 'He had the same interest in human anatomy as I do, but I regret that he didn't have the same skills. He once ordered a hundred pregnant women cut open with spears, just because he was momentarily interested in embryology.'

'Great-Uncle *Tee*,' protested Sara, setting down her cup.

'I do apologise, my dear,' said Sir Thomas. 'I'm always doing that. I forget that the more sanguinary details of medicine make other people squeamish.'

After tea, Sara walked Barney down to the gate. 'I've been greatly encouraged,' said Barney. 'Thank you.'

'I suppose you'll be staying in Durban for a while, until your brother is better?'

'As long as necessary.'

'What about your diamond mines?'

'They'll have to wait.'

Sara smiled. 'You really do strike me as a most straightforward and determined person. I should very much like it if you could come to supper one evening. I shall do what I can to persuade Papa.'

'Your father doesn't object to Jews?'

'Why on earth should he? My mother's mother came from a very aristocratic Jewish family in Russia. You'll have to meet my mother. She's so beautiful, and quite adorable.'

'Qualities which *you* seem to have inherited in full measure,' said Barney.

Sara Sutter made a funny little face, and then giggled. 'I love to be flattered,' she said. 'One gets so few compliments, out heah.'

'By the way,' asked Barney, touching the nameplate on the gate, 'what does Khotso mean?'

'It's Basuto for "peace",' said Sara. 'I suppose you would say "shalom."'

Barney took her hand. 'Yes,' he told her. 'I would say shalom.'

Barney spent Christmas Day alone in his suite at the Natalia Hotel. On Sunday morning, Christmas Eve, four black porters from the Durban Military Hospital had arrived with a stretcher and carried Joel away, so that he could be examined and bathed and prepared for his operation. Later that day, a messenger had come round with a letter for Barney written in an almost unintelligible copperplate, and this informed him that Sir Thomas was to operate the day after Boxing Day, Tuesday, and that he had high hopes that Joel would be walking again within two or three months, given that his internal injuries were not too serious. And, by the way, a merry Christmas.

Most of Christmas Day, Barney spent dozing on his bed, or reading. He even read the First Book of Samuel again, from the Bible which The London Missionary Society had left on his bedside table. 'The Lord maketh poor, and maketh rich; he bringeth low, and lifteth up. He raiseth up the poor out of the dust, and lifteth up the beggar from the dunghill, to set them among princes, and to make them inherit the throne of glory.'

At lunchtime, the management sent up on a tray a traditional Christmas lunch, with turkey and sausages and roasted potatoes. There was even a sprig of holly on the side of the plate. Barney ate his meal in silence, sitting on the end of his bed. He had never celebrated Christmas at home, of course, and out at Oranjerivier it had only been marked by Monsaraz getting drunker than usual. But even though it was not a festival that meant anything to him religiously, or in his memories, the whole of Durban was celebrating today, the church bells were ringing out across the rusty corrugated-iron rooftops, and echoing from the forested hills, and he could not help feeling more lonely than ever. He had celebrated Chanukah somewhere in the mountains, by whispering prayers to himself as he lay in his blankets. He was beginning to feel the need of his God again, and of his religion, and he was also beginning to miss Mooi Klip.

On the writing-desk under the window was a dried-up pot of ink, and a small sheaf of writing-paper with the printed heading 'Natalia'. He lifted up a sheet of paper and touched the word with his fingers. Natalia. Then he laid it down again. The Lord bringeth low, and lifteth up. Oh Lord, he prayed, lift me up. Oh Lord, lift me up.

At five o'clock, he decided to go for a walk. But he was just crossing the foyer of the hotel when the deputy manager called to him from the registration desk, and held up a small brown-paper parcel.

'For you, Mr Blitz. It was left only a few minutes ago.'

Barney took the parcel across to one of the leather armchairs, sat down, and untied it. Inside the brown paper was a red leather-covered box, and inside the box was a silver penknife, with the initials BB engraved on the side.

A small card was tied to the penknife. It read, 'To Mr Barney Blitz, wishing you the best compliments of the season, Sara Sutter.'

A knife was the most appropriate gift she could have sent him. That Christmas Day, she cut him to the bone.

Joel told him later that the pain he had suffered crossing the Drakensberg mountains had been nothing compared with the pain that Sir Thomas Sutter inflicted. But Sir Thomas Sutter had to break his leg and his hips again, and cut away all the superfluous bone that had formed, and reset everything as best he could. The ribs were all right, since the ribcage had formed a natural splint, but the collarbone had to be re-broken and re-set, and there was a severe rupture of the groin. When Barney was first allowed to visit Joel, on Wednesday evening, Joel was lying in traction, his face white, his senses still blurred by morphine, and all he could say was, 'How's Mama?'

Sir Thomas Sutter was waiting outside with two of his assistants. 'Your brother will live, God willing, and he will walk again; though never without a stick. I must say it was a most interesting and difficult case. It hardly ever happens in England, you see, that a man so seriously injured is brought to surgery so late as six weeks after his accident.'

'I'm very thankful,' said Barney.

'Well, I'm thankful to you for bringing him in,' said Sir Thomas. 'All this has made a very recreational end to my holiday, if you'll forgive me talking about your brother's misfortune as a recreation.'

'That's probably the right word,' Barney told him.

'Well, excellent,' said Sir Thomas. 'And you must come out and have a meal with us this evening. My grand-niece absolutely insists, and so do I. I expect they'll be serving cold turkey again, but as a matter of fact Gerald was so extravagant that he shipped in a turkey the size of an ostrich, and we'll be eating it as curries and croquettes until March, I shouldn't wonder. Well, the family will. I'm sailing back to London the day after New Year's.'

'Do I have time to change?' asked Barney.

'My dear chap, of course. I'll pick you up at the Natalia at six, when I've finished here. There's a frightfully interesting case upstairs, you know. An orderly from the 24th Foot was stepped on by an elephant. It's a miracle he's still alive.'

Barney walked back to the Natalia Hotel between lighted storefronts and decorated restaurants. There was a sea-breeze blowing, and up above him the sky was prickled with stars. A half-caste woman called out to him from the shadow corner of Commercial Street, but he shook his head without even turning her way. He could smell spicy East African food on the wind.

Sir Thomas was wrong: the Sutters did not serve up cold turkey that evening, but noisettes of lamb, and turtle soup, and a whole array of decorative moulds and jellies. Mrs Sutter, Gerald's wife, turned out to be just as beautiful as her daughter had described her – dark-haired, slender, and tall, with an endless white neck, and she immediately made Barney feel at ease by laughing at herself for forgetting what she had ordered the servants to cook that night. 'I was *so* sure that it was going to be fish,' she said, 'that my palate is quite disappointed at the prospect of lamb.'

The interior of Khotso was as pristine as its gardens. The dining-room was laid with a shining floor of polished English oak, and surrounded by mirrors. The drawing-room, to which they withdrew when the meal was finally over, was decorated in blue watered silk, and furnished in elegant turn-of-the-century mahogany. Mrs Sutter sat on a small French sofa, rising from the white satin petals of her evening-gown like the stamens of a flower; and Sara sat next to Barney, her hair drawn back and secured with strings of pearls, her dress as vivid and orange as the coral-tree blossoms which herald the South African spring.

Both Gerald Sutter and Sir Thomas were dressed in starched white shirts and white ties, with tailcoats; and Barney felt distinctly uncomfortable in his day suit, dark and well tailored as it was.

'Uncle is wonderfully pleased with your brother's progress,' smiled Mrs Sutter. 'I must say that we're all delighted.'

'Thought you had something of a nerve, to begin with,' said Gerald Sutter. 'But things have worked out rather well, don't you think? Uncle's had something to amuse him; your brother's on the mend; and Sara's found herself a new chum.'

'I was wondering if you'd like to ride tomorrow,' said Sara, touching Barney's sleeve.

'I'm afraid I don't have a horse. Nor riding clothes, either.'

Gerald Sutter grunted in amusement. 'My dear boy, we have something in excess of twenty first-class mounts here, apart from a collection of harmless hacks. You can borrow any of them you have a mind to. And, as for clothes, we must have enough to fit out the whole Zulu army.'

'Yes,' said Sir Thomas. 'It would be nice to see those blackies decently dressed for a change.'

They all laughed, and their servant Umzinto, who was dressed up for the evening in a yellow and white footman's costume, with a white pigtailed wig, leaned forward to pour them all some more coffee.

The following day, Barney and Sara took out a grey and a chestnut, and rode as far as the beach where the Umlazi River flows into the Indian Ocean. It was a humid, misty morning, and as Sara rode ahead of Barney through the sloping shallows, she was silhouetted against the pearly mist, tall and upright on her mare, her riding hat tilted fashionably forwards, her skirts carefully arranged side-saddle. They reined in their horses for a while, and listened to the foaming of the surf, and the occasional whistle of a mail-packet approaching Port Natal through the haze. Then Sara swung herself down into the sea, and led her mare back towards the beach, her cream-coloured skirts trailing in the water. Barney rode after her, and when he reached the beach, he dismounted, too.

'Sometimes this feels like the most distant, remote corner of the whole Empire,' said Sara. Her face was framed by the triangular space between her mare's chest and jaw.

'You're lonely?' asked Barney.

Sara looked at him. 'Aren't you?'

They had a chaperone with them, of course – an eLangeni woman who had brought up Sara since she was nine years old. She had stayed at a suitable distance all the way from the house, fat and very black, and perched on a shaggy pony so precariously that Barney had found himself looking back at her every now and then to make sure that she was still mounted. But now, the eLangeni woman found the surf so absorbing that she climbed down from her pony and gave the waves her unshakeable attention.

'This is wrong, you know,' said Sara, in a tone that gave away her feeling that she was glad that it was.

Barney said nothing, but released the reins of his horse and put his arms around her and held her near to him. In her riding-boots, she was almost as tall as he was, but everything about her was feminine and giving and warm. They kissed, and he tasted her perfume. They kissed again. Then he was clutching her so tight, so close to him, that he prayed he would never have to let her go. He closed his eyes and he could hear the ocean seething up the beach; he opened them again and he could see Sara's eyes in close-up, their dark brown irises folded like coral.

'You're so strong,' she said. 'You're weak. I can see you have weaknesses. But you're so strong, too. And that's what makes you so attractive.'

He pressed his forehead against hers, his hands linked behind her slender waist. 'Where can this possibly lead?' he asked her. 'I have to go back to Kimberley soon.'

She gently touched his lips with her finger. 'How can you think about the future? Tomorrow, the Zulus might rise and we'll all be dead. Assegaied in our beds.'

'What makes you think they're going to rise?'

Sara kissed him. 'They must do. It's in their blood. Everybody has to do what their destiny compels them to do.'

He let go of her, and turned away. His horse was tugging at some wild seagrass with its teeth.

'I'm not asking you to love me,' she said.

He nodded. 'I know. But right now, I think I could do with somebody to love.'

It was late February before Joel could walk again. Barney would go to visit him at the Durban Military Hospital every afternoon, and each afternoon Joel would gripe and sweat and swing himself around the ward on his walking-stick, before sitting down next to Barney in a thick sweat, his chest rising and falling with effort, and his hands trembling like an old man.

'I'll walk, just you wait and see.'

'Sir Thomas said you'd always have to carry a stick.'

'You think so? That shows what a *gonif* Sir Thomas is.'

'A *gonif*? And he's fixed you up so well?'

Joel leaned over to Barney and grinned at him. 'One day, my little brother, you're going to learn what life is all about. Life is all about taking, and not trusting. You live it any other way, and you're crazy.'

'I trusted you with our diamond claim.'

'And what happened?' gibbed Joel.

'I don't even know how you can look me in the face after what you did,' said Barney. 'And all that money. You must have been out of your mind.'

'It was the greatest poker game ever. I could have won fifty thousand. *Then* you wouldn't have argued.'

'But you didn't win, did you?' said Barney. 'You lost everything. And you lied. You told me you were going to put that claim fifty-fifty in our joint names. You never even went to the Diggers' Committee to re-register it, did you? You *momzer*.'

'Barney,' protested Joel. 'You're my brother.'

'Sure I'm your brother. And most of the time I wish that I wasn't.'

Joel gave an uneasy laugh. 'Well,' he said, 'I'm not sure that I blame you.'

Barney rubbed his eyes, and sat forward on his bentwood chair with his chin cupped in his hands. 'It's too late now, anyway. We've lost the claim and we've lost all of our savings and that's it. *Mechuleh*. Finished!'

The afternoon light fell across the parquet floor of the hospital ward. In the nearest bed, a British soldier with an amputated leg lay on his bed playing a board game called 'Lord Chelmsford's Revenge'.

Joel said, 'Sometimes I think I'm going mad.'

'For God's sake, you're not going mad.'

'But I *do*, Barney. Sometimes it feels like the whole world's pushing in on me from all sides, and all I can do is try to trick my way out of it, before I get caught. It was like that in Kimberley, when we were living with Mooi Klip. There was you, and her, and this everyday routine of getting up and digging the claim and sorting the stones, and I felt like the whole thing was crushing me to death. Every pound we put into the bank was like another brick in my tomb. Do you understand what I'm saying? The whole thing was crushing me, and the only way to get free was to throw it all away.'

Barney would not look at him. 'I should have let you die,' he said, bitterly. 'The only trouble was, you wouldn't.'

Joel was silent for a while. Then he said, 'No, I didn't die. And I don't intend to.'

He swung himself upright on his sticks, and pivoted himself away down the ward for another agonising exercise walk. Out of the corner of his eye, Barney watched him; and when Joel reached the end of the ward and suddenly cried out, 'Ah! Barney!' Barney was already out of his chair, and hurrying to support him.

He saw Sara two or three times a week. Usually, they went riding, with the Sutter's conveniently ill-sighted chaperone teetering along behind them; but occasionally it thundered, and then they would sit in the morning-room and talk, or play ludo, while the tropical rain clattered against the glass of the French windows, and the stone lions in the garden stared mournfully out across the lawns with drips on their noses.

They kissed as often as they could, and embraced. But there was no doubt that Sara considered herself a young lady of correct upbringing, and that the idea of going to bed with an admirer before marriage was quite out of the question. She was twenty and two months old, and a virgin, and the only reason she had not married before was because of the isolated life she led out at Khotso, wealthy and mannered and bored to distraction, a true daughter of the British Empire. When he talked to Sara, Barney was frequently electrified by her unshakeable certainty that whatever the British did was the work of the Lord, and that the Zulu and the Boer were nothing but clumsy mischief-makers who might one day upset the just and equable Scheme of Things so much that they would have to be Taught A Lesson. That was a phrase Barney heard time and time again since he had come to Cape Colony: they will have to be Taught A Lesson. The British seemed to regard the administration of the world as nothing more than an extension of their public-school geography classes.

For the first time, Barney began to understand the thinking of Cecil Rhodes.

By early March, his sabbatical ended, Sir Thomas Sutter had sailed back to London on the steamship *Agamemnon*, and Joel was limping around with the aid of a single stick. Barney was almost in love with Sara, to the point where he found it hard to go through a day without seeing her, or sending her a message; and when he did see her, and go riding with her, he would return to the Natalia Hotel in a mood that was half satisfaction and half frustration. One evening he came back from Khotso, went into the bathroom, and rubbed himself furiously until semen shot over his hand. He could have gone to a whore, but he did not want to. He did not feel like talking to any other girl but Sara. But he lay back on his bed afterwards feeling empty and resentful, and staring at the geccoes which ran over the ceiling in their own upside-down world where guilt and loneliness were unknown.

Then the money ran out. Sir Thomas Sutter had only charged 150 guineas for his surgery and after-care, but Joel's hospital fees had now topped £200, and the bill for Barney's suite at the Natalia Hotel took care of the rest. Barney had to go to Khotso on the morning of 11 March and tell Sara that he was returning to Kimberley.

It was hot and sunny on the steps outside the house, but in the distance, over the Indian Ocean, blue-black thunderheads had gathered, and lightning was licking at the sea.

Sara said, in a high, breathless voice, 'Shall I see you again! Ever?'

Barney nodded. 'If you want me to, I'll come back. But first I have to go see to my business.'

'Well,' she said, with a difficult smile, 'I suppose I can be brave.'

She walked a little way down the garden path, her hands clasped in front of her, and then she turned and looked at him with complete misery. 'Do you have to?' she asked. 'Do you really have to?'

Barney said, 'I'm sorry.'

'Oh,' she said, and her eyes flooded with tears. 'Oh, Barney.'

He held her hand. 'It couldn't have been any other way. I would have had to go back to Kimberley, no matter what.'

'But I could have come with you.'

'You? In Kimberley? Do you have any idea what it's like there?'

'The only think I know about it is that you're going to be there, and I'm not.'

'It's a madhouse. Rough, dirty, hardly any fresh water. Shortages of food. Nothing but diamond dealers and prostitutes and drunken diggers.'

'But I love you,' she squeaked.

Barney put his arm around her neck and held her face against his shoulder. 'I have to go back, Sara. And that's all. If I don't go back, then I might as well buy myself a ticket to New York, to the Lower East Side, and take up tailoring again. And you wouldn't want to follow me then.'

'Wouldn't I?' she challenged him. Her eyes were blurred with tears.

In the distance, the thunder grumbled aggressively. It sounded like Zulu *impi* rattling their assegais against their shields, and rumbling their warcry, 'uSuthu! uSuthu!'

'Give me time,' Barney pleaded.

She looked up at him. 'You'll give *me* time, too, won't you? You won't go off with anyone else? I don't mind prostitutes. I could stand that. But not another fiancée.'

'Fiancée?'

Sara's cheeks flushed pink. 'I naturally assumed –'

Barney took her hands, and held them between his own hands, tightly and safely and warmly. 'Sara,' he said, 'you're a Sutter. Look at this house, look at your background. You couldn't possibly marry anybody like me. I know you don't care that I'm Jewish, but I'm not even *rich* Jewish. As a matter of fact, I don't even own my own diamond-digging claim, just at the moment.'

'Barney, I don't *care*. What does money matter?'

He lowered his eyes, looked at her hands, and then released them. 'I wish it didn't matter at all. But I'm afraid that it does. Sara, I'm sorry. Maybe I've deceived you a little, just because I've enjoyed your company. No – I'm telling lies now. I've more than enjoyed it. I think I love you. But if we tried to marry ... it wouldn't work. You wouldn't have any horses or any servants or any gowns. I couldn't give you the life that you've been used to. The whole thing would be a mistake.'

Sara said quietly, and with an impeccable accent, 'I see.'

'I'll come back,' said Barney. 'I promise you that. When I've made some money, which by God I'm going to, then I'll come back.'

'And how long will that be?'

'I don't know. I'm starting from scratch.'

She was trying very hard to be offish; but she could not. She looked at Barney with tears sliding down her cheeks and all she could say was, 'Don't make it too long. I might be married to somebody else. And if that happened, and you came back too late, then I couldn't bear it.'

It began to rain, dark spots on the neat pathways of Khotso the size of pennies. English pennies, with the Queen's head on one side, and Britannia on the other. Barney kissed Sara quickly, and her mouth tasted of salt tears and rain.

*

They travelled more slowly back to Kimberley, arriving at the diamond mines in mid-May. The cosmos flowers had bloomed again on the veld, and the weather was cooler. They had ridden for days on the ox-waggon without speaking. Barney had been too preoccupied with thoughts of Sara, whom he had left behind, and Mooi Klip, who by now must have given birth to his child. I have a baby, he thought to himself, and I don't even know if it's a boy or a girl. I don't even know if it was born alive.

I don't even know if Mooi Klip's alive.

They were amazed, both of them, at the depth to which the Big Hole had now been dug. When they drove up to the east reef of the mine, they could see below them a scurrying ants'-nest of hundreds of diggers, all of them swarming over the hollows and hills and burrows with tireless energy, shovelling and hacking and walling up their claims with sandbags. The steel cables which connected each claim to the surface were now on three tiers of pulleys, the top tier bringing out the yellow ground from the claims in the centre of the mine, and the bottom two tiers serving the claims that were nearer to the rim. There were hundreds and hundreds of cables, shining in the afternoon sun like a giant spiderweb.

'We could have been a part of that,' said Barney, more to himself than to Joel. 'We could have been rich by now.'

'But we're not,' said Joel. 'So let's make the best of it.'

Barney cracked his whip, and the oxen trudged the last few yards towards their bungalow. Edward Nork was there, sitting on the verandah in his socks, trying to sew a patch on a pair of work trousers. He had grown a long gingery beard which made him look like a hermit, and he was wearing tiny wire-rimmed eyeglasses.

'The Lord in heaven,' he said, setting down his needlework. 'You came back. And you're better, Joel! I do believe you're better!'

Joel climbed down from the waggon and limped on his stick to the verandah steps. 'I'm not better, Edward. I'm worse. These days, I have to walk with a stick. But I'm still alive, if that's what you mean.'

Barney led the oxen through to the kraal, and Edward followed him. 'I'm afraid I haven't kept the house all that tidy,' he apologised. 'I'm not very methodical when it comes to cleaning.'

Barney said, 'At least you've kept it warm for us.'

With Edward's help, Barney freed the oxen from their harnesses, and then led them over to the trough to drink.

'Is there any feed?' he asked.

'I can get hold of some.'

'Thanks, I reckon these beasts deserve some kind of reward.'

Edward took off his eyeglasses and folded them. He appeared to be embarrassed. 'I heard from Mooi Klip,' he said.

'I was going to ask you if you had. Is she all right?'

'Oh, yes. She's doing very well. It was terrible, what happened between you and Joel.'

Barney said, 'The baby?'

'Oh, she had the baby all right. No trouble at all. It was a boy. She said she was going to call him Pieter.'

'Pieter,' said Barney. 'You mean like Pieter Retief?'

'I don't think so. More like Pieter Steyn. He was the Griqua who was praying for Joel, wasn't he, when you found him staked out?'

Barney nodded. 'She's still at Klipdrift?'

'As far as I know.'

'Well,' said Barney, 'I guess I'd better get over there and see her. And Pieter, too.'

'Congratulations,' smiled Edward Nork. 'You're a father.'

Joel came hobbling around to the kraal on his stick. 'Have you seen the inside of this house?' he demanded. 'It's a pigsty. In fact, it's worse than pigsty. Where the hell are we supposed to sleep?'

'Oh, yes,' said Edward Nork, uncomfortably. 'I'm afraid I had to dispose of some of the furniture.'

'You mean you had to sell our beds to buy yourself drink?' snapped Joel.

'If you like,' said Edward, with a touch of defiance in his voice. 'I didn't think you were ever coming back, to tell you the truth. Nobody did.'

'Do you know what's happened to Claim 172?' asked Barney.

'I heard that it was bought by an Australian. A fellow called McIntyre. He keeps himself to himself, though, and never buys a round of drinks, so I'm not at all sure how he's doing. He's not a millionaire yet, if that's any consolation.'

'I'm not sure that it is,' said Barney.

At that moment, there was a sharp rattling sound from the small stable at the side of the kraal. 'Oh,' said Edward, 'that's Alsjeblieft. I expect he's feeling hungry.'

'You've still got that mangy horse?' asked Barney.

Edward shrugged. 'I've grown rather fond of him, as a matter of fact. He's the only horse who's ever let me ride him. He's so docile, he even takes me home when I'm drunk. I think he'd put me to bed if I let him into the house.'

'Or if we had any beds,' put in Joel, sharply.

'I'll make it up to you,' said Edward. 'Don't you worry, my dear chap. I'll make it up to you.'

They spent the rest of the day sweeping out the bungalow and building up the fire. Then Barney cooked up a mess of beef and beans, and they sat on the floor in the living-room and ate it with their billy-can spoons. They talked for a while about diamonds, and Edward told them that the world market was slumping so badly that many of the Kimberley diggers were already selling up and moving on. Diggers were always searching for quick and easy fortunes, and there were rumours of gold having been discovered in the Transvaal.

The next morning, there was heavy grey cloud cover, and that fine persistent rain the Boers called *motreën* – rain as fine as mist. Barney woke up early, rolling out of the blankets that he had spread on the floor of the bedroom he had once shared with Mooi Klip. He lit the range to cook himself a breakfast of beef hash and eggs, and boiled up the coffee that he and Joel had made themselves the previous night. Then, while Joel was still sleeping, and Edward Nork was snoring away in the living-room in an alcoholic stupor, he opened the front door and went around to the kraal to saddle up Alsjeblieft.

The old horse shivered and snuffled in the rain, but stood there patiently while Barney tightened his girth, and clumsily swung himself aboard. This was not like riding at Khotso, where a black servant was always waiting with a portable step, and one's feet were inserted into the stirrups by the groom. But Barney had learned enough about riding with Sara Sutter to be able to direct Alsjeblieft out of the kraal and out through the early-morning outskirts of Kimberley, and point his nose north-westwards to Klipdrift. Barney had to blink from time to time, to shake the rain out of his eyes but there was a dreary familiarity about the landscape which made him feel at home.

The odd thing was, when Barney tried to ride around the De Beers Mine, where Cecil Rhodes was digging, the horse trotted to the north side of the mine without being bidden. Barney tried to tug his reins in the opposite direction, but he seemed to know exactly where he was going, and when he reached a rain-sodden tent, with pools of water collecting in its canvas sides, he stopped, and stood still, the rain dripping off his patchy hide, as if he expected Barney to dismount. Barney, wonderingly, climbed down.

The tent flap was flung back, and water gurgled on to the mud. A short, bearded digger in a checked shirt and a broad-brimmed hat and no trousers came struggling out into the daylight, snuffling and sniffing.

'I'm sorry,' said Barney. 'I didn't mean to wake you up.'

The digger stared at Barney and then at the horse. 'Screw me if that isn't Alsjeblieft,' he said, in a strong Irish accent.

'That's right,' nodded Barney. 'Alsjeblieft.'

'Well, that's a pity,' said the digger. 'I sell my diamonds to Dan Isaacs these days, ever since old Vandenberg passed over. But how are you, Alsjeblieft?' he asked, paddling his way through the churned-up mud, and rubbing the horse on the nose. 'I've got some sugar-lumps stashed away someplace. I'll find him one.'

'Dan Isaacs give you a good price?' asked Barney.

The digger looked up at him, and then shrugged. 'Good enough. Maybe not as good as old Vandenberg. But they say the market's going down the hill, you know? As long as I make myself enough to keep my body and my soul in the same tent.'

'Whatever Dan Isaacs gives you, I'll top,' said Barney.

The digger frowned uncertainly. 'Have you taken over from old Vandenberg?'

'I may have. I came here on Alsjeblieft, didn't I?'

'Well, sure. But can you pay me ready money?'

'Show me what you've got.'

The digger thought about that, and then nodded. 'All right. But let me put my trousers on first. I don't like to do business when I'm half-dressed.'

Barney waited in the drizzling rain while the digger dressed himself. Then the digger reappeared with a wash-leather bag, which he opened up and spread across the palm of his stubby hand. There were ten or eleven rough diamonds there, none of them less than two and a half carats. 'What would you pay me for these?' he asked.

Barney fished inside his waistcoat pocket for his loupe. He squinted at the stones one by one, and then he said, 'A hundred and fifty. Bearing in mind that we're going through a world slump.'

'All right,' said the digger, 'You're on. That's twenty more than Isaacs would have paid me. Can you pay me ready money?'

'Tomorrow. And that's a promise. I didn't come out here expecting to buy.'

'You came out on Alsjeblieft and you didn't expect to buy? Why, that horse would come out on his *own* and buy.'

Barney patted Alsjeblieft's wet flanks. 'I'm beginning to realise that.'

Barney rode on towards Klipdrift. The rain began to clear, and the sky was rich with white and stately clouds. He arrived on the banks of the Vaal River just as the sun was setting over the Kaap Plato, and the evening was alive with chorusing insects. He stopped at the first digger's hut he came across – a long, English-style cottage with a thatched roof and mud-plastered walls – and asked the woman sitting outside if she knew where he could find the Griquas.

She pointed, dumbly, to the northern part of the settlement. Barney raised his hat and followed her directions. The pale blue sky lay in the ruts of the dark muddy road like fragments of a broken mirror. Somewhere, someone was playing '*Rose of Ireland*' on a harmonica.

The Griqua houses were just like the rest – narrow and thatched and surrounded by mud. But somehow they seemed more permanent. Almost all of them were fenced, and most of them had vegetable gardens, neatly laid out in rows, the way the Boers always did it. One of the gardens even boasted a scarecrow—a sad-looking half-caste effigy with his body stuffed with straw.

He saw Mooi Klip before she saw him. She was walking ahead of him, her bare feet squeezing into the mud, her baby held around her in a sling of Indian cotton. She must have been walking down to the Vaal River to wash, or fetch water. In one hand she carried a large pitcher of terracotta clay. Barney dismounted from his horse, and followed her only two or three paces behind, leading Alsjeblieft by the reins.

Sudden sunshine lit up the houses all around them. Barney said, 'Mooi Klip,' in his softest voice. Mooi Klip hesitated, and then turned, and when she saw Barney all she could do was stand in that muddy street with her hand against her cheek, and stare at him as if he were a dream. A stray cat sprang on to a low mud wall beside her, and watched them both with curiosity.

'Barney,' she said. 'I didn't think I would ever see you again.'

'You called him Pieter,' Barney said, trying to sound steady. 'May I see him?'

Mooi Klip untied the Indian cotton sling, and carefully lifted Pieter out. He was only three weeks old, red and crunched-up and tiny, and his fingers groped at the air as if he were feeling for something that he could never reach. Barney held his hands out, and Mooi Klip let him hold his son for the first time.

'He's so small,' said Barney, breathlessly.

Mooi Klip nodded, and shrugged. Barney held Pieter up against his shoulder, and stroked his soft dark hair, and it was all he could do to stop himself from crying. This was his son, his small baby son, by the woman he loved more than anyone else.

'Joel's fine now,' Barney told Mooi Klip, swallowing the constriction in his throat. 'It hurt him a lot, that trip to Durban. But he survived, and they operated on him. He can walk now, provided he uses a stick.'

Mooi Klip said nothing, but turned away. Barney said, 'It wasn't my fault, Natalia.'

'No,' she said. 'It wasn't your fault. But you didn't really want to marry me, did you?'

'I don't know what you mean.'

'*Barney*,' she chided him, 'you loved me, but I was never right for you, was I? A Griqua girl. When you first met me, I could scarcely speak English. How can you introduce a black savage like me to all of your society friends, or to Agnes Knight?'

'Agnes Knight? She was nothing at all. Look at what you've produced. Pieter Blitz. My first child.'

'Pieter Marneweck.'

'I'm sorry?'

'His name's Pieter Marneweck. Not Blitz. We were never married, were we?'

'But, Natalia, he's my son. And, anyway, can't we marry now? What's to stop us?'

She gently took Pieter out of Barney's arms. The last light of the evening touched her curly hair, and sparkled in her eyes.

'I'm sorry, Barney, it just wouldn't work. There was a time when I thought it could. But you taught me more than English. You taught me that everybody in this world has their place, and that my place isn't beside you.'

'What am I going to do?' asked Barney. His throat felt as if it were coated in dust.

'You can live without me.'

'But how?'

'You've been living without me ever since you took Joel to Durban. And I've been living without you. It's easy. All you have to do is to pretend that pain is something that everybody has to live with, all of the time.'

Barney said, 'What about Pieter?'

'You can see him, whenever you like. I'll always be here.'

Barney lowered his head. 'And what about you?' he said, softly.

'I can manage,' said Mooi Klip.

Barney took a deep breath. 'I want to tell you something,' he said. 'I love you more than anybody else in this whole continent. I love you more than anybody else in this whole world. It's almost unbearable for me to stand here next to you and know that I can't have you. I want to get inside of your mouth and change the words that you're saying to me. For

God's sake, Natalia, how can you be so aloof? Haven't you missed me? Don't you feel anything for me at all? Don't you understand that nothing has any meaning unless you're right beside me to share it?'

'You want me to live with Joel?' asked Mooi Klip, raising an eyebrow.

'Natalia – that will never happen again – I can promise you that.'

'It happened once, and once was more than enough.'

'Natalia –'

She smiled. 'Why don't you call me Mooi Klip? The pretty stone. The glittering diamond you found in the mud, and then cast aside.'

Barney looked up at the evening sky. 'I don't know what to say to you,' he told her, throatily.

'Don't say anything. Not now. Come again when you want to. Perhaps bring a gift for your new son. I am not shutting myself away from you, Barney. I love you still. But the time is not ready yet, and neither are you.'

'I've brought a gift,' said Barney. And he took out of his pocket the wash-leather bag that the digger at the De Beers Mine had given him, crammed with rough diamonds.

Mooi Klip opened the bag carefully and stared at the gems with widened eyes. Then she said, 'No. You will need these. You can't.'

'Take them,' he said. 'One day, they're going to be worth a thousand times more than they are now. You can rely on diamonds to look after you, even when people can't.'

With an awkward heave, he mounted Alsjeblieft again, and raised his hat. 'This is ridiculously formal,' he said. 'I love you, and that's all there is to it.'

Barney tugged at the reins, and Alsjeblieft plodded back along the street between the shacks and the tin-roofed houses and the half-built wooden bungalows. Then, without any kind of urging, the horse turned south, and began to carry him along the banks of the Vaal River towards the nearest digger's settlement, under the willows.

'Do you know something, Alsjebelieft,' said Barney, 'I really believe that you know where you're going.'

The horse kept plodding through the long grass, leaving the twinkling lights of Klipdrift far behind in the Cape Colony night. Barney began to whistle a tune that he heard a street-corner violinist playing in Durban. The tune was called '*Will Ye No Come Back Again?*'

TWO

Edward Nork had left a message for him on the kitchen table. 'Am drunk, but can be found at Dodd's.' Barney read it, turned it over to see if anything was written on the other side, and then crumpled it up. Edward had been drinking so heavily lately that Barney expected to discover him dead one day in a ditch.

He could not entirely blame Edward for his alcoholism. The world price of diamonds had been depressed for years, and life at Kimberley was harsher and more lonely than the profits from a thirty-one foot claim could ever relieve. When the diamond diggers were not being chilled by torrential rain, they were pickled like walnuts by the sun; and the Big Hole was now so deep and treacherous that floods and slides and cave-ins were killing and injuring diggers by ones and twos every day. Hundreds of hopefuls abandoned their claims, either because the work was too hard for the profits they were making; or because they believed they had reached bedrock, and that their ground was all cleaned out. So many left that the restrictions on how many claims one man could own were finally lifted.

It was not difficult for a man to persuade himself that he had reached the bottom of the diamond bearing soil, particularly when he was grimy and exhausted and alone, and he had saved up just enough money to get back to whichever country he had first come from.

That was not to say that the town of Kimberley itself had not improved. Bricks and fancy building materials had reached the town from Durban and the Cape, including a fine collection of cast-iron balconies. The Kimberley Club was now an imposing edifice of red tuck-pointed brick, with iron-pillared verandahs, a mahogany entrance-door with engraved glass panels, and a billiard-room on the second floor, under a skylight. The effect was rather spoiled by the rusting corrugated-iron roof, but in north Cape Colony, shingles were even rarer than diamonds.

There was a new hotel, The Kimberley Palace, and a new whorehouse with private bathrooms and brown velvet drapes with tassels. There were countless new bars; and there was even a rudimentary racetrack, with wooden bleachers, where motley races were run on Saturdays between horses that rarely looked fitter than Alsjeblieft. Most of the bets were laid in rough diamonds, or claim deeds, and Joel went along there whenever he could, although Barney kept a tight check on how much money he took with him. These days, with ill grace, Joel was prepared to let Barney keep the company books, and to allow Barney to be the sole signatory to their bank account.

All in all, though, Kimberley remained a crude and un-civilised male society, where even the smallest luxuries like badger's-hair shaving brushes and scented soap were almost impossible to come by, and where there was very little else to do but drink, gamble, dig the ground, or go to prostitutes. There was a small library on Barkly Street, but most of its books were inspirational stories of Christian derring-do in isolated corners of the British Empire, or bound volumes of scientific periodicals of what Edward called 'exemplary dry-ness'. There was an amateur dramatic society, too, but Barney had been reluctant to join it because he knew that Agnes Knight was a member, and that she was now engaged to be married to its leading male actor, a tall Australian with wavy golden hair and a high nasal whine. His name was Robert Joy.

It was four years since Joel had lost claim No. 172 to Dottie Evans. The claim had been sold three or four times since then, and Dottie Evans herself had been so sick of a social disease that she had left Kimberley and gone to the Cape for her health. Joel still walked with a tilting limp, and his hips gave him pain when the weather was damp, or when the wind was about to change, but otherwise he was much better. He worked for Harold Feinberg most of the time, as a kind of clerk; for Harold had done so well that he had built himself a fine brick-fronted office on the main street, with an upstairs workroom facing the north light, and he now employed a staff of seven, mostly Jews from London's East End.

Barney had been practically pressganged by his horse Alsjeblieft into that occupation known as 'kopje-walloping' – riding from one diamond claim to another, buying up roughs. Every morning at six o'clock sharp, Alsjeblieft started to kick at the rails of the kraal, and would not stop until Barney had saddled him up. There was rarely any need for Barney to direct the horse at all: he would simply trot off on the same rounds that his previous master must have taken since diamonds were first discovered.

The veteran diggers knew Alsjeblieft by sight; and they soon made Barney's acquaintance, too. In a white sun-topi, a belted jacket, and loud check trousers and spats, Barney was welcomed wherever he rode, and he quickly learned to play up to the diggers' expectations of what a good 'kopje-walloper' should be. He brought news, and gossip, and sometimes he brought tobacco, and whiskey, and rude French playing-cards. If a new popular song had reached Kimberley from the Cape, he would learn it, and sing it to every digger he met.

His four years of 'kopje-walloping' did more to strengthen his resolve to be rich, and more to help him through the pain of losing Mooi Klip, than any amount of consolation from Joel, or starry-eyed dreams from Edward. He had lost a would-be wife, and a son. But he came across men who had left everything behind them – their wives, their children, and their homes, just to break their backs in the pits of Kimberley, or De Beers, or wash through gravel on the banks of the Vaal. He met hard men and bitter men; men who scarcely spoke, and men who wanted to talk to him all night. He sat by more camp fires than he could count, and shook more hands than he could ever remember. He learned to be patient, and bright, and above all he learned to be understanding. One digger had talked to him for three hours about his beloved wife Fanny, with whom he had lived in a small redbrick cottage in Streatham, in southern England. It was only later that the digger confessed that he had been found guilty of Fanny's manslaughter, and had only managed to escape to South Africa by a lucky chance.

'You don't know what it is, to love someone, and then to lose them,' he told Barney.

Barney did not argue. He had learned never to argue with the men from whom he bought diamonds. They had to argue enough with their kaffirs, and with the weather, and with the yellow ground from which they were struggling to make their fortunes. All they wanted from Barney were nods of encouragement, and a reasonable price for their stones, and a song or two, and maybe an ounce of British Pluck. They did not want to know that Barney had problems of his own, or that he was the father of a four-year-old child whom he hardly ever saw.

Barney did not pay much for his diamonds: in fact, he gave four or five shillings less than almost any other dealer. But he always paid on time and he was always square, and that was what the diggers liked about him. They felt he was one of them: a small man struggling against the world, and they would often sell him some of their best gems at bargain prices just because he had made them laugh, or brought them an envelope of dubious Egyptian photographs, or sang them two choruses of 'The Flowers of Loch Rannoch'. He was good at Scottish songs, because of his Yiddish accent. The 'Cheery Kopje-Walloper' was a part that Barney had to play as dramatically as Agnes Knight and Robert Joy were to play *Romeo and Juliet* in the Kimberley Dramatic Society's Christmas entertainment at the church hall, except that Barney had to play his part every single day, and with unflagging good humour, through thunderstorms and winds and droughts and days when the flies swarmed as thick as currants in a cake. His ambition depended on it.

During Agnes's play, he sat on a folding chair at the very back of the hall, his head lifted so that he could see over all the hats. Few men in Kimberley were in the habit of taking their hats off indoors, or even when they bathed, and some were known to keep them on even when they visited a prostitute. 'You only take your hat off to a lady, after all.' Barney thought how charming and spun-sugary Agnes looked, in her white diaphanous Juliet dress and her blonde hair plaited into medieval horns. And when she said clearly, 'I, a maid, die maiden-widowed,' he felt so affected that he had to go outside, and take a few deep breaths in the sweltering night air. He had lost her, charming and pretty as she was, and he knew that she would never have him back again. Wrong background, old chap. Sorry. The English had won an Empire by saying 'sorry'.

'Bored?' a voice asked him, out of the shadows.

Barney frowned. It was a girl's voice, and it was familiar. 'Faith?' he asked. 'Is that you?'

She emerged from the darkness of the church hall porch into the misty light of the pressure-lamp which hung by the door. She was wearing a pale turquoise evening-dress, and turquoise gloves, and her hair was tied up in dozens of tiny turquoise ribbons. Behind her, the moths plattered against the lamp, and there was a shower of applause from the audience.

'Actually, I came out to look at the stars,' said Faith. 'I've had more of Romeo and Juliet in two months than most people can stomach in a life-time. Agnes has been practising her lines every night since September. But soft! What light at yonder window breaks!'

'Excuse me?'

Faith smiled. 'That's a line from the play. I think I'm even beginning to recite it in my sleep.'

'I'm surprised you're still talking to me,' said Barney. 'You're not worried you might catch something, like a liking for matzo balls, or a chronic inability to work on Saturdays?'

'Jews have never worried me, I'm afraid,' said Faith.

'I see. Only your father and Agnes dislike us, is that it?'

'Agnes doesn't mind Jews either. She was only upset because she thinks you made a fool of her.'

'I guess I did, in a way. It was my own fault. I thought that if everybody took me for a goy, I'd stand a better chance of making a success of my business.'

'Well, you're right, of course,' smiled Faith, rather absently, patting at her ribbons.

'I used to believe I was right,' Barney told her. 'But these days, I don't think it matters a damn if you play billiards at the Kimberley Club or not. As long as you work hard, and make money, who cares?'

Faith nodded. 'I only wish people *didn't* care. But they do. Well, the sort of people that *I* mix with do.'

'The people that *you* mix with don't strike me as particularly pleasant or particularly tolerant or even particularly successful,' said Barney, sharply.

'No, I suppose they wouldn't. Strike you as any of those things, I mean. But ... they all went to the right school. And they all belong to the right club. And they've all seen service in the right regiments. And he who hath fagged at Eton, and been commissioned in the Blues ... yea verily, success and financial ease shall follow him all of his days.'

Barney said, 'It takes an exception to prove a rule.'

'And you're going to be the exception?'

He looked at her. She was a handsome girl, quite broad-shouldered, with a generous figure. He could not understand why she was not married; or perhaps he could. Out of all the English girls he had met since he had come to South Africa, she was the only one with a distinct and uncompromising personality. He knew that she liked botany, and walking, and collecting African artefacts; and maybe all of that was why the gentlemen of Kimberley stayed politely away. They expected from their womenfolk a very special combination of fortitude and subservience, a mixture of durability and feminine fragility. If a women could reload a Lee Enfield under ferocious attack from kaffirs, and still blush furiously at an inadvertent mention of turkey breasts at table; if she could give birth to children in a strooidak hut in 110-degree heat, and still flirt and coo when her husband came home from the diamond office; if she could wield a hammer and nails during the day, and then patiently allow her husband to go out gambling and drinking at night on his own; then a Kimberley man would propose without a moment's hesitation.

Faith was not that kind of a girl, and that was why nobody had asked her.

Barney said, 'I'm going to be rich one day. That's all I can say. And those snobbish friends of yours will tip their hats to me in the street.'

'I hope they do.'

There was a silence between them. The moths pit-pattered on the lamp. From inside the hall, they could hear nothing but the distorted voice of Juliet's nurse, bewailing her charge's death.

'When are they going to be married?' asked Barney.

'Who?'

He nodded towards the church hall doors. 'Those two. Robert and Agnes.'

'Oh, I don't know. They're talking about April.'

'Does she love him?'

Faith smiled at him, and nodded. 'I think so. He's just her type. All wavy hair and no intellect.'

'You sound like you don't approve.'

'Oh, I approve. Anything to keep Agnes entertained.'

Barney laughed. Then he said, seriously, 'Do you think your father would object if I asked you to step out with me? There's a cello recital next week, just after Christmas.'

'Me?' asked Faith. 'No, you can't ask me.'

'Why not?'

'Because.'

'What do you mean, "because"?'

She lowered her eyelashes. 'Because you would probably hurt me, in the end. I asked you to accompany me to church one day, remember? And what happened then? I wasn't hurt much. Please don't think that I was. But if I started to step out with you, then I would undoubtedly and quite ridiculously lose my self-control, and then I would lose you, too, and that would be rather more than I could tolerate.'

Barney reached out and took her hand. There were three strings of pearls around her gloved wrists, and they shone as pale as solidified tears.

'I don't want to hurt you,' he told her. 'All I want to do is take you out to a cello recital.'

She gave a sad, small smile. 'One think leads to another in my life. A cello recital would lead to a symphony; and I can't bear symphonies. They always have such melodramatic endings. They make me cry.'

'Faith —'

'Let's be friends,' she whispered. 'When we meet in the street, let's pass the time of day. Let's have coffee together, when we can. One day perhaps I'll show you my botany book. I have some lovely drawings of acacias.'

'Acacias?' he asked her, as if he could not understand what she meant.

That had been a year and a half ago, and he had only talked to Faith twice since then. Once in the street, when they accidentally met on the boardwalk, and once at a concert, when a stentorious singer called Daniel Napier had bellowed out thirty British patriotic songs, one after the other, without pausing for breath.

Barney liked Faith. He trusted her, and there were many times during those four years of kopje-walloping when he felt he could have proposed to her, and married her, if only Mr Knight would have allowed him. But as time went by, he began to understand that it would have been a mistake, and that Faith's estimation of their probable effect on each other was quite right. He would only have hurt her, in the end. He would only have made her cry.

He saw Mooi Klip once or twice a month, whenever Alsje-blieft decided it was time for them to plod up to Klipdrift. Mooi Klip's mother and father lived in a neat, white-painted strooidak house not far from the bend in the river, among a whole community of Griquas. They were quietly but firmly protective of Mooi Klip, and especially of Pieter, and whenever Barney arrived to see them, they would wait in the background, their arms patiently folded, and Barney could only talk to Mooi Klip in the most stilted way.

Sitting together on those riempie-thonged chairs, close to the shuttered window, Barney asked Mooi Klip time and time again to think of coming back to him, to consider starting again. But each time she would smile at him and shake her head. Even when he suggested buying out Joel, and paying for him to go back to America, Mooi Klip declined to think about marriage.

'I don't understand *why*,' he hissed at her. Her father was sitting in his big yellow-wood chair only three feet away from them.

'Because I am not ready to marry.'

'You were ready before. How can you possibly not be ready now?'

'You know what happened,' said Mooi Klip. Then, softer, 'It changed everything.'

'But I don't understand what's wrong. Is it because you don't love me?'

'No. You know that I love you.'

'Well, I love you, and I can't stand to be without you. So how can you stand to be without me?'

Mooi Klip brushed back her curls. 'Sometimes there are more important things than being together.'

'Like what? I can't think of a single consideration that could possibly be more important than our getting married.'

She looked at him straight. The washed-out afternoon light caught the side of her face, so that she looked like a sepia photograph of herself. But Barney did not even own a picture of her, let alone the real thing.

'It's much more important that you make yourself rich,' she said. '*That* is what is important.'

Barney let out a short, impatient breath. 'Do you really think that money matters to me that much? More than you?'

She nodded. 'It *must* matter.'

'And what about Pieter? I suppose I don't care about him? I suppose I'm not interested in being a father to him?'

'You are his father. Nobody can ever take that away from you, nor from him.'

'But how can I –'

Mooi Klip reached out and touched his cheek, stroking it gently, calming him down. 'You came here to Africa to make your fortune. You must make it. I have learned that I will only stand in your way.'

'You think I care about those narrow-minded Englishmen, and those prejudiced Boers?'

'You will do, when you are wealthy, and you have to do big business with them. What will they way, if you try to take a Griqua wife along to their garden parties, and their banquets? A wife who is as black as their servants? You are Jewish, and that is enough of a difficulty for you. Do not make it worse for yourself by marrying me.'

'Natalia –'

She raised her hand to hush him. 'I can only say that because I love you and because I know that it is best for you.'

They argued like that almost every time they met; but Mooi Klip was patient and adamant. She had been ready to marry him once, but not now. He could see Pieter whenever he wanted, and his fatherhood would never be denied him. But she would not marry him. Not when he shouted at her, and slammed doors; not when he tried to cajole her, or bribe her; not even when he cried.

Little Pieter was all that he could have wanted a son to be. He had his mother's dark curly hair, and dusky complexion, but by the age of four there was no doubt at all that he had inherited his father's chiselled face and big-boned physique. 'The little boxer,' his grandfather called him, which in itself was a courteous acknowledgement of Barney's rights.

Pieter spoke mostly in Griqua-Afrikaans, but Mooi Klip taught him English, too, and insisted that he should always speak English to his father. He only broke into Afrikaans when he was excited, or angry, and then Mooi Klip would smack him on the cheeks with both hands, as if she were playing the cymbals, and tell him not to be rude to his father. Barney told Pieter long stories about his adventures on Alsjeblieft, and on long cool autumn evenings he would sit him up in the old horse's saddle and walk him along the banks of the Vaal, with the sun spreading across the mud flats and the birds flickering up from the distant treeline like handfuls of cloves.

His occasional visits to Klipdrift were days of great calm, and of great joy; and also of bittersweet sadness. But in the extraordinary times that were to come, he would always look back on them as if he were looking through a series of lighted windows at landscapes made tiny by the perspective of the years, each of them rich with warmth, and with happiness, and with precious regret.

He found Edward in the far corner of Dodd's Bar, his head resting on his arms, a collection of smeary whiskey glasses assembled around his elbows. An Irishman in a green Derby hat and a green silk vest was sitting at the upright piano, playing an off-key song about Paddy O'Leary's party, and three other Irishmen had linked arms to dance a shambolic jig across the bare boarded floor. The air was thick with Empire tobacco, from cigarettes and pipes, since only yesterday an ox-waggon had arrived from Capetown with fresh supplies. The diamond diggers smoked what they could get, and sometimes, when the roads were barred all they could get was dried wild syringa leaves.

Barney sat down opposite Edward, seized his hair, and shook his head around to wake him up.

'What's the matter?' Edward protested.

'It's me, Barney. You left me a note.'

Edward raised his head and peered at Barney through eyes as bloodshot as garnets.

'A note?'

'That's right. On the kitchen table. You said you were drunk, but I could find you here.'

'Oh, did I? Well, that only goes to show what a foolish fellow I am.'

Barney beckoned the barman, who came across in his blue striped apron and stared at Edward with a face like a leg of pork.

'If you're buying any more for him, then it's up to you to drag him out of here,' he cautioned Barney.

'Just bring me a jug of water,' asked Barney.

'Five shillings,' said the barman.

'Just bring me the water, will you?'

The barman went off, and Edward gave him an inebriated wave. 'Never could stand that fellow,' he said. 'Too censorious.'

'You left me a note,' Barney repeated.

'Oh, yes. I did,' agreed Edward. 'Well quite right, too. Particularly since I've set you back on the road to fame and fortune, prosperity and wealth.'

'I see. And how did you manage that?'

Edward reached into his inside pocket, and then into his side pocket. Eventually, he found what he was looking for in his breast pocket – a sheaf of crumpled claim deeds. He held them up, and gave Barney an unstable grin.

'What are those?' asked Barney, sharply.

'These, my dear chap, are the title deeds for claims No. 203, 202, and 233, as well as half of 201 and half of 232.'

'Did you *steal* them?'

'My dear old fellow, of course I didn't steal them. I *bought* them. And what's more, I bought them on your behalf. Here,' he said, and pushed them across the table. 'They're all yours. Take them. Make the most of them.'

Barney, very slowly and cautiously, picked up the deeds that Edward had laid on the table. He leafed through them, and then put them down again.

'They're genuine,' he said. 'Four genuine claims.'

'Of course they're genuine.'

'But how did you pay for them? They must be worth forty thousand pounds!'

'I gave them an IOU. In your name, of course.'

'You did what? An IOU for forty thousand pounds? How the hell am I going to meet an IOU for forty thousand pounds?'

Edward waved his hand. 'My dear chap – wait. Hold your horses. The claims *are* worth forty thousand pounds, yes. But only in *our* opinion. The chaps who have been mining them have dug right down to the blue Norkite. They're all ready to pack up and go home, simply because they believe that they've reached rock bottom. They were willing to sell for a *very* reduced price.'

Barney stared at him. All he had in the bank was £3211 – the carefully-accrued profits from four years of kopje-walloping. 'How much?' he asked, in a thick whisper.

The barman brought their jug of water, and banged it on the table. He held out his hand ungraciously, and Barney gave him four shillings. He spat on them, and then walked off.

Edward poured himself a large glass with shaking hands.

'Three thousand, one hundred pounds,' he said, triumphantly.

Barney picked the deeds up again. Four claims, right in the centre of the Big Hole. It seemed like a hallucination, the reappearance of his mirage. 'Edward,' he said, 'you're a genius. One day, I'm going to erect a statue to you. In marble, like a Roman emperor, right on the reef of the Kimberley Mine. Edward, you're a *genius*!'

'Well, yes, I know,' said Edward, modestly.

'I must go tell Joel,' Barney said. He could hardly sit still. 'Lord above, this is marvellous!'

'The least you could do is buy me a drink,' remarked Edward.

'I'll buy you a hundred drinks. But first of all I want to go to the bank and draw out enough money to pay off this IOU. I want to know that these claims are actually mine.'

'One small snort of whiskey would do,' said Edward.

Barney snapped his fingers at the barman. 'Bring this gentleman another drink,' he directed. 'And treat him like the genius he is.'

*

Joel was dubious at first. He was quite comfortable working in Harold Feinberg's sorting-room, and a pretty young French girl had just come out from Natal to work with Harold on the commercial side. To leave the fine brick building on the main street and go back to the mud and the flies and the days of hard digging did not seem at all attractive, and he argued with Barney for hours before he finally gave in.

'I think those claims are a waste of money, mind you,' he said petulantly, once he had agreed to help Barney dig. 'If Johnson and Kelly have left them, how can they possibly be worth having? Johnson's the meanest man in the whole colony, if not the whole of Africa.'

'I agree with you. But Johnson's selling because he believes that his claims are all worked out.'

'But other diggers have kept on going, and still found diamonds. Surely Johnson knows that.'

'It's a question of soil break-down, that's what Edward says. The blue ground underneath the yellow ground gradually weathers into yellow ground itself when it's been exposed to the air. It's all the same kind of soil. But men like Johnson are usually in too much of a hurry to wait around and see that happen. They think they've reached the end of their claim, and they're only too willing to make a small profit and get out fast.'

Joel sniffed loudly, and tapped his walking-stick on the living-room floor. 'I still think Johnson knows what he's doing. I just hope you won't be too sore about losing four years of hard-earned money.'

'We'll never get anywhere if we don't take a risk.'

'A risk?' mocked Joel. 'Moses took less of a risk when he led the Children of Israel out of Egypt.'

'Moses had God on his side. Maybe we do, too.'

'I'll believe that when a divine Hand reaches out of the clouds and digs out a few cubic yards of soil for me. Get me a drink, will you? There's a bottle of port on the hutch.'

There was a cheerful rap on the bungalow door. Barney, halfway across the room, said, 'Come on in!' and Cecil Rhodes appeared, looking distinctly pleased with himself, in a creased cotton bush-jacket and jodphurs with mud-caked knees.

'What-ho, Blitz!' he said. He set his sun-topi down on the

table. 'I hear that you're back in the diamond-digging business again! No more kopje-walloping?'

'Not if I can help it,' said Barney.

'I always heard that you were a splendid walloper. Friendly, affable, and never wasted your time on dud claims.'

'I have my horse to thank for that. Alsjeblieft wouldn't go near an unprofitable claim, even if you filled it to the brim with oats and carrots.'

'How's life at De Beers?' asked Joel, sourly. 'I hear that you and your pals own half the claims there these days.'

Rhodes pulled up a chair, and sat down. 'Actually, now that the board have relaxed the rules on ownership, the whole show's going very much better. It was so unprofitable, with all those tiny claims! Now we've consolidated fifteen or sixteen claims together, and that means we can dig them all at the same level, and dig them deeper. We can serve them all with the same cables and buckets, too, and drain them all with one pump.'

'They tell me you're really quite rich these days,' said Joel.

'Wealth doesn't come into it, old boy. What we're doing here is extending the Empire, and making sure that we manage things the British way. Efficiently, profitably, and in the best interests of all.'

Barney brought them both a glass of port. 'Well,' he told Rhodes, 'you once told me that we might have a scrap on our hands. Let's see how we get on.'

'I'm looking forward to it,' said Rhodes, lifting his glass. 'I have to go back to Oxford in the spring. I'm studying for my doctorate in law. But I have a splendid fellow called Charles Rudd who looks after things for me when I'm away.'

'Well, I'm glad for you,' said Joel, finishing his drink in two quick swallows. 'It must be wonderful to be so rich, and surrounded by so many splendid chaps and fellows.'

Rhodes stared at Joel levelly. 'Yes,' he said, after a while. 'It is.'

The following morning, Thursday, Barney and Joel negotiated their way across the uneven, crumbling pathways of the Big Hole to inspect their new property. Edward had been right: the four claims had been dug really deep, right down to the blue ground, which in spite of Edward's constant efforts to christen 'Norkite' was now fairly generally known throughout the digging community as 'Kimberlite'. Joel limped around the claims, morosely kicking the ground with his boot-heel, and prodding it with his stick.

'Seems pretty well worked out to me.'

'That's what Johnson thought. But if Edward's right, this is only the beginning.'

'Edward's a drunk. I don't know why he impresses you so much. You wouldn't have been impressed by a drunk cutter, back at the tailor's shop, would you?'

Barney propped his fists on his hips and looked around. Right beside him, in the next claim, which belonged to the Compagnie Française des Diamants du Cap, a kaffir was loading earth into the buckets which hung from one of the steel cables. Since Barney had last dug here, the cables seemed to have multiplied, and everywhere he looked there were dangling buckets being jerked slowly towards the rim of the mine, and down again. Few cables were wound by hand any more: most of the diggers had set up huge horizontal winding-wheels on the edge of the mine, which were rotated by horses in harness. These wheels were called horse whims, and apart from being more powerful they freed the diggers to attack the soil of the Big Hole with even greater speed and ferocity.

'You really believe we're going to make ourselves rich?' asked Joel, dubiously.

'Why not? Rhodes has. And Rhodes isn't any cleverer than us.'

'He may not be cleverer,' said Joel. 'But he's English, and he's been to the right school.'

Barney walked across the claim and picked up an abandoned shovel. 'By the time we're finished,' he said, 'it won't matter a damn what school anybody's been to. It won't matter if they're Jewish or goyish. There's only one human currency out here, when it really comes down to it, and that's diamonds.'

He thrust the point of the shovel in to the hard blue ground, and dug some out. Then he crumbled it between the palms of his hands, picking out the pebbles and the gravel. He was left with three small diamonds.

'You see?' he said, holding the stones up to the sun. 'One of these is nearly a carat. And the other two are good-quality smalls.'

'What are you waiting for, then?' demanded Joel, with a smile. 'Go get some kaffirs, and let's get started.'

'You're sure?' asked Barney.

Joel made a face. 'You don't *have* to have me, you know,' he told Barney. 'I certainly haven't done you any favours, and I don't suppose I ever will. But we're brothers, aren't we, and I suppose that's a good enough reason for working together.'

'I think so,' said Barney. Then he made his way up the slope towards the edge of the mine, while Joel sat on the handle of the shovel and watched him go.

Diamond-fever caught them both. Every shovelful of blue ground they dug up from their four claims brought more gems, and more profits, and by the end of 1876 they were making more than £2000 a week. In 1877, on his twenty-ninth birthday, Barney reckoned that he was worth more than £75,000, and to celebrate he ordered an architect up from Durban to plan a mansion for himself and Joel on the outskirts of Kimberley, on a small kopje among the trees. He wanted a billiards-room, just like the Kimberley Club, even though he did not have the faintest idea how to play billiards; and a field for playing polo. He also wanted a long curving driveway, so that anyone who came to see him would have plenty of time to be impressed by the gounds and the house and the formal gardens.

He began to dress, at weekends, in well-tailored frock coats which he ordered from Capetown, with dark blue silk facings on the lapels. He also ordered ten smart double-breasted vests, and a dozen white collars, and spotted ties, and tweed trousers. Joel bought himself a small varnished brougham, and a pair of frisky grey horses, and spent his Saturdays trotting up and down Kimberley's main street in his smart white suits, raising his hat to all the girls.

The house began to take shape, and when the foundations were laid, Barney broke a bottle of champagne over its brown Cape bricks and named it Vogel Vlei. Joel, who stood a little way off with a red-haired Scottish girl called Mary, gave him an encouraging wave with his stick.

But even his money could not protect Barney from tragedy and violence. Two days later, without any warning, Alsjeblieft began to shiver and shake and foam at the mouth, and he had to call in Dr Schoeman to give him medication. 'He's old,' Dr Schoeman told him, coming out of the stable and tugging down his sleeves. 'The kindest thing you can do is to put him down.'

Barney said, 'But he did everything. He made my fortune for me.'

'All the more reason to be kind to him,' said Dr Schoeman, his eyes as blue and bulging as those glass marbles which English schoolboys called Sea-Blue Sailors.

'Let's wait and see,' said Barney.

Dr Schoeman shrugged. 'He's only going to suffer. His liver's gone.'

Later than evening, while Joel was laughing in the living-room with Mary, Barney went outside with his Shopkeeper's pistol, fully loaded, and walked around the house to the stable. The insects chirped and chirruped in the scrub all around him, and high above Kimberley the full moon was suspended bright and cold, the temptation of an age yet to come. He hesitated by the kraal gate, and then he went inside, and crossed the kraal towards the stable.

Alsjeblieft was lying on his side in the straw, his eyes wide, panting as he breathed. There were flecks of foam around his mouth. He raised his head slightly as Barney came in.

Barney tugged at his mane. 'How are you feeling?' he asked gently. 'Pretty bad, hunh? You have a *krenk*?' He was conscious of how nearly he sounded like his mother, on those winter days in New York when he had stayed home, in bed, with a snuffle.

Alsjeblieft whinnied, and his throat was thick with fluid. Barney stroked his shoulder, and thought of all the miles and all the days they had travelled together, Alsjeblieft and he, and how Pieter had sat in the old horse's saddle and pretended that he was a soldier, a Life Guard of Her Majesty the Queen.

'I hope you forgive me,' said Barney, and raised the muzzle of his revolver so that it pointed directly between Alsjeblieft's ears. Alsjeblieft seemed to sense that something was wrong, because he shifted on his straw, and almost tried to get up on to his knees.

'Forgive me, *alsjeblieft*,' Barney asked him, and then there was a very loud, flat shot, and the horse collapsed on to his pallet with a sigh that sounded human. Maybe it was a sigh of relief. Barney stood up, with the heavy pistol hanging in his hand, and looked down at the horse with a choking feeling in his chest. Then he left the stable and walked outside, breathing with as much difficulty as a man who has run a quarter of a mile in his veld boots.

Joel came hurrying out with his shirt tail flapping out of his trousers. 'What's the matter? What's all the shooting about?'

Barney nodded towards the stable. 'Alsjeblieft,' he said. 'Dr Schoeman said it was the best thing to do.'

'I see. Well, I'm sorry. I know what that horse meant to you.'

'And to you, too, Joel. Without that old horse, we never could have afforded those four claims.'

Joel clapped his arm around Barney's shoulders. 'You know your trouble, Barney? You're too sentimental. You saved up the money for those claims by working your backside off, and that's all. If you weren't so sentimental, maybe you would have found yourself a decent woman by now.'

'Like Mary?' asked Barney, sarcastically.

'Mary's all right. There's nothing wrong with Mary. And you can take my word for it that she's a genuine redhead.'

Barney irritably twisted himself free from Joel's arm. 'I'm not in the mood, Joel. That's all. I don't forget anybody who's done me a favour, whether it's a human or a horse.'

'Meaning that *I* do? Meaning that I should have to spend the rest of my life being humbly grateful to you for dragging me halfway across the Orange Free State in an ox-waggon, and having me operated on by some halfwitted British surgeon, so that I could have the privilege of walking around like a cripple? God, you're sanctimonious.'

Barney stopped, and seized the front of Joel's shirt. 'Listen,' he breathed, his jaw protruding with aggression, 'one more word out of you and I'll break your other leg.'

Joel pushed him away. 'One day you're going to stop threatening me, young Barney. The trouble with you is, your intellect gives out too early and then all you have to fall back on is your fists. All these fancy clothes, all these pretensions. A mansion you want, called Vogel Vlei? Why don't you call it Knishes?'

Barney rubbed the back of his neck, easing his wired-up muscles. 'Just leave it, will you, Joel?'

'Come on, now, you threatened to break my leg. I should leave? Let you walk away forgiven? I shouldn't say my piece about what kind of a hypocritical bastard you've turned out to be? And don't try to say that you're not. You're so damned hypocritical that you keep your little black woman tucked away in Klipdrift, as well as your half-caste son; while at the same time you prance around Kimberley complaining to all those goyish cretins about the kaffirs, and how primitive the Bantu are. You should *realise*, Barney – those goys don't respect you, whatever you say. They think that you're just as untouchable as the blackies. So don't try to match your prejudice with theirs. You'll never win.'

Barney listened to this in silence, and then stopped by the verandah steps. 'You've got me wrong, Joel. All wrong. There's only one thing I want out of life, and that's money. You see that mine out there? I want all of it. Then, I can do or say whatever I want and it won't matter.'

'You can do or say whatever you want right *now*.'

Barney shook his head. 'Not now. But the time will come.'

'When? When you're rich enough? You're pretty rich now.'

'When the whole of that Big Hole belongs to me. That's when.'

Joel gave him a sardonic grin. 'I see. That's when you're going to declare that you were born a Jew, that you've always been a Jew, and that you're always going to go to the synagogue and say your prayers, until they bury you in the ground. But not before then, right?'

'Get out of my way.'

'Or what? You'll hit me? You've got the gun this time. Why don't you shoot me?'

'I should have shot you a long time ago. You've been sicker than Alsjeblieft for years.'

'Oh, come on, now, Barney,' said Joel, hopping towards him on his one good leg. 'Don't tell me you're going to act the outraged little brother? Because of that black woman? Is that it? There are twenty black women at least as good as her down on Main Street right now, and you could have any one of them

293

for two pounds ten. I saved you that day! I saved you from yourself! Why, if you'd been married now –'

Barney raised the Shopkeeper's pistol and fired at Joel point-blank. He deliberately aimed to miss, of course, by more than three feet. But the sharp report of the gun stopped Joel right where he was, wide-eyed, his hands raised up to his chest in the posture of a frightened animal, and when Barney turned around to climb up the verandah steps, he was still standing there, his mouth opening and closing noiselessly, and the echo of the pistol shot was still racketing around the Kimberley kopjes like a shout of hatred that could never be forgotten.

Later that evening, Barney took the small ox-waggon and drove up to the site of Vogel Vlei. It was past ten o'clock, but the moon had not yet set, and the outlines of the foundations could clearly be seen in the darkness. He stood there with his hands in his pockets, the wind blowing his curly hair, and he could imagine for a moment the dinners he would hold here, in the dining-room; and the games of billiards he would play with Kimberley's diamond-dealers; and he could imagine the dances he would arrange on summer evenings, with the rows of French windows open to the lawns, and the waltz music wafting out over the trees.

Then he thought of Mooi Klip, and the moon as it sank was reflected in perfect miniature in the tear that formed in his eye.

By the winter of 1878, Vogel Vlei was almost completed. It was an E-shaped, symmetrical mansion in the English country house style, with a stables for eight horses, a kraal for oxen, and a magnificent gravelled courtyard in front of the main entrance, with a fountain which Barney's architect had bought in Ravenna, Italy, and which had been laboriously carried on ox-waggons across the Great Karoo in sixteen separate pieces. It did not matter that there was not enough water on Barney's estate to make the fountain actually work. He had a fountain, and that was impressive enough on its own.

Mooi Klip allowed Barney to take Pieter down to Kimberley one weekend, to inspect the new house. She declined to come herself, although Barney tried hard to persuade her. She was being cautiously courted these days by a young Griqua farmer, a very tall young man with noticeably Dutch looks about him called Coen Boonzaier. He and Mooi Klip were going to take advantage of Pieter's absence to visit friends along the Vaal River.

Barney took Pieter's hand and led him in through the carved oak doors of Vogel Vlei to the pillared hallway, with its shining parquet floors, and its decorative and sweeping curved staircase. Pieter was six now, a composed and dignified little boy, and his mother had dressed him in cream and beige union suit, with a brown bonnet. He was tall for his age, with big feet, and he had a very grave way of talking which amused strangers but which Barney always found touching.

As he grew older, Pieter was changing more and more to look like his mother; and Barney would sometimes sit him on his knee and stare at him for minutes on end, remembering the brown wide-apart eyes, the smoky-coloured curls, and the lips which had once parted to kiss him, and to tell him that she would marry him and love him for ever.

'Well, what do you think of the house?' Barney asked Pieter.

'It's fine,' said Pieter.

'Fine? It's magnificent! It's the best house in Kimberley! It's probably the best house in the whole colony!'

Pieter looked around the empty uncarpeted rooms, echoing and bare. So far, Barney had not decided on any drapes or furniture or decorations. He had not been entirely sure what to do. His architect had suggested a few names of decorators in Capetown – the man who had furnished Sir Henry Sarkly's house for him, and the company of designers who had converted the old Quinn house from a model of Georgian serenity into a confusion of Victorian over-indulgence. But Barney had demurred. He had vague and persistent memories of Khotso, and he wanted Vogel Vlei to have the same atmosphere. Elegant, immaculate, but also relaxed.

'Can I go home?' asked Pieter, in his strong Afrikaans accent.

'This *is* your home,' said Barney, laying a hand on his shoulder. 'Well, it's one of your homes, at least.'

'It doesn't feel like home.'

'No, not yet. But it will, I promise you. And I promise you

something else. You will always be welcome here, no matter what. You're my son, my only boy, and my first boy, and I want you to remember that, because it's important. If you want to tell people that Barney Blitz is your father, then it's all right by me. In fact, I'll be proud of it. In fact, I'll be more than proud of it.'

'Mama won't marry you,' said Pieter, flatly.

Barney looked down at Pieter, and Pieter was so much like his mother that it gave him a strange sensation of unreality. 'She *says* she won't.'

'Is it because of Uncle Joel?'

'Uncle Joel?' asked Barney, and his voice echoed across the oak flooring. He could see a reflection of himself and Pieter in the long line of French windows opposite, two pale figures in a huge sunlit room. 'Well – I suppose it's partly because of Uncle Joel.'

'She doesn't like him.'

'How do you know? She never told you that.'

Pieter blushed. 'I know. But I just know she doesn't like him.'

'I see.'

They inspected the first floor in silence. The ballroom. The library. The dining-room. The kitchens, with their cold black ranges, and their bare beams. Everywhere they went, there was a sharp smell of newly-cut wood, and plaster.

Upstairs, looking out of the landing window over the few straggling trees which formed the southern border of Vogel Vlei, Pieter said suddenly, 'I love you.'

Barney looked at him cautiously. 'You love me? You really mean that?'

Pieter turned towards him, and Barney could see that his son's eyes were tight with tears, and his mouth was down-turned. 'Mama says you're good. And I know you are. But she cries. Why can't you stay with Mama, instead of going away every time?'

Barney knelt down, and held Pieter tight in his arms. He tangled his fingers into the baby curls at the back of Pieter's neck, and then he said gently, 'Sometimes things happen whether we want them to happen or not. I was going to stay with your mama once, but things went wrong. It wasn't my fault. It wasn't your mama's fault, either. But they did, and now we don't seem to be able to get back together again.'

'Can I ask her?' said Pieter.

'Can you ask her what?'

'Can I ask her to have you back with us, to stay?'

Barney stood up, his hands on his hips, and looked around the deserted living-room. 'You can ask her if she wants to come and live here.'

Pieter looked away.

'You don't want to ask her?' Barney queried. 'Or is it that you don't want to live here yourself?'

Pieter said, 'It's not home. Mama won't think it's home. Your other house is home.'

'The bungalow? But that's just a – well, it's just a bungalow.'

'This isn't home,' insisted Pieter.

'Of course it's home. It's the biggest home in the whole of Kimberley. Come on, Pieter, I haven't even moved in yet. But when I do, then you'll see how friendly it is. I promise you.'

At that moment, Harold Feinberg's voice called, 'Hallooo? Anyone at home?'

'There you are,' Barney told Pieter. 'I told you it was home.'

Harold came squeaking into the living-room on soft black-leather pumps, and took off his sun helmet. He was breathing rather noisily, as if he had walked all the way from his office.

'Home?' he said. 'This place will never be home to anyone, least of all you.'

'You want to make a bet on that?'

'If you like. I bet you *my* best diamond of the day against *your* best diamond of the day, that on New Year's Day, next year, you won't even be living here.'

'Jewish or Gregorian New Year's Day?'

Harold Feinberg pulled an expression of mock outrage. 'Jewish, of course. Just because *you've* given up your religion, that doesn't mean to say that *I* have.'

Barney laid his hand on Pieter's shoulder. Harold said, 'That boy's growing, you know. I don't know what his mother's feeding him, fertilizer, maybe? – but he's growing.'

'Of course he's growing. He's six years old.'

'Your son and heir, huh?' asked Harold.

'That's right.'

'So why don't you marry the mother?'

Barney took a slow breath. 'I would, if she'd have me.'

'No, you wouldn't,' retorted Harold, pacing across the bare floorboards with exaggerated steps. He stopped, silhouetted against the sunlight that flared in from the uncurtained window. 'You wouldn't marry her for *nothing*.'

'What do you know about it?' asked Barney, more cuttingly than he meant to.

'What do I know about it? I'm a diamond dealer. And if you want to know about human nature, I'm your man. Come on, Barney, you've seen it for yourself, when you were out kopje-walloping. Greed, you've seen, haven't you, and despair, and hopelessness, and ridiculous optimism? You've seen all of those.'

'Sure.'

'Well – you may recognise those things in other people – but maybe you don't see them in yourself. When I look at you, do you know what I see?'

'I don't know,' said Barney, brusquely. 'What?'

'I see ambition. That's what I see. I see ambition, and I see one thing more.'

'Oh, yes?'

'I see you burning yourself out before you're forty-five. A young death. Because, believe me, you've already got the kind of house that most people can only dream about, and you're making more money in one week that most English people make in a year. Do you know how much they pay a butler, these days, a fully-trained butler, in an English household? Seventy-five pounds a year. A year! And you're making two thousand pounds in a week.'

'You're not doing too badly yourself, Harold.'

'You think I'm in the business for money? I'm in business for satisfaction. I'm in business because it's good for my digestion. But let me tell you something. You won't ever live here, not happily, anyway; and that poor boy won't ever be your son and heir.'

Barney said, 'What the hell gives you the right to say something like that?'

Harold Feinberg lifted his hands in pretended innocence. 'I say it because it's true.'

'It's true, is it? Well, let me tell you something. This boy is my son, and my heir, and when I die everything that I own will belong to him.'

Harold Feinberg came across to Pieter, and took a half-crown from the pocket of his grey vest. 'You hear that, my boy? he asked. 'Your papa's just bequeathed you everything. His house, his diamonds, his broken heart. They're all going to be yours.'

'Harold,' warned Barney.

Harold stood up straight. 'I'm sorry. I was brought up in Whitechapel. It makes your tongue a little sharper than it should be.'

'You didn't come here to give Pieter a half-crown, did you? Or to spend your afternoon baiting me?'

'No, I didn't. I came to tell you that the Belgian Company right next to yours want to dispose of their claims, provided they can get a reasonable price.'

'Westerlo? Are you sure? But they own eight and a half claims.'

'With your money, you should be able to afford them.'

'What are they asking?'

'Two hundred thousand. Cheap at the price, I can tell you.'

Barney pushed his hands into the pockets of his trousers, and made a face. 'I'd go to one-eighty, but no more.'

'They'd probably accept that. I'd have to talk to them for a while, though.'

'Then talk to them. I'll pay your commission.'

Harold said, 'There's more than commission involved in this. Waterlo have business connections with Ascher and Mendel, in Antwerp.'

'The cutters?'

'That's right. And, believe me, they're the very finest. They specialise in odd-shaped stones . . . getting the best out of a gem that most cutters wouldn't even know what to do with. They cut the Orange Diamond last year, as a seminavette. Seventy-one carats.'

'I remember. But what are you trying to tell me?'

Harold laced his fingers over his camel-coloured vest. 'What

I'm trying to suggest is a three-corner partnership. You mine the diamonds, I market them, and Ascher and Mendel's cut them. Between the three of us, in time, we could control almost every major diamond that Cape Colony can produce.'

Barney eyed Harold thoughtfully. 'You're talking a lot of speculative hot air, Harold,' he said. 'But you're also talking a lot of sense. The only thing that disturbs me is why Waterlo want to sell.'

'They invested too much money in diamonds before the slump. Now they need capital. It's as simple as that. And – let's be truthful – diamonds were never a good investment, were they?'

Barney ruffled Pieter's hair. 'You know what Rhodes said to me once?' he asked Harold. 'As long as women go on falling in love, he said, the future of the diamond industry will be assured. Four million diamond engagement rings are required each year, and that means that four million diamonds are required.'

'Rhodes is a cynic, when it comes to women.'

'I wish I were, sometimes,' said Barney.

'I'm glad you're not,' smiled Harold. 'The day that you're not desperately in love with one lady or another, that's the day I will call for the rabbi.'

Barney linked arms with Harold and led him through to the library. The only piece of furniture in the entire house stood there: a small chipped Pembroke table, clustered with bottles of South African sherry and sweet white wines. There was also a bottle of whiskey.

'Do you want a drink?' asked Barney.

Harold shook his head. He sat on one of the windowsills and watched as Barney poured himself a small measure of Scotch.

'You never used to drink,' he remarked.

'I never used to be a millionaire,' said Barney. 'It's a responsibility, being a millionaire.'

'What do you think of my partnership, then?' asked Harold. 'You want to try?'

'I'm not sure.'

'You're going to have to do *something* dramatic, sooner or later. Have you seen how Rhodes is buying up claims at De

Beers? In a few years, he's going to have control of the whole mine. Then he's going to start looking at the Big Hole.'

'He won't find it easy, taking over Kimberley.'

'He will, unless you're strong enough to resist him. And that means buying up as many claims as you can, and controlling the price of diamonds. You won't win out against Rhodes unless you control the price. That's why I think it's worth your forming an alliance with me, and with Ascher and Mendel. If we're clever, we can keep the price of diamonds high when Rhodes wants to buy, and low when he wants to sell.'

Barney poured himself another whiskey. Across on the other side of the library, Pieter was scuffing his foot across the oak parquet flooring to make curving marks, like giant eyebrows, or scimitars, or unsmiling lips.

'Maybe you're right, Harold,' he said, softly. 'Maybe we should get into the cutting side, and the marketing side, and the retail side. After all, it's the retail side that counts.'

'Well, sure,' said Harold. 'It's on the retail side that they make most of the profit. You think *you* make a profit when you sell a rough diamond to me? You think *I* make a profit when I sell a rough diamond to a dealer from Europe? You think *he* makes a profit?' Harold pouted his lips, and shook his head. 'Not a chance. What we make is piffle. The people that make money are the jewellers. They mark up those diamonds a hundred, two hundred, three hundred per cent! And the poor fellow in the street pays two hundred pounds for that glassy stone you sold to me for ten pounds. Then he goes waving it around, telling all his friends what a wonderful investment he's made! A two hundred pound diamond! What an investment! He should try to sell it back to the trade and see what he gets for it. Diamonds are the worst investment since the South Sea Bubble.'

'The South Sea Bubble?' asked Barney.

Harold waved a dismissive hand. 'Take it from me, a bad investment. But for you and me, diamonds could be tremendous – as long as we control the business right from the mines to the shops.'

'And as long as we own enough claims to keep Rhodes out of Kimberley.'

'That goes without saying.'

Barney finished his drink, grimaced at the taste of it, and then held out his hand for Pieter. 'Pieter, *kom*.' He said to Harold, 'I'll talk to you later, when I've had a chance to discuss things with Joel.'

'I thought everything was yours. The claims, the house. What do you have to ask *his* permission for?'

'He's my brother, and he does half of the work, at least. I wouldn't presume to change the whole of his future life without talking it over with him first.'

Harold set his hat on top of his head, and tilted it a few degrees backwards. 'All right. It's your funeral. But don't wait too long. The French people have got their eyes on those claims, too. Let me know yes or no by morning.'

Barney lifted Pieter up in his arms, and said, 'Pieter – say goodbye to your Uncle Harold.'

Harold raised his hat, and leaned forward with his moustache puckered up to give Pieter a kiss on the cheek. 'You're almost a lucky boy,' he told him, and then he gave Barney a brief and sideways smile that was friendly and sad and a little bit sour, all at the same time.

At noon the following day, in the offices of the Board for the Protection of Mining Industries, amidst the aromatic dust of cedar pencil-sharpenings and barathea business suits, Barney was handed in silence the titles to all of the eight and a half claims belonging to the Waterlo Diamond Coy. In return, he passed to the clerk of the board, a bespectacled Englishman with a face as pale as calf's-foot jelly and a disposition to match, a cheque for £185,000 and a few pence. This cheque was duly passed to a short freckly Belgian called Mr Wuustwezel, who waved it in the air in jolly celebration, only to be peered at by the clerk with an expression of dire disapproval.

'This is a solemn trading matter, Mr Wuustwezel, not a carnival.'

'For you, maybe,' smiled Mr Wuustwezel, irrepressibly.

Afterwards, they all gathered at the Kimberley Hotel, where Mr Wuustwezel ordered French champagne and cigars, and where they sat around highly varnished yellow-wood tables, surrounded by smoke, and talked of diamond prices and diamond digging and, most important of all, of Cecil Rhodes.

'Against a man of Rhodes' determination, you will never win,' attested Mr Wuustwezel. 'He will take over every diamond mine in South Africa, simply because he believes it is his divine duty to do so.'

'Just because he's a religious zealot, that doesn't mean he's going to get what he wants,' said Joel, testily.

'Do *you* have such inspiration? Such ambition?' asked Mr Wuustwezel.

Joel eased his mended leg into a more comfortable position, and pulled a face. 'I have a taste for riches, if that's what you mean.'

'I suppose you have to,' put in Edward Nork. 'Morphis is expensive, out here in the back of beyond.'

Joel drained his glass of champagne, and set it down on the table with a sharp click. 'I have pain,' he told Edward. 'Particularly in damp weather, and in the company of idiots.'

'You don't change, do you?' smiled Edward, reaching down beneath his chair to retrieve his bottle of Irish whiskey, and top up his glass.

Barney said, 'We can really start to mine on a large scale now. That's if you don't mind my interrupting your personal vendetta with a little business talk. We can level off our own four claims to the same depth as the Belgian claims, and drain them all with one pump. The Belgians have two horse whims, if I remember, and those two can serve to carry out all of the blue ground from all twelve claims. We'll have three times the mining area and yet our daily expenses will scarcely be increased at all.'

'You'll need more kaffirs,' said Mr Wuustwezel, raising his champagne so that one of his appeared to be grossly magnified through the glass.

'Kaffirs aren't expensive,' said Joel.

'Not your run-of-the-mill kaffirs. But there's one kaffir I recommend you take on in particular. His name's Jack, and he's a Ndebele. He'll cost you twice the price of your usual kaffir, because he's educated, and he knows what's what. He's a good foreman, too. Takes care of all your workers for you, keeps an eye on all the stones they find, and makes sure you don't get trouble.'

'How much did you pay him?' asked Barney.

'Nineteen shillings a month. And when you think this mine's losing fifteen or twenty thousand pounds a week through pilfering, that's a worthwhile investment.'

Joel reached across the table and poured himself some more champagne. 'Nineteen shillings a month?' he asked, wrinkling up his nose. 'Don't you think they'll start getting ideas, if you pay them as much as that?'

'Jack's a Christian, Mr Blitz,' said Mr Wuustwezel, his round face suddenly solemn. 'He's honest, and temperate, and he has no ideas other than to do good work so that he can earn himself good wages.'

'I always suspect fellows who don't drink,' said Joel. 'Even blackies.'

Barney stood up. 'I think it's time we went,' he said. 'We have a great many arrangements to make. And besides, I've decided to go to Durban in two weeks' time to buy furniture and furnishings for Vogel Vlei.'

Joel looked up. 'You didn't tell me that.'

'I've only just decided.'

'I see. I suppose you want to go sniffing around that Sutter girl again.' He turned to Mr Wuustwezel and said, 'My brother is not a man for whores. He likes his relationships to be difficult; even tragic, if possible. He is a man who is aroused by hardship. Girls who simply lie on their backs with their legs in the air just will not do.'

Mr Wuustwezel reached for his grey Derby hat and carefully put it on. 'I think I, too, must be leaving,' he said.

'The party's just started,' protested Joel. 'What about some more champagne?'

'If you want more champagne. I regret that you will have to pay for it yourself,' Mr Wuustwezel told him. 'After all, you are now the part-owner of one of the largest diamond mines in Kimberley, aren't you?'

Barney reached across the table and shook the Belgian's

hand. Mr Wuustwezel said, 'Thank you for everything, Mr Blitz. I hope that you will make much profit out of our mines, and I hope that your problems will not prove too great a burden for you.'

Joel raised his head. 'What problems?' he demanded.

Mr Wuustwezel touched his hat, and walked away across the polished boards of the hotel lounge.

'What problems?' Joel shouted after him. 'What problems?'

Then he turned around and saw the look on Barney's face, and he seized his champagne glass and emptied it in one exaggerated swallow.

Jack, the Ndebele, turned out to be one of the suavest black men that Barney had ever come across. He had tight curly hair, a broad, handsome face, and he wore a gold and ivory earring in his left earlobe. But there his resemblance to his brother kaffirs ended. He spoke almost perfect English, in a Shropshire accent, and he always wore a white collar and a grey morning suit. He was known around the Big Hole as 'Gentleman Jack'; but although his civilised manners would normally have aroused suspicions that he was trying to ape the white man, and pretend that he could be the white man's equal, Jack's devotion to his work and his reputation for honesty were enough to quell the fears of those diggers who liked to make sure, for safety's sake, that they kept their kaffirs overworked and underpaid. 'There is no more dangerous nigger than a nigger who has tasted kindness,' a Boer farmer had once told Barney, back in Oranjerivier. 'You must keep them without hope that they will ever know anything better; because hope is the first ingredient of unrest.'

Jack met Barney the day after the titles to the eight and a half Belgian claims had been handed over, out by the North Reef. It was a cool morning, and Barney was wearing his blue covert coat, and his cap. Work had already started on most of the claims, and the clatter of picks and shovels and the squealing of winding-gear had frightened away the birds which came to pick over the freshly-dug earth whenever the miners were away.

305

'Good morning, Mr Blitzboss,' said Jack, climbing out of the steepsided claim in his grey suit and rubber galoshes.

'Good morning,' nodded Barney. 'I see no kaffirs here.'

'I'm here, Mr Blitzboss. I've worked here since they first broke ground.'

'I've seen you. And Mr Wuustwezel recommended that I take you on.'

'I was hoping you would, Mr Blitzboss. I am a worker of exemplary character. Excellent references from all my places of employment. Orphan from three years old, Mr Blitzboss, both parents died of the cholera. Taken in by Wallington, an excellent missionary and his family, and taught the exemplary manners of British people. I wear underwear, Mr Blitzboss, clean every week.'

Barney gave him an uneasy smile. 'Good. Well, I'm glad to hear it.'

Jack tugged at his tie, to straighten it. 'Without a necktie, Mr Blitzboss, no man is properly attired. That's what they taught me when I worked for Mr Jones. He sold pianofortes and religious music, sir, and it was my part to sing Psalm 23 at a position of attention while Mr Jones demonstrated the pianoforte from the back of his waggon. Later I got work building houses at Klipdrift, and then mining. Now I am here, if you wish to take me on, sir.'

'Sure I'll take you on. Mr Wuustwezel paid you nineteen shillings the month, didn't he?'

'And fourpence, Mr Blitzboss.'

'What was the fourpence for?'

'A special extra emolument, sir. For keeping Mr Wuustwezel's cook cheerful. You see, if she wasn't kept cheerful, she cooked badly, and Mr Wuustwezel was a stickler for good food. So, three times in each month, he would say to me, "The soup's getting thin, Jack," or "The cutlets are burned again, Jack," and off I went that night to make his cook cheerful. A fine big Basuto woman, Mr Blitzboss – well, a quarter French, but black like tar. I can tell you that I earned my fourpence.'

'It sounds as if you did,' smiled Barney. 'Perhaps I ought to pay you a pound a month, just to make up for what you'll be missing.'

Gentleman Jack's left eyelid trembled into what was almost a wink. 'A pound will be satisfactory, Mr Blitzboss. You will get excellent work from Jack for a pound.'

'Let me tell you something,' Barney told him. 'In a few days, I'll be leaving Kimberley for a month or two and going to Durban. You've seen my house, I expect – Voegl Vlei? Well, it needs furnishing, and decorating, and I'm going to Durban to find someone to do it for me. When I'm away, my brother Mr Joel Blitz is going to be in charge. So – no matter what he does or says, I want you to make sure you obey his orders and do exactly what he tells you. He's a Blitzboss too.'

'I understand,' said Jack, simply.

'Well, make sure that you do. I don't want to come back from Durban and find there's been trouble.'

'No, sir. You won't find any trouble.'

Barney looked down at the cluster of diamond claims that were now his. There was nearly enough space how to use a steam-shovel, and excavate the rock at three times the speed. The sides of most claims were now collapsing so regularly that more and more debris had to be dug out than ever to reach the diamond-bearing soil. Rhodes had been right. The sooner all these hundreds of individual diggers could be bought out, and their claims amalgamated, the sooner the mine could be prospected by largescale, mechanised methods. Barney determined to order two steam winding-engines while he was in Durban, and more rotary trommels for sorting the soil once it had been dug out.

'I'll leave you in charge, then,' Barney told Gentleman Jack. 'I want this mine working at top speed by eleven o'clock this morning, with the best kaffirs you can find. You can tell them that if they work extra hard, they get extra rations.'

'You think that's a good idea, Mr Blitzboss?'

'What do you mean?'

Jack smiled. 'Mr Wallington always taught me that black men should be satisfied with their lot. They should work hard because it's good for their bodies and their souls, not because a white man has offered them more rations.'

Barney stared at him for a while. 'You really believe that?' he asked.

'Mr Wallington said it was so, sir.'

'Well, if you think Mr Wallington was right, how come you're happy to take a pound, instead of nineteen shillings?'

'And fourpence, sir.'

'Yes, and fourpence?'

Jack gave an enigmatic shrug. 'Maybe, Mr Blitzboss, I am ahead of my time.'

'Maybe,' said Barney. 'And maybe you're a damned rascal.'

It took two weeks before the Blitz Brothers Diamond Mining Company was bringing up diamonds in sufficient quantities from their new possessions to be able to show a profit. The sides of the Belgian claims had collapsed, from weeks of neglect filling them with tons of worked-out debris, and Gentleman Jack spent five days clearing it all away. Even so, the claims were dug so deep that frequent cave-ins were unavoidable, and there were some days when they had to shovel out three tons of rock and debris just to extract one ton of diamond-bearing blue ground.

Barney, impatient, had no choice but to wait until the excavations were going smoothly before leaving for Durban. But Joel and Gentleman Jack seemed to get along quite well with each other, which was one comfort; and Edward Nork was devising a way of shoring up the sides of the claim with discarded iron girders which he had rescued from the construction site of the new London & South African Bank; and so by mid-July, Barney was able to take his two best horses, Boitumelo and Moonshine, and load them up for a journey across the plains of the Transvaal and the mountains of Natal.

Mooi Klip was rolling out dough in the kitchen of her parents' house in Klipdrift when Mr Ransome rapped at the door and called, 'Anybody at home?'

Mooi Klip pushed her curls away from her eyes with the back of her hand, leaving a floury white smudge on the dark skin of her forehead. 'Come in,' she said. 'There's only me.'

Mr Ransome came through the open doorway with his hat clutched in his hands the same way a small and timid animal clutches its food. He looked around the kitchen with quick, jerky smiles; and then beamed at Mooi Klip appreciatively.

'What a wonderful sight,' he said. 'Surely this is how God meant a family home to look. The gentle woman in her place, preparing food. The fragrance of baking. And those pies! There is nothing to me more holy than a pie!'

'You can take one if you want to,' said Mooi Klip, amused. 'But they're hot.'

'Well, no, I won't at the moment,' said Mr Ransome. 'But if you have a glass of milk, I would appreciate that. I've been driving around all morning, and I'm feeling quite tired with the heat. It's unseasonably hot, don't you think.'

Mooi Klip wiped her hands on her blue-checked apron, and went across to the dented metal churn in the corner, where her mother kept the goat's milk. She poured out a glassful with a dipper, and set it on the plain oak table. 'You can have a pie if you want to,' she said. 'I won't be cross if you change your mind.'

Mr Ransome eyed the pies thoughtfully. Then he said, 'No, no. I must abstain. I must show some self-control. I do try to perform at least one conscious act of self-control every day.'

Mooi Klip went back to her pastry-rolling. The sun shone in through the open door, and glittered in the dust and the flour, and crossed the white-washed wall of the kitchen in a long triangle. The room was simple, but its simplicity, and the simplicity of Mooi Klip's work, made it curiously restful; so that Mr Ransome found himself saying nothing at all, but leaning back in his riempie chair and watching her through drowsy eyes as she rolled and turned the dough, and cut it into ovals for those small vegetable-filled pasties which the Griqua people called 'little birds'.

It was on days like this that Mr Ransome felt close to his God. He had been educated as a child with pictorial Bibles, in which he had seen the boy Jesus in His father's carpentry shop; and he was still enchanted by sunshine and honest work. If he was ever asked about conscience, or complicated struggles of the spirit, he would smile vaguely and look the other way, his bland face transfigured by thoughts of those crisp and curled-up wood shavings around the Messiah's youthful feet. Oh, to have been there, to have actually been there, and helped Our Lord with his chamfering, and his planing!

Mr Ransome was a missionary; a former curate at St

Augustine's Church, in Kennington, near London, and now the sole propagator of the Word for hundreds of miles around. At the age of twenty-nine, he still looked boyish, with an oval face like one of Mrs Beeton's pie-dishes, and a long pointed nose, and thick brown hair which defied combing. He was wearing his cassock today, as always, and his dog-collar. He believed in the simple symbols of Christian stewardship, especially when he was making the rounds of the Griqua community, whose beliefs were fierce and direct and fundamental. The Griquas combined the earthly magic of the Hottentots with the abrasive simplicity of the Boers, and Mr Ransome often thought (secretly) that they spoke about their religion with even more conviction than he did.

He had been to see Mooi Klip several times since Pieter's birth. He had christened Pieter in the stone font of St Margaret's Chapel, a corrugated-iron building by the banks of the Vaal. He found something noble and yet pathetic in Mooi Klip's predicament, and he had tried to bring her the comfort of companionship and words from the Bible. She had told him about Barney, and about Joel; and about Coen, too; and they had knelt on the brown tiles of the kitchen floor and prayed together several times.

'Mr Ransome – I've been worried,' said Mooi Klip, sifting flour on to the table.

'Worried?' asked Mr Ransome. 'Why?'

'I don't know. I shouldn't worry. But Pieter came back from seeing his father at Kimberley not long ago, and he told me that his father wanted me to think about going to live with him, in his new house.'

Mr Ransome tucked his fingers together. 'Surely that's good news.'

'I don't know. What about Coen?'

'You feel more strongly for Barney than you do for Coen, don't you? At least that's the impression you've always given me. It was only a sorry accident that you didn't marry him.'

Mooi Klip glanced at Mr Ransome and then shook her head. 'It wasn't an accident, Mr Ransome.'

'You still haven't forgiven him?'

'I don't think I could.'

Mr Ransome scratched his ankle vigorously. 'I really don't know what to suggest. If you hate Joel so intensely, and if you feel that Barney has betrayed you by sticking up for his brother rather than cleaving to you; and if you are still not sure of your feelings for Coen ... well, then, I can only suggest that you work and pray a little longer, that you seek further guidance from the Lord. It would be very unwise to do anything precipitate, particularly when you have Pieter's happiness to consider, as well as your own.'

Mooi Klip laid down her pastry knife. 'I feel so sad sometimes,' she said, softly. 'I think of Barney, and how things could have been between us. Then I think of Joel, and I can only feel hatred. I know that hatred is not Christian, and that I should try to forgive him. But I will never find happiness with Barney as long as his brother is there.'

'And Coen?'

She lowered her head. 'Coen is good and kind, and I could learn to love him. But I would hate to hurt him, and I think that if I married him, I would.'

Mr Ransome considered what Mooi Klip had said, and drummed his fingers on the table. Then he picked up his glass of goat's milk, and drank half of it. Wiping his mouth, he said, 'How would it be if I spoke to Barney myself? If I were to intercede on your behalf?'

'I don't know whether that would help,' said Mooi Klip.

'Well, it might not,' Mr Ransome admitted, 'but on the other hand it might. You never know. Jesus was always trying the impossible, and succeeding. Think what an impossible task it must have seemed in those days to redeem the sins of the entire world!'

'There's only one person whose sins need to be redeemed to make me happy,' said Mooi Klip.

'Ah yes,' signed Mr Ransome. 'The dreadful Joel Blitz.'

He stood up. He looked across at the pies. 'I have to go to Kimberley at the end of the week,' he said. 'Perhaps I should call on him then.'

'You won't upset him? I don't want him to think that I'm pressing him to take me back.'

'My dear Natalia, I'll be most discreet.'

311

He took her wrist and gave it a confident squeeze. With dabs of flour on her cheeks, and her curly hair brushed back, Mooi Klip looked as pretty as an Italian painting. There was a golden, fragrant aura about her which Mr Ransome found strangely disturbing. It was only the mid-afternoon sunlight in her hair; only the fragrance of a young woman at work; but he found himself glancing covertly at the way that her breasts pressed so tightly against the flowery fabric of her dress, and at that shadowy crevice where her silver crucifix hung, and he knew, he just knew, that his ears had turned bright red.

Mooi Klip smiled at him, and then kissed his cheek. 'You've been such a friend to me,' she said.

He did not know how to answer her. He felt as if there were no words in his vocational vocabulary to describe exactly how he felt. No words to say how attracted he was, or how elated, or how ironic he felt it was that he should have volunteered to go off to see Barney on a mission of reconciliation when all the time he wished that he could have this disturbingly attractive Griqua woman for himself. He felt confident, yes: but also profoundly depressed, and yet excited, too. God, his feelings were so maddening! He did not realise that he was actually in love, nor that he had been for almost two years.

He remembered the moment, though, when he had noticed Mooi Klip as a woman, instead of nothing more than an unfortunate ewe in his Christian flock. He had seen her in the yard outside her parents' *strooidak* house one hot November morning, washing clothes in a wooden butt, rubbing them on a corrugated washboard with kitchen soap. Her hair had been tied back, and the sleeves of her white cotton dress had been buttoned up. He had reined in his small spidery black carriage to wish her good day, and ask how she was; and she had looked up at him, shielding her eyes against the sun, a picture of the tender savage, one dark nipple visible through the wet material of her dress like a kiss through gauze.

Mooi Klip said, 'Why don't you give in to temptation?'

'I beg your pardon?' Mr Ransome blushed.

'Give in to temptation. Have a pie. I'm sure you can practise your self-control on something else.'

Mr Ransome's lips felt dry. He ran his tongue around them,

and then he nodded. 'Yes, you're right. I shouldn't be too ascetic, should I?' He took one of the pies, and held it up in a gesture of appreciation. 'It looks good. I shall save it for my tea.'

She watched him from the kitchen doorway as he walked back to his carriage, where it was tied up to a nearby fence. He turned around twice, and raised his hat to her, and as he climbed up on to his seat, he called back, 'I shall let you know about Barney as soon as I can! I promise!'

Mooi Klip waved and smiled, and then returned to her pastry. Mr Ransome hesitated for a moment, reining back his horse. He felt like jumping down again, striding down the garden path, taking Mooi Klip in his arms and telling her that he was passionately fond of her. But unstead, he said 'gee-up', and flicked his whip, and his horse obediently began to carry him off along the rutted pathway.

'I mustn't,' Mr Ransome whispered to himself, as he reached the outskirts of Klipdrift. 'I am a missionary of God. I mustn't!' And his self-denial that afternoon was more painful than the refusal of a thousand pastries. He munched his pie as he drove, and he cried as he munched, and halfway back to his house he had to stop the carriage and thump his chest, because he was almost choking.

On the night that Barney crossed the border into Natal, five hundred miles away, Joel was sitting in the dining hall of Vogel Vlei, with empty gunpowder boxes for chairs, and a large ship's trunk for a table, playing Pope Joan with Gentleman Jack and an old-time Kimberley character called Champagne Charlie. All around them, scores of candles swayed and dipped, stuck to the polished parquet flooring with their own wax. The three men's voices and laughter echoed from one deserted room to another; and even up the uncarpeted stairs into the upper landings.

Champagne Charlie was a small florid man with a gingery moustache like hanks of a horse's tail. He had earned his nickname in Dutoitspan, in 1874, by scattering broken-up fragments of the bottoms of champagne bottles over a worthless tract of dry farmland, and selling it for £3000 to a guillible diamond digger. He was known as a gambler, too, and an addict of unlikely bets.

Jack eventually threw in his cards, and stood up. 'I believe I've had enough gaming for one evening,' he said. 'Would either of you two gentlemen care for some more port-wine? Mr Blitzboss?'

'I never thought the day would come when I would sit down on a wooden box and play Pope Joan with a kaffir,' cackled Champagne Charlie. 'But he's a smart player, ain't he, Joel? A smart player. And he drinks now, too! It only goes to show that you can teach a monkey a trick or two, if you try hard enough.'

Joel played a queen and a jack, winning 'Intrigue'. He looked tired, and his face was greasy and pale. 'Some monkeys learn quicker than others,' he said, and there was a touch of caustic in his voice.

'Oh, you mustn't let Barney get you down,' said Champagne Charlie. He knew what Joel was talking about. After all, in every saloon and gambling house and brothel in Kimberley, wherever diggers and engineers and diamond dealers met to drink and talk and win money, Joel had tirelessly complained about Barney, about how righteous Barney was, and how super-cilious, and how Barney deliberately kept away from black women just to show off his moral supremacy.

'Barney does a good deal more than get me down,' said Joel. 'Barney makes me wish that one or other of us had never have been born. I wouldn't have minded which. It would have been better for me not to have existed at all than to be obliged to live out this preposterous life with this intolerable brother.'

'He doesn't seem like such a bad fellow to me,' said Jack, bringing over three glasses of port. 'He paid me extra money, right out, and he's always been straight.'

'He wouldn't even let me *die*,' Joel complained. He stared at Champagne Charlie with citric intensity. 'I was hurt, I was going to be carried away to my Creator. I was finally going to be released. But would my wonderful younger brother let me go? Oh, no. He had other plans for me. Six weeks of sheer agony on the back of a waggon. And then six hours of hell in an operating theatre, while my bones were broken and re-set. Now look at me. Worse off than ever, with a stick and a limp, like a cripple. Half-owner of a diamond mine that *I* know and *he* knows I don't even deserve. "What do you think of *our* mine, Joel?" "How shall we decorate *our* house?" When all the time he knows damned well that I did nothing to contribute to either of them. That's the salt he keeps grinding into my open wounds. He knows I hate him, he knows that I deliberately tried to ruin his life, and yet he still forgives me.'

'Ain't you pleased?' asked Champagne Charlie, relighting his cigar. 'I'd be pleased, if I'd done what you'd done, and my brother still forgave me. I'd be downright delighted.'

Joel lurched off his gunpowder box, and kicked it over with a loud slamming noise. Then, leaning on his stick, he stalked around the huge dining-room, weaving in and out of the candles that were stuck to the floor, his face ghastly in the guttering light.

'Being forgiven,' he said, 'is the most terrible punishment of all. I cannot endure it.'

Gentleman Jack, standing tall and black in his grey frock-coat, turned his eyes towards Champagne Charlie, and rolled his lips downwards like a comical mask. Champagne Charlie let out a nervous snicker.

'One day,' said Joel, his voice distorted by the bare walls, 'one day, I dream that Barney will do something to me that requires my forgiveness.'

He paused, breathing hard, the ferrule of his cane vibrating against the hard oak floor, *tip-tip-tip-tip-tip*, his right shoulder hunched and his crooked left leg bent beneath him as if it had been drawn by a child. 'Oh, I dream of that,' he said, under his breath. 'I dream of the moment when he has to come to me and say, "Joel, I'm sorry, please forgive me."'

'And then you can spit in his eye!' cried Champagne Charlie, slapping his thigh.

Joel shot him a quick, triumphant look. 'Oh, no, Charlie! I'd never do that! I'd forgive him! That's what I'd do! I'd forgive him!'

Gentleman Jack finished his port. 'I believe I'm going to get some sleep now,' he said. 'That's if you'll excuse me, Mr Blitzboss. We have an early start tomorrow. A whole lot of earth to move.'

'Don't worry about that,' said Joel. 'Pour yourself another drink.'

Gentleman Jack shrugged. 'Whatever you say, Mr Blitzboss.'

Joel took two or three ungainly steps through the candles. 'You know something Charlie,' he said, thoughtfully, 'I do believe I love Barney. I do believe that, in spite of everything, I love him. He was my father's favourite, you know. Not my mother's. My mother always preferred me. But then I think that all mothers have a special soft spot for their first born. Yet ... in spite of everything, I do believe I love him.'

'He's always been regular with me,' said Champagne Charlie.

'Ah, well,' Joel told him, dismissively, 'that's because you're not his brother. But I do love him. I love him still. The only thing that irks me about him, the only thing that enrages me about him, is that he always believes that he's better than me. He always has. Even though he's always been younger, and always will be. Even though he's always had less experience. He – *assumes* – as if it's a direct gift from Our Lord – he – *assumes* – that he's better. And that's what makes me feel like dragging him down, and breaking everything he believes is precious. Can you understand that? I used to break his toys. I tore pages out of his bar-mitzvah Torah. But it's good for him, you know. He mustn't always believe that he's superior. You know that? He has to understand that he's just as weak and as human and as sinful as the rest of us. Because if he doesn't, you know – are you listening, Charlie? – if he doesn't, he's going to be very, very, seriously hurt.'

Champagne Charlie pursed his lips in discomfort. 'Well,' he said, 'do you want to play some more cards?'

'I feel more like drinking,' said Joel and lifted his empty glass at the end of a stiffly raised arm. Gentleman Jack came across the floor on tapping heels and poured him another port-wine.

'No women tonight?' asked Champagne Charlie.

'I don't know. I'm tired of blackies. I'm tired of those French whores too, that cackling collection of stinking women they brought in from Algeria. Only God knows how many niggers and donkeys *they've* fucked, in their lifetime. I'm tired of everything.'

Champagne Charlie ceaselessly shuffled the cards, his podgy

fingers pouring fountains of fluttering pasteboard from one hand to the other, over and over and over. 'I hear that Agnes Knight is playing it a little fast and quick these days.'

'Knight's daughter?'

'The blonde one. The pretty one. The one who married that thick-headed Aussie.'

'Agnes Knight, hey?' asked Joel. 'Yes, I remember her. I thought she was going to leave Kimberley, and go to Cape-town.'

'Her husband was thinking of it, but in the end Agnes didn't want to go. The story goes that she was having a little slap-and-tickle with the surface manager of the Beaconsfield Diamond Mining Company. She didn't want to give him up.'

'And her husband didn't suspect?' asked Joel.

'He's an Aussie. Aussies never suspect anything, not until they climb into bed one night, and try to put their arms around their wives, and another fellow's voice says, "Hold on, chum, you've got to wait your turn!"'

Champagne Charlie burst out laughing in deep, breathy gusts, so that his yellow-cheked vest went in and out like the bellows of a home harmonium. Joel, leaning on his cane, allowed himself a dry smile, and waited until Champagne Charlie had finished. Then Joel said, 'Barney used to be struck on Agnes Knight at one time, you know. I believe he would have married her, if he could have done.'

'Knight wouldn't have let his favourite daughter marry a Jew-boy.'

'Well, that was exactly it. That was exactly why they didn't get married. But if she's playing a few games these days, maybe we can cajole her into helping us with Barney.'

Champagne Charlie stopped laughing, and cleared his throat. 'Don't get you, old chap. What do you mean by "help-ing us with Barney"?'

Joel slashed his cane around in an whistling arc, and lopped the top off one of the candles. Then he hit another one, and another one, until the dining-room began to grow shadowy and dark.

'Have another drink,' said Joel. 'Have another drink. You'll see what I mean when it happens. You'll see!'

*

317

They sat in the rose drawing-room at Khotso taking tea. Gerald Sutter stood with his back to the fireplace, one hand cocked under his tailcoats, his other hand holding his teacup across his chest as rigidly as if he were the standard-bearer at a military church-parade. His wife sat on a small crinoline chair, looking a little tired from a recent headache, but as elegant as ever in a pewter-grey silk dress, and silk slippers.

Sara, flushed, sat on the sofa next to Barney, her neck wound with pearls, her pale pink dress embroidered with flowers. The rose-coloured upholstery of the furniture and the pink moiré silk on the walls lent her even more lightness and grace. She made Barney, in his best black suit, feel as severe as a mortician.

'*You're* a surprise, you are,' Gerald Sutter told Barney, loudly.

'Isn't he just!' exclaimed Sara. 'I do love surprises!'

Mrs Sutter could not resist smiling, and she lifted her arm towards her husband as if she wanted him to take her hand; although he did not. He was too busy trying to compose a suitable response to Barney's proposal.

'Over the mountains you come,' he said, with a tight wave of his teacup. 'Cool as a cucumber. And, damn me!'

'Gerald,' protested Mrs Sutter, mildly.

'Well, it's true,' argued Gerald Sutter. 'You can't say the fellow's got anything but nerve. Damned, outright nerve!'

'Gerald, my dear, you don't have to curse to convey your feelings.'

'Curse? If I were to say out loud all the curses that came into my head when this fellow knocked at the door and told me that he'd decided to marry Sara, the damned plaster would fall off the damned walls at the sound of it!'

'You know that Sara was engaged to be married last year,' said Mrs Sutter gently, inclining her head towards Barney.

'She told me,' Barney nodded.

'It was so sad. A young boy from the Colonial Office. Tall, and straight. An Eton boy, actually. You wouldn't have thought he had a care in the world, to look at him. Disease strikes so quickly!'

Sara said, 'Really, Mother, I didn't love him. I was heart-broken when he died. But I didn't truly love him.'

'How can you say that?' demanded Gerald Sutter.

'Because it's *true*, Papa. That's how I can say it. He was good-looking and enormously polite. He could ride, and play bridge. He would have made a terribly suitable husband. But I didn't love him, and that was that.'

Gerald Sutter puffed out his cheeks. 'Well,' he said, 'if you didn't love a chap with all of those qualifications, then I don't know what love is.'

His wife touched him again, with gentle fingers. 'Of course you do, my darling. You could hardly stay in the saddle when I married you, and you could never concentrate at bridge. But I still loved you.'

'The point is,' said Gerald, 'does Sara really love Barney? *That* is the point.'

Sara turned towards Barney and took his hand. 'I haven't been able to forget him since I first met him,' she said. 'I fell in love with him then, and I love him still.'

'It's all very irregular,' said Gerald Sutter. 'Especially since he wants to marry you so damned quick.'

'Papa – I'm twenty-four years old. That's quite old enough to make up my mind, and *very* much too old to be still a maid.'

Gerald Sutter looked as if he were going to say something, but then he pouted, and puffed, and jerked his shoulders in mute acceptance. He did not want to have Sara on his hands for the rest of his life, after all. And what if Barney's proposal had been irregular, and sudden, and sprung on the family with all the abruptness of an opening cosmos flower – well, at least the chap had money, and at least he could ride, and at least Sara actually professed to love him.

And who was he, Gerald Sutter, to stand without reason in the way of true love? Especially when it was going to save him the cost of Sara's upkeep.

'Well,' he said, at length, 'very well. I'll agree to it. But against my usual principles.'

Barney leaned across the sofa and kissed Sara's cheek. 'There,' he told her. 'I knew that he'd be reasonable.'

'Reasonable!' exclaimed Gerald Surter, in mock indignation, while Mrs Sutter raised her hands and laughed. 'Damn me! *Reasonable!*'

Barney's proposal of marriage to Sara Sutter had come almost as much as a surprise to Barney as it had to the Sutter family. He had missed her painfully when he had left Durban six years ago to return to Kimberley, and he had often thought about her when he was kopje-walloping on Alsjeblieft. But he had always assumed that Sara would marry, and that somehow he would find a way to get back together with Mooi Klip; and after a year or two those rides by the shores of the Indian Ocean had become little more than restless images in the photograph-album of his mind. Sometimes he had woken in his bungalow and heard the desert wind, and thought it was the sea. Occasionally, a letter had arrived from Durban from a pump company, or a diamond-dealer, and he had thought for a fleeting moment before he opened it that it might be a letter from Sara. But love is unable to survive on memories alone, especially for a busy man, and the flowers that had been ruffled by the wind in the gardens of Khotso had long ago been dried and pressed between the pages of *Pilgrim's Progress*, and forgotten.

It was only when Barney had come to decorating Vogel Vlei that he had thought of Sara again. He had resisted the thought at first. He still believed that Mooi Klip might come back to him, and that there could somehow be a happy life for them together. But his sense of ambition told him that he would ever allow it to happen, not for real, not now. Mooi Klip would be nothing but an embarrassment, when it came to business. It was all right for a chap to have had a bit of black on the side, and quite acceptable to have sired a half-caste son. But to *marry* a darkie – well, that was something different. And from that excuse, it was an easy step to the next excuse, which was that he could not possibly marry Mooi Klip, in case he hurt her.

He had given their love a last chance. He had asked Pieter to tell Mooi Klip that she was welcome at Vogel Vlei. He had waited and waited for an answer. He had even pretended to himself that he needed to stay an extra week in Kimberley to make sure that the digging at the Belgian mines was going properly. But there had been no reply; and the date that he had set himself for leaving Kimberley had eventually arrived, as fresh and windy as any other winter day in north Cape Colony, and he had been obliged by his own pre-arranged plans to go.

He had quite convinced himself when he first set off for Durban that he was going to do nothing more than refresh his memories of the Sutter house, and ask them where they had bought their furniture, and how they had arranged for their drapes and their carpets to be made up. Vogel Vlei's white-washed exterior was a conscious imitation of Khotso, and its rooms were in similar proportions, and all Barney needed now was the upholstery and furnishings that would turn it into an elegant yet friendly country house.

But as he had ridden alone across the vast horizons of the north colony, under skies that dreamed with clouds, he had thought with increasing excitement of Sara, and their days together in the summer of 1872, against a remembered background of loss, and pain, and thundery monsoon clouds. He had been sure that she would have married. She had gone back to England, more than likely, and even as he rode eastwards across the plains of the Orange Free State towards his half-forgotten image of her, she was probably walking her terriers across the green and rounded Downs of Sussex, in her ribboned bonnet and her sensible boots. And yet, he could still think of her.

Barney was richer now than he had ever been in his life before -- richer than anyone he had ever known. But Mooi Klip's continual refusals to consider marrying him, and his lonely, ramshackle life at Kimberley, had convinced him that now was the time to find a companion. He needed a wife, desperately; someone he could decorate with diamonds, and adore. Someone he could wake up next to, and with whom he could share his silliest and his most serious desires. He was twenty-eight, and he was wealthy, and he was also Jewish, despite his renunciation of the ideals of his faith. Twenty-eight and not married? he could hear his father saying. What's wrong with the boy? He doesn't like girls?

What had happened with Mooi Klip stayed as a sad and complicated thought at the back of his mind; but what he had looked forward to more and more as he crossed the Drakensberg into Natal had been meeting Sara again. Sara was more than pretty; she was educated, and she was English. She would be an asset to him in the diamond business, as well as a good wife. And if she wasn't there ... well, he would face up to the bitterness of that when he came to it.

She had opened the door, herself. She had looked six years older; more elegant, more self-assured. Her voice had been less clipped, as if she no longer felt the need to assert herself. And she had peered at him myopically for a moment the way a gardener peers at a caper spurge which has unexpectedly seeded itself in another part of the flowerbed.

'Barney,' she had said. '*Barney.*'

He had hesitated on the doorstep, breathless. 'I want you to tell me something,' he had said, trying to keep the urgency out of his voice. 'I want you to tell me if you're married.'

'No,' she had told him, straight away, puzzled. 'No, I'm not. But don't just *stand* there, come in.'

'Thank God,' he had said. 'Will you marry me?'

She had blinked. 'I'm sorreh?'

'I said, will you marry me? I've just arrived here from Kimberley and I really think that's all I want to know.'

There had been a moment of strange hesitation. 'What will you do if I turn you down?' she had asked him. 'Will you ride straight back again?'

He had shaken his head. 'I shall hammer on the door until you change your mind.'

'Well,' she had told him faintly. 'I'm not sure. I mean yes, probably. But not on the doorstep. You'd better come in.'

They had talked furiously for a while in the hallway, in whispers. Barney had been able to watch himself in a gilded Dutch mirror, and it had reminded him disconcertingly of van Eyck's fifteenth-century portrait of a newly-married couple, all stiffness and piety. At last, Mrs Sutter had appeared, and looked at them as curiously as a peahen, her head on one side, and said, 'If it isn't Mr Blitz!'

Now, over tea, it seemed as if they were actually engaged. It had been less than an hour since he had knocked at the front door, and a purplish calotype of Sara's unfortunate Old Etonian still stood on the maplewood bureau by the window, smiling with brave inanity. But she was Barney's now, and they would be married within the month, and Barney's life would take on the style and the peace and the English elegance of Khotso. He had proposed marriage to more than a wife: he had proposed to a home, and a style of life, and parents-in-law who were prosperous and acceptable. If only his mother and father could have seen what a rich *machuten* he was going to have. Who needed the Kimberley Club?

'I've built a house out at Kimberley,' Barney explained to Gerald Sutter. 'I call it Vogel Vlei, which is Afrikaans for "Bird Marsh". It's the grandest house for five hundred miles, and it's all been built with diamonds.'

'Prospecting for diamonds always seemed like rather a *grubby* game to me,' remarked Gerald Sutter, laying down his teacup and patting the pockets of his coat to find his cigarettes. 'All that shovelling, and sorting. And they're an odd lot, aren't they, the diggers? I hope you'll keep Sara well away.'

'Of course. Vogel Vlei is a good mile away from the mine itself.'

'Glad to hear it. Healthy, is it, out there? No cholera?'

'As healthy as anywhere else in Africa.'

'Well, that's not saying much. Have you finished your tea? I think I could do with a snort of whiskey, to tell you the truth. It's not every day your daughter decides to get married. We must talk about a *lobola*, too, although I don't suppose you've much use for ten head of cattle.'

Barney grinned, 'I thought I was supposed to pay *you* the *lobola*, for losing a daughter and a worker.'

'A worker! My great-grandfather's rear quarters! Only if you think that riding and spending money constitute work! That girl pays more for one silly hat than I pay my groom for the whole year, did you know that? Fifteen pounds for a hat, and there's this poor fellow trying to bring up a family on twelve pounds six shillings a year. If it wasn't just, it would be positively scandalous!'

Later, after dinner, Barney sat with Sara on the patio overlooking the sloping lawns of Khotso. Peace, they called this house, and he felt that he might have found it. The diamond business was going well, the world price of gems was rising at last; and here he was with this tall, good-looking girl, about to be married.

'You know, at the Passover *Seder*, Four Questions are asked,' said Barney. 'The first question is, "*Mah nishtana ha-leila ha-zeh mikol ha-laillos?*" and that means, "What makes this night special, compared with any other night?" If I were to ask that question tonight, then I'd know the answer.'

'I was quite resigned to living the rest of my life as a wizened old maid,' said Sara, leaning her dark hair against his shoulder. 'I read my palms, you know, and my heart line was frightfully fragmented. As for my Lower Mars and my Mount of Venus ... well, you only have to see for yourself.'

She opened her hand and held it out to him. Barney took it, and stared at it for a while. Then he bent his head and kissed it. 'I don't know about palmistry,' he told her, hoarsely. 'All I know is that I should have proposed to you when I first met you.'

'I missed you, when you left,' Sara told him. 'I suppose I shouldn't admit it.'

'I missed you, too. I'm not ashamed of that.'

'Then why didn't you come back sooner?'

Barney held the open palm of her hand against his cheek, and kissed that part of her hand which she would have called her Upper Mars. 'There were other things I had to take care of, apart from my diamond claims ... I had old problems ... difficulties that had to be taken care of, one way or another.'

'And are they all taken care of?'

He looked towards the sea. It was too dark to make out anything but the dim white lines of the breakers, but he could hear it and smell it and feel its wind against his face. 'Yes,' he said. 'They're all taken care of.'

'There's good riding at Kimberley, I suppose? And a club?'

'Well, the riding's good. You can gallop flat-out for twenty miles and not see so much as a tree.'

'What about social life?'

'There's a dramatic society. They put on a special play at Christmas.'

'And a club?'

Barney made a face, and nodded. 'Sure, there's a club.'

'Well, that's all right, then. Somewhere to ride, somewhere to meet one's friends. A place to dance, and a house for entertaining in! I look forward to it!'

Barney stood up, and walked across the springy, close-cropped lawn with his hands in his pockets. Sara watched him, her scarf fluttering in the evening breeze. 'You're very handsome, you know,' she told him. He turned around. 'You're very beautiful,' he answered.

From inside the house came the steady, resonant sound of a Beethoven piano concerto, as Mrs Sutter began her practice. Sara left the garden seat and crossed the grass towards Barney and took his hand. In her evening slippers, she did not seem so tall, and she rested her forehead against him so that her hair blew against his face.

'I will love you, and I will be devoted to you,' she said. 'I shall never forget how you came back to rescue me after all these years.'

Gently, and yet not without confidence, Barney placed the outspread fingers of his left hand over her breast. She raised her head, and looked at him questioningly, as if she needed to know whether this was the correct thing to do. But he simply kissed her, twice, and nuzzled his face against hers; and in the shadows of the orange trees he eased down her light silk evening-gown, and then the cotton of her bodice, and held her warm heavy breast in his hand as if it were a prize, its crinkled nipple against his palm between his head line and his line of fortune, and caressed and squeezed it in time to the chords of Beethoven.

Sara closed her sapphire-painted eyelids, her lips slightly parted, and sighed as softly as the wind. Barney kissed her neck, and felt that he desired her and loved her more than anyone; which at that moment, on the lawns of Khotso, may well have been right.

They were married within three weeks, while the bells of St Paul's Church in Durban rang above their heads, and Mrs Sutter scattered rice, and the amateur brass band of the Durban Colonial Office played *The British Grenadiers* five times over, in dogged discord. Later, they went to the Oxford Road synagogue, where they were married again by a rabbi. This time, according to tradition, Mrs Sutter threw barley, and wept twice as copiously. She said she was pleased, though, that Sara had not had her head shaved, and adopted a *shaytl*, or wig. 'My great-grandmother wore one, and all I can remember about it is that it looked like a lopsided loaf of bread.'

In bed on their wedding-night, in the purple velvet-hung guest bedroom at Khotso, they made love in silence, their breath as quiet as the birds that slept in the branches of the coral trees. For a moment, they held each other so tight that Barney did not know if they were one person or two. Then Sara kissed him matter-of-factly on the forehead, and struggled to pull her nightdress down.

'You don't want more?' Barney whispered, kissing her cheeks, and her eyes, and her lips.

She hesitated before answering. Then she said, 'Well, it's all very well, isn't it? But it's not everything.'

Barney stayed where he was for a moment, leaning on his elbows. Sara lay absolutely still, watching him.

'We're married now,' he told her.

'Yes,' she said. 'Isn't it jolly?'

He dipped his head forward and kissed her once more. Then he rolled over on to his back and lay with his hands behind his head, staring up at the dark drapes of the four-poster bed.

She reached over and pressed her lips against his ear. 'I do love you, you know, Barney. I do love you an awful lot.'

He turned and looked at her. 'Yes,' he said. 'I love you, too.'

There was a fragrance of Mansion House pot-pourri in the air, and Sara sneezed.

Early the next morning, Barney woke up and found Sara's face only an inch away from his. Her mouth was open, and she was snoring softly. He looked at her for a long time, at the way her dark hair curled on the broderie-anglaise pillow, at her long shining eyelashes. She was a beautiful girl by anybody's lights, and he touched her cheek with his fingertips as gently as a man touches anything precious.

The French clock on the commode said a quarter to eight.

He eased himself out of bed, and padded naked across the room to the wardrobe, where his clothes had been hung. He struggled into a pair of sharply-creased trousers, and a white shirt, and buttoned up his suspenders. Then he quietly left the room, and tip-toed along the corridor until he reached the stairs.

It was only when he reached the morning-room that he realised that somebody else had been up before him. The French windows were open on to the dewy lawns, and Gerald Sutter was standing by the sundial in a lavish Chinese dressing-gown, smoking a pipe. Barney ventured out after him, and stood a little way away, his slippers stained by the wet grass.

'Up early,' remarked Gerald Sutter, taking his pipe out of his mouth and prodding at the tobacco with his finger.

'I just wanted a little fresh air,' said Barney. 'I think I drank too much champagne yesterday.'

'Well, you're entitled, on your wedding-day. Come to think of it, you're entitled whenever you please.'

'I want to thank you for a marvellous wedding. Well – *two* marvellous weddings.'

'Don't give me any credit for the ceremony at the synagogue. That was all my wife's affair.'

'It was appreciated, all the same.'

'Good. Good show.'

Barney said, 'I just want to tell you that I love Sara very much, and I think we're going to be very happy together.'

'Excellent. I'm glad to hear it.'

'Perhaps you'll come out to Kimberley to visit us soon,' suggested Barney.

Gerald Sutter swung around with his pipe in his mouth and gave Barney the sort of puckered-up look that Englishmen tend to give everybody who says anything nice, but manifestly silly. 'Very decent of you, old chap, but I must say I'm pretty much tied up in Durban. A shipping line to run, don't you know.'

'It's very exciting out there. The Kimberley mine is worth a visit.'

'Well, I suppose it is,' said Gerald Sutter, in a tone that implied that he supposed it *was not*, not for the least moment.

There was an uncomfortable silence between them for almost a minute. Then Barney said, 'Well, I'd better be going back in.'

'Ha, ha,' replied Gerald Sutter, without taking his pipe out of his mouth.

'I'll see you at breakfast, then,' said Barney.

'Good show. Kedgeree today, I wouldn't be surprised.'

'Good,' said Barney, and found himself back inside the house, at the foot of the staircase, suddenly uncertain of what he was doing here. I'm married, he thought to himself. A wealthy, well-heeled, properly married man. I might even have children in a year or so.

A Bantu servant walked past him, bearing a silver dish of steaming kidneys. Barney nodded to the servant without knowing why. For a moment he felt just like the small boy who had hidden under the summertime pushcarts of Hester Street, playing house with Leah Ginzburg.

The breakfast gong sounded, as if it were ringing in the start of his new life.

'Mr Blitzboss!' called Gentleman Jack, when he was still more than a hundred yards away. 'Mr Blitzboss!'

Joel shifted himself around on the woven chair that he had dragged out on to the bungalow's verandah, his face tight with pain. His leg had given him a difficult night, and now he was sitting out in the early sunlight with a bottle of whiskey and two packets of Dover's powders, trying to ease the cramps which crawled up and down his left thighbone like incandescent crabs. His drugs were running low, and that did nothing to improve his temper.

'What are you getting yourself so excited about?' he asked irritably, as Gentleman Jack slid off his dusty horse and tethered it quickly to the rail. 'Can't a man drink his breakfast in peace?'

'Mr Blitzboss – eureka!'

'What are you talking about, you damned black dressed-up monkey?'

'Eureka, Mr Blitzboss. Nothing less! Absolutely eureka!'

Joel ran his fingers through his straggly hair. His years of suffering had turned him grey, and he had a wide bald patch which he usually tried to cover up by brushing his hair straight back. This morning, though, he had not tried to conceal it. He had nobody to impress but himself.

'Just pass me that bottle, will you?' he said, reaching out his hand. 'I haven't slept all night with this damned thighbone of mine. And losing fifty pounds to you at poker hasn't made me feel any better, either.'

'Don't worry about the bottle, sir,' said Gentleman Jack. 'Here – look at this!'

He tugged out of his pocket a greasy leather rag which the kaffirs used to protect their hands when they gripped hold of the steel winding-cable. He laid it on the wicker-topped table, and unfolded it. One flap, two flaps, and there it was. A huge rough stone, still half-embedded in Kimberlite, measuring more than an inch by three-quarters of an inch by an inch. Most of the stone's surface was covered in dull and pitted earth, but at one corner the earth had been knocked off, and the trans-lucent point that emerged from it was immediately recognisable as diamond.

Joel stared at it for a very long time in absolute silence. Gentleman Jack watched him, panting slightly from his hard ride, his expression fixed in an irrepressible grin.

'Give me the bottle,' Joel said at last. Gentleman Jack handed it over, and Joel poured himself a full tumbler of whiskey. He drank two or three mouthfuls, and gagged. Then he set the tumbler down, and continued to stare at the stone on the table as if he expected it to move, or to speak to him, or to disappear in front of his eyes.

'This is a joke,' he declared. 'Edward Nork put you up to this. Edward Nork and Champagne Charlie. This is a melted-down lump of wine bottle, that's what that is, covered in mud.'

'Certainly not, Mr Blitzboss,' said Gentleman Jack, vigor-ously shaking his head. 'Absolutely not. That stone we found fifteen minutes ago, on the claim No. 202. The kaffir they call Ntsanwisi dug it up with the point of his pick.'

Joel, wincing, leaned forward and examined the stone more narrowly. 'You're sure? You're telling me the truth? Because, by God, if you're not, then I'm going to tie you up by your balls and let the vultures peck your stupid brain out. I'm not in any kind of a mood for jokes.'

'This is no joke, Mr Blitzboss,' Gentleman Jack protested. 'This stone was found just like I've told you.'

At last, cautiously, Joel picked the stone up, and felt the weight of it in his hand. 'This is enormous,' he said. 'It can't be diamond. No diamond comes this big. Have you ever seen a real diamond, this big?'

'Not me, Mr Blitzboss.'

'Give me your knife,' said Joel. He took Jack's penknife, opened it up, and scraped away at the dry Kimberlite on the sides of the stone. Jack continued to grin as little by little. Joel laid bare the dull, ground-glass facets of what looked exactly like a giant diamond. At last, when most of the earth had been picked and worried away, Joel gave the stone a perfunctory rub with the leather cloth, and laid it down on the table again.

Rough and wrinkled as it was, the stone possessed a shine so extraordinary that it made Joel's skin tingle just to look at it. Beneath its surface, it seemed to be harbouring a magical brilliance, a brightness as sharp and dazzling as a star, and whichever way Joel turned it, he caught glimpses of rainbows and scimitars, sequins and teardrops. It was a diamond – inconceivably large, impossibly beautiful, and probably worth more on the open market than everything that Joel had ever owned in his whole life – clothes, books, rings, hats, shoes, horses, and oxen. For more than 100 million years, which was the age of the diamond deposits at Kimberley, this stone had held beneath the ground a living fire, an almost animate light, and for all of those 100 million years it had been waiting for release, waiting for the one spectacular moment when it could stun the eyes of anybody and everybody who looked at it. The dealers gave diamonds names when they were as huge as this one: but Joel could not imagine a name for anything so remote, and so ancient, and so brilliantly cold. It rested eerily on his wickerwork table, this diamond, as if it had silently arrived from another star, and Joel found it impossible to take his eyes away from it.

'It's a diamond,' he whispered. 'It's an enormous, preposterous, incredible diamond.'

'Yes, Mr Blitzboss,' said Gentleman Jack.

'Jack – it's a *diamond*. Do you see the size of it? Do you see the *size* of it, Jack? It must be – what – three hundred and fifty carats. Three hundred and sixty! Look at the size of it! It's like a dream! I can't wake up! Jack, it's incredible!'

Gentleman Jack, uninvited, sat down. He wedged his stubby black fingers together like the dovetailed joints of a mahogany bureau, and stared at Joel with serious and intelligent eyes. 'You know what, Mr Blitzboss? If that stone isn't flawed, it will probably fetch more than half a million pounds. Maybe more. Maybe a million.'

Joel nodded. He groped for the whiskey bottle without taking his eyes off the diamond, and splashed out another glassful, wiping the table with his sleeve. 'Look at it,' he breathed. 'Look at that bastard. Three hundred carats, at least. A fortune! Listen – go get me the scales out of the kitchen. Kitty will show you where they are. Go on, hurry, I want to weigh this bastard!'

While Jack pushed his way into the kitchen to fetch the scales from the Griqua cook Kitty, Joel heaved himself out of his chair, picked up the diamond, and shuffled to the edge of the verandah with it, so that he could hold it up to the sharp morning sunlight. It felt cold to the touch, as a diamond should. He placed it right against his eye, and squinted without focusing into the very depths of it, through the smooth cleaved side where it had probably been broken away from another, larger piece of diamond. Edward Nork had been right about diamonds being formed by the intense heat of subterranean volcanoes: and the devastating force of the eruptions which had driven the diamonds to the surface had often broken and cleaved them. Two large stones of nearly fifty carats each had recently been dug up three hundred yards apart by kaffirs of the British Diamond Mining Company, and it had turned out that they fitted exactly together.

Inside the diamond, Joel saw white light of a strange quality that he had never seen before, even in some of the highest grade gems that they had dug up. It was tinged with the palest of exquisite lilacs, the colour of the morning sky when the last stars begin to fade. It was like a vision of purity, of unalterable truth. He could have stared at that light all day, until the sun set. He felt as if he could somehow transfer his consciousness into the actual interior of the stone – and that it was somewhere he could feel certain, clear of his intentions, strong, wavering, and true. Inside the diamond there was no pain, no drink, no morphia, no self-betrayal. It was a sharp and celestial world in which whiskey and gambling and pubic lice were unknown. Joel felt that to look inside that diamond was to know for a moment what dying was like. There could be nothing deader than the fused carbon of a diamond: nothing harder, nor more sterile. Yet the dealers talked about a diamond's 'fire', about its 'life', and they were right. In the deadest of all gems, the most vivacious of all reflections danced. In a diamond like this, all of his dreams could be resurrected; all of his confusions and his humiliations could be forgotten. This diamond was *certainly* incarnate, and he knew as he turned it, and turned it, and turned it, that it had to be his.

Not Barney's. Not even half Barney's. But *his*.

Gentleman Jack came out with the weighing-scale, a brass balance with an agate fulcrum, and set it on the table. He produced the small brass weights from his pockets, and set them out in a neat line. Joel lowered the diamond and came over to the table with it clenched tight in his hand.

'Feel that,' he said at last, dropping the stone directly into Gentleman Jack's outstretched palm.

'It's warm,' said Gentleman Jack.

'That's right. And that's one of the ways you can tell if it's a real diamond. It should be cold when you first pick it up, but it should quickly warm up when you hold it.'

'You learned something from Mr Nork, then,' said Gentleman Jack, a little archly.

'Don't talk to me about Nork,' retorted Joel. 'Balance the scale, and let's see how much this bastard weighs.'

It took them a few minutes to adjust the balance and weigh the diamond in the small curved pan. The scales were hardly accurate: Kitty usually used them for weighing out spices and herbs for cooking. But an approximation was all that Joel needed to satisfy his excitement. And when Gentleman Jack carefully lowered on the tiny brass weight that tipped the scales at more than two and a half ounces, Joel knew for certain that at 142 carats to the ounce, the diamond must be well over 350 carats.

He stood straight, his hands on his hips, and looked at Gentleman Jack triumphantly. 'Half a million?' he said. 'Three-quarters of a million, easily. Maybe a million.'

'Yes, Mr Blitzboss. That's right.'

Joel picked the stone out of the scales and walked along the length of the verandah, juggling it in his hand. 'Mind you,' he said, 'it won't be worth selling it here, in Kimberley. We'll obviously have to take it to Capetown. Maybe to Antwerp, or Amsterdam, to have it cut. If you have it cut first, you can ask twice the price.'

'Ascher and Mendel will do it, Mr Blitzboss. Mr Barney made a special arrangement.'

Joel inclined his head towards the eastern horizon, where the twisted branches of a camelthorn tree still clawed at the early sun. 'I wasn't actually thinking of Ascher and Mendel.'

'They're one of the best, Mr Blitzboss.'

'You're a Ndebele, Jack. What do you know from diamond cutters?'

'I know the business. Mr Blitzboss. I know Ascher and Mendel by name. Good cutters, that's what everyone says. Absolutely excellent with difficult stones.'

Joel gnawed at the side of his lip. Then he said, 'This Ntsanwisi. Can you trust him?'

'What do you mean, sir?'

'Can you *trust* him, that's what I mean. Don't you understand plain English?'

'Better than most white men understand plain Ndebele, sir.'

Joel limped back down the verandah. 'What I'm trying to ask you is, will he talk about this diamond? Will he spread it around?'

Gentleman Jack closed his eyes, and almost imperceptibiliy shook his head.

'You're sure about that?' Joel demanded.

'Yes, Mr Blitzboss. Ntsanwisi will never give you trouble. Maybe you should pay him money. Five, six pounds. But he will never talk about this diamond again if you tell him not to.'

'All right. And what about you?'

Gentleman Jack looked up warily. 'Me, sir?'

'Yes, you.'

'I don't understand, sir.'

Joel held the huge diamond up between his finger and his thumb, turning it in the sunlight so that it shone in soft prismatic colours. 'If you don't understand, Jack, let me put it clearly for you. This diamond is mine. It was found when Mr Barney was away, and that makes it mine.'

'Mr Barney is half owner, sir.'

'Maybe. But when this diamond was discovered, who was in charge? Me. And there's a little saying that goes, "Finders keepers, losers weepers". Or, "What the eye don't see, the heart don't grieve over."'

'Mr Blitzboss?'

'Don't act dumb,' snapped Joel. 'We're going to take this stone to Europe, under some pretext or other, and we're going to have it cut. Then we're going to put it on the market at a million pounds and make ourselves rich. And if that doesn't make any sense to you, then you're a damn sight more stupid than you look.'

Gentleman Jack clicked his knuckles, one by one. His handsome black face was expressionless.

'You taught me many things, Mr Blitzboss. Drinking, Pope Joan. All those things you taught me.'

Joel nodded. 'That's right. That's perfectly right.'

'Well, Mr Blitzboss,' said Gentleman Jack, 'the trouble is that I was brought up by good missionary people. They always said to me, be honest. Don't cheat. Don't lie. Don't consume the alcoholic spirits. Don't fornicate.'

Joel narrowed one eye suspiciously.

'I didn't always stay pure,' Gentleman Jack went on. 'I liked fornicating. I liked it very much. So, lots of times, I fornicated. No matter what it said in the Bible, I enjoyed it, and the women I took, they seemed like they enjoyed it, too. One Venda woman I know, she only likes it when church choirs sing, so when you fornicate, you have to take her to the back of the chapel, and hide in a bush. But that can't be wrong. Fornicating for joy, and listening to God's music.'

'What are you getting at?' Joel wanted to know.

'Only one thing, sir. This diamond mine is righteously half belonging to Mr Barney, even if he's in Durban. And not to tell him that we have found this stone – well, sir, it seems to me like stealing.'

Joel said, 'Hmmph,' and rubbed his left thigh with his hand. His face was fixed in a sour, abstracted mask.

'I fornicate, Mr Blitzboss,' said Gentleman Jack. 'I drink, too, and play cards, ever since I come to work for you. But diamond-stealing – never. No diamond-stealing, sir. Don't ask me.'

Joel picked up his cane, and poked it towards Jack's chest, two or three emphatic prods. 'I'm not asking you, Jack. I'm telling you.'

'It's not right, sir. God's punishment.'

'You think God cares about one single piece of rock? God doesn't cafe about rock. All His rocks are the same to him, granite or salt or diamond. Only men give them value. Look at this,' said Joel, and raised the diamond in the palm of his right hand. 'I could throw this diamond out into the bush, and you could never find it again. How much would it be worth then? Nothing. Nothing at all. And that's the point I'm trying to get into your thick woolly head. This diamond is valuable only because Ntsanwisi found it, and because you brought it to me, and because I know how to market it. Mr Barney didn't give it any value. What did he do? He wasn't even here. This diamond is ours because it's ours, and that's all there is to it.'

Gentleman Jack said slowly, 'You're going to take the whole thing? You're going to have it cut, and you're going to sell it, and you're never going to tell Mr Barney what happened?'

'You're a perceptive man,' smiled Joel. 'I like perceptive men.'

Gentleman Jack lowered his head. 'Supposing *I* tell Mr Barney about it?'

Joel stared at him coldly. 'You wouldn't.'

'But, supposing I did.'

'You're a kaffir,' said Joel. 'You have no rights, no legal standing, no soul. You may speak pretty fancy English, and you may dress up like a Capetown dandy, but that's as far as it goes. Inside of that tailored vest you're nothing but a primitive savage, and nobody's going to credit your word for one single moment, not even if you swear to God that you're going to cut your throat. But I'll tell you one thing. If Barney gets to hear about this diamond, and he gets to hear about it through you, then cutting your throat is going to be one thing you'll wish that you'd done.'

Gentleman Jack stared at Joel wide-eyed. Then he let out a breath of resignation, and looked away, and smeared at his mouth with his hand.

'You got that straight?' asked Joel.

'Straight?'

'You understand what you have to do?'

'I know,' said Gentleman Jack. 'I have to go back to work and I have to keep my mouth closed.'

Joel held up the diamond again, angling it this way and that in the rapidly brightening sunshine. 'You have to do more than keep your mouth closed. You have to tell yourself that you never saw this stone before in your whole life.'

'I want my share, Mr Blitzboss.'

'Your share? Your share of what?'

Gentleman Jack's expression remained unaltered – polite, subservient, restrained – but there was a barely perceptible tightening of his stance, a tension in the set of his shoulders.

'My share of the diamond, Mr Blitzboss. You know that.'

Joel dropped the diamond carefully into the pocket of his shirt. Then he looked at Gentleman Jack with the steadiest of impudent gazes and said, 'What diamond?'

'Come on, now, Mr Blitzboss. I got proof. Ntsanwisi will say he found that diamond.'

'You call that proof? What Ntsanwisi found was nothing but a worthless lump of Kimberlite and quarts.'

'Mr Blitzboss, I warn you, I want my share.'

Joel limped around the table, and then grinned. 'Of course you'll get your share. You think I'm going to cheat you? You brought me the diamond, I'll pay you. I'll pay you for keeping quiet, too. How does five hundred pounds sound?'

'Seven hundred and fifty, Mr Blitzboss.'

'Five hundred and that's it.'

Gentleman Jack slowly nodded his head. His ivory earring flashed in the sunlight. 'All right, Mr Blitzboss. Five hundred. But you have to pay me now.'

'I'll pay you when I sell the diamond.'

'No, Mr Blitzboss. Now. Otherwise, I tell the happy tidings

to Mr Barney Blitzboss, when he comes back. Good news! I'll say. The Lord has smiled on you. A giant diamond!'

'All right,' said Joel, easing himself back into his chair. 'I'll pay you when I go to the bank. You want a drink?'

'I don't really think I've got anything to celebrate, Mr Blitzboss.'

Just then, Kitty the Griqua cook came out to see if there were any dishes or glasses to collect up. She was a plump, friendly woman, a widow who had lost her husband and her two children from cholera more than six years ago, and who had worked as a servant in white people's households ever since. She had come to cook and clean for Barney and Joel after her previous employer, Mr Oliver Peters of the British Diamond Mining Company, had hurried home to England to take care of his paralysed mother in Eastbourne. Joel hated her with considerable vigour, more for her Christian hymns than her pot-roasts, although he hated her pot-roasts, too.

'I hear you talking about diamonds, sir?' she said, tidying up the wickerwork table. Her head was tied up in a tight green scarf, and she wore a simple Empire-line dress in dyed green percale.

'I'm always talking about diamonds,' said Joel, loudly and slowly, as if he were addressing a backward child. 'They're my business.'

Unabashed, Kitty grinned at him with her gappy teeth, and let out a wheezing laugh. 'I know that, sir. Diamonds are your business all right, sir. But they're not your *principal* business.' She held up the half-empty whiskey bottle, and shook it so that it sloshed. 'This here, this is your *principal* business.'

'Don't be so damned impertinent,' Joel told her, but without obvious anger. 'Go and make me some poached eggs before I kick your fat bottom out of this house for good and all. You hear me? And make sure they don't come out like bullets, the way they usually do.'

'Whatever you say, Mr Blitz,' smiled Kitty. 'I expect you've got yourself a whole lot of diamond business to talk over.'

Joel scowled. He would have dismissed Kitty months ago if the decision had been his. He would not even have hired her. But Kitty was a distant friend of Mooi Klip's family, and

337

Barney liked to have her around because her Griqua accent reminded him of Mooi Klip, and she could remember the days when Mooi Klip had been a small girl, and because he liked to think that whatever happened, Mooi Klip was not irrevocably lost to him, or too far away.

Joel thought Barney was showing all the signs of being soft in the head. One day, Barney would suffocate himself in the self-propagating kapok of his own sentimentality, and it would serve him right. Barney did not seem to be able to see that his skills at business and his showy determination to lick Cecil Rhodes at his own game were nothing more than superficial tricks and varnish. Underneath it all, he was still a dewy-eyed Clinton Street Jew-boy, all bread-and-*shmaltz*, and hugging your *mama*, and hot plates of *tsimmes* on Sabbath eve. He had ambition, sure; but his ambition would always be limited by his boyhood. The Lower East Side was not easily forgotten, even out on the plains of Cape Colony. The kaffirs' candles, as they dug during the long-drawn-out evenings, would always remind Barney of *menorah*, glittering in the darkness of New York.

Gentleman Jack said, 'I'll go back to the Hole, then.' It was more of a question than a statement.

'Sure, go back,' said Joel. 'I'll see you later on. After luncheon, maybe.'

'Are you going to want lunch today, Mr Joel?' asked Kitty, turning back, and keeping the screen door open with her foot.

'Maybe a meat pasty, or some cheese,' said Joel.

'There's some cold beef, Mr Joel. You could have that, with pickles.'

Joel looked up. 'Whatever you like. Now, will you let me get on with this diamond-talk that you think so little of?'

Kitty inclined her head, so that her double-chin rolled out like a shiny bratwurst. 'You know that the Griqua people say, Mr Joel, about where those diamonds came from?'

'No, Kitty, I don't.'

'Well, whenever I hear any of those diggers squabbling about who owns a diamond, who it actually belongs to, I think of the old Griqua story; and that story says that a long time ago there was pain and sorrow and hunger in this land, and so some kindly spirit brought a basketful of diamonds down from

Heaven, and decided he was going to scatter them all over the land hereabouts, to make people happy. So this spirit came flying across the Vaal River, throwing out diamonds, until he reached Colesberg Kopje, at the place they call Kimberley; and in those days there were plenty of tall camelthorn trees at Colesberg Kopje. The spirit caught his foot in the branches of the camelthorn trees, and dropped all of his diamonds in one place, right there on the hill, and that's where the white people found them.'

'Yes,' said Joel, testily. 'It's a very pretty story.'

'It sets me to thinking, though,' Kitty interrupted him. 'I think to myself, if it was *really* a spirit who scattered those diamonds, then which man can rightfully say that any of those diamonds belongs to him? They were a gift from Heaven to the people on earth, and I believe they really belong to all of us, don't you?'

Joel tapped his fingers on the table. Gentleman Jack glanced at him, uncertain of what he was thinking, and bit his lip.

'People have had all kinds of misconceptions about diamonds for hundreds of years,' Joel said at last. 'In India, they still believe that diamonds grow like crystals, and that every twenty years they're going to be able to dig up a fresh crop. Even here, it wasn't too long ago that some people thought they might be solidified dewdrops, congealed by the rays which emanated from a particular conjunction of the stars.

'The truth is, though, that diamonds aren't any of those things. They're nothing more than lumps of carbon which have been heated up by volcanoes; and they're lying around on the ground for anyone to claim as their own. They're not magic, and they're not mysterious. They're just lumps of carbon. And now I'd really appreciate it if you went in and cooked my eggs for me. And don't use too much vinegar.'

'Anything you say, sir,' nodded Kitty, and went inside. The screen door banged shut behind her.

Joel lay back in his chair and looked at Gentleman Jack with his eyes as neutral as pebbles, his hand crooked in front of his mouth.

'You know what I think, Jack?' he said.

'What's that, Mr Blitzboss?'

339

'I think it's a mistake to educate the blacks. I think it's the beginning of the end, when you educate the blacks. They're happier when they're ignorant, and living the life of savages. They used to sing *ihubo*. What do they sing how? Dreary Anglican hymns. You mark my words, Gentleman Jack, nothing but strife will come out of educating the blacks.'

'She's not a bad woman,' said Gentleman Jack, nodding towards the bungalow.

'You don't think so? She's inquisitive, that's what I don't like about her. And what was all that stuff about spirits and diamonds, and who they belong to?'

'I don't know, sir.'

'You think she overheard us?'

Gentleman Jack shrugged.

Joel monotonously stroked his bald patch, over and over again, and stared at a knothole in the verandah floor, through which he could see the sunshine glittering on the dust and the chaff beneath.

Then he placed his hand on his breast pocket, where the diamond nestled already warm with the heat of his body; and he smiled at Gentleman Jack with widening amusement.

'How soon should I leave for Capetown?' he asked. 'Next week, maybe? Edward Nork can take over the mine until Barney comes back, can't he? Edward's drunk, most of the time, but he knows what he's doing.'

'What would you say was your reason for going?' Gentleman Jack wanted to know. 'Just remember – if *you* get caught with this diamond, then *I* get caught too – and you know what they'll do to me.'

'I would say I was going to buy pumps,' suggested Joel.

'Pumps? You wouldn't have to go to Capetown for pumps. Mr Rhodes has plenty of pumps at De Beers.'

'Then I would say that I was going to find myself a wife.'

'A *wife*, Mr Blitzboss?'

Joel caught the tone in Gentleman Jack's voice, and laughed. 'Yes,' he said, softly. 'We all have to think of getting married at some time or another, don't we?'

*

The train of ox-waggons which brought Barney home to Kimberley with 54 chairs, 18 tables, 16 beds, a mile and a quarter of carpet, 23 Persian rugs, 31 paintings, 11 wardrobes, two miles of curtain fabrics, as well as an assortment of clocks, bureaux, sofas, birdcages, and tallboys, was generally considered by all who saw it pass, Boers and Basutos and diggers alike, to be one of the greatest spectacles of 1878.

The *Colesberg Advertiser* described its arrival in Kimberley as 'the nearest we have ever seen in this town to the visit of a travelling circus', and its slow procession towards Vogel Vlei was accompanied by dancing barefoot black boys, jeering layabouts, and two Irish prostitutes who were eager to make the acquaintance of the drivers.

The waggons brought more than furniture, though. They also brought Barney's new bride, sitting ahead of the train in her polished brougham, shaded by a tasselled parasol of cream silk, tall and straight-backed and more composed than any woman that Kimberley had ever encountered. 'The new Mrs Barney Blitz is a ravishing beauty!' exclaimed the *Advertiser's* social column. 'She is Junoesque; she is feminine perfection incarnate! We *eagerly* await the privilege of her acquaintance!'

While the drivers and the porters unloaded the waggons, Barney showed Sara in silence through the rooms of Vogel Vlei. Their footsteps echoed from dining-room to morning-room, from kitchen to stairs, from landing to landing, until they reached the main bedroom suite.

Barney sat on the wide windowsill in his smart dove-grey suit, took off his hat, and watched Sara twirl around the polished wooden floor.

'Well?' he asked her, setting his hat down beside him.

'Barney, it's going to be entrancing! *Far* more entrancing than Khotso.'

'I'm glad,' he said. 'I knew you'd like it.'

She swept over towards him, her arms outstretched, and then she kissed him on the tip of the nose. 'It's wonderful,' she whispered. 'It's like a dream. Wait until Nareez sees this beautiful room you've given us!'

'I think Nareez is too busy unpacking,' said Barney.

'Unpacking? Where?'

'In her own room, of course. Now, what would you say to a cold bottle of that French champagne, and some antelope pie?'

Sara was frowning. 'Nareez is my *amah*,' she said. 'Nareez brought me up from the cradle, from the day I was born.'

'Yes?' said Barney, puzzled.

Sara moved Barney's hat and sat down on the windowsill beside him, spreading her skirts of her pale-blue travelling dress. Her plumed bonnet had such a wide brim that it almost touched Barney's forehead, and he had to lean back a little to talk to her.

'There's nothing wrong, is there?' he asked her. 'The way you talked about Nareez just then, I got the feeling –'

Sara's expression gave nothing away. She blinked twice – two feminine, exaggerated blinks – the pupils of her wide-set eyes as dusty-brown and dewy as the undersides of mushrooms in those first cold moments of morning. But she allowed Barney's sentence to remain in the air unfinished, and unanswered, and when he inclined his head to one side, trying to show her that he expected some kind of response, she simply pursed her lips and continued to stare at him like the innocent, coquettish heroine of a bad amateur play.

Barney attempted a smile, but he found it difficult. The whole trek from Durban to Kimberley had been difficult. It had thundered all through Natal, and their slow processional climb up the foothills of the Drakensberg had been constantly halted by mudslides and broken traces and collapsing axles. One Sunday afternoon, under a sky like splintered slate, they had found their way through the mountains blocked by a huge slanting landslip; and in torrential rain they had been obliged to dismantle the ox-waggons in the way the old voortrekkers had done, and 'toboggan' the hulls down the slippery rocks until they could rejoin the road. All through the journey Sara had been composed and English and almost completely unapproachable. She had slept in one of the furniture-waggons with her Bengali *amah* Nareez, a small woman with a ruby in her left nostril who drenched herself in musk and swaddled herself in crimson silk, and who insisted on setting up her spirit stove every evening, no matter where she was, to stir up rancid *bhuna ghosth*, and to fry *parathas*. Nareez may have smelled like *brinjal bhaji* soaked in cologne, but Sara adored her, and treated her as if she were her own sister, or even her mother. And during all of those weeks it had taken to cross the mountains of Basutoland and the plains of the Orange Free State; even on those nights which had been heralded by the most gorgeous and romantic of sunsets, with the clouds on fire and the syringa trees blazing with scarlet light, Barney had never been allowed near Sara's 'travelling apartments' as she called them, and had never even seen her in her underwear. When he knocked on the tailboard of her waggon one morning, when the dew lay on the bushgrass like diamonds, he was greeted only by an indignant Nareez, who poked her head out of the canvas and cried out, 'Go away! Ladies' quarters only! No Peeping Toms!'

Barney had hoped that once they arrived at Vogel Vlei, he would be able to curtail Nareez's influence, and to assert his authority as Sara's husband and lover. He had planned weeks ago that Nareez should be assigned the smallest bedroom in the east wing of the house, which looked towards Kimberley and the Big Hole. The main bedroom suite took up most of the upper floor of the west wing, and faced out over the scrubby acreage which was Vogel Vlei's garden.

'If you don't tell me what's wrong,' said Barney, 'I can't possibly put it right.'

'I thought you would have *known* what was wrong,' said Sara.

'I'm not a mind-reader. Maybe you should have married a mind-reader.'

'There's no need to be ridiculous; nor offensive, either. I was simply saying that I expected more sensitivity from you, and perhaps a little more *savoir-faire*.'

'I don't happen to know what *savoir-faire* is. I'm American, not German.'

'*Savoir-faire* is French, as a matter of fact, and it means knowing how to do things properly.'

Barney lifted his hands in resigned acceptance, and let them drop back to his knees again. 'Okay, I don't have any *savoir-faire*. Now, what in particular makes you say that?'

'Well, the bedroom,' said Sara. 'The arrangements. I'm a lady, after all, and yet you seem to expect me to spend my entire life in your personal presence.'

Barney looked at her for a moment, and then said, 'Yes, I do. Isn't that the whole point of getting married?'

'But *Barneh*,' she said, clasping her hands together like an exasperated little girl, and exaggerating her English county accent so much that, for the very first time, it made Barney wince to hear it. 'A lady has to do so many private and intimate things ... things that she can't possibly do in front of her husband. I mean, good Lord, you don't expect to see me at my toilet, do you, or dressing? A woman should be the perfect mystery ... that's what mother always said ... she should appear as a vision of prettiness without ever giving away the little secrets which made her so. And, besides, it's *embarrassing*.'

'You're *embarrassed* I should see you dressing?'

Sara blushed, and lowered her head so that the brim of her hat obscured her face. Barney cupped her chin in his hand, and raised her face towards him again, frowning into her eyes in disbelief.

'How can you be embarrassed, if we're married?'

'Barney, my darling, that's part of being a lady.'

'But you've never said anything before. You weren't embarrassed on our wedding-night.'

'I didn't undress in front of you on my wedding-night. And, in any case, I *was* embarrassed.'

'You *were* embarrassed? Embarrassed by what?'

She turned her head away from his hand, and presented him with a profile that was as classic as a sculpture by Donatello, and equally cold.

'I can't talk about it,' she said. 'It isn't proper.'

'Between husband and wife, it isn't proper to talk about love? Between husband and wife, it isn't proper to talk about sex? If it isn't proper between husband and wife, then when *is* it proper?'

Sara licked her lips with the tip of her tongue, as if the actual words that came out of her mouth were distasteful to her. 'Men discuss it in clubs, and in the polo changing-rooms.'

Barney, was so stupefied that he felt as if someone had

punched all the breath out of him. He stood up, and walked across the bedroom floor, and then turned around on his heel and came back to the window again.

'In clubs? And in the polo changing rooms? Is that what your mother told you?'

'Barney, my mother brought me up to be a complete lady. To ride and to sew, to speak French and to play the piano, and to run a household. She also instructed me in marriage, and what any normal husband would expect from me. She wasn't a prude. Her lessons did include the duty of sexual intimacy, and in some detail.'

'Sara,' said Barney, gently, but with great intensity, 'sex isn't a duty. It's a pleasure, and the best way there is of showing somebody that you truly love them. It's one of the greatest joys of marriage.'

'You seem to have forgotten that sex is mainly for the purpose of bearing children. I *will* have your children, Barney. I won't fail you that way. Nor, I hope, in any other way.'

'Sara – I don't think you will. But you have to understand that I don't only want to see you when you're dressed up, or when you're bathed and ready for bed. I want to see you the way you really are. I want to see you night and day, whether your hair is combed or uncombed, whether you're wearing evening-gowns or underwear, with or without powder, in or out of make-up.'

Sara tittered, but without much amusement. 'That's nonsense,' she said. 'My parents never shared a bedroom. How could *we* possibly share a bedroom?'

'We shared a bedroom at Khotso.'

'That was our honeymoon. Of course we shared a bedroom on our *honeymoon*. But now we're talking about normal life.'

'*Normal?*' expostulated Barney. 'You call it *normal*, a man tip-toeing down the corridor with his slippers in his hand, every time he wants to make love to his own wife?'

'But, Barney, we *can't* share a bedroom. What about Nareez?'

'Nareez? What in hell does Nareez have to do with it? I married *you*, not Nareez!'

'Nareez is my *amah*, Barney. She bathes me, and dresses me, and does my hair. She brings me water in the night if I'm thirsty. She sits up and talks to me if I can't sleep. She rubs my forehead if I've got a headache. It can't possibly work out, the three of us in one bedroom. It's just not the thing.'

Barney stared at her. 'Oh,' he said, flatly. 'It's not the thing. Why didn't you tell me in the first place? If I'd only realised that it wasn't the thing, that would have saved us all of this squabbling. For the love of God, Sara, what are you talking about? This is our bedroom, yours and mine – husband and wife. Do you seriously think I built this bedroom so that you could share it with some fat greasy Indian woman, while I sleep in another bed, in another room, without even the consolation of being able to hold you and kiss you whenever I so desire? The thing! If sleeping apart is the thing in England, then I'm not surprised they're all so damned eccentric!'

'The English are *not* eccentric and Nareez is *not* fat and greasy! How dare you!'

'I dare because it's true, and I dare because you're talking like a middle-aged spinster, instead of a passionate young wife. And I dare most of all because I love you, and I'm not going to sleep without you.'

Sara sat rigidly upright, not moving. The sun had moved around the house so that it was shining through the window in which she sat; and her hair with highlights of red and bronze. But the brightness of the light behind her also concentrated the shadows on her face, so that her eyes, already dark with tiredness and displeasure, grew darker still.

When she next spoke, she was back to her airy patronising again. 'You will realise, Barney, when you've had longer to acquaint yourself with the habits of society, that there is a time and a place for everything. Passion included.'

'What a smart girl you are,' Barney told her, his arms hanging by his sides as if he were exhausted to the point of collapse.

'There are times when affection can be properly expressed, and times when it is better held in check. There should be just as much etiquette between man and wife, after all, as there is between friends or strangers.'

'Did your mother tell you that, or did you read it in one of those twopenny books on manners?'

'Barney! You're being so unpleasant!'

Barney loosened his necktie and dragged it out from under his collar. Then he wound it around his fists like a garotte. 'I seem to remember a time on the lawn at Khotso when you weren't so worried about etiquette,' he said.

Sara said, 'You're very bad-mannered, to remind me of that, especially now that I'm so upset. But just because I believe in doing everything the proper way, that doesn't mean that I don't love you, or that my feelings towards you aren't passionate.'

Barney glanced at her. 'Well, then,' he said, 'if that's the way you truly feel about me, Nareez can stay where she is, in the east wing, and you and I will share this bedroom. If you like, I'll have a bell installed so that you can call Nareez if you really need her. But you might remember that *I* can fetch water, just as competently as Nareez; and that *I* can talk to you, when you can't sleep, and without a Bengali accent, too; and that *I* can rub your poor aching head if you're suffering from the neuralgia, just as soothingly.'

'And what about my toilette?'

'We have a private dressing-room, and a private bathroom. You can close the doors of both, if you really don't want me to see you in your corset-cover and your hairpins.'

'I don't wear a —' Sara began, with indignation, but then she realised that the subject was indelicate, and she angrily got to her feet, and stamped. 'You're impossible! Why are you insisting on being so impossible? Why do you have to be so piggish about telling everybody where they might sleep, and where they mightn't?'

Barney came over to the window and held Sara's arms, so tightly that she gave a little cry. 'Barney!' she begged him.

He smiled at her, but there was no softness in his voice at all. 'I'm being impossible because I have a right to be. This is *my* house, and you are *my* wife, and like any good bride, Jewish or Christian, you are going to do what *I* tell you.'

'And if I defy you?'

He kissed her, first on the cheek, then on the lips. His kisses were quick, and light, but they betrayed his urgency. 'You won't defy me,' he told her. 'You love me too much.'

He tried to kiss her more deeply, on the mouth, but she plucked her face abruptly away and said, 'No!'

The echo of that 'No!' was heard in ten rooms at once, and even downstairs, where four kaffirs were sweating and grunting as they carried in through the front doors the huge solid-mahogany marriage bed.

Joel appeared, unshaven, hurriedly dressed in a pair of grubby twill trousers and a mud-splattered shirt. 'I didn't know you were going to come back so soon,' he said breathlessly, limping after Barney across the hallway. 'I didn't expect you back until the middle of next month, at least.'

Barney directed a kaffir to carry a gilded French chair into the dining-room. 'Neither did we. But the way the weather was, we decided to set out as soon as we'd gathered the bulk of the furniture together, in case we were caught by the rains. We still need more furniture, of course, but this will get us started. At least we'll be able to entertain.'

'I wish you'd sent a message on ahead of you,' Joel complained. 'I've decided to leave for Capetown on Monday.'

'Capetown? What for? I need you here.'

'Well, I know you do.'

'Then stay. You don't really need to go to Capetown, do you? The journey will half kill you, in the middle of summer. Besides. I'm having a special dinner next Wednesday night, and you *must* come to that. Even Rhodes is invited.'

Joel snapped his fingers at another kaffir who was carrying a chair on top of his head into the day-room. The kaffir set the chair down on the floor, and Joel perched himself on the edge of it, his aching back kept straight, his weight supported on his cane. 'The truth is, Barney, I'm going to to try to find myself a companion, among other things.'

'But you've got plenty of friends here in Kimberley. And servants. And by the way, we're going to have to train up a butler, no question about it. Maybe we can find a digger with domestic experience. And Kitty's going to need some more kitchen staff, now that we're moving in properly.'

'As long as their principal qualification is that they don't know how to cook pot-roast, then I quite agree with you,' said Joel. 'But to go back to what I was saying – I'm going to look for a wife.'

Barney had been beckoning frantically to a lone kaffir who was wandering around with a bronze statue of a dancing cherub, looking for somewhere to put it down. But now he turned around and stared at Joel, and said, 'A *wife*?' as if Joel had suddenly announced that he was *geshmat*. 'You want a wife? With all the girls here in Kimberley?'

'Girls are girls, Barney. What I need now is somebody who's going to look after me. I'm getting older, my leg and my hip give me agony most of the time. I want somebody to share the rest of my life. That's all. A true companion.'

'There's nobody here in Kimberley?'

'The decent girls are married; and none of the indecent girls are Jewish. Besides, I don't want a wife who's had as many diggers shovelling away at her as the Big Hole. I want somebody quiet, don't you know. Respectable. *Zaftig*.'

Barney said, 'You're really serious? You want a wife?'

'Why do you sound so surprised?'

'I'm not surprised. I guess I'm just pleased. And in any case, that'll make two of us.'

Joel's expression altered with such subtlety that only someone who knew him very well could have detected the difference. But the lines in his face, which had bitten deeper into his skin since his accident, like acid into a steel engraving, grew straighter, and tenser, and more pronounced. It was as if he had aged five years in the time it took for the sun to brighten as it came out from behind a cloud; or a *lammergayer* to wheel on the wind.

'What happened in Durban?' he asked, with corrosive quietness.

Barney had not expected him to react so sharply. 'What happened? Can't you guess what happened?'

'Tell me what happened. I want to hear you say it.'

'Well ...' said Barney, defensively. 'What happened was, I got married.'

'You got married? You just went to Durban and got married?'

'Have you any objections?' snapped Barney.

'I don't know. It's done. What's to object about? It was that Sutter girl, I suppose. You've been having polluted dreams about her ever since you visited Natal the first time. Either her, or some nigger.'

Barney retorted furiously, 'What the hell gives you the right to say something like that? I *did* marry Sara, as a matter of fact. She's my wife. And if you've got anything smart to say about it, you'd better be ready to have your other leg broken.'

'Or to be shot at,' said Joel, dryly.

'She's a beautiful, gentle girl,' said Barney.

'Sure. And she's a *shikseh*.'

'After all the whores you've paid for, you can say that?'

Joel pulled a face. 'At least I didn't marry any of them, did I?'

Barney slowly rubbed his cheeks with his hands. 'All right, Joel,' he said. 'Let's stop arguing about it, shall we? Whatever you say, it's not going to change the fact that Miss Sara Sutter is now Mrs Sara Blitz, and that you have yourself a new sister-in-law. Neither is anything you say going to divert me from asking you to join us on Wednesday night for our celebration dinner.'

'I've arranged to leave on Monday, with Henk van der Westhuizen.'

'Why can't you leave next Friday? You could go with Harold Feinberg, when he takes his diamonds down.'

Joel looked around at two kaffirs carrying a ponderous carved wardrobe through the polished hallway, like two black ants shouldering a matchbox a hundred times their size. 'Well,' he said, uneasily, 'I just think I'd prefer to go with Henk, that's all.'

'What difference are three days going to make?' asked Barney. 'You're going to catch a wife, not a train.'

'I don't know,' said Joel.

'Well, I do,' Barney told him, slapping his shoulder. Joel closed his eyes in pain. 'I know that you're going to stay and have a really good time. Look – here's Sara now.'

Sara came down the curved stairway in a pale green day dress and pearls. On her left breast she wore a darker green ostrich plume, and an array of diamonds, an engagement present from Barney. Her dark hair was fashionably plaited, and arrayed with turquoise combs. Barney went across to meet her at the foot of the stairs, and take her arm. 'Come and say hello to Joel,' he said. 'You haven't seen him since he was in hospital.'

Joel painfully forced himself to stand, and took Sara's hand. He dropped his head forward and kissed her fingers, and then he turned her hand around, palm upwards, and traced the tip of his finger lightly along her line of health, her line of heart, and her line of life. She watched him with a little curiosity, a little pity, and a little repulsion. He looked more twisted and haggard these days, and he smelled of stale whiskey. But he still had a little of his old charm about him, and he was still able to flatter a woman with his old sense of fancy.

'You have a long and wealthy life ahead of you, I see,' he told her.

'I didn't know you read palms,' she said.

'I don't,' smiled Joel. 'But I like stroking any pretty woman's hand, and I'm not so stupid that I can't tell that any woman who marries into one of the largest diamond companies in Kimberley is going to be ridiculously rich for the rest of her life.'

'You're teasing me,' said Sara. 'Barney, your brother is teasing me.'

'Yes,' Barney told her, with enthusiasm.

'You're coming to our celebration dinner, of course?' Sara asked Joel.

Joel's eyes flickered sideways, towards Barney. Barney responded by looking sideways at Sara.

'Well,' said Joel, clearing his throat, 'I was thinking of leaving for Capetown on Monday.'

'That's quite out of the question,' smiled Sara. 'You must come along on Wednesday night, and dress yourself up like the nob I'm sure you can be, and make a speech, too, telling everybody that we're married!'

'I'd really like to –' Joel began, but Sara shushed him.

'That's quite settled then,' she interrupted him. 'Now do come and help me re-arrange some of these pictures upstairs, Barney, my darling. I must have mixed and moved them around twenty times, and they still don't look quite right!'

Joel looked at Barney appealingly, but Barney simply shrugged. And at that moment, Nareez came downstairs, slip-slopping in her silk mules, and frowned at Joel so contemptuously, in his scruffy shirt and dirty trousers, that he raised his stick to Barney, said '*shalom*', and hobbled out of Vogel Vlei as quickly as he had hurried in.

'*Shalom*,' called Barney.

351

'Is that another devil?' asked Nareez, in her dense Bengali accent.

'That's my brother,' Barney told her.

'That's what I said,' replied Nareez, folding her arms. 'Now, Miss Sara, time for your oils.'

'I thought we were going to re-arrange the paintings,' said Barney.

Sara blew him a little kiss. 'Soft skin has to come first, my darling. And Nareez is *marvellous* when it comes to massage. Anyway, I'm very tired, and I think it will calm me down. Nareez will massage you, too, if you care for it.'

Barney shook his head. 'I think I'd rather go out and be trampled by elephants, thank you. What time will you be down?'

'For tea, of course. I'll tell that cook of yours to have it ready on the back terrace. Now, you will take care, my love, won't you, and you won't work too hard.'

'Come along now, Miss Sara,' said Nareez, taking Sara's arm. Behind Sara's back, Barney gave the *amah* a teeth-gritting scowl that made her gather up the hem of her sari and shuffle up the uncarpeted stairs as fast as she could, all bangles and chiffon and big bustling bottom.

Barney was sitting in the day-room in his green dressing-gown reading a three-month-old copy of the London *Morning Post* when Gentleman Jack knocked at the door. It was the day after their arrival back at Kimberley, and Sara was still asleep, her hair in curl-papers, her lashes prettily closed. Barney had come down early for a cup of tea and a dish of Kitty's chicken livers and onions; and now he was relaxing with a second cup of tea, a basket of fruit, and some stale news from England.

'Jack,' he said, affably, as Gentleman Jack ventured into the room. 'It's good to see you. How are things at the mine?'

'Excellent, Mr Blitzboss, thank you. Absolutely excellent. Since you went away, the average week is three thousand, seven hundred pounds. And some good fine gemstones, sir. One was twenty-three carats.'

'That's good news, Jack. How did you get on with Mr Joel?'

'No trouble, sir. Very fine. A most amenable relationship, I must say.'

'Well, that's a relief, anyway. Do you want a cup of tea? Kitty has some brewed in the kitchen.'

'No, sir. I just came by to say welcome back.'

'That's very good of you. I'm pleased to be back. Did we get those new steam-engines yet, for the winding-gear?'

'Two arrived, sir. One damaged. But I believe we can have the first one running in two days.'

'Good, fine.'

Barney went back to his newspaper, but after a minute or so he became aware that Gentleman Jack was still standing there, in his grey morning-coat and his muddy shoes, and that he was rotating the brim of his hat around and around in his hands as if he had something to say.

'Yes?' asked Barney, lowering his paper again. 'Was there anything else?'

Gentleman Jack let out a short hiss of breath, like a man who is irritated with himself. 'The truth is, Mr Blitzboss, I am not very sure.'

'You're not *sure*? What is it that you're not sure about?'

'Well, sir, it's to do with diamonds, and God, sir. And who is it who owns a diamond, once it's found.'

'That's easy,' said Barney. 'A diamond belongs, in law, to the man on whose claim it's discovered.'

'No matter who finds it, sir?'

'Of course.'

There was another awkward silence, and then Gentleman Jack said, 'If a man owns a diamond-mine, sir; and there's a diamond lying in the ground in that diamond-mine, and he never digs it up, then who does it belong to then, sir?'

'Jack – whether a man decides to dig up his diamonds or not – they're still his.'

'Even if he doesn't know that he owns them, sir?'

Barney set aside his *Morning Post* and stood up. He walked across to the doorway where Gentleman Jack was standing, his hands plunged deep into his dressing-gown pockets, and he stared intently into Gentleman Jack's face. The Ndebele was almost six inches taller than Barney, but he shied back, and gave Barney a foolish, apprehensive grin.

'What's happened, Jack?' Barney asked, quietly.

'Nothing, Mr Blitzboss. Everything is absolutely fine. I was just seeking clarification, sir. Legal clarification, you understand, and moral clarification. That's all, sir. It says in Deuteronomy, sir, that the law requires perfect obedience. And to obey the law, you have to know it.'

'You're sure nothing's happened? You seem like you're unhappy about something.'

'Everything's absolutely top notch, sir.'

Barney stared at Gentleman Jack for a moment, and then went back and picked up his newspaper. 'You know something, Jack, I spent the larger part of my childhood years, and most of my time as a young man, not knowing what it was that I wanted from myself, nor out of my life, nor the people around me. These days, I'm making a great deal of money, and I know exactly what I want to do, and how I want to do it.'

He folded the newspaper with careful, exaggerated gestures. Then he said, without looking up, 'I want to own the entire Kimberley diamond mine, personally. I want to be a member of the Kimberley Club – not because it will help me to get on, but because I'm going to be so wealthy and so powerful that they won't have any option but to admit me. I want to lead a happy married life, with lots of children. And I want to find my religion again, which I lost when I came out here to Cape Colony, and which seems to have been eluding me lately, like a ghost.'

'Yes, sir,' said Gentleman Jack.

Barney sat down again. 'How about you, Jack?' he asked him. 'Do you know what you want out of your life?'

Jack examined his hat as if he expected to find the answer to Barney's question written on the grey silk hatband. 'I just want to be a good foreman, sir. That's all.'

'You're sure?'

'It's the most that a black man can hope for, Mr Blitzboss.'

'It's more than most black men can hope for. A whole lot more.'

'I know that, sir.'

'All right, then. As long as you understand. Now, you'd better get back to the mine and get those winding-engines repaired.'

'Yes, sir. Oh – and, sir. There's a gentleman waiting for you outside, sir, in the hall. Mr Ransome, he says his name is.'

'A white man?'

'Yes, sir.'

'Why didn't you tell me before? You mean to tell me you've kept a white man waiting all the time you've been engaging me in this ridiculous conversation about legal clarification?'

'I'm sorry, Mr Blitzboss.'

Barney tightened his mouth in annoyance. 'You're lucky I don't sack you on the spot,' he told Jack. 'Go out there at once, and ask Mr Ransome to come through. And apologise for keeping him waiting. Do you happen to know what he wants?'

'He didn't say, sir. But he's a reverend, sir. The white collar, and the black dress, sir.'

'Very well. Now, go get him.'

'Yes, sir. And thank you.'

After a minute or two, there was a timorous knock at the door-post. Barney said, 'Come in!' and a small shabby man in a clerical cassock stepped into the room, and removed his hat in a visible cloud of dust.

'Mr Blitz?' he asked, in a voice as uncontrolled as that of a pubescent boy.

'That's right. Mr Barney Blitz. And you must be Mr Ransome. I'm sorry my foreman kept you waiting. I had no idea you were out there.'

'I, ah, well – it doesn't matter. Waiting always gives one an opportunity to meditate, don't you think? Really – you must excuse my dust. It was such a dry day, and I rode over from Klipdrift rather *hurriedly*.'

'Sit down,' Barney told him. 'Would you like some tea?'

'That's most kind. My throat feels like the Sinai desert must have done, to the Children of Israel.' He said 'the Children of Israel' with noticeable emphasis.

Barney lifted his head. 'Are you trying to tell me something, Mr Ransome?'

Mr Ransome blushed. 'Please – really. I didn't mean any offence. I was simply trying to delineate our differences, as it were. I mean, me being an Anglican, as it were, and you, well, being Jewish.'

'That requires delineation?' asked Barney, sharply.

'I'm not very sure. I just thought I ought to stake out the ground before I told you why I came here.'

Barney tinkled the brass handbell for more tea. Then he folded his arms across his chest and inspected Mr Ransome with undisguised directness. Mr Ransome picked at a stray thread on the arm of his chair until he realised with some embarrassment that he was pulling apart his host's furniture fabric in front of his eyes; and then he sat up straight, his fists clenched, and let out an involuntary whinny that reminded Barney of Alsjeblieft on a cold July morning.

'I've actually come here to talk to you about Natalia Marneweck,' said Mr Ransome. 'I'm not sure why, not entirely. I personally think that she's better off without you, if you'll forgive my saying so. But in six years she hasn't forgotten you, not completely, in spite of having tried. And before she marries her new fiancé, whom I understand you know of, Coen Boonzaier, I thought it worth taking the trouble to ask you if you still harboured any ... well, *affectionate* feelings towards her.'

'Is this a joke, Mr Ransome?' asked Barney. 'Because if it is, it's in pretty poor taste.'

'A joke?' said Mr Ransome. His ears were very red in the morning sun light, with a tracery of crimson veins. 'Why on earth should I perpetrate a joke, especially of such a nature, and especially on you, whom I scarcely know?'

'You tell me.'

'Mr Blitz,' protested Mr Ransome, 'I *revere* Miss Marneweck. She is not only a young woman of considerable personal beauty, but a character of extraordinary fortitude, gentleness, and religious purity. By most, she is considered to be a fallen woman, particularly since she has conceived and borne a child out of wedlock. But even though she may have fallen, she has risen again, by virtue of her simplicity, her straightforwardness and her love of God.'

Barney pulled reflectively at the skin of his cheek. He

thought, for one kaleidoscopic moment, of all those days he had spent with Mooi Klip in the bungalow; of their nights together in that squeaking brass bed; of their kisses and their whispers and their walks along the dry tracks of Kimberley on those evenings when the sun was magnified by the day's heat and inflamed by the day's dust. He thought of their wedding-cake, and of all those days of happiness when Mooi Klip had been busying herself to marry him. He thought of the wedding-breakfast, smashed on the bungalow floor, and he thought of Joel.

'Mrs Marneweck loved me once, Mr Ransome,' said Barney. 'But I spent six hopeless years trying to persuade her that *I* still loved *her*, and that we ought to get married; and every time she turned me down. I admit that she was hurt by me and my brother, Mr Ransome – hurt very badly. But she hurt me, too. And that's why I was so suspicious when you asked me if I still felt any affection for her.'

'You still love her?' Mr Ransome asked, throatily.

Barney went across to the window, and stared out at the rough uncultivated ground of Vogel Vlei's gardens. One day there would be flowerbeds here, and gravel paths, and orange trees. One day there would be neatly-clipped topiary to amuse the children. One day there would be children. He turned around to Mr Ransome, and said distinctly, 'Yes. I still love her. I will probably love her for the rest of my life. But I'm married now. I married more than two months ago, when I was in Durban.'

Mr Ransome's mouth opened and closed silently, and he looked around at the day-room as if he expected to see a thunderoulsy vengeful wife materialising out of the upholstery or bursting out of the drapes. 'You're married?' he squeaked and growled, in his breaking voice. 'I had no idea. I don't know what to say.'

'It's not your fault,' Barney told him. He wished, unconditionally, that the painful tightness that was congesting his chest would go away. He also wished more than anything that he had never found out that Mooi Klip still loved him. *She still loved him* – after everything she had said, after all those arguments and all those rebuffs, after all those visits and all. *She*

357

still loved him, after all these years. He felt raw all over, flayed. This stuttering clergyman might just as well have come into the room and lashed him with wire, until he bled.

He loved Sara, he knew it. But the love he felt for Sara was part of the love he felt for his own career, and his own future. Sara would help him get into the Kimberley Club. Sara would act as the perfect hostess, the wife who knew that 'don't you know' was fashionably pronounced 'don't-chi-know', and that nobody of any breeding said 'doin'' or 'thinkin'' as if they had 'g' on the end. She was also quite aware without having to be told that soup was never helped twice, that gentlemen who called at lunchtime and were invited to join the meal should always take their hat and their cane in to the dining-room, and that a visiting card must be *exactly* three inches by one-and-one-half inches, and printed in italics.

She was almost beautiful, too. Her face was well-boned, and her body was trim from all those years of riding. Her hair was soft. Her eyes were extraordinary. Her nipples were like azalea peatals that had fallen into bowls of cream.

Sara was everything a rich diamond-miner could want; except that she was not Mooi Klip.

Mr Ransome said, unhappily, 'I think I'd better leave. I'm sorry that I came.'

'What will you tell Natalia?' asked Barney.

'Simply that you're married. You wouldn't want me to say that you still love her, would you?'

'No,' said Barney, 'I suppose not.'

'It wouldn't be proper,' Mr Ransome insisted. 'After all, whatever your emotions, you have now made a lifelong commitment to your new wife.'

'Thank you, I'm aware of that,' said Barney.

'I'll go, then,' flustered Mr Ransome. 'My horse could do with a drink.'

'I'll have one of the blackies take it round to the trough for you.'

'Thank you. And, well, I'm very sorry to have troubled you this way. I thought that my errand was all for the best; but as it turned out, it was all for the worst. I'm sorry.'

Barney showed Mr Ransome to the door; but, as he opened

it wider, he thought he heard the squeak of a sandal on the polished hall floor outside. He looked quickly around to see if there was anyone there, but the hall was deserted. All he could detect was the faintest aroma of musk, and curry, and sweat.

'Nareez?' he queried. His voice echoed across the hallway. Mr Ransome gave him an uncomprehending smile. 'There doesn't seem to be anybody there, Mr Blitz.'

'No,' said Barney. 'But perhaps when there isn't anybody there, that's the time to start worrying.'

One of the servants came across the hall, a thin-legged Malay with spectacles so thick that they made his eyes look like two freshly-opened oysters. 'You were ringing, Mr Blitz? More tea?'

Barney turned to Mr Ransome, but Mr Ransome gave a modest little shake of his head, and raised his hand in an unconsciously Jesus-like gesture of polite refusal. 'I think it would be better all around if I just went quietly back to Klipdrift, don't you?'

That night, when Barney came back to Vogel Vlei from a long meeting with Harold Feinberg, frayed and tired, he found the bedroom door locked against him. He shook the handle once or twice, and then knocked.

'Sara? It's Barney! Come and open the door!'

There was no answer, so he knocked again, and rattled the handle more furiously. 'Sara! Please! What's going on?'

He listened for nearly a minute, but still there was no response. He shook the handle again, and finished up by giving the bottom of the door a thunderous kick with the toe of his veld boot. 'Sara! You must be in there! Open up at once! You're not still sulking about sharing a bedroom, are you? Sara?'

He stood in the darkness outside the door and waited. Whatever the reason, Sara was plainly not going to answer, nor was she going to open up. Still, there was a spare key to the bedroom in the butler's pantry downstairs, and since the workmen had not yet been around to fit sliding bolts to any of the doors, he would be able to open the bedroom up without any trouble. Tired and angry, he stamped downstairs again, crossed the hall, and pushed his way into the kitchen.

Kitty was still there, slicing beef for tomorrow's breakfast. So was Gentleman Jack and their new groom John Gcumisa, a laconic, woolly-haired Zulu who had originally cared for Jan Brand's horses in Bloemfontein. The two blacks put down their teacups and stood to uneasy attention when Barney walked in, and nodded to him in bashful deference. 'Good evening, Mr Blitzboss, sir.'

'I want the key to the master bedroom suite,' said Barney.

Kitty laid down her knife, wiped her hands on her apron, and went into the butler's pantry to find it. Barney waited in the middle of the blue and white tiled kitchen floor, his shoulder muscles crowded with tension, while Gentleman Jack and John Gcumisa stood silently staring at him, their tea steaming in white enamel mugs, and all the paraphernalia of the private evening which Barney had so suddenly interrupted lying on the table all around them: buttons, thread, playing-cards, matches, and a blue paper packet of tobacco.

'Here,' said Kitty, laying the key in Barney's hand. Barney looked at it, and then squeezed it in between tightly closed fingers.

'Everything's all right, Mr Blitz?' asked Kitty, although she posed the question in such an oblique tone that anybody else would have thought it was a statement of simple fact.

'Thank you, Kitty,' said Barney. 'Just – get on with what you have to do. You too, Jack.'

'Yes, sir, Mr Blitzboss.'

As Barney went to the door, Kitty said, gently, 'I saw the Reverend Ransome this morning, Mr Blitz. I used to know him, when he first came to Klipdrift.'

'Yes?'

Kitty kept her head down, wrapped in its black and red scarf. Her gold hoop earrings swung in the lamplight. 'He didn't tell no tales, sir. But he explained to me why he came here. And he said he was very sorry that things worked out the way they did.'

Barney laid his hand on Kitty's shoulder. 'I think I understand what you're trying to tell me,' he said. 'But you know that I'll appreciate it more if you keep it to yourself.'

'Yes, sir, I know that.'

Barney climbed the curved stairs to the upper landing again, holding the key to the bedroom door so tightly that it made a scarlet impression on his palm. Before he tried to open the door he looked down at his hand and thought: what would a palmist make of this? The key line? The line that showed which doors would open and which would close? Which doors would bring happiness and which would bring tears?

The worst part of it was, he already suspected why Sara was refusing to let him in. If Nareez had overheard his conversation this morning with Mr Ransome, there was no question at all that she would have told Sara all about it. And if Sara had believed that he still loved a Griqua woman, a woman who had given birth to his only child, her English sense of moral indignation would already have been stirred beyond any hope of reasonable recovery. Sara had been brought up, like all good colonial girls, to be a brick in times of native attack or malaria, but a swooner and a locker of doors in times of marital difficulty.

'Sara!' Barney shouted. 'I've got a key and I'm coming in!'

He unlocked the door, and pushed it. Sara had wedged one of the bedroom chairs under the handle but not firmly enough; and Barney had only to tussle against it with his shoulder, grunting, and the chair fell away. Then he threw the door wide, and burst in.

Sara was sitting up in bed, the sheets clutched to her breasts, her eyes wide with hysterical indignation and fright. Next to her sat Nareez, her hair wound up into a calico mobcap, equally wide-eyed, and equally frightened.

'You've no right!' shrilled Sara.

'No *right*?' Barney demanded. 'I built this house out of my own sweat and blood. And you're trying to tell me that I have no *right*?'

'Not after what Nareez heard you saying today, no. You brought me heah under the falsest of pretences. You gave me to believe that you loved me. You lied to me. You tricked me. And I believed you.'

'Oh, sure,' said Barney. 'It was all a practical joke. I travelled more than five hundred miles to Durban, and more than five hundred miles back, just to get a cheap laugh. You stun me

361

sometimes, Sara. You stun me! Yesterday, you were arguing against our sleeping together. Today, you're convinced that I was lying to you when I said that I loved you. What do you want? What do you want me to say? I thought I said it all already in the church, and in the temple. I said I wanted you for my wife, if you can remember, that I was going to love you and cherish you from this day forth. Cherish! What a promise that is! And now you're trying to tell me that you don't believe me? That you don't think I actually meant it?'

Sara, her voice shaky, said, 'You told that clergyman that you were still in love with a woman called Natalia.'

'Who told you that?' snapped Barney.

'Well,' said Sara, petulantly, 'Nareez.'

'Nareez,' Barney nodded. 'The *kibitzer* from Bengal.'

'She wanted to *protect* me, that's all,' Sara protested. 'You can't possibly blame her for that. She was passing the day-room, so she told me, and she couldn't help overhearing.'

Barney walked around the bed until he was only inches away from Nareez. The *amah* pulled the bedspread right up to her chin, and stared at him in hypnotised alarm.

'I did know a woman called Natalia,' said Barney, much more quietly, 'and, a very long time ago, I did love her. Didn't *you* have other loves? How about your old Etonian?'

Sara looked across at him sharply, but then she flinched, and looked away. 'I wasn't to know that you would come back for me, was I? And I certainly wasn't to know that poor Trevor would die.'

'No, quite,' said Barney. 'But just like it was for you with Trevor, that's the way it was for me with Natalia. Everything else you've heard about it is gossip. Eavesdropping, maliciously misreported.'

'You can't say that!' babbled Nareez. 'What you are saying is slander! What I heard was quite by accident, from open door. If you do not closet yourself in secrecy, then you must expect people to listen. This is open house.'

'You think it's an open house, do you?' Barney demanded. 'You think you can wander where you please, listening in to private conversations, and meddling in other people's marriages?'

'Miss Sara is not other people. Miss Sara is my charge.'

'Don't interrupt me, you fat Indian *shtunk*. Just get out of my bed and don't let me catch you in here again.'

'Barney, this is awful!' Sara exclaimed. 'Poor Nareez was only –'

'Get the hell out of my bed!' Barney bellowed. 'Get your big fat smelly carcass out of my bed!'

Nareez, incensed, threw back the covers, picked up her lopsided silk slippers, and pushed past Barney to the door. 'You haven't heard the very last of this, you devil!' she cried, wagging her finger at him. 'You certainly haven't heard the last! I know what I heard in the day-room! I know what you said, about loving that girl! Well, Miss Sara is my charge! Ever since birth I have nursed Miss Sara, and not you nor anybody will hurt her! I'll see to that!'

Barney took a deep breath. 'I want you to leave my bedroom, Nareez,' he said, in a voice that trembled like a telegraph wire under gradually increasing tension. 'I want you to leave my bedroom and I don't want you ever – *ever* – to set foot in here again. And there's something else, before you go. I never want you to call Mrs Blitz "Miss Sara" again. Her name, to you, is Mrs Blitz. And – wait – there's one thing more. I want you to go downstairs and tell Kitty to come up here and change the sheets. Tell her they were inadvertently soiled.'

Nareez glared at Barney with hatred. In her mob cap and her voluminous nightgown, with her long black braid hanging down her back, Barney thought that she looked like an enraged caliph out of the Arabian nights. She slammed the door behind her, and left Barney and Sara alone.

Barney walked across to the bureau, unfastening his gold and diamond cufflinks.

'You're undressing?' asked Sara, rather shrilly.

'You prefer me to get into bed with my clothes on?'

'I prefer you not to get into bed at all.'

Barney made a deliberately patient performance of putting his cufflinks and collar-stud back in their red velvet box, and closing the drawer of the bureau. He could see Sara in the mirror, sitting upright in bed with her arms crossed over her breasts. The oil-lamp beside the bed lit her face in an odd way, and made her look different. She could have been her own sister; or a stand-in from the theatre.

'If you must know, Sara,' said Barney, enunciating his words with exaggerated care, 'I am extremely tired. I have been talking business most of the evening with Harold, and all I want to do right now is get into bed and sleep.'

'Nareez was right, wasn't she?' asked Sara.

'Right about what? Nareez is never right about anything. She's a fussy, jealous, stupid, greedy, superstitious harridan.'

'How can you say such a thing?'

'I can say it because it's self-evident. Ever since we've been married, she's done nothing but interfere. She's always trying to make me look as if I'm some kind of lustful monster, intent on ruining your virtue. And the worst of it is, you let her.'

'I have to listen to her, Barney. She's my *amah*. She loves me.'

'Only children have *amahs*, Sara. You're quite old enough to look after yourself, without the help of some ignorant *platke-macher*. If I had anything to do with it at all, I'd pack up her bags and send her back to Durban on the next waggon. *Biryani* and all.'

Sara watched Barney as he unbuttoned his underwear with an expression that he could not quite understand. It was more concerned than remote, and yet Barney was not at all certain if the concern she was feeling was for herself, or for Nareez, or for him. There was also an almost imperceptible tightening of the muscles around her eyes that reminded him of the way a young child looks when she anticipates a smack.

As he stepped out of his drawers and stood in front of her naked, it suddenly occurred to him that she might be afraid of him. Not afraid that he would hit her, or abuse her. But simply afraid of his ambition, and his Jewishness, and his growing self-assurance in a world which, to her, was unfamiliar and uncomfortable.

He was partly right. Sara came from a family that had brought her up in the traditional English colonial manner, and while she had been excited at the thought of marrying a man who had trekked five hundred miles to find her, and of living in a grand mansion on the brink of a diamond mine, she was quickly discovering that her romantic fantasy had betrayed her. Life in Kimberley with Barney Blitz was not going to be anything but difficult, isolated, and deprived. Barney was rich, all right, but what on earth was the use of being rich when there were no luxuries to be bought, no theatres to go to, no smart parties, no hunts, and none of the feverish social intrigue that made colonial life so absorbing. What was life without five o'clock tea, and supper dances, and the regular arrival on one of Papa's steamers of the season's modes from London? How could she survive without coddled eggs, and opera? And how she missed those evening chats with her mother, over hot chocolate and mint cake!

Her feeling of alienation from her new surroundings made her feel alienated from Barney, too. Watching him talk to heavyweight diamond dealers like Harold Feinberg and wild-eyed geologists like Edward Nork, seeing him barking out orders to the thirty mud-caked kaffirs who dug with picks and shovels at the Blitz Brothers' diamond claims, all this placed him in a strange and rough environment which Sara felt she could never possibly enter.

And what was more, as he stood naked in front of her, watching her with an expression which, to her, was just as incomprehensible as her expression was to him, there was the most significant symbol of his strangeness. His penis, with its bare, plum-coloured glans; the seal of God.

'I think I'd rather sleep alone tonight,' said Sara. 'Please ... if you don't mind too much.'

'You still believe that Nareez was right?' Barney asked her.

'I don't know. I'm confused. I just want to lie here on my own and work it out for myself.'

Barney sat down on the edge of the bed. Sara, keeping the covers tight under her arm, turned away from him.

'Sara, there's something wrong between us, isn't there?' asked Barney, his voice as soft as the shadows that surrounded them.

'What could possibly be wrong?'

'I don't know. That's what I want to find out. I'm beginning to believe that perhaps you don't love me any more. Sometimes I find myself thinking that maybe you never loved me at all.'

Sara whispered, 'Do *you* love *me*?'

'Of course I do. You know it.'

'And you're sure you don't love anybody else? No girls called Natalia?'

Barney laid his hand on her shoulder, but she resisted his attempt to pull her towards him. 'You're my wife, Sara, that's the most important thing.'

'Is it? None of the colonial staff seemed to let their wives get in their way when they went chasing black women in Durban.'

'I'm not like that. And, in any case, I love you.'

She sat up in bed and looked at him intensely. 'Are you sure? You love me, and me alone?'

'Would I lie to you?'

'Make an oath,' she told him. 'Swear to me on the Bible that you love only me.'

Barney lifted his hand and touched her hair. 'Do you have to ask me to swear on the Bible to know whether I love you or not?'

'If you really do love me, it'll be easy.'

The bedroom seemed suddenly airless to Barney, and sweltering hot. He could still smell *jeera* on the sheets, too, from that Bengali woman. He stood up, and went to the window to open the white-painted shutters out wider.

'I took a solemn oath in church, and in the synagogue,' he told Sara. 'I'm not going to go through the rest of my married life being forced into reaffirming it. I love you, and that's all you need to know.'

'I see,' said Sara, with unexpected crispness, as if she had just been told by a servant that he had taken two sacks of brown sugar home without permission. 'In that case, Nareez wasn't mistaken.'

'For God's sake!' Barney flared up. 'How much longer am I going to have to live under the regime of that sow of an *amah* of yours?'

Sara thrashed her way out of the bed-covers, went to the wardrobe, and took down her long white robe with a rattle of clothes-hangers.

'What are you doing?' Barney shouted. 'Just because I happen to object to having my marriage messed around by some –'

'It's nothing to *do* with that,' Sara burst out, going to the door and opening it as furiously as Nareez had slammed it. 'It's all to do with love, and trust, and taking care of me. You don't have the first idea, do you, how strange and horrible this place seems to me. I'm miserable already, and I've only been here two days. You haven't done anything to comfort me, or make me feel at home. You've done nothing but shout at me, and shout at Nareez. Well, I think your behaviour has been utterly beastly and I'm not going to stay with you one moment longer!'

'Sara –'

'I won't listen! You're hateful!' And with that, she ran off down the corridor on bare feet, mewling like a self-pitying ghost.

Barney stood still for a moment, staring at the open door. Then he walked over with a tired sigh and closed it. For the first time in a long time, he felt like a drink. He sat down on the end of the bed, his chin propped on his hands, and wondered abstractedly how Mooi Klip was, and how much Pieter had grown since he had been away.

He slept on Sara's side of the bed, but he still slept badly. At five o'clock he woke up after dreaming a dream about Gentleman Jack tracking mud all over his new rugs, and climbed stiffly out of bed. He knelt in front of the window, while the incandescent rim of the sun came edging over his window-ledge from the other side of the world, and he said *schachris*, the morning prayer, with more entreaty in his voice than he had ever said it before.

He was given the first hint by Harold Feinberg, two days later, early on Friday afternoon. They had met for three hours with the unctuous, stiff-collared lawyers of the Rose Innes Diamond Mining Company, negotiating the purchase of six more claims. Normally, Joel would have joined in the negotiations, too, but it was one of those odd days when the barometric pressure drops, and the skies of north Cape Colony grow soft and grey, and fretful dust-storms whip up on the veld. On days like these, Joel would retreat to his private suite of rooms at the back of Vogel Vlei, and lie on his bed with the drapes drawn, his whole existence decaying with pain.

On days like these, not even whiskey and morphia would help. The cramp in his bones seemed to attack him like a wild beast. When he heard that a kaffir had been attacked and mauled by a lioness, he simply laughed. 'I've been eaten by lions a hundred times over.'

Harold had looked tired during the meeting. He was several stones overweight these days, and he had been complaining that his heart had been slow-dancing like an elephant in a Hungarian ballet. 'It's the work,' he complained, although Joel thought it had much more to do with the pretty young French girl from Natal, the girl he had once fancied himself, and who had recently been seen on Harold's arm on Kimberley's main street, and sharing supper with him at the Woodhouse Restaurant.

By three o'clock, Barney had come to an arrangement with the Rose Innes lawyers that Blitz Brothers would purchase four of their claims for £75,000, and take out a two-week option on the remaining two. The lawyers offered handshakes that were as reticent and scaly as turkey claws, and then left. Harold went to the rolltop desk in the corner of his office, took out a bottle of brandy, and poured himself a large glassful.

'You want some? Just to celebrate?' he asked Barney.

Barney, standing by the window, shook his head. Below him, in the street, he had just caught sight of Agnes Joy, *née* Knight, in the company of two tall young diggers. He recognised the diggers as Hugh Johnson and David Mackie, the successful young owners of the Cape Star Diamond Company. Apart from Barney himself, Johnson and Mackie were two of the richest men in town. Agnes threw her head back in silent laughter, and Barney saw Mackie give her a quick, saucy squeeze.

Harold joined Barney at the window, sipping his brandy. 'That's Agnes, isn't it?' he asked, and Barney nodded. 'She ought to be more circumspect, that girl. She's getting herself a reputation.'

'What for? Walking along the street laughing?'

'You know what I mean. I shall never know why she married that thick Australian from the drama club. He couldn't even act.'

Barney said, 'I guess I'd better be going home. Sara was planning on an early supper tonight.'

'How's she settling down?'

'Not too bad. It's a little rougher here than she expected, but I guess she'll get used to it.'

Harold gestured towards the window, with its view of brick façades and corrugated-iron rooftops and chimneys. 'In five years' time, she won't even recognise the place. It'll look like the West End of London. Do you remember what it was like when you first came here? That terrible old shack I used to work in, with the Irish whore next door? Those were the rough days!'

Barney took his hat from the hatstand, and brushed the top of it with his sleeve. 'I'm pretty satisfied with the Rose Innes arrangement,' he said, 'But I want to start pushing the Octahedron Company as soon as I can. We've got the capital; it's about time we started building up some momentum. We've been too slow lately, don't you think? I know I've been away, but Rhodes has already bought up a third of the De Beers mine, one way or another, and I'm damned if I'm going to let him outstrip me.'

'I heard that Rhodes has teamed up with Alfred Beit,' remarked Harold.

'Alfred Beit? Didn't he work for Lippert & Company, in Hamburg?'

'He used to. But then they made him a partner of Jules Porges, and as everybody knows, they're the wealthiest diamond merchants in the whole world, bar none. He's a genius. You think I'm a genius? Beit can remember almost every stone he's ever handled. One of Duncan's men tried to sell him some stolen gems, and he recognised them straight away as the same gems that had passed through his hands seven years ago.'

Barney raised his eyebrows. 'So we're in for some stiff competition, then?'

'From Beit, sure. Beit once told me that his only aim in life was to own every single diamond mine in Africa.'

'Looks like he and Rhodes are going to get on well.'

Harold accompanied Barney downstairs to the front door of the office, so that he could lock up. On the way down, he said off-handedly, 'By the way, did you hear about the giant diamond yet?'

Barney opened the front door of the office, and the noises of the hot afternoon came in — waggons, and laughter, and the distant *shuggg-shuggg-shuggg* of steam-powered winding-gear. A Bantu was sitting on the boardwalk outside blowing a soft, monotonous tune out of an instrument like an ocarina. 'Giant diamond?' asked Barney, shaking his head. 'What is it, a leg-pull?'

Harold leaned against the door, sweating. He loosened his tie to take some of the pressure off his throat. 'I'm not sure,' he said, 'I heard a garbled kind of a story from one of the kaffirs who works out at Isaacs' claim. All he said was, 'Boss, how much a gemstone worth as big as this?" and he made a circle with his finger and his thumb, like this, so that the tip of his finger and the tip of his thumb just touched.'

'Diamonds don't come that big,' said Barney. 'Not here in South Africa, anyway.'

'Why not?' said Harold. 'There was the Koh-i-Noor, wasn't there — one hundred and eight carats. And the French Blue, sixty-seven carats. And, I forgot — the Florentine was one hundred and thirty-seven carats.'

'Sure, but all of those diamonds were Indian, weren't they? And a diamond as big as your kaffir tried to describe would be twice the size of any of those — twice the size of the Florentine. It's just a fairy-story, Harold, that's all. You know what the kaffirs are like when they've been at the whiskey.'

'I don't know,' said Harold, 'he didn't *seem* to be drunk, and he didn't seem to be trying to spin me any kind of yarn. He just said, "How much a gemstone worth as big as this?" and when I told him it would depend on who you could find to buy such a stone, rather than the current market price of diamonds, he said, "Difficult to sell, then, boss?" and I said, "Yes, of course," I mean — if he was seriously talking about a diamond in excess of three hundred carats, then my own guess is that you could ask over a million pounds for it. Perhaps more, if you could persuade a government to buy it.'

Barney swung the door backwards and forwards, feeling the draught against his face. There was something about this tale of a giant diamond that irritated his consciousness in the same way that grit can irritate a clam. There was something about it which seemed to make other feelings that he had been having since he returned from Durban fit uneasily into place.

'What else did this kaffir say?' he asked Harold. 'Did he say that he'd actually *seen* a diamond as big as the one he was talking about?'

'No,' said Harold. 'But I can't think why he asked me, unless he had. And where could he have seen it? That was the question I asked myself.'

'Isaacs only borders on to three other claims. Francis and Company, the Griqualand Diamond Mining Company, and mine. So, we've got a choice of four.'

'Yours included,' said Harold.

'Yes,' agreed Barney, 'mine included.'

'What worries me is the implications of someone discovering a stone that size,' Harold said, patting his forehead with his bunched-up handkerchief. 'They might get themselves a million pounds, personally, but you know what effect it'll have on the market, don't you? The diggers will start producing twice as fast as usual, all trying to dig up the big one, and the market's going to be flooded again, just like it was in '74. It's taken us almost four years to get the prices up from '74, and if they go down again, well, a lot of diamond dealers are going to be ruined.'

Barney laid a hand on Harold's shoulder. 'I shouldn't worry. It's probably only a wild rumour. Maybe somebody dug up a hefty piece of quartz.'

'I don't know,' said Harold. 'I just don't know. But keep it to yourself, won't you? An imaginary diamond can cause almost as much of a panic as a real diamond.'

'Well – you can console yourself with one thing,' said Barney. 'What we did this afternoon, buying up most of Rose Innes, that's a step in the right direction. One day, you'll have just two or three diamond companies controlling the whole of South African mining, and then we can fix the prices as high as the public will pay.'

Harold held his hand over his chest. He was short of breath now, and he was sweating so much that his face looked as if it had been basted in honey. 'I don't suppose I shall live to see it.'

371

'Are you all right?' Barney asked him, frowning.

Harold nodded. 'Too much work,' he said, and each word was an abrupt gasp. 'You get along now. I'll see you on Wednesday, for your celebration dinner.'

Barney stood in the doorway until Harold had climbed heavily back up the stairs to his office. Then he stepped out into the dull, humid afternoon, adjusted his hat, and walked slowly along the boardwalk to the sidestreet where his carriage was waiting. His new black driver, Michael, was sitting up on the box in shirtsleeves, ragged trousers, and a formal black opera hat. The staff uniforms had yet to be ordered from Capetown.

'Back to Vogel Vlei, boss?' asked Michael, twitching his whip.

Barney said absent-mindedly, 'Yes.' Then, 'Michael?'

'Yessir, boss?'

'Has anyone spoken to you lately about a diamond?'

Michael whistled at the horses, and they wheeled edgily around in a semi-circle. 'Diamond, boss? One diamond special, boss?'

'That's right. One diamond special.'

'Well, boss, I did hear something.'

Barney sat back in his seat, his legs crossed, trying to appear relaxed. 'What did you hear, Michael? Did someone tell you about a giant diamond? Big as an eagle's egg?'

'You heard it too, boss.'

'Was that all you heard? You don't know who found it, or where?'

'No, sir, boss. But what I did hear was that someone was paying money to keep the story quiet.'

'And you don't know who that "someone" was?'

Michael drove the horses out along Main Street until they cleared the last of the offices and houses and lean-to stores. The day was as dull as a photograph. 'If I knew who that "someone" was, boss, I'd be round to his door myself, asking for hush-me-up money. Not that you don't pay me good, boss. You pay me goodest in Kimberley.'

Barney did not answer. He was trying to remember something that someone had said to him during the past two or three days. A word, a fragmented phrase. A feeling that something extraordinary had happened, and that he was being deliberately kept in the dark about it.

Joel was out of bed when Barney returned to Vogel Vlei, but still in a difficult temper. He had ordered tea once and then sent it all back because it was cold, and because there were not any spongecakes. Now he was sprawled on the couch with his left leg propped up on heaps of cushions, drinking whiskey out of the neck of the bottle and humming to himself in an oddly threatening way.

Barney came into the drawing-room and crossed the Indian carpet to the open French windows without even glancing at Joel. In the middle distance, like a scene from one of those perpetually enchanted landscapes by Claude Lorraine, two kaffirs worked at the stony ground with hoes, levelling the wide area which Barney eventually hoped to use as a paddock. There was a dry, aromatic smell in the air; a smell which, years later, would always remind Barney of Africa. The sun gilded the dusty furrows, and flashed on the blades of the kaffirs' uplifted hoes, and Barney could hear the men talking from almost a quarter of a mile away.

'Your lady wife is preparing her hair for supper,' announced Joel, in a blotchy voice. 'No!' he giggled. 'That's wrong! She is *not* preparing her hair for supper – that is, she is not preparing her hair for us to *eat* for supper – she is – preparing her hair – in *time* for supper.'

Barney closed the French windows and locked them. 'How much have you drunk?' he asked, flatly.

'In proportion to the intoxicating effect of the Dover's powders I have consumed, scarcely anything. This is only my second bottle, as a matter of fact, and I puked up most of the first.'

'Give it to me,' said Barney, holding out his hand.

Joel clutched the bottle to his chest, and slowly and emphatically shook his head. 'Not on your life, little brother.'

'All right,' agreed Barney. 'But if you want to go on drinking, go back to your room. I don't want you lying here, making an exhibition of yourself.'

'Exhibition? Me?' protested Joel.

'Just get upstairs,' Barney told him.

'Oh, you can talk about exhibitions. You're a fine one! As if the whole household doesn't know that you kicked Nareez out of your bedroom the other night, and that you and Sara haven't slept together more than once since you've been back! Exhibitions! You can talk about exhibitions!'

'Just get out,' snapped Barney.

'I'm going,' Joel cautioned him. 'I'm on my way. But if I were you, I'd really try to keep my personal life a little quieter. I would, really! It's not good for staff spirit, you know, all this argy-bargy upstairs.'

'Get out of here before I kick you out,' Barney ordered him.

Unsteadily, hobbling and hopping from one piece of furniture to the next, clutching at the moulding on top of the cream-painted dado for support, Joel made his way to the stairs. Barney followed a few paces behind him.

'You're a fool, you know,' gasped Joel, at the foot of the stairs. 'The most contemptible fool I've ever come across.'

Then, gripping the bannister rail, hand-over-hand, Joel began his agonising climb to the second-floor landing. Barney, tight-mouthed with anger and frustration and sheer despair, stood at the bottom of the stairs and watched him, not moving, not once attempting to help. The terrible part of it was that he *wanted* to help, he *wanted* to run up those five or six stairs and take Joel's arm; he wanted to show that in spite of everything they were still brothers, borne by the same mother, *alevasholem*, and raised in the same tenement on Clinton Street. But Joel at last had reached the upper landing, and was leaning over the bannisters with a face as grotesque as a dried-clay gargoyle.

'You hear me, *gonif* !' he shouted. 'You should keep your marital failures to yourself!' And with that, he shuffled and stumbled back to his bedroom, colliding with the brassbound linen-chest as he went.

Barney mounted the first stair, intent on following him; but then he stopped himself, and lowered his head, and turned back. He had followed Joel too many times after too many arguments, and he knew only too well how illogical and fierce his brother could be when he was drunk and drugged. Even if

Barney did succeed in calming him down, and settling all of their differences, Joel would usually have forgotten by the following morning what they had talked about, and he would sit at the breakfast-table white-faced and incommunicative, eating nothing but dry toast, painfully attempting to overcome both severe morphia withdrawal and a pounding hangover. Dr Truter, who came to examine Joel every two or three weeks with his untidy brown leather bag and his green-corroded stethoscope, had whispered to Barney on several occasions that it was 'an Act of God' that Joel was still alive.

As Barney crossed the hallway on his way back to the sitting-room, Michael came walking quickly towards him on slapping slippers, and said, 'Mr Blitz, sir?'

'What is it, Michael?'

'Someone to see you, boss. In the kitchen.'

'In the *kitchen*? What do you mean, in the kitchen? Who is it?'

Michael hesitated, and then glanced cautiously up the stairs. 'An old friend, sir,' he said, in a confidential tone.

'An old –?' began Barney, but then he looked at Michael's meaningful expression, and he realised who it was. At least, he *thought* he realised who it was. 'Lead the way,' he said, brusquely. Michael turned immediately and slip-slapped back towards the servants' quarters. 'One of those funny days, boss,' he remarked.

'Yes,' said Barney, without even hearing him.

She was waiting for him at the far end of the cluttered kitchen table, posed on a spare bentwood chair as if she were having her portrait painted. The dull daylight shone through the lacy curtains behind her and blurred the outline of her severe black travelling-coat and her small fashionable hat, so that Barney felt as if he were seeing her through tears.

'Natalia,' he said, walking forward and taking her hands. He kissed her fingers, and then he bent down and kissed her cheek, which was still just as soft, and perfumed with that same elusive musk.

'Well,' she said bravely, 'I hear that you're married.'

'Yes,' he told her. He cleared aside a tin cheese-grater and half of a red cabbage, and perched himself on the edge of the

375

kitchen table. 'I was married in Durban, to an English girl.'

'Kitty told me.'

Barney looked up at Kitty, who was ostentatiously keeping herself busy by scouring the baking-trays and clattering the milk pans. He smiled, and then turned back to Mooi Klip. He thought she looked tired. There were dark shadows under her eyes, and she seemed to have lost weight.

'You can't keep a secret long if you tell it to Kitty,' Barney confessed. 'But how are you? Did you just arrive from Klipdrift?'

'This afternoon. One of the diggers had to come over here for equipment, pumps and shovels, and he gave me a ride.'

'And Pieter?'

'He's staying with Mama and Papa.'

'He's well?'

'He's wonderful. He's starting to read.'

'You're a good mother, Natalia.'

There was a moment's silence. Mooi Klip twisted the diamond engagement ring on her finger around and around and around, and did her best to keep up a collected smile. But Barney had lived with her long enough to know how unsettled she felt, and that she had something else to tell him. So he sat on the edge of the table and waited for her to come to the point. His father would have said abruptly, 'What's the *tachlis*, my friend?' – 'Let's get down to the nitty-gritty.' For Barney, it was enough just to wait.

'I had a visit from Mr Ransome yesterday,' said Mooi Klip, at last. 'That was right after he came back from talking to you.'

'You knew he was coming here? I mean, before he came?'

Mooi Klip nodded. The sun caught the curls on the top of her head, and made them shine like the shavings of lathe-cut copper. 'It was his idea, to begin with. But I didn't do anything to stop him. I didn't know you were married, you see. Neither of us did. If I had – well, I don't know what difference it would have made.'

'I didn't think you loved me,' said Barney, quietly.

'I *didn't*,' she said. 'Not for quite a long time. I was frightened of you, believe it or not, and I was frightened of Joel, and

376

I was also frightened by the things you used to say. You used to talk of owning the whole of Kimberley. That was too much for me. Too heady. Do you know how rich a man would be, if he owned the whole of Kimberley? He would be like a god. I used to lie awake, thinking about that. If you became as rich as that, I would have had to meet princes and maharajahs and even kings. We would have had to hold banquets! An uneducated Griqua women like me would have done nothing but shame you.'

'I don't know how you can talk like that,' said Barney, standing up, and walking around to the back of her chair. 'I loved you that day when I was going to marry you, and I love you still. You could have faced up to princes and maharajahs as well as anybody. In any case, don't talk to me about maharajahs. It's closed season for Indians in this house, right at the moment.'

'Kitty told me about Nareez.'

'Well, you'd better believe what she says,' grinned Barney. 'Nareez is a human curry. Better out of your system than in.'

'I still wasn't right for you, Barney, was I?' said Mooi Klip, in the gentlest of voices. 'At least, you didn't think I was. I know you loved me, and I believe you when you say that you still love me, even today. But you didn't try too hard to get me back, did you? That was what I was afraid of, that was why I always chased you away. You were always willing to admit defeat a little too early; you were never willing to come back and back and back until I didn't have any choice at all but to say that I was going to be your wife.'

Barney blew out his cheeks. 'I tried as hard as I knew how. How can you say I didn't try?'

Mooi Klip turned around in her chair and took Barney's hands. Her eyes were dry of tears, but there was a look of such hopelessness and regret on her face that Barney felt as if he wanted to vaporise everything around him, dissolve Vogel Vlei, and return to those months in the bungalow when there was nothing but laughter and lovemaking and evenings around the fire. The months before Joel's rape, and Sara Sutter.

'I just came down here to make sure that you really *were* married,' said Mooi Klip. 'Well – I knew that it had to be true if Mr Ransome had told me. But I wanted to say goodbye, too. I shall probably marry Coen Boonzaier, I suppose, and spend the rest of my life in a *strooidak* farmhouse, speaking Afrikaans and baking soda bread.'

'I promised I would drape you with diamonds, didn't I?' said Barney, sadly.

She ran the tip of her finger across the four bruised hills of his knuckles. 'Don't worry about keeping promises. Promises are only a way of saying that you love somebody, and that you want to give them everything. Lovers don't expect their promises to come true.'

'Natalia . . .' said Barney, but Mooi Klip rose from her chair, and took hold of his arms, and shook her head to show him that she did not want him to say any more.

'You're married now. You love your wife. Don't spoil everything.'

Barney could not look at her. It was only now, seeing her here, that he realised what a catastrophic mistake he had made. He felt as if the walls of the house were slowly collapsing in on him; as if every second of every minute for the rest of his life had now become a claustrophobic burden. He had married Sara with such confidence and happiness, and he knew that it had been the right thing to do. Sara had been a little 'mature' for marriage, but unquestionably pretty, and still a good colonial 'catch'. She would guide him and grace him through countless business receptions and dinners and political soirées, her big breasts rising from her low-cut evening-gowns with patriotic buoyancy, her hair fussily plaited with ribbons and clips and pearls, and her voice as sharp and cultured as the diamonds on which her fortune depended. She and Barney would make love, once or twice, in tolerant breathlessness, and she would probably be fertile enough to bear him a son, and a daughter, and a second son with a penchant for breaking windows. They would travel widely, on steamers, in separate staterooms, and reach a wealthy and honourable old age, white-haired, forgetful, and eccentric, their memories of Africa fogged by time and distance and their own preposterous anecdotes. It had been the right thing to do; to marry Sara; for Queen and Empire and personal fortune.

The only agony was: he loved Mooi Klip.

'What I told Mr Ransome … that was all true, you know,' he told her 'I still love you. I would still have you back.'

'You can't. Think of your wife.'

'Natalia, I don't know what to say. I just didn't believe that you felt anything for me any more. I was lonely. You don't even know how lonely. And, well, I thought that I loved her.'

He found that his throat was blocked with rising grief, and that he could not even tell Mooi Klip how much he wanted her. But he held her close to him, and through the linen of her travelling-suit he felt the body that he had loved on so many nights, and which had once been swollen with his own baby. A body that the laws of marriage and adultery now decreed that he should no longer touch. Lord, he could remember her naked shoulders, and the dark twin moles on either side of her spine. He could remember the way her neck felt, under her hair, when he stroked her. He could remember her nipples, wide and brown, and the softness of her breasts. He could feel in the palms of his hands the ghostly and half-forgotten sensation of her whole body, in the same way that an amputee can feel a ghostly image of his lost leg.

He could remember lying next to her in bed, their foreheads touching, doing nothing at all but talking for hours. He could remember teaching her the English for 'passion' and 'heady' and 'adorable'.

He had lost it all now, and he felt as shattered as if somebody close to him had died.

'I'd better go,' said Mooi Klip. 'I can't do you any good here. But I will write to you, and tell you how I am; and you can see Pieter whenever you want. He misses you.'

'I miss him,' said Barney, with tears in his eyes.

'Ssh,' whispered Mooi Klip, touching his tears with her fingertips. 'You are a rich, successful, proud, well-married man. Don't let your servants see that you are human, too.'

He gave her an unhappy smile. 'I guess you're right. Well, you *are* right. There's no use crying over – mismatched marriages – is there?'

'There's one thing more,' Mooi Klip told him, her voice so soft that he could scarcely hear her.

'What's that?'

'It's to do with diamonds. Kitty told me, but she wanted me to make sure that she wouldn't be punished, or sacked.'

'What is it?' asked Barney.

'First you must promise that you won't be angry with Kitty.'

Barney dropped his head down in resignation. 'Okay, if it's really necessary. I promise.'

'Kitty says that Gentleman Jack found a huge diamond on your property. It happened while you were away in Durban. But this diamond is so big that Kitty says it looks like the sun. As bright as the sun, she said.'

Barney looked up, startled. 'She's actually *seen* it?' he said, louder than he meant to. 'She's *seen* it, and it's *mine*?'

'You've heard about it?' asked Mooi Klip.

'Well, sure I've heard about it. Harold Feinberg told me this afternoon. I was probably the last to know, though. It sounds as if every diamond trader and every digger and every gossipy kaffir in Kimberley has been talking about it.'

'Kitty said that Gentleman Jack brought it along to the bungalow, a few days before you came back. He showed it to Joel, and Joel told Gentleman Jack to borrow Kitty's kitchen scales, so that he could weigh it.'

Barney glanced towards Kitty, but Kitty was scrubbing a tea-towel on her corrugated scrubbing-board with almost maniacal violence, determined not to hear what was being said about her at any price at all.

'Did Kitty hear Joel say how much the diamond weighed?' asked Barney. He felt extraordinarily light-headed, and his voice seemed to echo flatly inside his ears. So the giant diamond was more than a drunken kaffir's fantasy: it was real. And what was more incredible about the whole story, the diamond was *his*. Or it would have been his, if Joel had not taken charge of it.

Mooi Klip turned to Kitty and asked her something in Afrikaans. Without looking around, Kitty said, 'Twee en 'n half ons.'

'Two and a half ounces,' said Mooi Klip. 'They were careless enough to leave the weight on the scales when they brought them back into the kitchen.'

Barney made a quick calculation. Then, awed, he mouthed to Mooi Klip, 'Two and a half ounces is *three hundred fifty-five carats*. Do you know how much a stone like that could be *worth*?'

Mooi Klip shook her head. 'I don't care what it's worth. It's *your* fortune, Barney. It's all yours. But when Kitty told me, I couldn't resist passing it on. It isn't very often that you get the chance to take your revenge on somebody who's done you wrong; and I do think that Joel deserves everything he's going to get.'

'God, I should have married you the first day I set eyes on you,' said Barney.

She reached up and kissed him. 'Don't say any more. Please.'

'But this diamond –' he said, spreading out his hands. 'Why didn't Kitty tell me as soon as I got back? Or Gentleman Jack?'

'They're servants,' said Mooi Klip. 'All they want to do is get through the day without problems. They don't want trouble. Even when it's not their fault, they know they might lose their jobs. So, they say nothing. Anyway – who are they to tell tales on Mr Joel Blitzboss, really? They're employed to do what they're told, that's all. And Mr Joel Blitzboss told them to keep their mouths shut. He probably even paid them, too.'

Barney paced across the kitchen, and them smacked his fist into the palm of his hand. 'It all makes sense now! Joel wanted to leave for Capetown on the first possible waggon. Gentleman Jack wanted to know all about the legal rights of ownership of diamonds. It all makes complete sense! They found a giant diamond, and Joel decided to keep it a secret!'

Mooi Klip watched Barney with cautious respect. 'You won't hurt him, will you, Barney?'

'Who, Joel? I'll break his back!'

'Barney – don't even think of it. That's not the way you are. Why do you think I still love you? I know that you honour your loyalties, that's why. I want Joel to lose that diamond, but I don't want you to hurt him.'

Barney looked at Mooi Klip, and then abruptly pulled over a chair, and sat down. 'I'm broken apart,' he told her. 'Lord God, I'm broken apart.'

Mooi Klip knelt on the floor beside him, and grasped his hands tightly. 'I know,' she said, gently. 'I know you're upset. But try to be strong. Remember I love you, and that Pieter loves you. Remember who you are.'

Barney looked at her wryly. 'I'm a tailor, that's all. Blitz, Tailors, of Clinton Street, New York.'

'No,' she said, 'not to me. To me, you're Barney Blitz, the grand diamond millionaire. And you're Barney Blitz, the gentle lover, too. Think of both of those things when you talk to Joel. Remember that you're both of them; the strong and the sensitive. Then you won't think of hurting him. Only *pitying* him, for everything he's done.'

The kitchen door opened suddenly, and Gentleman Jack walked in. When he saw Barney and Mooi Klip together, he hesistated for a moment; and when Kitty flashed him a quick and cautionary look, he retreated towards the pantry.

'Jack,' said Barney, without looking around.

'Yessir, Mr Blitzboss?' said Jack, freezing in alarm, like a partygoer caught in a game of 'statues'.

'Jack, a funny thing has happened.'

'What's that, Mr Blitzboss?'

'Well,' said Barney, sitting up straight in his chair, but still keeping his head turned away from Gentleman Jack, 'it turns out that somebody has found a diamond on my property – a quite considerable diamond.'

'Mr Blitzboss?'

'You don't have to act stupid, Jack, You can save that for the Kimberley Dramatic Society. I understand that they're sorely in need of a black individual for their Christmas production of *Robinson Crusoe*.'

Gentleman Jack said nothing, but stood up sheepish and straight, and placed his hat on the draining-board.

'I'm not the kind of man who likes to punish people for innocent mistakes, Jack,' Barney continued. 'I believe that everybody's entitled to an error or two. I make them myself.' (And here Mooi Klip squeezed his hand.) 'But when it comes to stealing, that's different; and all I can say about people who steal is that they're breaking the eighth commandment which was given to Moses by the Lord Our God.'

'Yes, sir,' said Gentleman Jack, tentatively.

'So – when it turns out that somebody has found a diamond on my property – a quite considerable diamond – and when I haven't yet had any sight of that diamond, regardless of the fact that I've been back here at Vogel Vlei for more than a day or two – well, I can only assume that whoever found that diamond is hiding it from me.'

'I'd say that, yes, sir,' said Gentleman Jack.

'I didn't ask for your comments, or what you'd say,' said Barney, coldly. 'All I'm asking you to do is to pass it on to whoever is hiding my diamond from me that I intend to search this house from attic to basement, even if it means tearing up the floorboards, and that I'm going to unearth that diamond no matter what.'

'I don't know who took it, sir, I promise,' said Gentleman Jack.

Barney suddenly turned around and stared at him. 'I know you've been paid to keep your mouth shut, Jack, and I know that you're worried about your job. But let me tell you this: I have enough evidence to implicate you in the disappearance of this diamond, and if you don't co-operate by flushing it out for me, than I'm going to pass you over to the soldiers and have you hanged from a camelthorn tree, frock coat or not.'

Gentleman Jack reached for his hat, and smirked in terror. 'Whatever you say, boss.'

'That's right,' said Barney. 'Whatever I say.'

There was a frigid pause, and then Gentleman Jack tugged open the kitchen door, and rushed out.

When he was gone, Mooi Klip stood up, and kissed Barney's forehead. 'I have to be going, too.'

'At night?'

'I'm staying with some Griqua people in Kimberley, then I'm going back to Klipdrift tomorrow.'

'I'll come up to see you soon. I promise.'

'Don't make promises, Barney. Just think about the love we used to have, and the child we gave birth to, and that will be enough.'

'Natalia, don't go.'

'I have to, Barney.'

'Don't. Stay with me here, tonight.'

She shook her head. 'Our stars may have said that we should have been happy together; my almanac says that we should. But stars aren't everything. Time is more important, isn't it, and circumstance.'

'You've learned some long words.'

'Mr Ransome taught me. He said, "It's a question of circumstance."'

'Yes,' said Barney, reaching out for Mooi Klip's hand. 'I guess that Mr Ransome is right.'

Mooi Klip kissed him again, with great tenderness. '*Ek het jou lief*, Barney, *wat ookal gebeur*.'

Joel was almost asleep when there was a furtive scrabbling at the door of his bedroom. He opened one eye, and listened. The room was filled with a warm and dusky radiance as the sun set over the veld, and there was a noisy chorus of birds outside on the trees. The scrabbling was repeated, and then a stage whisper said, 'Mr Blitzboss, it's me, Jack. You have to open the door, Mt Blitzboss.'

'Jack?' said Joel. 'What in hell do you want? I'm trying to sleep.'

'I'm sorry, Mr Blitzboss; but it's urgent.'

'Come in, then, it isn't locked.'

Gentleman Jack opened the door, and stepped into the room in one long-legged stride, quickly closing the door behind him. 'Mr Blitzboss, we have absolute problems now.'

'What problems? Pass me that glass of water, will you?'

Jack handed over the water, and then stood beside Joel's bed flustered and fidgety while Joel drank. When he was finished, Joel handed him the empty glass.

'Now, what's so urgent that you have to wake me up?' Joel wanted to know.

'It's the diamond, Mr Blitzboss. Mr Barney's found out.'

'Found out what? What are you talking about? He's found out that someone discovered it, or that we've got it?'

'He's found out everything, sir. He knows when it was picked up, and how much it weighs, and he knows that you probably have it hidden, sir.'

384

Joel pulled himself upright in bed. 'Who told him? Who the devil told him? Was it you? I'll cut your worthless black ears off, if it was you!'

'Not me, sir. That Griqua girl Natalia Marneweck. She was here this afternoon, sir, talking to Mr Barney.'

'Of course, damn,' breathed Joel. 'She's a cousin of Kitty's, isn't she? Or something like that. That damned Natalia. What was she doing here anyway? Didn't she know that Barney was married?'

'I don't know, sir.'

'Well, she probably did,' said Joel. 'That's probably made Barney seem all the more attractive. She was always one of those snooty *schwarzehs* who only want what they can't get.'

Joel swung off the bed, reached for his stick, and then walked across to the ugly rosewood bureau at the side of his room. He fished a small brass key out of his vest pocket, and opened the second drawer down. Inside, wrapped in a blue silk scarf, lay the huge 350-carat diamond. Gentleman Jack looked at it nervously.

'Mr Barney said he was going to search the house, sir. Top to bottom. Rip up the floorboards, he said.'

Joel picked up the diamond and clutched it tightly in his hand. He had held it like this over and over again in the past few days, since Gentleman Jack had brought it from the mine. Sometimes, when the pain in his hips and legs had kept him awake nights, he had sat in his straight-backed armchair by the window with the diamond cupped in both hands, feeling with a kind of silent passion the way it absorbed his warmth. It was *his* diamond, and nobody else could have it. Nobody else could understand the mysterious grandeur of its incredible size, or the glittering dreams that were secretly crystallised within its depths. Joel had kissed it, and licked it, and held it against his heart. He had even caressed his penis with it, his eyes closed, his mind aroused with fantasies of riches and beautiful women.

'We're going to have to say that Kitty was lying,' said Joel.

'Lying, sir? But what would she lie for?'

'Just to get her own back, that's what for. She never liked me. We're going to have to say that she heard rumours about someone in Kimberley digging up a giant diamond, and that she thought she'd get me into trouble by saying it was me. We're going to have to deny everything – deny it completely.'

'But what if Mr Barney searches the house, Mr Blitzboss? That's a big diamond, difficult to hide.'

'There are plenty of places where he'd never find it, Jack. I could bury it in the garden.'

'They're hoeing the garden right now, Mr Blitzboss. Someone would see you; or maybe they'd even dig it up. And, anyway – how are you going to be sure that you can recover it in time to take it to Capetown with you? Mr Barney's going to be absolutely suspicious, sir, especially when you leave. You're going to have to be careful he doesn't insist on searching your luggage.'

'He doesn't have any right to search me, or my luggage.'

Gentleman Jack said warningly, 'I don't think Mr Barney's going to be too concerned about that, sir. He knows there's a fancy diamond around, sir, and he knows that it rightly belongs to him, and this time I don't think you're going to be able to put him off.'

'A *choleria* on him.'

'Sir,' said Gentleman Jack, 'you have to do something, sir. Maybe you should hand the diamond over, and say it was all a mistake. If Mr Barney finds that diamond hidden, sir, he's going to have me hung.'

'Don't be ridiculous. My brother doesn't have the guts to hang anybody.'

'Please,' persisted Gentleman Jack. 'I have people who depend on me, sir. And even if Mr Barney doesn't have me hung, sir, or flogged, I'll never be able to find good work again, sir.'

'You should have thought about that when you were so insistent about getting your share of the tainted proceeds,' Joel retorted. 'You make me sick, you mission-school niggers, you really do. It takes more than a white collar and a tailored grey coat to turn a four-legged animal into a man. I should know, I used to be a tailor myself. So you speak like a white man, and know your letters, and believe in Jesus Christ? I could train a dog to do the same, Jack, and at least a dog wouldn't come whining back to be sick on my rug, the way that you have, just because the meat got a little too rich for it.'

386

He held up the gleaming diamond in front of Gentleman Jack's wide-eyed face.

'Jack,' he said, 'this is *my* diamond. That's all I'm going to say. And if you breathe one word to Mr Barney about where it is, or where it's going, or if you even so much as admit that it *exists*, then God help me I'm going to murder you, and I mean it.'

Gentleman Jack gave an involuntary shiver. 'Mr Blitzboss,' he began, 'I really wish you'd –'

Joel whipped the diamond away, and clenched it in his fist, close to his chest. 'Don't say anything,' he warned. 'Don't appeal to my better nature, because until I've got this diamond out of Kimberley and safely on its way to Capetown, I can't afford to have one. Now, get out of here.'

Gentleman Jack backed away to the door. He opened it an inch or two, peered through to make sure that nobody was about, and then slipped away on tip-toe. Joel closed the door behind him, and turned the key.

The trouble was, Gentleman Jack was right. He could not hide the diamond inside the house, because no matter how clever he was, there was always a chance that Barney might actually find it; and if Barney found it, and took it away from him, Joel was not at all sure if he was going to be able to survive, physically or emotionally. The diamond promised endless luxury for the rest of his life; all the drugs he needed; all the comfort he craved; and freedom from Barney for ever. To lose it now would be unbearable. He might just as well blow his brains out and have done with it.

He sat down in his armchair and held the diamond up in front of him. A new life, made out of fused carbon. Fiery and vivid and endlessly tantalising, like a glimpse of the future seen through an elaborate arrangement of rainbow prisms.

He could not swallow it, like the kaffirs swallowed roughs out on the claims. It it did not choke him, or lodge permanently in his stomach, he would excrete it out within a day, and he would have to keep on swallowing it, again and again, until next Thursday, just before he left for Capetown. The very thought of it made him gag. He opened his mouth wide and tried to get the diamond inside, but it was impossible. It wedged against his teeth, and he knew that it would never go down his throat, not without suffocating him, or tearing his larynx to shreds.

He could push it up inside his anus, he supposed, but that was another kaffir hiding-place that was too well known, and if Barney was really convinced that he was concealing it somewhere, Joel did not doubt that he would try a forcible body search.

Joel stood up, and went to the mirror. He stared at his reflection as if he expected it to tell him what to do. But what ideas could anyone give him – let alone this tired, pain-racked man in the shadowy room beyond his bureau? He was alone, as long as he wanted to keep this diamond for himself. Friendless, loveless, and running from both his brother and the law. He stared at his unsmiling image and wondered what it was that had brought him here, to this final fatal collision of temperament and greed.

The answer was probably his mother, whose problems were long since over but he could not think about her any more. There comes a time in everybody's life when resentment finally crumbles and flakes away. A sort of forgiveness by default.

Downstairs, Joel could hear voices, and clattering footsteps across the hall. Barney must be starting his search already, turning the house upside-down in a bustle of righteous possessiveness. God, that he should have been born into such a family. God, that he should have been born at all.

He looked towards the half-open bathroom door, and then a thought occurred to him. He remembered an evening about two years ago, when Barney had invited Harold Feinberg around to the bungalow for dinner, and the stories that Harold had afterwards told about the lurid histories of several famous Indian diamonds. One of the stories had concerned the discovery of the Regent diamond, a huge 410-carat rough, in the Parteal Mine on the Kistna River, in 1701. It had been picked up by a slave, who had smuggled it out of the mine, and had then made his way to the coast, where he had tried to buy his passage out of India by offering half the value of the stone to a British sea-captain.

It did not matter that the slave had been murdered by the sea-captain and his body flung overboard. What did matter was the way in which the slave had smuggled the diamond out of

388

the Parteal Mine. He had inflicted a deep wound in his own leg, and tucked the diamond into his flesh.

Joel turned back to the mirror, and his reflection turned to meet him. He had a limp already, from his bone-setting, so if he limped a little more, who would notice? especially if he said that his leg was playing him up. He always wore his left leg strapped in bandages, so a few more bandages would not attract any undue attention.

My God, if he carried the diamond in his leg, then he could openly challenge Barney to search him all over, up his backside, anywhere he felt like it. You can even degrade yourself by combing through my shit, little brother. You won't find what you're looking for.

He stood quite still for a moment, drumming his fingers on the rosewood veneer of the bureau. Then, taking his stick, he limped into the bathroom, where his cut-throat razor lay neatly on the shelf under the looking-glass, next to his shaving-brush. He picked the razor up, and opened it. He would have to strop the blade until it was sharper than ever, and sterilise it by passing it through a flame. He would have to have bandages ready, and a towel for the blood, and plenty of whiskey. He took a shallow breath, and made his way back into the bedroom.

Outside his door, he could hear Michael and some of the other kaffirs running up and down the stairs, and Barney's voice ordering them loudly to search the attic. Barney must have guessed that the diamond was in here, in Joel's room, but he had to go through this whole showy performance just to frighten Joel into handing the diamond over voluntarily. That would be the ultimate humiliation for Joel: to have stolen the chance of a wealthy future, and to be obliged to surrender it like a small boy who had misbehaved himself.

'Whiskey,' Joel whispered to himself. He went across to his night-cabinet, and took out a full bottle of Scotch. He wrenched out the cork, and swallowed three or four mouthfulls straight from the neck. Then he set the bottle carefully upright, and began to unbutton his trousers.

His preparations were careful and over-elaborate. This was partly because he refused to be rushed by the melodramatic searching noises that Barney was making all over the house; and partly because he was afraid of what he was going to have to do. But, after ten minutes or so, he was sitting on the end of the bed, with his china washbasin on the floor beneath his leg, and his trousers off, all prepared to begin his operation.

He suddenly realised that he had left the diamond on top of the bureau, and he had to hop over and get it. Once he had dug a hole out of his leg large enough to take it, he probably would not have the strength or the inclination to hobble around the room looking for it. He took another large swig of straight whiskey, and decided he was ready.

There was a crisp knock at the door.

'Who is it?' he asked, his razor poised above the white hairy skin of his left thigh.

'It's Barney.'

'Go away, I'm tired. I'm trying to sleep. Go and annoy your wife for a change, instead of me.'

'I want to talk to you.'

'Well, you can't. We've said enough already.'

'This isn't about that argument we had earlier. That's forgotten. This is about something different.'

Joel paused. Then he said, 'Whatever it is, it can wait. I'm tired, and I'm drunk, and I don't want to talk about anything.'

'It won't take more than a minute or two, I promise.'

Joel looked down at the huge rough diamond lying on the bed. His hand, still holding the razor poised a quarter of an inch above the skin of his thigh, began to tremble. 'We can talk about it later. Right now, I'm not in a very amenable mood. Now, go away.'

He could hear Barney shuffling outside the door, and he closed his eyes in utter tension. Make him go away, O Lord, Make him go away.

Eventually, though, Barney said, 'All right. I'll come back in an hour or two, when you've slept off that whiskey. But I'm going to talk to you then, Joel, I promise you, even if I have to break your door down to do it.'

'I always told you that you were too violent,' said Joel.

Barney did not answer, but stayed outside the door for a moment before walking off down the landing, to the head of the stairs. 'By the way,' he called, in a challenging voice, 'we're having an early supper tonight, so we'll expect you down at seven.'

Joel did not answer, but waited until he heard Barney go down the stairs, and start talking to the kaffirs who were milling around in the hallway. It sounded like a circus down there, all shouting and whistling and shuffling feet. Joel smiled wryly, and cut into his thigh with the razor before he had fully realised what he doing.

The razor was very sharp, so it sliced through the muscle and the fat without any trouble. It hardly hurt, but what made him shudder was the way the blade seemed to stick to his flesh, as if it wanted to carry on cutting him, all the way up; and the way the muscle of his thigh opened up like a bleeding and expressionless mouth. He laid the razor with trembling fingers on one of his hand-towels, pressed a handkerchief against his thigh to stem the bleeding, and quickly reached for his bottle of whiskey.

'Oh, my God,' he said to himself, trying not to look down at his leg. Then he guzzled at the bottle until his stomach burned with liquor.

Gradually, he lifted the handkerchief away to see if the wound was deep enough to lodge the diamond inside. There was so much blood that it was difficult to say; so he was obliged to press the diamond against his sliced-open skin, and force it into the raw flesh as far as it would go. He bit his lips in anguish as he saw that only about a third of the diamond could actually be concealed inside his first incision. He would have to cut deeper.

His next cut was shaky and uncontrolled, and he had to take the razor away and take five or six steadying breaths before he could bring himself to continue.

'You've started it,' he told himself, angrily, 'you might as well finish it. You hear me? You're going to have a scar anyway, so you might as well make it a useful scar.'

Watching his own hand with horrified fascination, as if it belonged to somebody else, Joel saw the razor cut right into the wound until the tip of it touched his bare bone. Then the razor sliced quickly from side to side, cutting out pale and blood-stained pieces of muscle, until there was a huge and massively bloody hole.

He dropped the razor on the floor. He was juddering and shaking now, like a man in the throes of a fit. Blood was running down his leg in uncontrollable streams, and into the china washbasin. He bundled up one of the hand-towels into a large padded bandage, and held it on top of the wound as hard as he could. It suddenly occurred to him that he was going to bleed to death, and that Barney would break the door down in an hour or so to find him lying on the floor as white as a *kosher* calf, and the diamond on the end of the bed.

Pursing his mouth in pain, he grasped the whiskey bottle again, and swallowed a large mouthful. The rest of it he was going to use to clean out the wound. He lifted away the soaking red towel, and splashed scotch all over his thigh, letting it run right into the blood.

That was the only time he actually cried out loud. He felt as if his leg was actually alight, as if the bone itself were burning. But within a minute or two, the pain had died down to a deep, excruciating numbness and he was able to open his eyes and look around him and realise that only a very short time had elapsed since Barney had come knocking at his door, and that nobody would be suspicious about what he was doing, not yet.

Now he picked up the diamond, rubbed it all over in whiskey to clean it, and pushed in into his raw flesh. It created a lumpy bulge in his leg, but he tightly wrapped a hand-towel around it, and then bound the wound together with bandages.

He sat for more than ten minutes without moving, trying to cope with the shock of what he had done to himself, and with the extraordinary sensation of having the huge diamond buried in his thigh. He thought for a while that he was going to go mad; that he might have gone mad already. But gradually his hysteria subsided, and he was able slowly to gather up the bloody towels and the basin, and clean the blade of his razor.

Unsteadily, cursing as he went, he lurched into the bathroom and replaced the basin on top of the marble-topped toilet stand, and dumped the towels into the tub. He caught sight of his face in the bathroom mirror, and it seemed no different than before:

no greyer, no more agonised, but no less ridiculous, either. He ran the taps so that he could rinse the blood out of the towels before they were too badly stained. He could always tell the servants that he had suffered a severe nose-bleed. He drank so much that he had them regularly.

Then he dragged his throbbing leg back into the bedroom, to take another bottle of scotch out of his night-stand, and drink almost a third of it without taking a breath. Half of it came gushing back up out of his nostrils.

Downstairs, he could hear laughter, as the servants searched through the coats and boots in the hall-cupboard. To think that there was still something in this world worth laughing about. To think that there was still something in this world worth living for. He jumped and shuffled across to his wardrobe, and opened it. He would have to dress himself for supper tonight: he did not want any of the servants to see the bloody bandages on his thigh. He wondered if he had the courage to be able to sit through the entire meal with the diamond buried in his leg, eating soup and game and sweet puddings, and pretending to listen to Sara's inane conversation about the gels she had known in Durban. He wondered if he were going to be sick.

The bedroom began to tilt sideways, and he had to sit down abruptly to stop himself from falling.

When Sara came down for supper, she looked like a European princess. She wore a dress of pale cobalt-blue silk, and her dark hair was tied up with three strings of Indian Ocean pearls. Her bodice was cut surprisingly low, so that her breasts were bared right to the pink tinge at the edge of her nipples, and an emerald and diamond cross rested in her cleavage as if to suggest that here was buried treasure. Her perfume was rich and intoxicating, civet-oils and vetiver and verdigris, and her lips were painted red.

Barney, in his tailcoat and black tie, put down his drink and stood up as she came into the drawing-room, and held out his arms. She came across to him willingly, and kissed him.

'You look beautiful tonight,' he told her, with undisguised admiration.

'Don't I always look beautiful?'

'Of course you do. But especially beautiful tonight.'

She kissed him again, and then raised a blue-gloved hand to wipe the lip-colour away from his cheek. 'I wanted to dress up for you. I think it's the only way I can think of to tell you that I'm sorry.'

'You don't have to be sorry. If anybody should apologise, it's me. I behaved like a gorilla.'

Sara sat down on the sofa and spread out her gown. The edges were embroidered with silk braid, in a slightly darker blue, and dozens of seedpearls, stitched on like flowers. Her feet were bare, which Barney found unexpectedly provocative.

'I think I expected too much from you,' she said. 'I certainly expected too much from Kimberley. It was rather a shock for a girl like me to find that there was no formal social life, except among a very few people from the London exploration companies; and that there was hardly anybody whom one might ask for five o'clock tea.'

'There will be, sooner than you think,' said Barney, with his back to the fluted marble fireplace. 'Harold Feinberg says that the town is going to grow as big and as sophisticated as London's West End, in a year or two. They you'll have a social life that anybody in Durban can envy.'

'I'm sure you're right,' Sara smiled. 'But whatever happens, I always want to be your adoring wife. I'm sorry for all our silly arguments, and Nareez has asked me to say that she's sorry, too, She knows that I've been afraid. This is rather a wild place, after all! And she's only been trying to protect me. She's protected me all her life.'

Barney took Sara's hand, and pressed it against his cheek. He looked her straight in the eyes, and the oppression that he had been feeling ever since he had talked to Mooi Klip began to lift. Perhaps Sara was going to turn out to be a happy choice for a wife after all. Perhaps all these wrangles had been caused by nothing more than home-sickness and belated wedding-night nerves.

'We might retire after supper,' Sara suggested, blushing slightly. Barney leaned over and kissed her, first her forehead, then her cheeks, then her lips.

'I shan't have any lip-colour left,' she whispered.

'Can you think of a better way of losing it?'

Just then, their new manservant Horace came in, wearing ill-fitting knee breeches and a draped brown riding-coat. He offered them sweet sherry from a silver tray, and then retreated from the room backwards on squeaking boots.

'I think Horace has heard about royalty,' said Sara. 'He always bows whenever he sees me, and he never turns his back on me, ever. It's rather quaint, isn't it? But I hate to disillusion him.'

They drank a silent toast to each other, and Barney said a *broche* in his mind for Sara's beauty, and also for her new warmth. It was going to take months of difficulty and pain for him to forget all about the love he felt for Mooi Klip, but if Sara was going to be as gentle and as alluring as this, he was going to find it far less harrowing.

'There's been an awful fuss in the house tonight,' remarked Sara. 'I asked Nareez what was going on, but she said she didn't know, not exactly. She said she thought it was some kind of a *search*, though. I couldn't think what on earth we could have lost that could have set off such a disturbance.'

'Ah,' said Barney, running his hand through his curly hair, 'that's rather a long story.'

'Well, I'd love to hear it, especially since it's turning my own house on its roof.'

Barney could not think why he felt reluctant to tell Sara all about it; but somehow he did not quite trust her enough. There was no particular reason why she should not know. In fact, she had every right to. But he found himself hesitating and hedging, and telling her almost nothing.

'The truth is, 'he said,' that I've lost something valuable. At least, I *hope* it's been lost, and that it hasn't been stolen. But I've organised a search for it, as openly as possible, in the hope that if anybody's hiding it, they'll feel constrained to hand it back; or, if it's really lost, and not stolen, that it will soon be turned up.'

Sara looked around the room as if she were appealing to an equally baffled audience. 'Really, my darling, you should have been a colonial governor. I don't think I've heard anybody make such a long speech and say quite so little since Papa invited Sir Henry Barkly to dinner. To begin with, you haven't told me what this valuable thing is, or how you lost it, or whether it's worth stealing.'

'Well ...' said Barney, but at that very moment Joel appeared in the doorway, crisply dressed in a boiled white shirt and tailcoats, but frighteningly haggard. Barney felt his heart beat a slow bump as Joel stared at him, leaning heavily over his cane, obviously waiting for him to finish what he was saying.

'Don't let me interrupt you,' said Joel, hoarsely. 'I'm just as interested as Sara in what this valuable thing might be. After all, how can we help you look for it if we don't know what it is?'

'Well, quite right,' said Sara. 'You *do* seem to be playing games, my darling.'

'Have a drink,' Barney told Joel. 'You look as if you need one.'

Joel heaved himself awkwardly across the room towards the nearest armchair, and sat down. 'Thank you,' he grimaced. 'My leg's been giving me sheer hell today. The weather, I suppose. Down goes the mercury, and I'm done for.'

'Is it a letter?' asked Sara.

'Is what a letter?' frowned Barney.

'This lost or stolen thing! This valuable property that everybody's looking for! Letters are always valuable, aren't they, in love stories, especially when they're passionate, and incriminating.'

'Well, it's not a letter,' smiled Barney, giving Sara an amused nod of his head. 'I'm not very good at writing letters, either passionate or incriminating – or even readable, for that matter.'

'Is it a piece of jewellery, perhaps?' Sara proposed. 'A tiepin, or a pair of cuff-links?'

'Or a clip?' put in Joel, very softly. The English-Afrikaans pun was not lost on Barney, and he fixed his gaze on his brother very steadily.

'You're nearly right, Sara,' he said, in a flat voice. 'The truth is that it's a diamond. Not just an ordinary diamond, either. But a diamond of unusual size. A real monster, from what I hear.'

'But how exciting! Has someone stolen it?'

Barney gave Sara a wry smile. 'I don't know, to be honest.

I can't prove anything at all until I find it. It was supposed to have been dug up on one of my claims while I was away in Durban. But even though there's been a lot of rumour and gossip about it, nobody has yet admitted that it actually exists, and nobody has yet admitted that they have it ih their possession.'

'It's just another one of those kaffir yarns, I expect,' said Joel, with a smile that was more teeth and muscle than anything else. 'They're always making up stories like that, just to keep the white boss hustling and bustling around like a dog after his own tail. One of them told me that he knew where King Solomon's treasure was hidden. Fifty metres deep, he told me, through solid bedrock. I would have had him flogged to death, if I could have caught him.'

'But this is a diamond, Joel,' said Barney, suddenly serious. 'This is a giant-sized diamond, anything up to 400 carats, and it was supposed to have been found on our claim.'

Joel shook his head, and let out a dry laugh. 'When you were away in Durban, little brother, I was in charge here. And let me tell you something, my supervision of what goes on in this mine is always ten times as strict as yours. If they so much as spit on the ground, those kaffirs, they get cuffed; and if I ever caught any one of them stealing, then God help me I'd strangle him with my bare hands.'

'What you're trying to tell me is that you don't believe this monstrous diamond actually exists? You think it's all a story?'

Joel looked up at Barney keenly. 'It may exist, Barney, but if it does, I haven't seen it. Don't tell me you don't believe me – because what do you think I would have done if I *had* seen it? I would have turned it over to you, wouldn't I? as soon as you got back from Durban? I'm not a diamond thief, whatever else you care to call me. And I'm your brother, too.'

'I'm glad you said that,' Barney replied. 'Because while you're down here, your room is being searched. I've even told them to cut open your cakes of soap.'

Sara was shocked. She said, '*Barney*! I can scarcely believe it!'

'All right,' put in Barney, calmly, 'you can scarcely believe it. But I've heard enough about this mythical diamond today to think that it's worth looking for it; and the first place that I've been looking is inside this house. We're talking about a gemstone that could be worth more than a million pounds here, Sara; and when you start talking about a million pounds, I don't think you can talk about loyalty in the same breath. Family loyalty, servant loyalty, any kind of loyalty. Most people have their morals, sure; and most people have a sense of duty and honesty and good old shoulder-to-shoulder comradeship; but a million pounds is more than most people's honesty is worth. A million pounds is enough to convince most people that it's time to forget about their duty, and their friends, and even the people they love. A million pounds is even enough to persuade most people to forget about their God.'

There was a momentary silence. Joel made a painful face at Sara, and shrugged, as if to say that *he* might not believe me, but I know *you* do.

'Maybe you think I'm crazy,' said Barney. 'Maybe you think that it's just as wicked to suspect your own family of theft as it is for them to steal. Well, maybe you're right. But let me tell you this: when there's a million pounds at stake, I'm as greedy and determined as anyone else, particularly when I know that it's *my* million pounds, and that it's being taken from under my nose.'

'So, you're accusing me of taking a giant-sized diamond, are you?' asked Joel. 'You're accusing me of stealing the largest gemstone that anybody has ever dug up at Kimberley – in fact, one of the largest gemstones that has ever been heard of in the history of the whole world?'

'I didn't say that,' said Barney, in a level voice.

'You didn't have to,' Joel retorted. 'It's enough that you ordered your black monkeys to look through my room. And to cut up my *soap*? You're as mad as Mama.'

'What would you have done?' demanded Barney.

'If *I* had suspected *you* of stealing some fictitious diamond – and by God, Barney, I emphasise *fictitious* – I would at least have had the decency to *ask* you first. I mean, you'll make sure they look through my underwear, won't you? And through all of my personal possessions? My letters, and my pictures of Papa and Mama? You'll make sure that they desecrate what little dignity I have left?'

Barney set down his drink on the small inlaid wine-table beside him. 'I'm sorry, Joel,' he said, quietly. 'But that's always been the difference between you and me.'

'What has? What are you talking about?'

'I'm talking about bluster, that's what I'm talking about. Hot air. You've been appealing to my conscience ever since you could talk; and now you're always appealing to justice, and to God, and to the tides of fortune, and to whatever comes into your head. But you've never actually gotten anything done, have you? You never cultivated the farm at Derdeheuwel. You lost all your money at Klipdrift. You got yourself accused of stealing diamonds at Kimberley. It's no use appealing to the powers that be, Joel, because there's only one reason you're sitting in this drawing-room in evening-dress waiting for a well-cooked supper, and that reason is me.'

'Is that my cue to pack my bags and leave you?' asked Joel, whitefaced and fierce.

'No, it isn't,' said Barney, plainly. 'But it's certainly a cue for you to tell me whatever you know about this diamond, don't you think, and to stop playing ridiculous charades?'

'Charades!' shouted Joel, although his shout was strained and weak, and thick with phlegm. 'You're the one who's playing charades! You spring this story about a monster diamond on me, the very first time I've ever heard such a thing in my whole life, and then you immediately accuse me of having stolen it! It's madness! And then you accuse me of playing charades!'

Sara turned to Barney appealingly. 'Don't you think we ought to drop the subject, darling! I don't want a row just before supper.'

Barney continued to stare at Joel with an expression of deep distrust. 'I just want a straight answer, that's all. There *is* a diamond, I know it. Harold Feinberg told me; and so did one or two other people who ought to know what they're talking about. And if Joel doesn't know anything about it, then I can only say that his memory is proving as inconstant as his loyalty.'

At that moment, Michael came to the open doorway of the drawing-room and gave Barney a quick shake of his head.

'Aha,' said Joel, shifting himself in his chair to make himself more comfortable, 'I suppose that means I've been vindicated.'

'It means they didn't find the diamond in your room, that's all,' said Barney.

'*Diamond*,' mocked Joel, with a sharp laugh. 'If you ask me, Barney, you've been out here in Kimberley far too long. You're getting the fever.'

'There *is* a diamond,' insisted Barney. 'It weighs more than 350 carats, and I'll bet money that it's somewhere in this house.'

'Do you want to reveal the identity of your informant?' asked Joel, raising an eyebrow.

Barney glanced towards Sara. He had already been given enough trouble by Nareez over his continuing affection for Mooi Klip. If Joel provoked Sara's suspicions even more by telling her that Mooi Klip had been round to the house this evening, it would take more than a day or two to persuade Sara that his affair was all over, and that Mooi Klip had returned to Klipdrift for good, to marry a farmer, and rear chickens. Without taking his eyes off Joel, he said quietly, 'All right. Let's forget about diamonds for the rest of the evening. Let's talk about love instead.'

'Love!' sputtered Joel.

'I think it's a very good subject,' enthused Sara. 'Dryden said that love is the noblest frailty of the mind.'

'Yes,' said Joel, 'and Phineas Fletcher said that love is like linen. The more you change it, the sweeter it is.'

Sara did not know what to reply to that; and Barney was too furious with Joel to say anything; so when Horace walked solemnly into the very centre of the drawing-room and rang a little hand-held gong for supper, both of them were more than ready to go through.

'Can I take you in?' Joel asked Sara, heaving himself to his feet, and offering her his uptilted elbow. Sara looked back at Barney, to see what he thought about it, but Barney simply made a face that meant 'go ahead'.

Neither Barney nor Sara could have guessed at the agony that Joel went through, just to walk the length of the hallway to the dining-room. He did not falter once, or cry out; but by the time they reached the dining-room door his face was deep grey, like a victim of angina, and he was crowned with sweat. When he took his place between them at the dining-table, he appeared to be unable to speak, and he shuddered from time to time so violently that he displaced his knives and forks.

'Are you all right?' Barney asked him, gravely.

'What?' said Joel.

'I asked you if you were all right. You look like death.'

Joel opened his linen napkin with fingers as clenched as claws. 'Of course I'm all right. It's the weather, that's all. It gives me a little twinge, now and again.'

'Well, as long as you're sure,' said Barney. 'We don't mind excusing you from the table, if you'd rather have your supper upstairs.'

'Wouldn't that interrupt your searching?' asked Joel, acidly.

'Joel,' said Sara, in a gentle voice. 'You really mustn't take everything so much to heart.'

'Oh, no,' said Joel, with a jerky smile. 'I forgot.'

It was a light supper of liver pâté, toast, and roasted fowl. Horace crept solemnly around the table and poured them chilled Austrian hock, which had been a gift to Harold Feinberg from a diamond dealer in Vienna. Sara talked about Fanny Brewbaker, a débutante she had known in Durban, and how Fanny had attempted to elope with a chump called Watkins, and how she had finished up dangling from the branches of a sausage tree, instead of in Watkins' arms.

Joel forked his food listlessly from one side of his plate to the other, saying nothing at all, and eating scarcely anything. Barney looked at him once or twice expectantly, but he would not even raise his head. What Barney did not know was that the walk from the drawing-room to the dining-room had opened Joel's wound, and that Joel was bleeding thickly into his left sock.

Before the coffee, Joel stood up, dropped his napkin, and said, 'You'll have to excuse me. I've had a bad day.'

'Wouldn't you care for a brandy before you go up?' asked Sara. 'I'm sure that you and Barney could settle all your differences over a drink.'

Joel leaned against the table to support himself. 'Thank you,' he told her, 'you're very kind. But you know what brothers are. Arguing one minute; and the best of friends the next. I'm sure that Barney didn't mean what he said.'

'You look bad,' said Barney, 'you'd better go lie down.'

'It's nothing much,' Joel told him. 'Fatigue, I think, more than anything.'

Horace brought him his cane, and he made his way slowly to the dining-room door. 'I'm sorry you didn't find your imaginary diamond,' he said, without looking around. 'It would have been wonderful if it had been true.'

'Yes, wouldn't it,' said Barney, without any inflection in his voice at all.

'Goodnight, then,' said Joel, and painfully made his way upstairs.

'He seems very *ill*,' remarked Sara, when he had gone.

Barney peeled himself an orange. 'I think it's the morphia, and the whiskey. He's going to kill himself unless he's careful.'

'He's not a bad man, you know, underneath.'

'I never said that he was.'

'No, I know you didn't,' said Sara, 'but you give him such a difficult time sometimes. He's very much gentler than you, you know. If you ask me, he'd be better off as a painter, or perhaps a musician. He doesn't have the head for all this diamond-digging and all this business. He thinks he ought to, just because *you* have. But he doesn't, at all; and I wonder if that's what makes him so unhappy.'

Barney chewed orange, and carefully spat out the pips into his hand, practising that social legerdemain that he had seen in Capetown and Durban. 'What makes Joel unhappy is his inability to face up to his own shortcomings. He lives in a world of utter fantasy – a world in which he thinks that he's rich, and successful, and unfailingly attractive to women. The simple truth is that he's not, and that he's never done anything to make him that way. He's not capable of it.'

'But you still love him, don't you?' said Sara, reaching out her hand across the damask tablecloth, and touching Barney's wrist. 'I wouldn't want you to fall out with him.'

'I don't know,' Barney told her. 'I used to believe that he and I would always be together, and always love each other, no matter what. Now, with this diamond business –'

'You really believe that there *is* a diamond, and that Joel has it?'

Barney nodded.

'Can I ask you how you found out?'

Barney looked at Sara for a moment, and then reached for some grapes. 'One of the blackies told me. That's all.'

'And you believe the word of a blackie against the word of your own brother?'

Barney did not answer that question, but continued to pluck grapes from the stem which he held in his hand, and eat them as methodically as if he were saying a silent rhyme to himself – she loves me, she loves me not, she loves me, she loves me not.

That night, when he climbed into bed, Sara was naked except for a small lace bodice, and she held out her arms for him almost immediately. He kissed her, and her mouth pressed as hungrily against his lips as if she were devouring a pomegranate. Her sharp-nailed fingers ran down the length of his spine, and around her bottom, and at last cupped his balls with threatening delicacy, caressing them most of the time with infinite care, but now and then squeezing them tightly, which made him gasp.

She opened her thighs for him without question, and guided him towards her parted lips. He felt as if the inside of his head were crackling with electricity, like one of those windy frightening mornings on the Drakensberg. Her desire for him was so unexpected and so aggressive that he was aroused more than at any time he could ever remember in his whole life. To be attacked in bed by a slut was one thing; to be savaged by a girl who was proper enough never to say 'mantelpiece' and to consider that name-cards at a dinner-table were rather 'low' was quite another. She gasped his name over and over again, until he shivered, and reached a climax of three distinct and intensive ejaculations. Yet she wanted more; and as he rolled over on to his back, she rolled on top of him, and gripped him with sticky hands, and whispered words in his ear which even an Australian digger might have coughed at.

'Barney,' she cooed, 'we must be the most marvellous lovers that ever were.'

Barney said nothing. He was too intoxicated by her eager submissiveness and her lewd whispers. It seemed like a dream in which even the most buried of all erotic desires had suddenly become possible. He turned her on to her stomach on the bed, and she raised her bottom urgently towards him, her thighs stretched as wide apart as she could. Barney pushed himself into her, gripping the soft flesh of her hips, until he could push no deeper. He felt extraordinary, dreaming, praying, or drunk.

He did not hear the door open one single inch. Nor did he see Sara, her dark hair spread wildly over the pillow, her face flushed, turn her head towards the doorway and stare with eyes that were incongruously calm and thoughtful at her Indian *amah* Nareez, who stood in the darkness of the hallway like one of the ancient and mystical Rakshasas, the night-stalkers.

Sara lay awake until dawn, listening to Barney breathing and murmuring in his sleep. She felt ashamed of herself, in one way for her lustful lovemaking; but in another way she felt far more settled, and more decided about the course which her life was now going to have to follow. She was sure, particularly now that the tensions of her body had been spent, that she did not really love Barney at all, not in the way in which her mother had loved her father, or in which she believed a woman ought to adore and respect her spouse.

Barney had attracted Sara right from the very first day she had met him. He had a beautiful slow masculinity about him which she still found disturbing. She had often watched his profile in the gilded evening sun and been unable to take her eyes away. But he did not understand her at all, nor did he have any real grasp of what was important to her, and why. Because of that, he plainly saw her abrupt changes of mood as unpredictable and unsettling swings in her character, whereas in truth everything that Sara did and said conformed to the great logic of the British colonial daughter.

It was not Barney's fault. He didn't have any experience at all of the ordered and ritualistic society of the English Abroad. He was an American, and a Jew, and so he was doubly handicapped in his comprehension of God, Queen and Country; of the Raj-like protocol of what to wear, and how to behave, and where to be, at what particular season; of the extraordinary complexities of visiting, and why it was so desperately embarrassing actually to come face to face with the person at whose house you were leaving your visiting-card.

Barney would never know what a *burra mem* was (a phrase that Sara's mother, a true *burra mem*, had fondly borrowed from India); and he would never be able to penetrate the mind of a girl who had been brought up in a world of clubs and polo and flannel underwear and formal picnics, a world of native servants and annual gymkhanas; a world where the rivalry between the Collector's wife and the Colonel's wife could have a whole city quivering for weeks; and where a man who was forgetful enough to put on a solar topee after sundown was generally considered to be guilty of ghastly bad form.

Sara had been swept away by Barney's dramatic proposal, and impressed by his wealth. She had felt passionate about him, too, and still did, although not so completely. After all, it was not only protocol and charm that characterised upper-class English ladies in the colonies, it was also that fierce Hot Weather carnality which had led one old hand to describe their lives as a perfect circle of tea-parties, durbas, picnics, and adultery. In one way, it was only the strictness of their self-imposed etiquette which kept their isolated and outdated world from collapsing into a stew of drunkenness, moral breakdowns, and despair. It was not done to take a drink before the sun went down, nor to continue to drink after dinner. Neither was it done to fornicate so brazenly that anyone (especially one's husband) actually knew. Conforming rigidly to what was done saved many of the Empire's finest ladies from coming catastrophically undone.

But out here in Kimberley, none of this mannered society in which Sara had been raised existed at all, moral or immoral; and although she had believed at first that she could survive without it, she had quickly discovered that she could not, and it was a severe handicap to the possible success of their marriage that Barney was unable even to imagine what it was that she missed.

But – Sara had decided – she was not going to mope over it. The greatest quality of the *burra mem*, apart from her exact social tone and her overwhelming feminine instincts, was her resilience under Trying Conditions. She would do her best to be a good wife to Barney; she would love him whenever she felt she could; she would seek his body when she needed it. But she could never lose sight of her ambition to be socially glittering, the belle of South Africa, and she would take whatever opportunities to achieve her ambition that offered themselves to her.

She began to feel inside, still half-developed, a capability for ruthlessness that would have given Barney nightmares, had he guessed that it was there. This was the only child that she would bear him.

Joel stayed in his bedroom throughout *Shabbes*, and through most of Sunday. He kept the door locked and asked only for a little chicken broth to be left outside on the landing. Barney went upstairs to speak to him two or three times, but until late on Sunday Joel refused to let him in.

When he finally did open the door, Barney found that the room was gloomy, with all the drapes drawn tight, and that there was an unpleasant smell around, as if Joel had not been washing. Joel was wearing his dark blue bathrobe, and sitting in his upright armchair, reading a book about country houses in New York State and Long Island.

'Are you all right?' Barney asked him. 'Do you want me to open the window?'

Joel shrugged, as if to say that he did not mind one way or the other. Barney drew back one of the drapes, and pushed open the window that overlooked the back of the house. A cool flow of fresh air flowed into the room, and ruffled an untidy sheaf of paper that had been strewn across Joel's desk. Barney picked one of the papers up and saw that it was covered in sketches of a large imposing house, with a pillared portico and formal gardens.

'Are you thinking up more ideas for laying out Vogel Vlei?' he asked. 'I'm glad that you're interested.'

Joel said nothing, but leaned forward to pluck the paper out of Barney's hand, and tuck it down the side of his armchair. Barney stared at him for a minute or so, and then sat on the end of the bed with his hands clasped in front of him, the way a parent addresses himself to a schoolboy who has just been caught behind the orangery, doing something embarrassing.

'Joel,' he said, 'I believe you found a diamond, and I also believe that you still have it hidden someplace.'

'You do, hunh?' said Joel, turning the page of his book.

'Joel – listen, we're fifty-fifty partners in this diamond-mining business, aren't we? If you *have* found a diamond, and it's really worth a million pounds, then you'll still get five hundred thousand. You're going to turn up your nose at five hundred thousand?'

Joel closed his book, and looked back at Barney challengingly. 'What diamond?' he demanded.

'The diamond that Harold told me about, and that Mooi Klip told me about, and that Gentleman Jack is too damned frightened to tell me about. You know damned *well* what diamond!'

'Did you find such a diamond, when you searched the house? Under the floorboards, maybe? In the soap? Why don't you look up my ass, and see if I'm hiding it there?'

'If I don't find it by the time you leave for Capetown, I intend to. And don't think I'm joking.'

'God forbid I should ever think you're joking, Barney. God forbid! Trying to get humour out of you is like cupping a corpse.'

Barney stood up. 'I want that diamond, Joel. That's all I'm going to say.'

'Diamond, diamond, diamond! You're driving me mad with your *tsutcheppenish* about this diamond!'

Resignedly, Barney left Joel's bedroom, closing the door behind him with quiet emphasis. Click. That's it. If that's the way you want it. Then he went quickly downstairs and called Michael to make the carriage ready: he was going to Kimberley to talk to Harold.

Harold was sitting on the verandah of his bungalow, rocking backwards and forwards in a cane rocker, and dozing. His French assistant, slim-wristed and pretty in a Parisian way, with plaited hair and unplucked eyebrows, was embroidering a cushion, and she called out to Barney as he stepped down from his carriage, '*Bonjour*, Monsieur Bleats!'

'This is unexpected,' said Harold, waving Barney towards a

small wicker armchair. 'What brings you *chez* Feinberg on a day like this? Would you care for a drink? Or a cup of tea? How about a *latke*?'

'I've come to pick those brains of yours,' Barney told him, crossing his legs to reveal his loud yellow and red Shetland socks. 'You know that huge diamond we were talking about the other day?'

'Yes?' asked Harold, suspiciously.

'Well, just supposing it was real, okay? And just supposing that a fellow was trying to smuggle it out of Kimberley, and off to the coast. And just supposing this fellow was under pretty close scrutiny, so he couldn't simply carry it in his pocket, or hidden in his luggage. Now, what do you think he might do?'

Harold rocked backwards and forwards and thought about the matter carefully. Then he said, 'First of all, there are plenty of traditional hiding-places which you could rule out straight away, because of the sheer size of this stone. It's as big as that, right – as big as the gap between a finger and a thumb, and that's *big*. So you couldn't swallow it, and you couldn't hide it in your hair. You might be able to tape it under your armpit, but of course that would lay you open to immediate discovery, if you were stripped. The Mogul emperor Mohammed Shah hid the Koh-i-Noor for fifty-eight days in the folds of his turban after he was conquered by the Persian shah Nadir, in 1739. But a harem girl gave Mohammed's secret away; and the next time Nadir invited him to a feast, Nadir insisted that they observe the age-old custom of exchanging turbans. Mohammed couldn't refuse, could he? So Nadir rushed back to his tent, and unwound the turban, and there it was. "It's a mountain of light," he said, and that's what they've called it ever since. "Koh-i-noor."'

'That's all very interesting,' said Barney, 'but nobody in Kimberley wears a turban. Nobody that I know of.'

'I'm going through all the hiding-places I can think of,' protested Harold. 'You want hiding-places, I'll tell you hiding-places.'

'All right, go on. Where else do you think someone could hide a diamond?'

'Well, when it passed to the Afghan princes, the Koh-i-noor

was hidden for *years* in the plaster of Shah Zaman's cell wall, when he was imprisoned and blinded by his brother Shuja.'

'That's a possibility – buried in a plaster wall.'

'It could be,' said Harold, 'except that this fellow you're asking about, he's trying to get it out of Kimberley, right, to sell it? He's not really interested in hiding it away for a year or two.'

'That's right,' nodded Barney.

'The Regent diamond, which Marie Antoinette used to wear in a black velvet hat, *that* was hidden in a hole in a beam in somebody's garret, after it was taken from the treasury during the French Revolution. Have you tried beams?'

'I've taken up floorboards.'

'Well, try beams. Try anything that you can dig a hole in. A mattress, perhaps; or a pillow.'

The French girl came up, and said, 'Would you like some tea, Monsieur Bleats? I will make some, if you like.'

'I'd like that,' said Barney.

Harold said, 'Remember the story I told you about the way the Regent was first discovered, and how it was smuggled out of the Parteal Mine?'

Barney's attention had been briefly distracted by a tall Hottentot girl passing with a clay pot balanced on top of her head, and a baby hanging between her breasts in a loose scarf. 'What did you say?' he asked Harold. 'The Parteal Mine?'

'That's right. A slave came across the Regent diamond on the Kistna River, and cut a hole in his leg so that he could smuggle it out without being detected. A little extreme, wasn't it? But a slave like that would have a lot to gain and nothing to lose.'

'I remember you telling us about that,' nodded Barney. 'I remember Joel remarking that a man would have to be mad to do a thing like that.'

Barney was about to say something else, but then he paused, thinking. Joel had heard that story, too; and if Joel had been thinking of ways to smuggle the diamond out of Kimberley, wouldn't that story have crossed his mind? Joel limped already, from his old fractures. Supposing he wanted the diamond so much that he was prepared to –

That would account for his sudden worsening on Friday night, wouldn't it? And the way in which he had kept himself locked away in his room for the past twenty-four hours? And if he had actually mimicked that poor desperate slave at Parteal – if he had actually dug a hole in his leg that was deep enough to accommodate a 350-carat diamond, wouldn't that also account for the strange stench in his room – the stench of dried-out blood and infected bandages?

'*Riboyne Shel O'lem*,' he said, under his breath.

'What did you say?' asked Harold.

'Nothing. But I have a terrible feeling that I know where I can find that diamond.'

Barney sat staring into space while the French girl brought tea. The cups were Minton, gold and green, and the tea was purest Darjeeling. Harold's fortunes were improving these days, and he was thinking of opening another office at Bultfontein. He did badly want an heir, though: and perhaps that was why he was being so attentive to this girl whom Edward Nork called 'Harry's little froggy'.

'If you do find the diamond,' said Harold, carefully, 'why don't you come and tell me first. We don't want to upset the market, do we? It wouldn't be good for anyone, least of all you. I'm too old and too sick to take another downturn in world prices. I want to leave something behind me, a thriving business. Feinberg and Son.'

'Or Daughter,' suggested Barney.

'If that's what God wills. But, excuse me.'

While Harold went inside to the lavatory, Barney talked for a while to his 'froggy'. Her name was Annette, he learned, and she had been educated in music in Paris, but when she was only sixteen she had run away and lived with an extraordinary eccentric in Navarre, the man who had first fired her interest in precious stones. He had taken her on a voyage to Capetown; but halfway there he had suddenly and for no accountable reason thrown himself overboard. She had been left in Capetown with hardly any money, and nothing but a small talent for playing the piccolo. In despair, she had taken a job as a maid; but later she had found employment as an assistant for a large Capetown diamond dealer, and she had made it her business to learn whatever she could about diamonds.

'Do you think that you and Harold will ever have children?' Barney asked her. 'It means a lot to him, you know, having someone to pass his business down to.'

The girl slowly shook her head. 'I know Harold wants children, but a child would kill me. Maybe not really kill, but destroy my liberty. I will never have children, you can be sure of that.'

Barney shrugged. No girl that he had ever come across had been quite so sure that she would not conceive, although he knew that Dr Tuter had a reputation for providing cheap, ir erratic, abortions.

'Each month, I push diamonds into *ma matrice*,' whispered the girl. 'Five gemstones, one carat each. They are enough to keep me from conceiving.'

Barney opened his mouth to answer her, but at that moment Harold reappeared with his shirt tail protruding from his unbuttoned trousers. He sat down with a smile, and picked up his cup of tea. 'Let's drink a toast in good Indian tea,' he said. 'Let's wish you wealth and happiness, and let's look forward to the day when I can invite you to a circumcision.'

The French girl looked at Barney and smiled; and Barney knew for Harold's sake that he would never give her secret away. He doubted, quite honestly, whether the practice of pushing diamonds into her womb would have any effect on her ability to conceive. Diamonds had always been attributed with the oddest of medicinal properties: the Hindus had crushed them up and drunk them, to give them strength, while the czar Ivan the Terrible had been quite sure that they were deadly poison. All Barney knew was that Harold's heart was unsteady, and that if he found out that he was being deceived, the unhappiness of it could kill him.

'What are you going to do about this monster diamond?' asked Harold, when they had finished their tea.

'Right now, nothing,' said Barney. 'If I'm right about it – if it really is where I think it is – then I believe that it will make itself known soon enough.'

'You sound peculiarly vengeful,' said Harold, laying his hand on the French girl's arm with proprietorial absent-mindedness.

Barney gave him a tight smile. 'Tell me about Ascher and

Mendel, in Antwerp,' he asked him. 'Do you think they'd be up to cutting a 350-carat diamond?'

By six o'clock on Wednesday evening, Vogel Vlei was all decorated and lit for the Blitz's first party. Twenty hired kaffirs lined the driveway with smoky torches to guide the carriages around to the front of the house, and Michael stood at the door in a footman's costume which Barney had borrowed from the Kimberley Dramatic Society. Inside the hallway, all the lamps were lit, and the floor had been polished until it seemed as if the guests were walking through to the drawing-room on the utterly still meniscus of a lake. There were black waiters with wide white grins and white gloves, and a string quintet of five doleful Boers whom Barney had first met in his kopje-walloping days in Dutoitspan. There was champagne, and South African wine, and there were more handsome women that Kimberley had ever seen together in one place at one time, at least since the French whorehouse had opened on Kopje Street. The talk was of diamonds, and of last year's British annexation of the bankrupt state of Transvaal, and of Cetewayo, the Zulu king. The accents were English, Dutch, Afrikaans, and Australian, and the laughter was very loud: it was not often that Kimberley saw such a grand occasion, and most of the less illustrious guests were effervescent with delight that they had been invited at all.

There were some conspicuous absentees: gentlemen and ladies whom Sara had particularly invited, and who had courteously but firmly declined. Sara had only been here a week, and she was not yet aware that the 'billiards-room chaps' of the Kimberley Club did not accept social invitations from Jews, or coloureds, or anyone else whose accent and background weren't quite up to the expected mark, don't-chi-know. She was not yet aware that Barney was not actually a member of the club, nor that it was only her own stainless social grace that had led most of her middle-class English guests to accept her invitation and shake out their old-fashioned tailcoats for the sake of one of the Chosen.

There were some eminent guests, though – mostly diamond

dealers. Cecil Rhodes had come over, and before the buffet dinner he stood stiff and wavy-haired in one corner of the fireplace, tugging intermittently at his starched white cuffs and trying to make silly conversation with a tiny woman in a fringed dress whose laughter would have peeled a Jerusalem artichoke at ten feet. Barney knew how uncomfortable Rhodes felt with women – he had seen him in their earlier days together, escorting girls around the reverberating wooden floor of the Kimberley Dance Palace, his back straight and his chin held so high that he looked as if he were composing a patriotic sonnet as he danced, or thinking about diving off a cliff. Rhodes had always chosen the plainest women to dance with, and once he had fulfilled the duties on his card he had always rushed immediately home.

Alfred Beit was there, dark and shy, casting an expert financier's eye over Barney's house and possessions. Sir Joseph Robinson, now Mayor of Kimberley, put in a brief and disagreeable appearance just after eight, because he obviously felt it was his civic duty to drink three glasses of Barney's champagne and eat five of his smoked antelope canapés and not talk to anyone, except to grunt, and blow crumbs off his straggling moustache. Francis Baring Gould had almost turned down his invitation, but changed his mind at the last moment, and arrived with a saucy young Dutch girl who was not his wife. Edward Nork was there, making a considerable effort not to drink too much champagne too early, in the company of the brightest new star at the dramatic society, a soft-faced young girl called Fanny Bees. Harold Feinberg came, proudly escorting his French girl.

Sara was delighted. This was not quite Durban; but then Durban was not quite Capetown; and Capetown was not quite London. It was far more glittery and social than she had expected, though, and she went bright-eyed from guest to guest, as tall and elegant as a swan in her white satin dress, trimmed with white feathers, and she received their compliments and their congratulations with joy. Barney watched her, smiling, and nodded his head to Edward Nork to point out how happy she was.

By eight-thirty, there was still no sign of Joel, even when the

413

guests went through to the buffet. Joel had emerged from his room from time to time during the past two days, but he had been thinner and sicker and less steady on his feet than Barney had ever seen him – even when he had been recovering from Sir Thomas Sutter's surgery in Durban. He spoke as if his mouth were always dry, and his eyes appeared to roam around the room in search of something that he might have forgotten. He had shaved only once in three days, and there was a sickly odour about him which made even Nareez wrinkle up her nose as he passed.

Barney knew what was wrong; or at least he had a pretty good idea. And he had throught seriously about ending Joel's agony by telling him what he suspected. But Joel's destiny was his own. Joel had decided to live his life this particular way, and he had come to this self-imposed Purgatory of his own free will. Over the years, he had hurt Barney too often and too cruelly for Barney to want to relieve his suffering now.

Barney had no intention of remitting his pain.

Gentleman Jack had seen how calm Barney had suddenly become, and how he had stopped searching for the diamond, and Barney's calmness frightened him so much that since Sunday he had made any excuse to avoid him, particularly when Barney made his regular morning visit to the diamond mine. Barney said nothing: he would decide how to punish Gentleman Jack when the diamond at last came to light.

During the buffet, Harold Feinberg came over and said, 'I believe this is the best party I've ever been to. And what a charming hostess Sara has turned out to be.'

'Thank you, Harold,' said Barney, taking a chicken roll from the table, and popping it into his mouth. 'I'm delighted that so many people came. Even if they did come out of curiosity, and nothing else.'

'You've, er – you've found the diamond yet?' asked Harold, glancing around to make sure that nobody could overhear them.

'I have some ideas,' Barney told him, offhandedly, with a smile that was deliberately vague.

'What ideas? You mean you know where it is?'

'I think so.'

'So what are you going to do?' asked Harold. 'Barney, listen, this is important.'

'Of course it's important,' said Barney.

Just then, through the open double doors of the dining-room, at the turn of the staircase, Barney saw the tip of Joel's cane, and then Joel's feet, in shiny black kid evening shoes. Step by step, Joel made his way down to the hallway, and Barney watched him with detached pity and with sharp regret; but not with sadness. What Joel was suffering now was entirely his own fault.

Harold said, 'This could turn the whole industry on its back. You know that, don't you? And it won't help you, either, when you're trying to buy up so many claims, all around you. The price will shoot up like a skyrocket.'

Barney did not once take his eyes off Joel, as his brother made painful progress through the hall and into the dining-room. Harold turned around once or twice to try to discover what Barney was looking at; but it did not occur to him that Barney was reserving all of his concentration for his own brother.

Joel looked like a corpse which at the very last minute had refused to be buried, and which had heaved itself out of the casket, and back to the banquet. His whole body appeared to have dislocated itself, and he dragged himself along by means of a complicated ritual with his cane, which involved shifts of grip and tilts of balance. He was only thirty-four, but he could have been a man of seventy.

'You'll promise to tell me, won't you,' said Harold. 'You won't go off half-cock and take the diamond straight to Cape-town?'

'Harold, I'll *tell* you,' Barney soothed him. 'Now go back to the party and enjoy yourself. You worry too much about things that haven't even happened yet.'

As Harold left, Sara came over and took Barney's arm, and kissed him. 'It's wonderful,' she said. 'Everybody's so kind. I don't know why Kimberley alarmed me so much, when I first came here.'

'It's a hard place,' said Barney. 'But the people here are only people, that's all.'

415

'I met that *nice* Mrs Forsyth,' Sara enthused. 'She was telling me about the monthly ladies' evening they have up at the Kimberley Club. I'd love you to take me to one! I'm sure I could outshine all of them!'

'Maybe next month,' said Barney.

'But you must! If we're going to live here, we must socialise. Particularly now that you're going to be a millionaire!'

Barney took his eyes off Joel for a moment, and stared at Sara in bewilderment. 'Who said I was going to be a millionaire? I'm nothing like a millionaire! I only wish that I was.'

Sara looked flustered; like someone who has made a scene with a stranger in a restaurant in the belief that the stranger was trying to walk off with their coat, and then discovered that it was not their coat, after all – that it had a different label, and unfamiliar gloves in the pocket, and that it even *smelled* like somebody else's. 'The diamond will make you a millionaire, won't it? That's what you said it was worth.'

'Sara, I don't *have* any diamond. If it exists, it's still hidden. You know that as well as I do.'

'But you know where it is. Or don't you?'

'Who *told* you that I know where it is?'

'Nareez. She was talking to that kaffir called Gentleman Jack.'

Barney slowly turned back to keep an eye on Joel. Joel was leaning against one of the buffet tables now, with a small private *kraal* of champagne glasses, downing drink after drink in steady succession, and muttering to himself.

'What else did Nareez tell you?' Barney asked Sara.

'Nothing. She just said that Gentleman Jack was worried, because you'd stopped searching for the diamond; and if you'd stopped searching for it, you must have discovered where it is.'

'Quite an efficient spy you have, in Nareez.'

'It's not spying, in my own house! How can it be? You should have told me yourself!'

'Yes,' said Barney, 'maybe I should.'

'Of course you should! You're so secretive, and then you wonder why I behave so defensively. It will be wonderful if you're a millionaire! Think of all the horses we'll be able to buy! We'll be able to travel to Capetown, and to London, and we'll be able to dress ourselves in all the latest fashions!'

'Sara,' Barney told her, patiently, 'even if we do find the diamond, and even if we do sell it for anything like a million pounds, it's going to take months for the money to come through; and then I'll probably invest the larger part of it in more diamond claims.'

'Of course you won't,' Sara teased him. 'Don't you have enough diamond claims as it is?'

'I want to own the whole of the Kimberley Mine personally,' Barney replied, in a flat voice. 'That's all I'm interested in.'

'That's a fine thing to say to your wife at your wedding celebration party.'

Barney took her hand, and squeezed it. 'Come on, you know I didn't mean it like that. I'm just a little preoccupied this evening, that's all.'

'With fond memories of Natalia Marneweck, I suppose?'

'Of course not! What the hell is that supposed to mean?'

Sara's expression went through as many changes as the drawings in a children's flicker-book. 'You *do* have fond memories of her, don't you?'

'Why shouldn't I? Any less than you have fond memories of Trevor, or of any other gentleman friends you've known?'

'At least I don't continue to meet my gentlemen friends in secret, in the servants' quarters of my new husband's house.'

'What are you saying?' Barney demanded, trying to keep his voice down. He was still holding Sara's hand, but now he was clutching it so tight that she wrestled to get it free.

'I'm saying nothing, except what is true. Nareez happened to go to the kitchen to bring me warm milk, when she saw you talking to Natalia Marneweck. She heard everything you said, and she told me that it sounded most affectionate.'

Barney looked at Sara for a long time, the muscles around his mouth bunched as if he were considering hitting her, or walking out. But then he said quietly, 'Why didn't you tell me before, that you knew?'

'I suppose I was afraid to. In any case, Nareez said that if you were going to be a millionaire, I should be careful. I should be nice to you, and try to make you forget Natalia.'

'Are you really that naïve? Or is this some kind of ridiculous prank? Whatever I felt about Natalia, I'm married to you; and, believe it or not, I want our marriage to be happy. That's all I can say about it. I didn't want to tell you about Natalia coming here because I thought it would only upset you. Nothing happened – except she went back to Klipdrift to marry some farmer. *Adonai El Rachum Ve-Chanum*, did Nareez really listen in to all that? So you knew about the diamond right from the beginning? And you thought I was going to be a millionaire? And that's why you –'

Sara blushed fiercely, and at last succeeded in tugging her hand away.

'Sara?' whispered Barney, intensely. 'Is that why you turned so passionate? Is that it? Because Nareez told you to make me forget about Natalia, in case you lost your share of my million pounds?'

'Don't,' pleaded Sara, mortified.

'Don't *what*? Don't try to get the truth out of you? Are you trying to tell me that all of your passion is faked? That you've been prostituting yourself for this diamond?'

'I'm your wife,' hissed Sara. 'How can you possibly dare to call me such a thing?'

Barney stood with his arms by his sides and looked at Sara with a feeling inside him like dropping off a mountain. 'I suppose I can call you such things because they appear to be true.'

'You're such a stickler for truth, aren't you? You're so noble, and so right, and so compassionate. The trouble with you, my deah, is that your compassion is like a curse. You're so indomitably strong that you crush everybody around you, without understanding your own strength. Did you ever think for a moment, my love, what your ambition *does* to people? You want to own the whole of the Kimberley Mine, and the terrible thing about it is that you will. Nareez understands what you're like, and she was trying very hard to save me from being crushed underneath your charity, and your sense of duty, and the guilt you feel because you married me. But why feel guilty? We probably don't love each othah; but nor do *thousands* of married couples, any more than we do. I'm just as responsible for what happened as you are. You excited me, the way you came to claim me. I'd just lost a fiancé, and I was bored to tears with living at home. I rushed into the wedding as eagerly as you did. Perhaps I've been cold to you sometimes, and unpleasant. Perhaps I've been stiff. Well, I'm that kind of a girl, I suppose, although not always. I've got a fractured life-line, that's the trouble. One day I feel that I'm fond of you, other days you get on my nerves so much that I can scarcely bring myself to speak to you. But, for God's sake, Barneh – don't pity me, and don't blame yourself, and don't try to make everything all right. If you do that, you'll bury me alive, the same way that you've buried your brother alive, and the same way that you've buried Natalia Marneweck alive. You don't realise what a powerful man you are, Barney – not for one second. You're like a landslide – a high-principled landslide that won't be diverted because of its conscience and its responsibilities and its un-wavering, impossible ambition.'

Barney opened his mouth and then closed it again without saying anything. He still felt as if he were dropping off that mountain, suspended weightless in empty space for that long vertiginous moment before the ground below begins to expand like a rapidly-rising load and suddenly slams into you.

'This isn't the place to talk like this,' he told Sara, at last.

'I know,' she agreed. 'But it had to be said.'

He nodded, distraught, off-balance.

'Do you think we can –?' He couldn't find the words. He said instead, 'I'm sorry.'

'No sorrow,' warned Sara. 'Now, I'm going to circulate. I feel rather shaky, as a matter of fact. I need some light conversation to settle me down.'

'Just answer me one question,' said Barney, taking her hand again, but gently this time. 'Were you really so afraid that I'd make a million, and that you wouldn't get a share of it? Afraid enough to –'

Sara thought for a moment, and then gave an ambiguous nod that did not quite seem to mean that she *had* been afraid; but that being afraid was the nearest way she could think of to describe it.

'Then why –' Barney began, but at that moment there was a high-pitched scream, and a smashing of dishes, and a chiming of fallen tureen-covers, and Joel rolled over on to the floor with a ten-foot linen tablecloth wrapped around him, bringing down apples and plums and knives and forks and half-sliced hams. A yellow Gouda cheese rolled across the dining-room and disappeared behind the velvet drapes as if somebody had sent it off on an errand.

'He collapsed!' cried Fanny Bees, the actress, who had been standing close by. 'He swayed like a tree, and then he simply collapsed!'

The quintet music died away in a straggle of discordant notes as Barney knelt down beside Joel and tugged away his necktie. Joel was blue around the mouth, but still breathing, and his left hand kept twitching and trembling from the muscular effort of leaning on his stick. He opened his eyes for a moment and peered at Barney like a man straining to see down a well.

Barney looked up at the gathered guests. 'Somebody help me carry him through to the drawing-room. We can lie him down on the couch.'

'Don't touch me,' breathed Joel. 'Whatever you do, don't touch me.'

'Joel,' insisted Barney, 'we can't leave you lying here.'

'Don't you think you've hurt me enough already, you *putz*?'

Barney untwisted the tablecloth and wrenched it from underneath Joel's back. 'Just keep your filthy language to yourself,' he said, his voice shaking with anger and emotion. He felt as if he could punch Joel and embrace him, both at the same time. God, what he must have suffered, to bring him to this!

A stocky red-haired diamond-buyer called Nathan Golden squatted down on his haunches and offered, 'All right, Barney. I'll take his arms.'

'Don't you lay one finger on me,' cautioned Joel.

Barney reached down and grasped Joel's ankles. 'You can say whatever you like, Joel – you can't stay here on the dining-room floor, surrounded by fruit. You're sick, and we're going to carry you through to the drawing-room. Now – you got him, Nathan?'

Nathan forced his thick-fingered hands under Joel's armpits, and half-hoisted him off the floor. 'Barney!' shouted Joel. Then, in a screech that paralysed everybody in the whole dining-room, and sent cold prickles dancing all over Barney's back, '*Barney! For the love of God! Barney!*'

Wide-eyed, terrified, the veins bulging on his forehead, Nathan Golden stared at Barney in mute alarm. Barney looked down, and Joel's face had the appearance of a rubber carnival mask that had been pulled mercilessly inside-out. Joel was in such agony that he could not speak any more, could not do anything at all but lie on the floor and pray that Nathan and Barney would not try to pick him up again.

Barney said to Nathan, 'Put him down, gently.' Then, to Sara, 'Bring me some cushions, will you, to prop up his head – and, Horace, go find me some sharp scissors from the kitchen, quickly, and some towels.'

Sara brought two or three silk-xovered cushions and lifted Joel's head on to them carefully. Joel was almost unconscious now, and saliva was running from the corner of his mouth. Every now and then, though, his whole body would jerk with a muscular spasm, and his eyes would flicker open and stare at Barney with that strange inhuman neutrality that you only ever see in the eyes of the nearly-dying or the just-born.

Horace came at a bow-legged run, and handed Barney the scissors they used for clipping chickens' wings and parcel-string. The party guests stood in utter silence as Barney took hold of the cuff of Joel's left trouser-leg, and sliced it all the way up to the crotch. Some of the ladies turned away, but most of them stayed where they were, fascinated by the sight of Joel's circumcised penis, and by a sense of impending horror. These were not Capetown ladies.

The fabric of Joel's trouser-leg was already stuck to his thigh by a crust of blood and dried lymph. When Barney tried cautiously to pull it away, Joel crammed his hand into his mouth and uttered a single gargling sound. He kept his hand between his teeth: he obviously understood that there was worse to come. Barney picked up one of the towels that Horace had brought from the kitchen, and tucked it under Joel's thigh before trying to peel the trousers back any further. Then he said to Nathan Golden, 'Whiskey. Bring me a whole bottle of whiskey.'

Everybody waited like a collection of well-dressed tailors'

dummies while Nathan went over to the liquor cabinet on squeaky shoes and came back with a bottle of scotch. Barney said, 'Pour it down his throat. Get him as drunk as you can,' and Nathan hesitantly held the neck of the bottle to Joel's lips. Barney snapped, 'I want him *drunk*, for God's sake, not merry,' and reached over to press the bottle roughly against Joel's teeth, tipping it upright so that the liquor gushed down Joel's throat, and all over his shirt front. Joel coughed, and made a loud retching noise, but he managed to keep most of the whiskey down.

Then, with a single unhesitating tug, Barney pulled away Joel's trouser-leg, along with a makeshift bandage made of torn linen, and revealed his wound. There was a cry of '*Oh!*' throughout the whole room, and almost all of the remaining ladies retreated from the dining-room with their faces as white as the walls. One or two of the men stepped back, too, particularly when the stench of gangrene rose from Joel's leg, and they saw the hideous extent of what Joel had done to himself.

Halfway up Joel's thigh, there was a moist and gaping wound, swollen, tinged with green, and clustered with watery blisters. The wound was weeping effusively, and the smell of rot was almost more than Barney could stand. Out of the wound protruded the pointed corner of what looked like a large fragment of glass.

With the points of the scissors, Barney touched the edges of the wound and the piece of glass. Surprisingly, Joel scarcely flinched. The flesh that formed the fishlike lips of his self-inflicted incision was dead, and the pain that he felt came mostly from the reddened area further around, where the gangrene was just beginning to attack.

Barney had suspected for days what Joel had done, but the reality of it shocked him so much that he found himself unable to speak, or to do anything but lay down the scissors on the towel, and kneel in front of Joel with his head bowed and his eyes closed.

Rhodes said, 'I'll send a boy to bring Dr Tuter.'

Barney raised his eyes. 'Thanks. I don't think I can handle this on my own.'

'Is that what I think it is?' asked Rhodes, nodding towards the wound.

'You've heard the rumours, too,' said Barney.

'They make jokes about the bush-telegraph,' Rhodes said, 'but if you keep your ear to the ground you can get to know almost everything. My kaffirs have been all of a-twitter for weeks about a giant diamond that was found on the Jewfella's claim at Kimberley.'

'It seems like the Jewfella was just about the last person to know,' said Barney.

'That scarcely matters,' smiled Rhodes. 'He who laughs last, don't you know. And there it is, it's all yours, if you care to dig it out.'

'Joel is my brother,' said Barney.

'Haven't you heard Harold's wonderful stories about brothers who blinded other brothers and locked them away for the rest of their miserable lives, simply for the sake of diamonds?'

Barney nodded. 'I guess I have.'

'Well, there you are,' said Rhodes. 'There in front of you is the living proof of what men will do for the sake of a large lump of crystallised carbon. Not only to each other, but to themselves.'

Barney knelt in silence for a minute or two, with Rhodes watching him with the very slightest smile on his face – the kind of smile that would have had him caned for smirking, if he were still a schoolboy. Then Barney picked up the scissors again, gripped Joel's leg just below the knee to steady it, and slowly inserted the points in between the lump of glass and the bleb-smothered edge of Joel's skin. Joel was practically unconscious now, and as Barney thrust deeper into the soft, dead flesh, Joel did nothing but whistle softly between partly-closed teeth.

At last, the huge stone dropped out on to the towel. Barney took his handkerchief out of his breast pocket, and disgustedly wrapped it up. Rhodes gave a small grunt that could have been amusement, or irony, or simply relief that it was all over.

Barney stood up. Dr Tuter was walking unsteadily through the doorway, led by the sleeve by a small barefoot Hottentot boy. Dr Tuter blinked at Barney as if he did not quite recognise him.

Over in the corner, Sara was standing with her hands clasped in tension, her face set like plaster. Not far away, in an emerald green sari, stood Nareez. Barney held the handkerchief up, not in triumph but in that ordinary human gesture that means, here it is, I've found it.

Rhodes said, 'Well done,' with unexpected smugness, and pushed his way back through the crowd of guests with his hands in his pockets, to rejoin Alfred Beit, and to help himself to more champagne.

Mr Ransome was sweeping his small back yard when Mooi Klip walked up to his fence in a wide summer bonnet, a basket of okra and purple kale under her arm, and stood watching him in the dusty, dappled sunlight. He propped his broom against the wall, and wiped the sweat from his forehead with the back of his arm. 'Natalia! It's good to see you.'

Mooi Klip smiled. 'I've been meaning to come to talk to you for days,' she said.

Mr Ransome opened the gate, and ushered her in. 'I try to keep the place tidy, but there are so many other things to do, so many souls still to be converted. Mind you, I think we're going to find it easier to bring all of South Africa into the Christian fold when the new Governor has done his stuff.'

'I didn't even know there was a new Governor,' said Mooi Klip. 'That just shows how ignorant I am.'

'There isn't any particular reason why you should have known,' Mr Ransome replied. 'But do come in and have some tea. I had some excellent Keemun sent up from the Cape.'

He led her across the overgrown verandah of his bungalow, under a tangle of creepers and bougainvillaea, and in through the open door to his modest sitting-room, which had been furnished strictly according to a Church of England budget. There was a clutter of dark, cheap chairs, and a mock-Jacobean sofa with sagging cushions. Twine-bound bundles of missionary Bibles and hymn books were stacked up untidily against the side of the bureau, which itself was surmounted by a tea-stained doily, a wooden cross, and a tin of Huntley & Palmers' Albany biscuits.

The only personal touch in the whole room was a water-colour of a redbrick suburban street, planted with trees. 'That's a view of my home,' said Mr Ransome. 'My mother painted it when she was recovering from the scarlatina.'

Mooi Klip laid down her basket, and sat on the sofa. The sun lined her profile in light, and poured two careful measures of shadow into the hollows of her collarbone. Mr Ransome looked at her with his hands slightly raised as if he had been going to say something emphatic, but had completely forgotten what it was.

'I've come about Coen,' said Mooi Klip.

'You want to fix a day, I suppose?' asked Mr Ransome. 'Well, let me get my diary, and let me put on the kettle. I gave Elretha the day off to visit her cousin. Very family-minded, Elretha. A good Christian.'

'I've decided not to marry Coen,' said Mooi Klip.

Mr Ransome stared at her. 'You've decided *not* to marry him? But, my dear Natalia, why? Has something gone terribly wrong?'

She looked up, and gave Mr Ransome a small, brave smile. 'We decided it together. He's a good man, and he's gentle like a lamb, but he's not for me. Barney did so much to bring me out, to show me what I could make of myself. If I married Coen, I'd be nothing but a farmer's wife; and I'd probably never speak English again for the rest of my life, except to you.'

Mr Ransome sat down next to Mooi Klip and took her hand. 'My dear, there is no *shame* in being a farmer's wife. It is one of the holiest of occupations, farming. It says in Proverbs that "he who tilleth his land shall be satisfied with bread: but he, or in this case she, who followeth vain persons is void of understanding."'

Mooi Klip turned and frowned at him. 'I'm not sure that I know what that means,' she said.

Mr Ransome's face, inspired by his recitation from the Bible, gradually subsided, until he was frowning too. 'I'm not sure that I do, either.' He stood up. 'I'd better make some tea. You'll feel – calmer – after some tea.'

'I'm calm now,' she said.

'Well, excellent,' said Mr Ransome. 'But what are you going to do? Have you thought about that? Here you are with a six-year-old son, unmarried, and having to depend entirely on your parents. Surely the life you are living now is even more imprisoning then being a farmer's wife would have been: and it will grow even more burdensome to you when your parents grow old.'

Mooi Klip said nothing, but brushed out her flowery skirt with her hands.

'I don't usually say this to young women,' Mr Ransome went on, in a more cautious tone. 'You see – the official line is that it is most desirable for at least one daughter to remain at home, unmarried, to care for the parents in their dotage. That is what the bishop approves of. But, in your case, I think things are different.'

'Why should they be?' asked Mooi Klip.

'My dear girl, they are different because *you* are different. You are a Griqua, a living symbol of this country's oneness under God, the mixing of the black and the white races. Did you know that one of the very first Christian marriages ever solemnised at the Cape in the seventeenth century was between a Hottentot woman and a white employee of the Dutch East India Company? You are an inheritor of that wonderful tradition, the acceptability of one race to another. And apart from that, you are beautiful; and for you to let your beauty wither away unseen in your parents' house for the rest of your life would be a criminal waste of God's bounty.'

'I'm still not sure what you're trying to say,' said Mooi Klip, gently.

Mr Ransome clapped his hand to the back of his neck in exasperation, as if he were swatting a mosquito. 'I'm trying to say, Natalia – I'm trying to say that you are a most exceptional young lady. I'm trying to explain to you that you ought to be married. Your son needs a father, after all. And you need to express, in the fullest proportion, your beautiful and intelligent womanhood.'

He stopped, and licked his lips. 'I hope I haven't embarrassed you.'

Mooi Klip shook her head. 'I'm not embarrassed by compliments. I'm very pleased for them. But why are you so angry? I've never seen you like this, not even when you're preaching. You don't have to be angry about me. I can find a way to live my life happily, you know that.'

'I'm angry because you've been so badly treated,' said Mr Ransome. 'It seems to me that your Barney didn't know a good thing when he saw one. To give you a child like that, and to throw you on the rubbish heap!'

Mooi Klip looked aside. 'Mr Ransome,' she said, 'that kind of sad affair happens all the time. It hurt me. It *still* hurts me, after all these years. Perhaps it wouldn't if I didn't have Pieter to remind me. But we can't cry over spilled milk. We can't be angry just because a man has done to a woman what men have been doing to women since Adam and Eve.'

Mr Ransome lowered his head, and when he spoke his words were very indistinct. 'It's never happened before to somebody I love.'

The small sitting-room was silent. Outside the open door, the leaves on the creepers rustled in a breeze that was as gentle as a secret whisper. The bar of sunlight which had been illuminating the crucifix on the bureau gradually crept across to the tin of Albany biscuits.

Mr Ransome looked up. Mooi Klip was gazing at him in the pose of a dark-skinned madonna. Her bonnet formed a halo.

'The new governor's name is Sir Bartle Frere,' said Mr Ransome, abruptly, loudly, in a violent change of subject. 'He's an old India hand, the bishop tells me. They've given him the job of gathering together all these ill-assorted colonies and native kingdoms and individual Boer states, and forming a single dominion, subject to the British Crown. And to British religion, of course.'

'What did you say?' asked Mooi Klip.

'I said, "subject to British religion, of course," ' Mr Ransome stammered, stepping backwards and stumbling over a heap of Bibles, scattering them all over the floor.

'No, before that. Before you started telling me about the new governor.'

'I didn't say anything. Did you hear me say something?'

'Mr Ransome, you're a man of God. You shouldn't tell tales.'

Mr Ransome hiked up his cassock, and got down on his hands and knees to pick up the Bibles. 'I said something out of turn, that's all. I promised my mother years and years ago, when I first entered the church, that I would abstain, that I would keep myself pure, and so what I might have said was quite improper of me, and I would prefer it if you would kindly forget I ever opened my mouth. My mouth was given to me in order that I should sing the praises of the Lord: not for making indecent proposals.'

'You said you loved me,' persisted Mooi Klip.

'Then I was quite out of order. Please forgive me.' Mr Ransome had disappeared behind the sofa now, and all Mooi Klip could see were his black worn-out shoes and his black laddered socks.

'Mr Ransome –' said Mooi Klip. 'Do you have to ask forgiveness for loving someone? Didn't you always tell me that love is the mainstay of the Christian religion?'

Mr Ransome scuffled and snuffled for a moment, and then emerged from behind the sofa red-eyed, with tears sliding down each cheek.

'Mr Ransome, what on earth is the matter?' asked Mooi Klip, reaching her hands out for him. 'Why are you crying?'

'I'm crying because I'm unhappy,' he said. 'I'm sorry, it's quite ridiculous. I shouldn't have said anything at all, and then none of this would have happened. You won't tell anyone, though, will you? If it gets back to the bishop ... I mean, they chose me for Klipdrift because of my self-avowed celibacy. They thought it was advisable to send out somebody chaste ... as a sort of example.'

Mooi Klip smiled. 'An example of what? Of an unhappy man? Of a man who believes in marriage but doesn't practise it?'

Mr Ransome stood up, and poked around under his cassock to find a handkerchief. He blew his nose, and wiped his eyes, and then he said, 'I'm sorry. I can't tell you how sorry I am.'

'Stop telling me you're sorry. I was fond of you long before I met Coen Boonzaier. I liked you the day you first came to

Klipdrift. You always seemed like a breath of the outside world. We can be friends, can't we?'

Mr Ransome cleared his throat. 'Of course. Yes. I mean, we always were, weren't we?' He put the Bibles back against the bureau, and came around to sit down beside Mooi Klip, leaning forward, with his knee clasped in his hands. 'I'm surprised to hear you thought so well of me.'

'Why? You're good-looking. You know all kinds of interesting things. I always thought that if you hadn't been a priest, you would have made a perfect husband.'

'Natalia . . . you really mustn't speak this way. I'm – well, I'm susceptible.'

'I don't know that word.'

'It means that you affect me, in a physical manner.'

Mooi Klip stared at him seriously. She was so feminine and soft and pretty that Mr Ransome could hardly bear to look at the way her chest rose and fell as she breathed. He knew this was all absurd. He was being tempted by the flesh. But the trouble was that Mooi Klip was so direct and innocent in the way she spoke to him, so frank in the profession of her affection, that he found it impossible to believe that what he was feeling was the work of Satan. He closed his eyes, but all he could think of was that moment when he had seen the dark shade of Mooi Klip's nipple through her gauzy blouse; and of the native women he had seen by the Vaal River, their big breasts bare and their Hottentot bottoms protruding through the brightly-coloured wraps they wore around their waists; and of the curious time when he had happened to glance down a side-alley in Klipdrift and seen an astonishingly beautiful long-haired girl of no more than thirteen or fourteen, a half-caste, quite naked except for a chain around her ankle. He had dreamed of that girl afterwards, as he had dreamed of Mooi Klip, and her slanting eyes had followed him unblinking down a thousand wretched and sweaty struggles with his chastity.

'Perhaps I'd better go,' said Mooi Klip, softly.

'I haven't made the tea yet,' said Mr Ransome, awkwardly standing up.

'You don't have to trouble,' Mooi Klip told him. She stood

up, too, and picked up her basket of vegetables. 'I really just came to tell you about Coen.'

'Yes,' said Mr Ransome. 'Well, I'm sorry that you decided not to go ahead with your marriage plans. I, er, I . . . I can only give you consolation from the Bible. As it says in Ecclesiastes, "Sorrow is better than laughter: for by the sadness of the countenance the heart is made better!"'

Mooi Klip stared at Mr Ransome for a moment or two, and then giggled. Mr Ransome laughed too, in an odd staccato way that made Mooi Klip giggle even more. She reached up and kissed his cheek, and said, 'You've consoled me already. I think you're a very fine missionary, Mr Ransome.'

'You ought to call me Hugh.'

'That is your name? Hugh? What does it mean?'

'I'm not honestly sure. My mother knows. She's good on things like that. You know, folklore, history. She embroiders rather well, too. She sent me a whole set of embroidered antimacassars for my birthday, I –' he looked around his cheap and crowded little sitting-room, 'I really haven't had time to put them out yet.'

'You talk of your mother,' said Mooi Klip. 'Why don't you tell me about yourself?'

'There's not a lot to tell, actually.'

'Why don't I make us a picnic, for you and me, and on Friday we can go along to Blaauwkopje and talk? My mother will look after Pieter.'

Hugh Ransome looked at Mooi Klip carefully, and smoothed back his hair. 'I should say no,' he told her. His voice seemed suddenly more mature, quieter. 'Do you really want me to come?'

Mooi Klip nodded. 'I want to hear all of your life, from the day you were born.'

'I'm afraid that the life of a man who has never known a single woman is not very interesting listening.'

'You never know,' said Mooi Klip, and turned around to go. A mongrel dog was barking loudly in the next-door yard.

'Natalia!' said Hugh Ransome, hastily.

'What is it?'

'It's – well, it's nothing, really. I just wanted to say "Natalia". I think the name is as beautiful as the girl.'

'Thank you, Hugh,' said Mooi Klip, and walked out across the verandah into the brilliant early-afternoon sunshine, as if she were a dissolving vision. Hugh Ransome stayed still in the middle of his sitting-room for a long time, embracing himself in his own arms; and then he felt the need to sit down.

'"Discretion shall preserve thee, understanding shall keep thee,"' he recited, under his breath. '"Wisdom shall deliver thee from the strange woman, even from the stranger which flattereth with her words; that thou mayest walk in the way of good men, and keep the paths of the righteous."'

He stared at the worn-out rug on the floor, and thought again of Mooi Klip with her sun-hat halo. 'Damn wisdom, and damn discretion,' he said, and then sat up straight and looked quickly around, to make sure that nobody had heard him.

Barney was working in the library at Vogel Vlei when Horace rapped at the doors and put his black face around it at an alarming sideways angle, with only his eyes showing. Barney looked up from his papers and said, 'What is it, Horace?' without even remarking on the servant's odd posture. He was used to Horace, after six months of living at Vogel Vlei. Horace was entirely individual. He had once tried to warm up a visitor's bed by coaxing a black nanny-goat to lie under the blankets until it was time for the visitor to retire.

'A gentleman from Capetown to see you,' said Horace. 'He presents his card.'

'Very well, then,' said Barney, 'where is it?'

Horace's head disappeared like a badly stage-managed Oriental conjuring trick. Then his right hand emerged, holding the card between two fingers.

'Bring it here, will you, Horace?' asked Barney. 'My eyes are reasonably good, but I can't read a visiting card from fifty feet away.'

Horace withdrew the card, and then remained in hiding behind the door. 'Come on, man, I don't have all day,' Barney demanded.

'I can't, boss.'

'You can't? Why not?'

'My uniform trousers, boss, have torn badly.'

'Then just read me the name on the card.'

'Can't read, boss.'

Barney threw down his pen in impatience, stalked across the library floor and plucked the card out of Horace's hand. It read 'William Hunt, Trade Attaché, Government House, Capetown.'

'It's me!' exclaimed a sharp voice, and Horace stood back against the door to admit the diminutive Hunt; still bearded, though now touched with wiry silver hairs, still immaculately dressed in a greyish-lavender suit, and still smelling strongly of French cologne. 'My dear Barney, it's such a pleasure to see you! After all this time!'

Barney grasped Hunt's hand, and shook it. 'I'm amazed,' he said. 'What can bring a city fellow like you all the way out to Kimberley? Listen – you must have a drink. Horace – bring us two glasses of schnapps, will you.'

Horace, with his back pressed to the open door, said, 'Now, sir?'

'Yes, Horace, now.'

Horace awkwardly shuffled around, and then hurried off across the hallway as quickly as he could, grabbing behind him for the errant triangular flap of fabric that had torn from his trousers. Hunt watched him go with a look of almost professorial interest, and even took out a pair of wire-rimmed spectacles.

'Fine brown bum your man's got,' he remarked.

'He's something of a clown; but he's good-natured,' said Barney. 'And I see that *you* haven't changed.'

'Would that I could, my dear chap. The truth is that all the new fellows that Sir Bartle has brought in from India are rather a supercilious lot; or, if they aren't supercilious, they're spotty. I'm not sure which I can tolerate the least – haughtiness or hives. Each of them has their own disagreeable poison.'

Hunt walked over to a large brown leather armchair by the fireplace, and sat himself down as if he had lived at Vogel Vlei for most of his life. He leaned his cane against the hearth and tugged off his gloves, one finger at a time, and flopped them over the arm of the chair. 'I've been hearing some very interesting stories about you,' he told Barney. 'They say you're almost a millionaire these days.'

Barney walked around his wide partners' desk and cleared away some of the papers he had been working on. He was entering the final negotiations for buying seven more claims, two of them crucial diggings right in the centre of the Kimberley pipe. Apart from the fact that both claims had been yielding scores of high-quality diamonds every single week since they had first been excavated, they stood right between Blitz Brothers and the French company which owned most of the claims on the Big Hole's southern side. Their owner was asking £360,000, and Barney was doing everything he could to persuade him to bring down his price. Barney was a millionaire, all right, but only on paper.

The trouble was, everybody in town now knew that Barney owned a 350-carat diamond, and even in the local dry goods stores his servants were being charged twice the going price for any supplies that were ordered for Vogel Vlei. Barney was finding that his liquidity was dwindling fast, just when he had the most need of it. He could have stepped up diamond production, but he was anxious not to stir up the whole of the Kimberley mine into a furious burst of digging, in case they flooded the market again and brought the world price down. Whenever he was asked about the monster diamond in public, he said again and again that it was one of a kind, a freak, and that the chances of anyone finding another one of that size were practically nil. Harold Feinberg during the summer of 1878 and 1879 lived on heart flutters, patent antacids, and the dogged sexuality of his little froggy girl. Barney could not even mention the diamond to him without him turning white.

'Owning one fancy diamond doesn't actually make me the richest man in the world,' said Barney.

'No, I understand that, of course,' said Hunt, 'And so does Sir Bartle.'

'Sir Bartle's taking a personal interest in me? I thought Sir Bartle was busy being friendly to the Zulus.'

'Well, he's *not*, actually,' said Hunt, 'and that's part of the reason I'm here. We're in a spot of bother with the Zulus, as a matter of fact. You know how they were always haggling with

433

the Boers over their borders with the Transvaal ... Well, Sir Bartle set up a commission last year to settle the matter, and – rather bad luck – the commission actually found in favour of the Zulus. Bit embarrassing, really, what. But Sir Bartle's trying to sort the whole thing out by insisting that he will only ratify Zululand's border if Cetewayo disbands his army.'

Barney listened to that, and then pulled a face. 'I don't know much about Zulus, but from what I hear of Cetewayo, that's about the last thing he'll do. How can he disband his army and still stay independent? The Boers will have him for breakfast.'

'Between you and me, old chap, you're quite right. But that's just what Sir Bartle's counting on, Cetewayo saying no. And unless Cetewayo disperses his army within a week, Sir Bartle's going to send Lord Chelmsford and two thousand soldiers into Zululand to teach him a considerable lesson. That way, Sir Bartle can keep his promise to honour his commission's findings, *and* crush the Zulus, both at the same time.'

Barney rubbed his eyes. He had been working late almost every night for the past three weeks, and he felt exhausted. 'You Colonial Office monkeys really enjoy this kind of thing, don't you?' he asked. 'But where do I come into it? I know as much about Zulus as everyone else around here, and that's nothing at all.'

Horace came into the library with two glasses of schnapps, and a jug of water. He was wearing his usual black tailcoat, but this time, underneath it, he wore bright yellow riding breeches. Hunt gave him an amused, provocative look which perplexed Horace completely. He turned to Barney for reassurance, and Barney waved him out of the room with a grin.

'It's your diamond we're interested in,' Hunt told Barney. 'It's already been written about in the London papers, of course; but I must say that you kept the press very short of detail. The *Morning Post* said nothing more than that they had heard a "rumour" that a particularly large gemstone had been dug up at Kimberley, and that it was "estimated" to weigh in excess of three hundred carats.'

'I'm not announcing anything else until I'm ready,' said Barney. 'It's taken us years to build up this diamond industry the way it is today, people like Rhodes and Gould and me. The

434

very worst thing that could happen to us now is an old-style diamond rush, and a collapse of diamond prices on the world market.'

'Well, you're right, of course,' said Hunt. 'But I must say that Sir Bartle came up with an excellent idea in his bathtub the other day. He suggested that he should announce the discovery of your diamond right away, in a really dramatic fashion, all champagne and trumpets and God Save The Queen – and that he should then arrange for a special presentation of the diamond to Her Majesty in London. He suggested that you might think of christening the stone the Victoria Star, in her honour.'

'And what would be the point of that?' asked Barney.

Hunt raised a finger. 'The point, my dear chap, is that the attention of Her Majesty and Her Majesty's ministers of State would be diverted long enough by this patriotic charade to allow Sir Bartle to overwhelm the Zulus and capture Cetewayo before anyone in the Government could start squeaking about fair play, and cricket, and all that nonsense.'

Barney sat back in the buttoned armchair behind his desk, and looked at Hunt thoughtfully. Barney had changed a great deal since Hunt had first met him on the deck of the *Weser*, and Hunt, who was sensitive to men, had already been alerted by the flamboyant style of Barney's well-cut tweed suit and by his careful but abrasive mannerisms that Barney was now stronger, and much more aware of his personal power, and that he was going to be far more difficult to handle than the peaky-faced Jewish emigrant whom he had tried to seduce off the coast of equatorial Africa.

What Hunt did not know, although he sensed it, was that Barney had lost at last those youthful sympathies which had made him so gentle and so spontaneous in New York and during his first years at the Cape. He had abandoned his unquestioning devotion to his brother, and to the memory of his mother; and he had grown wise to the papier-mâché *hauteur* of the British colonial classes. Barney had become less pliable, but also more perceptive, and he had begun to organise his business and his household on his own terms and very rarely on anybody else's.

435

All those nights of guilt and all those splattered visions of his mother's blood had long since faded away. Now, he slept dreamlessly next to a well-bred woman who had agreed to say what she was told, and lift her nightdress when she was required, and to smile and be pretty whenever it was called for. In return, he was faithful to her, and he brought her diamond bracelets and necklaces by the handful. Nareez came and went on shuffling silk slippers, and scowled at him whenever she passed him on the landing, but Nareez no longer upset him, because there was no longer any weakness in him for Nareez to pick at. He had come to terms with an attractive woman whom he did not love, and who did not love him in return. He had bought nearly a third of the Big Hole at Kimberley. And to crown it all he owned one of the largest rough diamonds ever found anywhere since the recorded beginning of diamond mining.

'The Victoria Star, huh?' said Barney. 'I'm an American, why should I consent to my diamond being called the Victoria Star?'

'We're friendly, aren't we, Americans and British?' said Hunt.

'I don't know,' Barney told him. 'Are we? Wasn't it Queen Victoria's grandfather who fought against us so bloodily only a hundred years ago?'

Hunt smirked. 'You're pulling my leg. You're German Jewish. You couldn't care a less about George III. Besides the Queen's mostly German herself. As one Kraut to another, you should be glad to give her the Star.'

'*Give?*' asked Barney, ignoring the gibe about his nationality.

'I don't mean *give* in that sense, my dear chap. There will of course be the matter of reasonable payment.'

'By whom?'

'By a consortium of British businessmen who are quite anxious to see South Africa organised into one profitable and easily-administered dominion, and to see that Zululand is All Sir Garnet as soon as possible.'

'All Sir what?'

'Oh, sorry, old chap. Fashionable expression in the colonial service. After Sir Garnet Wolseley, who crushed the Ashanti in '73. It means "shipshape!" '

'You British have a jolly phrase for everything, don't you?' said Barney. 'What's your expression for get the hell out of my house?'

Hunt made a *moue*. 'I think "bugger off" should do nicely for that.'

'Good. Then bugger off.'

Hunt sighed. 'You really don't understand, do you? I'm here to offer you almost anything, within reason, provided you sell us the diamond and make a big splash about how you found it, and how proud you are to hand it over to Her Majesty.'

'I haven't had the diamond valued yet,' said Barney. 'My dealer's still doing tests on it.'

'What have your tests discovered so far? Is it flawed? Is it coloured? I mean, I've really come up here on something of a blind man's errand. It may not be worth handing over to Her Majesty at all.'

'It's an exceptionally fine lilac-coloured stone of exactly 356 carats and two points. There are no flaws. That's all I'm prepared to tell you.'

Hunt tipped back his schnapps glass, and took out his handkerchief to wipe his mouth. 'I'm empowered to offer you £750,000, in gold and notes.'

Barney said, 'It may be worth more, it may be worth less. I can't tell until we've finished our tests. Besides, I don't think I'm particularly keen on the idea of using the diamond simply to take the public's attention away from one of your squalid native wars.'

'Steady on,' said Hunt. 'You can hardly call the spread of the British Empire squalid. Everywhere that Britain rules, there is justice, freedom, stern fair play, and so much gin and adultery that those who aren't down on their knees are flat on their backs.'

Barney gave Hunt a wry smile of amusement. But then he said, 'I'm not selling. Not yet. I want to see this stone through every single stage of its cutting and its marketing, and I want to see that it's bought for the right person for the right reasons. The Victoria Star? You must be joking.'

'I can offer you a million,' said Hunt, with a grin.

'Just like that? Sight unseen?'

'Subject to proper examination, of course. But if the stone turns out to be what you claim it to be, a flawless rough of 356·2 carats, then we won't have any difficulties, will we? It will be *worth* a million.'

'I'm not selling,' said Barney.

'A million, two hundred thousand,' said Hunt. 'That's my absolute limit!'

'I just told you that I'm not selling.'

'Then you're a fool, my dear chap. Where else in the world would you get nearly one and a quarter million pounds in gold and notes, even for a flawless 350–carat diamond? This is the best offer you're ever going to get, and I can promise you that if you don't take it now, you'll spend the rest of your natural life regretting it.'

Barney reached across the green leather top of his desk, and picked up a small brass bell with an imp's face on it. He tinkled the bell between his finger and his thumb, keeping his attention unwaveringly on Hunt.

'I'm not selling,' he repeated.

Hunt sat where he was for a second, drumming his fingertips tautly on the arm of the chair. Then he stood up as quickly as an unfolded clasp-knife, picked up his cane and his gloves, and said, 'Very well. If you're not going to sell, then you're not going to sell. It's been nice talking to you again.'

Horace opened the door, and said, 'Yes, boss?'

'You can show Mr Hunt to his carriage now, Horace.'

'Yes, boss. This way, Mr Hunt, sir.'

'Oh, Barney –' said Hunt, as he reached the door. 'There was one more thing I forgot to ask you.'

'What's that?'

'Your brother Joel ... well, I gather you must have located him, from what the report in the *Colesberg Advertiser* said.'

'Yes, I did.'

'They mentioned that he wasn't well.'

'He's not. He had some kind of infection. He lost his left leg.'

'I'm sorry to hear that,' said Hunt. 'Does he still live here, with you?'

'He has a suite of rooms upstairs. He keeps himself pretty

well secluded these days, though. He plays a lot of chess. I hardly see him from one week to the next.'

Hunt thought about that, still smiling, and then he said, 'There was some suggestion, you know, that your brother found the stone first, and that he tried to keep it hidden from you.'

'Was there?' asked Barney.

'Well, that's the way the chaps over at De Beers tell the story. It could all be nonsense, of course.'

'Then I expect that it is nonsense,' said Barney, in a level voice. 'Now if you'll excuse me, I'm very busy. Are you staying in Kimberley long?'

'A week or two. Just long enough to justify my scandalous expenses.'

'You must come to dinner, then. I'll speak to Sara about it.'

'My dear chap,' said Hunt. 'You were always a gentleman. I'm most obliged.'

After Hunt had left, Barney stood behind his desk, looking tall and grave in the diffuse oval of light that shone from his green-shaded lamp. He felt disturbed by dozens of inexpressible questions – questions about himself, about his happiness, and about his dim, grotesque world of manipulation and money into which his ownership of the huge lilac diamond was beginning to draw him. He remembered the rich people he had seen in New York, in their sleep top hats and their astrakhan-collared coats, sitting back on the seats of their phaetons with immaculately-groomed whiskers and faces as neutral as minor gods. Now he knew why they looked the way they did. They were groomed because they were rich, and could afford to keep servants; but the neutrality of their expression came from the uncertainty they felt that they deserved any of this attention and equally from their determination not to show it. Barney remembered thinking years ago that it must be wonderful to be wealthy: but the truth was, now that he actually *was* wealthy, in this stately library lined with thousands of unread books, that he felt off-balance and unsettled, and that his need for love and for family friendship was still as demanding as ever.

He had no urge to return to Clinton Street, and the Lower East Side. He still preferred to be a diamond magnate, rather than a bespoke tailor. But he was beginning to feel again that excruciating loneliness that he had felt when he first crossed the Atlantic Ocean to Liverpool, and he realised that, apart from those months he had spent with Mooi Klip, it had never once left him.

He left his desk, and walked across the library to the steel and cement Union safe which was installed under one of the bookshelves. He took out his keys, and unlocked the double doors. There, on the top shelf, wrapped up in soft gazelle-skin, was the diamond. He took it out, and carried it back to the lamplight, where he opened up the leather, and let the stone lie exposed and shining, an embodiment of pure fact.

Several merchants had already approached him with offers for the diamond. Most of them had been acting on behalf of governments or wealthy collectors. The Russian court had been showing particularly enthusiastic interest, and had twice sent the Belgian dealers Leopold & Wavers around to see him with offers that were cautiously close to a million. But Harold Feinberg had advised caution. The diamond was so rare and enormous that it would be a political influence as well as a spectacular piece of personal property. It had been discovered on ground that the British were quite sure was theirs, and there had already been letters in *The Times* asking when the diamond was going to be seen in the country of its ownership. It would not help Blitz Brothers with the Board for the Protection of Mining Industries, nor with Government House, if Barney were to let the diamond go to the Czar, or to the Prussians, or worst of all, to the Dutch. There were too many Boer sympathisers among Amsterdam's diamond merchants who might be tempted to restore it to the Orange Free State on a lease-land basis as a symbol of Boer independence, and what the Boer republic considered to be its rightful title to the diamond mines.

Barney had kept the diamond in his safe ever since his wedding-celebration party, although he had allowed Harold to come around to test it and inspect it. Harold had spent all day with it, only stopping for ten minutes to drink a cup of coffee and eat a plateful of beef sandwiches, and even then he had continued to stare at the diamond as if he were bewitched. At four o'clock, Barney had finished his paperwork and come into the conservatory to watch.

'I'm almost finished,' Harold had told him. 'It has a few tiny inclusions on one side, but those will be lost when they cleave it. It's a remarkable diamond. Just remarkable. I wish my old father could have seen it. It would have brought tears to his eyes.'

'What tests have you made?' Barney had asked him. 'You're sure that it's a diamond? I mean, one hundred per cent sure?'

'No question about it,' Harold had said. 'I tested it for hardness, by scratching another diamond with it. Also a sapphire. That's not a test you should ever do with a polished diamond, because you can damage the edges. But there wasn't any doubt about this one.'

'I thought the standard test was to hit the diamond with a hammer,' Barney had remarked.

'They used to. But the trouble is, diamonds are brittle, as well as hard, and you could end up with more than a handful of smashed pieces. I know a couple of East End merchants who used to encourage diggers to test if their stones were genuine or not by banging them with a hammer, and when the stones were all broken up, and the diggers went away disappointed, all the merchants had to do was to scoop up the bits and sell them as industrials, or pointers, for shopgirls' engagement-rings. They made themselves a small fortune.'

Barney had picked up the diamond and turned it over. 'What other tests have you done?'

'Surface tension, although it's difficult to get an accurate result with an uncut rough. If you leave a drop of water on the table of a diamond, it will stay there much longer than on any other kind of stone. And then there's conductivity. You've already noticed how quickly this diamond warms up and cools down when you hold it in your hand, or leave it alone on the desk.'

'What's it worth?' Barney had asked him. 'Do you have any idea?'

Harold had rolled down his sleeves and looked at Barney tiredly. 'This diamond is worth as much as anyone in the world will pay for it. If I were you, I wouldn't take less than a million pounds, in gold.'

Now, in the library, Barney sat with his head in his hands staring at the diamond and thinking. It was the most fabulous possession he had ever owned, clear and bright and so un-compromising that it was almost holy. If all the laws and truths of the *Torah* could be crystallised into an object that could be held in one hand, this is what they would look like. It was so enormous that it was worth far more than money. In fact, it was so enormous that Barney knew that it would be impossible to own it for very long: the financial and political claims that the outside world were making on it were too strong.

But for the time being, and especially while he felt as lonely as he did, he found the diamond strangely consoling. He could stare at it for an hour at a time, turning it this way and that way to catch the different lights in the lilac-pink depths of its brilliant interior. For Joel, the diamond had represented dreams of luxury and riches and women. For Barney, it was more like a statement from God that He did exist, that here in the shape of a giant crystal was the adamant and irrefutable evidence, and that Barney had not been forgotten, for all of his desertions, for all of his doubts, and for all of his unsaid prayers.

Under his breath, alone in his grand library, Barney recited the words of the *Kol Nidre*, the prayer that is recited on the eve of Yom Kippur. Then he turned down the wick of his desk-lamp so low that the massive diamond in front of him gleamed with an unearthly pink light. He did not cry. It was far too late for tears. And, besides, he had on his desk the most incredible symbol of man's greed and God's ingenuity that the world had ever seen.

At nine o'clock, Barney went upstairs to see Joel. It was a reluctant duty, because ever since the wedding-party the two brothers had scarcely been able to speak to each other: Joel because of his shame at having been caught, and his chagrin at not having got away with the diamond after suffering so much, and Barney because he no longer trusted Joel to tell him the truth.

Sara was in Joel's bedroom when Barney knocked on the door. She was sitting on the end of the bed playing cards with him, for mint bon-bons. As usual, she was fashionably dressed, in a steel-grey satin tea-gown, with a diamond corsage garland strung beneath her breasts, and her hair was plaited and combed and studded with diamond clasps. All of her diamonds were presents from Barney: the corsage garland, which was valued at more than £22,500, Barney had given her the week after she had discovered that he was not a member of the Kimberley Club, and that being Jewish he probably never would be.

Joel was looking almost rudely healthy. Since Dr Tuter had sawed off his left leg on the evening of the party, an operation in which both surgeon and patient had been almost incapably drunk, he was far fitter and more optimistic than he had ever been before. Dr Tuter had treated his amputation with boric acid ointment, which had prevented the further spread of gangrene, and Joel had slowly but steadily recovered. Once the pain of the operation had faded, Joel had found that the nagging agonies of his reset left leg had left him for ever; and although his hip still felt uncomfortable on stormy days, he slept better, and ate better, and even teased the florid-faced English nurse Betty whom Barney had brought in from Capetown that a lone-legged man could do things to a girl that a two-legged man would find impossible. The kaffir servants, of course, found that it was now far easier to distinguish between their two employers in their conversation. Their orders these days came either from 'Mr One-Leg Blitzboss' or 'Mr Two-Leg Blitzboss'.

'I came to see how you were,' said Barney, standing uncomfortably at the door.

'He's losing badly at farmer's joy, if that's any indication of his health,' said Sara.

'I see,' said Barney, with one of those smiles that came and went as quickly as a trick.

'I enjoy losing to your lovely wife,' said Joel, handing Sara three more mints. 'I like to see her excited, for a change.'

'Do you?'

Barney went to the window and drew back the drapes with one hand. Outside, the sky was as black as plums, with only a single streak of red to show where the sun had gone.

'You're not pensive again, are you, my deah?' asked Sara, shuffling the cards between sharp pink fingernails.

'Mmh?' asked Barney, turning around.

443

'I said, "you're not pensive again, are you?" You seem to spend all your time these days in a brown study.' She dealt from the bottom of the deck, as rapidly and as efficiently as only an English colonial daughter knows how.

'Either a brown study or a diamond-studded library,' chuckled Joel; and Sara caught his eye and laughed.

'I've had an offer for the diamond from a consortium of English colonial businessmen,' said Barney.

'I hope they offered more than those awful Belgians.'

'They did. They said they could put up a million-two.'

Joel looked up – first at Barney and then at Sara. 'That's a lot of money,' he said. 'Even *half* of it is a lot of money.'

'Are you going to sell?' asked Sara. 'Joel, my darling – you *can't* do that. That's cheating.'

'I enjoy cheating,' said Joel. 'Cheating is almost as good as drinking.'

Sara collected two more bon-bons from him. 'Cheating is only enjoyable if it's undetectable, or if it's only discovered when it's far too late.'

'I'm, uh, thinking about it,' put in Barney. 'The offer, I mean. The trouble is, they want the stone for political reasons as well as financial ones. Sir Bartle Frere is intent on invading Zululand, apparently, and he wants to present the stone to Queen Victoria at the same time, to damp down any unpleasant reactions he might get from the cabinet.'

'What a *chozzer*!' Joel remarked. 'Do you know what his nickname is? "Sir Bottled Beer!"'

'Do you have to use language like that?' asked Barney irritably. 'This is a house, not a pigsty.'

Sara tittered. 'I *adore* it when Joel speaks Yiddish. The words are so absolutely expressive. He taught me what *pisher* meant, this morning.'

'Kimberley's a rough place,' said Barney, 'there's no need for either of you to make it any rougher.'

'Oh, Barney,' protested Sara. 'You're getting so stuffy these days!'

'I'm not stuffy, Sara,' Barney retorted. 'I just don't happen to like the sound of a woman using foul language, that's all. Especially when it's a woman who seems to regard herself as a doyenne of society.'

'My *dear* Barney,' said Sara, slapping down her cards, 'I couldn't regard myself as a doyenne of society in this ramshackle little town even if I *wanted* to, since my beloved husband doesn't happen to belong to the only half-decent club for hundreds and hundreds of miles. The only party I have ever given was utterly ruined by his insistence on tearing open his brother's gangrenous leg in front of all of my guests, and in any case I can't afford to give any more parties because he's invested all of his money in those ridiculous diamond mines and he won't sell the only worthwhile asset he's got, which is that stupid oversized diamond.'

'I'm going to sell it, but I'm not going to sell it for the wrong reasons!' snapped Barney. 'And nobody is going to *pressure* me into selling it, either! I'll sell it when I want to, and to *whom* I want to, and at the right price!'

'By the time you get around to selling it, you'll have worn it down to a half-pointer, just by staring at it!' said Sara.

'You don't even understand, do you?' Barney demanded. 'I suppose you want the blood of Cetewayo's Zulus all over your hands, just because you need a few thousand pounds for dresses, and for parties? They're thinking of sending two thousand troops in, and you know what that's going to mean? Well, you obviously don't – a massacre!'

Sara stood up, her fists clenched and her face distorted in utter fury. 'How *dare* you say that to me! How *dare* you! Do you think I'm going to put up with year after year of this obscenely boring place with no money and no social life and no friends, just for the sake of a handful of black savages? And what other excuse are you going to find for keeping me short of money, after the Zulus? The Hottentots, or the Xhosa? You've got to sell the diamond, and that's all there is to it!'

'I'm not selling,' said Barney, quietly.

'They'll send the troops into Zululand anyway,' said Joel, placidly gathering up the scattered cards and mint bon-bons on his quilted bedcover. 'Whether you sell the diamond or not, there's still going to be a massacre.'

'At least I won't be part of it,' Barney declared.

'Listen, Barney,' Joel told him, 'every diamond that was ever dug out of the ground has blood on it. It's the way that diamonds are. This diamond has blood on it already – mine. You don't

445

think a few hundred dead Zulus are going to make any difference?'

'That's the way that people have talked for centuries about the Jews,' said Barney, and his throat was thick with suppressed emotion. 'What does it matter? A few hundred dead Jews aren't going to make any difference! Well, let me tell you something, Joel. I don't know very much about the Zulus, but I do know that they're proud and that they're independent and that they have a culture and a social life of their own. I also happen to know that Cetewayo has tried to keep the peace with the British. But what we're talking about here is betrayal – deliberate betrayal – and deceit – and murder. And the Governor wants to use my diamond to lend his reputation a little spurious lustre, at a time when his reputation is going to be pretty well completely drowned in blood. You can think what you like. You can think I'm stuffy, and you can think that I'm ridiculous. But I'm not allowing that diamond to go to London as the Victoria Star.'

Sara's nostrils flared, like a mare, but she kept her peace. She sat down on the bed again, her back straight, and reached for Joel's hand. 'If you're absolutely determined that you're not going to sell it, then the least you can do to amuse me is to let me hold another party. Perhaps this time you'll be able to resist the temptation to tear Joel's trousers off, and display his stump to all of our guests.'

'I think I can manage that,' said Barney. 'How about the last day of January?'

'I don't suppose anybody will come,' said Sara. 'Not after the last fiasco.'

'Tell them that I'm going to put the diamond on open view,' said Barney. 'Then they'll come.'

'You mean you'd actually let other people ogle your precious diamond, *breathe* on it, just for my sake?' asked Sara, sarcastically.

'Sara,' said Barney, 'I'm doing my best to please you. Do you understand?'

Sara held her breath for a second, and then let it out. 'Yes, my dear,' she nodded. 'I'm terribleh sorreh.' Her over-emphasised accent betrayed the boredom she felt, and the contempt in which any experienced Africa hand would have held a chap who was soft on the natives. Bit of a square peg, don't-chi-know.

446

Barney waited in the bedroom for a moment longer, but by the way in which Joel and Sara sat like children who were impatient for an adult to leave so that they could carry on with their game, he knew that he was not welcome. He said, 'I'll go down and tell Kitty to make us a light supper.'

'I'm not eating,' said Sara.

Barney looked at her, and then at Joel. He had seen that smug expression on Joel's face before. 'In that case, you'll just have to sit there and watch me, won't you?' he said. 'I'll have Horace ring the gong when it's ready.'

He left the bedroom, leaving the door slightly open behind him. At the far end of the landing, in the shadows, he saw Nareez. The Indian *amah* had slipped away before he could say anything, but her perfume lingered on the stairs like an unsettling memory.

'I never thought that clergymen could cook,' said Mooi Klip, sitting back in the cheap varnished armchair by the frosted-glass oil-lamp.

'It wasn't much, I'm afraid,' said Hugh. 'Boiled beef and onion dumplings is really about my limit. Would you care for some tea, to follow it? Or coffee?'

'Later,' said Mooi Klip. 'Come and sit next to me. You've worked so hard to make everything nice.'

'I was a bit worried about the onion dumplings,' Hugh told her, frowning back at the remains of their dinner on the small dining-table. 'I've only made them for myself before, and of course when you're cooking for yourself you don't worry too much if things turn out rather odd. They weren't *odd*, were they?'

'No,' smiled Mooi Klip, taking his hand. 'They weren't odd at all.'

Hugh looked pleased, and dragged across one of the dining-chairs so that he could sit beside her. They had a special closeness now, Hugh and Mooi Klip. They had gone out on picnics together with Pieter, sitting on top of the small hay-coloured hills around the valley at the Vaal River, while clouds puffed past them like the steam from unseen trains, and the air had grown so hot that they had been unable to do anything but stay under their wide parasol and watch each other perspiring. They had gone to a fancy-dress dance run by the Presbyterians. They

447

had walked hand-in-hand, and talked, and once they had gone all the way out to see Coen Boonzaier on his farm, and he had been quite friendly and cheerful, and offered Hugh a suck at his pipe.

Hugh had declined, but with a smile.

Now, with Elretha gone for the night, Hugh had invited Mooi Klip around for one of his home-cooked dinners, and he had decorated the table with wild flowers, and carefully set out his mother's antimacassars as napkins.

Mooi Klip said, 'Will you stay here for the rest of your life? In Griqualand, I mean?'

'It depends on my bishop, rather,' said Hugh. 'But I wouldn't have thought that he would have made me stay here for ever. I would love to take you back to England with me, and Pieter too. Kennington can be very pleasant, you know, in the summer. And I'm sure mother would adore you.'

Mooi Klip looked at Hugh fondly. She reached out to touch his face, to show him how affectionate she felt towards him; but he caught her hand first, and squeezed it tight. Rather too tight: she said, '*Ow*,' and he hastily let go.

'I'm afraid I'm not very good at this,' said Hugh. 'But when I say that I want to take you back to England with me, well, the truth is that I do. The truth is, Natalia, that I've been thinking about this for weeks now, and I want most desperately to marry you, to make you my wife. The truth is, that I love you most awfully.'

Mooi Klip did not appear to be at all surprised. She simply smiled at him, and said, 'Hugh . . . you have always been good to me.'

'It's my job,' he said, flustered. 'It's my job to be good to people. It's what I get paid for.'

Mooi Klip shook her head. 'How could your stipend cover all of the affection that you have shown me, and all the understanding that you have given me, and how fatherly you have been to Pieter? It can't. Not twenty years of your stipend could do that. What you have been to me, Hugh, nobody could ever have saved up enough money to pay for.'

'Stipend, eh?' remarked Hugh, furiously scratching at his leg. 'That shows you've been walking out with a clerical fellow!'

'Hugh,' said Mooi Klip, 'I want to be honest with you. I don't ever want to lie to you.'

'Well, no, of course,' said Hugh. 'You can't possibly have any kind of a marriage if you lie, if you're not completely straight. Quite right.'

'Barney Blitz will always remain as the man I loved the most,' Mooi Klip told him, with infinite gentleness. 'It happened that way, I don't know why. Each of us brought out the best in each other. Barney made me feel like a woman, but he also made me feel strong. He protected me, but he didn't keep me on a chain. He was jealous, but he gave me freedom. He was a warm lover and a good friend.'

'I see,' said Hugh, white.

Mooi Klip reached out for Hugh again now, and held his right hand between both of hers. 'What I want you to know, Hugh, is that neither time nor the love of anybody else can ever make me forget what Barney was to me. It is a fact of what I am. I can never forget. But I am sensible enough and feminine enough to know that I can never have him back, and that I cannot live without a man beside me for ever. I love you, Hugh. Not the same way that I loved Barney. But I love your friendship, and how gentle you are, and I love to see Pieter playing with you and calling you by your name. If you can take me as I am, knowing that I still have a deep-buried love for someone else, then I promise you that I will always be a good wife to you, and that I will love you and care for you and honour you. If you really want me to marry you, Hugh, then all I can say is yes.'

Hugh was so overcome that the tears sprang into his eyes, and he was incapable of saying anything. He stood up, and then he sat down again. Then he went across the room, and let out a peculiar noise, like a sneeze and a sob mixed up.

'I'm so delighted,' he said. 'I'm so delighted I could cry.'

Mooi Klip smiled. 'You look as if you're crying already.'

'What?' he said, a little fiercely, wiping his eyes. 'Why should I cry when you've just made me feel so happy? Natalia! I can scarcely believe it! My dear Natalia, I love you so much!'

Mooi Klip stood up, and Hugh took her into his arms. 'I feel quite extraordinary,' he said. 'But I feel as if God approves! In fact, I'm sure He does! I can serve Him equally well as your husband as I could as a single man. In fact, I can probably serve Him better.'

He kissed Mooi Klip, at first with great tenderness, so that the sound of their lips was as moist and as quiet as the opening wings of a newly-formed butterfly. But then he held her tight, as close as he possibly could, and he was trembling with the excitement of her. They kissed again and again, saying nothing, their eyes closed, and Mooi Klip lifted her hands like a blind girl to touch his face, to feel his hair and his cheeks and the curve of his lashes.

At last, Hugh opened his eyes, and looked at her. 'There is a great deal that you are going to have to teach me,' he told her, in an unsteady voice. 'I am a knowledgeable man, in my way; but I am also an innocent one.'

She did not speak, but took his wrist and led him towards the door. He hesitated at first, with a questioning expression on his face, but then she said, 'Come,' so warmly and so softly that he followed her.

The bedroom was crowded with shadows. An engraved-glass lamp burned low on the chiffonier beside the bed, its flame dipping from time to time in the slight draught that blew from the slightly-open window. The bed itself was as plain as a bed could be: unvarnished oak, dovetailed and pegged, and spread with a patchwork comforter of paisleys and chintzes and dimity. On the wall above the head of the bed was a lurid lithograph of the Garden of Gethsemane. Hugh turned to Mooi Klip in obvious indecision, his voice breathless. 'You are the first woman who has ever been in here, apart from Elretha.'

'You're afraid?' asked Mooi Klip.

'I wouldn't be telling the truth if I said that I wasn't. And I'm not at all sure that we shouldn't wait until we're married. It's really wrong, you know, to –' He stopped, and then 'Well,' he said, in a very low voice, 'it's technically fornication.'

'Are you committed to me?' Mooi Klip whispered.

'You *know* I am,' said Hugh.

'I am committed to you, too. I wouldn't have come here tonight if I hadn't been, because I knew that you were thinking of asking me to marry you. If I hadn't have been committed to you the thought of going to bed with you wouldn't even have entered my mind.'

'I know,' Hugh worried, 'I know. But it still seems so sinful.'

Mooi Klip lowered her eyes. 'We'll wait, then, if that's what you feel we ought to do. You are a man of God, after all.'

She went to the bedroom door and opened it again. Hugh stayed where he was, his face bursting with pent-up emotion, his fists squeezed tight. Just as she was turning away towards the sitting-room, he shouted out, '*No!*'

Mooi Klip looked back at him. In a gentler, less controlled voice, he said, 'No. I don't want to wait, however sinful it might be. I will just have to ask for God's understanding of how much I love you. Do you hear me? I don't want to wait. I can't, a moment longer.'

Slowly, Mooi Klip came towards him and took both of his hands. 'Is there a word for how you feel?' she asked him.

'A word?' he frowned.

'That's how I learn, by asking people how they feel.'

Hugh laughed, rather desperately. 'Well, I can only think of one word, and that's turbulent. I am the original turbulent priest.'

They kissed again, a slow kiss that seemed to Hugh to take whole hours, hours in which pictures from old postcard albums appeared and faded in his mind; the Oval at Kennington, the horse-drawn buses clustered around Piccadilly Circus; the divinity school at Caterham; and then the views of West Africa and the Cape of Good Hope; and the grass huts; and the heat-distorted deserts; and the naked Hottentot women with gold bangles around their arms. The nude child in the alleyway.

Mooi Klip let him go, and then sat down on the bed. 'Come on,' she said, 'it will be beautiful. Come on.'

Clearing his throat as if he were just about to begin a sermon, Hugh stepped forward and started to unbutton her dress at the back. Mooi Klip sat still and graceful while he lowered the dress down to her waist, and while he bent forward to kiss her shoulders. 'What do I do now?' he asked her, anxiously. 'I'm not very good when it comes to women's clothes.'

'Here,' she smiled, and held up the pale blue silk ribbons of her white cotton bodice. Hugh cautiously tugged them, and her bodice slipped down to one side, baring her breast.

451

'Oh my God,' said Hugh, and reached out to touch her with shaking fingers. Her nipple knurled and stiffened, and she touched his cheek in return, and kissed him.

Together, clumsily but lovingly, they took off their clothes. Soon Hugh was lying on his back on the comforter, his face and hands red from the sun, his body white, while Mooi Klip knelt beside him, stoking the dark crucifix of hair on his chest, and humming to him one of those haunting and repetitive Griqua songs that you can never remember and never forget. 'Their music is like a sad cry on the wind,' Hugh Ransome told the Bishop of Bath, years later.

'I love you,' said Hugh, intensely. 'I can't even begin to describe to you how much.'

Mooi Klip pressed her finger to her lips. In silence, he watched her hand as it coursed through the thicker hair on his stomach, and at last clasped the stiffness of his erection. She stroked him tantalisingly, up and down his virgin penis. Then she rose up on her knees, her large breasts swaying, and mounted him, sitting down on him as slowly as she could, so that he could feel very single tenth of an inch of himself as he was gradually deflowered.

'Natalia,' he breathed. 'Oh Christ Jesus, Natalia ...'

He climaxed almost straight away, but she stayed where she was, smoothing his chest with her hands, touching his nipples, kissing him, soothing him, until he began to uncurl himself again, and rise.

They made love three times before the chiming clock in the sitting-room told them that it was ten o'clock, and time for Mooi Klip to leave. She climbed off the bed, and took her dress from the back of the bedroom chair, and quickly buttoned herself up. Hugh lay where he was, his hands laced behind his head, watching her unwaveringly, as if he were quite convinced that she would vanish through the whitewashed wall, like a ghost.

She leaned over the bed and kissed his forehead. 'I hope you're at peace,' she murmured.

He kissed her back. 'I'm at peace with myself, and I'm at peace with you, and I'm at peace with God. Only God could have given me such ecstasy as that. Only God could have brought you here. Natalia, you are the most wonderful thing that has ever happened to me.'

'Shall I come round tomorrow?'

'I'll come round to you. I promised Pieter that I'd try to finish that kite.'

'What about the wedding?' she asked.

'I shall have to write to the bishop, of course. But there is no reason at all why we shouldn't be married by the end of February. I'll receive an increased stipend, too, you know. Not a fortune, by anybody's standards, but enough to keep us both in moderate comfort.'

'As long as we have enough of your boiled beef and onion dumplings, I shan't mind,' smiled Mooi Klip.

Hugh wrapped himself up in his comforter like a very white-skinned visiting sheikh, and escorted Mooi Klip to the door. She said, 'Don't come out on to the verandah. You know how much people gossip in Klipdrift. I wouldn't want to spoil your reputation.'

'You'll be safe walking home?'

'Of course. Goodnight, Hugh. My love.'

He gave her one last kiss. 'I think I shall sleep better tonight than I have for twenty-nine years.'

Hunt was at his most waspish when he came around for dinner on Thursday evening: he told a complicated and decidedly off-colour story about a diplomat in Capetown who had attended a reception for the French Ambassador dressed as Marie Antoinette, with two wriggling black monkeys crammed down the front of his borrowed gown for a bosom. Barney found Hunt inexpressibly irritating, and he sat at the head of the dining-table petulantly toying with his chicken casserole and wishing that he had never invited him. But Joel, who had swung his way downstairs on his crutches like a human pendulum, and who was now sitting opposite Hunt with his stump firmly wedged against the table-leg, thought Hunt was perfect, and kept calling him his 'pitseleh', his little baby. Sara appeared to enjoy Hunt's company, too, although from the way she looked at Barney whenever she laughed, her eyes sparkling and hard,

Barney felt pretty sure that she was exaggerating her amusement just to annoy him.

'The funniest thing that I've ever seen in all of my years in the colonial service was Sir Bottled Beer trying to lower the flag on the back lawn of Government House, and tugging at all the wrong strings,' said Hunt. 'The flag became so hopelessly entangled at the top of the mast that they had to send a kaffir shinning all the way up to the button with a pair of scissors, so that he could cut it free. Poor old Sir Bottle went storming inside and wouldn't come out of his office for a week.'

'You *do* sound as if you have an amusing life,' said Sara. 'I'm absolutely dying to go to Capetown, but of course we're so busy here, aren't we, Barney?'

'Desperately busy,' put in Joel. 'We have to supervise the sunrise and the sunset, and we have to count all the shovels at the end of the day in case any of the kaffirs have tried to smuggle them home in their loincloths; and then we have to decorate this mausoleum of a house in case anybody more important than a member of the Board for the Protection of Mining Industries decides to pay us a visit. It's a full life, *pitseleh*, I can assure you.'

Hunt, with a mouthful of grapes, glanced mischievously along the table to where Barney was sitting, and giggled. 'They're teasing you, Barney. But I can't say I blame them. You're not the same chap you used to be, when I first met you. You were hopeful, then, weren't you? Hopeful and happy. Or as near to happy as anybody can ever be when they're Jewish and penniless at the same time. It's this diamond. It's made you morose. I've heard they do that, you know. They're really rather depressing stones, when all's been said and done.'

'And I suppose the only way to shake off this moroseness is to sell it to you?' asked Barney, finishing off his glass of wine.

'Of course,' said Hunt, winking at Joel. 'You'd be a million pounds better off, and you'd be rid of whatever baleful influence that stone has been having on you. Where's your sense of fun, old boy? You've been chasing that same forkful of food around and around your plate for the past twenty minutes, and you look about as cheerful as a choirmaster in a nunnery.'

Sara said airily, 'It's no use trying to persuade him. He's

quite determined to handle this diamond on his own, even if it makes him no money whatsoever. It's his upbringing, I suppose. Poverty affects different people in different ways; but it's evidently made Barney a hoarder. You know, like those old tramps you see with paper parcels packed with rubbish and pieces of string.'

Joel honked like a wild goose with hilarity, and almost lost his balance, tipping a salt-cellar all over the tablecloth. 'Sara has her husband summed up to a T, doesn't she? Oh, Sara! Oh, God, my poor aching *kishkas*! She'll kill me!'

Barney stood up, and tossed down his crumpled napkin.

'Not staying for the brandy?' asked Sara, sharply.

Barney shook his head. 'I'm afraid you'll have to excuse me. I'm going to be obliged to spend the rest of the evening in the library, finishing off some paperwork. We're making a bid for those three Quadrant claims next week, and I still have all the surveys to go through, as well as Harold's reports on their gem samples.'

'It's all right, Barney, *bubeleh*,' grinned Joel. 'I'm sure we can find some way of entertaining ourselves while you're gone. How about some brandy, William, and a game of cards? Sara?'

Sara was watching Barney through the dazzling flames of the silver candelabra, and there was an expression on her face which he had never seen before. He thought at first that she was smiling at him, smiling at the way she had teased him this evening, and he smiled back. But then, narrowing his eyes against the glare, he realised that she was looking at him with *unfamiliarity*, as if she could not quite decide who he was, and where she could remember him from. It was the expression of a woman who no longer feels any affection for her husband at all; a woman who looks at the man at the head of her table, and beside her in her bed, and sees only a stranger. Barney knew that their marriage was formal and remote these days, but until now he had not realised just how much of an outsider he had become in his own house. He looked at Joel, who was lifting his glass in a mocking toast to Hunt; and then he looked back at Sara, and all he could do was push his chair back under the table and walk out of the room.

Once inside the library, with the doors closed behind him,

he stood for a long time with his hand held to his mouth, thinking. He had been able to cope with Sara and Joel separately; when Joel had been irascible and alone, and Sara had been aloof and alone. But now they had formed a relationship from which he was being increasingly excluded, a relationship of shared dissatisfactions; of mutually-felt isolation and inadequacy, particularly in the face of Barney's success. He had thought they looked like children, the other night, when he had seen them playing cards, and in a way they were behaving like children, too, keeping secrets from him, stopping in mid-conversation when he came into the room, exchanging glances and smiles. He did not think that they were in love. Love was not what they needed from each other. But he did believe that they were able to share their fears and their uncertainties with each other, far more intimately than they could with him.

During the slow summer months of Joel's recovery, while Barney had been digging and supervising out at the diamond claims for ten to twelve hours a day, and then coming back to eat a hurried supper before working three hours longer with Harold Feinberg, Sara and Joel had been playing whist together, either in Joel's bedroom suite, when his leg was hurting him, or out on the patio, in the sparkling shade of the newly-planted cherry trees. Sometimes they had argued, and if Barney had been at home he had lifted his head from his paperwork in the library to hear Sara snapping at Joel with the accents of a cultured poodle, and he had smiled, and gone back to his surveys. But a man and a woman only argue with such persistence when they are trying to get closer to each other, trying to tease out the real sensitivities behind the prickly manners and the aggressive charades.

On some evenings, sweating with heat and pain and frustration, Joel had talked to Sara about his boyhood on the Lower East Side, and about the way his *papa* had always favoured Barney, giving him rides on his shoulders and sitting him on his knee. He had told her about his *mama*, too, and how she had suffocated him not only with affection but with more and more responsibility, until he had felt that it was impossible for him to breathe. He told Sara about things that he had done and things that he had failed to. He told her secrets that he had never confessed to Barney. He told her what Meg his red-haired lady mistress had done for him, and why he had paid her so much money not to stop.

Sara, in her turn, told Joel all about her stilted upbringing; about her erratic mother and her laconic father. She told him about a life that had always seemed elegant and attractive on the surface, but which had at last proved to be empty of meaning.

And so both of them sat together in the vast, empty rooms of Vogel Vlei, one with a brother to whom he owed everything, including his life and his disfigurement; and the other with a husband who kept her in fine gowns and beautiful diamonds and endless discontentment.

Barney turned up the wick of the oil-lamp, and went to the safe. He hesitated for a moment, but then he unlocked it, and took out the diamond. It lay in the darkness, the diamond, its light unlit; but when Barney laid it down on his desk, on a sheet of white paper, it sent out flares of brilliant iridescence all around it.

'I'm going to name you,' he said. 'No gemstone as magnificent as you are should go without a name.'

He picked the stone up, and clasped his fingers around it, as if he were holding a human heart. 'I name you the Natalia Star.'

It was more than five minutes before he put the diamond down again, and sat at his desk, and then he kept staring at it. He knew that he had just put his deepest and most painful feelings into words; but he did not want to think about it any more. His sense of loss was too complicated and too complete.

He worked for a little over an hour, studying the Quadrant surveys and writing a long letter to Ascher & Mendel in Antwerp, asking them to send a representative to Capetown to discuss the cutting of the Natalia Star. On an impulse, he also wrote to Leah Ginzburg in New York, telling her that he was working hard, and that he was married 'to a very charming English girl from Natal'. Somehow he felt that if he told Leah about his marriage, it would improve things. His life with Sara was not *that* difficult, was it? They still kissed. They still made love. They talked over breakfast. What more could there be to any marriage?

He glanced at the diamond again, and remembered for one brilliant moment a night in the bungalow with Mooi Klip when she had whispered '*I love you, I love you, I love you*,' over and over again.

At last, he laid down his pen, lowered his lamp, and stretched. He was about to return the Natalia Star to the safe, when it occurred to him that it might be amusing to tantalise Hunt with it, and so he wrapped it up in its leather cloth and took it through to the drawing-room.

Sara and Hunt and Joel had just finished a three-handed game of cards, and they were laughing over another of Hunt's outrageous stories – this one about a new recruit to the colonial service who had been served up on his first morning in Africa a boiled ostrich egg, and told that it was frightfully bad form not to finish it. They all went quiet when Barney walked in, and Joel reached over to the bell-rope to call Horace to bring them some more brandy.

'Have you finished, my dear?' asked Sara. Her cheeks were flushed from drinking and laughing.

Barney nodded. 'Just about. I'll have to get up early tomorrow and write two or three more letters before I go to the mine.'

'You poor overworked darling. To think that all we can do is sit here and amuse ourselves while you have to go out and support us. But never mind, it's *Shabbes* the day after tomorrow, and you'll be able to put your feet up.'

'You celebrate the Jewish sabbath out here in Kimberley?' asked Hunt, lifting an eyebrow.

'The sabbath is the sabbath whether you're in Kimberley or Potter's Bar,' said Barney. 'I didn't use to observe it, when I first came here; but life is different now. I have time to remember my background, and my God.'

'He usually has at least five minutes to say a few prayers in between the mine and the library,' said Joel. 'He can say *shachris* while he's shaving; *mincha* in between mouthfuls of lunch; and *mairev* while he's washing his teeth before he goes to bed. Then he's just got time to say *Shema* while the kaffirs reload the mechanical *trommel* with more blue ground; and his Silent Devotions he can recite whenever the whims break down.'

'I didn't know you were so devotedly Orthodox,' said Hunt.

Barney sat down. 'I'm not. I think I forgot about God altogether when I first came to the Cape. My religion didn't seem to be enough to carry me through. But now I'm trying to get back to Him; and the only way I can do that is through prayer. Jews are great prayers, William. They believe that their whole life is a running conversation with the Lord. And why shouldn't I pray, when I've seen such evidence that He really exists.'

With that, Barney opened his hand, and held up the diamond. Joel, on the sofa, turned immediately away, as if Barney had slapped his face. But Hunt stood up, stunned, and stared at the stone as if it had materialised by some kind of magical trick.

'My God,' he said. 'I had no idea.'

Barney continued to hold it up, and Hunt approached it with his eyes wide. When he was close enough, he said, 'May I?' and picked it up carefully from Barney's palm.

'I have never seen anything like this in my life,' Hunt said. hoarsely. 'It makes me feel ridiculous. I mean – I can absolutely see why it has restored your faith in God. My dear chap.'

'I should take a good look at it,' said Joel. 'You won't see it again, ever. Old Shylock here is going to keep it locked up in his coffers until he dies, if you ask me.'

Hunt held the stone up to the lamplight, and rainbows curved across his face. 'It's astonishing. I really don't blame you for wanting to keep it. Look at those colours!'

Sara said, 'I keep telling Barney that it's too beautiful for us to lock away; but he won't listen, will you, my dear? I think the whole world should be able to admire it. But, oh no. Barney wants it for himself. He wants it in his safe, where it's worth nothing at all.'

'This stone has a destiny,' said Barney, holding out his hand for Hunt to give it back to him. 'I just want to make sure that it's the right destiny.'

Hunt turned the diamond around in his fingers one more

time, and then dropped it back into Barney's hand. 'You can't control destiny, old fellow. When you're dead, which you will be one day, that stone will pursue its course through history according to greed, and finance, and politics, and human passion, and you won't be able to do a damned thing about it. So what does it matter to you, its destiny? I'll give you a million-three.'

'I'm not selling,' said Barney.

'A million-four, and that's how confident I am that my backers will like what they see.'

'You're wasting your time, William,' said Joel, his eyes still turned away from the diamond. 'Barney is never tempted by money, only by the chance of proving his ineffable superiority. We used to have a name for people like him back in New York, but I won't repeat it here.'

Hunt looked covetously at the diamond as Barney wrapped it up in its leather cloth again. 'I'm staying in Kimberley for another day or two,' he said. 'Why don't you think it over? A million-four, in gold and securities.'

'There's nothing to discuss,' Barney told him, quietly and firmly. 'Now have some more brandy. Sara, do you know if Kitty made any more of those Dutch sugar cookies? Perhaps William would like a sugar cookie.'

Hunt sat down again. 'I just hope you realise what a difficult time Sir Bartle is going to give Blitz Brothers mining company after this. I wouldn't be surprised if he makes moves in court to have your licences revoked.'

'No,' smiled Barney, 'that wouldn't surprise me, either.'

Later that night, as they lay in bed, with the dim moonlight transfiguring their rooms into ice, Sara said, 'Will you *really* not sell?'

Barney had been dropping into sleep, and it took him a moment or two to understand that she had said something. 'What?' he asked her, blurrily.

'The diamond. Will you really not sell it to Hunt?'

'I've told you. I don't want to sell it to anybody until it's cut. That way, it will be worth even more.'

'But we're so short of money. And life is so tedious here. Don't you understand how bored and unhappy I am?'

'Sara,' sighed Barney, 'I don't want to start that argument all over again. I've already written to Ascher & Mendel, the diamond-cutters in Antwerp. In six months or so, we should be able to send the diamond to Europe, and have it cut. Maybe we'll take it to Belgium ourselves. Wouldn't you like to do that?'

'We could go anywhere we *liked* if we sold the diamond to Hunt. And Belgium's such a dreary place anyway. Besides, there's the whole question of patriotism. This *is* a British colony, and any really spectacular riches that are found here ought to go to the Queen, simply as a matter of courtesy. If you don't sell the diamond to Hunt, and allow him to call it the Victoria Star – well, that's a snub to the British throne.'

Barney propped himself up on one elbow and punched his pillow back into shape. 'For one thing, Sara, I'm an American, and I don't feel the slightest obligation to the Queen. And for another thing, I don't trust any of these colonial wheeler-dealers, nor their motives, nor their so-called "gold and securities."'

'Oh, you're so suspicious. Why on earth don't you just sell the diamond and have done with it?'

Barney did not answer, but wrestled himself into a more comfortable position in bed and closed his eyes. He had three letters to write to Quadrant's lawyers in the morning, and if he was going to get them done, he would have to wake up at five o'clock. Digging at the mine started at six, and he wanted to be there early. His kaffirs were finally going to excavate their two newest claims down to the level of all the rest of the Blitz Brothers diggings; and, with luck, Barney would now have sufficient space to bring in a steam-shovel. That would speed up the mine's rate of production more than ten times.

He did not know that Sara lay next to him for the rest of the night without sleeping. Nor did he know when he left the bedroom in the morning, and leaned over the bed to kiss her forehead, that she was still awake. Most poignantly of all, though, he was completely unaware that he would never kiss her again.

He was out at the mine with his foreman, eating a cheese pastry and drinking a mug of black tea, when he first realised that the key to his safe was missing from his key-ring. It was a grillingly hot afternoon, and when they sat down to eat their lunch at an old scratched kitchen table, with upended toolboxes for chairs, Barney took off his vest, and hung it on a nearby shovel handle.

'I shouldn't leave your keys in there,' said the foreman. 'We've got some light-fingered kaffirs these days. Jackdaws, I call 'em. They take anything as long as it shines.'

Barney unfastened his key-chain from his buttonhole and dropped the keys on to the table. Then he sat down and opened up the paper bag that Kitty had given him after breakfast to take to the diggings. The foreman, a short squat Australian with forearms like sides of beef, was already munching his way through a doorstep sandwich of sausage and mustard, mostly mustard.

'I saw Gentleman Jack late yesterday,' said the foreman, with his mouth full. 'He was sitting outside of Dodd's Bar, on the boardwalk, and he was pissed out of his mind. You know that fancy grey suit of his? It had holes in the knees and holes in the elbows, and it was so darn filthy it stunk.' He reached over and took a generous swallow of tawny-coloured tea, to wash his bread and sausage down. 'I'm darned if I know why you never handed that nigger over to the Board, and had him hung.'

'It wasn't entirely his fault, that's why,' said Barney. 'And besides, he won't ever get work in the diamond fields again, not from anybody.'

'Stafford Parker would have had him castrated.'

'Maybe he would. But I'm not Stafford Parker.'

He glanced down at his keys, and pushed them a little way across the table because the sun was being reflected by the oval brass name-tag and was getting into his eyes. The keys sprawled apart on the ring, and it was then that he saw the safe-key was missing. He set down his mug with a frown, and picked the keyring up, sorting through it key by key to make sure that he was not mistaken.

'Something wrong?' asked the foreman.

Barney jingled the keys in his hand. 'I'm not sure. Listen, I have to go back to the house for a while. Will you make sure they don't bring that side wall down when they start digging out the last of the debris? I don't want half of Tennent's claim collapsing into ours.'

'Sure. Aren't you going to finish your lunch?'

'You have it, if you're hungry. Now, where's Michael?'

He did not know what to think or what to feel as Michael drove him briskly back over the stony roadway to Vogel Vlei. He took his key-ring out again and again, and searched the pockets of his vest, but the safe key was indisputably gone. And not just lost, either. The key-ring was made out of sturdy steel and Barney practically broke a fingernail every time he tried to twist a key on or off it. The safe key had been taken deliberately, and since he wore the key-ring all day long, it must have been taken at night, when he was asleep.

It could not have been Hunt, because Hunt did not know where he kept his keys at night, under his socks in the drawer of his bureau. It could not have been Joel, either, because Joel could only walk with crutches, and he could not have swung his way into Barney's bedroom without waking him up, no matter how deep Barney had been sleeping.

He did not want to think of the other alternative, but there was no way in which he could stop his mind from turning it over. He closed his eyes as the carriage jostled its way up the tree-lined driveway that led to Vogel Vlei, and all he could see were pictures of Sara. Sara smiling, Sara frowning, Sara sad. The large white house stood silent and dazzling in the heat of the afternoon, and after Michael had turned the horses in front of the main door, and applied the brake, there was no sound at all except for the distant *pick-pick-pick* of the kaffirs who were preparing the gardens.

'You going back to the mine, Mr Blitzboss?' asked Michael.

'I don't know,' said Barney. 'Give the horses a drink, but don't unharness them yet.'

'Yes, sir.'

Barney tried to restrain himself from running as he walked through the open front doors of the house and across the hallway. As he reached the library door, Horace came out of the door to the servants' quarters, and frantically waved. 'Mr Two-Leg! Mr Two-Leg!'

463

'What is it, Horace?'

'They all gone, Mr Two-Leg. I'm sorry, sir. I told them they should wait. But they said, not to worry, old chap. They said maybe you could catch up with them later. Maybe not.'

'Gone? Who's gone?'

'Mr Hunt, sir; and Mr One-Leg; and the missis; and the *amah*.'

Barney gripped Horace's sleeve for a moment. 'Wait there,' he told him, and pushed open the library door. He crossed quickly to the safe, and tugged at the handle. The heavy door opened on its thick oily hinges to reveal what Barney already knew. The Natalia Star was gone. In its place was propped a letter, addressed to 'Barney Blitz' and marked 'Private' in Sara's schoolgirl handwriting; all loops and curlicues and self-indulgent whorls.

With unsteady hands, Barney took the letter out of the safe and opened it. On a single sheet of fresh notepaper, printed with the letterhead 'Vogel, Vlei, Kimberley, Cape Colony', Sara had written *'Vincit Qui Patitur*, Love Sara.'

Horace was still waiting by the door, nervously scuffing his feet on the marble. Barney called to him, 'What time did they leave? Early?'

'Just about one hour after you went to the mine, sir. They took the landau, sir, and six horses – four in harness, two running behind. They said they were going to Klipdrift for a day or two, to show Mr Hunt the diggings. I asked them if I should tell you where they were, sir; and they said certainly. "Certainly, old chap," they said, sir. "Off to Klipdrift to show Mr Hunt the diggings."'

'Is that all? They didn't say anything else?'

'No, sir, Mr Two-Leg. But they were in high spirits, sir.'

'Yes,' said Barney. 'I expect they probably were.'

He felt shocked, and cold, even though the library windows were all closed to keep the flies out, and the air was stifling. He stood where he was for a moment, by the open safe, with Sara's note in his hand, and then he walked around his desk, opened the top left-hand drawer, and took out the Shopkeeper's revolver with which he had almost shot Joel once before. Lord God, he should have done. Then he would never have married

Sara, and he would have been rid of Joel for ever. He released the catch on the revolver's chamber so that it fell open, took out his single box of cartridges, and loaded up with five rounds. He doubted if he was actually going to shoot any of them. He could not imagine killing Hunt, or Nareez or even Joel; and he certainly could not think of shooting Sara. But the simple action of loading the gun made him feel that he was doing something positive to get his diamond back.

'Horace,' he said, beckoning. Horace came over to the desk and stood to attention. 'I want you to pack me a saddlebag. Pack it as quick as you can. I want a couple of clean shirts, shaving tackle, socks, underwear. Roll me up a pair of blankets, too. And tell Kitty to pack me another saddlebag with bread, and *biltong*, and beans.'

'I understand, Mr Two-Leg.'

'I'm going to be away for at least a day,' said Barney, 'maybe two. Make sure you lock the house properly at night. Don't allow any trespassers in nor kopje-wallopers, nor tinkers. You got that? If anybody wants to knows where I am, tell them I had to go to Oranjerivier, in a hurry. All right?'

'Yes, sir.'

'Right. Then get a move on. They're only five or six hours ahead, and none of them know the roads really well. I should catch them at Modderivier.'

'Mr Two-Leg? I thought they were going to Klipdrift, sir? Different way.'

Barney shook his head. 'There's only one way those four are headed, and that's directly to Capetown. Tell Michael to saddle up Jupiter, if they haven't already taken him. I want to get going as soon as I can.'

In half an hour, the chestnut horse was saddled and ready, and Barney had changed into a khaki veld-jacket, riding-breeches, and wide-brimmed hat. Michael, who was holding the horse's bridle, said, 'You want me to come with you, Mr Blitzboss?'

Barney said, 'No thanks. What I'm going to say and do to those four people when I catch up with them, I'm going to do on my own, with no witnesses. Besides, I'll ride faster by myself.'

'God take care of you, Mr Blitzboss.'

Barney clicked to his horse, and it trotted down the driveway between the trees to the road. His black servants stood watching Barney go; and they walked across the hot gravel back to the house, saying nothing. It did not occur to them that there was nobody in this huge classical mansion now except them, that there was nobody to call 'boss'. Horace solemnly closed the front doors behind them, and locked them.

He rode south-west across the scrubby veld, and the wind plucked the dust from every step that Jupiter took, and blew it westward. The sun was beginning to sink now, and the landscape was taking on a grainy, inflated appearance, like a coke furnace seen through a muslin curtain. In the distance, on the western horizon, pale gazelles fled through the camelthorn trees, ghosts of their own forthcoming extinction.

They would have needed supplies, he thought. They could not have considered crossing three hundred miles of veld and desert in a horse-drawn landau, two women and a cripple and a pint-sized city-dweller like Hunt, not without water and food and not without a guide. Of course, Hunt had probably brought a guide with him when he came up from Capetown, and there were plenty of shiftless Afrikaners around Kimberley who would have been willing to take them across the Great Karoo for a few pound notes and a drink. But a guide meant one extra person for the horses to pull, and wheels that were going to get bogged down when they forded rivers, or whenever they crossed tracts of soft sand.

There were too many of them, and they were too in-experienced; and if they believed that Barney had swallowed their story and ridden across to Klipdrift to catch up with them, they may not even be hurrying. If he did not overtake them at Modderivier, about twenty miles to the south-west, then he would certainly stop them before they got to Belmont. He thought about what he would say and do when he confronted them, and even rehearsed it all in his head. He knew that Sara would give him the most difficulty. By stealing the Natalia Star from him she had virtually declared herself divorced.

And what made it worse for her, although she was unaware

466

of it, was the fact that she had taken the stone that Barney had named after the woman he felt he really loved.

Just before darkness, when the sun had dipped below the distant mountains, but the sky was still suffused with a pale bluish half-light, Barney reached a small farm settlement, no more than a whitewashed house with a corrugated-iron roof, and a cluster of barns and huts and straw-strewn *kraals*. He dismounted, and led Jupiter to the drinking-trough by the fence. There were mosquitoes in the air, and the last light in the sky was reflected in broken ripples in the trough as Jupiter lapped up his water.

Across the farmyard, a door opened, and Barney saw the orange glow of lamplight. A voice called, 'Who's there?'

'I stopped to water my horse,' Barney called back. 'I'm on my way to Modderivier.'

'Do you want a drink yourself?' The voice was distinctly Afrikaans.

'Thanks. I'll just tie up the horse and I'll be right over.'

Inside the farmhouse, at a plain wooden supper-table, sat a family of ten – a sun-wrinkled Boer farmer, his sturdy wife, and a collection of eight girls and boys, all blond-haired, and all alike as skittles, with angular cheekbones and snubbed-up noses. The wife took a blue Delft plate down from the high yellow-wood dresser, and ladled out Barney a generous helping of game stew, with floury potatoes. The farmer himself brought out a bottle of johannisboombeer brandy, and filled up a small thick-rimmed glass with it.

'This is very generous of you,' said Barney. 'I was expecting to have to eat my supper on horseback.'

'Bad for the guts, man,' said the farmer. 'My old father always used to say that you could do anything standing up except eat.' He reached across the table to shake Barney's hand. 'My name's Marais Brink, by the way, and this is my wife Elsa, and these are all the little Brinks. Well, not so little these days. Barend, my eldest, is twenty next month. Marietjie is three.'

'I'm looking for four, maybe five people,' Barney said, tearing off a piece of bread. 'They were headed this way in a four-in-hand, with two spare horses running behind.'

Marais Brink forked a large chunk of meat into his mouth,

and Barney had to wait patiently for an answer while he thoroughly chewed it, and took a sip of brandy, and then cleared his throat.

'There's been nobody like that past this way, man. Not today. It was today they were supposed to come by?'

'This morning, maybe eleven or twelve o'clock. They would have been hard to miss.'

'I'll ask my foreman, but I was out in the yard myself all morning, repairing a plough. I wouldn't have missed a rig like that.'

'This is just about the only way they can come, isn't it, right past the front of your farm?'

'Well, that's right,' nodded Marais Brink. 'They can't come around the back of the farm, not in a carriage, because of the ditches. And they can't go far beyond the track in the other direction, because it's all trees, and stones, and after that there's the river. Everything comes past the front here, man. I don't miss a thing.'

Elsa Brink offered Barney another spoonful of stew, but he raised his hand and said, 'Thanks, really. But no thanks. I don't have much of an appetite. Not while I'm still chasing after those people.'

'They took something from you?' asked Elsa Brink, clapping the lid back on the stewpot.

'You could say that.'

'Well, times are difficult, man,' said Marais Brink. 'There's been more thievery than I can ever remember. There was a time when you could leave your horses out at night; but not these days. I had a mule taken about a month ago. As if life isn't difficult enough already.'

Barney stared at him. Then the farmer's words at last sank in, and he blinked, and nodded. 'You're right. It's very difficult.'

After supper, the Brinks invited him to stay; and he sat preoccupied on a riempie chair by the fire, drinking johannis-boombeer brandy, while the children sang songs, and the eldest boy Barend played the fiddle. He thought of the tenement on Clinton Street, and of Leib Ginzberg practising his *mazel tov* dances upstairs. He thought of Leah and Moishe, and the thumping of wooden buckets outside the Brink farmhouse sounded so much like the thumping of bolts of cloth on the cutting tables at Blitz, Tailors, that Barney had to make himself sit up straight, and remind himself where he was. Thousands of miles away from the Lower East Side, in the middle of the night, in a small Boer farmhouse in Africa, with everything lost. His wife, his brother, the woman he loved; and the largest diamond ever discovered on the whole sub-continent.

There was something else, too. Tonight was *Shabbes* eve. He turned to Marais Brink, and said, 'Would you mind if I recited something? We call it the *Kiddush*. It's a kind of a prayer for the sabbath.'

'You're Jewish?' asked Elsa Brink.

Barney nodded. 'A Jew from America, a long way from home.'

'It's not unusual for a Jew, is it, to be a long way from home?' asked Marais Brink. 'You go ahead and say your prayers. We both have the same God.'

Later, as Barney lay sleepless in a hard wooden cot in one of the outhouses, with the waning moon watching him sadly through the uncurtained window, he repeated the words that he had spoken, the words that began the *Kiddush*, and he tried to take comfort from them. 'Thus the heavens and the earth were finished, and all the host of them. And on the seventh day God ended his work which he had made; and he rested ...'

But Barney found that rest was impossible. The moon sank behind a bank of early-morning clouds, and the sky began to lighten again, and on the other side of the farmyard a cockerel began to crow. He climbed off the cot, and went to the window, unshaven and exhausted.

If they had not gone to Capetown, where had they gone? Not to Klipdrift, surely; there was nothing for them there, and no escape to the coast. Not east, to the Orange Free State, or across the mountains to Natal. What would be the point of that? No point at all, unless Sara thought her father could help them to escape from South Africa with the diamond or sell it on the IDB black market. But they wouldn't be able to sell it for anything like a million pounds on the black market, not a diamond as huge and as distinctive as the Natalia Star; and Hunt's consortium of British businessmen, if they had ever actually existed, had apparently only been interested in putting up a million-four if they could be sure that the gem was going to be presented to Her Majesty as the Victoria Star.

So where had Hunt and Joel and Sara gone with the stone, and why? There were plenty of unscrupulous merchants and collectors who would pay anything up to £300,000 for it, credentials or not. But it would only take Harold Feinberg a month or two to alert the newspapers and the diamond trade all over the world that the Natalia Stone had gone missing, and anybody who wanted to resell it would either have to choose their client with great care, or else cut the stone up into twenty or thirty anonymous and far smaller diamonds, to be marketed separately. Either way, Sara and Joel would receive only a fraction of the money they might have been able to ask if they had been able to sell the diamond legitimately.

There were always buyers for diamonds of dubious background, but the stones had to be sold and re-sold before they acquired a new respectability. After he had killed the slave who had taken the Regent diamond from the Parteal mine, the British sea-captain who had promised to give him passage out of India had later sold the stone to the Indian diamond merchant Jaurchund for only £1000. Jaurchund had been obliged to put it around discreetly that he had 'exceptionally large diamonds for sale'; and when he was approached by Thomas Pitt, the grandfather of William Pitt and the governor of Fort St George, close to Madras, Jaurchund had been easily beaten down from his asking price of £80,000 to less than £20,000. Pitt sent the Regent to England to be cut into a flawless $140\frac{1}{2}$-carat brilliant, and sold it in 1717 to the Regent of France, the Duke of Orleans, for £135,000; but that did not help the slave, or the sea-captain, or Jaurchund, and Hunt and Sara and Joel were in the same position as the sea-captain.

But however little they were paid for it, and however alert the merchants were, the Natalia Star could still be lost to Barney for ever. As Hunt had reminded him, a large diamond has its own destiny; and unless Barney could very quickly intervene in the destiny of the Natalia Star, it would be out of his reach – cut, sold, mounted, and locked away in some private collection on the other side of the world. Barney thought about the stories he had told the newspapers about the Natalia Star being one of a kind, a once-in-a-lifetime discovery, and the ironic part about it is was that he had been right. It was. He might acquire the whole of the Kimberley mine, and excavate it as deep as it was possible to dig, and never find another diamond as huge as or perfect again.

He felt as if his wife and his brother had taken not only his diamond but his reason for staying in Africa, his reason for battling against Rhodes, his reason for trying to rediscover his religion, and his God. The Natalia Star may have embodied absolute truth, but it seemed to Barney as if absolute truth could too easily be slipped into a thief's pocket, and carried off.

In the morning, he breakfasted with the Brink family at six o'clock, and left them a five-pound note tucked into the blue milk jug on their dresser. Then he rode slowly back to Kimberley, and to Vogel Vlei, where his servants were awaiting his return with domestic patience. Somebody else was awaiting his return, too; and with a game-rifle.

It was Alf Loubser, the sheep-farmer from Beaufort West, looking as fierce as he possibly could. He had drawn his eighteen-ox waggon up outside the front doors of Vogel Vlei in a wide curve of horns and yokes and reins and idly-flopping tails, and he was sitting in the driving-seat with his long-barrelled gun resting across his knees. Beside him, in a gingham dress and a poke bonnet, her hands demurely clasped in her lap, was Louise, his daughter, the girl who had taken Barney's virginity all those years ago on that warm starry night on the Koup.

Barney climbed down from Jupiter wearily, and walked across to the ox-waggon leading the horse on a loose rein. 'It's Alf Loubser, isn't it?' he asked, taking off his hat and shielding his eyes from the sun with his hand. 'And that's Louise. My, you've grown, haven't you, Louise?'

'She's not as grown now as she was after you visited our farm,' commented Alf Loubser, harshly.

Barney stopped where he was, and squinted up at Loubser

awkwardly. The sun was right behind Loubser's head, shining through the canvas top of the waggon, and it blotted out the taut, narrow-eyed expression on the farmer's face.

'I'm not sure what you're saying,' said Barney.

'You're not? I'll suppose you're going to deny it, are you?'

'If I knew what I was supposed to be denying, then maybe I would. Listen, why don't I ask my boys to feed and water your beasts, and then you can come inside and talk this all over in a civilised way, whatever, it is. Did you come all the way from Beaufort?'

'Leg by leg. I have cousins in Hopetown, I was visiting them, too.'

'Well, come along inside. You look like you could use some refreshment, and I know that *I* could. Let me help you down, Louise.'

Alf Loubser reared up the muzzle of his rifle. 'She doesn't need any of your help, man. Leave her alone.'

'I was only trying to be friendly.'

'Well, we don't need friendship like yours. Friendship like yours, we can do without.'

Michael came out of the stables and took Jupiter's reins and Barney told him to fetch four or five of the boys to look after Alf Loubser's oxen. When they were pulling a full-sized eighteen-foot waggon, oxen could manage to plod only at an average of five miles a day, and they usually needed a day's rest after a long haul. It was just as tiring for the driver: a full waggon and its team could stretch 120 feet from the first oxen to the last wheel, and it could easily and frequently be halted by mud or sand or rough ground.

'It's a hell of a place you've got here,' said Alf Loubser, as his team were released from their yokes and led around to the side of the house to graze and drink.

Barney looked around at the dung-strewn driveway. 'You haven't done much to improve it, though, have you?'

'Although he was trying to be fierce, Alf Loubser could not help laughing. 'Don't you know that gravel needs fertilising, man, just like anything else?'

'One day, the Afrikaner sense of humour will penetrate my thick Jewish skull,' said Barney. 'Come along inside. Oh – and you can leave your gun with Horace.'

Alf Loubser frowned at Horace, who was standing attentively by the door and then turned back to Barney. 'I can't leave my gun with him, man. He's one of your boys.'

'You mean you came here with the intention of shooting me?'

'Why shouldn't I shoot you, the way you left Louise? You see this poor girl, three months after you left her belly was out here, and nine months after you left she gave birth to a baby girl.'

Barney looked first at Alf Loubser, with his red sweating face and his eyes as pale as a bleached blue workshirt; and then at Louise, who was still pretty in a white, transparent kind of a way, but who had not improved in the years since he had slept with her. Her figure was slipping under that cheap gingham frock, and there were purplish circles under her eyes. Her ankles were thickening, too, and there were dark blue veins in her legs. In a year or two, she would look like any other hard-worked Dutch farm woman on the Koup.

'The baby was yours, Barney,' she said. 'I didn't go to bed with anybody else for a month before, or a month after.'

'Give Horace the gun,' said Barney. 'I'm not going to talk about this while you're waving a loaded game-rifle at me.'

Reluctantly, Alf Loubser handed the rifle over, and Horace took it with a solemn nod of his head. 'Come inside,' said Barney. 'I'll have some tea and cold meat sent up. Are you hungry?'

'*I'm* hungry,' said Louise, but her father shushed her, and gave her a glare.

Barney led the two of them into the drawing-room. To Barney, it seemed silent and inhospitable without Sara; but Alf Loubser and Louise looked around it in awe, at the blue moiré-silk on the walls, at the ormolu clock with its flying cherubs, and the spindly-elegant French furniture. Barney went to the windows and opened them wide so that a warm breeze could blow in from the back of the house.

'So, you're trying to tell me that I'm a father, are you?' he asked.

'There's no question,' said Alf Loubser. 'She even looks like you. Dark, with curly hair.'

'How old is she?'

'Nearly nine. She's a pretty young girl, too, and clever.'

473

Barney stared across the fields towards the trees. 'Was it really nine years ago? I don't know whether it seems longer or shorter.'

'We call her Heloise,' Alf Loubser told him, not without pride. 'Me and my wife, we've been raising her like our own daughter. Everybody in Beaufort believes she is. She'll be a good worker!'

'Did you bring a picture of her?'

'A picture?'

'Well, how do I know that she actually exists, unless I see a picture?'

Alf Loubser pouted out his lower lip. 'What do you mean, how do you know that she exists? Of course she exists! I kissed her myself in Beaufort, not two months ago!'

'That's scarcely proof. The kiss will have dried by now.'

Louise touched her father's arm, and said, 'You have the birth certificate. It's in the Bible box, on the waggon.'

'All right,' said Barney. 'I'll have Horace bring it in.'

'No, you don't,' put in Alf Loubser. 'That blackie of yours could just as easily take it and burn it, and then you'd say that we didn't have any kind of a claim at all. Louise – you get it.'

Louise left them, and Barney indicated to Alf Loubser that he could sit down. The sheep–farmer squatted awkwardly on the very brim of a small gilded chair, his thighs wide apart, and folded his arms over his chest.

'I suppose you've come here for money,' said Barney.

'Well,' said Alf Loubser, most of his ferocity abated. 'I wouldn't have pursued you for it normally. I know that Louise has had a man or two, although not so many these days, and I suppose babies are one of the risks. But I do believe that Heloise is yours, and now she's growing up the child needs clothes, and shoes, and we're trying to give her some schooling. So, when Simon de Koker said that you'd found that ruddy great diamond, well ... you can't blame me, can you, for thinking that it was worth asking for a small contribution?'

Barney rubbed his eyes. 'I see. So I've got my old friend Simon de Koker to thank for this, have I? When did you last see him?'

'Two months ago, just about. But that was the first time for

474

years. He hasn't worked as a guide since '70, or maybe '71 at the latest.'

'What's he doing now?'

Alf Loubser pressed to his lips a stubby finger, stained with sheep-dip. 'Hush-hush, man. Mustn't say.'

'Something secret?'

Alf Loubser shifted his chair an inch or two closer, and leaned his cropped head forward confidentially. 'Between you and me, man, he's a secret agent. Would you believe that? He works for the old Pretorius government people in the Transvaal. Trying to overthrow the British, you see, and restore the independent Boer republic. But don't tell anyone I told you.'

Barney shook his head. 'I won't tell a soul. But what was he doing all the way down in Beaufort, when he's working as a secret agent in the Transvaal.'

'Don't ask me! What he does, that's hush-hush. He won't even tell you what colour hat he's wearing these days. All I can tell you is that he came past the farm two months ago, and he had a little English fellow with him – a little mannikin, not much taller than Heloise, but smart-looking, a good suit, if you know what I mean. They were on their way to Kimberley, they said, to see about some business, and that was all.'

Horace came in, and Barney ordered tea. 'I thought you said that Simon de Koker told you about my diamond?' he asked Alf Loubser.

Alf Loubser shrugged defensively. 'They were downstairs in the kitchen, talking till twelve o'clock at night. I went down to see if they wanted anything, that's all.'

'And you accidentally overheard what they were saying?' said Barney, raising an eyebrow.

'It's my house!' protested Alf Loubser.

'Of course it is,' agreed Barney. 'You had every right to listen. So, tell me, what did you hear them saying?'

'They didn't say much. Simon de Koker was worried about the weather. But then the little English fellow mentioned your name, and said something about this diamond you'd found, and how much it was worth. He didn't say anything else about it, and after a while they went to bed. But in the morning I talked to the pastor at the church, and he said he'd read in the newspaper about the diamond, so I knew that what the little fellow had said must be true. I talked it over with *mevrouw* Loubser, and we thought I ought to pay you a visit in Kimberley and ask for something to help bring up Heloise.'

Barney stood up, and walked to the open French windows. Then he stepped right out on to the patio, with Alf Loubser watching him uncomfortably from inside the drawing-room.

'You won't tell anybody that I told you?' Alf Loubser called out, anxiously. 'Some of these Boer snipers, they're very promiscuous with a gun!'

Barney shook his head, although he did not know if Alf Loubser could see him or not. He was thinking too hard about what the sheep-farmer had just told him. If Alf Loubser had seen Hunt in the company of Simon de Koker, and Simon de Koker was now an agent for the Boer resistance in the Transvaal, then it was highly unlikely that Hunt was still working for Government House in Capetown, as he had claimed he was. All those stories about Sir Bartle Frere tangling up the Union Jack on the lawns and raw young diplomats being forced to choke down whole ostrich eggs were almost certainly fictitious, dashes of invention that Hunt had put in to add believability to his story about wanting the diamond as a glittering diversion from the Zulu war. He had probably hoped that they would irritate Barney, at the same time.

Now that Barney could think about it more logically, the odds against Hunt still being employed by the colonial service were slight. After all, there had been several changes of Governor since Barney had first met him, and Hunt had probably lost his job years ago, when Sir Philip Woodhouse had returned to England. Apart from that, his homosexuality would always have made his career in the foreign service precarious: especially since most of the public school chaps who staffed Government House were very dull, and straightforward, and were not the sort of chaps who cared to be caught inside some other chap's mosquito-net with their ducks around their ankles.

Barney had no proof of it, but it seemed more than likely that the Natalia Star had been acquired for the Boers – either as a provocative symbol of their independence, and their rights in West Griqualand; or as a means of financing an armed rebellion against the British – or both. Perhaps Hunt had never intended to pay for the diamond at all. Perhaps the 'consortium of businessmen' was all invention, too; and he had come to Vogel Vlei with his extravagant offers of 'a million-four' simply in order to find out how difficult it was going to be to steal the diamond out of Barney's safe. If that was so, Hunt must have found Sara's discontent and Joel's simmering anger to be gifts from Heaven.

Louise came back into the drawing-room with the birth certificate. She offered it to her father, but he indicated with a wave of his hand that she should take it outside to Barney.

Barney took it and read it while Louise stood by his side, occasionally pushing her wind-blown hair out of her eyes. It announced simply that a female child had been born to Louise Stella Loubser at Beaufort West, and that the child had been baptised in the Kleine Kerk in the names of Heloise Petra Loubser. Barney folded the paper up again and handed it back.

'Do you really think the child was mine?' he asked Louise.

'I always hoped it was,' she told him.

He looked at her for a while, so young and pale and unsmiling – a girl who lived in a world that was mostly fairy-stories and simple dreams. She had remembered him after all these years, although she probably saw him as somebody quite different from the broad-shouldered diamond digger that he really was. She was the kind of girl who saw stars even on cloudy nights, and who could make a prince out of a kopje-walloper.

'I'll give you some money,' Barney told her. 'I can't admit that the child is mine. My lawyers would burst a blood-vessel. But I'll give you a hundred pounds a year for five years to take care of her clothes and her schooling, and that's just because I like you.'

Louise gave a vague, pretty smile. 'I look at Heloise sometimes and I can remember your face exactly,' she said.

'You'll take care of her?' Barney asked her.

Louise nodded, and then reached on tiptoe and kissed him on the cheek.

Alf Loubser came outside, his hands firmly pushed into his pockets. 'You've seen the certificate? What do you think?'

'I've already told Louise that I'll give her some money. Not much, because even a birth certificate isn't convincing proof that the baby was mine. But enough to make sure that you can educate her, and keep her well fed.'

Alf Loubser scanned the grounds of Vogel Vlei, his eyes wrinkled against the bright sunlight. 'I came up here feeling angry,' he said. 'Well, I'm sorry. You've behaved like a gentleman. I thought I was going to have to frighten you into helping Heloise. But it wasn't necessary. I feel like a bit of a pig, and I just hope that you'll shake my hand on it.'

He took one hand out of his pocket, and held it out. Barney shook it, and then smiled. 'Why don't you stay here the night?' he asked. 'There are plenty of empty rooms.'

'You live in this huge place all by yourself? No children?'

Barney shook his head. 'You know what children are like. They have a way of growing up, and leaving you.'

He took Louise Stella Loubser's arm, and escorted her back into the drawing-room, where Horace had spread a crisp pink cloth on the side-table and was laying out plates of cold tongue, and cold salt beef, and potato salad. Alf Loubser rubbed his hands hungrily, and gave Barney a wink of approval. Neither he nor Louise knew how desolate Barney felt, just at that moment, nor how much he appreciated their simple, unaffected company. Louise leaned her white-blonde hair against his shoulder and Barney touched it the way a child touches anything irresistibly silky.

Later that evening, while Alf Loubser and Louise were having their supper in the small parlour at the back of the house, Barney held a meeting with Harold Feinberg and Edward Nork in the library. Harold was not feeling at all well: his little froggy girl had been upsetting him by threatening to take another lover, and with the discovery of two new pipes at Dorstfontein, the market price of diamonds was looking what Harold always called 'distinctly tremulous'. The sooner the South African diamond industry became a monopoly, Harold grumbled, the better it would be for all of them. Then they could turn the flow of diamonds on and off like a tap, and control the price down to the last farthing.

Edward Nork was somewhere between yesterday's hangover

and tonight's bender, and he kept blinking and coughing and wiping his spectacles on his shirt, and excusing himself to go to the lavatory.

'Sara's out this evening?' asked Harold. 'What is it, crochet circle? Drama group?'

Barney took off his coat and hung it over the back of his chair. 'That's the whole reason I've asked you to come here.'

'What is?' Edward frowned. 'You want *us* to take up crochet, too?'

Harold coughed, clearing a barrowload of phlegm from his throat. He looked pale and unhealthy these days, as if part of him had already started to die. Barney was not at all surprised that his French girl was thinking of taking another lover, although it would not be easy for her to find anyone who could so regularly supply her with her favourite contraceptives.

'You're thinking of selling the diamond, is that it?' he asked. 'Leopold and Wavers have finally come up with an offer that you can't resist? You have that kind of look on your face.'

'Really, Harold, I don't know why you're so nervous about Barney selling this stone,' Edward put in. 'He's got to dispose of it sooner or later, and *later* is going to be just as bad for diamond prices as *sooner*. You should be pleased that he's going to sell it through Feinberg, and that you're going to get a healthy commission. Supposing he took it to Manny Greene?'

Harold slapped his hand on the leather arm of his chair; the same chair in which, only a few days before, Hunt had sat with his legs prissily crossed and proposed a purchase by his 'consortium of British businessmen'. He snapped crossly, 'It's the wrong time to sell. And, besides, I think Barney's original idea of having the diamond cut first, before we put it out to auction, is much better. It will give all of us experience of handling a big stone, all the way along the line; and it will increase our profit three hundred per cent. And don't talk to me about Manny Greene, that *shnorrer*.'

'You're so *cautious*,' Edward retorted. 'If Barney doesn't act quickly on the offers that Leopold and Wavers and all the rest of them have already tabled, he might end up with a stone that's worth three times as much that nobody's actually prepared to buy.'

'Why don't you stick to your geology?' Harold barked at him.

'What do you know from diamond dealing? Most of the time you're *shikker*.'

Edward sighed, and took off his spectacles to prod at his eyeballs with his middle finger, as if he were testing plums to see how ripe they were. 'You Jews exasperate me,' he said, with his eyes still tightly closed. 'A chap only has to disagree with you, and you break out into a rash of incomprehensibility.'

'*Shikker* means drunk,' said Barney, in a quiet voice. 'And, in any case, there isn't any future in you two arguing.'

'What do you mean?' said Edward. 'We always argue. It's good for our livers.'

'There you are,' said Harold. 'I'm talking world diamond prices, and he's talking offals.'

Barney said, 'It doesn't matter any more. The diamond's gone. It's been stolen.'

There was a curious silence, interspersed only by Harold's laboured breathing. Edward put on his glasses again and peered at Barney like Galileo trying to distinguish through his foggy seventeenth-century telescope whether the planet Saturn had rings around it, or ears; and hoping for the sake of his sanity that the evidence would not favour ears.

'It's been *stolen*? My dear chap! But how? Didn't you have it locked in your safe? I can't believe it!'

Harold said nothing, but let his chin drop forward on to his chest. His breathing sounded as harsh as the old harmonium bellows in the *strooidak* church in Klipdrift.

'I had a visit from someone I used to know in the colonial service at Capetown,' said Barney. 'He made me an offer for the diamond, saying that the British wanted to present it to the Queen. What I didn't know *then*, but what I've found out *now*, is that he probably no longer works for the colonial service, and hasn't done so for years. He's working in co-operation with a Boer scout called Simon de Koker, who apparently acts as a secret agent for the resistance in the Transvaal.'

Harold raised his head, his eyes protuberant with shock and shortness of breath.

'It's gone to the Boers? The diamond's gone to the Boers?'

'I suspect so,' Barney told him.

'Pitiful God, I can't believe what you're telling me,' said

Harold. 'You know what's going to happen if the Boers lay their hands on it? Either they'll hold it to ransom, and ask for their independence back. Or else they'll sell it to the Russians and buy themselves enough rifles and enough ammunition to push the British out of the diamond fields and back to the Orange River.'

Barney shrugged. 'I know that, Harold. Although I still don't know for sure that it *was* the Boers. There isn't any firm evidence one way or the other. But it seems to me to be the most likely thing that's happened. The Boers would have more to gain than anybody else by stealing it, and more to lose if it were cut and sold abroad.'

'How did they . . .?' asked Edward, nodding towards the safe.

'I'm afraid to say that Sara gave them the key,' said Barney. 'She's gone with them, along with Joel, and Sara's *amah*.'

'Motley sort of a crew,' remarked Edward.

'Motley or not, they've got the Natalia Star, and I don't know where they've gone.'

Harold said, 'I think I'm going to have to trouble you for a glass of water.'

Barney rang the bell for Horace, while Harold loosened his tie and sat in the armchair mopping his forehead and gasping.

'So, you called it the Natalia Star,' smiled Edward. 'Is that one of the reasons why Sara was so keen to help them?'

Barney looked down, and re-arranged some of the pens and pencils on his desk. 'Let's just say that our marriage hadn't been running particularly smoothly. But I was still shocked when I found out what she'd done.'

'When did this happen?' asked Harold.

'Yesterday morning, while I was working at the mine. I didn't find out that my key had been stolen until early afternoon; and then I made a complete fool of myself and chased them along the Hopetown road, thinking they'd made a run for the Cape. There wasn't any sign of them.'

'From what you've said about this Simon de Koker, it's far more likely that they've headed for the Transvaal,' said Edward.

Horace came in, and Barney asked for a glass of water for Harold and a cup of strong coffee for himself. Edward said that

481

he would 'make do' with the whiskey decanter on the library table.

When Horace had gone, Harold said slowly, 'The most important thing of all is to prevent the bastards from cutting it. Once it's cut, you'll have no chance of proving that it's yours. In the rough, we can identify it. I've got photographs of it from all sides; and drawings; and a plaster-cast.'

'They won't have any great difficulty getting it cut, though, will they?' said Barney. 'There must be a dozen good cutters in Amsterdam who would do it for them, no questions asked.'

'Well, you're right,' sighed Harold. 'But it could take anything up to eighteen months to cut a stone as big as yours – the Natalia Star, if that's what you've really decided to call it. And until they've bruted off all the rough surfaces, we've still got a remote chance of proving that it's yours.'

'That's if it actually goes to Amsterdam; and that's if we can find it once it's there. They could just as easily sell it in the rough to the Russian court; or the Austrians; or send it over to America.'

Harold drank his water, and then patted his mouth with his handkerchief. 'The only way we're going to find out where it's gone is if I put out feelers in the trade. One thing's for sure: they won't take it to a second-rate cutter. They're going to have to go to the best, and that narrows their options considerably. There are only three cutters I can think of who could do it justice – Josef Van Steenwijk, who works for Coster's, in Amsterdam; Levi Baumgold, at Annen's, also in Amsterdam; and Itzik Yussel, who's the head cutter at Roosendaal's in Antwerp.'

Barney leaned back in his chair and sipped disconsolately at his coffee. 'They might keep the diamond for years before they send it out for cutting. They might sell it as a rough, and not bother to have it cut at all.'

'Well,' said Harold, 'there's always a chance of that ... in which case, you'll never see the diamond again. But I'm crediting anyone who has the nerve to steal the continent's biggest diamond from out under the nose of its owner with the intelligence to make as much money out of it as they can. As a rough, it's too easily identifiable, and too difficult to sell and re-sell.

Remember that Thomas Pitt did with the Regent ... he sent it straight to London to be cut, so that nobody else could claim it was theirs. For my money, that diamond is going to be smuggled to Amsterdam or Antwerp within the month.'

Edward Nork had helped himself to a generous glassful of whiskey, and he noisily stoppered the decanter before coming back across the room and standing by Barney's desk, his spectacles propped up on his forehead, his shaggy eyebrows tangled in thought.

'What you're going to have to do is send copies of Harold's drawings to all the major diamond-merchants, explaining that the diamond is stolen. That won't stop anybody really unscrupulous, but it might frighten some of the more respectable houses off. Cheers!'

He swallowed whiskey, and then coughed until he was grey in the face.

'All right,' said Barney. 'If that's the best we can do, let's do it. I can tell you something though: I would rather have lost that diamond down a hole in the ground than lose it to those people.'

'I know,' Harold told him, understandingly. 'But that's the way it is with diamonds. They bring out all of your most possessive and jealous feelings, no matter how much you try to resist them. They make you slightly mad. And why not? Carat for carat, they're worth more than almost anything you can think of. Nearly twice as much as emeralds. A hundred times more than gold.'

'They're not worth anything at all if you've lost them,' put in Edward, with an exaggeratedly rueful face, and hiccupped.

Barney's guesses about Hunt and Simon de Koker had been mostly accurate, although Hunt had actually resigned from the colonial service only two months ago, the day after de Koker had approached him in an hotel restaurant on Adderley Street and suggested that he might care to help him lay his hands on the Natalia Star. De Koker had not particularly wanted to involve Hunt in a secret Boer mission, but he had needed someone who could get himself admitted to Vogel Vlei without arousing suspicion. He had also been worried that Barney might already have heard that he was working as an agent for the Boers, and might have him arrested by the British as soon as he turned up on the doorstep.

Hunt, for his part, had been more than eager for a little excitement, and a little peril, and the chance to play the starring rôle in a domestic and criminal double-cross. Once inside Vogel Vlei, he had been delighted by Barney's dogmatic insistence that the stone was not for sale at any price – particularly since he had only £36 os 2d in his Capetown bank account, which fell somewhat short of 'a million-four'. But he had particularly relished Sara, bored and irritated and bourgeois, and he had tried to exploit her frustrations for all he was worth by telling her how beautiful she was, and yet how neglected she was, an English rose flowering unseen and unappreciated in this dry and dusty tailing of the Empire. Joel had been easy to recruit: his resentment of Barney was so intense that in Hunt's words 'it could have burned holes in the carpet'.

After they had stolen the stone, though, they had not headed for the Transvaal, as Barney and Harold had supposed, and they had never intended to. De Koker's instructions from Swartplaas, the farm on the Witwatersrand that the Boers were using as a resistance headquarters, were to take the diamond out of the country as quickly as possible, from the port of Lourenço Marques, where a Dutch steamship would be waiting in the third week of March. Their journey to the coast would be difficult and possibly dangerous, but de Koker had arranged for a small escort of Boer volunteers to meet them at Wesselstroom and guide them through the Drakensberg pass to New Scotland, as far as Lake Chrissie, where they would turn eastwards again and follow the course of the Impellus River into Portuguese territory, and then down to the sea.

To begin with, to put Barney off the trail, they had headed northwards out of Kimberley on the track that would have taken them up along the valley of the Vaal towards Klerksdorp, and right into the heart of the Transvaal. But after a few miles they had turned directly eastwards across open country; and spent their first night camping by a smoky fire on the open veld, not far from the settlement of Boshof. When morning came, they had started off early, and made for Bloemfontein, the capital of the Orange Free State. It took them two days to get there, travelling as rapidly as they could; but when they arrived there they rested for another two days, so that Sara could bathe and buy herself two or three new dresses to travel in, and Joel could stock up on the medication he needed, Dover's powder and boric ointment. Simon de Koker exchanged their elegant but impractical landau for a horse-drawn waggon, which he stocked with beef and ham and smoked cheese, and eight kegs of water.

Edward had been right about them: they were a motley band, and from the very beginning of their uncomfortable flight across the Orange Free State there were violent disagreements about who should sit where, and who was in charge, and most crucial of all, who the Natalia Star now belonged to. Sara, who had taken the key from Barney's bureau, and had actually removed the stone from the safe, was quite sure that the diamond was now hers. Simon de Koker said that if the diamond was now hers, then why was he bothering to drive her all the way across southern Africa? The diamond was now the property of the true government of the Transvaal, the Boers, and it would be cut and auctioned in Amsterdam for the sole purpose of financing a Boer campaign against the British oppressors. Joel claimed that the diamond was fifty per cent his, since the mine in which it had been found was fifty per cent his. Hunt argued that the stone should be sold in the rough, as quickly as possible, and the proceeds divided four ways, with a few hundred pounds for Nareez. Nareez was suffering from heatstroke, and said nothing at all, but chewed coriander seeds, and stared at the mirages of lakes and rivers that shimmered on the horizon as if they were visions of the Ganges at Rājshāhi, on the hot days of her childhood.

What none of them knew, as they toiled their way towards the foothills of the Drakensberg, was that Sir Bartle Frere's invasion of Zululand had already started, and that only two hundred miles to the east of them, Lord Chelmsford was advancing towards the Zulu capital of Ulundi with three columns of regular soldiers and volunteers. On 11 January, the week before Sara and Hunt had stolen the diamond, Lord

Chelmsford's central column had forded the Buffalo River at Rorke's Drift and on 20 January, a few miles further on, he had established a new camp in the shadow of the odd sphinx-shaped mountain known as Isandhlwana.

On 22 January, the Wednesday after Sara and Hunt and Joel had stolen the Natalia Star, and when they were a day east from Bloemfontein, twenty thousand Zulu warriors attacked Lord Chelmsford's camp and slaughtered nearly 1400 soldiers and Natal native recruits, leaving the sloping hillside littered with burned-out tents, looted waggons, and stiffened bodies. The six companies of the 2nd Warwickshire regiment died to the last man, and the broken ground down to the Buffalo River was splattered with the blood of grooms, cooks, waggon drivers, and bandsmen, all of whom had tried to escape when the Zulu *impi* broke through the front lines of soldiers. On the same day, the British mission station and hospital at Rorke's Drift was successfully defended against 4000 Zulus by only 104 British soldiers. But Lord Chelmsford had been obliged to withdraw, and call for reinforcements, and to re-assess his previous contempt for Cetewayo's army.

It thundered for three solid days when Hunt and Sara and Joel crossed the Drakensberg mountains, great dark barrages of bumbling noise, with rain so harsh and torrential that it stung their faces. The horses shied and reared, and their hooves kept slipping on the wet rock. Six or seven times in every mile they managed to cover, their waggon wheels would lodge in a groove or a gully, and Simon de Koker and Hunt would have to lever the wheels free with shovel-handles, or push the waggon out with their backs. Joel, cursing and complaining, would have to be lifted out into the storm by Sara and Nareez, to lighten the load, and the three of them would be obliged to sit on a nearby boulder like drowned cats while the waggon was heaved back on to the track again.

'Every now and then, one is given a severe lesson in life that one should have been content with what one had,' Sara remarked, with a drip on the end of her nose, on the day they reached the highest point in the Drakensberg. She was sitting by the side of the road with a khaki canvas kitbag upturned on her head, her waterproof cape drawn around her shoulders, her

486

white leather boots hopelessly muddied and stained with water. The rain was sloping across the pass in sheets of bitterly-cold spray, and the waggon had got jammed again, this time in one of the old narrow tracks that had been gouged out of the rock by the heavy ox-waggons of the Boer *voortrekkers*.

'*Content?*' asked Joel. 'How could you ever have been content with Barney? Even this is better than sitting in that tomb of a house, trying to remember what human dignity was.'

'Do you think you've found your dignity now?' asked Sara, tartly.

Joel looked down at himself. Under his wide wet bush-hat, which was drooping down on all sides, he was dressed in a muddy brown overcoat and frayed grey trousers. He had wound a blanket around his waist to keep his hips warm and the stump of his left leg dry; and inserted his right foot into a leather saddle-pouch to prevent the rain from running into his shoe.

'At least I'm free,' said Joel, although he did not sound very convinced, even of that.

Sara took out a sopping handkerchief and wiped her face. 'I'd give up any amount of freedom for a hot bath.'

'We've got the diamond,' said Joel. 'In a month, we'll all be well on our way to Amsterdam. Then, when it's cut and sold, and we get our share, we'll be rich enough to do whatever we like. By this time next year, we won't have any worries about anything, *helevai.*'

Sara stared at him for a while, the raindrops clustered on her eyelashes. 'Do you really think I'm going to share the diamond with the Boers?'

Joel looked back at her warily. 'What do you mean?'

'Exactly what I say. I didn't take the diamond for the sake of the independence of the Transvaal, I can tell you that. I don't care for Boers one bit. They're crude, and they're uneducated, and they spend all of their time smoking pipes and eating dreadful varieties of cheese. Just look at that Simon de Koker. He smells like a mule, and I shouldn't think he's combed that beard of his for weeks.'

Joel picked up a pebble, and juggled it in the palm of his

hand. Only a few yards away, Simon de Koker was trying to wrestle the iron rim of the waggon wheel out of the rock with a crowbar, and there was a grinding noise of metal against wet sandstone. Hunt, almost purple in the face, was trying to push the waggon forward.

'He won't let you run off with it,' said Joel. 'He didn't travel all the way to Capetown and back, and then across to Lourenço Marques, just to watch you wave him goodbye.'

'*He* may be going to Lourenço Marques, but *I'm* not,' said Sara, emphatically.

Joel tossed the pebble up, and caught it again. 'Where are *you* going?' he asked, in a bland voice.

'You'll betray me, if I tell you. You'll probably betray me anyway.'

'Why should I betray you?' asked Joel, trying to sound surprised.

'You betrayed your own brother.'

Joel sniffed. 'Is that what you call it?'

'What do *you* call it?'

'I call it survival, most of the time. Sometimes I call it justice.'

Simon de Koker snapped his whip at the horses, and, 'Yip! Yip! Yip! Come on now, pull up! Pull up, you bunch of bonebags!'

'I don't think insulting them is going to help,' Joel called loudly, over the cold clattering of the rain. Simon de Koker looked around and gave him a flat, sour stare. Joel grinned back at him, and said, 'Don't mind me. What do I know from horses?'

As the team of horses strained at their harnesses, their hooves skidding and sliding and their flanks steaming with rain, Sara said quietly: 'A million-pound diamond for one would be ideal. A million-pound diamond between two would be almost as good. But a million-pound diamond between four? It's just not enough. Particularly when I suspect that our smelly Boer friend has no intention of giving us anything more than a token reward for our troubles. He's a political zealot, and political zealots are usually even more untrustworthy than common criminals. So Papa said, anyway.'

Joel kept on juggling his pebble, until at last he reached his arm back and tossed it away down the track, back towards the Orange Free State. 'You're going to have to think of a way of getting rid of him, then, aren't you? And Hunt.'

'Hunt won't be at all difficult. He's like a child. It's de Koker that's going to be a problem.'

'What are you thinking of doing? Knocking him on the head with a bottle, and tying him up, and leaving him for the *lemmergayers*?'

Sara's lips were blue from cold. 'We're going to have to kill him,' she said. 'He knows the land far better than we do. If we don't kill him, he's bound to get free, and come hot in pursuit. Anyway, for all we know, he's planning to do the same thing to us. If you were he, would *you* drive a whole waggon-load of cripples and women all the way to Lourenço Marques, when you could make it in half the time on your own? He's probably waiting for nothing less than a convenient place in the mountains, so that he can cut the horses' traces and push us all over a precipice.'

'Your sense of the melodramatic is over-developed, to say the least,' said Joel. 'And less of the "cripples", if you don't mind.'

'If you weren't a cripple you could deal with him yourself,' Sara retorted. 'As it is, it'll have to be me.'

'What are you going to do?' asked Joel, with hopeless jocularity, 'get Nareez to hug him to death?'

'Nareez is my companion,' Sara reminded him, sharply. 'She didn't ask to be dragged halfway across Africa, and she's been very brave.' She hesitated, and then she said, 'I'm going to shoot him.'

'What with? You don't even have a pistol.'

'De Koker has a rifle. That will do.'

'He sleeps with it. He carries it around all day. When do you think he's going to give you the chance to take it away from him?'

'We'll see,' said Sara.

There was a distant mumble of thunder, and lightning illuminated the sky behind the mountains like the scenery of a cheap opera. After a few minutes' pause, the rain began to fall even more heavily than before, and water foamed down the rutted track and sprayed around the wheels of the waggon.

Simon de Koker called, 'Yip! Yip! Yip!' and at last the waggon's back wheels reared out of the rutted track, and the whole rig rolled forwards six or seven feet, its wet canvas top wobbling on its frame.

'There's just one problem,' Joel whispered to Sara, as Simon de Koker and Nareez came across to help him back over the tailboard. 'If we kill de Koker, how do we find our way to wherever we're going?'

'The road's easy from here,' said Sara; and then realising that Simon de Koker had overheard her, she smiled, 'Isn't it, Mr de Koker? Quite easy?'

Simon de Koker picked Joel up as roughly as if he were a broken scarecrow, and with Nareez holding his one remaining leg, which made Joel tilt unnervingly sideways, they carried him over to the back of the waggon.

'The road to Lourenço Marques from here is very difficult,' Simon de Koker said. 'I don't even know it very well myself – which is why we pick up extra guides at Wesselstroom. On purpose, we're not going the easy way. If the British catch us, and take the diamond, it will be years and years before we can afford to fight for our independence again.'

'It's easy to get to Durban from here, though, isn't it?'

'Durban?' asked de Koker, suspiciously, beckoning to Hunt to let down the tailboard.

'I used to live there,' said Sara, smiling as attractively as she could with a wet canvas kitbag on her head.

Simon de Koker grunted, and rolled Joel into the back of the waggon. Hunt, his wet hair stuck to his face, the shoulders of his coat stained dark with damp, locked up the tailboard and said, 'Let's see how far we can get before we have to do this all over again.'

They drove in silence for another four miles, crossing into Natal and descending into the Sand River Valley towards Ladysmith. The rain at last began to ease off, and dissolve into a fine grey fog, which gave the mountainous landscape the silent and eerie quality of another world. Simon de Koker sat up in front of the waggon, driving, with Nareez sitting beside him in

490

her Indian shawl. Joel lay in the back, his head resting against a flour sack, snoring. Hunt and Sara faced each other across the waist, saying nothing, but continually addressing each other with their eyes. Hunt would give Sara a provocative, questioning look; and she would either stare at him with feigned disinterest, or turn away.

'When are you thinking of getting rid of ...?' Hunt asked her, as they rumbled noisily down an incline beside the Klip River.

Sara frowned, but Hunt vigorously nodded his head towards Simon de Koker's hunched-up back.

'I don't know what you're talking about,' said Sara.

'Of course you know what I'm talking about,' Hunt replied, with a teasing smile. 'Tomorrow morning, we turn north, to Ladysmith, and then to the Wakkerstroom, and then in three weeks we should be in Lourenço Marquès. This is where the road divides. This way, Lourenço Marquès; that way, Durban. Come on, Mrs Blitz, I've seen your mind ticking like a carriage-clock. All those cogs going round, all those jewelled mountings! I've seen you muttering to Joel, too. You're not going to let the Boers get away with your precious diamond, are you? Especially when they're going to use it to fight the British. De Koker may have judged your perfidy exactly; but he's forgotten about your patriotism. A fine colonial lady like you. Capetown's teeming with them; so I should know.'

The noise of the metal-rimmed tyres was just loud enough to prevent Simon de Koker from hearing what Hunt was saying; all his years in the colonial service had given Hunt a particular talent for gossiping about people only two or three feet away from where they were standing, without arousing their suspicions. He liked to call it the 'embassy murmur'.

Sara glanced at Joel, sleeping with his cheek pressed into a sausage-like fold, and his mouth hanging open. 'I *have* been considering alternatives,' she said.

'Of course. Just like de Koker must have been, too.'

Sara pressed her hand over the gazelle-skin bag which was now hanging around her neck, tied to her gold and diamond necklace. 'He's going to have to kill me first. Surely he knows that.'

'I'm quite certain he does. I'm not really sure why he hasn't killed all of us already.'

'I think I know,' said Sara. 'He's one of these men who needs a moral justification for everything he does. It's quite common among Calvinists, and political enthusiasts. They can't act unless they believe that they've been wronged. They're stern people, the Boers – very stern, but also very religious. And that's why Simon de Koker won't try to get us out of the way until *we* make the first move.'

'Well,' said Hunt, pursing his lips, 'it's an interesting theory.'

'I only hope that it's a theory that works,' replied Sara. 'And I hope that when we *do* make the first move, we make it effectively enough for Mr de Koker to be rendered incapable of retaliation.'

'Um, what do you have in mind, in particular?' asked Hunt, with a smile.

Sara looked towards Joel, still snoring on his flour sack. 'That's what *he* wanted to know.'

That night, they drew their waggon off the main road and tied up their horses by a stand of evergreens. It was still foggy, and when they lit their campfire to make tea and cook up a pan of salted beef and beans, the flames were blurred by a smudgy orange halo. They were ten miles short of Ladysmith, and the turning which would take them north to Newcastle and Wesselstroom, and eventually to New Scotland and Lourenço Marques, but the horses were exhausted and shivering, and Joel had been bawling complaints to Simon de Koker for almost an hour about his leg. At last, taciturn and reluctant, Simon de Koker had said, 'We halt here,' and jammed back the waggon's ironwood brake-handle.

They hardly spoke over their meal. They were all exhausted and cold; and since they had crossed the summit of the Drakensberg a noticeable feeling of mutual suspicion had settled amongst them. Simon de Koker sat well away from the rest, his rifle propped against a sapling close beside him, humourlessly stripping the skin from a *weinwurst* with his clasp-knife.

At last, Joel said, 'I'm tired out. Nareez – will you get me my blankets?'

The *amah* made a show of finishing her tin plateful of beans before getting up and bringing Joel's bedding. She considered herself nobody's servant, except Sara's; and even to Sara she was more of a mother than a hired woman. Hunt went to find his own bedroll, and made himself an elaborate little tent under the branches of the trees with the canvas flap which usually covered the boxes and barrels that hung from the sides of the waggon's hull. It was not long before only Sara and Simon de Koker were left by themselves, sitting ten feet apart from each other on opposite sides of the campfire in wary silence. The fire crackled and spat in the damp air, and all around them there was nothing but slowly settling silver, like the particles on a photographic plate, until Sara began to feel that this was the only existence there was, here in this suffocating and unfocused world of fog, and unseen mountains, and ghostly trees.

'I think soon that I will take charge of the diamond,' said Simon de Koker, without looking up.

Sara raised an eyebrow. 'You think so?'

'*Jaha*. It's for safety. A woman shouldn't carry anything so valuable.'

'I think I'm quite capable of looking after it myself, thank you,' said Sara. 'I was brought up in Natal, after all. I know my way around.'

'Well ... that's what I'm worried about,' said Simon de Koker, cutting off another piece of sausage, and pushing it into his mouth from the blade of his knife.

'You're worried that I'm going to run off with the diamond, all on my own?'

Simon de Koker chewed methodically, and then he said, 'It crossed my mind. Don't tell me it didn't cross yours.'

'Of course it did. But then we all went into this little affair together, didn't we? Each of us is equally culpable. Each of us will equally profit. I expect you're going to ask for rather a large percentage of the proceeds for the resistance in the Transvall, but then I can't say I blame you. The British have always been pigheaded about the Boers, and I'm sure that you're not going to give them any more than they deserve.'

493

Simon de Koker watched Sara carefully, his eye glittering orange in the firelight. 'I thought you were a strong British patriot,' he said.

Sara smiled at him. 'I'm afraid that profit comes before patriotism. It always has done in my family. My father is Gerald Sutter the shipper; you've probably heard of him.'

Simon de Koker nodded.

'The truth is, Mr de Koker, that you're a very brave man,' said Sara. She waited a moment or two for that remark to have its full effect, and then she added, 'You're brave because you're risking your life to overthrow a tyranny; and no matter whose tyranny it is – you have a moral and religious right to struggle against it. For once, I'm on the side of the Boers.'

'Are there many English people feel like you?' asked Simon de Koker, warily.

'Some. Mostly the old-time Africa hands – those who have seen for themselves how hard the Boers have had to struggle for their independence. We're not all insensitive, you know. We admire what you're doing, and we know that one day you'll be successful.'

'Hm,' said Simon de Koker, trying to sound suspicious, but clearly pleased.

Sara stood up, and walked around the campfire, so that she was standing only two or three feet away from Simon de Koker, her face softened and blurred by the fog, and by the shadows from the dying flames.

'Unless you've been ignoring me on purpose, you will have seen that I am a woman of great passion,' Sara told him.

'Yes,' said Simon de Koker. He closed his clasp-knife, and then realised that his hands were greasy with *weinwurst*. He wiped them assiduously on the wet grass while Sara came two or three steps closer, and gathered up her skirts so that she could kneel down beside him.

'You mustn't be afraid of me,' she said. 'This is one of those things that happens in war, and during great adventures. Men and women meet in desperate circumstances, and they take whatever they can from each other; not caring about their responsibilities, not caring about the future. You are a Boer agent, and I am an English lady. I should be taking care of my husband, and thinking of my propriety. You should be guarding me, and keeping me prisoner, and not listening to any of this. You should be thinking of the Transvaal.'

'The Transvaal?' frowned Simon de Koker, as if he could not understand what she was saying. He was hypnotised by her perfume, and her femininity, and the way that she spoke so suggestively in such a glacial English accent. The last woman he had slept with had been a big, black, broad-bottomed Kaffir girl in Dutoitspan, in the back room of Maloney's Bar, and that had been well over three months ago.

Sara reach out and tugged gently at Simon de Koker's fringe of a beard. 'Ask me no questions,' she whispered. 'Don't expect anything – least of all that this will ever happen again. I will always deny it, to my dying breath. But go to the waggon now, and lay out the blankets; and in a while I will come and join you.'

Simon de Koker slowly, hesitantly, reached up and held her wrist. His fingernails were embedded with crescents of black dirt, and both he and Sara glanced simultaneously at the contrast between the pale, blue-veined skin of Sara's arm and the grimy calluses of Simon de Koker's fingers; but then Sara laid her other hand over Simon's hand, and said *sshh*, as if to reassure him.

'You're a hero,' she said. 'And there never was a hero, not a real hereo, with clean hands.'

Simon de Koker said thickly, 'When this is over – tonight – you will let me have the diamond?'

Sara's eyes were wide and sincere. 'If you can prove you trust me ... then I can show you just how much I trust you in return ...'

'The diamond, though?'

'Anything,' she murmured. 'Anything at all.'

Simon de Koker looked round at the huddled blankets all around the fire, where the others were sleeping, or trying to sleep. Then he eased himself up, collected his rifle, and stood for a moment in the fog, still indecisive.

'Just a few minutes,' said Sara; and to encourage him, she lifted her gold neck-chain, so that he could glimpse the leather bag in which she kept the diamond. He nodded, and walked across to the waggon, a tall spindly shadow in the fog, with a wide-brimmed hat.

Sara waited five or six minutes, watching the fire sparkle and subside. Then she lifted the diamond from around her neck, and took it across to where Nareez was already sleeping, and tucked it in between Nareez's blankets. Carefully, she stepped over Joel, and tiptoed towards the waggon.

Simon de Koker was waiting for her, on the blanket bed that he had made up on the floor of the waggon, in between the biscuit-boxes and the kegs of water. As he sucked at his pipe, and the dottle glowed, she saw his sweaty bearded face and the flat herringbone pattern of his ribs, decorated with a pattern of moles and stray curly hairs. He had hung his hat from one of the hooks at the side of the waggon cover; and beside him, as close to his naked body as he could comfortably wedge it, was his Mauser rifle, greasy and dark.

'You took your time,' he smiled.

'I wanted to make sure they were all asleep.'

He took his pipe out of his mouth, and knocked it on one of the water kegs. 'That lot, they fall asleep as soon as they look at a blanket. They're just tenderfeet. I've buried more people like that on the Great Karoo than you could count on ten fingers and ten toes.'

Sara unclasped her cape, and folded it up. Then she began to unbutton her blue flowered dress. Simon de Koker noisily cleared his throat. 'You're not frightened, are you?' asked Sara.

'Frightened?' grinned Simon de Koker, and his Afrikaans accent was so strong that he pronounced it, *'frartened?'*

'I'd understand, if you were,' said Sara. 'We're so different, you and I. It's not just a question of two people sharing the same blankets. It's like two enemies, in the same bed.'

'I'm not your enemy,' said Simon de Koker.

She leaned forward, the front of her dress unbuttoned to reveal her white camisole, and kissed him on the forehead. 'I'm not your enemy, either. And I hope that God forgives us.'

Simon de Koker watched her in silence as she lifted her dress over her head, and then stood up under the blue-willow hoops of the waggon to step out of her underwear. Only the dim flickering light from the campfire, shining through the linseed-treated twill of the waggon cover, lined for him the curve of her body, and showed him for one fleeting second the complicated swaying of her bare breasts.

He threw back the blanket as she climbed on top of him, and reached up for her with both hands. He felt the wiriness of her pubic hair against his thigh.

'Simon . . .' she breathed in his ear. 'You mustn't ever think that this shouldn't have happened. It was fate. I saw it in your hand, in the lines of your palm, when you first took up the traces of Barney's carriage. I saw a broken life-line.'

Simon de Koker kissed her cheek, and then her mouth, and then said, 'What?'

'Your life-line,' she said. She kept on kissing him, little kisses all over his forehead and cheeks that teased him at first, but very quickly irritated him. 'A broken life-line almost always means sickness, you know, or bereavement. Sometimes it means an accident.'

'You're a strange lady,' Simon de Koker breathed. He touched her shoulder, and ran his fingertips down her arm.

She sat up; and in the darkness Simon de Koker thought that she was preparing herself to sit on top of him, and he craned his neck to see. But there was nothing but a dull rattling sound, and then a rapid series of sharp metallic clicks, like castanets. At the very same instant that his mind registered that she had been dragging his rifle towards her, lifting it, and releasing the safety-catch, she pulled the trigger, and with a deafening bang she blew half of his stomach across the waist of the waggon.

Outside, Joel shouted, 'What's happened? *Sara*! What the hell's going on in there? *Sara*!' and Hunt wrestled his way out of his blankets and came scampering around the campfire to see what was going on. He threw open the waggon-cover to see Sara crouched naked, except for her muddy white stockings, with Simon de Koker's rifle under her arm; and Simon de Koker lying back on the floor of the waggon with his eyes wide open and his body plastered in blood.

'Oh my God, it's murder,' said Hunt. 'Oh my God.'

Simon de Koker looked up at Sara with an expression of surprise. His lips moved silently for a while, but then he managed to speak. 'You've shot me,' he said.

Sara was incapable of saying anything. She had been quite

sure that if she shot him, he would die, with a small round puncture as his only wound. She had been totally unprepared for the violent ripple of shock that had shaken his belly like a tent in a storm, and the bucketful of red paint that had splashed over him from nowhere. And he was still alive, and talking to her!

'You've shot my guts art,' Simon de Koker told her, in a liquid whisper. He breathed out through his nose, and a bubble of blood came out of his nostril.

'I – I –' she began, but she was trembling too much to say any more. She felt freezing cold, and when she covered her breasts with her arm, the nipples were as tough and tight as buttons.

'You've got to finish the job,' said Simon de Koker. 'I'm not going to die like this. Not bleeding my guts art.'

'I don't know what to do,' Sara told him, in a hot colliding rush of words. 'Oh my God, I'm sorry. I don't know what to *do*.'

Simon de Koker slowly turned towards his coat, which he had left on top of the salt-barrel. 'In the left-hand pocket, you'll find some more shells,' he told her. 'Take one out, that's it, and I'll tell you what to do next.'

In the gloom, Sara dropped his coat on to the floor, and two or three of the shells rolled away between the boxes of provisions. But she managed to catch one of them, and clutch it in her hand, and sit up straight again, facing Simon de Koker with a feeling of such anguish and shame that she could not do anything but hold it up, and blurt, 'Here.'

Simon de Koker nodded. It took him a few moments to catch enough air in his lungs to be able to say anything. Then he whispered, 'Pull back the bolt on top of the rifle . . . to eject the empty . . . Then insert the new cartridge . . . that's right . . . wait, I can't see you very well . . . Then push the bolt back in again . . . The action of pulling back the bolt . . . will have . . . the action of pulling . . . will have cocked it again.'

Sara's arms seemed to have lost all of their co-ordination. She felt as if she were trying to load the rifle with wooden butter-pats. But at last she managed to jiggle home the bolt, and lift the muzzle again, and say to Simon de Koker in the most haunted of voices, 'It's done.'

With the deliberate slowness of someone who feels very tired, or melancholic, Simon de Koker reached up with one blood-spattered hand and guided the rifle towards his mouth. He closed his lips around it, and then turned his eyes towards Sara, neither pitifully nor appealingly, but in simple resignation at what had to be done. Sara could hardly see him through the tears which suddenly sparkled and danced in front of her eyes.

Hunt said, '*Sara* –!' and that was all she needed. A word to break the spell of her own horror. A word to remind her that she could not sit here a fraction of a second longer, undressed, in the company of a hideously wounded man. She tugged at the trigger, and Simon de Koker's face vanished as abruptly as a china pot knocked off the top of a wall. She did not even hear the bang this time.

Hunt had blankets ready for her as she stepped down from the waggon. There was blood on her knees where she had been crouching down, and she was shaking as uncontrollably as an epileptic. Hunt glanced into the darkness of the waggon cover, and then followed her across to the fire. 'More wood,' he said to Nareez. 'Let's get this fire burning up really decently, shall we? And brandy.'

Joel was sitting up in his bedroll, his face strained and white. 'He's dead?' he asked. It was an irrelevant question, but he had to hear the answer.

Hunt said, in a citric voice, 'A casualty of war. It was quite monstrous, anyway, the idea of selling that marvellous diamond to pay for arms and ammunition, especially since they were going to be used against the British. We must have some principles, mustn't we? *Some* sense of honour, and love of the country that gave us our birthright.'

'*Shah!*' Joel told him, venomously. 'Sara – are you all right?'

Sara lifted her head up and down like a marionette. 'It's the shock,' chipped in Hunt. 'A little brandy, a little sleep, and she'll be perfectly all right.'

Nareez had ignored Hunt's orders to go for more firewood, but she came across with a half-bottle of Napoleon brandy, which she poured into an enamel mug and placed carefully between Sara's shivering fingers. 'You drink now,' she cooed, gently, stroking Sara's hair. 'Don't think about anything at all. Just drink.'

'Well, I think she deserves congratulation,' said Hunt, with his hands perched on his hips, like a dapper little school boy admiring a cracking good innings at house cricket. 'She said she was going to knock the fellow for six, and she did. I think she's an absolute brick.'

'For the love of God, who is understanding and merciful, will you please stop behaving as if this is the snooker-room at Government House?' Joel pleaded. 'Go get some wood. That would be useful. The *amah*'s not going to do it.'

Hunt sighed, misunderstood but unabashed, and started circling around in search of logs. 'Always thought Indians were rather keen on this kind of thing,' he mumbled to himself, as he disappeared behind the line of tethered horses.

Sara finished her brandy, and then threw her head back, and closed her eyes, and stayed silent and still for two or three minutes, the fog prickling her face as it was slowly and wetly precipitated across the valley of the Sand River. Joel looked questioningly at Nareez, but Nareez gave him a little shake of her hand as if to say that he should not worry. A dog barked, somewhere far off in the darkness; or perhaps it was an ape.

Sara opened her eyes. Joel watched her a moment longer, and then said, 'I didn't think you'd do it.'

Sara lowered her head, and ran her fingers into her hair. 'I had to,' she said.

'The world needs more women like you.'

She turned to him, and made a bitter face. 'Does it? Or is it just that men like you need more women like me?'

'You're being unfair to both of us,' said Joel.

'And you don't know what you're saying. If there were more women in the world like me, then I don't think you would care for the world very much, and neither would I. You see only what you want to see, don't you, when you look at me? You never see the struggle that goes on beneath the lace and the jewellery.'

'Struggle?' said Joel. 'Why should you ever have to struggle?'

Sara stood up, keeping her blanket wrapped tightly around her. 'I have to struggle because I'm strong. At least, I could have been strong, if my background and my upbringing had allowed me to be. Can you imagine what it's like, to be born into a wealthy colonial family? Well, I don't suppose you can. It's the most privileged, marvellously idle life you can think of. I loved every minute of it, and I'd be lying if I said that I hadn't. I liked the riding, I liked the parties, I liked the gossip. And it was just as well that I did; because if I chafed against the life, like some women do, then I probably would have ended up mad.'

She was quiet for a little while, and then she said, more gently, 'I had freedom, of course, and money, and whatever dresses I wanted. But it was not considered proper for me to express a political opinion; or to show interest in anybody whose station was below mine; or to be too "enthusiastic". I was quite amazed that my parents consented to my marrying Barney; but then he did own diamond mines, and he had travelled halfway across Africa to find me; and he was Jewish. Mama found him rather romantic.'

Joel rubbed the back of his neck. 'Yes, I suppose you could say that," he mused, with obvious sarcasm, 'He *is* rather romantic. I don't know what else he is, but he *is* rather romantic.'

Sara drew a deep breath, and looked back towards the waggon. 'Anyway,' she said, 'my strength finally overcame my upbringing, and look how violent it turned out to be.'

Joel held up the gazelle-skin bag, dangling on the end of her gold chain. 'You won't forget the whole reason you did it, will you? You left it in Nareez's blankets.'

Sara came over and took the pouch, and hung it around her neck again. 'Thank you,' she said. 'I think you're the only one who really understands what I feel.'

Joel smiled at her, and kissed her cheek.

It was left to Hunt to drag Simon de Koker's stiffened body out of the waggon at first light, and bury him in a shallow depression by the stand of trees. He was still panting and perspiring as Sara and he stood by the grave and said a prayer for Simon de Koker's departed soul. Nareez was busy swilling blood from the planks of the waggon's floor; and Joel was sitting by the ashes of the campfire, trying to shave in icy cold water.

They had decided by default rather than by general consent to make straight for Durban, where Sara believed that her father could help them market the diamond, perhaps to one of his Indian or Persian business friends; and where Hunt could board a steamer for England and for anonymity. Sara was sure that Barney would eventually discover that she was back with her parents, but by that time the diamond would be long gone, and Gerald Sutter's lawyers would be quite capable of dealing with any infamous suggestions that Barney might level against Sara that she had taken the Natalia Star. She had left him because he had wrongfully deceived her about his social status in Kimberley, and because he had been intolerably cruel to her. He had been an ogre, and a Jewish ogre at that. Now he was showing his obsessive cruelty even more openly, by accusing her of stealing a valuable diamond!

This was their plan, anyway. At least, it was mostly Sara's and Hunt's plan. Joel had not yet completely decided what he was going to do; or if he had, he was not telling any of the others what it was. He remained smiling but uncommunicative as they heaved him up on to the freshly-scrubbed waggon, harnessed the horses, and prepared to head eastwards through the morning fog.

'I must say it's all gone rather well,' remarked Hunt, brightly. 'But I pity those poor Boer chaps at Wesselstroom. They're going to have a frightfully long wait if they're expecting *us* to turn up in a day or two!'

'I pity de Koker,' said Sara, baldly; and Hunt could not think of a reply to that. He grimaced like a disgruntled child, and stayed quiet for the next half an hour.

By mid-afternoon, they had reached Colenso, where they stopped to water and feed the horses, and to buy smoked bacon and bran from one of the small farmhouses there. There were a few British Army tents pitched five or six hundred yards away on the banks of one of the tributaries of the Tugela River, among the scrub and the trees, and a cooking-fire was sending up a lazy spiral of smoke into the fog. After he had brought out a thick side of bacon for them on his shoulder, the farmer told them about the massacre at Isandhlwana, only fifty miles or so to the north-east, and about the defence of Rorke's Drift. He was a red, grizzled little Afrikaner, who had decided in 1842 that the trek back across the mountains to the Transvaal was too much for him. He gave bacon and fresh eggs to the British soldiers, and in return they left his farm and his daughters grudgingly alone.

'So,' said Hunt, as they sat around the waggon by the roadside, and ate a scrappy lunch of biscuits and bacon, 'it seems as if Sir Bottled Beer finally went ahead and made a right royal mess of things!'

'They'll crush the Zulu in the end, though, won't they?' asked Sara.

'Of course,' said Hunt. 'The Zulu are terribly fierce, but they don't have any idea of what they're up against; or even why they're up against it. They only have one tactic, too: the "chest and horns", and even Lord Chelmsford should know how to cope with that. God knows what went wrong at this Isandhlwana place, but you can bet your boots that Sir Bottle will want his revenge. I wouldn't be sitting in the royal kraal at Ulundi now for all the tea in China. Not me!'

'Talking of tea,' said Sara, quietly, 'we seem to have run completely out.'

'Didn't that farmer have any?' asked Hunt.

Nareez said, 'I forgot to ask him. I'm sorry. I'll go back and see.'

Sara stood up, rather quickly. 'It's all right. I feel like a ride. I'll go down and ask those soldiers. They're bound to have some. The British Army survives on tea.'

She untethered one of the spare horses from the back of the waggon, threw a blanket over its back, and mounted it. 'I won't be a minute!' she called, and rode off down the rocky slope at the side of the road towards the Army encampment. Her horse slipped and hesitated, but eventually made its way down to level ground.

'Well,' said Joel, 'there she goes.'

Hunt frowned at him. 'What's that supposed to mean, precisely?'

'It means, there she goes. That's the last we'll see of her. Isn't that right, Nareez?'

Nareez looked cross. 'She went to fetch tea. That's all.'

'Oh, she went to fetch tea, did she? Well, you watch her. She's going to skirt right around those Army tents, and ride parallel to the road until she gets two or three miles further east; and then she's going to rejoin the road again and ride like all hell until she's so far ahead of us that we can't catch up, not with a waggon.'

'That's not right!' protested Nareez. 'She will not betray you!'

Joel shook his head. 'She's been thinking about it all day. I've been watching her face, and I could tell. First of all, with Simon de Koker dead, it seemed like a good idea to take the diamond to Durban and split it three ways. But then she probably began to think, why split it at all? I killed de Koker, I did all the dirty work, why should I share the diamond with anybody? Especially with a nancy-boy like Hunt, and a cripple like Joel. And they won't hurt Nareez, those two, so she can meet up with me later.'

'I am telling you, Mr Blitz, she went for tea!' said Nareez.

Joel lifted himself up a little, and then pointed down the valley of the Tugela. Sara had already passed the military encampment; and through the fog they could hear the soldiers whistling at her. Now she was following the course of the tributary north-eastwards, with her horse stepping carefully over the rocks, and she was almost invisible in the greyness, a disappearing ghost.

Joel grinned. 'There you are, Nareez, she's gone, just like you knew she would. All that ridiculous play-acting about tea! "I'm sorry, Mrs Sara, I'll go back and see if there's any tea." "Oh no, Nareez, I'll just get on my horse and trot down to get some from the soldiers. The British Army thrives on tea!" Tea! You women make me choke.'

Nareez said, 'It is rightfully hers, the diamond. It is a small thing, to compensate her for the suffering she has been through.'

'What suffering?' Joel demanded. 'A few boring months at Kimberley? And Barney never mistreated her, did he? Whatever you say about Barney, he always behaved like a gentleman, and a husband, whenever Sara would let him. He didn't love her. That was plain enough. But he didn't make her suffer.'

'I like to hear brothers standing up for each other,' said

Hunt, prissily. Joel ignored him, and twisted himself over sideways, so that he could dig his hand deep into his overcoat pocket. Grunting, he tugged at the lining, until at last he was able to withdraw his fist and sit up straight again.

'She may think she deserves all kinds of things, your charge and mistress,' said Joel. 'But what she thinks she deserves and what she's actually got are two different things. Look.'

He opened his hand, and there on his palm was the Natalia Star, shining dully in the dull afternoon light.

Hunt, in delight, applauded. 'Joel, you're a positive genius! I thought the diamond was around her neck!'

'What she has around her neck is a stone I picked up near Mont aux Sources, when we were crossing the Drakensberg. Every time the waggon was held up, I sorted through the pebbles beside the road until I found one that was almost the same size and shape as the diamond. Yesterday night, when she shot de Koker, she left the pouch in Nareez's blankets; thinking that I was asleep. I took out the diamond, and substituted the stone. A rock for a rock.'

Nareez clenched her fists. 'You are a teef! You are a terrible teef!'

Joel laughed in her face. 'I'm not as much of a thief as Sara; or as any of you. This diamond is legally half mine, in any case. I shall share some of the proceeds with you both, for helping me get to Durban; but I warn you that if you try to betray me to the authorities, you won't get very far. I shall simply say that you kidnapped me, and tried to steal the diamond which rightfully belongs to me and my brother. At the very worst, I shall be forced to share the diamond fifty-fifty with Barney. At the very best, you will both be hung for abduction and theft.'

'I suppose there's a Yiddish word for this kind of ruse,' said Hunt, cuttingly.

Joel held up the diamond, and a single piercing star of refracted light caught Hunt's eye. 'We call it a *chachma*,' said Joel. 'A wily trick.'

Nareez, who was looking the other way, spat noisily on to the ground.

*

Even in bright sunlight, the valleys formed by the tributaries of the Tugela River can be hopelessly misleading. In unrelenting fog, they are an endless nightmare of twists and turns and blind alleys, a Chinese puzzle in different shades of grey.

Sara knew that the tributary of the Tugela which flowed north-eastwards from Colenso joined the main river about fifteen miles downstream from Ladysmith; and that if she followed the main river about thirty miles further, she would cross the Newcastle-to-Durban road at Tugela Ferry. All she would have to do then would be to ride hard through Ugg and Greytown, following the road for two or three days until she reached Durban.

She had chosen to ride by a completely different road in case her horse went lame, and Joel was able to catch up with her; or in case they sent Hunt riding on ahead.

What had seemed like a simple escape in principle, though, became more and more confusing and frightening as the day went on. For some reason, around the tiny settlement of Stendal, she began to believe that she had lost her way; and after she had taken a short cut across the brow of a foggy kopje between one tributary and another, she mistook the Tugela River itself for the tributary that ran into the Tugela from Empangueni. She forded the Tugela on her horse, and continued to ride north-eastwards, wet and shivering, when she should have been riding south-eastwards.

Later in the afternoon, the fog began to clear, and the sun came out, wan and yellow at first, but then brightly enough to finish the day with long shadows and a pottery-blue sky, and birdsong. Sara felt better, and stopped to rest her horse and drink from a small stream. She had no food or bottled water with her: she had been counting on finding the Greytown road before dark, and stopping for supper at a farmhouse or an Army encampment.

Now, with the landscape thick with shadows, she made her most foolish mistake. She decided to keep on riding until it was too dark to go on. Refolding the horse's blanket, she mounted up again, and keeping the fading light of the sun on her left, and slightly behind her, she continued north-east. The heavy pouch around her neck walloped regularly against her breastbone as she rode.

There was still a chance for her to find her way: but she crossed a tributary that joined the Tugela from the north-west, believing it to be the Tugela, and carried on riding north-east by the light of the thumbnail moon, trying desperately to find the tributary that she had just forded. Exhausted, hungry, and panicky, she crossed the Newcastle-to-Durban road in the darkness, without realising it.

She was last seen alive on the following morning, a considerable distance away, through the binoculars of a scouting party of the 17th Lancers. They could do nothing else but return to their encampment with a dismayed report that a European woman had been seen riding at the gallop through the bushy ravines close to the Buffalo River, a few miles south-east of Rorke's Drift. She had appeared to have no weapons, no provisions, and no guide; and either she had not heard the three rifle shots that the scouts had fired into the air to attract her attention, or else she had ignored them.

Five days later, scouts of the Natal Native Contingent found the body of a brown-haired white woman by the side of the waggon road which led south-eastwards from Isandhlwana to the Inkanhlda Bush. She had been disembowelled by assegais, the short stabbing spears of the Zulu warriors, and badly mutilated. Around her neck was an empty leather pouch; and in her right hand, clenched so tightly that the scouts had been unable to remove it before they buried her, had been a large jagged pebble. A label in her riding-dress had identified her as Sara Sutter, of Durban.

Joel, Hunt and Nareez arrived in Durban on a humid, irritating day when it seemed as if the only thing worth doing was having a bath and then getting gradually drunk on gin-and-bitters on a cool verandah somewhere. At first, Joel was reluctant to let Nareez go; but when Hunt pointed out that all the *amah* wanted to do was scurry off back to Khotso and rejoin her mistress, who had probably arrived there by now, tearful and tired and not one penny the richer, Joel at last agreed to pay for a hackney carriage to take her out there, and good riddance.

Joel's sense of irony did not leave him, even though he had escaped with the diamond as far as Durban. Remembering his first visit here, with a crushed pelvis and broken legs, he booked rooms for himself and Hunt at the Natalia Hotel, signing his name 'Blitz' on the register with an aggressive flourish. If Barney ever followed him here, the evidence that he had come and gone would be bombastically obvious. He swung his way upstairs on his crutches, and was able at last to lie back on a soft bed, with his shoes off, and close his eyes; while the jumbled sounds of street-peddlers and trotting horses and carriage-wheels wafted in through the slats of his half-open jalousie like noises from a half-forgotten dream.

Joel slept, and then woke. There was a salty taste in his mouth, and he had dribbled a little on to the pillow. He heaved himself up into a sitting position, and then dragged the cheap linen coaster off the bedside table, so that he could wipe his mouth with it, and mop his forehead. He sat still for a while, thinking about Barney, and Sara, and the diamond, and then he seized his crutches from beside the bed, and hopped his way over to the bathroom, so that he could draw himself a deep tubful of hot water.

The bath was running, and steam was drifting idly out of the open window, when there was a sharp knock at the door. Joel said warily, 'Yes?'

'Mr Blitz?' asked an unfamiliar voice.

'Who is that?' Joel demanded.

'It's the manager, Mr Blitz. Charles Pope. Would you mind if I had a word with you, just for a moment?'

'Come on in,' said Joel.

The manager unlocked the door with his pass-key, and stepped into the room with the stiff, mannered movements of an old soldier. He was a short round-headed man, with a clipped moustache, and cheeks that were bright with broken veins, both from sun and brandy. He stood to attention in his black suit and his boiled shirt and his startlingly-elevated white tie, and faced Joel with flustered boldness.

'I saw your name in the register, Mr Blitz, and I was alarmed.'

Joel was sitting on the side of the bed, leaning on his crutches. 'Alarmed?' he asked, with a grin of surprise. 'Why?'

'Well, sir, it's an inheritance, sir; some years old; but an inheritance that I can't really afford to ignore. Not for my own sake, sir; nor for the sake of my family.'

'Why don't you get to the point?' asked Joel.

'Well, sir, the point is that before I took over the management of this hotel, sir – that was when I retired from the Army, sir, Royal Engineers –'

'Yes, yes,' said Joel, impatiently.

'Well, sir, the point is that someone called Mr Blitz stayed here before, some years ago.'

'That's right. It was me, and my brother Barney. What of it?'

Charles Pope clenched his bright yellow false teeth together and managed to look even more embarrassed than he had before. 'It was the way you settled the bill, sir, apparently.'

'You mean we didn't settle it? You're asking for money?'

'Oh, no, sir. The bill was settled quite satisfactory. Well, as far as I know, anyway. The difficulty was that it was paid in five-pound notes of awkward origin, sir.'

'Forged?'

'No, sir, not forged. But one was later passed in change to a particular gentleman from the Durban commercial community, sir, when he came to dine here one evening, or at least that's what I'm told. And this particular gentleman from the commercial community was able to identify the serial numbers on the note, for the reason that he was making concerted efforts to trace a certain quantity of notes that had gone missing, so to speak, from a merchant bank in Portugal.'

Joel nodded towards the bathroom. 'Would you mind turning those taps off? I'd hate to flood your lovely hotel.'

Charles Pope went next door, and turned off the water. When he returned, he said, 'You do follow my drift, don't you?'

'I'm not sure that I do. You're trying to tell me that the money we used to pay our hotel bill, nearly eight years ago, was stolen?'

'That's the drift of it, yes.'

Joel shook his head dismissively. 'You're going to have a difficult time proving it, my friend. And anyway, the bank has probably written the money off by now.'

Charles Pope clapped his hands together, louder than he had

obviously meant to. 'That's the problem, sir! The *bank* probably has. But the gentlemen who were looking for the money most certainly have not. They are gentlemen of unusual persistence.'

'I think you'd better tell me about this straight,' said Joel.

'Well . . .' said Charles Pope, 'I can only give it to you second-hand, because when you first stayed here, I was still manager of the old Muharrik Hotel in Cairo. But the manager who was here at the time, he told me that a bank in La Coruna, in Portugal, had been swindled some years ago of hundreds of thousands of pounds. It had been done by a whole gang of people, this swindle. Accountants, lawyers, bank officials, registrars. It cost the bank every last penny it had, and it almost brought down the Portuguese government.'

'So what does any of this have to do with me?' asked Joel.

Charles Pope pulled a series of rubbery faces, as if he could not quite decide which expression suited this explanation the best. But then he said, 'It has practically everything to do with you, sir; because the five-pound notes with which you paid your hotel bill were part of the haul of notes which were taken from the bank during this swindle. And the only way in which you could possibly have acquired them was from the one man in the whole gang of swindlers who double-crossed his associates and disappeared with everything, at the crucial moment. Six of the gang were caught and sent to gaol for life. Two more were shot while trying to escape from police custody. There were eight more, who are now living under false names in different parts of the world. Five of them run an export business in Lourenço Marques, in the Portuguese Territory; and one of them acts as an agent for his colleagues here in Durban. It was he who came to the hotel for dinner just after you and your brother had stayed here, and identified one of the stolen notes.'

'Well, this is all very interesting,' said Joel. 'But you have no form proof whatsoever of what you are saying, and for all I know you are lying through those artificial teeth of yours just to frighten me. I don't know anything at all about any stolen money, or any Portuguese swindlers, or anything at all. I'm an ignoramus, and you can't hold a man responsible for that.'

'Mr Blitz,' said Charles Pope, patiently, 'you and your brother paid over hundreds of pounds to this hotel, all in the same five-pound notes. Mr Salgadas will be most interested to know that you are here.'

Joel thought about this for a moment, blowing his cheeks in and out reflectively. 'I suppose you're going to tell him that I'm here? Is that it?'

'It would be my duty, sir. For the sake of my family. If Mr Salgadas were to find out that you had visited, sir, and that I had omitted to inform him ...'

'I see,' said Joel. 'It's extortion, is it? How much do you want?'

Charles Pope made a self-deprecatory face. 'Five hundred pounds, sir, should do it easily. Five hundred pounds for two weeks of silence, that's a fair rate.'

'How much does that work out per minute?' Joel demanded.

Charles Pope pressed one finger against his forehead and closed his eyes. 'Almost sixpence, sir,' he said, after a while, and then exposed all of his grotesquely artificial teeth in a wide grin. 'I used to be an accountant, sir, before I went into the hotel trade.'

Joel gathered up his crutches, and swung himself across to the window. 'Open these shutters for me, will you?' he told Pope, and Pope came across and unlatched them for him, so that he could look out over the tiled and corrugated-iron rooftops.

'I'll tell you what,' said Joel, 'I'll make a deal with you. But the problem is that you're going to have to take me on trust.'

Charles Pope took out a handkerchief, and solemnly stared at Joel while he explored the inside of his nose.

'The man who double-crossed the Portuguese swindle gang was called Monsaraz,' said Joel. 'I knew him very well. In fact, I used to run a farm with him out at Oranjerivier, in the north colony. The problem was, he was dying of lung disease. Consumption, probably, that he'd picked up in Portugal. You know what a filthy lot they are there.'

Charles Pope scrutinised his handkerchief. Then he said, 'Go on. I'm listening.'

Joel smiled. 'Before Monsaraz died, he entrusted all of his swindled money to me, and to my brother Barney. He told us to send most of it out of the country, back to Portugal, for his relatives. We disguised it as parcels of dried fruit. In return, he gave us fifty thousand pounds each. You might be interested to know that I invested most of mine in the Sutter Shipping Company, and that I have today almost seventy thousand pounds, just lying in the bank, waiting to be spent.'

Charles Pope said huskily, 'What are you proposing? You're not proposing that I should get myself involved in this, too?'

'I'm not proposing anything of the kind. I'm simply trying to put it to you that if Mr Salgadas were to get hold of the wrong end of the stick – if Mr Salgadas were to take his revenge on somebody in the sincere belief that he was finally getting even for the Monsaraz double-cross, even though that somebody may not be exactly the *right* somebody, then all of my problems would be over; and yours would be over, too, because I would pay you twenty thousand pounds in untraceable banknotes to help me.'

Outside, in the streets of Durban, a water-seller was calling out his high-pitched song in a voice that reminded Joel strangely of the way in which Simon de Koker had encouraged his horses. 'Yip! Yip! Yip!' Beside him, Charles Pope slowly stuffed his handkerchief back into the pocket of his tight hotel-manager's trousers and frowned at the far corner of the room, as if he expected a prompt-card to appear there, and tell him what to do.

After a long ruminative silence, he said, 'What do you mean when you say "that somebody may not exactly be the *right* somebody?"'

The following morning, at eight, Hunt was taking breakfast in the dining-room of the Natalia Hotel – toast and Oxford marmalade, with the morning newspaper propped up against the silver marmalade pot – when two men in off-white tropical suits and dark moustaches hurried through the swing doors, hustled a waitress to one side, and produced revolvers.

Hunt did not even see them. He was too engrossed in a

gossipy paragraph in the paper about Lieutenant Kenneth Ogilvy of the 2/24th, and how he had delayed his engagement to Miss Patricia Penrose, of Marianhill. He was still munching toast when the two men rushed up to his table, went down on to one knee, and aimed their revolvers at his face. Unlike Lieutenant Ogilvy they looked as if they were about to propose.

There were five shots, four more than necessary, and a lot of blue smoke, and broken glass, and blood. Then the men hurried out again. One of them even raised his hat in apology to the waitress he had jostled on the way in. Nobody screamed, or cried out, or even moved. Hunt bent over his newspaper, as if he were examining it from only a quarter of an inch away, and then he flopped back his head and rolled on to the floor.

At the same time, on board the London cargo ship *Wallasey*, which was two miles out from Port Natal off Umlazi, and still visible from the front lawn of Khotso, Joel was drinking whiskey from a flask, and leaning against the windy rail like a seasoned one-legged mariner.

The first mate passed him by, and said, 'Fine morning, sir. Make sure you don't fall in.'

Joel gave him a vague smile, and screwed the top back on his flask again. He had other things on his mind, apart from the sharpness of the morning and the smoothness of the sea. He was thinking of Hunt; and of Sara; and of Charles Pope. It was the thought of Charles Pope that he savoured in particular – and how Pope must have knocked on the door of his room with a tray of tea and a morning paper, only to find that his bed was unslept in, and that even his single bedroom slipper had gone.

The extortionist gets what the extortionist deserves, he thought; and that's nothing.

Barney did not get to hear of Sara's death until 5 July, the day after Lord Chelmsford had advanced on the Zulu capital of Ulundi with an impenetrable square of British troops, mowing down 1000 natives with rifles and Garling guns, and finally setting a torch to the royal kraal.

The letter from Gerald Sutter had been sent mistakenly to

Oranjerivier, and from the brown circles on the envelope it looked as if someone had left it on their mantelshelf for a week or two, and rested their tea-cups on it. It had been re-addressed twice, once to Colesberg and then to Kimberley.

Barney opened it in the drawing-room where he was having coffee with Harold. They had been working since seven o'clock on a deal to buy out three important claims from the Standard Diamond Mining Company, and he was still wearing his blue silk bathrobe. There were papers all over the floor, and even papers propped up against the coffee-pot. Harold had just taken out his tobacco-pouch to light his first pipe of the day.

'It's from Durban,' said Barney, turning the envelope over. On the back flap, embossed into the vellum paper, was the crest of the Sutter family, a ship flanked by pelicans. He tore the envelope open with his thumb, and opened the letter. He was silent for two whole minutes while he read it.

'Is that news about Sara?' asked Harold, thumbing tobacco into his pipe.

Barney folded the letter up, and laid it carefully on the birdcage coffee-tray, on top of all the other papers. It had been a sorrowful letter, perplexed, and gentle. Nareez had arrived at Khotso to say that she and Sara had been on their way to visit the Sutters in the company of a Boer guide and a friend of Barney's. There had been trouble on the way, and the guide had accidentally been killed. Sara had ridden off on her own to get help, and had never been seen alive again.

Three days after Nareez had reached Knotso, the Sutters had advised the British Army garrison that Sara was missing in the area between Colenso and Tugela Ferry. The Army had made enquiries, and ten days later had turned up the report from the Natal Native Contingent that they had buried the mutilated body of a white woman not far south of Isandhlwana.

'I cannot think that she did not die without dignity, or grace, or without opening her heart to the God who understands the Essential Rightness of being English,' wrote her father.

'Are you all right?' Harold asked Barney.

Barney nodded. 'That was from Sara's father,' he said, with a catch in his voice. He cleared his throat. 'She's dead. Or, at least, they found a body who answered to her description.'

'What happened? Oh, Barney, I'm so sorry.'

'Here,' said Barney, and handed Harold the letter to read. Harold put on his bifocals, and scanned it carefully, his lips moving as he read, his hand trembling slightly. 'This is a shock,' he said, at last, putting the letter down. 'I don't know what to say to you.'

'You don't have to say anything,' Barney told him. 'I think I began to get over my love for Sara the day after we came back here to Kimberley. I don't think either of us ever found out what it was that we actually wanted from each other. We were better off apart. I'm just sorry that we had to part the way we did, and I'm sorry that she's dead.'

Harold folded up his spectacles and sat back. 'It seems as if they were making for the east coast after all,' he said. 'And from what Mr Sutter says in his letter, it seems as if your friend what-was-his-name, the Boer, was also unfortunate enough not to survive the journey.'

Barney was pouring them each a small brandy from the drinks table by the window. 'You make that sound as if his death wasn't accidental.'

'My dear friend,' wheezed Harold, 'when you have lived in proximity to diamonds for as long as I have, you get to know that they are very dangerous stones to be near; and the nearer you are to them, the more dangerous it is. A stone like the Natalia Star has around it a circle of influence, if you like, and as soon as you step into this circle you are at risk. You remember you told me that you felt the Natalia Star was evidence of God's existence? Well, not everybody feels the same way about diamonds as you do. Not many people are so spiritual about them. But everybody invests them with equally extraordinary importance. And for something that is as important as the physical evidence of the power of God, people will kill.'

Barney handed Harold his brandy, and murmured, '*Mazel tov,*' under his breath. Harold sipped a little, and then put his glass down, and said, 'The question is, if two of the people who stole the Natalia Star are now dead, what has happened to the others? We know about Nareez, of course, but where are Joel and Hunt?'

'Most important of all,' said Barney, 'where is the diamond?'

515

'Well – there are several possibilities,' Harold told him. 'If Sara was murdered by Zulus, then the diamond could have been taken by the natives and given to Cetewayo.'

'That sounds a bit far-fetched,' Barney remarked.

'Maybe it does, but the history of large diamonds is always far-fetched. I'm more inclined to think that Joel and Hunt still have the stone, but if Sara *was* carrying it, and if it *has* gone to Cetewayo, then we may not be so unlucky after all. I heard from the post office this morning that the Zulu Empire may not last very much longer. The British forces surround Ulundi on three sides, and so the diamond might soon be recovered. We ought to write to Lord Chelmsford's chiefs of staff, and put in a claim, in case the British Army find it in Ulundi.'

'Well,' said Barney, 'if you really think it's worthwhile.'

'Of course it's worthwhile. We're talking a million pounds. Even more, if we can say that the diamond once belonged to Cetewayo. We shouldn't ignore any possibility, no matter how unlikely it seems.'

Barney was quiet for a moment. Then he looked at Harold, and said, 'I'm sorry. I wasn't really listening.'

'It doesn't matter,' Harold told him. 'You've had a bad shock, unpleasant news. Perhaps it's better if I go.'

'I'd rather you stayed,' said Barney. 'I want to settle this Standard Diamond Company purchase.'

'Let's leave it for today,' said Harold. 'The Big Hole will still be there tomorrow morning.'

'No, we'll settle it now. I might have lost my wife, and my brother may be missing, but I've still got my business. How much do you think they'll take for 170 and 160?'

'Barney . . .' protested Harold, spreading his hands wide.

'Don't mother me, Harold,' snapped Barney. 'I've been through just about enough.'

'All right, you want to finish the Standard Diamond Company business, then we'll finish the Standard Diamond Company business. And no mothering. I suggest you try to pay them £27,500 each, for 170 and 169, and £20,000 for 168.'

'That's less than we paid Stewart.'

'That's right. I'm trying to save you money.'

Barney walked across to the fireplace with his hands in his dressing-gown pockets. 'You know something, Harold?' he said. 'I thought I had everything, with Sara, and the diamond, and this house. I thought that I'd almost made it. Now, it's all gone, except the house, and what's the use of a house with nobody in it but yourself? And you know something, for all of the struggle, for all of the arguments, none of it really meant anything.'

Harold took his pocket-watch out of his vest pocket and went through an exaggerated performance of winding it and holding it up to his ear.

Barney said, 'You'd rather listen to your watch ticking, than me complaining about my unfortunate fate?'

'I'd rather not tell you what I think, that's all.'

'So tell me.'

Harold turned around in his chair. 'You really want to know?'

Barney looked back at him, just as sharply, and then looked away. 'Not really. I know it already. I should have tried harder with Natalia. I should have been less forgiving to Joel. I should have realised that only God blesses unions, not English society.'

Harold nodded, his double-chins going in and out like an accordion.

'But damn it, Harold,' said Barney, 'it's bad enough being Jewish. It's bad enough being an outsider because of your race and your religion, without marooning yourself twenty miles out from the rest of the human race because you've married a *schwarzeh*!'

'You still think about her, don't you?' asked Harold. 'After all these years, you still think about her.'

Barney turned his back to Harold and rested his head against the mantelshelf. 'She's got my only son,' he said.

'But more than that,' put in Harold, gently.

'Yes,' said Barney. 'More than that, I still love her.'

He lifted his head and looked at himself in the looking-glass above the fireplace. His short and unhappy marriage to Sara had aged him. There were three or four grey hairs around his ears, and his eyes had a dullness about them which only somebody else who had been through the same kind of loveless

517

struggle would recognise. He thought of Sara and he felt like crying for her, although he found it impossible to squeeze out any tears. He hoped, desperately, that she had not suffered too horribly. And he hoped too, that wherever she was, she would be able to forgive him for being the wrong man at the wrong time, trespassing in a society for which only his diamond mines had given him any right of entry at all: not his class, or his race, or even his ambitions.

Harold held out his glass. 'Give me some more brandy,' he demanded. 'And have another one yourself. You should drink. It's sad, but you're a free man again. Did you think of that?'

A week later, Cecil Rhodes came around to the house and brought Barney a bottle of single malt whiskey and a letter of condolence edged with black. He had put on weight, and his fair wavy hair had receded a little, but he was sunburned and healthy, and he was wearing a putty-coloured suit that was well-tailored to fit his rather broad-bottomed proportions. Barney was still in the habit of assessing people's wealth and personality by the clothes they wore, and from Rhodes's suit he gathered that he was doing very well these days, and that he was gaining confidence and skill.

'I was *frightfully* upset to hear about Sara,' said Rhodes, pacing around the library, and tugging out books now and again to inspect their bindings, and peer at their titles. 'I say – you've got Appelbo's *Complete Gemology* here – no wonder you're so knowledgeable about gemstones. Oh – the pages aren't cut.'

'I'm, uh, having a memorial service soon,' said Barney, taking the book from him, and pushing it back into its place. 'I hope you'll be able to find the time to come.'

'Of course, my dear chap,' said Rhodes. 'Business isn't quite so hectic just at the moment. Did you know that we now own more than fifty per cent of the De Beers mine? Next year, I believe that we're going to set up our own company, the De Beers Diamond Mining Company Limited; at least that's what Alfred Beit has in mind. In a year or two, the whole of the mine should be run as a monopoly, with all of the advantages that a monopoly can afford us.'

Barney went back to his desk. 'I suppose then you'll start turning your avaricious eyes towards the Big Hole'.

'Well,' said Rhodes, 'you have to admit that it's in a bit of a jolly old shambles.'

'We're sorting it out,' Barney told him. 'When I first came here, there were 1600 separate claims. Now the whole mine is owned by twelve companies; with just one or two stubborn individuals clinging on around the reefs.'

'Twelve are still far too many,' Rhodes replied, shaking his head like a bullock trying to shake away a fly. 'You're down to six hundred feet deep in places; with flooding, and collapses, and mudslides. You need to excavate the entire mine as one, under the auspices of one company.'

'I agree with you,' said Barney. 'Well, I agree with you that the mine should be owned by one company. I think our opinions only differ about whose company that should be.'

Rhodes picked up his hat. 'Britain, one day, shall control the whole of Africa and her wealth. That was my avowed intention when I came here and it remains my avowed intention. However, let's not talk diamonds any more. I have to go, and I want to tell you how cut up I was about your late wife.'

'Thank you,' said Barney. 'I appreciate your coming.'

Just as Rhodes was about to leave, Horace knocked at the library door, and popped his head into the room. 'Excuse me, Mr Two-Leg, sir.'

'Mr *Two*-Leg?' frowned Rhodes.

Barney gave him a fleeting smile. 'My brother has one leg. Or *had*.'

'You mean he's lost the other one as well?'

'No. He's gone missing, that's all. We're not at all sure of his whereabouts.'

'My dear chap, I had no idea. What a dreadfully trying time you must be having.'

Barney looked down at the papers on his desk, and said, 'Yes,' with as much patience as he could manage. Rhodes could see that he was outstaying his welcome, so he called, 'Cheery-bye. I'll see my own way out. Drop me a line when you've arranged the memorial service.'

Barney gave him an absent-minded wave, and he left. Horace piped up, 'It's a lady for you, sir. Mrs Agnes Joy.'

'Agnes? Is she alone?'

'Yes, sir. Excepting her coachman, of course. He's in the kitchen having a smoke, sir.'

'Oh, he's having a smoke, is he? He must have been pretty sure that his mistress was going to be staying.'

'I don't know, Mr Two-Leg,' said Horace. 'I wouldn't presume.'

'All right, Horace,' Barney told him. 'Show Mrs Joy through to the drawing-room.'

Agnes was sitting on one of the small gilded French chairs when he came into the room, her chin proudly uptilted, her blonde curls tucked up under a severe but fashionable little hat. Because the weather was turning colder now, she wore a blue riding-coat, and buttoned-up boots, and in her hand she held a pair of pale blue gloves. She turned her head towards him as he came in, and smiled the kind of smile that makes an innocent man wonder what he's done to deserve it, and a guilty man feel worried about what he might do next.

'Agnes!' said Barney, coming across the room and taking her hand. 'This is the most happy surprise I've had for weeks.'

'I'm sorry I took so long in coming,' she said, her voice a little throatier than he remembered it. 'But I didn't hear about your wife until last week, and today was the first day that I was able to get away. Robert's gone to Hopetown for a day or two, to talk to somebody about a job.'

'Would you care for a sherry?' asked Barney.

'I'd adore one,' she said. 'A very *sweet* one, if you have any in stock. I don't eat candies, but I do adore very sweet sherry.'

Barney sat down opposite her. 'How have you been?' he asked her. 'I've seen you around Kimberley from time to time. How's Faith? And your family? You haven't decided to have any children yet.'

Agnes pouted. 'Robert wants children, of course. All Australians do. There are so *few* Australians, compared with the size of Australia, that they believe they have an historical duty to increase their numbers as rapidly as possible. But the truth is that I had an infection when I was a little girl, a sort

520

of scarlet-fever, I think; and that the doctor said then that it would be very unlikely that I would ever be able to bear children.'

'And Robert doesn't know?'

'Why should I disillusion him, poor dear? He's very handsome, you know, but he's not particularly passionate; and if you ask me the only thing that ever arouses him is the thought of making me pregnant. So for my own sake it wouldn't be very wise to tell him that he never will.'

Horace came in, and Barney asked him to bring him another brandy, and a glass of oloroso for Agnes. 'How's Faith?' he asked, trying to change the subject from the sexual shortcomings of Robert Joy to something a little more general.

'Oh, she's well, although she's more old-maidish by the minute. She thinks I should have left Robert *years* ago. In fact, she thinks I was an absolute idiot for marrying him. She's quite right, of course. Robert has no money at all, and he's such a fool. Father's grown tired of telling me that I would have been better off marrying you, for all that you're Jewish. He calls you the "Chosen Chump" for some reason that I can't really work out. "You should have told me to mind my own business and married the Chosen Chump," he keeps telling me. "At least he owns half of Kimberley. That Robert of yours doesn't own half a share in a lavatory seat." Actually, do you know, I think Father's going rather, you know, what do you call it, addled.'

'I see,' said Barney. 'Well, maybe your father's right. Maybe we should have married. But he didn't exactly make it easy for us, did he? Or even possible.'

'You can't tell him that, not now. He has a most selective memory. He still doesn't like Jews, of course. But in view of his own rather wobbly financial situation, and in view of who's holding most of the purse-strings in the diamond business, he's prepared to make exceptions. Do you know that he even acts for Yosel & Farber?'

'Well, *they're* pretty Jewish,' smiled Barney.

Agnes smiled back at him. Age and experience, if anything, had emphasised the fine Nordic shape of her face, and taken a touch of colour out of her eyes, so that they looked paler, and more translucent, like opals. She was prettier than Barney remembered her, probably because he had tried to persuade himself when Mr Knight had broken up their flowering relationship that she was not really so attractive after all; that she was just another watery English girl with nothing to recommend her but an accent that could splinter your best glassware.

'I was surprised by your letter, though,' said Agnes. 'I don't know whether you were just feeling upset with your wife at the time, or whether you'd seen me in Kimberley with Robert or somebody else and you thought about the life we might have had together ...'

Barney was staring at her with such a baffled expression that she trailed off. 'The *letter*,' she repeated. 'The one you sent me two or three months ago. That was the whole reason I said I was such a long time in coming. I wasn't sure if you meant it.'

'You weren't sure if I ...'

Agnes opened her small blue-eyed crocodile purse, rummaged around amongst the rouge and the rice-powder, and at last produced a crumpled letter written on Vogel Vlei note paper.

'Read it to me,' said Barney.

'You don't remember what you said?'

'Just read it to me!'

Agnes fussily closed her purse, straightened out the letter, and then read it out loud to Barney in a clipped, precise voice that was not at all suited to the flowery passion of the text. 'My dearest darling Agnes, I am writing to tell you that my desire for you has still not waned, and that if you can ever find a way to come to see me again, to bring your lips closer to mine so that I may once more press their rosebud beauty with my own lips (she hesitated and stumbled over this part) then I shall be more than fulfilled! Let us forget the differences of our past ... let us cast aside any thought that both of us have entered into vows with people whose company we sought because of loneliness, and because of confusion. Come to Vogel Vlei on the evening of 26 January, if you can. My wife will be away, and I am sure that you can find a believable excuse to make to your husband. Yours as always, Barney.'

Barney held out his hand for the letter and Agnes gave it to

522

him, her forehead peaked into a tiny frown. Barney only had to glance at it to recognise the handwriting as Joel's; and it only took him a few ticks of the ormolu clock on the mantelshelf to realise why Joel had written it.

All through his convalescence, Joel had been trying to play Sara off against Barney, to stir her discontentment into out-and-out dislike. When he had been crippled and bedbound alienating Sara had been the only means at Joel's disposal of getting his revenge for the loss of the Natalia Star; and his only possible hope of winning the diamond back again. He had still legally owned fifty per cent of the diamond: perhaps he had thought that if he could persuade Sara to divorce Barney on the grounds of cruelty or unfaithfulness, he might also be able to convince Barney that to give Sara the other fifty per cent of the diamond in full settlement would be cheaper than having to assign her a large proportion of the earnings from his diamond mines. Then, Joel would have been left with nothing more difficult than the problem of cajoling her share of the stone out of Sara, and that probably would not have taken him too long. Perhaps he would have told her that the market price of large gemstones had drastically dropped, and offered her a title in one of Blitz Brothers' claims instead. Claim No. 176, perhaps, which was the smallest and the poorest of all of them.

This letter to Agnes must have been part of his ploy. Joel had obviously hoped that Agnes would turn up on the doorstep of Vogel Vlei, dressed in her most provocative gown, on the night of Sara's birthday celebrations, 26 January. One more nail in the coffin of a stillborn marriage.

'I didn't write this,' said Barney, tearing the letter in half.

'I don't understand you,' said Agnes.

'I said, I didn't write it. I didn't invite you here, not on 26 January nor any other day.'

'But that's why I came!'

Barney reached out and took her hands. 'I know. And I'm glad that you had the poise and the consideration not to come before you heard that Sara was dead. You're much more of a lady than any of those gossipy stuck-up *yentas* at the Kimberley Club, with their social mornings and their ladies' nights.'

Agnes asked quietly, 'If you didn't write it, who did?'

'Joel, my brother. It was a kind of a nasty joke.'

Agnes stared down at their hands for a long time. Each of them was wearing a wedding-band. 'I suppose you want me to go, then?' she said.

'Agnes –'

'I can't very well stay, can I, when I've thrust myself on a man who hasn't even invited me? I don't even go out with diggers unless they ask me first. I'm not a fallen woman. Not quite, anyway. I still read the *Morning Post*, and pour my milk into my tea last.'

Barney lowered his head. 'Agnes, I'd like you to stay.'

'You're just saying that to preserve my dignity.'

'I think I've been through too much to start worrying about dignity, either yours or mine.'

'Dear Barney,' she said, lightly kissing his eyebrows, and the bridge of his nose. 'I was so fond of you. I wish Daddy hadn't made such a fuss about your being Jewish.'

Barney kissed her back, at the side of the mouth, and then softly on the lips. 'I suppose everybody has to cling on to something. I cling on to my ambitions, and your father clings on to the Kimberley Club, and the important of being English.'

Agnes looked him straight in the eye. 'I ought to go,' she whispered.

'Doesn't your husband know how discontented you are?' asked Barney. 'Doesn't he know that you walk out with other men?'

'I tell him lies. I don't know if he believes them or not.'

'I don't know how you can stand it.'

Agnes smiled sadly. 'I can stand it because I can't think what else to do.'

Barney held the pieces of letter up, and then let them fall again. 'I almost wish that I *had* written this letter myself.'

Little by little, Agnes released her hands from Barney's; and then stood up. She touched the top of his hair, and bent forward to kiss him again on the forehead. 'I can't take any more heartbreaks, Barney. I made up my mind at Christmas that I would try to stay faithful to Robert; not because I'm so very concerned about hurting him, but because I can't bear any more of these casual attachments myself. In the past six years,

I think I must have fallen in love a dozen times. But each time my love has come to nothing, and each time I've ended up with nobody. I was infatuated with you when I first met you. I suppose you've been a little dream of mine ever since. But I can't stay with you. I couldn't bear the pain of being hurt again, and especially by you.'

Barney looked up at her. Her face was so concerned and so pretty; and in the shafts of sunlight that fell across the drawing-room she looked like an angelic showgirl, a poised and erotic equestrienne, the soiled but beautiful star from a travelling carnival. Perhaps she could never give all of herself to anyone, not even to him; and perhaps that was why she would always be frustrated and unhappy. But the love of a girl who asked no questions about the past or the future, a girl whose sexual appetite was demanding and immediate, and who played no tortuous games of etiquette and manners, – the love of a girl like that might be just what Barney needed. It might also be short-lived. He could not tell. But as Agnes stood before him in her riding-coat that afternoon, he knew that he was going to ask her to stay with him; for the simple reason that he had nobody else.

'Stay,' he told her.

She did not answer him for almost a minute, watching him with her pale and reflective eyes. 'If I stay, I'm going to have to ask you for a commitment. I warn you now.'

Barney held out his hand for her. 'Stay,' he repeated.

They made love that night with a ferocity that, at times, frightened them both. Quite naked, they clawed and plunged and thrashed, kissing until their lips were swollen and raw; tearing and tugging at each other as if their passions could only be satisfied by vandalising the flesh that inflamed them. Barney remembered for years later an instant when Agnes was underneath him, her head thrown back on the pillow, and how his fingers were clutching her breast so savagely that she screamed at him to stop, but not to stop, and how she held her own hand over his to prevent him from releasing his grip.

The next morning, he opened one eye and looked across the twisted sheets. The carriage-clock beside the bed said six-thirty. The sky was light, but the sun was not yet up, and the bushveld was oddly silent. Agnes had already gone. She had left a note downstairs in the library in writing that was as pretty as she was. It said, 'I will not hold you to any commitment. Love, Agnes.'

Barney quickly dressed, and called Michael to bring the carriage out. When it was ready, he climbed aboard, and sat back on the button-backed leather upholstery.

'Where to, boss?' Michael asked him.

Barney stayed upright in his seat, his morning hat tilted at a slight angle, his cane held rigidly in front of him. As the sun rose, the carriage was silhouetted against the golden haze that shone through the camel thorn trees; an essay in spindly wheels, calligraphic springs, and elegant horses. They could have been posing for an eighteenth-century painting.

'Boss?' Michael asked, turning around on his seat.

Barney took off his hat. 'I don't think I'm going anywhere this morning, Michael, thank you. I'm sorry to have put you to all this trouble.'

'No trouble, boss,' said Michael, and climbed down from his perch once again, to open up the small curved carriage door, and let Barney alight.

On the last day of August 1879, the steam-vessel *Mulhausen* docked at Antwerp, in Belgium, under a humid grey sky. The bells were ringing dolorously from Our Lady's cathedral, and flocks of gulls were keening and crying as they circled around the spires and rooftops and flat-fronted façades of the city, and then sloped out over the wide silvery reaches of the river Schelde.

Joel was all ready to disembark as the *Mulhausen* noisily reversed its screws and nudged up to the grey-cobbled Noorderterras. He was wearing a soft grey hat, a light grey cape, and a rather old-fashioned day suit which he had bought in Dieppe when he had changed ships. His leather valise was packed with two spare shirts, some cotton underwear, a bottle of whiskey, and his single right-footed slipper. He had grown a dark beard, and a full moustache, and if it had not been for his missing left leg, even Barney would probably have passed him by without recognising him.

He had been careful to make his journey from South Africa to Antwerp as misleading as possible to anyone who might be following him. He knew that Barney would soon have learned from Nareez that he had managed to reach Durban, and from then it would have been relatively easy for Barney to discover what ship he had sailed on: even though he had bought his ticket in the name of 'Leonard Matthews'. Only two ships had been sailing from Durban to Europe that day: and one of those had been headed for South Wales.

The *Wallesey* had docked at Lisbon, where Joel had disembarked and bought a fresh ticket to Dieppe under the name of 'Henry Lester'. He had then left the ship for good at Dieppe, and stayed for a week at a small pension off the Rue de Varengeville, in a gloomy high-ceilinged front room with a blotchy cheval mirror and a creaking bed, and a view through dingy lace curtains of the Épicerie Auffay, and a wrought-iron bench where stout old ladies with long black dresses would sit and gabble all afternoon.

Joel had taken two hundred pounds in cash with him when he had left Kimberley, but he was already running short. He had his own company chequebook, but the problem was that if he drew out any money, Barney would eventually be able to trace his whereabouts. He had tried to persuade the shiny-headed manager of the Crédit Seine-Maritime to give him a hundred pounds on his passport and his identity papers alone; but after a long whispery discussion with his chief clerk, the manager had smiled and shook his head. Joel had been forced to write a cheque and hope that Barney did not think of looking through the company bank statements for a few months.

Now he had arrived in Antwerp, on a close and silent Sunday, with the uncut Natalia Star wrapped up in green tissue-paper in his coat pocket, one of the wealthiest men in the city, and one of the most isolated. A shabby carriage with a patched leather hood carried him on clattering and grating wheels across the wide square of the Grote Markt in front of the Town Hall, and all around him people walked on their way to Mass, heads bowed, in scarves and clogs, and from the dusty energetic rawness of Kimberley Joel felt as if he had entered a stale and colourless world of widows and seagulls and narrow flat-fronted buildings, a world in which reality seemed to be affirmed only by greyness and solidity, and through which human beings hurried as indefinitely as shadows.

'You want cheap hotel?' the Flemish cab–driver asked him, drawing up the carriage in a street not far from the Town Hall, The street was only wide enough for one carriage to drive down it at a time, and it smelled sharply of sewage and Javanese tobacco and cooked meat.

Joel looked up at the flaking doorway and the sign which announced that here was the Grand Hotel Putte. 'This will do,' he said. 'You can give me a hand with my bag.'

The Grand Hotel Putte was dark and elderly; a building of panelled landings and windowsills where dead bluebottles lay undisturbed amongst the dust. A plump young Flemish girl in a white apron and white cap showed Joel to his room on the top floor. She smelled of ripe underarms and carbolic soap. Joel opened the window and stared out over the steeply-pitched roof tops while she turned down the bed.

'English?' she asked him, standing by the door.

Joel gave her an uneven smile. 'That's right, English. Here's a franc for your trouble.'

She took the money and dropped it into the pocket of her apron. She was trying to think of a word, and Joel found that he could not turn away until she managed to remember it.

Eventually, she said: '*Je lijkt zo eenzaam. Heb je geen vrienden hier?*'

He shook his head. 'I'm sorry, I don't understand you.'

She waited a little longer, and then she managed to blurt out, 'My – name – is – called – Anna.'

'Good,' said Joel. He couldn't think of anything else to say. Anna hesitated for a little while longer, and then left the room, leaving the door slightly ajar behind her. Joel swung himself across on his crutches and banged it shut. Then, breathing heavily, he struggled back to the bed and sat down. After a

528

minute or so, he opened his valise, and took out his bottle of whiskey. There was no mug in the room, so he drank straight from the neck, tilting the bottle back until he almost choked himself.

The travelling was over: now he was going to have to find someone who could cut the diamond for him, secretly but perfectly. It takes a whole variety of extraordinary skills to cut a diamond, and a stone the size and value of the Natalia Star called for the very finest cleavers, cutters, blockers and brilliandeers, as well as all the facilities that only a major diamond-cutting company could provide. It would be almost impossible to conceal the diamond's whereabouts for very long, and Joel knew that the risk of Barney finding out where it was being cut was dangerously high. But the risk was worth running: if he tried to sell the Natalia Star in the rough, he would probably make no more than £300,000 – maybe less. If he had it cut, however, and then gave it a 'legitimate' history by selling it and re-selling it through any agent or private individual who was interested in earning themselves a commission, he could sell it off for four or five times that amount, or as much as anyone was prepared to bid for it.

He had a list of names, some of which he had taken from Harold Feinberg's files; others which he knew simply by reputation. The cleaver would be the most important figure in the whole cutting operation. It would be the cleaver who would study the stone to decide where the planes of cleavage lay, the lines along which the diamond would be split, and on the skill with which he eventually cleaved it would depend the whole value of the finished gem. The cleavers were the élite of the diamond business, and many of them were driven to the diamond district each morning in their own carriages, and owned fine houses in the centre of the city. The undisputed best in Antwerp was Itzik Yussel, of Rosendaal's; but Joel was reluctant to approach him because he was the first and obvious choice. He had heard that a younger cleaver called Frederick Goldin was beginning to make an impression in the industry with his remarkable talents for saving as much carat weight as possible while shaping his diamonds to a 'make' of almost ideal proportions.

What Joel did not know was whether Goldin would be willing to cut a rough diamond of 350 carats without asking where it came from.

That evening, as the cathedral bells rang again, he lay on his bed and finished off his bottle of whiskey. From where he was lying, he could see a kite-shaped piece of sky, in between the dormer window and the roof of the building next door, and as he watched it, it gradually darkened, until it was black. The air was soft and warm and slightly sour, and riddled with mosquitoes, which bred in the marshy flatlands around the wide curves of the Schelde.

At ten o'clock, there was a gentle knocking at his door. He said slurrily, 'Come in,' and Anna appeared, in a black dress with a white lace collar, her wispy mouse-coloured hair pinned up with jet brooches and pins. She held up a brown glass bottle, and indicated by mime that he should rub it on his arms and his body. Then she circled her finger around in the air and made a buzzing noise.

'Ah,' said Joel, in a thick voice. 'Mosquito repellent.'

Without a word, she came and knelt down beside the bed, tugging back Joel's sheets and blanket. Joel watched her blurrily as she lifted his nightshirt, and unstoppered the bottle. He said, 'What are you doing?' but she did not answer.

Her hands were pudgy but firm, and she applied the lotion to his chest and his stomach as busily as if she were waxing a table. The lotion was cold, and smelled of camphor. She rubbed it on his back, and around his buttocks, and down his leg. He began to feel a tight, tingling sensation between his thighs, but he could not make up his mind if she really wanted to touch him there or not. He opened his eyes wide and stared at her; and she stared back at him, young and ruddy, with glistening drops of perspiration clinging to the blonde hairs on her upper lip.

Just as matter-of-factly as she had massaged the lotion on to the rest of his body, she held him in her fist like a broom-handle, and rubbed him up and down. It was only a matter of seconds before he snorted out loud, and anointed the shoulder of her dress. She stood up, corked her bottle of lotion, and looked down at him with a face that was too plump and expressionless for him to be able to read. She could not have been much older than seventeen.

'Anna,' he said. It was partly a question.

'Sleep,' she told him.

'But why? Why did you do that?'

She looked sideways. She probably did not understand him. Then she went to the window and closed it.

'Sleep,' she said.

Hours later, he woke up, awkwardly tangled in his sheets and smelling so strongly of camphor that he was practically sick. He had been dreaming about Kimberley, and the Big Hole, and the night he had fallen and broken his leg and his pelvis. It was hot and claustrophobic; so hot that he thought for a moment that he was back in Africa; but then he reached out and grasped the edge of the bedside table, and he remembered where he was.

For the first time in a very long time, he said a prayer.

They met at last in Frederick Goldin's workshop on the third floor of de Pecq's, an airy room with high windows facing northwards across the rooftops of the Antwerp diamond district. It was the third week in September, and it had taken Joel all of that time since he had arrived in Antwerp to arrange for an interview. For the first week, he had done nothing but visit the cafés and the restaurants most frequently patronised by diamond merchants, sitting in a corner by himself with a glass of cassis and a plate of stuffed veal, and listening to all of their talk about market prices, and quality, and make, and cut. Most of the dealers were Orthodox Jews, and they huddled around their tables in their *shtreimels*, their black broad-brimmed hats, with the *payess* or side-curls which most young New York Jews had long since cut off. It was an odd but reassuring feeling for Joel, to be back amongst his own people after so long in South Africa; and for the first day or two he had felt like interrupting the merchants' murmured conversations to take them by the hand and tell them how good it was to see them.

Deals in the diamond business were always arranged by

understandings; by word-of-mouth; with no written contracts. Hundreds of thousands of francs would be committed to the purchase of a parcel of diamonds without any paperwork at all, and with nothing to regulate the sale except the integrity of the merchants themselves. That murmuring that Joel enjoyed so much was the means by which a glittering torrent of diamonds passed from the traders to the merchants to the cutters, and then to the retailers.

At last, during the second week of his stay, Joel had got into conversation with an English-speaking dealer called Joseph Mandlebaum, a small pot-bellied man in his late forties, bespectacled, with the appearance of a Jewish gnome. From the way Mandlebaum had spoken, it had seemed to Joel that he was more of a wheeler-dealer than many of his colleagues in the Antwerp diamond business: he spent almost half of his time in London, in Hatton Garden, and he regularly sold diamonds to American dealers.

'If you happened to have a very large diamond that you wanted to have cut, very privately, who would be your best man?' Joel had asked him, as they had sat in a booth in a café called Boom's.

Mandlebaum had been sipping tea out of a glass, blowing on the surface to cool it, but he had paused with his cheeks still inflated, and then set down his glass, and looked at Joel through the tiny lenses of his spectacles with slitty-eyed sharpness.

'What do you mean when you say "very large"?'

'I don't know. This is only supposition. But, say, three hundred carats plus.'

Mandlebaum had stared down at his tea. 'That's a big diamond. Where would you find a diamond like that?'

Joel had sat back on his hard wooden seat. 'I don't think you're hearing me right. What I was asking was, where could you get such a stone cut *very privately*, and *very privately* would presuppose that nobody would ask such a question like, where would you find a diamond like that?'

'Umh,' Mandlebaum had said, also sitting back.

'I would presume that whoever arranged such a cutting would expect a fairly large commission, wouldn't you?' Joel had asked. 'And I would also presume that they would get it, without any argument.'

'You'd have to go one of the finest cutters,' Mandlebaum had said, reflectively. 'Someone like Yussels, or Steinberg, or maybe Frederick Goldin. To take a three-hundred carat diamond anywhere else would be – well, if you'll pardon the expression, criminal.'

Joel had grinned. 'I understand. But tell me, out of those three cutters you've just mentioned, which of them would be most likely to take on the job without asking any questions or spreading the word around? I mean, just out of interest?'

'Frederick Goldin, no doubt about it,' Mandlebaum had said. 'All he cares about is what he cuts. A stone like that, he'll see as a challenge, a step forward in his career. He's very jealous of Yussels, you see. He thinks of himself as some kind of prodigy. He believes he can keep more of the original weight of a diamond than Yussels, while still matching Yussels' make.'

Joel had nodded. 'You know him well, Goldin?'

'As well as anybody.'

'All right, then. Why don't you ask him the same question that I've asked you? Just out of interest.'

Mandlebaum had sipped some more tea, cautiously. 'Also as a matter of interest, perhaps I should tell you that a reward of one per cent is being offered throughout the trade for a very sizeable South African diamond of 350 carats known as the Natalia Star.'

Joel looked Mandlebaum calmly in the eye. 'I'm offering a commission of two per cent,' he said. And that was why, a little over a week later, he was helped into Frederick Goldin's workshop, hopping on one crutch, and given a ladderback chair to sit on beside the well-worn bench where Frederick Goldin himself was studying a parcel of diamonds through his 10 × loupe.

'Mr Deacon,' said Mandlebaum, introducing Joel, and then stood back with his thumbs tucked into the tight pockets of his black vest.

Frederick Goldin laid down his loupe, wrapped up the parcel of diamonds, and then turned to face Joel with a lean, rather dog-like face. He was tall, with frizzy gingery hair, and a complexion as freckly as bread-and-sultana pudding. His wrists seemed to be so loosely articulated that his large hands flapped this way and that like slapsticks.

533

'So,' he said, 'you're Mr Deacon, the man with the very large diamond.'

Joel coughed. 'Correction. I'm the man who's interested in knowing whether you might want to cut a very large diamond, and that's all.'

'You don't have to play word games,' said Frederick Goldin. 'I know what you want, and why you're here. You want a huge stone cut as near to perfection as possible, but instead of having to endure the usual publicity that accompanies such an event, you want it done silently.'

Joel said nothing. However much Goldin committed himself, Joel preferred to wait until he was absolutely sure of Goldin's trustworthiness before he admitted that he actually had the stone in Antwerp with him.

'All I can say to you is that you have not only come to the right man, you have come to the *only* man,' said Goldin. 'You could have gone to Itzik Yussels, and he probably could have done you a fair job, but sooner or later he would have let the cat out of the bag. He is a vain and pompous old man, and he would not be able to resist telling the world how wonderfully he had cut your stone.'

'And you?' asked Joel, quietly. 'You're not vain at all?'

'Of course I'm vain. Anybody who possesses as much talent as I do will always be vain. But I am an outsider in the diamond industry. They do not care for my methods; and they do not care for the way in which I challenge their traditional ways. I have spoken out for years against the second-rate cuts they impose on some of the beautiful gems that pass through their hands. There is a famous cut, a twelve-facet cut called the Antwerp Rose. Most of the cutters here won't hear a word against it; it is Antwerp's own, after all. But it is one of the dullest and most lifeless cuts of all, a cut that not even a topaz deserves.'

'Hmm,' said Joel, 'that's all very well. But what guarantee could you give that you wouldn't change your mind – that once you'd cut the stone, and made a really beautiful job of it, you wouldn't be tempted to win some professional kudos by letting it slip that you'd been responsible?'

Frederick Goldin leaned forward over his worktable. 'Mr Deacon,' he said, 'let us speak quite frankly. I believe that the diamond you have brought here to Antwerp for cutting is the diamond that went missing earlier this year from the Blitz Brothers mine in Kimberley – the diamond they now call the Natalia Star. De Pecq's have had at least two letters about it, one with a sketch showing approximately what the diamond looks like. The letters warn that the diamond will probably be in the possession of Mr Joel Blitz, whose most noticeable feature is that he has only one leg.'

Joel rubbed his chin, slowly and thoughtfully. 'All right,' he replied, 'if you know that much, then answer me one question and one question only. Will you cut the diamond, and will you cut it in complete secrecy?'

'That's two questions.'

'If you don't cut it in secrecy, then you don't get to cut it at all.'

Frederick Goldin stood straight. He looked across at Joseph Mandlebaum, who simply shrugged.

'It will be a considerable risk,' said Goldin.

'Not that much of a risk,' Joel told him. 'Fifty per cent of the diamond already belongs legally to me.'

'You want me to cut half of it only?' joked Goldin.

'I want you to say yes or no – will you cut it for me or won't you?'

There was a moment when Joel genuinely feared that Frederick Goldin was going to turn him down; when the diamond cleaver's face seemed to be collecting itself into an expression of regretful refusal. But then Goldin looked a little more whimsical, and mischievous, and then he nodded, and kept on nodding.

'Very well,' he said. 'If anybody finds out what I am doing, it will probably shock the industry to its very roots. But it is the kind of diamond that every cleaver wants to get his hands on before he dies. A diamond that only occurs once in a lifetime. I say yes.'

Without another word, Joel reached into his coat pocket and took out the package of green tissue paper. He set it on Goldin's work-table, and sat back.

Goldin stared at the package as nervously as if it contained a live snake. But then he reached forward with his long loose fingers, and tweaked the tissue open. At last, the Natalia Star lay exposed, brilliant and jagged; and next to the five- and ten-carat diamonds that were scattered on Goldin's table, it looked improbably huge.

Goldin sat down. 'Why didn't you show me this diamond the moment you walked in?' he asked. 'It has a morality all of its own.'

Joel smiled self-deprecatingly, and glanced at Joseph Mandlebaum in amusement. But Joseph Mandlebaum had his eyes on the diamond, and his mouth open and Joel had the feeling that he would have had to let off firecrackers to divert his attention away from it.

Frederick Goldin picked the diamond up and turned it one way, and then the other. 'This will have to be my sole occupation for the next two years,' he breathed. 'But what an occupation!'

'Won't de Pecq's get suspicious if you don't turn out your regular number of gemstones?' asked Joel.

Frederick Goldin said, 'No. Not at all. In any case, I will still be able to carry out two-thirds of my routine cleaving. They give me a free hand, you see; partly because I am so talented, and partly because I am so obnoxious to them. Besides it will take me six or seven months just to study this diamond and mark it out for cutting.'

'And two years before it's finished?' asked Joel.

'Maybe a little less. But cutting a stone like this can never be hurried. It is a question of *exact* degrees, *exact* angles, and inspired cleaving. Properly cleaved and cut, this diamond should yield one stupendous gemstone and anything up to five others, all of extraordinary size.'

Frederick Goldin went to the window, and held the diamond up in his hand as if it were a piece of the moon. 'To feel the weight of this diamond in my hand is a privilege in itself,' he said. 'I have never, ever, seen anything like it. I doubt if I ever shall again.'

Joel spent the rest of the day with Goldin, while the cleaver explained how he would study the diamond and determine which way its cleavage planes ran so that he could split it. No matter how talented the cleaver might be, he told Joel, there was always a danger that an invisible stress point inside the diamond would cause it to split the wrong way, and ruin it. But if the cleaving was successful, the stone would then be bruted into outline shape by rubbing another rough diamond up against it – a process which also required remarkable skill. Then, the stone would go for grinding or blocking. The blocker would mount it in a metal arm called a tang, and press it against a revolving wheel dressed with olive oil and diamond dust, gradually grinding down the flat top of the diamond, the table. After that, the blocker would grind the crown facets that slope from the side of the table to the middle of the diamond, the girdle. He would then turn the diamond over and grind the pavilion facets below the girdle; and finish up by grinding the culet facet at the base of the diamond, which had to be precisely parallel to the table.

At last, the diamond would be passed to the brilliandeer, who would cut all the remaining facets. Even on a straightforward emerald cut, there would be fifty-eight of them, and each of them would be checked to within fractions of a degree by eye, lining up edges precisely with other edges, and with reflections of edges.

That evening, Frederick Goldin took Joel for dinner at a French restaurant on Consciencestraat called L'Écstase. They talked nothing but diamonds, and drank four bottles of Chateau Hauteville between them. When Joel finally got back to the Grand Hotel Putte, Anna's father had to heave him upstairs, puffing garlic in his face with every stair.

Just before dawn, when the kite-shaped pieces of sky was already light, Joel's door opened and Anna came in, in her billowy white nightdress. Without being asked, without saying anything, she lifted the nightdress over her puppy-fat hips, and climbed on top of Joel with all the weight of an authentic Rubens.

By February of the following year, Barney controlled almost all of the Kimberley Mine with the exception of the L-shaped cluster of claims owned by the French Company; and, on the whole, he began to feel content. He felt he needed a rest, too, and to socialise more. He had been working so hard on modernising his mining equipment and buying up his competitors that he had not entertained anybody for dinner at Vogel Vlei for months; and he had neglected his visits to Klipdrift for nearly a year. Pieter must have grown beyond recognition.

Barney's friendship with Harold had grown offhand and unsatisfactory, although their increasing estrangement was not entirely Barney's fault. Harold was so ill with his hearing complaint these days that it was all he could do to climb the stairs to his office, and he frequently went home early. There were no more late-night business meetings, and no more five a.m. starts. Everything was done briefly and breathlessly in Harold's office, with the minimum of banter. Negotiate, sign, pay, and go.

Barney had seen Agnes now and again, once with her husband, and once in the company of a brawny young Australian, and he thought about her over and over until the inside of his head felt like a *trommel*. There was something about Agnes which stirred up a part of his personality which Mooi Klip had never touched; an inexplicable desire for sexual suffering and actual pain. He wondered if he harboured a secret need to be punished for his arrogance, but somehow that explanation did not seem to correspond with the excitement he felt when he remembered how Agnes had dug her sharp fingernails into the flesh of his buttocks. Nor did it correspond with his arousing recollection of hurting Agnes in return. He alarmed himself when he thought too deeply about that, and he made himself change the subject.

He thought about that Natalia Star more than anything else. He could close his eyes and remember it exactly: its soft and magical colour, its irresistible brilliance. It had been a symbol of his deepest love, and Joel had taken it from him, in just the same way that he had taken the first Natalia.

To have lost the Natalia Star was, inexplicably, to have lost his direction.

He left Edward Nork in charge of the mine one Thursday morning early in March and rode over to Klipdrift on his horse Jupiter. It was a dazzling day, with only a few clouds clinging to the far horizon, and Barney felt unusually good-humoured.

538

It had been nearly a year now since Sara had died and his official period of mourning was almost over. He had licked the Big Hole into good shape, so that his combined claims were bringing in more than £75,000 a week. Suddenly the years of work and argument and discontent seemed to be coming to an end, and he could look forward to travelling, and parties, and amusements. Vogel Vlei was almost finished, although he had missed Sara's good taste when he was decorating the guest bedrooms; and in Edward Nork's words the parlour looked like 'the anteroom to Lucrezia Borgia's outhouse'.

Barney reached Klipdrift a little after four o'clock, and rode around to Mooi Klip's house feeling sweaty and tired. He dismounted by her front gate, and to his surprise she was standing by the door, in a summer coat and a bonnet decorated with flowers, and carrying a parasol. Beside her, dark-eyed and solemn, with that short chiselled nose and wedge-shaped forehead that distinguished him as Barney's son, stood Pieter. Around them was a collection of chests and trunks, all locked and labelled.

'Natalia,' said Barney, tying Jupiter up to the gatepost.

She stared at him, her face flushed pink by the late sunlight which shone through her parasol.

'Barney ... why have you come?'

He opened the gate, and walked towards her across the yard. 'What do you mean, why have I come? I came to see Pieter, of course, I came to see you.'

Mooi Klip appeared to be partially paralysed, unable to move or speak properly. 'But *today*,' she said. 'Of all days, you had to come today?'

'What do you mean?' asked Barney. 'You're leaving Klipdrift? You're moving?'

'I sent you a letter,' she said.

'I didn't see any letter.'

'I only sent it today.'

He stepped up close to her, and looked around at all the trunks. 'You were only going to tell me you were leaving after you'd gone?'

She lowered her parasol. 'Do you think I could have had the strength to tell you any other way?'

Barney reached out and held her white-gloved wrist. 'Is this

539

Natalia Marneweck talking?' he asked her. 'The bold Natalia Marneweck?'

She raised her eyes. They were as dark as an owl's. 'No,' she said. 'This is Natalia Ransome.'

There was a very long silence. Barney released Natalia's wrist and stood with both hands clasped together in front of his mouth, the way the Bantu herdboys held their hands when there were whistling through reeds. Pieter clasped Natalia's sleeve uncertainly, seeking reassurance that everything was all right, but all Natalia could do was touch his hand.

'You married him, then,' said Barney.

Mooi Klip nodded. 'He's very kind,' she said, with a catch in her throat.

'Yes,' smiled Barney. 'That's what I thought about him, when he came to call on me.'

The sun was gradually nibbling at the tops of the trees on the far side of the Vaal River, and on the opposite bank Barney could see a diamond prospector bent over the slow golden shallows, dredging up yellow ground in a bucket. It seemed a hundred years ago that he had walked along the Orange River, and watched the diggers sorting soil on their rocker-tables.

He crouched down, and held out his arms for Pieter. 'How's my favourite son?' he asked. 'I'm sorry it's been so long.'

Mooi Klip coaxed Pieter forward. 'It's been a long time for all of us,' she said. 'The truth is, we're going to England.'

Barney was holding Pieter's hand. The boy seemed so gentle and serious, the same way that Barney had been when he was young. He looked up at Mooi Klip and said, 'England? For how long?'

She pursed her lips, and he knew then that she was going for ever.

'His church has sent him, I suppose?' he asked, and Mooi Klip nodded.

Barney stood up, resting his hand on Pieter's shoulder. Pieter obviously wanted to go back to his mother's side; but there was something about the way in which his mother was looking at him that made him stay where he was.

'I heard about your wife from the newspaper,' said Mooi

540

Klip. 'I was so sorry for you, but I knew that I couldn't come to see you. I would have to leave that to you. I thought sometimes that you might come. I even prepared myself for what I was going to say to Hugh. But you didn't come, and I had to honour my promises, and think of Pieter as well as myself; and so I married Hugh, in Hopetown, and now we're going to England.'

Barney touched Pieter's hair, and his thin childish neck, and his cheeks, and then let him go back to his mother. 'I left it too late, then,' he said, with less assurance than he'd meant to.

Mooi Klip could not take her eyes off him; any more than Barney had been able to take his eyes off the Natalia Star. The tears slid down her cheeks, and she had to hold her hand over her mouth to suppress her sobs. Barney could do nothing but look at those brown lambent eyes and think of the past, of all those days of love, and of all of those days of loneliness, and it seemed to him now that the past ten years had ruffled by like the leaves of a calendar, page after page after page, a whirlwind of white paper, and that nothing was left on this gilded March evening but regret.

'Kiss me once,' he asked Natalia. 'Kiss me once, the way you used to.'

And in the doorway of that whitewashed *strooidak* house in Klipdrift, they held each other for the very last time, and kissed like they always should have done, while the evening birds rustled up from the river, and the day began to fade.

On Wednesday, 14 July 1880, Harold Feinberg toppled down the stairs of his office on Kimberley's main street, as stiffly as a scarecrow. He died three hours later, in his own bungalow, in his own bed. Barney was at his bedside, and read for him as he died his favourite psalm, number 84, a psalm for the sons of Korah.

'How amiable are thy tabernacles, O Lord of hosts! My soul longeth, yea, even fainteth for the courts of the Lord: my heart and my flesh crieth out for the living God.

'For a day in thy courts is better than a thousand. I had rather

541

be a doorkeeper in the house of my God, than to dwell in the tents of wickedness. For the Lord God is a sun and shield: the Lord will give grace and glory: no good thing will He withhold from them that walk uprightly.

'O Lord of hosts, blessed is the man that trusteth in thee.'

Barney sat by Harold for almost an hour after he died, the Bible open on his knees. It was still morning, a few minutes before noon, and the sunlight shone through the blind in parallel stripes. A stray dog barked and barked, and yet Harold could not hear it. The silver hairs in Harold's ears still curled around his lobes; his nose was still as proud and fleshy and Jewish as always; his hands looked as if they were about to move at any moment. But he was dead, and he would never speak again.

Barney cried no tears for Harold, but he knew that Harold would understand. He simply stood by the window and looked out across the street and wondered on Harold's behalf why a God who was supposed to be such a model of humility should invest his children with so much ambition.

A week and one day later, a small spiky-haired boy in clogs came around to the Grand Hotel Putte and asked to speak to Joel. When Joel came out of the hotel dining-room, wiping sauce from his mouth with his napkin, the boy handed him a note. Joel gave him ten centimes and shooed him away. Then he swung himself back to his table, where his poached lemon sole was growing cold, and tore open the envelope with his butter-knife.

The note read: 'I am ready to cleave the diamond. I expect you by noon. Respectfully, Frederick Goldin.'

Joel finished his breakfast slowly, mopping up the last of his hollandaise sauce with torn-off pieces of breadroll. After his coffee, he asked for a schnapps, which he stared at for five minutes, and then drank with a flourish. Anna, who served as a waitress at mealtimes, dragged out his table for him so that he could haul himself out on his crutches, and make his way upstairs. She said, 'You're all right?', and he nodded at her.

He dressed with care, tying his necktie in a large butterfly bow. Afterwards, he felt so tense that he had to sit on the bed and pour himself a brandy from the bottle that he kept in his bedside table. He had been living on his own in Antwerp for a year now, so short of money that he had scarcely been able to afford to eat, waiting with badly-controlled impatience for Frederick Goldin to finish his preliminary studies of the Natalia Star and begin cutting.

Anna knocked on the door, and looked in on him. 'That was not bad news?' she asked.

'No,' said Joel. 'It was very good news. News that I've been waiting to hear for a long time.'

'You will have money soon? Father is worried about your bill.'

Joel drained his brandy glass. 'Father will just have to be patient for a little while longer. But don't let him fret. When I do settle up, I'll pay him twice over, plus interest.'

Anna came across and took his hands. 'I don't know if I feel frightened of you or sorry for you,' she said, in Flemish.

Joel grunted. 'I'd rather you didn't feel either way. I'd rather you just felt affectionate.'

She kissed him. 'You can *wish* me to feel anything; but how I will really feel, that will be private, inside of me.'

'Anna,' said Joel, quietly.

Before directing the cab driver to take him to de Pecq's, Joel asked him to stop at the small synagogue on Pelikaanstraat. He was thinking of offering a prayer before he went to see the diamond being cleaved. But when the cab actually drew up outside, Joel changed his mind. All he could depend on now was his own luck, the flukes and chances of his own destiny. He rapped his crutch against the side of the cab and told the driver to carry on.

Usually, the cleaving of a huge diamond would have been a well-publicised and well-attended event, and the workshop would have been jostling with dignitaries and journalists and artists. But when Joel arrived in Frederick Goldin's rooms a few minutes after twelve, Frederick Goldin and Joseph Mandlebaum and two assistants were the only people there. Outside the windows, the sky was relentlessly grey. Joel stood in the doorway for a moment, and then one of Goldin's assistants brought forward a chair for him, while the other closed the door behind him and, on Goldin's instructions, locked it.

The Natalia Star had been placed into a little wooden cup called a dop, and set there firmly with a cement of brickdust, shellac, and rosin, so that only the angle to be cleaved off was exposed. Goldin had already cut a small notch or kerf in the top of the Star with another diamond, and had wedged the dop into a tapered hole in his workbench. All he had to do now was slot a knife blade into the kerf, tap the blade with an iron rod, and the diamond would split along its cleavage plane. At least, it was supposed to.

'I intend to cut the diamond into an emerald-shaped stone of about 160 carats,' said Goldin. 'Then there will be three other major stones – a square emerald, a briolette, and a baguette.'

'You're only going to be able to get a 160-carat diamond out of a 350-carat rough?' frowned Joel.

'Believe me,' Frederick Goldin told him, 'that's a greater saving of weight than Yussels could manage out of the same stone. The Regent is only 140·5 carats, out of a rough of 410 carats. Weight is important, but not if it detracts from a diamond's brilliance. What I will give you out of this stone will almost be a miracle. So remember that.'

'Very well then,' said Joel. 'You'd better get on with it.'

Frederick Goldin rolled up his shirtsleeves, and dragged over a stool to sit down at his workbench. He positioned the long rectangular metal knife-blade in the kerf, resting it between his thumb and his index finger. It seemed to take him over half an hour to position the blade to his complete satisfaction, and Joel began to feel stiff and uncomfortable, and to wish that he had stayed at the Grand Hotel Putte instead of coming here to watch. To have to sit utterly still and silent while his whole future was put at crucial risk in front of his eyes was almost more than he could bear. He would have done anything for a drink. He wished he had brought his flask with him. But now Frederick Goldin was ready for the first cleaving, and the workroom was crowded with tension.

'This first blow will decide exactly how much of the weight of this diamond I shall be able to recover, and exactly how valuable the finished Natalia Star will be,' said Goldin, matter-of-factly. 'You can understand that the slightest error on my part, the slightest miscalculation, could result in the loss of thousands of francs of value. So, I will have to be careful, won't I?'

Without any further preliminaries, he tapped the iron rod on to the back of the knife-blade in a way that appeared to Joel to be absurdly casual. The rough fragment of diamond which was protruding from the cleaver's cement dropped neatly on to the workbench.

Joseph Mandlebaum let out a noisy sigh of relief. The two assistants gave Frederick Goldin a short burst of spontaneous applause. Frederick Goldin looked at Joel and grinned in pride.

'Is that all?' asked Joel.

Goldin's narrow face gradually cleared of self-satisfaction, like clouds moving away in front of a cold easterly wind. 'What do you mean, "is that all"?' he asked Joel.

'It took you nearly a year to get yourself ready to do that? Just one tap?'

'You're playing a joke on me,' said Goldin. His two assistants laughed, but not very happily.

'You think so?' Joel demanded. 'I'm beginning to wonder who's playing the joke around here, you or me. It took you nearly a year to cut one piece off the side of that diamond; how long is it going to take you to finish it?'

'Mr Blitz, with the greatest respect, you know that such a cutting just can't be hurried. That is why you brought the rough to me in the first place. To have it cut perfectly, not hastily. Now you're trying to tell me that I'm too slow?'

Joel took a breath. 'When I first brought you the Natalia Star, I had a little money left. Now, I don't have anything. I'm broke; and as you can probably understand, that makes a difference.'

'You really don't have money?' asked Joseph Mandlebaum. 'But you own half of the world's largest diamond-mine.'

'Sure I do. I'm a wealthy man. Except that as soon as I start drawing money out of my accounts with the Capetown banks, my brother is going to be able to locate me within a matter of weeks.'

Frederick Goldin looked across at Joseph Mandlebaum and

made a face. 'Maybe between us we could advance you a few thousand francs,' he suggested. 'Just enough for you to live on until I finish the diamond.'

Joel said sourly, 'That's just marvellous, isn't it? The poverty-stricken millionaire. When I first looked at that diamond, I saw dreams of incredible riches. Now look at me.'

Goldin held up the cleaved-off fragment of the Natalia Star. 'When this diamond is polished, my friend, you won't be poverty stricken any longer. You will be a king in your own right. You know that, don't you? And that is why you must give me the time that I need to do this job to perfection.'

Joel reached for his crutches. 'Come on, Mandlebaum,' he said. 'I believe you can start advancing me money by buying me a drink.'

On the morning of February 1881, Boer guerrillas shot and killed ninety-three British soldiers in a surprise attack on the crest of Majuba Hill, in the Transvaal. There were only a handful of them, but they abruptly and successfully halted a full-scale British advance through Laing's Nek to relieve British garrisons trapped in the Transvaal by a recent Boer uprising. The action was described by the British C-in-C as 'a rout almost unparalleled in the long annals of our Army.'

The Boers wept openly as they fired at the fleeing backs of the Gordon Highlanders and Northamptons; but by August they had won from the negotiations which followed Majuba a concession which they fervently hoped would be a first step towards fresh independence. The British government agreed to reconise Paul Kruger and his advisers as the legitimate leaders of the Boers, and to let them administer the Transvaal independently – although they were still to be subordinate to what was vaguely described as 'British suzerainty'.

The Treaty of Pretoria which guaranteed these concessions sent nervous ripples through the diamond industry – as any signs of Boer independence always did. The prime target for any act of Boer aggression against the British would obviously be the diamond fields at Kimberley, especially since the Orange Free Staters still bitterly resented their annexation.

For Barney, however, Majuba Hill had an immediate and startling effect. When the news reached Kimberley the following day over the new cable link, it was reported that among the 133 wounded was a young Australian naval rating named James McPherson. McPherson, as it turned out, was a cousin by marriage to Agnes Knight's husband, Robert Joy, and in their boyhood in Sydney they had been inseparable and loving friends, 'Bob and Jim'. After a week of indecision, Robert Joy decided with almost violent immediacy to travel to Durban, where James McPherson was in the military hospital, with the declared intention of bringing him back to Kimberley to recuperate.

Two months later, in April, Agnes received a telegraphic message from Natal saying that Robert had decided to take his wounded cousin straight back to Australia. His cousin had lost his right eye and the use of his left arm, and Robert wanted to take care of him. It was 'unlikely' that he would return. 'Kimberley is not really for me and I suppose neither are you really, my dear,' part of his message had read. 'You may seek annulment on grounds of desertion and keep whatever I have left behind. I am sure you will be much happier with somebody else; after all, you always were happier in other men's arms.'

Mr Knight was outraged that his daughter's honour should have been impugned over the open telegraph, but Agnes soon calmed him down. She was glad to be rid of Robert so painlessly, although she discovered that before he had set sail for Sydney he had drawn the last remaining three hundred and sixty pounds out of their bank, and left her with a few coppers.

It may have been for that reason that she arrived on the front doorstep of Vogel Vlei on a hot shimmering afternoon just before Christmas, 1881, in a wide white sun-bonnet and a white layered dress of silks and Brussels lace, and asked Horace if she might speak to Barney.

Barney came to the door himself, still carrying the copy of the Capetown newspaper he had been reading. He was wearing a pure silk shirt and a fawn-coloured vest and trousers that had been tailored for him in London. His dark brown silk necktie was held in place with a 22-carat diamond stickpin.

'Agnes?' he asked her. 'Won't you come in?'

Through the white veil of her hat she looked as if she might have been crying. She said, 'Only if you want me to.'

'Why shouldn't I want you to?'

'You know why. I've never been a faithful person.'

He folded his paper up, and smiled. 'I don't know whether I've ever been looking for a faithful person.'

'You heard about Robert?' she said.

He nodded. 'It was the talk of Kimberley for a whole month. I don't think I could have avoided hearing about it.'

In the distance, a farmcart trundled through the heat, and even from a quarter of a mile away, Barney could hear its iron-rimmed wheels on the road. Agnes said, 'The marriage won't be annulled for another six months, at least. But I couldn't wait to ask you.'

Barney lowered his head. He knew what she was going to say; and he knew, too, that it was what he wanted. But somehow on this warm and restless day, with the air like liquid mirrors, the words seemed to be magnified beyond any sensible meaning. Too obvious, and too overblown, and years too late. Yet what else could he do? Live alone in his decorated palace for another silent decade, in his fashionable suits and his opulent jewellery, eating alone in a dining-room that could have seated a hundred? He had been a prisoner of his own life when he was poor, and living in New York; but in Vogel Vlei he would be just as trapped, just as isolated, even though he was rich.

He said to Anges, 'Come back when they tell you your marriage is over. I'll be here.'

'Are you sure?' she asked him, her voice so soft that he could hardly hear her.

He nodded. Then he reached out for her hand, and held it against his cheek. 'Something tells me that we were made for each other,' he told her.

It was snowing when Joel laboriously mounted the stairs of Frederick Goldin's workshop in the last week of February 1882. Outside, he could see the grey flakes whirling down on to the rooftops of Antwerp, and transforming the whole city into an encampment of white.

It was today, Wednesday, that Frederick Goldin had promised him that the Natalia Star would finally be ready.

Joel had seen the diamond through every stage of its cleaving and grinding and polishing. The last time he had examined it, only two weeks ago, it had already appeared to be finished. A brilliant, flashing lozenge of pure light. But Goldin had told him that one of Antwerp's most talented brilliandeers was going to spend a final few days bringing it up to a perfect shine. To Goldin, everything had to be 'perfection'.

'I can never show the diamond to anybody, and claim credit for it, so my reputation is not at stake,' he had told Joel. 'But, I must satisfy my own pride.'

Joel knocked on the door of the workshop, and one of Goldin's assistants let him in. The light in the room was grey and unearthly, and from up here the view of the city seemed even more unreal. Even the rigging on the ships that were moored along the slate-coloured curve of the River Schelde had snared the snow, so that they looked like ghostly vessels from a nightmare.

Frederick Goldin was cleaving a small canary-yellow diamond in his dop; and Joel had to wait until he had halved the stone before he could approach him.

'Well?' Joel said, peeling off his damp leather gloves, and forcing them into his coat pocket.

Goldin looked at him for a long time. 'Well, what?' he asked, at last.

Joel cleared his throat. 'Where's the diamond?' he said. 'Is it completely finished?'

Goldin sat up straight on his stool and looked this way and that in obvious bafflement. 'I don't think I know what you're talking about.'

'What do you mean, you don't think you know what I'm talking about? I want to see the diamond!'

'I don't know what diamond you mean,' Goldin protested.

'The Natalia Star,' whispered Joel. 'What else do you think I mean?'

Goldin stood up. 'There's no such diamond,' he said.

'What the devil are you playing at?' Joel snapped. 'The Natalia Star. Three hundred and fifty carats of lilac-pink diamond. You've been cutting it for the past two years!'

Frederick Goldin turned towards one of his assistants, and the assistant shook his head.

'I've been in the diamond business long enough to know every major diamond,' said Goldin. 'It's my profession to know them. But I have never seen or heard of a diamond called the Natalia Star.'

'I brought it here myself,' Joel told him. 'It's my diamond and I want to know where it is.'

'You say *you* brought the diamond? It's yours?'

'You know damn well I did! By God, Goldin, I'm going to have you thrown in to jail for this! Where the hell is my diamond?'

'I'm sorry. You never brought me any diamond of any description,' smiled Goldin. 'And as for your threats of jail ... well, if you can prove that I took such a diamond from you, then obviously I will have to be arrested, and perhaps tried. But where is your proof? Where are your documents of provenance? What have you got on paper to say that the diamond ever existed, or that even if it did, it was yours?'

Joel closed his eyes, and swayed a little on his crutches. 'I don't think I can believe what I'm hearing,' he said. 'I'm going to count to ten, and when I'm finished, I want you to show me my diamond. Because if you don't ...'

'If I don't, what? You will strike me with your crutch?'

Joel opened his eyes again and stared at Frederick Goldin hauntedly. 'I went through agony and exile for that diamond, Goldin. I've suffered for that diamond for years. Don't think you're going to be able to take it away from me, because you're not.'

Goldin thought about that, and then smiled again. 'There was never any diamond, Mr Blitz. Come on, you're a sick man. You must have imagined it. You drink, don't you? Maybe it was something you hallucinated.'

'I'll kill you,' said Joel.

'No, you won't,' Goldin told him. 'You have no reason to.'

'I have plenty of reason. A perfect emerald-cut diamond of 158·4 carats, that's reason enough. The Natalia Star. It existed because I saw it. It shines like no other gemstone on the whole of this earth. It's mine, Goldin, and if you don't give it to me then I swear to you that you will die.'

'You're over-wrought,' said Goldin. 'Perhaps you'd like to sit down and drink a glass of water. Gilbert, would you bring Mr Blitz a glass of water?'

'I want my diamond,' repeated Joel.

Goldin shook his head. 'There was never any diamond,' he said. 'It was a dream.'

Joel stood on his crutches in silence while one of the assistants brought him a chair and a glass of water. He ignored both of them; although the assistant remained where he was, holding out the glass, one hand on the back of the chair, solicitous and still. Joel stared at the snow as it fell on Antwerp, on Jezusstraat and Twaalfmaandenstraat and the Oude Koornmarkt, on the Gothic spire of the cathedral, on the statues of Rubens and Quinten Matsys, on the Vlaeykensgang and into the river. He felt as if time had suspended itself, as if nothing else was ever going to happen, because the key to his future had disappeared as briefly and as completely as a star winking out behind a distant rooftop, a star by which he had desperately hoped to steer himself, but which had proved to be a false star, a wandering star, and a star too bright.

Agnes said, 'You know, my darling, I should have married you at the very first.'

Barney was bent over his desk, almost crouched over it, reading through a packet of letters that had arrived that morning from Kimberley. The light that strained into the drawing-room was autumnal and brown, and yet at four o'clock it seemed too early to call the servants to light the lamps.

'Hmh?' he said, as he pencilled a note into the margin of one letter. Then, looking up, he said, 'Well . . . that's a strange thing to tell me.'

Agnes smiled at him. She had been sitting contentedly for most of the afternoon in the small blue crinoline chair by the fireplace, tatting. The folds of her smock and her overdress revealed that she was heavily pregnant, and her face had that roundness and that light moustache of fine blonde hair that betrayed a woman whose body is enriching itself for that final moment of birth. Their second child was expected in ten days, perhaps sooner.

Barney put down his letter and stood up. It was five years since Joel had lost the Natalia Star to Frederick Goldin, five years and four months, and during that time Barney had worked more furiously than ever. Agnes thought he looked old, and very tired, but there was nothing she could do to woo him away from his desk and his diamonds. She tried to accept his work in the same spirit that she might have accepted the constant presence in their home of a crippled uncle: with patience, and endurance, and as much charm as she could. After all, Barney was very thoughtful, and very loving to her, and he adored their first child, David, as if he were a cherub.

'I don't give you much of a life, do I?' asked Barney. He touched the curls of hair that strayed over her ears. 'I'm surprised that you haven't asked me why I married you at all; not why I didn't marry you earlier.'

'You have to do what's right for you,' said Agnes.

Barney leaned forward and kissed her, first on the hairline, and then on the forehead, and then on the lips. The sound of their lips parting, in the stillness of that afternoon room, sounded like a mayfly falling on a still pool somewhere.

'Other married people see even less of each other,' said Agnes. 'I think we should just be happy for what we have.'

Barney looked at her for a while, and then kissed her once more to release himself from her loving but unwavering gaze. He went to the window behind his desk and stared out at the leaf-cluttered garden. They had been in London for three weeks now and already it was beginning to depress him. The heavy skies, the whirling leaves, the grey-shouldered buildings. London was a city of weight and law and majesty, but at the same time it was one of the most melancholy cities on God's earth. To be sad in New York could be maddening, maniacal, or even elegaic. But to be sad in London was to feel the shackles of history closing around one's ankles, shackles that one had to drag around from Regent Street to Hatton Garden, from Hatton Garden to Barnes, like the chains which Marley's ghost had forged for himself in *A Christmas Carol*.

Barney knew that he had very little to feel sad about. He had lost Joel, of course; and he had lost Sara. He had lost Mooi Klip, and he had lost the Natalia Star. But in April 1882, only three months after Joel had been tricked out of his diamond by Frederick Goldin, he and Agnes had been married, drawn together again by the same feelings that had first attracted them. She was fair-haired, and pretty, and coquettish, and for Barney she had all the temptingly unreliable qualities that so many Jewish girls lacked. He, to her, had been individualistic, even odd, even obsessed. But he was handsome, gentle, and he could touch her sensitivities in a way that no other man had been able to before. Perhaps it was the sense of fate that he carried around with him, of great events, even of doom, that attracted her. She always suspected that one day he would kill himself, and that he would never tell her why. There was a side of his mind that was always concealed from her – sometimes under the lock-and-key of direct refusal, at other times hidden beneath the dusty drapery of evasiveness and silence.

They loved each other, certainly, although it was impossible for either of them to tell quite how much. Not as much as they might have done if they had married when they first met. There had been too many painful encounters with too many other people since then. Not as much as they might have done if the Natalia Star had never been discovered, and if it hadn't burned its image into Barney's consciousness like the sun on his unprotected eyes.

They had married in Capetown in April 1882, first at the synagogue and then at the Anglican church. It had showered that day, and the quicksilver puddles had trapped the petals that their guests had thrown, and pasted them on to the wheels of their carriage. They had spent their honeymoon in Paarl, in a quiet and private *strooidak* house with an enclosed courtyard, and for the first two weeks they had talked and kissed and made love like two delirious young lovers. Barney could still remember the feeling of those warm afternoons on the old Dutch bed, under the thatched roof, with the windows open on to the flowering garden, and the distant clouds lazing their way across the mountains. He could remember the clock ticking in the corridor, the only sound in the silence after they had made love, and he could remember thinking that things could never be the way they were again.

The diamond business was too demanding, and Barney

wanted it to be too demanding. To reflect was to reflect on Joël, and the Natalia Star, and the dark and mesmerizing woman for whom the Natalia Star had been named. During the last days of their honeymoon, Barney began to have nightmares about his mother, about blood, and knives, and the old days on Clinton Street.

Once Barney and Agnes had returned to Vogel Vlei, Barney had worked harder than ever before. He would often rise before dawn, and have to bend over the washbasin and retch because his stomach was nauseous from lack of sleep. Most nights, he would return well after dark, too tired to do anything but eat a frugal supper of bread and stew, and then take a bath, and collapse into bed. Agnes had lain next to him, listening to him breathing, listening to him stirring and murmuring as nightmares raced through his brain, and she had often felt that she might spontaneously break down and cry out of frustrated passion.

There was a time, at a dinner party in Capetown, when Agnes had caught the eye of a handsome and straightbacked young British ordnance officer. They had danced twice, and at the end of the second dance, the officer had asked her if he could meet her again. She had been tempted, God knows, but she had refused, and kissed him once on the cheek as a consolation.

Agnes's married life had improved, however, after the birth of their first child, David, in 1884. Not long afterwards, Cecil Rhodes had introduced to Barney the son of an old school-friend of his, a smart and personable young man called Lance Pollock. Despite his public-school drawl, and his liking for loud cricket blazers and straw boaters and a monocle, Pollock was an astute and extremely hard young businessman, and he took over many of Barney's administrative chores and paperwork – apart from supervising at the mine. He was very harsh with the blacks. When he visited the mine, he always took a George Taylor riding-crop with him, and he never hesitated to use it. Barney always said that he would not trust Pollock with a single point; but Pollock was glib, and quick, and mercilessly efficient, and when Barney found that Pollock's management of the mine enabled him to spend whole days with Agnes and their tawny-haired baby boy, and even to take his first vacation, he began to rely on him more and more.

By the fall of 1887, Barney's accountants informed him politely that he was one of the wealthiest men in the British Empire. Together, he and Agnes had bought this huge country house in Barnes, along by the Thames; and another house on Fifth Avenue, in New York, cater-corner from Mrs Astor's house at Number 350. The demands of the diamond business took Mr and Mrs Blitz away from Vogel Vlei more and more often; until the popular name for it at Kimberley became 'the Ghost House'.

With his riches, came fame. Barney and Agnes Blitz were invited to all of the best parties, and were photographed with Vanderbilts and Huntingtons and even at Mount McGregor, with the dying President Grant. Agnes dressed in silks and velvets and lace, and for their third wedding anniversary Barney gave her a 120-carat diamond necklace. They financed one of New York's most memorable productions of *La Traviata*, with Gisella Fini. They met the Queen of England, and presented her with a Kimberley diamond cut as a teardrop, a silent crystalline memorial to her grief for Albert. They sailed from America to Europe and back again six times, and each of their sailings was noted in the London *Times* and in *The New York Times*. Some of their more lavish weekend parties in Barnes were described, in breathless detail, in the popular magazines bought by housemaids and governesses.

Agnes adored the parties and the riches and the unceasing attention she received. She was slightly sensitive about Barney's Jewishness; but he was never maudlin about his upbringing, and he never once took her back to see Clinton Street. He never went back himself. Clinton Street was the bottomless treacherous pool where his nightmare dwelt. It was a grave, rather than a memory. And besides that, it reminded him too much of Joel.

Agnes said, 'Would you like some tea now? Or would you rather wait?'

'We could have it now,' said Barney. 'These letters are giving me a headache.'

Agnes went across to the bell-pull to ring for the maid, but before she could do so, the door opened and their footman Edwards appeared. 'There's a gentleman outside to see you, sir. Mr Cecil Rhodes.'

'Rhodes? Here?' asked Barney, in surprise.

Agnes glanced at him quickly; as if to say, what's wrong? But Barney said, 'Show him in. Please. And tell Harriet to bring us tea.'

Rhodes strode confidently into the drawing-room. He was looking browner and plumper than before, and his grey Savile Row suit seemed to be too tight all around, especially across the front buttons, but he was in excellent humour, and he pumped Barney's hand with enthusiasm.

'Barney, my dear chap! And Agnes! How good to see you! I'm so sorry I descended without an invitation, but I'm only in London for two or three days, and time presseth. I hope I'm not interrupting anything crucial?'

'I'm just trying to catch up with my correspondence,' said Barney. 'I've always been a terrible letter-writer.'

'Well,' said Rhodes, drawing back the front of his coat and thrusting his hands into the pockets of his trousers, 'the reason I'm here is to save both of us a great deal of letter-writing. The fact is that I've put in a bid for the French Company, and if all goes well we're going to be neighbours in the Big Hole.'

Barney looked at Rhodes cautiously, but said nothing. Up until now, he had been quite content to share the Big Hole with the French Company simply because it would have cost him well over a million to buy them up, and because he had felt sure that they were far too expensive for anyone else to take over. The French Company had been peaceful and non-acquisitive, but if Rhodes took them over, Barney knew that it would only be a matter of months before Rhodes began to put pressure on *him*, too. For Rhodes, only complete control of South Africa's diamond industry would ever be enough. He had demonstrated that by the way he had voraciously acquired the whole of the De Beers mine, and he never stopped talking about a diamond monopoly to control prices of precious stones throughout the world.

Barney however, was emotionally tired. He had no dreams left, except to watch his children grow up happily. He had achieved wealth and success beyond anything he ever could have imagined in Clinton Street; and in doing so, he had lost everything that had ever fired his heart. With Mooi Klip, he had briefly experienced the vividness and strangeness of unconditional love. With Joel, he had just as briefly experienced unconditional hatred. With Sara, he had felt pride, humiliation, frustration, inadequacy and loss. He did not believe that he would ever feel emotions as turbulent as these again.

Nor did he believe that, for all the digging at the Big Hole, he would ever own another Natalia Star.

Rhodes stood with his hands in his pockets, his head slightly inclined to one side, waiting for Barney to say something. Agnes said, 'Would you like some tea, Cecil? I've just asked for some.'

'Well, yes. Capital,' said Rhodes. 'Although I'm afraid I've been overeating lately. Do you mind if I sit down?'

'I'm sorry,' said Barney. 'Go ahead.'

'The fact is,' Rhodes went on, as if he had been interrupted in the flow of a long financial monologue, 'the fact is that N. M. Rothschild's have put up a million, and that I myself have put up £400,000; and that the French Company seem more than interested. Well, you know as well as I do that they're losing interest in the diamond market. They don't have sufficient influence to be able to control it, the way you and I can. They're bound to sell, sooner or later.'

Barney went to the window again. A black and white cat was walking along the back wall of the garden. He said, 'It looks like rain again. It does nothing but rain here. I feel as if I'm drowning, sometimes.'

'You ought to come back to Kimberley,' said Rhodes.

'What for?' asked Barney. 'To be sacrificed on the altar of British imperialism?'

Rhodes laughed, and turned to Agnes. 'He *will* rib me, you know. He's always been a ribber.'

Barney attempted a smile. 'Whatever you bid for the French Company,' he said, 'I'll outbid you. I can promise you that.'

'I'm surprised,' said Rhodes. His voice abruptly lost its humour. 'I thought you'd be rather bucked. After all, you and I, we've been in it right from the beginning, haven't we?'

'Yes,' said Barney, 'and that's why I know you so well. And that's why, whatever you bid for the French Company, I'll outbid you.'

'You can't bid more than two million,' said Rhodes, suspiciously.

Barney sat down, and crossed his legs. He wished that he did not feel so weary, and so used-up. But he drummed his fingers on the arm of the chair, and smiled again, and said, 'I can bid whatever you bid, and more.'

The maid, Harriet, a pale girl with a face that always reminded Barney in its indistinctness of someone who had inadvertently moved during the taking of a daguerreotype portrait, brought in currant scones and Darjeeling tea. The steam rose in the afternoon light like the hair of a drowning woman. Rhodes smiled, and cuddled his stomach, and took two scones, which he spread with butter and greengage jam.

Eventually, Rhodes said, 'You can go on bidding *ad infinitum*, old chap, but we shall have it in the end.'

'You think so?' asked Barney.

'Sure of it,' Rhodes nodded. 'Absolutely sure of it.'

Barney stared at the small cluster of bubbles that circled in the centre of his cup of tea. 'It seems to me that you've come here with a proposition,' he said. 'You seem to have that air about you.'

'Well, that's true,' said Rhodes. He glanced at Agnes, and gave her a smile that was intended to be winning. Agnes patted the back of her upswept hair, and nervously looked towards Barney.

Barney said dryly, 'You'd better tell me what it is.'

'Barney,' Agnes protested. 'It's tea-time.'

'Cecil didn't come here to eat scones and drink tea,' said Barney. 'He came to talk business, and I think we'd better know what it is.'

'It's very simple,' said Rhodes. 'My suggestion is that you allow me to bid for the French company at my original price of £1,400,000, which I am quite confident they will accept. I will then immediately resell the French Company to *you* for just £300,000, plus a one-fifth share of Blitz Brothers.'

'You want only a fifth share in Blitz Brothers? And you'll let me buy the French Company from you?'

Rhodes nodded. 'You've overestimated my greed, I think. You've also overestimated how much of a monopoly I'm after.

As long as you and I control the price of diamonds between us, then what difference does it make? I just want the French Company to be out of it. They've been over-producing for years, and keeping the price down. What this business needs is careful control, and I'm sure that between us, you and I can exert it.'

Barney sipped his tea, and then set the cup down on the table. 'I'd have to talk to my accountants.'

'Of course,' said Rhodes. 'But in principle?'

Barney thought for a moment, and then nodded. 'In principle,' he said, 'it seems to make sense.'

Agnes caught the mood of relief from Rhodes, and the mood of cautious optimism from Barney. She leaned forward and said, 'Would you care for another scone, Mr Rhodes?'

Rhodes hesitated, and then took one. Barney watched him in silence as he pushed in into his mouth, devouring it in two or three bites, and then sucked the butter from his fingers with noisy relish.

'It's getting dark,' said Barney. 'I think, Agnes, you'd better instruct the servants to light the lamps.'

It was nearly six months before Barney saw Rhodes again, and by that time the Blitzes had left London and returned to South Africa. They were breakfasting at their bedroom balcony at Vogel Vlei one morning in April when one of their sixty black servants brought Barney a sealed envelope embossed with the seal of the De Beers Mining Company.

'It's from Rhodes,' said Barney, when Agnes raised her head. She had been embroidering a sun-bonnet for Naomi, their daughter, who had been born after twenty-three agonising hours of labour in early December last year. Agnes had sworn to God that after Naomi she would never have any more children. Not one. The pain and the humiliation had been too much.

Barney opened the letter. He knew what it would contain. Rhodes wanted to meet him that evening at the Kimberley Club, to talk over business. What Rhodes *really* wanted to do, as Barney was quite aware, was to ask Barney to sell out.

Since Barney had signed, late last year, the agreements that gave De Beers control of one-fifth of Blitz Brothers, Cecil had been working furiously to acquire even more Blitz shares. Rhodes had promised Barney's shareholders a glittering future, a future of diamonds and gold, and he was prepared to pay anything up to £40 for a £15-share to demonstrate his confidence.

At first, only a handful of shareholders had deserted Barney. But when Rhodes had increased his price to £45, and then at last to £50, there had been a mad scramble to sell out, and to take as much as possible before the price dropped again. By March, it was clear that despite Barney's protests, now Rhodes owned a substantial proportion of Blitz Brothers mining – a proportion that was large enough for him to be able to call on Barney by messenger and have him drive all the way along Kimberley's rutted high street at six o'clock in the evening to discuss what they were going to do about it.

Barney felt hot, and there was a red rash under his collar, and by the time the carriage drew up outside the clubhouse, he felt so irritable that he almost wished that somebody would accidentally trip him up, or poke him with their umbrella, so that he would have some justification for punching them very hard. As it was, he had to be content with squeezing the palms of his hands really tightly, and controlling his breathing.

The black coachman said, 'You want me to wait here, Mr Two-Leg?'

Barney said hoarsely, 'Yes,' and climbed the steps to the front door. The verandah below his feet was spread with a fine Indian carpet, and as he approached the entrance he was intercepted by a Persian doorman in a watered silk jacket and an amber silk turban.

'Mr Blitz, sir, pleased to welcome you. Mr Rhodes is waiting for you upstairs.'

His slippers squeaking on the polished floors, the Persian led Barney through the lobby to the main stairs, and then up to a small private room where Cecil Rhodes was sitting in a casual linen jacket, reading *The Field* and idly sipping a tall glass of brandy and seltzer. The shutters were wide open, because the Kimberley Club, for all its exclusiveness and all of its grandeur, still had nothing more than a corrugated-iron roof, and at this time of year it grew beastly hot.

'Ah, Barney,' said Rhodes, without getting up. 'My dear chap. Do sit yourself down. Would you care for a drink?'

'Tea,' said Barney.

'I can recommend the rum and hot milk,' said Rhodes.

'Very well then, I'll have one of those,' Barney assented.

The Persian squeaked off again, and Rhodes and Barney were left alone. Rhodes lifted his glass and tinkled the ice in it reflectively. 'Well,' he said, 'we've been having quite a struggle, haven't we, you and I?'

'I shall outbid you in the end,' said Barney.

'Perhaps you will,' Rhodes told him. 'But outbidding is not necessarily the crucial factor in this little skirmish. You can offer your shareholders whatever you like, in terms of pound notes. But I can offer them something far more valuable. I can offer them a monopoly of the diamond business, and the control of diamond prices on the world market; and that, my dear Barney, will make them rich beyond anything *you* could ever hope to offer them.'

Barney stared back at Rhodes, but said nothing. He was thinking of the day when Rhodes had first arrived in South Africa, like a plump and eager schoolboy, with his books and his cough lozenges.

'I shall win the day, you know,' said Rhodes. 'I have the historic tide of the British Empire behind me. I would annex the planets if I could. I have often dreamed of that. I shall win the day because I am on the side of *right*.'

'Well, that's your opinion,' said Barney. 'But, meanwhile, I'm not going to sell.'

'I knew you'd be stubborn,' smiled Rhodes. 'That's why I asked you to come here in person. I want to make you an offer which will make all this far easier for you to swallow. I mean, you must accept that a monopoly will protect all of our interests. At the moment, while we're still in competition, we're each of us vulnerable to the quantity of diamonds that the other decides to unload on the market. If I were to release next month all of the roughs that I have in Amsterdam and London, the price would drop through the floor. You'd be ruined; and it would take even me several months to recover.'

'I hope that isn't a threat,' said Barney.

'You know it isn't,' said Rhodes. 'Look, here's your rum and milk. I always find rum and milk excellent when I'm hungry, and my spirits are low.'

Barney took his drink from the black steward in the high-buttoned white jacket who had brought it up for him; and sipped it once before setting it down on the small brass table between them.

'What's your proposition?' he said.

Rhodes smiled. 'I may be misjudging you,' he said, 'but I don't think so.' And with that remark, he reached into the pocket of his white linen jacket, and produced a small envelope of dark blue tissue paper. 'Here,' he said, handing it across the table to Barney. 'Unwrap it. See what you think.'

Barney hesitated, but then took the tissue-paper package, and weighed it cautiously in the palm of his hand.

'Open it,' urged Rhodes.

Barney slowly unwrapped the tissue. He knew, with an intuition which made him tremble, what the package contained. It could not be, and yet he knew that it *must* be – otherwise Rhodes would never have offered it to him. It was the one single object on earth to which he was utterly susceptible.

At last, all the tissue was folded back; and there, in Barney's fingers, was a huge lilac-pink emerald-cut diamond, of at least 150 carats. It snapped at the evening light which bathed the room, as fiercely as a small dog, and turned the light into lances of orange flame.

Rhodes watched Barney's face with amusement. 'You recognise it?' he asked.

Barney nodded. 'It's been cut, of course. But there's no question about the colour. It's the Natalia Star.'

'These days, it's called the Rio Diamond.'

'Where did you get it?'

'It's only on loan,' said Rhodes. 'At the moment it belongs to the South American Diamond Company, and it was supposed to have been discovered four years ago in Brazil.'

'It's the Natalia Star,' whispered Barney.

'That's what I thought, when I first saw it,' Rhodes agreed. 'It *has* to be. There aren't any records of a diamond of any size

562

being discovered in Brazil, not for years. It's 158·4 carats, and if you calculate what it must have weighed in the rough, you come out with a figure very close to the weight of the Natalia Star. I'm not frightfully enthusiastic about emerald cuts, but whoever did this one was a genius. In fact, there are only two people who could have done it. Only *one*, actually, and that's Frederick Goldin, at de Pecq's, in Antwerp.'

Barney held the diamond up to the last ray of blood-red sunshine; and the facets of the diamond split the blood into light and fire. '*Natalia*,' he said, scarcely moving his lips.

Rhodes watched him, in satisfaction. 'I had my agent in Antwerp talk to Goldin,' he said. 'Of course, Goldin denied that he had ever seen such a stone. But Goldin is living in a new house in a well-to-do district these days, and there are rumours in the trade that he made the money from a huge black-market stone.'

Barney said, 'Is this stone for sale?'

'You're rushing me,' said Rhodes. 'I was going to tell you that my agent undertook further investigations, and took around to de Pecq's a picture which I had sent him. It was *this* picture, from the *Cape Courier*.'

He handed Barney a small yellowed piece of paper. On it, was a blurred newsprint photograph of a frowning man, and the caption underneath read, '*Mr Joel Blitz, of Kimberley*.'

Rhodes said, 'A man who looked like this – a one-legged man who looked like this – visited de Pecq's several times during 1881 and 1882.'

Barney allowed his hands to close over the Rio Diamond, tightly and possessively. 'Then this stone is mine,' he said.

'You can't prove it,' said Rhodes. 'The South American Company have all the papers of provenance.'

'Then how much is it?'

'They're going to auction it. It's expected to fetch two million.'

'Pounds?'

Rhodes nodded.

Barney understood at last the circle through which his destiny had turned. It was a destiny which he himself had determined, or, at least, which his passions had determined.

563

His life had revolved around this stone, the Natalia Star, and around the woman from whom he had named it, Natalia Marneweck, Mooi Klip. The stone was the symbol of the woman, and the woman was the symbol of the stone, and both were symbolic of Barney's hopes, and beliefs, and of his understanding of life and God. At last, with this diamond in his hand, he saw the pattern of his existence, as regular and as symmetrical as a well-cut diamond. The only trouble was, it was all too late. He had lost almost everything out of which the pattern was formed. The understanding was nothing without the substance.

'How much will you pay me for the Blitz Brothers mine?' Barney asked Rhodes.

'One million six hundred thousand,' said Rhodes, calmly. 'As well as which, you can have a life governorship in De Beers mines; you will always be guaranteed the largest individual shareholding; and you can become a full member of the Kimberley Club.'

'One million six hundred thousand?' asked Barney.

'The price of that stone,' Rhodes told him, with a self-satisfied smile. 'The South American Company have already agreed to sell it to me for that price, if I want it. All you have to do is say yes, and the stone's yours.'

Barney took the stone to the balcony, and held it up again, a star to the early stars.

'And you can guarantee my election to the club?'

Rhodes inclined his head, as if to say, you only have to ask.

Barney knew that he was going to agree. There was no point in fighting for ambitions which had already died; for affections which had already faded; for prizes which had already been won, and spent, and tarnished. And somehow, the thought that he would be able to come down here to the Kimberley Club every evening for a drink – a simple social pleasure from which his Jewish background had always excluded him – that seemed more of a temptation than anything.

Barney looked at the diamond in his hand. 'Very well,' he said. 'I don't think I can stand in the way of history any longer.'

Rhodes said, 'Have another rum and milk.'

*

She was hanging up the bunting for St Julian's Summer Fair when Mrs Cross came over and said that there was a gentleman waiting for her outside. She gave the end of her line of flags to Miss Hornchurch, and climbed as elegantly as she could down from the platform, her skirts and her petticoats raised just a little to reveal her white canvas summer boots, tiny and tightly-laced.

'He's in the lobby, Mrs Ransome,' said Mrs Cross. Mrs Cross was looking hot, and the fruit and feathers on her hat were in their usual disarray. 'Not an Englishman, though. A *colonist*, I'd say.'

Natalia crossed the floor of the village hall until she reached the lobby doors. There was a small window of hammered glass in each of them, and before she opened them, she tried to peer through one of the windows to see who this unexpected gentleman might be. Not far away, at the top of his ladder, Mrs Unsworth was singing '*The Old Hundredth*': 'All people that on earth do dwell ... Sing to the Lord with cheerful voice ...'

Natalia could just distinguish a dark and distorted figure through the glass, but she could not be sure who it was. So she opened the doors, and confronted the 'gentleman' with a polite nod of her head. 'Good afternoon, sir. Mrs Cross said you were asking for me.'

The man stood straight, his hands by his sides. He was wearing a grey morning-coat, and a wing-collar. He did not appear to have a hat; or, if he did, he had left it outside in his carriage.

He said, '*Mooi Klip*.'

Her heart bumped against her ribs. She stared at him in surprise and shock. And yet it was him. It was. He was older, and his hair was greyer, and he seemed to have put on more weight. But it was Barney Blitz, as handsome and solid as a prizefighter; as real as daylight.

She could not speak; neither could she move. But her mouth tightened with happiness and grief, and her eyes filled up with tears.

'Barney?' she asked. 'Is it really you?'

'Natalia,' he said, softly, and that was all it was necessary for him to say.

They walked together, arm in arm, up the sun-dappled suburban avenue. Once or twice, Barney had to step off the pavement to allow nurses to come by with baby-carriages, fringed and embroidered and protected by parasols. There was a dusty smell of lime trees and dried horse manure, the smell of transpontine London, south of the river, in the late 1880s, when Chiswick was still a village and people still moved out to Notting Hill for the fields and the fresh air.

Natalia said, 'Are you here for long?'

'I own a house at Barnes,' he told her. 'I've been here for a week, but I have to sail for New York on Friday.'

'I read about you in Hugh's newspapers,' she said. 'You're quite a socialite now.'

'Not really.'

He looked at her in the hazy sunlight. The extraordinary thing was that in spite of the brown summer dress she wore, and her veil, and her bonnet, she was still Natalia Marneweck, still as dark and as beautiful as that day when he had brought Joel into the Griqua encampment for help and rest. The years in between might have fled. But they had not: and now he was Agnes's husband, and she was Hugh's, and all the nights they had shared in Kimberley were nothing more than a remembered taste of sweetness; a taste of flowers and honey that could never quite be recaptured.

She said, 'Why did you come?'

'To make sure that you were happy.'

'Well . . .' she said, turning her face away. 'I'm happy.'

'Are you sure?'

'Yes, Barney.'

They had tea at a corner café, behind layers of net curtains, while outside the horses clip-clopped along the streets with drays and carriages. Barney did not even taste his tea. It seemed to be scalding hot and nothing else. But he remembered for years afterward the flypaper which hung from the ceiling, and the dead flies which clung to it.

At last, Natalia said, 'I have to go back. I can't leave Miss Hornchurch to do everything. It's our summer fair on Saturday.'

'I wish I could come,' said Barney, with a rueful smile. He

held her hand on the tablecloth. It was a useless gesture, except as a sign of his affection for her, because it could never lead any further. They were both quite aware that he would never leave his Agnes; and that she would never betray her Hugh.

'I'm running the cake stall,' said Natalia. 'We have home-made cakes for sale, and you have to guess how many sultanas there are in a large fruit cake.'

Barney tried to smile, but he could not. God, he wanted to hold her in his arms. God, he wanted her. He loved Agnes. Agnes pleased him and excited him and took care of him. But Agnes could never be Mooi Klip, any more than £1,600,000 could ever replace the Natalia Star.

He said, on the doorstep of the tearooms, 'I have a small present for you. It's only a keepsake. But you must promise me that you'll accept it, and that you'll keep it; and that you'll pass it on to Peter.'

Natalia said, 'Barney ... I can't accept anything.'

'I'm not asking you to compromise yourself. I'm not asking anything of you at all, except that you take this present.'

He took out of his pocket a small leather-covered box.

'What is it?' she asked.

'Open it when you get home. It's nothing exceptional. I just want you to promise me that you'll keep it for always, and that you'll pass it on to Peter.'

'Very well,' she said at last. She could sense how earnest he was. Then, 'Very well,' again, and she accepted the leather box, and put it without opening it into her purse.

Their lips brushed together. A whole lifetime of loving passed in an instant. Then Natalia was walking back along the street to St Julian's Church Hall, back to her bunting and her summer fête, and Barney was crossing the street to where his carriage was waiting for him, and the afternoon was as dim and misty as a memory, even before it had become one. It would become a memory, though, within three or four hours; and Barney sat in his carriage with his knuckles pressed against his mouth, to stop himself from crying; and the vicar's wife who had once in some magical time been known as Mooi Klip returned to her cake stall and her flags with all the composure of true grief.

It was only when the Rev. Hugh Ransome was sleeping that night that Natalia opened the small leather box, and discovered the diamond.